AIRSHIP 27 PRODUCTIONS

Published by Airship 27 Productions
www.airship27.com
www.airship27hangar.com

Interior illustrations © 2015 each artist as listed
Cover illustration © 2015 Doug Klauba

Editor: Ron Fortier
Associate Editors: Todd Jones & Jaime Ramos
Production and design by Rob Davis
Promotions Manager: Michael Vance

ISBN-13: 978-0692601136 (Airship 27)
ISBN-10: 0692601139

Printed in the United States of America

10 9 8 7 6 5 4 3 2 1

LEGENDS
OF NEW PULP FICTION

TABLE OF CONTENTS

Art-M.D. Jackson

v

Answering the Question for the Last Time

An Introduction by Tommy Hancock

Being a writer and a Publisher of New Pulp, there is a question I am often asked. Sometimes it is simply put forward as a polite query. In other situations, it's been almost put forth as a dare, egging me on to state an opinion someone can argue with. Regardless, it is a question that still comes up on a regular basis and this collection is finally the answer to this recurrent interrogatory.

What is New Pulp?

Now, normally I answer it with a pretty pat definition that I and around 40 other writers mostly agreed on a few years ago. But to me, personally, as a fan of Pulp of all types, there's a simpler answer.

New Pulp is about Heroes. Larger than life figures that go above and beyond the call of duty and many times go just as far beyond their own comfort zone. People who see a problem and instead of debating a solution or whose responsibility it is, they pull together and attack it, individually and as a team when a cross over event is necessary. Men and women of unique talents, both skilled in the specific and masters of the general enough to know a bit about everything and put it to use. Beings that can create entire worlds, even universes with just a thought and a little work. That is New Pulp.

And I'm not talking about the characters in the stories you're about to read. I am speaking of the writers and artists who make up what is considered New Pulp today, a massive number of them being represented in this book. A book put together...for me.

I was diagnosed with Congestive Heart Failure on June 8, 2015. Now, although CHF is not completely uncommon in this day and age, the reason for mine is a bit different. The nerves that feed my heart electricity are essentially dead and any power that was getting to my heart was just purely accidental. This means that my heart was not only pumping out of rhythm, but it was working harder than it should have to and, like any muscle, it grew bigger the harder it worked.

If you know me, then you may realize how devastating this was for me. Not simply the diagnosis, but the fact that the months, nearly year and a half before that I'd felt awful and couldn't understand completely why completely disrupted my usually pattern of being me. And to finally have a name on it, to know what it was and to hear a plan on how to fix it, that was both depressing and hopeful.

Because of my responsibilities as a New Pulp writer and publisher, I came home from the hospital in June and wrote a letter to the multitude of writers, artists, and publishers I work with and for, simply explaining what I had learned and what the next few months might hold. I received many more emails and well wishes than I thought I would and was touched by each one of them. What happened, though, that I in no way predicted and that completely floored me was the discussion and immediate commencement of a benefit book. For me, for my family, to help with medical costs and other needs. And that is the book you're now holding.

This collection, beyond being something that I am most thankful for and truly have no words to properly address how I feel, is potentially the penultimate gathering of the best creators New Pulp has to offer. Stories ranging across the Genre spectrum, each accompanied with an illustration by the top artists today, all beautifully packaged within a cover by the legendary Doug Klauba. Even if this were just another book, not a benefit, it would not be just any other book. And the fact that this terrific assembly of imaginations came together for me…truly does leave me speechless.

I thank each and every author and artist involved from the bottom of my now better functioning heart, surgery having been completed in late September. A special thanks goes out to Jaime Ramos, the originator of the idea, and Ron Fortier, Rob Davis and Todd Jones of Airship 27 Productions, who took Jaime's concept and molded it over months, gave their time and effort just like every author and artist in this book did, to make this anthology the best representation of New Pulp possible.

You want to know what New Pulp is? You're holding it in your hands right now.

Tommy Hancock
October 20, 2015

The Case with the Face
(An Ike Mars story)
by Fred Adams Jr.

People say lightning doesn't strike the same place twice. How about the same man? Just ask me. I can tell you all about it.

My name's Ike Mars; spell it like the planet. I've been hit by lightning twice. A friend of mine, a math wizard who works for the bookies on the South Side told me the odds of that happening are one in 790,000.

The first time, I was at a Pirates game sitting in the left field seats at Forbes field when a freak storm blew in. I was headed for the exit when I saw a bright flash then lots of darkness. I woke up in the ward in Mercy Hospital a day later with a burn on my wrist from my watch and one on my finger from a signet ring that mysteriously disappeared between the ballpark and the hospital. I found the ring in a hock shop three weeks later and the guy who pawned it a week after that. At least his dentist was happy.

The second strike happened last month while I was chasing a forger named Mikey Slavic across Schenley Park. It knocked me down but not out. My chewing gum was smoking when I spat it out and my ears rang for a week. Mikey thought it was his lucky day 'til he ran out of the park in front of an Iron City beer truck on Forbes. The driver slammed on his brakes, but the street was wet and Mikey was under the wheels.

My old partner from the Detective Squad Mason Cutter told me the second time was God saying "strike two." I said, "It means I'm chosen." He said, "Your ass is what that means." Eloquent as always.

Mason and I are two of the casualties of the new broom that swept like a tornado through the Pittsburgh City Police Department a couple of years ago when Cap Agronski was appointed Commissioner. People like us who didn't have the right last name or kiss the right butts for ten years found ourselves unemployed. So Mason and I made our own jobs. We became private investigators. We don't see ourselves as competitors, just little sharks swimming in the same tank with the big ones.

The trouble with Pittsburgh in 1938 is you can't pin down one trouble to blame things on. Guys I know in the FBI say for corruption, Pittsburgh's worse than Chicago. At least in Chicago the politicians wink and pretend they're on the level. In Pittsburgh the police don't investigate the police, and if you want to keep your private license, you better not either. So, I mostly chase bail skips, runaway kids, and wayward husbands. I'm still wearing last year's suit, but I'm eating okay, so who complains?

But back to the lightning.

About a week ago, I was catching a nap, something I've been doing more lately since the second lightning strike. I was head down on my arms at my desk in the office when Mason strolled in. I was dreaming about Benny Grillio, a bail jumper I'd been chasing for months when he shook me awake.

I raised my head and he pulled his gun. "What are you doing here, Benny? What did you do with Ike?"

"Who, whoa, whoa," I said, putting up my hands. "What's the matter with you, Mason? Are you drunk? It's me; it's Ike."

When he heard my voice, Mason's face twisted into a look of pure confusion. "I don't know what you're trying to pull, Benny, but it ain't working." He cocked the hammer on his revolver.

I thought fast. "September 4, 1937. The Wilshire. You and me when Paulie Brazzo died before his time." Something only Mason and I knew. We were working vice together and found Paulie the Pimp bleeding from a dozen slashes one of his girls put on him with a razor. He was leaking pretty good and his odds of living were just shy of fifty-fifty.

We decided it would be a shame to let this scumbag be sewn up by some emergency room doc and go back out on the streets, so Mason held Paulie's mouth shut while I pinched his nose. The coroner said he bled out, and nobody but Mason and I ever knew different.

"Okay," Mason said, putting down his pistol. "You're Ike Mars, but that's a hell of a disguise. Fooled me."

Now it was my turn to be confused. "What disguise?" I got up from my desk and crossed the room to the mirror beside the window. Benny Grillio was staring back at me. For one of the few occasions in my life, I was speechless. Then as I watched, Benny's features shifted around and my mug, with the scar on the left cheek and the mole on the right one took its place.

I turned around and Mason saw me. Now it was his turn to be speechless.

Mason and I talked about it for a while, trying to figure all the angles. We decided that the lightning did something weird to me that lets me change my looks. I was dreaming about Benny when my face turned into his. Did I have to be asleep to do it?

"Try thinking hard about somebody else," Mason said.

I screwed up my courage and concentrated on Cap Agronski. I felt my nose spread, my jaw push out into an under bite, and my forehead creep down a little over my eyes. I didn't need a mirror to know the change was effective. Mason's mouth fell open. Then it closed.

"Do I look like him?"

"So much I want to punch you in the teeth." I could see the wheels turning behind his eyes. He said, "You know what this means, don't you?"

I was already imagining the possibilities. I could pass for anybody; get inside any place on my looks. Get close to people I'm investigating and they'd never know it's me. Or make myself the image of some babe's husband and come home horny.

But then there was my voice, like a cement mixer full of gravel, and it didn't change with my face. Maybe if I whispered . . .

Enough about that. Like that Shakespeare guy wrote, "What's past is prologue." That's one of the few things I remember from high school English class because it's true. Now that you know how I got be how I am, let me tell you about the Hobbes case.

Lawrence Hobbes — Larry to his fans — was a nightclub crooner, and a good one by most people's standards. Popular. Tall, handsome, dark wavy hair, everything that made him a heart throb that women automatically swooned over and men automatically resented. He was stabbed to death one night six months ago by a guy named Bill Tenney, a backstage hand at the Red Parrot after Hobbes accused Tenney of stealing a pair of diamond cufflinks from his dressing table.

Tenney was caught red handed, literally, with Larry's blood on his clothes, the murder weapon in his hand and the cuff links in his pocket. He was little people on the power ladder, so after a fast shuffle of a trial off he went off to jail pending final disposition of his case.

That seemed to be that, as they say, until my office door opened and Mrs. Ambrose W. Pratchett walked in.

Lila Levitsky Pratchett, April-December bride of one of the 'Burgh's most powerful political fixers. He'd picked her out of the chorus line at Foxy's a respectable year after his wife died and he made her the respectable Mrs. P.

Five foot two, eyes of blue, and a lush head of blonde hair capping a physique like Venus De Milo with the arms left on. She was wearing a long raincoat, a big floppy hat, and dark glasses, as if that could hide her identity. She made the Society Page of the *Pittsburgh Press* so many times they kept a photographer in the trunk of her car. Funny thing about the *Press*, they loved to run her picture but always included her maiden name.

"Do you know who I am?"

"Sure, you're Mrs...."

She cut me off. "I said do you know who I am?"

"Uh, no ma'am."

"That's better. You catch on quick, Mars. I like that. Just call me Mrs. Smith."

"Mrs. Smith it is. What can I do for you?"

"I want you to prove my husband is guilty of murder." She fished a cigarette out of her handbag and before I could get around the desk to light it for her, she fired it up with a jeweled lighter.

"And who did Mister Smith kill?"

She frowned. "Oh, this is stupid. I'm Lila Pratchett. My husband is Ambrose Pratchett. I want you to prove he killed Larry Hobbes."

My turn to frown. "With all due respect, ma'am, there's a guy named Bill Tenneywho's looking at the chair for that one."

"I don't mean Ambrose stabbed Larry. He had it done for him, like all his dirty business."

"And why would Ambrose Pratchett want Larry Hobbes dead?"

Her eyes could have burned a hole through steel plate. "His jealousy. Larry and I were lovers years ago, and that's been over and done for years, but Ambrose was convinced that we were seeing each other again."

"I have to ask. Were you?"

"When? How?" she dissembled. "Ambrose watches me, his people watch me, and the newspapers watch me. It was all I could do to sneak away long enough to come here to see you. Ambrose is so possessive that he isn't satisfied with having me here and now; he wants to own my past as well and he believed that killing Larry would buy it for him."

She shuddered. "The morning after that Tenney fellow murdered Larry, I came down to breakfast and found Ambrose sitting at the table drinking coffee. Most mornings he'd be downtown at his office already, but that morning I suppose he wanted to gloat, to see my reaction. Do you know what he said? He said, 'See the paper?'"

I nodded. "You understand, Mrs. Pratchett that your husband is very powerful and very protected by the cops and the courts, not to mention other people. Making a case against him could be, shall we say, hazardous."

"Name your price."

I did. She reached into her purse and pulled out a roll of fifties and started peeling them off, laying the bills out like she was dealing a hand of solitaire. Based on the size of the roll, I probably should have asked for more. "I'll pay you that much again if you're successful." She scribbled on a scrap of paper from her purse. "Call this number when you have something. It's a friend of mine from Foxy's. She'll pass along the message."

"I'll start today. To protect your privacy and my hide, you might want to use the rear exit when you leave."

Lila Pratchett was right about one thing, City Councilman Ambrose W. Pratchett wouldn't soil his hands with something as sordid as arranging a murder. He'd have one of his henchmen take care of the details for him. The likeliest candidate was Hugo Blount. Blount was almost an appendage to Pratchett, Chang to his Eng, except when he was doing his master's bidding.

I'd seen Blount around but never got a really close look at him. A crazy idea was bouncing around in my head. To make it work, I'd need a photo or two of the nasty little rat. As far as I knew, Blount had never been arrested—suspected plenty of times but his ties to Pratchett kept him out of stir—so I couldn't get one of my old pals at the station to swipe a mug shot or two for me. I called my sometimes girlfriend Marge Conway at the *Press*.

"Ike Mars. Got a stiff neck from looking over transoms yet?" She cracked her gum.

"Naah, I wear goggles, Marge. All the pros do."

"Says you. Whaddya want? The only time you ever call these days is when you need something."

"Well, since you brought it up, could you find me a couple of decent pictures of Hugo Blount, Ambrose Pratchett's right hand man?"

"It's gonna cost you, bud. I want a steak dinner and at someplace with some class for a change."

"You got it."

"You gave in too easy, Mars. This must be a really big deal. I want champagne too."

"Only one bottle."

"Deal."

An hour later, I met Marge at Market Square. She bundled up against the cold in a long coat like Lila's but no floppy hat. She handed me an oversized envelope and I took her to Theo's for that steak. Tonight I could afford it.

Three glossy black and whites from the envelope showed Blount well enough for me to get a good handle on his features. "I had a hell of a time finding those three in the files. We have hundreds of pics of Pratchett, but most of the time, Blount's out of the frame or standing behind him."

"That's okay, Marge. These three will do just fine."

Marge smiled at me across the linen tablecloth. Her brown eyes always half close when she's had a few, and it makes her one of life's irresistible temptations. Then she always says something that kills the moment. "You know, Mars, if you'd marry me like any decent human being would do, you wouldn't have to buy me dinner tonight. I'd be cooking it for you."

"Patience, darling," I said, patting her hand. "All things come to him who waits."

"Shouldn't that that he who waits?"

"I forgot, I'm dating a proofreader."

"And furthermore, I never hear anybody say 'she' in that line."

"It's a man's world, Marge."

"For as long as he can hold onto it. If you're chasing Blount, that means you're chasing Pratchett. I hope you don't lose your grip."

Later that night, I studied the photos of Blount, taking note of the long nose, the thin eyebrows that looked as if they'd been plucked by a beautician and the crooked little scar like a fork of lightning across the chin. He was about my height, a little leaner, but I figured I could pull the masquerade off.

Since I learned about my new talent I'd practiced a little, but never tried it on the street. The process wasn't painful so much as it was uncomfortable. While I was changing it felt as if snakes were crawling under my skin, coiling in some places, uncoiling in others, and it left my face a little tender in spots once I turned back.

I closed my eyes and concentrated on Blount's mug and when I opened them a minute later, I was staring into his face in the mirror. Tomorrow would be interesting.

A call to one of my sources in the courthouse told me that Bill Tenney wasn't being held in the County Jail. He'd been moved to solitary in the Allegheny County Workhouse out in Blaw Knox. That was unusual, since the place mostly housed minor offenders who worked the onsite farm to pay their room and board. The Workhouse also served as an "inebriate rehabilitation" site, a fancy moniker for a long-term drunk tank.

It made sense in a way. If Tenney did the kill for Pratchett, he and Blount would want to keep him away from the mainstream where nosy guards and inmates couldn't pry the secret out of him.

The Allegheny County Jail was an intimidating place, a pile of limestone fashioned after a castle right out of the legends of King Arthur, but for sheer grimness, it couldn't beat the Workhouse. As you drove up, it looked like a ritzy boys' school from some Limey novel. High windows fronted the main building and ivy covered the walls and the towers. Then as you got closer, you saw the barbed wire stretched along the top and the guards aiming rifles from the turrets.

I pulled my car over a mile away from the Workhouse and changed my looks. When I drove up to the gate, the guard took one gander at me and said, "Go ahead, Mister Blount." So far so good. I got the same response at the sign in. I made my request to see Tenney in a hoarse whisper I blamed on laryngitis and nobody blinked. A guard led me to an interview room that was walls and a floor with a table, two chairs on one side and a third bolted to the floor for the prisoner on the other.

I had time for half a cigarette before another guard walked Tenney into the room. The guard cuffed him to the chair but didn't really have to. If they left the front door open and a taxi waiting for him, Tenney wouldn't have had the energy to walk out under his own steam. His sunken eyes stared at me from a face the same shade of grey as his uniform.

I offered him a cigarette to break the ice, and he started to laugh. His laugh turned into a deep wet cough, and when he took his handkerchief away from his mouth it was spotted with fresh blood. It all clicked at once. Tenney had cancer; maybe his lung, maybe his throat. Or maybe he had consumption. I could see he wouldn't live long enough to fry in the chair. Pratchett and Blount chose well.

"What are you doing here?" He mumbled.

"Came to see if you need anything," I said. "The Boss takes care of his people."

"He can start by handing that money over to my wife any time now. You said she'd get a hundred a month for her and the kids, but the last visit she told me she ain't seen a dime of it."

"Well, I'll get that moving and talk to the Boss and see if we can't give her a little extra, Christmas and all, you know."

"Yeah." He coughed again. "That'd be great. Any word on my appeal?"

That was a question out of nowhere. "Not yet." If I knew Pratchett, Tenney's appeal was already in some judge's wastebasket. "Anything else you need?"

"Maybe a decent pillow. Mine feels like it's full of sand."

"I'll see what I can manage."

My head was so full of ideas chasing each other around that I drove most of the way downtown before I remembered that I was still wearing Blount's face. I pulled into a Texaco station and a kid in a company uniform came out too quick for me to make the switch. "Fill her up, mister?"

"Put a buck in it," I said, forgetting for a moment the size of Lila Pratchett's retainer. He wiped the windshield with a rag while the pump ran. I couldn't change my face with him on the other side of the windshield, but then he asked if I wanted him to check the oil. As soon as he raised the hood, I started the change. I knew it worked by the confused look on his face when he closed it a minute later. He stared through the windshield at me.

I rolled down the window and stuck my head out. "Need oil?"

"Uh, no, mister. Oil's okay."

"Two bucks then, right?"

"Uh yeah, two bucks."

I was tempted to ask him to check the tires and while he did turn into Groucho Marx or maybe Boris Karloff, but thought better of it. I held out the cash, he took it from me, and as I drove away, I saw him staring after the car until I lost him in the mirror.

All the pieces swirled around each other like dead leaves in the wind, but they were starting to hook up one by one. I knew for sure that Pratchett through Blount hired Bill Tenney to kill Larry Hobbes. My word was hearsay, not enough to make it stick. I needed some way to rattle Pratchett into making some careless mistake that would tip his hand. That was going to be tricky, but I came up with a plan. It was nuts, but I thought it just might work.

Back in my office I dialed the number Lila Pratchett gave me. A woman's voice at the other end sounded almost as scratchy as mine, a lifetime of cigarettes and gin. "Yeah?"

"Got a message for Lila. Tell her to call Ike."

"Sure, pal." No questions. She hung up.

Ten minutes later my phone rang. "Mars? You called?"

"Yeah. I have a question for you. Does your husband believe in ghosts?"

The next afternoon I made a stop at the Red Parrot. The place had that sad empty look night clubs get when the neon lights are off, the bandstand and dance floor are empty, and the only sound is the clink of glasses and silverware from the kitchen. It reminded me of Kennywood Park in the middle of February. Two guys sat at the bar three stools apart nursing drinks and the bored bartender slouched at the end.

His posture didn't change when I walked up to the bar. "What'll you have?" He was new enough on the job to not know who I was.

"Nothing yet," I said, handing him my business card. "I'd like to speak to Sonny for a minute." He took the card. His mouth moved while he read it. I guess good help really is hard to find. He finally levered out of his slouch and ambled through a doorway at the other end of the bar. In a minute he reappeared and jerked his head for me to follow.

I knew Sonny Barnet from my days on the force. Cops were always welcome in the Red Parrot. People seemed to behave better when we were around. Sonny opened the Parrot two days after Prohibition ended and made a good living with it since. His waistline testified to that. Every time I saw him, his suit was always a half size too small.

He walked around his desk and stuck out his hand. "Ike Mars. Still ugly."

"Sonny Barnet. Still bald."

"Been a while."

"Too long, Sonny. I miss your prime rib."

He laughed. "Whose fault is that?"

"When you stick the word 'private' in front of detective, the salary goes down fifty percent. And nothing comes gratis."

He laughed again. "Come in one night next week. Let me know you're coming, and it'll all be on the house. Bring your girl. You still going with Margie?"

I nodded. "Who else would put up with me?"

He laughed again then put on his management face. "So, what brings you uptown?"

"Larry Hobbes."

Sonny frowned. "Hell of a thing that business. You know, I thought my trade would fall off without him. He really packed them in here. But I didn't lose one customer. In fact it got busier for a while. Everybody who came in wanted to know about the murder. People even asked me if they could see Hobbes's dressing room. I should've sold tickets."

"What I need is a photo of Hobbes, one of those eight-by-ten head shots you put on the posters."

Sonny swiveled his chair to a pair of filing cabinets behind him and pulled out one drawer then another. He said over his shoulder, "Mind if I ask what this is about?"

"Paternity, Sonny," I lied. "My client thinks her little boy bears a striking resemblance to the late Mister Hobbes. She's hoping to stake a claim on his estate."

"Tell her to get in line." He pulled out a file folder and laid it in front of me. He flipped it open and right on top was the picture I needed, a three quarter head shot of the crooner. "How's that?"

"Perfect." I held it up and studied it for a minute. "Was there anything Larry left behind in the dressing room? Personal effects, letters, mash notes? Or did the cops take it all?"

"Actually, they didn't take much of anything. They had an open and shut case with Tenney. I never figured Bill for a thief, let alone a killer, but," his voice took on an ominous overtone, "who knows what evil lurks in the hearts of men?"

"Keeps me in business."

"I think we still have a box of Larry's stuff back in the storeroom." He pushed a button on his desk and in a few seconds a refrigerator in a black suit came in from a side door. "Hey, Leo."

"Mars." Leo never said much; he didn't need to.

"Leo, go get that box of Larry Hobbes's stuff from the back and bring it in here, would you?" Leo disappeared the way he came and returned soon with a liquor case full of odds and ends.

"This all the stuff from Larry's dressing room. Take it out front and go through it. When you're done, leave it on the bar."

"Thanks."

"Glad to do it. And don't forget about that dinner."

"I wouldn't miss it. Thanks again Sonny."

I sat at a table near the dance floor and as I went through the box, the band members took the stage in twos and threes and began tuning up for a rehearsal. By the time they got through "Stardust," "I'm Confessin'," and "I'm in the Mood for Love," I'd pretty much seen all there was to see. There were a few photos, snapshots mostly of Hobbes in the Parrot with one dame or another, and a few steamy notes, but none of them from my client.

At the bottom of the box I found a chrome Zippo, a cigarette case, and a white silk scarf with the initials L.H. I looked at the night club photos again. In all three of them Larry had the white silk scarf draped over the shoulders of his tuxedo. It was a trademark. I folded the scarf and slipped it into my pocket. It would come in handy later.

I set the box on the bar and walked out into the cold. A few snowflakes were falling. Pittsburgh was dismal enough on its own without the weather chipping in. When you grow up here, it's a given. When you're a new arrival, it's kind of a shock. There is actually an old law on the books in Pittsburgh that's never been repealed that it's illegal to sell a Dutchman a rope on a cloudy day. Coming from the land of blue skies and tulips, Dutch immigrants found the perpetually mill-grey skies of Pittsburgh so depressing it made them suicidal. Makes sense.

Back at the office, I smoked through three Luckies by the time I had my plan worked out. It was risky; hell, it was crazy, but it was crazy enough to work.

I don't own a tuxedo, so I went to Sol Horowitz's shop to rent one. A cute little brunette stepped from behind the counter. "May I help you?"

"Mars!" Sol called out from the back of his store where he sat at a treadle sewing machine. "Did you finally decide to retire that suit?"

I nodded to the shop girl and headed to the back.

Sol sat in his shirtsleeves at the machine working his magic, his feet pumping the treadle and his head wreathed in smoke from the cigar in the corner of his mouth.

"This is the twentieth century, Sol. When are you going to get an electric machine?"

"When my feet fall off," he said around the cigar. "Electricity costs money. Feet are free."

"I need a tuxedo, Sol."

"Is it gonna come back looking like the last one I loaned you?"

When I was still on the force I borrowed a tux from Sol to wear to a hoity-toity reception for some bigwig where I was shadowing a team of pickpockets. I collared one of them reaching into somebody's hip pocket and instead of a wallet; his hand came out with a straight razor. I ended up busting his head with a chair, but not before he put a half dozen new vents in the coat.

"Hey, Sol, the city paid for it."

"But you and the city parted ways as I recall."

I pulled out my roll. "I'm good for it up front."

"What's the occasion, Mars? You getting married?"

"No, Sal, I'm not making a marriage; you might say I'm breaking one up."

"Spoken like a true gumshoe. I'll give you the works."

Sol measured me up and down. Based on the autopsy report on Larry Hobbes, I was an inch taller than he and outweighed him by about ten pounds, but the tuxedo would fit sell me well enough at night. Sol fitted me out with a cummerbund, a fancy pleated shirt with a wing collar and a bow tie. From the neck down I looked pretty good, and I felt pretty good too, like I was the proverbial canary-munching cat.

It was after five by the time I got back to my office. I stepped through the door whistling, the bag with the tuxedo under my arm. I threw the wall switch and the lights came on. I blinked when I saw Hugo Blount sitting behind my desk. Then the lights went out.

I woke up tied to a chair with Blount and two of his bruisers, Stan Hatfield and Sam Copley staring me in the face. My hands were tied, but if I could move them to the back of my head, I would have felt a lump as big as a golf ball. My files were scattered all over the floor.

"Funny thing happened yesterday, Mars," Blount said. "I visited the Workhouse and found out I'd already been there to visit Bill Tenney. The gate guard takes all the plate numbers when cars come in, so it was no stretch find out the car was yours. Two questions, Mars: how'd you pull it off, and why?"

I didn't have to pretend I was dazed. I was sapped by a pro. "Give me a minute. I need a drink. There's a pint of gin in the bottom desk drawer."

Blount nodded to Copley and the thug walked around my desk. He came back with the bottle and uncorked it. Sam split my lip shoving it between my teeth and poured enough down my throat to all but drown me. I coughed a lot and when I quit, Blount said. "The only reason you're still breathing, Mars, is you can't be in this on your own. Somebody put you up to the charade, and you're going to tell me who."

Hatfield rabbit punched me from behind and my head lolled to the side. Before I could catch my breath, Copley hit me square in the nose and blood sprayed down the front of my topcoat.

"Now, Mars, start talking."

I'd been in this situation plenty of times, but, always on the other team. I gave him a bloody grin. "I'm not telling you a damned thing. You're going to kill me anyway. Don't waste my time. Just get it over with."

After a considerable amount of applied violence with no results, Blount said, "He's not gonna talk. Take him to the river."

In ten minutes I was being hauled across a pier past a fleet of empty coal barges and looking into the dark water of the Monongahela River. Copley held me while Hatfield tied a concrete block to my ankle with a piece of rope. "Any last words, Mars?"

"If your momma charged money, she'd be rich."

Hatfield gut punched me to knock out my wind and before I could catch another breath, they picked me up to throw me in the river.

The beam of a flashlight shone down the pier. "Hey, what's going on here?" Hatfield and Copley heaved me over the edge. I hit the water with a splash and they took off as the watchman came running, blowing a whistle to call for help.

The Monongahela is deep, fast, and in November cold as a witch's tit. I figured I was done, but I was lucky the river was high that night. A second after I hit the water, the concrete block and I landed on a narrow lip sticking out of the pier below the surface. If the watchman hadn't come along, Copley and Hatfield would have seen me sit up gasping for air and finished the job.

They took the roll of cash from my pocket, but, being wise in the ways of the Underworld, I split the money up in every pocket of my suit plus both of my shoes. A twenty dollar bill persuaded the watchman to forget it ever happened.

I was shivering from the wet and the cold, but I walked six or eight blocks staying in the shadows in case Copley and Hatfield were watching and I caught a cab at the end of the Sixth Street Bridge. Instead of going back to my office, I went to Mason's place. I must've looked even worse than I felt, because as soon as he saw me, he said, "Holy Moses, whose husband caught up with you?"

I looked in the mirror over his bathroom sink and surveyed the damage. I'd done worse to other people and gotten worse myself once or twice. I closed my eyes and concentrated on my own face. It hurt like hell, but when the snakes quit crawling and I opened my eyes, my nose was its regular shape, my jaw was back in line, and the knot on my forehead was gone. I'd need a little makeup to hide some discoloration, but I'd pass muster.

"Mason, I need you to do two things for me: pick up a few items from my office and loan me your car."

I couldn't risk moving my car; it would give away the inconvenient fact that I wasn't dead. While Mason was gone, I called Lila's friend again and left a message for her to call me at Mason's number. It was a half hour before she finally rang back.

"You're alive."

"You sound surprised."

"Blount came here a while ago. I stood outside Ambrose's study and heard them talking. Blount said his men killed you."

"I'm glad they still think so. I have to move quickly before they tumble that I'm still breathing. Is there anybody else at the house with you?"

"Right now, only the butler and he leaves at ten."

"Tell me about your house."

Mason came back a few minutes after Lila hung up. I was lucky. Blount's boys didn't have time to tear up the tuxedo or search my car. I was even luckier that they didn't think twice about Larry Hobbes's scarf in my pocket. Mason found it lying on the floor beside my desk. I hung it over the lapels of the tux. "Give me the photo."

I stared at it for a full minute then closed my eyes. When I heard Mason say, "Hell's Bells," I knew it worked. "Don't try to sing," he said. It'll blow your cover."

My original plan involved letting Pratchett see me, just a fleeting glimpse at a window or as he drove by in his car to soften him up, but Blount sped up my agenda. I would have to go full bore and hope that the ghost of Larry Hobbes could scare Pratchett into a confession.

The pantry door of Pratchett's mansion in Shadyside was unlocked as promised. I stepped into the darkened kitchen and slipped black wool socks over my shoes to let me tread quietly over the hardwood floors. Up the back stairs and down the hallway to the door marked with a silk stocking draped over the knob.

I heard snoring from the other side of the door. I took more than a minute to turn the knob and another to ease the door inward making no noise at all. A faint light from an adjoining powder room bathed the place in a soft glow. A big four poster bed dominated the room and under a mound of covers I found Ambrose Pratchett. His shock of white hair lay against a satin pillow case, and his prominent nose and chin made the i.d. positive. Lila was nowhere to be seen; probably slept in her own room.

I tiptoed to the side of the bed and yanked off the covers then stepped back so he could he see me full height. Pratchett's eyes popped open, startled. "What—who?"

"Hello, Pratchett," I whispered. I lit a cigarette with Tenney's lighter, letting Pratchett get a good gander at my face in the flickering light. "Remember me?"

He slithered backward and up against the carved oak headboard, as if he were trying to push himself through it to escape. His eyes bulged in shock.

When humans are confronted with danger, their hands either come up swinging as fists, or they come up palms out as if to shield the eyes from a terrifying sight. Pratchett's hands were out like a traffic cop at a stop light. "Hobbes. You're not real. You're dead."

"Sure I am, Pratchett, I said, fingering the scarf. You killed me."

"No! No, I didn't! It was Tenney!" His eyes darted from one corner of the room to the other.

"Tenney stabbed me on your orders so you'll keep his wife and kids when he dies from cancer. You might as well have stuck me with the knife yourself."

"This is a dream," he gasped. You're not real."

"Guess again." I stepped forward, grabbed his ankle and yanked him out of the bed. He fell hard on the floor. He cowered against the night table.

"You killed me, Pratchett, and I'll be here to haunt you every night of your life 'til you come clean. Confess, Pratchett! Confess!"

He reached behind him and yanked open the night stand drawer. He came up with a .38 revolver and fired it at me. Once. Twice. I didn't flinch. He panic fired three-four-five. I took a step forward. Six. I took another step toward him.

Pratchett threw the gun. Lucky for me he wasn't much of a pitcher. It whistled past my ear. I heard it clatter in the corner behind me.

I leaned over the cringing politician, one of the most powerful men in Pittsburgh whimpering like a child and sitting in his own puddle in striped silk pajamas. "No! No!" he cried, crossing his arms over his face. "I'm sorry! I'm sorry!"

"Sorry for what, Pratchett?"

But he never answered the question. His hands dropped from his face and clutched his chest. Pratchett fell over sideways, rattled in his throat and died.

"Poor Ambrose. I guess the shock was just too much for his heart." In the mirror I saw Lila Levitsky Pratchett in the bedroom doorway with a small automatic aimed at my back. I turned and she gasped. "My God!"

Her hand wavered and she dropped the gun. Her hands covered her mouth. "Larry," she stammered. "You look just like Larry."

I walked over to the doorway and kicked the pistol into the hall. "You were going to shoot me, weren't you?"

"Yes—no—I mean . . ."

"What a nice little package. You didn't tell me the old geezer had a bum heart. Now he's dead, you inherit all his cash and you take me out of the picture. No loose ends. Cute."

"No, Mars, you've got me all wrong." She stared into my face—Larry's face, actually. "I was only going to shoot you if I had to. Yes, I planned on Ambrose having a heart attack, but if it didn't work, I was going to shoot him myself."

"And pin it on me?"

"Don't be stupid, Mars. If the cops hauled you in you'd crow like a rooster and I'd be in a cell next to you. I couldn't kill both of you with the same gun. Besides, didn't I switch the bullets in his gun for blanks?"

She had me there. "Speaking of cops, I guess I'd better get out of here before you call for the meat wagon." I turned to leave and she pulled at my arm.

"No. Wait." She framed my face with her hands. "You look so much like him. You are him." She rose on her toes and kissed me hard on the mouth.

"Hey, listen, I . . ."

Lila put her fingertips over my mouth. "Shh. Don't talk. It spoils the illusion," she said as her dressing gown fell to the floor. She took the ends of the scarf and pulled her face to mine. I never made love with a stiff in the room before, but I guess there's a first time for everything.

Later, we lay in the satin sheets blowing smoke rings at the ceiling.

"You know, Lila," I said I still have Blount to worry about."

"I think I can handle Hugo," she said. "You just lay low for a while. Shouldn't be too tough with your talent." She was quiet for a minute, but I could hear the gears whirring in her scheming head. "So, Mars, who do you know who has cancer?"

The End

Miami Misadventure
A Tale of the
Second Life of D.B. Cooper
by Nicholas Ahlhelm

Miami. I hate Miami.

As he made his way slowly up U.S. 1, Coop couldn't help but question how he found himself going back to a city with so many bad memories. Sure it was only a couple hours up from the town he called home. But Key West was filled with life: strange restaurants, colorful crowds and a penchant for ribaldry dating back to the age of pirates. Miami was all about money and coke. And most of the money came from the coke.

He knew he didn't have a choice. Grigori made that clear. While his old handler may not be with the feds anymore, he certainly could bring the kind of heat that Coop didn't want to see. He earned his nickname down in Key West due to his resemblance to the legendary hijacker. It wouldn't do to have anyone find out that he was actually the man that walked away with two hundred thousand dollars back in seventy-one. He did everything he could to cover up his youthful appearance at the time. It allowed him to go over a decade without attention. Grigori could end that with just a phone call.

I'm here because I'm over a barrel. I don't have to like it, but I do have to deal with it.

He pulled his seventy-seven Bandit up into a McDonald's parking lot and parked it as near to the building as he could. He didn't drive the car much back in the Keys, preferring a simple scooter on the narrow roads, but he kept the Bandit in case he needed to travel far or fast.

He looked around the lot as he walked towards the door. He saw no sign of his contact on the outside. Grigori told him to look out for a BRAT, the Japanese knockoff of the El Camino. He saw a couple trucks in the lot, but nothing like the tiny car-pickup hybrid.

Something doesn't feel right. He tried to push the thought aside as he opened the door and walked out of the fading summer sun and into the restaurant. He knew Miami made him uneasy. It was probably just that unease clouding his judgment. This was a simple pick up and transport job. Nothing he should have to worry about too hard. Grigori promised him.

He started up to the counter. He wasn't particularly a fan of greasy fast food, but he doubted he would have a chance to eat on the road. Coop didn't know what he was meant to carry, but he knew if Grigori was bringing him in, it was too valuable for any unnecessary stops.

The kid at the counter couldn't have been much over sixteen with a pockmarked face and the faintest hint of stubble on his upper lip. He dripped with sweat. As Coop met the boy's eyes, he could see the fear in them.

It wasn't fear of him. Coop doubted his beach bum shorts, baggy Hawaiian shirt and ragged Converses made him look like any kind of threat. No, it was something else. Someone else. Coop knew why his contact wasn't outside yet. He had walked into a trap.

"Get down," he said calmly to the boy. He focused his mind on the kid as he said it and felt his own power flow out with the words. The kid dropped to the ground, unable to do anything but comply to Coop's psychic nudge.

He threw his right hand past the unbuttoned top of his shirt. He found the holster inside and pulled the Hardballer from it. He didn't much care for pistols, but the AMT felt good in his hand. He knew how to use it, even if he had hoped his days of killing were long past.

The men came up from behind the counter, on either side of where the pock-marked kid disappeared. Coop didn't wait to take aim. They each carried Uzis, ready to cut him down. The government spooks recruited him for more than just his nudge. He was one of the best marksmen in Project Stargate. He dropped one of his would-be killers with three rounds to the heart before most men could even react.

He threw his body to the left as the other killer opened fire. The problem with modern thugs is they depended too much on their automatic weapons. The Uzi was a fine gun, but like any weapon on full auto, it offered little or no ability to aim. So the goon just sprayed it about where Coop was. A person quick on their feet could avoid death for at least a few seconds.

And that was all he needed.

Coop threw his body up and over a table. As he slid across, he sent another bullet straight into the skull of the other killer. But he didn't have time to take the shot and stop his own momentum. He kept going right over the far end of the table and crashed to the floor in a heap. He snapped right back up, glad no one was still alive to see that.

He ran across the room and leaped over the counter. The order-taker was still on the floor shaking. Coop ignored him, instead dropping two more bullets into the second gunman. He wasn't going to risk getting shot from behind while he talked to the kid. He took a second to check both bodies before he bent down next to the teen.

"Did they say anything to you, kid? Did they say what they wanted?"

The kid met his eyes, but didn't say anything. He was clearly in shock. Coop knew he wouldn't get anything else out of him.

"Calm down," Coop said with a nudge. "Take slow deep breaths. You shouldn't move from this spot until the cops come."

The kid nodded. He closed his eyes and took ragged but calming breaths.

Coop stood back up from behind the counter and stared straight down the barrel of another Uzi.

"Don't move or I'll blow your head off."

Coop couldn't quite believe his eyes. Espionage was a man's world. Sure, women would be recruited now and then, but they were mostly already in place, ladies with loose morals willing to sell out their dictator boyfriends or drug-dealing husbands. They weren't the type to perform wetworks. Apparently, times had changed.

The woman with the Uzi was absolutely stunning. She looked Puerto Rican, or maybe Cuban, with honey colored skin and flowing black hair. Her eyes were covered by solid black sunglasses, while her body was covered with a pair of daisy dukes and an abbreviated tank top. She was a thing of beauty—and also threatening to kill him right now.

"Hey, gorgeous, I'm not here for a fight. Your boys behind the counter picked it, not me."

She smirked at him. It wasn't a happy smile, but more a look of derision. "You are a fool, American. You think you are so much better than the rest of the world. Yet you oppress the people of my country; force us to be your 'protectorate'. I revel in watching your society crumble. I enjoy watching this city tear itself apart with drugs and violence. And I suspect I will enjoy watching you die once you've passed me the black box."

Coop couldn't help but laugh.

"I don't know what beef you're trying to make Puerto Rico have with Miami, lady, and I don't really care. But I can't help you here. I don't have anything. I'm here as the pickup man, not the delivery guy."

"You lie! Give me the black box now."

"I didn't even know I was here for a black box. I just showed up to meet my contact and your two dead buddies back there decided to ambush me." He let the nudge slip out with his next words as he focused on her. "Now why don't you lower that weapon and we can talk about this like rational people."

"You take me for some kind of fool?"

Always has to be the strong-willed ones, Coop thought. *Now I've got to try and talk my way out of getting shot.*

"Alright, let's start over here. We need to talk this out. My name is Coop. I was hired to pick up a package, take it across town and deliver it to the Palm Beach Airport where it will fly off to whatever covert endeavor it is needed for. I didn't ask what it was, because that's not in the job description. I'm just the transporter and I didn't want to be that in the first place. Mostly because I don't like to have Uzis leveled at my head. Now, you know me and why I'm here. It's your turn."

She lowered her sunglasses and met his eyes for the first time. Her eyes were noticeably different in color. One was a dark brown, the other a deep green. He understood now why she wore the glasses. It was far too obvious a physical trait for undercover work.

"My name is Valentina. I was told a delivery man would arrive at this time. I was told to intercept him. If you are not this man, then where has this delivery man gone?"

"That I don't know. I think we're at an impasse, darling. Maybe you should put the gun down."

Her grip tightened on the weapon. She certainly knew her stuff. Coop didn't mind—so did he.

"Look, lady. You can either stare me down with that gun until the cops come and arrest us both or we can get out of here and figure this out. I'm a bigger fan of the second option personally, but the balls pretty much in your court now."

Valentina glanced out the windows. Coop knew he had her. She probably had a record herself. Sure, it probably didn't involve hijacking a plane and a quarter of a million dollars, but she still didn't want to be caught.

"You make a good point. Your car is still outside?"

Coop nodded.

"Come on then."

She waved him along with her gun. Coop wasted no time in running across the empty McDonald's to the front door. She was a step behind him. *I could probably take her, disarm her and escape, but I need to see how this plays out. I am here to do a job and whether I like the way it came about, I still have to finish it.*

As they ran through the doors an overwhelming foreboding came over him. He glanced down the street and saw a black van pulling around the corner. The side door was open and as it closed, he saw the barrels of automatic rifles.

"Down!" Coop didn't wait for Valentina to respond. He grabbed her by the arm and yanked her to the ground.

Seconds later, glass shattered above their heads. The plate windows on the outside of the restaurant exploded into thousands of tiny fragments as hundreds of bullets riddled them. From this angle, they would have a hard time hitting Coop and Valentina, but he could feel the shards of glass cut up the back of his legs and arms.

"I am so tired of this crap," he mumbled to himself.

He turned to Valentina and saw the fear in her eyes. She was hard, but she feared death.

Coop reached out and yanked the Uzi from her hand before she could react. He bounded to his feet as he heard the screech of the van's tires. They were coming around again to make sure they finished the job.

He sent a three bullet burst into the front of the car. The driver swerved a bit, but he caught Coop's eyes.

"Stop!" Coop yelled, pushing every ounce of the nudge out in his words. The driver might have a hard time hearing the command, but the motion of Coop's mouth and the anger in its delivery would be enough to convey the point.

I just hope he's weaker willed than the girl.

The tires squealed as the driver slammed on the brakes. Coop wasted no time as he quickly started to circle the van towards the open door. He took aim with the submachine gun and let fly. Still off center from the sudden stop, the gunmen didn't know what hit them as the bullets cut them to shreds.

Coop turned back to Valentina. "You know any of these guys?"

She shook her head.

"Great, that means we've both been left out to dry. I don't know what this package is, but someone else has decided they want it and they're willing to kill everyone in the way."

"So where does that leave us? We're on a crime scene, the courier has stolen the box and we're left whistling in the wind."

"Maybe not," Coop said. "We should still have one would-be assassin to tell us."

He turned to the front of the van. The driver wasn't in sight. He knew he was outnumbered and hoped to get away with his life.

"Come out and surrender," Coop said. He already knew his nudge worked on the guy, so it was no surprise when the door opened. The driver climbed out, unarmed and with both hands in the air.

"Great, we have a prisoner," Valentina said. "How does that help us? It's not like he'll just tell us what we need to know."

Coop didn't bother to respond. His attention stayed focused on the driver and the nudge. "Who hired you to kill us?"

"Fernando Aguilar."

"No," Valentina yelled from behind them. "My Fernando wouldn't do that! He's as devoted to the cause as I am!"

Coop turned towards her. He put one finger perpendicular to his lips. Valentina looked angry but she fell silent.

"Why did Aguilar want to kill his own men? Why even bother with us if he's got the package?"

"He doesn't have the package," the driver said. "The C.I.A. offered him some kind of deal. They would get the D.E.A. and F.B.I. off our backs in exchange for his help in taking care of anyone else hoping to get their hands on it. The C.I.A. set up this meet to get rid of anyone else that would get in the way."

"What is it? What does the C.I.A. want so badly?"

"I don't know. That's need to know."

"Yeah, of course it is," Coop said. "What do you know about the courier? Where are they taking it?"

"I know they're heading north, to Boynton Beach. Aguilar has locked down a marina up there. I'm guessing that Half is going out that way."

"Half? Is that the courier's name?"

"I'm not sure. It might just be a code name or something. They don't tell us everything, man."

"I know that area well," Valentina said. "Fernando owns the marina he's talking about. I can take us there. I want answers to why he would let me walk into a deathtrap. He…" She turned away, unwilling to continue.

"Get back in the cab and wait for the police," Coop said to the driver. He didn't know how long Aguilar paid to keep the fuzz off the scene, but they could only stay away so long. He didn't wait to make sure the driver took his place, as the weak willed fool was easy enough to manipulate. He knew they needed to move. If they didn't hurry, they would never catch up with Half, whoever he was.

He walked towards the Bandit which appeared to have avoided the hail of gunfire. He grabbed Valentina as he walked and pulled her alongside him.

"Look, it's hard when someone you think loves you betrays you. But it happens, Valentina. You were dating a drug dealer. A man that imports cocaine into the United States while racking up millions of dollars, all at the expense of dozens—maybe hundreds—of lives a year. You can't expect a man like that to be all sunshine and roses. A man like that has only one interest, his own power. And

I'm guessing your little anti-American tirades were getting in the way of his profits."

She again glared at him, but said nothing. She followed him to the Bandit and hopped into the passenger seat. Seconds later, they were peeling out of the parking lot and heading north up the highway.

"We can make the wharf in maybe an hour," she said. "But this Half will be gone by then. What do you hope to do?"

"Press my luck," Coop said. He pushed the pedal to the floor. The Bandit accelerated quickly to ninety miles per hour as he whipped through traffic as fast as he could.

● ● ●

If Coop knew one thing, it was that a low profile paid off when you were playing secret operative. Half wouldn't want to draw any unwanted attention. He wouldn't break the flow of traffic or do anything blatantly illegal. Drawing the attention of the cops was not in his favor, even if he did have a friendly crime boss paying the police to look the other way.

Coop didn't care. He was a fugitive, but he had avoided more than one scrape before. The nudge always seemed to work well on beat cops, guys trained to comply on a regular basis. The occasional one strong-willed enough to resist it could usually be deterred with the right timing.

Or so he hoped as he sped through the middle of downtown Miami. But he suspected he had Valentina's former love or his C.I.A. contacts to thank for his good fortune. The police were nowhere to be found today. They were purposefully avoiding the route and that gave Coop and Valentina a chance.

By the time they cruised out of Fort Lauderdale, he caught sight of it. A brown BRAT moving along at a steady forty-five miles per hour. Coop started to slow as he came up on it. The car wasn't exactly everywhere, but he couldn't risk it being the wrong vehicle. Nor could he risk spooking the driver.

"Is that him?" Valentina asked from the passenger seat. "We need to stop him."

"We need to be sure it's him, first. If we knock some random BRAT off the road and it isn't our courier, we've lost any chance we've had to make up time. I want this guy as much as you, but we can't risk a huge mistake."

"Who are you? You know far more than just some hired wheelman. You aren't a government agent either or it would be you behind that wheel. So what is going on here? Who do you work for?"

"Sister, I wish I knew. I'm just a guy with a certain set of skills that I don't particularly like to use. Folks mostly call me Coop, and that's as good a name as any I suppose. And I wish I knew exactly who I was working for. It ain't the government and it isn't your syndicate. I know just as much about them as you do. But they've got me over a barrel and until I learn more, I work for them."

"I see," Valentina said. "I know what it is like to serve whether you wish it or not. My entire life has been built around one form of service or another. My parents made my sisters and I work from morning to night even as children. The heroin we grew brought the attention of your government. They came in with guns loaded. My parents died that day, as did my sisters. I only survived by falling into the ocean by my home. Fernando's father found me. He trained me for a new kind of service; one I suspect is not unlike your own."

"Same job, different bosses. It's a story as old as time."

Valentina said nothing for several minutes. She just stared out her window, glancing once in awhile back to the BRAT they trailed. "Americano, do you see the Suburban behind us to the right?"

Coop glanced in his own rear view window. He had passed the ugly thing when he was speeding towards the BRAT. It was a pretty typical vehicle on a road like this, decked out in white and red. It didn't seem out of the ordinary. "What of it?"

"They've stayed steadily behind us for the last ten minutes. Pretty much in the same spot at the same speed."

"You think they're watching us? A spotter vehicle for the courier?"

"I think it's a strong possibility."

"Well then, I guess we test it."

"What...?"

Coop stomped on the gas pedal before she could finish the question. The Bandit shot forward, easily closing the distance between it and the BRAT. He glanced up at the rear view mirror. He could almost hear the Suburban's engine revving as it sped up on them. It came up on them hard, faster than he would expect from something that huge. It would be a matter of seconds before they were on him and he knew what to expect then.

"I guess that answers that question," Coop said. "Take the wheel. I want you to stay on the BRAT. I'll catch up with you at the marina."

She reached over to take the wheel as he started to rise. "Wait, what are you planning to do?"

"You'll see."

Valentina knew what she was doing. They barely lost an ounce of speed as Coop climbed up through the top of the car and onto the back of his seat. She slid in behind him.

The Suburban was almost parallel to them. Coop watched the rear side door pop off. It flew back and away far faster than Coop found comfortable as he thought about exactly what he was planning to do.

He took a deep breath, before he took one bounding step onto the passenger seat and then threw himself out towards the other vehicle.

You're going to pay for this, Grigori!

He flew straight towards the opening, their slight lead on the Suburban just enough to give him the proper trajectory.

He smashed hard into the man nearest the door, knocking the AK-47 out of the killer's hand before he could raise it. If felt like he collided with solid steel, but Coop was mostly glad he was still alive. Now he just needed to stay that way.

His hand went for the AK on the floor as he rolled off the big man. He brought

it up off the ground just as another assault rifle was aimed his way. He pulled the trigger, hoping against hope the safety was already off.

The round went straight through the heart of the killer across from him. Coop followed with two more quick pulls. He didn't like to take chances.

His eyes went to the front seat just in time to see the Smith & Wesson 29 leveled his way.

"Miss," he screamed with the nudge, even as he dropped down to the vehicle's floor. As the bullet exploded above him, Coop wondered how many other criminals were cop movie fans like Dirty Harry here.

He didn't take any more time to contemplate it. Instead he brought up the stock of the AK and drove it hard into Harry's side. Harry lost his focus as the wind was forced out of him. Coop came all the way off the floor and swung the stock again, this time into the side of Harry's skull. Harry slumped over, dead or unconscious as Coop turned the barrel of the gun towards the driver.

"Hi there, name's Coop. You and me are going for a little drive."

The driver glanced his way, but didn't say anything. He just smiled.

"What makes you…?

A club struck him hard on the right side of his back. It knocked him off balance and into the rear seat. He looked up and saw Harry was on his feet still somehow, but Harry looked a bit different. There wasn't a bruise on his face where Coop smacked him. Instead there was a bit of torn skin and the metal beneath. He couldn't quite believe his eyes, but he didn't have time to figure out how Dirty Harry turned into the Six Million Dollar Man.

Harry came back at him, but Coop wasn't asking questions anymore. He brought up the barrel of the gun and sent three rounds straight into Harry's chest. Harry's body bounced back as each bullet impaled him with a sharp ping, but he slumped forward and off the seat when the damage was done. Blood spilled out over the floor of the van.

He swung the barrel back towards the drive. "What the hell, man?"

"You will die, American *schwein*."

"Alright, so German. Hans, what the hell are you?"

"I have no answers for you, American."

Coop stared at the other man as he continued to drive down the road. He could question the guy; make him answer with the nudge. But the nudge and ongoing traffic didn't mix, unless he nudged him towards driving.

"Alright, pal. You can sit silent if you want." He pushed out with the nudge as he spoke again. "Take me to your rendezvous point. Let's meet your boss."

Hans said nothing, but the Suburban accelerated as it sped to its destination.

● ● ●

The Suburban pulled into Aguilar Marina just as the sun hit its noon time peak. "Don't say anything," Coop said to Hans with just a hint of the nudge. He wasn't sure if it was the robotic parts or just a natural urge to follow the leader, but the driver was surprisingly easy to push.

He saw his Bandit and the BRAT parked in front of the marina, but saw no sign of either the courier or Valentina. It made sense. Any business they wanted to finish would be handled out back, where the boats were moored.

"Take a nap," Coop nudged one last time. Hans looked at him for just a second before he closed his eyes. Within a few seconds, he was snoring heavily.

Coop climbed over the remains of the other robot-men and climbed out the passenger door. He threw the AK's strap over his shoulder and let it dangle on his back. It would keep it out of immediate view but keep it close enough that he could use it.

He didn't bother entering the marina. It looked empty from out front and he could easily get around it from the outside. He started around it, staying close to the building in the hopes of avoiding any surprises.

Coop didn't much care for surprises, but he knew he was walking into a complete unknown. He didn't much like that either. He took short, quiet breaths to keep calm as he made his approach. He heard voices as he made his way around the building.

"I really am sorry about this, Valentina, but I knew you just wouldn't understand."

As he came around the corner, Coop saw Valentina near the edge of the pier. Two hulks held her tight. Coop could only assume they were more metal-men like Hans and his pals. Another pair of figures stood on the very edge of the peer, but both where clothes far too heavy for the Miami heat. One appeared to be a younger man, while the other was hunched like someone far too old to be here.

A boat was still docked in front of her. A heavy-set Hispanic man stood on the edge, flanked by two armed guards. A cocky half grin filled his face. This could only be the infamous Fernando Aguilar.

Valentina spit at him. Though she got surprising distance with it, it smacked the side of the boat beneath Aguilar. "You're working with these American *comemierdas*. You promised me you would stay true to the cause. You promised..."

"You were just a means to an ends, Valentina. No one works as hard as a true believer. And I won't pretend you weren't good in my bed. But in the end, business is business. I don't have time for any causes. I don't have time for you. You would be dead already if *Señor* Tundra didn't say he had a purpose for you."

"They aren't even human. I know why they called the courier Half now. Because he is only *half* man!"

The older figure beside her cackled. This must be Tundra. "It has been quite some time since anyone dared to call me that, my dear. Yes, my son and I are half human, half machine. The Fuhrer respected my creations during the war and the C.I.A. was only too willing to overlook my supposed war crimes in exchange for the technology I brought. And while my robotic men are quite formidable, I will return with a weapon of far greater power."

Fernando held up a box maybe six inches square. "Doesn't seem like much, but I trust *Señor* Tundra knows what he's talking about. Now stop struggling, Valentina. We have a ride to take and a delivery to finish."

The two big men pulled Valentina towards the deck of the ship. Coop knew this was his only chance. He needed to stop this and he needed to do it quick.

His nudge may have brought him into Project Stargate's purview two decades earlier, but they hadn't stopped there. They trained him to be an expert killer.

He pulled the AK-47 up and lined up the gun just below his eye line. He took a quick aim and let off a round. Coop moved the gun just a bit to the left and fired again. Then he lowered it a bit back to the right and fired a third and final round. Though it felt like an eternity as he pulled the trigger, he knew the entire act took just over a second.

The foreheads of the men on either side of Fernando exploded as the rounds landed perfectly in their skull. The third bullet was aimed for Fernando's hand, but it caught his shoulder instead. He stumbled forward and let the package slide out of his hand and on to the ramp between the ship and the pier.

He turned the gun towards the two brutes holding Valentina, but they were already throwing her to the side. They charged at him, each pulling a pistol from their pants. He let out a shot at the forehead of the first, but it reflected off his metal skull with a ping.

"Well, damn," Coop said as they drew a bead on him. He could fire back, but they had him cold and he didn't have any cover.

"You don't want to do this," he yelled putting the nudge behind it.

Tundra laughed behind the two gunmen. "We know of your psychic abilities, young man. My men have shut down their audio receptors. Whether you could assert your influence matters not at all."

"Well, I guess you've got me. Now where's that leave us?"

"I would love to dissect you. Perhaps I could find out something new for my robot-men, but alas there is no time. You will just have to die, Mister Cooper."

Cooper? They don't have Stargate's information on me, just the C.I.A.'s. Otherwise they would know my real name.

"Come on now. You've caught D.B. Cooper. Isn't that worth anything?"

"I'm afraid not," Tundra said. "End his..."

A red-winged jet shot over the marina. It moved at blinding speed as it rained bullets down on to the pier. Tundra's half-men didn't stand a chance. The rounds ripped them to shreds. A second later, the boom of its supersonic flight shook the entire structure.

I've apparently got a friend I didn't know. Let's not let his assistance go to waste.

"Valentina, get the package!"

The girl dived to the ground and grabbed the still intact package. As she hit the ground, Coop took aim at Tundra and his kid. He let fly with three quick rounds on semi-automatic. They took Tundra off the pier and into the water. He turned his aim towards the kid, but he was already diving from the pier beside his father.

"Go! Go!" Fernando's words cut through the chaos. The boat ripped away from the pier, the ramp tearing from its moorings. Valentina had one foot on it still and was sent spinning into the air.

Coop dropped the AK and ran towards her as she flew nearly ten feet up. He reached her just in time to catch her as she plummeted back down. She still held the box in her hands.

Her gaze flashed out to the water. "Fernando, he's getting away!"

"Not likely," Coop said as he lowered her back to the wood of the pier. "Look."

The jet, now going much slower, flew straight towards the boat. Coop watched as dozens of rounds ripped apart Fernando's ship before he could hope to make his escape. The ship almost immediately shifted in the water as the jet made another turn. It was taking in water fast and its engines were dead. Fernando wasn't going anywhere. He would have a good long sit until the harbor patrol could pick him up.

"Who is that?" Valentina asked.

"I suspect that's who is supposed to get this package," Coop said, "which makes me even more curious about what it is."

"Let's find out," she said. Only a simple latch held the package shut. It wasn't even secured by a lock. She flipped the lid open. They both stared down into the mysterious weapon Tundra and the C.I.A. wanted so bad.

All they saw was a patch of grass and moss sitting in some fresh soil.

"That was a bit anticlimactic," Coop said. "Any idea?"

"I've got nothing," Valentina said. "Is it some kind of trick from the C.I.A.? A bomb, perhaps?"

Coop shook his head. "Maybe our friend will have some answers."

The jet was moving slow as it struck the water just a few hundred yards in front of them. Coop hadn't seen any pontoons on the thing before, nor did he know of any jets that used pontoons, but they were there now. He suspected something was a bit off about the red-winged craft, but he only had so many questions he still wanted to ask today.

It only took a matter of a minute for the jet to come into the dock. It pulled up exactly where Fernando's boat had been earlier. The cockpit popped open and a young kid not much over twenty jumped up and out. The kid wore a red coat and a pair of jodhpurs right out of an old aviator flick. He climbed across a wing and dropped off it on to the pier.

"I guess you're the courier."

"Something like that," Coop said. "And you are?"

"Davy Nelson. It's a pleasure to meet you, Mister..."

"Coop. Just Coop. And that's Valentina. You understand how much trouble we've went through to get your bundle of grass for you? I'm not exactly a fan of fighting the C.I.A., let alone crime families and half-men."

"Half-men? Was Colonel Von Tundra here?"

"He called himself Tundra," Coop said. "I shot him. He'll wash ashore in a day or two."

"It makes sense. He's always had a thing for the mysterious. Though I doubt sincerely he's dead. I haven't managed to kill him in the past forty years. I would suspect he'll be back to bother me again." Nelson shook his head. "But where's my manners? Thank you so much for this, Coop. I would have come earlier if I suspected Half-Man was involved. That's the package?"

Coop nodded. He was still trying to figure out the forty year comment, even though he knew the kid probably wasn't even twenty-five. He didn't think Nelson would give him any satisfying answer. Instead, Coop just gave Valentina a slight nudge. With a reluctant sigh, she walked to the aviator and handed him the box of grass.

"I have to know," she said as she put the box in Nelson's hands, "why all this over some grass?"

"Believe it or not, that grass is an old friend of mine. In the wrong hands, I suspect he could be used for something horrific. I'll take care of him; see that he grows back among friends."

"Right," Coop said. Valentina only stared at the pilot.

"The police will be here soon," Nelson said. "We all should be going. Thank you for your help, Coop. Valentina."

He gave both of them a quick handshake before he turned back to his jet. He hopped back up on to the wing like a man born to fly. Perhaps he was, Coop thought.

Nelson turned back just as he dropped into the cockpit.

"If you ever decide to come back in, Coop, look me up. Just ask for Airboy."

Coop nodded as the jet slowly moved back into the water.

His dad told him Airboy stories growing up. Coop didn't quite know how the young guy was the same guy that fought in World War II, but he learned a long time ago this world was far weirder than anyone could ever hope to comprehend.

Instead he just turned to Valentina. "Looks like we're both back at square one. Care to get a drink?"

Valentina smiled. "I thought you would never ask. But this time, I'm driving."

Coop laughed as they made their way back to the Bandit, the carnage of the pier behind him.

The End

Moonlight and the White Mule

by Terry Alexander

Henry Cole's nose wrinkled in disgust. He stared down at the dirt crusted snoring man wallowing in the filthy mattress. Chuck Osborne reeked of stale tobacco and bad whiskey, his long unkempt hair matted to his head, particles of food embedded in his rough scraggly beard.

"Come on, Chuck." He kicked the bed. "Wake up. Get on your feet."

"What?" Chuck mumbled. He sat up, holding his head. He slowly rolled to the edge of the bed and swung his feet to the floor. "Who's there? Who is it?"

"It's Henry." He wrapped his hand around Chuck's wrist and pulled him to his feet. "Now get out of that bed."

"Leave me alone, Henry. Please leave me alone."

Henry kicked an empty bottle across the room. It clattered against the far wall. "It's time to crawl out of this pig sty."

"Quit shouting. My head's bustin' open." Chuck moaned.

"Good it's time to get back to living and climb out of the bottle." He manhandled Chuck across the room and threw him roughly in a hand made chair.

"Please, Henry. Please leave me alone."

"I've left you alone too long. It's time to rejoin the world. Lilly's gone and she ain't coming back."

"Don't talk about her like that." Chuck's fist thumped the table. "Lilly is a decent woman."

"Lilly's a trollop. She ran out on you." Henry's large hands fisted on his hips, a look of contempt wrinkled his face. "She ran off to the big city to find her a rich husband."

"Her family made her do it." Chuck's voice dropped to a whisper.

"She didn't have to go along with them. She could have said no and married you like she promised."

"Her people needed the money." Chuck stared at the trash littered floor, unwilling to meet Henry's eyes.

"We all need money." Henry poked at the dying embers in the wood stove. "Where's the coffee?"

"Why?"

"We're gonna sober you up, and then you're gonna get out of those nasty clothes and clean up."

"Henry, just leave me be."

"You ain't got a pinch of coffee in here. Get your shoes on." He threw a pair of brogans at Chuck's feet. "Come on we're going to Holson creek."

● ● ●

33

Chuck sat at the kitchen table hours later. He nursed a fresh cup of coffee. They had made a side trip by the general store and picked up a tin of Arbuckle's finest. Chuck's damp hair lay plastered to his head. "You nearly drowned me in the creek, you know."

"You weren't in any danger." Henry carried a bundle of clothes to the wash tub. "I'm boiling your clothes, kill out the lice."

"Why are you doing this?"

"I'm leaving in a few days, and I want you back on your feet before I go."

"Where are you going?"

"I know you're not up on the news, but Pancho Villa invaded two America towns, in New Mexico and Texas. The government is sending an army down there to get him, I'm joining up."

"You're joining the army?"

"I leave next week, going to Fort Polk, Louisiana for training."

Chuck shook his head, his gaze centered on a knot in the floor boards. "Do you remember that old story about the white mule?" He asked, lacking any other words. "I've seen it a lot lately."

"You've been drunk for months. It's a wonder you didn't see pink elephants."

"Maybe, but it looked so real. I swear a couple of times there was a woman riding that mule, real pale woman with white hair."

"The water's hot." Henry handed him a straight razor and shaving mug. "It's time to get that brush pile off your face."

"Hope I don't cut my throat." Chuck swirled the bristles in the hot water then in the shaving mug, applying the lather to his face. It felt warm against his skin. "You should have seen that white mule in the moonlight. I swear it was glowing."

"Leave that Elbindo mule alone. It's not a good sign."

Chuck scraped the razor across his jaw. "What did you call it?" "An Elbindo, a white mule with red eyes. An Elbindo."

Chuck shrugged, unwilling to correct his friend's mispronunciation. "I've heard the stories since I was a kid, sacks of buried Confederate gold and that mule watching over it, just waiting to show it to the right person, a special person. That mule would have to be fifty or sixty years old."

"I know of folks who went looking for that white demon, who never showed up again. Don't be one of them." Henry climbed to his feet. "There ain't any hooch left in the house. Do yourself a favor and eat some food. I'll be back before I leave."

"Thanks, Henry." Chuck toweled the remaining soap from his face. A tiny stream of blood flowed from his chin. "I'm out of practice."

"You're a good man when you're sober, Chuck. You need to stay that way."

A nod passed between the two men. Chuck daubed at the blood as Henry passed through the door. He glanced at the clutter in every corner of his small clapboard home. *God I could use a drink and a smoke.* He shook his head. *No, I ain't drinking. I'm gonna clean this place up.*

● ● ●

Hours later, Chuck sat in the same chair. His sweaty shirt stuck to his chest. He surveyed his handiwork. All the freshly cleaned dishes stacked in the cabinet. The floor swept and mopped and a sizable stack of clothes sat in the center of the kitchen table. Work kept the craving at bay. Now they assaulted him with renewed vigor.

He glanced out the single window. He estimated four or five hours of good daylight remained. *Brody could use a run. Old hoss hasn't been out of that pasture in weeks.* Brody stood fourteen hands high, a blue roan gelding wide in the shoulders and hips. He could go all day at a steady clip and not show any ill effects.

Chuck tugged his hat on his head; he grabbed a short length of rope from a peg by the door. Tall grass slapped his legs as he walked along the overgrown path. The roan came to him at the first whistle. Chuck slipped the rope over his head and led him to the barn. The saddle hung from the rafter boards by a rope looped around the horn. The smell of old leather and dried horse sweat wafted around his head, as he fitted blanket and saddle to the gelding. Brody took the bit easily. Chuck adjusted his hat; the leather creaked, as he settled in.

"Come on, boy." He patted the horse's neck. "Let's see what Blue Mountain looks like today."

Blue rises at a steep angle, and levels off for a short distance only to rise again to another flat area in a stair-step fashion. During the climb a person would believe he'd reached the summit, only to find more mountain remained to be conquered.

After an hour, the maddening desire for a drink returned in earnest. Like a physical thing gnawing away at his brain. He licked his lips, time to turn around and go home. His hands lifted the reins, when he saw a splash of white within the tree and brush cover. The mule, it had to be the white mule. Chuck's spurs raked the gelding's sides. The blue horse jumped forward, breaking into a gallop. Brody closed the distance, but still only glimpses of ivory met Chuck's eyes. A low hanging branch snatched the hat from his head, scratching his face.

"Come on, Brody. We're catching up." He rounded a bend in the trail, and caught a glimpse of the mule and rider, the white haired woman from his dreams. The pair disappeared around a large tree.

He lashed Brody's sides with the reins. The roan lunged forward, covering the short distance quickly. All thought of drink vanished from Chuck's mind. He circled the tree, yanking back on the reins. Brody's hind feet plowed the stony earth. Chuck stared in awe at the image before him.

The white mule stood twenty feet away. The most beautiful woman he'd ever laid eyes on sat on its back. Her clenched hands lay on the animal's neck. Brody sucked air greedily, filling his lungs. Chuck urged the horse forward. He reined up opposite the white haired woman.

The woman smiled, her hand rose to her lips, the fist opened. She blew a fine dust into Chucks face. Then wheeled the mule, her bare feet hugging its sides. Chuck closed his eyes against the miniscule particles. He coughed several times, his eyes watering.

Sweat immediately beaded on his forehead, coursing down his face. A wave

of dizziness overwhelmed his senses. Chuck made a grab for the saddle horn and missed. *What's happening to me?* His momentum carried him off his saddle crashing to the ground. He made one feeble attempt to rise and lay still.

● ● ●

The aroma of fresh coffee and sizzling bacon slowly invaded his numbed mind. His eyes blinked open. A sour taste filled his mouth. My God what is this?

"Breakfast is ready." Her pleasant voice grated in his addled mind. "You need to eat to get the taste out of your mouth."

"What happened to me?" Chuck sat up in the corn shuck bed, his boot heels banged on the floor. "What did you do to me?" His hands cradled his pounding head.

"The headache will go away in a few minutes. Come on you need to eat." Her voice held a musical quality. "The dust will wear off in a little while."

"Dust?"

"Leaves and roots, dried and ground down into a fine powder."

She raked her hair away from her face. Chuck looked into her dazzling pale blue eyes, like two orbs of freshly frozen water. "Who are you?"

"Marie Davenport. I'm the witch of Blue Mountain." She smiled showing even white teeth. "Now you really need to eat."

He stared enraptured by her beauty, her smooth skin, the graceful flawless neck and her smile, the most beautiful smile he'd ever seen. His hand pawed the table top for the coffee cup.

"Why are you staring at me?"

Chuck stuffed a slice of bacon in his mouth. "I've never seen a woman like you before." His full mouth mangled the words.

"The dust affects people like that sometime." Marie sipped at her coffee.

Chuck mimicked her actions, a plume of steam rose in his face. He caught himself stealing glances at her, averting his eyes when she looked his way. "How did I get here?"

"Believe me getting you on that big horse wasn't an easy thing. It was all I could do to get you draped over the saddle. Then me and Pappy brought you here."

"Your Daddy's here. I'd like to meet him."

"My Daddy's dead. Pappy's my mule."

"Folks say he's enchanted." Chuck sipped at his coffee.

"He is. He was born on the day my Daddy died. Been here ever since."

"You don't see mules like him everyday."

"It's the potions I use. My mama taught me. I can get any color animal I desire. My Mother and Grandmother were powerful witches and they taught me their secrets. Finish your breakfast. I'll show you around the place."

"Just give me a few minutes." He bit into another strip of bacon.

The sun shined brightly in the morning sky, the green grass bent under his feet. Chuck looked at the clearing, at least fifty acres of smooth clear land. "You know I've been all over this mountain and I've never seen this place before."

"I know. I've seen you riding this way. I wouldn't let you see it then. You're ready now."

"What did you want to show me?"

"My well. I want you to look in my well." She pointed to a stone ring above the ground; a crude slanted roof shaded the opening.

"What's in the well?"

"You'll have to look for yourself." She led him to the rock wall, moving the rope and bucket from a large nail driven into the support post. "Look in the water, tell me what you see."

Chuck leaned over the stone's, staring down at the mirrored surface ten feet below. At first, he only saw his own distorted reflection. The image clouded and slowly changed. "It's Henry. Me and Henry, we're wearing some kind of uniform and, we've got an odd shaped pot on our heads."

"Keep looking."

"We're in a forest. We're packing guns. What's that funny looking mask with a hose we're putting on?"

"You're across the ocean in France, fighting the Germans."

"We're not at war with Germany. Henry's going down Texas way after that Pancho Villa bandit."

"No, you and Henry go to France." Her hands fisted on her hips. "What else do you see?"

"We're on a ship, coming back home. It's not on ordinary ship, this one is special. There's a lot of wounded hurt men topside." He stared more intently at the water. "I see you. We're together."

"I looked in the water yesterday. It showed me the same things." She inhaled a deep breath. "You'll journey to a far away land. Fight many battles and see brave men die, but you will survive." Her eyes looked heavenward. "Then you will come back to me. We were meant to be together."

"I don't understand. What did I just see?"

"You can see the future in my well. This part of the mountain is enchanted." Marie licked her lips. "I know how you've suffered of late. I can ease the cravings for the whiskey and tobacco. I can't end your suffering, only time can do that. You will return to Blue Mountain." She handed him two vials of brownish liquid. "These will help during desperate times, use them wisely."

"I've just got here. I don't want to leave. We've just met, but I know this is right. I belong here." He stuffed the glass containers in his pocket.

A single tear streamed down her face. "I've loved you since I was a little girl. I used to watch you playing, wishing I could join you. Now you must go. Henry will die if you stay."

"Henry's gonna die?" he asked.

"If you stay, Henry will perish, he won't survive without you."

"I reckon I'd better go." He stared at the ground, trying to swallow the sudden lump in his throat. He licked his dry lips and met her eyes. "I'll be back."

Marie nodded. "Pappy will lead you back to your home. When you return, he'll be waiting to bring you back." The grass curled under her bare feet as Marie walked away. "Your horse is saddled and waiting in the barn. Please go now."

Chuck nodded, he turned toward the barn. Each step took a conscious act of will to complete. Pappy trotted up to his side and walked beside him like a trained dog. Brody waited in the barn saddled and ready to go. His left foot found the stirrup and he swung into the saddle. He didn't look back as he followed the mule down the mountain. Chuck knew he'd return to Blue Mountain.

The End

Against Fire and Stone
(A Grim Spectre Tale)
by Ralph L. Angelo Jr.

In 1937 the city of Riverburgh is a mere 40 miles north of Manhattan up the Hudson River. It is a small, but corrupt city. A city where life is as cheap as a ten cent bullet. Up until now there had been no hope in Riverburgh; there had been no one to fight for the citizen on the street, for the helpless. But that has recently changed, for you see Riverburgh has a new champion hunting its streets. They have the ghostly, terrifying creature called The Grim Spectre, and woe be unto any who would harm the helpless in his city!

The fire burned savagely all around The Grim Spectre. The apartment building he stood in was being consumed. The heat was staggering. The smoke-blinding and choking.

Across from The Grim Spectre stood a strange being. He was a big brute of a man dressed in a black vest and slacks. His chest was bare beneath the vest, and his skin color was reminiscent of granite. He smiled evilly at the Spectre, unaffected by both heat and smoke.

"Feeling the heat, Ghost-Man?" The gray skinned brute taunted.

The Grim Spectre said nothing; he merely stared from beneath his skull-faced mask's visage. He was as much a horror to behold as was his foe. He was athletically built beneath a bright white bodysuit. He wore a wide golden belt about his waist and a hood obscured his face for the most part, revealing only a skull face in a diagonal slash from left to right. Both his eyes glowed though, one hidden in shadow, the other terrifyingly visible set into his extremely realistic skull mask. A white cloak almost touched the floor behind him. On his belt hung two .45's as well as a whip on his right side. Beneath the folds of his cloak were hidden several throwing knives.

"Nothin' to say, Ghost-Man? That's okay, 'cause I'll let my fists do the talkin'."

The brute threw himself at The Grim Spectre, outstretched hands grasping for the ghostly apparitions throat.

But they went right through his neck, as if the Spectre was not there! The brutish thug fell chaotically through the intangible hero and stumbled to a stop before the wall of flame. He turned awkwardly with his eyes wide in surprise, facing The Grim Spectre once again.

"Y-You, you really are a ghost aintcha?"

"What I am to you, evil one, is fear," The Grim Spectre's hollow and horrific voice echoed through the burning room.

The Spectre stepped forward and threw a punch that would have shattered a normal man's jaw, instead the concrete colored foe barely flinched and The Grim Spectre cried out in pain and surprise.

He stepped back, grasping his right hand in shock.

"Surprised, Ghost-Man? My skin is like rock, that's why I'm called 'Stone'; I'm like a block of cement."

Stone again leapt for The Grim Spectre's throat with outstretched hands, but this time The Grim Spectre disappeared, as if he was never there.

Stone looked around the burning room in surprise.

The Grim Spectre rose out of the floor behind the seemingly cement-like foe. Favoring his injured hand, The Spectre reached his left hand out and grasped his enemy by the shoulder. Instantly the hand crackled with energy, sending a searing jolt through Stone.

In instant agony, the big man arched backward with his mouth wide!

"Arrrhhh!" he shouted in pain.

Even in agony, Stone spun about and back handed The Grim Spectre away.

"Ha! Gotcha that time, you damned spook. So you *can* be hurt."

"Can I, brute? That, you will have to endeavor harder to prove. But you, you I will make scream in both fear and pain. You will pay for the life of evil you have embraced."

The two antagonists faced each other and began to circle within the burning walls of the apartment building.

Stone lunged at The Grim Spectre and tried to batter him with his stone-like fists, but the Spectre merely became untouchable again and floated through his enemy.

Now they faced each other in opposite positions. Stone began to attack again shouting, "I'll tear you apart, you little spook!"

This time the Spectre pulled his left side .45 and fired repeatedly, each bullet finding its mark on Stones rock hard skin.

"Uggh, Unngg, Arrr," Stone growled with each bullet's powerful impact.

He raised his hands up, covering his face and began to stumble backward under the onslaught.

"So you can be hurt by such a small thing as mortal bullets," The Grim Spectre observed aloud.

"Mebbe so, Ghost-Man, but I'm still gonna send you back to hell."

Stone lunged again, just as the Spectre's .45 ran out of bullets. Tossing the gun aside, The Grim Spectre raised his uninjured hand and it began to crackle and glow again just as Stone collided with him, bowling him over. His left hand coruscated energy when he grasped Stone by the face, sending a powerful jolt through the bigger man's system.

'I can't turn intangible, the shocking touch doesn't work when I'm that way and this is the only thing that's affecting him,' The Grim Spectre thought.

Stone groaned loudly, "Aaaaahh!" and then pounded the Spectre across the collarbone, driving him to his knees, and effectively breaking The Spectre's grip on him.

"Y-You almost got me you damned spook, b-but I'm tough, r-really tough, an' you , I dunno if yer a ghost or just some guy in a costume, but now's the time ta send ya to hell any way you wanna look at it."

Stone grabbed the burning wall behind the downed Grim Spectre, dug his hands into it, and pulled it down on top of the deadly dark crusader.

"Good riddance to ya, ya bum," Stone growled. He turned and exited the burning apartment building, leaving The Grim Spectre seemingly buried.

• • •

Moments later and high above the street an invisible figure floated silently, watching the strange and terrible figure known as Stone exit the building and then enter a waiting limousine. As soon as he entered it, it sped away.

The Grim Spectre groaned as he touched his right arm tenderly, *'I think it's broken, if not for the magic belt's ability to make me immaterial he would have killed me.* The Grim Spectre began to float away, following the car from high up above the street, undetectable in his invisibility. *'I have to see where he came from, who sent him. I could just order Joey DeLuca to find out who hired this killer, but some things I have to do myself, even if I'm barely holding on to consciousness. Lead me to your boss, Stone. Once you do I'll know where to start.'*

The Grim Spectre continued to float above, keeping the limo in his sights. Finally after several agonizing minutes for the Spectre, the limo came to a halt at the highest point in Riverburgh, the area known as Mt. Olympus, where the jazz club called The Olympus Room sat, overseeing all of Riverburgh from its lofty position.

Stone exited the limo and casually headed up the granite steps of the place toward the entrance framed by two Greek style columns. The bouncers saw the powerfully built figure of Stone heading toward them and they wisely stepped wide, allowing him to pass, with a nervous glance at one another.

'He went in,' thought The Grim Spectre, still watching invisibly from high above the place, *'He has to be one of Zeus' thugs, sent to kill me. Only thing is that didn't work out too well so far.'* Touching his right arm brought instant pain to him. Beneath his mask, he grimaced for a moment as the pain subsided. Once it did, he turned and floated away, still invisible.

'I have to get home. The magic belt can heal me, but only if I get some rest. But the big question is, how do I beat this guy?' I can barely hurt him, even with a .45 firing almost point blank. My shock touch is the only thing that even slowed him.' He floated toward the wall of a non-descript apartment building and then quickly passed through it. Once within the place he became instantly visible.

The Grim Spectre looked around the room, making sure all the curtains were drawn. Once he was certain, he pulled back his hood and removed his mask, revealing the handsome good looks of trumpet player Bobby Terrano.

'I-I can barely keep my eyes open,' Bobby thought, *' I'm in so much pain, but my body just wants to sleep. If I hadn't of become immaterial and slipped through the floor of that burning building to the apartment underneath when Stone dropped the wall on me, I'd be dead right now.'*

Terrano stripped off the costume top along with the cape and threw it on the floor next to his bed. Then he dropped himself into the bed with little agility, and an instant later he was unconscious, the golden belt still wrapped around his waist.

• • •

Phylo Zeus took a large drink of the liquor within his glass, and then placed it down on the small table he occupied. Standing across from him was Stone, "So," Zeus began, "how'd it go? Is that ghoul burnin' in hell again?"

Stone met his gaze unwaveringly and then said, "I sent 'im there myself, Mr. Zeus. I dropped a wall on 'im. If he ain't dead now, then he really must be a ghost."

Zeus nodded and his mass of curly black hair atop his head swayed as he did, "Good, Stone, good. That's one less thorn in my side I have to deal with. I can't tell you how many guys I sent after this clown in the last few months. Every time I did, they'd end up either dead, or under arrest."

Zeus beckoned Stone to sit across from him. The gray skinned man did and then he said, "Well not this time, Boss; this guy ain't comin' back."

Zeus smiled, relieved, as if a huge weight was lifted off his shoulders, "Thanks, Stone. You earned a huge bonus for this."

Stone smiled and said, "Thanks, Boss. I hope this means you'll be callin' on me in the future to take care o' any similar situations you might have."

Zeus nodded and said," Yeah Stone, you can count on bein' the first guy I call from now on. You earned it."

A waitress appeared with a full glass of bourbon for Zeus, and he watched silently as she placed it on the table before him. He nodded and smiled at the pretty girl in the skimpy Greek style robes. She smiled sheepishly, turned around, and walked back to the bar.

"She's tasty," Stone commented, licking his lips lasciviously.

Zeus turned back to the hitman, his face suddenly hard and said, "That is one thing you do not ever do. You never under any circumstances mess with the staff here; are we clear on that? These girls are not your play things. They work for me and are an important part of my operation here. If you want to continue being my go-to-guy, you will take a 'look but don't touch' attitude when you are inside The Olympus Room. Do you understand me?"

Stone was stunned by the ferocity in Zeus' voice. After a moment he slowly replied, "Yeah Mr. Zeus, I got it."

"All right, Stone, see that you do and that you do not forget it."

Zeus beckoned the waitress over once again. She immediately returned with a full glass, which Zeus emptied this time while she stood there.

"Order yourself somethin', go on," Phylo Zeus offered with a wave of his massive hand.

"Okay, sure. Thanks, Mr. Zeus," Stone replied. He waved the waitress over and said, "Scotch, neat."

She smiled and said, "Sure thing, Mister." Then turned and walked back to the bar.

Stone turned and looked back at Zeus and saw him staring at him.

"So where is it?" Zeus asked.

"Where's what?"

"The body. Where's The Grim Spectre's body?"

"Body? The guy's supposed to be a ghost, Boss. There ain't no body. I dropped a friggin' wall on him. He's gotta be crushed flat under that, if he had a body. An' if he really didn't an' was a ghost, I sent 'im back ta hell with his tail between his legs."

Zeus looked at Stone silently; his face an unreadable blank and then said, "You didn't even check if there was anything left of him under that mess? Are you kiddin' me?"

"B-but, Boss, he's a ghost. How could there be anything under any o' that?"

Zeus slowly and carefully said, "Listen to my words, Stone. You will now slowly stand up and you will go back to the burning building. By now the fire should be out. You will go through the remains of the building and find me some scrap of evidence that says The Grim Spectre is finally dead. If you can't find any evidence that he was killed or destroyed or whatever he was, you should leave Riverburgh and never think about coming back here. Are we clear?"

"O-Okay, Mr. Zeus, whatever you say." Stone stood up slowly and turned toward the door. He walked away, practically feeling Zeus' gaze upon him the entire way. He opened the door leading to the outside and disappeared through it.

"Idiot," Phylo Zeus said as he slugged back another glass of bourbon.

● ● ●

Bobby Terrano tossed and turned, sleeping fitfully. His dreams were nightmares; nightmares of only earlier that evening.

Bobby saw himself leaving Bixby's a small jazz club he had been playing in. He was walking out the door for the night with his trumpet in its case and under his arm when he noticed people running past him. He looked on as a police cruiser roared past in the opposite direction. Then the acrid odor of something burning assailed his nostrils.

"What the hell?" he muttered.

Bobby turned and headed back into the club, walking to the bar.

"Hey Johnny, hold on to this for me. There's something going on out there and I want to take a looksee." He handed the bartender his trumpet.

"Sure thing, Bobby. You're back here tomorrow night anyway; I'll lock it up an' keep it safe for ya until then."

"Thanks Johnny. I may be right back, or I may not. See ya later," Bobby finished and dashed out the door.

'This is probably nothing, but it's definitely a fire. I don't know if any of the local thugs are involved or not, but if I can help out, either as Bobby Terrano or The Grim Spectre, I will,' Bobby thought.

He ran down the street and turned toward the direction the police car had gone, and then he pulled up short. Before him an apartment building was completely ablaze. Fire trucks had just arrived on the scene and the firemen were doing their best to contain the blaze, but even to someone who knew nothing about fighting fires, like Bobby, it was obvious that, *'The whole building is going to go down. They'll never save it.'* Bobby realized.

"Help me! Help!" a man's voice called from within the burning building. Bobby took a step forward then quickly backward into the deep shadows of an alley. He looked around once and made sure he was alone. Then he touched the magic belt about his waist and thought, *'Grim Spectre.'*

Instantly his garb changed from that of jazz musician extraordinaire to the ghostly, glowing white costume of The Grim Spectre.

His glowing white cape flowed behind him in the hot breeze as he floated upward, half of his skull-like mask forever hidden in shadow. Like twin orbs of molten steel did his eyes glow as he surveyed the scene of carnage before him. He floated bolt upright alongside and then through the wall of the burning edifice.

Within was thick with smoke and flame, and The Grim Spectre was unsure of where to go; where the cries for help had originated from.

But then he heard them once again.

"Help me, someone, I-I I'm trapped," came a ragged scream.

"Stay where you are," The Grim Spectre replied in his hollow sounding voice, "I will be there in a moment."

Floating intangibly through the burning structure he came upon a figure buried beneath a fallen, flame wracked beam.

"Help me, please," a fear filled voice called.

The Grim Spectre reached forward, touched the downed man on the shoulder, and said, "Do not be afraid, mortal. I am here to help you; not harm you."

The man's form became immaterial itself at The Grim Spectre's touch, and then the ghoulish defender of Riverburgh pulled the figure's arm, dragging the man out through the beam as if it were not there at all.

"Y-You made me a ghost now? Like you?" the man stammered, his face still hidden and held in such a way that The Grim Spectre could not see it.

"No, I merely sought to aid you, so we can escape this hellish place, and I can bring you to safety."

"Please, make me solid again, just for a moment," the stranger pleaded.

"Very well," The Grim Spectre replied, "but only for a moment. Do not breathe in too strongly. When I return you to your normal state you will be susceptible to the smoke and heat, and can be quickly overcome by it."

The man, who had yet to look in The Grim Spectre's direction, nodded his gray head of hair in silent agreement.

The Grim Spectre silently thought, *'Solid once more,'* and instantly both men returned to a fully solid form. It was only then that he noticed the strange color of the man's flesh.

"Your skin, it is gray," The Grim Spectre said aloud.

"That's right, Ghost-Man, it's like concrete, like stone," the man replied with a shout.

Before the Spectre could react the man batted his solid form away with his rock-like fist, knocking The Grim Spectre to the flame weakened floor with one powerful blow.

"I was playin' possum, waitin' for you to show up, Ghost-Guy."

"How foolish of you, human. Are you the one who set this fire? Did you cause all of this destruction merely to garner my attention?"

"Settin' the fire wasn't my job. I'm bein' paid ta take you out, and that's it. The rest o' this was done by somebody else."

Beneath his mask, Bobby Terrano grimaced. *'If this maniac didn't start this fire, then there has to be someone else out there who's just as corrupt and heartless, not to mention as insane and evil as this guy,'* The Grim Spectre thought.

"Who hired you? Who sent you here to draw my attention?" The Grim Spectre growled.

"What? Do ya think I'd actually tell ya? I ain't that stupid."

"Foolish dog, you trifle with powers you cannot possibly imagine. Surrender for your sins and leave this place as my prisoner and I promise you fair treatment while in my control."

"Can the ghost act, we both know you ain't the real thing. If you were, why wouldja need a couple o' .45's an' a whip?"

"Simply put, evil one, when in the world of men, one such as myself must use the tools of humanity to deal with those who would do harm to other mortals."

"Yeah, like I'm buyin' that," Stone laughed in reply.

"Whether you believe me to be what I am or not does not concern me, Stone, for if you wish to battle against the spirit of retribution upon the mortal plain then so be it. It will be your funeral, brute."

"We'll see about that, Ghost-Man."

Stone quickly lunged through the flames separating them directly at The Grim Spectre.

● ● ●

Bobby Terrano awoke with a sweat soaked start and said, "What a nightmare. That was everything that happened last night. I had to relive it all over again, but why?" Groggily he touched his forehead with his injured arm and then quickly realized, "It's healed," Bobby said aloud.

He gripped his formerly broken arm and touched it carefully.

"It's completely healed up. This magic belt is really something," Bobby said.

He touched the gold belt about his waist and slowly removed it, then said, "Become a regular leather belt again."

Instantly the belt complied and changed shape in an eye blink and a pulse of light into a plain leather belt. Bobby held it and marveled at it. Then he laid it down on his bed.

"I need a shower," Terrano said aloud.

He walked into the bathroom and a moment later the water began to spray.

Twenty minutes later Bobby exited his apartment and hailed a cab, "The Riverburgh Gazette," Bobby said simply to the cabbie.

The cabbie nodded and said, "You've got it, Chief"

Several minutes later Bobby entered the imposing old building and headed toward a particular reporter's desk. "Hey Tammy, got a minute?" he asked gregariously.

A girl with a mop of curly, flaming-red hair looked up at him and almost sneered, "What do you want, Terrano? You stood me up *again* last night. Why should I even talk to you?"

"C'mon honey; I was busy, I had an audition. A man's gotta work, right?"

Tammy looked at him and pouted a moment before finally replying, "I guess it's okay, as long as it was about a job."

"I gotta work to buy you nice stuff, Hon," Bobby said earnestly. He touched her chin and gently pulled her face upward by it until their eyes met.

"Okay Bobby, what do you need?" she sighed resignedly.

"You ever hear of a guy named Stone?"

"What the heck kinda name is 'Stone'? No, I've never heard of him. What is he? Another trumpet player trying to horn in on your turf?"

Bobby grimaced at her play on words and said, "Cute, but no. I think he's a hired killer and I think he's in this town."

Suddenly serious, Tammy shook her head negatively and said, "No, Bobby, I've never heard of him."

"Maybe she hasn't, but I have," a male voice interrupted.

Bobby turned toward the rotund man making his way toward them with a sandwich in hand.

"Hello George," Bobby said with a smile. He shook the big man's hand and asked, "So? What've you got? Fill me in."

"First, why do you want to know?" George Kowalski asked.

"Well," Bobby began thoughtfully, "Rumor has it he was seen fighting The Grim Spectre at an apartment building that burned down last night."

"What? How come you know this and none o' my so-called crack reporters know anything about it?" George asked in a wide-eyed frenzy.

Bobby took a step back and said, "Whoa George, calm down there big guy. I saw the fire and ran toward it, trying to help anyone who might be trapped in it when I heard all of this shouting coming from the building. I coulda sworn I heard two guys fighting in there and one of them was The Grim Spectre from what little I could see from the street through the thick smoke."

Bobby threw his hands into the air and walked around Tammy's desk in disgust, "Ahhh, it might as well all be a rumor, for what little information I have on this. What I got is useless. I don't even know why I'm asking questions about it; I'm not a reporter. It was more a curiosity thing because of The Grim Spectre."

"Maybe so Bobby, but most rumors have a strong basis in fact. So The Grim Spectre was fighting Stone, huh? That can only make matters worse for this city."

"Why, George?" Bobby asked.

Kevin Paul Shaw Broden '15

"Because he's a gun for hire who'd gladly work for the highest bidder. If he's in town it can only mean bad things for the citizens," George concluded.

"Wonderful," Bobby replied.

"So what happened in this fight? Did The Grim Spectre win?" George asked excitedly.

Bobby shrugged and said, "It was kind of a draw from what I heard. Both of 'em escaped with their hides intact."

"I ain't sure if that's good or bad," George admitted.

"How come?" Bobby asked.

"Because now Stone has some unfinished business with The Grim Spectre in our town. This could turn the city into a war zone overnight."

Bobby nodded, understanding George's fears.

"Do you have any info on this guy? Like who he really is? What's his real name, I mean," Bobby asked.

"That's just it, no one knows. He's some hideously deformed freak who became a hit man and that's it," George replied.

"So no one knows of any weaknesses he might have or how he became this stone hard killer?" Bobby asked.

"Naahh. In fact he probably doesn't have any. What do you want to know for anyway? Are you going to go fight him yourself?"

"Me? No way!" Bobby exclaimed excitedly, "I'm just curious to see what this is all about."

"Take this old man's advice, kid; steer clear of any of this. You could be sucked in and killed real easily. Stick to what you're good at, Bobby, your trumpet playing," the portly editor said.

"Thanks George, I intend to. I was just curious, that's all."

"You remember what happened to that curious cat, right? Keep that in mind: steer clear of those two. I don't know which one worse, the ghost or the rock hard maniac that is trying to kill him." George concluded.

Bobby nodded dejectedly, "You're right, of course, George. A guy like me could end up becoming a real ghost all too easily if I was caught between those two."

George Kowalski nodded and replied, "You got a good heart, kid, just make sure you keep it inside your chest."

"Will do, George, and thanks." Bobby turned toward Tammy who was still sitting there quietly listening to the whole conversation and said, "I'll catch up with you tonight? I'm playing Bixby's again; we can have dinner there and you can watch me play a set or two."

"Gee, you take me to all the nicest places," Tammy teased, "But I have to pass for tonight, hotshot. I have some investigating to do on my own."

"I hope you didn't get the really bad idea in your head to go after the ghost guy and this stone monster from listening to George an' me talking? Cause if you did, you better get that outta your head pronto. Got it?" he pinched her cheek playfully.

"What are you crazy? This stuff is way out of my league, and we both know it," Tammy answered, "Besides, George only trusts me with the fluff pieces."

Bobby exhaled a sigh of relief, "Okay good, because I worry about you getting all hot-headed and then doing something crazy."

"Hey! I may be hot-headed, but I ain't crazy!" Tammy snorted angrily.

"Yeah? Just remember those words if you *do* decide on trying something stupid. Something that could possibly get you killed," Bobby replied.

"All right, I get your point," she answered resignedly.

"Do you?" Bobby asked, while lifting her chin up so her eyes met his own.

She playfully knocked his hand away and answered, "Yeah, yeah I get it. I understand. But I still got something to do tonight, so I'll have to take a rain check on that five star cuisine you were offering me."

"Okay, just make sure it's something safe? I worry about you," Bobby said. He kissed her on the lips and then stood. "I'll talk to you later on, and George, thanks again for the advice."

George waved his goodbye with a hand filled with half a meaty sandwich, the other half was in his mouth, rendering him momentarily mute.

Bobby smiled and headed toward the elevator.

A few minutes later Bobby exited the building into the street and looked up and down the busy sidewalk carefully, then turned and headed toward his apartment, *'I have to play tonight, but I have plenty of time to pay a visit to a friend of mine or rather a friend of The Grim Spectre's,'* Bobby mused. He continued walking nonchalantly toward his own apartment.

● ● ●

An hour later Joey DeLuca was sitting in his dingy apartment wearing a dirty tank top T-shirt, sprawled out on his couch listening to the radio.

"DeLuca, I have need of you," a voice said that sent chills down DeLuca's spine. He turned about looking nervously around his dimly lit and empty room.

"W-where are ya? Show yerself. Is that you, Ghost-Man?" the low level thug called nervously.

"It is," replied The Grim Spectre. He suddenly appeared as if from nowhere. One moment he was nowhere to be found, the next he was standing next to the frightened Joey DeLuca.

"Geeze! You scared the bejeebus outta me!" DeLuca shouted.

"Quiet yourself, mortal, I require information from you. Have you heard of a man called 'Stone?'

DeLuca looked at the Grim Spectre incredulously, "Who? The hitman? That guy's like the most feared goon on the east coast. Why are you askin' about him? Wait, is he after you?"

Slowly The Grim Spectre nodded, "He is," was his only reply.

"Oh boy, cause ghost or not, this guy is hard to handle. Maybe you should lay low until he leaves town?"

"No DeLuca, you will tell me all you can uncover about the man. I need to know all there is to know about him."

"I'll find ya what I can, Boss," DeLuca replied, "But I got a bad feelin' it ain't much."

"Provide me what you can. This man, this Stone is unlike anyone I have encountered. He is a danger to this entire city and must be dealt with before he gets a chance to complete his mission."

DeLuca looked at The Grim Spectre and shivered, then said, "Meet me back here after midnight and I'll have what I can gather up for ya."

"Good," was the only reply The Grim Spectre gave in answer, "Do not fail me, DeLuca." The Grim Spectre turned to exit then stopped and looked back at his informant.

"What? What is it?" DeLuca asked, fear starting to tickle his throat.

"There may be someone else involved in this. A building was burned down last night; it was done to get my attention. Find me who did this evil deed. He must be brought to justice as well."

"Y-you think there's an arson guy involved?" DeLuca stammered.

The horrific being nodded once and said, "I do. Find him for me, DeLuca; I need a name, something to go by in stopping these men, if indeed a second one is involved. Many innocents may be hurt...or worse."

"I-I'll do my best, I p-promise," DeLuca nervously replied.

"See that you do," was all The Grim Spectre said.

Then, just as suddenly as he had appeared, The Grim Spectre faded away as if he was never there.

"Brrr," DeLuca shook involuntarily while looking about his dingy apartment and finally said, "That guy really gives me the creeps."

Hidden in shadow The Grim Spectre smiled inwardly, *'Good, let evil fear me. It is but another weapon in my arsenal against them.'* He turned and walked through the apartment wall, fading away as if he were never there.

● ● ●

Midnight came all too quickly to Joey DeLuca and none too quickly to Bobby Terrano, AKA The Grim Spectre, who in his normal identity played his set at Bixby's.

But come it did, and at precisely midnight Joey DeLuca was seated in his dark and grimy apartment staring at a blank wall, awaiting the return of the creature he both feared and was somehow growing to grudgingly respect.

"DeLuca," the familiar hollow voice said.

Joey DeLuca jumped out of his chair and turned toward the sound of the voice, his heart racing.

"Geeze! Don't do that! Ya scared me outta ten years o' life!"

"Perhaps I did, repentant one, but that may be the price you will have to pay for your former sins," the ghostly figure replied.

"Okay, okay I get it. I know I was a bad guy, I toldja I was tryin' ta make up for it all by helpin' you out. Anyway I got some info for ya; there's an arsonist from

Newark called 'Firebug' who's gone missin' in his hometown. Rumor has it he took on a contracted hit up this way, and that hit was you. Seems there's a growin' contingent that doesn't believe you're really a ghost. After seein' the stuff you do, I ain't one o' them, by the way."

The Grim Spectre merely nodded in understanding, and then said, "Go on."

DeLuca cleared his throat and then continued, "Rumor on the street has it that this here 'Firebug' and 'Stone' have teamed up figuring that it may take both o' them ta wipe you out an' send you back ta hell."

The Grim Spectre nodded slowly and fingered the grips of his twin .45's mounted at his ghostly waist. Then said, "I do not care what brought these two fools together. I will find them and when I do, I will end their reign of terror."

DeLuca quickly added, "One way or another, right? Cause if they kill you or whatever it takes to stop a ghost like you, that also stops them runnin' amok through the city, right?"

DeLuca didn't even see The Grim Spectre move, but suddenly he was being gripped by the front of his shirt by the spectral being and lifted upward until both his feet dangled in the air, and then The Grim Spectre said, "You fool! If they actually *do* find some way of disposing of me, it merely opens the floodgates up for them and their ilk to run amok through this city. The police cannot stop them. Most are too corrupt to even try."

"I-I know Spectre, I know," DeLuca agreed. He could not meet the gaze of the glowing eyes which were so close and cast upon him. Fearfully he turned his face away from the horrific skull which stared balefully at him.

Slowly, purposefully The Grim Spectre set DeLuca back down upon the floor, "Where can I find these evil men? Do you at least have that information for me this night?"

Before DeLuca could answer an explosion rocked the floor beneath their feet. Wordlessly The Grim Spectre turned toward the window and saw the glow of a fire a mere two blocks away.

He turned toward DeLuca and said, "Stay here; do not involve yourself in this. I do not want others to suspect you are aiding me. I do not want your worth compromised."

Wordlessly The Grim Spectre turned toward the wall and walked through it, fading from sight.

"Gee, thanks for the concern," DeLuca muttered.

● ● ●

Above the rooftops The Grim Spectre invisibly floated toward the burning building.

'I know what I'll find inside, but even if I take out Stone I still have to find this 'Firebug' and I don't even know what he looks like. But I have to start somewhere.'

He descended invisibly from above and passed through the rooftop of the burning building. Keeping himself invisible he slowly descended through floor after floor, searching for his foes, knowing at least one of them was going to be here.

Finally he saw the madman known as 'Stone' standing on a burning floor, halfway down the buildings height. The Grim Spectre surveyed the floor and saw no one else in sight.

This time he did not hesitate. He stood in front of his enemy for but an instant and then went from invisible to full glowing brightness instantly.

"Wha? What the...?" Stone shouted as he stumbled backward, his eyes blinded by the sudden explosion of searing light.

The Grim Spectre did not hesitate; he grabbed the bigger man by the face and sent his shocking touch coruscating through him.

"Aaahhh!" shouted Stone.

Any other man would have been rendered insensate immediately, but the big stone skinned brute snapped a powerful backhand across The Grim Spectre's face, knocking him across the room in one blow.

"Ain't gonna be that easy, Ghost-Man," Stone growled.

Fighting his way to his feet The Grim Spectre ducked a powerful right cross by his enemy, and retaliated in one quick movement. He jabbed something into the rock hard neck of his enemy, and immediately Stone howled in pain. He quickly snapped around seeking to smash The Grim Spectre away from him once again.

But this time his rock hard fist merely passed through his ghostly foe.

It was then that Stone realized he was, "Bleedin" You actually got somethin' that cut me?"

"Indeed, miscreant, something extraordinarily sharp to counter your inhumanly tough hide," The Grim Spectre replied.

Stone reached up and yanked the blade that was protruding out of his neck out and threw it to the floor angrily.

"I'll kill you!" he shouted and lunged at the Spectre once again.

Again he passed through him; once again The Grim Spectre turned and now slammed down twin knives from within his cloak, each on opposite sides of Stone's throat.

Stone dropped to his knees in pain and reached up to rip the blades free.

"No, villain, your reign of terror is over, as are your days as a killer for hire," The Grim Spectre grasped the handle of each blade and sent a withering blast of coruscating energy through them, and into the neck of the hired killer via his shocking touch.

"Aaaahhhh!!!" Stone howled in agony. This time there would be no stopping The Grim Spectre's terrible shocking touch. For while this madman had almost impervious skin, the flesh beneath was not near as well protective. Stone glowed with withering energy cascading about his form, his eyes wide and his mouth open in a never ending scream.

Then a blast of withering flame engulfed both men, and without hesitation The Grim Spectre ducked and rolled away, instantly becoming untouchable once again.

Wracked with pain he looked around the room for the culprit in this attack and when his eyes settled upon the doorway, he found his foe.

Framed in the doorway stood a man of average height, in a blood-red suit and white tie with a matching fedora atop his head. On his back was strapped the tank of a flamethrower and in his hands he held the gun and barrel assembly.

"Don't know how you ain't gone, Spectre, but I'll keep trying until you burn for good, I'll send you right back ta hell," Firebug exclaimed.

Firebug fired a withering blast of flame once more at The Grim Spectre, but the flames merely passed through him and then he faded from sight.

"Huh, I chased him away," Firebug said.

"I think not, foolish mortal," The Grim Spectre's eerie voice replied.

Instantly his whip snapped out of the darkness and wrapped itself around the barrel of the flame thrower. The Firebug pulled the trigger reflexively and sent a stream of flame across the room and out the side of the burning building.

The Grim Spectre tore the gun from his enemy's hand with his whip. Firebug was caught off guard and yanked to the floor.

"You ain't takin' me so easily, Grim Spectre," Firebug shouted. He pulled a gun from beneath his suit jacket and began firing toward the spot The Grim Spectre's whip had snaked away from.

Instantly one of The Grim Spectre's throwing knives flew from the darkness and smacked the gun from Firebug's hand

"Enough of this foolishness," The Grim Spectre's terrible voice roared from all about the room, "Your time of evil is finished, Firebug. You are finished. Surrender now and I will spare your life."

"Like hell, Grim Spectre, you're goin down, not me."

Firebug yanked on the hose for the flamethrower which was still attached to his back, and the nozzle, which had been lying on the floor after the Grim Spectre's whip attack, leaped up in his grip to his waiting hand.

"You fool!" shouted The Grim Spectre, his guns blazing. His bullets tore through Firebug, and one of them also tore through the incendiary tank mounted to his back. An explosion of flame and heat hurled the arsonist out the shattered wall of the flame engulfed building, leaving a flaming arc behind him to the ground fifteen floors below.

For a moment the firemen below who had been fighting the blaze looked up and were startled by what they saw. Framed in the hole shattered in the wall of the building stood a glowing, ghostly white figure, and held high above his head was the still form of the murderous Stone.

In a voice that filled their hearts with dread The Grim Spectre said to them all, "This man, and the other at your feet, have been setting fires in this city seeking to draw me into battle with them, and to sow fear and terror in the hearts of Riverburgh's residents. But while I, The Grim Spectre, exist in the mortal plain, I have sworn to protect the helpless and innocent of Riverburgh from the forces of evil that would seek to control and destroy your lives."

He heaved the limp body to the ground fifteen floors below, where it landed with a loud crash, leaving a small crater in the street.

The Grim Spectre turned his face skyward and floated into the night sky, glowing brightly, and then with a blinding flash of light he disappeared into the night.

Far below, behind the police and fire barricades the wide-eyed young reporter Tammy Thomas quickly scribbled notes into a pad and then turned to run into the night.

The End

You Will Not Descend
(A Sgt. Janus story)
by Jim Beard

My thoughts are quite jumbled, so much that I hesitated before setting pen to paper to write. Something needs to be said here at the outset:

Will you marry me, sir?

There. I have written the words, though they came uneasily, and now perhaps I should explain how I arrived upon them. It all began, of course, when I called you to my house, not three days ago.

(It seems foolish and silly and not a small part imprecise to write this down as if you were not aware of the events, or shared in them, either, but you have asked me for a document, and I find it hard to deny you anything.)

You arrived at my house at ten o'clock in the morning on September the 24ᵗʰ. The air was already cool as summer had departed quickly, and fall inserted itself in our lives. Seeing as I have no servants currently and live alone, I greeted you myself and invited you in. I had heard of the famous Sgt. Janus many times before, following your exploits in the newspapers, as I'm sure many citizens of Mount Airy have done the same over the years. When I looked upon your face while we stood on the threshold, I remembered then of a report that you had gone away for some time, that perhaps something untoward had happened to you, and that some feared you dead. I even recalled an article concerning a trial, a murder trial wherein you were cited as the one who'd been murdered.

It is possible that I misremembered those supposed events, but nevertheless, there you stood in my front hallway, somewhat Bohemian, but all together proper-seeming and professional. I warmed to you immediately.

(If I may digress again, allow me to say that a man in my house is not a common thing. I have few relatives, even fewer of them male, and they do not often visit. Furthermore, I am not in the habit of entertaining men in general. Oh, I know that the times have changed and women are freer to pursue gentlemen like never before, but though I come from a long line of Irish females with their own heads on their shoulders, I am not prone to inviting men to my house, or to offering them a proposal of marriage. Some might call me uptight, or closeted, or even a Sapphist, but the truth of it is that until three days ago, I had little cause to be interested in a man. There are so few of them, I have found, in the world today worthy of a woman's interest.)

I remember how polite you were, and well-spoken, belying the small band of copper in your right earlobe and your longish locks. Your eyes, though, were striking, and your steady hand in mine for that brief moment of greeting told me volumes of you. You were welcome in my house.

I began to tell you about my house, but to my surprise, you held up one hand—my eyes caught upon the small copper band on the smallest finger—and in a firm yet not unkind tone asked me as to what my concern was of it.

"Maybe I should simply show you, sir," I said, and laying a hand on your arm, led you further down the hallway and deeper into the house.

As we walked, you sketched out in a few brief sentences your profession as a "Spirit-Breaker." I remarked that it was exactly that for which I had contacted you. You nodded sagely and knowingly, as if you had already divined my problem and devised a solution for it. It was fascinating to see your composure concerning such a matter as the occult, but that would begin to change as I brought you to the foot of a staircase and we gazed upon it together.

"Miss Pilchard," you said, your brow creased minutely as you looked at me, "I believe I'm at a loss."

"We must go up, Sergeant," I told you, glancing at the steps. "You will see."

At the top of the stairs—they numbered seventy-seven, for I had counted them many times as a child growing up in the house—I kept hold of your arm and gently turned you around to face the direction from which we had come. You looked and then you smiled slightly, though your brow furrowed the more. After a moment's silence, in which I fancied you contemplated the mystery before you, you spoke.

"Ah, I see what you mean."

At the edge of the landing to which we had ascended, you stepped forward and swung one leg outward, as if to place it upon the top step, but you did not continue the movement for there was apparently no step on which you could tread.

The staircase *ascended*, you see, but it did not in turn *descend*. To our eyes, there was no flight of stairs there, only empty space.

● ● ●

You frowned slightly, taking in the queer sight of a staircase that went up, but not down. I was glad that you had viewed it all and reacted in any way, for it meant that someone else could see it, too, and that I wasn't mad. Then, expecting you to ask me to say something about the phenomenon or of the house itself, you surprised me by holding up a hand, just enough to signal for silence.

Your eyes, those unique, steely orbs, traveled over the surrounding area, over wood and stone and plaster, up and down, back and forth, missing nothing. I saw quite clearly their path, and that through them you satisfied something within yourself. Finally, your gaze came to rest on the missing stairs.

"Odd."

That was all you said, just that one word. In a way, I'm not ashamed to admit that you confused me at that moment. If you'll recall, I then said:

"Perhaps I was wrong to call you here. This may not be anything within your line of work."

You *smiled* at that. Oh, it was more a smile presented through your eyes than anything, but I saw the minute quirks at the ends of your mouth and the almost-imperceptible tilt backward of your head. I asked what might be amusing to you, assuming that I was erroneous in my call to you.

The smile vanished. You told me that, no, it was indeed in your line of work and that I was wise to involve you. You turned to look at me, voicing words that sent a chill down my spine:

"A spirit may reside here, Miss Pilchard. One that needs to be on its way."

It was the word "reside" that disquieted me, you see. When one lives alone, or when one believes she lives alone, and is used to it, news of an unknown border can come as something of a shock. I asked then how it was that this spirit manifested itself as a *partially* invisible staircase? Surely you didn't mean that the house itself was the spirit?

"No, not all," you replied, looking all around you again, though that time by turning your head and shoulders. "Though houses *have* a spirit of their own. How may we descend again to the main floor? Is there another way?"

I showed you to the servants' stairway, at the back of the house, long unused, for as I have said, I keep no servants. We made our way back to the main hallways and arrived presently at the staircase we'd ascended minutes before, hale and hearty and quite visible.

"Miss Pilchard, I will need to examine this occurrence further," you announced, not looking at me as you spoke. "It is…unusual, but not so far from my experience that I need claim defeat."

You turned to take me in your gaze once again. "We shall rid you of your spirit," you said resolutely. "And return to you the *full* use of your staircase…and your home."

I did not inquire as to the "we" you spoke of. I was not ready at that time to know more of your ways in your singular career, though I felt there was a certain *longing* I detected in your voice when you spoke of "home."

● ● ●

For the remainder of that day you conducted an examination of my house and of the area of the staircase. Much of it seemed to me to be simply walking around and around, on both levels, and observing the rooms and the construction of the house, but you told me later that one sees with more than just one's eyes, and that you had opened all your senses to the situation.

I had heard of such things as "extra senses" before, recalling an article I believe I perused once in a magazine, but at the time had dismissed it as horsefeathers. But after your description of such things, I began to change my mind. I began to believe that such things might be possible. Surely the absence, or partial absence, of my staircase was enough to at least set me on the right path to believing?

You told me, sometime in the late afternoon after many hours of observation (I prepared both a lunch and a dinner for you, which I was happy to do), that you had been conducting a series of tests. When I inquired as to whether these tests had proven valuable or conclusive, you remarked that they had—to a point.

"I have noticed that the phenomenon changes as the day wears on," you said. "And, in relation to your own proximity to it."

This revelation shook me somewhat, I will admit. I myself had noticed no real difference in the staircase in relation to the time of day, but I could not say if there was any change due to my own viewing of it. It transpired as I looked upon it, and I assumed it continued to transpire if I were away from it. If I understood you correctly, you meant to say that I had something to do with the vanishing.

"How extraordinary!" I said.

Lest you think I was prone to excitement or thrill over a supernatural occurrence in my own home, I assured you then and there of my reticence to fully come to terms with what you described. I added, too, that I had begun to grow quite weary, and glanced at the darkening skies outside the window. "Could we not reconvene in the morning?" I asked, ready to see you off after a long day.

"Oh, no, Miss Pilchard," you said in an earnest, forthright way. "I must stay the night if I'm to see this through to its conclusion."

● ● ●

You perhaps discerned little, if any, of my thoughts at that moment, but once you read this account of the events of those two days, you will know that I weighed them carefully before I spoke again. It was a troubling prospect overall.

I am not a prude, nor am I what might be called, if you'll pardon the term, a "free spirit."

The times are changing, owed to the war, of course, and the normal loosening of morality as the years advance and society continues to grow...and to experiment. But though I have already told you that allowing a man into my house unchaperoned caused me no concern, one staying the night was altogether a different matter. A woman alone in the world must rely on her reputation, at least to some degree, and talk of a man and woman—unmarried—staying in a house together through the night might prove quite damaging to the woman.

Still, I wanted the full use of my house back. And I knew of your standing and had already witnessed your professional manner and gentle nature, so I made up my mind and simply said, "Of course, Sergeant."

You smiled, told me to sleep well and to lock my door. I knew in an instant that the latter was to make me feel secure while you, well, did whatever it was that you do in a house that is being haunted. I bid you a good night and retired for the evening.

Once to bed, I fell asleep quickly. And dreamed.

For this next part of the telling, you will pardon me I'm sure, for it is difficult to put into words, though I related it in full to you later. But, more so than anything else that transpired on our "adventure," what I dreamed remains hard to credit. Or to grasp with mere words.

Stairs dominated the vision. Steps upon steps, but always going down, never up. What I remember most is the overwhelming urge or drive to descend stairs, as if my very life depended upon it, but being utterly unable to do so. In my dream, I walked through my house, which seemed much larger and sprawling than in the waking world, and came upon room after room which I did not fully recognize. The general construction and design appeared much as if it was my home, but surprises lurked around every corner—but nothing dangerous, or so I thought. Again, my house, yet not my house.

And stairs. Staircases appeared at every turn, but none that I could use...at least to go down. I tried; oh, how I *tried*, but something held me back each time.

Does that seem odd? I asked you the same question at the time I told you of my dream, but still the question nags me: is that altogether strange? Everyone at one time or another supposes that they may be losing their mind, I suppose, but do people question their sanity because of a dream?

Regardless, a force, if you will, of invisible yet frighteningly strong design restrained me from descending the stairs. There was no actual feeling of being touched or held, but I was unable to move, to step down upon the first stair below my foot, so strong was this force. Behind me, each time I attempted to descend, something—a force of another kind, I guess—urged me on. "Caught between a rock and a hard place," as the saying goes. It was, at times in the dream, maddening.

And then there was the figure that followed me.

It was a man, I believe, but there is some small doubt in my mind on that score. For a moment, here and there, I discerned it without hesitation as male...and a soldier. Yes, there it is, plain as plain. There can be no hiding it now: I believed it to be you, dear sir. That you had somehow come into my dream to watch over me, to protect me. Silly and overly romantic, assuredly, but there it is. I cannot deny it.

But at other times, I was not certain who or what it was, beyond a person. Always there, but always just out of sight, out of the prospect of realization. Fleeting and frustrating.

I awoke to the first rays of the sun at dawn peeking through the clouds. Feeling tired and uneasy, I dressed and went to find you, both timid and excited to tell you of my dream.

What would you think? I wondered. What *could* you think? I reflected.

● ● ●

Here is what you said after listening intently to my recitation, as near as I can remember it:

"The house you wandered through was your own mind, of course. The path you took was your own path to discovery, or more precisely, your undertaking to solve the riddle yourself. Very commendable. The stairs speak for themselves; a literal token of the actual phenomenon. I often dream in the same way, and under the roof of a house not too different from the one you describe in your dream. Remarkable.

Now, your approach to the stairs and the fact that you found yourself always above them, never at their foot, can tell us more than one thing. Firstly, and

simply, it speaks to your frustration over the problem we face here in reality. Completely understandable. But I believe there is more to it than that. I feel keen to believe that you are correct in describing your inability to descend the staircase as a 'force'—and an *outside* force at that. Very illuminating. It may be the key we need to solve this puzzle...and let us hope that it is not a Pandora's Box we open instead.

And the figure of the man? Or at least what you feel was a man? Problematic, but not too overly disturbing to me. Though my concentration throughout the night's vigil was focused and pure, I don't believe I was projecting at any time. I have been working to, ah, fine-tune the discipline these last several months, but again, I feel sure that the figure was not an echo of myself."

(I must insert a comment of my own here: I myself am not certain of this.)

"Where does this leave us, Miss Pilchard? It leaves us with a bit more than what we had at nightfall. Yes, a bit more. To wit: something or someone prevents you from descending your stairs, to the extent that this spills over into your dreams. It is an external force, not borne from your own psyche. You have a keen mind, and a good spirit—I am not concerned with those. This *is* a haunting, an intelligent mind from beyond that lingers in this house and is trying to tell you something—but what? Come; let us find out."

As we walked from the kitchens where I had made you breakfast, I asked of the nature of hauntings. Why would such things transpire? Do they not perhaps signal a break in the natural order? Why would the Almighty allow them?

"Many of those who I have aided have asked that same question, Miss Pilchard," you said, stopping in the hallway to take my hand and look me in the eye. "I cannot answer it in full, for I have spent much of my life trying to answer it to myself. Suffice to say, and in all honesty, we cannot fully know the ways of the Universe. It is not 'broken,' as you and others may divine, but rather it runs to a mechanism that is not truly understood by us mere mortals. We can merely observe it—and for a chosen few, try to make it run smoother."

"You," I said, catching a glimpse of it all. "You are one of those special persons. A 'Spirit-Breaker,' as you say. I think I see. And you have not broken my own spirit, Sergeant, but rather rallied it. I'm ready to see this through."

"Good girl," you called me, and though you released my hand, the warmth of it remained upon me.

We then approached the foot of the staircase in question, and you directed me to close all the shades and curtains that allowed the new day's sunlight into the area.

"It would have been best to attempt this at night," you explained, taking up a position at the foot of the stairs, "but we must make due with what we have. This cannot wait."

You called out then, in a strong, clear voice, the volume and strength of which surprised me, as mild-mannered as I believed you were.

"Spirit! Listen to me! We must communicate! You cannot continue to mount this campaign in this house! Come and tell me of your reasons for this action!"

The air grew colder for a moment, but nothing else manifested. I looked around me in the semi-darkness, expecting to see a shape or the slip of a figure, but I saw nothing but my furnishings. You paused, cocked an ear as if listening for something, then began to climb the staircase. It issued its normal minute creaks as you did so, but otherwise all seemed normal. At the top of the stairs you turned and looked down to where you'd begun your ascent, then to me. Your eyes widened a bit.

"Come up and join me, will you?" you asked.

Once settled next to you on the second floor, we looked together down the staircase, and as I expected, it was not there.

"It was there until you came up," you noted. "*You* are the key, of course."

You then asked me if I'd ever tried to walk *down* the steps when they'd disappeared. I assured you, maybe a smidge too coldly, that I assuredly had not. Please forgive me for that, but it seemed a foolish thing to ask me.

You very suddenly grabbed a nearby chair, and threw it out into space.

We watched as it impacted something invisible and then to clatter downward to the floor below…as if falling down a flight of stairs.

I apologized for never having thought of that before.

"Nonsense, good lady," you said, nodding as if you'd been shown the answer. "You're not qualified. Should have thought of it myself, long before. Stupid of me."

Before I could think clearly again, you called out once more in that commanding tone. "Spirit! I see your meaning! You have only Miss Pilchard's best interests in mind! Join me, and we will save her together!"

The cold air returned, but icier than before. It swirled around us, touching us, but then retreating. I hugged myself, and you put your arm around my shoulder. Almost instantly, the cold whipped at us, but seemingly directed at you, not myself.

Flinching against the arctic blast, you smiled. "Good…very well done. Another piece to the puzzle."

Before I could ask as to which piece it was, you bounded down the staircase. The staircase that wasn't there.

● ● ●

"It is almost finished, my dear," you called up to me. "Please descend and join me down here."

I resisted the notion and told you so in no uncertain terms. You made some comment about "Irish stubbornness," but insisted I follow your command. Something in your voice, something pure and good and assuring, broke through the barrier I'd erected, and I nodded my assent while placing one foot into space where a step ought to be.

"Barefoot," you said abruptly. "I will turn my back, of course."

As you did so, I doffed my shoes and then my stockings. Then, turning to the invisible staircase and to my Herculean task, I began my descent.

"*Feel* the steps with your feet," you directed. "You will know what is right and what is wrong. Let the essence of the house, its own spirit, infuse your skin. You will know when to take a step, and when not to. *Trust me*, my lady!"

"I do!" I told you, though at the moment I seemingly hung in space, floating several feet above my floor, where a staircase once was. I summoned all my strength, all my courage, and continued my journey into the Unknown. And I began to feel what you called the "spirit of the house." Not my ghost, not he who bedeviled me, but the essence of the structure around me.

Behind me came a pop and a hiss.

"Good Lord, no," you swore, and I turned my head to see bright sparks spring forth from an electrical outlet on the second floor. In an instant, tongues of fire licked at a nearby curtain and caught there. I blinked in surprise and shock, as in an instant, the entire length of material was immediately afire.

You sped up the stairs and past me, leaping at the fire. Whipping a small rug off the floor there, you beat at the blaze and then ripped the curtains down to smother them with the rug and trample any remaining tongues with your boots. Calling out to me again, you told me to finish my descent.

I took two more steps, and something felt very wrong. Before I knew it, something gave way below my foot and I was sucked into the abyss.

● ● ●

You were there at my side in an instant, pulling me free and explaining that a step had given way and my foot and leg had plunged within the open space. I clung to you for a moment and then you picked me up in your arms and brought me to the ground floor. Settling me in a chair, you turned to look back the staircase, asking me what was underneath it.

"Nothing that I know of," I replied. "There are no doors or entranceways to anything there, as you can see."

You asked if I had an axe, and when I said I didn't, you raced outside to your automobile and returned with one. I was much too taken aback to raise protest; I knew what was to come next.

Within a minute's twitch, you'd broken through the wall of the outer part of the staircase, and stuck your head inside the rent you'd made. A moment passed, then two.

"If you're able, and feel up to it," you said once you'd pulled your head out again, "I think you should come and see this, Miss Pilchard."

I steeled myself and joined you next to the hole.

When my eyes had adjusted to the darkness of the space under the stairs, I saw bones.

I did not truly faint. I have never fainted in my life. I did find myself slowly regaining a sense of reality after an indeterminate amount of time, with you standing over me, offering me a glass of water, and patting the back of my hand. You were a pretty sight for sore eyes, eyes that had recently viewed death at its most basic level.

"A skeleton," you explained, "of a man, yes, and the remains of his clothing tell me that he may have been a soldier."

"But how?" I asked. What was he doing trapped under my staircase? My family had owned the house for decades and decades. We had never heard even an inkling of such a tale or rumor. It defied explanation, or at least to my mind, but you made the attempt.

"A man of ill health, and somewhat elderly, from what I can see of his remains," you replied. "And for as to how he came to be under the stairs, I found a most ingenious mechanism that would have allowed him to lift up a portion of the stairs themselves and shut and lock them behind him."

"He did it to himself," I said, not as a question, but as a statement. Sick and perhaps even dying, he hid himself away from the world to leave it on his own terms. "But," I cried to you, "why did his ghost remain?"

You handed me a small object, dirty and dusty, a cameo with the image of a woman's head and shoulders at its center. She looked a little like me. You remarked upon that, in fact.

Cold realization flooded through me, drowning me in the truth of it.

"Come," you said, reaching out for me. "Let us send this gentleman on his way."

By candlelight, we kneeled by the hole in the wall of the staircase and you said these words:

"Go thee to thy rest, oh shade. Thou hast served well in life, now take thy reward."

I felt a stirring in the air, not cold, but warm. It lingered over me until you spoke again.

"Though you may love this woman, she is not for you, good soldier. She is set to continue in this life, while you are set to begin a new one of a different kind. You have *saved* her, as you always meant to do. Your warnings were heeded and the danger is past.

"I command you now to depart."

You did not issue the order in a harsh tone, but rather one of understanding. Still, it was as if an officer to a subordinate, suffuse with meaning and with no room for argument. The air swirled once more and then was calm.

"I'd like to bury him on the property, if you think it will be all right," I told you, and you nodded and helped me to my feet.

"Oh, Roman," I remember saying, "I just want to sleep...and not to dream."

● ● ●

There have been no more disturbances in the house, no invisible staircases, no fires, nothing amiss.

I found that while I missed he who had watched over me, and saved me from what might have been a very bad experience, for many days I could not think of anything to do with love or the depth of feeling that two people could have for each other. I had had my fill of it, and I felt as if I would be a spinster for the rest of my life, and happily.

But today, I cannot divorce you from my thoughts, Roman Janus, and so I propose marriage instead. I see you in my dreams now, simply and clearly.

Is that odd? Is that so strange? Or am I losing my mind.

Please, write back to me. Or come visit me, or allow me to visit you.

Let me know your own thoughts on the matter, dear sir.

The End

Nature of the Beast

by B. C. Bell

We should have known it was only a matter of time, what with all the trash of humanity, Mother Nature finally got pissed off. And Mother Nature's a bitch.

You've probably seen the videos of some moron trying to pet a moose, or a deer or something, the animal bashing his ribs in and chasing him down the road. Or the idiots trying to feed the bears at Yellowstone. Or the angry looking dolphins gathered around burning oil rigs. I think there's even one of a little kid getting swallowed by an alligator.

But nobody expected anything like this.

At first it was just coyotes, small packs of them wandering into the city, treating people like they didn't exist then skulking off into the night. I got a friend, works Animal Control in the city, told me some homeless guys got eaten. Newspapers never reported it, though.

Then some girl in California got attacked, and it was all over the news. Some teenage movie star fresh out of rehab and her bodyguards got mauled. Stories went from how vicious the animals were, to plastic surgery, and within a week we'd heard all we wanted to about the brave little starlet getting her looks sewn back on. It was the stuff of supermarket tabloids and had nothing to do with reality.

Then all the beautiful people leaving Luna Park were forced to lock themselves in their cars, afraid the gaping jaws of death might tear their Armanis. Within a week the people down at Denny's were on the menu.

That's when it became news.

Politicians and talk-radio hosts tried to write it off at first, saying these were just a few minor incidents where animals were overpopulated. But pretty soon the kids gathering up shopping carts at Wal-Mart were considered high risk employees, and Joe Six-Pack wasn't exactly taking the kids out to the petting zoo anymore.

Yup, all of nature's cute, little; fuzzy creatures had decided the human race was back in the middle of the food chain.

Dogs were the only animals that stayed loyal—millions of years of symbiosis ingrained. The big ones, even mutts, were selling for four-hundred dollars and up. Kennels would even send couriers to your house if you were dumb enough to sell your own. I saw an ad on TV where they'd take you to the grocery store and then bring you back home afterward, so you could stock up and not have to go back outside again.

The people in the country might have had more animals to worry about, but a lot of them already had the dogs. Channel 11 even interviewed Mac Healy from the greyhound ranch down the road the other day. 'Course, these days, hunters and survivalists are always on the news, talking about guns and gundogs, mostly.

My wife and I, on the other hand, had a four-ten shotgun, a twenty-two rifle, and a dachshund. None of them real high caliber killers. And we still probably could've sold the dog for a couple hundred bucks. I could see me now trying to talk that one up. "These dogs were originally bred to hunt badgers," and the dog would have taken a dump and run away from the guy I was trying to sell her to.

Her name was Asta. The dog, not my wife—her name's Joanie. We were big fans of the old Thin Man movies, and Asta was the most un-Asta-like dog you could imagine. She didn't do tricks, wasn't particularly concerned with being cute, and didn't solve crimes. She didn't like other dogs, but was constantly curious about what humans were doing. She had back trouble and slept a lot. Her areas of expertise were food scraps and cat droppings. Only now she didn't want to go outside anymore to search for the cat droppings.

Anyway, by the time the media admitted there was a problem, me and Asta already had us a system down. Used to be I'd let her out back in the morning, and she'd sniff around for about thirty minutes, walking in circles, looking for the perfect place to drop a load.

These days she went out on a leash and it was like the lightning round. She'd do her business in thirty sniffs or less, while I'd scan the lawn with the shotgun and make sure nothing snuck up on her. 'Course, she knew long before I did if anything was out there. Never stopped sniffing the air.

So this morning Asta had already staked out her loading zone and was getting into her batting stance—when this blue jay dive-bombs me. Got a handful of hair, which kind of pissed me off since I ain't got much left to begin with.

And then, before the dog's butt had a chance to pucker, this little blue jay bastard lands on an oak branch right next to the fence line—and starts cackling at me. I look up from clutching my scalp, and the bird's looking me right in the eye. Like he's laughing at me.

I'm thinking about raising the shotgun and the son of a bitch dive-bombs again before I even get a chance to get the barrel in the air.

I shoo it off, waving the butt of the gun, and the dog starts barking. Only natural, right? She's barking at the bird.

But she wasn't barking at the bird.

When I look down to pet her and tell her she's a good dog for barking and taking a dump at the same time, I suddenly realize we're surrounded by squirrels. A whole little platoon of them. And I say platoon because they've formed an arc around me and the dog, and they're edging around behind us to block the pathway back to the house.

We were being outflanked by a bunch of rats with fuzzy tails.

So I unload the gun on them. Two shot's, side by side. Break it open, throw the empty shells at them and reload. Fire again.

Well, the dogs barking, the rats are circling the wagons, I'm screaming, and it's like one of those cartoons where there's just a big ball of motion lines; and out on the edges there's the gun barrel, the dog pulling on the leash, and a bunch of bloody fur flying around. Oh, and that damned blue jay's still there, too.

I run back toward the door, kicking and screaming to clear a path, and I'm

pulling on the dog's leash behind me, and she's still trying to stay and fight the squirrels. So I drag her back inside and lock the door. She runs into the inside of it with her face, still barking. Finally, I get the leash unhooked.

And Asta turns and starts growling at me.

I figure she's just angry because I ruined all her fun. So I lock her in the utility room and the growling dies down. Then I go in and turn on the TV to see if they're saying anything on the news.

First thing I notice is that the news is actually on, which is kind of strange because it's ten in the morning and we don't get cable. News is never on at ten in the morning.

Second thing I notice is, it's Lester Holt—and he's the five o'clock guy, so it must be important. There's a newsflash streaming across the bottom of the screen telling everybody to stay indoors, secure your locks and windows. Out back, the dog stops growling and starts yapping like she's calling for help. I figure she's okay, just wanting for attention.

Meanwhile, Bryan's on the TV going on about wild animal attacks and they're showing videos one after another. Some lady's ferret is gnawing on her neck. A boa constrictor in Cleveland constricted some punk kid to death. Then they show some Rottweiler mauled somebody in the city, and I start to get worried.

I flip the channel over to Scott Pelley and he doesn't say anything about squirrels ganging up on people, but he says something else that gets my attention.

Something about "Neuro Aggressive Reactive Disorder, NARDS." And I almost laugh to myself because all them little critters sure grown some massive, big, brass ones. Nards I mean—or is that nads? Anyway, he says it's some kind of virus.

He goes on to say something about a Center for Disease Control press release and "neuroma, tumor cells of the nervous system." Only these kind grow "on the frontal lobes of higher mammals at a slower rate—and are now believed to be affecting dogs and humans."

I go back to check on Asta, and as soon as I turn that direction, she starts growling again. I open the door, she starts barking a fit. So I slam it in her face and head to the closet to get the twenty-two. Joanie hears me and comes out in the hall.

"Oh my God, Emmett. Did you hear on the TV?"

"Sure did," I say, and pull out the gun.

"What are you doing?"

"I'm getting worried, that's all," I say. "The dog keeps barking at me."

She gives me a funny look and I head down the hall to take care of the dog.

I almost hated to do it, but Asta just kept growling, meaner and meaner, the nearer I got to the door. When I opened it, she started barking and snapping at me. Never done that before. Least I was smart enough to use the twenty-two. Shotgun would've messed up the whole laundry room.

I go back to check the news and hear Joanie back in the bedroom on the phone. I can't tell what she's saying, but she's yammering on and on, and I can tell she's worried about something. Figure I'll just let her get it out of her system.

Meanwhile, Scott Pelley's on the TV rattling on about the boa constrictor Lester Holt already talked about, so I flip it back over to see what he's saying. "...symptoms may include rage, mania, psychosis..." And then there's something banging on the front door.

At first I think it's a goat or a deer trying to ram its way in, but something rattles the handle and starts hitting the door harder. I can hear the wood splitting as I'm turning around to grab the twenty-two. I'm reaching for the rifle and looking over my shoulder, and the only thing holding the door on is the chain. That's when I realize somebody's kicking the door in.

And damned if it isn't Mac Healy, the greyhound rancher that was on the news last night, standing there in his overalls with a .357 magnum pointed right at my head. And he's holding his family dog, Macy, a German shepherd, by the leash with his other hand. Moron.

"Drop the rifle, Emmett," he says.

I dropped it. "What do you want, Mac?" I say trying to keep him calm.

"Joanie just called and said you shot Asta."

"Had to. She wasn't right. Turned mean, even tried to bite me. She had that NARDs they're talking about on TV."

"Just calm down, Emmett. They listed the symptoms on the internet and..."

"I ain't got no internet..." And then all of a sudden his dog starts to growling at me, fur running a ridge straight down her back like she's got a body Mohawk. "Keep the mutt away, Mac, would you?"

"No problem here." Part of Healy looks like he wants to back off, and another part looks like he's trying to figure out how to reach out and grab me. And the whole time Macy's barking, spit flying through the air, practically foaming at the mouth. Mac keeps talking, but I can hardly understand a word he's saying.

Then I remember the shotgun's leaning on the wall, just inside the hallway entrance.

Macy's pulling on the leash, and Mac's trying to act all normal, except he's hollering over the dog, and I'm not really paying attention. My eyes shift just to the right, down on the floor where I put the twenty-two. And I get an idea.

And that's when Mac cocks the .357.

The dog's barking, and he's yelling, and I can't think. It's all too fast.

I lean down like I'm going to jump for the twenty-two. And when he looks down at it, I jump for cover in the hallway. He shoots the wall next to my shoulder, and I come up with the shotgun and pull the trigger.

Now, mind you, I'm maybe ten, fifteen feet away—and I can hear him hollering every vowel in the alphabet, so I know he's still alive. I sit behind the wall and wait for him or the dog to come around the corner, but it never happens.

When I do come out, I come out quick, ready to fire. But the dog's gone and Mac's lying there on the floor—in a puddle of blood—with his face peeled off. Still moaning.

I pick up his revolver and shoot him in the head with it. Put him out of his misery.

And I don't feel bad about it at all.

My own neighbor trying to kill me! If you'd of told me about it I wouldn't have believed you.

I go back to the closet to grab a pocketful of shells and start cussing myself for wasting Mac's .357 ammo. I'm thinking a handgun would be practical in a situation like this, and now I've only got five shots left. So I go into the kitchen to grab a knife, just in case, right?

That's when ol' Lester Holt on the TV turns to me and says "...paranoia, confusion, dementia..." and I start to think.

Joanie's got the bedroom door locked, and she's screaming something on the phone. Been hiding from me ever since I shot the dog.

Paranoid. Dementia. She's probably not even on the phone in there. Just talking to herself.

Looks like I'm going to have to take care of her too.

The End

Fifty

by H. David Blalock

Hank Straver was going to die alone.

It had always been his greatest fear. Since his fiftieth birthday, he had gone to extreme lengths to never be by himself. It was stupid. It was silly. It was unreasonable.

It was all that damned fortune teller's fault. The one he saw all those years ago.

When you're in college, the world is one big party. The real world is hulking over you just the other side of graduation and you get the irresistible urge to splurge your energy, money, and common sense in an effort to spend your last free days enjoying the things you'll never dare do afterward. It is the last time you will believe yourself immortal. Soon after that ceremony on the campus quad or in the auditorium, the creeping certainty of your own impending end begins its terminal growth.

Being an adult means coming to grips with your mortality. Hank became an adult the night he blew off Psych lab and went to the traveling carnival.

It was an unremarkable affair, full of dull-eyed barkers guarding worn tents boasting games of chance and skill Hank knew better than to try. The food wagons sold hard candies, cotton candy, and sweet drinks. The booth vendors hawked cheap trinkets and toys. The midway was littered with the debris of hundreds of carnival-goers. Blustering calliope notes rolled around the grounds. Over the whole hung an atmosphere of false gaiety, a facade of happiness clamped on the *ennui* of a life doomed to exist from day to day without hope for tomorrow.

The fortune teller's tent was a gaudy affair, tasseled in gold and decorated with esoteric symbols. It seemed odd and out of place, a bright spot in the surrounding twilight. The heavy scent of an exotic incense wafted from within. The gaily colored sandwich sign standing by the tent door said:

MADAME SERENA
SHE SEES ALL, TELLS ALL
FORTUNES TOLD
FUTURES REVEALED

He hesitated outside long enough to berate himself for a fool for even thinking of doing it, then pushed the tent flap aside and dove into the dark.

The incense smoke blurred the interior, muting the colors struggling to be seen in the murk. A hooded figure in a voluminous robe sat at a small square table - Madame Serena he supposed, gnarled hands gray with age protruding from the sleeves. On the table stood a glass ball. Hank nearly laughed at that. How much more kitsch could you get?

Wordlessly, Serena indicated the seat across from her and Hank took the hint. Her hand's emaciated fingers tapped the table twice, then presented themselves for payment. It dawned on him he hadn't seen what the fee was.

"How much?" he asked.

She tapped the table again, presented her hand once more. After thinking for a moment, he dropped fifty cents into the outstretched palm.

That's probably all this charade is worth, anyway, he thought.

Her hand disappeared long enough in the sleeve to stash the coins then reappeared to caress the curves of the glass ball. Hank wondered if he was supposed to say anything. Wasn't he supposed to ask a question or something? Close his eyes and concentrate? Chant?

"You will die alone at fifty," Madame Serena hissed from the depths of the hood.

"What?" Hank stammered. Wasn't she supposed to tell him he was going to meet someone and fall in love? Or that he was going to be rich and famous? Wasn't that what these so-called fortune tellers did? Lie? Tell the mark what they want to hear? "What kind of fortune is that?"

A low chuckle rattled from under the hood. "Be glad you didn't give me a nickel, ya cheap bastard."

"What does that mean?" Hank barked at her.

"Figure it out," Serena replied. "Now, leave."

"Not 'til I get my money's worth!"

That low chuckle rose again. "You really have no clue. Your money's worth is exactly what you'll get. Now, go!"

Hank bolted upright, started to shout an objection, but found his throat would not open to his command.

"Do not make me change my mind, Hank Straver," Serena said, her voice tense. She stood slowly, her form incredibly swelling from a frail robed hag into a looming, malevolent shadow that filled the rear of the tent, replacing the canvas with an impossible, incomprehensibly deep abyss. Hank gaped in astonishment as the darkness rose along the ceiling to hang directly above him. A rumbling began from within it, a sound so low it made the very ground under his feet tremble that ended in a single command.

"Go!"

An unseen hand pushed him violently through the tent flap and he stumbled out onto the midway. He stood there, stunned, a growing fear eating into his confidence. The reedy notes of the calliope grated on his nerves and the press of the midway traffic nearly spun him around before he could steady himself. A large man in a wife-beater chewing on a cigar shoved him roughly away from the tent, but he hardly noticed.

What had he just seen? A trick of the light from the globe? Some kind of sound equipment hidden in the back?

Yeah. That must have been it. These carnival people were always pulling shit on the customers. It was just some kind of scam. Nothing to get bent out of shape about. Just theater. A show. A damn good one, but just a show.

He shook himself, started to continue down the midway, but suddenly found he wasn't interested in the carnival any more. He wanted to go home and put the whole thing behind him. He didn't want to think about it. He wanted to walk away from the whole thing and get back to real life.

It was all he could do not to sprint for the exit.

Years went by and he slowly forgot about that visit to the fortune-teller's tent. The very peculiar nature of the visit helped him forget. The mind-numbing routine of the mundane settled over him like warm security. His life became filled with the minutiae of existence, the infinite details of simply being, the demands of a world uninterested in him personally and unconcerned with his continued presence within its fabric. He was absorbed into non-entity, comfortably anonymous. In a life ordinary, uninteresting and unremarkable, he found solace and consolation.

Only in his dreams was he sometimes haunted by the fading memory of an old prediction which seemed to have less and less to do with him specifically as time went by.

One day he was sitting at his desk in his nondescript job, poring over some meaningless forms that had piled up, nearly covering the morning paper. Around him the buzz of activity was a droning background noise, barely heard or even acknowledged. Hank was a part of the inner workings of a corporation, one of the little people who went unsung and unknown, and that was fine with him. He just wanted to live his life and be left alone. He had never been a people person. He could count the number of friends he had on the fingers of one hand and he avoided even them whenever he could. They had stopped inviting him to their gatherings after several failed attempts to get him to leave his Spartan apartment, to connect with humanity in at least a cursory way. He preferred his own company, sitting quietly on the couch watching reality TV and secretly laughing at the participants in the game shows for idiots.

He was wondering what to have for lunch when his eye happened to glance at the calendar on the wall. At first it was just an idle notation. In less than a week, he would celebrate his fiftieth birthday. His mind turned to what he might do to mark the occasion. Dinner? A movie? A little trip out of town? He would have to work that out later. Right now there was work to be done. He turned his attention back to it, but something in the newsprint partially covered by a company form caught his attention.

It was an announcement of a traveling carnival opening in a three days.

His heart skipped a beat.

The outside world paused and for the first time in years it looked at him, at him *personally*. The shield of anonymity, the comfortable obscurity of ordinary existence behind which he had hidden for so long dropped away. The confusion and anger and terror of that visit to the fortune-teller's tent slammed into him with almost physical force, driving the breath from his lungs. He felt naked before the scrutiny of that memory, that announcement, that prediction.

He looked again at the calendar. Maybe he read it wrong? Had someone put up the next year's calendar by mistake? Was somebody playing an odd practical joke?

But no, there it was. His birthday only a few short days away.

You will die alone at fifty.

The words thundered in his mind, echoing as if rolling toward him from mists of the past caught between walls of fate.

With an effort, he calmed himself. What was wrong with him? Did he really believe some moronic prediction by a carnival clown? Did he really think she could see the future? How stupid was that? He shook his head at his own foolishness. Such a reaction might be expected from a superstitious moron, but Hank Straver didn't believe that mumbo-jumbo. That stuff was for primitives and nuts, not businessmen. He was a professional, after all. That kind of medieval claptrap was for the movies.

He chucked the newspaper into the trash can and went back to work. Within an hour, immersed in the routine of the day, he forgot all about it.

The drive home that day took him past the fairgrounds where the carnival was preparing for their upcoming show. Gaily colored tents, the skeletal frames of carnival rides, swarms of workers and trucks moved and shouted and grew in the clearing. It was as if a great animal was rising through the surface with a low growl to look around for its prey.

What an odd thought, he said to himself. A chill went up his spine as he passed the carnival entrance. He hastily looked away and firmly concentrated on the road ahead. The familiar safety of his apartment was a welcome relief.

That night the dream returned. Once more he was in the fortune-teller's tent. Again she pronounced that sentence, but this time he wasn't pushed out of the tent. This time, he was swallowed by the growing shadow, lost in its cold and bottomless depths. He felt the warmth leave his body, the dark sucking his very breath into its void. Then, from deep within that abyss, something reached for him with claws meant to bury themselves in his soul.

He woke screaming.

Sweat nearly blinded him and he was dismayed to realize the terror had manifested in a wet spot under him. He cursed, climbing off the soaked mattress. Angrily, he stripped the blanket and top sheet, gasped at the sight of the large pool of blood sinking into the ticking. Hurriedly, he shucked his clothing to check himself for wounds, fully expecting to find huge gashes where those dream claws had gouged his sleeping, helpless flesh. Confused but relieved, he found he was uninjured. Where, then, had the blood come from?

He jumped at the jarring buzz of the alarm clock. He was expected at work soon. It was just a dream after all, a horrible nightmare. He looked at the mattress again. There was nothing out of the ordinary there. No trace of blood. If there had been any there, wouldn't it have left a stain?

He tried to put it out of his mind as he went about his morning routine. Like all dreams, the nightmare faded, but he couldn't shake that sense of dread. There was something very wrong. He could feel it deep inside and nothing he did could rid him of that feeling.

There was nothing for it but to go to the carnival, to show himself his fears were just phantasms, insubstantial phantoms bred of unfounded fear. He would walk the midway, see the fantasy world it bisected, its lane lined with entertainers, con men, and thieves. He would dodge the pickpockets, watch the rubes gaping wide-eyed at the gaudy booths, and laugh at the marks as they struggled to win at the fixed games. It would put things back in perspective, might even stop the nightmares.

• • •

The opening day Hank arrived early at the ticket booth. He wanted to get it out of the way as soon as possible. He'd spent the last couple of days in a bit of a fog much to the displeasure of his supervisor. Now, besides everything else, his job was on the line. He needed to get this sorted out not just for his peace of mind but for the sake of his continuing employment as well.

The midway hadn't had the time to fill with trash as he entered. The sawdust paving it was barely disturbed and the smell of food cooking filled the air. It was almost pleasant, he thought. Nothing like what he remembered. He slowly walked along, taking in the sights and sounds, absorbing the atmosphere so as to better understand the truth of how badly he had mistaken that prophecy. It was a piece of theater, a bit of dialog in a cheap fiction. The longer he stayed, the more convinced he became and the lighter his mood.

"Mr. Straver."

He lurched to a stop, a thrill running down his spine at the sound of that voice. Even after all that time, he could never have forgotten it. He turned and found he was standing across the midway from the fortune-teller's tent. Under the entryway, Madame Serena stood watching him from those black eyes. His throat went suddenly dry as she beckoned him to follow her inside.

He stood uncertain as people walked by between him and the dark maw of the psychic's tent. Part of him wanted to go ahead and face her, call her out on her lies. The other part of him wanted to run screaming to his car and scurry home to safety. He licked his lips, tasting cold sweat. A big man in a wife-beater slammed into him, sending him staggering toward the tent.

"Watch yerself, bud!" he bellowed without stopping.

He found himself standing at the tent-flap. The aroma of incense wafted from inside, its scent bringing the memory of his previous visit thundering into his mind. The shock, confusion, and fear hit him again as if it was happening for the first time. He fought off a growing paralysis and steeled himself against the terror, struggling to remind himself it was all a farce, a sham, a charade, a product of his own imagination.

He set his jaw and pushed into the tent's darkness, convinced he would find the psychic lurking behind her props, ready to jump out at him in a juvenile attempt to scare him. That was her speed, wasn't it? Frightening teenagers and conning people with "happily ever after" crap?

His eyes took a moment to adjust to the dim light. When they did, he discovered he was alone in the tent. There was no furniture, nothing at all. The air was

heavy with the odor of incense, but its source was a mystery. He looked around, trying to figure how the woman got past him to get out, but there was only the one entrance. Maybe it just looked empty. Like a magician's trick, done with mirrors.

"Hello?" he said, stepping further into the tent. "I know you're in here." He walked to the back of the tent and pushed on the canvas. It was solid and unbroken. He turned to either side, looking for a hidden flap but found nothing. "What the...?"

"Mr. Straver."

Spinning, he found himself facing Madame Serena. She looked exactly the same as the first time he saw her years earlier.

"Did you come back to negotiate?" she asked with a wry smile.

"Negotiate? What do you mean?"

She moved around to stand between him and the exit. "Happy birthday," she mewed.

He swallowed hard, his throat parched. In spite of himself, he stepped back once, felt the canvas of the back of the tent against him.

"You turned fifty today, didn't you? Happy birthday," she said.

"Uh... thanks."

They stood watching each other for a moment.

"Well?" she said.

He blinked. "What?"

"You came to say something to me?"

He opened his mouth, but found the words gone. He had meant to confront his fear, to prove to himself it was all a lie, but faced with the sight of the psychic, her ageless face, her dark presence, his courage failed him.

As if sensing his fear, she moved closer. Her lips curled into the semblance of a grin that might have been more of a sneer.

"Your time is running out," she breathed. "You're wondering how long, now. Days? Hours? Minutes?"

The incense odor was thickening around him. It was becoming hard to breathe. He felt the tent closing in around him. His blood thundered in his ears.

"Let me go," he said, cursing himself at how weak his voice sounded.

"I'm not holding you," she protested. "I thought you wanted to talk. I guess I was wrong."

He pushed past her and fled the tent. Her laughter followed him all the way to the ticket booth as he ran.

Any confidence he had was gone now. After seeing Madame Serena again, after seeing how readily she remembered him and hearing her voice again, he could no longer find the strength to ridicule her prophecy. Convinced, he began to eye everything in his life from the standpoint of whether he would ever find himself alone. He reasoned that if he could survive until his fifty-first birthday all would be well. But in order to do so, he needed to insure that he always had company.

First thing after leaving the carnival he sprinted to an all-night grocery and spent the first of several sleepless nights haunting its aisles, avoiding the puzzled, suspicious looks of the grocer and his staff.

His life became a waking nightmare. He never realized how isolated he had become from the rest of humanity until he had to find reasons to be around others. A committed bachelor, the thought of marriage so late in life gave him the shivers. He bought a dog, then two dogs just in case, hoping that would qualify as not "being alone". Then he had to get rid of them when he moved into an apartment building in the middle of town. He bought a parrot in such a hurry he forgot everything for it but the cage.

The days dragged by, filled with paranoid moments when he found himself alone in a room or riding an elevator suddenly solo. One day he stayed late at the office for a meeting. When it ended, he realized he and the client were the only people in the building. He hurried out beside the man, following him closely to the parking garage, making inane conversation to cover his fear. The client was at first a little annoyed, but became alarmed when Straver begged him not to leave, clutching the man's coat and nearly crying. The next day his boss called him on the carpet about harassing clients.

After the third incident, he got his pink slip.

Within three months he went through his savings and lost everything. He hung in to his apartment until the sheriffs came and kicked him out. For a while, he convinced a couple of his former co-workers to put him up, but eventually they firmly suggested he move along. He learned the hard way how to live on the streets, gaining more than one scar along the way. He traded his parrot for a new coat. For six months he drifted from one place to another, finally settling into a mission house, the only place he could be absolutely sure he would never be alone other than prison.

But not even the best efforts could guarantee he would never be alone, and as the last days of his fiftieth year approached, he began to believe he had made a mistake. A horrible, stupid, idiotic mistake.

The day of his fifty-first birthday came and went uneventfully. That night, he sat on the bunk in the mission, fury building as he thought of the last year and all he had lost. His life was a shambles. He would die penniless, ashamed to show his face anywhere he had ever lived before. Everyone he had known thought he'd gone insane. He had wasted his life, destroyed himself for the sake of a carnival clown's amusement. He was mad at himself for being a colossal fool, at his boss for not understanding, at the world in general for being always against him, but most of all furious at that damned psychic.

It was all her fault. She was the one who put the curse on him. She was the one who drove the nail in the coffin of his hopes. She was the one who started this whole thing.

She was the one who stole his life!

The carnival would be back soon, and all he could think about was how to get his revenge. He would make her sorry she'd ever met him. She was going to suffer for every single minute he'd lost. He amused himself developing a thousand scenarios whose only common factor was her inevitable death.

She took away his life. He was going to take hers.

The carnival returned and he was ready. He had spent hours working out every move in meticulous detail. He had even rehearsed it several times to be sure. He would snatch the evil bitch from the security of her fellow carnies, take her to an abandoned warehouse close by and extract every second of his suffering from her flesh before he killed her.

He couldn't wait until opening night, of course, but he had to be sure she was there. He staked out a hiding place and watched until her tent went up and he saw her moving near it. It was odd he didn't see her arrive, but he didn't think about that for too long. The sight of her walking around the midway brought back the red film over his eyes.

Night fell and he left his hiding place to strike out across the street. Nothing was going to stop him now. Everything was ready. He was set, determined, and committed.

He was so single-minded that he never saw the car round the corner, never felt the impact, and never saw the earth spin around him.

Through flashes of consciousness he saw red and blue lights, caught the smell of antiseptics, saw glimpses of figures in blue scrubs. Finally, a man in a surgical mask and cap came into focus leaning over him.

"Mr. Straver? Mr. Straver, can you hear me?" the surgeon asked.

He struggled to speak but could only manage to nod slowly. His entire body was afire with pain.

"We need to stop the internal bleeding, Mr. Straver," the man was saying. "We've started the anesthetic so you will feel a little fuzzy. Please count backward from sixty for me."

With an effort, he began. "Sixty...fifty-nine...fifty-eight...fifty–"

Of a sudden, he heard himself. What was he saying? He stopped, his heart pounding.

"Its okay, Mr. Straver. I'll count for you. Fifty-seven...fifty-six...fifty-five..."

"Doctor," a voice somewhere close by called. "Could you have a look at this?"

"Kind of busy here," the surgeon snapped.

"It'll just take a second."

The doctor disappeared from his sight. He was left alone. Inside his head that relentless countdown went on. No matter how hard he tried, no matter what he did, he couldn't stop it.

Fifty-four...fifty-three...fifty-two...

Was it just him, or was there a dark, shadowy figure rising over his head?

The End

Gridiron Second Down

by David Boop

Once a professional football player named Gordon "Gory" Burrell, a freak accident changed Burrell's skin to metal. Using his newfound invulnerability and strength, Burrell fights from the shadows against the Giordano family, Everett, Washington's #1 crime syndicate. Once the most feared man on the field, now he strikes fear into those who would do the innocent harm as... Gridiron!

Often reporter Terry "Pointer" Johnston found himself in a tight squeeze working for the Everett Herald.

CLANK-TINK-CRUNCH!!!

As the Lincoln Continental trunk compacted tighter by the second, Pointer, who lay bound inside of the trunk, realized this could be his final story.

Pointer covered the war between the local mob and the city's vigilante, the iron-skinned avenger, Gridiron. Hard to believe a year had already gone by since Gordon "Gory" Burrell disappeared and Gridiron showed up, but what a ride the year had been. While Pointer billed himself up as the impartial observer, "the eye in crime," he often used his network of informants to help Gridiron's unyielding quest to free Everett from the mob's ever-increasing grip.

CREAK-KIRICK-THUNK!!!

Scooting as best he could to the back of the trunk, Pointer knew there was nowhere he could crawl safely to. The vehicle had obviously been dumped into a car smasher at the local junk yard. Screaming wouldn't help. The hydraulic machine made too much noise to be heard over. This was it; his last story on the mob, never to be turned in. It was a doozy, too.

Rumors had Vito Giordano taking the reins of the mob after Gridiron took down Big Papa Giordano in a blaze of glory. Vito, a former enlisted man, needed the protection of the mob. While serving as an armory sergeant, Vito stole weapons for Big Papa and then went AWOL when the weapons were discovered missing. As the last remaining Giordano heir, the family circled around the young man tightly. His military training came in to good use, as Vito laid out new strategies to take over the city and stop Gridiron from interfering with their plans.

Pointer had left a series of clues after being discovered by a group of Vito's "made" men. He didn't have much time when it happened, and his only hope was that somehow Gridiron noticed and followed his clues. If he did, they should lead him to the goodfellows who'd stuffed Pointer into the rapidly deteriorating trunk.

But Gordon Burrell wasn't the brightest man even before becoming a superhero, nor had he gained any burst of brain juice afterwards. Like his days as a linebacker, Gridiron tended to lead with his head in a more... direct way.

CRINK-TINK-KIRICK!!!

Swallowing hard, Pointer pulled himself into the smallest ball possible. The effort was futile. Metal closed in on him from all sides. Sharp metal jabbed his ribs and the remaining air tasted of hydraulics, gas and fear. The trunk lid pressed against Pointer's face, pushing his head into the floorboards. The reporter tried not to think of his eyeballs shooting out from their sockets, or how his body would be discovered, if at all.

He thought briefly of June White, the gal he'd had a crush on for as long as he'd known her. She'd been Gordon's flame and continued to carry the hope that one day Gridiron could revert back to the man she and her daughter April adored. She knew of Pointer's feelings and while honored, there wasn't room for two men in her heart. Now, she wouldn't have any emotional conflict. Pointer was on cue to die. Right there. Right then.

He held his breath, not knowing what else to do and waited for the end.

● ● ●

Suddenly, all sound stopped save for the sound of a tightly wound spring.

CRANK! CRANK! CRANK!

The slow moan of gears moving backwards against their better nature. Next came the horrible rending sound of machinery being torn asunder as the crusher reversed its trajectory. Light streamed in from the holes where taillights used to be. The weight on Pointer's face abated and he could taste air again.

A familiar voice called to him.

"Johnston? You still alive in there?"

The words were stressed, as if spoken under duress. Pointer pictured the nigh-invulnerable Gridiron positioned on the edge of the crusher, lifting with all his might.

"Yeah, barely."

"Can you kick open the trunk?"

Pointer rotated as best he could. The metal had sprung back a little with the release of the crusher's unyielding fist. Using what leverage he could, he kicked. He also tried shouldering it. Luckily, the lock had popped under the crusher's onslaught and the trunk lid hung loose. Between kicks and shoulders, Pointer got the lid to bounce up and then drop back down, hitting him on the head.

"Ow!"

"Can you hurry? I'm not sure I can hold this thing much longer."

Panic touched the edges of Gridiron's voice, something Pointer hadn't heard before. Gridiron not only had iron-coated skin, but iron-laced bones making him able to lift very heavy objects. But those objects rarely pushed back with such force.

Pointer kicked up again, swinging his feet out through the small opening. He was able to sit up and stop the lid with his head once more. He inch-wormed himself out, falling beside the car. A small ladder lay nearby, so after getting his arms from around his back, he climbed for all he was worth.

Pointer could see the squatted legs of Gridiron as he gripped the edge of the metal slab. Fingers holding Pointer's fate were slipping. There were seconds left to finish his climb.

Once he got to the top, he rolled onto the junkyard's gravel surface and called out, "Clear!"

Letting go and jumping back simultaneously, Gridiron watched on as the giant crusher finished its ghastly work, crushing the Lincoln to a half an inch thick.

And then he turned to Pointer.

Despite knowing that Gridiron designed his outfit to intimidate bad guys, Pointer often recoiled reflexively when the mutated hero first arrived. Gridiron had incorporated a clown's grin to his facemask, leaving only his dark, angry eyes exposed. The horrific effect appeared as if an evil clown had clawed its way up from hell.

His outfit consisted of the tattered remnants of an old football uniform wrapped in a cloak made from a worn blanket. When seen, most people couldn't tell if Gridiron was hero or villain. That was okay with Gordon. He'd created the persona on the playing field and he had no problems taking it with him to his war on the mob.

Gridiron freed Pointer from his bonds.

"Cutting it close today, huh, Gory?" Pointer rubbed at his wrists and ankles.

"Call me Gory again and I'll toss you back in the crusher." There was no sarcasm in Gridiron's tone, and Pointer didn't know how serious the vigilante was... this time.

Gridiron hated it when he used Gordon's football nickname, but Pointer didn't care. Gordon occasionally needed reminders of the man inside the iron coat.

"Plus, you give lousy clues."

Pointer feigned mock injury. "Hey! Didn't have a lot to work with. I got nabbed getting a scoop for you. I know where the weapons shipment is coming in."

Vito had once again used his Army connections to get access to state-of-the-art military hardware. The Thompson M1s would give them an advantage over the Everett police department.

Gridiron crossed his arms and stared down at Pointer obviously waiting. It took the reporter a second, but then he got it. "Where are my manners? Thank you. You saved my life. Again. You'd think we'd just have an unspoken repertoire by now. I get nabbed while fetching you intel. You come save me. A 'thank you' from me. Chuck on the shoulder from you."

Gridiron, not seeming to be interested in Pointer's banter, turned and walked toward the junk yard's entrance. Pointer leapt to his feet and hobbled after him.

"Whoa. Wait a minute, big guy. What's up? You seem uncharacteristically moody today."

Gridiron said nothing.

"Was it something I said?"

Nothing.

Alarm worked into Pointer's conscience. "Is something wrong with June, or April? They weren't nabbed, too? I'll kill Vito myself if he's harmed them."

"No. *They* are safe." Gridiron stopped and spun on the reporter. "But then that's the point, isn't it, 'Pointer'? I'm starting to think you enjoy this too much. You put yourself in danger just so I'll have to rescue you."

Pointer froze, slack-jawed. After a moment, he stumbled a response. "Huh? What? You're making no sense. I'm no lovesick Gridiron groupie. Why would I—"

"To sell papers, that's why!" Gridiron stabbed a finger into Pointer's shoulder. Pointer tried not to let on how much it hurt. "Your stories about near escapes keep your readers coming back and you gainfully employed. It's like a drug to you. You know I'll show up at the last moment and pull your fat from the fire, but I almost didn't this time. You nearly died!"

Pointer laughed nervously, trying to wave the concern off. "But I didn't. And you did."

Gridiron growled low. "But what happens that one time I don't? I can't have more blood on my hands than I already have. It's one thing when it's Vito's men. It's another thing when it's a civilian, someone not part of the war."

Pointer understood Gridiron's concern was genuine. The hero of the gridiron, and the city of Everett, who was impervious to most forms of attack, got scared. Scared to let the Giordanos win. Or better put, afraid to lose. If Gordon didn't do well with losing, Gridiron made Gory seem like a pussycat in comparison.

Pointer nodded. "Maybe you're right. Maybe I have been taking too many risks of late. Probably why they want to kill me almost as bad as you. But you forget something."

Gridiron waited for Pointer's point.

"This *is* a war and I volunteered to fight in it." Courage welled in Pointer as he stood up to his reluctant partner. "If anything happened to me, I wouldn't be some innocent caught in the crossfire, Gordon. I'd be a soldier falling in battle. And I'm okay with that."

The speech did nothing to soften the iron avenger's stance.

"Maybe I'm not. Maybe I don't want to see June cry at your funeral."

"June? Heck, she'd be glad to be rid of me." Pointer laughed.

"NO! It's not funny!"Gridiron's shout reminded Pointer why he intimidated everyone around him, iron-skin or not. "She cares more than you know. And I count on you. If anything were to happen to me, you're the only man in this city I trust with her, trust to keep them safe. Understand?"

The hero turned and continued his trek through the junkyard. Pointer, however, held his ground.

"So, what? I'm supposed to hide while you do all the hard work? Nuts to that, buddy. I know you think you're going to die before this is over, and maybe you will. I'm doing my best to keep that a long way off."

Gridiron rounded a corner when Pointer called out, "Don't you want to know where the guns are?"

An exasperated sigh reached the reporter, so he raced to catch up to his friend.

● ● ●

The Giordano Family went from mansions and walking around the city unmolested to fortifying bunkers and guerilla tactics. The Everett P.D. had become more and more confident with each Gridiron success. While not officially condoning the actions of the vigilante, anything making their lives easier had their blessing. Then there were stories of rival organizations looking to fill the power vacuum left when Big Papa died. Russian, Mexican and even Oriental scouts roamed the back alleys looking for a foothold in the city. Vito's men sought them out and returned various body parts to their masters.

The pressure forced Vito Giordano to make brazen (or reckless) moves to keep the police and other mobs at bay. In some cases, he resorted to surprise attacks on local businesses they once received weekly protection money from. Street walkers never went to work without protection of a heavily-armed thug, rushing them from one John to the next in an effort to reignite the market. Extra levels of subterfuge had been placed on all illegal gambling joints, until even Gridiron and Pointer no longer knew where they were anymore. It made Pointer wonder if they made any money being so secretive.

"I mean," he told Gridiron as the slipped down the dark alley, "if so few people know about them, how do they do business?"

"An addict finds the fix, even if it's down in a sewer. Evil smells evil."

The reporter shuddered. His pal's dour mood took any fun out of fighting crime.

"Well, this mob armory was nearly as hard to find as a dice joint. I played dead to get the information."

"You need acting lessons then. You nearly had your final curtain."

Pointer hit the back of Gridiron's shoulder, unsure if the iron man felt it. "There you go again. I thought we settled that?"

"Shhh!"

"Don't you sh—"

Gridiron whirled around, simultaneously placing a hand over Pointer's mouth and pushing him back into the shadows. Pointer, who had indeed been hit by a speeding car in his pursuit of the truth, preferred the hit-n-run to Gridiron's tackle.

Peering down the alley, the reporter could see the back of a truck and three G.I.'s unloading weapons crates into a warehouse. Two still held the rank of Privates, but the third acted as if in charge. He wore Sergeant's stripes, so Pointer guessed he was Vito's replacement at the armory and maybe his co-conspirator.

The man himself, Vito Giordano, hovered over the shipment while five of his made men guarded the perimeter.

"Vito," Pointer whispered to Gridiron, "used to run the weapons depot out of Fort Lewis. Word is he called in a lot of favors to get those guns. If Uncle Sam got word Vito procured five crates of the new Tommy guns, he'd not only be court-martialed for the AWOL charge, but probably shot as a traitor."

Gridiron's metal brow furrowed. "Why now? Why take the risk?"

"Must be planning something big."

Pointer made to move in closer, better to hear what was going on, but Gridiron reaffirmed the spot he wanted the reporter to stay in by pressing him tightly against the wall.

"Careful. I'm no tackling dummy. I break, you know."

"I know. Stay here or I'll show you what I do to tackling dummies."

With that, Gridiron became the darkness, letting it envelop him.

Pointer watched impotently as the mob's men hauled their booty into the warehouse. Knowing where to look after so long following the hero, Pointer looked up to see a hulking silhouette open a skylight and enter the warehouse from above.

Vito excused his soldiers, as did the supply sergeant. Soon only two bosses remained and Pointer wanted, no needed, to know what evil they concocted.

He wasn't incompetent, no matter how Gridiron made it sound. Many a time he'd snuck into the back of a restaurant or pool hall unobserved, able to listen to the most private of conversations and leave without getting caught. If anything, hanging out with a superhero made Pointer more cautious; learning how to move with the wind, taking advantage of cloud cover over moonlight.

When the head thief pulled out one last box for Vito, Pointer had no choice but to get closer.

He crouched down and carefully placed his steps to be practically soundless. A dumpster lay near enough to the action to provide excellent cover for eavesdropping. Step by step, staying to the black, Pointer drew closer. Without a single mishap, he reached the goal. Breathing a sigh of relief, he tuned his finely trained ears to the secret dealings.

"I'm going to need this back in a week," the sergeant said. "They're taking it back out into the field for more tests. Everyone's anxious about what's going on in Germany and they want to make sure all our ducks are in a row. If the XR-1 came up missing…"

"Forgetaboutit!" Vito assured. "It's only going to take one shot to end Gridiron for good. Well, if what you told me over the phone is true?"

The thief waved his hands. "I wouldn't lie to you, boss. It's the only thing they salvaged from the wreckage of some weird airplane. And, boy, does it pack a wallop!"

Vito seemed impressed. "Heats metal up from a distance, eh?"

"Yeah. Like a flamethrower, but without any flames. No lights. No nothing."

"Then how do you know it's working?"

The GI smiled. "Oh, you know. Turns the metal bright red until it's dripping like candle wax. Try it out."

Vito scanned the area. "Okay, let's fry us a dumpster."

Coincidentally, it also happened to be the big metal dumpster Pointer hid behind.

Nodding, the sergeant hefted the gun-shaped object out of the crate and pointed it right at Pointer!

• • •

Just before the weird electric hum the weird gun reached its crescendo, Pointer flattened to the ground, making himself as thin as possible. Heat crossed his shoulder blades and tasted the acrid smell of molten metal as some invisible force punched a hole through the dumpster. Within seconds, the ray gun had finished its work, leaving a head-sized hole in its wake, the edges of which glowed and oozed like lava.

"Impressive," Vito said, not letting too much excitement into his voice. "Think that'll do the job?"

"Oh, this should do nicely. You'll have to thank the makers of this beauty for me."

"Not possible," the GI corrected, "there wasn't enough of them to pull from the wreckage. Whatever they were, they didn't look...human."

Vito clicked his teeth and said, "Takes monsters to kill a monster, I guess. Call it poetic irony."

Pointer thought it sounded like a future butt-kicking from Gridiron to him, but at that exact moment, a single drop of hot, liquid metal dripped onto his prone hand. He yelped and pulled it to his mouth quickly, both to lick the wound and stifle any further cries.

"You hear something?" the weapons thief asked.

"A rat!" Vito growled and grabbed the gun from his partner-in-crime hoping to flush out a spy, however, as the gun warmed up, a small object darted through the hole in the dumpster. The feline scrambled away, its tail a smoking stump.

"Not a rat, boss. A cat." The man laughed, but it quickly died away, when his former superior didn't join in. Vito kept staring at the area where Pointer lay holding his hand, his breath, everything, but his racing heart.

Finally, the Giordano head seemed convinced the noise was indeed just a pest. He turned away and walked into the warehouse, never relinquishing the weapon. Once both were gone, Pointer brought himself back to life. After sitting up and thanked the lord above for his continued existence, a single thought sent him scrambling after Vito.

Gridiron is toast if Vito gets his sights on him.

• • •

Slinking through the cobweb-laced warehouse, Pointer wondered why nobody ever cleaned them. With all the people out of work, you'd think companies could pay someone a penny a day just to dust the shelves. No one liked repeatedly pulling webs from their face.

Of course, he snuck in through the least used aisles as not to be noticed. So far, he'd heard no sounds of fighting or charging ray guns. Gridiron must be taking his time, accessing the situation; very un-characteristic for the vigilante. Maybe Pointer rubbed off on him some, just as his time with the hero had changed Pointer, too.

Once upon a time, the reporter would have sacrificed his favorite aunt Gertrude for a good story. However, after a year following Gridiron's exploits, he found himself helping more old ladies cross the street, donating his off time at missions and, as Gridiron suspected, putting himself in the line of fire. Gory had been wrong, though. It wasn't to make the front page, but to make a difference. A year ago, self-sacrifice would've been the furthest thing from Terry Johnston's mind, but Pointer couldn't think of a better way to die than trying to save the city.

Further introspections, though, would have to wait. Raised voices and gunfire alerted him to the news.

Gridiron had made his move.

Rushing forward, cobwebs be damned, Pointer reached an opening where he could see into an open area. A dozen men, mixed Mob and GIs, scrambled around for cover while firing blindly into the rafters. Obviously no longer wanting to be a sitting duck, Gridiron launched himself from above, cloak flowing behind him and landed on the pile of weapon crates. They crumpled under his weight, spilling the Thompson M1s across the floor.

One slid within ten feet of Pointer.

Fully in the fray, Gridiron cut loose. Bullets from guns old and new bounced off his metal hide as he charged the minions of evil. Scooping a gunman in each arm, Gridiron planted them hard onto the concrete surface, knocking the wind from them. Then, from a three-point-stance, he rushed forward, driving his shoulder into one, two, three different mobsters in a row. The assailants were falling like pins in a bowling alley.

All save for Vito Giordano, who cautiously hung back with his ray gun. Pointer could see hunger in the mob boss's eyes, a bloodlust for Gridiron to make a mistake like pausing just long enough for him to melt a hole through the hero's iron gut.

Pointer wasn't about to let that happen. Breaking cover, he scraped the M1 from the floor and fired in Vito's direction. The young mob boss ducked back into the racks at the sudden shower of hot lead. When he poked his head out to see who had the nerve to shoot at him, he mouthed the words, "YOU!" Vito turned his alien weapon on Pointer and the hum of the weird canon reached its peak.

Out in the open, Pointer wouldn't have time to find cover, so he kept firing, hoping his bad aim would eventual strike something. It would come down to who got hit first.

Vito pulled the trigger, fire blazing from the muzzle. Pointer braced for multiple impacts. Instead, he found himself air borne as he was blindsided from the right side. He and Gridiron tumbled down an aisle. The ray gun went off, melting shelving and crates as Vito's arc followed them. Pointer gasped for air when Gridiron placed a hand on his chest to keep him pinned down.

"Ribs!" was all Pointer could get out, yet it was enough for the hero to let up.

"I thought I told you—"

Pointer waved his to shut it and between gasps said, "Scold me...later...big gun...melts metal...you're in...danger."

Surveying the damage, Gridiron said, "I can see that now. Must have been an easier way to get my attention than attempting suicide."

"You were busy."

Pointer sat up against one of the numerous warehouse crates.

"So, what's next?"

Gridiron shrugged. "I'll do what I always do when a play goes to hell – improvise."

Pointer remembered Gory's improvisations on the field. He worried then more for Vito's safety than his own.

● ● ●

And without thought for his safety, Gridiron left the cover of the packing crates to face his deadly nemesis. He drew Vito Giordano's fire, but this was no foolhardy plan on the masked hero's part. Dodging between several tall shelving units, Gridiron let the futuristic weapon do its work, melting the supports holding the racks upright.

Like dominoes, the units Gridiron targeted fell forward in a pattern trapping the mob boss by his own machinations. They stood there, facing each other: Mobster versus monster. However, when Vito went to pull the trigger... nothing! Gridiron's tactics had left the gun drained of all its juice!

Vito was no match for the iron fists of justice. Gridiron laid the mook out flat. He still was unconscious when the United States Military Police arrived, aided by Everett's own P.D. The whole lot was packed up for jail while the XR-1 was quickly and quietly removed.

Once again, the unstoppable force of freedom, in the form of Gridiron, has protected this city in its darkest hour.

"Don't you think 'monster' is a little much? Aren't I 'sposed to be the good guy."

"It's all in the context, Gordy. You're a monster to evil doers. The innocent love you."

Gridiron furrowed his brow as he reread the passage.

"How about next time I describe you as 'an iron version of DaVinci's David'? An image like that will get some hearts beating faster." Pointer egged his companion on by elbowing him. They sat together on a rooftop enjoying the night air.

The snake that had been the Giordano family withered in the wake of Vito's arrest. The streets remained safe for the time being and Gridiron could take a break. He even visited June and April a couple times, thought he still kept the visits short, not wanting to let himself want more than was possible.

Gridiron tossed the paper aside, no longer interested.

"It's too quiet here."

Pointer shrugged. "And that's a bad thing?"

"Nah, but it doesn't give a guy like me anything to do. I need a fight. I want action."

"Maybe it's time for you to travel some. Visit some bigger cities. There're baddies everywhere, not just in Everett."

"Yeah, but how will people see me? A monster, as you just described?"

The reporter waved it away. "These metropolises have their own heroes and villains, some just like you, or so I hear. Men and women with all sorts of powers."

Gridiron put his fist to his chin in deep contemplation. Pointer couldn't help but think he looked like Rodan's *The Thinker* when he did this. After a few moments, Gridiron did something Pointer hadn't seen the big man do since before his transformation;

Smile.

"If there really are others like me out there, then I could finally cut loose. I have no idea what I'm capable of. I might finally get to be the 'me' I was made to be."

And though it would be sad to see Gordon go, Pointer understood. Gridiron helped the reporter become the person he'd dreamed about being, and that feeling should be experienced by everyone, especially by iron-clad superheroes like the one known as…

Gridiron!

The End

Chase the Darkness Down
(A Gunfighter Gothic story.)
by Mark Bousquet

"What day is it?" Jill Masters asked.

"The day where it's too hot for Hell," Hanna Pak said, taking off her gambler's hat to wipe her brow with a white and green bandana.

"No, the 10th? The 11th?"

"It's August," Hanna said, annoyed. "What does it matter?"

"Because," Jill said, pointing to the smoldering town a mile ahead of them in the sands of Arizona, "I think we're going to want to remember the day we rode into that town."

Hanna said nothing, but gently dug her boots into the side of her horse, spurring him on. Jill's horse joined them, and the two women moved across the hot desert of the Arizona Territory in silence. It was almost a year since they left Boston, and they'd gone from being a white merchant's daughter and her Korean servant to gunslingers for hire, solving the wild and the weird for coin as partners in Gunfighter Gothic.

"We Shoot the Weird in the Face," their business cards read, and they were good at it.

The Bostonians had little desire to return to Boston anytime soon.

The women wore boots, jeans, shirts, and cowboy hats. Hanna preferred her shirts to be green and her boots, vest, and gambler's hat to be black, while Jill's boots, vest, and poncho were brown, and her hat was a Stetson. They'd spent their whole lives together, but it was only in the past year they had become equals, and as they passed mutilated Indian bodies on the road to the frontier town, there was a shared comfort in being here together if they had to be here at all.

"Indian raid gone bad?" Jill asked.

Hanna pointed to a few white bodies sprinkled amidst the twenty dead Indians, and noticed both races had been killed by being hacked to death. "Looks like they were fighting something together," Hanna said, and looked behind her. "Something that came the way we did. What are you thinking?"

Jill pointed to the sun.

The horses stepped over and around the bodies, disturbing the flies that had come to feast on the easy meals. The smell in the air and dried blood in the sand told them this had happened two, maybe three days ago. Before them, the settlement consisted of a squat water tower and eight one-story buildings, four on each side of the street, and likely existed for no reason other than it was situated far enough from Tucson that people needed a place to refit and refuel. All of the buildings were smoldering or smoking. The four closest to them were burned black, while the further four were in better shape.

Without having to explain what she was doing, Jill took her black horse around the right side of town, so they could enter from opposite ends. Hanna watched her go, thinking how far they'd come in under a year. She was no longer the love-struck, eternally pining sidekick/servant, but an equal part of their endeavor.

Her distracted thoughts almost cost her a bullet wound.

There was a flash of light between two buildings on her right and she pulled the horse hard to the side as a bullet whizzed past his chest. Her gun was out and a bullet was sent hurtling in the direction of her attacker. Her bullet slammed against the side of the blackened wood and an old voice cried out in pain.

"Shoot at me again and you won't leave that alley," Hanna said, putting up a hand to halt Jill as she rode up from the other side of town.

In response, a gun was tossed out into the street.

"How do I know that's your only gun?" she asked. "Come on out, old man, nice and slow."

The old man did as he was told, crawling forward in slow, clunky movements. Hanna and Jill's eyes took in his naked, blistered body and knew in an instant Jill's first guess had been correct.

"Sun Chasers," Jill said, looking up at the sun. "Damn."

● ● ●

"The Chasers came out of the east, three mornings ago," David said. The third building on the right had been a whorehouse, and they'd placed the old man on a bed and covered him with wetted sheets to cool his body temperature. They'd brought him water from the tower and shared some of their jerky with him, breaking it into tiny pieces they soaked in water, which he sucked on before swallowing. "I had heard the stories about them, but I never believed them," he admitted. The Chasers had shaved off his hair to assist in the burning, and the women wondered how much longer he would have lasted.

Hanna and Jill had crossed paths with the Sun Chasers on two previous occasions. They were a band of sun-worshipping cultists who wore nothing but heavy boots and yellow and black kilts and spent their days chasing the sun. They rode hard to the east in the morning, then hard to the west in the afternoon. When the sun went down, they stopped for the night, and prepared their captives for the following day's conversion.

The conversion was simple: they stripped you naked, tied you to the ground, and let the sun roast your body. If you joined them, they let you up to ride with them; if not, you stayed lashed into the dirt until the elements claimed your soul.

"You refused to join them," Jill said.

David shook his head, every movement sending ripples of pain across his blistered skin. "It never came to that," he said. When he told them his story, his words came out in wheezes and gasps, slowed by his mouth's need for water. "They were wild men. The Indians showed up three hours before the Chasers. They were Paiute, I think, but no one really paid them any attention, except you could tell they had been run ragged. You know how it is out here," he said, and Jill fed him more water, which the old man gladly let run down his throat.

"How many Chasers were there?" Hanna asked. "How many were in this town?"

"And not to put too fine a point on it," Jill said, "but where's all the bodies? There's plenty outside of town but I didn't see anyone lashed to the ground. Not even you, it comes to it."

The old man looked to the window. "The dead men you saw to the west of town sacrificed themselves so the women, children, and elderly could get away," he said. "I stayed here … did my part … was supposed to be the last to leave, but they caught me and left I tied to a horse post. These Chasers … they weren't interested in converting anyone."

The Bostonians exchanged a glance, that last part not sounding like any Chaser story they'd heard.

"You're telling us the townspeople got away?" Hanna asked.

David nodded. "But," he said and looked to the door, his dry tongue calling out for more water, which Jill provided.

"But what?" she asked as he sipped and slurped.

"They haven't come back," he said. "Someone needs to go get them and tell them it's safe to return." He reached out and touched Jill's wrist. "Fill your canteens before you go," he said. "It's a long walk."

● ● ●

They left David in his bed, their canteens filled and a full pitcher of water left for him and moved across the street to one of the blackened buildings.

"It's a church," Jill said as they entered and she got sight of the pews and pulpit. "Your atheist butt will probably burst into flame at any second."

"Do you think God hates me more for thinking He doesn't exist," Hanna asked, "or you for not seeing the inside of a church in almost a year?"

Jill couldn't think of a comeback better than that, so she kept her mouth shut and led Hanna down the center aisle to stand before the pulpit. Together, they pushed the wooden stand to the side, and then opened the hatch in the floor the pulpit hid from sight.

"You can come out now," Jill said, kneeling by the hole in the floor and seeing a set of wooden steps leading down into the basement.

No one answered her.

"Into darkness, then," Hanna said, walking down the steps. A small oil lamp burned beneath them, providing light but not answers. The room was small, not more than ten feet across, and cut out of the Earth. For a moment, Hanna couldn't understand how it was supposed to hold an entire town, but then her boots stepped on wood and she realized there was another hatch, with another staircase leading down into an underground tunnel.

"I hate this," Jill said, crossing her arms and rubbing her elbows at the stark contrast in temperature.

"Yup," Hanna said, getting her bearings. They were at the end of the tunnel that led away from town, so there was only one way to go. The tunnel was narrow, cut right out of the ground and offering no other support. Oil lamps could be seen in the distance, but while there was enough light to see the next lamp, there were pockets of darkness in between, so one had to take it on faith the tunnel went where it looked it went. "Pull that hatch shut," Hanna ordered, and started down the tunnel.

"Remind me," Jill said, following orders, "just how much we're getting paid for this?"

Hanna didn't answer. They were good enough on money that it wasn't a concern, and she hated when Jill made an issue of it. Curse of being a rich girl's daughter, Hanna figured. Even if they were dead broke, they would not have turned down helping people, but helping people and getting paid was the better option.

The tunnel was hastily cut, designed for substance, not show. The floor was uneven enough that Hanna walked slowly, keeping her guns on her hip to allow her to use her hands for support along the walls. She heard Jill pull the hatch closed and start to follow after her, complaining every other step.

"If there's nervous people down here," Hanna said, glancing back, "you might not want to tip them to our arrival."

Jill made a face but fell silent. She kept the distance at fifteen feet between them and couldn't stop from continually looking behind her. Something was wrong here and she felt it in her heart as much as she'd figured it out in her brain. The Sun Chasers lived to convert people to their cause, and the scene they'd left upstairs didn't feel right. The Chasers weren't above killing, but...

"I've got something," Hanna said, motioning for Jill to join her. By the time Jill had closed the distance to where Hanna was, her partner had entered a large cavern and turned to her left. Unlike the tunnel, the cavern wasn't man made, but had been formed naturally. Several oil lamps burned around the outer wall, but just as many had already burned themselves out.

"Whoa," she said, seeing fifteen to twenty old women sitting on the floor of a round room.

Hanna was on one knee, staring hard into the face of the nearest woman. "Her eyes are milky," she said as Jill joined her. Hanna put a finger in front of the woman's eyes and moved her finger back and forth, looking for a sign of acknowledgment, but the woman kept looking forward, her head gently rocking forward and back as she wheezed out her breaths.

As Hanna continued examining the woman, Jill quickly walked around the room to check out the others. "They're all the same," she reported to Hanna, who had not been successful in getting the woman to recognize her presence. "All the same," she clarified, "in not only state of mind, but that they're all old women."

"You've got a theory?"

"If a group of people were running for their life from something, who runs the slowest?"

"You think the Chasers came down here?"

Jill shook her head. "I'm not convinced the Chasers were even upstairs," she said, "but they certainly didn't come through this room. They would have dragged these women back into the sun and taken them for conversion, not left them mumbling in the dark." The merchant's daughter looked around the room as the oil lamps neared their completion. "Gonna be dark here soon," she said. "We need to keep moving."

"Let's feed the women first," she said, and used up the bulk of her canteen to pour water into the mouths of the women, before tilting their head back to let the cool liquid sink to their stomachs.

"You're gonna waste it all," Jill said.

"Good thing we've still got yours," Hanna said, moving to one of the lit oil lamps to douse the light, leaving only one of them burning. "Better to save the oil then waste it," she said. "Let's go."

"No theory about what happened to these women?" Jill asked. There was a series of oil-soaked rags on sticks and she took one for herself and one for Hanna, and the women lit them before leaving the rocking, milk-eyed women behind.

"No theories," Hanna said, shaking her head after taking one last look at them, and moving forward. The extended cave system was wide open and in descent. The Bostonians walked down, feeling the cold increase as they went.

"No chance the Chasers came down here," Jill repeated. "They stop moving in the dark and we haven't tripped over them."

"Yet."

"Pessimist."

At the bottom of the descent, a small pond awaited them in a cavern, and across the forty foot expanse of water, a group of old men huddled together on a rocky beach in the far right corner of the room. A small fire was burning in the center of their circle, and they kept their eyes focused on the orange flames.

"I don't see a boat," Jill said, looking to her left and right. "Think it's safe to walk?"

"Yes," Hanna said, rolling her eyes, "a spooky pond beneath the earth is going to be totally safe to walk across."

"Don't be a baby. It doesn't even look that deep," Jill said. "Besides, look at them. If those old Dicks made it across, surely we can do it."

Hanna pointed to the far end of the rocky beach. "They had a boat," she said, and then looked around for a rock bigger than her hand, which she picked up and tossed towards the center of the pond. It hit with a big splash.

"It's deep," Jill said. "Let's keep…"

The splash had caught the attention of the old men. Those who were looking in their direction began to point and the ones that were facing the opposite wall tried to turn around but did little more than fall on their backs and point, their fingertips splashing in the shallows of the pond.

"Unnn unnnn unnhhhhh!"

"Come on," Hanna said, tugging at Jill's elbow as the men became increasingly excited. One of the men accidentally kicked over the fire, sending sparks into the air. "Let's keep going. We're not going to learn anything from them."

They skirted the edge of the pond and passed through a small opening to enter a large cavern system. The walls on the far left and right were solid, but ahead of them there were four different tunnels moving deeper into the darkness. Unlike the previous portions of the tunnel, there were no artificial lights down here save for the torches they held in their hand. There was enough water in the stream that ran from the third tunnel to them and bits of glassy rock in the walls for the light from their torches to magnify enough for them to get a good view of the room.

"What's the plan?" Jill asked.

"Don't drop your firestick in the water," Hanna said.

"This is why I let you make the plans," Jill said, looking back to the tunnels. "How do we approach them? I'll tell you right now…"

"Agreed," Hanna said, not needing Jill to finish. "No splitting up. Let's take them one at a time and see what we find."

They walked across the floor, the slow-moving stream moving away from them to the right, and entered the first tunnel, which bore no signs of being man made or altered. The tunnel was wide enough for six people to walk comfortably beside one another, and it veered off to the left almost immediately. Hanna and Jill walked in silence for ten minutes before Hanna stopped.

"I feel like we're just chasing the darkness," she said, "and these makeshift torches aren't going to last forever. Let's go back and…"

"Shh!" Jill snapped, looking ahead of them and straining her ears to listen intently. Hanna trusted Jill enough to tell her what she thought she heard when the time was right, so she didn't bother to ask. Instead, she closed her eyes concentrated on the sounds of the underground. She heard nothing coming from ahead of them, but when she cocked her concentration in the other direction; she could hear the old men by the fire still moaning away.

"They're in the water," she said, hearing the faint sounds of splashing.

Jill shook her head and pointed forward. "I don't care about them," she whispered. "I hear growling."

Hanna strained her ears, but couldn't discern anything, so she crept forward ten feet, the tunnel still arcing to their left, and then stopped. Closing her eyes, she concentrated again, and this time she could pick out the unmistakable sound of ... something. "Is it growling?" she asked Jill in a low voice. "It almost sounds like ... mumbling."

"Only one way to find out," Jill said and moved forward. As they moved ahead, the tunnel narrowed and straightened out as the sounds of animalistic grunting and growling grew louder. When the women realized there was a light source up ahead, they put their torches down and against the wall before proceeding. Another two hundred feet brought them into a room roughly the size of a hotel lobby. The room was round, made out of a metal wall that was lit with hundreds of torches and oil lamps, arranged haphazardly from floor to ceiling wherever there was space on the wall. It took more than a moment for their eyes to become even semi-accustomed to the brightness, and neither woman were ever not squinting while they were in the room.

"Jesus," Jill whispered when she could look around, as her eyes finally tool in the center of the room:

Several dozen babies were lying on the floor, wrapped in cloths of various colors and styles, and arranged in a three-body deep circle.

Standing in the middle of them was a naked man with severely sunburned skin that looked like melted red and pink wax, wearing nothing more than heavy boots and a black and gold plaid kilt.

"Sun Chaser," Hanna whispered.

"Get away from those babies!" Jill yelled, drawing both of her Colts.

"No!" Hanna yelled, but it was too late, and Jill fired both guns in a right-left-right-left firing pattern. All four bullets slammed into the Sun Chaser's torso, and the religious zealot screamed in pain as he took a step backward.

He would have tumbled into the sleeping babies, but a heavy, metal chain that was attached to his waist caught him. The Chaser dropped to a knee, wailing in pain as he looked to the wounds in his chest that were gushing blood.

"Brilliant," Hanna snapped, lowering Jill's guns as she jogged forward.

"You're regretting me killing a Sun Chaser?" Jill asked. "Have you forgotten what it was like to be their prisoner?"

"No," Hanna said, pointing to the chain, "but maybe you've forgotten what being a prisoner looks like."

Jill cut short the retort that was ready to fire to study the chain. It connected the floor to the Chaser's waist and was heavy enough to stop a rolling train. The Bostonians stood on the edge of the ring of babies, grim looks on their faces as the badly injured Chaser began growling and snapping at them from his knees, too injured to rise to challenge them. At no point did he talk in anything resembling his human tongue, and not just because it had been cut out years earlier. The wildness in the man's eyes told Hanna and Jill he'd been a Sun Chaser for a long time, driven mad by the quest to chase down an abusive god.

"I can't watch this anymore," Jill said, carefully stepping through the babies to put a final bullet into the zealot's chest.

"Does it feel good to shoot a prisoner?" Hanna asked.

"It feels good to kill a Sun Chaser," Jill said, and the women left it at that. "What do you make of this room?" Jill asked, stepping back outside the ring of babies. "Metal walls, a couple hundred lamps and a few torches …" Her squinting eyes caught one lamp near the entrance that was out but didn't think it was worth mentioning. She wished a few more of them were out so it wouldn't hurt her eyes so damn much just to look around.

Hanna didn't answer right away as she was busy studying the infants. Gently pulling up the eyelid of an Indian girl, Hanna discovered a milky eye. Rising to her feet, she saw that a stream of blood from the Chaser was about to run into a baby. Hanna reached down to move the child, when a scream came to them from the tunnel.

"Something's being attacked," Jill said.

Hanna shook her head. "That sounds like something issuing a challenge."

"Something's noticed there's company in the tunnels," Jill said. "We'd better move out."

"And leave these kids here?"

Jill flashed an annoyed look at her partner, who stood between her and the babies. "Need I remind you they were doing fine down here with a living, breathing Sun Chaser standing in the middle of them? I think they'll be fine said Chaser no longer breathing. We need to get out of here and figure out what's going on."

"Just hold on, dammit," Hanna said, grabbing Jill's arm. "Don't go off half-cocked for once. Think. What have you noticed about the three people we've…?"

"You want to play riddles in the dark so you feel smarter than me, Hanna?" Jill asked, growing agitated. "Fine. But let's skip past the part where I look stupid and get to your brilliance."

"The old women, the old men, the kids," Hanna said, waving behind her. "Who was the most active?"

"There you go," Jill grumbled, "doing just what I told you not to do."

"This is the brightest room," Hanna said, "and the least active people. The old men were in the darkest room and were the most active. If there's something bad crawling around down here doing something to the townsfolk, it's at its worst in the bright rooms."

"All the more reason to get out of here."

"All the more reason to stay with the children," Hanna countered. "There's more kids here than could have possibly been living in that town."

"The lesbian has mothering instincts now?" Jill asked. "Time to admit we're in over our heads. As awesome as we are…"

"I won't argue that."

"…whatever we're facing is strong enough to take out a whole town."

"We don't know that."

"We do know that we found all the old women in one room, the old men in another, and the babies in a third," Jill countered, glancing down to look at the kids. "Do you think the

others let that happen? Do you think the Sun Chaser allowed himself to be caught?"

Hanna frowned.

"Exactly," Jill said, noting the blood from the Chaser was being soaked up by the towel of one of the babies, who was beginning to stir. Knowing mentioning it would harden Hanna's resolve to stay, she didn't mention it. "So let's get above ground and call in some help from the nearest military fort or Indian tribe. We need…. Hell!"

Before Hanna could ask what had caused Jill's eyes to go wide, her partner had stepped forward and pulled her away from the ring of babies. Jill pointed to the baby with the blood-soaked blanket, who had just rolled over onto his stomach. "It's moving," Jill said, and the Bostonians watched in disgust as the baby lowered its face into the blood and began to drink.

"Vampires?"

"Baby vampires?"

"You … should not … have come …"

Hanna and Jill turned to the doorway, guns drawn, to see a ragged middle-aged woman holding herself up by bracing her arms against the tunnel walls.

The woman's body started to drop forward into the room when a blistered arm reached out of the darkness to grab her hair and yank her backwards. The sounds of munching and screaming could be heard before the woman's body was tossed back into the room with a hunk of flesh torn from her neck, followed by Old Man David, grinning as he chewed what he had taken from her. The woman's body spurted blood as it lurched forward, landing near the infants. Blood from her neck fired out across the sleeping children, but as the droplets of blood hit their faces, they awoke, crying and lapping their tongues into the air, desperate to catch the red liquid.

"It was the Indians who figured out what we were doing," David said calmly, no longer seeming to be bothered by the damage the sun did to his body. He wore a pair of jeans and boots, but he had no shirt on. His blistered skin bled from open wounds and he peeled off his bubbled skin to feast on it. "They had sent a band of white men to infiltrate our ranks and spy on us. It was those men you saw dead in the dirt."

"What are you doing here?" Jill asked, glancing back at the awakened children. "What about the Sun Chasers? Were they even here?"

David nodded, stepping back into the darkness of the tunnel to limit the light from the lamps and torches that touched his body. "It was the fates that brought them. They rode down the Indians and their white allies and killed them all for us. The fight gave us time to flee beneath the Earth, where we prefer to live."

"Who are you?" Hanna asked, her gun still pointed forward.

"We are the Darkness Eaters," David said. "We poison visitors to our town with waters from the underground stream. With each passing cup, their disgust for the light and hunger for the darkness grows stronger until their days turn inside out. Soon, even the moonlight and the stars are too much, and their eyes turn milky to keep out the light and offer them peace. It is then we take them into the dark to let them become one with the emptiness. There are dark things in the bowels of the Earth, and these long-forgotten creatures give us strength unimaginable!"

"What about the old women?" Hanna asked. "And the old men?"

"We hunt in packs," David said. "The youthful and strong hunt deep inside the earth, bringing us sustenance, while the elderly wait by the entrance to serve as a warning."

"Warning?" Hanna asked.

David cocked his head to the side and ran his tongue over his teeth. "The packs are on their way back from the bottom. You will not see the top of the world again."

"Where are the prisoners?" Hanna asked, wanting desperately to run but unwilling to do so without knowing the full cost. If there were innocents down here, they would try to save them.

David looked surprised. "Prisoners?" he asked. "The damned Indians took our would-be prisoners away before we could complete their transformation." He smiled. "The captured Sun Chaser will feed the children. You will feed the elderly. The light keeps us placid, you see, but in the dark our hunger for flesh and blood becomes almost unquenchable."

Jill looked to the babies, who were all up and active, lapping up the spilled blood and crawling over the Sun Chasers' body to bite away at the dead man's flesh. "Good thing the lights are on then, I guess," she said. "Not that I'm going to get this image out of my mind anytime soon."

David licked his lips. "We do like our food to squirm and scream," he said, and then jumped into the room to grab the one metal and glass oil lamp that was not lit and pulled it forward. A screeching of metal on metal preceded a heavy thud. The oil lamps flickered for just a moment before their supply of oxygen was choked out, plunging the room into near darkness. Only a handful of torches remained lit.

The darkness brought unholy wailing from the children, who began to turn rabid with lust for the blood and flesh of the Sun Chaser.

Hanna and Jill shared a look that said, "Time to go," but David was upon Hanna before they could exit. His burned fingers clawed at her shoulders, driving her backwards and knocking her into the squirming babies. She fell backwards on the floor and David fell with her, snarling and snapping at her face as Hanna held him off with her hands.

Jill stepped in, put a gun to his temple, and blew his brains out over the rabid children. Their screams grew louder, their hunger more frenzied. Reaching down, Jill pulled Hanna to her feet.

"We should..."

"We're getting out of here," Jill insisted, kicking a baby away from them. "Come on."

The two women ran out of the room, the sounds of the feast continuing to haunt their ears long after their eyes were locating the torches they had left behind. Hanna picked hers up without incident, but Jill accidentally kicked hers forward, and the flame went out when the rags separated from the stick and hit a pocket of water.

"Gives you an extra hand to shoot," Hanna said, driving them forward. Before they were out of the tunnel, three old women from the first room shuffled towards them. In the lead, Hanna collided with the first woman, sending them both to the ground. Twisting her body to make sure she kept the torch elevated, she fired her Colt revolver into the woman's arm because that was the part of her closest to the gun. Jill stepped in behind them and shot the other two women in the head, then grabbed the back of Hanna's shirt and helped her to her feet.

Hanna took aim at the woman but Jill stilled the shot. "I've got a better idea," she said and waited for the hungry woman to rise to her feet.

"Any time with that great plan," Hanna said.

Jill took the torch from her and pressed it into the woman's clothing, setting her on fire. "Jesus," Hanna said.

"Said the atheist," Jill said, handing Hanna her torch back and sliding around the woman, pushing her to walk in the direction of the babies. "Come on," she encouraged, "catch the scent from that feast."

Whether it was from the searing pain from the fire that enveloped her clothing or the orgy of devoured flesh, the woman rambled back the way they had come.

"I believe in Jesus," Hanna said, getting them moving forward again.

"You can't believe in him," Jill said, following behind at a quick jog.

"God's fake," Hanna said, "but Jesus is real."

"So, what, you think he was just a regular guy?"

"A regular guy who did amazing things," Hanna said. "Like healing the sick, feeding the poor," Hanna said, pausing to shoot at two more elderly women who appeared in the tunnel before them, "playing nice with lepers and whores."

"I don't want to discuss religion right now," Jill grumbled as they emerged back into the cavern to be greeted by the rest of the old ladies. "Or ever if you're going to turn it into poetry."

"Seems as good a time as any," Hanna said, noting that behind the ladies were the men from the underground pond. "Reload your gun," she said. "I've got a few shots left."

Hanna did, putting her torch down and refilling as Jill took the lead. The elderly women were a curious lot; they moved faster than zombies but slower than vampires, and it was only when one particularly spry elderly woman came at them almost too fast to be shot by the two of them than she realized these Darkness Eaters were only moving slow because they were old, not because of some causal condition.

"Jill," Hanna said, but Jill was already nodding.

"I saw it," she said. "Cover me," she ordered, and Hanna took the lead, firing away with one gun as she held the torch in the other, giving Jill time to refill her revolvers. By the time Jill was ready to start shooting, all of the old women were dead, and the pond men were coming at them. The two women were fifteen feet away from the men, giving Hanna time to reload before they were set upon. The men were old, but there was more vigor to their movement than the women, and they proved to be harder targets. While the women were generally too slow to be much of a challenge, the men spread out, trying to advance past Hanna and Jill's flank.

"Let's stick to the wall," Hanna said, moving to her right to take out the Darkness Eaters and create and escape route. They fired on the men when they got within ten feet of them, not wanting to waste their bullets. The men understood what they were doing and held back.

"Huh," Jill said as Hanna looked back to her. "Must be too slow from all the fire light. Let's hit the pond room and get out of...duck!"

Hanna obeyed, falling to one knee as Jill fired a shot over her head to hit a snarling Mexican in the face. Both women watched him fall but took little solace in their victory because they knew what this meant...the hunting pack had returned.

"Come on," Jill said, moving past her to step over the dead body. "We've got to move fast to get back to the surface so I can tell you what a horrible idea you had coming this way."

"I'm gonna need both hands," Hanna said, though she knew if this torch went out, all the light in this room went with it.

"Find someone, shoot someone, burn someone," Jill said, moving into the room with the pond to find eight men waiting for them. Jill didn't hesitate, firing with both guns as she advanced.

Hanna came into the room hot on her heels, firing two shots back through the doorway to keep the old men at bay as long as she could. The men of the hunting pack were much stronger than the previous Darkness Eaters, and none of them fell with one shot unless the Bostonians hit them in the head, which was damn near impossible in the flickering light.

The rocks beneath their feet were slippery now, too, as they'd become wet with the exit of the elderly men from the pond, and it was hard for Hanna and Jill to keep their balance. Hanna saw there was a small bit of fire left on the opposite shore, so she moved alongside Jill to assist in killing the next man up. He fell forward onto his knees, and Hanna kicked him square in the chest, knocking him onto his back. As she stepped over him, she placed her torch down on his chest, setting him ablaze.

"Why do you think Hell is hot instead of cold?" Jill asked, refilling one of her guns.

"Because Christianity didn't begin in the Arctic," Hanna quipped. She'd taken a few moments too long to make sure the torch lit up her last victim and the next pack member was on her, grabbing her shirt and hair as he opened his mouth to bite her neck. She heard Jill swear behind her.

Hanna fired her gun into his stomach, which knocked him back, but he kept his hands tightly wrapped in her hair, and pulled her with him. A second man grabbed at her and Hanna fired into him, too, until her gun click-clicked, signifying it was empty. "Little help!" she yelled.

Jill swore again, dropping bullets as she finished her reload, but stepped in to empty her gun into both men instead of picking them up. They were in a spot where the pond came close to the wall next to them, giving them little room to maneuver, and with a groan saw some of the bullets roll into the water.

"Thanks," Hanna said, pulling herself free.

"Don't thank me," Jill said. "I dropped half my remaining bullets back there into the pond."

Hanna nodded and turned toward the exit. "Three men left in front of us," she said as the flames rose higher behind them, "and a bunch of old men coming at us from behind."

"I wish you'd phrased that differently."

"Me, too. I…ah!"

Hanna was yanked to the ground and dropped her gun. It took Jill a moment to realize that Hanna had been grabbed by something in the pond. Dropping her guns to grab Hanna's hands, Jill struggled to keep her partner from being pulled into the water by a slimy, gray tentacle. "Do I really need to tell you to shoot it?" she yelled.

The momentary panic from being grabbed subsided now that Hanna realized Jill had her. "I still have the gun on my left hip," she said, "so let go of that hand."

Jill nodded, letting Hanna's right hand go and grabbing her left with both hands.

Hanna wanted to scream at Jill but she bit the retort down, not wanting to distract Jill from keeping her out of the water. She was already knee deep into the pond and didn't want to go any further; it wasn't hard to surmise that whatever this nightmare was, it was responsible for poisoning the water. It wasn't easy, but she took the gun off her left hip with her right hand, placed it against the tentacle that had wrapped around her legs, and fired.

A gigantic, bulbous head rose out of the water, its face covered with a thousand milky eyes, and a host of tentacles wriggled in the air as Jill pulled Hanna back from the edge. The two women were transfixed by the creature and the three members of the pack had their opening, rushing in to kick at the Bostonians.

Swearing harshly enough to offend the first six levels of Hell, Hanna went for the knife on her boot and hacked and stabbed at the men above her. The presence of their own blood only seemed to spur them on and they rained kicks and punches down on her.

Jill rolled away from the attack to buy herself a moment's respite to come back hard, but when she did so she rolled right into the feet of a handful of the old men as they stepped over the burning body. Moving hard and fast, Jill put her hands on the rocky ground and swung her boots around hard, knocking the first man back into the second man and giving her enough time to reach for one of her fallen guns and shooting one of Hanna's assailants in the back of his head. She turned back just in time for one of the old men to knock her gun to the floor, where it skidded into the pond, lost forever.

The loss of the weapon gave her an idea, and she grabbed the old man and hurled him into the pond. The tentacled beast immediately returned, attacking the old man in a lustful anger. The sight of what was being done to their fellow Darkness Eater caused the other men to back away, and allowed Jill to concentrate on Hanna's attackers. Pulling her own hunting knives off her hips, she stepped in and jammed one up through one man's chin, and drilled the second knife into the final man's brain.

"Yuck," Jill said, helping Hanna to her feet. "You're covered in blood."

"I'll let you wash it off me when we get topside," Hanna said, and the two women moved back the way they had originally come before the pond creature could realize it was eating one of its worshippers. The light from the fire behind them faded before the lights from the oil lamps in the first room made themselves known, but the two women moved up the slight incline steadily, sacrificing speed for security. By the time they reached the original room, they heard the screams of new Darkness Eaters behind them.

They didn't hesitate to climb up and out of the room and back into the church, where they were met by a band of ten Indians, arrows pulled tight on bowstrings.

"The bad guys are coming," Jill said to the leader, "so don't waste your arrows on us, Mr. Paiute."

The lead Indian looked at her with an odd expression on his face, before breaking out into a wide smile. "We're Mescalero," he said, but took Jill's idea to heart, and saved his arrows for the Darkness Eaters who ventured into the room where they had first left their humanity behind. When no more Eaters approached, Hanna and Jill helped the Mescalero toss wood from the church down into the hole and set it ablaze.

By the time the church had stopped burning, they stood two miles out of town, watching it burn and ensuring no one crawled out of the dark and into the night.

"Thank you," Hanna said to the lead Mescalero.

"Don't thank me, yet," he said. "There's a band of Sun Chasers who need killing for what they did to ours three days ago. You're going to help us find them and kill them."

"Are we gonna get paid for doing it?" Jill asked.

"You're breathing," the Indian said, "so you already have."

The End

Came a Demon
(a Bartholomew Sylvaine story)
by Forrest Dylan Bryant

They found Bartholomew Sylvaine in the library of Wooltemere Manor, motionless on the floor with a ring of books around his head. His body lay stiff and straight as a tailor's mannequin, but a smile graced the curve of his pale lips. He looked strangely happy.

"Horrible," breathed the Vicar. "I told you we should have waited for the Bishop to arrive. Now look what's happened. First Lord Wooltemere, now your so-called ghost hunter. How will we explain this?"

Gray light angled in from the tall windows, highlighting the soft fabric of Sylvaine's impeccable Savile Row suit, the blood-red cravat around his neck, and the halo of dusty books. Beyond the square of light, stage magic paraphernalia filled bookshelves and tables, corners and walls. Skulls grinned down, trick daggers threatened. The room looked more like a sacrificial altar than a gentleman's library.

Lady Margaret Wooltemere could feel her courage failing, perhaps even her sanity. She had never wanted to come here in the first place, to live as a peer's wife in the middle of nowhere. And now it appeared the manor didn't want her either, or her husband.

She was looking right into Sylvaine's beatific face when his eyes snapped open. "Lady Wooltemere!" he scolded. "You promised not to interfere!"

Margaret jumped. The Vicar squawked. And Bartholomew Sylvaine, Investigator of the Unseen, sprang upright with the agility of a circus acrobat.

"I asked you to remain upstairs with Lord Wooltemere while I examined the house. Instead you've gone blundering about like a pair of bull elephants." Sylvaine paused and tilted his head, as if listening for something in the distance. "Alas," he sighed. "The vibrations are quite disrupted now. I'll learn no more here." He leaned against a vanishing cabinet — another magician's prop — and drew a clay pipe from his vest pocket.

"I do apologize, Mister Sylvaine. We thought…"

"You did *not* think. That is the problem." Sylvaine pointed the pipe at Margaret and scowled. The pipe's bowl, shaped like a dragon's head, scowled along with him. "So, do you want the manor cleansed or not? The source of the disturbance is here, in the library. I'm quite certain of it."

"Ah, the… *disturbance*. So it's true, then? We are haunted?"

Sylvaine turned his attention to the fireplace, making small but violent gestures at it with his free hand. "Haunted? Goodness no, dear lady," he called over his shoulder. "The manor isn't haunted. Not at all."

Margaret and the Vicar let out sighs of relief.

"No, no, no," Sylvaine added. "This is *much* worse."

● ● ●

Three hours earlier, Sylvaine had sat alone in the taproom of the village pub, listening to the locals moan about the weather.

A pall hung over North Devonshire that week. On the rickety train that had carried him here, Sylvaine had watched the passing landscape with a heavy heart, feeling far older than his thirty-five years. Something strange was at work in those rough, rolling hills, something that made him feel like the last man on earth.

Wooltemere Village was a forlorn collection of dingy houses on a rocky shore. The hamlet angled down to a rough stone wharf, as if ready to tumble into the sea at any moment. It was a fitting place for the last man on earth to end up.

He glanced at the black mourning crepe above the bar, hung to frame a stern portrait of Queen Victoria. More images of the late monarch glared down from the side walls. They only enhanced his sense of doom. If even *she* could go after all these years, was anything permanent? Was anything real? The scene felt uncanny, like a play staged for his benefit, or a dream. He ran a hand through his mane of dark hair and took another sip of port.

Seagulls screamed splitting the air as the pub's ancient door swung open. A beautiful young woman swept in. Her delicate features, filtered by a black veil, were creased with worry. It was a look Sylvaine had seen on the face of many a client.

"Lady Wooltemere, I presume? It's a pleasure to meet such a divine creature on such a dismal day."

Margaret frowned for a moment, still unused to hearing herself addressed as Lady Wooltemere. She didn't care for it. Margaret was twenty-two years old, three months married, and four weeks a resident of this place that bore her husband's name. "Lady Wooltemere" should be a gray-haired matron, she thought, not a vibrant young bride from Chelsea. Yet here she was. She offered her hand to Sylvaine with all the grace she could manage and did her best to return his charming smile.

That smile twisted a bit when Sylvaine saw Margaret's black-clad companion. "The local Vicar? Well, this is a surprise. You fellows usually disapprove of my line of work."

The Vicar was thrice Margaret's age and craggy as the surrounding cliffs. He eyed Sylvaine with undisguised contempt.

"Indeed, sir! But her Ladyship insisted. And I must admit I'm at a loss to explain the... er, situation." He ruffled the thin strands of white hair that crossed his scalp. "I've sent word to the Bishop, but he is away in Canterbury..."

"So you decided to have me take care of it instead. Well done." He winked at Margaret. "But for heaven's sake, where have you brought me? This is a charming seaside village..."

A fisherman went into a coughing fit, sending the results flying into a spittoon. "As I say, a charming village, but where is the house?"

"It's about two miles from here," said Margaret, "out on the moors. I can tell you all about the situation as we go."

"By all means, my lady, let's away. And do tell me you keep a better class of port in your cellar than this rot." Sylvaine pushed his glass across the table, scowling.

● ● ●

Rain drummed against the carriage windows as they made their way inland. The gray, rocky vista of Bristol Channel gave way to silent, scruffy fields on which sheep stood about like woolen haystacks. There was no sign of human habitation.

"Dreary, isn't it?" moaned Margaret. "And it's all ours, they say." She inclined her head against the window, crushing her bonnet against the glass.

"I've lived here all my life," sniffed the Vicar. "It is a peaceful place. Contemplative. An ideal land for hard work and communing with God."

"Hm. One can commune with a great many supernatural beings in a place like this," said Sylvaine. "As Lady Wooltemere has learned. Tell me everything from the beginning, my lady."

Margaret considered her visitor. She and the aged Vicar occupied one bench, while Sylvaine and his traveling bag sprawled on the opposite side, riding backward. Yet even in these cramped circumstances, the Investigator of the Unseen gave off an aura of elegant mystery and arcane knowledge. It was as if he knew what she would say, and was just waiting for the recitation.

"George — Lord Wooltemere, I mean — took up his seat only a few weeks ago," she began. "I'm a complete stranger here, and he may as well be; George hadn't set one foot in Devon since he first went up to school. We never imagined he'd have the title. But two months ago there was a telegram. Half the family had succumbed to influenza, the barony was his, and George owned everything from here to Cornbrough. Just like that."

"Quite a shock, I suppose?"

"Indeed, Mister Sylvaine. We were just gaining our bearings. George had graduated from University and I from the Women's College. We married straightaway and he went to work as a junior partner in his cousin's firm. The world was ours. And now we're running a drafty pile of stones in the middle of nowhere. Think on it, sir. It's a new century, unlimited progress beckons, and yet we've been thrust back into a bygone era to play squire and lady."

Margaret shot a cold glance out the window. "The only thing I can say in its favor is that there's plenty of room for our magic equipment. It's a sort of mania with us, you see. We even considered taking the stage professionally at one time. I designed most of our tricks myself. Mirror japes, those were our specialty." Sylvaine smiled at her, but the message was unreadable.

They passed through a crossroads, with muddy tracks stretching away on either side. To the left, the rutted road wound its way to Cornbrough, Bideford, Barnstaple, and onward... ever-larger towns leading eventually to London. On the right, the tracks disappeared into the hills, ending somewhere among the cliffs. Ahead lay Wooltemere Manor... and nothing else.

"There's magic in this place too," said Margaret. "But it's the wrong kind. I walk these hills and feel like I'm at the far end of the world. One wrong step and I may fall right off."

"I feel it too, my lady. And take care, for I believe you might."

Margaret saw the twinkle leave Sylvaine's eyes. He was not speaking in jest.

"Tell me about your husband," he said. What happened that night?"

"We were bored! George wanted to break the monotony, that's all. When he found those queer books in the library, he was naturally curious..."

"And so he decided to dabble in spiritualism, as so many bored people do nowadays. Quite understandable, especially for an amateur magician. But *what did he do*? Please be specific."

"I don't know! I wasn't there. It was the night of the seventeenth. George had the books and decided to hold a séance in the library. Two pals of his were passing through — that would be Arthur Hempley and his brother, Francis. They joined him. I declined to take part."

"Quite right!" interjected the Vicar.

"I thought it sounded like *fun*," countered Margaret, "but I had a headache, so I took to bed with a book. All at once there were shouts from below, then a scream. I leapt up, but at that same moment every oil lamp in the house went out, *poof!* It was extraordinary. I fell over a chair in the dark, and by the time I got a candle lit and found my way to the library..."

"Lord Wooltemere was as he is now," said the Vicar. "Struck dumb by the wrath of God. He does not speak, does not write, does not answer any question put to him about his dalliance with Satan. He sleeps and sits and stares into space, and that is all."

"The local doctors are useless," added Margaret. "They say it is a severe mental strain and he may recover given time, or not at all. I wrote to a brain specialist in London, but he cannot come until next week."

There was silence for a few moments. Sylvaine, frowning, titled his head back in thought.

"A singular tale. And his friends, the Hempley brothers, they are the same?"

"N-no," said Margaret. "I found them unconscious under the library windows. George was opposite, near the fire. When the brothers awoke, they claimed to remember nothing. Nothing at all."

"You believe them?"

"They seemed sincere. They remembered arriving at the house, sharing whiskeys and soda with George, but nothing else until the moment I found them."

"May I speak with them? Or your servants?"

"They've gone. All of them. The Hempleys decamped for a relative's home in Somerset yesterday, right after I sent for you. As for servants, we only had two, and they wouldn't stay. There have been strange sounds and... and... *smells* in the library each night since the séance. The servants refused to spend another night in the house unless I called in the Vicar."

"I performed the standard rites, although I admit to being a bit rusty," added the Vicar.

"At first that seemed to settle things, but two nights ago the housemaid went to light the fire in the library and found a bright blue glow filling the room. There was an awful moaning noise, too. I heard it myself. That was the last straw. The servants left within the hour."

"A pity. Eyewitness testimony would have been useful, especially the brothers."

"But they do not recall..."

"Oh, they do, even if they do not know that they do. The mind has layers upon layers, my dear, and each contains multitudes."

The carriage stopped. Just ahead loomed a dark, hulking mass; a great stone house where no house should be, seemingly as old and forsaken as the land itself.

"Wooltemere Manor," said the Vicar.

• • •I.

Sylvaine asked for leave to examine the house alone, sending the others upstairs to attend Lord Wooltemere. Margaret and the Vicar sat and paced and fussed as the minutes lengthened into an hour or more, but Sylvaine did not reappear. The ticking of clocks became intolerable. They were everywhere — in the bedroom, in the corridor, drifting up from the parlor downstairs, all rushing to count the seconds that piled up into a mountain of inaction.

Finally they could wait no more. Patience gone, they went off in search of Sylvaine, and that was how they came to find him in his strange attitude upon the library floor.

Once roused from sensing the "vibrations," Sylvaine leapt into action. "Haste, friends! I must see Lord Wooltemere without delay. He may have done great damage. No fault of his own, of course, but now he stands upon a precipice."

They rushed upstairs, Sylvaine leading the way as if he owned the place. "Third door on the left!" called Margaret, but somehow he already knew where to go.

• • •

A casual onlooker, beholding Lord George Wooltemere for the first time, might well have mistaken the young man for a waxwork figure. He sat up straight in his padded chair but showed no other sign of life. His wide blue eyes stared at nothing. Margaret adjusted the blanket over his lap, stroked his lanky brown curls, and kissed his cheek, muttering kindness all the while.

"Darling, I've brought Mister Sylvaine, the... the..."

"Investigator," said Sylvaine.

"Demonologist," muttered the Vicar.

"Sometimes, yes. But such instances are rare, and for that you should thank my many predecessors, Vicar."

"Humph!" The Vicar stalked to the window and fiddled with the drapes. Sylvaine drew a second chair alongside Wooltemere's and looked into the young man's unseeing eyes.

"Lord Wooltemere. George. I am going to ask you some questions."

But Sylvaine did not ask questions. He didn't say another word. Instead, he laid his fingertips on either side of Lord Wooltemere's head. Margaret and the Vicar looked on, astonished.

A pained whimper escaped Wooltemere's lips, and something broke inside Margaret's heart. "See here!" she said, striding to her husband's side. She seized Sylvaine by the shoulder, and her world spun away into nothingness.

● ● ●

The bed, the window, and the Vicar all vanished from Margaret's vision as if swept away by a conjurer's trick, giving way to empty space. All that remained were George, Sylvaine, and herself. A kind of blue smoke curled between them in long tendrils, writhing like a living thing.

"Who are you?" Sylvaine was saying. "Where have you taken Lord Wooltemere? I command an answer!"

George opened his mouth, but the voice that replied was not his own. It was cold, malevolent, echoing through the emptiness with a serpentine hiss.

"*You know me, Sylvaine. Waited for you. Lured you. Have you now.*"

Margaret gasped in horror, and now Sylvaine was confronting her. The smoke swirled, suddenly thicker.

"This place is not for you, my dear. You are in grave peril. Leave immediately, or join George in his doom!"

The smoke reached for Margaret's head, smothering Sylvaine's frantic warning. "*Another sacrifice...*" hissed the strange voice. "*Two. What now, Sylvaine? What now?*"

Margaret reeled as the smoke wrapped itself around her. An abyss yawned below: a frozen place of eternal, dreamless sleep. It pulled at her, called to her. But something else — was it Sylvaine? — told her not to look down, never to look down into that darkness. She felt herself dropping… dropping…

Sylvaine's mind grabbed hold and began hauling her upwards, fighting the downward drift. For a moment, she balanced between two equal and opposite forces, and then…

She was back in the bedroom, flat upon her back. The Vicar stood over her, holding a wet cloth to her face and making "tut-tut" sounds. Bartholomew Sylvaine paced before the window, lost in thought. Lord George Wooltemere sat in his chair, motionless as before.

● ● ●

"I don't understand. What do you mean, it's a trap?"

Sylvaine's scowl deepened as he stroked the cravat around his neck. "This is no random possession, my friends. It is a trap, carefully laid. Lord Wooltemere is merely the bait. *I* am the target."

"That makes no sense. The target of what?"

Sylvaine puffed on his pipe, and the dragon's eyes on the bowl glowed red. "You must understand," he said, "Ninety-nine out of a hundred ghost stories or possessions are mere rubbish, exaggerations or disorders of the mind. At the worst, some nosy deceased aunt seeking to glean gossip from the living. Nothing to worry about."

"As I told her Ladyship," muttered the Vicar. "Nothing we cannot handle."

"Ninety-nine times out of a hundred," repeated Sylvaine. "But manifestations of elder demons are something else, and that is what you have here."

"A demon?" cried Margaret. "Are you serious?"

"Deadly serious. And among demons, the Ka'ti'i are ranked among the very worst. They hardly ever visit this world — once a century at the most — but when they do they can leave vast destruction in their wake. Set loose, it could ravage the countryside, and wipe Wooltemere Village off the face of the earth."

"An actual demon," breathed the Vicar. "Why, I've never…"

"Ah, but *I* have, Vicar. I fear we've tangled before, this being and I. Long ago, before I occupied this body. I have no memory of it, but the Ka'ti'i never forget. This one isn't here to destroy your lands; it wants to destroy *me*, personally. Not just in body, although it will tear me limb from limb. No, it wants to demolish my soul."

"And it's taken George simply to… to lure you here?"

"It didn't have to be Lord Wooltemere, my lady. It just took the first person foolish enough to read from the books. What mattered is that I would come to investigate; I and no other. How did you come to summon me here?

"I remembered Professor Carruthers from University. He always had an interest in hauntings," said Margaret. "So I wrote to him, and he replied with several names. But when I saw yours… Well, I'm not sure. I just knew I had to send for you. It seemed… *obvious*. Even the Hempley brothers urged me to contact you. I couldn't rest until you'd agreed to come here."

"Hm. I thought as much. The moment your husband and his friends held their séance, the trap was all but sprung. You've been under a subtle diabolical influence since that night."

Sylvaine drew a line in midair with his pipe. "A door has opened between our world and that of the Ka'ti'i demon. Just a crack, mind you, but wide enough for it to steal Lord Wooltemere's consciousness away. It then planted the idea that you should seek me."

"Another world… So that place I saw, the emptiness… it was real?" Margaret shook her head in confusion.

"As real as this one, my dear. Your husband's body remains here, but his mind is down there. For now he is merely asleep, but with each passing moment, the door opens wider. His spirit falls deeper into the rift, and the horror on the other

side comes nearer to us. That explains the sounds your servants heard, the smells, and the blue light."

"God have mercy," breathed the Vicar. "What comes next?"

"The endgame. It has been eight nights already, under a waxing moon. Tonight the moon is full, the door will be fully open, and the Ka'ti'i will come to claim its prize."

"You mean George," said Margaret.

"Or me. I am forced to choose. I can leave here and abandon Lord Wooltemere to die... or I can stay and let it take me instead."

"Madness! Let's all leave right now, and never return to this cursed house. If the thing cannot come until tonight..."

"Ah, but that is the trap. That is the fiendish brilliance of it. Lord Wooltemere must not leave this house. The threads connecting his mind and body are stretched too thin. If you remove him from this place now, he will die. Do you understand?"

Margaret collapsed into a chair. "Oh, George!" she cried.

"And you as well, my lady. You interfered when I reached out to him, and entered the other realm without any protection. A part of you is trapped there as well, bound to him. If you try to leave this house, you will most likely go mad. No, I must surrender to the demon. Or I can leave you both to your fates, and have your young lives upon my conscience evermore."

"That is no choice at all," said the Vicar. "There must be a way to defeat this abomination."

"No human being can destroy it. But perhaps we can out-think it. If we can get it to release its grip on Lord Wooltemere before we close the door, you will both be free. That is the challenge before us. We have until nightfall to find a way."

● ● ●

The first order of business, Sylvaine explained, was to learn the nature of the rift between realms. And for that, they would need a secure place, out of the demon's view.

Sylvaine daubed salt water across the doors and walls of Lord Wooltemere's study— sealing the room against outside mental influences, he said — and set the Vicar to work.

"Here are the books Lord Wooltemere read at the séance," instructed Sylvaine. "Look for any references to specific entities, formulae, numbers... I can use those. But do not read any of these texts aloud," he warned. "Not a single word." For himself, the ghost hunter took up an assortment of aged volumes from his leather bag.

Margaret remained with her husband in his bedchamber, watching for any change. She detected a furrowing of his brow after a time and rushed to report it to Sylvaine.

"It's the protections I've placed on this room, I'll wager. The Ka'ti'i senses them and realizes we intend to fight."

"Is George in danger?"

"No more than he already was. The monster cannot attack until the full moon reaches its zenith."

"I feel so damned useless!" blurted Margaret. "I don't know anything about demons or sorcery. Mirror tricks and parlor magic won't be much help much against the real thing. I don't suppose we'll have an opportunity to capture the beast bodily? I could rig a trap..."

"Touching a Ka'ti'i manifestation would mean instant annihilation. Your living organs would be strewn across the countryside. But you can help, yes. I believe we can immobilize the creature long enough to send it back where it came from, but only if we create an unbroken circle around it. We must build our trap in the center of the library and get it to enter of its own free will. Can you think of a way to do that?"

Margaret pondered this for a moment, picturing the scene, and a light of triumph came into her eyes.

"Mister Sylvaine! Have you ever heard of a trick called the Vanishing Lady?"

• • •

Evening came early under the dark clouds, bringing a howling wind that redoubled with each passing hour. Inside the black bulk of Wooltemere Manor, the storm of activity was equally intense.

First they cleared the center of the library. Some of the furnishings had not been moved in a hundred years. Shelves, rugs, tables, and chairs were piled up to create a pair of makeshift walls, with Wooltemere's gaudy stage props heaped in front.

In their place, Sylvaine drew the signs of true magical power. Three concentric circles were set down: one of chalk, another of salt, and the third of some dark, greasy fluid he'd cooked up in the kitchen. Slow-burning candles ringed the innermost circle. Around each candle, Sylvaine sketched curious signs with a lump of charcoal. Holy water, sprinkled over the whole despite the Vicar's strenuous objections, completed the defense.

Sylvaine moved to the center of the enclosed area, sealing himself in by drawing an eight-pointed star from edge to edge. Again he used the greasy liquid. He did not speak to the others, but muttered to himself in a stream of harsh, indecipherable phrases. The Vicar could discern neither English nor Latin.

Margaret, dragging a large mirror, joined her husband and the Vicar behind one of the twin piles of furniture. She positioned the glass so as to reflect three other mirrors angled at strategic points around the room. To test her handiwork, she lit a match and held it aloft. Answering lights bounced back from the correct positions. "Ready," she reported.

They settled down to wait. Sylvaine sat with self-assured calm amidst the ciphers on the floor and closed his eyes. The Vicar, however, was restless. He could not quite accept what was happening. Every village cleric hears the odd ghost story from time to time, but this was madness. If Sylvaine was right, not only the lives but also the very souls of four people were in imminent danger, his own among them. His watery gray eyes peered into every corner of the room, and he jumped as a crash of thunder echoed across the hills.

Something terrible was coming.

● ● ●

It was as black and foul a night as anybody could remember; and in that part of the world memories go back a long way. The full moon rose, invisible, behind the clouds. The rain came down in great, undulating sheets, and wave after crashing wave slammed into the rocky coast as if to demolish the land. In the village, an old woman said that Devon was caught between the wrath of Heaven and the chaos of Hell.

The moors were a pandemonium of screaming winds and thrashing water. But if one could silence that chaotic onslaught, another sound might have been heard that night. It was a low, chattering moan that shivered on the air, rising and swooping like something out of a nightmare.

Wooltemere Manor stood black against the darkness, yet a few windows were alight. A sickly blue glow grew and ebbed in time with that weird, moaning cry, as if the house itself were breathing. If Heaven and Hell were colliding this night, there could be little doubt which side had claimed Wooltemere Manor.

Hell's ambassador arrived at midnight.

● ● ●

The blue glow had been visible for hours, rising from deep within the unlit fireplace. Then came the eerie, chattering moan and a nauseating stench like rotting meat. By the time the Ka'ti'i entity appeared, rising up through the stone floor of the hearth, the room was a reeking riot of light and noise.

It was hideous. The demon slumped and oozed around the cold hearth, a pulsating, almost shapeless apparition. Its flailing limbs, ever moving, shifted in size and number. Its hide was shimmering and gelatinous. It radiated evil.

Bartholomew Sylvaine stood proud and defiant in his magic circle, but the others crouched behind their wall, pale and wild-eyed. Margaret looked ready to faint or flee, and the Vicar was no calmer. He clutched his Bible to his breast and began chanting every prayer he'd ever learned.

"Steady!" shouted Sylvaine. "Hold your ground. You are all protected so long as I remain within the circle and all the candles are lit."

The Ka'ti'i shuffled back and forth, fixated on the dapper man in the circle as it probed his invisible shield, searching for weakness.

"Demon! We meet as foretold. Now release Lord Wooltemere and take me... if you can."

The demon made no reply.

"We made a bargain, demon. Wooltemere's life for mine."

"*We bargain now.*" When the demon spoke, its hissing voice echoed from the unconscious body of Lord George Wooltemere, lying behind the barricade. "*Leave circle and Ka'ti'i will release him.*"

"No. Wooltemere goes free first."

Wooltemere's throat issued a strangled noise, full of bile and hatred.

"*Take you all,*" hissed the demon. "*All die.*"

"Your greed will be your undoing. But you can try," said Sylvaine. He closed his eyes and began to hum a merry tune, as if he had not a care in the world.

The standoff continued for hours. Margaret found the strain unrelenting, despite Sylvaine's nonchalance. The Vicar kept up his steady stream of prayers, and she joined him for the few she remembered. But Sylvaine never moved, and the demon never stopped probing the magic circle. The candles burned low, and one of them flickered ominously. Sensing victory at last, the Ka'ti'i focused all its evil will upon that one tiny spot.

The candle sputtered and hissed.

The flame died.

The circle was broken.

"*You lose, Sylvaine,*" crowed the demon. "*All die. ALL DIE!*"

The horrible thing leapt from the fireplace with all its limbs extended, grabbing at the dank air. It soared over the impotent marks on the floor and slapped down in the center of Sylvaine's magic circle like a monstrous wet hand.

"*Now!*"

Sylvaine's voice rang out — not from within the circle, not from under the demon's mass, but from behind one of the great piles of furniture. His face beamed triumphantly from four well-placed mirrors. For Sylvaine had never been in the circle at all.

Two lines of bizarre green flame sprouted along the floor at lightning speed, converging upon the greasy third circle of the elaborate pentacle. The demon spun in place, searching for Sylvaine, but it was too late. The pentacle exploded, surrounding it on all sides with searing green light. The Ka'ti'i screamed with a venomous anger that shook the walls, but it dared not touch the dancing, mystic flames.

"Trapped! We've got it!" the Vicar cried. Margaret watched her husband in silence.

The demon screamed once more through Lord Wooltemere's body, and Margaret made a terrible realization: *It would not let George go.* Their triumph was no triumph at all. The doorway would close, but without George it was all for nothing.

Margaret grabbed his stiff body and held it close. And just like that, she was no longer in the library.

● ● ●

Forrest Dylan Bryant

The world spun away as it had before, and Margaret was back in the weird, empty dream space. But this time there were only the two of them, her and George, and the coils of smoke that jumped and constricted like angry snakes.

Lord Wooltemere's mind embraced his wife through the smoke. "Maggie, darling, is it you? Here? But how?"

Margaret remembered Sylvaine's warning. A part of her mind was trapped here, he'd said, bound to George. Perhaps that's how she'd been able to return. Perhaps the doorway between worlds had not yet closed. And that meant there was still a chance.

"We've trapped the demon, my love. Sylvaine is about to close the door. We have to find a way out."

"There's only one way out. Up. But so long as the demon holds me here, I cannot go that way. There's only down… down… into the dreaming." The smoke twitched and constricted around him.

"No, George, don't look down!" Margaret felt the inexorable pull of the frozen abyss below them. She'd faced its gravity before, but Sylvaine had brought her back. Could she bring George up the same way? Could the Ka'ti'i, trapped in the magic circle, stop them from leaving here? There was only one way to know. She grabbed George as tightly as she could and pulled upwards. They somersaulted, spinning round and round… and *up*.

When the spinning stopped, she willed herself upward again, gently this time. And they flew. Margaret didn't understand how they did it, but she could sense their motion, growing faster the higher they went. She could hear the Vicar's distant voice, calling to them, and she aimed for it. The emptiness grew lighter as the tendrils of smoke fell away. And she could feel a warmth that she knew to be their bodies, somewhere just above them, growing closer, closer…

● ● ●

Bartholomew Sylvaine strode up to the magic circle, close to the spot he had pretended to occupy before. His elegant gray suit smoldered as he neared the flames. He held a tattered book in his left hand, its pages yellowed and creased from centuries of use.

"Vicar," he said, "please guide our friends home. I will deal with this creature." Sylvaine read aloud from the ancient tome, chanting in an eerie, singsong voice. The spell's words, written in a lost tongue, were meaningless to a modern ear, but they held a terrible power. The Ka'ti'i howled in agony as each spiked syllable lashed into its body. It quivered and cowered as if physically beaten, pulling its limbs inward for protection.

Sylvaine repeated the chant twice more, each time louder than the last. At the end of the third reading, he dashed the book to the floor and thrust a damning finger at the squealing demon.

"Begone!" he bellowed. "Flee from here ye foul spawn of Hades, and tread not upon this Earth again. In the name of serene Vas Nak'ath, in the name of the Twelve Sages and all that is holy under the gods, *I banish thee!*"

The flames collapsed into a perfect sphere that spun and shrank, falling into itself until it was the size of a pumpkin… an apple… a pea. And then it was gone, taking the hideous Ka'ti'i with it. Only Sylvaine and the feeble light of his candles remained.

The Vicar emerged from behind the pile of furniture, leading Lord and Lady Wooltemere by the hands. They were woozy, shocked, but quite alive.

"You've killed it," he breathed. "It's a miracle. Thank God!"

"I thank all of them," said Sylvaine. "But no mortal can kill such a beast, even with the power of gods behind him." He picked up the book and cradled it in both arms. "We have sent the Ka'ti'i back to the invisible realm from whence it came, that is all. But it will not return to this world in our lifetimes. Our struggle is ended."

● ● ●

Sylvaine sprawled across a divan in the parlor, exhausted. His suit was ruined, frayed at the sleeves and charred at the lapels, but the mischievous twinkle had returned to his eyes.

"So, Lady Wooltemere. I see magicians do indeed 'do it with mirrors.' Imagine that." He lit his pipe and the dragon puffed out a strange, sweet smoke.

Margaret gave a weary laugh. "So, Mister Sylvaine. You really do banish demons with musty incantations and magic circles. I always thought that was the domain of the penny dreadfuls."

"My work is a shade more respectable than that, I hope! What was it Hamlet said? More things in heaven and earth than are dreamt of in your philosophy?"

"And the darkest hour is just before the dawn. Who said that one?"

Sylvaine glanced at the window. The clouds had lightened to morning gray. The howling winds and torrential rains had gone, leaving only a smattering of drops against the pane.

The Vicar set to work with whiskey and siphon as he weighed Sylvaine's words. "More in heaven and earth, yes. We've seen that with our own eyes. The bishop and I must go over it in detail when he arrives tomorrow. I took careful note of everything you did, Mister Sylvaine. I am keen to know how well your methods tally with those of the Church."

"Hm." Sylvaine said no more to that.

"So, what did I miss?" All applauded as Lord Wooltemere staggered into the room, freshly dressed and smiling weakly.

"Mister Sylvaine," he said, "I remember you from my dream. Thank you, sir. I regret that when first we met, you did not see me at my best."

"My lord, we are always at our best, and our worst. But in you the best is greater. I can see it every time Lady Wooltemere looks at you. Her love shines like a beacon in the dark; much like her face shines now." Margaret blushed as she sat down beside her husband.

"What was it like, darling?" she asked. "How did it happen? What else did you see?"

"I… I'm not entirely sure. I need to gather my thoughts. Right now it's all so raw, so… terrifying."

"Perhaps a nip of this will take the edge off," said the Vicar, offering the whiskey.

"I have something better," said Sylvaine. "Round up four glasses. I'll be just a moment." The Investigator of the Unseen went back to the library to retrieve his leather traveling bag. From this he lifted a small bottle of purple liqueur.

"Just the stuff for getting over a night like the one we've had, believe me. A wee dram of this and you'll all feel like it never happened." He poured an ounce into each glass and handed them around.

"You've done this before," quipped Margaret.

"Many times, my good lady. But never with so much at stake. You have no idea how close we all came to losing that battle. Without your mirror trick, it's possible that none of us would be here now."

A silence fell over the room as Sylvaine's words struck home.

"Come, why such gloomy faces? We are alive and whole. Drink up!" Lord Wooltemere and the Vicar held their glasses aloft with shaking hands and gulped down the liqueur. Margaret brought the glass to her lips and paused, giving Sylvaine a quizzical look. He had not raised his glass. He nodded and smiled, and she understood.

Margaret drank. A warm, happy sensation spread along the length of her body, wrapping itself around her brain. This was not the terrible, cold drowsiness of the nowhere place and its dark abyss. It felt welcoming, friendly, and safe. The horrors of the night grew dim. Through drooping eyelids, she saw a slow smile creep across her husband's face. The Vicar was already fast asleep.

"Yes, in a moment you will all feel as if it never happened," said Sylvaine. "Do you understand? It… never… happened."

Margaret could feel herself sliding down into her husband's lap. Sylvaine was still speaking, but she lost track of the words. Something about imagination and superstition. A fire in the library. Speaking to a bishop. It all slid away before she could make sense of it. All she could focus on was the cadence of his speech, the musical way it rolled off his tongue. But his voice was changing now, growing deeper and more commanding. At the last, a few words cut through the fog.

"Now forget. Forget. And sleep."

The blackness took her.

The End

In the Forest of Sorrows

by Richard Lee Byers

The gold and ivory foliage rustled, announcing the advent of another threat. Ryan and his companions—Kunu, the little plant man with his own crown of gleaming yellow leaves in place of hair, Dosembrian Ros, the elderly telekinetic "magus," T'chok of the mountain giants, who with his long horns, towered over Ryan as the Earthman towered over Kunu, and Velenna Leona, princess of Saer Zin and for the past six years, Ryan's wife—lifted their weapons and made ready.

Halkan Shen spoke, seemingly from the empty air, no doubt in reality from a hidden speaker quite possibly bioengineered to grow as an inconspicuous part of a nearby tree. "Enjoy the fight, David Ryan. It is the last such victory you will ever know."

Kunu laughed. "He always assumes that this time he's finally going to kill us. That's what I like about him: the optimism!"

Ryan grinned, but inwardly he was puzzled. Halkan Shen was the megalomaniac who'd discovered the scientific secrets of a lost civilization and used them to enslave a planet, and he was indeed prone to taunt his enemies with the assurance that they were about to die. But this gibe had been different. The tyrant seemed to be saying that his foes were about to win, but it wouldn't do them any good. What did *that* mean?

The stalkers broke cover. Charging on six legs, the vaguely lizard-like things had scaly, mottled white-and-golden hides and spindly many-jointed arms that rose from their backs and terminated in jagged blades. Ryan had never seen their kind before, which might mean Halkan Shen had bioengineered them too. But they could also simply be creatures native to the legendary Forest of Sorrows that surrounded the tyrant's secret citadel. Since crash-landing on Wyla a decade before, the Earthman had encountered an abundance of bizarre and predatory life forms.

The gaunt, old Dosembrian raised his staff and struck the lead reptile with a burst of invisible force that stopped it as if it had slammed into a stone wall. Kunu gave a trilling call, and a tree swatted a second beast with one of its branches.

So far, so good; but the rest of Halkan Shen's guardians kept coming.

T'chok met one of them with a stroke of his battle-axe that sheared off two of its stabbing, lashing extremities at once. Giving ground, Velenna twirled her saber in a complex figure that riveted a lizard-thing's attention, and then with her other hand she threw a dagger that pierced one of its several eyes.

Dodging, parrying when necessary, Ryan advanced through a reptile's slashing arms. He had to if he was to come within striking distance of a vital spot. His blade clanged with the repeated impacts.

Sweeping low, one of the creature's arms nearly hooked his ankle, but he spotted the threat and sprang above it just in time. He laughed as he sometimes did at a particularly close call and split the lizard's skull.

He killed a second beast, and then Velenna cried for help. He whirled.

She'd killed her first reptile, but another had knocked the saber from her hand. Now she was frantically defending with a dagger.

Ryan shouted to distract the lizard-thing and then rushed it. It pivoted to meet him with a swirl of arms. Without breaking stride, he parried a slash, a stab, and then Velenna dived onto the creature's back and drove her knife into the base of its neck. The beast collapsed.

Ryan looked around. His friends were finishing off the last of the reptiles. He helped Velenna to her feet. "You had me worried for a second."

She brushed back the bronze curls that had fallen across her azure forehead and jade eyes. "Why? You're always there when I need you."

He wanted to kiss her, but Dosembrian cleared his throat. "May I suggest," the magus said, "that you wait for a more suitable occasion?"

Ryan snorted. "May I suggest that you and your telepathy stay out of my head? But maybe you have a point. Is everyone all right?"

T'chok grunted. "Yes. Good fight." He wiped gore from the edges of his axe.

They hiked onward. To Ryan, the Forest of Sorrows seemed an endless living maze, and he was glad he hadn't tried to march an army through it. Not that he'd had a choice. The Alliance had smashed Halkan Shen's legions in the Valley of Crimson Stones, but it had been a costly triumph that left them in need of time to regroup.

Ryan would have been happy to recover with them if he hadn't stumbled across a document indicating the location of the tyrant's hidden lair, to which he'd likely fled after his defeat. The Earthman meant to catch his enemy there before Halkan Shen moved on again, and his closest companions had insisted on accompanying him.

Fearing surface-to-air artillery, they'd landed their giant moths outside the forest and entered on foot. Where, Ryan suspected, they would now be utterly lost if not for Kunu's woodcraft and ability to commune with the slow, deep consciousness of the trees.

They made camp at dusk. The campfire jumped and crackled, and one or another of Wyla's three moons occasionally peeked through the tangled branches overhead. T'chok took first watch, and Ryan and Velenna sat cuddled together beneath a blanket. Had they been alone, they surely would have made love, but for now, it was enough to murmur, hold hands, and gaze into one another's eyes.

After all these years, it still amazed Ryan that such a wonderful, beautiful woman—and royalty to boot!—had fallen in love with the surly stranger he'd been when he first arrived. In those days, he'd been obsessed with getting home to the Human Confederation, and she'd waited him out, waited for him to realize that everything he truly wanted was right here on Wyla for the winning.

Something fluttered. Then a net fell over T'chok. He snarled and flailed, and several monkey-sized creatures with bat-like wings swooped out of the darkness to light on him.

Ryan threw off the blanket. He seized the sword lying on the ground at this side, drew it from its scabbard, and sprang to his feet. Then he hesitated.

This combat felt different than the scores that had preceded it. He couldn't say how, but it did.

He scowled the uncertainty away. The only thing that mattered was that T'chok needed him. He raced in the mountain giant's direction. As he did, Dosembrian seized one of the winged creatures in his psychokinetic grasp and pulled it away. The beast had a writhing proboscis like a shorter version of an elephant's trunk, the needle tip now dipped in T'chok's blood.

Ryan tried to pick a target, one he could attack with minimal chance of cutting or stabbing T'chok my mistake. Then more flapping sounded overhead. He threw himself aside and banged into a tree trunk. A net thumped down on the ground beside him.

Hissing—in frustration, perhaps—more winged creatures dived out of the darkness. They had curved claws on their wings and could evidently fly and slash at the same time.

Ryan dodged the first, cut, and the creature avoided the sword stroke by dipping under it before streaking out of reach. Damn, they were fast!

He pivoted, and the next little beast was right in front of him, the talon on its outstretched wing poised to take out his eye. He bellowed, cut, and sheared the wing in two. Shrieking, the flying beast thudded to the ground.

Three more whirled above him, each no doubt hoping to assail him while he was focused on another. He kept them from maiming him but couldn't tag them either. Angry, he attacked harder and harder, though still to no effect.

Then the tree he'd bumped into seized one of the winged creatures in its leafy grasp and crumpled it like a piece of paper. Dosembrian's telekinesis pulled the wing off a second. Now free of the net, his upper body spotted with round little wounds, T'chok charged, leaped, swung his axe, and split the last one in two.

Panting, Ryan looked around. The fight was over. Velenna and his other companions were staring at him.

"What 's wrong?" he asked.

Everyone hesitated. Then Velenna said, "You didn't fight like yourself."

Ryan frowned. "I would have killed the three of them eventually, if Kunu, Dosembrian, and T'chok hadn't gotten them first."

"Perhaps so," Dosembrian said, "but your mental state was different. Normally, you're energized but calm. This time you were tense and tenser still as the battle progressed and victory didn't come easily. Even though I too was busy fighting, I felt the agitation building inside you."

Ryan drew breath to argue. Then he realized the magus was correct.

"You're right," he said. "I don't know what happened."

"May I?" Dosembrian closed his eyes, and stood motionless for a while. His psychic probing and sifting tingled inside Ryan's skull.

Finally the old man said, "I wondered if Halkan Shen had recruited a master of the Whispering Art to tamper with your mind, but I find no trace of any such influence."

"Bend down," Kunu said. When Ryan did, he wiped a drop of sweat off the human's forehead with his fingertip and put it in his mouth. "Hm. If you have something strange in your system, it's not pollen or spores from the forest or any drug that comes from plants."

"We're all tired," Ryan said. "I was just having an off moment."

Velenna smiled. "No doubt."

The others murmured in agreement.

But Ryan sensed their lingering worry, and he couldn't blame them for doubting. He hadn't succeeded in reassuring himself either.

They hiked on at daybreak. Big two-headed snakes attacked them while the sun was still climbing, and shambling bear-like beasts with quills ambushed them when it was past zenith.

In each fight, Ryan struggled. When a foe pushed him hard, frustration and perhaps even anxiety tightened him up. He had trouble thinking of the tricks and tactics he hadn't attempted yet and instead repeated ones that had already failed. The moves grew wilder until he overcommitted and left himself vulnerable to counterattack.

He still managed to kill an opponent or two. But the warrior acclaimed as Wyla's greatest swordsman, the man comrades counted on to rush to their aid when they found themselves in trouble, was gone. In fact, in the clash with the bear-things, one of the creatures knocked Ryan's blade out of line, lunged, and would have driven a fistful of spines into his heart if T'chok hadn't rushed in and split its head.

Ryan looked around. All the quill bears were dead. "Thanks," he panted.

The horned giant shrugged. "Is how we do."

In a sense, that was true. He and T'chok had saved one another's lives on numerous occasions, but always when they were outnumbered. Ryan shouldn't have needed his friend to protect him from a single adversary.

"It's a bad idea to linger where we raised a commotion," Velenna said. "Let's move on."

"On toward Halkan Shen's citadel," Ryan said.

She cocked her head. "Of course."

"I realize that was the plan. But at this point, we have to admit the truth. Somehow, he's taken something from me, and I'm not the fighter I was. I don't want to let the rest of you down."

T'chok's brown lips quirked upright. "We fight pretty good ourselves."

Kunu nodded. The golden leaves that grew in place of hair rustled around his head. "Better than anything Halkan Shen can throw at us."

"Indeed," Dosembrian said, "and despite the added risk, it's worth trying to put an end to the despot forthwith, before he can devise a new strategy and raise a new army."

"Lead us as you always have," said Velenna to Ryan, "and we'll come through all right."

He took a deep breath. "Let's go, then."

It stormed during the night. Rain hammered down. A dazzling, deafening, blue thunderbolt blasted a tree not fifty paces from the spot where he and his companions had made their camp.

In the morning, vines and bushes had put forth red and orange blossoms, water dripped from white and yellow leaves, and the boggy ground sucked at a traveler's feet. A haze hung in the air.

Gradually, so gradually that at first Ryan didn't register that it was happening, the haze thickened into mist. Finally he realized that if the obscuration grew any worse, he might lose sight of Kunu, who was taking point, entirely.

He started to call to the little plant man and then faltered in confusion. It was difficult to bring the proper words to mind, as well as to arrange them grammatically.

"Hold up!" he shouted. "Let's close up the gap!" Had that come out right? Had he pronounced all the words correctly?

"What?" Kunu answered. "I don't..." The rest of the response was just as loud, just as clearly articulated, but Ryan somehow missed the sense of it.

The fog continued to thicken, the process now so accelerated that only Halkan Shen's technology could be responsible. Lost in muggy grayness, Ryan couldn't see any of his companions anymore.

"Help!" Kunu cried.

Ryan drew his sword and then felt something sliding over his toe. Expecting another serpent, he looked down and discovered a woody stalk sprouting from the ground with preternatural speed. It twisted around his ankle, tethering him, while it continued coiling up his leg.

He trusted Kunu to master any plant, even one created in Halkan Shen's laboratories, so long as his friend understood the problem. "There's a kind of... of...*vine*...attacking me!" he shouted. The words stuck in his brain and throat as they had before.

Kunu yelled back, but Ryan failed to grasp the meaning. T'chok bellowed something, too, something about the danger being at their feet.

Ryan's vine wrapped itself around his leg nearly up to the hip. Then the end of it curved away from his body and, forking repeatedly, divided into half a dozen stalks. Each swelled into a pod, which then split and opened lengthwise to reveal rows of thorn-like fangs.

It was awkward to hack at the vine with a sword. It was too close. But Ryan cut at a point below the first branching, sheared through, and all the sets of jaws fell gnashing to the ground.

By that time though, a plant was winding its way up his other leg. He stabbed the point of his sword into the base of it, right where it was emerging from the boggy soil. The resulting convulsion drew it tourniquet-tight around his limb, but only for a moment. Then it slackened, and he managed to tear it away. The same process rid him of the first vine.

His companions were calling out in the mist, but he couldn't understand most of the words. He suspected the agitation manifesting in his rapid respiration and pounding heartbeat hindered his comprehension as it did his swordplay. Trying to calm himself, he took a deep breath.

Somewhere behind him in the fog, Velenna shouted. Ryan recognized the word *help* if nothing else. He charged toward the sound of her voice. Another predatory vine burst from the ground before him, and he lopped it into two wriggling pieces.

His next stride revealed a shadow in the mist. Two more, and the shape resolved into his wife. To his surprise, she'd already disposed of whatever plants had attacked her.

She peered back at him. "Were you *something something something?* I'm *something.* I said *something* help Dosembrian!"

Saber in hand, she dashed in the direction of a series of croaking cries, and Ryan followed. They found the magus lying entangled on the ground and pulling with both hands at the loop of vine that sought to garrote him. Apparently pain or panic was hampering the use of his telekinetic abilities.

Together, Ryan and Velenna rescued Dosembrian, and then the three of them found T'chok free and unscathed. By then the fog was thinning, and it was easy enough to locate the caterwauling Kunu. The plant man had sunk to his shoulders in quicksand, and a glistening thing like a man-sized amoeba had slithered across the top of the morass to assail him. Apparently it wasn't susceptible to sinking, and the trees that had bent over to bash at it splashed its substance but without seeming to do it actual harm.

Dosembrian's telekinesis yanked Kunu from the quicksand and set him on solid ground. Then, glaring, the magus churned the pit, rolling the amoeba and the slippery earth over and over together until the substance of the former was lost in the greater volume of the latter. His task accomplished, he swayed, and T'chok caught hold of his arm to steady him.

Ryan looked down at Kunu. "Now I understand why you didn't order the vines to leave us alone. You had your own problems."

The plant man swiped mud off his forearm. "It wasn't just that. I *something something* not understand you. I'm *something* trouble understanding *something.*"

"We all are," said T'chok.

"And I'm having trouble understanding you," Ryan said. "God damn it!"

Velenna put her hand on his shoulder. "Easy. *Something* Halkan Shen's doing to you, it's not *something* all that well. You can still fight, and we can still *something,* just not quite as well as before. And we'll find the *something* in his *something.*"

Ryan put his hand over hers. "Of course. We always come out all right in the end."

He clung to that thought. But through the rest of the day and the evening that followed, it galled him that the others were choosing small words and arranging them into simple sentences in the hope that he would understand, just as it scraped at him that he had to struggle to make himself understood in turn. It made him feel stupid.

But there was more at stake than his pride. Velenna had said she and the others looked to him to lead. Whether commanding an army or directing a small band of friends, he'd always had the knack. It was he who'd ordered the diversion of the river in Aeklinth, and in High Gilzalan recognized that the Pale Colossus was seeking the scroll, in each case turning seemingly certain defeat into victory.

That however, had been when he was clearheaded enough to come up with tricks and tactics under pressure, and spoke fluently enough to ensure that his orders were instantly understood. He couldn't help wondering how well he'd manage in his current diminished condition.

The next day brought them within sight of Halkan Shen's castle. Its mosaic walls and minarets rose on an island in the center of a lake, and a causeway linked the isle to the forest.

Peering from a stand of trees on the shore, Ryan said, "I don't see any guards on the..." He couldn't think of the Wylan word for *battlements*. "The walls. But I'm sure somebody's keeping watch."

Dosembrian nodded. "And I'm more *something* still that someone would *something* us if we tried to cross the bridge. I *something* we *something* a boat instead."

"And cross after dark," said T'chok.

They withdrew a little way into the forest and found a fallen tree and some other deadwood they could fashion into a raft. The mountain giant set about the task of constructing it with his usual tireless tenacity. Since Ryan didn't have an axe, he judged he'd be more useful watching out for Halkan Shen's minions.

As he prowled from one patch of cover to the next, he spied an asymmetrical figure, one shoulder higher and one arm longer than the other, with ridged brown hide and whorled mold growing on top of that. Its head bulged on one side, was flat on the other, and sported three round black eyes. Symbiotes or parasites, tiny beetles crawled up and down the creature's limbs.

The thing was no bigger than a child, but that didn't mean it wasn't dangerous. Ryan eased his sword out of its scabbard. Then, sensing his presence somehow, the creature turned and spoke his name in Kunu's voice.

It's a trick, Ryan thought. But if so, it was a poor ruse that disguised the thing's voice but left its appearance unaffected.

"You're *something* at me," Kunu continued. "What's wrong?"

"You look different to me. Really different."

"Let's go back to the others," the plant man said.

Ryan shivered. Though he wasn't sure why, he dreaded going back. But it was the only sensible course of action.

When he saw the group gathered at the half-completed raft, he flinched.

T'chok looked less like a horned man than a horned leprous ape, but he was by far the easiest to look at.

Dosembrian more closely resembled a human, but that only made the differences more jarring. There was something nauseating about the eyes placed too high on the head and too far to the sides of the flat nose with its single nostril. About the beard of wormlike tendrils. About the arms that were too short with the elbows set too high, and the truncated, twisted feet.

Being of the same species, Velenna naturally displayed similar characteristics. Ryan told himself she was the love of his life, and truly, that hadn't changed. Yet at the same time, it was surreal, almost unimaginable, that he'd ever regarded her as beautiful.

He swallowed. "Somehow, Halkan Shen has..." Damn it, what was the word for *hypnotized?* "Tampered with my mind again. You don't look like yourselves. I could have attacked Kunu."

"Let me see." Dosembrian peered at Ryan. Then his eyes widened. It had suddenly become difficult to read his companions' expressions, but Ryan still recognized surprise.

"What is it?" he asked.

"The way you saw us before was the illusion," the magus said. "What you see now is the *something*. I never before realized your *something* was *something* because I never had cause to *something* your mind in this *something* way."

"That can't be true! Halkan Shen's tricking you somehow! We'll fix it when we fix the other things that are wrong!"

"I hope so," Dosembrian said, but in the manner of someone saying whatever was necessary to soothe an agitated friend. Ryan could tell the telepath didn't actually doubt his own opinion.

With his sight altered—screwed up, damn it, whatever Dosembrian believed— Ryan didn't trust himself to play sentry anymore. He sent Kunu to patrol the woods and sat down with his back against a tree trunk. After a time, Velenna came and sat beside him.

"Am I truly ugly to you now?" she asked.

He wanted to spare her feelings, but they'd never lied to one another. "Like I told Dosembrian, we'll fix it."

"You've always looked strange to us." Velenna's tone was bleak. "But to me, otherness is not the same thing as ugliness. I suppose that's a way our two races differ on the inside."

Some hours after nightfall, Ryan and his comrades dragged the raft to the lake. Two of the moons reflected in the black water as well as a few scattered lights burning from within the castle on the island.

Together, the crude paddles T'chok had fashioned and Dosembrian's psychokinesis sufficed to propel the craft. Occasionally a splash sounded as a fish or some other aquatic creature broke the surface.

When the infiltrators landed, the magus's power floated a rope up the wall and knotted the end around a merlon. Ryan climbed onto the battlement, checked for immediate danger, and then whistled for his companions to follow.

All the wall-walks within view appeared deserted. So too did the shadowed courtyard below. The intruders descended a staircase and skulked onward.

An archway led to a larger courtyard. On the other side, in front of the entrance to the central keep, sat a house-sized tapered metal cylinder with the words ANTARES MINING AND EXPLORATION emblazoned in English on the side. Ryan froze in amazement.

Meanwhile, Kunu was the last to pass through the arch, and as soon as he did, a portcullis dropped with a rattle of chains to clash against the flagstones. The several doors ringing the courtyard flew open, and blades and armor gleamed within.

"Make a circle!" Ryan shouted. That way, no one could attack him or any of his companions from behind.

But the enemy didn't come streaming out to engage them. Instead, the prospecting ship's airlock opened and Halkan Shen stepped forth. Ryan only recognized him by the rubies that studded his robes like beads of blood. Otherwise, the blue-skinned tyrant looked as grotesquely transformed as Velenna and Dosembrian did.

"Do you understand me?" asked Halkan Shen. He was speaking English.

Ryan answered the same way. "Yes."

"Good. Since you're no longer fluent in my language, I thought it might be easier to converse in yours. Behind those doors are the few survivors of my Holy Legions. They're eager to avenge their defeat."

"We're ready when they are."

"Understand that when I say 'few,' I mean compared to the host I once commanded. There are more than enough to overwhelm you, the princess, and your friends. Admittedly, with the aid of his trusty allies, Wyla's finest swordsman might have stood against them, but he's no longer with us, is he?"

Ryan swallowed. "What did you do to me?"

"I intend to explain. Just promise me that you and your companions won't do anything rash until we finish talking."

Ryan reverted to the tongue of Velenna's people. "Keep your guards up, but don't make the first move. Halkan Shen and I are parleying." He shifted back to English. "Go on."

"Perhaps," said Halkan Shen, "I should start at the beginning, although I suppose some of what happened is obvious. Once I realized you were a traveler from another world stranded on this one, I went looking for your vessel. I found it, brought it here, and when time allowed, studied the secrets within."

"That's how you learned English."

"English was the least of it. I learned what human doctors do to infants."

"I don't follow."

"Because in your civilization, you've been doing it so long that the average person doesn't even think about it anymore. You're full of nanites and bioware, David Ryan. Enhancements that maximize health, accelerate learning, and in a crisis, suppress fear and sharpen your reflexes. Very helpful to an Earthman marooned on a more primitive planet. It equips you to play the hero, when in reality, all your triumphs amount to a cheat.

"Fortunately," Halkan Shen continued, "I eventually figured out how to reduce you to a mere mortal like the rest of us. Once repaired, your ship's computer proved capable of communicating with your internal machinery and even switching it off. Which didn't *completely* cripple you. At this point, you've slashed your way through too many sword fights and spoken our Wylan languages for too long. But if one pulls the foundation out from under a structure, the edifice atop it cracks and crumbles."

"That doesn't explain what happened to my eyes."

"I was getting to that. Naturally, your own people can adjust the bioware, too. Do you recall giving your employer permission to do so before embarking on your voyage?"

"The doctor said a couple tweaks would help me."

"He was right. Apparently, if sentient beings are sufficiently alien, Earthmen find prolonged contact stressful, particularly if there are no other humans around. The mechanisms in your brain protected you by editing your perceptions of the natives of Wyla into something more palatable."

"Until you turned off that function, too."

"You should thank me if you value truth."

Ryan raised his sword. "I'll value the sight of you bleeding out on the ground."

"Don't be hasty. I warned you, if you insist on a fight, my soldiers will kill you. But that would be a waste when I need your help."

"What are you talking about?"

Halkan Shen sighed. "I should have prioritized my investigation of your ship. If I'd realized it contained a means of crippling you...but I didn't, and so you had time to cast me down from my throne. It won't be easy to re-conquer this entire world with the resources I have left. But if the champion of the rebellion repents of his treason, if he grovels to me and begs my forgiveness, that should demoralize your fellow malcontents considerably."

"You can't really believe I'd ever do that."

"Why not? The past ten years amount to a dream from which you have now awakened. You can't play the hero anymore. You can't enjoy the company of your friends and certainly can't love the princess as a husband loves a wife, not now that all Wylans stand revealed as monstrosities. But happily, I was able to repair your *whole* ship, just not the machinery I used to strip you of your unfair advantages. Do as I ask and I'll let you go home to your own people."

Ryan hesitated. "Before I did anything to help you, Velenna and the others would have to go free."

"That...is a lot to ask. However, none of them can provide the propaganda victory that you can, so I agree—for now. The next time they fall into my hands... well, you know. Do we have a bargain?"

"Yes." Ryan turned to his companions and in their language said, "Halkan Shen is letting you go. Get far away before he changes his mind."

Dosembrian frowned. "You don't mean you're staying."

"It's the only way that any of us survive."

T'chok hefted his axe. "The way is to fight."

"Not when there are no plants here for Kunu to command. Not when I'm...sick. We'd lose."

Velenna took Ryan's hands in hers. "We said we'd cure what ails you."

"There is no cure. I beg you: go. If not for my sake, then for Saer Zin's. Your people need you to finish the work we started. To make sure Halkan Shen never terrorizes them again."

Their wings a humming scarlet blur, four huge moths flew over the battlements and landed in the courtyard. The soldiers astride them climbed down from the saddles and held the steeds by the reins.

"There's your way home," Ryan said. "Go. Please."

Velenna took him in her arms and kissed him. Her lips were rough and tasted sour, but he made himself ignore the differences and return the kiss as he always had.

Then, with a sob, she wrenched herself away. She, Dosembrian, T'chok, and Kunu mounted the moths and soared up into the sky.

"Now," said Halkan Shen, still in English, "it's time to fulfill your end of the deal."

"Wait until they have more of a head start."

"If that's what it takes to satisfy you. Meanwhile, my servants will fetch the cameras. You and I are going to introduce video to Wyla. Our little movie will play everywhere, repeatedly, until everyone who believed in you has seen it."

The servants also brought a rubber sword. Apparently, even though Ryan had lost much of his prowess, Halkan Shen was too wary to let him approach with a real blade. The tyrant told him what to do and say, and then it was time to begin.

Ryan walked to Halkan Shen, dropped to his knees, and laid the mock weapon on the ground between them. Then he kissed the conqueror's feet.

"You are the rightful ruler of Wyla," he said in Velenna's language, "just, kindly, and wise. I'm ashamed of my rebellion and the traitors who rebelled with me. I renounce them and beg your mercy."

"You don't deserve it," said Halkan Shen, "but in the hope that it will help to bring peace, I grant it *something*. Fly away in your *something* and trouble this world no more."

"May all the gods bless you," Ryan said. He kissed Halkan Shen's feet several more times, then rose and entered the exploration ship.

Though it felt strange to be back aboard in front of the controls after so many years, he still remembered how to pilot. He activated the J-drive, and one of the screens showed the courtyard dropping away beneath the ship. Over the course of the next minute, all Wyla shrank to a blue and white disk.

Ryan tensed. It seemed the logical moment for the spacecraft to explode, but after a while, when he was still alive and all the instruments were still showing green, he decided that maybe Halkan Shen hadn't sabotaged it after all.

Perhaps he shouldn't be surprised. Throughout their conflicts, the tyrant had sometimes misled him but had never lied outright, and it was conceivable that he regarded Ryan's humiliation as vengeance enough.

In theory, though, it was a revenge that left Ryan free to continue their war. He didn't know how to use the equipment aboard the ship to restore his bioware, but doctors back in the Confederation would. And then...

Then, how would he return to Wyla? The ship was the property of Antares Mining and Exploration, not his own personal vessel.

But suppose he did find a way back. By then, Halkan Shen would likely have rebuilt a power base. He'd surely have the technology ready to switch off Ryan's enhancements all over again, and as if that weren't bad enough, the Earthman's former allies would despise him as a turncoat.

Still, despite all those handicaps, what if Ryan did find a way to win another protracted struggle with his foe? What would be his reward?

Even if at that point, he was still peering through a veil of comforting illusion, he'd remember how Velenna truly looked. He'd also know that his own appearance had posed no obstacle to her desiring him, and although perhaps that should inspire him to a similar transcendence, it wouldn't. Rather, it would underscore differences of mind as profound as the variations in their physicality, differences to which he'd once been blissfully oblivious.

Now that he recognized how alien she and her people actually were, how could he live among them and feel anything but alone, no matter how many accolades they bestowed on him?

Perhaps Halkan Shen was right. Maybe he needed to accept his defeat and return to his own kind.

Maybe. But he wasn't going to.

The love he and Velenna had shared was real. His friendships with T'chok, Kunu, Dosembrian Ros, and scores of others were real. If the truth had blighted his ability to take joy in them, that was a defect in his nature, not theirs. He still owed them his loyalty.

Besides, for years they'd been proclaiming him a hero, and heroes didn't let the villain win.

He turned the ship around, accelerated, and aimed it at Halkan Shen's citadel like a sword.

The End

The Hidden City
of Ru-Don

by Wayne Carey

"Thank you, everyone, for coming. My name is Henry Baker and I'm about to take you on the adventure of a lifetime, to the hidden world of Ru-Don. Even today, in 1949, much of Africa is unexplored and there are strange and wild places where modern man has never set foot, places lost for centuries to the outside world. One of those places is Ru-Don."

I looked over the crowd from my place behind the podium on the little stage. Chicago's YMCA auditorium was not large, but the dozen people scattered among the sea of seats made it seem cavernous. Not a very good showing. Still, if half of those bought my book after the lecture, I'd break even and be able to have a decent dinner. There was a pretty redhead in the front row, with a pleasant smile and attentive eyes, a copy of *The Hidden City of Ru-Don* resting on her lap. She probably brought it for me to autograph, as some readers did.

Two men entered the auditorium and took seats in the back, catching my attention not because they were late, but because they were not your typical reader. Both were big guys in dark suits that cost more than what I make in a year, which isn't saying much. Men you would not want to run into in a dark alley. Or even a sunny park.

I ignored the two thugs and launched into my spiel. I'd done it so many times that it rolled of my tongue without any thought, so I could concentrate on the redhead. A little background came first: degrees from Northwestern University, working on digs in Egypt before the war, the discovery of the ruins of a lost civilization on a pacific island when I was stranded after my ship was attacked. The island was bombed by the Japanese during a hair-raising adventure, all chronicled in my first book, which had done well and had cemented my reputation. The island never actually existed. Sure, I was in the Pacific Theater and was on a ship that sank, rescued a day later from a sand bar. But the facts didn't matter. I had come up with a story that sounded good and might have sold, but would never have made a splash … unless it seemed real. So I made readers believe in it, and I've been writing "real" adventures ever since. The latest was the discovery of Ru-Don, which came from an old map I had found in a curiosity shop in Dar es Salaam. I showed the map at my lectures to add a bit of realism to hook the audience. It was a ratty old thing, maybe a hundred years old, with fading ink and questionable origin. I told them that to ensure that the people of Ru-Don were left in peace; the map was not printed in the book. Actually, it was to insure that no one else tried to find the place, since I made up the whole adventure. The map had sparked my imagination and I wrote the book while hitting some tourist sites in East Africa, never venturing further into the interior than Nairobi. It was my best book yet.

"And now," I said after an hour of teasing the audience, "for those of you interested in more details, I have copies of my book for sale and I would be happy to personalize them for you."

I sold five books before the crowd started to leave. The redhead hung around, but before she had a chance to approach, the two guys in expensive suits came up to the table in front of the stage.

"Dr. Baker?" the one said.

"Our boss would like to speak with you," the other said. He made it sound like a threat.

I had never been to Chicago before and couldn't think of anyone I might have insulted. The only thing that came to mind was that their "boss" had read my books and had discovered that they were utter fiction. Others had done the same, but none of them had carried guns, which these guys did.

I stood on week legs and shoved my remaining books into a cardboard box. "I'd love to, gentlemen, but I've got to catch a train."

"Boss said we should drive you to wherever you had to go. After," said the first one.

That made it sound a little better . . . that there actually would be an "after" after. And I didn't seem to have much choice.

I cradle my box and tried to smile. "Then let's go meet your boss."

The redhead peeked around the guy on the left. "Excuse me, Dr. Baker, I'd like to have…"

"Sorry, sister," the other guy said, "the Doc has an appointment."

I smiled apologetically at the young woman as the two well-dressed goons led me away, one on either side. I would have preferred to spend some time with her, but destiny called. I just hoped it wasn't for the last time.

"And just who is your boss?" I asked while they hustled be out of the auditorium.

"Carmine Carrino," the first one said.

Even I had heard of him. His exploits had reached national renown. The authorities just have never been able to pin anything on him.

I sat in the back of the '48 Cadillac with Joe, while the other guy, who was of course named Vinny, drove. They took us out of the city into a neighborhood with mansions squatting behind high walls. Through a huge iron gate, down a winding drive, to one of these sprawling brick monstrosities. The front door was opened by a man dressed like a butler, but he was as big as my escorts and carried a thirty-eight shoved into his waistband under his tailed coat.

A squat, middle-aged man with thinning hair and thick arms waited for us in the library. He wore his shirt sleeves rolled back and sat in an easy chair near a fireplace large enough to garage a Pontiac. As we entered, he stood up and set a book down on the coffee table. He reached out and crushed my fingers in an exuberant handshake.

"Dr. Baker, so good of you to come. Please, sit down. Joseph, have Maria bring some coffee."

So far so good. He did not act like he was about to accuse me of being a fraud. He seemed pleased to see me, although he didn't smile. Which I didn't mind because I heard somewhere that mobsters smiled when they were going to have someone whacked.

The maid brought coffee and sandwiches, and even she looked like she was packing.

"I suppose you wonder why I asked you here," Carrino began.

I shoved a sandwich wedge into my mouth so I wouldn't have to speak. Besides, I hadn't eaten all day.

"It's because of my sister. She's worried about her boy, Frank. Now, Frankie's a good boy, don't get me wrong. His father is my lawyer. Takes care of a lot of my business." I did not want to know anything about his business. "Frankie's in law school. Good grades, but he's not happy. Then he reads a book."

He glanced at the coffee table between us, to the book he had been reading. My book. *The Hidden City of Ru-Don.*

"I checked up on you, Dr. Baker ..."

I stopped chewing, my stomach acids erupting.

"... and as incredible as your stories are, you seem legit. I got friends in the publishing business. Frank, he was obsessed with your books. Read them all. He saw you at one of your lectures in New York. So he ups and quits school between semesters and heads off to Africa on his own. He wants to explore this Ru-Don place himself."

I took a hard swallow, the sandwich falling like a cannon ball. *But Ru-Don isn't real.* "I never published the map," I said. "He'd have no way of finding it."

Carrino tapped the side of his head. "Ah, but Frankie's smart. Perfect memory. What you call photographic. He saw your map at your lecture. After looking at it once, he went and made an exact copy. Then he emptied his bank account and sailed to Africa."

"I'm sorry," I said. "I doubt he'll actually find it, even with the map. It's ... pretty well hidden."

"My sister tried to read your book when she found out what happened. All those dangers you went through. Hostile natives. Fevers. Lions. Treasure hunters. Those Nazis. I hate Nazis. I didn't fight in the war like you did, but I did my part, and I'm glad you took care of those Nazis trying to destroy Ru-Don. But my kid sister is worried, and when she's worried, I got to do something. Promised my mother on her death bed. You understand, don't you? You ever make a promise to your mother?"

I nodded slowly. I had promised never to return home and I have kept that promise, to her relief.

"Then you can understand why I brought you in on this. I'll spare no expense. We have a plane ready to fly to Africa. Everything has been worked out. All you have to do is lead the expedition into the interior, to Ru-Don, just like you did before, like in your book, and find Frank. Bring him back safe and sound."

"I have commitments," I said. "With my publisher. I can give you the map..."

"Like I said, I got friends in the business. I'll take care of everything. Do this, and you won't have to worry about selling another book. I'll take care of you."

Implying: If you don't do this, I'll take care of you.

I put on a big smile. "When do we leave?"

My plan was simple: disappear. I had no choice but to take Carmine Carrino's proposal and fly to Africa. I would follow through, outfit an expedition, and march into the interior, and then I would disappear. I had enough money hidden away to last a couple of years. I would head to Egypt; lay low in Cairo for a year or so. I knew some people. Eventually, I'd be able to show my face in the States again, probably under another name and with a new scheme, but at least I'd be alive. Unfortunately, Joe and Vinny were tagged to join my little expedition. They would not be so easy to shake.

Carrino chartered a plane to California, another to Hawaii, and eventually to Nairobi. A train would take us into the interior. Trucks would carry us and our supplies to the mountains, then we would walk. He gave us unlimited expenses to outfit the safari. The problem was that I had never outfitted an expedition. I had never been on a safari of any kind. I had been to Nairobi two years earlier, while writing my book, but that was the closest I had gotten to deepest darkest Africa.

My first act was to feign a flare-up of malaria, which I never had. I told Joe and Vinny that after a dose of quinine and a little rest, I would be as good as new. When I was certain they had retired to their own rooms to rest after the long trip, I headed to the bazaar.

Paul Onyango claimed to be the grandson of a Maasai king. Were that true, he had been disowned by his family long ago. Something we had in common. He owned some shops in the bazaar. I found him in one that sold "artifacts" that were made in Asia and shipped in. It was also filled with local junk and reminded me of the place in Dar es Salaam where I had bought the map that had started this mess.

"*Jambo*, Paul!"

He glared at me from behind his cluttered counter, his dark eyes stabbing over the edge of glasses with an attached jeweler's lens as he worked on the opened back of a gold pocket watch.

"What you want?"

"Good, you remember me."

He slammed the watch down, causing springs to fire in three directions. "I remember you owe me twenty dollars American."

I reached into my pocket, pulled out a bill, and slid it across the counter beside the ruined timepiece. He looked through the jeweler's lens at the picture of Ben Franklin.

"What's this?" he asked, picking it up as though it might bite in retaliation.

"It's real. And there's more where that came from."

He pulled off the glasses and one eyebrow curled up in suspicion. "Who you want me to kill?"

"No one. Not yet, anyway. I need your help. I have to outfit a safari."

His laugh boomed through the shop. "You've never been on a safari. You don't know the first thing about it. Look at your shoes. Those things would fall apart the first day."

"Yeah, but I got a powerful backer who thinks I do know, and that's why I need your help. You can find me the right person to outfit the expedition and a guide to take us in, without me looking like an idiot."

"Too late for that."

"I mean in front of the two guys the backer sent along to keep an eye on me."

He thought for a moment, rubbing his chin. "Where you want to go?"

I reached into my back pocket, pulled out the cloth map, and then unfolded it, laying it over the watch parts. I stabbed a finger at the script that said "Ru-Don." At least, that's what the faded ink looked like.

He slipped the glasses back on, bent over the counter, then straightened, lifting the map to study it in the sunlight streaming through the windows. "This is real. Where did you find this?"

"In a shop like this, in Dar es Salaam, three years ago."

"You mean, like in this?" he asked. He reached under the counter, took out a battered book with a torn dust jacket, and set it down.

I grinned. "You read my book. That's great. It's a mess. What did you do, beat your wives with it?"

"Ru-Don isn't real," he said.

"I know that."

"Nothing in that book is real."

"I know that."

"Who would ever believe such a thing?"

I told him, in excruciating detail. He had a concept of American mobsters from movies shown at the local Nairobi cinema.

"You, *rafiki zangu*," he said, "are in deep dung."

"Tell me about it. Can you help?"

He looked over the map. "This is real. Whether Ru-Don is a lost city, someone's name, or a hole in the ground, who can say? I don't even think it actually says Ru-Don. Could be something else. But based on the other landmarks, I believe we can find it. As for outfitting your safari, I have a cousin. But I will come with you."

"Not a good idea."

"You need a guide and an interpreter. I can do both. And you need someone to keep your secret. I'll do that, too, for a price." He gave a wide grin.

"Deal."

We made arrangements and I left the shop, bumping into a woman who hovered outside in the dusty street. She wore khaki clothes and sturdy hiking boots, a wide brimmed hat pulled down over short red hair.

"Excuse me," I said. "Wait. Don't I know you?"

She pushed the brim back and looked up at me.

I wagged my finger at her. "Yeah. Chicago. Last week. You were in the audience at the YMCA. What are you doing here?"

"Dr. Baker, I need to talk with you."

"Don't tell me you came thousands of miles to get me to autograph your book. Say, how did you get here? You weren't on any flights I was on. What are you up to?"

"Ah, well, it's a long story. Can we go somewhere a little more private?"

An Arab jostled me as he passed by in the narrow street. I quickly checked for my wallet, relieved to find it.

"No we can't. Out with it, sister."

She scowled at me. "Okay. I know you're here on behalf of Carmine Carrino. Do you know he's a mobster? Do you even realize what crimes he's committed?"

Yeah, and I'm trying to prevent him from committing one more murder. Mine. "What are you?" I said. "FBI?"

"No. I'm …" She glanced around at the crowd. "… a reporter."

"Seriously? You followed me from Chicago to get a story? Are you nuts? What kind of publisher would throw away that much money?"

Her hands balled into fists. "You mean because I'm a woman?"

"No. I mean because you're stupid. You have no story here, sister. Go home and beg for mercy from your publisher."

"Editor. My editor agreed to this."

"Why?"

"Well, he's my father."

"Just go back to Chicago."

"I know you're organizing an expedition to go back to Ru-Don. I picked up that much. I just don't know why."

"Because Carrino's nephew was stupid enough to read my book and wanted to find the place for himself."

She grinned. "Really?" Then she lost the grin and looked hopelessly disappointed. "Oh. You mean it's not some criminal venture. No treasure hunt or something like that."

"No. There's no treasure in Ru-Don."

She looked puzzled. "You said in your book that there was."

I had forgotten about that. "Oh, yeah, but that's sacred to the people of Ru-Don. I'd never take it from them. I kept the map to Ru-Don out of my book for the express purpose to keep people from going there and robbing them."

"Like those Nazis tried," she said.

"Exactly. But Carrino's nephew saw my map and decided to strike out on his own. This is more like a rescue mission."

"Then take me with you." She moved a little closer.

"What? Are you nuts? Oh, wait, we already established that you are."

I turned to disappear into the crowd before she could follow me, but she called out instead.

"I know there is no Dr. Henry Baker!"

I stopped dead in my track, got bumped by two Maasai women, and nearly fell over a goat. I didn't turn back around. I didn't have to. She came to me, a smug smile on her pretty face.

"I'm Henry Baker," I said through clenched teeth.

"I did my research. There were only two Henry Bakers who went to Northwestern. One is a medical doctor in California, the other died ten years ago at the age of seventy. Which one are you?"

"Your research is faulty," I said. She had done a better job than Carrino and his people.

"Nope. If its one thing I'm good at, it's research. You may be Henry Baker, but you didn't get a doctorate at Northwestern. What else did you lie about?"

"Northwestern, Penn State, what does it matter? I'm not here for a job interview; we're here to find some kid. Now get lost."

"You take me along so I can write the story about the kid's rescue, or I'll tell Carmine Carrino."

I thought over the consequences. Joe and Vinny would not be happy either way. But the one alternative ended with me dead a lot sooner.

"Fine."

Her name was Anna Kramer and I told Joe and Vinny she was my cousin who happened to live in Kenya. They didn't like the idea of her joining the expedition, so I threw in the story that she worked for the government and that they occasionally assigned people to watch over safaris to make sure they didn't wipe out animal populations or burn down villages. They accepted this and didn't even bother to question why an American was working for the British government in Kenya, but then we're not talking about intellectual giants here.

True to his word, Onyango made arrangements for the expedition, only charging us twice the usual cost. He knew people, and they provided supplies, booked train fairs, reserved trucks at the end of the rail lines, and found bearers to carry the supplies once the roads ran out. A week's traveling took us deep into the highlands of central Africa. During my brief time while writing the book, I had been no further than Nairobi. I was surprised at how beautiful the country was. Wide grassland dotted with herds of animals. Snow capped mountains. Valleys thick with forests.

We came to a village of twig huts and camped far enough away so as to not annoy the residents. Joe and Vinny wanted to avoid them all together. They had both watched old jungle movies, but Onyango, who tried not to laugh at them, insisted the locals were friendly. He went ahead alone with some cheap gifts he had packed among our supplies, returning hours later.

"They have seen your boy," he said as we sat around our camp fire, swatting at bugs.

"They saw Frank?" Vinny asked.

"Yes," Onyango said. "He was here two weeks ago. He had a small group and a guide named Mburu. I know him. Not the best guide."

"You think he robbed the kid?" Joe said. "Took his money and left him in the middle of the jungle?"

"No," Onyango said. "I mean he is not very good. He gets lost easily."

"Where did they go?" Anna asked.

"East, toward the *iburunga*. The mountain range Europeans call Virunga. But we are not the only ones looking for the boy. A group of Europeans came through about three days ago, guided by Yego. Now he would take a persons money and leave them stranded in the bush."

"Did the villagers say why these Europeans were following Frank?" I asked.

"No."

"Any idea where in Europe they're from?" Anna asked.

"All whites are Europeans. Doesn't matter," Onyango said.

"The kid's in trouble," Vinny said, "and we're more than a week behind him. We got to get moving."

I actually had more hope than I started with. From the beginning I doubted our ability to even find Frank at all, let alone find him alive. Now we actually had evidence that we were on his trail. If we could catch up with him, then Carmine Carrino would be appeased and Joe or Vinny wouldn't have to put a bullet in my head.

We had a couple of men who were good at tracking, and we soon came upon signs of people having passed this way.

A few days later, our camp was attacked.

We had settled in for the night, everyone exhausted after pushing hard, Joe and Vinny anxious to make as much progress as possible. Food was scarce, but Onyango was able to bring down a buck antelope and his men prepared it for us all to share.

The gunshots tore through the camp, scattering our bearers.

Joe and Vinny drew their revolvers and Onyango grabbed his rifle.

I pushed Anna down near the crates that carried some of our dwindling supplies and tried to look manly, but I had no gun to shoot back at our unseen attackers.

Shadows appeared among the sparse trees. Weapons flared and gunshots rang out.

Joe fired in one direction, Vinny in the other.

A torch hurtled through the air, landing on the slope of one of our tents, the canvas bursting into flames.

Bullets ricocheted off pots, tore into canteens, ripped through the second tent, broke one the lanterns hanging from a pole in front of the tent, spilling fuel that ignited and caught the canvas aflame.

And then no more shots. No more lurking shadows. As we crouched among the ruins, with the tents smoldering, silence fell over the camp.

I turned toward our stack of crates, which had escaped fire, and Anna was gone. A quick look around, and she was nowhere to be found.

"Those dirty mugs must have nabbed her," Vinny said.

When morning came, the four of us sifted through the remains of our camp. No bearers. They had all vanished. No Anna. She had been kidnapped. We gathered what we could and pushed on, trying to find the trail of our attackers, but only Onyango knew how to track and he admitted to not being very good at it. The better trackers were among those men who had fled during the night raid.

We followed the trail into the rocks, and even I could tell we were walking into a trap.

Sure enough, bullets pinged off of the rocks around us. Men with rifles hid among the boulders above us. Onyango went down as he raised his rifle to shoot back. Joe pushed me down and took a bullet in the chest for his trouble.

I caught the big man as he crashed down on me. Blood soaked his bush jacket. One bloody hand caught my shirt.

"Find the kid!" he said, staring up at me. "Get him home."

I took hold of that hand and squeezed back. "I will," I promised.

He sank back and his fingers went limp.

"Drop your weapons!" demanded an accented voice from just above us.

Vinny looked at me as I eased Joe's body down and stood up. I nodded to him and he raised his hands, dropping his revolver.

"You too," said the voice. "Drop your gun."

I lifted my hands. "I don't have a gun."

"No gun? What kind of idiot comes to Africa without a gun?"

The man stood just above us, Anna held in front, a Luger pistol pointed at her temple. He was tall and thin, a narrow face of an undertaker with a pencil thin mustache and a thinning hairline that made is forehead look overly large. He stood stiff, making the wrinkled khakis look like a uniform.

"What do you want?" I asked. I looked into Anna's wide, terrified eyes and tried to appear reassuring. Covered in another man's blood, I don't think it came off very well.

"I want you, *Herr* Baker."

Germans. You have got to be kidding.

They allowed us to bandage Onyango's wounded arm before they tied our hands. Vinny asked to bury Joe, and they refused. His rage boiled underneath. If his hands hadn't been tied at this point, he probably would have torn into them, killing half of them with his bare hands before joining Joe. But he held his tongue and helped me support Onyango as the German's marched us over the rocky slopes to the sparse grass on the other side, where a small camp had been set up.

They sat us in a line on the ground among the cluster of small tents and I expected to be executed.

The leader studied the cloth map they had found in my pocket when they had searched us.

"So this is the famous map that led you to Ru-Don?" the German said. He looked down at me. "I am Major Dieter. I have been an admirer of your adventures."

"Really?" I said without enthusiasm. "You've read my book?"

"All of them, actually. You are quite the adventurer. But this last one particularly intrigues me. You defeated my own countrymen before they could fulfill their mission to revive the Third Reich. Now I make it my mission to complete their task and take revenge."

"Oh," I said. Execution time, over something that never even happened.

"You will help us enter Ru-Don," Dieter said.

"What makes you think I'd help you?" I demanded, not going into the little fact that there was no Ru-Don.

"Otherwise, I will shoot the girl," he said, drawing his Luger and touching the muzzle to Anna's red hair.

"Okay," I said. "But you have the map. Why do you even need us?" Then I realized how stupid that was to actually say. Much better to say something about all of us being of value to him.

"I have the map," he said, holstering the Luger. "You have the experience. You have been here before. You know the people; you know where their treasure is hidden. My predecessors were unable to procure the treasure to resurrect the Reich, thanks to you. I will succeed and become the new Führer."

He folded the map and buttoned it into the breast pocket of his bush jacket.

"I have been living in Egypt when word came to me that the young American was searching for Ru-Don. Apparently he tried to be secretive, but when he hired men for the expedition, those men talked. Word spread. I have ears everywhere. He had a copy of the map. I had believed only you possessed that and I have been planning to travel to America to confront you about it. I missed the young man by a week, but set out after him. How fortunate that you have come along. I thought it a coincidence that someone followed us, but then I spotted you from a distance and recognized you from the picture on your book cover."

The publisher had insisted. I should have gone with my instincts.

We weren't given any time to rest. The Germans struck their camp and we marched on. When Dieter figured out that Ru-Don did not exist, that there was no treasure, we were all dead. Until then, there was at least hope that we could escape. If I could delay the inevitable long enough, we might be able to set Vinny onto them. He was ready to rip each one of them apart. And I was developing a personal dislike for Dieter.

More marching. We were exhausted. The Nazis cursed us, beats us, and drove us on. They were particularly vile toward Onyango, calling him every vile name they could come up with. He was weak from loss of blood, but he kept on. Vinny watched over him, supporting him as best he could. I believe he would have carried Onyango on his back if it had come to that.

We made a grueling climb up the slope of an extinct volcano. Dieter, looking like a field marshal, stood at the crest, surveying the crater.

"Ah!" he declared in triumph. "Behold, Ru-Don."

I stumbled up beside him, trying to keep my balance with my hands bound together; coming up with excuses as to why there wasn't a hidden city. It's actually in the volcano one over. Oops, they had been in an active one and all died. The city is really, really hidden. Maybe I could get close enough to shove him over the edge, though he probably wouldn't die from the fall.

Then I caught sight of what he was looking at.

The crater was carpeted in lush green. Thick jungles around the edge of the crater, then cultivated fields. In the center was a sparkling blue lake. Surrounding the lake were buildings. They weren't modern skyscrapers, but they weren't primitive huts, either. Stone structures, some large. And smaller buildings of wood.

Beside me, Anna whispered, "It doesn't look like what you described in your book."

"Ah," I said. "I used some literary license."

We found a path that wound down the slope to the crater floor and cut through the trees and tangled brush and vines. Small animals scampered through the foliage. There was the occasional grunt of a wild boar. The forest was filled with game.

When we reached the fields and could see the city in the distance, people tending the crops scattered before we could get a look at them.

Then a group of men approached. Armor glinted in the sunlight. They carried spears and swords sheathed at their sides. Bronze helmets hid their features.

Dieter grabbed me and shoved his Luger into my side.

"Talk to them. Tell them who you are. You became their friend, *yah?*"

"Right."

I waved my bound hands and smiled at them. "*Jambo.*" All I knew was a little Swahili. Probably not any use in a lost civilization.

There were a dozen of them, in armor that resembled ancient Egyptian. The leader slid off his helmet. His skin was a deep brown, with feature possessing qualities of many races. I suspected that his heritage was more Egyptian than anything.

He looked at us with curiosity, particularly narrowing on Anna. His eyes darting to her bound hands, then to those of the rest of us. Suspicion clouded his features and he spoke to his men. Swords were drawn.

"Tell him we're friends," Dieter said, punctuating his demand with a jab of his pistol into my kidney.

The leader of the soldiers demanded something in reply, his men fanning out. Unfortunately, none of us understood him.

Dieter pulled his gun from me and aimed at the Egyptian officer.

I pushed his arm up before the gun fired, then swung my bound fists into his face.

One of the German's fired his rifle and an Egyptian soldier crumpled. The other Egyptians closed in, one stabbing the killer through with his sword.

Vinny took advantage of the diversion and threw his arms over the head of one German about to use his Luger. The gun fired into the dirt and Vinny choked the man to death.

Another German took a spear to the chest; one got his head caved with the haft of a spear. Two remaining Germans dropped their weapons at sword and spear point. Dieter, blood streaming from his nose, released his Luger and lifted his hands.

Surrounding us, they lead our group toward the city.

"*Unazungumza Kiswahili?*" I asked the leader.

He had replaced his helmet and turned to look at me. "*Ndio,*" he said.

Thankfully he could speak Swahili. But I only knew a few phrases, and had forgotten a lot of the past two years.

"Onyango," I said, "tell him that we are friends to his people. The others made us prisoners and forced us to come here."

"And ask him about Frank," Vinny said.

The Egyptian glanced sharply at Vinny but seemed to ignore what Onyango translated. He walked ahead, putting an end to any kind of conversation.

As cities went, it wasn't big. There was one larger building at the edge of the lake, flanked by smaller ones of stone, the wooden homes in clusters. Brown-skinned people paused in the packed dirt streets to watch our procession. They all wore white clothes reminiscent of Egyptian paintings. Our escort marched us to the largest building, through huge wooden doors, and down stone halls that looked centuries old. Down a circle of steps, and then into a large room lit by small windows near the ceiling. The floor was covered with straw. The iron door banged shut, locking us in.

"Hello?" said a small voice from the shadows.

"Frank?" Vinny said, crossing the room.

"Vinny? Is that you? How did you get here?"

The young man in dirty, torn khakis reached out and took the big man's hand. He untied the cords around his wrists while they caught each other up.

I undid Anna's bonds. She returned the favor, then we helped Onyango. We replaced his bandage as best we could with shreds of a torn jacket. He was weak, his complexion gray. I feared that if we didn't get him help, he would not make it.

"I thought you were their friend," Anna said.

"Yeah, well, it's been a couple of years," I said.

She frowned. "You've never been here before, have you? God, I am so stupid! I sought you out to expose you for being a phony scientist. I had no idea that you were a complete charlatan. When I found out you were working for a famous mob boss, I let the bigger story blind me. I had no idea you were such a con artist."

Dieter and the remaining two Germans huddled in the corner, whispering.

The Egyptian officer returned after about an hour, accompanied by another, older man. They entered the cell and approached Anna, the older man speaking to her. She shook her head to indicate that she did not understand. The officer spoke to me in Swahili, but I only caught a few words. I tried to make him understand how little I knew and that Onyango was our translator, and he was unconscious.

He motioned to his guards. They entered and lifted Onyango, carrying him away.

Then he took Anna by the arm and led her to the door.

"Hey!" I said.

He turned, a short sword in his hand and pointed at my middle. He barked a few words that I did not need to translate. Then he left with Anna.

"Well that ain't right," Vinny said. "What we goin' do, Doc? You're the expert."

An expert of getting people into trouble. First Frank, then Joe. Now Anna. The poor kid only wanted a story for her paper, now she was the prisoner of ancient Egyptians.

"Dr. Baker," Frank said, "it's such an honor to meet you again. I had no idea you would come all this way for me. You know, this place isn't much like you described in your book."

"That's because I've never been here before, kid. The book was fiction. It was all a lie."

Confusion clouded the young man's face. "But I don't understand. I made a copy of your map. It led me here. I just didn't figure my guide and bearers taking off at the first sign of trouble."

"The map was real," I said. "I made up everything else. I'm sorry, Vinny. I got Joe killed. Do whatever you want with me."

The big man ground his jaws together and furrowed his brow. "Seems the Nazis were the ones that killed Joe, and they're goin' pay for that. If it weren't for you, we wouldn't have found Frankie. Now, we just need to get the lady and get outta here."

He slapped my shoulder, which really hurt. I avoided the fact that if it wasn't for my book, Frank wouldn't have come to Africa in search of Ru-Don.

"Then let's get out of this cell," I said. "We've got a lot of work to do. Give me your belt."

He undid his belt and handed it to me without hesitation, though with a puzzled look.

I went to the iron door and studied the lock. It was a simple mechanism. Reaching through the bars, I pushed the prong of his belt buckle into the key hole. It took longer than I thought. Light through the windows was beginning to fade as the sun set. Fifteen perspiring minutes and finally the lock clicked and the door swung open.

The Germans were on their feet.

"Let us call a truce, *Herr* Baker," Dieter said.

Vinny's face burned with rage as he balled his fists. I touched his arm and shook my head. Then winked at him.

"Sure," I said to Dieter. "Why don't you go looking for the treasure stash? We'll find Anna and Onyango."

The former Nazi major nodded. "Perhaps we can find our weapons," he said, then waved his men out of the cell and down the hall.

"What did you do that for?" Vinny demanded. "I want to kill them."

"They'll provide a diversion," I said. "Now let's find Anna."

"She ain't too happy with you," he said.

"She's not the first."

"Excuse me, Doctor," Frank said as we hurried down the corridor. "How are we going to find the young lady and your friend in the city? Do you actually know where they were taken?"

"Nope. I'm just making this all up. Something I'm good at."

We surprised a soldier when we turned a corner near the stairs. He drew his sword. Vinny shoved me aside and threw a bucket-sized first into the man's face.

I picked up the unconscious man's sword and handed it to Vinny. Then I slapped the soldier to bring him around. Vinny bent down and sneered, pointing the sword at the man's bloody face.

"Where's the girl?" I said.

He shook his head, not understanding.

"Girl," I said, forming a feminine shape with my hand. "With the red hair. Hair. Red." I pinched my hair.

He still looked confused.

I touched blood from his cheek to the tip of my finger and showed it to him. "Red!"

Then I touched my hair. "Hair!"

He nodded and pointed.

Vinny grabbed him by the collar of his armor, lifted him up, and pointed him in the right direction, sword in his back.

Night had fallen, so the halls were deserted. The guard took us down the corridors to a set of double doors. We shoved them open, ready to rush in and face death. We were immediately surrounded by armed guards, swords and spears pointed at us.

The chamber was large, the only furnishing being a throne on a dais at the far end, on which sat the older man who had been present when Anna was removed from the cell. Soldiers lined the walls among pillars that supported the high ceiling. A fresco behind the throne depicted hieroglyphics and illustrations similar to those in Egyptian temples and tombs. Statues between the pillars represented the Egyptian pantheon. The man on the throne did not, however, wear a pharaoh's crown, nor was his head shaven. He probably held an office more akin to governor or military leader rather than king. Standing before him were the Egyptian captain who had captured us and Anna, with Onyango laying on a litter beside them. The Maasai prince had been cleaned and his wound cared for by expert hands. His deep color was beginning to return. Anna had bathed and was dressed in one of the local white gowns, looking very fetching as a red-haired Egyptian maiden.

"What are you doing?" she hissed at me as the guards disarmed Vinny and brought us together before the throne.

"Rescuing you," I said.

"Yeah, well, that isn't working too well. Besides, I've got this covered. They like my hair. They think I'm some kind of goddess or something."

I didn't like the sound of that. "No, don't do that."

"Why? You lie all the time. What's the difference?"

"Because I'm a heel and you aren't. Onyango, tell them she isn't a goddess, that sometimes red is the hair color where we come from."

Onyango looked from me to Anna, then to the man on the throne who seemed to be growing impatient. He spoke in a quivering voice, hesitating near the end.

The older man stiffened, then spoke to his captain, who drew his sword.

I stepped between him and Anna. "Wait!"

Then I had Onyango translate: "It's my fault she's here. It's my fault any of us are here. I take full responsibility. Don't punish them for what I did. Let them leave. Take my life instead."

Anna looked at me, her eyes glistening with moisture. "Henry, you don't have to do this."

"Yeah, I…"

The doors burst open and three Nazis fired rifles and pistols into the chamber. "*Wo ist der Schatz!*" Dieter shouted.

I threw myself over Anna. Together we fell onto the floor, knocking over the guard captain.

Vinny sprinted toward the dais and threw himself at the man seated on the throne. The chair and both men tumbled backward as bullets ripped the fresco on the wall behind them.

The Germans fired blindly, their leader screaming. Bullets ripped into stone and tore through decorative armor.

Crawling across the marble floor, I grabbed a spear from a dead guard. With all my might I hurled it. The blade plunged into Dieter's chest.

The two remaining Germans hesitated, giving the Egyptian guards an opening to swarm over them and cut them to shreds.

● ● ●

Djehuti, the governor of Ru-Don, showed his appreciation by not killing us. In fact, he awarded Vinny with a necklace of a golden eagle for saving his life. The jewelry must have weighed ten pounds but he wore it proudly. They allowed us to stay for a week while Onyango regained his strength, providing rooms for us. Inaros, captain of the guard, showed us the city. Anna made notes for her big story.

Inaros was taken by Anna and asked, through Onyango, if she would stay in Ru-Don. She graciously declined.

He asked what Dieter was after, why he wanted to kill so many people.

"Treasure," I told him.

"But we have no treasure," he said. "Just a little gold mined from the mountains."

Long ago, Egypt had established the colony to produce gold. When the mines no longer produced, the colony was forgotten. It became self-sufficient and continued, isolated from the rest of the world with a little contact with local tribes. Over the centuries, small amounts of gold were pulled from the mines, but Egypt never came back for it. Inaros showed us the storehouse that hadn't been opened for decades and presented each with Ru-Don coins, which were worthless to the people of the crater valley. To Anna he gave a gold ring inscribed with hieroglyphics. He wanted her to remember him.

When Onyango gained his strength, the people of Ru-Don filled packs with supplies and sent us on our way.

"Sure you don't want to stay?" I asked Anna as we crested the crater and headed down the slope.

"I've got a job to do. This is one heck of a story. Maybe a Pulitzer."

"Will anyone believe it?" I asked.

"They believed yours," she pointed out.

"You can't tell anyone," Frank said. "Other people will come hunting for the gold. That will ruin Ru-Don."

"We just won't tell them where it is," I said.

"Yeah, that didn't work last time," Vinny said.

"Well, I lost that copy of the map I made," Frank said.

"And Dieter took my original one," I said. "It was probably on him when they burned the bodies."

Anna stopped. "Without the map, how are we going to find our way back?"

Frank tapped a finger to his temple. "Photographic memory."

"Let's just get back," I said. "I've got a new book to write. This time, it'll actually be true."

"Good," Anna said. She wrapped herself around my arm. "No more lies between us. We can't build a relationship with lies, can we, Henry?"

"Ah, yeah. About that. That isn't actually my name."

The End

Werewolves in the Park

by Peggy Chambers

They came out of nowhere surrounding her as she walked down the dark street. She was turned around after exiting the subway…new to the city, they were still unfamiliar to her…and it became dark much quicker than she imagined. Sarina found herself suddenly pushed and shoved into the alley as they laughed at her dilemma. She tried to resist but they were much stronger than her. Three young hoods wore matching jackets with a picture of a wolf with glowing yellow eyes on the back. It read "Gray Wolves" under the picture. She was thrown to the ground, kicked and punched in the damp, grimy alley screaming in pain. Her screams went unanswered.

"Ah, Chica!" The one with the scar on his face taunted her. "She's a pretty one. I think I'd like her on our side."

Sarina was held to the damp concrete by the hoodlums. Scar Face leaned over her then fell to his knees, one on each side of her body. His putrid breath on her face, she thought she would die when he sank his teeth into her shoulder. Unluckily, she did not. She screamed again, but still no one heard. Or no one listened. His teeth burned through her like a white-hot poker. She heard a howl…then passed out.

Waking in the dark alley hours later, she sat up painfully and took inventory. She was dirty, bruised, and there was dried blood on her shoulder. But she was fully clothed. Welcome to New York City. Standing was pure agony. Every bone in her body hurt. She did not remember swallowing battery acid but her throat said she must have. She had no idea how she found her way back to her apartment, but once inside she bolted the door and fell on the bed. Finally she was safe.

The next morning Sarina stumbled into the shower. All she found from the night before were a few fading bruises. Looking over her shoulder in the mirror, she realized she was almost healed! It was not possible to have imagined that level of terror and pain. Those injuries were real. She knew they were. But there was no evidence. Until the next full moon. The terror of the alley was nothing compared to what happened then.

● ● ●

Sarina looked out the window again. Summer nights started later in the day, thankfully. The pile of paperwork on her desk was never ending. Three mergers in one day were more than she could ever hope to complete. She ached. Her pumps were too tight and when she scratched her leg (were her nails growing?) she knew she needed to shave. She remembered doing that in the shower that morning when she washed her hair, but damn! Already?

"Sarina, Josh sent more documents to finalize before you leave." Ernestine

151

stood before her with paperwork in hand. The short, busty, woman was named after her father. Sarina had never met Ernest, but if he was anything like his daughter, he must have been a drill sergeant. She was a whiz in the office and she could spot a typo a mile away. She was also the office gossip. Nothing got past her.

"Then maybe he needs to do it himself." Sarina snapped unnecessarily at the woman who assisted her daily. Once a month her emotions became raw.

"Girl, you have an attitude today. Must be the moon or something." She turned on her heels and walked away after dropping another pile on Sarina's desk.

Sarina sighed as she dialed Josh's number. "Can't do it today, bud. Need to leave early." He was her supervisor, but first he was her friend. He let her slide sometimes because of their friendship. He knew she would get the work done, and then some. They even went out for a drink now and then and the last time he told her in confidence he had the hots for a woman in Acquisitions. Not that he would ever act on it. One drink and he chatted about everything. Sarina was sure she knew all Josh's secrets. He only thought he knew hers.

But, she would owe him forever. He covered for her when she was sick for a couple of months. The gestation period for a wolf was 63 days. She had Googled it.

During the pregnancy, she came into the office as often as her body would let her. She lied about seeing a doctor. She was sick most mornings and lost a lot of weight, unable to keep food down. Her clothes hung on her body, thankfully hiding the bump in her womb. It was Nate's, she was sure of that. The one night stand before he left. He was her one weakness. But now he was gone and she kicked herself for being so stupid to get knocked up at this time in her life...or any time for that matter. She was not the mothering type.

Labor came quickly and luckily she found a cave in the park where she ran daily. Becoming a werewolf wasn't enough of a problem; becoming a mother was worse. Her problems were just beginning.

"Where do you have to go? You have no social life and there's no one at home. Are you feeding the homeless or something?"

"Yeah, that's it. Just can't today, Josh." Was it getting darker or was it her imagination? She looked at the mirror she pulled from her purse and could see no evidence of what was to come, but her tongue ran over her teeth constantly feeling for sharp points. They would be a dead giveaway.

It was already after seven and only the die-hards remained at their desks.

"Alright, I guess it can wait. See you in the morning." He sighed as she quickly hung up the phone and grabbed her purse, shutting down the computer.

Running for the curb Sarina flagged down a cab. "Central Park," was all she said.

By dark she was in her element, running freely. Pads feeling the moist soil beneath them as claws dug in and provided traction. This was not like jogging in the morning in spandex and running shoes. This was real life! This was a life she had never experienced before the assault. Her eyes could see things in the dark that no infrared night-vision goggles could ever see. The wind blew on her body raising the hair that would not be there in the morning. It couldn't be. The daylight brought changes.

Most people were home snug in their beds or sleeping through re-runs on TV. She was hunting dinner. She was hungry for meat and so were the little ones. It was time she taught them to hunt too. But not the two-legged prey. That was her rule. The two-legged variety was off the menu. She still had a little humanity left in her. Besides, she didn't think she would make it in prison on a murder charge when the moon turned full.

The rabbit hid behind the foliage, its nose quivering. She drooled uncontrollably as she stalked her prey, able to see it with distinct clarity in the dark. It would be just enough to feed a growing family...maybe. The boys' appetites were increasing daily. They had to learn to hunt too, but she was afraid they might be seen. That was where Tara came in. Tara was a neighbor in the park that had no litter of her own. She offered her services one night when Sarina was exhausted and trying to nurse the litter. Coyote milk was a good substitute for wolf milk. Tara agreed to babysit in exchange for part of the kill while Sarina went to the office in her other life. Otherwise her babies would have starved. Sarina had to keep up appearances during the day if they were all to survive. She wasn't a real wolf and she wasn't a real human anymore either.

Warm blood dripped from her fangs and pooled between her claws. She stood still crushing the windpipe of the tiny creature quickly. She would create as little pain as possible for one so willing to give its life for her and her family. Glancing behind her, she made sure she was not seen and then ran through the park to the cave.

"They're hungry tonight, Sarina. They have to learn to hunt soon."

"I know, but how can I teach them what to hunt?"

"They're wolves. They know what to hunt." Tara licked the smallest one bathing him after his evening meal.

"That's what I'm afraid of."

The full moon shone in through the opening of the cave and called to her again. She pulled herself away from its magnetism and lovingly licked the largest of the three. She had to name them. He snuggled against her and she noticed his bare haunches. His legs had lost their fur, and at the bottom of his legs there were feet. Human feet! She watched in astonishment as his body transformed under the moonlight into that of a human baby. He sucked his thumb serenely. All he needed was a diaper. She stopped licking and caught Tara's eye. She nodded to the baby on the dirt floor of the cave and the hair on Tara's back stood up. A whimper escaped the coyote. Sarina's babies were human! Now the trouble would really begin.

● ● ●

Without a knock, the door swung open and Josh walked in carrying two Grande-sized coffees. A bag hung from one hand.

"Close the door, were you raised by wolves?" Sarina looked up with red-ringed eyes from lack of sleep.

"Tough night?" Josh sat the coffee on her desk with a flourish then turned and closed the open door.

"I didn't get much sleep."

"I figured."

"What does that mean?" She was quick to growl at Josh. He was an easy mark; always setting himself up for her harassment.

"Nothing, just that I saw you come in this morning. Is that the same outfit you had on yesterday and what's smudged on your blouse?"

Sarina looked down and remembered dressing in the cave before dawn; her babies sleeping soundly on the floor next to the coyote.

"I fell asleep on the couch. If you didn't work me so hard, I'd have a real life."

"I wonder."

A noise escaped her throat like a growl and then was soothed by the hot coffee. Two creams one sugar. He knew her well.

"Bagel?" He held out two whole-grain bagels with cream cheese.

"No Lox?"

"They were out."

Sarina ripped off a chunk and chewed it hungrily. She remembered the bleeding rabbit the night before and suddenly choked.

"Eat slowly and sip the coffee." Josh smiled with cream cheese stuck to his chin. "How about some lunch today; maybe a nice salad?"

"Maybe a rare steak." Sarina wiped Josh's chin resisting the urge to lick it.

"Carnivore."

"Okay, but I want to go by that book store down the street. I need a story book." She stammered realizing how out of character it seemed for the dragon lady in the office. "A friend is having a shower…you know, a baby gift."

"Sure, a baby gift. You bet." He winked and turned to walk away. "By the way, you might want to shave your legs before you wear a short skirt again."

Slowly reaching down she felt the downy covering of her legs that she was sure she shaved yesterday. How could he see that with her legs under the desk? She remembered she had yoga pants in her gym bag.

Browsing through the children's section of the book store, Sarina looked for children's books to read to the litter. Her fondest childhood memories were of her mother reading her a bedtime story. Mom died when she was young and Dad tried, but he never read them the way that Mom had.

"Three Little Pigs and the wolf, Red Riding Hood and a wolf, the Boy Who Cried Wolf! What is the deal with all the nursery rhymes and wolves? Were they trying to scare the kids to death? And why are wolves always the bad guy!" Sarina tossed the books back in to the pile.

"Fairy tales were meant to scare children. Most people lived a rural existence and they didn't' want the kids wandering off into the woods and getting hurt, or worse. I think wolves just fit the bill." Josh followed behind her as they walked around the book store. He never once mentioned her yoga pants paired with the blazer from yesterday.

A noise near the front drew their attention as a gang of young thugs pushed their way into the store. They seemed out of place with the Musak piped in and the smell of coffee in the air. Sarina froze in place when one of them walked to the other side of the aisle and looked up and over directly into her eyes.

He smiled.

"Hey, Chica. Do I know you?" There was a gleam in his eyes and a scar on his cheek.

"Let's go." Josh pulled her away from the books.

"Don't leave." The hood smiled showing yellow pointed teeth. "I'm sure we've met before."

Josh pushed her to the front door and out onto the street.

● ● ●

The large wolf padded through the park searching the dark. His eyes glowed in the night. He saw everything. The mouse that hid under the leaves, coyote families searching for scraps, and the three sets of tiny eyes that peered out of the small cave carved from the rock under the oak's spreading roots. He watched those tiny eyes nightly. Sometimes the larger eyes of their mother appeared and pulled them back inside. He saw that too. Nothing escaped his gaze.

Tonight the moon shone brightly. That meant there were many sets of eyes out. Some were sentries while others were looking for trouble. It was time. He needed to let her know who he really was. He sniffed the air. Yes. She was there like every time the moon was full. Silently he padded to the cave. He knew she smelled him too and it was a scent she recognized. She would be confused at first.

Without warning, the smaller wolf sprang from the cave knocking the much larger wolf to the ground. They tumbled over each other, the smaller one snapping and scratching. A female wolf, though smaller than a male, could be a formidable opponent when she had little ones. He pinned her to the ground and the look of terror in her eyes quickly became confusion. He lessened the hold he had on her, and she sat up. A whimper escaped her throat and she backed away. The moon shone down on both of them and the big wolf could see her shiver in its light. He took a chance. Quickly his pads turned to feet and the hair on his face disappeared. He looked like her friend from the office standing in the moonlight without the shirt and tie he normally wore. Her eyes grew large as she recognized the man who transformed in front of her. Sarina stepped into the shadows and also morphed back into her human body but remained hidden.

"Josh?" She peaked out from the leaves of the bush.

"Who else?" He smiled thinking how long he had wanted to show her what he really was. He blew a tune she heard him whistle at work sometimes. She was unsure what it was.

"You're one of them!"

"You mean one of us?" Josh smiled again at her surprise.

She stepped back into the moonlight and quickly turned back into the wolf. The pull of the moon was too strong for her to resist. He changed back into a wolf to match her transformation.

"I've wanted to tell you, and I kept thinking you would figure it out by yourself. We have very sensitive noses."

Sarina looked toward the cave. "I've smelled something on you for some time, but I didn't know what." She stepped protectively in front of the cave entrance.

"Can I see them?" He tried to smile but it turned into a show of teeth; maybe not a good idea under the circumstances.

She growled.

"Come on Sarina, you know I wouldn't hurt you or the pups."

"How did you know about them?"

"I've been watching you. Is Raoul the father?"

"Who?"

"You know, Scar Face. He was in the book store the other day."

"No! I mean no, he was the one that did this to me. He is not the father of my children."

Josh pawed the ground. "I just assumed. Who is the father? I don't want him angry that I'm here."

"Their father left. He's not around anymore. He doesn't know about them." Sarina looked shyly at the ground.

"I see."

"It was Nate. Nate is their father. It happened just before he left. I never thought about getting pregnant and it certainly never occurred to me I would have wolves!"

"You were already a werewolf when you hooked up with Nate. What did you expect?"

"I didn't expect anything! I didn't expect to get assaulted as I got off the subway in New York City. We don't have subways in Oklahoma. I didn't expect to fall in love with Nate, and I sure didn't expect to end up like this!"

"You're in love with Nate?"

"Maybe. What does it matter? He's gone and not coming back."

A limb popped in the distance and both heads turned. They were not alone. "Go, take care of the babies."

Sarina trotted into the cave and Josh stood sentry outside.

"Hey, Chica, you home?" The wolf stepped into the moonlight from the shadows. Even in his present state, the scar on his face could be seen through the hair. He stared at Josh.

"What do you want, Raoul?" Josh stood his ground in front of the cave.

"The girl. Is she home?"

"You have no business with the girl. Leave."

"No, I'll leave when I'm ready. I'm not here to see you. Where is the girl?"

Sarina stepped into the light from the cave entrance. The hair on her back bristled.

"I don't want to see you. Go away." She bared her teeth growling.

"There you are. I've wondered where you ended up after our first meeting. But I see you hang out in book stores and with this guy. You and I have a history. We belong together. Come with me tonight."

"No, I don't want to be with you. You've done enough already. Go away."

In the distance, Josh could smell the other wolves of Raoul's pack coming closer. A fight was sure to happen tonight and he was only one to protect Sarina and her pups.

The wolf pack advanced circling around behind him with their skinny leader in front.

"Nail, haven't seen you in a while. Still eating good, I see. How did you get to be so skinny with all these guys to do your dirty work for you?" Josh hoped to be able to put off the confrontation as long as possible. Maybe he could think of something to save them all.

The skinny, shaggy wolf stepped into the light and showed his teeth. "Don't you worry about me, I get along fine. You however, are alone tonight. That could be a bad place to be in."

Sarina stepped from the cave and howled. Maybe Tara would hear the call. Raoul pounced on her as the rest of the pack attacked Josh. Growling, Josh bit and scratched all within reach. The wolf pack retreated and then regrouped advancing from another direction. Josh could not hold out forever as he received injuries from the group. Suddenly there was a yelp. He looked up at Sarina and found hundreds of yellow eyes in the dark. The coyotes were here to help. This was their park and they defended it against all comers. Especially the Gray Wolves. And tonight they had the Gray Wolves outnumbered. They swooped in with one mind barking their shrill bark and chased the wolves out of the park, biting every wolf haunch they could make contact with.

It was over in an instant, but Josh knew the wolves would return.

Sarina stood over Raoul baring her teeth. The wolf lay on the ground bleeding from her bite on the neck, but still breathing. He would be found in the morning by joggers and only look like someone who was in a brawl and lost.

"We have to move the pups. The Gray Wolves know where they are now." Josh stood beside Sarina looking in the cave entrance. They had saved the pups this time, until the wolves came back.

● ● ●

Luckily no one saw them take the box of puppies in the back door of her apartment. Management had no tolerance for pets. It was going to be a long night, what was left of it. The pups were learning to howl.

"You did a great job staying in your human form walking home with the full moon tonight." Josh picked up the smallest pup and it curled instinctively into his lap and closed its eyes.

"It wasn't easy. I don't think I could have done it for anyone else than these little guys."

"Maternal instincts are very strong."

"Yeah. I guess I'm calling in sick tomorrow, boss. I don't have a sitter now. Bringing a box of puppies into an apartment is one thing, but bringing their coyote babysitter is another."

The largest pup stood in the box that was much too small for them and stretched. A high-pitched howl escaped his lips.

"Shhhh." Sarina picked him up and cuddled him soothing his fur. He curled into a ball and slept in her lap.

"We can't keep them here." Josh smoothed the fur of the one still sleeping in the box. "We have to find another place. We'll stay here tonight and tomorrow, I'll get us someplace new."

"Is it normal for them to be wolves most of the time? I mean will they always be wolves? One of them turned human one night when the moon shone through on him." The pup snuggled closer and Sarina ran her hand the length of his body. He wiggled. He almost looked like he smiled.

"I think they will be like us. Well, not just like us. They were never bitten. They started their life as werewolves. That has to be different. I think I know someone I can ask. He's been around a long time and seen a lot of things. What's his name, by the way?" Josh stroked the baby in his lap.

"I haven't named them yet. I've been busy."

"Well they have to have names."

"I was kind of waiting to see if I had boys or wolves."

"What's the difference? They still need names. "

"I mean do I name them John, Bill and Paul or Spot, Rags and Snoopy?"

"If one of them changed, they will probably all change. You've got three sons on your hands to feed and educate and then there is the werewolf problem. They have to be taught to control it. You know how boys are on a playground. They can't be showing off to the girls and stuff. This is serious. But luckily there is an underground network and there are many more like them. They won't be alone."

"How many?"

"There are over eight million people in New York City, and we make up a small portion. I don't know how many exactly but enough to protect the city from the likes of Raoul."

"Protect?" Sarina lay down on the floor with the pups curled up against her.

"There's a network. I'll introduce you. Like in any culture there's good and bad. But we take care of things. Werewolves have been around for a long time and we aren't going anywhere."

Sarina's eyes fluttered and she strained to hold them open.

"Get some sleep." Josh handed the third pup to her and stood. "Tomorrow I'll show you something new."

Sarina woke to the morning sun shining in the window and a baby boy crawling over her. He was hungry. And he was human.

● ● ●

Josh knocked on the door early with coffee, bagels and deli meat from the shop around the corner. The pups would want meat. He told her before they left

the apartment where they were going. She tried not to look like a tourist and attract any more attention than a young couple with triplets already did.

"West 91st street on the Broadway line is under the west side of Central Park. The subway was abandoned there in 1959. We'll have plenty of help once we get there."

Abandoned subway systems? What had she gotten herself into? Then again, she didn't know what she would have done without his help.

Sarina and Josh walked to the subway station with babies swaddled to their chests. She pulled the corner of the sling up to cover the baby and keep the sun off his face. No one would see him if he decided to change back at the wrong time. Walking down the street she became aware of the scents of people who passed them. Some were familiar…wolf like…not quite human. She looked into the eyes of a woman whose scent was particularly strong and the woman nodded almost imperceptibly. They were everywhere!

From the subway he led her down a hall where no one stood waiting for a train. Looking both ways they carefully slipped into the door marked Maintenance after they made sure no one saw them. Josh pulled a flashlight from his pocket. "Follow me and be careful. It can get slippery sometimes." She followed him down the cavernous hall that once ran with subway trains.

Stepping through the opening they were met by an old man. He sat on a stained mattress and looked like just another of New York's homeless population. Someone Sarina would never associate with. He smiled an almost toothless grin and stood on shaky legs.

"Josh!" The man ambled their way leaning on a cane for support. His shoes showed toes through the holes in the front and he appeared to have had a bath sometime this century. His scent was unmistakable. He was a wolf.

"I see you brought company." He smiled at Sarina and then studied the sling on her chest as it wiggled and stretched.

"This is Sarina. She was bitten by the Gray Wolves."

"Nice to meet you, Sarina." He moved as if to shake her hand but instead lifted the cover of the sling. Sarina instinctively stepped back not wanting him to touch her son.

"Sarina this is Adolph. He has been here for many years and helps to keep the werewolf populations in order. He was my teacher and protector. He has helped many in our condition over the years."

Sarina attempted a smile as the man once again reached to lift the cloth covering her son's head.

"It's okay, he won't hurt them." Josh stepped forward and uncovered the two he had snuggled against his chest. They were both human…at least for now.

"Beautiful babies." Adolph leaned over the slings inhaling deeply. "All babies are beautiful, don't you think?" Once again he reached for the cloth over her baby's face and this time she let him. "Full blood?"

"No, their father was human," Josh answered for her.

"No matter. Wonderful, wonderful children. Come and sit." He gestured to the stained mattress. Sarina balked thinking of the germs her children would be exposed to and then remembered serving them raw rabbit meat. Their immune systems were not normal.

They spent most of the morning talking to Adolph. Other people came and went…some looking for guidance, others bringing food. He was the king of the werewolf group in the New York City area even though he never acted like it. His actions were more like a sweet grandfather.

"Josh has told you that we protect New York City?" Adolph formed the sentence like a question. Sarina nodded. "Did he tell you how?" She shook her head no.

"We patrol the streets in groups, or sometimes just alone. I find it safer in groups. We patrol especially on nights the moon is full. There is always trouble. You can ask any policeman or any emergency room worker. Full moon nights are the worst. The coyotes are in charge of Central Park. They live there anyway so we let them patrol their neighborhood. We can use the help. You and your children are welcome to stay with us. We will help you learn to be a werewolf and not let the average man on the street ever suspect a thing. We will also teach your children. Wolf babies mature much faster than human babies. I guess you've already seen that. We will get you ready to go back up onto the street and be a normal human being except when your services are needed. Then we would expect you to help the pack."

"The bad wolves, the ones that bit you, are our bitter enemies. We work hard to control our abilities…they are abilities, not disabilities. And once you have mastered those abilities, you can help in our quest for a cohesive society where everyone is working for the greater good. Does that seem like a good thing to you?"

"What about my job? I need to show up each day and bring home a paycheck. After all I'm a single mother now." Sarina caressed the soft head of the child that snuggled next to her chest.

"Josh will help you there."

"Adolph, she is learning to control the urges. We brought the babies out of the park and into her apartment last night. She walked down the street like a normal person. And the moon was strong."

"Impressive! Must be the maternal instinct."

"Do you agree, Sarina? Do you want to join us?"

"I think I need to. I can't handle myself and the babies alone. So, yes."

"You'll never be alone, Sarina. Welcome to the pack. By the way there is someone I want you to meet. You may already know her, but she will be great to work with the babies."

Out of a shadow stepped a short woman with dark curly hair. "Ernestine!" Sarina stood and embraced her assistant. She was also a werewolf. How could she have missed that scent all this time?

"I've been waiting to see the babies, Sarina." She stepped forward and brushed her hand over the cheek of the sleeping child in the sling and smiled. The child lifted his chin and howled low and quietly eyes still shut.

"Oh this one has his mom's attitude! May I?" Ernestine reached for the baby and Sarina surrendered it carefully.

Sarina felt she was home maybe for the first time since she arrived in New York. She had a family.

● ● ●

On Sarina's first nightly patrol she left the kids with Ernestine who promised Tara would come by soon to help her. They would all be okay and in bed early.

She looked behind her several times thinking of her litter and Josh nudged her.

"Mind on the present," he scolded.

"I know, I just . . ."

"We start out on the roof tops. We can see it all from there. The muggings, robberies and worse. If we can stop it we do."

"So we're not just protecting people from the Gray Wolves?"

"No, anything bad that happens and we can stop it, we do. The police can't be everywhere all the time. I like to think of us as super heroes. We get in and we get out and most of the time no one is the wiser. Or if they are, they don't talk about it to their friends. They don't want to be considered crazy."

"Yeah, I'll bet. I remember a time I thought all this was crazy. What's that?" She nodded toward the street.

On the ground a woman dropped her car keys as she stumbled from the bar. Leaning over to pick them up, a man ran up behind her and snatched her purse. He kept running.

"Help! Someone stop him! He grabbed my purse!" she shouted into the wind… no one heard her…the noise of the bar overtook her voice.

Josh was instantly leaping across rooftops chasing the robber from above. Sarina followed. Suddenly Josh disappeared. Had he fallen? No! She ran to the edge and looked down but all she could see was the robber, then Josh pounced on him from behind. Josh looked up and nodded at Sarina to look left. There it was; the fire escape that led almost to the ground of the building. It was a small leap to the alley from there and she was on the street beside him. He stood looking at her with a wolfish grin, a purse hanging from his teeth.

"Let's take this back to its rightful owner." They trotted off down the street.

Sarina glanced behind her at the running suspect who turned at the same time…their eyes locked. She bared her teeth. Sarina could tell by the look in his eyes, he wouldn't be telling anyone about his encounter with a wolf in the middle of the street. No one would believe him anyway.

Josh dropped the purse beside the car and the wolves hid behind the trash cans outside the bar.

"Oh there it is! I must have dropped it," the drunken woman giggled as she picked up her purse and absent mindedly wiped the saliva from the handle on her jeans.

"Your first patrol." Josh nodded at Sarina and they walked back to the darkened alley together. "You did good."

● ● ●

"I just think if we had an apartment together, we could look after the boys better." Josh opened the door for his co-worker.

Sarina's eyes narrowed. Her friend from work…her boss…was asking her to move in with him? Sarina and Josh traveled in to the office daily on the subway system. She was sure people were beginning to talk since they always arrived together.

"Do I look helpless to you?" They stepped into her office and he closed the door.

"No! Of course you're not helpless. I mean look at everything you have done, moving to New York, taking on a job in a city you didn't know, becoming a werewolf, even if you didn't want to, and becoming a mother. You've had an eventful few years."

"Yeah, my dad told me to stay in Oklahoma. But then I wouldn't have the boys." She unconsciously sighed. "I don't know how I will ever be able to take them home to meet their grandfather."

"Maybe we could do that someday. Look at how they are growing; so much faster than normal kids. With Adolph and the other wolves to teach them, they will be ready for school soon. And how are you going to explain that you suddenly have three school-aged kids when yesterday you had none?"

"Yeah, that's the problem. I've been thinking about telling my co-workers they are my nephews. I could say they were my sister's kids and she died or something. I still don't know what I'd tell Dad."

"We could say we adopted them."

"We, again. These are my kids and I am raising them, remember?"

"I'd like it to be us. Think about it. I'm not asking for the moon, no pun intended, just to be close to you and the boys. I can be of some help and it would be good for all of us."

"Maybe. We'll see." Sarina stared at her feet and when she looked up, she saw Josh standing with his chest puffed out and smiling. "What are you smiling about?"

"You said 'maybe.' That's as close as I ever got before!" He walked off whistling a tune she had heard from him many times before. She was sure it was "Blue Moon."

Sarina ran through the daily log, checking her calendar and returning phone calls. Her head was not really on her business these days. Her boys were always in the back of her mind. Rex, Hunter, and Rusty took up most of her time and energy. Josh was right. Adolph was a great teacher and with Tara helping out, they were growing up quickly. It was about time to introduce them to the world. She could say she adopted them from her sister and Josh could play their father. Maybe. She did need the help. She also needed to check out good schools close to work and then find a proper home to raise her boys. Somewhere with a park nearby to play in.

● ● ●

Riding the subways, Sarina picked up her boys and took them to and from school. They became familiar with the art of hopping subways and getting into the werewolf lair. Still too young to be left alone they always had an adult by their sides.

"Now remember to stay together and well, you know the rest. Adolph told you under no circumstances . . ." Sarina attempted to smooth the hair on the head of the smaller boy.

"We know, Mom. Respect the teachers, don't show off, we know." Rex scuffed the toe of his shoe in the dirt. He was the biggest when they were born and instantly took the lead in anything they did.

"I know you will. Now, who picks you up after school?"

"Josh, Ernestine or you," they repeated in unison.

"Right. Remember no one else takes you home."

Rusty gave his mom a hug and ran for the steps of the building, his brother in tow. Hunter, always with a faraway look like he wished he was somewhere else, followed the other two. Their futures awaited them.

She smiled and waved. Normally she would have smelled the scent of Raoul behind her, but not today. Her maternal instincts were in high gear.

Raoul slinked out from behind the trash can and watched Sarina as she walked away and headed to her office.

● ● ●

"Mom's late," Rusty looked in to the distance. "I hate waiting."

"She'll be here." Rex stood next to his little brother in front of the school.

"You boys are here every day. Waiting for your mom?" A man with a scar on his face walked up to the boys as they waited for Sarina.

Rusty looked up and smiled, then back at the picture he had drawn in school that day. He was keeping it for his mother.

"You boys want something to drink? I have a place right over there and I have sodas of all kinds. You can see your mom from there."

Hunter looked up at the man standing in front of them and sniffed.

"You smell strange. Not like me and my brothers."

Raoul took a step back.

"No thanks, Mister." Rex stared at the man in front of him. He knew trouble even at an early age. "We'll wait here."

"I'm thirsty." Rusty looked at his big brother.

"No, Rusty. Mom said to stay right here."

"But, I'm thirsty and we can see Mom from over there. Come on, Hunter." He grabbed his brother's arm and started to move when Rex stepped between the man and his brothers.

"No."

"Hey boys!" Ernestine bounced down the street waiving. Her nose twitched and she searched the street. She knew she smelled him. Raoul! He was close. Had he seen the boys? "Everybody okay?"

"I'm thirsty." Rusty still held his mother's picture.

"Well, let's do something about that before we get on the subway then." She looked around for the man whose scent she picked up, but could not find him.

"I was going to go with that man to get something to drink but Rex wouldn't let me."

A low growl escaped Ernestine's throat. "We don't go anywhere with anyone except me or Josh or your Mom, got it?" She directly looked into Rusty's eyes.

"I know."

"Never."

"I know!"

"Okay, let's get something to drink. Mom will be home from work soon."

● ● ●

Slipping in the Maintenance door in the subway corridor, Sarina could smell her pack. She could even single out the scent of her pups. It was amazing the things she never used to smell. The damp tunnels held no fear for her anymore, they were home. This was where her children were taught how to be wolves and where she met the people she now called family. An occasional rat ran past but kept to its side of the tunnel. The abandoned rails were slick with water and she had learned not to walk on them. Her sensitive ears could hear the play of her children in the distance and then it hit her. She smelled something new. No, it was something old. Something that brought fear and hatred to her and the hair on the back of her neck stood up. Raoul was in the tunnels and he was not alone. She could smell many wolves and none of them smelled like her family. She was followed.

Slowly she turned around and thought she heard footsteps behind her. She could not lead the Gray Wolves to her pack. There had to be other tunnels she could follow. She had to make them follow her and not go in the direction of her children. Her feet picked up speed and she could hear the feet behind her. She could move faster as a wolf and without the trappings of shoes and office attire. Quickly she changed into the wolf that sometimes roamed the streets at night under the full moon. It was amazing how far she had come since the first time she painfully turned into a wolf against her will. Now she was practiced enough to change any time she needed to. But was she good enough to draw the pack away from her family?

She turned left and trotted ahead listening for the sound of footsteps behind her. Where could she lead them? She hit an intersection and turned right, away from the light hoping the wolves would follow her. What she would do when they caught her, she did not know. Then left again, and the footsteps kept up. They seemed to have multiplied and then she realized they too had changed. Instead of walking on two feet, now they had four and they could see as well in the dark as she. Left again, she found a door that she had not seen in the past and hopped through it when suddenly she was in the middle of the lair where Adolph and the others were. She had led them directly to her family! She tried to turn around but it was too late and she was quickly overrun by hundreds of wolves with hungry eyes. They barged through the doorway and across the dusty room.

"Ernestine! Get the kids!" Adolph shouted from his dirty mattress as he rose on shaky legs. Josh ran toward Sarina and she barely saw Ernestine shove her children through a door before she was hit from behind.

"Mom!" She heard her son call her, but all she could hope for was that he was safe.

Knocked to the ground, she smelled him first and then turned to see Raoul, Nail, and more Gray Wolves than she knew existed running through the door into the lair. They had brought the whole army.

But Adolph's werewolves had an army too. They came from all directions, leaping, growling, and snapping at the other wolves. Teeth bared, wolves ran headlong into each other. A ferocious battle was taking place all around her. She saw Josh only once with a Gray Wolf on each side of him as he ripped with claws at each of them and bit the one that still got past his claws. They were being overrun.

An old wolf was backed into a corner and was knocked down by large claws, blood running from his mouth, his breathing shallow. When Sarina looked up, she saw the wolf standing over him was Raoul. The old wolf had to be Adolph, the leader of her pack. She was unable to calm her fury. The old wolf breathed once and then ceased. Raoul howled in triumph. He had killed Adolph!

Sarina sprang onto his back without thinking. He instantly slung her off and then advanced on her as she lay on the ground. The incident seemed familiar, like the first time he jumped her. But she would not be surprised by him again. When he leaned over her, she swung her clawed paw and connected with his windpipe, this time ripping it out of his throat. He stumbled back holding onto his neck and fell to the ground. Without thinking she leaned over Raoul on the floor and holding his head in her paws she twisted and yanked. A horrible crunching sound of bone splitting echoed as she ripped his head from his shoulders. Raising the head like a trophy, blood running down her arm, a prehistoric howl came from so deep inside her she didn't recognize it. But it reverberated off the tunnel walls. All movement stopped and hundreds of yellow eyes were on her. She had killed the man that made her what she was. The Gray Wolves instantly stopped. Slowly they looked at one another just as the coyotes ran in from across the room. The Gray Wolves scrambled for the doors back the way they came. Adolph's werewolves and coyotes sprinted after them and the yaps could be heard down the corridors. She had protected her family. She made the Gray Wolves retreat.

● ● ●

"You know, Nail will run away now without Raoul to back him up?" Josh walked beside her on the rooftops overlooking the city on their nightly patrol.

"So Nail was never really the leader?"

"In name only. Raoul was the power behind the throne."

"They'll reorganize." Sarina could see everything around her with her wolf eyes.

"That's okay, we have a new leader too and she is smart."

"I don't know about that. I still wonder how I let them talk me into taking over Adolph's place."

"You're the right person for the job." He smiled a toothy grin in the full moon light. "Smart, sexy, and a great mom."

"Whatever."

"You are. You'd make a great mom to another baby too you know. Have you ever thought about having another?"

"More pups? You know wolves have litters, not just one."

"Maybe a girl, like her mom."

"Oh you're funny. I'd ruin this figure."

"That figure is just fine. I don't think it is going anywhere. But really, how about one little girl with me?"

"In your dreams. No thanks, I have three kids."

"I think I'm wearing you down." Sarina could see Josh's smile in the moon light.

They walked off together with the full moon rising. Josh nuzzled Sarina's neck and she let out a wolf-like giggle. In the distance, the sirens sang a song of trouble on a moonlit night when the orb was full. Her strong back legs sprang into action leaping from one rooftop to the next.

The End

You'll Laugh When I Tell You

By Adrian Cole

Nick Nightmare, Private Eye, Public Fist, at your service. I run my one man agency from a two-bit office in downtown Manhattan. My real moniker is Stone, but the Nightmare tag sticks on account of the weird stuff I often get tangled up in. I'm a victim of my own success. I used to think the worst thing in the world was spiders. Now I'm not so sure. I'll tell you about it.

I was sitting in a quiet bar one evening, just chilling out with a shot or two of whiskey and reading my latest literary acquisition, *Stiletto Sister from Hell*, when I found myself looking into the wide grin of Police Chief Rizzie Carter NYPD. I knew his full range of grins and this wasn't a happy one - more of a grimace. Which meant he had a problem and he wanted to enlist my peculiar talents to exorcize it.

"Have a seat, Chief. You look like you could do with a beer or six."

"One will do, Nick," he said. Even that was unusual for him while he was on duty. Must be an even bigger headache. Alarm bells were starting to give me one, too.

"Problem?"

He shrank down across the table in the booth—as far as that was possible for a man of his size and weight. The Chief was a very big guy. I do mean big. He ate hamburgers and fast food for his country.

"You know I'm a sceptic when it comes to the weird stuff," he growled quietly. Also unusual for him. You could normally hear him two blocks away. He really was spooked.

"Why else would you enlist my help? My middle name is weird. So what have you got this time?" I'd investigated more than a few very bizarre cases for him and earned my soubriquet because of it.

"I guess we all question our own sanity sometimes. With me, it's more a case of thinking it's the world I live in that's cracked and I just have to navigate it the best I can. I'm a simple detective, Nick. I deal in facts, cold and hard. I'm not interested in the weird and wonderful. They just clutter up the truth: usually someone's idea of a blind or a smoke screen. Fine for the movies, but in my day-to- day grind I don't have time for that crap."

For him, that was quite a speech.

"Consider my interest piqued," I told him, slipping my pulp novel away.

"Where do I start? Facts: a murder, an ugly, one-off killing that's got the forensic boys shaking their heads in disgust. Sure, they love anything bizarre, and this is as off-the-wall as it gets. Right in the guts of the city, and I do mean guts. What started off as a blockage to a sewer, a compacted mass of turds and other unintentional binding agents - discovered by a couple of drainage workers who were just doing their job - turned out to be something else altogether. Okay, putting it bluntly, it was a turd, but I tell you, this was no ordinary dump."

Another long speech. Whatever happened to Mr Staccato?

The Chief wrinkled his nose as though the offending item had been dropped down on the table in front of him. "Ordinarily the sanitation boys woulda shovelled the thing into a few sacks and disposed of it however they usually shift that kind of gunk. But the torpedo-shaped, human-sized mess intrigued them. Gave them a few laughs. Maybe you need to be a sanitation worker to appreciate that."

"I think you're probably right, chief."

"Yeah, well, they showed it to someone higher up the chain, and he did the same, until someone smelled a rat. Except that no rat ever dropped a pellet that big. In fact, nothing they knew about dropped a pellet that big. Because it wasn't a compressed mass of dozens of turds like they often deal with - it was one single payload."

I tried not to grin. "Must have made someone's eyes water," I said.

He didn't look amused. "Word got through to my department. We've been investigating disappearances in the area above the sewer where this thing was found. Weird things were going on there. I like to keep an open mind. Lucky for me I was spared the job of examining the thing. It's now in an outside shed, where the lab boys are doing the dirty work. I just saw it from behind a glass screen."

I could see now why he wasn't chewing on his customary fistful of hamburgers. I nodded.

"It was stretched out on a slab, fussed over by three men in special suits and masks, like it was some biological nightmare. It was the size of a body and boy, it oozed and must have stank unbelievably. Jeeze, I'm glad I was screened from it.

"Karson, the guy in charge of the physical investigation, confirmed it was a human body. Or, it had been. A person, can you believe that? I asked him if he knew who it had been and he said, yeah, it was a scientist, Ray Dawkins - one of the men we'd been looking for."

"Murdered and tossed into the sewer?"

"Kind of. How did Karson put it? He said Dawkins had been ingested, digested and excreted."

I stared at him. This was no joke. "*Eaten?* You're saying, he was eaten? Since when did we have a T Rex running around the streets of New York?"

"Karson asked me if I'd ever seen what a snake does to its victims. A constrictor. He said they wrap their coils around their prey and slowly crush it, breaking it down to a manageable chunk. He said goats and small horses can be victims of boas, pythons and anaconda."

"Constrictors have remarkable jaws, almost elastic," I said. "They swallow their prey whole and then spend days, even weeks, digesting it. Eventually they excrete the remains."

"Yeah, Karson said that."

"Chief, you're telling me that a *snake* swallowed Ray Dawkins and that mess

was all that was left? An entire person? That would be one very big snake, Chief."
I gave him my sceptical look.

"Karson reckoned these snakes can stretch, many times their width. But he reckoned this one would have to be as big a specimen as any known to science. Possibly a mutation. A python, or a green anaconda. The green ones are the big ones."

"Two things occur to me," I mused. "One, where did it come from, and two, more to the point, where the heck is it now?"

"Probably back in the sewer system, somewhere relatively warm, according to Karson. As for where it came from - I woulda said a zoo, but we checked that out. No big snakes missing. They woulda noticed."

"Maybe it came from the docks? A ship?"

"Someone would have raised the alarm. We got a sort of lead. This guy, Ray Dawkins. He worked for a scientific big noise by the name of Doctor Vermeillen."

"I've read about him," I said. "Celebrated biologist, right?"

"You got it. His staff were the ones helping us with the disappearances in the area. One of which was Ray Dawkins. So what else do you know about Vermeillen?"

I sat back and dug into my mental filing cabinet. "He's spent years in South America." Something was clicking into place. "That's right - often in anaconda country. He's probably the world's foremost authority on constrictors. So that's your lead?"

"You wanna follow it up for me?"

There was no point answering.

"Vermeillen runs a pharmaceutical factory," he went on. "He's head of research. I've done some investigating there. During the interviews I saw behind the main workings of the company. The staff told me that these places have their side-lines, pet projects that sometimes lead to breakthroughs - for the benefit of mankind."

I grinned. "Always for the benefit of mankind. I daresay a few pockets are getting heavily lined to boot, especially Vermeillen's."

"He has some very rich connections in the city. I think we're talking a whole lot of money here. A lot of vested interest."

"So anyone poking their nose in too deep would not be person of the month. I get the picture, Chief. So how am I supposed to get in there? My guess is the place will be a fortress."

It was his turn to grin. "No problem, Nick. I'll get you a badge and everything else you need. You can be one of my team, a member of the NYPD."

"Remind me, how long do you get in the slammer for impersonating a police officer?"

"Don't worry about that. Oh, I almost forget—one of Vermeillen's big buddies is someone you crossed a while back."

This was not something I wanted to hear. "Now you're really going to spoil my day. Who?"

"Lucien de Sangreville."

I sat back and groaned audibly. De Sangreville and I had indeed crossed swords—not to put too fine a point on it, the man was a Satanist, a very powerful one, at that. Sometime previously I'd been involved in a fracas with him and his acolytes that had almost resulted in disaster, right here on the outskirts of the city. Somehow my team had won out and de Sangreville had bolted, not seen since. The last thing I needed was to get mixed up with him again.

"You think he's involved in this case?" I asked the Chief.

"It's unlikely. Just thought you ought to know the kind of people you'll be dealing with. But there's no reason to think that Vermeillen will know who you are. He knows I'll be following up my investigations. He'll be expecting the cops to show up again. You could be anyone."

"That makes me feel so much better."

• • •

I was led in to a brightly lit office, dead in the heart of the pharma-ceutical set-up, all steel and glass, bright and brash. The far end was all windows, overlooking an area that could have served for a set on the latest Hollywood jungle epic. Late afternoon light streamed down over the rampant greenery within it, creating a tropical effect and I wouldn't have been surprised to see a couple of raptors pacing about, looking for meal on its floor, a couple of storeys below.

It was damned warm in here.

My fake ID had got me into the place, just as the Chief had promised and I was cleared to meet its top man. Vermeillen rose from his desk and offered his hand. It was probably the only cold thing in the place. Firm grip, though. He looked about forty, very muscular, whereas I'd expected a more cerebral type, and his skin was unblemished, his face smooth, and his weirdly colored eyes bright. His hair shone as though he'd just stepped out of a shower and combed it, still wet, back over his head and ears. He spoke in a soft, vaguely European voice.

"You must be Chief Carter's man. Thank you for sparing more of your time. I won't insult you by offering you alcohol on duty, but the iced water is very refreshing."

I accepted the drink and sat in one of the high tech seats, sipping the cold water. On one of the gleaming steel shelves that lined a wall, there were several arty sculptures in colored glass, and a row of small jars with glass stoppers—they looked to me like medicine bottles, brown and a tad incongruous. Mind you this was a pharmaceutical factory, so what the heck.

"We've found Ray Dawkins," I told Vermeillen.

He nodded. "That's good. Has he explained himself? Why such a brilliant scientist should abandon us is beyond me –"

I gave it him straight about Dawson's death. "Our forensic team are confused, Doctor. They have this crazy idea he was eaten by a snake. That would have to be a very big snake, right?" I gave him more details and even showed him a photo or two.

He remained calm, but his face monitored puzzlement. "People have been swallowed by snakes before. Usually children, though. I have seen green anacondas that grew to almost forty feet. They are not the sort of creatures you would want to capture and bring back to civilization."

"Could there be one, out there in the sewers? Have you any specimens here? Could any have got out?"

"We do have constrictors here, yes. However, they are very carefully monitored. Most marvellous creatures. They have a unique strength, you know. For their body weight, the amount of power they generate is extraordinary. In India, there are places where they call the bigger pythons, elephant killers. Can you imagine what it would be like for a human to possess the equivalent power?"

"Are any of your snakes missing?"

He shook his head, his eyes almost closed. The oppressive heat of the office had made him languorous and if I had to spend much longer in here, I'd be dozing off as well.

"I checked this morning with my technicians. All secured."

"Could one survive out in the sewers?"

"Yes, I should think so. The anaconda is a water snake and likes heat. The sewers would be warm enough, and large enough to accommodate one. It would need food regularly. Once every few weeks, if it had sufficient."

"Dawkins is the only missing person we've found. Are you saying the others could have been taken by the same snake?"

"Very possible."

"You don't find that odd?"

He fixed his cool, unwavering gaze on me. "I don't follow."

"Five of your staff, including Dawkins, have gone missing. Why should the snake select them as victims? If it's down in the sewers, wouldn't it be more random?"

"Oh, I see—you think it's coming here to hunt? But how could it get in and out? By all means inspect the entire building. You simply will not find a means of ingress."

"With your permission, Doctor, I'll need to do just that."

"They're very intelligent, you know. Not just strong. The South American Indians are convinced that they are evolving. Some tribes worship them as gods. Man's relationship with them goes back into the dawn of time."

"Why do you keep them?"

"Apart from the fact that I find them utterly fascinating, we do conduct experiments. Just as venomous snakes provide science with invaluable products, so, too, the constrictors. I couldn't discuss details with you, of course, but I can assure you everything here is ethical."

"I'm sure it is. Well, if you could perhaps get someone to show me around, particularly the lower levels."

Vermeillen was obviously bored with the questioning and it looked like he'd bought my false credentials. If anything out of order was going on here, he was confident it wasn't going to implicate him.

The young man who was picked to give me the guided tour was called Krezni.

He was a nervous, ascetic type, eager to show me anything of interest, though not very forthcoming if I tried to dig deeper about the kind of research that they carried out. After an hour or so of checking, I couldn't find anywhere that breached the tight security of the buildings. If there really was a big snake on the hunt outside, there seemed to be no way in for it.

I talked to Krezni about it over a cup of coffee. "How long has Doctor Vermeillen worked with snakes?" I asked him.

"Must be years. He founded the company about thirty years ago and he was visiting the Amazonian jungles even before that." Krezni couldn't keep a hint of hero-worship from his voice.

"Thirty years? Are you sure about that?"

"Of course." Krezni turned to a white-coated assistant. "That's right, isn't it, Louisa? Doctor Vermeillen started the company up thirty years ago. Your father worked here."

The girl came over, smiling thinly, as though slightly bored by the whole business. "Sure. What about it?"

Krezni introduced me and then excused himself and went back into one of the labs.

"So how old is Vermeillen?" I asked the girl. "He doesn't look older than forty."

I saw at once that the question had caught her unawares. She seemed to be weighing up an answer. "He's a lot older than that. I can't talk here. But I can give you something." She collected the empty coffee mugs with feigned casualness and spoke so that only I could hear her. "Make your way to the rear of the factory, where the trash is stored, you'll see a blue tarpaulin. Check it out, but make damn sure you're not seen."

She moved off, yawning as if I was of no interest to her. But I knew the smell of fear when I got a whiff of it and that lady was scared of something.

● ● ●

I did as the lab assistant, Louisa, had told me and made my way to the rear of the factory, using the deepening shadows to mask my presence, knowing I was probably being watched by the internal security cameras. They would have known though, that a cop would want to snoop about.

I opened an outside door that showed a wide yard, walled in on three sides and with big steel gates at its far end. There were a lot of discarded boxes and sacks of what I took to be trash heaped up out here. I studied the walls—there were lights, but I couldn't see any cameras apart from a pair fixed so they could monitor the gates.

I took a chance and slipped outside. I don't smoke, but I pulled a pack from my coat and lit one up—an old trick. Anyone watching me would be thinking I'd sneaked out for a drag or two. I walked about randomly until I saw, in one corner, what must be the blue tarpaulin Louisa had mentioned. I went over to it and casually checked the cameras. Not watching.

The tarp had a big symbol emblazoned on it in red—a bio-hazard warning. Stooping down, I tugged a section of it aside. There was a box, loosely taped. I pulled back the lid and found a dozen of those brown medicine bottles inside. I slipped some gloves on and pulled one of the bottles out, unscrewing its lid. The bottle felt empty. Very carefully, I sniffed at it. There was a strong, sweet smell, but nothing I recognised. I re-capped it and shoved it in my coat pocket, pulling the tarp back further.

Something long and thin was under there. It had been wrapped in some kind of shrink-wrap, like it was a mummy. Closer inspection showed that the shiny material was an integral part of the object. I noticed the heavier appendage at one end. Even more like a mummy, with a shrunken head. I tugged at the main bulk, but it was too light to have been a body, more like a bound-up pile of cardboard, as if kids had been making a dummy for a bonfire. The stuff was shiny, slightly slippery to the touch. Then it came to me.

Scales. Or more precisely, snake-skin. I was no expert, but I knew snakes shed it from time to time.

And this was a very large specimen. Something clicked into place. Big snake. Maybe this was shed by the thing that took Dawkins - the anaconda.

I ran my hands carefully over the skin, pausing as I reached the top end with the appendage. I undid the squashed layers of scales to reveal a bulbous, wrinkled mass and eased the last of the enfolding tissue away. It was like a crumpled mask. The mask of a man aged about eighty.

Except that it wasn't a mask, it was a face.

Discarded, with the skin, in favour of something much younger, much more vital. A face I knew.

The face of Doctor Vermeillen.

I drew the tarp back over the disgusting object and made my way back, as casually as I could across the yard, dropping the cigarette and stubbing it out for any watcher's benefit. The implications of what I'd seen hammered inside my skull like a bunch of hysterical imps. Vermeillen? He was—what? Some kind of mutation? *He'd* shed his skin? And with it, a lot of years.

Back inside the factory, I slipped along the corridors until a movement ahead brought me up sharp. I was still feeling phased by what I'd seen.

It was Krezni, my guide of earlier. "Thought I'd lost you," he said anxiously, as if it meant he'd be in deep water with his boss.

"Just needed a quick smoke," I quipped. "Anything else you want to show me?"

"I think you've seen everything."

Yeah, he got that right. "This is the ground floor, right?"

He nodded. "There's a car park under us, but that's all. Do you need to see it?"

"Sure. Just a quick once over."

He led us to a set of steps down to a steel door and unlocked it.

"Leave this open and I'll come back when I'm done."

He seemed relieved to agree. I went down into the car park, which was almost full. There were other stairs and lifts to it and as I wandered about, people came down from above and got into their vehicles. It was the end of another working

day for most of the staff. Everything seemed normal, just people going about their business. Except for that thing among the trash. If anyone knew about that, they were keeping very quiet about it.

There didn't seem to be any leads down here, so I was about to go back up into the building, when I saw the lab assistant, Louisa, about to get into her own car. I walked casually over to her.

"You find what you were looking for?" she said quietly.

"Yeah. You want to tell me about it? Some other place would be fine."

She shook her head. "He'll kill me. But if you need another lead, there's another level. Red fire door, security only. I don't have a key." It was as much as she was going to tell me. She sat at the wheel and pulled the door shut, switching on the ignition. I let her drive off.

Didn't take me long to find the fire door. Steel, well secured. Another level. My guess was a snake pit. I was going to have to come back much later and do some serious snooping. If I dragged the Chief and his merry men along with me, Vermeillen would make darn sure we wouldn't find anything. This was going to have to be more subtle. And very dangerous. Getting keys to open that fire door was the easy bit. I was also going to need some very special protection.

● ● ●

I clued up the Chief with one phone call.

"If anyone else was telling me this," he growled, "I'd say they'd lost their marbles. Now you want to go back in there alone? You've done some crazy things for me, Nick, but this is too risky. You don't have to do this."

"Let's just say my appetite is whetted. Just get your back-up team ready. If I get in too deep, I'll ring you."

He was right. This was nuts. But I like a challenge. I made sure I was about as protected as I could be. I started with the body paint, using protective designs from one of my private manuals, an old tract given to me some years before by a *houngan*, a voodoo priest I had some friendly dealings with—but that's another story. I also wore a few charms, a necklace and in one pocket I had a small, shrivelled monkey's skull. You don't want to know about that.

Naturally I took my twin Berettas, as well as a few stilettos. I'd feel naked without them. Lastly, I took a set of keys that would open most doors this side of Hell. I'd selected black clothing, including a thin raincoat, so overall I looked something like a ninja on patrol—maybe a slightly baggy one. Whatever, it would take a keen eye to spot me.

It was long gone midnight when I got back to the pharmaceutical factory. During my tour earlier in the day, I had picked out a couple of weaknesses in the surveillance set-up where I could do my Spiderman impersonation and shin up over the external wall. On the inside, I slipped up a fire escape, just another shadow in the night, and selected a window that opened up easily enough. I was inside.

I didn't waste any time going down to the underground car park. It was silent and empty and best of all, unlit. It could have been a tomb, hopefully not mine. No one felt the need to monitor it. Even so, I was careful as I made my way, using a narrow beam flashlight, to the door I knew led down to the other floor. As I crossed the car park, I heard something, a deep throbbing. I thought it must be power transformers, but as I got to the steel door, it sounded more like—drums. The ground beneath me vibrated. I was putting the pieces of this puzzle together and my suspicions about it were being realized. I'd made the right choice when I protected myself.

The key slid into the door lock and I played around with it for a while until I heard it click obligingly. I pushed the door very slowly inwards, one of the Berettas in my right hand. Two things came pulsing out of the crack the open door had made—a thick cloud of fog, hot and clammy, with a stench of incense and a few other unsavoury smells as well as the thunder of those drums. Someone was having a party and it was well into the swing of things.

I risked a peek around the door. Dark corridor—steps leading down to the source of the noise. No one there, though, so I slipped in and re-locked the door behind me. There was a deep red glow ahead and I inched my way down the steps. At their foot the corridor turned and opened on to a surprisingly huge chamber that looked like it had been carved out of the bedrock. There were a couple of tall, fat columns nearby, so I got in behind one, where I'd get a good view of the proceedings and still be unnoticed.

When I looked, I thought I must have beamed out of New York and on to Haiti. And Cecil B. de Mille was having an absolute ball. Lights, mostly reds, pinks and purples, flooded a central area, where scores of writhing bodies, apparently wearing little more than a bead or two, were cavorting and prancing about in time to the insistent rhythm of the drums. While the women were mainly young, the men were of all ages and my guess was, if I'd taken a real good look, I'd have recognised a lot of the city's business moguls. Some of the crowd were helping themselves to food and drink from the long trestle tables where there was enough to feed an army for a month's campaign.

There were a lot of huge braziers, pouring smoke upwards to where there must have been air vents to take it away; otherwise everyone in the place would have choked, in spite of its size. Streamers, ribbons, exotic plants, including a few potted palms and giant ferns had transformed the setting. Like I said, a veritable Haiti. I saw the drummers now—about two dozen of them—huge Negroes, as big as anything you'd see strutting their stuff on the New York Giants football grid. Sleek with sweat, they pounded those huge drums like there was no tomorrow.

I looked at the pillars and realised with a slight shudder that each of them was sculpted with fat snakes, writhing around them. In the lurid glow, those critters looked alive, their jewelled eyes gleaming. I felt like they were all looking my way. Well, I wasn't going to be able to mingle with the crowd—not in my present regalia—I'd have stood out like a bear in a nunnery. And there was no way I was going to divest myself of a single stitch.

Maybe I'd just keep an eye on things and slip away. If I called on the Chief and he broke in here with his gang, there was nothing much they could do—maybe a few arrests for disorderly behaviour, drugs, and so on, but this was just a riotous big bash. The people here had connections.

So I watched. Beyond the central area and the manic drummers beside it there were long steps leading up to a higher level and on this there was a big fat block of stone. It had the look of an altar, so maybe this was where things would really hot up, if there was to be a sacrifice. In which case, I would have to take some kind of action. Orgies are all well and good, but I draw the line at human sacrifice.

Below me, the wild dancers started a chant going, the words of which were meaningless to me, except for one word. It cemented the last piece of the puzzle in place—Damballah. Voodoo god. Not necessarily a bad guy, but I wasn't ready to bet my shirt on that.

In answer to the chant, a number of figures appeared above the steps. I would have given them full marks for outfits. Feathers seemed to be the main order of the day, that and snake-skins, combined with bone necklaces, knives, spears, dramatically colourful clothes. Two men in particular stood out and one of them raised his arms. Slowly the mob below came to order.

"We gather to praise Damballah, the Great Master!" called the prominent guy, and I knew the voice at once—it was Vermeillen. I wondered about the other guy, but couldn't see his face—he wore a thin mask, wood daubed with white symbols.

"Bring the slave of Damballah!" Vermeillen called to a group of people to his left. They dragged a woman out on to the raised area and even from this distance I could see who it was. Louisa, the lab assistant who had tipped me off. She was in big trouble and it looked like I was going to have to repay a favour.

I watched as three guys, naked as babes in a bathtub, pulled Louisa to the stone block—the altar—and stretched her over it, snapping steel manacles on her arms and ankles so that she was unable to move. I had both Berettas out. Even at this distance I reckoned on taking out a thug or two if I had to. The one advantage I had was that no one else hereabouts had a gun handy—that much was plain to see.

Vermeillen stood over the woman and below him the mob had started shouting again. This was getting ugly. The other guy brought Vermeillen a golden goblet and handed it over like it was the Holy Grail. Vermeillen held it aloft and spouted more of the mumbo-jumbo that turned the drunken mob on. He lowered the goblet and drank whatever was in it.

"Let Damballah be praised! Let him savour this offering we bring!"

Everyone on the raised area stood well back, leaving Vermeillen alone with the distraught woman. I drew a bead on him. If he got nasty, I was going to let him have it.

What happened next took everyone by surprise, not least of all me. Vermeillen shook, twisting and contorting, writhing about as if he'd swallowed poison. He fell to the stone floor, jerking this way and that. No one made a move to help him. They seemed to be expecting this. I had a sneaking suspicion I knew what this was all about. I was right.

Man into snake.

Not for the first time, Vermeillen was transforming. Here was the evidence we had been looking for. Here was the huge anaconda that had swallowed human victims whole. Because that's what was happening—Vermeillen's arms and legs seemed to slide up into his torso, which began to fatten and elongate. His head modified itself and became swollen and wedge-shaped, the long, shining head of a huge constrictor. By the time that monster had finished the change; it was twenty feet or more long, its body as wide around as a human torso.

"Damballah! Damballah!" screamed the mob, surging forward, like they wanted to touch their revolting master.

The serpent raised its head, weaving from side to side, eyes gleaming in the mottled firelight, long, pink tongue flicking this way and that like twin lashes. It touched the body of the woman, caressing it. I knew what was coming.

No time for niceties now. I took careful aim and fired off three rounds. One hit the golden goblet that Vermeillen's second in command had taken back and it went spinning. I was sure the other two shots had hit the big snake. Its ugly head snapped back like it had run into a tank and it did seem to be dazed—but not killed. I realized that I'd need a bazooka, or maybe even a real tank if I was going to do that.

The mob were screaming and shrieking, not with terror, but with fury. A lot of the people turned and looked in my direction. I may have been wrapped in shadows, but I heard a shout from up on the raised area. My number was up and the dogs were loose. I could only hope that I'd done enough to distract attention from the unfortunate Louisa. I got that right—one last glance showed me the big snake sliding quickly down the steps, heading in my direction.

I ran back to the steps that led up to the steel doorway out of here. It took me a few moments to fumble with the key—my nerves were falling apart, knowing that the huge snake was going to be closing in on me in no time. I dropped the goddam key. Bending down, I heard the hiss, like a steam engine, right behind me, though out of sight round the last turn in the stairs. The walls rocked as the snake hit them with the force of a loco. It was only when I understood that the stairwell was far too small to let the snake through that I got myself reorganised.

Quickly I unlocked the door and went into the car park. I didn't look back. Sooner or later that big beastie was going to batter its way into the area. I made it to one of the elevators and prodded the door pad. I got in and punched the button for the top floor, the fifth. My aim was to get on to the roof and swing my way out of this place by an aerial route.

That may have been fine, but half way up the ascent, the elevator stopped. On the third floor. The floor that contained Vermeillen's office. This was not looking good.

I banged the buttons—any one would do—but nothing worked. They'd trapped me. I had my Berettas ready. I didn't have long to wait.

The doors hummed aside to reveal a carpeted corridor, brightly lit on both sides. A dozen guys, fully dressed, complete with sub machine guns, were waiting for me. I could have taken out a few, but they would have riddled me with slugs. Behind them, a tall figure spoke and I knew the voice at once.

Lucien de Sangreville. Still wearing his robes of office as a voodoo sidekick to Vermeillen, sinister as Christopher Lee at his most menacing. So it had been him down at the ritual, my former satanic adversary, who had every reason to want to see me hung, drawn and quartered.

"Take off your mask," he said in that measured British accent. There was a hard, cold edge to it. Slowly I did as instructed. You win some, you lose some.

"Mr Stone. Or Mr Nightmare, if you prefer. I did wonder if it were you. Delightful to see you again. Still meddling in affairs that don't concern you, though. Would you please be very sensible and give one of my colleagues here your guns, unless you want to be shredded where you stand."

"No need to get testy," I said. Reluctantly I gave one of the gunmen my Berettas. I made a good note of the guy's face as he tucked them into his belt.

De Sangreville led the way along the corridor to the suite of offices at its far end. I had a dozen guns trained on me, so I didn't get heroic. The protection I was wearing would have warded off most kinds of juju, but they wouldn't have stopped a hail of lead.

We entered Vermeillen's main office, where I'd interviewed the scientist. De Sangreville dismissed his men, all but two of them, who hung by the door. There was one other person in the room—Vermeillen himself. He looked a mess. Like he'd been for a ten mile run through bad terrain. He was breathing heavy, his clothes dishevelled and his face and hands slick with something akin to hair gel. At least he wasn't in his big serpent guise. He must have changed back, and probably far too quick for comfort.

His eyes narrowed and fixed on me—here was hatred personified.

"Strip down and put all your weapons on the table," said de Sangreville.

I didn't have a lot of choice, so I unloaded my knives, my cell phone and a few charms, including the monkey's skull. The guard who'd taken my Berettas stepped forward and dropped them down among the stuff.

"Very thorough, Mr Stone," said de Sangreville.

I had one last item to add. A small brown medical jar with a glass stopper. Both Vermeillen and de Sangreville stared at it as though it was a bomb about to go off.

"I thought I'd take a sample of the merchandise," I said, nodding to the shelf where several other bottles gleamed.

"Did you," hissed Vermeillen. "Well, since you're so interested in our work, we'll oblige you with a demonstration." He came forward awkwardly, obviously in pain, and I tried not to look smug. My bullets must have done some damage after all.

Vermeillen picked up the jar. "Since you interrupted the ritual, you can help us complete it now."

"I had a feeling you might say that."

Vermeillen stood back from his desk, unscrewed the top of the jar and tilted it, drinking its contents, thirsty as an addict. He banged the jar down on the desk and grinned at me, waiting for the serpentine transformation to begin.

There was indeed a transformation, but not quite what mine host was expecting. He'd assumed—as I thought he would—that I'd stolen the jar on my visit earlier. That was correct. It was the jar I'd picked up among the trash outside. Only I'd filled it with something fresh. Let's just say, it wasn't the same gunk that was in Vermeillen's usual jars. And it sure as hell wasn't going to transform him into a snake, big or small.

He bent over double and began to wretch, his hands clawing the air. He dropped to his knees, then rolled over onto his belly, wriggling squirming—about as close to a snake impersonation as he was going to get with that nasty potion inside him.

De Sangreville rushed forward, alarmed, and tried to get Vermeillen to his feet. The scientist's mouth foamed, like he was having the mother of seizures. Blood started oozing from his eyes. The two guards stepped forward, unsure what to do. I was less hesitant. I went round the desk, ducking down, and grabbed both Berettas. I left the charms and monkey skull.

"Shoot him!" snarled de Sangreville, but I was far too close to him and Vermeillen for either of them to risk a shot.

I loosed off a few rounds at the tall glass window behind us and it instantly shattered into a million pieces, glass rain. Before anyone could stop me, I leapt through the wreckage and out onto the ledge beyond where the thick fronds and branches of the trees in the central garden welcomed me. I did my very best Tarzan impersonation and swung out on to the nearest tall growth. The first of the sub machine gun bullets whizzed and whanged among the foliage, but I was climbing fast. It was dark up ahead and there were enough places to screen me.

The gunmen fired away randomly, fortunately without success until de Sangreville screamed at them to get after me. I doubt that they had a lot of practice at this sort of thing, so their progress wasn't that hot. In fact, I found a place to secure myself, waited and then let the first of them have it right between the eyes. His body crashed noisily through the big fronds and didn't stop until it hit the paving stones down on ground level. My guess was he was dead long before he splashed himself over them.

His companion was more cautious, which was fine by me. It gave me all the time I needed to haul ass out of there. I got to the roof and scurried over it, leaping from one building to another until I got to the boundary wall. Maybe there were night cameras that picked me up, but no one was able to do anything about it.

Well, not until I got outside. I was dusting myself down, congratulating myself on a good job well done, when a door in the wall swung open and three armed thugs burst out, guns trained on my chest. My guess was, they wouldn't shoot to kill. They'd want to take me back to de Sangreville. Maybe I should just make a run for it and let them shoot me.

Lights suddenly flared up all around me, as if the noonday sun had decided to put in an appearance. I was caught right in the beam. Beyond the glare, I could see a half dozen police patrol cars.

A solitary figure, big as a walrus, shuffled into view.

"Chief," I said. "This is a pleasure."

Rizzie Carter pointed to the three gunmen, who were looking more than a little embarrassed. "You bozos got licences for them things? And what were you thinking of shooting at this time of night?"

The gunmen were bright enough—just—to lower the guns as a bunch of cops moved in on them.

The Chief turned to me. "So what happened to, I'll ring you if I get in a tight spot?"

"They took my cell phone."

"And Vermeillen?"

"He won't be bothering you again."

"I won't ask." The Chief knew well enough that I had my own methods of dealing with the kind of nightmares I fetched up against. He took the view that, if the job got done, there was no need for details. "You okay?"

I slipped my Berettas into my belt. "Sure. I'm not concerned about the cell phone. But when you've finished cleaning up in there, I'd like my monkey skull back."

"Right," he said. But as he led me to the patrol car, he was—understandably - shaking his head.

The End

Dangerous Client

by Lisa M. Collins

I'd been watching this dame for weeks…every night, every show was exactly the same. She'd slink out center mast of the stage, and belt out a blues moan and cry, singing about her lost love and how he did her wrong. About half way through the show she'd swing her right leg out of the slit of her tight red dress, slid it up and around and down the microphone pole. Every man in the room was suddenly a fan. It didn't matter what she was singing. Who the hell cared? And all the women, they were interested one way or the other, half leaning forward taking mental notes, and the other half leaning back contemplating her demise.

"Barkeep, hit me a double," I said.

"Brown or white?"

True to my religion, Irish Catholic, I said, "Brown."

The bartender slid me a highball half full of Jameson. There is nothing like triple distilled barley elixir to set a man right as rain.

A pert blond with short ringlet curls bounced into my vision, "Cigars? Cigarettes?"

"Two packs of Lucky's"

"Sure, Mister. You want some matches?"

Nodding affirmatively, I craned my neck around her to catch the end of the show.

"She's quite lovely, isn't she?" the cigarette girl blocked my view.

"What?" I was losing patients with this Betty.

"Veronica Lovelace, the singer, she's lovely."

"Sure," I took the girl by the arm and physically moved her out of my line of sight.

"Sorry, Mister." She evaporated in a whiff of rose perfume and curls.

I knocked back the last of my drink and lit a cig, taking a long drag. Exhaling the smoke through my nose, I contemplated how to get close to Veronica. She was my only lead on Anton Tolland. Word on the street was she'd been seen downtown numerous times in the last week with Tolland. And if he was true to his dossier he would dump this broad for greener pastures soon, and be splitzville.

Tonight I had to make my move, and since it was Friday all the dolls from the show would stop by the bar to pick up their scratch. I stretched my six foot frame out to the side and propped my feet on the stool to my left. It wasn't the best seat in the house but it was by the cash drawer. Let the fly come to the spider.

"Last call!"

People were starting to drift out on to the street for other late night pursuits. I ordered another double and nursed it waiting for Veronica.

And she didn't disappoint. She had traded her red number for a black one.

183

The seams were stretched tight over her curves you could see them strain as she breathed. Slithering between me and the now vacant stool to my left, she leaned her ample bosom over the bar.

"Jake, I need my money, hon."

Turning to her smoky voice, the bartender cracked a smile at the goods on display. "Sure, Sugar. Be right with yah."

Veronica tapped the toe of her satin shoe.

I leaned toward her and tapped out a Lucky, "Care for a smoke?"

She turned to me, giving me an eye full of her wares. "Sorry, Doll. I'm in a hurry."

Jake headed our way and started counting out the cash. "Oh, Vee, your old man called and left this number. He said call him on the double." Jake handed her the phone.

I watched her dial the number with her scarlet clad nails and memorized the digits.

"Hey Carl, Anton wanted me to call. He's late."

Whatever Carl said didn't make her happy, and her shoe went to tapping again.

"Don't Baby me, Anton…I…fine, but what am I supposed to do? Amuse myself!" A muffled but strong voice murmured over the line. "Why you rat bast…what? For tomorrow?"

The change in her tone was like fire and ice.

"OK, I forgive you. How did you swing tickets? All right, Darling, send the car for me after four. Good night."

Hanging up the phone she turned toward me, "You know if the offer is still good, I'll take that cigarette now, Doll."

"The name's Mack." I held out the pack and lit hers as she moved close.

Sliding her nails up my forearm she said, "That's a nice strong name."

This dame was good. "I couldn't help but overhear your conversation. I was going to hail a cab. You want to share a ride? It's not good for a beautiful woman like you to be out alone at night."

She moved her hand up and gave my bicep a firm press, "And so chivalrous too. I would love to Mack, and I know how to make a mean martini."

I slipped on my coat over her bare shoulders and snapped the brim on my fedora with a slide of my index finger. "My favorite," I lied.

• • •

Our cab stopped outside of a gated uptown brownstone. I paid the cabby and followed Veronica to the door.

"Nice house."

"Thank you," she said unlocking the solid oak door.

I took off my hat and placed it on the tree by the door.

"I'll get those drinks started, make yourself at home."

I grabbed her wrist and hauled her back to me. I cut off her gasp with my lips and kissed her long and hard, twisting her arm around her back, not leaving a breath of air between us.

When I released her she slowly smiled up at me, "I should slap you where you stand."

I leaned down and nipped her neck right below her ear and whispered, "Be very sure about you next move, Princess, if that is how you want to play."

Veronica melted against my chest. "Well, we will just have to play that one by ear. Like I said, make yourself at home."

"I was." Surveying the room it looked upscale for a singer from downtown. Every surface seemed to glitter with silver and crystal.

"You like it?" Veronica handed me a martini and swept her hand around the room, "It's my boyfriend's."

"It's real nice, Doll, so when does the old man come home?"

"Oh, he doesn't live here; this is just one of many properties." She slinked back over to me, "Anyway, we don't have any plans until tomorrow night."

"Really," I pulled her down to sit next to me on the couch in front of a cozy fireplace.

Giggling, Veronica murmured, "So we have all night."

• • •

I woke with a start. Veronica was draped over my chest. I eased her off and sat up. My head pounded. I stretched and went to the bathroom to find some aspirin and got dressed. When I came back out Veronica was propped up against the headboard, hair all mussed, with the sheets barely covering her chest.

"Don't you want to stay for breakfast?"

"Can't, Doll, got to hit the street."

"Oh, Mack," she let the sheet slip. "Please."

I knew why Tolland had kept this filly on the line for so long, she was one good looking broad.

"Sorry, Princess, but I got some business I got to take care of." I leaned down and traced her collarbone, making the skin goose bump.

"Fine," she pouted.

Sitting on the edge of the bed I pulled her into my lap and kissed her until I felt her arms come around my neck, "This was great, Doll, but you have an old man, and I'm not getting caught in the hen house."

"Oh, Mack!" She laughed and pecked my cheek. "So I'll see you around."

"Yes you will, Princess," I said sliding her back to the bed.

Little did she know that I would be sticking closer to her than a shadow. One night with her and I had Tolland's phone number and schedule for the next twenty-four hours. She had definitely never heard the adage loose lips sink ships.

• • •

It was just past nine when I got to my office downtown. As soon as I hit the door I knew, Millie, my receptionist, was not in a good mood. Of course her mood was subject to change.

Millie was on the phone, "Mr. Ivy, you haven't paid for the last job..."

I walked up to the desk and took the phone from her. "Listen," I cut into his litany of excuses, "I don't care. If you need help call the Salvation Army." I slammed the phone down.

"Mack!"

"Millie we have work to do. I need to get a date for this evening's show at The Palace Theatre."

Millie gave me her best rendition of the Mona Lisa, "Are you saying," she snapped her gum, "that you need me to find you a willing female?" She lifted her perfectly arched right eyebrow, "Is this for business or pleasure?"

Sitting on the corner of her desk I tucked a curl of her long sable brown hair behind her ear. "You know me." I winked.

"You're a bad, bad man, Mack Stevens." Millie poked me with a pink lacquered fingernail. "So what kind of lady are you looking for this time, an eye catcher, a smooth operator, or a girl next door?"

"Let's go with a girl next door with the ability to keep her trap shut, and hold her liquor."

"That's a tall order on short notice. Do you already have tickets? That show's been sold out for a week."

"No, but I know someone who can help me out with that bit. You just get the girl and have her dressed and ready to go by six." I boosted myself off the desk and squeezed between the file cabinets and into my office, "Oh, and if Ivy calls back, tell him I am not taking clients this week. Call back next week and have money, this isn't a charity."

"Sure thing, Boss."

● ● ●

I sunk down in the soft leather of my desk chair. My plan was coming together, but tonight would have to be flawless. I dreaded making the call for the tickets. My current employer was a real piece of work, all business, no excuses. I fortified my coffee with a shot of the good stuff and dialed the number. The connection was made on the first ring. Mr. X spoke without greeting or prompting, making me wonder if I was the only one who ever called this number.

"Stevens, Nice to hear from you on such a beautiful fall day. Since I know you can't possibly have what I want, how can I be of service to you?" His voice was muffled like spoken from far away.

"I have a bead on your mark. I need two tickets for The Palace Theatre, tonight's showing at seven."

"My mark will be there?"

"Yes, from what I have uncovered."

"Why do you need two tickets?"

"It will be less conspicuous if I arrive without a date."

"Very well, I will have the tickets waiting for you at the door."

After five years of working with X, not to question how he managed things. "Thanks. I hope to have the location of the mark in a few days."

"Good. Be sure your companion to tonight's show doesn't screw things up," he hung up.

Nothing on Earth would make me happier than the day I would no longer owe Mr. X. I had sold my soul to the devil and I knew it.

You know what they say about hindsight. How X even knew I was behind on my gambling debts, I might never know. All I had to do was be on retainer for some missing persons cases. I had already begun to wonder what X did with these men as I tracked them down, but, honestly, I didn't want to have my curiosity confirmed. A light rap on the door jolted me out of my thoughts.

"Yeah?" I bellowed.

The door cracked open, "Boss, I think I got you what the doctor ordered."

"Already?"

"She walked right in the door. I looked up and, well, she's perfect."

"This I got to see, Millie. Bring her in."

Millie shoved the door open and in stepped the pert blond from Ramon's.

"What are you doing here, cupcake?"

"You two know each other?" Millie eyed the short blond.

"Well, we met briefly over at Ramon's," I said.

"Oh," Millie turned to me, "Well, what do you think?" Millie grabbed the blond by the arm and spun her around giving me a whirlwind tour of her assets.

"I don't know Millie, I don't think…"

"What are you two talking about?" The girl caught herself on the door frame, looking a bit green from her spin.

"You said you were looking for work, Doll." Millie popped her ever-present piece of gum.

"I am but I'm a respectable kind of girl," she said.

"Oh, sure, Doll, aren't we all." Millie rolled her eyes at me.

"All right, I didn't catch your name, Sweetheart." I indicated the visitor's chair in front of my cramped desk, "Thank you, Millie. I'll conduct an interview."

Millie rolled her eyes even more dramatically and gave me one her rare double snaps on her gum, "Right, Boss."

After the door clicked shut the blond answered my question, "The name is Amy O'Malley."

"Amy, what kind of work were you hoping for? As you can see my office is fully staffed and we couldn't possibly fit another desk in here."

"Well, I was hoping I could do some freelance stuff."

"Freelance? Not sure I'm following you, Doll."

"It's Amy…I could you know, keep my ear to ground for you at the club and around town."

It was cute how her curls bounced around her head, but this dame was crazy if she thought I would pay her on the regular for information I could get for free.

"That's not really how things work."

"Oh, I could really use the money. Do you have anything? I can clean and file." She batted her big blues at me.

Crap…I'm a sucker for pretty face. "Ok, Doll, listen. I don't have any steady work for you, but…"

Amy clapped her hands.

"But," I continued holding up a finger to calm her down, "I have this onetime thing tonight and need a dame on my arm. I am doing some surveillance so you'll have to do exactly what I say when I say."

"I can do that."

"Good, Millie, will get you all set up. We are going to a Broadway Musical, so make sure you wear something nice, but not showy. We need to look like we belong, you know, blend into the crowd. Got it?"

"Sure, but I don't have anything like that in my wardrobe."

I came around the desk and opened the door. "Millie, put something nice on my credit down at Macy's. Now ladies, I do have some work to do. Be ready to go by six. We'll leave from here."

Through the shut door and sat at the desk. The dossier on Anton Tolland troubled me. Mr. X had done a lot of homework on this one. Usually the files were a few sheets with a couple of photos, but this one was full of photos, Tolland with dames, playing golf with notorious gangster types, dinner with a judge, and cards with the mayor. This photo time line was a new twist to X's usual intel. Each photo told a story in tableau. The key to Tolland's weakness were there in black and white. No matter where the man went he had a smoke in one hand and a scotch in the other. Mr. Tolland was a gambler. Now that was an obsession I understood.

God help me, but I'm so tired of owing my existence to another. Between the Chicago Outfit and Mr. X, I barely had room to breathe. I needed be my own man again. Some days I want to slip off to the track and burn though payroll. Only the thought of Millie destitute and her old man making mincemeat of me, made me turn right out my front door and not left and straight on to Atlantic City. But to get out of this mess I had to complete this last job, Tolland was the last name on the list.

I swept the photos into the top drawer along with the notes, and hit the street. The cool fall breeze tugged at my hat and whipped the lapels on my camel hair overcoat. I walked down the stoop steps, across the sidewalk, and beheld what was perhaps my only true love, my Atlanta Sports Tourer. I slid my hand along the fender caressing the steel warmed my cold heart. Hopping in and turning the key, the engine roaring to life, always made me feel like there was at least one thing right with the world. This was the one thing I wouldn't let my loan shark take. I may hate Mr. X but he paid the bills and kept the Tourer safe and sound.

● ● ●

Amy may have been a demure little cigarette girl in the club, but she knew a thing or two about the feminine arts. Millie had her outfitted in a swath of emerald green satin that left plenty to the imagination. What really captured my attention were the rocks around her neck, Mercy, if I had paid for that they had better be paste.

"Ladies," I said marching into the office. "What part of keeping a low profile didn't you both understand?"

Millie gave me that look that says she knew exactly what she was about and didn't give one hoot or a lick if anyone else cared or not.

"Millie?" I gave her my best Clark Gable stare down.

She cleared her throat, "Well, Boss, she had this fabulous necklace, so we worked around it."

"Yeah, speaking of that. Those rocks for real?"

"Of course!" Amy's pale complexion flushed at her neckline.

"Sorry, Doll, didn't mean to offend you, I just wanted to know what a girl like you was doing begging for work with rocks like that at home."

Amy's hand fluttered across her bosom drawing my eye. She stuttered, "I ah...I could never sell them; they're my grandmothers." As her flush began to glow in earnest under my inspection, Millie came to the rescue.

"Boss, you're going to be late if you don't get a move on."

"Speaking of being late, I got a last minute task for you." I stepped back in my office with Millie and shut the door. Holding my finger to my lips, I motioned Millie to sit down. I pulled two files out of my top desk drawer, and the newspaper from yesterday.

"Millie," I whispered. "I think that the guy we found on the last case turned up dead."

Millie gasped. "What?"

"Shhh. I want you to follow up on a hunch, but I think that all of the gentlemen in these cases may no longer be in as good a health as when we found them. I want you to do some check for me. If I'm wrong, then great, but if I'm right, then we have a serious problem."

Millie took the files from me. Her eyes were wide. "You think we might be helping someone find their hit list?"

I nodded. "Mum's the word to anyone but me, and I need the info as fast as you can. If we are right then the guy that I am looking for tonight may not have long on this side of the grass. I'll call you from the theater during Intermission."

"Right, Boss. Be careful."

I headed out the door finding Amy leaning against Millie's desk. I jammed my hat on my head and held the door for the still rosy Amy.

"Shall we?" I cocked an arm out for her to take. Her hand trembled as I tucked her in tight by my side. Almost made me feel like a cad, but if she was going out in public wearing that dress and an easy twenty-five grand about her neck, she would need to get used to the perusal.

We arrived at The Palace Theatre in time for cocktails. We each had a glass of Champagne as we made our way to the private box Mr. X had provided.

"This is fancy," Amy purred running her white opera gloved hand over the back of the burgundy velvet chairs.

I pointed out the second row of the box. "We want to sit where our faces will be in the shadow so we don't draw any unwanted attention."

"Mack, come sit with me." She patted the chair.

For a moment I wanted to give in, "Not right now. I'm here to work, Doll."

"I'm not your, doll, Mack." Amy put on a pretty pout.

I leaned in close, trapping her in the chair by placing my hands on either side of her lovely neck. I whispered in low growl in her ear, "No, not yet." I turned on my heel. I needed another drink. "Stay here, Sugar. I'll be right back." I called over my shoulder.

Finding an accommodating bartender I drained a double and surveyed the other attendees.

"You want another, Sir? We close the bar until Intermission."

"No, best not."

"Ah, the little woman will give you a hard time?"

"Something like that." I turned to go back to my seat.

"Hey, your name wouldn't happen to be Mr. Stevens?"

"And if it is?" I eyed the bartender whose name, Reggie, was embroidered on his shirt.

"So are you?" He eyed me back with that inscrutable look all really good bartenders learn.

Perhaps I should have had that other drink after all. "Yes. Stevens, Mack Stevens."

He reached under the bar, at that I slipped my right hand on to the Enfield in my pocket.

"I have this letter for you," he said pulling out an envelope.

Taking my hand off the revolver I said my thanks and walked to the grand staircase. Casually leaning against the banister I opened the missive under the light of the chandelier. Inside was a short note on Crane & Co.'s finest ecru stationery. It said, simply, *Lovelace is in private box #7, X.* I pocketed the note as the lights flicked off and on, indicating the start of the show. I hustled my way to the box.

● ● ●

By the end of the first act I had a bead on Tolland, and Veronica was on his arm. She was all trussed up in Paris's finest and had enough jewels on to outshine the Queen. It made you wonder who was really getting the raw end of the deal when she and Tolland would inevitably part ways. At least the jewels looked real. In the shadows of the second row were Tolland's muscle. Of course if my hunch was right, he was going to need them.

As the first act was well underway I leaned over to Amy, "I have a small task for you."

"Ok, what do you want me to do?"

"Don't point. You see the seventh box."

Amy peered out and counted the boxes under her breath, "Yeah, the one with that woman with half a diamond mine hanging around her neck?"

I chuckled, "That's kind of high and mighty of you," I looked down at her museum quality specimen hanging on her neck. "I want you to blow this whistle one time if you see anyone leave that box." I handed her a small gold whistle.

"But, Mack, won't they kick me out?"

"No. You are sitting where no one can see you. One quick burst if anyone leaves. Then put the whistle in your bag. Just act like everyone else. Like you don't have a clue who would be so crass."

"Fine, but I don't like it."

"You don't have to like it, that's what you're getting paid to do."

When I was almost at the doorway Amy turned around in her seat. "Mack, be careful."

I gave her a mock salute, "Always am, Doll."

● ● ●

The coat check for the private box holders was at the end of the hall on the left of the grand staircase. A sweet little chit with hair black as night was brushing the coats. I needed to get rid of her for a few minutes in order to search through Tolland's coat for clues.

"Hello, miss?"

"Yes, Sir, How can I help you?" She stepped back to the front of the booth.

"Reggie, the bartender said he needed your help, something about a lady in the front parlor being under the weather."

"Oh, my. Thank you." I continued on around the corner until I heard her heading down the stairs. She had locked the door behind her so I vaulted over the counter. The check on box seven's cubby said one mink stole and one black wool overcoat with white cashmere scarf and black leather gloves. As quick as I could I looked through the pockets. Nothing on the right, gloves on left. I heard someone running up the stairs, so I frisked the inner pocket and came away with a matchbook and scrap of paper. I jumped the counter and ran down the hall. Now how the Sam Hill was I supposed to get back to my box without passing by the coat check.

TWEET

I was caught between a rock and a hard place. Go forward and I might get made by either Veronica or Tolland. Go back and I might draw unnecessary attention to myself from the coat check girl and security. Decisions, decisions, back; the coat check girl would have to catch me first. I spun and headed back the way I came.

As I pass the coat check the girl nailed me with a hard stare, "Sir, you were mistaken. Reggie didn't need any help."

"Is that any way to speak to one of your betters?" Veronica's smooth voice iced down the raven haired girl.

"Sorry, Ma'am" The coat check girl ducked back into the booth.

"Mack, what kind of trouble are you causing now?" Veronica ran her gloved hand down my arm.

"It wasn't me. Some girl was upset in the women's parlor I guess they are trying to keep it hush-hush."

"Really?"

"She must be somebody of note."

"How delicious, a scandal at the theater!" Veronica twittered. "So what brings you to the finer end of town? You on the job?"

"No, just hanging on the arm of a socialite playing hooky from her set."

"Now, Mack, be careful that's a snake's game."

I grinned, "Well, I know when to hot foot it."

Veronica laughed devilishly and pulled a cig out of her handbag and tapped it into a long jade cigarette holder. "You got a light?"

I pulled the absconded matchbook out of my pocket, and lit a match. Veronica pulled a long slow drag.

"O'Rourke's?" She tapped the matchbook cover with a red nail. "I've wanted to go there since the grand opening last month, but my Anton says that it isn't the kind of place for a lady of distinction. Whatever that means," she chuckled.

I wondered what other secrets Tolland was keeping. "Well, it probably is better to let the crowds die back a bit. You know how crowded new clubs can get."

"True, well, see you around, Mack"

"Good night." I watched her sway back to her box, and then headed back to Amy.

Taking my seat I settled in to watch the last bit of the 2nd act. Amy turned on me. "Oh my goodness. I thought you might have got caught. Here I was all worried and you are perfectly fine. Oh my goodness!"

I patted her hand that clutched the arm of her seat. "Doll, everything is going according to plan. Just relax and you did great."

She huffed and looked like a deflated balloon. I raised an eyebrow at her, "What'd you expect gunfire and explosions? This is detective work. We like to keep things quiet and low key."

"It's just so…so understated."

"Seriously, that guns blazing, riot police stuff is just for those pulp rags you buy down at the drug store. If my life was like that I'd be gray haired and put in a home by now." I chuckled at her lack of enthusiasm for the job at hand.

She settled back in her seat and didn't say a word until Intermission. As the curtain settled she perked up, "So, Boss, what do you want me to do now?" Now she was interested in detective work.

"You saw that woman who was in box number seven, right?"

"The one in the slinky dress?"

"Yeah, the red one. She will most likely have a drink at the bar. I want you to chat her up. Nothing too particular, just keep her talking and at the bar. I have business with her old man."

"So one of those gentlemen in the box is who we are here for?"

"Exactly. Can you handle that, Doll?"

"If you stop calling me that." Amy flounced out of her seat toward the door.

"Amy."

She looked back over her shoulder at me. The way the low lights of the hall framed her silhouette in a halo it made her look like an angel from on high.

"Mack?"

I closed the distance between us, and she let go of the curtain. The darkness engulfed the box as I tipped her chin up and her lips met mine. I just wanted a little taste, but her body pressed into mine and lit a fire too hot to be caused by any angel. I pulled my scorched lips from hers and took a step back. A man could lose his soul in that dangerous territory. I swallowed hard. "That was for luck"

Her fingers were at her lips, "Luck?"

"Go on, time's wasting." I took her by the shoulders and turned her around, shepherding her out the door toward the bar, even though I was the one in need of a stiff drink.

"What are you going to do?"

"Oh, you know super-secret spy stuff." I laughed at her expense.

"Funny, Mack." She rolled her eyes heavenward.

"Fine. Detective stuff, you feel more informed now?"

She drew her pretty mouth into a frown and pouted her way down the staircase. Who knew maybe she might be useful to my operation after all. Turning toward the phone booth at the right of the grand staircase I squared my shoulders. Hopefully Millie would have the info I needed.

I dialed up the office and a man answered the phone. "Who the hell are you?" I asked.

"It's Mark. Listen here Stevens; I don't like my Millie mixed up in this kind of…"

Millie's voice cut him off, "Mark Jacob Winston! Give me that phone."

"Sorry Boss." Millie exhaled into the phone.

"Stevens, I'll have your ass if she gets hurt!" Millie's old man yelled at the receiver.

"Hush. Sit down." Millie wasn't having any of that.

"Millie, I take it the good news I wanted is more like bad news?"

"Yeah, Boss. Your hunch was right. I looked up news about those files. All of them, Boss, every single one died of natural or violent causes in the last year to six months. You know that mystery client could come after us if he figures out we are on to him."

"Give Mark that gun I keep in my top desk drawer. It's loaded so be careful. I have a bit more to do here. Just lock everything in my top drawer and go on home, and I want you take tomorrow off."

"What are you up to?"

"Nothing, I just think it would be a good idea for us to keep a low profile for a few days. If we draw attention to the office then our mystery client just might think we know more than we do."

"Night, Millie."

After she rang off I spotted Amy at the bar. She and Veronica were deep in discussion. I headed out to the glassed in balcony where traditionally the men smoked cigars and relaxed during the break. Tonight it looked like a small wager over cards was the going thing. I snagged a Cuban and a snifter of Hennessy. Tolland was playing five card stud. I took a club chair with a view of the table. From my angle it didn't take me long to see just how Tolland was so good in the cards. His index finger was set on the front of the card stack and with a quick practiced flick he was dealing the second card to his opponents and keeping the top card for himself. He must have marked some of the big cards, but all these silver-spoon-fed boys would never know they were being swindled by a master. I wondered if the mob types he was playing poker with in the dossier photos knew he was such a skilled cheat.

The lights flickered to announce the end of Intermission, which sprouted several grumbles from the men around the table. Tolland assured them that they could win their money back this weekend at O'Rourke's. So Tolland would be at the club this weekend without Veronica. Now it made one wonder just who he was seeing there or if it was just business.

After the final curtain call Amy and I made our way to the main lobby, trailing twenty feet or so behind Tolland and company. They stopped along the way to make conversation, but for the most part continued toward the exit and Tolland's waiting car. I practically dragged Amy to the car so we could follow them and almost lost them at the corner of Garfield and Michigan. We hung back and followed them through Hyde Park to a brownstone. It had three floors and an iron gate with wicked looking spikes. With all the lights on in the home it was like watching fish in a bowl. The fog obscured my car in the shadows and haze, but every movement in the house was clear as day.

Tolland and Veronica walked hand in hand up the staircase to the upper floor and disappear behind an oak door. One of the goons made a sandwich. His partner spread a newspaper on the Chippendale dining table and unloaded, cleaned and reloaded his hardware.

I took Amy back to her place once I was convinced that Tolland planned to stay. I dropped by my apartment changed into street clothes. By the time I made my way back to stakeout the brownstone a full moon was rising over Chicago and the fog rolling in from the harbor was like a thick suffocating blanket.

After a few hours of watching the brownstone, my toes were numb with cold and I wanted a cuppa Joe. Finally there was some activity beyond the goon sleeping off his sandwich and the gunman playing solitaire. Tolland and Veronica emerged from the second floor bedroom and the sandwich guy jumped up and brought the car around. Veronica kissed Tolland goodnight and Sandwich drove her home. That left Tolland and Gunman in the house. Tolland said a few words to Gunman and went to the third floor office.

I had Tolland dead to rights. The only problem was now that I knew where he was hiding. I would have to pass that information on to Mr. X. More than likely X wanted Tolland dead. I didn't want that on my conscience. On the other hand if I didn't tell X the debt I owed to The Chicago Outfit wouldn't be paid in full, and I would be the one sleeping with the fishes. There was only one solution. I would tell X, get the debt paid, and play guardian angel to Anton Tolland. Driving home the fog and moonlight cast a silver glow over the city and washing out colors, fading everything into shades of gray. Gray was a color I seemed to be having a lot in common with lately.

● ● ●

I was on my second Irish coffee of the morning when I called up X.

"So, Mr. Stevens have you found the man I am looking for?"

"I have."

"Good. Tell me and I will see that your debt to the Outfit is wiped clean."

"785 East Hyde Park Boulevard. It's a three story brownstone, with an iron gate."

"Very good, Stevens, this now ends our arrangement." The line went dead.

Ends our arrangement…our arrangement? What the hell did that mean?

Thirty minutes later Millie burst into my office without a knock. "Boss, Big John Tucker is here."

As the words left her mouth a huge looming shadow blocked the office doorway. "You, Mack Stevens?"

I swallowed hard and gripped the handle of the Enfield I had holstered to the desk. "What of it?"

"Are you or are you not." The deep baritone filled the space between us.

It seemed like the better part of valor to be direct at this juncture. "Yes."

The big man reached in his pocket and handed me a hand written receipt signed Al Capone. No numbers just the name.

"We good?" I asked.

"Yeah." He tipped his fedora to Millie, "Ma'am," and headed out the door.

When the door clicked shut Millie flung herself into my guest chair. "Oh my heavens, Mack, I thought he was here to kill us."

I handed her my coffee. "Drink a few sips of this. You look like you need it."

Millie choked down two sips. "Is there any coffee in this cup?"

"Oh, a splash or two." I laughed at her grimace.

"So now what Boss?"

"I have to protect Tolland."

"How are you going to do that without drawing attention to yourself? It's not like you can sit outside his house all hours of the day or night without someone noticing. What if our mystery client figures out that we know he's a killer?"

"I don't know. I need time to think."

"Well if the timeline of the other murders are any indication, you have less than three days. Otherwise Tolland will be singing with the choir."

Millie looked tired and scared.

"Here is what I want you to do." I said turning the dials of the safe. "I want you and Mark to take the kids to your mom's in Minneapolis." I pulled out a couple hundred dollars.

"I will clean up this mess."

"Mack, you want me to leave town?"

"You've been talking about seeing you mom and now you can. I don't need the money now that my debt is erased. So please go. If things here get dicey I don't want you or your family in the way."

"But, Mack, who will watch your back?"

"Don't worry."

After another round of please and go's I finally convinced Millie to head home and pack. Tolland didn't know it yet, but I was his very own ace in the hole.

● ● ●

O'Rourke's was not your typical nightclub destination. Located near the docks in a well maintained warehouse, the club occupied the top 3 stories. In the loading dock cars drove into the building to drop off passengers out of the public eye.

I pulled the Tourer up to the valet and paid through the nose for him to keep it near and ready to go.

The first floor loading dock had been transformed into a lobby where a bouncer was the first hurdle for access. With a flick of greenbacks in a well-timed handshake the bouncer let me up the staircase. Thankfully I remembered my receipt from The Chicago Outfit. I flashed Al's John Hancock to the second hurdle, a hostess with a sharp heart shaped face and a no nonsense twisted bun of pale blonde hair. Passing muster, she lifted the velvet ropes and I stepped into a gambler's paradise.

Every table held some game of chance or cards. The glint of the roulette wheel spinning reflected rainbows cast from the crystal chandelier overhead. I had to pull myself away. I had a murder to catch, and so far I hadn't seen Tolland. I knew he was somewhere in this building. His Nash Lafayette 400 was parked in the VIP section of the loading dock.

I made my way through the throng to the back bar where I could get the lay of the land.

"What'll be?" The gray haired barman asked.

"I take a double Jameson, no rocks."

The bite of the whiskey was soothing. Now I was fortified for whatever Mr. X had in store.

After one too many, I finally saw the break I needed. The north side of the building had a series of floor to ceiling windows with heavy red velvet drapes. The fourth one up the side had a small stand for the cigarette girls. Four hid a low key doorway to the ultra-private section.

I need to get into in there if I wanted to find Tolland before Mr. X made his move. This would be just the place to try an assassination. There were plenty of people to pin the murder on and there was no way any cops would be called. It was perfect.

I settled into a game of craps. The dice were medium rare. I was up and down and then back up again. After giving the house a decent cut of my cash I went over the cig stand.

"Can you get me pack of Lucky's, Doll?"

A bright red head said, "Sure, Mister. That'll be twenty cents."

When she bent over to grab a pack from the lower shelf I took the bowl of matchbooks and dumped them into my jacket pocket.

"Hey, Doll, you got any matches?"

"Right here...I'm sorry it looks like we are out." She frowned. "I'll be right back with some."

She took the bowl and went into the back by the bar leaving me alone. I slipped through the curtain and was brought up short by the biggest man I've ever seen.

"May I see your ticket, Sir?"

Ah Hell! I pulled out my Outfit receipt with Capone's signature and showed it to the bouncer.

"Very good, Sir, enjoy your evening."

In the center of the low lit room were clusters of club chairs in sets of four. Men I recognized only from the newspaper were dispersed in conversation. Most had a lovely lady or two draped provocatively on the rolled arms of the club chairs. With the scent of hand rolled stogies and whiskey in the air the place reeked of money and sin. I felt right at home. The back wall had three rooms set with high end poker tables and uninformed dealers. This must be the no limit games I had heard about at the track.

A gent in a butler's uniform approached me. "Welcome to Euphoria. Currently all the tables are full, but I can procure you a drink and put your name on the list. As members cash out a new member is selected to replace the player."

"First can you direct me to the restroom and second I'd like a glass of your best triple malt, sir." I said putting on my manners.

"I'll put your order in and the washroom is right down the hall first door on the right."

I entered the hall that ran along the back side of three private poker rooms. Behind each was a doorway that opened up into the hall. There were also three doors opposite. Up ahead I heard a familiar laugh, Veronica Lovelace. Perhaps she had talked her man in to bringing her here after all.

I crept toward the doorway. Veronica was in no laughing mood she was tearing into Tolland.

"Vee, baby it isn't what you think. This is just business!"

"Just business...just business!" Veronica yelled.

The doorway was cracked open enough I could get a glimpse. Vee's back was to the door and she blocked the view into the room.

"Just where do you think you are going?" Vee asked.

"Don't shoot Vee, I can explain. I swear," Tolland begged.

Veronica brandished a small silver derringer as she moved closer to her prey.

"Oh, I've heard these stories before, you two-timing rat!" There was murder in Veronica's eyes. "Tell me you're busy...that you can't see me tonight. Just so you can play with this little floozy!"

Now I could see Tolland on a loveseat next to Amy!

Amy? What the hell was going on here? Was this the new job she got, playing the harlot for the Outfit?

Tolland started gasping for air! Clutching his throat he began foaming at the mouth.

"Anton! Speak to me baby!" Veronica rushed to his side and threw her purse and the little gun on the coffee table.

Amy grabbed the gun and I rushed through the door, but she was too fast.

"Stay right where you are Mack!"

"Mack?" Veronica twisted around with Anton in her lap. "Mack, get help. Anton's been poisoned!"

Amy motioned me over to Vee with gun pointed at my heart. "No one is going anywhere and if you yell again I will kill you."

Backing up to the door, Amy used her foot to click it shut. "These rooms are soundproof. The men who come back here don't want anyone to know the vile, nasty things they do."

Anton gasped his last breath. Vee went into hysterics.

"Mack, pick up the body and sit him up on the couch."

"I'm not going to help you!"

"Yes you are or I'll kill Vee. Simple as that."

I did what she asked, and helped Vee stand up. "Now what, Amy?"

"Well I'm not taking the wrap for this." She pointed the gun at me.

Vee jumped Amy. They wrestled for control of the derringer. One shot fired, and then a second and they collapsed in a heap.

I pulled Vee out from underneath Amy. "Vee, please open your eyes!"

"Did we get her?"

I turned to Amy. She was bleeding out onto the carpet. I helped her raise her head.

"Why Amy?" I asked.

Through spurts of blood she said, "They killed my family. Experimented on them in the war. They had to die." She started to fade. "Mack, I'm so sorry," and she was gone.

I laid her head down on the floor and went to the door. I whistled loud, and the butler gent came running.

"How may I be of service, Sir?"

I opened so he could see.

"Not a problem, Sir. I'll handle it. This is a discrete establishment. The emergency exit is at the end of the hall."

● ● ●

The cops found all kinds of files on the dead men in Amy's flat. All of them were former Nazis hiding in the US of A under phony names. Apparently that misguided girl had been chasing them for several years to get her vengeance. Looking back on the case I had hoped to save Tolland, but in the end he got what he deserved.

The End

Challenge of the Lost World

by Percival Constantine

Elisa Hill opened her eyes and found herself staring out the window of the small plane, looking directly at the foliage-covered ground. They were suspended quite far off the ground, nose-first. She reached for the buckle on her seatbelt and used the seat to help her fight against gravity pulling her towards the plane's console.

It wasn't clear just how they were being suspended in the air, but if Elisa had to guess, she would say they'd crashed into a pretty strong tree. But the tree wasn't likely to support the plane's weight much longer and she had to step carefully so as to not trigger a fall.

She moved gingerly from her seat to the pilot next to her. He was slumped over and if not for his seatbelt, would be splayed out on the flight stick. Elisa approached him carefully, reaching a hand out to him.

"Smith? You okay?"

Smith didn't answer. Elisa gripped the back of his seat and pulled herself close enough so she could lay two fingers on the side of his neck. She couldn't feel a pulse and she sighed.

The plane started to move and she heard the sound of wood cracking. Her fears were confirmed, the tree wouldn't hold her much longer. Elisa braced herself against the seats to move from the cockpit and into the small cabin. Her backpack sat on one of the passenger seats and she picked it up. Slowly, she pulled the straps over her shoulders and fastened the belt around her waist. Elisa went to the door and the plane dipped. She grabbed onto the open doorframe, the plane now almost completely perpendicular to the ground. Elisa used both hands to pull herself out of the plane and onto the surface.

The cracking and snapping of wood was like an alarm bell for her. There was another branch that seemed to be within jumping distance. The massive branches that held the plane finally gave and the vehicle fell from its position.

Elisa jumped, reaching her hands out for the closest branch. Her right hand missed, but she caught on with her left. She dangled from there, hundreds of feet in the air and watched as the plane crashed beneath her.

With her right hand, she reached behind her back. Elisa gripped the gold-lined handle and drew the kukri dagger from its sheath. Pulling up with her left hand, she jammed the curved Nepalese dagger into the wood.

Once Elisa reached the branch, she gave herself just a minute to rest as she stared at the twisted wreckage of the plane. It was her way into this place and now she had to find some other way to get home. That was her first priority.

Elisa pulled the dagger from the tree and sheathed it while surveying the area. There was a cliff ledge not far from her and a line of trees she could follow to reach it. Elisa moved from one branch to the next, never staying on one for more than a few seconds before jumping to a new perch. She swung from a vine and released, falling until she landed in the soft grass on the cliff's ledge.

Now on solid ground, Elisa removed the backpack and set it on the ground, bending down over it. She dug through the supplies and until she found the satellite phone. Elisa quickly attempted to call, but all she got in response was static.

"Goddammit…" She looked at the phone and tried another number. Still nothing. One final attempt. She tried to call her mentor, Max Finch back in the States, but that also was met with nothing but static.

There was some sort of interference in the area. That could be what caused the plane's instruments to start going out of control and led to the crash. There was indeed something strange about this island and if Elisa was going to have any hope at getting out of here alive, her first course of action was to figure out just what this place was.

She turned off the phone and returned it to her pack, then geared up and began the hike down the cliff. As she walked, she thought back to how she'd gotten roped into this mission in the first place.

● ● ●

Elisa was led into a massive meeting room where a man in a suit stood facing the window, overlooking the city of Seattle. When he heard the door closed, he turned and smiled at Elisa, approaching her and offering his hand.

"Ms. Hill, thank you for accepting my invitation." He had short, silver hair and a mustache, as well as piercing blue eyes. "Philip Ryder, we spoke on the phone."

"Nice to meet you, Mr. Ryder." Elisa returned his handshake and her eyes fixed upon the large, gold ring on his finger. Engraved in it was the Masonic symbol of the square and compass with the letter G in the center. "Although I'm a little surprised. If the Freemasons wanted to get in touch with me, why not go through Shroud?"

Ryder released the handshake and gestured over to the board table and Elisa followed. Ryder sat at the head of the table and Elisa sat at the first chair to his right. He folded his hands and laid them on the table's surface, right beside a computer tablet.

"Jason Shroud's a little busy in Europe at the moment," said Ryder. "But we've discovered something that we feel is well within your purview."

"And what's that?"

Ryder picked up the tablet and turned it on. He laid it on the table and used his fingers to zoom in on a portion of the map in the Pacific. "Do you recognize that island?"

Elisa pulled the tablet closer to her and stared at the small island in the middle of the ocean. She couldn't quite tell its location, so she zoomed out on the map to see the surrounding area. But that didn't help and her brow furrowed in confusion.

"No, I don't."

"That's because it doesn't exist," said Ryder.

Elisa looked up from the tablet. "Excuse me?"

"The island you're looking at doesn't exist, Ms. Hill. It's not located on any map."

"Where'd this image come from?" she asked.

"A government satellite picked it up. As I'm sure you've guessed, we've got sources from within who were able to pass it on to us. But the question is what is this island doing there?"

Elisa shrugged. "Why come to me?"

Ryder sat back in his chair. "I know a lot of people within the myth hunter community were suspicious of your claims about Lemuria, those of us within the Freemasons aren't among them though."

"I appreciate that, but I don't see what Lemuria has to do with this. Lemuria's a continent. This island is maybe a tenth of its purported size."

"True, but from what Jason's told me of your experience, you entered Lemuria through a kind of dimensional gateway, correct?"

Elisa gave a nod.

"I wonder then if this is related to that gateway. Perhaps the island is somehow phasing between the different planes of reality, emerging into our own."

Elisa frowned. "Mr. Ryder, I'm not really one to call anyone else's theories crazy, especially after some of the stuff I've seen recently, but my gut tells me that's a little far-fetched."

Ryder tightened his lips. "Probably won't surprise you to learn you're not the first person who's said that to me. Although one thing's for certain, this island is there when it shouldn't be."

"What do you propose?" asked Elisa.

Ryder leaned forward and pointed at the screen. "I'd like you to investigate it for us. Discover just what this place is and see if you can get some clue as to why it's appeared out of nowhere."

Elisa looked at the map. She wasn't very comfortable working for the Freemasons without dealing with Jason Shroud. But at the same time, she had a natural curiosity. And since leaving her position at Burroughs University, she was getting a little antsy.

She smiled as she looked up at Ryder. "Shall we get down to business then?"

● ● ●

Once she reached the forest after descending the cliff, Elisa circled around and passed the wreckage of the plane. She pulled her compass from the backpack and examined it. The needle spun around and she sighed, closing the lid and sliding it back into her pocket. Whatever interfered with their instruments worked on her compass as well, it seemed.

She needed to get a lay of the land and figure out if there was some way she could make it off the island. Or at the very least find a spot where the interference was light enough so she could make a call.

Before any of that, the first priority was finding some food and a safe place to set up camp. Judging from the position of the sun, she only had a few more hours before dusk and Elisa didn't want to be caught out here without knowing just what she was up against.

Elisa walked carefully through the forest. She'd been in numerous jungles and forests all over the world, but the flora here was completely alien to her. It made her wonder just what sort of fauna she'd discover.

The myth hunter found herself wishing that she'd brought her partner, Asami, on this job. It was rare that Asami didn't accompany her on a job, but Elisa felt after what she went through in their hunt for the Necronomicon that she deserved a break. Plus, this seemed like a simple enough job.

She mentally kicked herself for that decision. The superhuman senses Asami possessed as a result of being a fox changeling would have definitely come in handy out here. Of course, she also would have complained endlessly about being led into another life-or-death scenario, so Elisa figured it wasn't a total loss.

Elisa could hear rustling in the distance. Just past the forest was a clearing. She moved towards the edge of the forest and quickly ascended one of the trees so she could have a better vantage point. It also had the benefit of keeping her hidden in case the animal was something too dangerous for her to take on, or provide her ample opportunity to strike without warning.

The animal's footfalls were heavy, but the leaves obscured most of her view. The only thing she could make out was a shadow cast across the plain. It was fairly large, whatever it was. The shape reminded her of a rhino, which was bizarre enough. She saw the shadow of one of the horns on the grass and figured that's what it had to be.

Then the creature came into view and Elisa had to clasp a hand over her mouth to prevent an audible gasp from escaping. The creature had an earth-tone body and certainly bore a resemblance to a rhino. But its head consisted of a beak-like mouth, a bony frill near its neck, with two long horns protruding from its brow and a smaller one perched on its elongated snout. Despite sharing many similarities with the rhino, the creature was certainly a reptile.

Elisa pulled her hand away from her mouth, though her crystal-blue eyes were still wide with shock. She didn't think it was possible but what she was looking at was none other than a triceratops. An actual living, breathing dinosaur was on this mysterious island.

The triceratops moved across the plain, turning its head from side to side to scan the area. It moved closer to the forest and began to tear off leaves from one of the smaller plants within reach. Elisa just stared at it in a transfixed state.

Once she recovered from the initial shock, Elisa reached carefully for the digital camera in her backpack. She held it up and lined up the triceratops in view, recording it as a movie. As she stood mesmerized, recording every movement of this long-thought extinct creature, she almost didn't notice the slight tremor.

But she certainly heard the roar that accompanied it.

The triceratops did as well and turned as fast as it could to view the source of the danger. Elisa followed its movements, recording off in the distance as she witnessed a larger shadow descend on the plain.

With each step, this predator took, the ground quaked. Elisa remained frozen in the tree, but didn't stop recording. The triceratops, for its part, tried to run off. But as it was in escape mode, the great beast descended upon it.

Elisa watched as the tyrannosaurus came at the triceratops, its huge jaw biting into the triceratops's back. The smaller creature yelped in pain and the tyrannosaurus went to work on it, quickly devouring its prey.

All Elisa could do was sit there transfixed. She watched as the tyrannosaurus finished off the beast and then let out a roar of satisfaction, shouting towards the heavens. It turned its head, its yellow, lizard-like eyes staring right in Elisa's direction.

Popular culture said the tyrannosaurus had vision based on movement, but in reality the dinosaur's vision was far greater than that of a hawk. It wasn't hard for it to spot Elisa in the tree, nor the blinking red light on the front of her camera.

The tyrannosaurus charged towards her. Elisa stuffed the camera into her pack and turned her back to the beast, jumping from one tree limb to the next. She kept moving, jumping from tree to tree as fast as she could manage.

She chanced a glance over her shoulder and saw the tyrannosaurus charging into the forest, knocking the trees over. Elisa looked forward again and continued her ascent. She tried to move further up the trees, hoping she could reach the cliff near the plane's wreckage, but she'd already passed the plane and the tyrannosaurus had already destroyed most of the forest in its pursuit of her. More than that, doubling back seemed like suicide to her.

Elisa was quickly running out of trees. The forest ended at the mouth of the valley and she jumped off the branch, landing in a crouch on her hiking boots. The sound of trees being knocked down was still behind her and so she ran at breakneck speed, pumping her legs as hard as she could.

While looking over her shoulder to see how close the tyrannosaurus was, Elisa's leg caught on a fallen branch and she tripped. She landed on her face and flipped over just as the tyrannosaurus slowed down on its approach. It roared at her and Elisa instinctively unsheathed her twin kukri. It was highly unlikely she could defeat a tyrannosaurus armed only with these, but if she was going to go down, she was determined to do it fighting.

Something flew from above the tyrannosaurus. Like a shooting flame. It struck a nearby brush and it erupted into flames. That drew both the attention of Elisa and the tyrannosaurus. While the creature turned to investigate, another ball of fire shot from the sky and this caused the tyrannosaurus to move back in surprise.

Another flaming projectile and Elisa could see it was an arrow. This one struck the tyrannosaurus' tail. That sent the creature into a panic and it charged off, waving its tail frantically to extinguish the fire, having fortunately forgotten all about its prey.

Elisa breathed a sigh of relief, then her natural curiosity re-asserted itself and she wondered just who fired those arrows. She wondered if there was someone besides the Freemasons who knew about this island, or maybe they managed to send a rescue party when Elisa didn't report in?

"That was a close one."

Elisa turned at the sound of the deep, baritone voice. She was shocked to see a man standing there, leaning against a long, makeshift bow. His clothing was made of dinosaur hide and he had a long, straggly beard and hair that were both a deep, black shade. His chest, visible from the top of the vest he wore, also had curly hair that matched the color of his whiskers.

"You're lucky I happened along, my dear."

Despite the man's ragged appearance, he spoke with the tone of an educated man and possessed an English accent. He even offered his hand to help Elisa to her feet. She accepted it, but still stared at him like he was even stranger than the tyrannosaurus that nearly killed her.

"Who are you?" she asked.

"Pardon me, where are my manners?" He offered a burly hand to her. "Professor George Edward Challenger at your service."

● ● ●

Elisa's mind was still whirling with all the new information that had been thrown at her feet. First, was the revelation that dinosaurs still walk the earth on this mysterious island and then the appearance of a man claiming to be Professor Challenger. The same man who now led her into a cave that he'd set up as his own home.

She was amazed at how lived-in the place was. Hand-made furniture sat out with rugs and covers crafted from animal skins. Hunting weapons were mounted on the walls and makeshift lanterns hung from the ceiling. Challenger lit each of them and motioned to a chair for Elisa to sit in. He took his seat in a larger chair beside her and settled his massive frame into it, the wood creaking with every movement.

"Now miss, tell me who you are and what you are doing in the Lost World," he said.

"My name's Elisa Hill. I came here…" Elisa paused for a moment before speaking, running the words he spoke across her mind. "Wait, did you say this is the Lost World?"

Challenger rolled his eyes. "My first companion in years and she's a dullard?"

Elisa frowned. "Hey look, this is a lot to take in. Forgive me if I'm a little shaken, but the Lost World is widely regarded as a hoax."

"Yes, I remember the response. At first celebratory and then later the intellectual gnats decided to discredit the work performed by myself and my compatriots. It's why I returned, to prove definitively once and for all that the Lost World exists."

"Right, that was in 1930. And you never returned."

"Obviously."

"So how come you don't look a day older than when you left?" asked Elisa. "You've been missing for over eighty years."

She'd expected more of a reaction from him at that news. Instead, Challenger

just reached for the small table beside his chair and picked up a wooden pipe. He stood and walked over to a far wall with a table in front of it and, taking a small stick, lit the tip in the lantern's flame. He used that flaming stick to light his pipe and returned to the chair, puffing on one end.

"Did you hear me?"

"I'd suspected a great deal of time had passed," said Challenger. "I stopped keeping track of the days around the end of my first decade here. It all feels like something of a dim memory now."

"So how are you still alive and young?" asked Elisa. "And if this is the Lost World, then why is it on an island? I was always told that it was a plateau in South America."

"The Lost World is not a fixed location, Miss Hill. I have seen it flicker between many different surroundings in my time here. Whatever strange science is responsible for that may also be the reason why I haven't aged a day in over eighty years."

"Ryder was right, this island moves in and out of sync with our dimension," said Elisa.

"Pardon?"

"Forget it," said Elisa. "So tell me, why are you still here after all this time?"

"After the last of my party perished, I thought I'd try to find some way to return home. Unfortunately, there was no way off the island. I became trapped out here. You are the first person from the outside world who has set foot on this island since my party and I arrived."

"That means this island has been out of sync with reality for decades," said Elisa. "Maybe it's based on some kind of cycle. If that's the case, we may have time to get off before it phases out again."

Challenger chortled. "You truly know nothing of this place."

Elisa leaned back in her chair, crossing her legs and arms. "So tell me what I'm forgetting."

"The ape-men," he said. "If you wish to reach the coast, you must first cross their territory. But doing so would be suicide. They would find you and kill you."

"Then we go another way. This *is* an island after all, isn't it?"

"Of course, if you'd like to contend with that tyrannosaurus once again. Or any other number of predators." Challenger took a few puffs on his pipe. "It all comes down to which you'd prefer, being eaten or trampled, or simply murdered with a spear. And of course, once you reach the coast, you have another issue; how will you cross the ocean?"

"And what's your brilliant plan to get out of here?" asked Elisa.

"Quite simple, I have none," said Challenger. "I plan to remain here."

"What?" Elisa's eyes widened at the statement.

"You yourself said that over eighty years have passed. I would be a man completely out of time, even more lost in that world than on this island. Here, I know my place. I know what I am to do."

"Fine," said Elisa, rising up. "Then will you help me get out of here?"

● ● ●

It was before dawn when Elisa found herself hiking up the mountain-ridge that separated the ape-men's land from the rest of the dinosaurs. As she did, she muttered curses under her breath about Challenger, who had refused to raise a hand to help her more than he already had.

Once she reached the summit, she set her pack down on the ground and opened it, pulling out a pair of binoculars. Holding these up to her eyes, Elisa scanned the area. She looked back from where she came and saw the tyrannosaurus still out there searching for food. Elisa turned the binoculars to the other side of the mountain.

Down below was the land of the ape-men. It was far more advanced than she'd imagined. Still rudimentary, but it seemed like they'd built a small city of sorts. They appeared more evolved than the accounts given in Challenger's famous expedition to this land. There were some triceratopses among the town with saddles affixed to them. Apparently the ape-men had managed to domesticate some of the animals.

But no boats. In fact, the settlement seemed to end quite a bit before the coast. Almost as if they feared the water. Elisa assumed that had something to do with the island originally being located on a plateau. That water represented the edge of oblivion for them. But the borders extended to the base of the mountain. She would have no choice but to cross into it.

Elisa lowered the binoculars and knelt down beside her pack. She placed them back inside and spotted the satellite phone. Drawing that out next, Elisa turned it up, attempting once again to call Ryder.

"Elisa?"

She laughed with relief when she heard the Freemason's voice on the other end of the line. "Oh my god, it worked! Must have managed to find a spot unaffected."

"What happened?" asked Ryder. "We lost track of the plane before it even reached the island."

"There's some kind of interference out here, it screwed up our instruments and brought down the plane."

"Did you find it?"

"Yeah, and a lot more besides. Ryder, this island is the Lost World. Professor Challenger himself is here, too."

Ryder was speechless at the mention of Challenger's name. Elisa called out to him again to make sure the line didn't go dead.

"Yeah, I'm still here," he said. "Oh my god, you mean *the* Professor Challenger? How's that possible?"

"It's a long story. I've got some documentation, but I need to get out of here and quickly."

"I'll get a plane out there right…"

"No! If that interference is still there, it might bring it down just like it did to ours. You know where you lost contact with the plane, right?"

"Yeah, we have the coordinates right here."

"Good, get a boat out to that area and start patrolling. I'll come to you."

"But Elisa, that's at least a good five-mile swim from the island."

"It's also the only option," said Elisa. "Just do your part, and I'll do mine."

She heard footsteps and looked to the side to see ape-men approaching. Thick, reddish hair covered their entire bodies and they wore animal skins similar to the ones worn by Challenger. There were three of them, each holding spears with stone heads. They barked at her in some unfamiliar language.

"I'm gonna have to run, Ryder. I've got some gentlemen callers."

"What? Elisa, are you okay?"

"Do what I said and I'll take care of myself." Elisa turned off the phone and as the lead ape-man barked, she held her arms out to the side. He gestured at the phone and Elisa held it out to him.

The ape-man approached slowly, looking at his men. They seemed just as perplexed. He came closer and reached one careful hand out. He growled at Elisa right before he grabbed the phone from her and quickly backed off.

The three inspected the strange device, pushing buttons and growling and screeching when they found the power switch and saw the display light up. Immediately they dropped the phone and backed away from it, aiming their spears at the mysterious, oddly-shaped box.

While they were distracted, Elisa drew the kukri from their sheaths, held them in reverse-grips, and pounced. She crossed her arms in front of her head just as she approached the first of the ape-men, cutting into his throat.

She saw another ape-man rushing her. Elisa bent backwards, the spear passing over her body. She snapped back to attention and spun to the side to avoid another attempted stab. Elisa charged in when she saw an opening, dragging the kukri across his belly, disemboweling him.

The third and final ape-man roared in anger at her, a bellowing cry that pulled his lips back and bared large fangs. He charged at her with the spear. Elisa jumped over his head and hurled a kukri into his back.

He lurched from the impact and collapsed on the ground. Elisa approached him and pulled her weapon from his back. She wiped the blood off both kukri and sheathed them. Elisa took the binoculars out again and inspected the town below and the coast. Taking careful stock of the situation, she started to make a plan. If she used the homes for cover and moved along the outer edge of the settlement, she should be able to reach the coast without too much trouble. From there, it was just the simple matter of a five-mile swim and then treading water until Ryder's boat finally managed to find her, and who knew how long that would be?

The only thing to do at the moment was to wait, at least a few hours. Get something to eat, maybe. Give Ryder time to get his people out here. Although she would feel a lot better if she had the time and the resources to assemble a raft of some sort.

● ● ●

After some lunch, Elisa checked in with Ryder once more. The ship would be in position soon, which meant it was time for her to move. She donned her pack and began the trek down the mountain. The ape-men had left tracks on their way up and she followed those, moving down a well-worn path. This must have been how they typically moved across the mountain to venture into the more dangerous realms for hunting.

The village was even larger up close than it seemed from above. Elisa reached it after about an hour of walking. She used the brush for cover and moved closer, staying low to the ground. She'd watched from the mountain as most of the men went out to hunt, mounted on the saddled triceratops she'd seen. That meant only women, children, and the elderly were left in the settlement. Even with the hunters gone, Elisa knew that those left behind were still part-ape and strong enough to tear her apart with their bare hands.

Elisa moved carefully to the first house, officially crossing over into the ape-men's territory. She stayed low, creeping along the edge of the stone structure and peered around the edge. The path was clear and she moved swiftly across to the next house and regained her cover. As she moved along this place, she didn't notice until too late the ape-child in one of the trees staring right down at her.

Her blood froze and she locked eyes with him. The child tilted his head to the side, watching her with curiosity. Then he heard another voice and looked to it. He responded in their language and pointed.

Elisa readied her kukri and the ape-child's mother stepped up to the tree and followed her son's finger to see what he pointed at. As soon as she saw Elisa, she cried out with a loud, booming voice.

The myth hunter moved away from the house, not wanting to hurt any more of these creatures if she could help it. They were just defending their home after all. But they quickly gathered, pouring out of their homes and staring at the interloper.

"Dammit," she muttered. "I don't suppose any of you could spare a raft, huh?"

They bared their fangs and snarled at her. But then another noise came, a loud roar. Elisa looked up as did the creatures to see a tyrannosaurus rampaging into the settlement. The ape-women turned their attentions to the immediate threat as the tyrannosaurus came charging into their village, swinging its tail and attacking the inhabitants.

Elisa for her part took cover behind one of the houses. She waited there, listening to the screams as the tyrannosaurus did its work. She felt a hand on her shoulder and instantly spun, holding up her dagger. Professor Challenger stood there, calmly holding up his hand.

"Come, we have to move now!"

"But these people!"

"Miss, if you care to join them within that monster's belly, then be my guest," said Challenger. "Otherwise we must move, now!"

Elisa took one last look at the T-Rex but then followed Challenger's lead. He charged alongside the outer edge of the village and Elisa was right behind him. It wasn't long until they finally reached the coastline and Challenger turned one final time to look upon the village.

"It's done," he said. "This is as far as I go."

"Why did you come back?" she asked.

"Perhaps because I have something of a soft spot for lost causes," said Challenger.

"And the tyrannosaurus?"

"I led it into the village. Knew it would be the only way to cause enough of a distraction."

Elisa's open palm connected with the side of the old professor's face. The slap was so hard, the sound echoed slightly in the air and threw Challenger's massive head to turn. He rubbed the red spot beneath his thick beard and looked at her in surprise.

"Those people did nothing to anyone," she said.

"They are savages, Miss Hill. It was either them or us and that is the reality of life on this accursed island."

Elisa fixed her eyes on his. She wanted to hit him again, or maybe stab him, but she thought against it. Being trapped in this place seemed like a suitable enough punishment for him. "Just get out of my sight," she said.

Challenger gave a simple nod, "As you wish." He turned and returned the way he came. Elisa wasn't sure if the tyrannosaurus would still be there when he had to cross the ape-men's village. Part of her hoped it was and that Challenger would meet the same fate he delivered onto the women and children of the village.

Elisa took the pack off and moved into the water, holding it out in front of her and using it as a make-shift flotation device. She swam out, away from the coast of the Lost World. It was a place of savage beasts and Challenger had become just like those he'd lived amongst for the better part of the century.

The End

Fire & Blood of Innocents

By Dale Cozort

Two bullets left. One for me if it comes to that, which it probably will. They're all around me. No place to run. No place to hide.

They call this The Sanctuary, but it's overrun by wolves, both the human and animal kinds, if the manikula are really animals.

The human wolf: Josh Rocheforte. He runs things here, snaps his fingers and people die. And I invaded his private world with just a pistol and my wits.

Wits. I wouldn't be here if I had any.

Oh I can escape. All I need to get back to the real world is fire and the blood of an innocent. But if I go, the wolves will follow me.

● ● ●

My path to The Sanctuary started when these United States, in their wisdom, voted in prohibition, not long after I got back from the Great War.

I drifted through jobless, hungry times, then traded an old shotgun for moonshine, and sold the 'shine for more money than I made honestly that month. Those sales led to others and in two years I was head of the Black Gang, named after me, Roy Black. Ironically, Mom was in the Christian Temperance League, the one adult in Boone's Crossing who didn't know I was a moonshiner.

Boone's Crossing was moonshiner territory, surrounded by hills too steep for crops or cattle. Walnut Bluff towered over town, letting us track Sheriff Silver. He was a former classmate of mine, honest, but uninterested in moonshiners.

My bootlegging life started downhill when Josh Rocheforte returned to Boone's Crossing in September1926.

That fall and winter, nothing seemed to change, but hidden forces ate at my world, like a river undermining its bank, getting it ready to collapse.

I saw hints of those forces. In the fall, three heavily loaded trucks rumbled up a rutted logging road to the Rocheforte place. Nobody saw them leave. Then, four months later, in early spring, dozens of trucks, none of them the same make as the first three, rushed down that road.

The Great War taught me that curiosity gets you killed, but not knowing what the enemy is doing is more dangerous. Not knowing what Josh Rocheforte was up to worried me, but it would take days to search his place on foot, the only way to search it, so I spent more time than usual on Walnut Bluff, watching his place.

I loved sitting on Walnut Bluff with my binoculars and a Great War surplus bolt-action rifle, watching ant-sized people and horsefly-sized cars below me.

The mystery of Rocheforte's trucks kept me watching. We thought Rocheforte was moonshining, and looked for a still but didn't find one.

He was doing something illegal. I knew that because I knew Josh. We grew up together. Girls thought he was handsome. I didn't see it, but he *was* smart, evil too, poison mean, a bully and manipulator. I stayed away from him, but watched him like I would watch a wolf lurking outside the fence.

Josh graduated and left Boone's Crossing. I figured the city got him and they deserved each other. Then he came back to the Rochefort farm shortly after his dad died. His sister cared for the old man when he got sick, but left when Josh came back.

People grow up around Boone's Crossing, then they either stay or leave for the city. If they don't come back in six months, they never come back. City life grabs them like a drug and they need the lights, noise and people.

But Rocheforte came back eight years after he left. I knew he was up to something far worse than schoolboy bullying.

● ● ●

April on Walnut Bluff brought long sunlit days, budding leaves and animals stirring from winter hideouts. It also brought the manikula. They were three gray dots when I spotted them, moving through the forest like the wolves I saw in a zoo on my way to France.

Wolves in southeastern Illinois seemed unlikely, though wolves are great wanderers. Seen through my binoculars, the animals had fur and muzzles like wolves, but other features matched no animal I had heard of. No wolf had that forehead and no wolf switched easily from four feet to two like these creatures.

They abruptly disappeared into a gully that led to the side of Rocheforte's place nearest the bluff.

I waited for them to reemerge, wondering what they were. Curiosity pushed me to climb down to the gully, maybe a quarter mile from where the animals disappeared.

I kept a lookout for Rocheforte. He showed up in town alone to buy supplies at irregular intervals, but we never saw anyone on the place. Yet three trucks had come and more departed. There could be dozens of men up here.

I trudged down the gully. A creek usually ran here during the spring thaw, but surprisingly it was dry.

Birds took panicked flight from the trees in front of me. So the mystery animals were close. I climbed out of the gully. Where were they? I dodged behind a tree when a gray shape bounded over the lip of the gully.

When I peeked around the tree, the animals had gathered around a bare spot where the soil had subsided in a twenty-foot circle, standing comfortably on their short hind legs, as tall as a big man, then two dropped to all fours, where they seemed equally comfortable. Two dug in the soft dirt, while the third studied the forest and sniffed the breeze. Its eyes suddenly focused on my head and it uttered a weird growl/hoot. I wanted to yank my head back, but I kept it motionless, inching my rifle up.

The animals spread out like human hunters, pinning me against the gully's side. I fired at the closest one, but it moved between my trigger pull and the muzzle flash. Then the clearing was empty. I chambered another round, the motion practiced, but shaky.

An explosion like an artillery shell sounded in the distance. I tried to ignore the echoes, listening for the animals and wishing for a revolver. The animals could all attack at once, from short range, too fast to work the bolt action.

The echoes subsided. In the silence, I felt the ground shake. I thought my legs were trembling, but then a wall of water swept down the gully, overflowing its bank. I took two steps, then water slammed into me like a truck. I glimpsed one of the strange gray animals in the flood, legs thrashing.

A branch gouged for my eyes before raking across my forehead. The flood tossed more debris at me. I curled into a ball, helpless in the current. I fought to keep from breathing dirty water until my lungs ached, but finally the water slowed and my head broke the surface. I gulped in air and found myself floating through Boone's Crossing's elementary school playground, within arm's reach of a swing set. A teacher clung to a swing, looking horrified.

I stood up in waist-high water and said, "I'm okay." I felt relieved for a second, then I saw the bodies.

● ● ●

My body screamed pain at me. I kept finding new injuries, ranging from scratches and developing bruises to a deep gash across my forehead. I made it out of the flood without major injuries, though I felt like I had been in the grandfather of all drunken brawls. I pushed the pain aside and concentrated on getting bodies out of the water. They were all young women, ice cold and dead. I carried seven to the dry ground by the school, but there were more.

I turned and saw Sheriff Silver standing behind me. I remembered him as a short grammar school kid, eager to hang around with the big kids and grateful when my friends and I tolerated him. Now he looked every inch a sheriff: tall, broad shoulders, clean shaven, in his mid-twenties, two years younger than me.

"What did you do?" he asked.

I spotted one of the mystery animals washed up among the debris. "What did it do?" I pointed to the beast.

The sheriff pushed it onto its back with his foot. "What is it?"

The creature looked dangerous even in death, though not as dangerous as the three looked when they stalked me.

"Teeth that would make a grizzly jealous and a forehead that would make a gorilla jealous," the sheriff said. "What did you get us into to?"

"Why was there a flood?"

"Old Evan Berry's son blew a beaver dam. You washed out with the dam and some things that need explaining."

"I didn't kill it, whatever it is."

"What about the girls?"

I told the sheriff about the clearing where the ground had sunk, along with what I knew about the creatures. He looked grim when I mentioned three of the animals.

"You have a problem," he said. "A bootlegger, washed out in the same flood with ten bodies. Girls, young ones...ten to fifteen years old, probably buried late last year so they stayed cold most of the time. That's why I can still tell they had the blood drained out of them."

"No blood? People will talk nonsense," I said. "Vampires. If anyone around Boone's Crossing is a vampire, it's Josh Rocheforte."

"Well there you go," the sheriff said. "I'll dunk him in holy water or whatever kills vampires." His face got grim. "They all have burn marks and parts of the skeletons were cut off cleaner than autopsy guys could cut them."

That added yet another mystery to a long list. Animals from a nightmare. Blood, fire and girls with missing body parts.

Josh Rocheforte had to be behind this, I thought, but why would he drag girls here to kill them?

I told the sheriff about the mystery trucks. I wouldn't normally share so much with the law, but this needed to get solved fast.

"The beast is an ape," the sheriff said. "But no ape we've ever caught. I need to find these critters, and that will take a man who knows those hills the way only you do. Take me where you saw them."

Josh Rocheforte strolled up as the sheriff said that. He still had the thick, wavy blond hair the girls made such a big deal over, the big sincere-looking smile and broad shoulders that didn't look like he got them by hard physical labor the way most men around Boone's Crossing got broad shoulders. His waist was thin. It emphasized his shoulders but made him look like a wasp. A stinging insect. That fit him.

He turned to the sheriff. "What's going on here?"

The sheriff gestured at the dead girls. "Washed out of a grave, probably from your place."

Rocheforte's expression didn't change, but then he caught sight of the mystery animal and his face seemed to freeze. "What is that thing doing here?"

"You know what it is?" The sheriff asked.

Rocheforte didn't respond immediately, but finally said, "It's a world of hurt come to this little town."

I felt the slow, gentle rhythm of Boone's Crossing, a rhythm with time to chat with neighbors and linger over a meal. Why was this man here? He almost vibrated with impatient energy.

"Three things don't fit here," I said. "Murdered girls, an animal out of nightmares and you."

"You think you fit here?" Josh asked. "You went to France in the Great War, got a metal or three."

"Uncle Sam borrowed me. I always belonged here."

Rocheforte walked away without saying anything more, a cold man, formidable. He had been prepared for the girl's bodies, but the dead beast had shaken him.

What would Rochefort gain from ten dead girls? Contract killings? That seemed unlikely. Why would he mutilate the bodies and hide them here? Was he a vampire? Vampires were legends, not a reality of rural America. Then again, werewolves were legends too, and the coroner was about to autopsy one.

"You know the hills better than anyone else," the sheriff said. "And you know about the other two creatures. What people know will get them stirred up bad enough. If they know two of those things are still out there, things will get out of control ugly."

"Any idea where the girls came from?" I asked.

"I know they're city folk from their clothes and their hands. No calluses. Only city people have hands like that."

How did they get here? Why was their blood drained? What did fire have to do with their deaths? Why the strange amputations?

An ancient man in bib overalls and a white shirt with a deputy's badge pinned to it walked up after Rocheforte left.

"I saw young Rocheforte strut away," the old man said. "Bad seed there. He has river pirates in his family, going back to frontier days."

The old man eased himself down to look at the animal in slow, painful-looking stages. "Rochefortes are an old family in these parts. Rivers were how the settlers moved big stuff before the railroads and pirates squatted on the banks grabbing what they wanted."

I almost asked if he was old enough to remember those days. Actually, the old man's grandfather could have told him about the pirates. There were still living links to those times a hundred years ago.

River pirates were history though, and their presence in Josh Rocheforte's ancestry seemed to matter no more than me having horse thieves in mine.

Why would anyone bring girls here and kill them? Actually, I wasn't sure they had been killed near Boone's Crossing. Carting mutilated bodies around seemed risky, but bringing them here alive posed its own risks. What if one escaped on the way?

"If that Evans kid got rid of those beavers before the water built up we would have been better off," the old man said.

I couldn't say as he was wrong. None of the victims was local. No one around Boone's Crossing was affected until the bodies were uncovered. That sounds callous, but we care about those we know and reserve only token pity for the deaths of strangers.

Three heavily loaded trucks went to the Rocheforte place around the time of the murders and disappeared so even I couldn't find them. The girls would have fit easily in one of those trucks. If they came in on the trucks, what else came with them?

With enough time I might find out, but I didn't have time. I felt the same way I felt when I saw the flood racing toward me, knowing what was about to hit me but with no time to stop it. What could I do before a flood of reporters and camera bulbs and state police hit me?

"I can figure out where the other two animals ended up," I said. "We can track them from there." But would that solve the mystery of the dead girls? Were the animals even related to the girls? They seemed to have been discovering the mass grave when they spotted me. Two strange, unrelated events so close to the same time and place seemed unlikely, but what could the animals have to do with the girls? The animals' jaws were powerful enough to tear off limbs, but the wounds wouldn't have been clean.

"The state police are going to come to my town strutting like they're better than us," the sheriff said. "They'll pretend to investigate, then grab you and strut back out of town, acting like they did us yokels a favor. Then when they leave, I'll still have a murderer in my town and monsters from a bad movie lurking in the woods, with the trail trampled by idiot reporters and idiots with state police badges. We need to find those animals and solve this."

I hesitated, knowing something of the animals we would be tracking. Even the bravest man wouldn't hunt them without fear. But still, I followed the sheriff through Boone's Crossing's quiet streets, to the sheriff's car, with the spring sun warming us, with me knowing this might be the last time I walked those streets as a free man.

● ● ●

I lost my rifle in the flood, but a battered long-barreled forty-five revolver in a western-style holster and a box of ammunition appeared on the seat of the sheriff's car beside me. I touched it tentatively, then buckled it on when the sheriff didn't comment. It felt solid, reassuring, but I still felt fear lurking. I proved my courage against machine guns, gas and artillery in France, but these animals struck fear in me.

We drove as far as we could, then hiked to where the flood had washed out the bodies. The flood had receded, leaving only a trickle in the gully and debris on the banks, with mud seven feet high on the trees.

The sheriff let me take the lead. The flood had wiped out the animals' footprints, so I tried to see the forest as they saw it and guess where they would have gone.

As I studied the water's path I realized the animals would have been carried to the same place I had if it caught them. Could they have climbed trees fast enough to escape? Maybe, if they saw the water soon enough. I spotted tracks that looked like handprints, complete with short fingers and thumbs. Blood droplets along a set of tracks showed that one animal was injured.

The early afternoon sun filtered between the branches, warming my battered muscles. I pushed scrapes and strained muscles out of my mind. None of that could matter now.

The trail got harder to follow because the beasts seemed as at home on the ground or in trees, but the blood kept us on the trail, getting fresher with each step. We found marks where the wounded creature dragged its hindquarters, apparently getting weaker.

Then one of the creatures was on me, bowling me against the sheriff. It grabbed the sheriff's arm in its jaws and slung him into a tree ten feet away.

I grabbed the revolver and fired, spraying bark over the creature. It flinched and disappeared into the forest.

I ran to Sheriff Silver. He was breathing but unconscious. I couldn't leave him, but I couldn't let the creatures get away. I lifted the sheriff over my shoulder, and staggered on.

Apparently the unwounded animal had circled back to attack us, desperate to protect its companion. I thought about the beast's strength, and speed. If it attacked again, I had to kill it, but more bodies would tell us little.

I kept on the trail, desperate, battered, with the unconscious sheriff on my shoulder, with no plan. Then I stumbled into a clearing, not forty feet from the animals.

● ● ●

Smoke rose in front of the beasts. No animal could make fire, yet these beasts had. Part of me wasn't surprised. The way they stalked me before the flood was unlike an animal, no matter how crafty.

The wounded one sprawled on its side, blood seeping from its hip. Its companion fanned smoke toward the rock face, smearing red liquid on the surface. Blood? Probably. The rock behind the smoke disappeared, revealing a circle of leaves and a tree trunk. It was as though I was looking through a culvert at a tree on the other side, but the hillside should have been hundreds of yards thick, yet the tree was only a few feet from the opening.

I stood undetected, but with no idea what to do. If I shot the animals the murders would still be a mystery and I would still be the main suspect.

Then the sheriff groaned. The beast snarled at me. I fired, clipping the rock above its head. It grabbed its companion and dragged it through the hole, then disappeared.

I lurched to the hole through smoke with a burnt flesh smell, still carrying the sheriff. He whispered, "Go through." I realized I had no choice if I was going to clear my name. I eased him down and crawled through, my revolver poised, expecting the unwounded animal to be waiting for me.

I found myself by the only trees among knee-high grass stretching in every direction. A coal-black castle stood high above the plains, dominating it. I saw no sign of the animals, but the blood trail continued.

An almost uncontrollable urge to scramble back through the hole shook me. I turned and saw the hole contracting toward my foot. I jerked forward, but felt a tug on my shoe. The shoe's toe disappeared, a clean cut like the ones on the bodies.

That solved one mystery, but added more. What lurked in the castle? How did I get from Boone's Crossing to this vast plain? How could I get back?

Dozens of the beasts loped toward me. Two newcomers carried the injured animal away, standing easily on their back legs. The animals were out of pistol range, but I leveled the revolver at one. It snarled and moved aside, then moved again when I shifted my aim. The animals started a strange almost musical howling chant, brutal, threatening. They didn't come closer and as the beasts carrying the wounded one moved away, the others retreated too.

I kept the revolver poised but didn't shoot. Two of the animals were a big enough challenge. Against dozens, I had no chance.

I wondered why they didn't charge. They could certainly overwhelm me. Were they afraid of guns? They seemed to know my revolver was dangerous. Had more of them been to our world? I caught myself at that thought. This was not our world. But where else could it be? It didn't look like any description of Mars or Venus I had seen, yet it didn't look quite like Earth either. It felt older, worn-down, used up.

The beasts kept backing away. They didn't move toward the black castle though, but glanced warily toward it. That wariness wasn't misplaced. Several dozen riders in dark brown clothing emerged from the castle, spurring their horses toward us.

The beasts moved between the wounded animal and the newcomers. They seemed ready to charge the horsemen, teeth bared, chant/howls getting louder, more defiant.

The horsemen rode forward, taking no precautions against attack, ignoring the snarling beasts.

I recognized their leader. "Rocheforte."

"The gun won't help." He gestured at the beasts. "But they won't bother you if you stay close. Follow me. I may have a use for you."

He and his men rode toward the castle, not looking back. I followed, through a cloud of metallic-tasting dust.

The manikula drifted away, carrying the wounded one. The chant/howls died away, leaving the vast plains silent except for horses' hooves.

The castle towered over us like a skyscraper, with walls like black glass. Muted sunlight passed through it, casting gray, half-hearted shadows on the grass.

I glanced back longingly at the trees. Every minute I stayed here made it harder to go back. My absence would focus suspicions about the murdered girls, with my enemies pointing the tide of fear and suspicion toward me. I felt as though I had abandoned the sheriff, injured and bleeding.

I have to get back, I told myself, but could see no way to do it.

● ● ●

The castle's doors were massive, and when they opened the passages inside felt like they were made for something bigger than men. I thought the manikula might have built it, but it would have dwarfed them too.

Rocheforte laughed. "You look like you slipped on a banana peel and landed neck deep in crap. Haven't you seen a castle before?" He stood in the doorway, suddenly seeming exuberant, expansive. His smile seemed genuine for the first time, boyish, enthusiastic. "This is all mine. Duke Rocheforte. It has a ring to it."

I felt more helpless here than I had in the Great War's trenches. The revolver seemed useless here, with no way home even if I got past Rocheforte's men.

"They call this The Sanctuary," Rocheforte said. "And say it's a place where people flee injustice. I don't see it." He pointed to a dot on the horizon. "Indians there lost a war with the Five Nations Iroquois and would have been slaughtered, but fled here and lorded it over the locals until my river pirate ancestors came. That's the way it goes. You conquer and strut around until someone tougher knocks you down." Rochefort gestured at the plains. "Little globs of people throughout this country, but never many. Pequots in New England, maybe some California Indians. They don't spread because of the manikula."

Rocheforte led me to a huge open room where several hundred men dressed in buckskins or frayed blue jeans ate around crude wooden tables. Nervous-looking serving women moved among them, mostly Indians but with teenage girls in modern clothes mixed in.

"They're good fighting men," Rocheforte said. "Not good at anything else, but they don't have to be. They take what they want from the Indians."

I tried to make sense of this place. Some of these men could be descendants of river pirates. They had the look of outlaws. But they didn't build this castle.

So Rocheforte came here recently to rule the place. Who ran it before him? Some of the men had dark skin and Indian features, but I saw no sign of tension between them and others. The men seemed genuinely glad to see Rocheforte. He moved among them like a politician, addressing everybody by name.

How did his popularity fit with recently toppling older leadership? Where did that leadership go?

I felt shell-shocked, but my mind still worked, shoving aside questions of how or where and concentrating on the fact I was in the power of a merciless man willing to kill young girls and undoubtedly willing to kill me.

I didn't waste time wondering if I was dreaming. The smells and sounds and feelings of this place were too sharp for a dream.

Other than the serving women, the crowd was all male between twenty and forty-five years old. I wondered where the wives and children were. The men were all armed, some with modern revolvers, others with flintlock pistols and long, sharp knives, an array of weapons that told me these men had enemies in this strange world.

Rocheforte swung by me and asked. "Aren't you going to ask how I ended up in charge here?"

"Would you tell me?"

"I would tell you something. It might not be the truth. "

"What are the manikula?"

"They're apes that became hunters like wolves. Indians claim they were here before the Indians came. Maybe our ancestors trapped and burned them out of our world, but some made it here, grew strong and made this place a nightmare."

"But you control them."

"If I snapped my fingers they would tear you apart. It's handy owning a world. If I killed you, no one would care."

"Why didn't you bury those girls here?"

"I thought they would keep until spring. Second biggest mistake I've ever made."

Was anything he said true? His explanation of the manikula made sense, though I doubted that he had the power he claimed over them. His explanation for the bodies also made sense. He probably didn't know how to get here when he buried them. He didn't deny killing the girls and showed no remorse about them, which didn't surprise me.

"River pirates and street toughs," I said. "Quite a crew. Old-timers say your family were pirates."

"Long ago," he said. "We all have pirates or horse thieves in our families if we go back far enough. Kings and dukes too. "

"What are river pirates doing here? Or should I bother asking? You'll lie about that like you've lied about the Indians and the manikula."

That was a shot in the dark. I couldn't tell Rocheforte was lying, but his story didn't fit. The manikula looked at us like meat, but some invisible leash kept them from tearing us to pieces.

The Indians were another mystery. They came here well over two hundred years ago. Why didn't they spread? The manikula? That didn't seem likely. Humans, including Indians, hunt down any animal that kills them, even beasts as formidable as the manikula. Indians should have wiped out the beasts, or the manikula should have killed off the Indians. But the manikula remained, confident, unafraid, yet not harming people here.

"The manikula are waiting for a signal," I said. "But I don't think they're waiting for your signal."

I watched Rocheforte's face. It went grim.

"I knew you were smart."

"What do you want from me?" I asked.

"Maybe nothing. Or I may need you help me keep the manikula from flooding into Boone's Crossing and the rest of our world. The Indians get more restless the more men we bring in, but we could handle them. The manikula are another story. You're right. I don't control them. Something keeps them from attacking us here. Go twenty miles from the castle and you're fine, but go another step and they'll kill you. Forty-five miles due north another gate takes you straight to downtown Chicago. Bring people through that gate and they're safe as long as they don't go more than twenty miles from it. You see the problem."

"Five miles in a truck," I said. "Guards with Thompson submachine guns against animals. No. I don't see the problem."

"I didn't either at first. When I found out about this place…old family secret dad kept until he died…it looked like easy money. A still here. A castle. A route to Chicago no law can find. The castle was a fortunate accident. I had to figure out how to get over here in an isolated spot, so I brought the blood donors, shall we say, to Boone's Crossing. It took a while, but I figured it out."

"You killed a dozen little girls." I stared at him, seeing no sign of remorse.

"Seventeen, actually. I'm not a nice guy. Don't tell me you're shocked."

I realized that I wasn't.

"Once I figured it out, I did the same thing in Chicago. It looked perfect: make shine at the castle, then ship it to Chicago through Sanctuary."

The first three trucks must have brought girls, still, and men to help Rocheforte take over the castle.

"What happened to whoever was in charge here before?" I asked.

"The Duke and his family? What do you think? Shallow graves for all of them."

Something about the way he said those words felt a little off. "Did you really get them all?"

"They all died." He sounded confident this time. "The operation went as planned for a while, but those five miles got more dangerous each time. The last two convoys didn't make it. I rerouted the booze through Boone's Crossing to Chicago, but that gave up the biggest advantage of the operation. Then I gathered guys and guns in Chicago to wipe out the manikula from the Chicago side and the castle side, but the bodies washed out before I got enough guns and men here. Now I can't bring guns through Boone's Crossing because the state police and reporters will swarm the place. So they have to come from Chicago through those five miles."

"What about the manikula getting to our world?" I asked.

"It raises the stakes, but either way they have to die, and soon. The guys from Chicago will meet us, fighting their way through the last five miles to bring more guns."

"Why can't you just find some other spot some in the twenty safe miles and bring what you need through there?"

"It doesn't work that way. We can only go back in certain spots and they take you where they want to, not where you expect. We'll kill all the manikula within fifty miles. How to open gates won't have spread further because they have their own quarrels." Rocheforte looked grim. "If I have to send someone into the death zone to meet the Chicago boys, I could use a famous bootlegger, a war hero who outran and outwitted the law in the lead, and my men think that's what you are."

"Why should I help you?"

"The girls were more useful to me dead than alive," he said. "Stay more useful alive."

We drove the twenty miles to meet the Chicago convoy in seven rugged Ford pickups with improvised armor of heavy metal strips woven together, leaving gaps wide enough to fire a rifle through. Thick screens covered the windows and shielded the tires. Manikula tracked us.

Thirty guys rode in the trucks, some armed with Thompson submachine guns. Manikula massed on the other side of the twenty-mile border, musical chant/howls echoing.

Rocheforte swung by. "Still think this will be easy?"

I pointed to the submachine guns. "Got one for me?"

"If we had Thompsons to spare we wouldn't be here."

The chant/howls died away, leaving ominous silence. A long, grassy hill on the other side of the twenty-mile line blocked our view.

"The birds are here," someone muttered. They swirled over us, huge and black, like gigantic crows.

"They work for the manikula," the same voice said.

Rocheforte got on a radio built into one of the trucks, but raised only static. He climbed on top of a truck, trying to see over the hill, then pulled me aside. "The Chicago boys passed their twenty mile mark ten minutes ago. Now nothing. No radio. No truck sounds. They're in trouble."

"If they're in trouble we should hear gunshots," I said.

"We'd hear gunshots even if they aren't in trouble," Rocheforte said. "The manikula will attack. No shots means the convoy is already lost or it turned back."

"Or it never started." That was a shot in the dark, but it made sense. The Chicago operation didn't really need Rocheforte and the more new gunmen he brought in, the more likely someone would see that.

I could tell the idea wasn't new to Rocheforte. In the silence, gunshots sounded from over the hill, a lot of them. They got closer, then tapered off.

Rocheforte swore. "We need a distraction. Drive west as fast as you can. Get up the hill as soon as you're clear of manikula."

I thought about refusing, but from the sound of it, men were in desperate trouble on the other side of the hill. They were moonshiners, but then again so was I.

I hopped in a truck full of guys and jolted across the plains with another truck following. Manikula loped alongside us, fast as trucks over rough ground. They didn't have the endurance of an engine though, and we outpaced them after half a mile.

I turned, crossing the safe line. The manikula redoubled their efforts. I crested the hill and turned it to race along the crest, pulling the manikula further from where the Chicago convoy should be crossing to Rocheforte. I saw no sign of the convoy, but heard shots echoing from where it should be coming across.

A huge brown form rose from the dirt in front of us. I swerved to avoid it, sending the truck down the side of the hill away from the safe zone. The beast looked like a bear, but one out of a nightmare, nearly elephant-sized and covered with bony armor. The beast bulled into the truck behind us, overturning it and tearing away its armor. Men fired their guns into the beast at point-blank range, but the bullets had little effect. Manikula swarmed over the overturned truck, pulling men out and tearing them to pieces.

I had to turn back to driving, dodging a boulder that loomed in front of us. Guys in the back of my truck fired back at the beast. Another one like it appeared in front of us, forcing us further from the safe zone.

Rocheforte yelled over the radio for us to pull back, that Indians were attacking the castle.

I dodged another huge beast, but had to turn further from the safe zone, then gunned the truck, trying to circle past the 'bear' to the safe zone. It sprinted toward us and bowled the truck over with one massive arm.

I flew from the truck, landed hard, staggered to my feet and ran, while manikula swarmed the truck, tearing apart my companions, leaving me alone, on foot, at least a mile from the safe zone, with a sea of manikula between me and safety. I still had my revolver and used it, desperately dodging a closing net of manikula and giant 'bears', using up my ammunition. Two bullets left now, one for me. Wits. If I had any I wouldn't be here.

● ● ●

At first I thought the woman was a manikula. She was dirty, with tangled black hair, dressed in remnants of a gown its owner might have worn to a dance. Two knives made of the same black glass as the castle hung from her belt. She came at me with a wave of manikula then said something guttural. The manikula stopped as if on command. She said in English, "Do you really want to die for Rocheforte?"

I paused, the revolver poised. Two bullets left. "I don't have a choice."

"Maybe you do," the woman said. "Let us talk."

I remained ready to shoot, then turn the revolver on myself. The plains were quiet now, with no gunshots or truck noise.

"You hate Rocheforte," the woman said. "I could see it in the way you stood."

"I don't hate him enough to let manikula loose on our world."

"I showed them how to get there," the woman said. "You let Rocheforte come here, kill my parents, drive me from my home. I gave you back death."

Her English sounded rusty, as though she hadn't used it in a long time, but her voice sounded younger than she looked.

"Who are you?"

She drew herself up, looking both regal and ridiculous in her rags."I'm the Duke's daughter," she said. "The real Duke. The castle belongs to me."

"You escaped and the manikula didn't kill you."

"They will after I help them kill Rocheforte." She said that matter-of-factly, accepting it.

"They'll kill me then too, and invade my world. Rocheforte isn't worth it."

Her face turned grim, with a hint of madness. "He tortured my family. Days. Weeks. But I will kill him, his men, and the people he turned against us. Then I'll have no reason to live. You hate him too, I can see it. Help me."

"What do you need me for?" I asked.

"Manikula can't go into the castle, but I have to," she said. "You could help me."

Rocheforte held the castle, but the family he overthrew took secrets to their shallow graves. Among those secrets, a hidden passage and a secret chamber that controlled the castle. The woman told me that much, but wouldn't tell me what she planned to do when she got to the chamber, beyond killing Rocheforte.

She did give me her name, Adelita.

The manikula formed a loose circle around us. One of the huge armored bears ambled over and exchanged complex guttural sounds with them.

"It talks," I said.

"As much as the manikula, "Adelita said. "Not like people. Rocheforte knows nothing of this place. When the herds come through in the spring and fall, manikula, bear and crow hunt together, actually more war than hunt. When the hunters gather, men can no more live outside the safe places than at the bottom of an ocean."

I had no choice but to go along with her for now, surrounded by manikula and huge bears. A bear lifted us on its broad back, with her behind me, our legs touching. She leaned close. "If you betray me, I will slit your throat quicker than the manikula could tear it out."

I turned, my face inches from her dirt-covered one, her brown eyes holding my gaze, her expression unreadable, then she grabbed my waist as the bear jolted into motion.

It cantered across the plains, fast for its size, though manikula easily outdistanced it.

Manikula chant/howled in the distance and the bear picked up its already fast pace. "The Indians are losing," Adelita said. "We must get to the castle before Rocheforte beats them. We can only get to the chamber during the confusion of battle."

The bear kept up its pace and soon we heard gunshots. It let us down behind a rolling hill outside the castle.

Adelita pulled a trapdoor open and led me through a tunnel to the empty dining hall. She opened a hidden door into a well-lit chamber with black chairs arrayed around a black glass table. The walls came to life, with each showing moving pictures far clearer than any I had seen.

The pictures showed views both inside and out of the castle. Manikula by the thousands gathered near the castle, with dozens of huge bears. They stood watching a battle playing out between Rocheforte's men and clusters of Indians, some inside the castle, others supporting them from outside.

The Indians were clearly losing. Moonshiners had them pinned down inside the castle and trucks roved outside, overrunning Indian positions.

One of the screens showed us in the hidden chamber. Adelita stared at it. Her hands flew to her tangled hair.

"Don't look at me!" she said fiercely. She seemed ready to break into tears. "That wasn't me," she said those words over and over, as if saying them would make them true. "Rocheforte. He did this. Now it's his time."

Her fingers moved and hidden doors opened along the castle. The manikula and bears surged toward the doors. Bears charged into Rocheforte's trucks, bowling them over, sending men flying. The manikula swept in. Rocheforte's men fought back, spraying bullets into the manikula. In spite of their speed, the animals couldn't avoid all the bullets and dozens fell. More charged into the castle though and the battle became chaos, with the beasts and men lurking, ambushing one another.

Manikula and bears attacked Rocheforte's men and Indians alike. Both fought back savagely.

"You turned off whatever was keeping us safe," I said.

She didn't respond, staring at the screens with a mixture of horror, fascination and joy.

I pulled my pistol. "Turn it back on."

She tore her eyes away from the pictures. "He's still alive."

"What did the Indians do to you?"

"What did anyone in any of the sanctuaries do to me? The manikula can kill in all of them, everywhere in this world." She held up her hands. "Can't you see the blood?"

"Turn it back on. It's not too late."

She pointed to a screen. "Rocheforte is still alive. If I turn it on, he'll still win."

Rocheforte seemed indestructible, escaping a dozen skirmishes that should have killed him. He had a destination in mind and moved ruthlessly toward it, his men dying around him. The manikula tore apart fighting men, women and children.

Adelita ignored my revolver. I stared at the table, trying to figure out how to reverse what she had done, but the black surface gave me no clues. I could shoot the woman, but couldn't reverse what she had done.

She sagged in the chair, her eyes following Rocheforte from picture to picture. "Die, you bastard!" She yelled.

I found myself torn between hoping the manikula would drag him down and admiring his struggle. Manikula were dying by the hundreds, as were Indians and Rocheforte's men, but Rocheforte's life seemed charmed.

He disappeared off the edge of a picture and suddenly we couldn't see him on any of the screens. Adelita's fingers tapped the table again and again, changing pictures from one part of the castle to another. Finally, we spotted Rocheforte, alone, crouched in a bedroom and stashing greenbacks in a duffel bag. A manikula silently opened the door and charged. The two went down in a spray of blood, with Rocheforte stabbing and the manikula tearing at him. Finally, both lay still in spreading pools of blood.

"He's dead. Please, stop this now."

She stared at the man and beast. Finally she touched a spot on the desk, then another. The hidden doors closed and the manikula stopped attacking. The ones outside the castle loped away, followed by gunfire from Rocheforte's few survivors. The ones inside the castle dashed frantically for an exit, only to be shot down by Rocheforte's surviving men and the Indians. They made no attempt to defend themselves, trying only to get away. Even the ones that didn't take bullets died, collapsing on the castle floors.

Rocheforte's surviving men and the Indian survivors didn't resume their battle. The Indians drifted away, a pitiful remnant. Only a few dozen wounded river pirates lived.

Adelita slumped in her chair, head down, and tears streaming down her face. The tears subsided, then she stared at the screen where Rocheforte and the manikula had fought. The room was empty except for the manikula's body and the duffel bag.

"Something got his body," I said. "He wouldn't have left the money."

"He isn't dead until I see his body," Adelita said.

I agreed. We tramped through blood and bodies to the room. The duffel bag was still there. It looked as though someone had dragged Rocheforte's body away, leaving a body-sized swathe of blood. We lost the trail in the hall.

Survivors were getting organized, threatening to trap us in the castle. I talked Adelita out of continuing the search, grabbed the duffel bag and a submachine gun, then we fled the castle. We wandered to the tree where I crawled through from my world.

When we got there, a dozen manikula were fanning smoke toward the rock face. The rock disappeared. I raised the Thompson and fired until they lay still.

"Congratulations," Rocheforte's voice came from behind us. He held a Thompson gun, his face bloody, skin hanging from his cheek. "You brought my money, killed the manikula and now you die."

Adelita whipped around and threw one of her knives, charging behind it. The knife hit Rocheforte in the throat. He fell, struggled to raise the weapon, crawling toward the tunnel. Then Adelita, was on him, stabbing with her other knife until he died. She collapsed across him in the mouth of the tunnel.

I dragged her and the duffel bag through, pushing Rocheforte's body through to get it out of our way. The tunnel closed behind us.

● ● ●

The sheriff recovered from his wounds. Adelita passed herself off as an orphan girl from Chicago and told the state police that Rocheforte had tried to kill her. True, though she didn't mention that the murder attempt happened in a different world. She cleaned up, cut the tangles out of her hair and turned into a beautiful, though lost and confused, twenty-year-old woman. She carries a lot of guilt, but she is strong and she fits in to Boone's Crossing well. We spend a lot of time together since I got out of the moonshining business and bought a general store with Rocheforte's money.

My last act as leader of the Black Gang was blowing up the rock face the manikula came through. I hope that keeps the two worlds apart. As to the Chicago gate, all I know is that a bunch of Chicago moonshiners disappeared. Hopefully, the manikula wiped them out. Sheriff Silver hid the manikula's body, leaving only rumors of its existence.

The Sanctuary still has its mysteries. Who built the black castle? Not river pirates or manikula. Why fire and the blood of innocents? Most importantly, did the secret of how to get to our world die with those last manikula?

The End

'Pather

By Gordon Dymowksi

Fire.

Placing the dermapatch on his neck, Tyr Walton squinted as he tried to ignore the fiery sensation coursing throughout his entire body. As the patch delivered its soothing payload through the skin of his neck, Walton slumped on the bench, peering out of the park's transparent dome at the Martian sky.

As the multitude of whispers in his mind faded, Walton attempted to reconstruct the events of....well, just how *long* had it been? As Walton closed his eyes a variety of images flashed in his mind: he and his colleagues breaking out. Stowing away on the transit shuttle from Earth. Large plasma displays announced WELCOME TO URBPLEX BURROUGHS. Breaking away to find supplies and shelter. Never feeling centered even despite the slight lag of Mars' artificial gravity. Hiding and avoiding law enforcement.

But those feelings slipped away with every dose of slyde. Acquiring it wasn't easy – all of the medical facilities had it under lock and key, so robbing dealers was his only option. Despite TerraGov's controls, Mars had a thriving black market for slyde and a variety of other drugs.

Rising from the bench, Walton approached the transparent wall of the dome. Through the dome Walton saw the long tunnel that connected this terraforming park to the Urbplex. In the distance, Walton caught lights from the various transport shuttles and planet skimmers landing and taking off. With Earth healing after a long illness, Mars provided a great opportunity for a second chance. For those wanting to build a new life on the red planet, Urbplex Burroughs– the oldest, most elaborate Martian settlement – could either provide a new home or a first step towards building a farm, a startup colony, or some other endeavor.

Catching his reflection in the dome, Walton realized how shabby he looked: tousled brown hair which stood up, framing a slim, triangular face. Straightening the sleeve of his jacket, Walton looked like he was wearing a dead man's clothes. Fitting his already slim frame loosely, they reminded him that he had one priority: *survival*. Everything else was secondary.

Walking down the path that led out of the park, he noticed a woman wearing clothes which showed their age. As she stopped, she looked at him with dark-circled eyes, and her long, ragged blonde hair draped over shoulders hunched from carrying some huge emotional weight. She turned, regarded him for a moment...

Perhaps you should invite the man home for a meal.....

As she waved him over, Walton felt himself getting warmer as he approached her….

• • •

"You mean she died from a fast, *backwards* heartbeat?" Natan Bodaway asked.

Standing in his commander's office, Bodaway could not believe what he saw on the holographic display. Running his fingers through his jet-black hair, Bodaway felt warm despite the temperature-controlled office. Like his commander and fellow officer, Bodaway was wearing regulation TerraSec uniform: grey bodysuit and burgundy-colored jacket with the pyramid-shaped yellow TerraSec emblem on its right lapel.

"I believe that's what the phrase 'reverse tachycardia' *means*," said Nik Kragin – Bodaway's commander – as he rose from his desk. Both men regarded each other with caution, seeing the other as the complete opposite. Bodaway had the jet-black hair and the light-brown complexion of his Apache heritage; Kragin contrasted with a pale complexion, bald head, and slightly bulkier figure.

Stepping in was Michelle Beaumont, Bodaway's partner, whose uniform slightly lightened her dark-brown complexion. "Bodaway was not at fault, Commander – he was acting with appropriate force."

Kragin waved his hand, "*Neither* of you are under review. In fact, after reviewing Mr. Masterson's forensic results, I examined his companion's results to double check…and the both of you need to see this."

As Kragin poked at a square hovering in one area of the room, Bodaway and Beaumont watched as the display expanded in front of them. In one corner of the display was a young woman identified as Deo Kwelin. As text and photos popped into view, all three checked out Kwelin's lifestream. Except for her status as one of the first TerraCorps officers born and raised in the East Asian Collective, nothing about Kwelin stood out. Noticing the words FORENSIC ANALYSIS hovering in one corner, Kragin poked at it with a finger. As the text-filled window popped in front of them, all three officers read in silence for a few moments.

"Neuropathic damage due to long-term hypermeth use," Beaumont read aloud, turning towards both men. "Makes sense – Bodaway and I discovered an illicit lab on Upper Level 12, Grid 17. Former pharmaceutical market converted into a processing lab for hypermeth, slyde, charlymore…."

"Funny thing," Kragin noticed the word TOXICOLOGY floating in the air, poked at it. "Read this…."

"*Despite damage due to long-term use, no evidence of hypermeth usage found,*" After reading out loud, Bodaway turned to his two colleagues. "So Masterson dies from an unusual heartbeat *allegedly* caused by my weapon and Kwelin has severe nerve damage from using a substance she hadn't used. So I'm in trouble because…. why again?"

Kragin sighed. He hated when Bodaway pulled this act – despite being one of the best TerraSec operatives in Burroughs, Bodaway had a bit of an attitude. Perhaps growing up on Mars was a bad influence on Bodaway. Perhaps TerraSec's status as the *only* law enforcement agency on Mars—a planet that questioned whether the Terran Cooperative *should* have jurisdiction – had an influence. Especially given Earth's efforts to establish startup colonies and agricultural cooperatives on other planets – and asteroids – had failed miserably in the past few decades. Earth's lunar colonies shared Mars' resentment of Earth's near pathological need to interfere in various affairs. Perhaps Bodaway's rebelliousness was some mixture of those factors, or maybe Bodaway simply thrilled at any opportunity to straddle the line between policy and police work.

"You're not in trouble, Natan," Kragin said. "Far from it – there's plenty to warrant your…..unusual investigative style in this case. Switch to verbal interface."

"Verbal interface established," a feminine voice too smooth to be natural announced.

"Computer," Bodaway spoke aloud. "Please provide appropriate background records for Deo Kwalin and Shen Masterson."

"Unable to comply," the feminine computer voice responded. *"Proper Security Credentials required."*

All three Operatives looked at each other. Stepping forward, Bodaway's aquiline features looked even harsher lit by the display.

"Please define parameters of security clearance," Bodaway snarled, frustrated at the constant bureaucracy of the Cooperative. Especially the need to say *please* to a computer.

"Files on recent search strings require TerraCorps clearance status Triple Blue or greater."

Bodaway, Beaumont, and Kragin stared at each other, surprised at the computer's announcement. Triple blue status usually meant the upper echelon of Earth's military as well as government officials only a few levels below the Coordinating Council.

"Data lag?" Beaumont asked, wanting to break the silence.

Kragin scratched the back of his head, "Unlikely – checked the data routers between here and Earth; only about 30 milliseconds lag for commercial channels. TerraSec channels show a 10 millisecond lag. This isn't a tech glitch…and before you ask, both of these people had *no* prior charges before today. No listing on the transit shuttle's manifest, no relocation papers – nothing."

As he and Beaumont turned towards Kragin, Bodaway grinned at the opportunity to investigate this puzzle. Amongst his colleagues within and outside of Burroughs, Bodaway had a reputation of diligence and recklessness. However, Bodaway would argue that knowing when to be diligent – and when to be reckless – is an art form.

"So here's the sitrep," Kragin scolded both agents, with Beaumont regarding Bodaway with some disdain. "The two of you are going *back* to that lab to find potential leads. I'm going to do my best to play dumb with TerraGov and somehow get a hint of what they're hiding."

"OK, chief," Bodaway mumbled, following Beaumont out of the door.

"Bodaway, a moment, please," Kragin's voice had a tone of counterfeit politeness. "Beaumont, wait outside."

Turning back, Bodaway approached Kragin's desk, standing between it and the holo display. Rising from his chair, Kragin folded his arms and gave Bodaway a nasty look.

Raising his hands defensively, Bodaway stepped back, "Why the look? You *just* said that I used appropriate force..."

"And thanks to the vid record, I *know* you were ready to go past that. So much so that you may have been called into..."

"I haven't yet, have I?" Smiling, Natan Bodaway guessed Kragin's game. "But you're protecting yourself. I understand all about protecting your ass..."

"And ass protection is *not* part of a TerraSec officer's duty. Things between Mars and Terra are not easy: Earth's written off the lunar colonies, and they want to expand further onto Mars. The Colonial Board wants nothing further to do with Earth. Right now, our home planet..."

"Hey, I grew up on Mars," Bodaway countered. "This *is* my home planet."

Plus, Bodaway thought to himself, *Earth's too hung up whether it's called Earth or Terra. Mars is much easier to remember.*

"Despite that, you're working with Beaumont on this – and yes, you're working with a partner because we're in enough trouble as it is."

"Isn't trouble part of the TerraSec Mission Statement?"

Pursing his lips, Kragin bent his head, hoping Bodaway wouldn't catch his increasing frustration. Raising his head again, Kragin looked Bodaway in the eye. "We are in a very tense political situation. The *last* thing we need is a TerraSec operative acting as if we're back in the Wild West."

Clenching his fist, Bodaway tried to dismiss his growing resentment – after all, four hundred years ago his ancestors were fighting Kragin's over land. Despite centuries of progress for all the NorthAm First Nation tribes, comments like that were unnecessary...especially since many of those tribes established some of the first Martian colonies.

"Look, if you're thinking I'll shoot first and ask questions later," Bodaway countered. "I won't. That's not the Apache way. But if provoked, I *will* fight back."

Hoping for a clever retort, Kragin paused but sighed when he realized Bodaway wasn't going to change. He didn't even bother giving permission for Bodaway to leave as the junior officer took the opportunity.

● ● ●

Removing the fork from his mouth, Tyr Walton paused thoughtfully as he chewed. "Is this *real* bacon?"

Around him were the dingy white walls of a standard residential unit in the western end of mid-levels. Sitting across from Walton was Ayva Kartyr, the woman he had met in the park. As he ate, he felt calm and serene as the burning throughout his body subsided. He hated when that happened – that constant crossing of personal lines – but when it came to survival, he had no other choice. He had never intentionally killed anyone....and hoped to avoid it whenever possible.

"No," she answered before taking a bite off her plate. "It's actually textured, synthesized protein from…"

"Sorry I asked," Walton grumbled, then took another forkful of synthetic bacon. As he chewed, he swore he could taste the processing.

"Eggs are natural, though," Ayva responded. "My cousin has a small patch of land in the Endeavor CoOp. Raises chickens, some basic vegetables – he sends me a monthly care package. No meat, though – most of that comes through Terra, and with export and import fees…"

Turning away, Walton thought he heard a voice in the back of his head. No, not heard….*felt*. He didn't like that, but sometimes his gift asserted itself. It always meant that the return of the fire, starting in the back of his head and spreading throughout his body as his nervous system readjusted. But for some reason, his mind focused on the same repeated phrase:

Leader, Thinker, Soldier, 'Pather
Leader, Thinker, Soldier, 'Pather

Glancing around the small kitchen area, Walton realized that he had failed to complete his task. There was one more person who would complicate his efforts. He had wished to avoid hurting the other two….but some choices were avoidable and others were inevitable. Tyr Walton prided himself on knowing the difference.

As Ayva looked up, Walton saw so much promise in her eyes, in her face…. that he felt close to guilty about his past actions, and his further plans for her. Part of him even wished that someone would try to stop him…but that was crazy thinking. Rising from his seat, Walton regarded Ayva with some compassion.

Smiling at her, Walton ran his hand through his hair, "I'm gonna have to go… some last minute business. What's the fastest way to get to Level 24, Grid 10?"

"Transit tube up three levels, across five," Ayva responded.

"Thanks, baby," Walton leaned forward and kissed her on the cheek. As he left, Ayva forgot all about him, drowning her sorrows in black coffee.

● ● ●

"So where were you assigned before Burroughs?" Bodaway asked.

Entering the burnt-out pharmaceutical facility, Bodaway and Beaumont scanned the walls burnt black and gray through amateur chemical processing. Strewn throughout were a few warped metal tables, a variety of jugs and packaging for chemicals, and cracked and broken equipment. Both were midlevel in the Urbplex, whose retail and various business structures separated the well-to-do in lower levels from the poor and transient on the upper levels.

"Deimos Psychiatric, five years, first assignment," Beaumont placed her hand on the blaster holstered on her hip.

"Deimos, huh? Don't get too many operatives with experience there. Usually they serve on one of Earth's lunar colonies or penal asteroids."

Beaumont shrugged. "First assignment. Wanted to do it—felt I could do more with psychiatric patients than stranded with criminals. Greatest risk on Luna would be a paper cut."

"Or carpal tunnel," Bodaway turned his head. "Wasn't this a pharmacy..."

"Old branch of PharmaTech before they went out of business..." Looking around, Beaumont thought aloud. "Looks like they were cooking hypermeth and charlymore, with equipment for processing slyde..."

"Can you speak to me in English?" Standing in the center of the room, Bodaway glimpsed the variety of broken tables and equipment strewn around the facility. Catching some passers-by gaping into the facility, Bodaway flashed his best don't-mess-with-us look. Shuffling away, the passers-by found other distractions.

"Hypermeth's simple – old Earth methamphetamine chemically bound with a synthetic anabolic steroid," Beaumont's voice had all the warmth of a diagnostic text. "Charlymore is a derivative of peyote, but with the kick of Luomasine. Slyde is...well, it's short for *philoslydrophine*. Synthetic neurotransmitter used in treating diseases like Parkinson's disease and Jesselex Syndrome. Usually a gateway drug for middle schoolers..."

Both operatives heard a woman mumbling from a far corner of the room. As Beaumont drew her sonic blaster, Bodaway reached down towards his hip, felt the handle of his weapon, and then removed his hand.

"Engage SmartSuit Interface," Bodaway's voice activated the microtech sensors and commlinks in his uniform. Although it felt awkward, Bodaway knew the microtech handled the finer forensic work. Beaumont followed suit, with both recording and integrating all sorts of data. All they had to do was keep their eyes open and act accordingly.

Drawing her pistol, Beaumont took the lead as Bodaway paused for a moment. Reaching into his hip holster, he grasped the handle and withdrew a long, black baton with a collar of mesh at the far end.

"Wow, a baton," Beaumont muttered. "Aren't regulation blasters good enough for you?"

Shushing her, Bodaway pointed into a far corner. Moaning and muttering emerged from under a barely-lit cubicle. With a twist of his arm, the end of his baton glowed as semi-transparent collar collected around the mesh. As Beaumont held her pistol steady, Bodaway approached the source of the sound.

Out of the cubicle sprang an older woman wearing torn, disshelved clothes. Her brown hair had streaks of gray, and her sunken eyes made her appear older. Shaking her head, Beaumont realized that the woman must have been exposed to chemical fumes, and that the TerraSec Operatives who closed this place down failed to engage clean-up protocol. Grasping Bodaway by the shoulders, the brown-haired woman looked at him as if he was her potential executioner. Stepping back, Bodaway broke her grasp and used his baton as a barrier between them. Cowering, the woman fell to her knees and pleaded with Bodaway.

"Please, no! Save me!" As the woman spoke, Bodaway couldn't see any obvious trace of drug use....but *something* was affecting her. "Save me from the black horde!"

Feeling his heartbeat quickly slightly, Bodaway shifted and remembered his TerraSec training, "I am Natan Bodaway, this is my partner Michelle Beaumont. We are TerraSec Operatives, and can have TerraMed within…"

"Leader! Thinker! Soldier! Pather! Beware the tear in the sky!"

"Who tore the sky?"

Lunging forward, the woman grasped Bodaway's shirt, nearly knocking him to the ground. "You don't get it…seven years gone to the rip in the sky. The rip where nothing escapes. The voices on the other side of the tear—you must keep me from them. The 'pather, he thrives, he stole pieces of my mind, he killed the solder and the thinker…"

Moving forward, Beamont drew clear aim as Bodaway tensed his arm to strike, "I am sorry, but you need to step away. Terran Cooperative Mandates recognize our authority to…"

'No! No authority!" Releasing Bodaway's shirt, the woman's eyes showed fear as she turned towards Beaumont. "They'll come! They want to tear the sky more! They want to…"

"*Please cease and desist,*" An electronic voice buzzed. "*This is now a Terran Military Corps initiative.*"

All three turned to notice three soldiers wearing TerraCorps' distinctive maroon-and-gold body armor. Only the obvious feminine shape of the middle soldier distinguished her from a pair of male counterparts. All three had right arms raised, particle weapons attached to their forearms and aimed at the two TerraSec operatives and the woman.

In response to the soldiers, Bodaway lowered is baton, "OK, there's no need to fight. TerraSec has propriety over Martian internal affairs…"

"*You will step aside,*" one of the male soldiers aimed his weapon at Bodaway, who flexed his wrist as the collar of his baton grew thicker.

"Halt!" Beaumont aimed her blaster at the woman who ran away from them.

Rushing towards the entrance, all six saw the shabby woman approach a thin, wiry-haired man.

"Walton!" Cradling Walton's head in her hands, the woman began sobbing, "I'm sorry…I….I…."

"You did all you could," the wiry-haired man responded, placing his hand on the woman's shoulder.

"We…we're not going to make it. We…we're going back, aren't we? Into the void…"

"No, we're not," Walton responded. "In fact, I have a plan…"

For a few moments, everything stood still despite the buzz of passers-by deciding that this *was* worth seeing. Turning his head but staying in his defensive position, Bodaway mumbled, "Open channel – full feed to Kragin. Options needed. Process."

Feeling a slight buzzing on his lapel insignia, Bodaway knew that his SmartSuit was collecting data from internal sensors and Urbplex monitors and sending them back to headquarters. Kragin would advise him via subdermal commlink, but it was merely for show – Bodaway had no intention of following protocol.

Addressing the three soldiers, Bodaway's voice filled with confidence, "Look, guys, this is simple: *we* have jurisdiction. *You* don't. Now go away and play elsewhere – I hear Singapore Luna is quite enjoyable…"

Stepping forward, the female TerraCorps officer raised her arm, *"You will shut up and listen. We are TerraCorps. One more word and we will use force."*

Out of the corner of his eye, Bodaway glimpsed the wiry-haired man back away. As Beaumont covered Walton with her pistol, Bodaway glanced at the woman, then Walton, then the trio of soldiers. Tightening his grasp on the handle of his baton, Bodaway ran his thumb over a small glass oval on the handle. As he felt a neutral interface in his arm click into gear, he stood ready to strike out.

"Please put down your weapon," the female-shaped soldier warned.

"You first," Bodaway countered. Switching her stance between the shabby woman and the soldiers, Beaumont never noticed the way Walton's eyes gleamed as they slanted in concentration. As Beaumont faced the soldiers, she didn't notice the woman rushing to lift a plastic bottle from the floor. "You're all serving the 'pather! You're all serving the 'pather!" Hurling the plastic bottle at a soldier, the woman screamed as a bolt of energy hit her square in the chest. As she fell to the ground, the bottle hit the soldier, splashing liquid down his front and spilling into the power-packs that lined his waist. Sparks shot from the soldier's waist and he fell to the ground, yowling as he removed his armor.

Standing his ground, Bodaway snarled, "This is *over*. You have one chance. Walk away *now*."

"Or what?" the sole remaining male soldier said facing Bodaway as the female soldier turned to confront Beaumont. *"You're going to hit me with your sex toy?"*

His lips curling into an arrogant grin, Bodaway simply examined the soldier. Both soldiers moved with the slight wobbly nature most native Earth-borns had when moving within enhanced gravity. *This is going to be easy*, Bodaway thought as he caught Beaumont adjusting the level on her sonic blaster.

"It's an Apache war club," Bodaway said. "Know the difference."

As he lunged towards the soldier, Bodaway swung the slightly translucent head of the war club directly into the soldier's side. As the power pack smashed and sparked, the soldier moved into a corner as Beaumont fired at the female soldier. Air appeared to crumple in a straight line from Beaumont's pistol to the female soldier's armor, bouncing harmlessly off of the chestplate.

Turning towards Beaumont, Bodaway yelled, "Intensity level four, Beaumont! Open channel – we have Situation 57, Option Alpha! Request backup!"

As the soldier removed the broken powerpack, Bodaway fought the temptation to give the soldier a lecture on Martian weapon policy. Strict TerraGov requirements—and obscenely high prices—kept the Urbplex somewhat weapon-free. Plus, most high-end projectile weapons were prohibited because one good wall puncture would result in atmo-leak…and that wasn't good. Most TerraSec operatives could opt for the regulation sonic blaster or a custom weapon….and Bodaway chose the latter: a weapon that reflected his heritage. His grandfather told stories of the Apache as noble warriors, and Bodaway wasn't going to rely on a blaster. His war club – powered by "sonic compression" technology, whatever *that* was – could serve as a club, tomahawk, or a variety of other weapons. Bodaway could switch gears and modes quickly due to touch-sensitive controls in the handle and a neural link implanted in his arm. Combined with muscles conditioned in both Martian and Terran gravity, Bodaway knew how to fight when the time came.

Watching the soldier who had removed his chemically damaged armor, Bodaway was not impressed. He was a plain-faced blonde man, regular musculature, wearing a black undersuit. As the soldier took a fighting stance, Bodaway held his war club in his right hand and made a "bring it" gesture with his left. As the soldier crouched and lifted a metal bar from the floor, Bodaway kept him in his line of sight. The other male soldier was clicking arm controls rerouting power as Beaumont was handling the female soldier. Lunging with the metal bar, the soldier attempted to spear it through Bodaway, who moved aside and swung the war club directly into the soldier's gut. As the soldier crumpled to the ground, Bodaway caught Beaumont cornering the female soldier and firing a shot from her blaster. As the air crumpled in front of the gun, a dent suddenly appeared in the female soldier's chest piece.

Feeling something hit the side of his head; Bodaway stumbled and staggered as he realized the soldier had risen back up, getting the jump on him. Catching the soldier in a defensive position, Bodaway made a feint with his war club and delivered a devastating side kick into the soldier's knee. As the soldier stumbled, Bodaway swung his war club, the collar of solidified sound delivering a harsh blow to the soldier's jaw.

Both pairs – Bodaway and the unarmored soldier, Beaumont and the female soldier – stood within the empty facility, each expecting the other to make the next move. The third soldier had begun removing his armor. Within moments, the familiar cloister sound of TerraSec reverberated throughout the section, a mixture of TerraSec and TerraCorps operatives arriving and aiming their weapons at the facility. Through that cluster two men walked – one was a smallish man wearing old-style spectacles and the maroon-and-gold uniform of a TerraCorps officer; the other was Kragin who sped towards Bodaway.

As all four lowered their defenses, Kragin approached Bodaway and stood by the operative's side.

"Don't argue," Kragin mumbled. "You are off active duty. You are to remain in your office until further notice."

Bodaway started to protest, "Come on – you know policy in this matter. They shot – and killed – a potential inform…"

Kragin scowled and grit his teeth, *"Don't argue.* Just stay in your office. Maybe play on the dataNet…"

Sighing, Bodaway shuffled behind Kragin as both men left the broken, burnt facility.

● ● ●

"Now, we'll chalk this little escapade up to poor judgment," Glancing at Kragin, the maroon-and-gold uniformed man's mustache seemed to dance as he talked. "After all, we understand the strained relationship between the Terran Cooperative and the Martian Colonies..."

Standing at attention in Kragin's small office, the man looked past the lenses of his spectacles at both Kragin and Bodaway. Both men didn't appreciate having someone from Earth *military* interfering with their work. It also didn't help that this man looked rather meek….almost like a librarian. The kind of man who sat on his front porch, yelled at playing children, and talked about "the good old days."

"Now, Colonel Ronson," Kragin gestured with his hands as he spoke. "We understand the situation…and that is why I opted to not have Operative Beaumont at this meeting, and insured that Bodaway was confined to desk duty until we met…."

…And until you had enough to cover your ass, Bodaway thought but avoided saying. Sure, he had spent time in his office, but he had worked with Kragin long enough to know that "office duty" meant *I'm buying you some time to do some digging.* Although it would be tough to justify, Kragin would avoid making Beaumont the point of blame in this situation. Besides, Bodaway knew that he would be more than likely to be let go as senior officer, but had to play this straight.

Interrupting Kragin, Ronson leaned over and poked his finger on Kragin's desk with each word, "Listen, having your officer stay in his office to fill out paperwork and watch porn…"

As the familiar feeling of courage and recklessness kicked in, Bodaway stepped forward, "I'm sorry, sir, but that's not possible."

As Kragin glared at Bodaway, Ronson growled, "What's not possible?"

"Watching porn. TerraSec has dataNetfilters on those channels. Besides, Martian porn's pretty boring – it's mostly TerraCorps blowhards making vague threats."

Surprised at this outburst, Ronson turned and adopted a wide stance facing Bodaway. Through squinting eyes, Ronson regarded the officer for a moment.

"Don't push me, boy," Stepping towards Bodaway, Ronson poked at the operative's chest. "You have *no* idea who you're provoking."

"Actually, I do, sir." Turning towards Kragin, Bodaway saw him nod his head. Turning back towards Ronson, Bodaway announced, "You're Colonel Nigel Ronson of Terran Military Corps. And this is all about the wormhole."

Stepping back, Ronson failed to hide his surprise, "What do you mean, *wormhole?*"

"You know—the wormhole that was discovered about …fifty years ago?"

Before Ronson could respond, Kragin said, "Yes, Operative Bodaway, tell us about the wormhole. This ought to be *good.*"

Straightening himself, Bodaway caught Ronson's gaze and flashed a cocky grin. "Since I was benched, I downloaded my SmartSuit's data into our computers. Turns out the woman in the old pharmacy on mid-level? Her name's Joan

Lindstrom – higher-end academic with experience in sociology, anthropology, linguistics – in short, she can figure out an entire society from a simple relics. Wrote several gigs of academic studies."

"I don't see your point," Ronson quickly dimissed, hoping to avoid the topic altogether.

Nodding towards Kragin, Bodaway explained, "But since I *couldn't* use TerraSec datastreams to investigate – I was benched, you know – I used public domain streams for news, highlights, etc. So I investigated the two people who had died in a previous raid: a soldier named Deo Kwelin and – as it turns out – an experienced Exploration Corps officer named Keeta Masterson. So this is interesting – three people who are the least likely to need illicit drugs are found dead around a particular shop. But again, I can't use our secure streams….so I decided to go public…"

"…which are routed through the Collaborative's relay bots." Holding his gaze on Ronson, Bodaway's tone grew slightly darker. "So that TerraGov knows *precisely* what we're doing…"

Although Ronson's face grew slightly ashen, he held his defiant stance.

Undaunted, Bodaway continued, "But all three of them had one thing in common: their lifestreams ended about seven years ago. Vanished – maybe even deleted from the net – without any indication of path. So I researched what was going on seven years ago. Found a couple of interesting items."

Looking upward, Bodaway spoke aloud, "Open Bodaway File 656-99, Voiceprint password *Gray wolf warrior*"

In front of all three men, the holographic display kicked in, with a variety of text floating in front of them. Poking at a corner marked HIGHLIGHTS – 2282, Bodaway stepped back as a variety of images arranged themselves in front of the men. One was a video portraying a purple-and-gold whirlpool against a black backdrop; the other was a green-and-gray logo for something called *GeneTech*, and the third was a news item with the headline TRANSLIGHT IN OUR LIFETIME.

"Headline refers to TerraGov's research corps had determined that they were about ten years' away from workable faster-than-light propulsion. Meaning that…"

"You could get from Earth to Mars in fifteen minutes." Crossing his arms, Ronson kept his rigid posture. "Rather than ten hours. Every school child knows *that*. Now, are you going to keep wasting time or do I need to remind you of TerraCorps authority?"

"Authority you *don't* have," Kragin pointed towards the ceiling. "Our meeting's being monitored – and recorded – by the Martian Coordinating Council *with* my and Operative Bodaway's express consent. Everything's legal, so any action you take will be considered a violation of territorial agreement. Understand?"

After two long strides, Ronson brought his face close to Kragin's, "And what will you do if I *don't*?"

Grateful that he *wasn't* the troublemaker, Bodaway moved Ronson away from Kragin, "He'll invite you to a game of Martian Roulette….and you *really* don't want that."

As Ronson loosened his posture, Bodaway pointed to the holographic display. "What's also interesting is that, around the same period of time our three people disappeared, GeneTech announced a partnership with TerraCorps – something about nanomanipulation of human genomes. Using microscopic machines to enhance a soldier's capabilities – but you know all this already, don't you, Colonel?"

Remaining silent, Ronson merely scowled as Bodaway continued, "But what also happened was the wormhole from the Terrinsky array – or Lindstrom's *tear in the sky* – was emitting some kind of signal. Rumor at the time was that it was indicative of possible extraterrestrial life...but how could *anything* live in a wormhole?"

"Unless they were transmitting *through* it." Catching on, Kragin nodded in assent. It also helped that Bodaway had sent him the files before the meeting.

"What's also interesting," Bodaway said. "Is that most wormholes are microscopic or subatomic....but this one, out in the middle of interstellar space – about four light years away – has an estimated diameter of 700 meters. Just enough to fly a small ship through..."

"You have no idea what you're talking about," Ronson fumbled in his bluff of Bodaway and Kragin. "That would....what would our reason be..."

A small red square popped up in a far corner of the display. As Bodaway poked at the square, all three men watched it expand into a profile named WALTON, TYR. Next to it was text which announced LINDSTROM – FORENSIC ANALYSIS. Pressing his fingers against the latter set of words, a full set of text and video appeared before the three.

"*Cerebral damage due to excessive neurotransmitter buildup.*" As he read aloud, Kragin pursed his lips in thought. "Hmmm....Lindstrom wasn't crazy due to hypermeth fumes – someone messed with her brain. Deliberately."

Regarding Ronson with little respect, Bodaway exhaled, "Now, in theory, if you're going to send a ship into a wormhole – because let's face it, probe data takes too long to process, and we need new ground to tread on because there aren't too many planets in our solar system to colonize – you'll need at least four people when dealing with possible new life forms. Masterson's the leader, familiar the exploration game. Lindstrom's the thinker with experience in cultural and linguistic analysis. Kwelin's the soldier, and Walton's the *pather*...."

Sensing the opportunity to mock Ronson, Kragin spoke in an overly theatrical voice, "So does that mean he's the navigator, Operative Bodaway?"

"That's what I thought, at first." Poking at Walton's name, a large series of dates and text with a TerraSec banner running across the top. "After pulling data from local cameras and my SmartSuit, I ran Walton's name along public databases...."

"...which TerraSec red flagged, since it filters for known criminals," Kragin countered. "Bringing the search to my attention."

Losing his military composure, Ronson allowed a brief flash on shame on his face. Both Kragin and Bodaway regarded him for a moment – there was an ancient joke about "military intelligence" being an oxymoron, but both men knew better. Ronson was the exact *opposite*.

"Precisely – because I would *never* violate TerraSec policy." Both Ronson and Kragin heard the wink in Bodaway's voice. "Turns out our good Mr. Walton has a previous record of petty larceny, smuggling, racketeering, extortion – in fact, he somehow managed to disappear from Lunar Penal seven years ago…"

"But not before some psych technical evaluated him for high levels of empathy and understanding, right?" Kragin asked. As Ronson regarded him with disbelief, Kragin shrugged, "Hey, I'm only assuming here."

As Ronson regarded him with reluctant respect, Bodaway continued, "So if you're going to explore new worlds, language is an issue. After all, take my name…."

"Can we please get on with this?" Shifting on his feet, Ronson glanced around. "All of this is nice, but…"

"But nothing," Bodaway snarled. "TerraCorps either drafted or abducted four individuals. They were gene modified for possible higher functions. But one of them –Walton – became almost superhuman. He's a telepath or "pather". We've managed to track him – basically, facial ident – through a variety of incidents, and we think he's hiding out in one of the mid-level residential units…"

"Good." Lifting his left arm, Ronson spoke into a wrist communicator, "Attention…"

Grasping Ronson's wrist, Kragin snarled, "You do *not* want to do that."

Snatching his wrist away, Ronson shuffled a bit as Bodaway spoke, "Walton actually developed some rudimentary telepathic abilities. The ability to 'push' people and possibly read their thoughts. Walton's capacity to cold read, combined with your nantotech, makes him an almost unbeatable adversary. Perhaps he and his three colleagues arranged to go off-world together…but things happened. Perhaps Walton thought he could stem the damage with illicit drugs or perhaps he didn't care. Whether his companions would suffer the same fate was irrelevant. They ended up dead because Walton moved mind reading to some kind of control over their modifications, maybe even their bodily functions…we may never know. All that matters is that he's out there—and we're taking him in."

"And putting him *where*, exactly?" Regaining self-respect, Ronson strode towards Bodaway. "If he's that powerful, you're going to need a high quality facility like Murdoch, a high security facility twenty hours from here – only TerraCorps has the ships that can transport him without incident."

"But *we* make the collar," Kragin said. "After all, this is a Martian Colony effort with TerraCorps assistance."

Biting his lip, Bodaway hated Kragin's suggestion. However, Phobos was not an option – it would be too easy for Walton to break out and return. Compromise wasn't what Bodaway signed up for when enlisting in TerraSec, but this time… it was necessary.

"Agreed," Ronson grunted. "You'll excuse me if I don't shake your hand."

"That's fine." As he sat down, Kragin waved Ronson towards the door. As Ronson began to depart, Kragin cleared his throat.

Wanting to have the last word, Ronson asked, "Is there anything else you wish to add?"

"Only that TerraGov – and the media – are going to have a *field* day with this." Flipping the monitor on his desk on, Kragin appeared nonchalant. "Bodaway's idea – that way, there are more eyes on the military when they attempt this kind of thing in the future…"

Turning and striding forward, Ronson clenched his fist ready to strike Kragin. Stepping between the two, Bodaway grabbed Ronson's wrist.

"Oh, and before you interrupted me: language is a funny thing. My name in Apache – I'm not sure which dialect – means: *you just got served, bro."*

As Bodaway released Ronson's wrist, the Colonel stormed out of the office. Avoiding an interplanetary war was the *easy* part; apprehending a possible telepath….well, *that* was going to take planning.

● ● ●

"You know….I don't need telepathy to know what *you're* gonna do."

That damn Urbplex vidcast offering the reward for information on Walton's whereabouts was a dumb move….but dumb moves tended to work on Mars. Damn nosey neighbors were the first to reach out and narc on Walton and Ayva. Standing in the terraforming park where he met earlier, Walton was surprised that a sole TerraSec operative – a tall man with dark hair – was there to arrest him.

Grinning, Walton felt confident. This was going to be easier than he expected. Noticing the weapon holstered on the Operative's hip, Walton kept silent to see how the situation would play out.

"Natan Bodaway, Terran Security Services," the dark-haired man announced. "I know why you're running. Come with me and you'll be safe."

As Bodaway approached Walton, he heard a subtle *pinging* from his collar. Glancing at the display running down the length of his sleeve, he read GIRL IS SAFE – PROCEED WITH CAUTION: KRAGIN. Things were going according to plan, but Bodaway quickly glanced at the pistol-shaped device Walton was holding.

"I don't think so, Natan." Standing his ground, Walton aimed the large, pointed tip of the device at Bodaway. "I know you have your weapon set to emit subsonic waves – too low to hear, but enough to make reading you muddier – but I hold the winning hand: Dead man's drill."

Stopping in front of Walton, Bodaway scanned the surrounding area filled with trees and foliage imported from Earth. He wondered if he could evade the dead man's drill—after all, if it could pump the oxygen out of a spacesuit so quickly that reserves wouldn't kick in…

Holding his hands in the air, Bodaway stopped and regarded Walton, "OK, you win. I get it – TerraCorps recruited you because you were desperate." *Not that I believe that…*

"And you *shouldn't*," Walton held the weapon steady as Bodaway lowered his hands. "You *really* think TerraCorps took us in out of the kindness of their hearts? Oh no, son – in fact, we were all desperate to sell our bodies – our souls were second-hand. Masterson couldn't pay off his debts, Kwelin was close to dishonorable discharge, Lindholm took her coffee with a charlymore chaser..."

"And you're hooked on slyde, right?" Bodaway smirked. "Be still my beating heart."

Grimacing, Walton tightened his grip on the weapon, "No, Natan, I was never hooked on slyde – hell, no dealer should *ever* use his own stash. I'm not *that* stupid. But after TerraCorps stuck those whatevers in our bodies...hell, every time I push someone or read their mind, my nerves get all shot, and it *burns.* My thinking gets rewritten with every effort. Slyde makes me feel normal."

*As if you ever were....*Bodaway thought.

"You really *are* an arrogant prick, aren't you? News flash: TerraCorps was gonna send the four of us on a one-way trip through the wormhole. Oh, sure, we might have sent a probe or two, but Mother Earth's desperate. We're failing *miserably* at the colony game. Mars is this close to breaking ties, Luna's a hot mess, and Venus is falling flat on its ass. Only Earth's prisons are working...and they're on asteroids too damn far to reach. So our effort was gonna be simple: find out who's sending the signals and send back intel, or find an empty world and recreate the human race. Or both, given the nature of faster-than-light travel."

Flashing on two memories, Bodaway focused on a memory of his grandfather, hoping to confuse Walton, "My partner tells me that one of slyde's side effects is paranoia..."

"You just don't get it!" Embarrassed at his outburst, Walton relaxed his aim. "All the four of us wanted was to get away – to build new lives. We even swore to each other that if things went wrong..."

Moving forward a few steps, Bodaway stood face to face with Walton. "Oh, cut the crap. I've read your record: you're a petty grafter artist who got caught with his hands in the cosmic cookie jar. You killed your fellow – colleagues, conspirators, whatever – simply because you're too damn selfish to share."

Bowing his head for a moment, Walton appeared ashamed of himself. Lifting his head back up, Walton flashed Bodaway a sincere, cynical smile.

"You're right – I am selfish," Walton aimed the drill at Bodaway's chest. "But let's face it – I am who I am. I'm a 'pather."

Before Walton could act, Bodaway shot a quick kick to Walton's knee, causing the 'pather to drop the weapon and fall to the ground. Lifting himself up, Walton threw a wild punch that barely missed Bodaway. Throwing a sharp, quick jab to Walton's throat, Bodaway stepped back as the man stumbled. Spinning on one foot, Bodaway delivered a roundhouse kick that knocked Walton to the ground.

As he stepped on Walton's chest, Bodaway reached beneath his jacket and withdrew his blaster. Normally, he relied on his war club, but now seemed right for good old-fashioned TerraSec justice. Aiming the pistol at Walton's head, Bodaway sneered, "Ever play Martian Roulette?"

Shaking his head, Walton's breathing took on a fearful rasp as Bodaway spoke. "Simple really – most blasters have five intensity settings: one is stun, five blows a hole in six inch fleximetal. TerraSec standard is level two. Forgot what setting I left my gun on....wanna find out the hard way?"

*Better watch out there's someone behind you....*flashed in Bodaway's brain.

As Bodaway turned his head, Walton stuck the side of Bodaway's leg. As the TerraSec operative rose and released the pressure on Walton's chest, the telepath scurried on his back.

"Damn!" Bodaway muttered under his breath, regaining his composure. From a brief distance he heard Walton declare, "Nice bluff."

Turning towards Walton, Bodaway saw the man standing in front of a tree, yielding a knife that must have been hidden up his sleeve.

"Now, now – I didn't even need to read your mind to know you were bluffing." Squinting, Walton regained focus as he spoke. "You rely on your war club – you're so proud of it. You hold that pistol awkwardly....and thinking of your Injun grandpa ain't gonna help you now."

"That's funny." Throwing the pistol towards the ground, Bodaway shook his head at Walton. "Nobody's used that word in....oh, four hundred years? If you're going to insult me, try something unique. Make fun of my hair, or my clothes, or my commander or even or that my war club isn't big enough. Try harder, Walton. You're failing."

Feeling a warm, tingling sensation in the back of his head, Bodaway stayed calm as Walton hissed, "See, you underestimated me...your subsonic waves and grandpa issues are like background music. See, I don't just read minds willy-nilly...I gotta *push* to do it, and it *hurts*."

Pressing his forearm against Bodaway's throat, Walton marched the operative back against a tree. As Bodaway pulled his right hand into his jacket sleeve, Walton paid little regard and looked straight into Bodaway's eyes.

"Now that feeling in the back of your head," Walton hissed. "That's me reaching in and moving some neurons around. Soon, you're gonna find it harder to breathe, and when your colleagues find you – *if* they find you – it'll look like you overcranked on hypermeth. Because I not only can read thoughts...I can manipulate brain patterns. My job was to work with Masterson on interpreting language, but I found I had a side benefit....unfortunately, it causes something the docs call *neuropathy*...and unlike most slyders, the drug *helps* me."

Feeling something fall into his right hand, Bodaway squinted as pain shot through his head. Relaxing his focus on Bodaway for a second, Walton could swear he picked up a stray thought.

"What? You still think you're gonna take me down, Injun?" Knowing that odds were with him, Walton raised his eyebrows in disbelief. "You're gonna be the hero in this story?"

As Walton pressed his forearm into his throat, Bodaway felt the 'pather's presence in his head. Since he couldn't speak, he collected his thoughts into a single sentence, hoping that Walton would pick it up.

I'm not playing the hero, dumbass – I'm merely a distraction.

Feeling something hard jab into his abdomen, Walton heard the familiar *hissing* of a hypospray. Releasing his grip from Bodaway's throat, Walton stepped back and felt a cooling, calming feeling that seemed all *too* familiar.

Holding up the hypospray, Bodaway jeered, "There's enough slyde in your system to keep one of the startup colonies going for a week. With a nice side order of nanobots to rewrite your nervous system. But that's not the best part."

Hearing a loud *whump*, Walton felt something sharp enter his back. Falling to the ground face down, Walton tried to stave off the cloak of darkness that enveloped him....and failed. As he approached Walton, Bodaway saw a long, white tube sticking out of the man's back. Removing it, he noticed the needle at the end and placed it in his jacket pocket.

Moving out of the grove of trees was Beaumont, holding a large, open-ended cylinder in her right hand.

"Great plan," Beaumont muttered, holding up the cylinder to Bodaway, "You jack him with the slyde, I follow up with the sanity cannon. Delivering enough tranquilizers to keep Walton under wraps until Ronson and his soldiers arrive."

"You *sure* Deimos knows you have that?" Bodaway asked with a knowing grin.

Beaumont kept silent, but grinned back.

Seeing Colonel Ronson appear with three other TerraCorps soldiers, Bodaway leaned towards Beaumont, "Think he's a little upset at us?"

"He trusted you with that hypospray..."

"He did, didn't he?"

"And of course....this whole matter becomes classified and we keep quiet."

"All part of the job."

Both Operatives walked away from Walton's body, passing Ronson and his soldiers. Neither side said anything, but both knew too much had happened. All that mattered in the aftermath was how well they cleaned up this hot mess.

In other words, another typical day on Mars.

The End

Chance of a Ghost
(A Green Ghost story)
By Win Scott Eckert

June 1945

I looked into the clear blue eyes of one of my best friends in the world, and saw fear.

I bent down and chained the irons clapped around Ned Standish's ankles to the steel hook which was, in turn, welded to the interior of the prison transport van.

I stood and looked him in the eye again. It wasn't that Ned was a coward. Ned was a brave man.

But even a brave man faces his impending execution with a degree of fear. Ned was no different. A bead of sweat hung precariously from the tip of his patrician nose. His dirty blonde hair, shot through with gray, was plastered to his skull. His breathing was labored.

I turned from Ned and descended the steps at the back of the van. My partner, similarly attired as I was in the blue garb of a prison guard uniform, stood waiting.

"All set?" Gawronsky asked. He was a short, squat pit bull of a man, with forearms as thick as melons. He looked like a guy who could tear the proverbial phonebook in two without breaking a sweat.

I nodded. "Yeah, snug as a bug. He's goin' nowhere. 'Cept the chair, like he deserves."

Oh, how the mighty had fallen.

Ned Standish, headed from the Big House to the Big One.

Edward "Ned" Standish, of the Kingsport Standishes. *Summa cum laude* graduate of Miskatonic University with a bachelor's in Political Science, and a Harvard Law grad. A rising star among the city's elite movers and shakers, but with keen sense of justice for all and for the plight of the common man—despite his very blue blood.

And most recently the Police Commissioner of the City of New York.

Okay, that last was a tiny exaggeration.

It had been a bit of a running joke between us, back in the day. After all, how many Police Commissioners could New York have? The truth was, Ned was—ahem—Ned *had been* an Assistant Commissioner for one of the boroughs. As were Weston, Kirkpatrick, Woods, Foster, Quistrom, Gordon, Warner, and Hombert, and all the rest.

Now he was reduced to this. His reputation in shambles. His name disgraced. His career trajectory cut off in its prime. There would be no mayorship for Ned Standish, no seat in the governor's office.

Just a cold, hard, metal chair, straps around the ankles, wrists, and waist, two electrodes, and a heart-stopping 2,000 volts of electrical current. Followed by a cheap wooden casket under six feet of damp loam and an unmarked grave.

Murder in the first degree, the jury had said.

The penalty is death, the jury had said.

Gawronsky chuckled at my remark about the Big Chair. I slammed the heavy rear door with a resounding *clang* while he went to report to a small group of prison officials who were standing off to one side, looking proper and somber in their dark double-breasted suits and hats. A clergyman dressed in black stood with them.

I went around to the passenger side of the heavy transport vehicle, climbed in, and pulled the uniform cap down lower on my forehead. I could imagine Ned breathing heavily in the back cabin of the van, counting down the minutes.

Gawronsky got into the driver's seat and pressed the starter. The big engine roared to life. He put the truck in gear and we started rolling. We were headed to Ossining Correctional Facility about thirty miles north of the city, where Ned had a date with "Old Sparky." The officials followed us in a large blue sedan.

Ned had received a special privilege, courtesy of his family standing. He had been granted a private visit with family members outside of the prison walls. Truth to tell, it was more for their benefit than Ned's. The visit spared the family the embarrassment and press coverage of a trip to the notorious prison.

Now he was on his way back to Sing Sing, to spend his last day in the so-called "Dance Hall" chamber, and then walk that last mile.

Gawronsky kept up a steady stream of snorting and hacking as he drove. It was annoying, and made me want to smash the little pig nose, beneath the beady piggy eyes, from which sprang the nasal cacophony.

We were about ten miles out of town.

This was a good a time as any.

I slipped my right hand into my pocket and depressed a button on a small metal box. Behind us, the dark blue sedan blew a tire. I didn't see it, but I knew it was so. I coughed and hacked as loud as I could to cover the noise of the blowout, on the off chance that Gawronsky might be between snorts and hear it. He glanced over at me and I kept up the hacking; better he look at me than in the rear view mirror.

"You makin' fun of me?" he asked, narrowing his eyes even further, if that was possible.

"No, no, I'm okay, I'm okay," I said after a half minute, "just swallowed wrong." After that, he kept his eyes on the road.

Which was just fine with me.

I buried my face in my hands and kept up the light drama of the telltale mucus. I did miss the stage, although I hadn't been an actor. I always looked forward to the final reveal.

Now it was time to deliver it.

I looked up sharply and screamed at Gawronsky.

He screamed back, and I didn't blame him; set squarely between my blue uniform cap and the collar of my prison guard's jack was a gaping, glowing death's head. My skull-like visage was stark white, tinged with a faint greenish luminosity. My eyes were black pools with dark grayish rings encircling them, set over gaunt, bonelike cheeks.

Caught by surprise, Gawronsky screamed again.

I punched him hard on his piggy nose—the brass knuckles sewn into my dark green gloves were bound to add some additional *oomph* to my blow—and it bloomed brightly with blood and snot and gore. His head lolled to the side, and I was relieved. I didn't want to have to fight the guy and his tree branch arms off, and was glad I had taken him by surprise.

I grabbed the wheel and reached a foot across to tap the breaks. I brought the lumbering vehicle to a halt at the roadside and killed the engine.

Before getting out, I removed a small glass vial from a special pocket sewn into the inside of my jacket, broke it open, and let the fumes waft around piggy's broken nose and gaping mouth, thus ensuring an extended slumber. I tied his wrists behind his back with a thin, super-strong cord for good measure.

I checked my watch, got out, and loped around to the back of the prison van. As I unlatched the hinged metal door, I glanced to my left and came up short.

A vision drifted there, raven-haired and cherry-wood-eyed. A blue-sequined evening gown, with a plunging neckline that exposed a pre-Code hint of dark areola circling each firm breast, clung precariously to her magnificent curves.

"Angel . . ."

I blinked, and the vision was gone.

I heard a car rolling to a stop behind me and turned to face it. As planned, the car was not dark blue, and was not filled with prison officials and a clergyman.

A stunning brunette with a hundred-megawatt smile and penetrating green eyes was behind the wheel of the black sedan. Next to her sat a small man with a round, cherub's face and a fat cigar stuck in the corner of his mouth. A small black bowler hat perched on top of his bowling ball of a head.

I turned back to the prison van, threw open the rear doors, and thrust my skullfaced head inside, eliciting a small yelp of surprise from Ned Standish.

Then: "Where the hell have *you* been?"

● ● ●

It was a good question, and Ned Standish wasn't far off, though he didn't realize it at the time, when he asked where the *hell* I had been.

Where the hell had I been, indeed?

Let's back up for a moment.

My name is George Chance. I've sometimes been known as The Ghost, or The Green Ghost, though only a select few were aware of that.

Ned Standish was one of the select few.

So was Merry—sorry, Meriem White. She's asked me to ditch the "Merry," and who am I to argue? She's my fiancé and I'd like to keep it that way.

The little guy in the bowler hat was Tim Terry, a longtime friend from my circus days.

Yes, I said "circus." I may have the air of the suave sophisticate around town, with my stage magician's tuxedo and top hat, but I definitely traded up when Meriem agreed to marry me; she's the one with the high class background. Now, Meriem has helped me—The Green Ghost—out of a bad spot more than once, and she says that she has "intuitive flashes" which let her know to come running. I don't necessarily buy it, but as I said, I like being engaged to her, so that, as they say, is that.

Anyway, George Chance. You may have heard of me. More than likely, if you *have* heard of me, you've probably forgotten it all, and I wouldn't blame you one bit. Your life has been turned upside down by three-plus years of a little thing called World War Two, and mine has as well.

Before the war, I was an up and coming stage magician. Some would even say that I had "made it." I was raised in a traveling circus, where my father was an animal trainer and my mother wowed the audiences as a daring trapeze artist. I picked up a lot of other skills, and friends, back on those days. When I had the chance to study with the greatest, Harry Houdini, I grabbed it. Some have said that I eventually came to match the great Houdini in the art of escape. I'll never believe it, personally. There was only one Houdini.

Still, there were those who saw something in me. Police Commissioner "Ned" Edward Standish, for instance. While I mastered the arts of makeup and disguise, knife throwing, picking locks, creating illusion, and everything else required in a top-notch magician's bag of tricks, Ned knew I had the potential for something more. And when the opportunity arose, he brought me in on a baffling case where he thought my skills and background could help.

Thus was born George Chance, amateur criminologist.

Soon after came the disguise.

Well, perhaps it seems silly to you, but at the time it seemed as if everyone was doing it. The Black Bat, Captain Midnight, The Phantom Detective, The Domino Lady. Heck, there was even some guy calling himself "Ki-Gor" who was making the jungle safe for everyone. The war put a stop to a few of them, including me, but many are still going strong.

So, with Ned Standish's help and encouragement, I graduated from a mere "dabbling criminologist" who occasionally aided the police, to the crime buster known as The Green Ghost.

I gathered together my merry band of helpers and set out to tackle the criminal element: upper crust poisoners, underworld mobsmen, fake psychics, financiers who swindled the desperate masses, wives who murdered their lovers or their husbands, stepfathers who strangled their charges for inheritances…any and all "impossible crimes" were my bailiwick.

And above all, like my mentor Houdini, I made it my calling to debunk the charlatan mediums who preyed on the grieving, despondent, and weak-minded.

Which made my wartime experiences in Europe all the more…disturbing.

I had made it my mission, as The Green Ghost, to fill criminals' and mobsters' hearts with dread—*cue dramatic pipe organ*—when I went forth into the night with my dreadful skullface and supposed supernatural abilities, putting my expertise to use as a—*cue dramatic pipe organ*—relentless crusader for justice.

So, how did I, the great Green Ghost, fare against a real occult threat?

Reasonably well, I'm happy to say, and even more happy to be here to tell you so. Though I frankly still have some doubts as to whether these instances were really supernatural, as inexplicable as they were.

Meriem would say just what she always does when she urges me to accept her flashes of insight. She'd say that I need to overcome my scientific and rational biases, and get on with the business of protecting those who need protecting, and battling whatever dangers need battling, be they weird menaces or mass murderers.

Before the war, evildoers had quaked at the prospect of tangling with me. When I "turned on the Ghost," they went scurrying back to their dark corners rather than face The Green Ghost, the remorseless tracker of wrongdoers. But during the war, I admit I had quaked a time or two. Or three.

Before the war, I had been aided by a loyal band of assistants and partners. The aforementioned Ned, Tim Terry, and Meriem, as well as a few others. Of all my helpers, I'd only had contact with Meriem over the ensuing three and a half years. Those brief moments of respite with her helped me retain my sanity— even as she sometimes tested my sanity by insisting on joining and assisting on my missions.

As to the wartime missions themselves, they began simply enough—if you call "simple" an OSS request to liberate a noted archaeologist, one Horatio Smith, from a supposedly unescapable Nazi war camp. Smith has been something of a modern-day Scarlet Pimpernel, rescuing many from the clutches of the Nazis and helping them get out of Germany and other occupied territories. Getting Smith out and back in action was a big propaganda win for the Allies, and the OSS rewarded me accordingly…I was now working for them full time. "Drafted" may not have been the exact word, but it may have as well have been.

My missions were invariably behind enemy lines and involved disguise and misdirection. My superiors outfitted me with the latest and greatest equipment, much of which I've leveraged for my own use now that I'm bringing back The Ghost.

For instance, the gasmask.

Gone is the old rigmarole of painstakingly applying the Ghost makeup disguise. In the old days I'd descend to my underground lair and apply the makeup in a brightly-lit chamber, standing in front of a three-paneled mirror. This involved meticulously inserting wire ovals into my nose to elongate my nostrils, which I then darkened with pigment. I followed this up with dark makeup smudged across the lower eye sockets to give them a hollow look, and then applied light powder on my whole face to give it a sallow appearance. I finish it up with old, yellowed caps of ivory over my teeth. This whole process took twenty minutes, easily, to get right.

When I was operating in New York, as The Green Ghost, laying my traps for already-known criminals and charlatans, I had the luxury of twenty minutes to prepare.

Behind enemy lines, when disguises needed to be doffed and donned in five minutes, or less, there was no such luxury. The OSS experts provided pre-made rubber mask disguises, to which I added my own special touches.

The new Ghost mask is derived from a gasmask I had used on various OSS missions. It glows with phosphorous, and the black eyeholes are outfitted with one way lenses that glow on command, softly but eerily. It works just as well as the old makeup and it's on in under a minute rather than the prior fifteen or twenty. It has a few other tricks, courtesy of wartime spy agency technology, but I won't get into those now.

As the newly-returned Green Ghost, I still wear a slouch hat puled low over my skullface, and a dark suit, the jacket of which is packed with small but effective magic tricks, gas bombs, and other OSS toys.

I still have a double-edged throwing knife sheathed on my right forearm. I still carry a flat automatic underneath my suit jacket, and I am still not a stellar shot, which is a strange thing for a former spy to say, but it's true.

Spy.

The war in Europe had changed me. I had witnessed the depths of human evil, and perhaps skirmished with the supernatural. Emphasis on the perhaps. I am still a skeptic at heart. But what if I was wrong?

There was that strange encounter with a hideously wriggling whitish worm at an abandoned chateau in northern France . . . The skirmish with the pack of wolf-like men in the Balkans . . . The revolting frog-mouthed, tentacle-lipped creature that accosted me in the sewers of Paris . . . The nameless dread I felt when traversing the Baltic Sea on a mission to slip into Berlin . . .

Now that I had returned to New York, would the supernatural menaces I had confronted in France and Germany—or I had dreamed I confronted—follow me home?

● ● ●

Home was an abandoned church rectory on East 55th Street, my lair and safe house. I owned the building through a dummy corporation and had carefully encouraged the reputation it had as a haunted edifice.

Befitting a ghost-ridden church, the place was run down and crumbling—or at least the exterior was. The subterranean chamber which comprised my sanctum sanctorum was comfortably furnished and modern. It was the perfect warren for perfecting my latest tricks and disguises, and for holding planning meetings with my circle of aides, who also had access to the den, coming and going via various secret entrances and tunnels.

Ned was with me now, as were all my agents and friends.

Meriem White sat to my left in an easy chair, her magnificently distracting legs casually crossed, her green eyes shining with happiness.

Joe Harper, world-weary and yet with a trace of fading sophistication about him, sat to her left. He has been many things—a pitchman, a booking agent, a gambler, and a bookmaker. He knew Broadway like no other.

Dr. Robert Demarest, New York's Chief Medical Examiner, was next in the circle. His face was long and gloomy, causing others to underestimate him. His skills as an expert physician, pathologist, and scientist were matched by few others.

Tim Terry sat to Demarest's left. Tim was a top notch investigator, irrespective of his association with The Ghost, and he and I went back farther than anyone else in the room.

Next was Glenn Saunders. By a strange chance of fate, a along with a little plastic surgery, Glenn was my exact double: six feet, one inch, broad-shouldered, with a lean waist, blue eyes, and wavy blonde hair. Glenn had once taken my place on death row after I had been framed, giving me the chance I had needed to find the real killer. He was that kind of guy.

They all were, really. Loyal and steadfast, talented and accomplished.

I was a very fortunate man, and happy to be back home.

"...weird you've both been on death row now," Joe Harper said, snapping me out of it. I was happy to be back home, but there was work to do.

"It's bizarre," Demarest said, "but Ned's still on it, we've got to clear him."

"Right, we can play old home week later," I said, and turned to Ned. "Tell me what happened, how this got pinned on you."

Ned, sitting directly to my right, shrugged and wrapped his fingers around a steaming cup of coffee, as if his hands were cold. It was plenty warm in our little hideout, but I didn't blame him. "I'm not sure where to start," he said.

"Pick the first incident that comes to mind, that started you down this sorry path," I suggested. "Let your mind go and don't worry about logic. Just start wherever it makes sense."

"Okay, I'm game," Ned replied. "Well, I was having an early evening meeting with the District Attorney. We were putting together the file on the Toby Basinger case, and I poured us each a finger of whiskey to celebrate."

"Basinger," I repeated. I went a little cold at the name. I remembered that case. It had hit a little too close to home.

Meriem watched me intently. "Toby Basinger," she said. "Wasn't she that little flapper girl that...liked girls? She offed that nightclub chanteuse, what was her name again . . .?"

I tried to ignore Meriem's question and asked Ned one of my own: "What were you celebrating?"

"Why, catching her, of course," Ned replied.

"Catching Toby?" I asked.

Ned nodded and took a long gulp of coffee.

"Okay, back up a moment," I said. "When was this?"

"About a year ago," Ned replied.

"But she killed the...the nightclub singer back in '40, wasn't it?" I asked.

"Right," Ned said. "Rejected lover scenario. She escaped shortly afterward. We finally caught up with her last year. The D.A. and I were preparing the case that night."

"All right," I said, "I'm with you now. Go on."

"D.A. Skinner left about half an hour later, maybe around seven-thirty. It was late, but I had more paperwork to catch up on. It was probably around nine o'clock or so when they all came busting in." Ned's voice was starting to shake.

"Who, Ned? What happened?"

"The police captain on night duty and the jailhouse chief burst into my office, followed by four boys in blue. Everyone had their guns drawn, and the next thing I knew I was slammed on the floor, cuffed, and under arrest!"

Ned buried his head in his hands for a moment and then looked back up.

"They said I went down to visit the prisoner, Miss Basinger. They said I ordered them to let me into her cell and leave us alone. They said they heard a scream, five minutes later. They said when they opened up the cell, no one else was there but Toby Basinger, lying stone dead on the floor with a knife in her heart. They said there were multiple witnesses, there was no doubt it was me, and that no one other visitors had been in the cellblock at that late hour.

"But I swear to you George . . ." Ned Standish looked me straight in the eye. "I swear to you...*It wasn't me.*"

● ● ●

We took a breather from the questioning.

Meriem had gone to freshen the coffee. Glenn had volunteered to take care of it but she had insisted, saying she'd needed a bit of air.

"That was quite a start you gave when Ned mentioned Toby Basinger, George m'boy," Tim said. "Looks like Meriem's bent over it."

"Bent?" Glenn asked. "Why?"

"Girl trouble," Tim said.

"Tim, knock it off," I warned, but it was too late, and Glenn wouldn't be put off.

"What do you mean? The Basinger girl? Didn't she like...other girls?"

"Yeah, she liked one girl so much she killed her," the tiny crack detective said. "George's ex, the nightclub singer" he added meaningfully.

"Oh boy," Glenn said. "I think I'm starting to get it, now."

"Angel de la Ruse," I said, so low they almost couldn't her me.

Tim put a small, meaty hand on my shoulder. "She was bad business, m'boy."

"Yeah, and I'm probably in for a bit more bad business later tonight," I said, nodding toward the small kitchen where Meriem was brewing a fresh pot of joe.

"The whole thing is bad business," Demarest said. His long horse face was more somber than I'd ever seen it.

"That it is, that it is," Tim said, chewing on his unlit cigar thoughtfully. "We certainly haven't been able to crack it. Here's hopin' you can solve it, George."

"It's an impossible crime worthy of the great George Chance," Joe Harper said. He lit a Red Apple cigarette and took a long drag. "Almost seems like only you could have pulled it off, George."

"What? Me? Stop yanking my chain, I was out of the country a year ago, I've only been back a couple of weeks."

"Besides," Glenn interjected, "George had no motive."

"No motive! No motive, he says." Joe Harper was smirking. "Saunders, you never saw this Angel de la Ruse dame. She was built, and I mean built, and was hot for a reunion with our pal George, here, if you know what I mean. She was his ex! Who wouldn't want to rub out the little flapper in return for offing that magnificent dame? No motive, he says. Geez."

"Well, who cares about some imaginary motive anyway, Harper," Glenn retorted. "Like you said, it was an impossible crime."

"Maybe *too* impossible." Joe looked pointedly at Ned.

"Now wait just a goddamn minute—!"

"Hang on boys, hang on," I said, cutting off Ned's indignant reply. "I believe Ned, without question."

"Aw, I do too, boss," Joe replied. "I'm just blowin' off steam." He turned to Ned. "Sorry."

"Coffee's on, boys!" Mereim called as she walked in from the kitchen.

I grabbed my mug and looked up…and almost dropped it in my lap. My jaw went slack and I'm sure my cheeks went five shades of crimson.

Why am I sure?

Because the other five men in the room had the same combination of red-faced embarrassment and dumbfoundedness.

Meriem White stepped into the room, nude from the waist up. Her perfectly rounded, firm breasts bobbed slightly as strode forward. She was smiling cheerfully. The pot of fresh-brewed coffee was clutched tightly in her right hand.

The sheath dress she'd worn earlier in the evening was gone. She wore only a white satin garter belt with lacy straps. These stretched down to secure the white silk stockings which clung tightly to her marvelous legs. Legs which ended in perfect little feet encased in glitzy high heels.

Meriem marched brightly around the room, as if she hadn't just stopped all conversation dead in its tracks, and poured the dark brew into my outstretched cup.

"Black, just the way you like it, isn't it, dear?" Her green eyes were radiant. I nodded dumbly.

She marched around the small circle of seated men, blissfully unaware of their astonished, and frankly admiring, gazes. Looking back on it, perhaps I should have been jealous, but at the time I was frankly too stunned to react in any other way.

Stunned, and, like the other men, perhaps just a bit dazed.

Going around the circle, she reached Ned last. "Here go, Ned, you poor dear, you've been through so much, I hope this helps."

I saw the knife flash and was moving without thought. As I tackled Meriem she became a raven-haired beauty. Her eyes were of Cherrywood brown. The blue-sequined evening gown she wore ripped as we tumbled over Ned's chair and landed hard on the floor. My breath gusted violently upon impact.

While I struggled to catch air, Angel de la Ruse mounted me, her knees pinning my shoulders, her torn gown hanging from one shoulder, reminding me of what I had had so long ago.

I tried to focus. I'd have my strength back in a minute, but I didn't have a minute.

Angel's coal black hair hung in my face. I melted into her deep brown eyes. Her lips, ruby red and glistening, parted expectantly—as they had so many times years before.

Her olive skin rotted off in small chunks, exposing the ivory cheekbone below. She grinned, and a yellowed tooth fell out of a gumless cavity. A scent of dirt, not unpleasant, came from her gaping mouth.

She raised the knife and hissed. *"You should have saved me, George."*

I wondered where everyone else was and why weren't they helping me, and saw my closed fist hammering toward her skull.

Somehow I connected.

It felt like punching something squishy and wet and not all there, and then it was gone.

The knife clattered to the floor and the empty evening gown deflated and collapsed, draped across my body like a spent parachute.

● ● ●

"So," Mereim said, "Angel was able to take the form of others, and become corporeal, for at least short periods of time. As she did so, people around her seem to almost enter a trance state, a light hypnosis."

My lovely Meriem—thankfully—was unharmed. She had also been dazed by Angel's presence.

I shook my head in disbelief.

"All right then, George, how do you explain it?" Meriem challenged.

"I've spent my whole career debunking stuff like this," I said.

"Debunk away, if you can." She was getting angry. "For my part, I've always been more open-minded than you. Angel was a fetch, or a doppelgänger."

"And she came back and killed Toby Basinger," Ned said, "as revenge for killing *her.*"

"Yep," Meriem said, "now you're catching on."

"But why take Ned's form to do the deed?" Tim asked.

"Ned is one of George's closest friends," Meriem said. "George was out of the country and had a solid alibi. No one would ever believe he had done it. Pinning it on Ned was the next best revenge."

"Yeah," Joe Harper pitched in. "Imagine how George would feel knowing one of his best pals went to the chair and there was nothing he could do?"

"Okay," I said. "Then why another appearance tonight?"

"Easy," Meriem said. "You messed up her revenge by rescuing Ned, and she was going to get her payback one way or another. If you hadn't fought your way out of that daze, we might all be dead. I think she meant to kill us all and make you watch, and then kill you. You were never as deep in it as the rest of us—maybe because your illusionist background helps you see through other illusions. You saw the knife where the boys here saw a simple coffeepot, and when she was on you, you were able to fight back, whereas everyone else was essentially paralyzed."

"I have to hand it to you," I said, "It makes a sort of weird sense. And . . ."

"Yes?" Meriem wasn't going to let me off easy. "Go on."

". . . I think I saw her, outside the prison van, as we were about to break Ned out."

Meriem came over, put her hands around the back of my neck, pulled my head down, and lightly brushed my lips with hers. "There now, that wasn't so hard, was it? There's hope for you yet."

● ● ●

Several months had passed.

There was no way the authorities were going to buy the Angel de la Ruse ghost story. Heck, I still only half believed it, myself.

What they did believe was that George Chance, master illusionist, demonstrated that a similarly-skilled prestidigitator could have pulled off the Toby Basinger killing. I was in the clear because, as verified by the government, I had been on deep cover assignment in Europe.

With enough new evidence to justify a retrial, and more than enough reasonable doubt in play—investigators had never been able to connect Ned with the murder weapon, and had no way to place him at the scene other than the word of the now very unreliable witnesses—Ned Standish was a free man, and well on his way to being reappointed to his old position as Assistant Police Commissioner.

"I was beginning to despair that there was a chance, any chance at all, that you'd come," Ned said as we descended the courthouse steps. "Thank you, my friend."

"Come on, Ned," I said, a twinkle in my eye. "There's *always* a chance of a Ghost."

The End

Voodah
of
Thunder Mountain

By Derrick Ferguson

Based on the character created by Matt Baker and this story is dedicated to him with much respect and affection.

Mornings in the central village of the N'risi were usually pleasant, with much laughing, joking and singing as the men, women and children of Akahachi went about their daily routine. A new dawn was always welcome here and greeted with gratitude and joy.

But not this morning. This morning was greeted with screams of terror and fear. Men shouted and cursed as they fought against an enemy both strange and terrifying. Women snatched up children and ran for safety as the enemy raced through the wide, dusty streets of the village, the harsh, inhuman laughter coming from their bulging throats rising above the wails of the injured and the dead.

Ever since the first raid five days ago, guards had been doubled and a strict curfew observed. But after a few days had passed and no further attacks came, the guards relaxed their vigilance and the N'risi gradually stopped looking over their shoulder at every strange sound they heard. It was now obvious that the enemy had merely been biding their time, waiting for them to start to believe that first raid was just a one-time thing and unlikely to re-occur. Such was not the case.

The village center was a scene of outright terror. Several bodies lay on the ground, being torn to bloody, ragged ribbons by the misshapen claws of the enemy. They looked like men, but with elongated arms and legs that ended in hands and feet that were more like paws. They were hairless save for tufts of fur running down their spines, the backs of their forearms and the backs of their lower legs. The communicated with each other in a strange language that sounded like demented laughter. Due to their savagery, greater strength and agility they made swift work of the humans who were unprepared for the hideously aggressive man-beasts. One N'risi warrior was still on his feet, desperately swinging the light spear in his hand at a man-beast, half his scalp torn from his head. Blinded by the torrent of blood pouring down his face, his defense was ineffectual and the man-beast seized him with both hands, lifted the warrior over his head with both hands and dashed him against the side of the nearest building. The screams of the dying man competed with the sound of his own bones shattering. A woman ran at top speed through the village center, two man-beasts in hot pursuit, her back slashed so badly the whites of her bones showed clearly. Oya alone only knew where she was finding the strength to run.

Her salvation came in the form of a muscular mahogany form that seemingly plummeted from the sky. A savior more dangerous and more deadly a killer than the man-beasts themselves. A cry of challenge burst from the savior's lips as he landed on the back of one man-beast, his brawny right arm wrapping around the thick neck. The man-beast stopped laughing in delight and started squawking in surprise. So lost in a primal orgasm of blood lust that it had no idea of what was happening to it. The savior buried his knife up to the hilt in the man-beast's chest and by the time they both hit the ground, the man-beast was dead.

The savior dropped the dead body and looked around for more foes to slay.

The second man-beast hooted his war cry and charged the savior, his long right arm whistling out. If it had landed where the man-beast intended, the savior would have been disemboweled in an instant.

But he whipped backwards, getting his torso out of the way of that slashing attack and as the man-beast's other arm came around to try and slice his throat, the savior's hunting knife sliced cleanly through that arm, taking it off just above the elbow. The cleaver-like design of the knife greatly added to the weight of the blade and backed by the immense bicep of the arm that held the knife, it was a task that looked frighteningly simple. The man-beast howled and toppled over on his back, the stump gushing blindingly red ichor. The savior ignored him. He would not survive another thirty seconds losing blood like that.

A warrior staggered drunkenly in the savior's general direction. He couldn't have known which way he was going due to the amount of blood pouring down his face. But he caught the attention of two man-beasts crazed with the smell of so much fresh blood. One of them covered an amazing twenty feet in one spectacular bound and came right down on the back of the warrior. Bones snapped and popped like breadsticks. The sounds were nothing compared to the shriek that burst from the lips of the warrior as the man-beast drove his paw right into the warrior's back. There was a ripping and rending of muscle and sinew and the man-beast's hand came up with the warrior's still beating heart clutched tightly in those thick fingers.

Then the savior hit the man-beast in a near full speed charge and the creature's back broke from that incredible impact with a thick, meaty snap. It hit the ground, the lower half of its body twisted in a grotesque angle. The warrior's heart fell from its hand into the dust.

Seeing what had happened to his comrade, the second man-beast hooted in dismay and simply bounded away, covering ten feet or more in every spring.

The savior went over to where the woman had collapsed. His expert eye told him that she was dying. It was nothing less than a miracle she had survived this long with those hideous wounds. He knelt next to her, took her bloody hand in his.

Her eyes opened. And seeing who held her hand, she amazingly managed a last smile. "Voodah...thank you for trying..." Her eyes closed and she was gone.

Voodah slowly stood up. Six feet of pure muscle hardened by life lived in a jungle where there were more ways to die than there were stars in the sky. A headband of braided leather dyed red and white served to keep sweat out of his eyes during his exertions in the heat of the day. And such eyes they were. Amber in color. The color of a wolf's eyes. He flicked the foul man-beast blood from his foot long blade with a simple twist of his wrist. The foot long blade was unlike any had ever seen. Voodah's mother had given it to him on his fifteenth birthday, saying it was a gift from his father. The keen edge of the blade had not lost its sharpness in all the years Voodah had used it. It was quite unlike any knife seen in that country and many coveted it. Many had died trying to take it from Voodah. His hands and forearms were wrapped in leather bands also dyed red as were the leather bands on his feet and lower legs, up to his calves, leaving his fingers and toes free. The loincloth of white and red he wore appeared to have been woven from some sort of metallic fibers. A coiled ten foot length of good rope and a shepherd's sling hung from his belt.

He sheathed his knife and turned away. There was nothing he could do for the dead. His thoughts now had to be for ensuring that the living stayed that way.

The attack appeared to be over. The man-beasts had withdrawn, leaving death and grief in the wake. The sounds of weeping women and wrathful men now filled the air.

Voodah found the village chief at the village's main gate. Aged he might be but Gahni still stood ramrod straight and the spear he held tightly in his sinewy right hand was encrusted with the blood of the enemy. For forty years had he been chief of all the N'risi and for twenty years before that he had been the foremost warrior of his people.

Voodah and Gahni clasped forearms in greeting. "I came as soon as I could, Chief Gahni. When word of the first attack reached me I was in the land of the Ranu, visiting friends."

Gahni nodded. "I understand. And when these creatures did not attack us again, we thought that one attack would be the only one. We thought they were migrant creatures and had continued on their way." Gahni pointed with his spear at one of the creatures on the ground. "Have you ever seen the like? I know you have travelled far. Further than any N'risi ever has. I was hoping that you had seen these creatures in your travels. That was why I sent for you."

Voodah hunkered down next to the creature. He carefully examined the heavy, misshapen jaw and broad teeth. The snout like nose and the bulging red eyes. He took one huge paw in his hand and felt the muscles in the forearms and shoulders. He stood up, shaking his head. "Never have I seen the like. I have never even heard of anything like it. This is a creature completely new to me. They just came and slew? For no reason?"

"Some of our women and children were missing. At first we thought they were dead but when a count was made, that is when we knew for a fact that they were gone. A rescue party was formed immediately and set out after them. But they returned a day later. They could not pick up any trail at all. That is another reason why I sent for you. You can track a snake across stone."

"You exaggerate my abilities, Chief Gahni."

"And you insult my intelligence. I have known you for many years, Voodah. I have seen you do things that no man can do. But you have long been a friend to the N'risi and have never failed to give us your aid when we asked for it. So I have never spoken of what I have seen. I ask you again for your aid. If these were men as I know men, I would send every warrior under my command after them. But this…" again Gahni pointed with his spear. "This is a foe I cannot fight."

Voodah started to answer but was interrupted by a shrieking that sent clouds of birds from their perches in the trees into the sky. Gahni's wife Banga burst through the crowd of villagers encircling Voodah and Gahni. She fell at her husband's feet, screaming; "they have taken Dalili! They have taken our daughter!"

Gahni bent down to take his wife in his arms even as he snapped orders to the warriors of his personal guard. "Search everywhere!"

No more needed to be said. The guard spread out in all directions. In this the villagers and the rest of the warriors assisted them. Dalili was the youngest of Gahni's seven daughters and much beloved by all.

With so many searching it did not take long to verify that Dalili was indeed nowhere in Akahachi. Banga was taken away to Ghani's dwelling where the servants could look after her and care for her.

The look in Ghani's eyes decided Voodah's course. "Take care of your people, Chief. I will find these creatures, I swear. I will find where they live and I will ensure they will not attack you again."

Ghani nodded. He did not make Voodah promise to bring back his daughter alive. That would not have been fair to Voodah. Ghani knew full well that his daughter could be dead by now. But he would settle for Voodah delivering his vengeance. "You may have as many of my warriors as you wish to assist you."

"I go alone. I can travel swifter by myself."

"You will need help when you catch up to them, surely!"

Voodah smiled. "Did you not yourself say that you have seen me do things other men cannot?" And then he turned and ran. The villagers parted as Voodah increased his speed and soon he was through the gates, through the clearing on the other side of the village wall and into the dark, brooding greenness of the jungle.

● ● ●

Once away from the eyes of the N'risi, Voodah allowed himself to run at his full speed. If any of the N'risi had seen him they would have gasped in amazement. Ghani had seen Voodah run the first time they had met many years ago and it took Voodah some time to convince him that he was human. At least he thought he was. His mother had never told him who his father was or what people they belonged to. She had raised him on The Mountain of Thunder with only old Kose and his wife Saada to aid her. Despite his age, Kose seemed to have a bottomless well of woodcraft, combat and survival skills that he passed along to the boy. It was Saada who taught Voodah languages and how to write in those languages. She also taught him the art of medicine, how to brew potions, make poultices and which herbs and roots would cure and which ones would kill.

Voodah's nostrils flared. He had noticed the odd smell of the man-beasts and that was the trail he followed. The musky, heavy scent lingered in the air. Even as a boy Voodah noticed that he seemed to be able to see, smell and hear better than any of the boys he played with in the village at the base of The Mountain of Thunder. When he asked his mother about that, she did the same thing she always did; she smiled enigmatically and said that they were gifts from his father.

Voodah knew he could cover more ground if he took to the trees. He was confident of the trail the man-beasts had taken and even more confident that he could pick it up once he had covered a significant distance. Going by way of the trees would close the gap between Voodah and his quarry.

He scrambled up the nearest tree, using fingers and toes with the agility of an ape. He held onto to no branches or vines but shimmied up the thick bole of the tree with a grace both powerful and elegant. Once in the upper levels of the tree, Voodah ran along branches that were barely wider than his feet.

Voodah flung himself out into thin air, tumbling through the air over and over. He landed on a thick branch that bent like rubber and then firmly sprang back, flinging Voodah up into the air in a soaring arc. He appeared to be heading right into a sold tangle of leaves, branches and vines but Voodah twisted his body in such a way that he sailed through the tangle as if it weren't there.

He reached out his hands to seized hold of a vine and then swung in a dizzying arc. Voodah let go of the vine and sailed through the air as if he could fly. There was nothing but the rustle of the leaves and the humming of the wind and a shaft of bright sunlight that haloed Voodah.

Voodah reached the end of his arc and plummeted toward the jungle floor, arms outstretched as he picked up speed rapidly. His arms went out and his hands seized a branch, twirling around it twice like an Olympic gymnast on a high bar and then he came to rest on top of the branch. He paused a few seconds to get his bearings and then dropped fifteen feet to a thicker branch. His nostrils flared as he sought the scent. And he caught it. Satisfied, he dropped twenty feet to the spongy ground, his powerful leg muscles easily absorbing the shock of landing. He could have dropped from twice that height with no harm at all. His strength was yet another gift from his father, according to his mother. Many gifts had Voodah received from his father. And while he was grateful for all of them, he had never received the one gift he valued above all others; the name of his father.

Voodah followed the heady scent for another half a mile, loping along at an easy trot that ate up distance without tiring him out. His sharp eyes picked up tracks in the ground. There was a hunting party following the same spoor he was. A party of ten warriors. Voodah suddenly stopped as he picked out another, smaller set of footprints. He crouched down to take a closer look. Yes, they were the footprints of a woman. He was sure of it. In fact, it appeared that the woman was leading the warriors. Intrigued, Voodah increased his pace so that he would catch up to them.

Presently he came to a gorge over which a huge fallen tree formed a natural bridge. Voodah saw the ten warriors just starting over on their side, clambering up the long petrified roots that made for hand and footholds to provide access. And on the other side of the gorge, Voodah saw the beast-men. At least a dozen and each one of them held a squirming N'risi captive. Sharp as his eyes were, Voodah still could not make out if one of them was Dalili. Voodah increased his speed, his intention to join up with those ten warriors. Together they could catch up to the beast-men and rescue the…

One of the ten warriors screamed. His sandaled feet slipped on a patch of moss and he lost his balance. His arms waved wildly, his spear and shield falling into the gorge. The other warriors, taken by surprise, stood petrified.

But not so Voodah. Even as he hurried onto the tree bridge, his right hand seized the length of rope at his belt. One end was already fashioned into a noose and as the warrior fell, Voodah hurled the rope outwards. The eyes of the other warriors opened wider in astonishment as the noose encircled the falling warrior's wrist. It pulled tight as Voodah braced himself so that he would not also fall. The warrior screamed against as his shoulder was yanked out of the socket. But he still lived.

Voodah pulled the man up and handed him over to his comrades. Then they all made their way across the tree bridge until they were safely on the other side.

One of the warriors stepped forward. As impressively muscled as Voodah himself with skin the color of a mountain cliff, the elaborate markings on his shield, his bronze greaves and the ivory horn on his helmet identified him as the leader of these men. He eyed Voodah with no trace of fear at all but suspicion. "Be you demon or human? Never in all my years have I seen any man perform such a feat."

Voodah extended his hand. "Take my arm and see for yourself that I am a man, just as you are." He slapped his chest with his other hand. "Hear that? Flesh and muscle, just like yours."

"Who are you?"

"I am Voodah."

A ripple murmured among the warriors. The leader nodded and clasped Voodah's arm. "I thought so. Many are the tales told of Voodah. I can see for myself that they were not exaggerated."

"You are men of the Mkhulu. You are far from home. Your lands are at least six days travel that way." Voodah pointed to the east.

The leader nodded. "I am Mordu, war chief of the Mkhulu. The man-beasts raided one of our villages six days ago. My chief charged me with the task of finding them. We did." And here Mordu allowed himself a wolfish grin of satisfaction. "After we slew them, I sent their captives back home with half of my men. The other half stayed with me as our guide found another trail of man-beasts. I decided that we should continue to track them and find out where they come from. Maybe we can destroy them all and put an end to their raiding."

Voodah nodded. "Then we are on the same mission. The beast-men raided Akahachi just a few hours ago. They took the chief's daughter. I have given him my word that I shall find the lair of these beast-men and put an end to this."

"Just a few hours ago you say? That must have been when I lost their trail."

The voice reminded Voodah of the music played by the Sisasei, that remarkable tribe of people who every waking moment was dedicated to music and always inventing and fashioning new instruments to give voice to the music of their souls. A woman stepped forth. Striking in height as she was just a few inches shorter than Voodah himself which made her taller than some of the warriors. Her terra cotta skin was utterly flawless in its exotic beauty. Eyes the color of desert sand regarded Voodah with cool interest. Her brightly colored kanga flattered and accentuated the curves of her slim body.

"You track for these warriors?" Voodah asked. "But you are not Mkhulu. What is your interest in this?"

"You can tell just by looking at me that I am not an Mkhulu woman? How can you do that?"

"I am Voodah."

The woman smiled. "I was stolen away by Ichebayn pirates from my people when I was but a girl. I was sold as a slave to a Mkhuluan prince. Thanks to my gifts and skills I rose up in stature in his household and was able to buy my freedom."

"Gifts and skills, eh? And what would those be?"

"Not what you are thinking, I assure you. My name is Jano."

"Jano sees with The Sight That Is Not Sight. She has been of use to our king and my warriors many times," Mordu said. "And we waste much time with all this talking. Are you with us, Voodah?"

"As I said before, we are on the same mission."

"Then let us be perfectly clear: I am in command." Mordu's voice and the way his hand tightened on his spear emphasized his words that this was not a matter on which there could be a compromise.

Voodah salaamed in respect to Mordu as Voodah understood quite well that Mordu needed to keep face in front of his men. "I am content to provide what aid and assistance I can unto you, O Mordu."

Mordu visibly relaxed. "Very well, then. Let us resume the pursuit then."

The warrior whose arm had been dislocated was back on his feet, two of his comrades having helped him to place the shoulder back in his socket. He was sore but alive. He walked over to Voodah and clasped forearms with him. "My name is Makena. My life is yours for all the rest of my days no matter how long or how short the gods see fit."

"Your life belongs to your king, Makena. I am but a stranger who saw a man in distress and helped. That is all."

"As you say. But as for me, I shall lay down my life for Voodah if and when it becomes necessary."

And the group started off in pursuit of the beast-men with Mordu and Jano leading the way. There was a trail of sorts here on this side of the gorge that made the walking easier. Voodah walked a bit closer to Jano so he could speak to her without all hearing his words; "I beg your pardon if I spoke out of turn when you spoke of your skills and gifts."

Jano favored him with a dazzling smile that washed over Voodah and suddenly made him feel warm inside. "It is the nature of a man to think in such a manner. I do not take offense. I have heard much about you, Voodah. I do not think it is in your nature to offer insults just to be insulting."

"It is not, I assure you." Voodah replied. "I am curious. Once you bought your freedom, why did you not return to your people?"

Jano shrugged. "My master did not mistreat me. In fact, the Mkhulu treat their slaves very well in comparison to some other tribes such as the Sohtreh or the Orphi. I have seen what they do to their slaves. And I was taken so long ago that I barely remember my people and their ways. I was much more comfortable with the Mkhulu and once I bought my freedom I was treated and regarded as a member of the tribe."

Voodah nodded. "And you truly have The Sight That is Not Sight?"

Jano gave him another smile but this was one tinged with a hint of mischievous mystery as she replied; "Let us just say that much like you, Voodah, I can do many things that are remarkable to others and leave it at that for now. We have much walking to do and I need to concentrate."

● ● ●

"Have you ever seen this before, Voodah?"

"Never. And I have been through this region before. I am certain I would have seen that. It is not something I would not have noticed."

"Jano?"

"There is something not quite right about this region. I have felt it for the past few miles. I suggest we formulate a plan of action quickly."

Voodah, Jano and Mordu stood on the crest of a hill overlooking a majestic clearing in the middle of the jungle. In that clearing was something none of them expected to see; a small town, encircled by a high stone wall. The buildings were constructed from wood and stone and not in the fashion of any of the tribes Voodah was familiar with. And like Jano he sensed there was something not right about this region. What it was, he could not say for sure. But Voodah had long ago learned to listen to and trust his instincts. They had kept him alive more times than he had had hot meals.

Mordu motioned to his warriors who waited at the bottom of the hill. They joined their leader who said; "We are going to enter the town and speak to whoever is in charge. Stay alert!"

"Would it not be wiser to send a man on ahead to scout the town and bring back a report?" Voodah said. "It might be a mistake to reveal how few we are to a town that looks as if it has a goodly number of warriors to defend it."

Mordu leveled a baleful gaze on Voodah. "We have seen no signs of life, no lights in the windows, no smoke from the chimneys. Either the beast-men have slaughtered the townspeople or they have fled, abandoning the town. In either case, night is coming. We have but two hours of good daylight left. I would not like to waste them explaining my orders to you."

Voodah salaamed. "I am yours to command, O Mordu."

Mordu grunted and nodded. He gestured with his spear and they all set off at an easy run through the knee-high grass of the clearing. Voodah strained his eyes and ears, hoping to spot any signs of danger. But he saw nothing. And that worried him even more. There should have been guards stained on the wall at regular intervals and gatekeepers manning the watchtowers on either side of the main gate. It was their job to challenge any visitors and to open the gates if in their judgement the visitors were legitimate. The watchtowers stood empty and silent.

The gates of the town stood wide open. Mordu went first, followed by Voodah and Jano, then the ten warriors. Wind whistled through the deserted streets. Windows were shut tight. There were no dogs barking, no commerce being done. No women going about their errands or men doing their work. The nameless town was devoid of people.

"The trail of the beast-men leads here," Jano insisted in answer to Mordu's questioning look.

Voodah slipped away from the group and in a thrice climbed up to the roof of one of the buildings. He could search much faster on his own. Making no more noise than a leaf falling from a tree branch, he ran from one rooftop to another, easily leaping the gaps between the roofs. His blood pounded hot in his veins and his muscles felt good as he sprang and leapt with an agility that could only be matched by by the great apes themselves. As he ran, Voodah's eyes scanned the town. Still no signs of life anywhere. This was a mystery that was quickly deepening from strange to frightening. Could the beast-men truly be involved in the disappearance of the population of an entire town?

Whatever had happened to them hadn't been violent. Voodah saw no blood, smelled none either fresh or dried. In fact, there were none of the smells associated with human beings dwelling in a community together at all. There should have been smells of cooking, of waste, of numerous body odors mingling together. Smells of fire, of vegetables. The range of smells he should have smelled was too many to count but they should have been there.

And they weren't.

But there was light and sound and it was coming from the multi-storied red sandstone building in the center of the town. Voodah did not hesitate for a second. He resumed leaping across the rooftops toward the domed building. He couldn't waste time going back for Mordu and his warriors. And Voodah was fairly certain that if he did go back, Mordu would not be happy that Voodah had found what might be the lair of the beast-men before him. In any case, Voodah would better be able to slip in by himself.

A long flight of steps led up to the entrance of the domed building. No guards were in front. Voodah crouched on a rooftop, letting his senses do their work and provide him with information. There was no way to get in through the roof, which was obvious. And he could scout around for another way in but his instincts were telling him that he might as well just go on in through the main entrance.

Voodah sprang from the roof and landed lightly in the street. Adjusting his sheath so that he would have no trouble getting to his knife when he needed it, Voodah brazenly strode right up the stairs and pushed open the gleaming, inlaid doors and stepped inside.

The interior was as lushly decorated as any of the fabulous palaces of the southern kingdoms which Voodah had been to as a boy. He and his mother had made several journeys to the lands of Makeda, Ronga, Bimaro and Jimangi during his growth from boyhood to manhood. His mother had presented him to the kings of those nigh legendary lands and they had simply placed their right hand on the boy's head and said; "He is Voodah." And that was all. Voodah had asked his mother why they did that and all she would say was that they owed much to his father.

The marble floor of the entrance hall felt cool underneath Voodah's toes as he made his way through. Huge chandeliers with candles as thick around as Voodah's thighs provided ample illumination. At the other end was another set of tall inlaid doors that Voodah shoved open. Before him was a magnificent room ablaze with light that reflected from the tapestries woven with gold and silver thread. Two huge hand-carved wooden chairs rested on a dais at the far end of the room.

Also in the room was a dozen of the beast-men, snarling and roaring at Voodah. But they did not attack. And he highly suspected that it was because the man and woman who sat on those throne-like chairs had not given the word for them to attack.

Both the man and woman were splendid specimens of near-human perfection. Both of them had tawny umber skin and this, along with their distinctive facial features led Voodah to think that they were brother and sister. The man's words confirmed with when he stood up, his leather garments creaking as he did so. "See, my sister? A suitable male for you has arrived! And you were afraid that the men our servants have brought us would not be strong enough to survive your affections!"

"Who are you?"

The man folded heavily muscled arms across his wide chest and laughed. "As an uninvited guest in our town and our home, it is upon you to introduce yourself first, I would think."

"I am Voodah."

"You say that as if we are supposed to know the name," the woman said. She had not taken her eyes off Voodah since he entered the chamber. Her eyes roamed freely over his impressively muscled body.

"I am indeed well known in the jungle. But perhaps you are not of the jungle? I do not recall any town ever being here and I know the jungle well. Where are you from?"

"I am Darius and this is my sister Lesi. We are the last of our people. Lesi brought us here so that we may repopulate our village and become the mother and father of a new race. One hardier and stronger."

"And what happened to your people?" Voodah asked. He kept his eyes on the beast-men but they still did not make any move toward him. Once Darius and Lesi began speaking, their snarling and roaring subsided into a low rumble.

"Does it matter?" Lesi stood up. Silken robes of shimmering silver and gold slithered over her long arms and legs as she walked slowly down the steps of the dais and approached Voodah. "You are truly a man unlike any I have seen. Tell me...have you fathered many sons?"

"That is none of your business. What is my business is that I have come for the N'risi people you have taken against their will. Produce them so that I may return them to their families."

Lesi came closer. Her eyes bored into Voodah's and he found it impossible to look away. They shone with inner golden lights and her voice seemed to both increase and decrease in volume as she said; "That cannot happen. We need these people so that we may create a stronger race. Our people were strong, yes...but not strong enough. We took them, one by one until only Darius and I were left."

Voodah tried to move his legs but could not. It was as if they were rooted to the ground. All he could see was Lesi's eyes and all he could hear was Lesi's voice as she said; "You *are* different. I can sense it. I can *feel* it. You will give me many strong children. But first..."

It was seeing the teeth that snapped Voodah out of the spell.

He swung his arm and it connected against the side of Lesi's head, sending her sprawling. Darius roared, opening his mouth impossibly wide, his incisors lengthening. Upon hearing that roar, the beast-men charged, loping straight at Voodah.

Voodah was no fool. As strong and as swift he was he knew that he was no match for a dozen of the beast-men attacking him all at the same time. He turned and sprinted from the throne chamber, his powerful legs easily increasing the distance between him and the beast-men. He ran back through the entrance hall and then to the outside.

"Voodah! What do you here?"

Mordu, Jano and the ten warriors stood at the bottom of the stairs, just as surprised to see Voodah as he was to see them.

"We have been searching for you!" Jano said. "We..."

"No time to explain! Prepare yourselves for battle!" Voodah shouted, drawing his own knife. The beast-men burst from the domed building in a wave of claws, teeth and screaming, savage bloodthirsty rage.

The men of the Mkhulu were men indeed. Brandishing their weapons they uttered ear-shattering war cries and met the charge of the beast-men with one of their own. Gleaming spearheads were soon covered in blood. Claws tore at flesh and crushed bone. The beast-men were not used to warriors who gave as well as they got but soon the smell of freshly spilled blood filled their nostrils and drove them into frenzy.

Voodah was right in the thick of battle, weaving and bobbing, ducking under the swipes of huge paws that would have crippled him if not outright killed him if they had landed. His huge knife was no longer shiny. From tip to cross guard it dripped with the blood of beast-men. Voodah uttered his own war-cry, a howling ululation that sounded like something that had no business coming from a human throat.

He leaped onto the back of a beast-man who already bled from a dozen wounds inflicted by two dead warriors who lay at the beast-man's feet, their heads crushed. Voodah reached out a hand, yanked the beast-man's head back and with one swift movement, sliced open the beast-man's throat. A torrent of steaming blood spilled out to splash on the bodies of the warriors.

Voodah spied Jano running into the domed building. "Jano! No!" Voodah ran after her. She had no idea of the horror inside and she would be helpless against the spell-making of Lesi.

Or so he thought.

He re-entered the throne chamber. Darius was nowhere to be seen but Lesi and Jano appeared to be locked in a staring contest. Lesi was no longer beautiful. Her lower jaw had elongated to accommodate the overlapping sets of razor-sharp teeth that had burst through her gums. Voodah could plainly see Lesi straining to attack Jano but she could not. It was as if invisible chains held her.

"Go!" Jano commanded. "Through that door behind the dais! The man ran through there! I can deal with this witch!"

Voodah did not hesitate. Time later for explanations. There was only time for action now. Swift, terrible, bloody action. He ran around the dais and saw that there was a circular door with a handle in the middle. The door was ajar and Voodah's swift, forceful kick opened it all the way, tearing it loose from the heavy brass hinges.

Over two dozen men, women and children cowered in a corner of the room. Beds were knocked over, indicating that this was the place where Darius and Lesi had kept them. The still rank smell of fear and despair in the air also told Voodah that.

Upon hearing the door being kicked open, Darius whirled around. His eyes had swollen to twice their size and were now like huge lanterns as they glowed with orange heat. His mouth was a grotesquery, resembling that of a lamprey's. His elongated fingers sprouted ragged claws.

Darius hissed and in reply, Voodah let loose with his war-cry and sprang at Darius. Darius slithered out of the way of Voodah's spring as if the floor were ice. He gripped Voodah by the arm and shoulder and with a surge of muscles, tossed Voodah at the nearest wall.

But Voodah twisted in mid-air like a gigantic panther and struck the wall with his feet. Again displaying a near superhuman co-ordination, he propelled himself off the wall, right back at the startled Darius. Taken by surprise, Darius couldn't get out of the way in time. Voodah's right hand seized him by the throat. Man and monster crashed to the floor with an impact that seemed to shake the room.

His transformed mouth was incapable of speech but Voodah could hear Darius 'speak' in his mind; *Join us! You have more in common with us than you do with the mewing rabble! Join us and we can be kings of this land! Who could stand against you, my sister and I if we join forces?*

Voodah said nothing. He raised his knife as far back as it would go and brought it down right in that terrible, gnashing obscenity of a mouth. Darius screamed as his blood sprayed into the air. Voodah withdrew the knife and removed his hand so that he could sever Darius' head with two swift strokes. Darius lay still but his eyes still glared and his mouth still moved for a long minute until those baleful eyes closed and the mouth stopped.

Voodah got to his feet, wiping Darius' stinking blood from his face. He turned to the still cowering captives. "You have nothing to fear from me. I am Voodah, a friend to the N'risi. Some of you know me, do you not?"

"Voodah!" from somewhere in the crowd a girl of about thirteen summers burst forth and ran to embrace him, ignoring the blood on him.

"Dalili! I dared not hope that I would find you alive. The joy your mother and father will feel upon seeing you again will fill their hearts to overflowing."

"I want to go home, Voodah!"

"And so you shall, little one. And so you shall." Voodah lifted his head to smile at the others. "All of you will."

Voodah led the way out of that horrid room and came upon Jano standing over the body of Lesi. Blood had poured from Lesi's ears, eyes, nose and her eyeballs were globs of pulp running down her cheeks to mix with the blood. Voodah said nothing, merely looked from Lesi to Jano. Back to Lesi and then back to Jano. "Gifts and skills indeed."

Jano merely smiled.

● ● ●

At last the work was done. The bodies of the brave Mkhuluan warriors who had died in the battle were laid in a row. Their shields and spears lay on their chests. Only Mordu and Makena survived the battle. The bodies rested on biers of tree branches and now Mordu set fire to the branches. He and Makena said prayers for the souls of their dead brothers in arms.

The bodies of the monsters Darius and Lesi along with their beast-men had been carried into the domed building and dumped unceremoniously in the throne chamber. This building was then set on fire. No one said any prayers for them.

Mordu walked up to Voodah. "My thanks for your help. The name of Voodah will be an honored one among the Mkhulu and you will find friendship and honor in our village."

"Peace and long life unto you, war chief of the Mkhulu. It has been an honor to fight by your side and I am proud to call you comrade." The two men clasped forearms. Makena stepped forward to also clasp forearms with Voodah. The two men smiled and nodded at each other.

Mordu gathered together his people and they started their long trek back to the lands of the Mkhulu. The N'risi stood apart and surprisingly, Jano stood with them.

"Why are you not returning with Mordu and the the others?"

"I told him that I wished to visit for a time in the land of the N'risi. I have not seen much of the world and the gods did not mean for a woman to live her entire life in one place. I can always return to Mkhulu when I wish. And you will need help in returning these people home, am I right?"

Voodah threw back his head and for the first time in days enjoyed a good laugh. "Somehow I have the feeling that you are right most of the time, Jano! Very well, then! Come, all of you! It is time for you to go home!"

● ● ●

"I will never be able to thank you for returning my daughter to me, O Voodah. And for bringing me a new one!"

Voodah and Ghani stood on the porch of his dwelling. It had been three days since Voodah had returned Dalili and the others to Akahachi. It had been three days of celebration and jubilation that had not been seen in Akahachi for some time. And as the guest of honor, many were the gifts given to him by the grateful families of the people he had rescued. Voodah merely instructed that they be placed in the simple cottage that had long ago been set aside for his use when he came to visit. Voodah had many such cottages in the villages of the tribes he befriended. Wherever he may go, he always had a home.

As Jano came out of the house to join them, Voodah raised a questioning eyebrow in her direction. "I take it you mean Jano?"

"Indeed. Once you told me about how she aided you in rescuing Dalili and the others, I could do no less than ask her to stay with my wife and I and join our family. For as long as she wishes to stay with us, Jano will be our daughter and we will treat her as such."

Jano curtsied slightly. "An honor that is too great for one such as me, O Chief of the N'risi."

"None of that! I have told you to call me father! Must I make it a command?"

Jano giggled. "No, you do not have to make it a command...Father."

"And what of you, Voodah? Will you stay with us a while longer?"

Voodah shook his head. "It has been long since I have visited my mother on The Mountain of Thunder. I will go and spend some time with her." Voodah turned to Jano. "Peace and long life to you, Jano, daughter to Ghani, Chief of all the N'risi."

Jano curtsied again. "May the gods guide your steps, Voodah."

Voodah nodded and turned to go. He started off at a jog, waving at the villagers as they bade him farewell. He soon was out of the gates and crossing the lush, green plain to return to the jungle.

"He will return, will he not?" Jano asked.

"Of course he will." Ghani placed an arm around her shoulders. "Whenever we need him....whenever any and all who need his aid and protection from evil... Voodah will return."

The End

Dash and the Dangerous Dame
by Kevin Findley

The Southern Pacific Sunday run from Los Angeles to San Ysidro and back was considered a milk run. For the most part, it's about getting weekend vacationers back home and drunken idiots back to their jobs, wives and girlfriends. The round trip is eight and a half hours, to include taking on and off-loading cargo and passengers. It's also ideal to let new company detectives get their feet wet.

For James Walter 'Dash' Dasher, that meant a quiet ride with a trainee just out of the classroom. If he was lucky, perhaps even a chance to meet a secretary or a script girl on the way back from a Mexican weekend with her girlfriends.

"It's eight o'clock Mr. Dasher; time to check in with the engineer. Do we both go or should one of us stay here to keep an eye on the passenger cars?"

"Go ahead and check on the engineer Sid. I'll try to hold back this riot without you."

"Yes Sir! I'll be back ASAP." The recently discharged Corporal Harriman executed a perfect about-face and almost double-timed to the front of the train.

Dash chuckled and started walking back through the passenger cars. In the third was a group of four young women. Two were badly sunburned and being fussed over by a third. The fourth girl kept looking behind them at a man near the back of the car. Dash looked at who was keeping her attention and recognized the fellow immediately. He quickly forgot about the girls and walked up to introduce himself.

"Excuse me Sir. Are you Nigel Bruce?"

The mouth under the bushy mustache smiled. "Why yes I am."

Dash put out his hand. "It's a pleasure to meet you Mr. Bruce. My name is James Dasher; I'm a detective with the Southern Pacific. I just saw you in *Charge of the Light Brigade* and I enjoyed your character, Bertram Lynch, in *Murder In Trinidad* a couple of years ago. He was a pretty accurate investigator for a movie; most aren't."

Bruce laughed and shook Dash's hand. "Thank you, Mr. Dasher. I just wish more people had enjoyed the film as much as they did good old Bertie."

"Well I certainly did, thank you for the performance." He hesitated a moment and then pressed on. "May I ask what brings you on the train tonight Sir? Another movie?" The Southern Pacific had a relationship with all of the major studios, but Dash hadn't been told of any scenes being shot on the train for this run and didn't see a film crew.

"No, I was visiting family friends in Mexico for a few days. I was born in Ensenada while my father worked there with an engineering company in '95."

"So is this area as much home as England?"

The actor laughed, "Not quite, Mr. Dasher, but it's certainly more comfortable for me than many British citizens in Hollywood." He gestured to the padded bench in front of him. "I was about to order a drink. Sit down and join me if you have a moment and please, call me Nigel."

"Thank you, Nigel. Make it James if you'd like."

The waiter came immediately at Nigel's gesture. "Two whiskies please." He nodded and as he turned to leave, Dash spoke up.

"Make sure you pour from the good stock, Murray."

"I'd never give you the cheap stuff, Dash." Then he made a point of winking at Nigel and rolled his eyes at the detective. Both men laughed.

"So tell me about the exciting world of railroad detectives, James."

"It's a lot like the Army, Nigel. A big book of rules and a whole lot of hurry up and wait. What's better though is you get to throw any troublemakers off at the next stop." Dash told a few of his more interesting stories, catching politicians getting friendly with constituents in the baggage car, a bobcat escaping it's cage and scaring a group of nuns in the middle of the night and an honest to God train robber who picked a carload of Marshals coming home from a convention to try and rob.

Sid Harriman came back for new orders while they were laughing over the hapless thief. The young ladies had already joined them by this time and the fourth one easily convinced Sid that she had loved trains since she was a little girl and wanted him to show her everything this one had to offer. As the other three returned to their seats to apply more sunburn cream, Dash pointed to the cane by Bruce's hand.

"Were you injured in the war, Nigel?"

"Yes, at Cambrai back in 1915. What makes you ask that?"

"You drop your hand just above that knee and massage it fairly often. I make that gesture every time a train gets up in the higher elevations."

Nigel smiled and shook his head knowingly. "Where were you wounded?"

"Chateau-Thierry; 1918."

"Ah." Both men sat silent for a time after that, each remembering good and bad days. The mood lifted again when Murray brought another round of drinks.

"So tell me James, why does our friend Murray here call you 'Dash'?"

"It depends on who you ask, Nigel. There are a few sore losers that claim my hands are so fast they can't tell if I'm dealing off the bottom of the deck or not."

"What do the rest say?"

"Most of those are women who say I convinced them to move too fast."

As they finished their drinks, the engineer blew the whistle letting everyone know they were approaching Los Angeles. Dash got up and explained that he and Sid needed to get back to work.

"It's been a pleasure meeting you, Nigel."

"The pleasure was mine James. If the timing is right when I see you again, I should have a couple of tickets for you to my next picture."

"Thank you Nigel; that'd be great!"

● ● ●

"OK Sid, everyone's off the train. The conductor should be here in a minute. You work your way up the train with him and make sure no one and nothing is still here that shouldn't be."

"Aren't you supposed to show me how to do that, Sir?"

"According to the book, yes. The truth is a conductor knows his train better than us and can show you where the hiding places are for a person or a package that no one else would even guess existed."

Sid quickly scribbled that in his notebook. "I'll make sure he points everything out."

Dash shook his head. "That's a great way to get left off a train someday. He'll show you what you need to know. Keep your eyes and ears open and your trap closed."

Before the younger man could execute another about-face, he did his own and began working his way toward the baggage car. He had his own set of master keys while Sid depended on the conductor to lock each car after they cleared it.

The last passenger car contained two private compartments. The one on the right was clear, but Dash opened the one on the left to find a man bloody and unconscious. The case at his feet was torn open at the hinges and empty.

Dash made certain the man was still breathing and then ran back to the dining car. "Murray! Grab the station master and get a doctor! We've got a guy in bad shape in the rear passenger car; move!"

● ● ●

"I should have been told we had a company courier on the train Ed. Security is what I'm there for."

"We didn't want to take away from the passengers' safety."

"That's a crock. I had that new kid on the train; he could have covered a bunch of sunburned, hung over weekenders blindfolded."

"The courier didn't know that." Ed Yoblonski was starting to get irritated.

"That's my point exactly! I've never met Dan Haskell and he should have identified himself to me or Harriman the moment he stepped on the train!" Dash was on his feet now, ready to punch a hole in the nearest wall.

The man leaning against Ed's filing cabinet spoke up. "Careful there Sport; that temper of yours nearly got you fired last year. I'd hate to see that happen now."

"Who is this guy Ed? He looks like the math teacher I used to hit with spitballs back in grammar school."

"I'm Parker Newton, Mr. Dasher. The Director for Transportation Security for Southern California."

"In other words, the guy who can fire me right now."

Newton smiled brightly and nodded. "That's me."

'What the hell,' Dash thought, 'in for a penny, in for a pounding.' "What was this guy carrying that you let him ignore every courier rule the company put in place to keep this kind of thing from happening?"

"Does it matter?" Yoblonski interrupted.

"Yes Ed, it does. This wasn't a payroll obviously. If it was, Sid and at least one armed, uniformed guard would have been in the car with him at all times and another posted outside."

Newton interrupted. "What if I tell you it was diamonds?"

Dash snorted in derision. "At least you didn't try to tell me it was gold certificates. Hoover's goons would have confiscated the whole train by now if there was that much money involved."

"All right, you proved you're not stupid." Newton sized him up another moment and then decided. "A number of the stolen documents were bearer bonds. They aren't the main concern though. That's the sheaf of contracts for right of ways and other property issues to run another line down to Mexico."

"Another line? There are still Hoovervilles out along the tracks, Mr. Newton."

"Yes, but we're coming out of it. Southern Pacific has repaid its bank loans and we're even back in good standing with the Reconstruction Finance Corporation. No one's planning to start a new line this year but we are looking to secure the future with a little seed money."

Dash shrugged. "OK, so the money's there after all. So now you have to get more copies signed. Who is going to benefit if you don't get it done?"

Ed began ticking them off on his fingers. "Union Pacific, the Mexican railway companies, trucking companies pushing for better highways and a bigger piece of government freight hauling, even some Feds who want to nationalize the rail system. Take your pick, Dash."

"To address your first point Mr. Dasher, copies were already signed for the most part and are being collected now. The problem is that we only have to the end of the month to get them all in the Governor's office; that's Thursday, three days from today. If we don't make that deadline, we lose our exclusive option and it goes out to everyone."

Newton continued, "A rival doesn't even have to buy every stretch of land to stop us. If they grab up just a few key parcels, we won't even be able to move the line left or right, it would have to go through an entirely new corridor."

"So how are you getting the copies to Sacramento?"

"Once we get them here in L.A., we'll run them up on the first train; this time with all the armed guards we should have had the first time. A representative from Governor Merriam's office will meet us at the station."

Newton paused, lit a cigarette, offered one to Dash and smiled. "Guess who gets to head up the security detail?"

"I expected that. If I'm running security this time, I also want to know who spilled the beans about last night's fiasco."

"I'm looking into that now. I can't promise you'll know before we make the run to Sacramento."

"Great, more good news."

● ● ●

Dash knocked on Ed's doorframe and walked in. "You bellowed fearless leader?"

"The last copies are on the way. They'll be here in time tomorrow for the 10:15 up to the Capital. Have you got your boys ready?"

Dash nodded. "Two armed guards, one in and out of the compartment. Sid Harriman will be in the compartment with the courier as well. Any word about who put the finger on Dan?"

Ed nodded. "You're going to love this one. Turns out Haskell had just got himself a new girlfriend. Some gorgeous redhead who nobody can find now."

"You got a name to go with that ginger?"

"Loretta Loy."

"Great, Loretta Young and Myrna Loy." Dash shook his head. "There are times I really hate Hollywood."

● ● ●

Once the courier and his guards were settled in the first passenger car, Dash went back to the platform to watch who boarded. Five minutes before departure, two ugly thugs walked onto the platform with a yapping dog in a carrier ... and its beautiful, redheaded owner.

She turned her head suddenly, letting him know she was aware of him and stared at him straight in the eyes. Miss 'Loy' smiled with all the promise and malice she could muster, daring him to come closer. Then just as quickly, she turned it all off and stepped onto the train.

Dash blew a low whistle. "OK, I see it now. I'd have named her Loretta Loy too." He went to the back of the train and waited for the conductor to arrive. Thomas Danvers used to teach languages in college until the Depression and he still had a perfect ear for accents and dialects.

"Tom, do you have anything on the two men hanging around with that redhead up in the second car?"

"They give you the heebie jeebies too James? The dark haired guy called the other one 'Vilho' in German, but that's a Finnish name. I don't know if it's his real name, but with that blonde hair and blue eyes, he's sure the biggest Finn I've ever seen. I didn't catch a name for the other one."

"Anything else?"

"The German keeps his jacket buttoned, so I'd guess he's got a gun in his belt or under an arm. Vilho kept reaching down toward his right foot. I'd bet he's got a knife or maybe a little snub nose down there."

"Thanks, Tom."

"Anytime, James."

● ● ●

As Dash opened the car door, he saw the armed guard facing the compartment with his hand on his sidearm. Sid leaned out of the car to look at him.

"Mr. Dasher, we got a problem."

"What's happened?"

"We just went to the restroom and after we got back, I remembered what you said about the conductor knowing the trains better than anyone. Herman here," he pointed to the very rumpled courier, "has a brother who's a conductor."

"Don't keep me in suspense, Sid."

"This is one of the refurbished cars, so I went back to the W/C and started banging on the new panels by the sink. I remembered last weekend the conductor told me some of them weren't nailed in properly and leave space underneath and behind the basin where you can hide a big package. I found this." It was an empty train case identical to the one on the courier's wrist.

"That proves nothing and no one except the station master has a key for this one."

Dash looked inside. "I don't need to open your case, Herman. Before the contracts were placed in here, I took a grease pencil and put my initials on the bottom." He held it up so the nervous little man could see them clearly.

"I don't know what ..." SMACK! The case bounced off Herman's forehead, cutting open the skin over his left eye. Dash leaned in, grabbed him by the throat and slapped him twice.

"I don't care what you were paid or even who paid you right now. Tell me where the contracts are or I bounce you under the train."

"I don't know!" He nearly screamed. "I was just paid to leave the case behind the sink! I swear!"

Dash dropped him, turned and handed a key ring to Sid. "Find out what's in that case; it might be useful. I'm going after that redhead and Mutt and Jeff."

"Hey! You're not supposed to have a key!"

"I'm the boss Sid, I get to make up the rules as I feel like it."

● ● ●

Miss 'Loy' and the German weren't in the car, but the Finn was sitting there, nice as you please. Up close, the blonde man was even uglier. The broken nose had obviously been poorly set and there were scars on his cheeks and around his eyes; in fact, his only undamaged features were his blue eyes.

"Get up ugly, I found the switched case and you're going to tell me where you stashed the papers."

It wasn't just women and losers at the tables who nicknamed the detective 'Dash', there were also the men who woke up on the ground that swore they never saw the punch. Before the big Finn had the .32 more than a few inches up out of the ankle holster, the detective's left was on it, slamming it and the hand holding it into the side of the car. His right buried itself twice in the once again broken nose, flattening it and causing Vilho to lose his grip. The pistol bounced under the seat.

Unfortunately, the big Finn knew how to take the punishment. The thug roared, got his left hand on Dash's neck and shoved him against the side of the train car. With a grip like a vise; he'd have broken his neck if Vilho had gotten both hands on him. Even so, the left one alone was making Dash's vision start to swim. The other passengers began yelling and pushing their way into the next car.

Memories began blurring Vilho's face into the German who had gotten over the wire, jumped into the enemy trench and right on top of then Staff Sergeant James Dasher back in '18. Dash shoved his right thumb under that crushed nose with two fingers on top and got ready to tear it off like he did back then.

CRACK! He saw Vilho's eyes roll up and then shoved the blood covered face away to find a familiar one behind it.

"Nigel?!" was all he could gasp out before he started coughing.

"Good afternoon James." He waved the recovered .32 in the air. "I do hope I haven't struck the wrong man."

Coughing turned to laughter and didn't stop until they had Vilho handcuffed to a tie-down ring set in the floor of the passenger car. Dash went forward to inform Sid and have him to grab Tom to keep their prisoner upright and make sure he didn't stop breathing. Then he returned to the waiting actor.

"I'm not complaining mind you, but how come you're on this train?"

"I'm meeting a director in Sacramento. If I get the job, I'll be filming in San Francisco for several weeks."

"Well, if that doesn't pan out, how would you like a job as a railroad agent?"

"Are you sure this won't be a problem?" He tapped his cane against his leg.

"That's the great thing about trains, Nigel. Cough! You can't run for any more than twenty-five or thirty feet at a stretch. Cough!" He began to tell Nigel what was going on when the whistle blew, letting everyone know they were pulling into the Sacramento station soon.

"Come with me and bring Bertram Lynch with you."

● ● ●

"So that's the story, once she gets off the platform, I can't touch her and I don't have enough to push the local cops to stop her unless she has those contracts in her hands."

"Can't you get them to at least follow her?"

"Not a chance, Nigel. The precinct captain is a guy named Vickers. He likes running our guys in for carrying a concealed weapon even if they have their license and permit on them; he thinks we should leave them with the station master before we get to the street."

"A strict law and order type?"

Dash snorted, "If a cop doesn't like the average, honest Joe carrying a gun, it's because he's dirty, lousy at his job or both. Unfortunately, Vickers is just dirty, so he knows how to work the system." He pointed with his chin. "There's 'Loy' now, stepping off the train."

"Perhaps I can give you a little more time James." Nigel smiled at him and then went off to intercept the young woman. Dash noticed she didn't have the dog carrier with her. 'The bodyguard must be getting it.' Then the light bulb went off and he raced back to the baggage car just as Nigel intercepted the redhead.

"Excuse me Miss! Do you have a moment?" He planted himself directly in her path and turned on the charm. "I'm Nigel Bruce, the actor, and if you don't mind, I wanted to speak with you about paying a visit to the director I'm seeing tomorrow. I'm certain there's a part in his movie for a stunning woman such as yourself."

Dash jumped onto the baggage car, skipping the steps. "Dante! Where's that yappy mutt that was brought on board in LA?"

"Some big goon came and got it. He had the right ticket; is there a problem?"

"How long ago?"

"Just as we stopped, you missed him by a minute. He's probably on the platform now."

Dash ran out and called back over his shoulder, "I owe you a beer!"

"You owe me a keg by now you cheap gumshoe!"

● ● ●

On the way back to the front of the platform, Dash pulled a leather sap from his back pocket and watched ahead for the other thug through the windows. He stayed close to the outside wall once he spotted him. As the goon hit the first step, Dash swung up; hitting him across the knee and knocking him to the platform.

The carrier hit the ground with no bark or yelp. As the other man tried to get up on one leg, Dash quickly cracked the sap over his head, putting him down until the cops could be called. A quick look in the carrier confirmed what the detective guessed; no dog, just a large stack of contracts.

"I'll take that carrier, Mr. Dasher." He looked up to the see the beautiful girl walk toward him while pointing a very ugly pistol at him. "Please move over with him, Mr. Bruce. I'm certain now your offer of a movie role was a ruse."

Nigel only moved a half step. "The compliments on your beauty were certainly no ruse, Miss."

"You ain't taking anything, Red."

"Yes I am, and you'll make it quick before the other detective gets off the train and I have to shoot all three of you."

"The governor's representative will be here any moment with a police escort."

"No he won't, his office was informed that the train would be fifteen minutes late."

"So who are you working for? Union Pacific?"

"I'm independent. With no more war, corporate spying is the only game left gentlemen. I guess you can call me the Mata Hari of the Boardroom."

Nigel jumped into it. "I once saw Mata Hari perform during the War. You're not a patch on that beautiful woman's slippers ..."

"You tell her, Nigel!"

She turned her head to fully look at Dash. "Be quiet you ... Ahhh!" She never saw Nigel strike out with his cane, knocking the pistol from her hand. Dash quickly stepped forward and grabbed the .38 off the platform.

"... or those of Greta Garbo." Nigel finished.

● ● ●

Several weeks later, Dash met him again on the Friday train down to San Ysidro. Both men greeted each other warmly and caught up; Nigel had just completed his shooting schedule in San Francisco and wanted to spend a few days in Baja.

"Is Mr. Harriman still working with you?"

"He is, doing fine too. Do you recall the group of young ladies we met on the train last month?"

"Yes, especially the one that took quite a fancy to Harriman."

"She certainly did, they got engaged last week."

"Ha! I suppose we'll see more of that with the world coming out of this Depression." Nigel pointed a finger at Dash. "Speaking of young ladies, did you ever find out who our Mata Hari worked for James?"

"Miss McGillicuddy ... quit laughing Nigel, that's her real name, never squawked. Her two companions were only rented muscle and didn't know anything. If anyone else found out something, they're not telling me about it. We still don't know who tipped her off about the run to Sacramento either. It's no coincidence she knew which courier to bribe."

"At least she's behind bars."

Dash shook his head. "Last week her attorney showed up with his secretary for a pre-trial visit. Fifteen minutes later, the jailer found the secretary knocked out, tied up and stuffed under the cell bunk and our little spy gone with a lawyer that no one ever heard of down at the Sacramento courthouse."

Nigel chuckled and smiled at Dash, "This is just like the movie serials, James."

"How do you mean, Nigel?"

"You now have a recurring nemesis!" Nigel began roaring with laughter.

"There are times I really hate Hollywood and just for that you Limey gimp, I'm telling Murray to only pour you the cheap stuff from now on."

The End

Bloodlines

by Andy Fix

A blood red sun set on the fog shrouded battlefield. A lone figure strode through the dead and dying as the last rays of the day's sunlight glinted off his battered armor. He stopped at the side of a fallen knight and hung his head in grief. After a moment of silence, the knight doffed his helm and slowly lowered himself to his knees, letting the axe that he carried fall from his weary hands.

The exhausted knight tore at the tattered remains of the surcoat that hung from his waist. With this crude rag he wiped at the dried blood and gore on the pallid face of his fallen comrade.

"Alas, Sir Ronan! So many of us have fallen here this day; so many good knights lost." No tears streamed from his steel-colored eyes, but the crestfallen look on his face betrayed the grief he felt in his heart.

The sound of hooves drew his attention away from his mourning. Off in the distance, he glimpsed three horsemen moving slowly through the unnatural fog that still clung to the field. One of the men carried a lance adorned with a pennant, but the he couldn't yet make out the details. They headed straight for his position. Hefting his axe on his shoulder, the knight stood to his full, towering height and faced the oncoming men.

As they drew closer, the coat-of-arms became clearer: a gold device on a purple field, the arms of House Orkney. These, then, were enemies.

The men halted twenty yards away. Two men-at-arms wearing coats of mail and armed with sword and shield situated themselves in front of the third horseman. This one wore mail and plate and carried a war lance. Such expensive equipment marked him as a nobleman.

"Hail, sir knight," called the mounted lord. "Lay your weapon aside and yield."

"And why should I be the one to yield, Orkney," asked the lone knight as he twirled his massive axe in front of him. All exhaustion left his body as the rush of the impending fight filled his heart.

"We have you at an obvious disadvantage, sir. There are three of us, and mounted. There need not be any further bloodshed this day."

"Only three of you? I believe it is you, then, who are at a disadvantage. If you want my axe, I will gladly give it to each of you in turn."

"Your boasts ring hollow, sir," said the mounted knight. "Your king is dead, your Order has been sundered, and your comrades lay slain around you. Even as we speak, my cousins lay siege to Camelot with a vast army. Your cause is lost." After a pause, the Orkney knight continued, "But if you pledge me your axe, you may join us in victory."

The lone knight scoffed in disbelief. "Why, in the name of all that is Holy, would I fight for you?"

"Your surcoat is shredded, sir, but even without a coat-of-arms to know you by, still I know of you," replied the nobleman. "You tower over the battlefield as a giant, speak with a vulgar accent, and wield that great axe as if it weighed nothing. You may have forsaken your heritage, but your Saxon blood betrays you. There is only one Saxon knight who fights for Camelot: Sir Axel of Mayfair, called "The Axe", Knight of the Rose and of the Order of the Round Table."

"Aye," responded Sir Axel, "you have the right of me, but you fail to explain why I should pledge my arms to you." Axel rested his axe on his shoulder. Despite what the Orkney knight may think, the great axe was a damn heavy weapon, especially after a long day of battle.

"All of the Saxon ealdormen in Britain have sided with us. Our armies swell with Saxon warriors, and you would be first among them."

A sneer spread across Sir Axel's face. "You speak wrong of me now, Orkney!" He hefted his axe and moved towards the horsemen. "Aye, I was born to a Saxon father, but he pledged his fealty to Uther Pendragon, King of Britain, and to King Arthur after him. And like my father before me, I fight for Camelot!"

The Orkney knight nodded towards his men and both spurred their horses. They charged towards The Axe, swords raised.

Axel stood his ground as they galloped towards him. At the last instant, he dropped to one knee and ducked his head as the first horseman's sword stroke passed just over top of his tightly cropped hair. The knight then jumped back to his feet and thrust the butt end of his axe up towards the second horseman. The butt-spike caught the man under his upraised sword arm and pierced into his exposed armpit. The horse's momentum drove the spike deep into the rider's chest and lifted him out of the saddle. Axel threw him to the ground, and the knight angled the axe shaft downward and thrust the spike into the man's heart.

He yanked the shaft out of the corpse and turned to face the first horseman. The knight spun out of the way of the charger as it bore down on him. As he moved, Axel swung his weapon out in a wide arc. The heavy axe head struck the rider in the back as he passed, crushing through the mail and severing the man's spine. The limp body slid off the saddle and fell lifelessly to the ground.

Sir Axel stood defiantly and pointed his weapon at the other knight. "Are you ready to yield yet, Orkney? Lay down your arms and give me your horse, for I seem to have lost mine."

It was the Orkney's turn to scoff. "The only thing I will be giving you, Saxon, is a better death than you deserve!" The mounted knight spurred his horse into a charge and lowered his lance towards Axel's chest.

As the knight bore down on him, Axel stepped inside the thrust and brought the underside of his axe down on the lance's shaft. Using his weapon as a hook, Axel forced the lance down and drove the tip into the ground.

The force of the impact shattered the lance and knocked the shocked knight off balance. Axel thrust his shoulder into the knight's hip as he passed, knocking him off of the horse. The nobleman fell heavily to the ground and rolled to a stop. He struggled to regain his feet, and he fumbled with his helm to face it in the right direction.

Axel waited for the knight to get situated and draw his blade. The knight slowly circled his foe and fended off the smaller man's feints and jabs. Frustrated, the

Orkney knight lunged at Axel with a desperate overhand swing. The Axe blocked the stroke with a thrust of his axe head that struck his foe's wrist, shattering the bones of his forearm. The knight screamed in pain and dropped to his knees as his cradled his broken arm to his chest. He saw Axel's weapon raised high and brought his shield up over his head. The powerful blow crashed down on the wooden shield, smashing it to pieces and breaking the Orkney knight's shield arm, as well.

"Mercy, Saxon," whimpered the helpless knight.

"Aye, I am a Saxon," replied Axel. "But though I may have Saxon blood in my veins, and though you slay my King, murder my brothers in arms, and even usurp the throne I swore my oath before, I will always stand for Camelot!"

The Axe looked around the battlefield. This was what was left of King Arthur's idyllic Camelot. The chivalry of the Round Table lay dead in bloody heaps. Sir Axel clenched his jaw tight as anger overwhelmed his grief, and he found no mercy in his heart. With a powerful stroke, his weapon came down on the top of the Orkney's helm, cleaving it and the skull inside in twain.

"To the very end."

● ● ●

The sun had already set below the horizon by the time the knight managed to approach the Orkney's horse. There was little fight left in the exhausted animal when Axel finally grabbed the reins. Once he hoisted himself into the saddle, the horse seemed resigned to its fate.

Axel wanted to put the battlefield as far behind him as possible before darkness made travel impossible. The foul stench of the battlefield sickened him, and the raucous squabbling of the crows as they feasted on fallen friend and foe alike tore at his nerves. The ghosts of the fallen were already rising; their faces peered at him from patches of swirling fog and their voices whispered his name on the breeze.

"Axel, m'lord, please..."

This last voice, as faint as it was, was no ghost. The knight pulled up abruptly and peered into the darkness. "Who speaks?"

"Please, m'lord, some water," pleaded the hoarse voice again.

Axel could barely make out the ethereal form of a man standing in the midst of a fog-shrouded copse of trees. As he approached, he saw that the man wasn't standing freely, he was held to the tree by daggers pounded through his hands.

The knight dismounted and rushed to the stricken man's side. "Good God, who did this to you?"

The man moaned in pain as Axel pried the daggers from his hands as gently as he could and lowered him to the ground. He was young, barely more than a lad, and probably a squire to one of the fallen knights. He was stripped to his waist, and his exposed skin had been nearly flayed off.

Axel poured some water he into the squire's mouth. As he peered at the grisly face, he came to a sudden stop. The knight gasped and repeated, "No, no, no, no!"

"I came back to help you, m'lord," said the young man weakly.

"Myles, you young fool, I sent you away! That battle was not for you to fight or die in! God in Heaven," Axel implored, "why did you curse me with such a disobedient squire?"

"I'm ready to take my vows, sir, you know I am," replied Myles with some defiance strengthening his voice.

""Tell me, lad, who did this to you? Was it one of Orkney's men?"

"No, m'lord," replied Myles, his voice weakening again. "T'was Saxons. They recognized my surcoat, sir. They knew me to be your squire."

Axel's face reddened and his jaw tightened. "Tell me, lad," he said through gritted teeth, "what arms did they bear?"

Myles' breathing grew shallower now, and his eyes struggled to focus. "Two... two black wolves, sir, on..." He whispered, but his strength was ebbing quickly.

"On a field of gold. Aye, lad, I know it well. Those are the arms of Wulfgar, brother to my father, Aelfgar. As vile and cruel a Saxon as there ever was."

"I fought like a true knight, sir. I'm ready to take my vows, I..." A bloody coughing spasm interrupted the squire.

"Aye, that you are. Rest easy now." Axel stood and drew his sword, a weapon that rarely left its scabbard. Holding the blade in both hands, the tall knight dropped back to one knee and held the blade for Myles to see.

"I'm ready..." the squire managed to say again.

"Myles of Salisbury," began Sir Axel, his voice quavering with emotion. "In the name of God, St. Michael, and St. George," he touched the blade first to the squire's left shoulder, and then his right, "I give you the right to bear arms and the power to mete justice." The knight laid the sword on the boy's chest and folded his cold hands over the hilt. "I now name thee Sir Myles, knight of the realm."

The Axe looked to Myles' face and saw the boy's unfocussed eyes stared off into nothingness. With a heavy sigh, he reached down and brushed the eyes closed with his fingertips.

"Rest in peace, sir knight."

● ● ●

The weary knight slumped low in the saddle as his mount picked its way along the darkened road. He buried Sir Myles beneath the boughs of the rowan tree a full day ago. But if Sir Axel hoped to catch up with Wulfgar's warband before they joined the Orkney host besieging Camelot, rest would have to wait.

The crackle of a fire and the smell of roasting mutton caught Axel's attention. His belly grumbled angrily, reminding the knight that he hadn't eaten since the night before the battle. He then heard a man's pleading voice, while other voices responded with laughter and cruel taunting in the Saxon tongue.

He dismounted and grabbed his helm and axe from where they hung on the saddle. Horse and lance were the weapons of the Britons, and Axel never felt comfortable fighting from horseback. With axe in hand, the giant Saxon was as formidable as any mounted knight.

Several of the warriors jumped in surprise as Axel strode into the ring of firelight, and a few of them managed to raise their swords or spears. A man in friars' robes and bound with rope huddled dangerously close to the fire.

"You are a bold man, Briton, I'll give you that," said the largest of the warriors in the British tongue. He leveled his spear at Axel's chest and took a step towards him.

"I'm no Briton," replied the knight in Saxon, "I am Axel, son of Aelfgar, son of Heahwulf. And you had best drop that spear before I shove it up your arse, point first."

The Saxon warriors looked from Axel to the spearman in confusion, and the Saxon warrior dipped the point of his spear towards the ground. "Ealdorman Wulfgar is also the son of Heahwulf," said the spearman. "Are you his kin?"

"Aye, Wulfgar is my father's brother. He raised me after my father was killed in battle when I was a child."

The spearman smiled broadly. "Then well met, Axel, son of Aelfgar," he said. "I am Cuthbert, son of Cuthred and thane to Ealdorman Sigebryht. Any kin of Wulfgar is welcome at our fire. Join us! We were just about to roast a Christian."

The rest of the warriors broke out into laughter as the tension eased out of the situation. The bound friar, however, whimpered anew as the hope of rescue evaporated. Several of the Saxons poked again at the terrified man with the butts of their spears, nudging him ever closer to the fire pit.

Axel took off his helm and accepted a shank of mutton handed to him. He seated himself by the fire and rested his axe within easy reach at his feet. "Tell me, Cuthbert," he said as he worked his way through the meat, "How close am I to catching up with Wulfgar's warband. I lost track of them during the battle."

Cuthbert sat on the log next to him and took a long draught from a wineskin. He spat the wine into the fire behind the friar and laughed when the poor man yelped in terror at the resulting burst of flame. "You're heading the wrong way if you're seeking to rejoin your warband, Axel. Wulfgar's headed north, towards Gloucester."

"Gloucester," asked the knight. "Is he not joining the Orkney army at Camelot?"

"He was supposed to, but he decided to seek glory elsewhere. He has a personal axe to grind, it would seem."

The knight counted the number of Saxons in the camp, noting their positions and how inebriated each was. "A blood feud?"

"Ealdorman Wulfgar doesn't share his business with me," answered Cuthbert, "but his warriors made mention of taking a keep. Mayfair, I believe they called it."

Axel bit hard once again into his mutton in an attempt to hide his reaction. After taking a draught from the wineskin, he said, "I know of it. Mayfair is a sturdy castle; he can't have enough warriors remaining to take it alone."

"Oh, he's not alone," said Cuthbert with a chuckle. "His witch summoned up a fomorian, a cursed monster from the Other Side. Wulfgar was supposed to send the giant against the walls of Camelot, but why waste such a gift for the Orkneys, eh? Let the Britons kill each other off."

Axel put the remains of his mutton on the ground and grabbed his axe. "Cuthbert, I thank you for the food and drink," he said as he rose to his feet. "Your hospitality does honor to your father. But I've lost much time already, and I must make haste to Mayfair if I am to catch Wulfgar."

"No need to leave just yet. You need rest from the looks of you, and the evening's entertainment has yet to begin."

A grim smile spread across the knight's face. "Oh, things are about to get entertaining," said the Axe as he lowered his helm over his head. "Just not for you."

● ● ●

"Are you able to ride, priest," asked the knight as he cut the ropes binding the man's wrists and ankles.

The friar stared up at the armored form standing between himself and the bonfire that was so recently about to consume him. The giant knight's armor glinted orange and red from the flame behind. He was the Devil himself, limned with Hellfire and covered with the gore of the damned. "God help me," said the holy man as he crossed himself.

"He just did," replied the knight. "He set my path to cross yours. Now, can you ride a horse?"

"Y-yes," stammered the priest. "I'm just bruised, and maybe a bit singed." He glanced around at the six dead or dying Saxons scattered on the ground and crossed himself again.

"Good, we need to get going. These woods are sure to be crawling with more Saxons with their bloodlust up. You would be safest with me."

"Who are you? Where are we going? What's happening?"

"My name is Sir Axel," answered the knight, "and we are going to Mayfair keep in Gloucester to prevent my uncle from attacking my home with a giant monster summoned from the faerie realms by a Saxon witch. Any other questions?"

"Sir Axel the Axe," gasped the friar. "You're a knight of King Arthur's Round Table! Shouldn't you be joining the king to defend Camelot?"

"The king is dead, man, as are his knights. I am all that is left of the Order of the Round Table. Camelot is lost, but Mayfair might still be saved. If we hurry."

The friar blinked for few heartbeats as he tried to process all of this information. "V-Very well, sir knight. I will join you."

"Good, now grab one of the horses..." Axel paused for a moment. "What is it I'm to call you," he asked.

"I'm Brother Thomas," said the friar as he grabbed a broad-brimmed farmer's hat that was folded in his belt and slid it on his head, "from the village of Hancock."

"Then mount up, Brother Thomas," said Axel. "Ealdorman Wulfgar and his warband are two days ahead of us. We have a lot of riding to do."

● ● ●

The rolling hills of Cotswold fell behind them as they rode through the flat valley of the River Severn. To his credit, Brother Thomas managed to keep up with Sir Axel. He even tended the Saxon pack-horse they liberated from the Cuthbert's camp, and he worked wonders with their meagre provisions to provide them with palatable meals.

"How much further until we reach Mayfair town, Sir Axel?"

"Mayfair hardly qualifies as a town," replied the knight. "It's more of a hill-top keep with a handful of buildings around the hillside and some farmsteads scattered about nearby. It lies on the far banks of the Severn and about a half day's ride north towards the Forest of Dean. I hope to reach it before nightfall tomorrow."

"And you have family there?"

"Aye, my wife, the Lady Alba, and my twin children, daughter Ari and son Broderick," answered the knight with a hint of a genuine smile. "This winter will be their second."

"Oh, named after the Lady Arianna, the Lady of the Rose, I presume. And for your companion Sir Broderick, also for the Lady's Order of the Rose."

Axel looked over at the friar for a moment before nodding. "You do know your tales, Brother Thomas."

The friar beamed and said, "Oh, I know all the tales of the Knights of the Round Table, Sir Axel. I listen to the bards retell them at all the fairs and markets I visit. They're all so exciting and romantic!"

The Axe scoffed. "Listening to the tales might be exciting and romantic, but living them tends to be uncomfortable, violent, painful, and occasionally terrifying. Tell me after tomorrow how much fun you are having."

● ● ●

Brother Thomas clamored to the top of the low hill and stood next to the tall knight. "What is it you spy?"

Sir Axel pointed north to a distant column of smoke rising to the low clouds. "I can't say for sure, but that is about where Mayfair lies. I fear Wulfgar and his warband have beaten us there."

The friar crossed himself, saying, "Then I pray for your family, sir knight. May God preserve them."

"Pray not for my family, friar," replied the Axe, "for they will find their way to Heaven, if it comes to that. Pray instead for Wulfgar and his dogs, for when I find them, even God will not be able to save them."

● ● ●

They encountered first signs of the Saxons' savagery just after mid-day. The mill a few miles outside of Mayfair was utterly destroyed. It wasn't burnt to the ground, it had been torn asunder. No two stones stood intact, and huge pieces of lumber could be seen laying a good bowshot away from the foundation. What remained of the millers who had lived and worked there were smashed and rent beyond recognition.

Brother Thomas paused to cross himself, too shocked to utter a prayer out loud. Axel fixated on the column of smoke that hung in the air up ahead like a grave marker.

"Come, friar," said the grim knight as he kicked his horse into a trot. "We'll attend to the dead later."

By late afternoon, they discovered the source of the smoke. The few buildings that made up the small Mayfair marketplace at the foot of the hill were gone, their contents scattered about the square. Atop the hill, what remained of the keep still smoldered and burned, belching forth the cloud of greasy black smoke that had guided Axel home.

Brother Thomas looked to speak words of comfort to the knight, but Axel's visage filled him with dread. A mix of shock, grief, and barely controlled rage darkened the knight's face, and his jaw was clenched so tightly that the friar thought the man might be grinding his teeth to powder. Brother Thomas feared to even draw his attention.

The friar dismounted his horse and picked an object out of some debris. He stood, holding a large iron crucifix in his hands. "Heaven help us, this... this was a house of God. Axel, what kind of monsters would do this to a church?"

A man pushing a cart full of bodies and body parts through the square overheard the friar and looked up. "Axel? God be praised, is that you, m'lord?"

The knight reined his horse to a stop and dismounted in one fluid motion. "Gerhard, good man, it is I! Tell me..." He paused as he approached the cart. "Is she... are they..." he managed, staring at the contents with dread in his eyes.

Gerhard bowed his head. "M'lady is... she's gone, m'lord." He glanced up at the smoking ruins at the top of the hill. "She fought like a lioness, m'lord; she would not be taken alive. They turned the keep into her funeral pyre."

Axel flinched and took a step back as if the man had physically struck him. He shook his head a few times as he tried in vain to form words. Finally, he asked, "And my children? What of Arianna and Broderick?"

"The Saxons took them and fled, m'lord, after they lost control of their monster."

Sir Axel instantly regained his composure. "Fled? You must tell me everything that happened, Gerhard."

The weary man sat on the edge of his cart. "It was horrible, m'lord, just horrible. The giant was just tearing everything and everyone in sight to pieces. Poor Clegis was torn in twain right in front of me." Gerhard bent his head and began weeping uncontrollably.

The lord of Mayfair placed a hand on his man's shoulder, and after a few moments, Gerhard began again. "The giant started battering the gate of the keep, but we managed to drive it off briefly with burning oil. A well-aimed shot from Idris the Huntsman killed their witch. Free of the Saxons' power, the monster decided it wanted no more to do with us."

"Hurrah," shouted Brother Thomas as he thrust his fist in the air, but his celebrating was cut short by withering glares from the other two.

"The beast killed a few of the Saxons on its way back down the hill," Gerhard continued. "But the damage had already been done. There were too few of us left to defend the walls, and the gate was too battered to stand. The Lady Alba and a few guards nearest to her shut themselves within the great hall, and m'lady herself took up a sword. I saw her slay one of the Saxon dogs with my own eyes."

Axel smiled grimly and said, "A woman after my own heart."

"You would have been proud of her, m'lord. We all were. We tried to fight our way through to them, but there were too many Saxons and too few of us. And when one of their warriors showed up carrying the twins, they put the hall to the torch and fled."

"Where to," asked the knight.

"The giant headed up north towards the Forrest of Dean, m'lord," answered Gerhard. "As for the Saxons, they headed west, probably to hole up in the ruins of the old abbey."

Sir Axel smacked a gauntleted fist into his palm. "Gerhard, gather what men remain. First, we'll go after Wulfgar and get my children back. Then we'll track down the fomorian before it ravages the farms in the countryside. I will have my vengeance!"

Gehard looked up forlornly, then motioned at the contents of the cart. "Most of your men are in here or already in their graves, m'lord. The others left to protect their homes. I have been lamed and would be useless in a fight."

Axel's energy evaporated with a sigh.

"I'm sorry, m'lord, but I'm afraid that you are all that you have left."

● ● ●

Sir Axel and Brother Thomas halted outside the ruins of the abbey just far enough away to remain out of bowshot. They marked this distance by the arrow that thudded into the ground just a few yards in front of them a moment ago. The early morning sun hung high enough that they could see several Saxon warriors peering over and around what remained of the low wall that surrounded the courtyard. The Axe could probably take the place if he had a dozen good men beside him. Unfortunately, his force consisted of just himself and the friar.

"Come no further, knight, unless you seek your death," came a heavily accented voice from behind the wall."

"I am Axel, son of Aelfgar, son of Heahwulf, and kin to Ealdorman Wulfgar," he answered in the Saxon tongue. "I seek to parley."

After a few moments, a large man wearing chain and plate stepped out from behind the wall and walked to the midpoint between arrow and the ruins. His beard and hair had grayed and thinned, but he looked as strong and healthy as a man half his age. "Axel, my son! Come greet your kin!"

The knight dismounted and approached the Saxon lord. Wulfgar stood at an even height with him, and his steel-colored eyes looked evenly into Axel's own. The man's smile, however, did not reach his eyes, and Axel had to restrain himself from physically smashing the smug grin off of his face.

"Uncle," said Axel through gritted teeth. "I am not now, nor ever was I, your son." He noticed six more Saxon warriors approaching to stand just a few feet behind Wulfgar. Each was nearly as tall, and armed with sword, spear, or axe. These would be Wulfgar's most loyal thanes, and likely his fiercest warriors. The knight eyed each of them up and determined that he could likely handle no more than two of them at once, possibly three. There were also, of course the men still behind the wall. This could be difficult.

"So, you are not here to rejoin my theod, then," asked Wulfgar. He sounded genuinely disappointed. "You spent years as one of us; there is still a place for you at my side."

"Are you mad, uncle," demanded Axel, his face reddening with anger. "You destroyed my home, slaughtered my people, murdered my wife, and abducted my children!"

"This is war," replied Wulfgar. "That's what we Saxons do to our enemies! That's how I raised you to be. Instead, you go prancing about like one of these Britons, playing at war by knocking each other off your horses with sticks, with your flowing ribbons and shining armor." Wulfgar looked Axel up and down and sneered. "Of course, your armor isn't looking so fancy now. What happened, did you misplace your squire?"

With a roar of rage Axel hefted his great axe back to strike. A gentle hand grasped his arm, and a calm voice said, "Remember your children. They are the reason we are here."

"Your priest speaks wise words, Axel," said Wulfgar. "Even if you managed to strike me down, you wouldn't live long enough to make it to the walls back there, much less see your children again."

With great effort, the knight returned the axe to his side. ""I want my children, Wulfgar; you have no claim to them."

"They are my kin," said Wulfgar as voice rose with his ire. "They have Saxon blood running through their veins, and they will be raised as part of my theod! I don't know where I went wrong with you, but I swear by my father and by his father, I will do right by your children."

"Where you went wrong with me, uncle" said Axel as he placed his face close enough to Wulfgar's as to practically touch noses, "is when you slew my father and ripped me from my mother's arms!" The knight felt Brother Thomas' grip tighten on his arm as a reminder to hold his temper.

"And I should slay you right now," hissed Wulfgar, not giving an inch to Axel's advance. "You have become as soft as he was! My fondness for you when you were a child is the only reason you still draw breath before me. Leave now, before I take that from you, too."

Axel stepped back a pace and took a deep breath. As he slowly let it out, he looked from his uncle to each of the thanes standing behind him, impressing each of their faces into his memory. He squared his shoulders and stood tall and straight.

"Hear me now, all of you," said the knight in a loud voice. "My name is Axel the Axe, son of Aelfgar!" He held his weapon up high for all to see. "I swear upon my ancestors that one day I shall come for my children, and on that day each and every one of you shall die!" He stared hard into Wulfgar's eyes and added, "I will wash my axe in your blood, uncle." He spat on the ground at the old Saxon's feet and then turned and headed back to his horse.

● ● ●

"Sir Axel, where are we going," asked Brother Thomas. "Mayfair lies to the east, yet we are headed north."

"I will not return to Mayfair without my children," said the knight.

"But that's madness, Sir! Without any men to help, you cannot defeat the Saxons. It would take an act of God!"

"Then you had best begin praying, friar, for I have no men back at Mayfair, or anywhere else. We head north to the Forest of Dean."

The friar shook his head in dismay. "Please tell me we aren't going after that fomorian. That monster is from Hell itself!"

Axel looked at the friar and smiled that grim, cold smile that chilled Brother Thomas to the bone. "Fear not," he said, "for I have a holy man at my side. 'Though I walk through the valley of the shadow of Death, I shall fear no evil.' Isn't that how it goes?"

Brother Thomas shook his head again and crossed himself. "God preserve us," he prayed, just as the first shadows of the Forest of Dean fell across them.

Axel stopped his horse a few paces inside the trees. "Friar, I want you to stay here and wait for my return."

"But... but, Sir Axel, I would stay by your side. You said yourself that you need my protection."

"Whether God protects me or not is up to Him, friar. Your safety, however, is my responsibility. My blood is up and I need to kill something. If you pray for anything, pray for the giant." Axel turned his horse and kicked it into a trot. In just a few moments, the knight had disappeared into the shadows of the woods.

"May God protect you then, Sir Axel," said Brother Thomas as he looked around at the towering oaks, "for I know not the way back home."

● ● ●

The warhorse picked its way along a path that was little more than a game trail at points. Shafts of sunlight penetrated the dense canopy in few places, and a green-tinted twilight only dimly lit the rest of the forest. Patches of dense fog billowed between the trees, shrouding everything beyond a dozen yards.

Felled trees and monstrous footprints in the moss-covered earth marked the path of the beast. The faint breeze carried the smell of death on its breath, and Axel spied the occasional human limb, gnawed to the bone by gigantic teeth, littering the sides of the path. It certainly wouldn't be difficult to find this giant.

As Axel approached a clearing, he heard the sound of wet, smacking lips of the slobbering monster as it devoured yet another of the knight's folk. Axel dismounted and slid his weapon from his saddle. He worked his way on foot down an uneven slope from behind the fomorian, taking his time to pick his footing.

A moss-slick rock betrayed him, and Axel lost his balance. Thrusting the butt-spike of his axe into the ground, the knight saved himself from tumbling the rest of the way down the slope, but the noise of his armor banging against the stone drew the giant's attention.

The beast turned and rose to its full height. It easily stood over twice as tall as Axel's nearly seven foot frame. The monster's shoulders were as wide as a castle gate, and long sinewy arms hung down to its knees. A rotting cowhide loincloth draped its hips. When the monster reared back its head and roared, gore dripped from the two sword-length tusks that jutted upwards from its lower jaw.

In one hand the giant still held the half-eaten peasant leg it had been working on, and in the other, a boulder the size of a mead cask. With a grunt, the giant flung the rock in Axel's direction. The stone crashed into the slope just feet away from the knight.

Axel jumped to his feet and rushed headlong towards the monster. He didn't feel like dodging any more boulders, and he had nothing to throw at his foe in return. At close range, his axe would come into play.

The fomorian grabbed a fallen tree from the ground and swung it like a club. Unable to check his descent down the slope, Axel could do little to avoid the blow. The tree smashed into the knight's side, crushing the breath from his lungs and flinging him to the ground. Though he wore a coat of plates over his torso, Sir Axel felt at least one of his ribs crack from the impact of the club.

Quickly regaining his senses, he rolled away as a second blow smashed into the ground where he had been. Without stopping to think, the knight ran directly under the monster's tree-trunk thick legs.

Unable to use its club, the giant raised a massive foot up to smash it down on the knight as he passed underneath. Instead of rolling out of the way this time, Axel raised the butt-spike towards the bottom of the monster's foot. As the beast brought its foot down, it let out a yelp of pain and stumbled backwards. The spike had found a soft spot between the toes.

Sir Axel pressed his advantage and swung his weapon at the giant's shin directly in front of him. This part of the monster proved tougher, however, and the axe head didn't bite very deep into the rock-hard flesh. The giant responded by reaching down and grabbing the knight by the shoulders and flinging him towards the trees.

Axel flew an impressive distance through the air. The thick boughs of a pine tree broke his fall somewhat, but he still hit the ground hard enough to rattle his head.

The knight reached for his dropped weapon and looked around for his horse. If he kept this up much longer he'd be smashed to bits. Axel spied the battle-hardened charger holding its ground at the edge of the clearing where he left him.

The fomorian was lumbering up the slope towards the Axe, so the knight quickly regained his feet and made a break for the horse. The monster bellowed in rage, and Axel heard him ripping another boulder from the earth. The knight ducked and rolled just as the missile whistled over his head and shattered the thick trunk of a nearby tree.

This was too much even the toughest of warhorses, and the charger reared and turned away from the charging giant. Axel caught the reins as his frightened mount thundered by, and he swung himself up into the saddle without the horse missing a step.

He threw caution to the wind and gave his mount free rein. He trusted the terrified beast not to stumble and break a leg, and he held tightly to its neck to avoid getting unhorsed by any tree branches. The knight heard the giant smashing through the trees behind them in pursuit.

● ● ●

Brother Thomas leaned towards the forest with one hand cupped behind his ear. He thought he had heard something a moment ago, but wasn't quite sure. The friar yelped in surprise and almost fell off his horse when he saw the big warhorse come crashing up the game path.

"Ride, priest, now," shouted Sir Axel as they galloped towards him. Behind him, Brother Thomas could see treetops swaying and disappearing as trees were being toppled.

"What in God's name...?"

"RIDE!"

Brother Thomas' horse, spooked by the commotion, didn't wait for the friar's command. As soon as the charger galloped past, the frightened mount jumped and bolted after them. It was all Brother Thomas could do to hang on.

"Axel," screamed the friar as he caught up to the knight, "w-what is that?"

"That," responded the Axe with, "is our act of God!"

● ● ●

The setting sun painted the ruins of the abbey ahead of him the color of fire and blood. Beneath him, Axel could feel his horse's flanks heaving as it drew in labored breaths. He had pushed this warrior to its limits of exhaustion, but he needed just a bit more. He glanced again over his shoulder; the fomorian had gained a few more strides.

The giant loped along on all four limbs, using its arms and knuckles as an extra set of legs and feet. Its bulging, bloodshot eyes, filled with rage, were fixated on Sir Axel. A spray of spittle belched forth from its maw with every breath it took. After chasing the knight for hours, the monster was beginning to tire, as well. But not enough.

Axel was close enough now hear the Saxon warriors within the walls shouting and laughing as they sat around their bonfire. The knight saw just one lone spearman standing at a gap in the crumbling wall, but he stood facing the courtyard as he watched the antics of his comrades.

The charger was frothing at the mouth now, and it was slowing noticeably. "Just a few more yards, my friend," Axel said, "then you can rest." The knight could feel the gusts from the giant's breath now. He may not have a few more yards.

The Saxon guard heard the pounding of the warhorse's hooves at the last instant. He turned as the horse leaped over the low ruins of the stone wall. Eyes wide, the warrior ducked and barely avoided getting brained by the massive hooves. As he stood up and grabbed his spear, a giant fist smashed his head down into his chest cavity. The fomorian stepped over the ruined wall and announced itself with a roar.

Axel rode through two dozen stunned Saxon warriors in the courtyard. Ignoring the knight completely, the thanes rushed to grab their weapons and shields. In an instant, the monster was upon them, and the courtyard became a slaughterhouse.

The Axe dismounted and smacked his horse on the rump. With the last of its strength, the beast bolted for one of the gaps in the wall and disappeared. Axel moved towards the lone building that still stood and saw a figure exiting the shadow of the door. A curtain of mail attached to the Saxon warrior's helm hung down to his chest like a steel beard, and a long gray braid swung from the back of his neck.

With a wordless shout of rage, Axel charged towards Wulfgar. The ealdorman held his ground and flung his hand axe at the knight's head. The heavy iron axehead struck the knight's helm a glancing blow, but it was hard enough that he blinked away stars. He regained his senses as his uncle smashed into him with his shield.

Few warriors were large enough to bowl the Axe over, but Wulfgar matched the knight pound for pound. Axel screamed in pain as he landed on his damaged ribs. The Saxon warrior laughed and raised his sword for the killing thrust, but Axel quickly rolled inside the blow, sweeping Wulfgar's legs out from under him and knocking him to the ground.

Both men grabbed their dropped weapons as they scrambled to their feet. Wulfgar adjusted the shield on his arm and Axel straightened the helm on his head as they circled each other. Behind them, the sounds of combat and the screams of dying men filled the courtyard.

"You will pay for the lives of my thanes," snarled the Saxon ealdorman.

"I gave you fair warning, Uncle," replied knight. "You should have heeded me."

With a roar of anger, Wulfgar lashed out with his sword. Sir Axel deflected the blade with his axe-head and in the same motion brought the butt-spike up and thrust it at his foe. The spike pierced the mail on his foe's shoulder and plunged deep into the flesh. The old Saxon screamed in pain and brought his shield edge up hard under Axel's chin.

The knight shook his head clear and tasted blood on his tongue. He felt the tip of a sword slide between the plates of his armored tunic, but there wasn't enough strength behind it to finish the killing stroke. Axel shoved the Saxon away with haft of his great axe and both men stumbled apart.

Axel's ribs burned with pain, his side bled freely, and his head rang from all the blows it had taken today. Wulfgar's sword arm hung weakly at his side, and he too was battered from recent battles. The fomorian continued savaging the remaining thanes in the courtyard.

"Yield, Uncle," said the knight. "Your cause is lost."

"Join me, Axel," replied the older man with desperation creeping into his voice. "Together we can unite the Saxon theods and conquer the Britons. I would rule has high-king with you, my son, as my heir."

Axel feinted with his axe, drawing a counter strike from the wounded Saxon. The knight side-stepped the expected thrust and brought his great axe down hard on Wulfgar's exposed shoulder. The axe cut through mail, flesh, and bone, catching deep within the chest and cleaving Wulfgar's cold heart in twain. The Saxon's lifeblood washed over the knight's axe and poured out onto the broken cobblestones at his feet.

"I am not your son."

All was silent for a moment, then Axel heard the deep, heavy breathing of the giant behind him. He turned around and saw the gore streaked monster standing amidst a pile of partial bodies and torn limbs. Arrows, broken spears, and axe-heads adorned the beast's flesh like macabre decorations. Its eyes, still so full of hate, glared down at Axel as it raised a giant fist for one final kill.

"Stop," cried a voice from behind the giant. Brother Thomas came rushing into the courtyard holding in his hands the iron crucifix from the rubble of Mayfair. The iron glowed red hot in the holy man's grasp, but his flesh did not burn. "In the name of God, I banish thee back to Hell!" Wielding the cross like a sword, Brother Thomas thrust the crucifix into the fomorian's calf.

The giant roared in pain as the now white-hot iron pierced its flesh. The skin of its leg burst into flames, and the entire limb, flesh and bone, burnt to ash. The monster fell to the ground with a crash as the flames spread over its entire, massive frame. Within seconds it was consumed. Nothing remained but a fomorian-shaped pile of ash and the foul smell of burnt flesh.

From the ruined building came a child's cry, and without a second look at the carnage in the courtyard, Axel turned and ran through the doorway.

● ● ●

Axel stood with his children in his arms and allowed emotion to overtake him. He wept long and without shame, letting his tears wash over all that remained of his bloodline.

"Are you sure about this, Axel," asked Brother Thomas.

"Aye." The knight handed both of his children to the friar one at a time. "I am a warrior born, and a hunted one at that. These two would never be safe with me, no matter where I might try to hide. Will the gold from the Saxons' loot be enough for the Church?"

"The Church will keep them safe, Sir, I swear to you." Brother Thomas paused for a moment. "But when will you come for them? They will want to know their father."

The Axe mounted his horse and looked towards the rising sun. "Not in this life time, Brother Thomas."

Without another glance at his children, Axel guided his horse down the road. He wept that they would never know the pain he felt in his heart.

The End

The Hideout
(A Brother Bones story)
by Ron Fortier

It was long after midnight and most of the patrons in Old Town's Gridiron saloon had long since packed it up and gone home; wherever in Cape Noire was home to each of them. Of course there were always the night owls who hung around till whenever owner Butch Hammer decided to lock up.

On this particular muggy summer night, three of Hammer's regulars were seated around one of the dozen of round tables that filled the small bar. Similarly dressed in worn, dark suits and fedoras, the three sat drinking bottle after bottle of Wyld Ale, the new beer recently bought from Alexis Wyld's new brewery acquisition on the outskirts of the city. Not that any of the trio were connoisseurs, they had decided on the new drink because it was being sold cheaper than most of the other labels in town. It was a promotional gimmick and by the number of empty soldiers scattered amongst the butt-filled ashtrays on the table's surface, was a mild success.

"Fifty thousands dollars to anyone who brings her the head of Brother Bones!" Michael Brown said and then made a fist, hit his chest and burped. "Can you believe that? Fifty thousand smackers for taking out one guy!"

"He ain't just one guy," corrected Mark Kalita who sat to Brown's right. "You know damn well Brother Bones is some kind of spook. She's been trying to bump him off for a couple of years now and come up snake-eyes every time." He grabbed his bottle and drained it in one swallow.

"How do you even know that's true?" asked the youngest of the three, long haired Gerald Kuster. "I mean, why the hell would a dame like Alexis Wyld put a bounty on a character like Bones? Don't make no sense at all." He lifted his hat and scratched his hair. His dandruff always made his scalp itch.

"What?" Brown, the older of the three snapped. "Where da hell you been hiding these past three years, Gerald?" No one called Kuster, Jerry. He hated that nickname. "It was Brother Bones who murdered her father, you know...the old crime boss of Cape Noire, Topper Wyld."

"Ah, I thought that was just a bullshit story some of the guys made up."

"Well, it ain't, pal." Brown twisted in his chair and held up one of the empties. "Hey, Butch, how about another round."

The bartender/owner nodded and went to the cooler as Kuster continued their discussion. "So where'd you hear she'd put out a bounty on him?"

"Ran into one of her top guns, Reed Vengel."

"You mean that rat-faced little guy who likes to use knives instead guns?" Kuster, like most of the criminal element in the port city, was all too familiar with the hood in question.

"The one and the same, Gerald," Brown concluded. "Ran into him while getting a haircut downtown. He and his crew are spreading the word all over town. Miss Wylde wants Bones' head on a platter and is willing to shell out fifty thousand gees to make it happen."

"Shit," Kuster nodded, dropping his fedora on the empty chair beside him. "That's a lot of freaking money."

"Agreed," Kalita chimed in. With straight black hair, he was the charmer of the group; a real lady's man. Fishing into his fancy suit jacket, he pulled out a pack of smokes and lit one up with his Zippo. "But you know what bugs the shit out of me, guys?"

"Nah," the older Brown played along. "What has your shorts in a twist, pally?"

"Simply this," Kalita blew out a puff of gray smoke. "For almost three years this skull-faced wacko has been running around all over this damn town putting the bloody fear of God in our criminal fellowship. And not only has he gotten away with it, but no one still has a goddamn clue as to who he really is—or where the hell his hideout's at! Now does that make any sense to you guys?" Kalita slammed an open hand on the table rattling the empty bottles.

"Well, gee," Kuster said. "Maybe his hideout is in that airship thingee he's always flying around in."

Kalita looked at his friend and tried to make sense of his statement. "Huh? What the hell are you talking about now, kid?"

"You know...the bone-ship or some such...that they talk about on his radio show every week."

Kalita couldn't believe his ears. Brown started laughing.

"What?" Kuster was confused. "You guys never heard his radio show?"

"God save me," Brown managed to get out between loud chuckles. "He thinks the freaking radio show is for real!"

Kuster looked at Brown with a hurt expression. "Huh?"

"Jezzuz, you moron," Kalita couldn't help himself. "And I suppose you think the Lone Ranger and Captain Midnight are real too?"

For a second, Kuster looked like he was about to either cry or get up and hit somebody. Before he could choose either reaction, Butch arrived with three fresh brews on a tray. He set it down, removed the bottles; passing one to each of his customers and then began setting the empties on it.

"Couldn't help over hearing your conversation," Hammer said, his mouth wrapped around a half-smoked, foul smelling cigar. "You wanta know where that Brother Bones is hiding out, you oughta ask Old Gus over there in the corner."

Brown, Kalita and Kuster all swiveled about in their chairs to look at the old man slumped over the table in the far back corner. Old Gus Reinerman was an established fixture in the Gridiron. During his youth he'd been a seaman who, according to his tall tales, had sailed around the world a dozen of times. When he lost his leg to a great white shark off the Philippines, he'd come home to Cape Noire to settle down. Hammer hired him as a janitor and let him sleep in the storage room located in the back of the bar.

"You're kidding, right?" Kalita asked scrutinizing the barkeep to see if he was joking with them.

"Nope. You know how Old Gus rants and raves all the time and spins his stories to get a free drink from the regulars. Well, a few nights ago while he was cleaning up the place, he told me he'd seen that Brother Bones guy come out of some nice brownstone somewhere here in the city."

Hammer picked up the now full tray balancing it with one hand and started to go back to the bar. "I didn't pay it no mind, but hearing you guys talk about that reward and all got me remembering it."

"You think he was telling the truth?" Brown asked Hammer's back.

"How the hell would I know," the big Irishman said over his shoulder. "Talk to him or not. It's no skin off my nose."

Brown looked at his mates. Neither said a word but eyed each other in silence. "Aw hell," he finally uttered grabbing his new beer. "What we got to lose?"

He pushed back from the table and got off his chair; Kalita and Kuster did the same. Together they sauntered over to the table in the back shadows.

"Hey, Gus," Brown called loudly. "Wake up, we wanta talk to you."

• • •

An hour later a fancy black sedan pulled up to the curb in the middle of a nice, well kept block. Streetlamps gave off a soft glow painting the brownstones and other apartment buildings a muted gray color. The expensive car, less than two months old, belonged to Michael Brown and he loved driving it. The few other parked sedans in this neighborhood were mostly rundown, second hand vehicles. As this was a blue-collar part of town, they were all the locals could afford.

"You sure this is the right place?" Mark Kalita inquired from the front passenger seat. He was looking up at the six story tenement building they had parked in front of.

"That's the number Old Gus said," Brown shut off the headlights and killed the engine. "The place he saw Brother Bones go into."

The old sailor, once they had shaken him awake, had related the story of how months earlier, while on a drinking toot with several of his old sea mates, he'd gotten lost and wandered through this part of town drunk as a skunk. He'd collapsed on the stoop of the building across the street, nursing a bottle of rum and then fallen asleep. Later that night he'd been awaken by the sound of a car pulling up in front of this very building and from it had emerged the Undead Avenger accompanied by a young man. Old Gus had seen them go into the building and a few seconds later spied the lights flash up on the third floor. After they were extinguished, he had passed out again.

Come the next morning he'd walked to the nearest bus stop and caught a ride back to Old Town and the Gridiron. It wasn't until weeks later when he'd seen a sketch of Brother Bones in the newspaper that he had remembered both the incident and, more importantly, the address of the place itself. He had told this to Hammer and some of the other Gridiron crew but all of them just ignored his claim as just another of his alcoholic induced fabrications.

Until now.

"I don't see no roadster," Kalita pointed out as he opened the door and exited.

Getting out of his own door, Brown looked up and down the street. Of the three autos on it, none was a roadster. "Hell, that don't mean nothing. Could be parked out in a back alley somewhere. If there's a chance this Bones spook is living here, then I'm gonna find out and then we can talk how we're gonna split that fifty gees."

At the same time Gerald Kuster had come out of the back seat and gone around to the rear to pull open the trunk. Brown came over to flank his left side while Kalita his right. The trio looked down at the weapons stored there; two Thompson submachine guns and one double-barrel shotgun. Brown and Kalita hoisted the machine guns while Kuster hefted the big shotgun and then quietly lowered the trunk lid. As the three moved away from the sedan, Kuster broke open the shotgun. He took two shells from his jacket pocket and slid them into the twin breaches before closing the chamber again.

Brown led the way up the cement stairs and jerked back one of the two doors and entered the small vestibule. Kalita caught the open door and followed him inside. Kuster held the door wide with the tip of his weapon and gave the deserted street a final look before doing the same.

Minutes later they were climbing the hallways stairs.

• • •

In the coldwater flat, the man who doesn't sleep sat in his chair looking out the window at Cape Noire. His black, lifeless eyes never stopped gazing out at the tall, high rise towers beyond the bucolic park only a few blocks away. Because he didn't sleep he also did not dream, but rather was himself the living embodiment of a nightmare.

He was Brother Bones, the Undead Avenger and he simply sat and waited.

He waited for the candle on the bureau behind him to flicker with light which was meant he was needed to bring vengeance to those who spread evil throughout his city.

And just as it had done so many times before, the tiny white hot flame miraculously appeared, surrounding the pitch black tiny wick. Light glowed in the small, square room and Bones turned his head at the flame's appearance. He silently got up from his chair and walked to the bureau where the candle was set. Next to it was a porcelain white mask. He stood and gazed deep into the heart of the fire.

"Bones, you are needed." Within the shimmering yellow flame he saw the tiny angelic face of his spirit guide; a teenage girl he'd shot to death in his previous life as gunman Tommy Bonello. Now she served the mysterious fates as their conduit to him in this zombie-like incarnation. He was not allowed the eternal rest of death until his mission for them had been fulfilled.

"What?" His was voice was deep, cold and without feeling.

"Three men are coming for you. They seek your demise at the bidding of Alexis Wylde."

The thing that was Brother Bones showed no reaction to the name of his enemy. He had too many to bother worrying about any of them individually—if, in fact, he was capable of worry. How does one worry a dead man?

"I will deal with them."

The lovely young face seem to smile whimsically and then faded away.

Brother Bones opened the bureau's top drawer where he kept his twin .45 silver plated automatics in their leather rig. He slipped it over his shoulders and made sure both were snug under his arms. Then he picked up the mask and placed it over the horror that was the remains of his one time handsome face. Rotted with decay, it had the power to make men go mad should they ever look upon it.

The candle flame winked out. Bones grabbed his topcoat and floppy slouch hat from the coat rack and then walked out of his room. He glided through the darkened kitchen in the apartment he shared with card dealer, Blackjack Bobby Crandall. His gloved hand grabbed the doorknob of the door leading to the outside hall and then stopped.

He heard footsteps rushing up the stairs.

• • •

"Which one?" Gerald Kuster whispered in the wide hall between the two apartments that filled the third floor; one to the west and the other to the east. A single light bulb shone down from the high ceiling above them casting very little illumination.

Brown looked from one door to the other realizing too late they had never considered the fact that each of these buildings always had multiple tenants on each floor. So, if Bones was actually in either apartment, they might lose their element of surprise by breaking into the wrong one. He looked to Kalita and Kuster and shrugged. He was just as much in the dark as they were.

"Aw, this is bullcrap," Kalita finally said and pointed with his Tommy gun at the door to his left. "Gerald, watch that one." Then he took two quick steps to the opposite door and kicked it with his right foot. Brown clutched his own machine gun ready for whatever happened next.

But the door didn't budge. In fact Kalita's foot almost had no affect on it whatsoever. He looked at the other two, growled and kicked it again, this time aiming for the area next to the doorknob. Supposedly that was the weakest spot. Or so he'd been told. He'd never actually kicked in a door before.

There was a cracking sound but the door remained solid and intact.

"SHIT!" He took a step back and gripping his Thompson against his side, fired a burst and blew the handle apart. The door slowly moved.

Then a woman screamed! "Aieee…who's there!"

"That's a woman!" Kuster stated the obvious, his shotgun still pointed at the other door.

The woman screamed a second time.

"That's the wrong door!" Brown said, now nervous. They could hear people moving around behind both doors. From the untouched one a man called out. "Whoever is out there, I'm calling the cops!"

Everything was falling apart fast. All they needed was for a bunch of folks to come storming out into the halls and see them.

"Let's get the hell out of here!" he ordered and started running down the stairs. Kalita held up his smoking machine gun and started after him cursing as he did. Finally Kuster held his shotgun against his chest and as ever, became the caboose.

"Hey, guys," he asked as they hurried down the stairwell. "What about Brother Bones?"

● ● ●

Brother Bones ripped open the front door and stepped into the hallway, both .45s held in his hands and ready to unload death. Now they were pointing at a very surprised Bobby Crandall.

"AGHH!" he screamed, his hands coming up to cover his freckled face. "Sonuvabitch, Bones! You scared the shit out of me! What the hades is going on?"

Crandall dealt blackjack at the nearby Gray Owl Casino on the night shift. It being a warm night, he'd walked to and from work.

Bones kept his pistols in his gloved hands and commanded his young ally. "I'll explain later. Go back down and out the back door to get the car. Then meet me in the street."

"The street?"

"Just do what I say. There's going to be shooting."

"Alright, alright!" Use to these kind of weird demands, young Crandall started back down the stairs with the Undead Avenger on his heels. "Looks like another late night, I suppose."

He received no answer. Again, that was no surprise.

On the ground floor, Crandall headed down the corridor for the back door while Brother Bones marched quickly out the front entrance.

● ● ●

The three fleeing hitmen didn't see him until they were almost down the cement steps from the building's front stoop.

"Good evening, gents," his voice brought them up short and they froze on the lower steps, their weapons still clutched in their hands. And then they saw him.

He stood across the street facing them, tall in his somber overcoat with his wide brimmed hat hiding most of his white façade. Still they could all see it clearly enough as the pure white porcelain seemed to absorb the streetlamps' light and glimmer. They were looking at a skull and within its sockets there was only blackness.

"I hear you were looking for me," he held up his twin automatics. "Well, here I am."

Brown, Kalita and Kuster were transfixed, each stuck to where their feet were planted as the apparition before them was indeed a nightmare come to full blown life.

Kalita broke first and pulling up the barrel of his Thompson, he marched off the sidewalk and opened fire at the figure in black.

"YEAH!! Bring it on, Bone Man! Eat lead!"

Brother Bones merely laughed louder and started walking towards Kalita. Despite his gut wrenching fear, Kalita managed to keep his Tommy-gun steady and was gratified to see several of his shots hit the bizarre avenger. Three bullets hit Bones in the chest and staggered him, his arms flailing outward.

"Hahahaha," Kalita laughed. "How do you like them apples, Bone Man?"

Brother Bones shook himself off like a dog that had just come out of the water, his head down while he moved his big shoulders about. Then he simply raised his head and at the same time brought up his pistols and fired each. The first bullet caught Kalita in the shoulder. He began to spin around when the second projectile went through his temple.

Seeing their pal shot down, Brown and Kuster came charging across the street, but only Michael Brown was firing. Kuster, in his rage, was holding his shotgun in front of him like some ancient battle-axe, momentarily forgetting what its real use was for.

As dozens of bullets tore up the tar in front of Brother Bones, he began laughing again, knowing fully well nothing these pathetic men had could truly harm him.

Then Brown's machine-gun was empty and he stood like a fool, facing the Undead Avenger as his body started to tremble. Bone's single shot plowed through his face and he fell over to lie next to his dead compatriot, Mark Kalita.

All the while Gerald Kuster kept running forward until he was right atop the skull-faced vigilante and then his sanity returned to him. His body bumped into Brother Bones and just like that they were face to face. Sweat rolled down Kuster's brows as he now looked into those two eye-sockets. There he saw the coldest black eyes he had ever seen; at the same time he felt Bones' automatic pressing into his gut.

With tears starting to stream down his face, he made a last feeble attempt to swing his shotgun out just as both pistols barked and together blew out most of his back. Like a deck of cards, Kuster fell in on himself with a whimper and dropped to the road dead.

Brother Bones calmly put his two guns back in their shoulder rigs just as the speedy roadster came rolling around the corner. Crandall brought it to a screeching stop just in front of Brother Bones and then leaving the engine running, jumped out of the car.

"Open the trunk," Bones told him as he reached down and with one hand took hold of Gerald Kuster's jacket and lifted him off the chewed up road. He walked over to Michael Brown and picked him up with his free hand. At the back of the roadster, Crandall stood with the trunk wide open. He'd seen Bones perform such feats of strength before and none of this was new to him.

Bones tossed Kuster in the big empty trunk first and then began to drop Brown over him. As he did so something fell out of the dead man's coat and hit the ground with clink.

Crandall bent down and scooped up car keys. He looked at Bones and then over where the fancy black sedan was parked.

"You think it was theirs?" he suggested holding up the dangling keys.

"Who else in this neighborhood could afford such wheels."

"So what do we do with it?"

"Take it to a car shop and sell it for whatever you can get for it," Brother Bones said as he went to fetch Mark Kalita's corpse. "Then take the money to St. Michael's and give it to Father O'Malley. I'm sure he'll put it to good use."

"Hey, right. That's a great idea. I'll do that." Crandall stepped out of the way as his supernatural boss deposited the final body with the others. "So what are we going to do with them?"

"We are going to take them to the harbor and drop them in the bay."

After Bobby Crandall had collected the trio's weapons and dumped them in the back seat, he slid back behind the driver's wheel. Bones was already in the passenger seat and remained quiet all the way to the harbor.

● ● ●

At the same time Brown, Kalita and Kuster were being uncere-moniously dropped into the warm waters of the Pacific, Butch Hammer was just finishing up his nightly routine in closing up the Gridiron and going home.

All the chairs had been set upside down on their tables and Old Gus was busy swiping a wet mop around the wooden floor pulling the bucket-on-wheels as he went. His peg leg made a tapping sound whenever he took a step.

"Well, I'm out of here," Hammer declared as he threw on his short-waist jacket and newsboy cap by the front door. "We'll see you tomorrow morning, Gus. Don't forget to lock up."

"Ain't done it yet," the cantankerous old sailor fired back. "Don't plan on starting now."

The old fellow stopped moving the mop for a minute and scratched his chin as if perplexed by something. "Butch, I been thinking about what I told them three fellahs earlier tonight."

"What, about where to find Brother Bones?"

"Uh-huh. It got me to thinking just now...you know, how they got house numbers done up a certain fixed way."

"What do you mean? Like all the even numbers are on one side of the street and the odds are on the other?"

"Right." Old Gus looked at his boss and said. "Been thinking I might have given them guys the wrong number, Butch. I told'em it was twenty-six. But the more I think about it, I think it was really twenty-seven."

"Oh, well, I don't think it's any big deal. You can tell them the right one next time they come in."

"Yeah, I suppose. Okay, boss. Have a good night."

"You too, Gus. Bye."

Old Gus watched his employer close the door behind him and through the plate glass window go walking off into the night. He shook his head for a second at how fuzzy his old brain got sometimes.

Then he began whistling a rowdy tune he'd learned when he was a young man in Calcutta. He danced with his swaying mop across the wet floor.

The End

The Pirate King
(A Mace Bullard Story)
by David Foster
Based on characters created by Paul Bishop

The moonlight shimmering off the still water was cut by the bow of a forty-foot long sailing coaster, which glided silently into the harbor. The *Prowling Tiger*, captained by Kingeroy Karter, had a low hull and two masts amidships furnished with lateen sails. Known as the *Pirate King*, Karter was feared along the length of the rugged Barbary Coast. With his band of corsairs, he was a slaver, raiding coastal towns for women to put in chains and later sell at auction. On this night, the city of Agadir was to be raided. Having recently sold his last shipment at a slavers market in Velara, he needed fresh cargo.

Karter stood tall on the quarterdeck as the sails were lowered and the anchor dropped. He watched as a longboat was put over the side. Laden with weapons and netting, the crew dropped down into the boat and started rowing for the shore. Each man was quiet as he went about his task. The routine well rehearsed, entering the city undetected was key to their success.

Karter smiled to himself as his cut-throats pressed toward Agadir. There was no doubt this would be another successful raid.

• • •

Sergent Mace Bullard of the French Foreign Legion was not so foolish as to go drink for drink with his stout-hearted comrade, François Mesmer. Mesmer, who was six-foot-four and impossibly broad shouldered, was putting away brandy as if it were lolly water. But Bullard did not begrudge his friend letting off steam. Their past two campaigns had been hard and rigorous. Many good Legionnaires had fallen along the way.

They sat at a table near the door in a dingy waterside bar, away from a group of Arabian musicians. The looping rhythm of the tabla echoed through the small room. To their left on stage, several belly dancers shimmied and swayed, their stomachs undulated teasingly in time with the music, much to the delight of the men assembled before them.

Mesmer paid the dancers no mind. He charged his glass. "Here's to Henri Moiret," he snorted.

Bullard nodded somberly and touched glasses. "To Moiret," he repeated.

They both downed the liquor.

Henri Moiret had been the Legion lookout at Fort Granuille. He was only eighteen years old when he had been cut down by El Hakim's brigands. He didn't deserve to die so young.

A hostess stopped at their table. "Can I get you gentlemen anything?" she asked.

Mesmer pointed at his glass. "Brandy," he slurred.

Bullard covered his glass with his palm. He had drunk enough.

It was like an explosion. The door splintered as it was cleaved through by a heavy ax. Pandemonium followed as a gang of pirates flooded into the bar looking for women to take prisoner. The hostess screamed as she was lifted off her feet and thrown over a pirate's shoulder.

"Whaaaa...?" Memser blurted.

The dancers and barmaids ran for their lives, scurrying for the back exit.

"Slavers!" Bullard exclaimed.

Bullard pressed to his feet to intercept the brigands. However, he was swamped in the charge and struck by a cudgel. He slumped to the floor, blood running freely from a wound above his brow. The blood streamed down his face. It looked like he was done for.

● ● ●

Mesmer saw Bullard fall and let out an almighty war-cry. Anger coursed through his veins. He kicked away from the table, upending it. He grabbed the two nearest pirates and slammed their heads together. The sound was sickening as their skulls collided. Mesmer bounded over their inert bodies and charged the next man in line. A cutlass swung toward his head, but he ducked under the blade and grabbed the brigand's wrist. With his free hand he punched the pirate in the throat. The pirate coughed blood as he sagged to the floor.

"Evant la Legion!" Mesmer bellowed as he moved on to his next adversary. He scooped a marauder up in his large hands, and then holding him aloft, hurled him across the bar. The brigand crashed into a shelf lined with bottles. His body slid to the floor amidst the shards of broken glass.

Another corsair charged Mesmer from behind. At the last second, Mesmer turned and unloaded a powerful right cross. It connected with the startled corsair's nose, the shattered bone driven back into the pirate's brain. The pirate toppled to the floor like a felled tree.

Mesmer turned quickly to counter the next foe, but no one came at him. The remaining corsairs took up positions just out of reach, surrounding him. With his senses dulled by alcohol, Mesmer never saw the threat. Before he could react, a heavy cargo net was thrown over him. He was instantly caught up in its toils, struggling to break free. He gritted his teeth as he pulled and tugged at the rope netting. It was no use, he was hemmed in tight. A pirate advanced; a heavy wooden cudgel in his hand. Mesmer tried to charge at him, but could not move. The club came down hard on his skull. As he buckled and dropped to his knees, he looked across at Bullard, still lying on the floor. Bullard did not move his face covered in a sheet of blood. Was he dead?

Mesmer was struck again. His head lolled forward, his eyesight blurred. A final blow put him down. He slumped forward as darkness washed over him.

● ● ●

The leader of the raiding party, a sallow looking man with high cheek bones, known as *Amir the Red,* lowered his cudgel. Standing over the fallen Legionnaire, he looked around the bar. Two men were dead, one had a broken back, and two lay unconscious. Such losses were unacceptable. His men had performed poorly.

As Amir considered what to do next, he was approached by his shipmate, *Tarjyn the*

Bold. Tarjyn was a slender man with heavily hooded eyes and a long beard. Amir didn't trust him. Everybody knew Tarjyn believed he should be leading the raiding parties.

"What are you waiting for? Kill him!" Tarjyn urged.

Amir nodded. He drew his sword and raised it for the death blow. Then he stopped. Why did Tarjyn want the Legionnaire dead? Amir lowered the blade.

"What is wrong? Have you lost your nerve for killing?" Tarjyn said.

"You know the law. It is not for men such as us to pass sentence. We must let the King decide. Bring him and the women and get back to the ship."

Tarjyn sneered, and threw back his head in anger. But he complied. With several of his shipmates he carried the heavy Legionnaire out of the tavern.

Amir heaved a sigh of relief. At Tarjyn's goading he had almost made a terrible mistake, one which would have cost him his life. The King's law was inviolate. The Legionnaire had to stand trial.

• • •

Bullard groaned as a damp cloth was mopped across his brow. He opened his eyes. An old woman with silver hair tied in a bun smiled down at him. She had been tending to his wound.

"We thought you were dead. You received a nasty blow," she said. "I have stitched you up."

Bullard nodded and pushed himself to his elbow. He was still on the floor of the tavern.

"Easy," she said.

Bullard fought off a wave dizziness and took in the scene. The tavern was a shambles. Furniture had been upended or destroyed, and the floor was covered in broken glass. Then he remembered his comrade.

"Mesmer?" Bullard groaned. His voice was hoarse. "Where is Mesmer?"

The woman seemed confused. "Who?"

"There was another Legionnaire with me, a big man. I need to know where he is."

She shook her head. "Wait here. Don't try to move. I will get Fareek."

The woman climbed to her feet and returned several moments later with a gentleman in a tattered red waistcoat and a bandage around his forehead. He took a knee beside Bullard.

"I am Fareek, the owner of the tavern," he said. "Magdalena tells me you are looking for your comrade?"

Bullard sat up. "Yes. Where is he?"

"I have bad news. I saw everything. He fought valiantly, but the slavers took him. They carried him out in a net."

At least Mesmer was still alive. "Where did they go? Which direction?"

"They sailed north, I believe."

Bullard nodded and pushed to his feet. Fareek took his arm to assist.

"I'm okay," Bullard said, shrugging off the hand.

Fareek stood back. "Is there anything else I can do for you?" he asked.

Bullard had already decided he would go after Mesmer. He had a four-wheel-drive vehicle but it wouldn't suit his needs. The road didn't follow the coast.

"I will need three horses, and provisions. Can you help me?"

Fareek scratched his whiskered chin. "Yes, it can be arranged, but I don't understand.

They are on water, you are on land?"

"They have to come close to shore some time, and when they do, I'll be there to greet them."

"But you are only one man. They are a small army. What can you do?"

Bullard gritted his teeth. "You'd be surprised."

● ● ●

Mesmer woke in a dimly lit room. His mouth was dry and his head ached. He wasn't sure if the pain was from the beating he received or the amount of alcohol he consumed. He tried to move only to find he was chained to a thick wooden beam. As his senses returned, he felt the room rise and fall and heard the creak of the timbers. He realized it wasn't a room at all, but the cargo hold of a ship.

"Eeeewww! Get it away. Get it away!" a woman's voice cried.

Mesmer craned his neck and saw seven women chained against the far wall. They looked frightened. He recognized three women from the bar. One of the dancers squealed as a rat scurried across her legs. It was like being locked in hell.

Mesmer knew he had to do something. Using all his strength, he struggled against the chains, attempting to break free. They held tight. He gritted his teeth and cursed.

For the moment he would have to be patient. But he knew his time would come.

● ● ●

Silhouetted against the moon, Bullard rode hard along the coast, resting each of the horses regularly. He could not leave Mesmer's fate to the corsairs. Mesmer was a friend. Bullard did not have many friends. As he pressed on, he thought back on the day they met in Rabat, one year ago. The day he *became* Mace Bullard.

He had regained consciousness in a filth filled alleyway with no memory of who he was. As he staggered to his feet, he found himself looking down the barrel of a gun. Three thugs from a Moroccan crime syndicate had him cornered, and under the threat of death, they kept demanding *the key*. He had no idea what they meant or why they were so determined to kill him for it.

Surprising even himself, he instinctively tumbled forward, rolling into a handstand, kicking the pistol from the would-be-shooter's hand. Back on his feet, he scampered away only to find the alley was a dead-end.

With the thugs hot on his tail, he had no time for thought, only action. Using only his hands and feet, he scaled the wall in front of him to a balcony on the first floor – not even wondering how it was he had the skills to do so.

As he had climbed, he passed a poster advertising a troupe of circus trapeze artists and acrobats. The featured performer, *The Great Vadim*, was displayed prominently, but the man with no memory moved too fast to notice his own startling resemblance to Vadim.

The building wall led to a balcony and a room beyond that was part of the Hotel Luxor. Desperate to escape his pursuers, the man with no memory stole an identity card and a Foreign Legion uniform laid across a chair in the room where he found himself.

Fortunately for the man with no memory, the absent Legionnaire – known as Mace Bullard – was drunk and passed out in the hotel bar downstairs.

On the street, posing as Legionnaire Bullard, the man with no memory eluded his pursuers by falling in with a bunch of 'fellow' Legionnaires. They asked no questions – he was wearing the uniform of the Legion, which was good enough for them.

One of the Legionnaires was François Mesmer, who, since that fateful day, had become a loyal and trusted friend. Bullard could not let him down. He urged the horses forward. He had to find the pirates.

• • •

At midday, François Mesmer was marched onto the deck, his wrists and head in a wooden yoke. The crew of the *Prowling Tiger* jeered and pelted him with rotting fruit and refuse. Mesmer stood defiant, despite his battered appearance. His Legionnaire's uniform had been reduced to rags; his hair was mussed and matted with blood, courtesy of a gash on his forehead.

The pirate called Amir pushed through the crowd and took control. Mesmer remembered he was the man who had clubbed him in the tavern. As their eyes met, Mesmer glared at him with hatred. Amir grunted and took Mesmer by the arm. He steered the Legionnaire to the mast, where he was chained.

Amir turned to address his shipmates.

"Quiet, *King's men*," Amir bellowed. "This court is now in session. All quiet for the King."

The cabin door opened and a tall man dressed in peacock-blue stepped onto the deck. The King looked like a throwback from a nineteenth century pirate tale. His dark hair was long and his mustache was waxed and curled at the end. He wore a sabre at his hip. Mesmer had never seen Kingeroy Karter before, but knew his reputation. He was as mean and as ruthless as they came. Karter sat down at a table that had been set up near his cabin door. He was clearly the judge overseeing proceedings, however as Karter began to peel and dissect a mandarin, he appeared noticeably disinterested in the outcome.

At the King's signal, Amir announced Mesmer's charges.

"The man standing before you today has been charged under pirate law for murdering two of your ship mates." The assembled pirates began to abuse Mesmer once more. Amir continued, raising his voice over the din. "Furthermore he broke the back of Augustus Grey, a fine man, whose service will be sorely missed. An attack on the King's men is equal to an attack on the King himself." More abuse flew. Amir turned to Mesmer. "How do you respond to the charges?"

Mesmer raised his head. "Not guilty," he snarled.

A rotting fishhead struck Mesmer's face, hurled by one of the crew. Laughter erupted on deck. Mesmer balled his fists and struggled against the yoke. If only he were free, he'd go down swinging.

"Order! Order in the court," Amir called. "Order. The King will now pass sentence."

All eyes turned to Karter. The King pushed away from the table and stood.

Karter's voice was deep. "Shipmates, I have listened to the evidence presented against the prisoner and after due deliberation I have no alternative to pronounce him guilty as charged. The sentence is death; to be carried out at sun-up on the morrow."

• • •

Bullard followed the corsairs north and found them anchored in Broadside Bay, a small protected inlet. As he sat perched high on the cliffs overlooking the bay, through a spyglass, he watched the proceedings. His Legionnaire brother-in-arms was dragged onto the deck. Bullard was relieved to see Mesmer still alive. Even from that great distance, Bullard could ascertain what went on; a *pirate court*. It was an old practice intended to terrify the prisoner. The sentence was always death.

But Mesmer would not die. Bullard would see to that. He had been through too much with his friend to allow him to die at the hands of pirates. Bullard would wait till dark, and then make his move.

● ● ●

Mesmer had been left on deck all afternoon under the baking sun. His skin was burnt, and he was dehydrated, almost to the point of delirium. What he wouldn't give for a glass of cool water. It somehow didn't seem right, like a cruel joke. Not that he was afraid to die. On the day he joined the Legion, he knew he would face death constantly, and sooner or later his luck would run out. But he always pictured himself dying in combat, not trussed up helplessly at the hands of a band of brigands. His head lolled forward.

Mesmer fought to remain conscious. He opened his eyes to see the setting sun hovering low on the horizon. Bathed in golden light, Amir and two other men came to collect him.

"You look thirsty, Legionnaire," Amir called as he threw a tin of water in Mesmer's face.

The water felt good on his burnt skin and chapped lips. He stuck out his dry tongue trying to catch as much precious water as he could. The pirates removed the yoke and took his arms. It was a good thing, Mesmer could barely stand. They dragged him unceremoniously below deck to the cargo hold once again.

Chained to beam, Amir squatted down before him.

"Legionnaire, sleep well tonight, for tomorrow you die," he said with a broad grin.

Mesmer didn't respond. He raised his head defiantly and stared at the pirate. The pirate's grin turned to a sneer. He broke eye contact, stood and walked away.

Mesmer cursed under his breath. The count-down to his execution had begun.

● ● ●

It was after midnight when Bullard made his move. From thirty feet up, he stood tall, puffed out his chest and dived out away from the cliff face. He hit the water cleanly, barely making a splash on the moonlit surface. After traveling fifteen-feet under water, he surfaced and with long strokes started swimming toward the ship. He covered the distance quickly and latched onto the anchor chain. Hand over hand; he hauled himself up till he was level with the hawsepipe. He placed one foot on the hull and then heaved himself up over the gunwale, landing on the deck.

His arrival did not go unnoticed. The night watchman approached and raised a lantern.

"Who goes there?" the watchman called.

Bullard didn't answer. He bounded forward and rolled into a handstand. As he came out of the roll, he kicked the startled pirate in the chest. The pirate fell back and cracked his head on a black-powder barrel. He was out cold. Bullard turned quickly to see if anyone else was on deck at this time of night. Not a soul, all was quiet. He scuttled across to his fallen foe and retrieved a flat throwing-knife, which was tucked into the man's belt. Now to find Mesmer.

Where would pirates keep their prisoners?

The answer was simple; the cargo hold. Keeping low, Bullard crossed to the hold and peered down through the wooden grate hatch. All he saw was darkness. Mesmer may have very well been down there, but he couldn't tell. And he couldn't risk calling out in case he was wrong. He'd have to investigate further. The grate was padlocked. He would have to find another way down.

Cautiously, he crossed to the hatchway and started down the ladder until his foot hit the deck below. Only a dim lamp lit the room. He turned and peered into the darkness. He was in the crew's quarters. The men were asleep, sprawled on bunks, or swinging in hammocks. Light on his feet, Bullard slowly and quietly made his way through the cabin, past the sleeping men. At the end of the cabin was an open doorway. He stepped through and saw a pot-bellied guard seated on an empty gunpowder barrel. Behind him was a heavy iron gate, which led to the hold. The guard opened his half-closed eyes. Confusion registered on his face. He did not recognize Bullard. He staggered to his feet.

"Who are you? What are you doing in this part of the ship?"

Bullard didn't answer. He sidestepped and kicked the pirate in the stomach. As the big man doubled over, Bullard elbowed him in the back of the head. The pirate slumped forward, unconscious, landing with a heavy thud. Bullard cursed silently. He hadn't intended to make so much noise. Had he given the game away?

He craned his neck back to the crew's quarters. Hidden in the shadow of the doorway, Bullard watched as one of the pirates raised his head and looked in his direction. The pirate shrugged his shoulders, yawned, and lowered his head, returning to his slumber. Bullard heaved a sigh of relief, and returned his attention to the iron gate. It was padlocked. He retrieved the key-ring from the fallen pirate at his feet and inserted the key into the lock. The bolt sprang open. Bullard pushed through the gate and stepped into the hold. He was almost overpowered by the smell of death and decay.

Through the darkness, Bullard searched for Mesmer. He saw him chained to a beam looking worse for wear. His head was bowed, eyes closed, and his chin rested on his chest. Bullard scrambled to his side. His friend didn't stir. Bullard reached for his shoulder.

"Mesmer," he whispered as he shook him. "Mesmer."

The big Legionnaire groaned and opened his eyes. *"Mon Sergent? ...* I thought you were dead. How did you..?"

"I followed along the coast. But we haven't a moment to lose. Let's get you out of here."

"You have keys?"

"Wouldn't be much of a rescue without them," Bullard replied as he unlocked his comrade's shackles.

"We need to rescue the women too," Mesmer added.

It was only then Bullard realized the women of Agadir were also in the hold; hidden and chained in the shadows.

Bullard nodded. "Indeed. We're *all* getting out of here." He helped Mesmer to his feet. "Steady yourself while I will release the women."

As Mesmer held the beam, Bullard crossed to the women who were huddled in a corner. He could see the fear in their eyes. They withdrew as he closed in, having suffered at the hands of the pirates.

"It's going to be alright," he reassured them, his voice little more than a whisper. "I am going to release you."

Bullard held his hands wide, allowing them to see the keys. He inched forward and took hold of the chain, moving along the links to the lock. With a turn of the key he released them. He knew he could not march everybody out through the crew's quarters. They would be sure to be discovered. That left one option. They would have to climb out through the wooden grate hatch above. There were rungs leading to the grate. Bullard wasted no time. He placed the key-ring between his teeth and scrambled up the rungs till he reached the hatch. He uncurled one arm, removed the key-ring from his teeth, and started working on the padlock. It came open easily.

He knew raising the grate would be far more difficult. Using his shoulders, he forced the hatch back a few inches and squeezed out of the narrow opening, careful not to make any noise as the grate closed behind him. On deck, it only took him a second to find a rope. He tied one end to the grate and looped the other end over the yardarm to use as a pulley. Putting his shoulders to the task, he heaved the grate open and held it tight. The women came through first, followed by Mesmer. As the big Legionnaire climbed onto the deck, Bullard heaved a sigh of relief and slowly let the grate close behind him.

Bullard straightened himself up after his exertion and crossed to the group now gathered amidships. They couldn't all swim back. Bullard's eyes darted around as he sorted a way to get everyone to shore. He saw something that would suit their needs covered by a tarpaulin.

"We'll take the longboat," Bullard said. He turned to Mesmer. "Do you think you're strong enough to help me get it over the side?"

Mesmer looked hurt that his *sergent* would think such a thing. "I can do it," he grumbled.

Bullard stifled a grin as he untied the ropes and removed the tarpaulin cover. Mesmer took hold of the winch and rolling his shoulders, raised the boat. Free from its cradle, Bullard guided it out over the edge.

Once it was clear, Bullard said, "Gently, my friend."

Mesmer lowered the longboat to the water, careful not to make a loud splash.

"You first," Bullard said to his comrade.

Mesmer nodded. He climbed down one of the guide ropes and balanced himself at the bow.

"Send them down," Mesmer called, careful to keep his voice low.

Bullard steered the first woman to the rope. He held it tight so it wouldn't sway.

"François will help you at the bottom," he said.

She took the rope and snaked her way down to Mesmer's waiting arms. Bullard kept watch as one by one the other women followed behind her. Mesmer caught the last one and helped her to take a seat. It was Bullard's turn. In moments they'd be away. However, as Bullard took the rope, a pirate holding a kerosene lantern aloft staggered from below.

"Intruder on deck! Intruder on deck!" the pirate yelled.

Bullard cursed. He spun quickly and in a smooth fluid movement, threw the knife he had taken earlier. It struck the brigand in the wrist, who yelped in pain and dropped the lantern. The lantern smashed and a pool of kerosene ignited the flame racing along the deck. Bullard bounded over the small fire and charged shoulder first into the pirate. The corsair was shunted toward the railing. He tried to fight back, but momentum was with Bullard. As they struck the side, the pirate toppled over the edge, landing in the water below.

Bullard knew they only had seconds before the pirates came for them. He scrambled up the rigging and called down to Memser.

"Go." Bullard yelled. "Get to shore."

He could see conflict in Mesmer's eyes. His comrade did not want to abandon him. But Bullard knew if he did not take the fight to the pirates, the longboat would be a sitting target as they rowed to shore.

"Get the women to safety. That's an order," Bullard yelled.

Mesmer reluctantly complied and released the guide ropes, then started rowing.

The pirates burst from their quarters below brandishing cutlasses and knives. Bullard grabbed a rope, and swung down bouldering into the first wave. They fell like ten-pins.

• • •

The fire continued to spread, its tendrils igniting one of the lowered lateen sails. The canvas was dry and went up quickly. The rigging was next to go, long thin fingers of flame tracing across the ropes.

A powder barrel at the foot of the mast ignited next, shooting into the air like a cannonball. The night sky lit up, sparks flew, and the crew ducked for cover as flaming debris rained down from above.

With multiple fires now raging, it was *Hell* on high water...

• • •

Bullard ducked under a flashing blade, and then rolled into a handstand, kicking the cutlass from the shocked brigand's grasp. Before the pirate regained his composure, back on his feet, Bullard balled his fist and smashed him on the point of the jaw. The pirate reeled back against the gunwale and toppled over the edge, falling back-first into the water below. However, there was no respite. Two more of the King's men set upon Bullard. He swayed out of reach of a slashing sword, and then dropped to his knees to avoid the second blade. As the pirates followed through with their lusty strikes, Bullard bounced back to his feet and slammed his fist into the back of the nearest pirate. The man cried out and arched his back, dropping his sword. Bullard scooped it up and raised it as the second pirate turned and swung his cutlass at Bullard's throat. Spark's flew as the blades met.

• • •

Tarjyn the Bold watched as Amir engaged the Legionnaire in battle. Overhead the fire raged, the yardarm engulfed in flame. Tarjyn figured it would come down upon them any second now. He could warn Amir, but that would also alert the intruder. If Amir should fall, Tarjyn knew by rights, he would become second in command; he would lead the raiding parties in the future. He chose to remain silent, letting chance decide Amir's fate.

The Legionnaire must have heard the timber snap. He leaped back as the yardarm and rigging crashed amidships. Amir and two other pirates had not been so quick to move. They were crushed beneath the fiery yardarm.

Then Tarjyn saw his chance. His right to lead would be cemented if he killed the Legionnaire. Tarjyn circled the flaming detritus quickly, moving in for the kill. He charged in with his cutlass raised high above his head, preparing to split the enemy from skull to sternum. The Legionnaire sidestepped as the blade came slashing down, and then threw a crushing right hand that caught Tarjyn on the point of the chin. The corsair shrugged off the blow. With anger in his heart, he turned and swung the blade at Legionnaire's midriff. The intruder jumped back, the blade missing by a fraction of an inch. Before Tarjyn could strike again, the Legionnaire bounded forward and acrobatically leaped into the air, wrapping his legs around Tarjyn's neck. Fighting for air, the corsair tried to break free, but he was dragged down to the deck, caught in the vice-like grip.

Tarjyn reached for his cutlass, which had jarred from his hand as he struck the deck. If only he could retrieve the weapon. His fingers clawed at the hilt, but he couldn't drag it in. Starved of oxygen, his vision began to blur, but he refused to give up. He stretched for the blade again. This time he snagged it. He drew it close. However, before he could strike, the Legionnaire tightened his grip and rolled his hips. Tarjyn heard his neck snap. It was over. As his life ebbed away, his last thought was the bleak realization he would never lead the King's men.

● ● ●

Bullard grabbed the dead man's cutlass and scrambled to his feet as another corsair charged at him issuing a blood-curdling war cry. The metallic *clang* as the blades met echoed through the choking smoke and ash. Bullard twisted and then brought his sword in, around and down. The pirate parried the blow and then swung his own sword, a wild slashing blow intended to take Bullard's head off. Bullard ducked under the blade, and then moved forward. Holding the hilt with both hands, he swung the cutlass in a savage arc, embedding the blade in his opponent's midriff. The corsair toppled to the deck, blood pooling around him as he died.

Bullard didn't have time to dwell on the man's death. Another pirate lunged at him knocking his cutlass into the fire. As the pirate raised his sword for the death blow, Bullard bounded forward, caught him by the wrist and slung him into the mast, which by this time was well alight. The brigand screamed as his clothes caught fire. He ran to the railing and hurled himself over the side.

Two other pirates descended upon Bullard. The Legionnaire pried a boarding pike free from a wooden rack and turned to face them.

● ● ●

Standing on the quarterdeck, through the smoke and flame, Kingeroy Karter watched as one by one his men were cut down. Karter gritted his teeth and balled his fists at his side. The Legionnaire had to be killed. Karter drew his sabre from its scabbard and made his way to the lower deck.

Karter's men drew back as their leader entered the fray. The intruder stood at the ready with a boarding pike in his hands.

"Legionnaire, you know there is no escape," Karter hissed. "I will run you through, and throw your body over the side for the sharks." He advanced and swung his sabre.

The Legionnaire parried the blow with the pike. "Do your best, Captain," he responded over the roaring flame. "Time is running out."

Karter didn't comprehend. He reposted. "I'll have time enough to dispose of you."

Once again, his opponent parried the blow. "That may be, Captain, but what of you? What of your men? The fire is too far gone. Your ship is done for."

Karter stood back on his heel and looked around. The enormity of the fire finally struck him. The ship had gone up quicker than he could have possibly imagined. The whole cabin section was now alight, flame billowing high into the night sky. The remaining pirates, fearing for their lives, leaped over the edge seeking the safety of the water.

Cowards, Karter thought.

"Well, Captain, what's it to be?" the Legionnaire asked.

Karter felt a white hot rage building inside his chest. He cried out and charged, thrashing his sword at the intruder. He drove the Legionnaire back toward the flame. As he pushed forward, his opponent tripped over a dead body, and tumbled to the deck. The pike was jarred free. This was Karter's chance. His opponent lay unarmed at his feet. The Pirate King raised his sword high above his head, and in a lightning fast move, brought it slashing down.

● ● ●

As the blade came screaming toward him, at the last fraction of a second, Bullard threw himself hard to his left, through a wall of flame. His hair was singed, and his clothes alight. As he rolled to a halt, coughing and spluttering, he swatted himself down, extinguishing the fire. He had no time to rest. Karter pushed through the flame, brandishing his sabre. Bullard lay on the blackened and blistered deck next to another fallen pirate. A sword lay at his side. Bullard scooped it up and raised it as Karter brought his own blade to bear, swinging it like an ax. Bullard parried the blow, but from his position couldn't go on the offensive.

Karter raised himself to his full height and drove downward again. Bullard scooted back, and the blade jammed into the deck between his legs. As the King hunched over, attempting to pull the sabre free, Bullard rocked forward and ran the Pirate King through piercing his heart. A bloody rosette formed on his tunic. Karter swayed, then pitched forward to his knees. With his last ounce of strength, Karter raised his head and nodded. As darkness came, his head lolled and he slumped forward in a heap.

Bullard heaved an audible sigh of relief and scrambled to his feet. He knew his ordeal was not over yet. As the mast burnt through and came crashing down through the deck, Bullard knew he only seconds to abandon the sinking ship. The ship rolled to port as the stern dropped, and the bow rode high. Water rushed into the hold. Bullard lost his footing as he clawed to the edge. The ship dropped back down, and Bullard was swamped as a wave washed over him.

● ● ●

From the shore, Mesmer watched as flame engulfed the *Prowling Tiger.* He sat on a sandy stretch of beach with the women he had rescued at his side. They treated him like a hero, though he didn't feel like one. It was Bullard who had rescued them all. He heaved a heavy sigh as the mast crashed down through the deck. The ship listed heavily to port. Almost burnt to the waterline, she was going down fast.

"Your friend was a brave man," a woman nestled at his side said. Mesmer turned to face her. He recognized her as the hostess from the bar in Agadir. "He gave his life for us," she added.

Mesmer shook his head. "No, he's not dead. I have no doubt. I am beginning to realize the *sergent* is a very resilient man."

"Surely, he cannot have escaped from the fire," she said skeptically.

Mesmer forced a smile. "Keep watching the waves. He'll join us soon enough."

"Suppose he does make it, what happens then? I mean, what happens to us?" she asked. She gestured to the other women around them.

"That's simple. We'll escort you back to Agadir where you can go back to your families. But most of all, you'll never have to worry about the Pirate King again."

The End

David Foster

Third Veneer Split
by Jeff "Venture" Fournier

Epicurious Locke shifted at his desk to answer the phone with more anticipation than a student of the Stoic philosophers should probably have shown but he was alone in his private office at home. The late winter air had lent a holiday quality to the estate and its pine wood environs. Excitement was all about as his house staff prepared for the holidays, but in the chamber of the house's master it was usually more tightly controlled.

"Locke speaking. Yes George. No, you didn't call too late. The special load I asked about went out? Good. The address? Got it. Oh? No reason, just tracking customer demand for our new inks. Thanks again. Merry Christmas to you too."

He hung up the handset of the phone and finished the doodle he was tracing while his shipping foreman at Dyna Inks had told him the last piece of the puzzle. His trap was working perfectly. If you want to catch rats you must bait with the finest cheese. If you wanted to catch counterfeiters you had so many more options. After he had made his decision to target the counterfeit and scam men of the underworld he had spent much of his time in his office here or his private workshop on the grounds. For years he had kept track of press sales to questionable persons through his industrial contacts overseas. He had paper mills report to men who reported to him about their stock levels in various better quality papers. Details such as who was buying and not reordering or who was making specific requests for specific stock. Then came the watching of the plate makers and engraving men. Learning those who were honest and those who were not so scrupulous. Eventually he had managed to have the plan come together.

If you engineer an ink that would make impressive counterfeit bills when mixed with an additive only certain companies supply and you tracked the movement of those disparate items eventually a pattern would emerge. They might put up a facade or thin veneer of innocence but no legitimate company would order ink and the solution in those quantities and ratios for any normal printing purpose. Coming up with the formula to the 'cheese' took most of his not inconsiderable skill in the arts of chemistry and engineering. Tracking the shipments and eliminating false leads took up the rest of his time. Thank God his manufacturing empire could practically run itself these days.

Nowadays he had the advantage of also being an ink supplier to the actual Federal Mint but those inks were all well tracked and accounted for by unsmiling G-men with Secret Service badges and bad suits. He had managed to get enough of a sample of it to engineer the 'cheese' but he had to be very careful. If his company had dangled the real inks in front of his prey's nose he would have been too blatant, too arrogant. They would have smelled a trap filled with 'too good to be true' and it would have gotten him a visit by the self same Federal agents. He liked to keep them out of it as much as possible but times were changing. It was only 1930 but soon nation states would become worried by the scourge of counterfeiting bills, stocks, and bonds and they would act. It would become an international problem. But they were slow if effective and most of the people capable of producing forgeries were very fast, high level criminals. They might be spies for foreign governments or even other governments themselves. If he knocked over that hornets' nest carelessly they would jump much more quickly, be more inquisitive and that might lead them to his door. He must deter that as much as possible. His continuing work to destroy the cheats and schemers who poisoned the world's economy and the common man's life with their own greed was his private war.

Tonight he had a destination from one of his contacts and from there he could follow them to wherever they were printing their phony bills and eating away at the hard work of honest men. Once he had found them, they would meet his old friend once again. It had taken a while for his alter ego to come together. Now he had the money, skills and time to devote to his fight exclusively.

He reminisced how far had he come from the meager beginnings of his life. A poor orphan living on the lawless streets until taken in by a most unlikely master to which he had eagerly became an apprentice of his trade. A printer and forger himself, old Kelovitch had been a caring man doing dangerous work for dangerous men. The criminals paid no mind to his young apprentice 'Pic', but Pic paid attention to everything. He wrote down names and dates and details each night after he had memorized them during the day. He could offer no other explanation other than that he liked to learn things. Young Pic did learn, and continued as he grew older, if not wealthier. Now he could have bought and sold that humble print shop a thousand times over. If it had not been burned to the ground long ago.

Epicurious had risen in his station in life after he had gotten vengeance against those who had destroyed the only place that ever felt like home. He had schooled himself and paid his way with their ill gotten gains. Blackmail was a noble term when it was applied against criminals. His new identity was simple to forge so he could disappear and no one had ever connected him to his past. University had made him a better man than he had been long ago when he had only been driven by survival or revenge for his own sake.

A classical education was his under the name he used today. While doing so he had not only become a different and better man on the outside but on the inside as well. The philosophies of the ages were his passion and he was never the same after taking their teachings into his soul. He felt regret for his part however small in the old forger's workshop. One did what one needed to survive, but atonement was a balm to the soul he had sought for a long time. When the idea for his great work had come to him, he threw himself into it with a will. Epicurious had planned big and started small on his pursuit of the false makers of the world.

Locke moved to the full bookcase and removed one of the volumes of philosophy and set it only half way back in. Five seconds later the secret door in his back closet opened allowing him passage into the darkened chamber to get ready. As he passed by he silently touched the head of a small statue that stood on a plinth by the door. It was the only thing he had taken from the shop so long ago. The leering devil's brow was polished to an almost silver sheen from such repeated caresses.

● ● ●

Ted Birch rolled up and got out of his car into the bitter Chicago winter. You would think he would hate the cold coming from down south but he liked to think it went hand in hand with playing in the big leagues up north. You wanted to play hockey for the pros you had to get out on the ice. You wanted to work for the mob setting up a funny money operation and you had better like the Windy City in November. The Mob figured money would pass faster in cities and in greater quantities. By setting up here they would shorten the time from getting the fake bills printed to putting them to use. Birch saw an opportunity and he took it.

Several other men were already milling about in the cold as he arrived. The last barrel of ink had been manhandled off the old Ford truck and was being rolled through the slush and mud to the side entrance to the warehouse. He motioned for the two stevedores to get the truck out of here and as they did he went over and talked to 'Big Bob' Luvik.

Big Bob and his two men were all the muscle he should need here as this operation was hush-hush. He had always been taught to keep the circle small. It helped to stop the snitches and squealers. If no one knew what he was doing he would be a million richer by next month. If the cops did find out he would move the operation in a few hours and be set up in another location a day after that. It was flawless, flawless.

He exchanged greetings with Big Bob, Ernie and Drew. He handed the gunsel a fresh bottle of Canadian. One of Al's crew had brought it in last night to the jazz joint they had been at. The gunman's eyes lit up and he laughed. "You always remember I got a taste for this stuff Mr. Birch, Thank you!" He pocketed the fifth and left it untouched for now. Mustn't get plastered in front of the management. Bob and his men had come highly recommended by those who would know. Each had a rap sheet and had done enough time to prove their worth as stand up guys. They were no choir boys, but they knew their trade and kept their mouths shut.

"Where are we at with the presses Bob?" Birch asked his underling as he fired up a dollar cigar. He would have to finish it outside as practically everything in the warehouse now was flammable to one degree or another. Paper, petroleum inks and solvents, it was a devil's brew waiting to happen.

"That guy you sent to do the wiring up for the power was slick Mr. Birch. No fuss no muss. The pressman fired 'em up an hour ago doing a test run for resignation or something. They said it was all good barring an appearance by the printer's devil."

Birch looked on uncomprehending. "The what?" he laughed.

Bob smiled and continued, "It's a term the ink and type guys use. It means any unforeseen problems with the works or the paper. If 'the printer's devil' is outta the shop everything runs smooth. We are all set as soon as they get the plates and ink up the presses."

"Let's see he stays out then Bob. I have to go give them these. Keep an eye on things out here." He gingerly handled the wrapped bundle from his other pocket. He had never let them leave his side the whole time he traveled up from Florida. The plates were a bigger investment than the Heidelberg Offset rig inside and that had to be imported from Germany. Birch had paid a small fortune to a cutter in the panhandle for a set of plates both tens and twenties, front and back. The old man had said it was his finest work and Birch believed him. The guy was hanging over a gator pit in the glades when he said so but Birch felt the engraver's dying words were true from what he had seen. Shame he had to off him, but when you lose all that money on the ponies and start talking where you got it something had to give.

The big loading door to the warehouse closed behind Birch after he entered. His men fanned out and began a lookout up and down the deserted road that passed by the place. No one seemed to be around. A typical Illinois winter had dumped inches of snow everywhere and the place was deserted. The back alley and streets to this run down Chicago neighborhood were untraveled in such weather by the natives.

Across the street in what was just another run down abandoned house a strange figure watched the men through a pair of unusually powerful opera glasses. He clicked them shut after studying the guards for a few moments more. He was dressed in what looked like formal attire with tails. He unfolded a strange devil mask of some flat black material from his pocket square. After concealing his face he donned a black silk top hat with a flourish and shoved over a rat eaten chair. The weird figure sat facing the window that looked out onto the warehouse from the darkened abode. As the hours passed the sounds of presses starting and stopping again and again could be faintly heard over the winds whistling through the alleyways. Still the figure in the abandoned house did not move. He sat watching the shadows grow with seemingly infinite patience.

On the other side of the street Bob and his men had taken turns sitting in the car warming up with an occasional pull off of Bob's bottle to fight the chill, as the evening began to roll into the artificial canyons of back streets and alleys. They seemed to be very predictable but alert. Just as the night took the evening the figure in the chair finally stirred. He adjusted his coat and something at his wrist and silently made his way out the back door of the flop.

"Hey Bob! We got somebody coming this way down the street." Ernie tossed his smoke in the snow and went over to his boss. Bob extricated himself from the car he and Drew were in and took a look where Ernie nodded his head. Bob knew he had a little of the sauce but he almost couldn't believe his eyes. Staggering down the way was some clown in a top hat, tails and a cape! The fog and the night air hid his face but the way the guy was staggering he had to be plastered on something. He was using that walking stick like a blind man to negotiate imaginary obstacles.

The theater district was in that direction but if the guy had wandered this far down the wrong street to here he must have tied one on but good. They couldn't have him wandering around. Bob walked up to talk to the drunk dandy before he got too close. He would offer the yutz a ride and send Drew to drop him off. Keeping a low profile meant being unnoticed.

No fuss, no muss and no cops.

"Hey Rockefeller you get lost?" he stepped up to the man as the tuxedoed guy staggered low and almost fell over. Bob could smell the bourbon wafting off the guy as he came close. He went up and grabbed the man to guide him by the arm. In one split instant he saw his mistake too late. The man's face was covered by a flat black devil mask. The arm he touched didn't tense but seemed to become more fluid and relax while the other arm did the opposite. The devilish figure's other hand arced up in a short sharp movement that ended at Bob's temple. The short devil bar of flexible lead, steel and leather connected with bone crushing force to leave the hoodlum senseless faster than anyone could react. Bob fell face first in the snow. The devil dropped his cloak and began to move.

To his men Bob had seemed to just keel over. It had happened so quick that it took a moment to register that he was in trouble. Shouting curses, Ernie got out his piece and started to take aim at the other guy. The figure tossed his cane at him while it closed the distance between the street and the gangsters. The night air was split by the crack of his .45 as Ernie's shot went wide. His aim had been spoiled by the impact of the cane hitting his gun. The figure in the tux and tails did not zig or zag but came straight on. He moved like a sprinter out of the block not some dandy on an icy street.

Suddenly the devil man produced a pair of .38 snubs from his jacket, one in each fist. He went into a low crouch and both of his guns chattered death as he stitched up the mobster from hip to head in a flurry of lead. Ernie fell back against a nearby tree and slid to the bloody slush. His last thought was that his mom had been right. The devil did come for him someday...

Drew had seen the whole thing from the running car. That crazy man had killed both of his mates in less than a minute. He threw the sedan into gear and silhouetted the freak in the headlights. The guy was doing a 'New York reload', dropping the empty guns in his jacket pockets and going for a pair of fresh ones from somewhere in his tux. Through gritted teeth the gunman hissed, "Welcome to Chicago pal!" Drew mashed the accelerator down and lined up to run over this night terror with the Detroit iron at his command.

His fresh guns thrown aside, the devil in formal wear leaped onto the hood and avoided the impact with the flying car's bumper. Drew was tearing down the street at 40 in the snow, swerving to shake the bastard off and leave him a crumpled heap of bloody rags. The dead black face of the devil masked never waived as the monster got a secure grip and used the cosh in his other hand to shatter the windshield into the drivers face. Blinded temporarily, Drew lost control of the car and spun out into a row of parked cars and trash cans slamming the Ford into the curb. When the car had hit the devil in black had gone flying and so had Drew's face into the steering wheel. The mobster rolled in stunned pain.

When he regained his sense a few seconds later he looked around for the menacing figure in black tails. Nothing! He must have tossed the guy into a ditch somewhere. He staggered as he opened the door and felt wetness streaming down from his head onto his face. "Christ almighty!"

Blood ran freely from the cut on his forehead, but he had had worse. He must look a mess but that other guy was chopped liver. He had to get back to warn the boss. Tell him what happened. Birch must have gone nuts when he heard the shots and the ruckus. As he stepped away from the car a foot lashed out from on top of the car roof. The mobster took a metal clad heel to the face and collapsed to the ground. Examination would show he had his face caved in by what coroners would later call 'a hard blunt object that left the shape of a cloven hoof'.

The dark devil slid off the roof to the ground next to the mobster for a moment and gathered his senses. He had not gotten through the ordeal unscathed. His quilted jacket lining had saved him from most of the scrapes and bruises but he had landed on his shoulder hard as he had been flung from the car and it pained him. Straightening his once formal suit as best he could he picked up his pistols from the road as he ran back to the warehouse. Taking spare ammo from his jacket stores he reloaded them as he moved. Absently he tugged the boutonniere and its attached mechanism from his lapel. It had dutifully sprayed an atomized puff of alcohol at fifteen second intervals to sell his deception. It had continued to merrily puff away through the fight. All of the heady fumes were starting to get to him.

With the guns loaded he began to eat up the yards with a fast run raising a metallic sounding racket as he picked up speed. The split hoof shaped metal cleats in his shoes allowed him to move at such a rate on the ice and snow without slipping. The fact that any footprints left in the snow would look like a goat's was just an added bonus to tonight's theater.

After hearing the shots from outside Birch was frantic. Bob and his boys would not have lit someone up casually. This must be serious. It could be cops or it could be a rival from Chicago who had gotten a crazy idea. He told the pressmen to scram out the back and they did. He had a moment of indecision as he tensed, waiting for the cops or whoever to bust in but nobody came.

"Ok, stay cool. Bob and the boys must be running interference." He would leave with the plates and... They were still in the press! He went over to the machine and tried to remember how the press monkey had done this, only in reverse.

Cursing he worked at the fasteners to free both sets of the tens from the inked up machine. He whimpered a little inside at the amount of money he had to leave laying on the pallet where the press's off put had been stacked, but he fell to the task at hand. Bad enough if he got caught in a room full of bogus bills. The feds would give him hard time in Sing-Sing. If he lost the plates there were other people who had invested in this little operation that would not be as gentle.

"You're not going to get away with them," a chilling voice echoed from the walls of the now silent press room. It seemed almost amused.

Birch left the plate half extracted and drew his automatic. He crouched low next to the shielding bulk of the press. Whoever spoke didn't sound like a cop. He didn't even sound like he was from Chicago. A shot rang out from a far corner and smashed into the machine. Birch ducked behind and heard the ricochet bounce around the warehouse. That had been close.

"Come on you rat bastard!" Birch yelled as he blew a magazine of hot lead into the dark corners of the warehouse. The shot had come from over there but it was barely lit. He paused to reload ignoring the echoing thunder in his ears and then reached up to the press to grab the last plate. His questing fingers found that it had been shattered by the single bullet that hit the machine. He realized that the shooter had not chosen him as his target but the smiling reverse face of Hamilton on the plate. The engraving was ruined.

Then the lights went out. Startled for a moment, calm came over him. Birch knew the breakers had been cut. The bastard must be in the corner by the switch box. He knew the layout of the place pretty well so he shifted position to drill the guy when he came out. Where were Bob and his boys?

The voice came again. It seemed farther away now. "What we call evil, it seems to me, is simply ignorance bumping its head in the dark."

Birch shifted his gun to his other hand and drew his cigarette lighter out of his pocket. He began to move towards the door on the wet concrete of the warehouse floor. Escape was his goal now. He would hunt this bastard down later and boy would there be a reckoning! Somebody had squealed and that guy was dead. He flicked the lighter alive and used it to see his way to the warehouse door. He stared for a moment at what he saw there. It was a man in a flat black devil mask wearing formal dress of some kind. He was holding a hand pump from a barrel in one hand which he dropped to the floor. The other arm leaned against the door at a jaunty angle. This wasn't no cop!

Birch pointed his gun at the Printer's Devil. He would blast this apparition to kingdom come and get out with the other plates he still had in his pocket. At the same moment the figure shown in the pale light of the lighter did a sweeping kick with his foot flinging water from the ground up at Birch's lighter.

Only it wasn't water.

The air exploded into fire and blew the masked man out the door as the raging inferno consumed the warehouse, the money, the plates and whatever was left of Ted Birch.

● ● ●

Later the next morning at the estate of Epicurious Locke the master of the house sat down gingerly with his cracked shoulder and slightly burned backside. These things had been factored into his plan but not explicitly. The staff at the hospital had accepted his story about the little "accident" at his personal lab out back. Just last month they had to treat a rubber tycoon with similar injuries from a racing mishap the nurse said. A few real hundred dollar bills would assure the discretion of the doctors in keeping the news of a major chemical company owner causing an accident on his own property out of the papers.

He waited for his butler to bring in his breakfast before opening the paper to read the morning news. The houseman had grown accustomed to his eccentric employer's bouts with injury and late nights. Personally he thought Mr. Locke was out at a speakeasy and had wrecked his car, but it was not his place to pry.

Taking the paper and his coffee Locke opened it to check the day's headlines. Far back in the paper was some disturbance in the warehouse district last night it seemed. Police thought it might be a gasoline smuggling operation and a few deaths were involved. Luckily the fire had been contained to only the one structure. After the Great Fire in 1871 the Chicago Fire department had become one of the most effective in the nation.

Once again he was shown that you couldn't always believe what was printed. After a moment of reading he had an inspiration about creating incendiary bullets. He quickly grabbed his note pad to write it down and noted that the doodle he had drawn last night was still there. It was the letter 'P' with two small horns at the top. Yes, that would do nicely. He made a mental note of it and threw it in the fireplace and watched it burn to ash.

The End

In the Shadow of Sand

by Adam Lance Garcia

I do not recall the day, only the sand. I still feel the grit against my skin, still taste pebbles on my tongue, still feel the granules crunch between my teeth.

I have often questioned my motives, doubted myself and my actions in the decades since, and I have yet to find a suitable rebuttal. I should never have thought myself brave enough—strong enough—to cross the dunes. How could I have dared to make the attempt, and in my audacity, my madness, sacrifice that which was most precious to me?

And yet… And yet there are days in which I convince myself that I was not to blame, that no fault could be placed at my feet. How was I to know what we would encounter amongst the dunes? How could I have ever guessed? So much of our culture is built upon stories, tales passed down through texts and the voices of our fathers, but there is no parable or ballad that speaks of what found us in the shadow of sand.

I had sent my wife and daughters away to the safety of my father's father in Aqaba days before the Christian of Europe invaded Jerusalem. In my naivety I believed that the Christian would remember that we were all children of Abraham, but in their blindness, in their stupidity, they believed they had a right to the Holy Land over all others. When their armies were first seen in the distance I had thought we could have fought them off, but as the days turned into weeks and they began to massacre every man, woman, and child, no matter their faith, I knew there was no hope left.

My son and I, along with a dozen or so other survivors, escaped the city in the dead of night. Seven of them were cut down before we made it the outer walls, and two more were speared some distance outside the city limits. By the time the sun rose there were only eight of us alive. We had lost most of our supplies during one of the attacks, with only some bread and a few bladders of water between us. Some broke off and headed toward Egypt, while five stayed with us on our journey toward Aqaba. They all died within the few days, either from Christians, bandits or starvation. By the time we reached the desert, there were only two of us left, me and my son. We had been traveling weeks without pause, days without food, and hours without water. The camels were dead. All we had were our cracked and battered feet, which bled into the sand, each step fire. Even the sun, which had for so long stared down upon us unrelenting, was hidden behind the orange and grey of the storm. It engulfed us, enfolded us, and cut us off from the world. The simple act of breathing had become a labor, despite the tails of my keffiyeh wrapped tightly around my nose and mouth, the sand fought its way into my lungs.

And then there was the deafening sound, at times a lion's roar, a snake's hiss, or the distant cries of a woman.

I kept my son close to me, our arms hooked as we blindly stumbled through the sand. Each step threatened to be our last, every breath an effort in agony. At times I would shout instructions or he would howl his pleas for rest, but the words were always lost, snatched out of the air before they could reach our ears. I had sworn to protect him, promised his mother I would keep him safe, my flesh and blood, and yet in my hubris, I had brought him into heart of desolation, where not even the faintest hope could endure.

But we kept moving forward, out of my own stubbornness than any desire to survive.

My son tugged at my sleeve. "Father," he rasped. Skin flaked off his face like rice paper, leaving red rashes in their place. His eyes lolled back in his head showing the spider's web of veins amongst the white. Without a word, I picked him up and carried him in my arms, finding him lighter than I expected. I do not when he had grown so frail, so thin. I pressed my lips against his forehead, said a silent prayer, and continued forward, deeper into the turmoil.

It was in the darkest point of the storm that I saw her, a form in the sand, without mass or weight. I first dismissed her as a hallucination borne of exhaustion, dehydration, and my wind whipped eyes. But as we continued on, I began to see her clearer, a woman, dressed in white, shining as a beacon in the distance. I called out to her over the wind. "As-salāmu ālayki, sister. Who are you that stands amidst the storm and sand?"

The woman did not reply, nor did she seem to be affected by storm. As I got nearer I could see the sand move around her body like currents in water. Her garments did not so much as flutter from the roaring wind. As my eyes struggled through the swirling sand I could make out a white boshiya draped over her head with the faintest definition of her features visible through the thin fabric. My son, seeing the woman's white garments in the corner of his eyes, weakly turned his head to face her.

"I see something, father," he rasped, disbelief filling his words. "A woman in the storm! She is…"

I wiped the back of my hand across my face, believing—hoping—the mirage would dissipate with the wind, but I knew, deep in the heart of me, that she was a solid as I.

My son turned his head back against my chest and looked up at me with dry eyes. "Who is she, father?"

I shook my head and whispered that I did not know and tightened my arms around my boy's fragile form. It was only a woman, I told myself, only a woman lost in the storm just like us. But as we approached I felt something shift both around and inside me, as if we had stepped through a threshold from one realm to another and an unreality had overtaken us; that we had moved from what was to what should never be.

I called out again and the woman did not reply. But I felt her gaze. Even at a distance it felt like a blade of ice aiming for my heart. My son wormed his way out of my grasp and took a tentative, clumsy step forward.

I put my arm in front of him and slowly pulled him behind me. "Do not approach her, child."

"But…"

"Do as I say," I hissed.

I raised my hand in greeting and took a half step forward, careful to keep my son hidden behind me. The woman did not respond, did not move and the stillness of her robes told me that she did not so much as breathe.

"Sister, we are travelers lost, seeking sanctuary from this storm. Are we near town or village?"

She turned her head slowly face to me, and the sensation of unbecoming grew stronger. The delicate shroud covering her face was as still as death. I could just make out her white pupil-less eyes through the sheer fabric, the orbs a pure milky white. I would have thought her blind.

"Sister! I implore you!" I sobbed. "Please tell us, are we near a town? Are we near sanctuary?"

"Father, she wants us closer," my son said, pushing against me with a burst of energy I had not thought him capable.

"Child, stay," I commanded.

The woman titled her head as she considered us, her white eyes were penetrating. I felt my hand move to my scabbard, my fingers kissing the gilded handle. It was an unconscious, instinctual motion, one which I have wished I had completed.

Then the woman spoke.

"Traveler." Her voice came to us from all sides, rasping, cutting, as if the sand itself was speaking, it was lyrical, feminine yet deep and masculine. It was screaming yet silent, a whisper and a shout. But her mouth, her face never moved. Her shroud did not move with her breath. It was as though the sand itself had deigned to speak. "Traveler, what do you believe your destination?"

For a moment my voice left me, caught in my throat like a hastily eaten morsel. At the time I blamed the arid state of my tongue, but it was fear, a spring of terror that welled in my heart with no bottom. "We go in peace. My son and I—we are making our way to Aqaba. To the home of my father's father. We, our caravan, had been set upon by Christians, Crusaders from Europe who ignore the peace of Allah. They wanted the sands to run with our blood. All our companions were murdered and we survived only by the grace of God. We thirst and hunger, and are in desperate need of rest and healing…We have walked for many miles. We have been lost since the storm. We have not drank or rested in days. Please, if you know of shelter—of sanctuary…"

The woman began to walk toward us and the wind and sand shifted around her, parting like an army for a king. The granules struck at my exposed skin, battering me as though they would break my skin. I pinched my eyes shut for a moment and tears pooled in the edges. My jaw began to chatter to despite the heat. I could feel my son quake in my grasp. I moved closer to my son while my free hand gripped at my blade. When I opened my eyes, the woman was standing right before me, traveling meters in moments.

"Traveler. There is no sanctuary," she replied with a gleeful purr. Her skin, barely hidden beneath the thin white robes, was as porcelain or marble, smooth without break or blemish, glinting subtlety in the dim orange light of the storm. She was beautiful and horrible, her visage shifting before my eyes like the water's surface.

"She loves us, father," I heard my son whisper behind me.

"Then where do you come from, sister? Where can we find respite from this storm? If you do not know then we shall continue until we have found shelter or… death."

The woman began to pace around us and I saw that her feet never touched the ground, but only brushed against the grains of sand. Her eyes never fell upon us and yet I could feel her gaze all around us. The sand swirled into a vortex, a rush of wind that threatened to steal my footing. My boy grabbed onto my leg but I could not give him comfort.

"Traveler. What is your name?"

"I am Liaqat." I said, gasping for air amidst the wind. "My son, Idris." I swallowed the lump forming in my throat, finding it drier than ever. "And what—what is yours, sister?"

"Liaqat. Idris." the woman said as with a sensual pleasure. Upon hearing her speak our names both my son and I collapsed to our knees, our breaths momentarily stolen from us, as if she reached into our chests and grabbed them with her ghost white hands. I gasped and my son let out a cry of pain. Spots formed in front of my eyes and my head tipped forward, consciousness threatening to be robbed from me. I gritted my teeth and held on, much more for my son's sake than my own. Whatever that woman—that creature—was, I swore that I would not let her overtake us.

"Traveler. You have the taste of the sand on your tongue," she said with a pleasurable sigh. "And the sand has its taste of you, as it has so many before. The sand remembers. It remembers the footsteps of men, of beast, and insect. It recalls the water and the sun. It recalls the nights and the distant lights. It remembers the time before stone monuments and straw huts. It saw the forests and the fires, the movements of earth. It recalls the mountains and the wind that cut them down. It has never forgotten the molten rivers, the beasts that swam within. It recalls when there was nothing but darkness, before the distant pinpricks of light."

I pulled my son close to me and wrapped my arms around his emaciated form. "We have no quarrel with you!" I cried. "Please, let us pass, sister!"

"I am no sister to you," she said without emotion. "I was old when the dunes began to form, old when the moon was but dust forming into rock."

"You are a Marid," I whispered. "A jinn, a curse upon this earth and an affront to the Great Allah!"

A small smile formed on her porcelain lips while the swirling sand erupted with a cackling laughter. I clapped my hands over my ears, screaming at the sound. My palms came away wet, coated crimson.

"I have no name known to you or your God. I have no name that you can speak with your clumsy tongue."

"Father..." my son whispered in a caked, dry breath. I brought him closer to me, yet he somehow felt more distant, thinner, as though he was fading from the world like light from the setting sun. "Father, please— Let me— She wants us to..."

Tears began to stream down my cheeks, drying before they could reach my chin. "Just let us go in peace."

"Traveler," she said sharply. "You have crossed into my dominion, a slight I cannot forgive. I demand immolation."

"What—Yes. Whatever you desire, we shall give. Name your price and we shall leave your realm and never return."

The woman stared at me for several moments before she spoke. "What would you give? Tell me what you would offer."

I gazed at my hands and my feet. I thought desperately for what I could give to this creature so we could gain safe passage. But I could think of nothing. We had no water, no food. Even our clothes had become rags. All we had was each other. For a second, for the briefest of moments, my eyes fell to Idris and I knew in that instance the woman had determined my choice for me.

I grabbed Idris by the shoulder and shouted, "Run, child! Run!" but his eyes were glassy, his gaze distant. He was alive and conscious, but his mind was gone. I let out sob then, which was really a scream. I tried to reach for him but the wind suddenly swelled and the sand blinded me. I wrapped my arm around my eyes and stumbled against the force which buffeted me like a ship on a raging sea.

"Please!" I cried. "Please! We meant you no disres..."

The wind dropped away suddenly and the sand hung suspended in the air. There was a crinkling sound and the sand shifted open, and the woman approached. She gave me her thin, mirthless smile and reached forward. Her pale white fingers slipped free of her robes, they brushed my sunburned cheek and cracked, bleeding lips, feeling like a spider's fang. Her skin felt cold and bloodless like stone. My open wounds stung at her touch and I felt my heart turn to stone. I have always been a man of faith; I have studied every line of the Holy Qur'an; the Great Prophet and Allah have ever been my guides. I lived all my life knowing there are jinn that walk this earth. I know they exist to test us, to deny our rightful place in Jannah. Yet the moment that the woman touched me, I felt all of my faith leave me, for I saw in my mind's eye what was truly beneath the being's porcelain skin. I saw a world, cold without sun or life, burst into flames. I saw beasts with bodies out of nightmares, the sky filled with wings and spears. I saw mountains

crumble into sand. And throughout it all I saw the woman, walking the world, holding the grains of sand in her hand like a blade, stabbing into the heart of all that trespassed.

I fell back as if struck and my son slipped from arms and rolled over beside me. He let out a soft sound that might have been a gasp or ecstatic sigh. I tried to make my way to my feet, but the sand broke open beneath and drew me in to my waist before stiffening like stone. I looked to my son. His eyes were rolled back in his head, his mouth wide open, letting sand pour in. No—the sand was pouring out, flowing like river from mouth. The woman raised her hand and Idris's body lifted off the ground, his arms slack at his side, his legs were bent awkwardly and holding no weight. He appeared boneless like a marionette on strings.

"Idris!" I shouted, clawing at the sand in futile effort to reach for him. I pulled my legs free of the sand, propped my knees on the surface and crawled over to him. I grabbed at his arms and tried to shake him free of his trance, to rescue my boy from the woman's embrace. "Oh my son! My son!!! Please! My son! Give—Let him go, nameless one!" I bowed my head deeply, my forehead touching the swirling sand. "Please. I would—I would give anything you—Any—Anything you desire. My life, my soul. But my son—"

"Traveler," Idris said in a rasping, dry voice that was at once his own and the woman's. His eyes remained unfocused as sand continued to spill from his mouth, nose, and ears. "Traveler. Do you hear me?"

"I—Yes. Son. I…"

"Traveler. You are not welcome here."

"NO!" I shouted. "Please, Idris, my son. Hear me. Hear the voice of your fath…" My stomach lurched violently and I fell to my hands and knees. A torrent of sand vomited from my mouth, dry as the desert. I tried to stem the flow, but the sand continued to pour without pause, cutting my throat and mouth, grinding down my teeth down to nubs. The sand began pile up over me, burying me up to elbows and waist, and soon my knees. I was able to free one of my hands and wrapped it around my boy's. I tried to pull him away from the woman—the creature—the beast—but he would not move. The woman turned her white eyes to me and I saw Jahannam. My grip loosened and I felt the boy slip from my right hand. As the sand overtook my eyes, the last thing I saw was the woman wrapping her white marble arms around my son, still weeping tears of sand. I fought to let out a scream…

…only to awake in the desert sun.

I do not know how long I was unconscious, how long I lay beneath the blazing, unforgiving star. My body was covered in sand, drifting over me in the light breeze. My skin was cracked and burnt. My lips broke open and began to bleed. My mouth and throat were dry. I ran the brittle sponge of my tongue over my teeth, all of which remained despite what I had experienced. I rolled over, shifting the small dune of sand off my body and weakly found my way to feet. I tried to call Idris, but my voice had left me, leaving only a dry croak. I turned round in a circle, searching for him even though I knew he was gone.

In the distance I saw a figure appear on the horizon and soon heard the galloping of horse hooves approach. I weakly raised my hand before stumbling onto my knees and waited for the rider. He was a young man, his face weather beaten but strong. I saw in his eyes a silent concern, as if he knew what I had endured. He jumped off his horse, ran over to me, and handed me a bladder of water. I grasped at the leather container and desperately drank its contents.

He placed one hand on my shoulder and the other over the bladder and slowed the flow over water. "Drink slowly," he said, quietly. "You will make yourself sick. The desert has drained you of your water. If you return it too quickly the desert will take your life."

I heeded his advice and carefully sipped the water. I trembled at its taste, the liquid acting as an elixir to my whole body. He fed me dried fruit and meat, which I chewed hesitantly; not daring to believe any of what I was experiencing, was real.

"Brother, how did you come to be here?" he asked after a time.

I told him of the invasion, how we escaped. I told him of the deaths, of the sandstorm, but when I began to tell him of my son and the woman, my voice hitched and I grew silent. Though I had faced the horror firsthand, the words that played in my head sounded like madness. There was a terrifying moment where I even began to doubt if I had truly experienced what I had.

"You met her," he said when I had fallen silent.

I nodded in silent relief.

"And she took someone."

"My son," I sobbed.

The man nodded knowingly, running his fingers over the sand. "As she has taken many others."

"You have lost someone as well?"

"My brother," he said after a moment. "Over two decades now, he has been gone." He peered out into the desert. "Sometimes I think I still see him, walking on the horizon along with so many others, approaching but never arriving. He is mirage, an oasis in the mind if not the sand....We have always known of her, as have you. You have seen her before and you see her now. She has many names and none. She takes the young, the old, the good and the wicked. She takes what we give, that what we cannot bear to be without."

"What...? What is she?"

He shook his head and gave me a sad smile. "She is death. She is the sand." He took a fistful of sand and let the grain runs through his fingers. "She is the desert. Or maybe she is just the spirit that lives there. Maybe she was once a soul like ours. Maybe she was one that was taken, like your son or my brother... I do not know what she truly is and I do not believe anyone shall." He placed a hand on my shoulder. "You have a wife and daughter who yet live?"

I nodded. "Yes. In Aqaba."

"Then I shall take you to them. You will see their faces and you will remember your son's. We can mourn those she has taken. We can wait until our time comes and she finds us. Or we can live. We can live as if we know we will see the next morning. Because we can fear her, we can fear death, or we can keep marching, keep moving and make sure that every moment we have between us and her is filled." He took my hand into his and helped me to my feet. "Come brother. Let us take you to Aqaba."

He helped me onto his horse and we rode into the night, making camp in the light of the white full moon. The next day we arrived in Aqaba, and I into the waiting arms of my wife and daughter, and I wept. I told them I had lost Idris to the desert and I thought that true enough. My wife took my face into her hands and forgave me. My daughter wrapped her arms round my leg and told me not to cry. I did my best to listen to her. And while the taste of sand lingers on my tongue to this day and the sound of wind still keeps me awake at night, I live my days as if I shall see tomorrow, because even if I don't, I know I shall see my son.

The End

Gears of Blood
(A Moth story)
by Don Gates

CELEBRATED SCIENTIST COMES TO THE JACOB'S LADDER QUARTER

Professor Patrick Fitzroy, noted scientist and mechanical engineering whiz, has decided to call the neighborhood of Jacob's Ladder home.

As many residents know, the Jacob's Ladder quarter of New Aspiria is home to a great many inventors and geniuses. National media coverage has given Jacob's Ladder the reputation for being a utopia for technologically-minded individuals and so when people of renown like Patrick Fitzroy come to town, tongues start wagging.

It's no surprise that the esteemed professor has chosen to make Jacob's Ladder his new neighborhood: Fitzroy has recently come to be featured on numerous newsreels, radio programs, and electro-broadcasts as being a pioneer in the field of mechanical engineering and so he fits right in with the gaggle of eccentric science buffs and machine designers in the area. "Jacob's Ladder has the right kind of atmosphere and attitude that I like to work in," he said to reporters recently. "My work – and my life – can only thrive in such a place. My wife and I are very excited to call it our new home and look forward to starting our family here."

Fitzroy's last comment is already coming to pass. Sources in the know say that the professor's wife, the lovely Rena Fitzroy, and the professor himself are already expecting a child. This is precisely the kind of wonderful news that New Aspiria and its residents love to hear. Welcome to the neighborhood, Professor and Mrs. Fitzroy! We look forward to seeing your family grow along with us and our proud city!

• • •

Night in New Aspiria: skyscrapers stretched into the air, their clean deco lines gave the spires a sense of strength and optimism, of man's indomitable strive and will. Here and there, like great looming mushrooms, the glowing forms of Tesla towers and their ever-present soft nimbus of blue-white light. Spotlights stabbed upward from the concrete and steel canyons, lighting the inky blackness with fingers of illumination as if trying to beat the starlight into submission.

In the bottom of one such city chasm, the wail of sirens split the night. Squad cars pulled up to the front of the Charterfield Arms building and screeched to a stop at the curb. The officers alighted from the cars and hastened through the throng of news reporters on the steps of the building without giving them a single word. Meanwhile, the streets were swept with lights shining downward from the sky as police airships combed the area with their searchlights. Gyrodrones buzzed around the premises, radio-controlled by unseen hands in the back of an unmarked police truck and searching with their peering camera eyes, looking for something to lead the search. So far, nobody had seen anything. All leads were dry.

Inside apartment 491, the young parents were in hysterics. The woman, a pretty blonde with a fashionable finger-wave hairstyle, was a visible wreck. Her cheeks were streaked with tear-smeared makeup and her eyes were reddened. Her bathrobe was rumpled, and a seemingly endless amount of used tissues spilled from its pockets.

The man was doing his best to hold up: he carried his slight build with an air of determination, despite the messed state of his hair and the look in his eyes that said the world was falling down inside of him. He held his wife gently by an arm around her shoulders. "Dammit, isn't there anything else that can be done?" he demanded from the policemen that were swarming the apartment.

"I'm sorry, Mr. Keyes, our men are doing their best. We've got air support and drones watching the street and our best men are out there beating the bushes, going door to door and trying their best to find her. If your little girl's out there, we'll bring her home." The head detective was a stern-looking man with a gentle voice. He was doing his best to project an air of confidence to reassure the young parents, but inside he was tired and doubtful. He'd seen this sort of thing before, and it rarely ever seemed to go their way. "Are you sure you don't remember anything else that could point us in the right direction?"

"Yes, yes, I've told you everything," Terrance Keyes said wearily. "We came home from the theater at ten o'clock. When we came in we found Rosemary..."

"Oh God," Ila Keyes moaned under her breath.

Her husband stroked her hair before continuing in a lower tone. "We found Rosemary in the living room. We rushed to Holly's room and she was gone."

The detective nodded. "I see. I'm going to take a look around again. Let me know if you remember anything, okay?"

As the detective turned away and the Keyes did their best to comfort one another, the coroner's team wheeled a sheet-covered gurney out of the apartment's door behind them. Beneath the sheet was the disemboweled corpse of Rosemary the nanny, the only person who knew for sure what had happened there that night.

Directly across the avenue from apartment 491, a lone figure in white crouched beneath the shadow of a huge streamlined gargoyle. In his hand he held a small box that was fronted by a small, shallow dish. A wire ran from the device to the man's ear.

The man in white finished listening in to the apartment conversations and began sweeping the officers and reporters in the street below with the dish. There was a jumble of conversations and murmuring conjectures. Nothing seemed to hold any interest. He kept sweeping...

"...no, it was a clean extraction," came an isolated voice into his earpiece. He stopped scanning and held the device steady. "They're wheeling the nanny out now. No witnesses. The cleaning crew outfits and truck, they did the trick. Nobody's mentioning that, if they even saw you. It was clean, very clean."

The man in white peered through the lenses of the mask he wore into the darkness below. The goggle lenses lit up the scene for him to see a telephone booth at the corner. A uniformed policeman stood there, within the dimly lit confines of the booth, confident that nobody could hear him. The man in white adjusted the goggles and his vision magnified. The uniformed man turned, the flash of his teeth glinting white and predatorily in the glow of streetlamps. Whatever the person on the other end of the line had said made him laugh, and it was a harsh sound.

"Alright then, I'm coming now. Gonna ditch the uniform and I'll be there as soon as I can. For the Eternal Dreamer." He hung up the phone and exited the booth, heading for a parked patrol cruiser nearby.

The man in white turned off the device he held and removed the earphone, placing them into pockets inside his overcoat. He stood and placed his fedora on his head. All his garments were white, even down to the strange gas mask he wore. Between the odd filtration system and the oversized crimson-lensed goggles over his eyes, he resembled an insect in human clothes.

The policeman's car pulled away from the curb and the strange white-clad watcher leaped from his perch. His leap sent him over thirty feet in the air, and at the apex of his jump his overcoat blossomed, revealing itself to be a set of wings with a nearly fourteen foot wingspan. He glided down the city street, eyes intent upon the patrol car moving within the late night traffic below.

The Moth was on the hunt.

● ● ●

JACOB'S LADDER'S RESIDENTS VOCAL IN OPPOSITION OF ORGANIZED CRIME

Despite New Aspiria's police denials, Jacob's Ladder residents continue to insist that not only is there a strong organized criminal element in their area, but that the criminals are also leaning heavily onto intimidation tactics to try and coerce them into paying them "protection money" to keep their property, families and homes safe. Those that don't pay claim they have been attacked or harassed, forcing them from their homes and places of business.

Those that live in the Jacob's Ladder quarter – a neighborhood known to be home to many scientists, builders, and thinkers – claim to have come under attack by men that represent various crime-families of New Aspiria. They claim that these criminal groups view these inventors and scientists as a source of ill-gotten income. Science and technology are widely known as New Aspiria's #1 exported products and services, and it seems these suspected gangsters want a cut of these profits. The most notable member of these suspects is Rudolph Morgante, reputedly the head of the Morgante crime family and who has gone on record before for being an aficionado of wireless electrical transmission research and has been accused of the kidnapping and extortion of several noted scientific figures. Many in Jacob's Ladder have claimed the Morgante family is one of the chief terrorizers of their besieged community, though none of the accusers wish to go on the record.

"These thugs need to know we will not cower in the face of their threats," said Professor Patrick Fitzroy. "I have a wife and a son and a life here, and I want to protect them. The police don't seem to be doing much to prevent this kind of bullying, so I encourage my fellow neighbors to stand up to them. Stand strong and don't give in to their pressure!" Professor Fitzroy – most recently the inventor of the Atlas Suit, a "powered body-frame" that assists the crippled and disabled in their day-to-day lives – is one of the more famous and noted citizens living in Jacob's Ladder, and has been one of her champions for the past four years.

New Aspiria police have declined to comment on this issue.

● ● ●

The Moth glided from perch to perch in the smoke-choked dimness of the city, careful not to lose sight of the car he tracked. It wasn't easy. The police cruiser zipped down the multi-lane avenues of New Aspiria with a speed that only a squad car could have. Traffic often parted for the vehicle, and if it came to a red light the driver would toggle his lights & siren on and was allowed to move unhindered through the intersecting street.

The white clad Moth followed the car into the middle-class Bronson Heights neighborhood, where the squad car pulled up to a small apartment block. The policeman got out of his vehicle and went inside while the Moth landed, his mechanical white wings folding down into their "overcoat" appearance. Climbing stealthily down several flights of fire escape stairs, he hid behind a buttress on the building across the way and watched, waiting.

After almost twenty minutes the policeman exited the building, this time in plain clothes. He furtively checked the street before climbing into another car, this time his personal vehicle. The car pulled out of the apartment parking lot and headed east.

The Moth climbed up onto the fire escape railing and jumped, once again his leap taking him up an astonishing distance before his wings snapped open. He glided again, following the trail of his quarry.

After several miles of city streets, the policeman's car turned southwest and headed toward the docks. Gliding after the car would be a problem with fewer traffic lights and not as many tall buildings. The Moth had been prepared for this. At the final traffic light, he had landed upon a low roof nearby. He'd launched a grappling hook from his wrist and hooked it onto the rear bumper of the car. As it sped off through the night, the Moth flew high behind the car like a kite, his line kept him tethered to the object of his pursuit, and if the driver knew it, he did a pretty good job of hiding it.

At last, the car turned down a fog-shrouded pier. There were men in the distance guarding the gate in a high fence that surrounded a huge, dark warehouse.

The Moth disconnected the grappling hook from the car's bumper and the line retracted itself up into his sleeve. He banked and glided down to a nearby roof and landed. Folding his wings, the Moth crouched and peered through his light-enhancing goggles.

The policeman's car stopped at the gate and he spoke to the plain-clothed guards. The Moth was too far away to hear the conversation and didn't have time to set up his electronic ear equipment. He saw the guards nod and open the chain-link gate to let the policeman's car into the area. Through the gate, the Moth could see at least a dozen vehicles parked ahead. The policeman's car joined the others and he exited the vehicle and went inside the warehouse.

Several minutes later the warehouse guards heard a shuffling through the fog and gloom. A figure shambled toward them, stopping to rest against a pier support post. They watched as the figure began slumping as it seemed to doze off, only to wake up and come shambling toward them again. The man was coming closer.

"Hey," one of the guards called out, "Get outta here, you. This is private property. Go sleep it off somewhere else."

The figure shrugged, continuing to stumble closer.

"Damn, didn't you hear him?" The second guard moved from his post and began walking toward the bum, who was heading toward the edge of the pier. "You better get the hell outta here, if you know what's good for you."

The man held up his hand in a placating gesture and started to turn; he stepped off the edge of the pier and disappeared.

"Oops," the first guard called, and laughed.

The second guard walked toward the spot where the bum had fallen. "Heh, guess that takes care of that." He stepped to the edge and peered down, then suddenly fell forward and disappeared off the edge too.

The first guard watched, now silent. "Hey," he called when his friend didn't appear again. He pulled a revolver out of his belt and headed toward the spot. When he reached the edge, he craned his neck, peering down into dark water.

"Hey," he called out again, this time in a voice small and nervous. He leaned further out over the water.

A shadow moved between him and the light post above and behind him. The guard spun around in time to glimpse a white monster with red eyes as it swooped down upon him. It grabbed him, muffling his screams before he'd had a chance to fire his pistol. White wings closed around him and his world descended into blackness.

● ● ●

ONCE THRIVING NEIGHBORHOOD OF SCIENCE NOW A NEAR GHOST TOWN
(electrocast)

At one time the quaint lanes and avenues of Jacob's Ladder boasted well-maintained trees, grassy parks, and beautifully kept lawns and gardens. Children played freely in its streets until well after dark, while the adults of the community met their peers and fellows to discuss the important facets of the day: politics, art, and above all the sciences. Jacob's Ladder was the heart of New Aspiria, the home of those who were pushing the boundaries of energy, mechanical, chemical, and theoretical research. The future was always the present in Jacob's Ladder and ground-breaking announcements were always just around the corner as residents would often meet and collaborate on their work. Jacob's Ladder brought out the best in people.

Unfortunately, Jacob's Ladder also brought out the worst in people. After years of being preyed upon by the criminal element, the quarter now lays in desolation and neglect. Most of the houses are boarded up and quite a few are burnt out. The lovely yards, gardens, and parks are now overgrown. There are no children playing in these streets now, only wary eyes that peer with concern from shuttered windows. Jacob's Ladder is now a corpse.

With that figurative corpse-state there are also literal corpses: the bodies of those residents that refused to give payment to New Aspiria's gangs for "protection" against violence, who stood up to them and refused to let them in on secrets that would make them rich. Jacob's Ladder is haunted by the victims of New Aspiria's shadowy underworld.

If one wished to put a face on this tragedy, it would probably belong to Professor Patrick Fitzroy. Fitzroy was once an esteemed gadgeteer, the creator of multiple patents that would help give sight to the blind, ears to the deaf, and legs to the crippled. Just four years ago Fitzroy relocated to New Aspiria from Sharpe's Bay on the West Coast and settled into Jacob's Ladder, an ideal home for the esteemed scientist and designer. Fitzroy and his young wife Rena gave birth to their infant son Adam not too long after settling in and life seemed good, at least for a while. The gangs of New Aspiria began to pressure the neighborhood and even though the police seemed to turn a blind eye to the crisis, Fitzroy and others began to rally. The professor encouraged his neighbors to "stand strong and don't give in" and for a while it seemed as though the bad guys were beaten. However, Fitzroy claimed the pressure increased, most notably from the notoriously fearless Morgante family. There were reports of vandalism, death threats and violence directed toward the professor and his family. When Fitzroy continued to stand up to the pressure, there was retaliation.

On the evening of May 23ʳᵈ of last year, Fitzroy walked his wife and son out to the family sedan. Rena and Adam were bound for the grocery store while Professor Fitzroy was going to stay at home to work on a project. As his wife turned the key in the car's ignition—a bomb exploded from underneath the vehicle. Rena and Adam were killed instantly in the explosion, while Professor Fitzroy suffered horrible throat injuries which resulted in the loss of his speech.

An arrest and trial followed for Rudolph Morgante himself, the reputed head of the Morgante organization. Professor Fitzroy gave a tearful and silent testimonial on the stand, communicating with a chalk board, about the ordeals he had experienced at the hands of Morgante thugs. However, the gang members and their leader all had alibis that placed them outside of New Aspiria at the time of the bombing, and thus the trial fizzled.

On the steps of the courthouse immediately following his trial, Rudolph Morgante gave a statement to the press: "These people keep trying to accuse me of all these things, but as you can see I am clearly not involved. Nobody cares about that hole in the wall. It's gonna rot, and eventually the only things there will be rats in the gutters and the moths around the streetlights. I say let the place die. Let the moths have it. Let them have the whole damned city. (laughs)"

Following the trial, Professor Fitzroy became a hermit in his old house. Rumors say that he's stopped working on his inventions, and without his leadership the neighborhood of Jacob's Ladder has indeed crumbled. Citizens have either given in and now hide in fear or have simply moved away. All that is left now of the once shining utopia of science is a ghost town, barren and utterly silent.

● ● ●

Darkness.

The gloom was nearly impenetrable. The Moth had picked the lock at the warehouse's side door and stepped inside from a world of dim fog to utter, stygian blackness. He closed the door behind him and, confident there was nobody in the antechamber with him, stood and waited. His eyes didn't adjust and the gloom remained a black wall.

The Moth reached up and toggled a switch on the weird goggles he wore as part of his mask. The device whirred softly to life and the lenses rotated as they tried to light the dark. It made very little difference: the goggles amplified any ambient light, even starlight, to a comfortable level for the wearer. In this place, there was no light.

It wasn't right. There was something beyond sinister in this warehouse. The Moth felt it, a pressure that was just barely there, but insistent—a pressing feeling.

Feeling his way slowly through the room, the Moth finally found a door. He cracked it and eased it open. There was more gloom beyond, but this was lightened a little bit by some distant light. The goggles barely picked it up but it was enough to give the Moth a little sense of where he was.

It was a long hallway. There were a few doors along it. Here and there were a few branching hallways, their entrances covered by tattered blankets and tarps that swung gently in an unfelt breeze. The weird pressing feeling intensified here. There was something foreboding about those branching hallways and rooms. The Moth made his way down the eerie passage. There were no sounds apart from the creaking of an unlit overhead light along the roof of the hallway as it swung back and forth.

A smell caught the Moth's nostrils. The odor made its way past the filtration of his mask. It was a charnel smell, something dead and rotting, masked behind the odor of… ammonia? The Moth pulled back one of the blankets covering the nearest doorway and found himself looking down into a concrete pit filled with bodies covered with lye. There were a few men and women among the corpses, but the majority were smaller.

Children.

The Moth's unseen eyes narrowed behind the lenses of his mask. There was nothing he could do for these victims. He gently drew the blanket back across the doorway as though he were covering the bodies themselves before turning and continuing down the hallway.

As the Moth approached the end of the hallway, a low humming came to his ears. It was a strange sound; as he felt it as much as heard it, yet it wasn't a vibration. He moved low, cautiously, along the hallway. In the distance he could see a pair of double doors. The dim light that was illuminating his way was coming from the cracks between and around these doors.

The Moth reached a four-way intersection in the hall and froze. To his left and right were dark halls, and lined up in the halls were rows of bald men wearing rags. The men had some kind of mark carved into their foreheads, long since healed into scars, and their eyes were rolled back in their heads. They were chanting some kind of low words. The Moth was reminded of recordings he'd heard of Tibetan monks. However, this sound was ominous—the humming of evil.

None of the men moved or even seemed to notice him. The Moth pictured the layout of the warehouse. It seemed like the interior was ringed with a maze of hallways and this weird collection of chanters could possibly form a ring around the central chamber. His skin crawled as he considered what was going on within the warehouse's depths. He continued on, drawing closer to the double doors.

As he reached the doors, the Moth could hear voices, faint but strident, coming from the other side. Some kind of call-and-response litany. He pressed his goggled eye to the crack in the door and the lens adjusted. He could see just barely into the room, and his blood chilled.

A group of robed men stood in a semi-circle, their faces hidden by the oversized hoods they wore over their heads. Other men stood around, as if an audience to watch the proceedings. And in the center of it all, a little blonde girl no older than six years old was gagged and bound to some kind of ceremonial table. Standing over her was another robed figure in an elaborate headdress, his arms raised to the sky. A dagger glinted at his belt.

The Moth grabbed the handles of the double doors and flung them wide. He stepped into the room as the men turned as one to look in his direction.

Suddenly something struck the back of the Moth's head and he crumpled, the world melting into darkness around him.

● ● ●

EXPLOSION DESTROYS HOUSE IN ONCE-PROMINENT NEIGHBORHOOD; SCIENTIST FEARED DEAD

A blast ripped through a mostly vacant area of the old Jacob's Ladder quarter of New Aspiria on Thursday morning around 1:30 am. Police and fire crews rushed to the scene to discover the boarded up brownstone belonging to Professor Patrick Fitzroy in flaming rubble. The only suspected casualty of the blast is Fitzroy himself, who has turned up missing since the explosion; all other nearby residents are all accounted for.

Investigators have yet to determine the exact reason for the blast, but believe that it may have been caused by chemicals and/or a mechanical apparatus belonging to the professor, who had been living as a recluse for the past two years since the deaths of his wife and young son. Fitzroy's neighbors in the dilapidated quarter had been seeing less and less of the professor recently and authorities are classifying this incident as an accidental explosion and death.

If anyone has any information regarding the incident or Professor Fitzroy's status or whereabouts they are encouraged to report to law enforcement officials as soon as possible.

● ● ●

The Moth's head lolled against his chest. There were stirrings of sensations around him, sounds that came to his ears. Voices.

"… I'll talk about that at tomorrow's council meeting. Somebody really should do something about those vagrants around the Bloomfield quarter, they're really a nuisance."

"I know: there were actually a few hanging around the Furstheim Museum last week. Can you believe it?"

"Wait, he's coming to."

The Moth raised his head and opened his eyes. Light flooded through his goggle's lenses, stabbing the back of his throbbing head. He wanted to rub his aching eyeballs but couldn't move his arms.

He was tied into a chair.

"Well, if it isn't our knight in white," a man said. He stepped forward and the Moth's eyes focused on him. He wore a robe, the hood thrown back to expose a clean-shaven face with impeccably parted hair and a smooth, firm jaw. Everything about the man bespoke money and power.

The Moth looked around. All the men in the chamber looked like the first. In this barbaric lair of the occult was gathered a group of cultured, intelligent, urbane men. Beyond them, the Moth could see the altar; the bound form of the little girl – the kidnapped Holly Keyes – was still lying upon it. She was still alive, her chest moving with her hurried, terrified breaths.

"I suppose this is the legendary Moth," said another man as he stepped closer. "The boogeyman has come to our lair on a special night."

The Moth's head swiveled from side to side. He remained silent.

"Doesn't talk much," said one man.

"Maybe we need to give him something to say," another voice murmured, and then a fist slammed into the Moth's ribs, followed by another punch to his gut. His head dropped but no sound came.

"Heh, he's tough," someone grunted. "Let me try…"

"Enough," a voice commanded. "He's already thrown the ceremony off enough as it is. We don't need further delays." It was the man in the headdress.

"If this chump has thrown the ceremony off, I'm gonna wear his eyeballs on a necklace!" A meaty-looking, thuggish man – an obvious gangster - had said this and he stood scowling at the Moth's bound form with disgust. "Hell, if there's enough left of him after we're done, I might just do it anyway." He grinned.

Beyond the gangster, the Moth noticed another altar for the first time. Upon this altar were photographs of each of the men along with other paraphernalia: campaign posters, badges, ledgers, wanted posters… these were all men of stature in the city, or at least men who *wanted* stature, or fame or infamy. Politicians, businessmen, policemen, gang-leaders; they were among the rich and powerful in New Aspiria, the gears that turned behind the scenes of the city. Gears that were greased with the blood of the innocent.

The Moth counted the men. There were thirteen of them in all, and a fourteenth had just entered the room.

"The channelers are all still in their throes," the newcomer said. "They haven't been interrupted."

"Excellent," said the man in the headdress as he checked his pocket watch. "Then we can proceed. Our friend here hasn't affected our timetable too badly at all." He grinned and snapped the watch shut, the sound like metallic teeth clacking together. The other men chuckled.

"Alright then, everyone, take your places in the Circle," the leader called out. He looked up at the stars overhead through a skylight in the warehouse roof. "The Anointed Star is at the apex. It is time."

As the men all donned their hoods again and got into formation around the altar Holly Keyes was on, the leader turned toward their new captive. "Mr. Moth, you're about to see something very few will ever witness, and something very few live to tell about. You, of course, will not be among them."

One of the hooded men—the police officer the Moth had followed—threw a switch. A strange machine that straddled the room hummed to life. A large metallic sphere was suspended by the machine high over Holly Keyes' body on its altar. The sphere began to crackle with electricity. The Moth felt the hair on his arms tingling beneath his clothes.

The group of men began chanting again, their strange call-and-response was in the words of a bizarre dead language. As they chanted, the strange murmurings of the weird men in the hallway outside seemed to get louder, and all the sounds and voices seemed to blend into one hideously thrumming pulse of malevolence.

In the air between the machine's electric sphere and Holly Keyes, something dark was coalescing from nothingness. It burbled into existence and began shaping itself as the leader of the cult raised the ceremonial dagger over the little girl's body...

The Moth managed to hit a switch on his forearm, and a pair of claw-like blades snapped into position over the back of his right hand. He sawed through the ropes binding his arms as though they were butter to a white-hot knife.

The priest's dagger fell, but something shot from beyond the circle of men, something that knocked the blade from the priest's hand while delivering a blast of electricity to the dagger's wielder. The priest jumped back and fell on his rear, eyes wide with surprise and shock.

The group's heads turned as one to witness the Moth, wraithlike in his white garments, the crimson lenses of his mask glinting with a fierce, triumphant challenge. The Moth reached a hand to a control box at his belt, turning up the battery power there to nearly its full charge. The exoskeleton he wore beneath his clothes powered up, his strength augmented.

The Moth raised his left hand and duplicate blade-claws popped from that sleeve as well. He motioned a challenge with his hand.

The cultists rushed him. The Moth dove headlong into the fray, but danced between the men, deftly avoiding their fists as he dove smoothly toward his goal: Holly Keyes.

The Moth sliced through the ropes that bound the girl and scooped her up with one motion. He raised his arm and fired a grappling line toward the ceiling. It smashed through the skylight above and caught on the roof. The line snatched the Moth and Holly upward, through the broken glass and onto the top of the warehouse. The cultists below scuttled for safety amid the shower of broken glass.

On the roof, the Moth set Holly on her feet. He quickly checked her for wounds. There were none, she had been unharmed by both the priest's dagger and the falling glass shards.

He placed a hand gently on her chest to signal her to wait there and then he leaped back down into the fray, his glider wings open like an avenging angel.

● ● ●

INFAMOUS GANGLEADER FOUND DEAD
(*electrocast*)

Rudolph Morgante, the notorious head of the Morgante crime family, was found dead this evening in one of his illicit gambling halls.

Morgante, along with a sizable number of his men, were found after what appeared to be the result of a violent shootout. However, none of the Morgante men had been struck by bullets and the only shots fired appear to have come from their own pistols. Instead, the gangsters suffered death from violent blows, burns, stabs or cuts, and other methods. Police detectives are at a loss, and as of yet, no eyewitnesses have come forward with an account of what could have happened.

The death of Morgante and his trusted lieutenants puts to rest a reign of criminal terror that stretches back at least twenty years. Suspected of having his fingers in every racket from gambling and prostitution to drugs and underground technology trafficking, Morgante was well known – and feared – by citizens of New Aspiria, as well as rival criminals both near and far. There is certainly no shortage of possible suspects, so police may have their hands full in determining exactly who is responsible for the deaths of the Morgante gangsters.

Keep watching this electrocast feed for updates to this case as they come along.

UPDATE (22 mins. ago):
It has been confirmed (by a secret but reliable source) that the only clue to the identity of the slayer or slayers of the Morgante family members may be a small jar containing a single live white moth. The jar was found on the floor of the gambling house in the center of the room where the most carnage had occurred and placed directly in front of the Rudolph Morgante's eyes.

More details will be posted as they develop...

● ● ●

The Moth landed amid the group of cultists and his limbs flew into motion. A kick to the midsection of one of the robed cultists sent him flying through the air to crash into a stack of wooden pallets. The Moth spun, his blades slicing through the throat of another cultist who had picked up a steel bar and was rushing in to bash his head. In a spray of red, the cultist went down and the Moth was already on the move as another cultist dove for his chest in a tackle. The Moth sidestepped the man and drove his elbow – reinforced by the steel exoskeleton – down upon the man's skull. His body slid to a stop and was still upon the floor.

A shotgun wielding man stepped from the shadows. He yanked the trigger and the gunshot boomed through the inner sanctum of the warehouse but the Moth spun, his body cartwheeling out of the path of the buckshot blast. As he landed, the Moth aimed a fist at the gunman and hit a button on his forearm beneath his sleeve. A quick jet of flame burst from the Moth's wrist and engulfed the cultist. Robes ablaze, the man dropped his shotgun and ran blindly, his screaming shriek echoing from the rafters.

There was a noise behind the Moth, and he spun around in time to skewer the pair of men who were rushing him from behind. The wrist-blades sliced them open as he withdrew them and they fell squirming, dying at his feet.

Another group charged at him, three men all coming from different angles. The Moth waited until they were nearly upon him before he ducked and rolled into a ball, rolling backward and out of the way. A burst of a white powder covered them, and then the Moth hit them with a blast of his wrist mounted flame-gun. They ignited as one and their cries went up among the din.

There was a booming howl, an unearthly and chilling sound. The Moth turned.

The coagulating darkness that had been forming above Holly Keyes was still there, but taking grotesque shapes. It writhed in rage and agony, a thing half-formed from whatever nightmarish fusion of magic and science had been used to unleash it. The Moth forced himself to look away from the monstrosity and instead he looked upon the cult's priest.

Wild-eyed, the man stood before that dark shape and screamed. "How dare you? *How DARE you?!*" He rushed the Moth, the regained ceremonial dagger held high.

The Moth reached up, his forearm colliding with the priest's with a bone-snapping blocking strike and the priest dropped the dagger. The Moth's other fist snapped out and collided with the priest's chest. His sternum shattered, the priest staggered back, gasping.

From his wrists the Moth launched a pair of electrically charged stun-rods which impacted with the frame and controls of the strange machine. A burst of voltage climbed up the wires and supports, overcharging the metallic sphere. Energy burst and crackled from it. The thwarted dark thing howled again and reached out, grabbing the priest off of the ground and drawing him into that pulsing shape in the air. The priest screamed and the machine began to fall apart. Bodies, debris, weapons, the altars... everything was being sucked into the dark star of evil in the center of the big room. The thing was collapsing upon itself and pulling the warehouse into itself as it did.

The Moth snatched up the ceremonial dagger to study later. There was no time to aim the grappling hook. The Moth - his exoskeleton's power nearly depleted - put everything he could into an upward leap toward the skylight. He burst through the opening and landed on the roof, which was shaking and starting to collapse. He scooped Holly Keyes up in his arms, her own arms wrapping tightly around his neck. The Moth leaped off the roof's edge, the glider wings snapping open as the building fell into itself, crumpling into a ball.

From the safety of a nearby roof, the Moth and Holly watched as the warehouse imploded. A line of police and fire vehicles headed toward the scene, but the Moth avoided them, fearing further corrupt officials. He would be following up on this cult and its members and participants, but not tonight. Not yet.

He carried the little girl into the darkness, heading off back into the city.

● ● ●

There was a sound. It wasn't loud but it was enough to rouse the dozing form of Ila Keyes, who had cried herself to sleep on the couch. Terrance Keyes had been reading a late edition newspaper and he put it down, ears straining to listen for the sound and not believing he'd heard it.

The sound came again. "Mommy? Daddy?"

Terrance and Ila Keyes looked at each other in shock and bolted from their seats, rushing toward Holly's room. They were the only two people in the apartment now; the police had all left about an hour before. This had to be Holly's voice, didn't it? They prayed and hoped, and turned the doorknob to their daughter's room.

And there she was, dirty and disheveled, but alive and clutching one of her teddy bears. She smiled as her mother and father grabbed her, embracing her in a tearful, loving crush.

"Oh, baby," Ila said to Holly between furious kisses to the top of her head, "Baby, where were you?"

"I was in a bad place, with bad men. They wanted to hurt me." Holly didn't know how to explain it all yet, so it came out simply. "But he saved me."

"Who? Who saved you?" Holly's father wiped a tear from his eye, perplexed.

"The man in white," Holly said, and she pointed to her window.

Terrance and Ila noticed for the first time that the window was open, the expensive curtains billowing gently in the night breeze. There was nothing to see outside except for the city, but on the windowsill was a small glass jar, its lid studded with air-holes. Inside the jar fluttered a little white moth.

● ● ●

The Moth hung up his white fedora. On a rack next to it, he hung the white overcoat/wings. He would service them later.

On a table filled with hi-powered microscopes and other evidence gear, the Moth set the ceremonial dagger down. It would take a lot of investigating and research, but he was determined to find the source of the weird cult and ensure it was crushed.

He removed his clothes – the white now streaked with blood and dirt. Then he took off the exoskeleton he wore beneath it. The batteries were completely dead now and the wrist weapons would need maintenance, but he would see to that later too. He hung the exoskeleton on a rack in the center of the wall and plugged the batteries into the charging station. The mask he wore sat on a mannequin head nearby, and he recharged the batteries for the headgear as well.

He stood before the mirror on his dresser, a sad-eyed man with a mangled throat and four days' worth of beard stubbling his cheeks. A photo of a man with a beautiful dark-haired woman and a smiling, chubby-faced boy sat on the dresser. After gazing lovingly at the woman and the boy, he considered the man in the photo. *The resemblance is only superficial*, he thought. *What would that man then think of me now?*

He stepped to the window; the sun was coming up over New Aspiria. The glow of the city lights and the Tesla towers was giving way to the golden glow of dawn. Out there, a child was safe and an evil group had been stopped, at least for the time being. But there would always be more people that would need his help. Outside, the city stirred in the birth and hope of another day.

His city.

The End

Burden of Guilt
(A Flying Dutchmen story)
by Joe Gentile

"**W**e cannot fight this Allied Meteor plane with what we have. We need to get this into production now!" The engineer was gesturing towards his creation with pride.

"Indeed, Herr Ochmann. Our prototype has tested beyond expectations. I had heard that the official word to proceed will be coming today."

Gabrielle adjusted her glasses and pretended to not hear the two engineers as she quietly moved away towards the metal lockers. She did not see them smile oddly at her as she went by. Nor did she see the smug satisfied look they exchanged after. If she had, she would have known that something was not right.

• • •

"The old factory is a sad testament to what we were, especially how desolate it looks here in the in the evening."

"Like much of Germany," was Gunter's soft response.

The blue-black night sky was still, and the pilots could see below them the soft glow of the town of Marienburg.

The two pilots, whose planes were practically wing tip to wing tip, were in close radio contact. This was just another night of patrol over Poland. There hadn't been too much activity here in a couple years. As far as Klaus and Gunter were concerned, they didn't understand why they had to patrol this dead zone at all. Until moments later...

"What the hell? What the hell?"

"Oh my God! Pull up! Pull up!"

First Gunter, then Klaus, stared in horror as a blinding glow-in-the dark fighter plane seemingly materialized soundlessly in front of them out of nowhere! It had a skeleton for a pilot—and it was poised to strike!

• • •

Earlier that day:

"I can't rescue." The Flying Dutchman said.

"Dutchman, you know this is important. We have no time." Christabel's voice crackled through the plane's radio.

"I can't."

"You have to. It's a job for one man. You are the best there is."

The Flying Dutchman did not respond. He sat looking at his radio as if he had never seen it before. He rocked with the rhythm of his twin-boom, twin-engine Fokker G.I. He had no choice; he knew that. Destruction he could do, as his nine guns could spray havoc to many targets at once. Revenge he enjoyed, as his heavy plane made dive-bombing a scream for his enemies. Fear he managed on every outing, as his neon plane and his skull head helmet scared the hell out of anyone who saw them.

But a rescue was too much of a risk, as his curse was just still too much for him to wrap his head around. Everyone he came near and everyone he was close to—died. He was convinced it was a curse for his own past stupidity and bravado.

"We have a man on the inside. It's now or never."

In a pre-arranged code, Christabel gave The Flying Dutchman the coordinates. Her complete faith in him and her daily radio calls were the only things that kept him going. He did have one deep burning commitment that superseded everything else though. It was his desire to wipe out the Nazi's, even one at a time if necessary. It was something he breathed in and out every second of every day, and it radiated through every fiber of his being.

He was the last of the Dutch Air Force; a single plane on an impossible bloody vendetta. Due to his past arrogance, not only were all the Dutch fighter planes destroyed, but his village…his family…his girl…all gone. Nazi strafing took care of all of that after he gunned down ten Nazi planes. They came after him next and shot him out of the sky. His memory was blurry after that. He was not sure if he was alive or dead, but he knew what he had to do.

● ● ●

Flying Dutchman's night vision was excellent. He pushed his heavy plane up smoothly. He was well versed in the handling of his customized aircraft. His instruments aligned and he knew he was very close to the airbase outside of Marienburg, Poland. This was the new home of the German Focke-Wulf aircraft factory. It had sustained heavy damage in two previous Allied raids. According to Christabel and the Dutch Underground, there were some rumors of advanced aircraft development still going on there somewhere in the rubble. They had been able to place a lone operative there under the guise of "research assistant". The last word received from that operative was that a new interceptor fighter, the Super Loren, was not only developed, but built and ready for testing. The plane was so advanced that it could change the tide of the air war; so it and everything associated with it had to be destroyed. He was to get to the factory, find this prototype, destroy it and all records of it, as well as rescue the Dutch agent.

The Dutchman figured if this ruined factory was in any way active, the Germans would not leave it completely unprotected. They wouldn't field an entire squadron of air protection because that would stir up too much attention. They needed some kind of warning system, likely a handful of patrol fighters, which would not seem out of the ordinary in German controlled airspace.

Flying Dutchman killed his engines. Gently, gracefully, the heavy plane tilted downward. Then, it dropped like an anvil, gathering runaway locomotive speed. The fuselage barely shook with the effort,and the Fokker remained mostly silent through its lightning descent.

He saw them in seconds. Two skinny looming dark shapes below: German Messerschmitts. These planes were used for every conceivable service by the Germans, but they were originally designed to be fighters. They were quick, nimble, well-armored, and had advanced engineering for firing weapons. Like almost every other plane, the Messerschmitts had their weaknesses as well, such as how high they could climb.

He started to pull up to slow his dive, for he wanted to be sure that the enemy pilots saw him first. He wanted them to taste fear, just like he envisioned his family had experienced as they were gunned down in cold blood.

● ● ●

"It's not real!" Gunter screamed. *"He is a corpse!"*

"Doesn't matter! Get out of the way!" came Klaus' anxious reply.

"But, there are no more Dutch planes…" Gunter mumbled quietly as his eyes caught a glimpse of the skeleton-headed pilot, but try as he might, his brain was failing in its attempt to send a message to his reflexes to move his plane. Both trained fighter pilots were spellbound and took precious seconds before finally reacting. That was more than enough time.

The Dutchman had been ready. His nine guns easily opened up the two German fighters like sardine cans. The element of surprise was all his as his weapons shattered the nice, peaceful sky into thunder. The Germans felt a giant vacuum of air pulling at them and their bullet- riddled bodies were sucked out into the night. Their planes began to move off of their flight lines, then fell, and began to twirl and release a heavy opaque black smoke. The increasing volume of a whirring sound as they gained speed acted as alarm to the Dutchman to stay alert. The momentum of the Dutchman's plane kept him moving downward, but he was an expert at that kind of sneak attack so he knew exactly how to handle it.

He didn't have the luxury of time to go through his usual after kill ritual. He took a deep breath knowing that would have to wait. The firefight, as brief as it was, plus the two downed fighters crashing into the ground would likely ruin any further chances of surprise, so he had to make an unexpected move. Like an eagle with its talons up, he pulled the Fokker up and skid-landed amidst the uneven grounds of the factory ruins. It was a hell of a put down and would never have been attempted by most pilots, but he was as one with his plane. He knew time was very short now. He saw one small house-sized building twenty yards away. It was the only thing within sight that was close to being intact. He kept his plane facing that direction as he opened the cockpit and jumped out. He reached beneath his black leather jacket and pulled out his two short shotguns that he kept strapped to himself at all times. These weapons were more than just guns. They were the only thing left from his home that wasn't demolished. Although he was an accomplished marksman, he didn't have to be in order to use these two little pocket cannons, as they would spray lead in a thirty degree arc. With one in each hand, he rushed to the house building. The dark covered him to an extent, but with his plane glowing in the dark like a beacon, there was only so much the dark was going to help him stay hidden.

Within seconds, a wall of light arose as a garage door to the house opened. German soldiers exited from within, shooting at him and his plane. Upon feeling the hot gunshots all around him, The Dutchman calmly strode into his attackers. He didn't fire a single shot, and oddly, not one of the hundreds of rounds aimed at him managed to hit him either. He had experienced this many times since his "death". Each time was exhilarating. Quickly, less and less gunfire was heard as the open-mouthed Germans became aware of their futility. Some ran after seeing the Flying Dutchman's skeleton head, and some just ran. Those who remained were transfixed in their tracks.

The Dutchman let loose with both shotguns and a storm of hot lead sliced into everyone and everything. Not a single German soldier got away, even those that were fleeing the scene. Dark crimson blood reflected intermittently in the moonlight. He was completely soundless as he walked into the open garage door.

Inside was a series of benches, lamps, circuitry, engine parts...and a single airplane. It had low swept wings at 45° mounted in the mid-fuselage. It had a wingspan of 7.6 meters and a length of 11.6 meters. There looked to be a rocket engine for take-off and two Lorin ramjets located on the tips of the sharply swept tailplanes which would be used for cruising. Its armament consisted of two 30 mm (1.18 in) MK 108 cannons.

Dutchman was quite an engineer in his own right as he had custom worked his Fokker way past original design specs, but this plane...was beyond anything he had ever seen. This would outrace and outmaneuver anything currently in the air. It could not be allowed to be mass produced.

The garage was very quiet, as if respecting all of the dead men strewn about outside. He did not feel anyone else's presence but did feel that he had little time to make this all happen. He harnessed his weapons and began to quickly look through this make-shift lab for any evidence of the missing Dutch agent. The more he looked, the more he knew what he would find.

He caught sight of a small trail of fresh blood. A couple of drops lead to a metal locker. He opened it and immediately caught a female body that fell onto him. She had been shot in the neck and the wound looked fresh. She was barely conscious. He kneeled while laying her down on the ground and stopped. He looked at her. She couldn't have been more than twenty years old, barely out of her teens. Blond hair and blue eyes with glasses, but even in this situation, she was quite attractive in an intelligent way. She was indeed the Dutch agent he had been told about.

She looked up at him with alarm.

"You must be the Flying Dutchman. Leave now! It's all a trap!"

"A trap? There are no survivors outside."

"They knew who I was the whole time. They waited to kill me until you landed. They want you dead. This crazy plane is years away from being ready to fly!"

"I will take you to safety. You will survive." But he spoke to no one; she had already lost consciousness and slipped into the great beyond.

Then he heard it. His attention had been on the girl, as they had planned all along. There were heavy footsteps outside. The German soldiers and two pilots he killed were expendable. They had let them be killed. Now their honorable deaths had been tainted by even more evil than war. He stood up and took out his two shotguns again. He had been fooled. That was a human trait. So perhaps he wasn't dead after all.

A loud whoosh went up, and a flickering bright light came from the outside: flame. His plane, he thought. They wanted him outside. He hated to disappoint. He walked calmly out there with both weapons aimed ahead, not making a sound.

As he reached the open garage door, he turned towards his plane and opened fire with both guns. He could see over the two men that his plane was on fire. The men had flamethrowers strapped to their backs that launched their heat death right at the Dutchman, enveloping him in fire. Apparently the Nazis knew that bullets might not harm him, but wanted him to think they didn't know until their surprise attack.

Even with his leather jacket and head aflame, he just kept walking towards them. He blasted both soldiers into atoms. Not enough pieces were left for identification later. Fountains of flames from their fuel tanks lit up the ground like the sun, and then just as quickly, extinguished themselves.

He went back into the garage, but he knew the Dutch operative was dead. She had given herself for the cause and no one would know. This didn't seem right, hell, none of

it seemed right. She had her whole life in front of her...until now. He had to make her sacrifice worth something. How would that even be possible?

Even though he had been on fire, the flame was out now and he was not damaged. He thought how odd that was. Perhaps it proved he was in fact dead. He picked her up across his arms and carried her outside to his plane.

Remarkably, the plane was no longer aflame either and it was also no longer glowing. Interesting, he thought. Good to know.

He carefully placed her inside his mostly empty cabin. He had never had a passenger before...living or dead.

Once in his plane, he turned his guns to the house, and let loose a bombardment that went on for a full thirty seconds. The new-fangled plane was nothing but a sagging frame when he was done. He got his Fokker in the air, and once there, made one quick pass over the house, letting his bay doors open to drop one of only a few small bombs he had on board. He watched it go down and strike the house full on.

Reaching to the floor of the cockpit, he pulled some white roses from a box. He let a couple drop to the ground from the air. That was his kill ritual. It calmed his bloodlust down to a manageable level. It made him remember his mother, who had her pride and joy white roses still in her hand when she was gunned down.

He was not tired of vengeance. That was his whole existence. He just could not understand how to come to terms with the death of the Dutch agent, Gabrielle. It was because of his personal war that she had been killed. He was now responsible for yet another death. How can he make up for this one? Just doing what he has been doing appeared to not be enough as his enemies were willing to sacrifice much to get at him. He had tried his best to not leave any loose ends, but it seemed that he was not completely successful as word of him and his exploits was known by the Axis. Someone had either witnessed him in action or someone in the Underground had loose lips.

Either way, it was reality, and he had to find a way to live with it—if "living" was something he was doing.

● ● ●

He spent as much time in the air as possible. When he needed an emotional reckoning, there was only one place he went. It was a small cement room. It was a ruin of a larger structure or series of structures. It sat in a field of scorched earth now, a lone survivor of some other purpose that would be lost to time.

This is where he remembered waking up after his so-called death. Was he brought there? Did someone come to his aid? His memory was completely gone on the event. He remembered being gunned down, severely wounded, and trying to wrestle his plane out of a nose dive to the ground. Then, nothing. He just woke up in this bunker, this crypt-like cement box. There was blood both inside and outside the cement walls. His plane was waiting for him right outside. It had looked brand new, but also very different. He could swear it was breathing. His vision had also changed. He saw every bit of movement in a slow motion. It was as if he was moving at a different time than everything else.

The cement tomb was barely seen as occupied from the outside as it had a portable wind up radio on a wooden stool and a small cot to lie down on. It was about time that Christabel would be listening. He wound up the radio and sat on the cot staring into nothingness.

"Mission finished..." he said barely audibly.

"Dutchman! Good to hear from you! Are you ok, over?"

"Operational."

"And what about our operative, Gabrielle?"

"I failed."

"Oh, I am so sorry. I am sure you did all you could."

He paused before responding. It was all his fault, no matter how he looked at it. The agent had died because of his existence.

"She will be returned to her homeland. She is owed that for her service."

"So the plane and plant?"

"Gone, but it was all a trap."

"What?"

"The plane wasn't functional. News of it was purposely leaked so they could draw me out."

"Oh my god. We didn't know. They shouldn't even know about you."

"That is of concern, yes."

"I suppose it was bound to happen. You have done a good job of hurting them from the inside out."

"Perhaps, but it is also possible that someone spoke who shouldn't have."

"I do not believe that anyone here would ever do such a thing."

She was probably right. If she was, that just meant his fault was even larger and he is doing more harm than good.

"I am having a hard time knowing what to believe about anything."

"Are you...ok? I am here. Please tell me how I can help? Let me come to you."

"No. I can't have another death on my conscience."

"I am willing to risk it, for you risk your life every day for us."

"I am not sure that is true as spoken."

"What do you mean?"

"I may already be dead."

"What?"

He did not respond. He was somewhere else...some when else. On his family farm, the cocky pilot, encouraging his friends to fight back against what would otherwise be the quickest takeover of any country in history. Pride, he said. We have the skill, he said. It would be unexpected, he said. They all followed him—to their deaths. In the end, the Nazis they shot down were just a spec on the radar. Their country was conquered in swift order and they had not made a single bit of difference. It was all so pointless, as everyone he ever loved was dead. Because of him.

"Dutchman? Don't give up. You are making a huge difference. You are a symbol for all of us."

Silence.

"Hello?"

The End

Moon Over Cairo
by Teel James Glenn

"Cairo," Bahj "Bobbie" El Fathi intoned as if he were saying a prayer. "Triumphant city of a thousand Minarets and the glorious capital of Egypt. Continuously inhabited for over 3500 years, with as many as nine different cities located on this very place. Hard to believe this nineteen hundred and Oh five of the Christian era."

The 'civilized Bedouin' as he called himself, was standing at the window of our hotel that faced out to the Khan al-Khalili market. He wore a newly purchased tropical linen suite and it only served to emphasize his tall, whipcord build. His brown skin contrasted with the light color of the suit and his jet-black hair with his bright blue eyes.

It had been a week since I met him on the Cairo Queen sailing up the Nile. Bahj, or Bobbie as he kept telling everyone, was the son of the Emir of El Kador, a protectorate of the Crown with newly discovered oil wells. Bobbie had been educated in Oxford by a far seeing father who wanted his son to understand his 'overlords'. We had come to Cairo only that morning.

My name is Horatio Venture and I am journalist, which Bobbie knew but I was also working as an agent of the Foreign Office of the Crown. Bobbie didn't know that.

He believed my 'running into him' on the Cairo Queen was a casual occurrence. It was not. I had been assigned by my superior to 'mind him.' It seems that his father was a savvy 'camel trader' when it came to negotiating the oil leases on his land and there were factions-on both sides of the deal that were not happy with his demands. It was felt that his only son might be used by those with interests against the Empire might use Bahj as a lever.

I had cultivated a friendship with him and we had visited the cafes and nightclubs on our first night in Cairo.

"You make all of us Europeans seem ravening beasts, Bobbie," I said.

"Are you not?" He said turning from the window with a quizzical expression on his handsome face. "Oh, you have the veneer of the civilized but really, would not the finest of English gentleman be indistinguishable from the cave man on a football pitch?"

"Ah," I countered, "so you are saying that people are people?"

"So you are saying there is a level playing field of greed and evil in the world?" His smile was a winning one, with no rancor in his statements, which, I must say, was an endearing quality in him.

"It is my contention," I said with some truth to my real feelings, "That we are all not much different in motives or appetites; it is only our minds that may rise above our base, wolfish instincts. Things like religion, family and concepts like honor make us more than the base beasts of jungle."

"Ah, an optimist," Bobbie laughed. "Let us see if your assertions are correct in the dance quarter, eh?"

"I suspect that is the best place to conduct a scientific study, "I said.

The two of us left the hotel for our second night of adventure in the exotic city with a deep sense of excitement.

The Khan al-Khalili was considered to be one of the largest markets in the world and if it was not it was certainly one of the nosiest and most colorful.

On the northern side of the bazaar the Mosque of Sayyidna al- Hussein was majestic and golden in the afternoon light of the desert sun. It was one of the holiest Islamic sites of Egypt and in part why Bobbie had chosen the hotel where we were staying. We wandered the market for a time as the hustle and bustle of the day flowed around us like a living beating animal.

Though there was a wild variety of skin colors in the mix of races I have never felt more a part of the tide of humanity.

Then the muezzin from the Mosque gave the uvular adhan, the Muslim call to prayer, and the market seemed to ripple as so many dropped to their prayer rugs all around us.

I exchanged a look with Bobbie and I knew he was feeling the same conflicting feelings of both connection and distance from the strange ritual all around us. He gave a smile that told me he only half felt the need to kneel and pray, for he was such a contradiction of facts, but he dropped like the rest and began to pray facing Mecca.

He drank and did drugs with the fervor of an Oxford student after passing exams yet he stopped five times a day to make his prayers in a religion that forbade both. He was a man who seemed to pick and chose his observances; a true contradiction.

I was not the only non-Muslims in the Khan al-Khalili market. There were the expected some Europeans in their tropical suits and dresses, though barely a handful but I had not expected to see so many native non-Mohammedans. Of that ilk there were two-dozen; some Berbers in their blue robes, Negroes in skins or simple cloths wraps, several Chinese who were selling silks at a large stall and three individuals who fit none of these categories. They wore robes like the Bedouins but something in their carriage set them apart.

Then I realized as I looked at them that they were looking at me. And at Bobbie. Their eyes were not Arab eyes, but were European ones.

When the tallest of the three, who seemed to be the leader, saw me looking at him he dropped to his knees as did the other two following his actions. They appeared to offer prayers toward the Mosque, but I had the distinct feeling that it was a mimed performance.

I cast a glance back at the Mosque that seemed to me to embody all the mystery of the city beneath its graceful towers and then at the three anomalies in burnoose before putting them out of my mind to go in search of a meal.

Would that I had studied them further in light of the trouble that followed.

● ● ●

Bobbie and I made our way out of the square and walked away from the market toward the center of the city. We were on the eastern bank of the Nile, where the modern downtown, built under influence of French architecture, was a center of commerce and popular with nightlife.

"The name Cairo means victorious in my native Arabic," Bobbie said.

"The same word refers to the planet Mars," I added. "Always the warrior beacon in any culture it seems."

"You are a witty fellow, my Horatio," He said with his wide grin. "You feed my mind."

"I seem to remember your body was hungry when we left the hotel," I said as we headed into the maze of buildings off the square. The shadows were lengthening and the browns and tans of the day were becoming purples and orange all around us.

"Touché', new chum," Bahj said with a smile. "You should know my now I am easily distracted by shiny objects and pretty women!" That started us laughing.

The sound of our laughter echoed off the walls of the narrow passage we were cutting through. There were other sounds as well, the scrape of dessert boots on cobbles and suddenly we were aware that we were not alone.

Ahead of us two figures stepped out from the shadows of the narrow street to block our path. A knife blade glinted in one of their hands.

"Looks like we got company, Horatio."

I looked behind us to see two more dark shapes materialize from the night.

"Seems we are surrounded." I said. I surprised myself that I felt no fear, just an icy sureness that I would not be an easy victim.

"It seems we are in what you folks call a sticky wicket, eh?" Bobbie whispered to me. "But I do have an old family heirloom under my jacket; a desert knife."

"I'm afraid all I have is my fists," I said with bitter self-recrimination.

As I spoke one of the figures behind me produced a cudgel and began to raise it.

I suited action to words and with a battle cry that would do a rugby pitch justice, charged!

As I expected my sudden frontal charge startled the thuggish figure before me into inaction. He was bigger than I but I rammed my shoulder into his gut with all my body weight and thus unbalanced him so that he actually slammed into his compatriot.

I continued past the two fallen men because I saw a pile of debris against the wall of the alley and rightly thought I could find a weapon there. Also, the two would certainly follow me to keep them from Bobbie.

I secured a damaged amphora from the pile of trash, spinning with a solid grip on the handle. The bandit that I had not struck directly was on my heels with his cudgel raised to strike.

I smashed the jar into his face so that the amphora exploded into a hundred shards. As he dropped unconscious I snatched up his club to head back toward my friend.

My Arabic friend had charged at the same time I had and I could see the first of his assailants had been taken by the same surprise as mine. That robber was down, wailing in pain where he had been slashed.

The second thug had produced a Khyber knife of his own and the two were faced off assessing each other.

My first attacker was on his feet now and I could see enough of his features to see that he was startled by the opposition we had presented.

"Not the ripe plumbs you expected, eh fellow?" I snarled at him with a ferocity that surprised even me.

"Leave, we will get him another time!" the man Bobbie had wounded yelled to the man facing me. He yelled in heavily accented Russian. I did not catch every word but I knew enough from my own travels to understand them a little.

"But we'll…" the man facing me stammered.

"Go!" the leader called.

My opponent backed away from me and grabbed the groggy fellow I had clubbed.

I let them go a little stunned by the explosive violence.

"Well, Horatio," Bobbie said after a moment. "I certainly have worked up quite an appetite now. How about you?"

We found a small café that had pleasant flute music calling to us and relaxed with a long and satisfying meal while exotic flute music played.

"I have heard that most of clubs are down by the banks of the Nile itself," he said with great cheer as he sipped strong coffee after out meal. "One particularly, The Golden Camel is supposed to be quite unique."

I knew there was no way I could dissuade my charge from his night of wild jaunts but I found myself wishing I had my trusty Webley pistol with me; I was certain that the attack in the alley was not random. One of the attackers had said they would "get him later' and I was sure they were referring to Bahj.

"I'm up for that, my friend," I said cheerfully," but let us stop at the hotel so I can change my jacket, first."

"Sounds smashing, Horatio," he said. "I shall do the same, I am all sweaty from our little adventure and I want to be fresh for the ladies!"

We put money on the table and rose to head out into the balmy Egyptian night. The moon was just rising but still bright enough for streets to still be active with both locals and tourists.

Our stop at the hotel was a short one, so that, less than an hour later (with me feeling the comforting weight of the pistol in a shoulder holster) we walked down the ubiquitous alley that led to the entrance to the Golden Camel Night Club.

We looked much like light and dark versions of each other as we entered the nightspot and attracted no little amount of attention for it in our almost identical linen suits.

The interior of the club was a smoky cave lit by scones on the walls whose exact dimensions were masked by the smoke and the darkness. There were several dozen tables, most occupied by couples, scattered around the room. It seemed an even mix of races, European and Middle Eastern with every manner of ethnic dress.

"This way to the best seats in the house, effendis," the swarthy maître d fawned over us as we entered the club. He escorted us to a table by a column under one of the curving arches at the corner of a small dance floor.

"This is a most fine table, effendis," he said. "You will have a jolly good view of the dancing girls. May I bring you some libation?"

"Libation," Bobbie smiled to me. "It makes it sound so very special, like liberty or liberal or with very little stretch, licentious!" He turned his beaming smile toward our host. "Most certainly my good man," he said. "Libate us with your best!"

The little man scurried off to comply with his mandate and the Emir's son settled in to a night of anticipated debauchery. He lit up a hookah that was at the table and handed me the one of the smoking pipes.

The waiter brought the drinks then and we enjoyed a fine Greek wine to warm our palate while waiting for the evening's festivities.

We didn't not have to wait long. A doumbek began to intone an ancient savage rhythm and the notes of a flute began to wind sinuously around the room calling up images of a primal past. Then the star of the Golden Camel slid out onto the middle of the dance floor; the alluring Yasmina!

She was dark and dusky and moved across the floor like liquid sin. She did not so much dance to the music but between the notes, wrapping herself in them as if they were a mink stole. She was dressed, if so strong a term could be used, in silks and jewels that did as much to reveal her voluptuous form as conceal it.

It seemed to me that in a very short time the brown skinned beauty fixed her attentions on our table and vibrated over toward Bobbie. She made eye contact with my charge and I could almost feel the sparks fly between them.

● ● ●

The tone of Yasmina's dance number changed from enticing to exciting with a shift up tempo. She shed some of the myriad scarves (one of which she draped across Bobbie's head) though never quite reached the scandalous state before the finale staccato explosion of the doumbek signaled the end of her solo. She bowed to thunderous applause and raced off into the darkness.

Bobbie sniffed the silk kerchief and laughed. "Ah, my Horatio," he said. "And the night has barely begun!" He sipped some wine and was about to speak when a strange figure materialized out of the smoky darkness of the club.

"Do the effendis seek after great artifacts?" The beggar asked. He was draped in so many layers of clothing it was hard to perceive his true shape. He had a beard and a motley-colored turban.

A waiter appeared and it was clear he was going to shoo the beggar away but my companion held up a hand. "No leave him," Bobbie said. "I am always interested in object-de-art."

"A thousand thanks, effendi," the beggar said. His beard parted into a smile that showed twisted teeth. "I am sure you will like what I have for you; a most rare treasure." He held out his dirty hand to show a circlet of brass and gold. In the dim and flickering light it appeared almost to glow as if on fire itself.

"A lovely trinket to be sure," Bobbie said. "But I have seen a dozen of it's like in the bazaars of many cities." He smiled effusively and slipped a hand into his pocket, I knew, to draw out a few coins for the ragamuffin.

"No effendi," the beggar said. "This is a very special ring; it is a wishing ring! Forged from the very heart of the earth by the fire hot breath of the djinn!"

"A wishing ring?" Bobbie asked.

"Yes, effendi, for the Djinn are creatures of smoke and fire and have powers."

"I am sure you think so, my friend," Bobbie said, "But if it were a wishing ring why have you not wished yourself to the caliphate?"

The beggar shrugged his shoulders somewhere beneath his layers of rags. "I have no such ambition, effendi. And I have made my wish upon it, the Djinn grant but one to each wearer." His beard parted again in a wistful smile. "I had my fortune from it and lost it in the most pleasant and sinful of ways. So now I hope to make enough to gorge myself at least one more time."

Bobbie arched an eyebrow and looked to me with a smile. "What say you, Horatio? Shall I be this fellow's means to a sore stomach on with the rise of the sun?"

I regarded my companion and the beggar with amusement. "Seems a jolly trinket," I said. "And how much can this fellow consume to be full?"

Bobbie laughed. "Indeed. How is this, my good fellow?" He pulled some paper currency form his pocket and the beggar eyes widened.

"You are most generous, effendi!" The beggar snatched the cash with speed that would do a cobra proud and placed the ring in Bobbie's hand.

The ragged man disappeared into the shadows of the club as if he were an apparition. Bobbie held the ring up to study it in the flickering torchlight, angling it this way and that to study the workmanship. His grin widened.

"Here, Horatio," he said offering me the ring to examine. "See the workmanship?"

I took the ring from him. I held it close to my eyes and studied it in detail. It looked like a simple wrought ring at first. Around the orange burnished band were incised words that were in some language that might have been Sanskrit. The simplicity of the ring masked a complexity of subtle etching within the band itself. There were the faintest of images there.

"I can't make them out," I said as I squinted and angled the ring to catch the light. "Wait...I can see desert scenes that the sands themselves seem to move in the light."

The scenes of desert splendor changed as I looked at them. A trick of the light made it seem as if the images were shifting and I saw figures moving; warring figures with raised swords and axes. War chariots and horses charging. And in the midst of the chaos I was a single figure bent over a forge. He was a wizened form and as I watched I saw him shape the ring, his lips muttering ancient incantations.

The ring blazed white-hot then faded to a bronze glow. That was when the withered smithy stood back and called to a beautiful, dark skinned girl. When she entered she stood above the glowing ring and with a swiftness that belayed his ancient look took out a knife and slit the woman's throat.

The blood spurted from her neck to bath the ring in a hiss of steam. A single drop her life's blood landed on the surface of the ring and coalesced into the red jewel that sat on the ring.

"Horatio?" Bobbie's voice called me from the vision and I shook myself with a shiver. Had I been hypnotized? Was it the wine and the incense? "You look a bit peaked?"

"Oh, I'm fine," I said. "Just a bit dizzy, I think from working too hard to keep up with your debauchery." I handed the ring back for him, oddly glad to be rid of the thing.

Just then Yasmina took the dance floor again and I was able to settle back, take another drink of wine and try to forget my flight of fancy. Still the images from the ring lingered in my mind and all but blotted out the sensuous gyrations of the exotic dancing girl.

My companion took no more notice of my strange mood, entranced by the dancer, but I noticed he slipped the ring on a finger on his right hand.

Yasmina whirled and spun with even more frantic sensuality than she had the first time on the dance floor but this time it seemed even more focused on Bahj. I had the impression that she was dancing mostly for him. So did Bobbie.

I found my eye wandering away from the wiggling hips of the siren and looked beyond her to notice two fellows who were also not watching the girl.

There were two of them and they were watching Bobbie.

"That is not a coincidence," I thought as I slipped my hand under my jacket to touch the butt of the Webley.

I split my focus now between the girl and the men until she danced off into a curtained doorway. Bobbie took another sip of his wine and leaned over to whisper to me.

"It seems that Yasmina is prepared to help me in my studies in debauchery, Horatio, old fellow. I do hope you don't feel slighted, but you just don't shake a leg nearly as well as her."

I couldn't object without tipping my hand as his minder, so I just laughed and said, "Well, I shall dull my pain at being jilted with some of this excellent Greek wine! Tally ho!"

He staggered off with an attempt to be graceful. The two watchers' eyes followed Bobbie's progress like sharks as he exited the clubroom after the girl. The two men followed, barely a heartbeat later.

"Just a bit obvious, gents," I thought as I rose and moved into the shadows to make my way to the doorway around the edges of the room so any other 'watchers' would not see detect me.

I was through the doorway barely a minute after the two men and not a moment too soon.

● ● ●

The doorway had disgorged me into a narrow hallway and in that corridor Bobbie and the two men were engaged in a struggle while the dancing girl stood by, obviously complicit.

The Emir's son was doing his best to defend himself but he was drunk enough that his coordination was off and the two burly assailants were all business.

I drew my pistol.

"Gentlemen," I barked, "you can leave upright or be carried out."

The two men turned brutish and startled faces toward me. I cocked my gun. "I am serious, gentlemen."

They did not believe me and one of them pulled a curved knife. I shot him neatly through the head and he dropped like a sack of laundry. The other man screamed, threw Bobbie into the girl and raced off down the hall.

The girl screamed, protesting her innocence as I ran to Bobbie and helped him untangle himself from her.

"Oh be quiet, woman," Bobbie snapped at her. He looked up at me with a half smile and real gratitude in his eyes. "That was not exactly the excitement I was hoping for. You are a very handy fellow to have around, Horatio."

"I think we had better head back to the hotel, Horatio," He said. His legs almost gave out underneath him so I all but carried him out of the club. "Horatio; I wish I could have wolf of a fellow like you around all the time to protect me."

"I've been called something of a wolf at university," I said with a smile. "I guess it's my destiny."

"And destiny is a powerful thing, my wolf," he snickered.

I smiled at him and noticed a glint of light off the newly purchased ring on his finger which made me think about what an eventful day it had been.

● ● ●

The next day, refreshed despite our encounter of the evening, we were both eager to see more of the wonders of the city. I had convinced him that the two attacks were just coincidence, but I did not for moment believe it. I knew I would have to be on my toes for all the time with him. And truth be told I had grown fond of him.

Also, truth be told, my toes were hurting; I had woken with cramps in my feet but I took some gin and aspirin and pushed on to be as cheery as possible to keep at my charge's side.

We went to The Royal Egyptian Museum of Antiquities which loomed over the busy square. The outside was impressive, but once inside the museum we were both overcome by the magnificence of the vanished glory that had been Egypt.

We moved through the museum as two men who were enchanted by the objects before us. The Emir's son seemed as enthralled by the mystic objects of the east as I. It was another of the contradictory things about my charge; for one who profaned so often against the tenants of his religion seemed to have so much reverence for the history of his people.

One obelisk, a dull red stone spire as tall as a man arrested our attention particularly. It had been found, so the card before it said, near the Ruins of Luxor itself. Its pitted surface was marked with faint glyphs worn almost to invisibility, but it might well have been an open hand that had once been lined out in white hues. It was Anubis, the Jackal headed god of the dead. It seemed to call to me. I found myself staring at it and I felt a strange premonition of something terribly wrong.

After a time we walked from the darkness of the lobby into the blinding bright light of the Egyptian noon. When we stood in the middle of square we looked back at the pink stone of the museum, still awed.

My feet were starting to hurt rather badly by this time so the two of us walked to a nearby sidewalk café enjoying the multiple cultures of the amazing city and have some lunch.

"You doing alright, old fellow," Bobbie asked me when we had ordered some appetizers. "You seem a bit off."

I was massaging my calves and flexing my feet to try and relieve my cramps. "I guess I must have pulled something or other." I didn't tell him of my fantasy when looking at the ring or the nightmares I had instead of sleep. Or for that matter the itch that had more recently started in my ears.

"You seem distracted, Horatio. Perhaps a good meal will set you right."

"Yes, Bobbie," I tried to shrug my feelings off. "Some good lamb and I'll be right as rain."

I was not, however, much improved by my meal. My feet kept bothering me and the itch of my ears was intensifying to the point that it was distracting me in my conversation with Bobbie.

"I think we had better head back to the hotel," the Emir's son said with concern in his voice. "We shall have the house physician take a look at you, old bean."

"I guess you're right, Bobbie. Maybe I just got some bad food or drink last night at the Golden Camel." If it had only been that!

● ● ●

"You are looking quite beastly, Horatio," he said to me as the elevator cage ascended at the hotel.

"You surely know how to bolster a fellow's spirits," I managed. By now my hands were cramping as well as my feet.

"Well I can't have my den mother out of commission just when I'm getting ready to sample the delights of Cairo this evening. We'll get a doctor to fix you up and then be off to a little place I heard of on the waterfront called the Salamander!" He was doing his best to be hail and well met but I could see he was actually concerned about me; another contradiction in this son of the desert.

We made our way to the suite we had taken together. Just as he opened the door a figure darted out of the stairwell across the hall from us and before we knew what had happened we were both shoved into the room.

"What!" I reached for my pistol but had no chance to draw it before two more men already inside the room beat me to the ground and overwhelmed Bobbie.

The last I was aware of before blackness overtook me was the sight of Bobbie yelling, "Horatio!" as the thugs swarmed him.

● ● ●

My journey up from unconsciousness was a slow swim through an inky pool. The throbbing in my head was a drumbeat played on timpani that faded to the beat of my blood pounding in my veins.

I was aware of strange smells before any sounds-sounds that seemed unusually loud. I could hear people walking in the hall, the elevator cage moving and even the sounds of the distant street.

I opened my eyes a crack in case my attackers were still around but the room ahead of me was empty, though a wreck as testament to Bobbie's struggles. Darkness had fallen outside and the full moon was up, casting concealing shadows across the room.

I was still on the floor in the sitting room that communicated to our bedrooms. I listened hard to hear if any of the assailants were still around but detected no movement in any of the other rooms.

I rolled from my side and felt every ache I would expect to from the beating I had taken but oddly enough, no pain in my feet. I got up on all fours and cautiously moved to each of the bedroom doors, peering into each room to be sure I was alone.

It was as quiet and lonely as the tomb. I pushed myself upright and stumbled against the doorway to my room rest.

That was when I noticed that my feet felt odd. I looked down and gasped!

Where my feet should have been were fur covered paws!

Paws like a wolf!

My mind whirled and I think I cried out, "Oh my God! I must be hallucinating this."

I was stunned. Numb with shock but I also realized I could not remain so for long; Bobbie might be counting on me to save him.

My thinking was that if the assailants had wanted to kill him they would have done so on the spot, hence they must have kidnapped him. It would make sense if they wished to put pressure on his father...it was exactly what the foreign office had feared. I had failed in my assignment.

And more, I felt I had let my new friend down.

"Snap out of it Horatio," I chided myself. "You are an agent and you have a job to do... you're just having hallucinations from a blow to your head!"

I pushed off the doorjamb and stumbled into my bedroom and to the water pitcher on the bureau. I reached for it to splash some water into my face to clear my head but to my horror the arm I extended had at the end of it not a human hand but another paw!

I screeched like a mouse in a trap and smashed both of my 'front paws' down on the bureau, knocking the pitcher of water and bowl over.

"No, this can't be happening!" I said aloud.

I turned and froze, horror piled upon horror! There in the looking glass beside the wardrobe, illuminated by a slash of blue moonlight was my reflection, but such a reflection, as I could never have imagined.

The image I beheld was something from Dante's outer ring: I was wearing remnants of my suit and my face was recognizably me but that was where the familiar ended. My face had pushed forward into a sort of short muzzle and my ears had elongated. Over all was a light coating of hair that looked almost like fur; I was a distorted image of a wolf!

I stared at the apparition before me for a hundred heartbeats trying to absorb the outrageous being that was staring back at me. My mind raced and I tried to find some clue that would prove I was in a fever dream but could not poke a hole in this new reality.

I found none.

Gradually I calmed myself and I was able to think and it occurred to me; the Wishing Ring! Bobbie had wished me to be his wolf!

"I guess this removes any doubt the ring works, old fellow," I said. "You've lost your charge, had your head handed to you and have bloody dog ears sticking up out of your head!"

I sniffed in disgust and was reminded of something that I had noticed when I first woke; my sense of smell seemed heightened. It gave me an idea.

I went back to the sitting room, maneuvering on my hind paws and sniffed. I concentrated and I was able to perceive a tapestry of scents. In my mind's eye I could see scent trails of three men and Bobbie as clearly as if I were watching a moving picture show.

My new form had given me new abilities and somehow, realizing that helped me to shake my lethargy. I began to make a plan.

I moved to my closet and found a loose-sleeved djellaba robe. The Berber robe was hooded and I pulled it up to hide my ears. Then, with a silent prayer headed out into the hallway and down a back stairs following the scent trail of the kidnappers.

Wish-curse or not, I was not going to fail in my duty to my country or to my new friend. Horatio Venture was on the trail and damn be any who got in my way!

● ● ●

My pursuit of the kidnappers was made simple by the fact that they were forced to use the back stairs and back alleys with their victim. The darkness of the city concealed my altered state and I found that my transformed body moved with a speed and, dare I say, grace I myself did not normally posses.

The streets of Cairo, even those around the four star hotels were canyons of darkness and not safe places in the dead of night. Off the main streets they were little populated. I progressed unchallenged, following a scent trail that was all but emblazoned in the very air before me.

The kidnappers had not chosen to drive, for which I was grateful, but as I raced along I found myself concerned for Bobbie's state. It was sure he would be battered and it made me angry. It was an irrational anger, after all what did I expect from kidnappers but still the anger added speed to my newly minted legs and paws.

The scent trail took me down toward the wharf area of the city where the streets were even narrower; little more than spaces between the buildings. Here even the moonlight barely penetrated so my odd look and altered feet did not draw attention to me.

The moon was at its apex when I reached the waterfront and a large warehouse where all the scents I had been following seemed to have come to rest. I had reached the kidnapper's lair.

I stood in the shadows of a stack of boxes while I rested from my run and assessed my options.

I was alone, unarmed and with no real knowledge of how many attackers might be in the building. "Well, Nelson at Trafalgar didn't have it so easy either," I thought. Most obviously I could not ask anyone for help vis-a-vis my appearance. So it was 'Damn the torpedoes' and that was that.

I shrugged off my hood for greater freedom of movement.

I moved up close to the building and used my enhanced hearing to listen.

Inside I could hear several men in heated conversation. They spoke a mix of Arabic and French, both of which I understood well enough to follow the talk. They were arguing over Bobbie's fate with one, louder voice than the rest in favor of killing the Emir's son outright. He talked of blood feuds and debts to be paid. The other voices warned him that someone called El Nassr had paid them good money to keep Bahj alive to put pressure on his father. For the moment the cooler heads were in control but it was clear to me that the Arab speaker was not to be placated for long.

I had to act, but I had to be careful to not act hastily. I had to locate exactly where Bobbie was and find a way to release him without endangering him with gunfire. To that end I prowled closer and listened and sniffed all the more.

There were four men in the main room but I could not divine Bobbie's presence so I moved along the side of the building. Near the corner of the building I had a sudden whiff of cologne that I recognized as my friend's. I listened at a small, barred window and heard the heavy, steady breathing of one man inside.

"Bobbie," I whispered. "Can you hear me?"

"Horatio, is that you?"

"Yes," I said. "I'm outside. What is your condition?"

"Worse for the wear," Bobbie said. "The rotters were not gentle with me, but I'll survive. I was sure they had killed you; it is good to hear your voice."

"Yours as well," I said. "Now to business; where are you in the building and where is the guard?"

"I am alone in this room, tied to a chair so there is no guard," Bobbie said. "There may be one outside the door, but I doubt it. I suppose this wish ring works; I prayed for your safety and to be delivered."

"Well talk about that when you are free," I said, not willing to dwell on my state." I have to contrive a way to enter quietly and affect your release. And do it without hands."

"Without hands? Are you injured?"

"I'll explain when I get you out," I said. "Let me look around, I'll be back." I set about to do just that and moved along the outside of the old mud-brick building till I located a door. It was locked and of thick, but old timbers.

I listened but heard nothing on the other side. I would not be able to manipulate the lock with my thumb-less paws but I could smash it. The noise of such a frontal assault would draw anyone inside and that was a problem.

Just as I stood contemplating what to do a steamship on a dock nearby blew its whistle to call the crew from their travels for the midnight curfew. Immediately I whirled and, before the long whistle blast was done, kicked back with my right foot/paw to smash the lock on the door.

The barrier flew inward leaving the dark maw of the portal to call to me.

I entered as quietly, sniffing my way to where I guessed Bobbie's cell to be. I kept listening hard for any sign that my explosive entry had been detected.

"Looks like I got away with it," I thought just as I rounded a corner and ran into a startled Arab sitting on a crate looking at the pictures in a Hollywood screen magazine.

The dark haired man was certainly more startled to see me in my current form than I to see him. This gave me the edge, I lashed out with my right paw and slashed him across the jaw, striking like Jack Sharkey with a preternatural speed before he could cry out an alarm.

I rolled the unconscious and bleeding guard behind some stacked crates and searched him. I found a key on him and, cupping it beneath my paws was able to get it into the lock on the cell door.

When the door swung out I slipped in to see Bobbie lashed to a chair in the center of the room. He looked up with a hopeful expression that quickly changed to shock when he saw me.

"Horatio?" He stammered. I saw his dusky skin go pale as he looked at my lupine form but I had to ignore it.

"I know this is hard to see, Bobbie," I said as I entered. "But imagine how I feel; your wishing ring has done quite a number on me."

Hearing my voice come from the apparition before him seemed to startle him even more but as I watched he took a deep breath and then grinned.

"Did I not tell you that my people have the secrets of the ages?" He was suddenly his old self.

He was indeed the worse for wear, his cheek bruised and his lower lip split and puffy. He saw me staring.

"I assure you, you look worse, Horatio."

I made my way across the room and applied myself to the knots, which was not easy with my non-human hands.

"Do be alacritous, my friend," he said. "They could be upon us any moment."

"Doing my best, Bobbie," I said. I finally resorted to gnawing at the knots with my razor sharp teeth and in a few moments had him free.

"This is most unusual," he said as he stared at me. He stood to get circulation going in his limbs and shook his arms and legs. "But I see why you did not summon other help."

"Let's get out of here," I said. "They may come to check on you."

We headed out into the hall and I pointed to the unconscious guard behind the boxes. "He had a gun on him," I said. "But I couldn't pick it up with these." I held up my forepaws.

Bobbie gleefully pulled a semi-automatic pistol from the guard's waistband, also securing out a curved dagger-in-sheath. "Now I feel complete again," he grinned. "See, the barbarous roots of my people have come to the surface."

"We better be leaving," I said. "I heard them talking they work for someone called El Nassr."

"The Hawk has been opposed to my father's policies," Bobbie said. "He would have our resources turned over to the Russians for his own gain."

"We can discuss that later," I said. "Right now the door out is over that way." I started to turn but he stopped me with a hand on my hairy arm.

"No, Horatio," he said. His grin now looked even more feral than my savage appearance. "They will only try kidnap me again; my people are not good at retreating; we are much better at attacking!"

Before I could stop him he headed further into the warehouse to hunt his kidnappers. I had little choice but to follow.

● ● ●

I moved to beside Bobbie and pointed toward where I knew the kidnappers were. "I can smell them that way," I said. "There are four of them." He nodded and moved off with a determination on his face that I had not seen before, as if the jolly Bobbie was a mask.

"A bit of Henry Five," I thought. "Seems he has stepped up to the breech!"

We moved between a large bales of cotton that made a narrow corridor along one side of the large warehouse. My sensitive nose led us to the room where the other kidnappers were still squabbling among themselves. The loud Arabic voice was still lobbying for simply killing Bobbie and keeping it a secret from his father so they could blackmail the Emir.

"I see why you rushed in," Bobbie said. "Some people are just impatient." He grinned at me like the old Bobbie and added, "I guess I'm one of them."

As he spoke he raced forward with a fierce battle cry and kicked the door inward.

The occupants of the room whirled at the intrusion and with the reflexes of men who spent their life living on the edge. Guns were in the hands of two men and knives in the others before Bobbie had passed through the portal.

The Emir's son fired his pistol and one of the gunman fell with a bullet through his head.

The other gunman returned fire but the bullets went wide and licked wood from the doorsill. Bobbie returned fire and a heated gun battle ensued.

While the bullets flew the two remaining thugs charged my charge with their knives. I charged as well.

My transformed lupine body propelled me into the two men, smashing into one with a hard rugby body block while I flailed a hind paws to slash the second in the arm with my razor-like nails. He dropped his knife.

I could not grapple in the conventional sense but the inner animal nature my transformation had released served me well in the fray. I mauled the man I fought, ripping into him with my jaws so that blood flew freely till he was mercifully unconscious. Then I whirled to face the now disarmed thug.

The gunshots had ended and the armed kidnapper was down, shot in the stomach. Bobbie turned to aid me but at that moment the remaining thug got a good look at me, screamed "Anubis!" and raced from the room.

"Well, that seems to be that," Bobbie said as he shot the moaning gunman through the head with casual calm that spoke of his Bedouin roots. "Shall we go get a drink? I am parched!"

• • •

We made it back to our hotel via the same route I had come, unseen and unopposed. Once there Bobbie had champagne sent up to the suite and we sat and sipped while we examined my circumstance.

"I have used my one wish, apparently," he said as he reclined on a divan. He drank with some delicacy as his cut lip was now badly swollen.

"Well, I can not put the ring on," I said. I held up a paw to illustrate my point. I had a silver punchbowl filled with champagne and was using both my paws to hold it and slurp the bubbly. "Perhaps we can find someone to wear it and wish me back?"

"Honestly, Horatio, even if I hand it to someone and tell them I will give them untold riches to make the wish; do you think they will do it or do you think they will wish to be Emir themselves?"

His argument was a realist's assessment of human nature but it did nothing to comfort me.

"Staying this way is not a very pleasant prospect, Bobbie," I said as I sipped my drink. He shrugged.

"Well, it could be worse, you might not have a wealthy compatriot who owes you a blood debt, eh?" His smile was devil-may-care. "Not to worry, after all, where is that British stiff upper lip?"

I touched my right paw to my mouth. "More of a muzzle." I leaned down and took a sip of champagne in a very lupine gesture then smiled back at him. "But if I don't change back when the moon goes down I know a fellow named Dr. Argent in England who might know a bit about my condition, in the meantime, my bowl of bubbly is getting low, do pour me a bit more, and while I'm thinking of it, I could use a nice rare steak!"

The End

The Lady Wore Vengeance

by Tommy Hancock

She cut a haunting silhouette out of the darkness of the office doorway, only the dull jaundiced glow of the single light bulb dangling in the hallway behind her. Her left hand rested on its matching hip, delicate, long fingers riding dangerous, deadly curves. Her right hand snaked elegantly up the doorjamb above her head, giving her shape the look of a sultry hourglass in repose. Hints of crimson along her form flickered in and out of the black of night seeping in through the windows of my office. A tight fitting, perfectly suggestive red dress, tailor made for her by some dowager on the outskirts of Paris, if I remembered correctly. It was the last thing I'd seen her wearing before her unannounced, but not wholly unexpected arrival a few minutes ago. The last thing she'd probably ever wear.

"As stunning as ever," I said, turning my back to my desk and shrugging back into the trench coat I'd nearly shuffled off seconds before. I'd only just opened the door, put the brown paper sack cradling my bottle of dinner and desert on the corner of my desk when those tiny little hairs, those holdovers from earlier states of evolution great minds tell us, stood up and did their 'Somebody's coming' dance along the back of my neck. No footfalls on the ancient stairs, no pained sigh of the third story hallway floor, no hushed whisper of skin and fabric against the wood of the door. No sound. Just a sudden chill running like the blood of a dying winter down my back. "Being dead and buried a month looks better on you than most."

"Aw," she cooed, her voice like thick velvet poured over melting ice. Just soft enough to breathe new life into old memories, but rough enough to remind me why the memories were from long ago. "I bet those are words you don't say often to old girlfriends."

"More than I'd like to admit." I stood, studied her as my eyes adjusted to the darkness. Familiarity allowed the shapes of the battered couch and the war scarred hat rack to solidify. The twin windows in the wall to the right gave off such little light due to opening on the dullest alleyway in the city, but still enough to pierce the black of a still unlit room. Yet as my eyes played along her exquisite road map of a body, a joyride I'd taken as a naïve boy who didn't know better and one I'd gotten off of as a jaded man who just didn't give a damn anymore, I saw more dark than light. Shadow danced around her like flickering streamers, allowing glimpses of the dress, a hint of thigh through the slit, the shimmer of her matching red heels. But unlike the rest of the room, the darkness around her seemed alive. And selfish.

I took a deep breath, the scent of lilacs and earth filling my nostrils. Lilacs I remembered. The smell of dirt laced with decay was new for her, but not unfamiliar. "So," I offered, "you just come back to be on display in my doorway?"

The shadows around her face shifted just enough to allow me to see those pouting scarlet lips, the bottom one making like the eaves of a roof over her chin. "Didn't you ever have manners? Too much to ask for you to invite a lady in?"

I stepped forward, crossing my mouse hole of an office nearly in one stride. Standing now only three or four feet from her, I still only saw hints and glimmers in the dark. It worked that way sometimes, I knew. I also knew a little more than I had minutes ago about who she now was. Or more, what she was on her way to becoming. "You carried being a lady like most men wear ties. Loose and long. But yeah," I said, my hands idly pulling my trench coat tighter, closed, "sure. I think there's just barely room enough in this hovel for two."

She laughed; something lost between a giggle and a purr, and slinked toward me. As she moved, the lingering black that had before clung and crawled over her like silken ribbons faded and the woman I'd known as Evelyn Passmore, never ever Eve or Evie, came into view.

She moved in the dress as if she flowed inside of it, all the grace of a lazy river ready to turn into raging rapids if just given enough reason. The frock itself still held much of its luster, only slightly dampened by a film of ashen dust spotting it. A random thread had begun to unfurl in one place or another, but not in ways that anyone who wasn't looking for it would notice. Hair the color of burnt amber still framed an almost doll-like, oval shaped face that ended in rather a sharp chin, the point softened slightly by the thickness of her lips. I let a sardonic smile curl my mouth as she stopped just inches from me, allowing me the once over. She really didn't look like someone who'd lain in a coffin for the last thirty days. A tease here, a lint brush there, and she'd be ready to rejoin the elite of the city in their nightclubs and society balls again. Except for her skin and the eyes. They were now more suited to the darker pursuits that Evelyn had always found fascinating.

Once vibrant, almost china white to go with the dollish face, her skin was now pallid, gray like burgeoning storm clouds. Her flesh was mottled, her face a uniform light shade, while her bare arms sported spots, almost like dark, deep gray bruises. What was revealed of her chest by the low cut of the dress also looked as if it had begun to pass from healthy to decomposing, but only slightly. And her eyes, the glittering green of dew heavy grass before, they had changed as well. Black, darker than starless nights, a shade heavier than whatever evil might lurk in hidden hearts. As black as the arts that Evelyn Passmore had more than dabbled in, but they weren't dead eyes. They simmered with life in a way they never had before. An unearthly, corrupted life, filled with a morbid electric hunger that would never know peace and only demand more.

She leaned forward and then draped herself on me, pinning her body to my chest like a quickly wilting corsage. I felt her breasts rise and fall; her lungs filling with air they no longer needed more out of routine than necessity. She stared ahead for a second, her eyes squarely planted at the base of my neck, and then she looked down, a throaty chuckle rolling out from her welcoming mouth. Her hands slid from around my neck and snaked their way down my chest, the right one hesitating about mid stomach on the right side.

"You were always glad to see me," she mewled, her fingers teasing the hard bulge, dancing along the length of it.

"Maybe," I said, "but you know nature didn't leave me that well armed." I pulled back slightly, forcing her fingers to fall away from their exploration. "Holster, is the same place it's always been."

"Okay," she replied, a gray tongue playfully wetting her scarlet lips, "Just seems… longer than I remember."

"World changes every day," I said, turning away, giving her my left profile, the one she said she always favored. "What keeps a man alive has to change with it. And that," I said, my eyes falling on the bagged bottle that sadly was not going to get my attention as I had planned, "begs the question. What's keeping you alive, Evelyn? Why are you here?"

I let silence rise in the room like a slow tide. Just as the quiet passed from uncomfortable to all encompassing, she breathed in sharply. Old habits died hard, apparently. Just like her.

"I died." She said it as if it was something I'd not known, something she was reporting for the first time. And I let her continue on, easiest way to get anyone to talk was to let them do it naturally, in their own time. "I know it wasn't much of a surprise to most," she looked down at the floor, her hands folded in front of her, forming a gray fleshy arrow pointing at the floor. "The way I was living. The parties, the drinking." She paused. "The men. And the women."

"But," her voice sounded different, almost as if an innocence that had never truly been there was edging its way in, "I was actually a little caught off guard by my death. I'd taken precautions, I thought. Dabbling here and there with the dark things," I grimaced at her familiar pet name for something so much more complicated than she made it sound, "That became more than just playing around. But you knew that."

She'd raised her head; I felt her eyes fall heavy on me. "Yeah," I answered because she expected it. "I never cared for magic. Have no use for it."

"I know. You made that quite clear when you walked out of my room two years ago. Funny," she mused, taking a step closer to my desk, to me. "That's when all that went from party games and silly little séances to...more." She waited, wondering if the guilt she'd slung at me had hit its mark. I didn't move a muscle. "And I got pretty good at it," she continued, disappointment tingeing her words. "Learning the right words, putting all the pieces together. Moving up in that world, so to speak. Didn't think anything could stop me. Or hurt me."

"Until it did." I turned to face her again. She had drifted to the corner of my desk opposite me, her fingers out, teasing the battered metal. "You were awful young, everyone said, for a heart attack."

"Is that what they said? Everyone?"

"No. The coroner said he didn't know of any reason your heart should have just exploded the way it did. Nothing left but tiny pieces scattered all inside your chest. Like confetti, he'd said."

Her head bobbed up and down, a shuddering nod. "There were reasons—and all of them far beyond highballs and spirit boards. I had made...deals, allied myself with others who went from playing to pursuing the dark things like I did. Eager to become a part of what made the world turn, what really makes everything around us move forward. You know," her words came faster now, a burst of passion behind them, "that it is what comes out of the shadows that fuels what light we have. You know that."

"No," I said flatly. "No, I don't."

Her face wrinkled in frustration. "Well, it does. And I wanted to be a part of that. I was tired of being just a person, just someone else for others to use, to move around. I wanted to be a force, a shadow all my own. And I was almost there. Almost there. But I couldn't do it alone. No one can access the dark things that way alone. They..." her words caught in her throat, "they demand too much for just one person to be able to give."

"So, you made deals. And someone, one of your partners, crawfished you. Made you a part of the process instead of one of the benefactors."

"Thought you didn't know anything about magic."

"Never said that, just said I didn't care for it. You were double crossed. Sacrificed."

As the word left my mouth, her entire body trembled. Violently shaking, sounds like sobs rippled out of her. I stepped toward her, and then stopped just as quickly. Her black eyes burned like ebony flames, raging fires fueled by hatred unquenchable.

"Yes," she seethed. "And that is why I am back. For retribution. They..." her voice was little more than a growl, although she struggled to keep the ladylike ring to it, "Someone used me. Killed me, knowing I would come back, wanting me to so a ritual could be finished. But the dark things, they were already in me. They made sure I came back, not mindless, not a thrall, but something else. Something that could take what I needed."

"Yeah," I barked, moving forward suddenly, slapping her hard across the face, "but what flavor?" She jerked back, staring at me, her eyes wide with shock. I slapped her again hard across the left cheek. "You were dead. You're not now." She was looking at me once more, her black eyes narrowed, her scarlet lips opened, her breathing short and ragged. "But the dead come back in so many ways on the side of the street you're walking. So, what are you?" I hit her again on the opposite cheek with my open palm. "Ghoul? Fiend? Somebody's undead plaything?" She glared at me now, anger creasing her gray face. Her eyes were little more than black slits and the red lips peeled back, baring startlingly white teeth. "For once in your life, Evelyn," I roared in her face, "be honest with me and yourself! Show me what you are!"

I raised my hand to hit her once more, but was stopped in mid swing. Her left hand now held my wrist, nails digging like tiny blades into my flesh. The rage in her features had gone from fury to something bestial, the wrath of an animal. Her eyes sliced through me, the black in them almost palpable, seeming to pour forth from them, threatening to envelop me. And her teeth glistened; especially the four canines. A little longer, sharpened to a needle point and wet with saliva and need.

"There you go," I said softly. "Whoever did this to you expected a dumb little lamb wandering to the altar, but you came back as the hunter."

As I spoke, her grip on my wrist relaxed. We both lowered our hands and I watched as her appearance changed once again. The teeth receded and her lips closed. Anger flushed from her face, leaving only sadness. Her eyes widened again, though still dark like the night, and looked woefully at me.

"It's…" she struggled to speak, "not like the book…or those silly movies. It takes time. My heart, it's even back together, though not like before. It doesn't beat, but it's there."

"I know," I said, almost soothingly. "Everything takes time, it's how corruption works," I smiled, "but Lugosi sure makes it look elegant."

"Elegant." The word had no meaning for her as she said it. "It is an existence, like anything else. I am controlled by the same emotions, the same needs. The same… appetite. Just for different food." She turned away, her head lowered. "And those I feed on, they don't change, they don't become. It's…not like that."

"No," I said reaching out to her, my hand falling gently on her shoulder. "That's all fiction and the fact is too terrifying to believe. The idea that a person, dying with hate and unfulfilled vengeance in their heart, is all it takes to come back as a vampire, most minds can't deal with that."

"Not all it takes, "she said quietly. "I opened myself up to this, up to all of it. And I can't stop it. I can't even find the one who did this to me, even though that is why…all of this." She spun around, her hands grabbing my coat lapels, desperation wracking her entire body. "I can't even get the bastard who did this to me! I get distracted! I get hungry and…"

"That's why you came to me," I said, knowing her words would have been something different. "You need a babysitter, someone to hold your hand."

She let go of my coat with her right hand and slapped my face this time. "Go to hell, Mason."

"No, not again," I said grinning through the stinging pain as I pulled away from her, "Alright, I'll play tour guide, make sure you don't dine on the regular folk." The smile never left my lips, "But I work pretty much like your 'dark things'. Nothing's free once you walk through that door, doll."

From somewhere around her waist I didn't see, she raised her right hand, fingers splayed out. In her palm rested two coins. Gold. "Something," she said huskily, "I had hidden away."

"Good thing for me the Ferryman didn't check your bags," I said, taking the gold from her hand. "Now, you may not be Pied Pipering your way back to your killer like they planned, but I bet you have an idea who the most likely candidates are."

She nodded. "I only worked in the darkest things with two people; William Bygard and Fineas."

"Okay," I said, already walking toward the door. "Your nightclub-owning boy toy and the milquetoast husband. Let's start with obvious and work our way to ludicrous, then."

● ● ●

Billy Bygard's Byzantine Club resembled the architectural love child of King Nebuchadnezzar and Pablo Picasso. The building towered over Eighth Street downtown, a facsimile ziggurat, complete with four step-like floors stacked one atop each other, the shrine, Bygard's personal residence and playground, crowning the obscene structure. The building was wrapped in off white and brick red chevrons, the zig zag motif playing hell with one's eyes. The odd look of the club was accentuated by the bursts of color scattered almost haphazardly along the walls. Resembling human figures, paintings dotted the Byzantine, images appearing in muted blues, yellows, and greens, people as if viewed through a prism. Twisted faces, cube like digits, elongated or truncated limbs. The Byzantine struck a chord with customers and passersby, somewhere between fever dream and freakish oddity. That, combined with Bygard's ability to book the best Jazz and Big Band acts in the country kept business booming every night of the week.

I held Evelyn close to me, not in the way lovers out for a night on the town do, but more like a man walking his feral dog, my right hand wrapped like a vise around her left arm. She was still early in her development as a revenant, vampire variety, but what made that problematic was how unpredictable her rather new needs might prove. Agitation, emotional aggravation, and physical aggression were all keys to making her true self, the one I'd provoked ever so slightly in the office, come to the surface. And we were very likely to encounter all three as we topped the last step and entered the Byzantine.

The door opened up on a foyer, no space wasted on a lobby that allowed customers to move from the hat check window immediately into the heart of the beast. Two bars lined the far walls of the first floor, both decorated in the red and white chevrons adorning the outside walls, their tops made from painted black mahogany. Along both walls just past the bars were matching staircases, each passing by the second floor, and an empty doorway on the left side of the building, a bare wall on the right, going past the nonexistent third floor, an illusion from the outside only, and coming together at the singular door into Bygard's home, the fourth floor shrine.

Bygard had been one of Evelyn Passmore's frequent pastimes for years, even back when she and I were teasing one another with talk of wedding bells and picket fences. A veteran of the Great War, Billy had returned to the States with more money than Croesus and a reputation that might have made Machiavelli tremble. Building the Byzantine his first year back, Billy reveled in the Twenties and had so far survived the first five years of the desolate Thirties as if poverty and desperation were good things. And for someone apparently as skilled in the hidden occult as Bygard was believed to be, that was likely true. He'd made quite a name for himself as being the man to get whatever someone mystically-minded might want or need, making the Byzantine his own personal occult black market. It was why he'd been a suitable 'friend' for Evelyn when she decided she wanted to go from parlor magic to more audacious pursuits.

I checked my hat with the precocious little blonde in the box, but kept my coat. I asked Evelyn if she wanted to check her shadow wrap, the rivulets of black back now and dancing about her. She ignored my question and led the way into the club proper. The light was low, cast from fixtures along the wall, each one resembling faces from the twisted, perverse figures painted on the outside. Looking up high, past the fittings, I noticed different lighting. Tiny pinpricks all through the air and along the roof, lining the stairs as well. Flickering little hints of multicolored light, from pink to blue to orange. No visible bulbs from where I stood. Not even like stars, just glimmering hints. Hovering.

I glanced around from our vantage point, a raised dais that marked the end of the entrance. Tables dotted the expansive floor before us and each one was full. The band, Gabriel Yellow and His Heavenly Horns if I knew my music, were staged at the far end of the building from where we stood, tearing into one of their original compositions. An affectation Yellow was known for, playing only his own music. 'Good Lord gave me a gift,' he'd said once, 'Who'm I not to make sure I use it?'

"I don't see him," Evelyn said, her voice low. "He's usually over there." She gestured at the table closest to us to the right. "Likes to stay near the bar."

"Maybe he's changed spots," I offered. "You have been buried a month, remember."

She shook her head. "No, he sat there for other reasons. People like us, we don't change practices easily."

I nodded, knowing she was right. Bygard would have sat at that table for more than quick access to whiskey. Ley lines and conjuring spots, among other possibilities. "Then, he's upstairs. Not home," I said, my eyes climbing the left side stairway to the second floor doorway, "not with the joint hopping. He's in the office."

Evelyn nodded and tugged me along, my hand still on her arm, toward the left bar. As we passed patrons, I recognized several faces and several faces recognized Evelyn. Some whispered about how amazing it was that someone resembled the tragically passed socialite so much. Others, those more into the dark things like Evelyn, either murmured incantations for protection under their alcohol heavy breath or slammed down their last shot and left.

As we turned and walked along the bar heading for the staircase, a man with aspirations of being a mountain, moved from where he'd been impersonating a statue at the bottom of the stairs, since we'd come in. He lumbered toward us, moving away from the bar, out into the open area between it and the tables. He wanted space.

"Mason," his voice was a ragged bass, with only one tone. Mean. "You look like a man wanting to go upstairs."

I stopped and turned, shifting Evelyn behind me, still holding her arm. I raised my head a tad to be able to look into the large man's face, seemingly carved badly out of a head that could have passed for a medium sized granite boulder. Big brown eyes sat nestled deep behind a rather prominent muzzle, his nose large and nostrils flaring as breath escaped them. The mouth was wide and sat atop a prominent chin that led to nearly no neck, only to a pair of shoulders that extended outwardly several feet in each direction. Flat, thick, and strong, punctuated with bulging arms, muscle wrapped like barbed wire spoiling the cut of the tuxedo his job forced him to wear. Hair the color of wet sand crowned the big man's head, thin strands of it slicked back with whatever pomade Bygard probably made him use as well. The same color hair oddly covered his face also, not in the usual fashion of a mustache or a beard, but all over his face. Not perceptible if you didn't want to see it, but there.

"Grierson," I said, "that is just where I am going."

"No." Grierson raised his arms, his bulky hands curling into pudgy fists. "Mister Bygard ain't taking visitors. Not you," his vacuous brown eyes drifted to just over my shoulder, "and especially not her."

Music played on around the little tableau we were beginning to play in and very few people turned from their companions or drinks to pay us attention. The Byzantine was that sort of place where, whether or not you came to drink or summon demons, you didn't ask many questions about anything you saw.

"She's here," I said harshly, "maybe because of Mister Bygard. And I'm here because of her. He'll see me."

"Not standing upright he won't!"

Grierson leapt at me with more grace than his body portrayed. I shoved Evelyn back, and both hands free, stepped into his charge. Just as he swung his hefty right hook, I dipped my shoulder and shoved every bit of myself into his midsection. Breath thundered out of him as he staggered back, bent over.

As we took our first steps in this dance, I noticed something else about Grierson's head. Two tiny bumps peeked out, one from each temple, from under the stringy, wet sand colored hair. Tiny black knots. Tips of horns.

Grierson charged again, this time both arms coming at me, hoping to smash me between the two mammoth fists. The left one grazed my shoulder, knocking me down to the floor. I rolled just in time to avoid the massive leather projectile of Grierson's left shoe pawing at me, sliding my hand into my coat as I moved. Coming up rather shakily on my feet, I shoved my .38 out in front of me. Bent over, ready to run at me again, Grierson felt the six inch barrel slam into the flesh just between his eyes.

A dumb grin worked it's away over his broad mouth. "Bet you don't load silver every day, flatfoot."

"Nope," I said my hand as steady as my voice. "Just plain lead. And that's all it will take with you, Grierson. You're still a baby, as far as werebulls go. Takes time, doesn't it?" My eyes passed over to Evelyn, still standing at the bar. She and Grierson and Bygard, and any of those who wanted the easy road they thought the arcane provided, they all learned too late most of the work in magic, like in anything, took time. "So," I continued, "my little lead slug will canoe your bovine brain just fine. Either give the high sign, Grierson," I had not been blind during our little spat to the number of other tuxedoed types melting from across the bar, all with hands in their jackets, "or I will spread your head like bad butter all over the floor."

Grierson, trapped in his bent position because moving might make my gun go off, raised his beefy right fist, and opened it, five sausage like fingers all pointing to the roof. Like any trained animals, the other bouncers and guards in the Club all returned to their posts, leaving me and the burgeoning minotaur alone in the crowded room.

"Now," I said, pulling the gun back, but keeping it pointed at him, "up we go."

"You," Grierson rumbled, "but not her."

I started to insist; shoving the gun into his prevalent midsection, but Grierson shook his head and pointed toward the staircase. I poked him, gesturing for him to walk that direction and I followed. As we stepped closer, I saw markings on the wooden stair railing. Carvings, shapes dug out of the wood. Each one different, but bearing one similarity. They were filled in with something crystalline, hard, and white.

"Runes." Evelyn's voice drifted from behind me as she looked over my shoulder. "For protection."

Grierson nodded. "He's been up there," he waved a fat hand at the office doorway, "for over a week. None of us…" he hesitated, "nobody like me can get up there. He's got one of the regular girls delivering food to him, but he won't leave."

I turned to face Evelyn, my gun still pointed at Grierson. "Can you stay here?" I asked. "Or is this like an all you can eat diner for you?"

She shook her head. "No, I'll be okay." I didn't waver. She smiled sadly. "I promise. I'll stand here, close to the stairs. The runes, they…they help. They don't hurt if I don't go any closer, but they keep things at bay."

I nodded and handed her my gun. I didn't have to ask if she knew how to use it, I'd shown her years ago. She nodded back and kept it aimed squarely at Grierson's chest. I turned and started up the stairs.

Music drifted up from below as I took each step slowly. I studied the carvings on the rail and the ones I now noticed on the wall to my left. These too were coated in white. A hardened salt mixture. I looked back out over the club as I was about halfway up the stairs. Some of the tiny points of light I'd noticed before were now below me, some of them actually quite close to the stair railing. A sound competed with Yellow's original tune in my ears as I walked up. A whirring, almost a buzzing, not quite like flies, but like something moving quickly. A whole lot of somethings. Tiny wings.

I stopped with just three steps left to go and leaned over the railing, my upper body now above everyone's head. Something whizzed by my ear, touching it. I instinctively slapped at the burning on my skin. Nothing too painful, just a hint of pain, like I'd leaned close to a hot light bulb. The dots of light nearest me moved on their own now, darting back and forth, frenzied, as if my presence upset them. One, the color of an overripe pumpkin flew past my eyes, almost bumping the bridge of my nose. And in that split second, I saw a tiny figure with glowing orange wings appear and vanish just as quickly.

I climbed the last three steps and stopped in front of the office. The doorframe was crowded with more runes, each one sparkling white with salt. A pile of regular salt ran along the bottom of the doorway, from one jamb to the other, stacked about an inch high. I paused a second as I studied the man I saw through the door.

Billy Bygard was a dirty, anxious, bedraggled shade of his usual self. The trademark white tuxedo and matching tie, with black shirt and shoes, was now stained with food, sweat, and fluids I didn't want to guess at. The tie was undone, lying on his ornate oak desk, nearly lost between half eaten meals, empty bottles, and stacks of books. Not pulp magazines or dime store reads, but thick tomes, bound in leather and various skins, some likely human if I knew Bygard.

The man himself was in no better shape than his wardrobe. Considered handsome, even matinee idol material by many, Billy Bygard's face was wan, his jowls sagging and flabby. His eyes, noted to be the bluest in the Byzantine, were murky, heavy lids half hiding them. His skin was dimpled, not in a way that made girls swoon, but more like a strawberry, covered in tiny bumps and divots, like bug bites.

"Stay out, peeper," Bygard snapped, raising his left hand from his lap, a pistol in it. "You're working for them, aren't you? Only reason you'd be here. Stay the hell out. I don't need nothing but this gun to kill you."

"No," I said, holding my hands palm up, "not working for the fairies, Billy. Whatever their beef with you, it has nothing to do with me. But, it seems like even those of the sugar plum variety are out here, and all waiting on you."

"Damn fairies," Bygard swore. "Don't understand how things work. Made a bargain with them, just the way you're supposed to. Not my fault," he kept talking, not really to me, just rambling, "that they don't understand modern talk. Wasn't my job to tell them that what I would get for what I gave them was…was…" I waited. The needle hit the groove on Bygard's mental phonograph again finally. "They owed me…fairies…for what I got them. Fairies, pure and simple, just a few hundred for whatever I wanted. And you know, Mason, you know what the best fairy is for someone like me?"

"Yeah," I answered. "Dead."

He nodded. "Especially the young ones, the kind I bartered for. Not my fault they didn't know that. But now, now they're here to get me. To kill me. They're mean bitches, those little bastards. Their heads are mostly teeth, these kind anyway. Long rows of tiny teeth." His body shook as he chortled, "But they won't get me. Not here. Got in my house upstairs about two weeks ago, almost devoured me then. Had to hide here, but I took care of it. They won't get me here."

I nodded back. "Not here about fairies, Billy. I'm with Evelyn Passmore."

"She's dead. In the ground last month."

"And now she's out of the ground. Downstairs at the bar. And she's mad, Billy. Mad about being killed. Mad about being woken up. Mad and hungry."

"Don't care," Bygard said, shaking his head. "Not on me. She wanted to do more, to go deep, but not with me. We talked about it, but it was pillow talk, if that. No—not me. I had my own plan." He waved the gun in his hand absent mindedly. "Damn fairies. She's not here for me."

"Who then?"

Bygard snickered. "The great Henpecked himself."

I cocked an eyebrow. "Fineas Passmore?"

Billy nodded. "Never met him more than socially up until about two months ago. Anything he needed to cast spells or conjure with he usually sent Evelyn for. Until about two months ago. Then he made a few purchases himself."

"What kind?"

Bygard sat up in his chair, put the gun on the desk and for the first time since I'd walked to the door and his eyes fell on me steady and unwavering. "The most heinous kind. He's after big things, Mason. Tired of just being big man on the block here. Wants to be the only man on the block. Anywhere. And that takes a lot of work. And lives. A whole lot of lives. But," he smiled, almost seeming proud of Passmore's ambitions, "it has to start with one."

"Not for you though, right, Billy?" I gritted my teeth, staring Bygard down. "You wanted to start with a few hundred. A few hundred young fairies. Kids, Billy, don't matter that wings sprout out their tiny backs. Still kids." I turned to walk back down the stairs, pushing my right foot out farther than necessary as I did. The line of salt at the bottom of the doorway scattered, my shoe kicking it down, leaving a broad bare spot of about four inches open. No salt. Just naked wood.

I heard Bygard scream like a little frightened girl and fumble for the gun on his desk as I started back down the stairs. As I walked, I felt the air behind me move; a whoosh filling my ears, like thousands of tiny little insects had just flown past. About halfway down, bloodcurdling shrieks trumpeted louder than anything in Gabriel Yellow's band and another buzzing sounded above. Not like flies, but like saws, like a thousand tiny sharp jaws cutting and tearing. And as I reached the bottom of the stairs, the entire Byzantine was deathly quiet, except for the whimpering coming from Billy Bygard's office, now suddenly aglow with a kaleidoscope of pulsating light.

A few brave souls worried about their paychecks and human enough shoved by me, bolting up the stairs. Grierson just stood stock still, his eyes locked on the office above.

I paused in front of Evelyn long enough to take back my gun in one hand and a firm grip on her arm with the other.

"Time for you to go home," I said as we walked toward the foyer.

• • •

"Come in, Evelyn, darling."

She glanced to her right at me, her left hand still in a fist, still raised after knocking on the door. I nodded and she pushed the lever down on the ornate brass handle and pushed the penthouse door open.

She walked in, with me a step or two behind her. I'd not been in the Passmore home, but it resembled almost every other penthouse I'd accidentally found myself in before. Ornate furnishings, a mixture of solid wood antiques and more modern steel and leather furniture. Dark paneled walls, black in the entryway and first living room, a rustic bark like brown in the den, dining room, and beyond, from what I could see. But no Fineas.

"The balcony, Evelyn," his tinny voice sounded as if he were in the same room with us. "You know how I enjoy conjuring in the night air."

She walked on, weaving her way through the house. I kept pace. There was little to worry about. Fineas had fully expected her, asked her in when she announced herself. He'd used one of the earliest tricks people of his sort learn, throwing his voice. We walked through each room and as we moved, I knew Evelyn's husband was no amateur. Little clues, like floating vases and flickering images framed on the walls, memories captured in some spell that played over and over like movies, filled the penthouse. Fineas Passmore was reveling in the dark things.

"Ah," he said as she rounded the corner. The sound that left his thin lipped mouth when I stepped into view behind her was somewhere between a grumble and growl. "Oh," he groaned, "Freeman Mason, the detective. What's the matter, love? Didn't you know your way home?"

Fineas Passmore walked into the second living room from the balcony through open French doors. He was a tall, gaunt man, a face of angles and corners centered around a vulture's beak of a nose. A ring of red hair circled from one temple to the other, no follicles adorning the top of his pate. He wore likely what he'd worn to work at Passmore Manufacturing earlier that day, gray business suit, white shirt. He'd put on a bit of weight since the funeral a month ago, but largely still resembled a poorly constructed scarecrow, only one with more stuffing about the gut now. His left hand was empty, held loosely against his chest. The right one clasped a silver goblet, a large mouthed chalice with a single black jewel set in its bowl and green tendrils of smoke curling up over its lip.

I had wondered when the nuptials between Fineas and Evelyn had been announced over a year ago just what had drawn them together. Everyone else took bets on the obvious. Money was all Fineas had to offer to anyone. But I knew how little Evelyn cared about money, or better, I knew what she wanted money for. She and Fineas had had to share other interests. And that had brought us all to this moment.

"I knew the way," Evelyn said, her voice erratic, jagged like broken glass. I watched her shoulders tense as she stopped walking about ten feet from her widowed husband. "But I didn't have to come."

"Oh," Fineas said, "but you did. Don't you remember?" He chuckled, the sound of fingernails on a chalkboard, and began walking in a small circle, waving the silver cup back and forth in front of him. "Of course you don't. You died that night. Died because it was your time." He laughed again. "Because I needed you to. You showed me, Evelyn, what power could do for us. You did. But I wanted it for me. Only for me. And now," he stopped his pacing, "you're going to die again to give it to me."

"You're not listening, Passmore," I said. "She didn't come here because of your summoning. She came back not knowing who'd killed her. She came back only for one thing."

Realization crept over Fineas Passmore's face like a death shroud. Hints of terror filled his beady hazel eyes as he said, "What do you know, Mason? You're not...one of us."

"Right." I nodded. "But look at her, Fineas. You'll know I'm telling the truth. Look at her face. Into her eyes if you can."

I watched as Passmore turned his gaze from me to Evelyn. Fear contorted his features as if he were having a seizure. His body shook as he staggered back, his empty left hand reaching behind him, feeling for the balcony railing. His right hand somehow clung to the cup, unwilling to release it at any cost.

"No!" he shouted as Evelyn moved after him slowly. "I...I did it all right! You were given! All the words, all the pieces were put together! You can't be...that! You were my sacrifice!"

The sound that erupted from Evelyn Passmore was without description. Shrill and deafening, it caused me to wince even as I rushed forward. She was already moving herself, her feet barely seeming to touch the ground. Her arms were in the air, her hands now little more than gray talons, long black nails extending from them. I ran at her back, throwing my coat open. Passmore's eyes somehow detached from Evelyn and passed to me as the light of the room caught the silver glint in my holster. I drew the blade from its scabbard, the one that hung just below my holstered gun from my shoulder, and with the shout of her name, stabbed Evelyn Passmore dead center in the back with a silver tipped short sword.

I reached around her body with my free arm as I pulled the blade out. She rolled in my grasp, turning over on her back. I dropped to one knee, lowering her to the ground. Every bit of beauty that had marked her as Evelyn Passmore was absent from her face. What looked up at me now with hellishly black narrow eyes was a manipulation of the occult, a monstrosity. Pointed ears, fangs that could not be contained by a closed mouth, and thick, strong lips as red as the blood they demanded. What had been a nose was only two nostrils now, holes set deep into charcoal gray skin.

"Why, Free?" she whispered. I'd dealt a crippling blow to her heart, sickening it with silver, but not a final one. "Why help him?"

"I'm not," I said, raising the sword up so she could see it, black ichor coating it, but barely dripping. "But you're no better than he is, sweetheart. Worse, in fact. You came to kill him, but you weren't going to vanish in a wisp of fog after that. You'd have stayed, kept feeding, and gone back to whatever it was got you into this."

Her lips twisted into what might have been a knowing grin around enlarged fangs. "You always said...you didn't have...much use for magic."

"I don't," I said. As I swung the sword down. "Doesn't mean I don't know how to kill it."

The blade sliced through her neck with one stroke, slicing flesh and bone like paper. I dropped her body as her head struck the floor, rolling over on its side. Her left profile was always her best, too.

I stood, looking at Fineas Passmore now framed in the open French doors. His green eyes stared as decay gripped his wife's body and head, skin began to peel, and a stench was filling the room. And then he looked up at me and smiled.

"Thank you, Mason," Passmore said, raising the goblet before him. "Death didn't have to be at my hand, she just had to die doubly. And with a few more words..."

The short sword clattered as it hit the marble floor. I drew my gun from its holster and pointed it at Passmore, pulling the trigger as I moved. His bald head exploded in a burst of vibrant pink matter as I fired three shots through it. He staggered, almost as if he were only drunk, the magic words just on the tip of his tongue as blood ran over them. The silver chalice tilted, and then tipped. A purple fluid started to fall to the balcony as Passmore stumbled back, but every drop evaporated into green smoke before hitting the ground. I walked forward, Passmore's already dead body striking the balcony railing. I knocked the chalice out of his hand with my gun hand and pushed him over the rail with my other.

I watched the corpse fall fourteen stories. Tumble ventilated head over heel, a stream of gore following it like the tail of a horrific comet. As Passmore thudded into the almost empty street below, someon from down there screamed. And I smiled. It was a real scream of surprise and terror. Of someone who was on her way home from a late shift at the diner two blocks over. Or a showgirl rushing to get to the stage door before she was fired. Or maybe a bag lady startled from her regular trashcan rummaging. Whoever it belonged to, it was a scream. And the first really human sound I'd heard since Evelyn posed in my doorway hours ago.

The End

The Sleeping Sun

by Nancy A. Hansen

Dark of hair and pale of countenance, Darya Valhoven, heir apparent to the realm of Elverune, Gateway to the Cold North, walked the blood-drenched battlefield in her bridal dress, though she wore it simply to be recognized by her own countrymen. The incursion of the fierce Nordi forces on the pass their castle protected had postponed any celebration. Now she feared both her father and her betrothed lay amongst the dead, for while the sleeping sun had finally risen for the season, it had suddenly turned black in the sky.

● ● ●

When word was brought that the Nordi were amassing on Elverune's border yet again, Raimo Valhoven had called his men to arms. Her beloved Nikko had ridden off proudly on his big black destrier with the other knights and their squires. Ranks of common soldiers marched behind them, leaving only their fortress home's wall guards and housecarls to protect her and the servants. The intention was to cut the invaders off before they could gather enough strength of numbers to build and drag siege weapons along behind them. Being the northernmost outpost in the cold lands of the long winter darkness, Elverune could not expect reinforcements for weeks, though messengers had been sent out to other realms to sue for assistance. The bottleneck canyon between sheer slopes that the gatehouse spanned could be held, were there sufficient numbers of troops in place *before* the enemy reached it.

Word had reached Darya that the conflict did not go well. Because they could not spare the guards, she had ridden out unaccompanied to see how the army fared. A lone person traveling fast could make the gate in two days of intense traveling. Wrapped in a dark cloak, she had galloped unremarked upon past many a bullock-pulled wain or overloaded donkey hauling the dead and dying home.

When she arrived, the deeper darkness of evening had fallen, and the fiercest fighting of the battle raged just beyond the pale illumination of the torch lit gate. She dismounted and tossed the reins of her winded mount to a surprised stable boy. Taking the spiraling stairs inside a tower two at a time, her heart thumped like a war drum in her breast. Screams of pain and terror from man and beast, vile oaths and cursing, the clang of weapons and armor, and grunts of laboring men, were deafening as they echoed off the steep rock walls around them.

Darya's fists were balled and her mind in a whirl as she stood atop the tower and tried to make sense of the half-seen knots of combatants struggling below, unable to pick out who was friend or foe. All night long she remained up there like a shadow, staring out over the shifting battlefield, her heart leaden with dread for loved ones and countrymen alike.

As day broke, the colossal doors still stood. Yet as the first hints of dawn struggled to light the mountainsides, she saw how steep the price had been. Even the gate guards were nearly decimated, for they had been forced to join the fray. Only the archers were left unscathed; a mere handful of men. She spoke heartening words to them as she watched the retreat of the enemy and the remainder of their own warriors giving chase, then hurried down as soon as it was deemed safe enough. At her insistence, the boy who had taken her horse into their empty stable the eve before retrieved her mount and led them through a curving passage and out the well-hidden sally port.

• • •

The cold steppes beyond the bottleneck canyon stretched between crags too steep and barren for anything bigger than a goat to climb. The battle itself had spread out for over a league. Their own army had taken grievous losses, but still had held the Nordi in check. Scouts brought word that the invaders were joining forces with the savage men who lived beyond the pass. They would come back in greater numbers with a battering ram, to try to bring the pass gate down. They had only retreated because they shunned the sunlight. The Nordi only attacked during the winter darkness, or at night.

The stink of putrefaction had already begun to fill the air, and Darya gagged more than once as she passed bodies that had bloated or been disemboweled. So many good men dead! So terrible to leave them thus. Yet, it would take time they didn't have to sort and gather the corpses, prepare remains, and sing their own onward to the hall of the gods, and dig a pit to toss the unconsecrated infidel into. They must regroup before the Nordi returned.

Where the fighting had been the most intense, the swift-footed courser she'd ridden could not wend his way through the destruction and slaughter without shying at the blood and gore. In a side-saddle, she'd be tossed if he reared and came down hard. She left the snorting gelding tied to a shrub, and doffed her cloak to cover his eyes, wandering through the battlefield alone. Oblivious to the cold winds sweeping down the mountainsides, or the mud, gore, and filth that darkened the hem of her once expensive dress, Darya was disconsolate and seething with foreboding thoughts.

Would not someone who had recognized her come forth? Were none of the best still alive? Would there be no one left to lead them in the next battle to protect their homeland? Did the long sleeping sun turning black foretell the end of her line?

The sky above roiled with clouds, for they were on the cusp between the long days of dark winter and the return of the season of light, and with that often came storms. When they cleared, the sun's face remained hidden from view. As if to accent the sense of doom and despair, the rusty cawing of crows, the wheezy croaking ravens, and the occasional screech of a scavenging eagle were the only living sounds for miles. Shadowy silent wraiths of the air, vultures wheeled overhead, circling before they flapped down to hop awkwardly about; yanking at the corpses, the big birds' naked heads splotched with ichor. Darya's stomach lurched at the thought of all those valiant men, as well as their bitter foes, becoming no more than a feast for the carrion pickers.

Their men at arms had died bravely, for while their wounds were grievous, they had fought until they dropped. Foot soldiers clad in dark leather with plating lay scattered about where they fell, pikes or axes and round shields of wood with dark iron studding dropped nearby, short stabbing swords still in many lifeless hands. Armored knights in bright surcoats marking their orders had either been felled with their mounts, or had died fighting on foot, their great destriers studded with arrows or run through by spears. No one had retreated to save his own skin. The soldiers of Elverune were staunch, and gave their lives freely to protect their land.

Nowhere though could she find evidence of her father or her beloved. Darya knew that they had either died or were too weak to rise. Had one or the other lived, he would have been on his feet, marshaling the few who survived to put up some sort of defense. Most of the dead had been killed on the spot, but many who had clung to life had been ruthlessly slain by the enemy before they withdrew.

Looking around, she did spot one lone creature who still remained upright. A single dark bay stallion, his head bowed and no more than a flank wounded lightly by an arrow, stood guard over his master. She picked her way toward him, and whistled. The horse's head came up, his ears pricked forward, and he whinnied eagerly. As she drew closer, she recognized him, and her heart gave a leap, for this horse was Rusko, Erno Eaglestone's regular mount! Darya stroked Rusko's head until the powerful and restive horse quieted, and then she snapped the shaft and gently tugged the arrow from his flank, avoiding his steel-shod reflexive kick. The wound bled, but it was shallow, so it would heal.

Always smiling Erno, his pale blond locks bloodied beneath a dented helm, lay senseless nearby, having been brained by a Nordi warhammer before Rusko kicked the enemy man's face in. As she drew closer, Darya noted that Erno still breathed, and her heart leapt. She knelt at the side of the first live man she actually recognized, one of her father's favored young guards; a friend and always a boon companion to her own Nikko.

"Erno, do you know me?" Darya asked in a deep and throaty voice choked with emotion as she gently eased the battered helm from his head. The scalp beneath had split open when the metal buckled, and the wound had bled copiously, but it did not penetrate the skull, though there was no way of knowing if his wits had been scrambled.

"A woman? Lady Darya?" he queried weakly with a thick tongue as his eyes fluttered open and he struggled to rise. Heedless of the blood staining her sleeve, she boosted his head and shoulders, and gave him a sip of watered wine from her own skin. "That helps, though my head throbs so.

"Gah...how I wish that was mead though!" he added with a crooked grin lighting his still boyish face as his blue eyes struggled to focus. "Am I not dead?"

"No, you live," she reassured him. "But what of my father, and Nikko?"

"I know not," he admitted without enthusiasm. "We were overrun, and the cursed Nordi brought wolf dogs to slow down the knights by hamstringing the horses. Many of the men were thrown or crushed when a horse went down suddenly. Old Rusko here was one of the few who managed to avoid them, but because of the dogs, we all got separated. I lost sight of the Lendmann and the others; it was such a brutal battle. I will help you look for them," he added, slowly pulling himself to his feet with her help. Erno was not tall, but he was solid and strong; well built and no lightweight. Yet he wavered and swayed drunkenly, and Darya had to curl her arm around his back so that he could concentrate on putting one foot before the other without falling. His sword lay nearby, and she picked it up, and handed it to him as he grabbed Rusko's bridle to steady himself before sheathing it. "I fear I can't ride yet," he said as his head spun.

"We'll lead him," she said, taking hold of the reins, but walking slowly, allowing the horse and his master to limp along at their own pace. Somehow, having at least one man she knew beside her made it seem as if all was not lost. Like her father before her, Darya was grim and realistic. They would likely all die when the Nordi came back with reinforcements, but if she could gather enough men to her side; they would hold the invaders off as long as possible.

The farther down the battlefield they wandered, the more living men they encountered. Many were badly wounded and some died soon afterward, but a few struggled to regain their feet at the sight of Darya. With a joyous shout from Erno, they found her father's lanky and taciturn squire Johan, who had taken an arrow to the off shoulder but fought on until pain and exhaustion had forced him to sit down with his back against the charred but still standing base of a wooden lookout tower. He heard them coming, and his blue eyes fluttered open. He lifted his head weakly, so that they could see the small clump of chin whiskers on his narrow face beneath his mail coif. "My Lady!" he said in surprise, his head bobbing tiredly in a nod of deference, "Tell me you have not come here to surrender to these troll-kin!"

"No Johan, I have come to rekindle the fight, and put the heart back in our countrymen," she said with feeling. "Can you rise?"

"I will, if that is the way of it," the young man said, and before they could get to him, he grabbed the arrow shaft protruding from his shoulder and broke it off without any more than a grunt and a grimace. Darya pulled the remaining part from the far side…at least it had not penetrated a lung. Before Erno could offer a hand, Johan was back on his feet and fumbling one-handed for his sword.

"My father…he is dead?" she asked him in trepidation. Johan sighed, and he pointed back to the left.

"Over there. We guarded him until they pushed us back here. He died bravely," he added, trying hard not to show emotion for the elder man he'd idolized. She turned before they could see the moistness brightening her eyes and made her way through the carnage to where their battle standard lay shrouding the broken body of Raimos Valhoven, last Lendmann of Elverune. He'd been run through by a spear, and lay pinned to his own gray warhorse, who had fallen half onto him. She knelt by his side with head bowed, hiding the tears that fell silently. There was no sobbing or wailing, no tearing of hair, for the only living child of such a man would not allow herself a public demonstration of weakness.

Even many hours dead and rigid from the cold, his face was as always serene, his grizzled beard bloodied but trimmed neatly beneath his coif. Someone had closed his eyes out of respect. His helm lay nearby, and his great sword was half buried beneath the horse's body. He had drawn it before he fell, and fortunately it lay undamaged; just out of sight, so it had not been taken as plunder. With some effort, she tugged it free, and held it in her hand, testing the blade, before she set it aside. She lifted the standard, the gold stitching of a mountain cat rampant on the red of the bloody sunrise of winter's ending, and waved it overhead, for here lay the greatest man she had ever known.

"Lady Darya!" called a man with a guttural voice from somewhere to her right, and she spun around. Marko Forkbeard was struggling to extricate himself from beneath a pile of men he had killed. He was covered in blood and gore, most of it not his own. Forkbeard was not her favorite of the men Nikko had surrounded himself with, for he drank hard and boasted much in coarse jests, and his hands ran free with ladies who were many stations above him. He was broad shouldered and blocky-built, all muscles and brawn, and he swung either sword or axe with deadly accuracy. He levered himself to his feet with his sword, and stepping over bodies, limped over to where she stood holding up their flag.

"Aye, that's the end of a good Lord," he said gruffly. He didn't seem surprised to see her there. "You'd best leave, My Lady; they'll be back, you know."

"Do *not* presume to tell me what to do, because I have come to lead the next battle," she said with venom, and viciously jammed the rod end of the standard into the ground. For some reason, Marko always infuriated her. She spun on him abruptly. "What news have you of Nikko?"

He shrugged as Erno and Johan made their way over to her with a knight's banner, their faces grim with weariness and pain. Other men dragged themselves and each other out of the dead, trying to reach her side.

"Unfortunately, I know naught of him. We fought separately, for he rode with the knights. I prefer my two feet on the ground," he added dryly. Marko was not known for his horsemanship, for he'd ridden more than one steed to death. "I last saw him when we were ordered to secure the gates. He blew the horn, and then he and his van went galloping hard at the flanks of the retreating Nordi. I can't even see their horses from here," he added, surveying the battlefield.

"I need to find him," Darya insisted, as she withdrew Erno's sword from the scabbard on Rusko and handed it off, shoving her father's blade in its place. "None of you are fit to ride, so take this time to get my father off the field, and then gather any men who can still fight. Someone give me a hand up first though!" She was trying to mount, but the war horse was taller than those she was used to, and the high pommel and cantle along with the long, full skirt of the gown impeded her from swinging a leg up to sit astride him. She nearly fell twice when the restive equine began to circle in his nervousness. In irritation, she took a fierce hold on his bridle and drew her dagger.

Erno started forward, but stopped when she bent over and slit the gown front and back, from knee to hem.

Marko knelt to offer his hands to help her up, but she spurned them. He'd see enough leg as it was, and Darya was not giving him a glance up inside her dress. With a strong grip on the bridle and high pommel, and a boot in the near stirrup, she finally managed to heave herself astride. Erno, ignoring his throbbing head, adjusted the stirrups for her and checked the girth straps while Johan handed up the knight's banner. She nodded her thanks, not trusting her voice, and then couched the pole of the banner in the crook of her arm before reining the big horse around. Digging the heels of her little low boots into the sides of the big horse, she headed off without waiting for anyone to tell her it was too dangerous to go out there alone, the banner snapping behind her.

"That is a special kind of woman," Erno said with a half-grin as he and the other three watched her ride away on the big war horse.

"She is a Valkyrie," Johan agreed as he looked around to see who might still be alive enough to fight.

"She just needs a strong man to tame her," Marko commented with something between a smirk and a sneer on his face.

"Don't ever let Nikko hear you say that," Erno commented as he slogged on after Johan, who was already trying to find a way to pry the dead horse off his late Lord.

● ● ●

Darya rode well, but the field was littered with bodies, so it was slow going. Rusko plodded his way around and through most of them as she scanned the field ahead, looking for men she knew. She was far more familiar with the knights, for they often came to her father's banquets to pay their respects, as well as to any war councils, and she'd been obliged to sit in on both. Now she was grateful for what she had learned.

Eventually she began to find armored bodies and horses wandering lost, with the occasional wounded man dragging himself along. None she recognized yet, other than one horse, the dappled gray gelding of Tomas the Fatherless, Nikko's squire. Harma shied as she approached, and she had to roll up the standard, which was spooking him, before leaning out over Rusko's broad neck and sweeping up his reins. The gray gelding lead fine after that, and she was able to hoist the banner again, allowing it to sweep overhead, cracking and fluttering as they trotted forth.

The field was less crowded here, though well trampled, and the bodies of the slain were farther apart. More Nordi were amongst them, but some knights and their mounts as well, and she mourned each of the men she knew well. She named them, and blessed them with a tear shed for lives given bravely, but went on. They passed through a wooded copse, her eyes searching all around her for possible ambush, and seeing naught but two dogs and a Nordi with a shaven head lying dead together, his spear broken at his side. Lances had taken them down. The men she sought had come this way, and her heart leapt with hope that Nikko was amongst the living yet.

Down a slope, she came upon the end of the battle, where equal numbers of her countrymen and their aggressors lay dead or dying. Only a few knights were still well enough to be on their feet, and they trudged through the carnage, killing whatever enemies they could still find alive, assisting the survivors of their rank, and praying with those whose end was near. Tomas was amongst the living, and he stood over Nikko, for the dusky black stallion Korppi had thrown her beloved after stumbling over the body of another horse and breaking a leg. Darya rode up and quickly dismounted, kneeling down beside Nikko, whose sightless eyes stared at nothing.

"He is dead, My Lady," the tall and slender squire said almost tearfully. "He hit hard and his neck was broken with the fall. He lived only long enough to beg me to put Korppi out of his pain. With his dying breath he told me he will wait for us on the bridge to the hall of the gods."

Tomas was well-known as Nikko's half-brother by a village laundress, and though Nikko's father had never accepted him, they grew up together as boys, and trained as warriors once they were of age to learn fighting skills. Only Nikko could become a knight, but Tomas was always his squire. He was the closest friend Nikko ever had.

"Your father?" Tomas asked her as he helped her up, his dark-rimmed blue eyes almost pleading.

Darya could barely speak, her throat wanted to close on itself. "Dead," she finally declared flatly. "So far, only Johan, Erno, and Marko of his guard still breathe, though all are wounded."

The tall young man with the long brown-black waving hair and neatly trimmed mustache and beard bowed his head in sorrow. "Then we are finished."

Darya touched his arm. "No, because I will lead our army now Tomas, for my life is forfeit anyway if we lose the gate. Gather whatever men and horses we have left to help you bring our dead back to the tower. Nikko..." she glanced down briefly, steeling her emotions. "Nikko goes back with me," she insisted.

● ● ●

Between the two of them, they loaded the tall and heavy body on Rusko, who was the more placid of the two mounts, and tied it in place. She handed the knight's standard off. "Take this banner so men may know you. We must hurry and regroup; the Nordi will be back at dusk," she warned, squinting at what little light the glowing sliver of sun threw into the noonday sky.

"I am not a leader or even a knight, My Lady. I don't have the right to bear it," he reminded her.

"Then we will amend that now," she insisted. She pushed him back down on his knees, and holding her hand out for his sword, jammed it into the ground before him. Tomas turned his eyes up to the heavens, praying that he be fit for this.

Darya gave him a few minutes to make peace with himself, but they were out of time, for rays of the gradually emerging sun beamed down on them both. She drew and raised her father's blade overhead, and tapped him on both shoulders. "Do well by your countrymen, Sir Tomas," was all she could choke out, for she remembered the pride she had felt at Nikko's knighting three years ago. There was no time for further formalities, and she had much to do.

"My sword is yours to command, My Lady," he told her with feeling as he rose and sheathed his own blade.

"Lead as Nikko would have," she answered huskily and turned away, brushing a tear from her cheek. Grieving could come later, if they survived.

She rode Harma, and led the burdened stallion behind, back up the hillock, through the copse, and onward across the field of death, letting the cold winds off the slopes dry tears on her cheeks.

• • •

The bodies of Nikko and her father were transported back down to the fortress via a commandeered oxcart. Darya's heart went with them, but she remained behind to hold a council of war with whatever knowledgeable men she had left at her disposal. Lightly injured soldiers had been sent out to the nearest villages to conscript any men and boys who had stayed behind to mind stock and guard their homes. They raised no more than a hundred all told, some of them very old, some far too young, but it was all they could muster in a single afternoon. Word had come from the fortress, where her motherkin cousin Kaarle served as regent in her absence that Duke Gustav was sending a contingent of knights and pikemen, and Baron Fleming had archers and infantry to spare. What few men of arms remained behind were already on the way, with any able-bodied villagers. It did not matter, for none of them would arrive in time. The gate would be overrun by dawn.

Candlelight and beer within the council hall did little to dispel the intense melancholia that had spread over the men sitting before her. Those who had needed medical attention had been hastily seen to, and what dead could be recovered were dragged back and piled in a great crescent-shaped heap well before the gate, along with their horses, and soaked in resin and tar. If things did not go well, the bodies would be fired, and hopefully the flames, the stench, and the smoke would keep the Nordi and their allies at bay for a while. What few mounted men they had left would then sally forth from the tunnel cave entrance, and the portcullis would slam down behind them, leaving all stranded out on the field with the invaders.

"The odds are against us," bemoaned the captain of the archers, a dolorous man named Ivari. "We waste our time here. We should fall back to the fortress, and try our luck there."

"And let them burn our people out, capture our women, and torture our children?" bold and brash Tomas said with anger in his voice. "Not while I've a life to spend!"

"We'd die just as fast before getting there as we will here," Erno agreed, and he wasn't smiling when he said it. "At least here, taking a stand means something."

"My Liege Raimo led the van, and he did not hesitate to fight, no matter his age," Johan agreed quietly. "When he fell, Nikko promised him to drive the Nordi back into the hills. He too never considered the cost of his own life. They both fought for even the lowliest of the farmhands. They fought for Elverune."

"And now they're dead!" Ivari said with a rising voice. "And we are even more woefully outnumbered! I have children I want to see grow up, and that won't happen if we stay here."

"Oh, spare us your maidenly mewling! Surely yes, we'll all die here tonight," Marko spoke the obvious, as he banged down his mug for the third time after draining it in two long swills, "But your children, and their children, and generations after them will sing our praises throughout the land. A coward dies many deaths, but a courageous man

lives forever if the skalds know his name and deeds by heart. It's a noble way to leave this world; still in your prime, wrapped up in a glorious moment," he added.

Ivari rose with the insult, drawing his long knife. Marko too was on his feet, a sneer on his face and the hilt of his short sword in his hand. Darya pushed between them, and glared them both back down into their seats on the rough benches, her blue eyes the color and intensity of the glaciers atop the highest mountains.

"My father…your Lendmann…and valiant Nikko," there her voice almost broke, and she swallowed hard before continuing, "They did not fight in vain. They did not seek for glory. They died that we may *live!* And we do live yet, so do not speak to me of defeat! Even I, a woman; while I still breathe and can swing a sword, or string a bow and nock an arrow… I will fight for my land and my countrymen too. You waste my time here, bickering like children. What I want to know is will you all stand beside me in the battle?"

"Aye!" came voices from all across the table. Men leapt to their feet and saluted their current liege with fists or drinking horns held aloft. Even Ivari, as skeptical as he was, could not deny this small and grim faced woman with the determination born of generations of cold northern blood.

"Well, I for one am not yet ready to die," Erno said with a lopsided grin. "I have a bet with Johan that I can drink more summer ale than he can without passing out. They haven't tapped those kegs yet," he added to many amused chuckles.

Darya flashed him a tight-lipped smile, before they got down to tactics and assignments. Tomas, though newly knighted, would lead the charge of what little cavalry they had left, a mere twenty seven mounted men, all knights and squires, including Erno on big Rusko and Johan on a riderless roan gelding. Marko would lead the footmen; mostly militia conscripts. Ivari and his archers, as well as several local hunters who had their own bows and keen eyes, would back them up with arrows, as well as flaming pitch thrown down on anyone trying to scale the gatehouse towers. Once the wooden gate was gone, and the portcullis breached, they would have no choice but to clamber down and fight in the alleyway.

If it came to that, they would surely die, but all would sell their lives dearly.

● ● ●

As the last sliver of the sun's disc dipped below the horizon, the blackness of the true night was at hand. The moon that had blocked the sun would not rise again till the morrow.

Curse this darkness that lingers day and night, and plays into enemy hands. When will we see our sleeping sun shine again? Ah, if we can just hold them off one more night, perhaps at least some of the reinforcements might make it through!

Darya's thoughts wandered as she strung a bow, and then laboriously wound a crossbow before placing it within reach. She had learned to hunt and hawk while still a girl, so was no stranger to such weapons. After her mother's death, her father had seen to it that his only heir was at least adequately trained in arms, and so she had been hefting a long sword for over a decade. She was no shield-maiden, but she'd at least give a good accounting of herself, as fair as any common soldier on that field of death below.

She fully intended on joining the fray once the pitiful remainder of the knights rode out, all of the men on horseback having been dubbed and given their titles. She had cut the long fluttering sleeves from her gown, and with strips of that cloth, bound the flaps of the skirt into rough leggings, so that she could move freely and mount or dismount without being hampered by it. She'd traded her own little boots for a worn pair of the stable boy's hobnailed ones, stuffed with a wad of hare's fleece to make them fit well. For armor, all they had that fit her was a mail coif with a hauberk that hung to her knees. She was as ready as she ever would be, and cared not a whit if she died this night, for her heart and soul had already gone to the grave with the deaths of her father and bold Nikko.

"Here they come!" said several voices around her, and she leaned against a merlon with an arrow nocked and ready, peering out the nearest embrasure. A quiver filled with more arrows hung on the belted baldric that lay diagonally between her small breasts and encircled her slender waist. She felt no fear, only a jangle of battle nerves and a dynamic state of mental alertness that kept her from dwelling on her loses. There would be time for grieving later, if she survived this night. For now, there was a ravening horde of invaders that needed to be stopped, and the painted and skin-clad savages that came charging ahead of the Nordi warrior band already outnumbered them ten to one. She raised the bow, sighted, and shot the first of many wild men that would die kicking and screaming that night.

● ● ●

It was, as Marko had predicted, a battle where heroic acts of bravery and steadfastness would spawn numerous ballads and poems.

What passed as infantry had already moved out to meet the shrieking devils who raced ahead of the Nordi tribesmen. These wild men were dressed in fur-covered skins, their long hair full of braids with clay beads and feathers, their faces made fierce with markings of ocher and lime dust smeared in grease. They brandished crude axes and clubs as they came barreling onward. Men and boys of the villages unused to the battlefield felt their blood turn to ice, but Marko who led them never hesitated. He charged in bellowing his own full-throated battle cry. His long-hafted axe swept up, down, and sideways; spraying blood in sheets of mist while mowing down every enemy combatant he encountered.

Soldier or farmer, miller or shepherd, graybeards and middle-aged fathers flanked by boys with down on their cheeks; none hesitated, but pounded in after their fearless commander, screaming in defiance. Some met their death quickly, yet so did many of their adversaries. The men of Elverune took to the field to protect their homes and livelihoods, their loved ones and the things they held most dear. No enemy was allowed to get through in that initial rush. Their attackers might look like hellspawn, but the common people of Darya's land fought as demons against them, and even as those in the forefront began to fall, the rest stood firm, and battled on without wavering.

Had she time to think on it, Darya would have shed tears of pride, for this was the tenacious spirit of her countrymen that her father had often bragged about. They held the line, and whittled the initial attackers down to a number which could be contained.

Yet these wild men were just the shock troops of the invaders; tribal chieftains and their warrior bands who had been coerced into throwing their lives away. The Nordi were barbarian warlords, and far more cunning. They allowed their erstwhile allies to whittle down the numbers of the defenders.

● ● ●

Up on guardhouse wall, bows twanged and arrows fell thick and fast amongst the enemy. The trick was not to shoot your own men; far easier said than done in the near darkness. At that level, they had a better view of the battlefield beyond the intense frontal skirmishes, and Darya and her archer cohort could see the Nordi moving steadily in behind, carrying with them scaling ladders and a huge battering ram. As they approached they loosed their war dogs again; tall, long-legged beasts with the bloodlines of wolves mixed with that of the burly domestic canines used for protecting sheep. Still half-wild, vicious and starving, a few of them stopped to feed on the bodies of the slain, tearing away chunks of flesh and gulping them down.

It was becoming nearly impossible to pick out enemy combatants in the press directly below, so Darya ordered Ivari to have his archers concentrate on bringing the dogs down, now that they were coming into range.

"Kindle the pyre too, for we'll need the light." She handed off her bow and quiver to the nearest person, which turned out to be the stable boy. He took her position on the wall, nocked an arrow, sighted carefully, and fired.

"Where will you be, My Liege?" Ivari asked as she clasped arms with him before heading into the tower.

"Out there," she said, and pointed to the battlefield. "I must ride forth with the knights, for they'll need every sword they can get. There are far more of the Nordi left than we expected."

"Go with the gods then!" he cried, and men and boys along the wall…along with several camp follower women who fought beside them…cried out similarly in acknowledgment as she passed by.

With their blessings ringing in her ears she was on her way, and the head archer turned back to his duty.

● ● ●

The knights were ready to go when she arrived, and smiling Erno was holding the bridle of Harma for her. Johan looked flushed and feverish, and he favored his injured shoulder as he picked up the reins of his mount. His wound was likely turning septic. No time to worry about that now.

She nodded to them all wordlessly, and mounted up, checking that her father's long blade was in the scabbard. She took her place at the head of the van beside Tomas, who had found another horse. "You might do better with this…at least initially," he said quietly, handing her a long-handled war hammer with a curved spike on the opposite end of the head. It was lighter than the sword, but swung well, and could be just as deadly.

"My thanks," she said with a slight smile in his direction. He was wise enough not to mention that she would struggle with a heavy long bladed weapon swung in just one hand while keeping the other on the reins. She had no experience with a lance, so did not ask for one. Darya was not afraid to die, for she had made her peace with that over the last few difficult hours, but she wished to take many enemies with her when she did. She flipped down her spurs, settled herself in the saddle, and nodded. Tomas raised his hand, and they started to walk their mounts down the torch lit tunnel. The first portcullis banged shut behind them.

They traveled two abreast in the echoing stone corridor toward the sally port opening. At the final turn, there were no torches, for they did not want to announce the presence of the opening to the enemy. The wooden and iron portcullis on that end was raised on greased lines so that it didn't shriek of its presence, and they sedately trotted their mounts out under the starry sky as it thumped down quietly behind them, effectively locking them outside the gate. Once all were clear, they gathered together for a final moment. The pyre had been lit, and billows of smoke wafted over the field of honor and horror, giving it an even more hellish look.

Tomas drew his sword, as did every other man, and brandished it on high. "For glory, for honor, for Elverune!" he shouted, and every voice around him picked up the cry as spurs were applied, and their mounts began to trot and then canter. They broke into gallops going down the slight slope, and fanned out as they charged. Some of them engaged with the final stragglers of the wild men of the hills, cutting them down as they went by, but the knights' main target was the Nordi, who were the true threat.

Though she had handled arms and sparred with other men on horse or afoot, Darya had never been in a battle before. There was no describing the sensation of galloping hard under the stars over a field already torn apart and littered with bodies, the chill wind off the mountains taking her breath away in misty clouds as she gasped for air. Dust and smoke swept by in choking swirls, and the metallic clash, grunts, oaths and shouts of fighting men vied with the thunder of hooves and her own heart pounding in her ears. Along with Tomas and the other knights, she slammed into the first line of Nordi invaders like an indomitable force of nature, and began laying blows all around her.

That is where instinct took over, for the Valhoven line had generated many a fine warrior. Darya did not have time to recall that she was the last one to bear the family name. She kept on fighting out of battle nerves and anger, swinging the war hammer at every shadow which leapt at her, braining some and bashing the faces of others. Every time a Nordi went down under her blows she felt a grim sense of satisfaction. Another foreign marauder sent to wander the frozen wastes as a wailing wraith.

The dogs were the biggest problem. Already several horses were down due to them, and knights were fighting afoot. A big and shaggy brindle beast leapt at Harma, and managed to get its teeth into the horse's haunch. Darya tried to twist and lean out to swing the hammer's spike into its face, but Harma kicked the dog at the same time, and unseated her. She fell from the saddle, landing hard, bruising her arm and shoulder. She lost her war hammer, and one foot was still tangled in the stirrup, dragging her around as the war horse kept kicking and bucking, trying to shake off his attacker.

One kick fell true, and the big dog somersaulted backwards to lay whimpering and twitching, with broken ribs and collapsing lungs. Before Darya could extricate herself, its Nordi master came running in with a spear. She just barely managed to break free and rolled beneath her mount to avoid being impaled. Darya dragged herself to her knees with hammer in hand as the snarling man lunged around Harma and came at her again. Before he could sink the blade home, Harma lashed out with front hooves and teeth, and the man dodged sideways. Darya lunged at him and smashed the hammer into his arm.

The man screamed in pain but he deftly lifted the spear shaft with his off hand and came rushing back at Darya one last time. Finally on her feet, she raised the war hammer in defense, but he had the benefit of a longer reach. Just as the Nordi began the fatal thrust that would impale her, his head popped off with a sideways spray of blood and rolled to her feet, still holding an astonished look. The remainder of his body crumpled and fell forward. Erno had seen her go down, and had ridden Rusko hard through the press to get to her side.

"I owe you a barrel of mead," she gasped out as she grabbed her reins.

"And Harma a bag of carrots! A good horse is worth as much as a man," he told her with a grin, which made the blood splatter beneath his helm look like mummer's face paint. She mounted again, and Erno was off, for the Nordi with the scaling ladders and battering ram were passing by, and they had to be stopped.

● ● ●

The rest of that foul night became a blur. Several times Darya came close to losing her life. Exhausted, she took a few cuts before a hard blow from a sling stone that was meant for her head hit her back instead. It knocked the wind from her and she fell off her mount again, losing the war hammer permanently.

Realizing they had a leader down and cornered, several Nordi rushed at her, and Darya was surrounded. There was no time to regain the saddle or find the weapon she'd lost, but she had the presence of mind to yank her father's sword from its scabbard and brought it into play, two-handed.

"Come test me, if you dare!" she snarled, her face a mask of defiance. "I am a Valhoven, and we don't kill easily!"

● ● ●

Darya gave a good accounting of herself, but she would have died there, had not Tomas battled his way to her side. He too was unhorsed, but together they fought like twin furies; thrusting, grunting, parrying, and slashing. It had become apparent to the Nordi that this warrior leader was a woman, and that the man in the surcoat with her was also someone of importance. If they cut them both down, the rest of the defenders might lose heart, and the gateway to the southlands would be overrun at last. They pressed forward mercilessly on all sides, backing the duo uphill.

Suddenly the sun rose over the mountain. A stray beam limned both defenders in golden halos. The sight of that stopped the invaders in their tracks.

Darya and Tomas stumbled forward and cut their assailants down as they turned to run away.

● ● ●

It had been a costly battle.

Brave young Johan died when in feverish dizziness, he collapsed in mid-swing. A hastily swung club smashed his face in. Marko was crushed to death with the last of the foot soldiers defending the gate from the battering ram. Their broken bodies managed to stop the charge. Ivari and several archers including one woman and the stable boy died on the wall as they fought off Nordi on scaling ladders. Many unnamed men in the field lay dying and crying out for mothers, sweethearts, or wives before they passed to the halls of the gods. An exhausted handful were left alive, all of them wounded, body and soul.

The few wild men that were left alive had deserted the Nordi during the fiercest fighting of the night. When those first tentative sun rays broke over the eastern slopes, there was a ragged cheer from the defenders, for immediately all Nordi began to break off their attack and retreated into the shadows. There were not enough horses or men fit to ride to chase them down. Why these invaders feared the sun, no one ever knew, but its late arrival after such a long sleep turned the tide.

● ● ●

Exhausted, bloody, and injured, Tomas and Darya walked their weary mounts side by side back toward the gates, which though battered, still stood firm. It was over, at least for another long summer.

"They will come again some dark day," she said wearily to the man at her side who reminded her so much of her Nikko.

"And we will be prepared. We know them well now; as well as your father and his men did," he answered.

Erno had joined them but had respectfully dropped behind, both he and Rusko limping heavily.

"Will we ever know peace here?" she asked sadly. "I tire of fighting."

Tomas was silent a while before he answered.

"As long as there is a sun in the sky, and our people love the land, believe in themselves, and do what must be done... yes, we will know peace. We will know it because we must sometimes fight to maintain it. That is the way of the world."

"Well I pray the sun sleeps no more in my lifetime, for I prefer to sing over horns of ale enjoyed *with* my companions, than while mourning their loss," Darya declared.

No one dared argue that point with a Valhoven!

The End

The Look of Love

by Greg Hatcher

"This is torture, Tony." Carol Baldwin glared at Tony Quinn over her martini glass. "You know how I feel about these things."

Quinn raised an eyebrow. His mouth quirked in a half-smile. "Would you rather have had the one without the olive?"

"Not the drink, damn it. You know what I mean." Carol waved a hand at the crowded hotel ballroom. "These... society affairs." She shuddered. "I don't think you realize how awful these people can be, Tony. Gossipy, malicious...."

In fact, Quinn did know. His preternatural hearing abilities allowed him to hear the muted whispers from around the ballroom, the wives of powerful businessmen speculating about him and Carol. The pitying comments about him, the catty remarks about her. *Look at that chiseling blonde, attaching herself to that poor blind man. How can she afford clothes like that? She must be into his money.*

None of those things were remotely close to the truth. Yes, Quinn had money enough, and yes, he and Carol were taking the first tentative steps toward something that was becoming more than mere friendship. But it was she who had rescued him two years ago: when Quinn had been a young prosecuting attorney whose star shone bright in the D.A.'s office until he was blinded and nearly killed by the mobster Oliver Snate. It had been Carol, together with reformed grifter Silk Kirby, who had nursed him to health and, more importantly, persuaded Quinn that there was still hope, the fight was not over. And it had been Carol that had engineered the experimental procedure whereby Quinn's blind and useless eyes had been replaced with new ones... and it was that experimental procedure that had somehow resulted in Tony Quinn not only regaining his sight but also acquiring other, new, abilities.

After the operation, Quinn could not only see, he could see into the infrared. This meant he could see in the dark, he could sense heat sources and movement even through solid walls, and the months of living as a blind man had trained his other senses as well; his hearing was far beyond normal ranges and his sense of touch was so refined he could read air currents with his hand with the same ease a normal man read a speedometer on a car dashboard. He was a creature of the night, most comfortable in quiet darkness. These newfound abilities, together with the renewed anger at crime and injustice that had fueled Quinn's career as D.A., had led to the creation of the Black Bat.

It was the Bat's business that had brought them to the banquet honoring Commissioner Warner; it was almost always the Bat's business that took Quinn out of his townhouse at all. Feigning blindness was exhausting, and even behind the dark glasses the ballroom lights were hard on his enhanced vision. But sometimes circumstances demanded it. Tonight was about shoring up his cover. It would have raised awkward questions if Quinn had begged off. Anyway, Jerome was a friend, after all.

It was rare for Tony Quinn to truly enjoy a moment of leisure. His work, the mission he had assigned to himself as the Bat, was dark, brutal, and dangerous. Most of the time, even in his civilian identity, his life was consumed by that mission. Working undercover gathering intelligence, or, like tonight, shoring up his public persona as a harmless blind attorney. It left little time for himself, or Carol for that matter, to be their true selves. The most they ever seemed to manage was an occasional stolen moment together, brief respites from the endless war to which Tony Quinn had pledged himself.

Suddenly Carol smiled back at him, a brilliant flashing smile that reminded Quinn how fortunate he was that she had chosen to continue at his side, even with the added burdens the Black Bat's crusade brought her. "Oh, I know. I was just grousing. Really, though, Tony, it's different for a woman. They pity you...but they judge me."

"I know." Quinn winced a little. "I can hear them."

"Really?" Now Carol was curious.

"You don't want to know. But they're as awful as you say. Landon likes your dress, though."

"Landon?" Carol sighed. "He's a pig. I'm sorry, Tony, but he is. I know you and Jerome think he's a good cop but whenever I'm in a room with him his eyes never leave my bosom. It's unnerving. And it doesn't seem to matter at all to him if his wife is there or not. Poor little mouse, I feel so sorry for her. Oh well." She squared her shoulders. "No sacrifice is too great for the cause of justice."

"That's my girl." Quinn patted her shoulder. "Anyway, we're almost done here, I promise. I just want a few moments with Jerome, and he's not here yet."

"What? I thought this bash was in his honor."

"It is." Quinn glanced up at the dais, behind which hung a banner reading *Congratulations on 10 Years, Police Commissioner Warner!* Though there were places laid for dinner at the table, no one was sitting there yet. "They were supposed to start the dinner seating ten minutes ago, though I daresay no one minds the cocktail hour being extended a little. But they can't start without the guest of honor. I suppose we could try and find out what's keeping him. Chief Landon's over there, he would know." He offered her his arm.

Carol rolled her eyes at the thought of talking to Landon, then she took his arm and together they wove their way through the other partygoers toward the cluster of police officials and their wives at the far end of the ballroom.

Chief of Detectives Thomas Landon looked up and grinned as they approached. "Hey there, Tony! How you doin'? You certainly are looking fine tonight, Miss Carol," he added. The grin turned wolfish, almost a leer.

"Thank you, and where is your lovely wife tonight?" Carol smiled sweetly.

She had put just enough of a point on it that Landon flushed a little. "She should be along soon," he said. "Had to drop the kids off at the sitter." But his embarrassment was only momentary, as his gaze drifted once again, almost involuntarily, to Carol's décolletage.

Quinn was tempted to snap his fingers under the burly chief's nose, as one would a dog's, to get his attention. But he had to continue the pretense of blindness, and blind Tony Quinn would not have noticed Landon's leer. "So where's our friend the commissioner? He wouldn't miss his big night, would he?"

"No idea," admitted Landon. "Just got here myself. Oh hey, here he comes."

Quinn stiffened. Even from across a crowded room he could tell that something had shaken Commissioner Jerome Warner very badly; breathing too rapid, and the acrid tang of sweat. *Something's wrong.*

Warner saw them and strode over. "Good, you're both here," he said, addressing Quinn and Landon. Then he remembered his manners and added, "Sorry, Carol, but I need Tony for a few minutes. There's been a murder. One of ours." Warner was grim. "Janice Salem. Found dead in her apartment an hour ago. A secretary, but she was still NYPD and by God I'm going to get the rotten son of a bitch that..."

"Oh, God." Landon looked sick. "Little Janice from the Ninth Precinct? Who would want...?" His voice trailed off. Tony Quinn heard a jump in his heartbeat, and a tiny, nearly imperceptible shudder went over Landon as well. Imperceptible to most people, but not to Quinn.

"An animal. He didn't just kill her, he worked her over first. Took his time from the look of it. And he..." Warner's voice dropped and he looked at Carol, then at Quinn. "He...Tony, it's not fit for a lady..."

Carol let out an explosive snort. "Jerome, really. I'm not a porcelain doll. Just say it. He raped her?"

"No." Warner's face was grave. "That would make a kind of sense, at least. No, this... I don't..." He hesitated and then finally said, "He tortured her. For hours. And then... he took her eyes."

No one knew what to say to that. Chief Landon had been looking more and more ill, and finally, with a strangled, "Excuse me," he sprinted for the men's room.

Quinn couldn't blame him. He felt a little sick himself. But more than that, he felt anger; the familiar outrage that fueled the Black Bat's work. He had to focus that anger, make it work for him.

"I was hoping you could come down with me to the crime scene, Tony," Warner was saying. "I really want this bastard, whoever he is... and you seem to have good luck with the weird ones. I could use your insight."

"Of course." Quinn nodded. "Just let me see Miss Baldwin home and I'll join you up there as soon as I can." Without waiting for an answer, he spun Carol around and took her arm, hastening both of them toward the exit.

Once on the sidewalk, Carol said to him, "You aren't really seeing me home, are you?"

"Sadly, no." Quinn allowed himself a rueful smile. He kissed her forehead. "Silk will have to see you back to the townhouse. The Black Bat has work to do." His face grew tense again. "In particular, I think I need to track Chief Landon. That was more than just reaction. He knows something about Janice Salem."

Carol was shocked. "You don't think... Tony, he's an oaf, but I can't see him as..."

"Nor I. He's not a killer." Quinn shook his head. "But that reaction...it was far too strong for a hardened police detective, even a murder as gruesome as this. I need to know what he knows. Silk's here, love," he added as the sedan pulled forward.

The driver's side window rolled down and Silk Kirby leaned out. "Home, boss?"

"Just Miss Baldwin. I'll need my bag, though." Quinn opened the trunk and pulled out the small traveling bag that held the Black Bat's disguise, the cloak and mask, along with the pistol and the grapnel gun. "Silk, have Butch meet me in Alphabet City... the Hightower Apartments. Avenue D." This was Butch O'Leary, the former heavyweight boxer that now served as the Bat's other aide.

"Something cooking, boss?" Silk looked eager. He had fought at Quinn's side many times, dating all the way back to when Quinn had first caught him in a burglary attempt and persuaded Silk to turn his talents to fighting crimes instead of committing them. Nominally he now served as Quinn's chauffeur, but like all who shared the Black Bat's secret, he was a fellow soldier, and even though he was no longer a criminal, he had never lost his taste for excitement. "I can..."

"Not necessary. Just get Carol back to the townhouse. Butch will be enough. Be sure he brings the Bat's sedan and not this one, though." Quinn had a special car he used for the Black Bat's work; a battered, nondescript sedan that housed a supercharged racing engine.

At that Carol straightened and put her hands on her hips. "Damn it, Tony!" she said. "First Warner and now you! You know perfectly well I'm no hothouse flower..."

"No, no." Tony Quinn laughed. "I have a different chore for you. You said you knew Mrs. Landon. I need you to telephone her. Find out what she knows about Janice Salem; what might have set off her husband. Maybe she can shed some light."

"All right," Carol said, mollified. "But it's better if we just go there in person. She's so sweet... if she knew Janice, this will be a terrible blow to her."

"As you think best." Quinn was already moving, disappearing into the shadows beyond the street lights. His voice had changed to the Black Bat's rasp. Carol knew that even before he donned the Black Bat's disguise that Tony Quinn was already gone, replaced by the cloaked avenger New York's criminal underworld hated and feared.

● ● ●

Doris Landon was a plump, brown-haired woman in her early thirties. Despite the fact that it was past ten P.M. when Silk and Carol arrived at the Landons' small bungalow in Little Neck, she insisted on serving them tea. "I just can't fathom it," she said, as she poured a cup for Silk, then for Carol. "I knew her, of course. Janice was a little bit of a thing. Surrounded by file folders piled on her desk all the time. Always so deferential to the officers. They had her buffaloed."

"Hmm." Carol sipped tea and thought it over. How best to get at the subject? She knew that Mrs. Landon would be horrified by the thought of any scandal touching her husband. But Tony was sure Chief Landon knew more than he was telling... if Doris knew anything, Carol was determined to get it out of her. "Buffaloed?" she probed, gently.

"Oh, well, she was supposed to be filing, you know, secretarial, but..." Doris Landon leaned in and whispered, "Sometimes she would type up the officer incident reports and things. The boys would always try and push off their paperwork on her. It's not right. They're supposed to do that for themselves."

Not right. Carol considered it. Something about the way Doris had said that....*Not right...*

Her vision swam. "I'm... not right," Carol said, blearily.

Something in the tea. Oh God.

Silk swore and rose to his feet, reaching inside his jacket for the gun he wore there in a shoulder holster. But the drugged tea had slowed his reflexes, as well. Carol watched in horror as Doris Landon whipped a snub-nosed pistol out of the pocket of her flowered housecoat and shot Silk point-blank in the chest. Blood sprayed the couch cushions.

Carol tried to scream but all that came out was a kind of squeaking gasp. The second-to-last thing she saw before she lost consciousness was Silk collapsing to the rug. The drug made everything look like it was moving underwater, in slow motion, as Carol saw him fall to his knees, then to one elbow, and finally flat on his back, a red stain blossoming around the hole in his shirt.

The last thing she saw was Doris Landon throwing her head back and laughing, loud and long. Carol tried to reach up, to strike out at that madly laughing face, but blackness took her.

● ● ●

The front room of Janice Salem's apartment was an abattoir.

Her body lay in the middle of the carpet, surrounded by sticky, still-drying blood spatter. The smell of it, which Warner had always thought was the same as freshly-sheared copper, permeated the room. Her hands and feet were bound, not with rope, but with twists of metal wire that had bitten deeply into her wrist and ankles. The murderer had not undressed her, but her clothing was shredded and falling away.

"The death of a thousand cuts," Warner muttered.

He had not meant to say it aloud, but the medical examiner looked up from where he was kneeling. "I'd say so, Commissioner," he agreed. "Have to autopsy to be certain but I'd guess that was cause of death. Blood loss. Whoever he was, he was damn careful not to hit anything important. He wanted it to last."

Chief Thomas Landon stood just behind Warner. At the M.E.'s last comment he let out a brief, nauseated gurgle of horror.

The commissioner turned and laid a hand on his shoulder. "I know, Thomas. It's bad," he said, kindly. "Step out for a minute and get some air, and then we'll talk about getting this son of a bitch."

Landon nodded, and without saying anything he stepped out of the room into the hall. The other residents of the floor had been sent downtown, where they would be questioned as possible witnesses and then sent to a hotel for the night. That just left his fellow policemen... and the press. Uniformed officers stood at either end of the first-floor hallway, blocking the crime-beat reporters and photographers from swarming the place. It didn't stop them from yelling questions, though. "What's the story, chief?" one of them called out. "Got any suspects?"

Landon just shook his head. Not wanting to run the press gauntlet, he headed upstairs to the roof. It was only three flights up, and he needed a minute to think.

He emerged out on to the tarred roof of the brownstone apartment building, and sat on the cornice, facing inward, away from the edge. On either side, the adjoining buildings rose above, leaving the roof in deep shadow.

For a moment he just sat, his hands on his thighs, taking deep, whooshing breaths. It couldn't be what he suspected... but... Janice. He had never meant for it to get this far.

"Chief Landon."

The hissing rasp startled Landon so badly he almost fell backwards off the roof. He scrambled to his feet, fumbling for his service revolver. "Who's there? Come out where I can see you!"

A cloaked figure stepped forward, not completely in the light, but enough that Landon could see a .45 automatic in his gloved hand. The face was masked, a cowl that covered the entire head. A scalloped, leathery cloak billowed around him like bat's wings. "You're covered, Landon. Put away your revolver or you'll regret it."

"The Black Bat!" Landon didn't holster the revolver, but he let his arm fall to his side. "I'm not afraid of you," he added in a quavering voice that was not at all convincing.

"No? You're afraid of something." The rasping voice sharpened, became accusatory. "Something about Janice Salem. Something you don't want others to know. But I will know it, Landon. You'll tell me."

"I don't know what you...?"

"You are *lying*. I know when you lie." It was true; Quinn's enhanced senses detected microscopic changes in heartbeat, breathing, and other minute indicators even more efficiently than an actual lie detector could have done. The Black Bat leaned forward. "Tell me the truth! You were having an affair with her. Admit it."

It had been pure guesswork on Quinn's part, but it worked. Landon sat heavily back down on the cornice. "No." He shook his head. "Not an affair. Just the one time. It was a party. I'd been drinking a little. You have to understand...Doris...she gets so... sometimes she... ah, God!" He let out a muffled, dry sob.

The Black Bat waited for a moment, then prompted, "Doris is your wife?"

"Yes." Landon wiped his eyes with his forearm. "She... you have to believe me. I didn't ever think she would...she threatened...but..."

Your wife killed Janice Salem?

"I don't know," Landon said miserably. "I think so. There have been other times... but they looked like accidents. I suspected, but I told myself I was imagining things... they coulda been accidents. But always girls I was, y'know... lookin' at. Doris gets crazy jealous," he added, as if that was justification. "I never even done anything, just looked. Flirted a little. Except the one time with Janice. I didn't think Doris even knew who she was."

"Your wife is a killer and you knew? You knew and you kept *silent?*" Quinn was so horrified that he forgot to speak in the Black Bat's voice. Doris Landon was the butcher that had bled Janice Salem dry and cut out her eyes. *And he had sent Carol over there.*

Landon didn't notice the Black Bat's horror. He just shook his head again. "It's over. It's all over. Everything. I'm finished as a cop. I know it. And my marriage is finished. Everything's finished."

*"Where is your wife now? **Where?!**"* The Black Bat roared.

Thomas Landon looked up at Quinn's masked face and smiled a horrible, ragged smile. "You know what's really crazy? I never cared nothin' about them other girls. Not really. I love Doris. Even now. I always did."

Then he put the service revolver in his mouth and pulled the trigger.

● ● ●

Carol came awake in darkness. There was sharp pain at her wrists and ankles. It was the pain that had awakened her. She was bound to a wooden kitchen chair with metal wire. She wrenched her arms, testing her bonds, and let out a yelp as the wire bit deep.

"Don't bother." It was Doris Landon's voice, but changed. No longer sweet and diffident, now it was confident and full of humor. "That's the wire Tommy uses to mend the fence up here. You can't break it."

"Where's here?" Carol subtly tested her bonds again. The wire hurt like hell, but she thought she felt the wooden arm of the chair loosen a little. *Careful. Don't let her see that. Keep her talking.*

"Tommy's and my vacation cabin. Up by the Shawangunks. I come here to do my work." Doris Landon's voice sharpened. "When one of you *whores* takes after my Tom. It happens."

"I never..."

"Don't lie to me!" Doris stepped forward and backhanded Carol, hard, across the face. "I see how he looks at you! I see it! You led him on!"

Carol could taste blood in her mouth. She glared up at Doris. "I wouldn't have your husband if you paid me. I have a man of my own...he's worth a hundred of..."

"You're lying!" It was a shriek. "You're a lying whore! Like that Janice Salem! And Frances Markham from the diner! And that little Negro bitch from the fruit stand! You all look at him! You sluts lead him on! My Tom can't help himself!"

Dear God. Carol felt acid rise in her throat. *She's killed before. She's winding herself up to kill **me**.*

But suddenly Doris Landon was calm and controlled again. "I fixed them all," she said, with a quiet pride. "People thought they was fires, or car crashes. But I did it. I took care of them. And I made sure they could never look at my Tommy again." She bent to a wooden cabinet and opened it, and pulled out a gallon pickle jar. Carol heard something slosh.

Then Doris Landon turned and held the jar out to Carol with both hands. "I make them say they're sorry. And then I make sure to remove all temptation."

The jar was full of eyes.

"I had you on my list anyway," Doris went on. "Janice and then you. But you made it so easy, coming to me. I felt bad about your driver, though. He seemed like a nice fella. Manners. Knew his place."

Silk, Carol thought sickly, and bowed her head. Then she straightened. *I won't scream. I won't cry. I won't give this horrid creature the satisfaction.* "He was worth a hundred of your ugly ape of a husband, too," she spat.

Doris Landon's face grew red with rage. Her hands shook. The only thing that kept her from hitting Carol again was that she had the heavy jar in both hands. "You'll be sorry you said that," she hissed. "I'll make you sorry. I'll make you sorry for everything."

She set the jar carefully on top of the cabinet, then opened another drawer and drew out a slender filleting knife. Then she turned back to Carol and smiled.

"And it will take a very long time," she added.

• • •

Silk Kirby wasn't dead.

Miraculously, Doris Landon's bullet had passed through the grifter's chest without hitting any vital organs or even an artery. It had been a small-caliber round and though it had nicked Silk's collarbone, the wound wasn't in and of itself lethal. Mostly he was in shock, and fading in and out of consciousness from the chloral hydrate Doris Landon had dosed them with earlier. Ironically, the drug was helping Silk hang on, lessening the pain somewhat. The blood loss, though, was becoming severe, and coupled with the sedative in his system, the valiant ex-crook didn't have long.

Stay conscious, he told himself. *Got to stay alive long enough to tell the boss...got to hang on... or she'll kill Carol...*

He tried to pull himself to a sitting position but dizziness overwhelmed him and he fell, hard. Fresh blood welled from below the red-crusted shirt. Inwardly, Silk cursed himself for a weakling. *Goddamn it you are NOT going down from one lousy bullet wound from a dumpy woman in a housecoat!*

He saw a telephone on a table by the couch. Again he tried to move but searing pain shot through his arm the second he tried to use it to right himself, and he fell back to the rug. The table with the phone was barely four feet from him but Silk thought it might as well be a hundred miles. He couldn't reach it; that was all. He was going to die here, bleeding out on this crazy woman's rug. *Stupid...stupid way to die...*

Then the door to the bungalow blew open. It was Butch O'Leary, brandishing a Colt revolver. At the same time, the Black Bat burst in from the back entrance to the kitchen, brandishing his automatic.

"Nice..." croaked Silk from the floor. "Two-pronger. Just like in the Army manual."

Instantly both the Bat and Butch were kneeling next to him. Butch opened the bloody jacket and tore strips from it to bind the wound. Silk's eyes closed for a moment, then opened. "Boss... she took Carol. Tried... she doped us...stupid...sorry."

"Where?" The Bat's voice was tight.

"Heard her say...vacation place... somewhere in the Gunks. All I got. Sorry..." Silk passed out.

The Black Bat nodded at Butch. "Get him to a hospital. Flag someone down. I'll need the roadster to get Carol."

Butch nodded, scooped Silk into his arms as easily as he would a child, and left.

The Bat knew Butch would do whatever it took to get Silk to medical care. Beyond that, it was out of their hands. They just had to pray Silk would pull through.

The Black Bat put it from his mind. No time to worry, no time to grieve. He had to find Carol.

A vacation home. Somewhere in the Gunks. The Shawangunk Mountains. Ulster County. Somewhere then there had to be an address. A utility bill, property tax record, a deed, something. He saw a large rolltop writing desk at the other end of the room. In a bound he was across the room. He tore the drawers out, rifled the compartments.

There! A bundle of envelopes secured with a rubber band. Bills and notices from a variety of utility companies. Gas, water, New York Edison... The Black Bat riffled through them like playing cards. Suddenly he froze. *Ulster Coal Oil!* And an address for where it was delivered.

Near Chadwick Lake. The Black Bat pulled up his glove to check his watch. Almost eighty miles. Even going all-out in the supercharged roadster it was going to be at least an hour. But it would have taken Doris Landon time to get there as well, and he would have to hope that the madwoman would wait until arriving at the cabin to start on Carol. She couldn't be that far ahead; it had barely been two hours since he and Carol had said their farewells in front of the Waldorf-Astoria, at Jerome's banquet. Though it felt like a lifetime ago.

Hang on, Carol. I'm coming. To rescue... or avenge.

• • •

Each time Doris Landon had turned away from Carol in the dank little room, to fetch her trophy jar or to put it away, Carol had taken advantage of the distraction to wrench furiously at the bonds that tied her to the cheap wooden chair. The wire was strong and it hurt like hell, but she felt the wooden dowels connecting the seat of the chair to the armrests loosen a little more each time. Now, as the Landon woman turned back with her slender knife at the ready, Carol wrenched her body back, then forward, in one final explosive, desperate effort.

The armrest dowels splintered and suddenly both her arms were free, though her wrists were still wired to the now-detached wooden chair arms. Carol instantly swung at Doris Landon's face and the wooden armrest, still tied to Carol's arm, whipcracked across her captor's cheekbone. Doris squealed and fell back on her ample behind, cracking her head on the cabinet.

"That's for Silk, you horrible old bitch," Carol spat, and tried to stand.

The bottom of the wooden chair was still intact and Carol kicked awkwardly out, trying to break the chair legs free as she had the armrests, but they were made of sterner stuff. She flailed her arms, trying not to fall.

Then Doris Landon was up off the floor and lunging at her with the knife. Carol lashed out at her face again and missed, hitting the knife hand instead. The knife flew out of Doris Landon's hand and clattered into a corner of the room. The woman's face was beet-red now and she was making an inarticulate keening whine through gritted teeth. She fell on top of Carol, pawing at Carol's face. "Your eyes...I'm a' take your eyes..." she wheezed.

Then there was a sharp crack. Doris Landon went limp, sprawled across Carol's stomach. Her face made a small, shocked O of surprise. Then the eyes glazed and a final huff of breath escaped the dying lungs as Carol struggled out from under the body.

The Black Bat holstered his automatic. His entire body shuddered, and even under the mask and cape of the Bat, suddenly there was only Tony Quinn, sagging with relief. He gathered Carol to him and held her for a long moment, then bent to untwist the wire holding her to the broken remnants of the kitchen chair.

In seconds she was free. The Black Bat peeled back his hood, revealing Tony Quinn's acid-scarred face. At that moment Carol thought it was the most beautiful thing she'd ever seen. She hugged him hard.

"Are you all right?" he asked after another long moment.

"I am now." Carol looked at the body on the floor and shivered. "Tony, it was her. She killed Janice Salem...and God knows how many others..."

"I know." Quinn pulled her closer to him. "But it's over now. Thomas Landon is dead too... killed himself. It's done."

"It'll never be done," Carol said, and Quinn just held her as her shoulders shook with silent sobs.

● ● ●

Two days later, the two of them were standing on the balcony of Quinn's Manhattan townhouse, facing each other. Quinn was leaning on the balcony railing, enjoying the respite from feigning blindness to the world, content to feel the afternoon sun on his face and watch how it made Carol's hair shine. He smiled and said, "Silk seems to be mending well enough."

"The nurses all like him," Carol said, laughing. "That always helps."

Quinn laughed with her, but there was sadness beneath it. After a moment, he asked, "And you? Are you all right?"

"Today's the first day I didn't wake up with a chloral hydrate hangover. Back to nine-tenths human." Carol shrugged. "Cuts and bruises. We've had worse, Tony. You were in time."

"I don't know, Carol." Quinn was pensive. "This one felt... too close. Silk getting shot like that, and you at the mercy of that woman... I don't know. What you said, that it'll never be done. That's stayed with me."

Carol smiled, "Oh, Tony. Don't torment yourself so. It was reaction, that's all. I just meant..."

"Let me finish, please." Quinn's face looked bleak. "I'm trying to say...maybe the Black Bat's mission...I think I'm asking too much of you. Of all of you," he finished, awkwardly. "It's one thing when it's me taking the risks. But I..."

Carol slapped him.

It shocked Quinn into silence. He stared.

"You damned fool!" She glared at him. "You think you're the only one that's made a choice? That has a mission? Do you realize how *insulting* that is? What, do you think Silk and Butch and I are too stupid to know what we're doing? Is that it?"

"No, of course not." Quinn looked away from her for a moment, then turned back to face her. "I mean...I think *I've* been too stupid to know what you were doing. What you were risking. What we might lose." He paused for a moment, then blurted, "I can't lose you, Carol. I can't."

"You're damn right you can't. I'm not leaving." Carol laughed ruefully and hugged him. Then she stood back and grasped him by the shoulders. "Tony Quinn, you listen to me.

This is important. When I said, 'it'll never be done,' that didn't mean I wanted out. Sure, lying there in that cabin with that wretched creature and her trophy jar, I was scared to death. But I've been scared before, it doesn't mean I'm ready to quit on you or what we do. I was trying to tell you... there is no safe place." She shook him a little, to emphasize it, and said again, *"No. Safe. Place."*

"But..."

She cut him off. "No, I mean it. Think about it, Tony. That horrible Landon creature... she was coming for me anyway. Not the Black Bat. *Me.* Carol Baldwin. And why? Because once upon a time her lummox husband ogled my breasts! That's all it took! That's all it took for Janice and those other poor girls to have their lives snuffed out. Who could have predicted that? How can you guarantee safety against something that... insane?" Carol sighed, and fell silent.

After a moment she added, "The world we live in...even without the Black Bat in our lives, Tony, it's still a dark and dangerous place. But even when guns are going off all around us, even when we're going hell-for-leather in that souped-up sedan of yours running after crooks or from the police....when I'm with you I know it's all right. Honest to God, the only time I ever *truly* feel safe is when I'm with you."

Quinn regarded her for a long moment.

Carol flushed. "Well? Say something."

Quinn swallowed. Finally, in a hoarse whisper, he said, "Carol...in the insane world we live in, the only time I ever truly feel peace is when I'm with *you.* Like this. Here. Now."

There was only one answer to that. Carol pulled him to her. After a moment's hesitation, he leaned down and kissed her hard.

And in Tony Quinn's world, for that brief, stolen moment, everything was all right.

The End

Gunn Takes a Gander
(A Bear Gunn Adventure)
By Nikki Nelson-Hicks

Bear Gunn sat across the street from his office, sipped coffee and watched a sour man in a beige coat pace angrily in front of Gunn Investigations. In the man's hands was a yellow piece of paper, an eviction notice, which he twisted as if it were a certain tenant's neck. Bear blew a cooling breath on his coffee and smiled at his landlord, Mr. Steinbaum's, annoyance. It was the second one in three months. This wasn't anything serious; it was a game between them. He only had to sit here until his landlord gave up waiting to confront his favorite deadbeat tenant and thumbtack the damn thing into the door so Bear could tear it off, wad it up and get this day started. He knew the guy loved him. Hell, everybody loved him. Who didn't love Bear Gunn? He was one lovable son of a bitch.

Bear leaned back in the chair and smiled back his best lopsided boyish grin. The one that dropped panties all across Europe a few years ago in the Great War. He knew he was handsome in a roguish way. He was blessed with a head full of curly, honey brown hair and hazel eyes that changed color with his mood. And right now his mood was a bit naughty.

Lillian, the waitress at Rudy's Café sidled up to Bear, wrote out the check and put it down beside him.

"What's this, honey?"

"Your bill. Don't think for a second you're going to skip out on it."

"Lilli, my sweet girl, what do you think of me?"

"I think you didn't call me after our date last week."

"Now, sweetie, sometimes I get caught up with work and…"

"And I think I saw you with Ruth at the movies two days ago."

"Well, let me just explain myself…"

"And I think you better pay up before I start waving Mr. Steinbaum over."

"Fine, fine!" Bear held his hands up in submission. Steinbaum was walking down the sidewalk, his hands pushed deep in his pockets. Bear watched him pass by the diner. *Ah, the game continues.*

"Lean down here, sweetie." She complied and he dug his fingers in her thick russet brown hair, pulled her close and kissed her. As she pulled away, he ran his fingers around her ears and made a show of pulling out a dime and a nickel out from it. He tossed them down on the table. "Here you go, precious. Now, can I get a piece of your delicious apple pie to go?"

• • •

Gunn Investigations was housed in a small office wedged in between a shoe repair and fruit stand. It was drafty, the walls were thin and it stank of the Big Muddy that flowed past the French Market. And that was on a good day. In the summer, the walls would become veined with mold and the flies that collected around Newman's Fruit Stand would attack and dive into any orifice that came close enough for them to take aim.Inside, there were two rooms. The first was the reception area. There was a couch, chairs and a small desk where Melinda Page, his secretary, received clients. She was a good bird, a bit of a Dumb Dora when it came to animals, but she worked cheap and was easy on the eyes.

The second room was his office and private sanctum, four walls and a window that opened to an alleyway. He had a simple oak desk, a chair that made obnoxious noises, a sink, a private toilet and a hot plate. Behind the desk were two metal file cabinets: one with a half a dozen files and the other served as a hidey hole. Next to the door was a bookcase filled to the brim with *Black Mask* magazines and books by Doyle, Chandler and Hammett. They were the Holy Trinity of Literature according to Bear Gunn. It was through their words and stories that he rebuilt his life on after the war. If a young man had the good luck to avoid bullets and poisonous gas, then that lucky son of a bitch had better use the rest of his life doing what makes him happy. Life is too damn short and most of that time it is too goddamn nasty to do anything else. With that philosophy lodged in his head and an Army pension in the bank, Barrington "Bear" Gunn decided to live the life of his pulp heroes and open up a private detective business.

He tore off the eviction notice, balled it up and unlocked the door. He whistled loudly as he entered.

"Is he finally gone?" Melinda came out of Bear's office. She knew the drill. When Steinbaum came by to collect rent, she hid until Bear gave the all clear. "I was beginning to have palpitations back there."

"Nothing to worry about, doll." Bear threw the paper ball and she caught it, one handed and tossed it back, hitting him square in the forehead. Melinda Page had reflexes like a panther and a wicked right hook. A native of the Crescent City, she was one tough cookie and had more talents than just being able to write short hand. She had saved his ass more than he liked to admit and she enjoyed reminding him of that fact.

"Well, I have good news." Melinda said. "We have a client."

"Oh?"

"Uh-huh. He's still back there in the hidey hole. A real scaredy cat. " Melinda sat down on her desk and crossed her long legs. She liked to wear tight green dresses that showed off her assets much to Bear's approval. She opened up her purse, pulled out her compact and readjusted her tight blond pin curls. She was always fussing with her hair, making sure every twist and twirl was just so. She powdered her cheeks and perky pug nose. "He nearly wet himself when he saw the ducks."

"Geez, Mel." Bear pinched the bridge of his nose. "Tell me you aren't keeping ducks in my sink."

"Where else do you expect me to keep them?"

"I've told you before that my office is a place of business, not a damn zoo."

"Oh, keep your shorts on, Mr. Big Business Man, it's just until I can get them to Jackson Square. What do you have against ducks anyway?"

"I don't like birds." He gave a quick shiver. "They give me the heebie jeebies."

"Don't worry your pretty little head." Mel blew him a kiss. "I'll protect you from the big bad birds."

Dames!

Melinda was a magnet for strays. If it slithered, flew or crawled, they somehow found their way to her and, by extension, into his office. It wasn't the first time he had ducks in his sink. There have been opossums under the heater, kittens in the cupboard and once she even asked to use one of his beloved *Black Mask* magazines as a liner for a parakeet cage. She learned quickly where Bear Gunn drew the line that day.

"Are you going to introduce me to our client? Or should I crack out a damn Ouija board?"

Melinda sighed and closed her mirror with a snap. "For crike's sake! Come out already, you mook!"

"No!" A muffled, squeaky voice shouted. "I'll wait in here."

"See?" Melinda shrugged. "Scaredy cat."

"We'd have ended up back there anyway. Hold my calls, doll."

"Let's see what little old me can do." Melinda took the phone off the hook and laid the receiver on her desk. "Whew. Nearly broke a sweat with that one."

"You know, I could get another skirt."

"Oh yeah, what girl wouldn't love a paycheck that is three weeks late? I'm sure you're beating them off with a stick. I worry myself sick just thinking about it." She pulled out a paper bag from the desk drawer and handed it to Bear. "Would you toss some popcorn to the ducks? It's nearly their dinner time."

Bear took the bag and shook his head. *Dames!*

• • •

The ducks quacked when they saw the door open. How two full grown mallards fit in his sink Bear didn't want to guess.

"Dinnertime, you nasty bastards." Bear reached into the bag and threw a handful of popcorn at them. They caught a few in mid-air, quacking, flapping their wings and spraying water and feathers everywhere.

The door of the faux file cabinet opened and the squeaky voiced man fell out. "Ahhh! The ducks are loose!"

"Settle yourself down, son." Bear helped him up to his feet. "Have a seat."

Gunn tossed the bag and his fedora down on his desk and did a once over on the fidgety little man in front of him. He was mulatto, very light skinned and could probably pass as a white in the right light. Young, maybe in his early twenties. His hands were soft and his nails were bitten down to the quick. His hair was chemically straightened like many of the boys who haunted the jazz joints over on Bourbon Street. He had a black eye and he reeked of reefer. His shoes were old but his pants, shirt and jacket were new, recently tailored by the faint blue chalk marks on the pants cuff.

Bear sat down and tallied up his marks: a reefer smoking mulatto who has come into money, probably stolen from someone who wants to make sure this young gentleman doesn't have the time to finish his ensemble with a nice pair of two toned leather Oxfords.

"I'm Barrington Gunn. You saw my name on the door out front. And you are?"

"Jackson Talley. I got your name from some of the boys at the harbor. They said you could help me."

"And what do you want me to do for you?"

"I need you to make me disappear."

Bear laughed. "Not really my area of expertise. Sounds like you need a magician, not a detective. See, I'm more in the business of finding people, not losing them. Sorry, I can't help you."

"My friend, Drake, down at the dock. He said you helped a guy, Bannerman, vanish. Got him a new life."

Bear took a deep breath and exhaled. "Bannerman was a long time ago and a different sort of case. Sorry. I'm not your guy."

The young man pulled his thumb away from his mouth and shook his head. "No, you don't get it. This is serious deep shinola. If they find me, I'm a dead man."

"What did you do, son?"

"Nothing, sir." Talley rubbed his earlobe and then brushed a hand over his pomade heavy hair.

"Really?" Bear raised an eyebrow.

"I didn't do nothing." Talley started chewing on his thumbnail. "But they think I did."

"Look, I'll give you a piece of advice, okay? On the house. Use the rest of whatever you have left from whatever it is you didn't do and get the hell out of New Orleans."

"You don't think I didn't try? You think I got his shiner shaving? They won't let me leave. That's why I need to disappear. I've got the money, see?" Talley pulled out a fistful of twenties. "Eighty dollars. It's all I got left and I'll give it to you, all of it, just help me disappear."

Gunn rubbed his chin thoughtfully. Eighty dollars could square the books with Steinbaum and Melinda and even have a few bucks left over for himself.

Gunn took the money, stuffed it in his pants pocket and pulled out a piece of gum. He sat back, unwrapped the Black Jack gum, and started chewing slowly. "You got my help. But I still need to know what I'm getting myself into so, tell me everything and start from the beginning."

Talley let out a huge breath and his shoulders dropped about an inch as the tension left him. "Okay, I'll tell you everything. God's truth, I swear."

"I appreciate that. It makes my job easier when clients don't lie to me."

"I play guitar around town. Not just shine boxes, I've played in white clubs, too. But I got busted for selling a pinch of reefer, lost my gig, and fell on some hard times. I had to hock my strings, and then I got tossed out of my old lady's house so I needed cheap digs to crash. Things were looking down and then I met Joe. I never got his last name. Everybody called him Easy Joe. He and a few friends shared a flat right there in the Quarter and he said I could stay there until I got back on my feet. He said he even had connections, you know, men he worked for who were looking for help. I thought I'd finally found some good luck for once, you know?"

"But these men he set you up with weren't working on the right side of the fence, I bet."

Talley started biting his thumbnail and shook his head. "They'd give us jobs, nothing big time. Just some smash and grabs; nickel and dime stuff. I only intended on staying until I made enough to get my guitar out of hock, you know? Or maybe get a new one."

"Or maybe long enough to get a new suit?" Gunn cracked his knuckles and put his hands behind his head, rocking for a moment as he stared at the water stained ceiling. "Yeah, I got the picture. Forget the particulars and get to what went wrong."

"Joe got picked to do a special job for one of his bosses, Mr. Mallone, a quick smash and grab. Joe said it felt hinky so he asked me to come along."

"Why did it feel hinky?"

"It wasn't the sort of job guys like us were sent on. We're usually just muscle in the back, yah know? And the fact it came from Mallone, well, that put up red flags in my head."

"Why?"

"It wasn't a well-kept secret that Easy Joe and Mallone's favorite girl had a regularly scheduled appointment, if you know what I mean."

"Dames." Gunn shook his head. "It's always dames. What was the job?"

"To break into a house and crack a safe. It was one of those big ones over in the Garden District. Mallone gave us the combination and all the information we'd need: the layout, what kind of security the old broad had, hell, he even knew the damn dog's name."

"What went wrong?"

"What didn't? First, the layout was all screwy and we couldn't find any kind of safe like Mallone said we would. Hell, there wasn't even a dog! But there was a very angry old man who did not appreciate us breaking into his home. He shot Joe twice, right in the gut. Joe shot back, hit the old man right in the forehead. I swear, to God on high, I didn't know Easy Joe was packing heat. A blackjack, a switchblade and some brass knuckles, sure, we both had that stuff but nobody said nothing about bullets."

"Then what did you do?"

"I stood there for a minute, not knowing what to do and then I heard police sirens. Something inside me just took over and I grabbed some stuff that looked expensive enough to hock. I knew once this hit, I'd need to get the hell out of town."

"Why? No one knew you were there."

Talley rubbed his ear. "I got seen. I was bagging the last of the silverware and this old lady caught me in the kitchen. She started pointing and screaming. I rushed out the way I came in but I figured she got a good look at me.

"So, I laid low for a couple of days. Once it seemed okay, I went and hocked my stuff figuring I'd use the money to get a bus ticket and get out of town."

"But first you stopped off to get a new suit."

"I didn't have anything but what I had on my back. Besides, a man needs to look presentable when traveling."

"So why aren't you gone?"

"They jumped me at the bus station."

"Who? Mallone's men?"

Talley shrugged. "I ain't seen these guys before. I just guessed it was but, now that I got time to think about it, it doesn't seem likely. They kept asking me about the box. Where was the box? How would Mallone know about the box?"

"What box?"

"One of the things I stole was a small jewelry box. Well, I thought it was a jewelry box but I never could get it to open. It was dark wood with gold curlicue designs all over it. I got ten dollars for it."

"Where did you hock it? We need to get a better look at this box to see why these men want it so badly."

"Odyssey Shop, over on Magazine."

Gunn picked up his hat. "All right then, let's go."

Talley shook his head. "No, sir. No. I'm not leaving this room. You go yourself, talk to Mama Effie, she runs the joint, and tell her that Talley sent you. She'll talk to you."

"Miss Page said you were afraid of the ducks. You okay with them now?"

"I'll take them over whatever is waiting for me out there, thank you."

Gunn stood up, put his fedora on and grinned. "Well, sir, you own my services for as long as your eighty dollars stretches. Feel free to make yourself at home. I'll be back shortly."

He left and closed the door behind him.

"I guess I'm playing babysitter this afternoon?" Melinda said.

"No, doll." He peeled off a pair of ten dollar bills. "Here's your back pay and a little extra."

"Extra?" Melinda took the money, folded the bills and stuffed them in her bra. She arched a perfectly arched brow. "What sort of extra, Mr. Gunn?"

"Research, sweetie, just regular old research. I need you to go and see if there have been any burglaries in the Garden District. Burglaries that went wrong. Like two dead men wrong."

"I have a girlfriend who part times as a police dispatch. She owes me for a bleach job I did for her. She might have some straight dope."

"Good girl, get on that."

"What about our guest? Are we just going to leave him here alone?"

"He's not going anywhere. Scaredy cat, remember?"

"You're the boss. So, where are you going?"

"I've got to go see a woman about a box."

● ● ●

With a few bills in his pocket, Gunn felt a treat was due and hailed a Yellow cab.

"Hello, friend, how much to the Odyssey Shop on Magazine?"

The cabdriver turned his head slowly and chewed on the stub of a cigar like a cow reconsidering its cud. "Around two bucks for the drive and another sawbuck not to remember your face should anybody ask."

"Sounds fair. Let's go."

The drive took less than five minutes. Bear got out of the cab, handed over the money and the driver handed him a stained business card: "Sawbuck Sam, any hour, any parish. No questions asked. 555-8790."

"Much obliged, Sam." Bear tipped his hat. Sawbuck Sam nodded and drove away. He stood outside the Odyssey Shop. There was a CLOSED sign hanging inside the door. He had heard crazy talk that it was a front for an underworld Mafioso gang that dealt in everything from booze to prostitution and everything they could fit into a hole in between. Bear smirked at the gilded logo above the door, "WE GO TO THE ENDS OF THE EARTH TO SATISIFY YOUR NEEDS!"

Gunn tilted his fedora back and took a peek through the opaque front windows that looked stained from cigar smoke. Inside, it looked like a junk store. Rows and rows of mason jars, knick knacks and all kinds of rubbish. A quick flash of movement alerted him to a woman walking across the floor. She was holding a large book. Gunn knocked on the window, loudly.

She stopped. Her face look distorted through the blurred window. "Go away." she shouted and waved him away. "Can't you read?"

"I need to see Mama Effie. It's important." Gunn said.

The woman came to the door. She was tall, a café colored Creole woman. She looked down on him, and judged him insignificant in a matter of seconds. "Come back tomorrow. We're closed for the day." She pulled down the blind and clicked a bolt closed. "Private affair."

Gunn knocked on the door. "Jackson Talley sent me. About a box."

There was a click as the lock turned and the door opened. The woman was just a wisp, thin as an alley cat, but the sheer force of *HER* filled the entire doorway. All six feet four inches of Bear Gunn shrank away under her gaze. "I am Mama Effie. You have five minutes."

"Thanks."

Bear followed her to the register. She wore a very slinky red dress and a double strand of pearls. Two bald headed black men dressed in suits sat nearby studiously reading the paper. She sat down in a high backed chair that swiveled and waved her long manicured blood red nails. "Introduce yourself."

"My name is Barrington Gunn. I'm a private investigator."

The two goons made a snorting sound which Bear decided to ignore.

"Jackson Talley was assaulted recently and be believes it may be connected to the box he sold to you. He said it was mahogany with gold inlay, about so big?"

"I have it here." She nodded and pulled the box out from a shelf under the register. It was about as big as a paperback, dark wood with strange symbols etched in gold. It made Bear's eyes hurt to look at it for too long. "It's a puzzle box. My grandmere had one but I can't figure out how to open the blasted thing." She shook it. "Hear that? There is something inside."

"Could be what Talley got his face busted in for. Can I give it a try?"

Mama Effie handed him the box. "I'd be very obliged if you could open it, sir."

Bear held it for a second, feeling the weight. "It's heavy." He turned the box, this way and that, held it up to his eye and squinted. "Yep. It's locked tight. Huh. Let's try this." he said and slammed the box, hard, onto the slab gray floor.

It split like a walnut. Bear picked it up, put it on the counter and cracked it open. Inside was a smaller golden box.

"Curiouser and curiouser. Look, there's a latch on this one." Bear said as he started to open it.

"Not to quibble but I'd like to remind you that possession is nine tenths of the law." Mama Effie said as she snatched up the golden box. "Ugh, it's leaking." she said and put it back down.

Bear pulled a penknife out of his pocket, opened it and used the blade to flip the latch. He carefully wedged the blade in between the lid, opened it and took a peek.

An eyeball looked back at him.

"What sort of madness is this?" Mama Effie cried out. The two goons shot up from the chairs and ran to her side.

Bear looked closer, poking at the grayish white orb with his penknife. "It looks like inside the gold box was another box, a glass one, that held the eyeball suspended in..." He sniffed the blade. "Smells like pure grain alcohol. Why would anyone want to keep an eyeball?"

"I suppose it depends on who it belonged to." Mama Effie mused. "Either way, I don't want it in my shop. Tell your client he can have it back. I'll expect a refund, of course, minus some wear and tear on the merchandise."

"I don't have the power to make that kind of deal." Bear closed the little gold box with its gruesome trinket and slipped it into his pocket. "I'll see what I can do."

● ● ●

Bear took another cab back to the office but this time without the anonymity surcharge. He found Melinda pacing and taking long, nervous drags on a cigarette.

"Uh-oh. What's wrong?"

"Where do you want me to start?" She stamped out the cigarette and lit up another one. "First, our scaredy cat client is gone."

"Gone?" Bear took long strides to his office, opened the door and saw an empty office. "He's gone."

"Is there an echo in here? That's what I said. I'm not blind. I'm just glad the ducks are safe."

"Well, as long as they are okay." Bear rolled his eyes as he closed the door. "When are they going to fly the coop?"

"Barb is coming by tonight to get them so don't get your britches in a bunch, okay?"

Bear sat down at Mel's desk. "So, what's got your knickers in a twist?"

"First, tell me this guy has paid his bill in full."

"He did. Cash."

"Good because if half of what I heard is true, I don't think he has time to wait for a check to clear."

"Spill it."

"Officially, there was an incident at a house in the Garden District but written up as vandalism. Unofficially, two bodies were taken to the morgue."

"How can that be unofficial?"

"Because it was at the address of Reverend Du Blanche. Heard of him? No? Well, according to Vicki, Du Blanche is a big roller. He pulls all kinds of strings in local politics, has a pocketful of cops and keeps his fingers sticky with all sorts of creepy, dark mojo. He even claims to have pulled out the eyeball of Marie Laveau to see the future. I ain't saying I believe in any of that sappy, crystal ball, mumbo jumbo but I'm smart enough to know that somebody who brags about plucking out eyeballs is bad news. I'm glad that scaredy cat is gone. We're lucky to be clean of him, if you ask me."

"Well, I don't know how clean we are yet, sweetheart."

Bear pulled the small golden box out and laid it on her desk.

"I'm guessing that's not an engagement ring in that box."

"Don't get your hopes up."

Her pale skin grew a shade greener. "Don't tell me you've got Marie Laveau's eyeball on my desk! Bear, for crying out loud, it's leaking! You're letting voodoo eyeball juice run all over my desk."

"Don't get in a twist, doll." Bear wrapped it in a handkerchief and put it back in his pocket.

"What are we going to do?"

"I've got a plan. We take this back to the owner and ask for a hefty reward. The Reverend gets his eyeball back and we get a double payday. Everything is golden."

"No, no, that's not how this sort of thing goes down, Bear. These people are crazy. It's an eyeball, Bear. *AN EYEBALL.* Do you know what kind of people dig eyeballs out of a dead woman's face? Crazy people, that's who! And worse than that, they are crazy voodoo people. Oh, Bear! They are going to come looking for it and find it here with us and, I don't know! Turn us into zombies? Oh, no…no, they'll turn you into a zombie. I'm too pretty. I'll be sold into white slavery." Melinda held her face in her hands and sobbed, "I don't want to be a voodoo sex slave, Bear!"

"Calm yourself down, woman. How in the world could they possibly track the box to us here?"

A sudden, heavy knock on the door answered him. Melinda cocked a perfectly arched eyebrow.

"That doesn't prove anything. Besides, I don't think they are the kind that would knock."

The knocking continued, louder and heavier.

"Say, you wanna get that, doll? I think that falls under your job description."

KNOCK KNOCK KNOCK

"I resign."

The door slammed open and a man stumbled in and landed at Mel's feet. She squealed and kicked him over to reveal a very bloody and battered Jackson Talley.

Bear rushed to the broken man.

"What happened, you damn fool? Why didn't you stay put?"

"I'm so-so-sorry, Mistuh Gunn." Talley sputtered through busted lips. "I didn't think it through."

"They never do, do they? I guess it is true what they say about good help being hard to get these days."

Bear looked up towards the velvety voice. It came from a dark skinned man in a flashy midnight blue suit with shiny shoes who was leaning against the door. He was bald, wore a black eye patch over his left eye and smoked a long white cigarette. He had a ring on each finger. Each ring, Bear mentally calculated would pay his rent for a year.

He looked down at the mush that was Jackson Talley and then back at the Man in the Midnight Blue Suit. He did a quick tally and knew what had to be done.

Bear hissed at Mel. "Go to my office. Lock the door. Hide."

For once, Mel did not argue.

"Very good call, Mr. Gunn." He entered the room gracefully like a cat. "I always feel it is best for men to do business without the distraction of beautiful women."

"Well, you have me at a disadvantage." Bear stood, flashed his winning smile and went to meet him. "I don't believe I've had the pleasure of meeting you."

"Ah, forgive my rudeness. It has been a busy day. First, my colleagues were lucky to find Mr. Talley at his favorite reefer peddler's. After some coercion, he confessed that he stole something precious from me. A box about so big but he had sold it to the Odyssey Shop. So, then we had to go all the way to Magazine Street. The lady of the shop was a tad hesitant but I am very persuasive. She gave me this."

Midnight Blue Suit tossed the broken box to Bear.

It was sticky with blood and Bear felt his face grow hot.

"I'm the most honorable Reverend Henri Du Blanche and owner of the contents of that box."

"It's empty."

"So it is."

"So, to me, it looks like you're the owner of jackshit."

"Ah, that is where I hope you could be of assistance."

"Me?" Bear tightened his grip on the box.

"You find things, yes?" Du Blanche said as he moved in closer. Bear saw two great hulking men in suits come in and close the door.

"Sometimes."

"Then, let's be professional. I want to hire you to find what was in that box. And, to be completely frank with you, I believe this will be an exceptionally easy job for you."

"Do you?"

"Yes, since I believe you already know where it is and most importantly," Du Blanche lifted up the eye patch to show Bear the gaping, red empty eye socket, "what it is."

"I don't know what you're talking about, bud." Bear swallowed down a wad of bile. "That looks nasty. Have you seen a doctor? Could be infected."

He replaced the eye patch. "Stop playing stupid. The woman at the shop screamed your name as I was cutting into her face." Bear's face reddened and his nostrils flared. Du Blanche smiled and took a step closer. "Speaking of pretty faces, where is your woman?"

"Leave her out of this."

He snapped his fingers and his goons came to his side. "Perhaps she knows something."

"Don't you even think about it, bud. I'm warning you."

"No! I won't let you hurt her, too." Talley got to his feet and grabbed Du Blanche, pulling on his arm. "I won't let you."

"Get off me, pig!" Du Blanche slapped the pitiful man. Talley went down in a heap and the goons went to work kicking and punching him to make sure he stayed down.

"That's it!" Bear exploded and decked the first goon with a haymaker that sent teeth flying across the room. "Leave the poor son of a bitch alone! Try taking me on for size!"

The second goon reached for his gun but Bear pulled him in close for a jab and grab, pulled the gun away and pistol whipped him until he fell unconscious. Huffing and red faced, he turned to go at Du Blanche who stood calmly to the side, holding a .38 with his finger on the trigger.

"If we're finished playing, shall we do business?"

• • •

Bear tossed Talley over his shoulder and took him back to his office. Du Blanche and his men followed behind. He carefully put the unconscious man down in his chair.

The ducks squawked and flapped at the sight of him and begged for dinner. Bear picked up the bag and tossed a few popcorn kernels at the ducks. He grabbed a handful more and stashed it in his coat pocket.

"Filthy birds." Du Blanche grimaced and swatted at the down that floated in the air. "Where is the woman?"

Bear shrugged. "Maybe she went out the window? Who knows dames?"

"Let's get down to business. Do you have Laveau's Eye?"

Bear sat on the corner of his desk and thrust his hands deep in his coat pockets. "Yep."

"Give it to me."

"Whoa, son, perhaps you don't understand the fundamental concept of a free market. See, it goes like this: I have something you want, you pay me and then I give it to you. I think you forgot about that second bit. You look like the sort that carries a big wad so I'm thinking about a five hundred dollars is a good going rate."

Du Blanche nervously rubbed the stones on his rings. "Show me first."

"A show of good faith? You catch on quick." Bear took the handkerchief out of his pocket. He unfolded it and held up the golden box. "See?"

"Open it."

"You hurt my feelings, sir. I don't think you trust me."

"I don't. Show me the Eye and then I'll give you the money."

"Okay, the customer is always right." Bear started to stand but slid awkwardly off the desk and toppled forward, the handkerchief flying up. "Oooops!" He grunted as he reached out with his other hand to catch himself, tossing popcorn everywhere.

"SQUAWK!" The ducks flew up and snatched up the kernels and the white handkerchief in midair. They gobbled and fought over each bit until only the stained, white cloth remained.

"No!" Du Blanche screamed, started chasing and shooting at the birds that flew deftly away from him, around the room and out the window. Du Blanche pounded his fists on the window sill, "Damn you! Damn you to hell!"

"Bad luck!" Bear came up behind him and slapped him on the shoulder. "You'd best get after them. I'd try Jackson Square. I hear ducks love that place."

"You bastard! You stupid son of a bitch! Do you know what you cost me?"

"I don't know about you but I'm out five hundred big ones."

Du Blanch screamed in anger and snapped his fingers. "Kill him!"

The beaten and battered goons swaggered up to Bear.

"Oh, now, boys, are you sure you're ready for another round with me?"

The goon on the left pushed his broken nose back into place and spit out a wad of blood. "Yeah, sure. I think I got my second wind back. How about you, Des?"

The one on the right nodded, pulled out a blackjack and slapped it against his beefy palm. "I got your back, Harry."

"Okay, okay. You got me." Bear put his hands up and pointed behind them. "But how about her?"

Melinda was standing behind them with two .38 revolvers, the hammers pulled back, her finger on both triggers, pointed at their backs. "Hello, boys. Miss me?"

"I'm not afraid of a woman." Du Blanche sneered and aimed his revolver at her.

Melinda swerved a few degrees to the left, pulled the trigger, shot the revolver out of Du Blanche's hand and was back on point in seconds flat. "You should be."

"Her typing sucks but, man, oh man." Bear stopped to pick up Du Blanche's gun, "She can hit a fly off a cow's tit."

Du Blanche spit in Bear's face "This is not over, Mr. Gunn. Mark my words, you have made a terrible enemy today."

Bear pulled the handkerchief out of Du Blanche's pocket, wiped his cheek and handed it back to him. "So, should I add the duck to the bill?"

● ● ●

Later that evening, Mel met with Bear at Rudy's Café.

"Will the scaredy cat be okay?" she asked.

"He's pretty banged up. I left him at the hospital." Bear laughed. "Told them to bill the Most Honorable Reverend Henri Du Blanche."

"You shouldn't laugh. I think you are going to pay dear for today's little shenanigans."

"Maybe." Bear stirred his coffee. "Sorry about the ducks, Mel."

"Ducks are ducks. There will always be more. I'm sorry it cost us a payday."

"Did it?"

Mel's eyes went wide. "What did you do?"

"Let's just say I have very nimble fingers. A quick bit of misdirection and, voila!" He fanned out his hands, clapped and produced a small golden box.

"Bear…is that?"

Bear flashed a smile. "Know anybody in the market for one magic eyeball, gently used?"

The End

Señor Tijras

by Joe Hilliard

C all Aguacate, he'll know what to do.
My first thought as I heard the scream.

Then, a piercing whistle filled my ears, and I thought no more. I rushed forward, instincts kicking in.

The girl screamed again. She looked fourteen; too much eye make-up and a gash of scarlet lipstick seemed to stretch her mouth ear-to-ear. The screaming only exaggerated her grotesque look. Like a demented doll for psychotic children. *Click* My eye took a quick shot of her as she turned. She ran, stumbling in her too tight too short skirt. She wasn't moving fast. Natural, inelegant strides. No augment work on her.

Not yet.

Only then I realized the fright I'd probably put into her. Maybe she thought I was her attacker. A masked man. A masked man on the streets of Tijuana.

I'd been down here three weeks on the wrestling circuit. El Asesino Americano. The American Assassin. I'd been on my way to the stadium when I'd heard the screaming.

I checked the girl on the sidewalk. She didn't look pretty. Not anymore. Once she could have been her companion's twin sister. Except now she wore a second red slash across her throat. Blood still pumped feebly out of it. *Click* My eye took another quick shot. Her clothes were the cheap disposable paper ones you could buy out of the vending machines on any corner. The poorest of the poor. There were no marks on her flesh. A quick flit of my eye confirmed. And no augment work. Nada. She was pure as driven snow. The snow that never fell in TJ.

She was too far gone. Her body was cooling. With a final spasm, her life ended.

I gagged inside the mask. It was too damn hot. The streets were too close together. I pushed the bottom of my mask up to breathe a little easier. The mouth slit too small, too tight, constricting my breath. Noxious fumes of an overcrowded city hit me. I fought back a second gag and pulled the mask back down.

Then, I heard that whistle again. Further away. I focused in on that instead of the girl on the pavement. Anything to fight the nausea. The Tijuana night was lit up garishly with neon advertisements for everything under the sun: cerveza, tortas, tequila, tacos, películas in glorious 4-D, lucha libre, and fútbol. You name it. And I saw ... it. Blurry motion on the horizon. Leaping into the air above the low-rise buildings, dropping down onto roofs before flailing into the air again. It was pushing its augments to the limits. I dialed my eye in, but it wasn't built for that strenuous of a workout. I figured I broke part of the mechanism. A steel parody of the human form dressed in a long coat. *Click* My eye caught what it could. The whistle faded away into the night with him. I ran the internal mapping to coordinate with what I was looking at. It was heading south, away from the border.

The sirens were almost upon me. Screaming. Everything was screaming tonight. I'd been too caught up in watching that thing flee. That's my problem. Always has been. One track mind. It makes you a good wrestler. A good jobber. It doesn't make you much else. You don't even have your own gimmick. You're just a replacement. It's what got me the job. Aguacate, the promoter, had needed a replacement for the original Asesino Americano. He'd taken a bad tumble off the ropes on a tour of the hinterlands, broken both collarbones and his guidance software. Taken one right in the sweet spot. I met him when I first got down from Pomona. Wanted some pointers on his gimmick. But he couldn't control his facial muscles. His whole face rippled with quirks and jerks. They had some software doc down from La Jolla, but it looked like he'd need some major re-wire work. That guaranteed one week contract was shaping up into a long haul gig.

I dialed in Aguacate's office. I needed quick advice. Tell me what to do, I can do it. But I'm no thinker. I'm no artist. I'm just a guy. Today, I'm the Asesino Americano. Tomorrow, quién sabe?

As long as it wasn't Jailbird Jim.

I felt the whisper of bullets around me. Los federales had arrived. I started running. Aguacate would have to smooth it over later. My legs were better engineered than that thing. Mine were designed for power drops from the tops of thousand foot arenas. I could leap two hundred feet straight up from a standing position. Give me a running start and I could go several city blocks. None of the shots came close. I doubted any of los federales were heavily augmented. They'd be working private sector instead if they were. The latest US-Mexico-Canada tripartite deal had split the border towns wide. Tijuana. Mexicali. Niagara. Detroit. All of them International Free Zones. Barely regulated. Teaming with people. Barely regulated. Barely contained. And anything goes.

I propelled myself six blocks east before taking a jump south. No one paid me much attention as I flitted by. I wasn't the only night traveler. I lit up my eye. 7:46 pm, Pacific Standard Time. I was set to go on in forty-four minutes at el Estadio Olímpico. El Asesino Americano had a match with el Espíritu Escarlata on the undercard.

You can't keep the people waiting.

Aguacate was waiting for me in the locker room when I arrived. His eyes glistened behind his thick permanent glasses. He shook my hand. Gently, fatherly. While I stripped down, I gave him a quick appraisal of what happened.

"Give me the shots of those girls. This thing. I'll take care of it." I downloaded the pics and he was gone.

● ● ●

April 1, 2037. All Fool's Day. My real muscles ached. My augments felt like they ached. Escarlata and I had gone the full three falls. The crowd ate it up. My shoulders burned like they'd gone three rounds with a meat grinder. Escarlata and those amazing augmented hands. Steel fingers. Vice grips. I'd never seen anything like them in all my years on the circuit. He was no jobber. He was on the way up the ladder.

I lay face down on the massage table. El Estadio Olímpico had the most updated facility I had seen this side of the Garden in New York. None of the Southern California venues measured up. The crawler worked its way across my back, applying heat and massaging out the kinks. A second crawler sunk itself into the back of my head and ran diagnostics through my eye. I sighed and flipped on the telepape unit inlaid under the table. Top story - more fighting on the Chiapas-Guatemala border. Opinion columns ran pro Mexico occupying northern Chiapas for its own security. After its succession a few years ago, that would be a major blow to Chiapas. War seemed imminent. The voices squabbled on the telepape. I flicked the volume down lower. I scrolled through to the local TJ section. If it weren't for a picture of the dead girl, I would have missed it. She had no make-up on, but I recognized the eyes. Her staring eyes.

"Hey, Mack! Qué pasa?" A deep booming voice interrupted my scan. Escarlata walked in. His scarlet costume was elegantly designed. Form fitting, with just a subtle teardrop eye-shape to the mask, making it come alive. El Asesino Americano had passed on some dull black and greys with a shocking electric blue and red skull mask. Sure, I'd worn worse, but this was still far from the crowning glory of my career.

"Xavier." El Espíritu Escarlata. Xavier Salomón Guadalupe Reyes. His voice was firm, commanding, yet not loud at all. Hypnotic. You listened to the tone and only later realized he hardly told you anything about himself at all. He wasn't boastful like so many of his wrestling brethren. Whispers from other luchadors hinted he came from a big wheel family out of Chihuahua. Educated up north somewhere. Probably USC. Not public school. With all the recent border upheavals, he could be making a real name for himself on the political scene. Maybe even governor. Locker room rumor had it he wore the mask to protect the family name.

What I did know: he was as pure-bred técnico as I had ever seen. Strictly first order. And I liked him. He'd made my three weeks enjoyable. Even though he had kicked me two days to sideways in three separate matches now. "I'm beaten down. Not the idol of the masses."

He laughed. "Pobrecito. You Americanos are never serious. Your predecessor was not. You are not."

"I can be, Xavier, I can be." I shook my head. I heard that whistle again. "I am right now."

Xavier lowered himself onto the massage table next to me. The crawlers quickly swarmed out over his body. He sighed and closed his eyes. The skin on his eyelids had been permanently etched the color of his mask. Eyeless. Another neat gimmick. "Are you, Mack? You look too relaxed to be serious. Decadence saps the seriousness from all men. Even a noble warrior such as yourself." And he laughed.

"I saw a murdered girl last night. Just before our bout."

Xavier slowly opened his eyes. He stared over at me. "You saw a murder? Before or after I rearranged your limited brains?"

"Now who's not serious? I didn't see a murder. I saw a girl die after her murderer left. Check out the pape. Ask Aguacate. I told him."

The telepape lit up as Xavier fiddled with the control. I could see the articles reflected on his mask as he ran through them. Finally, he stopped. "Esto? La puta?" He glanced over at me. Even under his mask, I could feel the raised eyebrow.

"She was no whore." Angered, I struggled to a sitting position, knocking one of the crawlers to the tile. "She was a girl. A little girl. Fourteen."

"Fourteen, unfortunately, is not a little girl here, mi amigo. Not here. Not anymore. You've been here long enough to know. Not since the Treaty. It's just a number. Meaningless." He closed his eyes again. "It's all meaningless." The crawler had climbed back up on the table and was trying to get me to lie back down. I slapped at it, then turned off the table. It waddled off to the recharging station.

"Meaningless? No life is meaningless. No life should be meaningless. She ... she died right in front of me."

"This is the first time you've seen someone die, Mack?"

"No. Before. In Houston. It was a hick town gig run by a small-time promoter. Things weren't rigged right. He cut safety corners. This jobber's name was Big John. He had a hillbilly gimmick. Real popular a few years ago. Up north anyway. He went in, tried to get a spring off the ropes. But they broke. He flew right through. His neck snapped on the floor. No blood. Just nothing. Nothing at all.

"But this wasn't like that. This was cold blooded butchery. Her throat was slashed."

"Slashed?" Xavier sat up, sending his own crawlers flailing. His eyes flared under his mask. "It does not say that here."

"It was. I was there. Someone had slit her throat wide open. I've never seen such a neat cut. Here." I plugged into the pape and downloaded my pic from the night before. "See for yourself. Clean. The murderer had metal hands of some sort. I didn't get a great shot of it."

"It?"

"Yeah. It. It was like a metal man. No, more like a bug. Like a metal bug shell. In a really ratty coat. Here." I shot the next pic into the pape monitor. "Like I said, not very good."

"Señor Tijeras!"

"Who's Señor Tijeras? Does he wrestle on the Mexico City circuit?"

"No. Not Señor Tijeras. Mr. Scissors. He's the boogeyman. Like Jack the Ripper. Or your Night Stalker. Your Hillside Strangler. He's responsible for at least ninety deaths in the past ten years."

"The pape doesn't mention any of that. They barely give any details. This could be anywhere in the City."

"Exactemente. They wouldn't. Here in Mexico, he is notorious. Beyond notorious. He revels in his notoriety. Any mention of his name would only invite another killing. And another. Why do you think they don't mention how she died? So no one will know." Xavier shook his head. "But people will talk." He stood and walked towards the locker room.

"The Free Zone has brought him back. It has raised the dead."

● ● ●

Neither Escarlata nor I were on the bill that night. Aguacate arranged so each luchador worked no more than three matches a week. Twice was ideal. He ran a large enough stable to work that most weeks. Bring in bigger crowds to see a lot of different gimmicks. Not like the Pomona gig I'd left where a few names ran the show. And a jobber could expect four to five shows weekly. Masked. Unmasked. Maybe three different gimmicks. TJ was spoiling me.

El Estadio Olímpico was packed to capacity. Como siempre. Eighty thousand people. Six days a week. Two shows Friday and Saturday. Three hour plus shows.

Escarlata and I were sitting in the third level upper deck. Part of the contract obligated you to attend several matches a week when you weren't wrestling. Aguacate liked to make his luchadors part of the fabric of the City. Celebrities. And the crowd ate it up, they loved sitting alongside their heroes.

I dialed my eye up a little to get a better shot of the gimmick on stage, a new guy that had just signed on. I hadn't caught him in action yet. Slim Chico. Some guapo off the Salvadorian circuit. He looked trim and fast. Really flying off the tope rope. Didn't seem heavily augmented. Maybe Aguacate had him pegged for the lightweight, less augmented, division. Interesting. The crowd was eating it up, yelling with every dive from the ropes.

For stadium duty, you needed to dress the part. Escarlata had a brilliant scarlet suit that perfectly complimented his mask. I had found a medium blue suit in el Asesino Americano's wardrobe that made the mask as palatable as possible, so had it tailored to my cut. I had bought a nice red and blue piped tie from a street vendor outside the stadium that made the suit.

I was enjoying a tamarindo between falls when I spotted her. Two sections over. The same too tight too short skirt. The same garish make-up. I trained my eye on her. *Click* She was sporting a mean shiner. It purpled into her skin.

"Mira!" I nudged Escarlata. He had been concentrating on the next fall. The crowd roared its approval of Slim Chico. Aguacate really knew his talent.

"Qué? What is it, Asesino?"

"Over there. Section 323. It's her. The girl." Escarlata squinted, his eyes weren't augmented.

"Are you sure?"

"Yes." I shot up the pic from my eye onto the display in my hand. "Looks like she's alone."

El Estadio Olímpico only looks old. It was designed to give off an aura of ancient times. Like the Coliseum in Rome. It's actually one of the most modern stadiums I'd ever been in. Aguacate used the Free Zone status to his advantage, picking global dollars from so many pockets. And los federales, preying on their fear. After all, security needed to be boosted to deal with all the new unknown elements pouring in. If you knew how to use it, the stadium could be as good a friend as any human staffer. Better. Aguacate had instructed all the luchadores on the use of the system in case of emergencies. The talent has to be protected after all.

Escarlata and I made our way into the concession ring behind the seats. I nodded to one of the cerveza guys and leaned over the counter. Each concession booth had a linkup to every other concession booth, the security system, even the announcer's booth. Trouble anywhere in the stadium could be contained almost immediately.

I accessed the security cameras for our deck easily enough. Escarlata peered over my shoulder, munching from a bag of chicharrones he had taken from the concession stand. I fed the system the pic of the girl, the section, and an approximate seat number. "C'mon, Escarlata. They'll have her downstairs in security by the time we get down there."

● ● ●

She sat on a cold metal folding chair. Barely. She was ready to bolt any second. Her hands gripped the corner of the table in front of her. Tightly. The two stadium security guards standing at the door didn't calm her any. Both were ex-military Aguacate had hired with some rather obvious armament augments. Probably just off a stint in Chiapas. She glanced up as Escarlata and I came into the room, then shrank back into the seat. She was shivering. It was cold in the bowels of the stadium.

I have to say, Escarlata fit the bill as a genuine caballero. He pulled his suit coat off and wrapped it around her bare shoulders. Up close she didn't even look fourteen. Just all dressed up in adult clothes. There was some scabbing underneath her eye, speckled into the discolored skin. I ran my eye over it. *Click* Interesting. There were patterns. Like those made by rings. Or some kind of machine. Escarlata bent down next to the girl and spoke quietly in her ear. She had stopped shivering, but still looked cold. And scared. She shook her head.

"Quieras bebida? Comida?" Escarlata suddenly spoke louder, cutting the quiet of the room. She nodded, but still did not speak.

I nodded to one of the security. "Go upstairs to the nearest stand. Bring down, uh, a torta, some tacos el carbon, uh, churros, and a tamarindo."

"Jamaica." Her voice was deeper than I thought it would be. Too much of that vaunted TJ clean air. I smiled and raised my hands in a shrug.

"Y una jamaica. Charge it to Escarlata's account. You better get a few more chairs too. We could be here awhile."

"This is Xochi. She lives on the streets. Near where you saw her." Escarlata's voice was even. Patient. Like he was talking to a child. I didn't know if that was for my sake, or hers. Nodding, I sat down on the edge of the table, at the far end from the girl. "Her family was from Chiapas. They came here during the revolution. The first revolution." He bent over slightly so she could whisper in his ear more. "She says you frightened her last night. She thought you were with him."

"Tell her she frightened me too." Xochi smiled and laughed at that.

Escarlata nodded.

"Where is her family?"

"Estan muerto." Her voice had a hollow sound to it. As dead as her family. I nodded.

"You understand, then? She has lived on the streets for several years now." Escarlata put a hand on her shoulder. "She and her friend had been living together about eight months. For protection."

"What...?"

Escarlata's eyes pierced me, stark black surrounded in crimson. "What do you want to know, Asesino?"

"What was her friend's name?"

Just then, the security guard returned with the food. Xochi's eyes lit up. She pulled the chair closer to the table, and hunched over her plate with her shoulders so that no one could take her food. Taco in one hand, churro in the other, Xochi tore into the food. I eased myself off the table and walked over to a corner. Escarlata joined me.

"She saw him. Señor Tijeras. He will be looking for her as well. He never leaves a girl alive."

"How do you know? It could be anyone, anything that killed her friend."

Escarlata shook his head. "It was him."

"How do you know?"

He turned to look at Xochi. She had devoured the tacos, the churros, and was almost through the torta. She looked up quickly, instinctively. She felt us observing her. Her lips parted into a smile. And she looked like a child. Finally.

"Qué recuerdas sobre él?" Escarlata's voice was cold, metallic. Her face fell. The smile vanished.

"Sus manos."

His hands.

● ● ●

We took Xochi back to Xavier's place. He had a split level penthouse atop the second largest tower in TJ. His robo-vacuum was finishing as we came in. He opened the curtains to let in the smoggy orange sunset. Muted flames leapt off the billows of smoke and soot. Xochi collapsed on the sofa and fell asleep almost immediately. Xavier went to the refrigerator and handed me a bottle of tamarindo. It was strangely quiet, here above the City. Peaceful. The sound of the streets failed to penetrate this high.

"We need to go to los federales."

Xavier laughed. It was a dark laugh. "Mack, do you really think they will help? This is the Free Zone. Any competent police force would have found both you and Xochi by now. You'd be in jail with that ugly mug of yours. Probably on your way to the gas chamber. Such a pretty scapegoat.

"But they aren't. They don't care. They want to make like it never happened. You know this. You saw the papes. If we took Xochi in, she'd disappear. They'd kill her. Or worse. Maybe they deport her back to that war zone. They don't want to hear about it."

"Aguacate?"

"I do not think he would want us involved. Bad for business."

I popped the cap off the tamarindo. "So? What do we do?"

Xavier took the bottle away from me, took a pull on it. "We? We go hunting."

"The hell we do."

"It is a devil we're after."

I took the tamarindo back from Xavier and drained it. "You act like you know this devil."

"Do I?" Xavier stood in front of the refrigerator again. His back to me. He piled a plate high with some shredded carnitas out of a bowl. His fingers carefully shredded it even more. "Perhaps it is merely the weight of my people. The weight I have always borne."

I snorted. The Asesino's mask didn't cover it too well. "Claro que sí, Xavier? Really?"

"Perhaps not so melodramatic, Mack. But yes, a burden that is mine."

Xochi stirred on the couch, cried out. I bent over her and stroked her hair. She continued to mewl in her sleep. Tears stained her cheeks. She shivered in Xavier's suit coat.

"You have something to cover her with?"

Xavier went to the closet underneath the stairwell and pulled out several woolen blankets. I took them from him and covered her gently. The tears had stopped. But her face had frozen tight. Even in sleep, she did not relax.

"So? What do you know about this Señor Tijeras?"

"Mañana, Mack. Mañana. I need some sleep now."

"Yeah. Sure. Mañana."

● ● ●

I slept in the guestroom. The bed was easily twice the size of the entire room Aguacate rented for el Asesino. The windows were draped in elegant green and gold curtains. Either Xavier had dipped into the family funds, or I seriously needed to renegotiate with Aguacate. Mictlantecuhtli, the God of Death stared down at me all night from the wall, his cavernous eye sockets drinking in the light. My night was filled with the shadows he left in his wake.

Xavier, on the other hand, seemed perfectly human in the morning sun. Well-scrubbed and well-rested, he was making eggs and chorizo for breakfast. Xochi piled her plate high with the first round. Xavier motioned a plate towards me, but I declined with a nod. My stomach had never adjusted to eating in the morning. Not since I'd started out in Niagara as a jobber back in '25. I made do with a tamarindo from the refrigerator. In this City of extreme need, Xavier's refrigerator was a cornucopia full enough to feed an army. Excess and extreme. Hell, there was more room in his refrigerator than my place.

The smog overpowered the morning sun, leaving only grey streaks out the curtains. Xavier sipped his café while rolling the pape through a monitor embedded in his marble countertop. Xochi continued to eat, ignoring us both. I leaned against the countertop, finishing off the bottle. Here we were, just the model of morning domesticity.

"There was another killing last night." Xavier didn't look up from the monitor.

"Where?"

Xavier sighed. "Does it matter? Tomorrow, the next, next week, and they will breathe

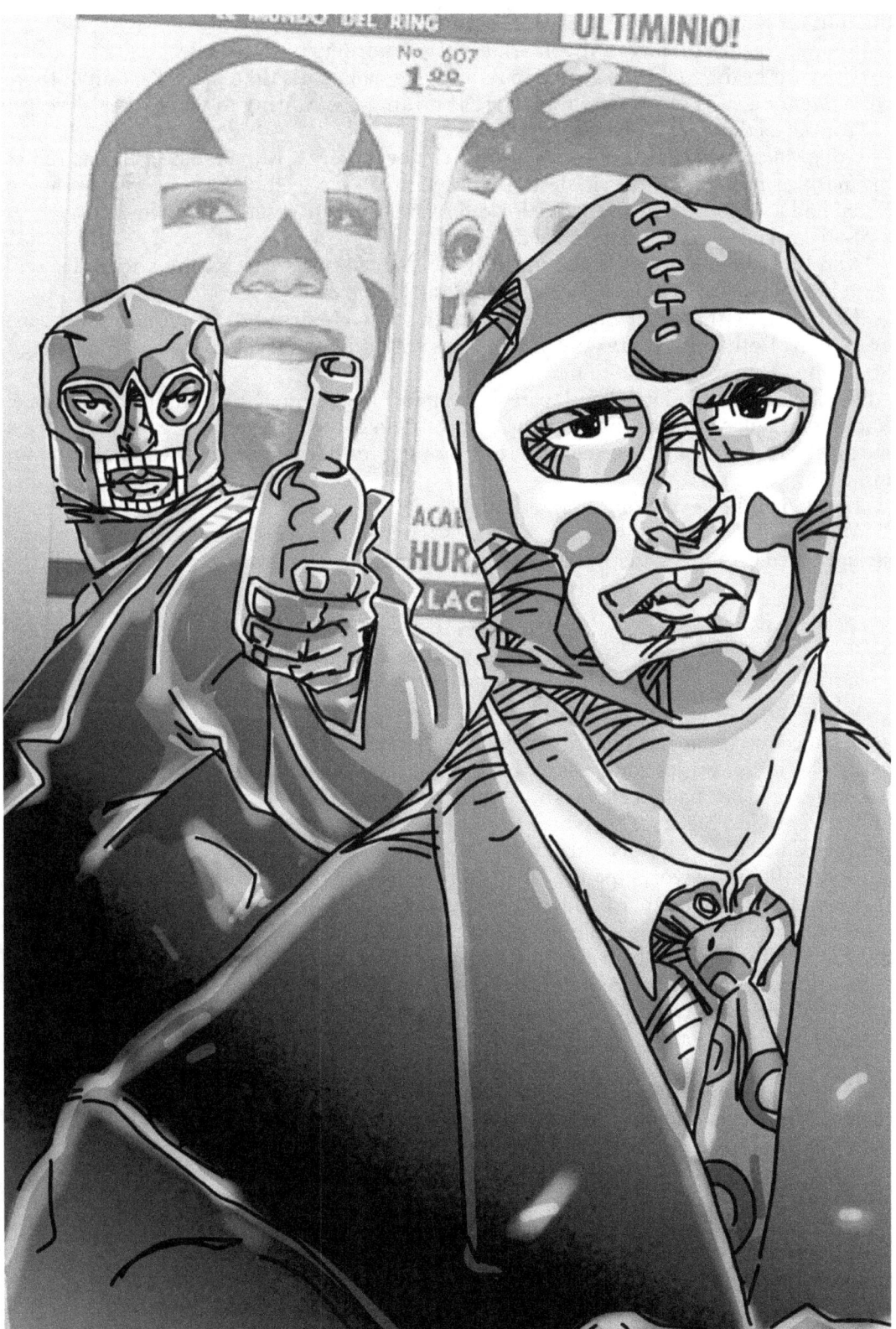

life into his name. He will come."

"Sounds like he already is, if you ask me. Two murders in two days."

"Use your brain, Mack. Here two in two days is nada. Less than nada. Last night there were twenty deaths in the City limits. He's building up. Waiting to truly come alive."

"You act as though you know him, Xavier."

"I do, Mack. I do." He looked up at last. His eyes were strained, bloodshot as red as his mask, as red as his tattooed flesh. "I know him all too well." He closed his eyes again. Xochi had finished all the food. She looked from Xavier to I, searching our faces.

"So?" I asked again. "What do we do now?"

"And I told you, Mack. We go hunting." He nodded imperceptibly at Xochi. "He will want her. No one sees Señor Tijeras and lives. No one. Not in years."

"Can we take that risk? She's been through so much already." As though she wasn't even there. Both of us. Just a pair of wrestlers with our faces hidden in masks. So tough. So strong. "Can we ask that of her?"

"We have to demand it of her. It can't be helped. I have to go to the Olímpico now. Take Xochi to her place. Grab whatever she wants. Then come back here directly." He tossed me an electro-static key. "Remember, he's looking for her as surely as we're looking for him."

I pocketed the key. "Comforting thought."

"What is comforting nowadays?" Xavier shrugged into his coat, adjusted his tie, and straightened his mask. "Just get back here as quickly as you can."

"Right."

● ● ●

Xochi lived in an assortment of cardboard boxes lashed together with string and assorted colors of tape. It's hot and dry in TJ. No wind. No rain. None in at least fifteen years. Her house was as solid as anything in the City. Maybe a little more low rent than the place Aguacate had set el Asesino up in, but then not so much really. It's all disposable.

We were a few blocks from where I had first laid eyes on her. A few blocks from where her friend had died. The smog still hung low; the sky hadn't opened up today. I scattered some rats that were worrying the outside of the place while Xochi clambered inside.

I bent low to follow her inside. My shoulders rubbed the sides. About halfway in, I gave up. It would be impossible for me to turn around once I got in. If I got in. I eased myself back out. I could hear Xochi throwing things around inside. I had no idea what she could have here. Pic chips of her parents? Movie magazine chips? Historietas? Make-up? What did a fourteen year old girl in Tijuana worry about anyway? A boyfriend? Getting too fat? Chiapas? Hell if I knew.

I had this sudden urge to smoke. I hadn't in years. Bad for training. The original Asesino hadn't such qualms. His suit pockets had been loaded down with books of matches from every go-boy club across the City, half packs of Luckys, and some tawdry brand of local smokes that reeked of cloves.

A few more minutes and Xochi scrambled out, a bag thrown over her shoulder.

"Todo?"

She nodded. I dug in my pocket and pulled out one of el Asesino's disposable lighters. My fingers were too fat, too gnarled to make it work. Xochi took it from me. Adeptly, she thumbed the igniter. And just like that, it caught. Everything she could not fit in a bag.

All her life. I thought back to my place and realized I didn't have much more to account for in my life. I had more of Asesino's possessions than my own.

The box house burned quickly and burned brightly.

● ● ●

Xavier had returned from the Olímpico before us. The floor of the living room was littered with video equipment and computer components.

"I got the idea from you, Mack. Last night. When I saw how the security system at the Olímpico worked. Perhaps I should have studied computer science instead of political science." He barked out a sharp laugh. "My father would have loved that. Only he would have found something so practical to be so useless." He shook his head. "So utterly useless. All of it. So utterly useless."

"So? What's the plan?" Xochi and I sat down on the couch. Xavier sat on the floor, holding up what looked like a button. He tapped a button on a remote and the television came to life. My face stared back at me. Xochi made rabbit ears behind my head. I scowled. She clapped and smiled.

"Bait."

"Bait?"

"Xochi."

"You're insane."

"No. We know Tijeras will be after her. He wants her. So we hook her up with this." He reached over and slipped a micro dot onto Xochi's collar. Xavier's face appeared on the screen. "And one for you." He hooked another onto the lapel of my suit coat. The screen split to show the view from both cameras; Xavier seemed to be staring at himself. "I can monitor you with these. He'll come. And we'll have him."

"We'll have him? I don't think I'll be able to handle him. Can you? Even together, I don't know..."

"Relax, Mack. Don't you trust me?"

Trust had nothing to do with it.

● ● ●

Several days passed. I followed Xochi from a relatively safe distance on the streets. We had hammered on Xochi that she was to go back to her regular life, as much as possible.

And I followed.

As she ate fifty-cent pastor at a taquería.

As she watched the boys parading down front of the Hipódromo Caliente, their pockets flush with cash.

As she skated at the roller park.

As she stood in booths at the local music shop, listening to the newest norteños.

As she stood on the Plaza Santa Cecilia listening to a guitarist spin a corrido about the bandit heroes of Chiapas.

I wondered if she even remembered Chiapas anymore. If it was any worse than what she was dealing with now. I stared at the reflection of my masked face in the plate glass window of the McDonald's. Did I look tired? Would I ever look as tired as her? El Asesino laughed back at me and shook his head.

I wrestled twice, beating some jobber just down off the El Paso circuit, then losing to Slim Chico. His technical skills were better than I had thought. Worse, I'd had my mind on other things. I wasn't sharp. Naturally, Escarlata won his matches while hardly breaking a sweat.

Señor Tijeras was nowhere to be seen. Not by us. Another murder took place. But the pape description was even vaguer than the first. It could have been him, it could not have been him. I even went out to the murder site. We ruled it out. Something didn't fit right about it.

As if anything could ever fit right about murder.

● ● ●

"I give up." We were back at the Olímpico. It was a large, loud mid-week crowd. Xochi sucked down her jamaica loudly through a straw. Escarlata had a crimson fedora tipped back on his head. My coat was off and my sleeves rolled up. We had an electrostatic map of TJ spread out on our laps. "This place is just too damned big for the two of us."

Escarlata pointed and the marks on the map highlighted a lurid pink. "Here's where we know he's been." Just two spots. Two little spots. "And Xochi." He traced the green lines crisscrossing all over. "He must be close. He must."

"Why? For all we know he lit out for Chihuahua or..."

"What? Chiapas?" Escarlata snarled. I pushed the map off into his lap. I plucked my tamarindo up off the floor and took a swig.

"You tell me, Escarlata. You tell me. You're the expert." I found myself snarling back. "You seem to be in his brain. But you aren't sharing. I'm," I pointed at the map, "just drawing circles in the sand. And I've had it. What we really need to do is get Xochi somewhere safe. Somewhere outside the City." I stood up. "C'mon, Xochi." I held my hand out to her. She took it, softly. Like a child. I grabbed my jacket with my other arm. Like a lamb to the slaughter.

● ● ●

In retrospect, we should have seen it. Escarlata should have anyway. Me, I was still too in the dark about too many things. But then, the spider never thinks he might be someone else's fly. I was angry. Too angry to think straight. Too angry to pay attention. The air outside was hot and dry. I just wanted to get Xochi away.

A whistle filled my ears as we walked away from the Olímpico entrance into the plaza outside. It filled my ears as I turned towards the scream.

Señor Tijeras was on top of her in an instance. I still held Xochi's hand, her sudden collapsing weight pulling me down. His eyes were deep set into his face, buried deep into his steel face. They looked familiar as they bore into mine. They paralyzed me. I couldn't rise.

Somewhere, I heard yelling. Escarlata had made it out of the stadium. With a snarl, Tijeras raked his hands across Xochi's back. Then he disappeared. I looked up. Escarlata had launched himself onto Tijeras' back, thrusting them both over and away from me. The two grappled in the plaza.

I bent over Xochi. She was sitting up. I reached out and felt her blood on my hands. Tijeras had split her back wide open. Her eyes were glazing over. I cursed under my breath. Escarlata's play had been all wrong. He had been wrong. I had been wrong.

Xochi was dying. It was dark. The lights had gone out. Tijeras and Escarlata were both gone. I laid Xochi down gently. She gasped as her back touched the pavement.

"Yvette."

"Qué?" I leaned in closer to her. I could feel the faintness of her breath.

"Mi amiga. Su nombre. Yvette. Remember her. Remember us." And she died.

I reached down my gloved hand and closed her staring eyes.

● ● ●

I tracked them. It wasn't hard. I dialed my eye up a few degrees. A blood splotch here, still fresh. I almost lost them in the multitude of blood trails outside a carnicería, but a brief splash of crimson cloth sent me back on the trail.

A few more blocks, and I realized that I didn't need to track them. I knew where they were going. I had always known where this would end. It shouldn't have been hard. But I'm a simple guy. Not too smart at all. Just a good jobber that could use his hands. Not his mind.

I still had the key Xavier had given me. It was dark inside.

● ● ●

I had never killed a man before. It was easier than I had imagined. What does that say about the capacity of man? Even a jobber like me. It was easy. So easy. He was still standing over Xavier, blood dripping from his metal talons. Even in the dark, I could see the deep wounds on both of their bodies. Flesh rent from flesh. I caught Tijeras from behind with a body blow. Before he could get to his feet, I kicked him in the abdomen. Once. Twice. A third time. I used the full power of my augmented legs. I could hear bones breaking, organs bursting, and the crunch of a body falling to pieces.

Xavier had wounded Tijeras greatly. I could see where his face was crisscrossed with deep cuts. I only threw the final blows. He was dead before I laid a hand on him.

It felt good. I thought about a young girl lying dead on the pavement. No one was there. I had been the only one, and even I had fled her death. Some hero. Just a jobber.

When I turned, Xavier was not to be seen. I caught the sound of his ragged breath. He had crawled behind the couch in the living room. He was bleeding severely. I propped up his head. His eyes opened and looked into mine. They weren't as bright as they used to be.

"Mack."

"I got here as quickly as I could. I'm not so swift sometimes."

"Swift enough, my friend, swift enough."

"I don't understand. What does it mean?"

"What does any of it mean, Mack?"

"Señor Tijeras?"

"Is my younger brother. I am sure you suspected. My parents—they paid handsomely to cover it up. They've tried to forget all about Armando. All about what he's done. What he's done to our family."

"Take it easy. Relax." I propped Xavier up on some pillows from the couch. I went to the refrigerator and brought back a tamarindo. He took a grateful swig. He was perspiring profusely. The torn collar of his crimson coat swam in it.

"No. Someone does need to know. You, my friend, need to know. My sister. Tamara.

She was the first one. She was twelve. He butchered her. Tore her to pieces. I can ... I can still see her. I can see what was left of her.

"I found her. I heard her screams. She begged for mercy. But Armando ... Armando did not care. Not for her. Not for me. Not for our family. Only for himself. His own pleasures." He coughed. "What can I say? He wasn't so different from father. From me. All we want are our own physical pleasures. Our own bitter pleasures.

"He laughed. That ... that bastard. He laughed.

"None of us knew. He'd been stealing money. My parents thought he'd been off getting high like any other respectable politician's son would. But ... he'd found a black market bone shop. He'd been cut. Cut good. Body and soul. They took away his soul."

"We all make our choices, Xavier. We all ... we are all responsible for our choices. You. Your brother. Xochi. All of us. Me. We are not owned. Not by the actions of others. Only by our own actions."

"There's that gringo optimism again." He grunted. "If I didn't hurt so bad, I'd smack you one. Just one more. One last lesson for the ring."

"I could use it. I think Aguacate's ready to cut el Asesino off."

"He better not. Absence only makes the heart grow colder." Xavier spit blood onto the floor.

"I don't think that's the way the saying goes." I didn't think Xavier would last much longer without attention. His blood was the same color as his costume. Escarlata. He was bathed in it. I sat him up at the table. He took another slug of the tamarindo.

"It should though, Mack. ..."

I watched as he slowly drained the bottle. He tried to set it down, but heavy fingers and it fell, rolling away from him on the table.

"Mack, you are my friend. You are my friend because you are here. No one else is here. Not my brother. Not my sister. Not my parents. Only you. You are here to witness my end.

"I have killed my brother. There is nothing left for me."

"I'll call los federales. They can get an ambulance here. Aguacate. He can take care of things. He'll take care of you." I touched my phone link.

Xavier shook his head. "I don't want him to take care of me. Don't you understand, Mack? I don't want to go back to that life. I don't want to go back to any life. I ... I just want to die. I killed Xochi. As surely as I killed my brother. As surely as I killed Tamara. All of them. I killed them. Their blood is on my hands." He banged his hands on the table. "My hands of steel. Oh, God, what have I done?"

And he died. Sitting there at a table in his apartment.

I reached down my gloved hand and closed his staring eyes. The body of Señor Tijeras, Armando Juventud Reyes, lay on the floor. The windows were broken. Furniture thrown everywhere. I could hear the dim sound of sirens. I sighed, then dialed up the number.

Aguacate's secretary put me through to him immediately.

And so ended the short, brilliant career of el Espíritu Escarlata.

● ● ●

Xavier's father parlayed the adulation into a new run for the governorship. The run he had originally meant for his eldest son. One son was given a state funeral. One son was dumped in an unmarked grave. I never met their father. He was there and gone in the blink of an eye. Just an image on the television.

Aguacate decided to retire the Espíritu Escarlata gimmick rather than have another luchador take it over. It was somewhat noble of him. Escarlata was a hero, a real honest-to-goodness hero. He could have made millions. The vendors were selling bootleg masks hand over fist outside el Estadio Olímpico. But he let sleeping dogs lie. Perhaps Xavier's father had spoken to him.

I tried to locate Xochi's body, but by the time I made it back to the Olímpico, los federales had picked her up. As in life, so in death, she simply disappeared.

I quit the Tijuana circuit a month later. Came back north. I found an opening on the Pacific Northwest circuit. I'm Mad Dog McGurk now. The money's not as good. But it's a nice friendly group.

My mask is covered in felt fur. With bulging eyes.

Mad Dog McGurk.

That's me.

The End

The Unfair Fare

By Lee Houston, Junior

There are things we do in life not because we want to, but because we have to.

Case in point: now that I was off for the night from my regular job, I would love to be home, nestled in the arms of my loving wife. Instead, I was driving a taxi cab trying to earn some extra money from this part-time gig because we were expecting our first child in a couple of months, and I wanted to get ahead on the bills before both they and the baby arrived.

Unfortunately, only the tenured drivers got the choice routes like the airport and downtown. The rest of us either had to wait around for calls or go out in search of fares, but I didn't want to waste the gas and run up a high fuel bill.

It was a dead evening. Weeknights usually were. To make matters worse, it was the middle of summer and still near ninety degrees in what little shade might be available. I was sitting in my cab with all the windows down and the engine off for the moment, hoping for a little breeze. After all, if I couldn't afford to go cruising, I certainly couldn't afford to sit idle with the air conditioner running.

Thankfully mine was the closest taxi available when the dispatcher radioed. What would be my lone fare of this shift was a pick up at the local university. At least now I had a valid excuse to roll up the windows and turn on the AC.

It took me a couple of minutes to find the Science Hall once I reached the campus, but found my rider standing on its front steps. The man looked like a clichéd characterization of a typical college professor with his graying hair, thick glasses, and tweed jacket with the mandatory elbow patches.

I tried to be polite when he first entered the cab, but except for telling me where he wanted to be taken, "I am not interested in idle chitchat. Just please drive me to my destination," was his only other comment. My passenger never said another word the whole trip.

That wouldn't be a problem. I preferred the silent passengers compared to the ones that could talk your ears off by the end of the trip.

I never found it odd that Mister Anonymous stayed slumped down in the back seat like he didn't want to be noticed, but it was curious that every once in a while he looked over his shoulder to see out the back windshield. A cautious eye on the rear view mirror revealed that we weren't being followed, yet I thought I understood his nervousness. He would be far from the first person I was either taking to or picking up from an illicit affair.

The cab's GPS system confirmed that the address he gave me was way out in the suburbs. Even if there was no tip, which happened a lot nowadays, I was anticipating a somewhat large fare. It wouldn't be one of my better nights, but it could have been worse.

In hindsight, I should have kept my big mouth shut.

We entered the residential neighborhood, but were still a few blocks away from my passenger's destination when I had to slam on the brakes. A softball had suddenly flown low across the street. As it hit the opposite curb and landed in somebody's front yard, a child came chasing after it.

I waved to both the kid and the angry father, who was yelling at his boy for not looking both ways before crossing the street, when I heard a sound that didn't make me happy.

My fare had bolted from the taxi without paying!

I hastily put the cab in park with the four way flashers on, unfastened my seat belt and ran out, hoping to catch the guy; but he was fast for an older man. My ex-rider had rounded the corner and was going down the cross street, as if the devil himself were on his tail.

All I could do was angrily slam the passenger door shut and get back inside the taxi.

This was the second time in my short career that somebody tried to stiff me, and there was no way I was going back to base empty handed on a thirty mile ride. As I re-secured my seat belt, I looked over my shoulder to make sure the path to the first open driveway behind me was clear. With the flashers off, I put the cab into reverse.

I made a quick three point turn using the borrowed driveway and gave chase. However, when I rounded the corner, my elusive fare was nowhere to be seen.

The whole area was just another part of your typical suburban neighborhood. Sidewalks running parallel to either side of the street in front of well kept houses with equally maintained yards. My cab was the only traffic on the road, for there wasn't even a parked car along either curbside. Approaching a late summer sunset, the only person in sight was a lady walking her dog.

Since she was on the opposite side of the street from where the cab should be, I turned my four way flashers back on as I pulled alongside her. Then I rolled down my window and asked, "Excuse me, but did you see a man running just now?"

"Yes. He almost ran into us and it was all I could do to keep Bruno under control," said the lady, indicating the big German Shepard on a leash with her.

"Did you happen to see where he went?" I asked.

"He crossed the street and ran toward that house over there with its porch light on." The place she indicated was two doors further down on my right. "However, I can't tell you whether or not he actually went inside," she added.

"That's okay. Thank you," I said, pulling away.

I parked in front of the house, intentionally blocking the four door black sedan that was sitting in the driveway in case the man tried to get away again. I stopped the meter at $79.50, shaking my head in disbelief. None of this made any sense. Was the address he had given me a phony, because he knew we would be passing his true destination along the way? The man didn't look to be either a thrill seeker or destitute, so why attempt to get out of paying?

I thought about calling my dispatcher, but didn't want to risk losing my job over this. I noted the address in a quick text to my wife, telling her that if she didn't hear from me again within two hours, to notify the police and let them know what happened. Then I hid my slimline cellphone back within the inner brim of the floppy cab company hat I wore.

With everything off and the windows up I got out, locked the taxi, and walked toward the front door. The place looked like all the other two story residences surrounding it, except for the fact that all the curtains were closed. I couldn't tell for sure whether or not anyone was home, but rang the doorbell anyway.

I heard the faint tone of fancy chimes originating from somewhere inside, but otherwise nothing.

I stood on the porch alone until reaching the point where I needed to decide whether to push the button again or try my luck at the house on either side of this one when the door finally opened.

There stood a man at least a couple of inches taller than me and seriously way more muscular than my average build. This guy looked like he bench pressed engine blocks for fun. He had slick black hair and a very heavy five o'clock shadow. His thick arms were spread out, with one behind the door and the other on the opposite side of the entryway. He tried to make the pose look casual, but he was definitely barring me from coming inside.

"What do you want?" he asked in a gruff voice.

"I had a fare who jumped out on me as we were driving by, and a witness said he came this way," I explained. "Did a man with gray hair, wearing a tweed jacket, come in here?"

"No," the man said tersely. "Anything else?"

I was about to reply when we both heard the noise. A loud moan heralded something heavy hitting the floor somewhere behind the guy. My missing rider falling to the floor?

We both instantly realized that my hearing that was a bad thing. Before I could get off the porch, the erstwhile doorman grabbed me by the front of my shirt and jerked me inside with one hand. As I stumbled into the house, I heard him hastily closing and locking the door.

Except maybe in a seriously unfair fight, there was no way I could face my unwanted opponent one on one and have any hope of victory. I took a quick look around what turned out to be a nicely decorated living room, but saw nothing I could use to defend myself with. My only available course of action was to put the large room sofa that was sitting in the center of the wall to wall carpeting, between me and the angry man who was now coming toward me.

On sheer instinct, I picked up a crystal paper weight from the end table next to the sofa and flung it at him.

Naturally the guy ducked. The paper weight flew over his beefy left shoulder and hit a picture hanging on the wall behind him. The display glass broke as both the frame and my makeshift missile fell to the ground.

Meanwhile, my potential assailant thought he'd try leaping over the sofa to tackle me. I stood my ground until he was committed to his jump, but then swerved around the opposite end from where the guy would land and ran back toward the front door.

Unfortunately that was when a man stepped out from behind a door near the exit. I hadn't noticed it during my abrupt entrance and had no idea where the door led, but there was no missing the fact that this new arrival now stood between me and freedom.

"What's going on here?" he asked. Except for not sporting a gold chain around his neck, the man looked like he just walked off one of those cheesy romance novel covers, wearing slacks and a partially unbuttoned collared shirt that exposed some of his toned chest. Not my type, but I could see where his suave looks and smooth voice could turn any woman's head.

"In a rush to get here, Pembrooke stiffed this cabbie," explained my first opponent, who was now coming up from behind, which put me in a squeeze play between the two of them.

"Dang! That's too bad, for both of them," said the second man, staring at me. "Tie the driver up with Pembrooke and then grab the cab keys. Pembrooke didn't have it on him, so it must be somewhere in the taxi."

"After I search it, do you want me to ditch the cab some place?" asked the first man, as he grabbed me from behind. He was far from gentle as he squeezed me within his two big arms.

"No. We'll use it as our getaway vehicle. Another cab in airport traffic will hardly be noticed. Meanwhile, I'm going upstairs to check on our other guest," said the second man, who was obviously the ringleader of whatever was going on, before he headed toward a staircase near what I presumed to be the back of the house.

The room that the big thug carried me into looked like somebody's den, with a large wooden desk on one side in front of a wall of bookcases, and a fireplace on the opposite side as part of the outer wall. Kicking the door closed behind him, the jerk threw me down onto the carpeted floor next to a body lying there.

Heedless of what was about to happen to me, I crawled over to check on the mysterious Mister Pembrooke, who just also happened to be my fare jumper.

Meanwhile, the thug had picked up a thick coil of rope that had been left in a plush guest chair near the room's lone door. The way he was holding the end between both of his large hands and the grin of evil intent on his face made me scared that the guy might have something more sinister in mind than just tying me up.

"Does whatever your plan is include murder?" I asked which actually stopped the man in his tracks.

"What do you mean?" he asked in return, with a genuine look of confusion on his face.

"This guy is dead," I said; crab crawling backwards away from the body lying on the floor.

Shocked, my foe went down on his hands and knees to examine Mister Pembrooke. That was when I rose and made a dash for the fireplace, grabbing the metal poker from the tool collection that sat to the far right at the base of the hearth opening.

I turned to defend myself as the thug started to get up again, but I noticed down was an easier position for him to obtain than up. I took advantage of the situation and moved to strike, but he tried to block my blow with his right arm. Thankfully I still had enough time to alter my swing enough to avoid his attempt to grab the poker away from me.

I took the opportunity to strike my opponent on his back as hard as I could, but the guy never so much as flinched, so I had no idea whether or not the blow had any effect.

He swung around on his hands and knees trying to grab me. I knew if he managed to grab me that would be the end, so I did the unthinkable and struck him on top of the head. The sound of metal hitting human flesh and skull was sickening, but the thug went down flat against the carpeting.

A noise made me turn my head. Mister Pembrooke was starting to stir. Hanging on to the poker just in case, I helped Pembrooke into a sitting position. At the time I examined him, the man was either unconscious or just dazed, but the distraction worked in my favor.

Pembrooke insisted on sitting in the chair behind his desk. I helped him over and into it, then gave him a moment to catch his breath before asking, "Want to tell me what the hell is going on around here?"

"What are you doing here?" he asked in return, surprised to see me.

"You stiffed me out of an eighty dollar fare and I tried to collect, not knowing I'd be stepping into a bigger mess," I answered.

"I tried to get away without paying you your proper remuneration in hopes that you would summon the authorities," Pembrooke replied. Until now, I never realized the man had a slight British accent.

"Afraid it doesn't work that way. Even if the police could be bothered to find you, what you did is just a very minor misdemeanor at best," I explained. "I'd be out the fare and maybe a job too."

"Oh dear. I was hoping the authorities would come because these two men kidnapped my wife and forced me to…"

Then we both heard the thug starting to stir.

I grabbed the poker from where I left it on Pembrooke's desk top and snuck up behind my foe. He had made it up onto his knees and was holding his head with both hands. Despite the hatred I felt toward him, I didn't want to hit the guy in the skull again, so swung the metal shaft down toward his shoulder blades.

The poker made solid contact, which forced the guy to fall face first toward the carpeting again. Yet as he did so, my assailant kicked back with one leg and knocked my feet out from under me.

I managed to hang onto the poker as I fell flat on my back. My cab company hat fell off in the process, but landed in such a way that even if it slipped out of the inner band, it still covered my cellphone. Meanwhile, the thug managed to crawl over to the guest chair and started trying to pull himself up, the coil of rope left abandoned for the moment on the floor between us.

"I don't know what the boss has planned for the Pembrookes," he said between wheezy gasps, trying to catch his breath, "but as far as killing is concerned, I'll certainly make an exception in your case."

I got into a sitting position as my foe turned to face me. If looks could kill, I would have been dead hours ago as he rose to his full height. There was no way I would be able to get back on my feet in time, and I did not want to feel those vice grip arms of his around me again.

My plan was to fake a poker swing to the thug's gonads, but actually aim for one of his knees. The way I had it figured out, if I couldn't hobble him further, at least I'd have a chance to get back on my own feet to face him better.

However, just as I prepared for the guy to attempt attacking again, a gun shot rang out!

I had to roll out the way as the man came tumbling toward me. From what I saw of the blood gushing out of his chest as he fell, the thug would not be fighting any more this day.

Perhaps not any others as well.

I stood and saw Pembrooke still sitting at his desk, only now the main drawer in the middle was open and there was a gun in his hand.

I honestly didn't know what to say at that moment. On one hand, the guy had just saved my life. Then again, there had to have been another way, although the thug didn't have any reservations about killing us.

Then a revelation struck me.

"That other guy had to have heard the shot and will probably be back at any moment to find out what happened. Quick, close the drawer and get back down on the floor where you were," I said, as I grabbed the rope off the floor.

Moments later my prediction came true as the second man came running into the study. What he saw was Pembrooke lying where he left him, apparently still unconscious on the carpeting, with his buddy's prone body next to him.

Meanwhile, I appeared tied to the guest chair. Actually, I had placed my feet within the coil of rope I left at the base of the chair and just kept my hands behind my back. They were holding the fireplace poker, which was pressed between me and the chair.

The man took one look at me, and then rushed over to check on his friend. That was when I stood up and hit him across the shoulder blades with the poker. The second villain started to fall to the right of the thug's body as Pembrooke stood up and pointed his gun at the guy's back.

"NO!" I shouted.

Pembrooke looked teary eyed as he said, "But he threatened to do terrible things to my wife if..."

"I know the feeling. I'm married too, yet we should let the police handle this. Help me tie him up and then you can go check on her," I said.

Our efforts may not have won any prizes, but they got the job done. It wasn't necessary to tie up the other guy. Pembrooke felt for a pulse on both the man's neck and wrist, but there wasn't any.

Afterward, my former passenger looked at me and asked, "You will corroborate my account of events with the authorities, correct?"

"There's no reason not to," I answered. Besides, never argue with a man holding a gun. "There is one thing you could do before you run upstairs, if you don't mind."

"Just name it and it's yours," promised Pembrooke.

"Please pay me the eighty dollars you owe me for the cab ride."

"Certainly," he said with a smile, before putting the handgun on the desk top. Then Pembrooke pulled out two one hundred dollar bills from his wallet. "I believe the proper adage is, 'Keep the change'."

"It is. Now go check on your wife."

With that, he smiled and left the study.

I collected my hat and cellphone. Neither were the worst for wear after what I'd been through. The phone on Pembrooke's desk had a dial tone when I picked up the receiver, so I used it to call the police.

It was about twenty minutes before my self imposed deadline from the first message to my wife. I was about to text her again when suddenly another gun shot echoed through the house.

Only this one came from somewhere upstairs!

I have absolutely no idea why I did it, but after I unlocked the front door to allow the police easy access to the house, I left the known villains in the study and ran for the staircase with the fireplace poker in one hand and my cellphone in the other. I could have grabbed the gun too, but I've never held one in my life. The last thing I wanted to do was accidentally shoot myself.

I was cautious enough to ascend as quietly as I could and didn't call out to see if Mister Pembrooke was okay in the process. Whatever happened, I saw no point in announcing my presence if there was another villain upstairs and I was approaching a trap.

I reached the top floor and saw the last door on the left open. The rest were all closed.

As I neared the open door I heard a woman's voice speaking, but it wasn't expressing the emotions I thought it should be under the circumstances.

"You stupid fool!" she said. "If you had just cooperated like you were supposed to, we would have just tied you up and have been out of the country before anyone was the wiser. Well, I could always say I managed to get free just before you came in, grabbed the gun from the nightstand, and accidentally shot my husband thinking you were one of the kidnappers. By the time they figure out otherwise, I'd be long gone. After all, I've already cleaned out our accounts while you were collecting the ransom."

That was interesting. Mrs. Pembrooke was a willing participant in her own kidnapping? The way these things work on television, she was probably planning to leave her husband and run off with that would be Romeo we tied up. Then again, if she already had all their money, what were the kidnappers expecting Mister Pembrooke to pay them with?

Yet it was what she said next that really made me angry. "Then again, I should have known better. You've never done what you're supposed to in all the years we've been married. What did I ever see in you beyond the prestige of being a professor's wife is beyond me? But I can continue carping you out later. Guess I'll just have to kill that cab driver and search the taxi myself. Who knows? Maybe I'll go to Rio without George and let him take the fall for everything."

I hugged the wall next to the open door as I heard her approach the hallway, but then she stopped in mid-step. Had she heard me out here after all?

Then I heard a rush of footsteps as she dashed into the hallway, weapon drawn and ready to use.

Unfortunately for her, I wasn't a cooperative target.

Instead of finding me standing in the hallway where she could take an easy shot at me, I had crouched down and was swinging the fireplace poker hard and fast at her legs.

I freely admit that the sound of her yelling in pain was quite satisfying as I stood up and punched her in the nose. The fact that I was still holding the poker in my clenched fist added to the impact as blood began to leak out of her nostrils.

Mrs. Pembrooke started to raise her hands, but whether to grab her nose or in another attempt to shoot me I'll never know, because I grabbed the gun out of her hand before she could react and threw it down the stairs. The weapon went off wherever it landed. Told you I knew nothing about guns.

● ● ●

"That was when you guys came in with your guns drawn, yelling for everyone to freeze and drop our weapons," I said to the police officer taking my statement. "I hope none of you got hurt."

"No. We didn't," replied the cop. "Now then, we discovered Mrs. Pembrooke's suitcases in the master bedroom where Professor Pembrooke's body was, all packed and ready to go. However, she claims that they were getting ready to go on a second honeymoon, but her husband didn't have a chance to pack yet. The black sedan in the driveway is registered to the other man, and his suitcase was in the trunk. Yet that guy you claim is her lover says he's just a family friend and was going to drive them to the airport because he happens to be catching a flight later tonight himself."

"As if," I said in rebuttal.

"Just between us, everything our crime lab techs found so far appears to support your story, but both of them are saying that the dead guy must have been a burglar with bad timing who her husband surprised, because everyone was running late to begin with. That is allegedly why Professor Pembrooke called for a cab to drive him back here, because his car is still in the garage. Do you have any other evidence that can support your statement?"

"Just this," I answered, before holding out my cellphone. "When she started talking, I activated the video recording function. You won't have much of an image unless you like beige walls and earth tone carpeting, but the audio track of her talking to her dead husband is crystal clear."

"Great. I'll get one of the tech guys over here to download a copy for evidence, but I wouldn't delete that for a while, just in case."

"Understood," I said. "Now, if you don't mind, I do have two questions. What did Professor Pembrooke hide in my cab that was so valuable? I figure that since he didn't have anything with him, it had to be something on his person."

"We found a computer flashcard stuffed in between the rear seat cushions," said the officer. "Not sure what's on it because its password protected, but Professor Pembrooke apparently did some important stuff for our government at the university."

"Really?" I said in disbelief. Geez, I wonder if that means the Feds will get involved in all of this.

"What's your second question?"

"I don't want to sound merciless, and I know you'll need it as evidence for now, but when can I have the two hundred dollars Professor Pembrooke gave me back? I still need to settle his outstanding fare."

The End

The Gentleman Thief and the Artist

by Emily Jahnke

As I was blindfolded, I couldn't see where the man with firm hands was leading me. I had to rely on my other senses.

I could hear my button boots scraping across a lush carpet. Sharp wood varnish. Cold air prickling the skin beneath my clothes. Hot bile rising in my throat.

Why the Hell did I accept his invitation? I wasn't brave. I wasn't like Frances and my other friends at the factory, marching and carrying banners. I wasn't like Aunt Bertie, going undercover and writing exposes for *The Herald*. Nor was I like Lucas as he chased the criminals of Washington City down.

I remembered Lucas' dark hair and pensive eyes. My exhausted mind spun like a top. My brother needed to come home. Frances needed him. *I* needed him.

The Gentleman Thief could help me.

I felt like I was drowning in fear. What if it *wasn't* him? What if it was the same person who had Lucas? Lucas had made many enemies.

I should've thought of this, I kicked myself. At least I left a copy of the invitation in my room for Lucas' partner to find should something happen to me. If Peter was as half as smart as I remembered…

I longed to run home and dive under the covers like I did whenever I read. At least I could close the book and return it to the library when it became too much.

It was too late though. Help me save Lucas, I prayed over and over.

A door opened before me. The firm large hands helped me over the threshold like a marionette. I heard the floor turn to hardwood.

This room was warmer than the winding passageway the man had led me through. Radiant heat hit my left side and I could see a warm bit of light through my blindfold. A snapping crackle confirmed that it was the fireplace. I winced and moved away from it. My body shook and I began hyperventilating.

"Deep breaths, Lottie." I heard Lucas' firm voice soothing me through an attack, running his fingers through my hair. "Just breathe. It'll pass in a few moments." My heart slowed and my mind cleared. I needed to stay calm.

"Leave us." A man before me ordered. I felt my guide let go of my arm. There was the sound of shoes crossing the hardwood floors along with an opening and closing door. I heard a rustling sound as a hand reached behind my ears and tugged on the blindfold. It fell off. "I apologize for the blindfold," he said, "but I can't take chances."

Startled, I almost fell backwards at his voice. "Understandable." I said blinking as my eyes took a few minutes to adjust to the change in light.

Standing before me was a lanky man at least a head taller than me and dressed in a tuxedo with leather shoes and gloves. His brown hair was slicked back and a red mask trimmed with gold braid covered the upper part of his aquiline face. The shadows cast from the fireplace made his brown eyes darker.

That's odd, I thought, studying him. Reports in the paper ranged from blonde curls and blue eyes to black stringy hair and green eyes. The hair could be a wig, but how could somebody change their eye color?

In any case, the only things that were consistent with the papers were the lanky figure, tuxedo and masked face.

"It's a pleasure to finally meet you." He said with a smile before bowing and kissing my hand. I felt the soft lips brushing the knuckles hiding beneath my kid gloves. "Why don't you have a seat, Miss Sawyer?" He said, gesturing to a couple of chairs.

"How…how'd you know my name?" I asked, still shaking.

"There isn't a lot I don't know." He said, a lazy smile crossing his face. "But back to the topic at hand. Have a seat and we'll chat."

I did as he suggested, sinking into a chair. It hissed as I sat down and I took off the satchel I carried. It landed next to my chair with a thump. The chair reminded me of Lucas' favorite chair back home. The one that smelled of tobacco, cologne and wood shavings; I had seen Frances curled into it when I left an hour ago, her tears staining the dark green velvet….

Miss Kingsley's lessons from years ago returned.

"Back ramrod straight."

"Folded hands in lap."

"Head level."

He was said to be a gentlemen to any lady he encountered. When Miss Julie Wordsworth begged him to not steal the diamond necklace her grandmother left her, he agreed to leave the necklace in return for a kiss. People's ears were still burning from the scandal…but Miss Wordsworth's already beautiful smile was said to be more radiant.

"Would you like something to drink?" He asked, turning to a small table next to the chair opposite me. Sitting on that was a glass pitcher along with two crystal goblets. "I have a fine Bordeaux claret."

I was still shivering from the cold April night. Frances always made sure a hot toddy was ready for Lucas on similar nights. Lucas said it warmed him up faster than just sitting next to the stove. Besides, I didn't wish to offend the Gentleman Thief by refusing his hospitality. "If it's not too much trouble," I said.

"Of course not. Otherwise I wouldn't have offered it." While he prepared the drinks, I studied my surroundings.

The paneled oak walls were covered with paintings. I recognized two of the pieces. *A Shepherd and Shepherdess in Pasture* by Watteau and *A Woman at her Toilette* by Van Gogh. They had been stolen from Mr. Adam Lewis some six weeks before. Mr. Lewis hired Pinkertons to guard the house, invested in strong locks and stayed up all night with a loaded hunting rifle. He had bragged that the house was locked up so tight that God Himself would've needed an invitation to get in.

Not that it stopped the Gentleman Thief from carrying out his threat. Lucas and Peter were still wondering how he pulled it off.

There was also a cherry oriental carpet on the parquet floors but no windows. A marble fireplace was to my right, a large bronze screen cut to look like a peacock with its feathers spread out.

I edged away from the fire.

"Here you are." He said, turning around and holding out a goblet filled with claret.

"Thank you." I said. My host sat down in the chair an arm's length away from me. Resting his left ankle on his right knee, he began sipping the wine.

"Good claret." He said. I was about to take a sip myself when something crossed my mind.

What if the drink was tampered with?

I looked down at the surface of the wine. There were no traces of powder on the sides or an oil coating the surface.

Then again, if he could change eye color, what else can he do?

"Are you afraid that I slipped something into your drink?" He asked. I nodded, putting my glass on the table next to my chair. "A wise move. I could be anyone. You needn't fear, though. Your brother would never forgive me if anything happened to you."

"I've been kicking myself enough, thank you very much." I snapped as I watched him take another sip, thinking of the jack-in-the-box Lucas had carved for my fourth birthday. At any moment, the spring would release, except I was unsure what the reaction would be. It wouldn't have been a puppet coming out of a box, that's for sure.

"There's no need to be curt. Speaking of the famous Detective Sawyer, that's why I invited you here." He said upon finishing, putting down his glass. "I understand he hasn't been at work for the last two days. Is he ill?"

My nerves snapped like an over-tuned violin string. My lower lip quivering, I bowed my head and felt the hot tears spilling out. Don't cry, I told myself, swallowing. I couldn't afford to lose control.

I thought of Lucas' stony face watching Father's casket being lowered into the moist dirt. He never shed a tear, even though his shoulders were slumped.

"Here." He said. I saw that he was holding out a crisp white handkerchief. I took it and wiped my face, smelling the faint traces of cologne. "What happened?"

"Lucas has been missing for the last two days." I said tasting my salty tears. "My brother will never forgive me for this but I need your help."

"Why should I?" He asked, leaning back in his chair. "Your brother is the one chasing me."

My hands balled into fists and I could feel my fingernails cutting through the material of my gloves. "You'd risk leaving his wife a widow and their child without a father?" My hiccupping voice rose as I shook.

"Calm down, Miss Sawyer." The Gentleman Thief said, holding up his hand. "I never said that I wouldn't help you. Let me rephrase that. What will you give me in return? I *am* a busy man after all."

"I have some jewelry my mother left me." I said opening my artist's satchel and taking out a small wooden box, a gardenia painted on the cover. Lucas had carved it for my last birthday. It felt heavy as I passed it to the Gentleman Thief. "I've also got a hundred dollars in there," I said my throat dry.

I can always earn that money back. I reminded myself. As much as I hated my job at the Hope Street factory for its long hours, low pay and Rick, Lucas encouraged me. "It won't be long before you have enough. I know it's hard." He always soothed as he rubbed my aching shoulders. "But it'll be worth it in the end."

The Gentleman Thief opened the box, taking out a ruby necklace. The stone glowed red in the firelight. Lucas and I had scraped our allowances for six months to buy Mother that necklace for Christmas. I remembered how she kissed us, tears in her eyes.

It was the last Christmas we spent together.

Shaking the memory away, I studied him. There was a spark in his eye as he appraised the necklace. That's when I noticed his gold and diamond cufflinks. Of course, I thought as my hopes sank. He could afford nicer jewelry. That is if he didn't decide to steal it.

"Very lovely." He said, returning the necklace, closing the jewelry box and returning it to me. I shoved it into the satchel, a little relieved that he didn't want it. "But they're nothing tempting. Besides, I've got plenty of money."

"I'm an artist." I said diving back into my satchel and taking out my leather bound sketchbook. "I can sketch or paint something for you." I swallowed. "I can create a forgery that you can use to swap. Make it easier to steal things."

My host took my sketchbook and flipped through the pages. I saw his face softening as he looked over my work. My hopes rose. I prayed that it would be enough.

"You're very talented, Miss Sawyer." He said after a while, closing the sketchbook and returning them to me. "However, the owners of the artwork could notice the forgery. Not everyone is perfect." The lazy smile on his face grew wider. "Besides, how will people know what I've done? I may appreciate fine art but I'd never use fakes in my work. You should know that by now."

My anger ablaze, I rushed him with my hand held high. His hand gripped my wrist with the speed of a striking rattlesnake. The Gentleman Thief stood up, looking at me while keeping my wrist in a tight grip. I winced but the pain in my wrist was nothing compared to the look he gave me.

It reminded me of the one Lucas gave me when he learned that Peter and I had gotten into a childhood scrape. "A lady never raises a fist where she can use her wits. You're almost twelve, Lottie." He scolded as he treated my split lip with his handkerchief. "Next year, you'll be a woman, just like Mother. You want to make our late mother proud of you, don't you Lottie? Then be a lady."

The memory calmed me down. What have you done? I scolded myself. You almost threw away your one chance at finding Lucas!

His eyes softened a little. "Miss Sawyer, I don't blame you for being upset." He said in a low voice. "And I'm sorry for saying that just now. But slapping me isn't going to bring your brother home. If you insist on hitting me, then I'll consider the conversation over. Understand?"

I nodded. He let go of my wrist and my hand dropped like a lead weight.

He said nothing. We faced each other. The only sounds were from the crackling fireplace. I was so close that I could see every thread of his tuxedo and smell traces of the cologne he wore.

Lucas used the same cologne…it was embedded into his favorite chair and all of his shirts.

And now I had nothing left to give.

All but one. My mind seized on an idea.

I shook, wanting to retch the supper I had eaten.

Anything but that! I longed to scream.

My late parents would turn their grave over and Frances would be horrified.

What if somebody found out? My mind tried to banish the shameful idea I had. There has to be another way.

More memories of Lucas flashed before my eyes. His long fingers stroking my hair and soft voice soothing me after a nightmare. His deep belly laugh as we played charades. His smiling eyes as Frances walked down the aisle at their wedding.

I had no choice.

For Lucas, I would've danced with the devil himself.

I turned my attention to the goblet I had placed on the table. Frances said that getting a little tipsy on her wedding day made her feel brave. I needed every inch of bravery I could get. Raising the glass, I took a swig. The full bodied wine burned as it went down my throat and I choked back a cough, putting down the goblet. The warmth filled me and I felt a little stronger.

Best get it over with; I thought as I bowed my head and began unbuttoning my blue jacket. Tears of shame and fear ran down my face and I swallowed my sobs. Everything counted on me tempting him.

The thought of him turning me down scared me more than him accepting it. This was my last option.

I'd never see Lucas again if this didn't work.

My jacket fell to the ground, pooling at my feet. I felt exposed to the world even though it was just the two of us and I still had my white shirtwaist and blue skirt on.

I squeezed my eyes shut to keep the tears from falling. A large hand touched my right temple, the fingers rubbing my scalp. I balled my fists and tried to keep from shaking.

I was disgusted with myself for not being more clever or brave.

Only a coward stoops so low…and that's just what you are, Charlotte Anne Sawyer, I scolded myself. You're nothing but a coward.

There was more I wanted to say but I didn't know if I could say it without losing my composure.

Please help.

"Charlotte, look at me," he said. I opened my eyes and looked up at him. A sob escaped from me as his thumb wiped a tear away. A soft smile crossed his face and his brown eyes were warm. "I'll help you."

Relief washed over me and I smiled, my knees knocking. "Thank you."

"No need to thank me yet." He said, putting his hand on my back with one hand, holding my hands in the other and slowly lowering me into the chair. "Your brother isn't home yet." He went back to his chair. "And in any case, I need your help."

"With what?"

"I need you to tell me everything about the day your brother went missing." He touched his fingertips together.

"Oh," I said, trying to laugh away the nervousness. "Lucas, Frances and I were having dinner…"

"Frances is your sister-in-law, correct?" He asked. I nodded, deciding to not ask how he knew. "Please continue."

"During dinner, an officer arrived with a message for Lucas. He read it for a few moments before picking up his pistol and badge. There was a lead at the Southern End and he was going to check it out." I said. "He kissed us goodbye and asked us to not lock him out. We didn't see him for the rest of the evening. I thought he had already left for work when I left for my job the next morning." I closed my eyes, remembering the sight that greeted me when I came home. "Frances was in a lather when I got home from work. Lucas hadn't shown up at work."

"Very unlike your brother?" He asked.

"Even when he was sick with the flu, he still went in," I said. "Chief Williams and the other officers promised to do everything in their power to find Lucas. The next day, a… gentleman…brought Frances and me Lucas' pocket-watch." I wiped at my face again and looked down at my lap. "Or rather what was left of it."

His large hand took mine. Without thinking, I put my hand on top of his, enjoying the warmth.

It reminded me of Peter's…

After a moment, he yanked his hand back. "Forgive me." He said, looking away from me, a flush crossing beneath his mask.

"It's all right." I said with a nod, swallowing my disappointment. Why was I…don't think about that now, I told myself. Stay focused on getting Lucas home.

"About the gentleman who brought the watch back, did he give his name?" He said, picking up his wine glass.

I tried to remember but my mind was drawing a blank. "I was too worried about Frances to pay attention to his name. But I do remember that he was missing his right earlobe."

His face darkened as he put the glass down again. "Did he have curly black hair and deep brown eyes?"

A chill settled over me. "You know him?"

"No." He said, not looking at me. He knew something. I could just *feel* it. "What about the lead your brother went to check out?"

Now I had a chance to test my hypothesis. I decided to lay my trap and see if he would fall into it. "It was about a group." I said, snapping my fingers and furrowed my face as I... tried...to remember. "Oh, it was an Italian word that began with S?"

"The Savonarola Society." The Gentleman Thief said, standing up and walking to the fireplace.

I *knew* it. I thought as I looked at him. The Savonarola Society was a name my brother had spoken in hushed whispers to Peter when they thought I was too busy embroidering or painting to pay attention.

I had never once paid much attention to it, but now that they may be responsible...

"What is the Savonarola Society?" I asked.

"Something you don't want to know." He said, resting his left hand on the marble mantle and standing with his feet shoulder-width apart. His head bowed down.

Something in his demeanor reminded me of Lucas...after our parents died and he would gaze at their dual portraits above the fireplace. Pity filled me and I almost wanted to get up and see what was wrong.

But the sound of a popping ember reminded me where he was standing and I held back.

In any case, I doubted he'd appreciate a stranger getting so close to him.

I had to know something though.

"Is Lucas in danger?" I asked.

"You won't like the answer."

"So 'yes' then," I said, wringing the handkerchief in my hands and looking down to hide my tears. He didn't respond.

I wasn't surprised. Maybe because, deep down, I knew that Lucas had gotten himself into some serious trouble. But I didn't want to say anything aloud for both Frances and me.

Lucas reminded Frances and me at least once a day that he may never come home. But he had come home unscathed night after night for so long that it had lulled us into a false security.

The reality that my brother may be gone forever threatened to pull me down. I had already lost Mother and Father. I didn't want to lose Lucas either.

"Frances wanted to go looking for him. She probably would've, had Dr. Morgan..." The words spilled out before I could take them back. I felt like a valve had been released and it felt...good...to express my fears. "If I was brave enough, I'd rip the city to pieces and not stop until he was home."

"I know you would." He said in a soft voice. Before I could ask him what he meant by that, I heard him turn around and walk back to me. He knelt and took my hands in his. I looked at his firm brown eyes. "Miss Sawyer, I can't make any promises in regards to your brother's life."

"I've lived with that fact for over ten years."

"But I give my word as a gentleman that I'll get answers for you and your sister-in-law."

I felt better. "If a true gentleman makes a promise, you can count on him to keep it." Father once told Lucas and me. "Always keep your promises and you'll be fine."

But he was a thief, I protested. He stole things.

He seemed to pick up on my thoughts as he nodded. "I don't blame you for not trusting me." He said before picking up my jacket and standing up. "As much as I enjoy our discussion, I have work to do and you best get home." He offered a hand to me.

I nodded, taking his offered hand. He held the jacket while I slid my arms into the sleeves. I felt his fingers on my neck as he smoothed down my jacket collar.

"I only ask for two things from you." The Gentleman Thief said.

I froze, unsure of what he would ask of me. "What are they?" I asked, turning around to see him holding up my satchel.

He smiled, passing me my satchel. "Nothing much. The first is that you don't speak to anyone about what happened to you tonight."

"That seems fair." I said as I rested the long strap over my shoulder and across my chest, hoping the second would be as simple. "I won't say anything to anyone. I promise. My father taught me the value of keeping my word."

"Excellent. The second is that you work for me." The Gentleman Thief said.

Dread returned, having been lulled to sleep by his behavior. I would have to do something illegal. What if Lucas found out...*if* he lived that long?

"What kind of work?"

"I won't have you breaking any laws and I'll contact you in my own time. Do you promise?"

I wanted to run. I wanted to get out of there.

But Lucas...

"You will be generously compensated for your time in addition to getting answers." My host said.

The idea intrigued me. The more money I had, the sooner I could leave my job at the factory and start my new life.

But Lucas...

"Will you give your solemn promises to help me should I ask it and never speak of this night?" He asked, eyes furrowed and voice firm.

It was the same voice Rick used whenever he cornered me at the factory for information.

I feared the consequences if I backed out. "May God forgive me," I said, holding out my hand.

"Then you agree?" The Gentleman Thief asked. I nodded. "Say it."

"I promise to keep this a secret and help you," I said before I could take the words back.

"I accept." He shook my hand with a firm hand before he took the blindfold out of his pocket. "And now I must blindfold you again."

I turned around and closed my eyes, feeling the soft cloth slip over my eyes. He tightened the knot in the back as another thought came to me. "Why are you doing this?" I asked.

"So that way you can't tell anyone where I am." He said, brusque. I winced at his harsh statement. "Oh, you mean why I'm helping you find your brother?" I nodded. He sighed. "Determination and courage are something to be respected."

I didn't doubt he was talking about Lucas. "I'm pretty sure he'd drag you away from the devil himself if that's what justice asked for."

The Gentleman Thief chuckled. "Yes, your brother has those admirable traits." I heard the door open. "Make sure Miss Sawyer gets home safely." He ordered. I felt my hand being lifted again and the familiar sensation of lips on my knuckles. "It was an honor to meet you."

"Thank you for everything." I said.

"You're welcome." He said as he let go of my hand. Different hands took my arm and led me through the snaking corridors. While I was worried about the promises I had made, I felt better than I had felt in two days.

Even if he was a thief, he was a gentleman first and foremost. And a gentleman always keeps his promises.

The End

Only I'm To Blame

by Ken Janssens

Jay Nicks thrust his head through the doorway to look up and down the fourth-floor hallway. Seeing no one but a thick-goggled Chinese man hopelessly attempting to open his door, Jay stepped back into his apartment. He rubbed the sleep from his eyes as he stared down for the third time at the note in his hand, the one that was slipped under the door less than a minute ago. "If you want to see your wife again, look under the payphone near the corner of Mason and Clay. No police." The words hadn't changed. Jay hurried to find his clothes.

The room was dark, the heavy curtains pulled tight to block out the morning light. That differed from his circumstances last week when the most shade he had from the sun were the branches of park trees. Jay currently lived, for the time being at least, in that adequate Tenderloin apartment with three other guys. He was a squatter now, having been invited to crash there by Henry, a guy he'd met while working at the soup kitchen on the outskirts of Chinatown. Jay didn't know where the owner of the residence was, and right now, he didn't care.

To get to where he left his jeans, Jay stepped over Pablo, the other man who slept on the floor like he did. The transgender male, who had claimed the couch for the night, was off who-knew-where at this time in the morning. When Jay bent over to pick up his only pants, a rush of alcohol-induced pain flooded into his temples and ears. This didn't shock him, as most of his mornings started this way. His drinking was the final straw that cost him his job, but oddly, it never interfered with his three shifts a week at the soup kitchen. Without fail, though not always without a buzz or a hangover, he showed up on time for his volunteer shifts. Jay needed his atonement more than he needed his Kentucky bourbon.

Frantically, Jay tried to mash on his tied shoes, not believing he had time to unlace. Then he stopped. The adrenaline, the only thing to have supplanted his self-pitying funk in months, began to lose its edge, and Jay's head fell into his long-fingered hands. His wife was dead. That's what the cops said, though he never saw the body. "The face was not in a recognizable state from the gunshot," they said. So this note had to be a prank.

Jay untied his laces, crammed on his shoes, relaced them, and charged out the door.

As he spilled onto the street, the bright sun beating into his eye sockets felt like it would cause his head to explode. Jay threw on the cracked sunglasses he had found in a park waste bin and marched up Leavenworth Street. The sea of people he had to continuously navigate through felt like walking against six-foot waves at the beach. The crowds in San Francisco were worse than they'd ever been. Not just gradually worse, but exponentially. Every time a stranger bumped into his shoulder, the base of Jay's skull held its throb for a few extra beats.

After walking eight blocks uphill, Jay's relief became palpable when he turned east to travel the three, level blocks to Mason Street. His eyes darted around, looking for a payphone. At first he panicked but then glimpsed a gray one through the crowd. The stand blended into the dusty cement wall behind it. Jay sprinted across the street, getting honks from the slow, continuous throng of cars. His fingers skittered across the bottom of the plastic covering that surrounded the phone to protect it from the elements. Finding nothing there, he slid his palm under the phone itself. His pinky licked electrical tape as it passed over, so Jay squatted down to get a better angle to pick at the edges and free the folded paper adhered there. Jay ripped the note free and unfolded it. His hands shook as he recognized the same printed scrawl from nearly half an hour earlier, despite the fact only digits were present. "415-555-7257."

Jay plunged his hand into his pocket for change. He didn't have much money to his name, but what he did have, was more of the coin rather than of the bill variety. As two quarters plunked into the narrow slot, he truly missed his cell for the first time since he sold it for forty bucks to a drug dealer on Geary. The phone rang... once... twice... three times.

Click. "Go to the wharf. Walk south until you see an old warehouse with a large, smiling crab on it in cracked paint. Go in. Look for the hole in the floor. You won't miss it. Don't bring anyone. Don't get followed." Click.

The voice was supposed to be a woman's voice but it was modulated to hide the speaker's identity; it was clearly a man on the recording. Jay scanned around as calmly as possible. He had no intention on calling the police, especially after the first note said not to, but it never occurred to him that anyone would be following him. He thoroughly did a complete three-sixty pan of his surroundings, but Jay couldn't spot anyone that was taking any particular interest in him. Not that he could see that far; the masses were cramped together as they strode down the sidewalks to their jobs or vices. The population density had become next to unbearable.

Convinced he was alone in his quest; Jay trudged his way over a block to Powell Street to catch a trolley. Though there were several people waiting at the stop, when the cable car pulled up, he was able to fight his way on. He had no time for niceties. His conviction burned hot from lack of use. When the conductor came around, Jay scrounged for enough coinage to pay the steep fare. Normally, if he couldn't walk to his destination, he'd take a bus as it was a lot cheaper. But the crowds slowed the buses considerably, and even today, nothing got in the way of the cable cars.

Jay hung off the side of the trolley as they rose to highest point of downtown and back down towards Fisherman's Wharf, one thought recurring every few seconds. It was of his first kiss with Katrina. He'd wanted to do it for days, but she'd just come out of a relationship. She wanted to take it slow, she whispered. Jay felt that she only said that because she thought she was supposed to. He knew that she wanted him as much as he did her, maybe before she even broke up with Neal. Jay could feel her thin but soft lips touch his. Katrina was the first to slip in the tongue. He grew hard, fast. Both back then and now. He opened his eyes to see his stop approaching a few streets down. Jay inadvertently tempered his excitement as he thought of the warehouse he headed towards. If this *was* just a prank, he would be okay with it. In fact, he might be relieved. The variety of horrible things his wife could have endured if she had survived all this time in captivity tore at his mind. But if it wasn't a prank... if it was something more sinister, he had to be careful when he entered the unknown building. Katrina's life would depend on it. So would his, though Jay didn't really care about that.

As the trolley came to its final stop before getting in line to turn around, Jay leapt off and pushed his way towards the wharf. When he reached it, the throng of souls was worse than anywhere else. Jay had to lead with his shoulder to squeeze through the sightseers and ne'er-do-wells, the hawkers and seafood lovers. Eventually he made his way to the shore and lurched south, swerving around aimless person after aimless person. His pulse quickened when he saw a happy crustacean peering over everyone only a few blocks away, seagulls crapping on its face from the roof above.

Upon finally reaching the warehouse, Jay halted to make sure he was prepared for what was to come. He thought about his possible adversary's motives. Why would he have done this to Katrina? Why would they have done this to him? He was no one, now more than ever.

Jay breathed heavily and moved towards the boarded-up front entrance. After determining that the door could be swung towards him despite the slats of wood nailed across it, he gripped the half-circle handle and tugged hard.

The inside of the warehouse was musty and decaying. The building clearly had been condemned at some point, regardless of signage stating so. "Look for the hole in the floor. You won't miss it." Jay didn't believe that to be true anymore. There were holes everywhere, in the floor, the walls, the ceiling... The holes differed in size from that of a fist to the height of a stool. Jay moved forward cautiously, trying to detect any movement. The floor creaked with each step, which made him cringe. The wide hallway eventually emptied out to the middle of the warehouse. Jay knew that he had found what he was looking for. The warehouse was like a hub, all hallways met in the middle. Where the hallways had a ceiling fifteen feet above, the hub's only limit was that of the building's roof, the floors having never been constructed above it. This was probably so that the crabs could be dumped through the retractable roof into this silo-like area. In the middle of the floor of the hub used to be two large trap doors, when opened they would allow whatever was on the main floor to drop into the basement, presumably where processing of the crustaceans occurred. Now, however, the doors were gone, leaving one giant hole. One unmissable hole.

Jay's first impulse to run up to the chasm trumped his better sense. He just had to know if she was alive... if Katrina was down there. His legs took him across the half football field of flooring to the hole. He threw on the brakes so as not to fall in, planting his right foot down; the toe of his shoe dangling over the pit. With a hand placed on his knee for balance, Jay stretched his body forward to look down into the chasm. It was a thirty-foot drop to the metal, basement floor. Squinting to understand what he was seeing, Jay realized that there was a pile of something in the middle of the basement floor. It was a pile of human beings! Men. Eleven of them. As his eyes adjusted to the darker hole, a small, almost-imperceptible gasp escaped through his pursed lips. All eleven men were exact duplicates of himself! The differing degrees of decomposition aside, they were genetically the same... despite some sporting different hairstyles...all having differing clothes...and one marked with a large, half-healed scab on his face.

Those cosmetic differences aside, they looked exactly like each other... exactly like Jay... exactly like me.

● ● ●

I repositioned myself slightly before I pulled the trigger, then let my finger contract on the metal. A 129-grain AccuBond Long-Range ripped out of my rifle and hurtled towards Jay. The impact with his head was almost instantaneous, causing his body to lurch forward into the pit. I could almost hear the thud from the halting of his descent but that could be any number of random noises that I'd heard in this large building over the last few weeks. For a few moments from my second-story perch, I stared at the massive hole where I'd sent now a dozen of my duplicates, and then I turned to the case for my Nosler M48 Patriot and placed the rifle inside.

From the thigh pocket of my cargo pants, I retrieved a flask of Canadian whiskey. Now that my day's task was complete, I could start into my oblivion. I needed it bad. The buzz as it touched my lips. The sting as it rushed down my throat. The comforting

heat as it pooled in my stomach. I couldn't wait for the haze to take its rightful place in my mind.

I'd been in such a haze for a while, relatively speaking in my existence. I discovered the benefits late in life, twenty-six-years old, and though I put alcohol aside for most of the first year Katrina and I dated, it had ventured back by... that night. The night that she died.

• • •

It had been just after eleven p.m., when Katrina woke me up on the couch, having passed out from a twelve of Old Milwaukee. Her acid reflux, which could get quite bad, was plaguing her like crazy and we were out of Zantac. She asked me to go with her to the corner store. I told her it was, like, ten houses down and that she'd be fine to go herself. I got pissy about it, too. It turned out that she wouldn't be fine. A diminutive cokehead who needed cash saw her as easy prey. Katrina resisted only a little. The druggie's trigger finger was twitchy. The blast went off in Katrina's face.

After that night, the haze turned into an all-out pea-soup fog. I waded in there for a long time. I couldn't recall the length of my stay in limbo, but a person can only do that to themselves for so long until one of two things happen: they die or they cut back. I cut back, but only to where I used to live, back in "Hazeland". I was in that fog long enough, however, to have missed when the change happened in San Francisco.

The population of The City by the Bay grew by a lot. I'd heard theories about how it started from what other people opined at the bus station, in lines at fast-food joints, outside the bars where people smoked, and mostly from the mass amount of homeless folks who roam the downtown streets. Some said that...and this is the one I heard most often...that a bunch of alternate universes fused together into one, causing everyone to have multiple duplicates. Others said that the government had been making clones of us for years and the Area-51-esque facility had a problem, allowing all the duplicates to break out. One guy, this massive Samoan dude, thought everyone had just split into two, then four, then eight. Like asexual reproduction. We were all freakin' amoebas.

Regardless of what was going on, I really didn't think on it too much. All my mind could put any focus to...the only thing I could latch any tendril of attention...was how I was responsible for Katrina's death. If I had gone with her to get her pills that night, the pint-sized stoner would have looked for someone else to hold up. Simple as that. Because I had rolled over and went back to my drooling slumber, Katrina was gone from the world. Gone from my life. She had been my everything. She still was. I missed her so much. I couldn't live without her, I knew that.

So I started to plot how I could kill myself.

I thought about it constantly. It took over the top spot of the charts in my head. The problem being, of course, was no matter how much I wanted to die; I was too much of a coward to take my own life. I'd never known what was on the other side of this existence and the thought of traveling to that place always terrified me.

What I did know was that the world around me was getting more crowded. But I never believed the whole duplicate thing, not until one day at a no-name convenience store in Chinatown. While at the counter paying for some fuel for the bad opinion of myself, I glanced over at a man who had walked in the front door. With a dramatic double take, I craned my neck to watch him go down the mostly-microwavable food aisle. This man didn't just look similar to me; he looked like he *was* me. I waited for him outside on the sidewalk, trying to cover my face by burying it in a discarded newspaper section, and then followed him when he exited. I was on him for most of the day. After awhile it occurred to me he was like me, but he was different... in one fundamental way. He didn't blame himself.

Oh, he was a depressed alcoholic just like me, worn down further by horrible circumstance, but he didn't believe that he was the reason that Katrina was dead. Not anymore. Maybe at the beginning, but now it was clear that he had come to terms that shit happens and that the druggie killed his wife. I didn't. I was to blame for my Katrina's death.

In the next few days, I began to see more of my duplicates, just walking down the street. And they all appeared the same. Depressed, drunk, but not at the bottom of the abyss. Not wishing it would all end. Not suicidal. Why was that? Why did they all take a detour in despair but eventually find their way back to a more manageable middle road, where my brain stayed on the road less traveled and retained the blame... retained the need for death. How dare they not feel the same?!

Then it all became clear. I still felt that I needed to die. I needed it. I needed it and now I could have it. So I found this abandoned place, this seafood-processing warehouse, and lured one of my doubles here. It was cathartic, but, as these bad habits usually go, once wasn't enough. I needed to die over and over again.

And I couldn't kill myself.

● ● ●

I walked down the stairs from the second floor and marched down the hall. I was going to stride to the front entrance, head out to my real life, if that's what one could call it. However, something stopped me. I turned towards the pit, a "what if" nagging at my brain. "...more of my duplicates..."

"My duplicates." What if they weren't my duplicates at all? What if I was one of their duplicates...? That couldn't be. I had a lifetime full of memories. Sure, they were adrift in a sea of liquor, but a lifetime's worth. But then, so did they, didn't they? Otherwise, how could they go about their lives like they had always been living them?

No! No, I was me. I had always been. Even if I didn't want to be me anymore, I was. I gave my head a shake, a brain-loosening one, then turned back to walk the long hallway to the entrance. As my eyes looked up from the floor, I glimpsed the muzzle of the gun pointed at me just before the trigger was pulled. I flew to the side, the bullet just missing my left shoulder. Out of reflex, I dashed back into the cavernous hub of the building, sprinting across the expanse as fast as I could. The rifle case jostled in my hand and against my side while my legs crammed into the floor below, propelling me forward. I circled the hole and floored it to the other side, hoping to make it to the winding hallways and staircases in the back half of the warehouse before a bullet lodged in my body. Whereas the last bullet missed my shoulder, this one connected with it. Damnit! Fire surged in the skin and muscle and meat.

Another piece of metal whizzed by my ear but luckily didn't find its target. When my fingertips were close enough to grasp the edge of a door frame, I whirled myself around and out of the open space that could have taken my life. Before I continued down the hallway towards the first staircase fifty feet away, I halted. I peeked my head around the doorway to see my would-be assassin's face. I shouldn't have been surprised to see mine racing through the hub to get to me. Blood had formed a path through his matted hair and down his neck onto his shirt. It was Jay... the most recent one. The one I had just shot in the head. Not well enough, I guess. And now, somehow he had a gun... pointed right at me. Plaster splintered near my face. That was enough gawking. I broke for the stairs.

I needed a few moments to get my rifle out of its case and load it. I wasn't going to get those moments any time soon. Another bullet drove into the rifle case just as I rounded into the stairwell. The case's metal shell probably saved me from losing my kneecap. What was that? Five bullets? I wasn't able to determine the make of the gun so I had no idea how many more rounds he could have left. Two by two I bounded up the stairs. When Other Jay entered the stairwell, he shot up through the spiral. I kept far enough against the outside wall that no bullet was going to clip me as long as he stayed half a floor behind. But I was lugging a heavy load and he wasn't. I decided to abandon the stairwell at the third floor; the higher I would have gone, the more it would have become a fish in a reverse barrel scenario.

I caught myself on the railing that separated the catwalk-like hallway and the open space of the hub, and then jogged breathlessly to my right. I had explored the warehouse a lot over the last few weeks, checking out the best vantage points to shoot from, and I knew that on the other side of the hub from where I was hobbling, a large, windowless room with a lockable door existed. In there, I would have the time I needed to ready my firearm and even the odds. Unfortunately, I'd have to run the gauntlet of more than a football field out in the open. Other Jay was going to have all the opportunity in the world to hit me, depending on how good his aim or luck was. One of them was pretty good.

After I turned the first corner, Other Jay's bullet crossed the hypotenuse over the open space and burrowed into the flesh of my side. Part muscle, part love handle, this gunshot wound bled greater than my earlier one. I switched the rifle case back over to my left side to act as some kind of shield, despite the further burn it caused in my shoulder. I took the second corner hard, almost losing my footing from exhaustion. As I approached the large room, no other shots were fired in my direction. I didn't know if that meant Other Jay was out of bullets, but I wasn't going to stop to find out. I reached the door to the room and whipped inside. Before I locked the door behind me, I saw my doppelganger come to a stop at the second corner. The race and the head wound finally seemed to be taking a toll on my assailant. He needed to catch his breath...or maybe regain his balance or something? We might have shared the same DNA...the same brain, technically...but we didn't share the same thoughts. I could only guess what was going on in his wounded head... just like I guessed his movements throughout the day to get here. Just like I didn't know he brought along a gun. We were *not* the same person.

As I removed the Patriot from its case, that phrase resonated in my head. "We were *not* the same person." No matter how much we looked alike or how similar our mannerisms were to one another, we were different people leading different lives. What had I been doing? I hadn't been killing myself all these months. These individuals were just that: individual. Separate from any other person. Even me.

The door knob exploded in front of me, causing the door itself to swing open halfway. Other Jay's gun turned the corner before he did. I still hadn't loaded my rifle by the time he stood in front of me, aiming right for my head, able to end me at any moment. When he spoke, it was eerie to hear the voice I had heard a few times before on recordings of myself. It's amazing that despite the identical twin appearance of Other Jay, his voice was not the one I perceived in my head on a day-to-day basis.

"I'm pretty sure I know the answer, but I have to ask," Other Jay seethed. "Katrina... she's not alive, is she?"

I pondered his question as I put down the Patriot on the desk beside me. I forgot about the bait I used to get him here. How could I ever have forgotten about her?

"No," I answered, dryly. "We killed her a long time ago."

"He killed her."

I smiled at him. I couldn't help myself. "That's the difference between us. At least, the one that finally got me."

"So she *is* dead. I guess that's that then."

Other Jay straightened his arm and focused down the barrel. He didn't want to miss.

"Don't you want to know why there are so many other ones of us?"

Other Jay kept one eye open behind the rear sight. "No. Did you ever?"

"Not really," I mumbled.

Other Jay breathed in slowly with pursed lips as he stood the fifteen feet away. He made sure his aim was perfect.

I squeezed the trigger.

The End

The False-Faced Killer

By Joel Jenkins

Monica Killingsworth walked from the Aguadilla airport, breathing in the thick, humid air as she threaded a mile of back roads to the off-site car rental agency. She had traveled light, with only a carry on which held a few essentials. Everything else she needed she could pick up with cash. This wasn't a pleasure trip, after all. At least, not until Lucas Santos-Banaez was dead.

The air inside the rental agency was much cooler and the interior somewhat dimmer compared to the blazing sun that drew high in the Puerto-Rican sky. Still, Killingsworth did not remove her sunglasses as she entered. Instead, her nose wrinkled at the heavy scent of bleach which hung in the cool air. She was the only customer so she strode directly to the counter.

"Hola," greeted the fair-skinned, and broad-faced woman behind the counter. Her hair was an orange-tinted shade of blonde which lay flat against her skull and came down in a wispy cascade around her sloping shoulders and heavy bosom.

Killingsworth's Spanish was fluent, but it turned out that it was entirely unnecessary for the clerk saw Killingsworth's pale skin and blonde hair and assumed that her customer was an English speaker. "How can I help you?"

"I'm looking for an SUV—something with a rack for a surfboard," replied Killingsworth.

"Ah, of course, we can help you," the clerk replied. She keyed a text into the face of her phone and turned her attention to the computer in front of her. "To start out with I'll need some ID and if you want to avoid paying the supplemental insurance, I'll need proof of insurance from your current carrier."

"I'll pay the supplemental insurance," said Killingsworth. For what she was being paid to off Lucas Santos-Banaez she could afford the outrageous insurance fees, and besides she had neglected to have her friend, Meg Cabot, in New York forge a proof of insurance. Though, to call Cabot a friend was perhaps a little bit strong. Killingsworth didn't really have friends in the way that most people have friends. She had associates and some of these she liked well enough to use their services on a repeating basis, and not to kill them...unless absolutely necessary.

Killingsworth produced a perfectly forged Alabama driver's license which identified her as Joan Dowdy. In addition, she also had a teacher's union card and her cover was that she was taking a surf vacation during Christmas break. It had been years since she'd been on a surfboard, but word was that Lucas Santos-Banaez had a weakness for blonde surfer girls. That would make it easy to get close to him.

Santos-Banaez was an up and coming drug dealer in the capital city of San Juan and apparently he was beginning to encroach on the territories of some of the other dealers who were unhappy about the increasing slice of the pie that Santos-Banaez was stealing away. These other dealers had pooled their resources to hire Killingsworth to put Santos-Banaez in the ground or in the ocean.

The clerk began a long litany of questions which Killingsworth answered with a studied nonchalance. She had memorized the pertinent information of her cover identity and the false details came easily to her tongue. Still, something about the situation made her feel uneasy.

The longer she stood within the rental agency's barren entry room, the surer she became that something was amiss. There was a lingering scent of something foul beneath the overpowering aroma of the bleach, and she thought she detected the scent of gunpowder—which was something of an aphrodisiac to her.

That was when she noticed the identity tag clipped to the blouse of the clerk. It identified the clerk as Angela Martinez and beside the name and the logo of the rental agency was a small snapshot which did not resemble the clerk in the slightest.

Instead of a pleasant-faced woman with straight hair that wandered between yellow and orange, the photo depicted a woman of narrow features, much darker skin, and a full head of curly black hair. It was certainly possible that the clerk had put on some weight and dyed and straightened her hair since the photo, but as Killingsworth surreptitiously studied the features from behind the tinted screen of her sunglasses she became convinced that the woman posing as the clerk and the woman on the identification tag were two entirely different people.

"And I'm also required to charge you a daily fee for the EZ Pass," said the clerk. "It's a $35 dollar initial charge, followed by a fee of six dollars per day. This allows you to pass through the toll roads. If you go to San Juan on the 22 you'll hit four or five tolls."

Killingsworth bent over and pried off her shoe. "I seem to have a rock in my flats." She made a show of shaking out her shoe, but as she did this she twisted the short heel, releasing a hardened ceramic blade which was concealed within the sole of the shoe. This was a special invention of the ShoeMaker in Milan, where Killingsworth liked to spend some of her ill-gotten gains.

"Do you think you'll be going to San Juan?" asked the clerk.

"Angela?" asked Killingsworth.

The clerk's expression was blank. She did not recognize her own name. Apparently, she had been in a hurry when she had killed the actual clerk. Probably, she had barely had time to hide the body and steal the identification clip—no time to study just who she was impersonating or even to realize that there was a telltale photo on the card. "Who?"

"Angela," said Killingsworth as she drew her slim figure erect, keeping the ceramic knife out of sight behind the counter. "That's your name isn't it?"

"Of course," smiled the woman. "You were behind the counter and I didn't hear you very well." She put some paperwork on the counter and began to point at a series of spots on the contract. "I'm going to need you to sign here, here, here, and here. Then you'll need to initial here."

"I'm in a hurry to meet somebody," said Killingsworth.

"Of course, Miss Dowdy," replied the clerk as she glanced at her personal phone, which rested beside the business phone behind the counter. "I'll do my best to push the process along. It's amazing how much paperwork the company makes me do for just one rental." She placed a key on the counter.

With the red-nailed index finger of her left hand, Killingsworth pointed at one of the contract's subsections. "What's this mean, here?"

The clerk leaned forward, and that was when Killingsworth shoved the ceramic blade through her neck. A shocked expression crossed her features and she gurgled as her hands spasmed and clutched at the counter. Killingsworth gave the blade a jerk to make sure the carotid artery was cut and then shoved the woman back so that she toppled to the floor behind the counter.

In a few moments, Killingsworth was behind the counter with the dying woman. She pulled out the flaps of the woman's blouse where they were tucked into her waist and she found a .22 semi-automatic pistol with a silencer screwed on the barrel. In most cases, all a silencer did was reduce the volume of a pistol from ear-damagingly loud to merely loud. However, a .22 went off with a fairly innocuous pop so, fitted with a silencer, it was actually a pretty quiet gun. It wasn't a very powerful round, but a well-placed bullet or two, especially from close range, could do the job effectively.

The imposter's blood made crimson pools upon the white tiles of the floor and eventually she ceased twitching and gave up the ghost. Killingsworth dragged the body into the bathroom, then moved into the brief corridor behind the counter and opened the door of a broom closet to find the dark-haired Angela Martinez slouched at the back among a mop bucket and broom. There was a pair of bullet holes in her head.

Killingsworth closed the door. She stepped back out into the lobby and glanced at the imposter's phone. A text message stared up at her from someone named Francisco. "OK," it read.

Passing a rack of keys upon the wall, Killingsworth went out the back door of the agency and into a parking lot packed with vehicles. She saw a man with tousled hair, wearing overalls and carrying a toolbox, retreating from an SUV. "Francisco!" she called.

He turned, hesitantly. "Si?"

Killingsworth spoke in rapid-fire Spanish as she held up her key. "Is that my SUV over there?"

He nodded. "Where is the clerk? She should showing you your car."

"Oh, well she had to visit the ladies room. She said that Francisco would take care of me."

"She did?"

"Oh yes," replied Killingsworth. "Angela was very helpful."

"Oh, yes," agreed Francisco. His free hand dipped into his toolbox. "Angela is a very nice woman."

Killingsworth drew closer and shoved her newly-acquired .22 into Francisco's side. "Let go of your gun!"

When faced with the prospect of a bullet in his spleen, Francisco quickly gave up the pretense of being the rental agency's mechanic. "Don't shoot! I'm letting go."

Killingsworth reached into Francisco's toolbox and withdrew an ugly looking .357 revolver with a scarred butt which looked as though it might have been used to hammer a few skulls in. Killingsworth dropped this into her carry-on bag which was slung over her shoulder. Inside the toolbox were a variety of detonators, remote controls and a wad of plastic explosives. "You and I are going to go for a drive, Francisco."

"This was nothing personal," said Francisco. "It was just a job."

"Who hired you?" asked Killingsworth.

"Lucas," said Francisco. "Lucas Santos-Banaez. He said an enemy was flying into Aguadilla—a chica with blonde hair and a bad reputation."

So much for getting close to Lucas. Somebody in Santos-Banaez's rival organizations had leaked the information of her arrival to Santos-Banaez. That was the way of things when too many people knew about a hit. "Tell you what, Francisco. I like how you've been cooperating. If you're helpful enough I might even let you live."

"I'd like that," said Francisco.

"Do you know where I can find Lucas?"

Francisco nodded. "Some days during surf season he stays at a cottage on the 413."

Killingsworth knew of the 413. It was nick-named 'The Road to Happiness'—famous to surfers because it provided easy access to a number of beaches known for good surfing. She handed Francisco the key to the SUV. "You're going to drive me to him."

Francisco swallowed hard. "We can't take this car."

"Why not?" said Killingsworth, even though she was pretty sure she already knew the answer.

"I placed plastic explosives beneath the carriage. When the car is started it will explode."

"That's a shame," said Killingsworth. "Perhaps you can do something to disconnect the bomb?"

Francisco nodded. "Of course. Do you want me to take the bomb off?"

"No," said Killingsworth. "For now, I just want you to disconnect it. If you play this right, Francisco, you and I are going to become very good friends."

"What do you mean by that?" questioned Francisco.

Killingsworth didn't immediately answer this question. "How much is Lucas paying you to kill me?"

"Fifty thousand to split between me and Agata."

"Were you close to Agata?"

"I never knew her before today," said Francisco.

"That's good," said Killingsworth, "because Agata isn't alive any longer."

"You said she was going to the bathroom," said Francisco.

Killingsworth shrugged. "She's in the bathroom, but she's never coming out under her own power."

Francisco's eyes shifted back and forth.

"How would you like to make a hundred thousand dollars today?" asked Killingsworth.

This sounded like a wonderful alternative to Francisco, who up until this moment had been thinking he was going to end the day like Agata. "I would like that very much." He hesitated.

"But you are wondering if you can trust me to keep my word," prompted Killingsworth.

"In this line of business no one tells the truth," said Francisco.

"I always keep my business deals," said Killingsworth. "It's the mark of a professional. When I say I'll do a job I do it. That's why I get paid the big money. Because I'm dependable. So, if I tell you I'm going to pay you 100k for a day's work, I'm as good as my word."

Naturally, Francisco was still skeptical. Just because someone said they kept their word was no reason to believe that they actually did keep their word. A liar had no qualms about lying about being truthful. "What do you want me to do?"

"First, we're going to close down the rental agency for the day. Then you're going to disconnect that bomb. You're going to drive me to Rincon so we can pay a visit to Lucas Santos-Banaez."

They drove with the windows down, the warm wind buffeting them, keeping them cool and dissipating the lingering stench of death. For the most part, Francisco drove in stoic silence, bringing them through the fast pass lanes when they reached the widening roads where toll booths stretched across the highway. Each time, Killingsworth pulled a cap low over her face and looked at her feet so that the cameras wouldn't pick up her visage. Finally, they left the toll highway and followed the 22 toward Rincon, where high, jungle-covered hills reached into the hazy, heat-filled skies.

Killingsworth might have leaned back, closed her eyes and enjoyed the heat and the wind gushing through the windows of the SUV if she had not been on the job. Instead, she kept a close eye on Francisco, who occasionally glanced at her apprehensively as he drove with both hands upon the steering wheel. He might have looked youthful except for the telltale lines growing at the corners of his eyes and the creases growing in his forehead—and then there was a bit of white in his sideburns.

"Tell me, Francisco. How did you learn to wire up a car with explosives?"

"The US military," said Francisco.

"The US military taught you how to wire up cars?"

"Not cars, specifically," replied Francisco. "But they taught me how to demolish bridges, bring down walls, and blow holes in buildings. When I got out of the military and came back to Puerto Rico I discovered it was the only marketable skill I had. Demolition jobs were few and far between and finally I gave in when someone showed up at my door and offered me a bucket load of cash to use my skills illegally."

"You mean to kill people," said Killingsworth, mincing no words.

Francisco nodded. "I'm not proud of it."

"Why not?" asked Killingsworth. "Your vocation requires a high degree of skill that only a few people possess. You should take pride in your work."

"I do...in a fashion," said Francisco, "but the guilt eats me up. I drink to numb my conscience and to forget about the people I kill."

"A conscience," mused Killingsworth. "I think perhaps I had a conscience once, but it died a long, long time ago."

"I try to console myself that my bombs are used to kill bad people," said Francisco. "Murderers, thieves, and assassins such as yourself."

"Whatever gets you through the day," said Killingsworth, who didn't seem to take offense at Francisco's characterization of her. "I kill plenty of bad people as well—mostly. I kill murderers, assassins, drug-lords, thieves, unfaithful husbands, and wives, but some are just in the wrong place at the wrong time and saw things they shouldn't have, or they're rival businessmen who have done nothing unethical, or occasionally I knock off an innocent beauty queen who has the temerity to be more talented and charming than her jealous competition."

Francisco shuddered at the thought and glanced with revulsion at the icy demeanor of the long-legged blonde which sat next to him.

"Take it easy, Francisco. You do just what I say and you're going to come through this a hundred thousand dollars richer. Whatever you might think of me, I'm always true to my bargains. You shoot straight with me and I'll shoot straight with you."

"As long as you don't shoot straight at me," said Francisco in all seriousness.

A smile cracked Killingsworth's icy expression. "See, Francisco? You and I are going to get along just fine."

They took the 115 and threaded through thick jungle growth and copses of mango trees, which shed their heavily laden boughs so that fruit dropped alongside the roadways. Eventually, they worked their way past the roadside pincho stands advertising pollo el carbon and through the small town of Rincon and up the 413, which wound up the jungle-heavy hillside. The road was really no more than a lane and a half and when Francisco met vehicles coming the opposing direction, both he and the other car were forced to drive into the narrow gutter to pass one another. This often brought the car in the opposing lane near the edge of a precipitous slope, but drivers in Rincon were used to such perils and took them in stride.

Here, residential homes built of stucco and surrounded by wrought iron gates clung to the hillsides. Mingled amidst these were auto mechanics, a gas station, bakeries, and pizzerias with no apparent rhyme or reason. Zoning ordinances appeared to be non-existent in such neighborhoods and it only added to the charm of the place when you could walk out your tropical hillside home and visit a bakery next door.

They passed the Lazy Parrot hotel and continued winding through the hills until Francisco eased the SUV onto a rare wide spot on the shoulder, which sat beneath a great tire tree with twisted limbs and heavy branches as big as tree trunks. He motioned to a large building which sat in a depression on the right. "That's Lucas Santos-Banaez's vacation house. It used to be a restaurant, but it was only open for a few months. It sat

there for years with the jungle growing over it until Lucas came in and paid cash for it."

It was a large building that sat on pillars like many of the hillside homes. There was a flat slab of concrete beneath it in which sat half a dozen vehicles. Broad stairs ascended the front of the building and a veranda encircled the entirety of the home. Here, mosquito netting had been stretched and lantern lights hung. Twilight settled upon the hills and the thump of bass traveled through the thickening air. Killingsworth could hear the jangle of music and she could see male and female figures mingling upon the veranda, most with bottles in their hands. Surfboards leaned against the railings of the stairways below.

"During surf season, Lucas likes to spend the weekends up here. During the week he goes back to San Juan to take care of business."

"Which is selling cocaine," observed Killingsworth.

"Those beautiful women on the balconies," said Francisco with a gesture, "they flock to Lucas like mosquitoes to blood, because he gives them as much Colombian Gold as they want."

"Coke whores," said Killingsworth. "It's too bad they might be collateral damage, but it can't be helped. You roll with the swine you get butchered with the swine. You see Lucas?"

Francisco nodded. "See there, with the two women in bikinis?"

Killingsworth saw a smooth-faced man of about thirty with an open shirt that displayed a hairless chest and a couple of gold chains. A gorgeous Puerto Rican brunette hung on one arm and a curvy blonde on the other. She recognized him from the many photos she had studied and memorized. "You bring Lucas down to look at my body and start running as soon he pulls back the tarp. I'll give you three seconds to get clear and throw yourself on the ground. I'll be listening, and if you double-cross me I won't wait for you to get clear. We have an understanding?"

Francisco nodded soberly, and then he hissed. "No, no, no! I can't do it. I can't do it."

Killingsworth's face hardened. "Why not? I thought we had an agreement."

"It's my brother. My brother, Manalo is here."

"What's your brother doing here?" asked Killingsworth.

Francisco clutched his face and head with both hands. "It is all my fault. My little brother, he saw I always had plenty of money and begged me to get him a job with Lucas. Finally, I introduced him and Manalo's been running errands for him. I didn't think he'd be here tonight."

Killingsworth was unmoved. "We still have a deal, don't we?"

"No, we don't have a deal!" said Francisco. "Do you think I would kill my own brother for a hundred thousand or even a million dollars?"

Killingsworth shrugged. "Many people have paid me to kill their relatives."

"I will not do it!" Francisco folded his arms to illustrate his adamant resolve.

Killingsworth lifted the silenced .22 to Francisco's temple. She was sure that Lucas Santos-Banaez and his fellow party goers would not hear the noise of its firing over the loud music. "Then I guess our association is about to come to an end. It's too bad. I kind of like you, Francisco. The fact that you won't kill your brother shows that you have some spine."

"Don't you have any family?" pleaded Francisco. "You must know what it is like to have someone you care for!"

Killingsworth shook her head. "I was an orphan."

"You must have had someone that took care of you. Who loved you and you loved back?"

"In a fashion," said Killingsworth, "but they're gone now. Someone in my line of work can't afford to have family connections. It's a weak spot enemies can exploit."

"I beg of you," said Francisco. "Do not kill my brother. I will..."

"You'll what?" asked Killingsworth.

"I'll trade my life for his," said Francisco. "I will send him out to you and you will keep him alive. I will make sure that Lucas Santos-Banaez dies. I won't run. He'll have no warning of what is about to happen. Your other plan was weaker, anyhow."

Killingsworth saw the wisdom of this and lowered her pistol. "I think we have an acceptable deal, Francisco."

Slipping out of the SUV, Killingsworth watched as Francisco pulled from beneath the clotting shadows of the tire tree and turned down the descending drive into the valley where the Lucas Santos-Banaez made his vacation home. A couple of guards approached the vehicle before it reached the valley and one of them motioned a submachine gun at the vehicle.

Killingsworth listened to the conversation on the open phone connection, which she had with Francisco. The conversation came in a staccato of Spanish, which Killingsworth had no trouble following, for she was just as expert in Spanish as she was in English, having learned both of them as a child in Colombia.

"This is a private party," said the guard with the visible machine gun.

"I'm invited," replied Francisco. "I've got something that Lucas will want to take a look at."

"You know Lucas?" asked the guard with the machine gun.

"I know Lucas," affirmed Francisco.

The other guard, hand on a pistol beneath the loose tails of his shirt peered into the SUV. "That's Francisco. He's the man that makes things go boom for Lucas."

The man with the machine gun looked upon Francisco with a new found respect. "You did the job that killed Boss Becerra?"

"That's right," said Francisco.

They quickly ushered Francisco through and he brought the SUV to a halt in the parking area beneath the home. From her vantage point behind the corner of a stone wall along the roadside, Killingsworth watched as Francisco climbed the front stairs, past grappling couples and heavily intoxicated surfers who sat on the steps or leaned against the rail.

Francisco greeted people as he went. He halted when he came to a man younger than him, but with similar features, who was engaged in conversation with a dark-haired woman clutching a beer bottle and smoking a cigarette.

"Manny," called Francisco. "I need you to do me a favor."

"Can't you see I'm busy, Francisco? Emigdia and I have a lot to talk about."

"I'm sure you do," said Francisco as he dragged Manalo away from the woman, "but this is very important."

Killingsworth could see the two brothers talking privately on the veranda and hear Francisco's low tones over the open phone connection. "A yellow car followed me from the plaza in Rincon, all the way up the 413. I want you to go up to the road and see if there's any sign of a yellow car."

"What make?" asked Manalo.

"I don't know the make," said Francisco. "But there's not that many yellow cars. Go up to the road and walk up and down it to see if you can spot it."

"And if I do?"

"Then come back and tell me," said Francisco.

"What are you going to do?" asked Manalo.

"I've got business with Lucas," said Francisco.

"What business?" pried Manalo.

"Its business you're better off having nothing to do with," replied Francisco. "In fact, I want you to do me a favor."

"Besides looking for a yellow car?" questioned Manalo.

"I don't want you going down the same road as me, Manalo. You're better than that. You're still young and you've got a lot of potential. This life here," he motioned at the party and commotion swirling all around them. "It's all going to come crashing down. You need to make a fresh start before it comes crashing down on you."

"Whatever you say, hermano," replied Manalo.

"I want you to take me seriously, Manny. I may not always be around to keep an eye on you and in this business; it's easy to get on the wrong side of somebody."

A hard looking man with a series of tattoos down his left arm and up his neck, a pistol thrust into the waist of his pants, spotted Francisco and beckoned to him. "Over here, Francisco. Lucas wants to talk to you...now!"

Francisco patted his brother on the shoulder. "Go take a look for that yellow car."

Manalo paused only to whisper a few things into Emigdia's ear and she nodded sagaciously as he descended the stairs. For a moment, Killingsworth watched Manalo as he left the home. As he climbed the driveway toward the road he was intercepted by the pair of guards armed with machine pistols and he spent a few moments explaining the situation to them.

Killingsworth couldn't overhear their words, but she knew it could be bad for her if the guards with the machine pistols decided that the news about the yellow car was worth investigating themselves. It was going to be tricky enough to handle Manalo, but add two guards with machine pistols into the mix and things were bound to get messy.

Fortunately, neither guard seemed too concerned about the possibility of a car following Francisco from the plaza at Rincon. Instead, they were satisfied to wave Manalo through and let him take a look by himself. As Manalo climbed the last fifty feet to the road, Killingsworth eavesdropped on Francisco as he spoke to Lucas.

"Tell me you have good news, Francisco," said Lucas as the explosives expert approached.

"Things didn't go quite as planned," said Francisco. "The assassin collared me in the yard behind the rental agency. I had to shoot her."

"For a moment there, you had me worried," said Lucas. "You know how much faith I put in you taking care of this job for me. And you know what happens to people who fail me."

Killingsworth thought she detected a slight quaver in Francisco's voice as he responded.

"It ended up being quieter this way," said Francisco. "And her body will be easier to identify."

"That might be a good thing," said Lucas, his teeth gleaming in the lantern light. "I want to drop her body on Desi Calderos's front doorstep as a message that he shouldn't screw with me. He thinks he's clever hiring a foreign assassin to come in and take me out, but I've got friends even in the Calderos Cartel. He can't even blow his nose without me hearing about it."

"You want to take a look at the body?" asked Francisco.

"Are you sick?" asked Lucas.

"What?" asked Francisco. "You're not squeamish about looking at a body are you?"

"No," scoffed Lucas. "I've seen plenty of dead men. I mean you're sweating bullets."

"Its nerves," explained Francisco, and he wiped the gathering beads of sweat from his forehead. "I get this way after every job. It's like some sort of delayed reaction."

Lucas laughed and clapped Francisco on the back. "Let's go take a look at that body. I hear the assassin they sent after me was a real looker. They thought she might have a better chance at getting close to me." He glanced at the curvy blonde who had been on his arm a few moments before. She and the dark-skinned brunette were engaged in an earnest conversation near the icebox. "If I have a weakness it is white women with blonde hair—but then, any color will do in a pinch."

From her hiding spot, Killingsworth watched as Lucas, his tattooed bodyguard, and Francisco descended the steps toward the SUV parked beneath the house. Then she glanced to the mouth of the driveway where she saw Manalo emerging onto the street. She hid in a knot of shadows, so Manalo had not discerned her yet, but after a pause he climbed the street in her direction. It wouldn't be long before Manalo discovered her hiding there in the darkness. If he raised the alarm too quickly Lucas might not be in range of her attack. She reached into her pocket for the device Francisco had given her from his box of tools.

Every moment brought Manalo closer, and Killingsworth's eyes darted between Francisco's approaching brother and the trio of men who approached the SUV. Francisco opened up the hatch at the back of the SUV and revealed a tarp, beneath which lay a body. "Here she is."

Holding his breath in to avoid inhaling the stench, Lucas leaned forward and pulled back the flap of the tarp. "But this is Agata! Where is Killingsworth?!"

"Right here," muttered Killingsworth and her voice came through Francisco's open phone line so it seemed that Agata's corpse was speaking. Killingsworth pressed the remote in her pocket and the signal detonated the plastic explosives planted on the underside of the gasoline tank of the SUV. There was a double explosion which burst the SUV into shrapnel and caved in the sides of the other vehicles beneath the home, shattering windows. The flesh was torn off Lucas, his bodyguard, and Francisco. Their bones were pulverized and the three of them died instantly.

A flaming ball scorched the underside of the home, and the pillars holding it aloft cracked and buckled so that the entire home shifted. The blonde woman in a bikini tumbled drunkenly over the rail and fell on her back in a scorched plantain bush, which likely saved her life. The others abandoned their beer and their cocaine and went shrieking from the off-kilter house, trampling each other in a rush for the stairs.

Manalo was just a few feet away from Killingsworth when all this happened. The only reason he failed to spot the blonde assassin was because his eye had been upon the road and the few vehicles that were parked alongside, farther up the winding route, which was overshadowed by palm fronds and the encroaching jungle foliage.

When the twin explosions incinerated the SUV, Manalo came up short and gave out a cry of horror. "Francisco!"

Killingsworth took the opportunity to rise out of hiding and shove the .22 against his liver. "Keep quiet and come with me."

Manalo was so overwrought with grief that he barely registered the prospect of being shot. "But...but my brother!"

"He's dead," said Killingsworth, her voice cold. "He traded his life so that you could live. Don't let his sacrifice be in vain. Do you have a vehicle nearby?"

"Down by the house," choked Manalo.

"Never mind," said Killingsworth. "We'll steal one."

She prodded Manalo, stumbling up the road, but turned just in time to see one of the guards rising from the dark, machine pistol in his hand. Before he could shoot, Killingsworth thrust out her .22 pistol and fired. The shot was from a good thirty yards away, but she put a single bullet through his eye. As he pitched backward his finger reflexively pulled the trigger of his machine pistol and a staccato of muzzle flashes lit the night as thirty rounds spat into the air.

"Faster!" urged Killingsworth. "Everyone saw you leave the property right before the explosion went off. They're going to think you did it."

"But I wouldn't have killed my own brother!" objected Manalo, and his anguished voice suggested that he was near tears.

"They're not going to take the time to think about that," replied Killingsworth.

As they sprinted into the dark the other machine gunner opened fire. Bullets scathed the narrow roadway, ricocheted from stone walls, punctured mailboxes and clanked against wrought iron fences, but they rounded the corner without being struck.

Killingsworth halted Manalo, lifted his shirt and passed her hand around the waist of his pants until she found the protruding butt of a pistol. She jerked the holster free from the waist where it was clipped and added this to her growing collection of pistols. Normally, she would have visited a black market arm's dealer and picked up a weapon appropriate to the hit she was making, but fate and Francisco had provided her with the means to kill Lucas.

"Are...are you the assassin that Francisco was supposed to kill?" choked out Manalo.

"Supposed to have killed," repeated Killingsworth, "but he and I came to an understanding. She struck the window of the small sedan with the butt of Manalo's revolver and shattered the glass. Then she reached inside and opened up the door. "Climb in."

"Where are we going?" asked Manalo.

Killingsworth cracked the steering column, yanked loose two wires and touched them together. The starter turned and the engine fired, then she climbed behind the wheel. "I had an agreement with your brother to get you to safety. I'm going to drop you off in downtown Rincon with one hundred thousand dollars. What you do or where you go after that is your business."

"A hundred thousand dollars? Why are you giving me money?"

"That's the agreement I had with Francisco. It seems he had high hopes that you wouldn't blow it all on a fast car and faster women. He says you're smarter than that. Here's your chance to prove him right."

"That's what Francisco said he wanted me to do." Manalo scratched his head, tears and bewilderment in his eyes. "I didn't think those were going to be the last words that he ever said to me. I didn't know...but he knew. He knew that his car would explode when he opened the hatch, didn't he?"

"He wanted something better for you, and he bought you a second chance with his life," said Killingsworth.

Manalo wiped away the moisture streaming from his eyes. The warm tropical air buffeted in through the broken window, drying the tears. "Why give me money? Why don't you just kill me and dump me at the roadside?"

"That wasn't the bargain I made," said Killingsworth.

The End.

The Shadow Men of Az Zibar
(A Donovan Pike Adventure)
by Mark Justice

"I don't believe it," Pug Benson said.

He and Pike were in a darkened room in what was once a small restaurant on the edge of Dahuk, not far from the border of Iraq and Turkey. The windows had been blown out months before by nearby explosions. The interior was trashed by looters. The pair had humped it here double time after learning of the rendezvous location from the PI that old man Ellerbee hired. Three of Pike's men failed to intercept the two girls when they landed in London. The meet was supposed to happen here, but Pike and Pug were growing skeptical; until the Mercedes drove onto the street and stopped fifty yards from the empty restaurant.

Dahuk was serious ISIS territory, though the terrorist group's presence was sparse in this rural section of the capitol of Kurdistan. The coalition had pushed them out of the heart of Iraq.

The gold two-seater idled in the street, its engine noise a soft purr.

"That's a freakin' 2009 McLaren SLR FAB Desire Design," Pug said. "I can't believe it's a terrorist car."

"So?" Pike watched the occupants through his rifle scope.

"So, it's worth like a million four."

Pike snorted. "For a car?"

"Can we keep it?"

"Sure," Pike said. "If it will fit on the boat."

"Crap," Pug said. "I always wanted one of them cars."

"We've got another vehicle."

It was a truck, impossibly old and flecked with rust. Two men were in the cab. Another man was in the bed, along with two young women.

"They're wearing burqas, but it could be them," Pug said.

"Five guys, counting the two in your dream car," Pike said.

"Want to wait for more to get here? Make it a fair fight?"

"I think we'll work with what we have," Pike said. He sighted on the man in the truck bed first. That foe posed the immediate danger to the girls. "I'll take the one in the bed as soon as the yahoos in the front get out. Think you can handle them?"

"You know, that attitude really screws with my self-esteem. Words hurt, Donovan."

Pike smiled as he laid the crosshairs on the man who held a machine pistol pointed in the direction of the two girls, teenagers who thought flying across the world to join ISIS would be a big, fun adventure. Pike saw plastic ties around their wrists. These two were going to be very popular with the terrorist group, unless Pike and Pug could hit their targets.

The driver and passenger doors opened and two young men climbed out. They were dressed in American t-shirts, jeans and tennis shoes. Not ISIS, Pike thought. Wannabes. Carrying out menial tasks to curry favor. The passenger had a handgun in the waistband of his pants. He had to assume the driver was also armed.

"Light 'em up," Pike said.

Pug fired twice from his M24 sniper rifle; the two slugs seemed to strike simultaneously, as the driver and passenger hit the ground together, dead from head shots.

The man in the back of the truck looked around in confusion, before he reached for one of the girls, presumably to use as a hostage. Pike didn't give him a chance. He fired his trusty Browning hunting rifle. The impact removed the top of the man's head and threw him out of the truck. The two girls made themselves as flat as possible.

The men in the car decided that retreat was a good option. The McLaren backed down the street.

Pug put four rapid shots through the car's windshield. The McLaren continued in reverse until it turned and rammed into the concrete wall of a squat building. No one got out.

"Still want the car?" Pike said.

"Nah," Pug said. "It's shot."

"I'll get the girls out of the truck. You call Womack."

● ● ●

Captain Charles Womack, an Aussie, was in charge of the coalition forces for this region of Iraq. He was accompanied by a uniformed Iraqi soldier. Womack surveyed the bodies in the street and the wrecked car, and whistled.

"The two in the car are middle management," he said. "Good work."

"What about the girls?" Pike said. The two teens, Kallista Farouk and Grace Ellerbee, granddaughter of the old man, didn't object to being sent home. Both were traumatized and Grace had soiled herself.

"On a plane to Germany. Doc'll check 'em out and send 'em to the states. I think their big adventure is over."

"Thanks, Chuck," Pug said. "We gotta catch a ride, too." *The Triton*, Donovan Pike's personal yacht, was anchored at the other end of the country, in the Persian Gulf. Ellerbee's influence netted them a helicopter ride back to the sea.

"Chopper's on the way," Womack said. "So what's it like for you two sand dogs on your own? Nobody giving orders. Nothing like the Gulf War, I bet."

"It's pretty sweet," Pug said. "But I can't wait to get back to Florida. I need some vacation."

"And if I remember anything about you, there's a woman waiting."

"A Cuban babe named Floramaria," Pike said. "She's really something."

Pug blushed, while Womack laughed. "What about you, Donnie? Ready to settle down, or are you happy being a soldier of fortune."

Pike grimaced. "That's not what I am."

"He's an *adventurer*," Pug said. "Like Indiana Jones, but with more money."

Womack smiled and shook his head. "You two never change."

In the distance, the whirring blades of a chopper could be heard.

"Love to stick around in paradise, Chuck, but we gotta run," Pug said.

An old man wandered into the street, along with a few others who went into hiding when the terrorists rolled in. Womack's Iraqi companion apparently knew the elderly man, and the two conversed in Arabic.

"You sure you don't want to stick around? The coalition could use you. We're gonna wipe out these rats sooner or later," Womack said.

"Sorry, pal, got things to do," Pug said, clapping the Aussie on the shoulder. He had to reach up to do it, since he was fully a foot shorter than Womack. Pug was built like a barrel-chested fireplug.

Womack's Iraqi compatriot strolled over to them and chuckled.

"What is it?" Womack said.

"Crazy old man. He has family in Az Zibar. He claims the area is being haunted by ghosts. Tall, dark ghosts."

Pug placed his hand in the center of Pike's back and gave a gentle shove. "Chopper's almost here. We have steak in the *Triton*'s freezer and a case of beer. Doesn't that sound good?"

Pike didn't budge. His back felt like a block of granite.

"Tall, dark ghosts?" he said.

Pug sighed and looked to the sky. "Sorry, Floramaria."

● ● ●

Womack let them use the chopper. It was a much shorter ride to Az Zibar, almost next door to Dahuk. But he made it clear they were on their own for a ride back to the Gulf. Womack did lend them the services of his Iraqi colleague, Jamail Al-Sameer, a captain in the Iraqi army. He spoke fluent English and he thought he would enjoy, as he put it, "a diversion with a couple of crazy Americans."

The chopper sat down in a lush, green field near a river. Pug later learned it was the Kabir. Mountains rose in the distance and a small town was within a short walk.

"Gentlemen," Captain Al-Sameer said with a great flourish of his arms, "welcome to the gleaming metropolis of Az Zibar."

Pug saw a smattering of small buildings, probably houses, and many goats. "Do they have a Holiday Inn?"

Al-Sameer laughed.

Pike stared at the town. "Do you know the name of the family of the old man back in Dahuk?"

Al-Sameer did. The trio grabbed their guns and packs and, as the chopper took off, they walked to town.

● ● ●

It was nearly dark when they found the right house. A thin man in his thirties spoke to them. Beyond the door, a woman of the same age cooked on a wood burning stove while three small children ran around their mother's legs.

Al-Sameer finished the conversation and turned to the Americans. "Barir will take us to the site after dinner."

"Tonight?" Pug said.

"That is when the shadow men appear."

"Oh, okay. What's for dinner?"

"Whatever you packed," Al-Sameer said. "He invited us to join them, but they can barely feed their children. I told them Americans could only dine on unhealthy food, and I would stay out here and stand guard."

"Thanks," Pike said.

"I may have also left him with the impression that the short one liked to steal goats and would not be a proper influence on his children."

"Hey!"

"Sorry, my friend. I was trying to conserve their meager supplies."

The three of them sat on the ground in the cool night air and ate beef jerky, MREs and drank bottled water. Finally, Barir emerged from the hut with a walking stick in one hand and a short sword in the other.

"How far is it?" Pike said.

Al-Sameer did a calculation in his head, and then said, "Six or seven miles, near the Shanidar Cave."

"Seven miles!" Pug kicked at the ground. "Man, all this hiking is why I got out of the army."

"And your little problem with following orders," Pike said.

"That wasn't just me, bud."

Al-Sameer laughed again.

• • •

The four men walked for an hour and covered a little more than three miles. Barir lead the way, with Pike and Pug walking side by side behind him and Al-Sameer bringing up the rear. The terrain had been flat for about a mile. Now they were going uphill at a slight grade.

"So what is this Shanidar place?" Pug's breathing was steady. He looked a bit on the chubby side, but he could march with the best of them.

"One of the greatest archeological finds in history," Pike said. "Ten Neanderthals were excavated in the late 1950s. Some of them may be 60,000 years old or more. Also, two cemeteries were discovered there, dating back 35,000 years."

"You know much about our famous cave, my friend," Al-Sameer said from behind them. Pike and Pug slowed and allowed the Iraqi to catch up to them.

"It's what he does best," Pug said. "Archeology, I mean. He thinks he's pretty good in a fight, but I have to watch his back."

Pike made a sound that fell somewhere between a snort and a cough.

Al-Sameer chuckled. "How did the two of you get into this line of work?"

"We got out of the army and we were both restless. We tried a lot of stuff. Treasure hunting. Deep sea fishing. Soldiering for hire. We hooked up with some other guys and now we travel around the world; a lot of time following up on a project for the Ravencroft Foundation."

"The think tank?" Al-Sameer looked puzzled. "I mean, no offense, but..."

"Yeah, I get it. We're not really the think tank types. Two things: number one is that the Foundation is involved in archeology, especially ancient tech. Number two, the Ravenscroft Foundation was co-founded by Pike's old man."

Al-Sameer stopped walking. It took Pug a few steps to realize the man was no longer next to him. He paused again, to allow the Iraqi to rejoin them.

"I'm sorry," Al-Sameer said. "I did not realize he was the son of Dr. Pike."

"It's okay," Pug said. "He doesn't look like the brainy type."

"I can hear you," Pike said from five feet away.

"Wait," Al-Sameer said. "Did you say *alien* tech?"

"I guess I should have said 'alleged' alien tech, 'cause it's never been totally proven that the First came from another planet. Right, Donovan?"

Pike sighed.

"The First?" Al-Sameer shook his head. "I feel I have walked into one of your American movies."

"They're real enough," Pug said. "They were here way back when we were crawling out of caves. The theory is they were here to guide us or something. Pike's dad and Old

Man Ravencroft disappeared a few years back looking for the First." He glanced at Pike and lowered his voice. "The First left behind some of their machines, too. We've come across some of them. So have this group of crazies called The Brotherhood of the First. We ran up against them a few times. They want all the tech for themselves. They hope to bring back the First or something. Evil nutjobs is what they are."

Al-Sameer seemed skeptical. "I think you pull my leg, my friend. My country has many legends and gods. I heard all the stories as a boy. Yet I've never seen anything, other than suffering and greedy tyrants."

"Hey, I'm no scientist," Pug said. "I'm just telling you what I was told. But I have seen some of their machines. And I shot a few of those Brotherhood yahoos—before they could shoot me, naturally."

"You have...interesting lives." Al-Sameer slowed his pace until he trailed the group again.

They walked another hour, mostly uphill, as the night grew cooler. The ground beneath them was now more rock than grass. Pug was about to declare a rest break when Barir shouted. He pointed to a small cave about fifty yards to the left of the path.

"He says this is the place," Al-Sameer said. "The home of the Shadow Men."

"Where are they?" Pike said.

Al-Sameer uttered a sentence in Arabic. Barir swallowed hard, and then ran toward the cave.

"What's he doing?" No one answered Pug.

Barir covered perhaps half the distance to the cave when the first apparition appeared.

It was suddenly, soundlessly standing in front of the cave entrance. Tall–much taller than a normal man–the faceless figure shimmered in the light of the moon. The shadow man was not black, really more of a dark blue shade. Pug saw the occasional flash of light within the form, as though the body of the shadow thing carried fireflies within it.

Barir, trembling and breathing loudly, backed slowly away.

When he had retreated ten yards or so, the shadow man vanished as quietly as it appeared.

"What the hell," Pug muttered.

"I don't believe it," Al-Sameer said.

"Let's all go up," Pike said. "See what happens."

Barir declined to accompany them. So Pike, Pug and Al-Sameer walked to the cave.

When they reached the halfway point, three shadow men appeared. The figures were identical. They had no features of any kind, save for the random flashes of light. The shadow men reminded Pug of figures cut from a schoolchild's construction paper.

"What are they?" he asked. "Holograms?"

Pike resumed walking in the direction of the cave.

Pug and Al-Sameer raised their rifles.

The lights within the shadow men flashed brighter and more rapidly.

Floating across the rocky terrain, the faceless figures moved closer to Pike.

"Put your guns down," he said. The two men complied.

The shadow men halted their advance. They did not return to their original position, but the flashing of the lights within their forms slowed, then stopped.

Pike stepped up to the closer figure. He extended his arm until his hand was within the shadow man's midsection. The faceless form did not react.

"I think we're looking at a security system," Pike said.

"You have seen this before?" Al-Sameer said.

Instead of answering, Pike walked through the shadow man. Pug could see his outline through the body of the apparition.

"Donovan, are you okay?"

"I'm fine. I'm going to see if this thing has an off switch."

"This is a machine?" Al-Sameer spoke softly, as if the dark forms would hear him.

"Well, it ain't ghosts," Pug said. "No such thing."

The Iraqi didn't answer.

Pike stood at the opening to the small cave. It was nearly circular, about the size of a large beach ball and the top was about as high as Pike's knees. Above the cave, trees rose, tall and thick. He squatted and ran his hands around the edges of the opening. He stopped beneath the top of the entrance. His hand lingered a moment. Pug heard a faint noise that sounded like a mosquito's buzzing.

The trio of shadow figures vanished.

"So you *have* encountered this previously," Al-Sameer said.

Pike stood and faced them. "No. But I have seen this tech before. I found a switch and took a chance."

"Wait a minute," Pug said. "If that was a security device, what was it protecting?"

"Let's find out." Pike said. He knelt at the cave entrance.

"Wait!" Al-Sameer stepped forward. "Barir should not miss this." He called out to the man from Az Zibar. Barir joined them, albeit reluctantly.

Al-Sameer put an arm around Barir's shoulders and guided him toward the cave. Pug walked in front of them.

"Without this man," Al-Sameer said slapping Barir on the back, "we would not be here."

He pulled a handgun from the holster on his belt, placed the barrel an inch from the back of Barir's head and pulled the trigger.

Pug jumped and uttered an expletive. He raised his rifle, spinning to face the Iraqi captain and the Glock in his right hand.

"I would make careful choices now, my friend."

Pug nodded. He raised his left hand and lowered his rifle to the ground with his right.

As he stood up, he spun counter clockwise and drove his right elbow into Al-Sameer's face. The Iraqi was a few inches taller than Pug, so he had to strike at an upward angle, reducing the kinetic force of the blow. Even so, he felt and heard Al-Sameer's nose flatten under his elbow. The Iraqi fell backward, dropping his gun on the way. He clasped both hands to his face. Blood flowed through his interlaced fingers.

Pug reached for the Glock. He heard the shot the same instant the dirt at his feet exploded into the air.

He slowly turned. On the wooded hill above the cave, several armed men emerged from cover. The lead man tracked Pug with an assault rifle.

Pug couldn't help noticing one other fact.

Donovan Pike was gone.

● ● ●

Al-Sameer climbed to his feet, wiping blood away from his broken nose. He said something to the other men and they climbed or jumped down from their perch.

Two men held Pug by his arms. Al-Sameer stood before him, nose bent at an ugly angle and oozing blood. There was a rage etched across the Iraqi's features. Al-Sameer drove a fist into Pug's gut, knocking the breath out of the smaller man.

Pug struggled to suck air in his lungs for a minute. When he could speak, he stared at Al-Sameer. "No matter where we go, you Brotherhood lunatics are never far behind."

The Iraqi attempted a smile, winced from the pain, and grimaced. "I was here long before you, fool. It was my job to get close to Womack, because of his relationship with

Donovan Pike. We knew he couldn't stay out of the fighting for long. He is an animal. As are you."

Pug was able to smile. "So you hang around in a freakin' war zone hoping Pike will show up to–what? Lead you to some old rusty artifact?"

"Once we collect all of the holy relics left behind by the First, they will return to guide mankind. And the Brotherhood of the First will rule at their side."

"Holy guacamole," Pug said. "You're even crazier than we thought. And believe me; we thought you were insane long before this."

Al-Sameer punched him in the stomach again.

The air left his lungs in a *whoosh*. When Pug could talk, he raised his head. "Besides, you'll never get all that old alien junk. A ton of it is locked..." He swallowed hard. "Aw, crap."

Now Al-Sameer endured the pain long enough to display a triumphant grin. "Exactly. Pike will tell us the access codes to the Ravencroft Foundation's storage facilities in Florida. After he extracts a certain item for us from the cave, now that he was kind enough to deactivate the safeguards."

"And why will he do that?"

Al-Sameer produced a long hunting knife. He held the blade in front of Pug's face, where it caught the moon light. "Because I am going to slice all the delicate parts off his best friend. Now where did Pike go?"

"Here," a voice called. Pike climbed from the small cave opening. He straightened up. He was holding a silver scroll. "I found what you were looking for."

Al-Sameer gasped.

"It's what the security system was protecting. I bet it's a log or a star map, leading back to the home of the First. I only glanced at it. We've never seen their writing before, other than the symbols on their machinery. But I know a very smart lady at the Ravencroft Foundation who can translate this in about a day."

"Hand it over or we will take it from your bullet riddled body." Al-Sameer uttered a command and rifle barrels were trained on Pike.

"You could do that," Pike said, "while I do this." Flame bloomed from his other hand. The dusk and distance had hidden the lighter. Pike set the scroll aflame and tossed it away from him. He dived to the ground and slithered back into the cave.

Al-Sameer screamed. He rushed to the flaming scroll to extinguish it. A rifle barrel appeared from the cave's opening. Pike fired once. The round entered Al-Sameer's left eye, spun him around and dropped him on the rocky ground.

His men were stunned for an instant. It was long enough for Pug to pull away from his two captors. He used his powerful arms to slam their heads together with a satisfying crunch.

"Pug! Run!"

Pug trusted Pike, so he spun and headed for the path. A couple of shots zinged by his head, but his zig-zagging lope kept him safe.

Behind him he heard screams.

He stopped and turned.

The shadow men were back. Four of the dark figures attacked Al-Sameer's remaining soldiers. The shadowy apparitions picked up the men and shook them like dolls. One shadow man tore a tall soldier in half. Pug backed up a few more steps.

When the last man was dead, the shadow men faded away.

"Pug!"

"Here! I'm okay."

"Come on back," Pike said. "It's just us."

Pug returned to the cave. Pike used a flashlight to illuminate the ground. He was right. No one else lived.

"What just happened?" Pug said. "You walked right through one of those shadow dudes. How did they tear those guys apart?"

"This." Pike handed a round metal object to his friend. It was about the size of a saucer for a tea cup. Six lights were arranged around its circumference. The one on the far right was glowing with a blue light that was almost purple.

"When I first reached the cave, the second button from the left was lit. I punched the button on the far left to shut things down. I guessed the opposite end would produce maximum damage."

"You *guessed?*"

Pike directed his light across the ground again. "I bet the sensors for the system are spread out underneath the ground. This will all have to be dug up."

The light caught the embers of the remains of the scroll. Pug pointed at it. "What about that? That could have told us so much about the First."

"The only thing it could tell us is when beef jerky expires. Which is never," Pike said. "I took the wrappers off a couple of MREs in my pack and rolled them up."

"So there wasn't a scroll?"

"No," Pike said. He reached into the cave opening and pulled out his pack. "There was this, though." He held out a rectangular piece of metal. The shape reminded Pug of a computer tablet, though much thinner. It was cool to the touch. The face of the metal was blank. Pug touched the center of it with a fingertip. An image appeared in mid-air in front of his face. It looked like the Earth, but something was off.

"There's one big land mass," Pike said, his voice brimming with excitement. "Before the continents."

Pug pulled his finger away. The image faded. He touched another portion of the metal. Something else appeared. It looked like a sky full of strange stars.

"It's a map, ain't it?"

"I think so. They left it for us. I believe it's an invitation," Pike said.

Pug handed the metal device back to Pike. "I can't wrap my head around this, Donovan. What are we gonna do?"

Pike removed a satellite phone from his pack. "You are going to call Gemma at the Foundation and arrange for a fast extraction. Then we're going to put some distance between us and this place, in case any more of the Brotherhood are lurking around."

Pug began to dial a number in Florida. Gemma Ravencroft was the sole offspring of the Foundation's other co-founder and she'd been involved in an on-again, off-again relationship with Pike since they were teens.

"Oh, and tell her to send someone who can speak Arabic, along with some money, preferably gold," Pike said.

"Okay, but she's gonna wanna know why."

"We're not leaving until we break the bad news to Barir's wife. Then we're going to make sure his family is cared for."

"Got it."

Pug made the call. Then the pair departed the area of the small cave and the dead men. They walked toward the moon in silence, carrying the future with them.

The End

Story-Land
Powhatan City Confidential

by Joseph Lamere

MARCH, 1970

PARKLAND COUNTY, KANSAS

Agent 42 waited until a lone light burned in the farmhouse before he made his move. This was his first solo mission for the Society. He still had two months left on his probationary period. If he succeeded here the White Coats had agreed to waive that period and make him a full-time agent with the Primary Source Society.

He had never wanted anything more in his life.

He had done his due diligence on the matter. He knew Mr. Clark stayed up late, struggling to put into words what had happened to him earlier in the month. Mr. Clark, a farmer by trade, wanted nothing more than to make a name for himself with the pulps. He figured "the incident," as he referred to it, was the perfect scenario.

Agent 42 knocked softly on the back door. He didn't want to startle Mr. Clark and he sure didn't want to wake the baby. Mr. Clark was a reasonable man, he told himself. He had to know there would be interest. He had to know sooner or later *someone* would come calling.

Mr. Clark set himself up on the kitchen table after his wife cleaned up the dinner things and put the baby to sleep. Only then would he allow himself to bring out the battered Underwood typewriter and sit up late into the night, gnawing away at his latest adventure.

At the sound of the knock, the clack of the typewriter stopped, but only after the telltale *ding* which told Agent 42 Mr. Clark had come to the end of the line. Mr. Clark didn't want to interrupt his train of thought. Agent 42 had read some of the farmer's offerings. They were amateurish exercises full of exclamation points and cardboard dialogue. Mr. Clark had a vivid imagination; Agent 42 knew what that was like.

The farmer came to the back door, his heavy work boots clomping on the linoleum, peering out into the darkness with a frown. He was younger than Agent 42 had imagined him to be. He looked about twenty-five when the dossier said he was almost forty. Agent 42 guessed there was something to be said for outdoor living, even in a place like Meteor Falls.

Agent 42 held out his badge and pressed it to the glass. On the way here he had prepared what he planned to say. He would take an official tack with Mr. Clark. He would mention "official state business." He would talk about "national security" and "the need for cooperation."

Mr. Clark scanned the badge, squinting to read the fine print. Mr. Clark had the looks of a man who wouldn't be bluffed by talk of the government. Agent 42 decided to extemporize a bit. This was Clark's home turf. Government business or not, the man had the right to boot him off the property. Clark looked the type to do it, too.

Clark opened the door a crack, his eyes alight with something like curiosity. "I can't say I'm surprised, you coming here in the middle of the night," he said, in his voice a measure of resignation. "I expected you boys about three weeks back though." He stood aside to let Agent 42 through. "Come on in and have a cup of coffee if you've a mind to."

"Thanks," Agent 42 said, surprised the farmer had put it together as quickly as he had. The White Coats had expected Clark and his wife to be suspicious. The White Coats had surmised rightly that Mrs. Clark had taken to the child so quickly because she couldn't have children of her own. That's why they'd insisted Agent 42 make the approach after the wife had already gone to bed. Mr. Clark seemed more pliable. "I will."

They sat down at the kitchen table, Clark careful with the Underwood typewriter and the stack of pages he'd already filled. He handled the pages carefully. He didn't want to get them out of order.

"I'm sorry to barge in like this," Agent 42 said.

The curiosity in Clark's eyes turned to something else; something less whimsical. "Oh, I doubt that's true. I imagine your bosses worked it out so you came to visit me about an hour after it's considered polite to do so, if only to get me separated from the wife." His eyes never left Agent 42's. "You'll have a fight on your hands, if you aim to take the boy away from her. My wife Edna is tougher by far than I'll ever be."

Agent 42 held up his hands. "I didn't come here to take the boy," he said. "I only came to draw some blood from him. My...superiors...they fully intend to allow you and your wife to raise the boy in the manner you see fit."

Clark considered this. "You're not going to dissect him or nothing like that?"

Agent 42 almost burst out laughing. Is that what people thought? But the farmer did read the pulps. He had that overactive imagination. Agent 42 considered the possibility that it was this imagination which had led him out to the south forty that night almost three weeks before after seeing that meteor—or what he'd taken to be a meteor—streaking across the sky.

"No sir," Agent 42 said. "I'm not going to dissect him."

THE FOGG

TODAY

Agent 42 explained how it would all go down. Somehow they'd managed to place a tracking device on him. The Fogg didn't even want to know how they'd done it. The Primary Source Society had always been resourceful. Basically it meant they owned his ass and they didn't mind letting him know it.

Things were happening in Powhatan City. The Citizen had gone missing. Draconian, army or not, was overwhelmed with work. The Primary Source Society was concerned. They wanted a man on the inside. The Fogg, a non-corporeal entity—little more than a collective consciousness in the shape of a man—was the perfect candidate.

So here he was, skulking around the Grantham estate, getting the lay of the land. He had been here forty-eight hours. On the surface Grenville Grantham led a life of leisurely excess. But he was deeper than the public perception of him as a millionaire playboy.

Grenville Grantham was Draconian's alter ego. No real surprise there—he had long been on the public's list of potential suspects, but never in the Number One position, a testament with which he surrounded himself. Grenville Grantham was careful not to spend too much time in the spotlight. In fact his mansion on the North Shore appeared abandoned, a fiction created by the public face of the Grantham Corporation, Elwood Noire.

Grenville Grantham had the resources to make Draconian work. Years before, during the height of Draconian's fame in the mid-eighties, he had been a one-man operation, but it wasn't like that anymore. Grenville Grantham was in the Draconian business these days, but he didn't spend much time wearing the cape and cowl. He had created an army of clones, all assigned different zones of the city. Draconian was everywhere and crime in the metropolis was down significantly, especially since the Citizen's disappearance a little over two months before.

An old Limey by the name of Gearhead, a Firm pensioner, was responsible for the clones. Blackpool, Grantham's butler, used to be a Firm operative during the Cold War, their number two man behind Supercool. The only other support personnel were the aforementioned Elwood, who operated as a sort of roadie and all-around fetch-it guy. Elwood made sure Draconian's trains ran on time.

The Fogg settled in. The Fogg made himself at home. He became part of the scenery. No one noticed, even Grenville Grantham, said to have an almost supernatural awareness of his surroundings.

At night Draconian's army went out onto the streets of Powhatan City. Grenville Grantham walked with a cane now. He offered up advice on everything from close quarter combat to remedies for sore knees. Grenville Grantham was the Draconian emeritus and the clones afforded him every respect. He had seen and done the things.

The Fogg loved being here, surrounded by all these fine things. He loved knowing the secrets of the multi-verse. Over the years he had collected these secrets. Over the years he had kept these secrets safe for the sake of the Primary Source Society. No more of that. The Primary Source Society had crossed the line. They had kept him prisoner for over three years in their basement "museum," kept on display like some kind of freak. No due process. No trial by jury. They had deemed him dangerous. Now, only because he was necessary, they had let him out of his cage.

They thought they could use him. They thought they could keep their secrets safe. No more of this. Somebody would pay for this information. He had a good idea who.

Somebody would always be in charge.

Somebody would always pay the freight.

THE OMNISCIENTIST

He reached out with his mind, looking for entertainment, looking for something to keep the werewolves of nothingness at bay. After a while you got tired of walking around inside your own skin. That's all it was really; wanting to taste somebody else's life for a while because you were bored with your own.

The boredom had gotten him in trouble on more than one occasion. That boredom had led him here, to Powhatan City, a place he hadn't visited for quite some time. He'd gotten himself in a spot of bother a while back. He'd found an entryway into the Citizen's consciousness. All he'd wanted to do was know what it felt like to fly through the sky, to feel that freedom, the wind brushing your hair back, that sense of weightlessness, an almost-death that thrilled and terrified him at the same time.

His mistake had been letting Philthy Phil Mac Nasty piggy-back on the experience. That was the racket Phil had been running then; piggy-back rides for regular Joes who didn't have *his* particular gift for sympathetic experience.

Unbeknownst to the Omniscientist, Philthy Phil had been recording the whole thing through a remote Narrator. Every time he had piggy-backed the Citizen, a virtual Philthy Phil had been right there, breathing down his neck. Sold on the black market the tapes made Philthy Phil a small fortune. Who *didn't* want to know what it felt like to be the Citizen, at least back then before his disgrace?

It wasn't long before the Citizen caught wind of what was happening. A guy like that, not from around here, he had sensitivities normal humans didn't. The Omniscientist should have known better, but he'd let his curiosity, or anyway his instinct for trouble, get the better of him. The Citizen, utilizing Draconian's investigative skills, tracked the tape's provenance back to the Omniscientist, serial experience thief.

It hadn't gone well for him.

The Omniscientist had never forgotten the look on the Citizen's face when he'd come to collect his dues. "I can't arrest you for what you've done," the Citizen had said in that lofty way he had, better than anyone else in the room. "But I can sure as hell run your ass out of town on a rail."

The Omniscientist had left town that night on a bus; he'd never looked back. He had taken what Philthy Phil had taught him. He had gone into business for himself. He sold second-hand experience tapes. As expected the sex tapes got big play. It wasn't too long before he was in business with Grace Face herself, the queen of the snuff films.

The Citizen wasn't around anymore. Word on the street was he'd gone to look for his home planet. Word on the street was the home planet had been destroyed by a rogue black hole sent through the galaxy by the Heckler.

The Omniscientist took a deep breath. He didn't want to admit it, but he'd missed this place. Maybe…maybe things would be different this time.

Man, he sure hoped so.

FROM THE FILES OF THE PRIMARY SOURCE SOCIETY INTERVIEW CONDUCTED BY: SPECIAL AGENT 42 SUBJECT: BLABBERMOUTH

Q: **Do you know why we've called you in today?**

A: You want to get the scoop, the skinny, the dope. You know I'm the guy to talk to. You know I can't tell a lie, like that one dude, what was his name…?

Q: **George Washington?**

A: I think we called him something else, but okay. Let's go with that. So…it's your dime. What do you want to know?

Q: **What can you tell me about the IM-MACHINATION SQUAD?**

A: You mean what can I tell you besides the fact they've got a stupid name? 'Cause that's a stupid name.

Q: **Be that as it may…**

A: The IM-MACHINATION SQUAD is this group of Narrators. They try to impose a sense of order on the world you call fiction. Supposedly they're the ones pulling the strings in the multi-verse. They decided who lives and who dies. On the one hand you've got the Third Person; he's the best of the Narrators, or at least he *was* before he fell out of favor a few years back. Everybody wanted to work with him: Draconian, Big Sir, everybody. He had an eye, if you know what I mean. He knew how to tell a story. He paid attention to the little details. Guys liked that.

Q: **And on the other hand…**

A: And on the other hand you've got the Omniscientist—another stupid name if you ask me. He's another of the Narrators. His deal is he can reach inside and read a person's thoughts. No, it's more than that. He can actually *live* the person's life for them. He can get inside your head and change things around. Like the Third Person, characters liked the fact the Omniscientist could make their decisions for them. He had that editor's eye for story. He knew what parts to leave out and what parts to include.

Q: **What else can you tell me about the Omniscientist?**

A: As you can imagine he was used by some of the criminal masterminds of the past few decades—the Heckler, Morrissey, even the Jester. They wanted him to remote-access their arch-enemies. The Omniscientist didn't have the scruples the Third Person had. The Omniscientist got inside the Citizen's head, he got inside Draconian's head. He laid these guys bare. Some say the Citizen still hasn't fully recovered.

Q: **But you said the Third Person "fell out of favor." How so? Did he collude with the Omniscientist?**

A: It was more like...have you heard the phrase "third personing?" Do you know what it means to do that to somebody?

Q: **No.**

A: It means you're getting the third person treatment. It means you stop seeing the world like you're used to seeing it. It basically means somebody is out to get you. You have been shanghaied. The whole procedure turns your world upside down. You go from living in the present tense to living in the past tense. You have to. That's the deal. After it's all said and done, you have to go back to the world again. You have to go back to first person narratives. People have trouble with the transition. *This* is what it means to "third person" somebody. The Third Person is the derivation of that phrase. *That's* why he fell out of favor. He neglected to talk about the fallout, about what happens after he moves on to his next character.

Q: **I believe one of our agents has been "third personed," as you say.**

A: Yeah, I heard that too. Has your boy come out of it yet?

Q: **We're still monitoring the situation.**

A: That's good. That's how you answer an uncomfortable question—with generalities. I'll have to remember that one.

Q: **How does the Omniscientist fit into all this?**

A: If you want my take, the Third Person trusted the Omniscientist when he shouldn't have. They'd gone to school together or some such nonsense. The Omniscientist ran some sort of game on him; the Third Person fell for it. Something about a dame...I don't know the details. I've heard a few other things, but that's the story I believe. The Third Person was always a sucker for a dame. Now they're sworn enemies or whatever passes for sworn enemies nowadays. They're both looking for work. They're both fighting the same characters for the same gigs; it's inevitable their paths are going to cross.

So these guys are the most prominent members of the IM-MACHINATION SQUAD, which has since disbanded, or so I've been told. What I heard is they grew too powerful. Characters were starting to rely on them too much. The Third Person was supposed to have this magic touch with narrative. Guys started getting lazy, started to think they didn't have to do anything original so long as they had the Third Person in their corner. They were wrong. And then when the third person curse caught up to them, that's when the backlash kicked in.

Other members of the Squad I've heard about are Type-O and Mr. Metaphor, but they've sort of fallen off the radar. They were the smart ones. Everyone these days are going to first-person narratives. They want to control the content. They want to have final cut. If they tell the story through their own eyes then they get to control who knows what when. Then there's the Fogg.

Q: **Tell me what you know about the Fogg.**

A: He's the fly on the wall. He's...he's the one who sees everything. The Omniscientist can reach inside your mind, but the Fogg sees it all. He keeps the secrets, all the stuff left on the cutting room floor.

Q: **He knows all the dirt?**

A: And then some.

Q: **Thank you. You've been very helpful.**

A: Like I have a choice, right? In my opinion, you guys shouldn't be so worried about what remains of the Squad. You have bigger fish to fry.

Q: **How's that?**

A: I heard a rumor on the street the other day. I'll note it is an unsubstantiated rumor, but still. You might want to check it out.

Q: **Okay, so?**

A: I heard Philthy Phil Mac Nasty has the Jinx stashed somewhere outside Powhatan City.

Q: **We were under the impression the Jinx was dead?**

A: I was too. But you're only dead when the multi-verse needs you dead, you know what I mean?

Q: **Yes. Yes, I do.**

THE THIRD PERSON

Over the years he had worked for some of the big names. Sure, he'd signed confidentiality agreements and what-not, but the statute of limitations had run out on all that. Besides, none of those guys were paying his bills anymore.

He had an eye was the thing. He had an eye for story. He had an eye for plot and character development. He didn't do like some of the other narrators and impose his will on the narrative. No, he let it flow naturally, going where it was supposed to go. Sure, you could cheat. You could try and take shortcuts to get a real page turner going, but he'd never done that. He'd gone deeper, into the psychological depths of the characters he'd worked for. Maybe this was why he had had such a successful run back in the late seventies and early eighties. They'd trusted him, sure enough, but it had also been a narcissistic thing, make no mistake. They'd worked with the Third Person because he knew what made his character tick. The Third Person noticed what other people didn't. He paid attention. He didn't just look at the *action;* he looked at the *motivation.* He and the character in question talked it over. They collaborated. What didn't fit was left on the cutting room floor.

The biggest name he'd worked with back then had to be Draconian.

But Draconian wouldn't have been possible without the work he'd done with Big Sir. People really took notice after Big Sir.

He had interviewed with the Citizen, who said he'd liked the work he'd done with the Tarantula, but there wasn't much to the Citizen. He was too perfect, and only the Third Person knew this perfection was a concoction. The Citizen sensed his reluctance. They'd agreed in the press their collaboration hadn't worked on account of "artistic differences."

Big Sir made his name. Big Sir distanced him from the other narrators. Until Big Sir he hadn't found his voice.

Big Sir should have been a Gothic knuckle-breaker. Big Sir should have been a bone-headed ass-kicker, making his way through the world with two fists and a lantern jaw. The Third Person gave him a human side. The Third Person made him more than just a tough-guy cliché. The Third Person made him more than the sum of his parts. When it was over, he turned Big Sir over to another Narrator, the Omniscientist. Big Sir wanted to go into a different direction. There were no hard feelings. Besides, Big Sir had begun to bristle a bit under the Third Person's influence. The big man didn't like all the credit for his success given to a third-person narrator. He'd decided—perhaps rightly so—to go with a first-person point of view. The Omniscientist gave Big Sir that freedom.

But then, about a month after the Third Person went on to work with Draconian, Big Sir had gone missing, a success the cognoscenti attributed to the Third Person's ministrations. This was maybe where the Third Person's relationship with the Omniscientist had started to go south.

Blame it all on Big Sir. All the good, all the bad. There for a while, before the backlash hit, he could do no wrong, and it all came from the work he'd done with Big Sir. Without Big Sir there was no way he'd have worked with Draconian. Big Sir might have made his name, but Draconian made his reputation.

After that run with Draconian, all the heavy hitters wanted to work with him. He'd had interviews with several, all offering good packages, trying to sweeten the pot with this or that fringe benefit. Maybe that was his mistake, thinking every subsequent situation would be like it had been with Draconian. It wasn't.

After Draconian he thought he could afford to be choosy about the kinds of jobs he took. Most of them were vigilantes who wanted what came to be known as "the Draconian Treatment." He knew what this meant, of course. This meant they wanted that brooding, self-reflective thing. They wanted gravitas. They wanted nobility. They wanted, in a word, to be Draconian. The Third Person didn't have it in him to try to replicate that success. There was only one Draconian—sort of.

But it was never the same after Draconian. He couldn't quite get that mojo back. They'd gotten along so well together. After a while it had been difficult to determine where Draconian ended and he began. You had to have that synergy otherwise it felt forced.

Yeah, the biggest name he'd worked with back then had to be Draconian. Sure, there had been a string of hits in the post-Draconian period. After three hits in a row, everyone wanted to work with him. He found he could almost write a blank check. Other narrators were jealous. He'd been lucky, they thought, that was all. The Third Person knew it wasn't luck; he paid attention when others didn't. He noticed the little details other narrators couldn't or wouldn't take the time to bother with. He and Draconian got along so well because they both put forth the extra effort. They both went that little bit further.

That was the life, living with Draconian. For one thing the guy had more money than he knew what to do with, more money than he could spend in three lifetimes. Everything was first class all the way: from the travel accommodations, to the meals, to the room Draconian gave him in the mansion outside the city.

So besides paying attention what was the key to success for a narrator? The Third Person echoed Draconian's life, walking in lock-step with him, never letting him go *anywhere* alone. (Save for the restroom, of course). That's the way you had to do it if you wanted to be successful in the narration business. You had to live the principal's life with him. Anything less was shoddy business. The Third Person knew guys who'd leave their principal alone for days at a time, phoning it in two or three days later, after the fact. It wasn't even first-hand information, for Pete's sake! He couldn't abide that.

All good things eventually come to an end. Such was the way with Draconian. That deal with the Omniscientist—a first-rate tool if the truth be told—and the Citizen really put fear into all the narrators. The Omniscientist had sold out the Citizen, pure and simple. The backlash began soon thereafter. The Omniscientist had sold out the Citizen, and in doing so he had sold out all the narrators. Most characters went to first-person narration after that. Draconian and guys like that didn't want the same thing to happen to him. Now, looking at it in retrospect, the Third Person couldn't blame him.

THE JINX

Philthy Phil said he knew where the guy was. He'd taken the precaution of hiding the Jinx out of town, somewhere no one would go looking for him, stashed at a no-tell motel on the other side of the river. So long as the Jinx was alone then he wasn't a danger to himself or anyone else.

Philthy Phil had done this kind of thing before, back when he was the Heckler's lead Henchman. He'd paid six months in advance and left the Jinx with enough money to maintain his lifestyle without getting too crazy. He'd left his quasi-sister-in-law, Chesty LaRue, in charge of the guy. She cooked him steak dinners and read to him out of the *Dirty Letters* section of *Playpen* magazine.

Cornelius, better known as the Gauntlet on account of his overripe forearms and swollen hands, drove the White Buffalo's Speed Demon; both of them hunkered down, expecting the worst.

Even so, Philthy Phil was shocked at what he found.

The no-tell motel was in shambles, a tumble-down shell advertising hourly rates and neon delights. Tall grass grew over concrete, aching through a rusted-out play set. Room doors stood open. Flies buzzed lazily, a stench of rot and death in the air. The place had aged twenty years in the month since Philthy Phil had deposited the Jinx here.

The Jinx had been hard at work it looked like.

Philthy Phil motioned for his men to spread out. They looked spooked, hardcore guys with an off-day mindset suddenly gone horribly awry. Philthy Phil felt it too, but he didn't want to let on. This was his caper.

The men lingered. They'd read the vibe. This was a nowhere place and whatever remained would haunt them.

Phil barked orders, sparking them into action. He toyed with the dials on the location device. The Jinx was still here, it said. He wasn't smart enough to play possum. He didn't have it in him anymore.

"Hey, boss!" a voice called. "Over here!"

With a weary sigh Phil kicked through the tall grass, headed toward the motel, a one-story deal built in a horseshoe shape. The stench got worse the closer he got. He understood why Van Owen wanted the Jinx on the team. Van Owen wanted the Jinx for the same reason the Heckler had kept the Jinx around all those years before; he took your special talent—whatever it was—and upended it on you.

Cornelius sidled up, wincing from the arthritis that had come in the wake of his transformation. His shoulders drooped from the weight of his hands and forearms. "You know something?" he said. "I never did like the Jinx, even after the Savings and Loan job."

"Me either," Philthy Phil admitted.

"If he could turn this place into a ghost town in one month's time, then..." Cornelius frowned, not wanting to say the words aloud. The Jinx was cursed, and the way he looked at it he wasn't going down alone. He'd take as many people with him as he could.

"Yeah," Philthy Phil said. "I know."

They found the Jinx in one of the rooms, clinging to the corpse of a female, at least a week old, her face a garish, mummified mask. From here she looked like an oversized doll. Perhaps that's how the Jinx thought of her in that jacked-up brain of his.

Phil gagged but held back. It had been tasked to him by Van Owen to bring the Jinx back to Powhatan City. You didn't cross Van Owen in the same way you didn't cross the Heckler.

This? This was worse than Phil had imagined. He knew driving over here it was going to be bad; he never thought it would be like this. The Jinx had laid waste to everything he'd seen in the past month. He knew the Jinx couldn't help himself, but this was *his* fault; he should have known better. People had a tendency to forget themselves around him. People had a tendency to die in his presence. He would tell you it wasn't his fault. He would tell you it was the cost of doing business.

"Alright, man," Phil said to the shadow curled up on the bed. "Put the body away and let's go home, what do you say?" Then, to Cornelius: "Call in the forget-me-not crew." These were the clean-up guys. They'd have to ret-con everyone in the area over this. "And try to find the Omniscientist. I heard he was in town."

Cornelius cocked an eyebrow. "The Omniscientist? What do you want with him?" It must have been a long night. Cornelius never usually questioned orders.

Phil looked away from the Jinx tableau. The Jinx French kissed the corpse—penance for violating her in this way. Whatever else he was, the Jinx was still a Jesuit school boy at heart.

Phil breathed in foul air. He held back a wave of nausea. So much worse than he'd thought coming over here. He motioned to a couple of the hardboys. A couple goons waded in and tried to pry him loose from the corpse. They were expendable. When they came up missing in a week or so no one will miss them. "I have a feeling he's looking for work."

GEARHEAD

Blackpool introduced him around. He was pleased to see the main man, Grenville Grantham, had given his clones actual names and not numbers, which had been the case on his last visit to the Grantham mansion. A name personalized them. A name gave them something of an identity.

Gearhead shook hands all around. The clones all met their maker's eye. They all said the same thing in unconscious imitation. "Pleased to meet you." They didn't remember him from the last time, a failing common to this particular model. They remembered only what they had been trained by Blackpool and Grantham to remember.

It had been Blackpool's idea to put a twist on the Firm's Supercool protocol. If Draconian was going to be truly effective like Supercool, he would need to possess a bulletproof reputation, and in order to do that then he'd need to appear to be everywhere at once. Blackpool realized that with his old friend Gearhead's help he could make that happen. Draconian's reputation among Powhatan City's underworld was fierce. In the fifteen years since Gearhead had last been here, they had only lost one of the clones, and that during a freak accident in the tunnels under the city.

Here they were; the fruits of Gearhead's labor made flesh. He had not considered the moral implications of his task, not then. It had seemed to him only a problem to solve, that was all. Now, faced with the practical reality of Draconian's battalion of clones, Gearhead felt sick to his stomach. *He* had done this; no one else. *He* had made this happen through the sheer force of his will and personality.

He shouldn't have created Draconian's battalion of clones. He knew that now. He shouldn't have given in to the whims of a petulant billionaire with a savior complex and a too-wise old friend with charisma to spare.

Grenville Grantham, the original Draconian, tapped his heavy wooden cane on the floor. The Draconians fell to. They knew who was in charge.

It was brutal to watch what happened next. They gouged. They bit. They tore flesh. They kicked knees and balls. Evenly matched, their combat was a moot point. They stopped just short of killing each other—killing was against Draconian's code. Couldn't have that now. They were each assigned zones of influence in Powhatan City. They were each scheduled according to a specific skill set. They would be needed on the streets tonight.

"Alright," Blackpool barked. "That's enough!"

The Draconians stood around in various stages of undress. They spat teeth and blood. Gearhead realized this display had been for his benefit. Blackpool and Grantham wanted him to see the success of their collaboration.

"What do you think?" Grenville Grantham asked. He looked older than the last time Gearhead had been here. He walked with a limp. Scars criss-crossed his face and hands. The life of a masked vigilante had been hard on him.

"They're fierce," Gearhead replied.

"They're warrior-poets all," Grantham announced to the room. He had the voice of a radio actor. He patted his stomach. "I was sixty years old this past birthday. The knees are shot; the back too." He looked wistful. "Can't do the things I used to do."

Gearhead collapsed to the floor. The world spun out of focus. The faces of Draconian's clones gathered above him, peering at him curiously. He realized too late they were the only children he'd ever know.

"Which one of you knows CPR?" Blackpool asked.

THE THIRD PERSON

The Citizen wanted to reinvent himself and he wanted the Third Person's help doing it. This required long conversations deep into the night, the Third Person nodding the Citizen along, taking mental notes for changes they could make later when the talking had been done.

As the Citizen talked, the Third Person's eyes wandered to the pictures displayed on the refrigerator. The Citizen's adopted parents were genuinely proud of their son, no matter his origins and no matter what had happened in Denton City back in 1988. His schoolwork remained taped to the fridge door. A picture of the young Citizen stared back, that take-on-the-world grin of his unmistakable. The Citizen was comfortable here. From time to time he would look up and gaze at the picture of his younger self. He smiled at some recollection. The Third Person knew he would hear about it eventually.

Judging by the background notes the Third Person had gathered together, the Citizen was almost forty-five years old, but he looked no older than twenty-five, his skin smooth and pale as marble. He was fit, his muscles bulging beneath the ridiculous farm boy attire he wore. He'd already explained about the glasses, which shouldn't have fooled anyone. The only reason they did, the Citizen explained, was because the glasses left a sort of psychic residue which messed with the minds of normal people. The Third Person could see the Citizen for who—and what—he really was only because he was allowed to.

"You want to know what I really look like?" the Citizen asked during one of these sessions.

The Third Person thought about it. He knew the Citizen was an alien, and as soon as he'd learned about the "psychic residue" of the man's glasses, he knew there would be more to the story. But if he was going to do his job effectively the Citizen would need to drop his masks. Big Sir and Draconian had dropped their masks; that was why they had been so successful.

"Sure," the Third Person said.

The Citizen removed his glasses and smoothed his hair. "It'll take just a second for the psychic residue to wear off," he said. "My parents couldn't be certain what galaxy I'd land in, so they placed a chameleon wheel in my genetic structure allowing me to blend in with most of the known planets." As he spoke the air around him seemed to deepen, the molecules becoming denser.

For the first time the Third Person saw the Citizen how he really was.

No doubt about it, the Citizen's home features were reptilian, his grey skin slick and mottled. A lizard-like tongue snaked out at the corners of his mouth. Only his perfectly coiffed hair remained the same, sitting atop his head like a ridiculous hairpiece.

The Third Person sat there smiling, wanting the moment to end. This wasn't the Citizen the public knew and loved. This was an alien, and if he had been found like that by the Clarks of Parkland County, Kansas then he would have never seen adulthood.

"Your parents knew what they were doing," the Third Person said trying to keep it neutral.

The lizard-thing smiled, the corners of its mouth creasing slightly. "You want me to go back to the way I was, don't you?" The smile broadened. "It's okay if you do."

"Could you please?"

The Citizen replaced the glasses, adjusting them at a jaunty angle. The process reversed itself. Again the air between them became denser. Slowly the Citizen returned to normal. The Third Person, relieved, tried to erase the image of the lizard-thing. He would have to edit this part out, he realized. The general public would never go for this.

The Citizen moved delicately, each gesture carefully measured. The Third Person imagined the Citizen had broken many things in his lifetime just because he'd forgotten how strong he was. Pens and phones and door handles had been built with mortal men in mind, not aliens from a planet long destroyed.

Yes, the Citizen had broken many things over the years. Cautiously, the Third Person touched on the subject of the Citizen's self-imposed banishment from his adopted city. The Third Person had heard all the rumors, of course. Pictures of the Citizen emerging from Chesty LaRue's cathouse on the Lower East Side had been published by a Denton City tabloid. Around about 1988 he had come to Powhatan City with the sole purpose of lying low and trying to rehabilitate his image. Draconian and his war with the Heckler had made it impossible for him. The stain of that time remained with him, though he had made his home in Powhatan City since '88.

No doubt about it, Powhatan City had changed things. Powhatan City had offered him a second act, a second chance. The Citizen hadn't been back to Denton City since '88. Powhatan City was his home now.

The Third Person probed gently. Exposition wasn't his thing. His old friend Blabbermouth was the exposition expert. Blabbermouth would have been able to get the back story without any blood spilled. The Third Person wasn't that good. He knew there was something the Citizen was dancing around, some subject about which he was as cautious as his movements.

The Citizen had come back to Kansas, he said, because his adopted father had died. He hadn't spoken to the man since the disgrace in '88. Tomorrow would be the dispensation of Mr. Clark's property. Nothing held him here anymore.

Nothing except...

They sat in the kitchen of the farmhouse in which the Citizen had grown up. As the Citizen spoke, the Third Person's eyes wandered to the refrigerator, where pictures and finger paintings were posted proudly. He stared. He remembered his own school pictures, black and white and smudgy. He and the Citizen were contemporaries. If the picture of that boy taped to the fridge was the Citizen then his would have been black and white too. But it wasn't.

The Third Person stared at the gap-toothed, ginger-headed young man who grinned from many of the photographs interspersed among the paintings. The boy looked no more than eight years old. His forelock jutted jauntily on the left-hand side of his head, just as the Citizen's did. The Third Person wished he could stand and walk over to the fridge to get a better look. Before the night was over he'd do just that.

The Citizen told his tales. The Third Person began to wonder. It wasn't much of a leap to full-on speculation. The gap-toothed boy was the Citizen's son.

THE JINX

Philthy Phil and Cornelius cleaned up the Jinx as best they could. They had blindfolded him in the hopes his perception wouldn't focus on them. The Jinx had a memory for faces. He and Philthy Phil went back to the days, but Phil knew none of this mattered. The Jinx was the Jinx. He couldn't help who he was.

Cornelius pulled up and Phil deposited the Jinx with a couple stray goons. The goons had no idea who the Jinx was. One of them wanted to know what was underneath the blindfold. Cornelius answered before Phil could. "Just do your job, boy-o."

Philthy Phil tapped out a rhythm. He still wasn't sure he ought to have brought the Jinx in on this thing. The Jinx was a monster, no doubt about it. The monster could turn on them all at any moment. The Heckler had used the Jinx's services, and the Smiler before him. But the Jinx had been sane back then. Phil knew there was no way in hell the Jinx was sane these days. He had been out in the desert for far too long.

Phil had a few plates spinning in the air. Besides getting the Henchmen back together he had the Citizen thing to worry about. The Citizen had gone missing. Draconian's army was out in force. Word on the street was the Citizen would return to action soon. He had had some family trouble. Nobody knew what it was.

Cornelius stood looking after the Jinx, his head bowed, his clothes in tatters. The two goons that book-ended him, were muscle-bound types with tattoos and shaven skulls. "Look what it's come to," Cornelius observed.

Phil, lost in thought, nodded in agreement. Way back when you could count on a decent class of criminal or at least the kind who believed a life of crime was the only way out of Powhatan City. The Citizen was an alien. Draconian had to be a multi-millionaire in order to afford all those gadgets of his. Bottom line, they weren't normal folks like the rest. They didn't know what it was like to come up the hard way. It created a class consciousness you could have counted on in the old days; not anymore. All these young goons thought the rules didn't apply to them. They were in it for the money and not the philosophy. Most of these morons couldn't even *spell* philosophy.

"I'm gonna go make some calls," Phil said. "You wanna...?"

"I'll lock it down for you," Cornelius said hunching his shoulders and heading toward the office.

Phil watched him go, those arms of his swinging from side to side in a way that had to be painful. Cornelius had worked at the City College back in high school. He was a janitor then, looking to outrun the life of crime his father had barely survived. There had been some sort of "hyper-serum" invented by this Dr. Sterling at the college. They'd asked for volunteers. A ten thousand dollar bonus had been promised. Cornelius' mother was going through a rough time. The ten grand looked good. Cornelius signed up. Two weeks later he'd come back to the Lower East Side on a stretcher, his arms strapped to his sides. Dr. Sterling and those White Coats at the college had created Cornelius. They had deposited him on the streets of Powhatan City like he was a stray that liked to bite. He could throw a punch, ole Cornelius.

Phil headed upstairs and made a few calls.

Chuck Nunn and some of the other old-timers had turned down Philthy Phil's offer. They were retired now or else on probation. They didn't want to risk another jolt inside. They wanted to live out the rest of their days in peace. Phil didn't blame them. They weren't cut from the same cloth as he was. He had well over ten million dollars socked away—what was left from the Powhatan City Savings and Loan heist—but it had never been about the money for him. It had always been about the action. He didn't want to die alone in some rocking chair. He wanted to go out in a hail of bullets.

He put in a call to the Third Person. He had worked with Draconian way back when, but he was on the pay-no-mind list now. He could stand to make a few bucks. Draconian's identity was a matter of much speculation on the street. Most guys had it narrowed down to three or four high flyers, big spenders from uptown. Phil had all of them under surveillance. Until now he'd never considered going right to the source.

It didn't take long for the Third Person to hip to the reason why Phil had called. A guy like that was always going to have his guard up. He'd been burned too many times in the past. The Third Person tried to put him off, but Phil knew how to turn on the charm.

He hung up the phone and sat there thinking. He could feel the rotten-at-the-center vibe the Jinx gave off. The warehouse felt *off*, and he could swear he smelled gas fumes. They had to get a handle on this Jinx thing. They had to...

Wait a minute. Wait just a minute here. The Omniscientist. He could call the Omniscientist and have him take a reading from the Jinx. If they knew what was coming then they could prepare for it.

THE OMNISCIENTIST

He didn't like this. He didn't like this one bit. But this was what happened when you ran out of options, you had to take the jobs you were offered.

He should have never come back to Powhatan City. The place was burned down for him. What, did he think just because the Citizen had disappeared that his luck would change? He was a fool if he thought that.

Not for the first time, the Omniscientist thought he'd made a mistake trusting Grace Face. But then again she was a clone; he should have known better than to trust a clone, especially one created by an Englishman. He had allowed her to run roughshod over him. He had allowed her to talk him into that Citizen deal. If it hadn't been for that then they never would have kicked him out of the IM-MACHINATION SQUAD. And if he had never been kicked out of the IM-MACHINATION SQUAD then...

He didn't want to finish out that thought.

"Alright," the Omniscientist said. "What do you want me to do?"

Philthy Phil walked him through it. Philthy Phil wanted him to be cautious. Philthy Phil wanted him to get out of this alive. This was the Jinx they were talking about after all. The Jinx scorched earth. The Jinx left a trail of bodies in his wake.

"For the record," the Omniscientist said. "I don't like this."

"You don't have to," Philthy Phil replied. "You're getting paid."

"You know what the bumper sticker reads on the Jinx?" The Omniscientist didn't wait for Philthy Phil to reply. "The bumper sticker reads *No one here gets out alive.*"

"That's sweet," Philthy Phil said. "It's got a nice ring to it."

Philthy Phil said it was Van Owen's idea to bring the Jinx into the mix. Van Owen was the new guy on the scene, the one who had taken over for the Heckler. Philthy Phil hadn't taken a poll or anything—he wasn't that kind of guy—but most of the Henchmen preferred the Heckler's stewardship. For one thing Van Owen was nothing more than a head; some intermediary carried it around in a Mason jar. For another, Van Owen was South African; he just didn't know how they did things in Powhatan City or if he did then he didn't give a shit.

A couple goons brought the Jinx out on a dolly, his head strapped to the back, his eyes covered with a blindfold. One of the goons coughed into his fist. The other one looked pale and sickly. It had begun. The Omniscientist recognized the Jinx's handiwork.

"I want you to take a reading," Philthy Phil said. "I want you to get inside his skull."

The Omniscientist nodded. He'd figured as much. He concentrated on the Jinx's face. Once he'd memorized it he closed his eyes. "Come on," he whispered. "Come on. Let's do this, what do you say, huh? Let's do this thing."

He opened his eyes. He realized he couldn't see too well, his eyes covered by something dark enough to keep the light from bleeding through. He sniffed the air—perfume. It smelled expensive, like something you'd give your mistress.

With a jolt of recognition the Omniscientist realized what was covering the Jinx's eyes wasn't a blindfold at all but a black stocking. Some connection begged; he ignored it. He had to concentrate. He had to remember who he was. He had to remember he was the Jinx. The usual rules didn't apply.

He settled down. He controlled his breathing. He could do this. He could be this guy. "Okay," he said with the Jinx's voice. "Okay, man. You're in. Now what are you gonna do?"

The Jinx's consciousness was a minefield. The Omniscientist tread carefully. He understood this land of metaphor and symbolism almost as well as Johnny Nocturne, the man of dreams. He knew where to step. He knew how to avoid the pratfalls and the pitfalls.

The Jinx's thoughts gushed blood and gore. The Jinx's thoughts reeked of death and destruction. The Jinx fed on secrets. The Jinx fed on the lies we tell ourselves.

"Okay," the Omniscientist said. "Okay, let's do this, huh? Let's do this thing."

Slasher tableaux: Faces with melted features emerged out of the gloom, reaching, recognizing him as an interloper. Skeletons cackled and cavorted. Two Roman centurions rolled dice. They looked up and the Omniscientist saw they were eyeless. They shrugged and went back to their game.

The Jinx knew things. The Jinx understood the underlying subtext of the universe was water. The river was muddy. The river was thick with viscous, vicious secrets. All he had to do was reach out and touch the water. All he had to do was...

The goons on either side of him had contracted malaria in their time with the Jinx. One of the goons had passed it along to his nephew. The other goon had given it to his step-mother. The goons were plague rats, deserting a sinking ship.

The Jinx knew things about Philthy Phil and Chuck Nunn. Philthy Phil had been the brains behind the Powhatan City Savings and Loan takedown. Chuck Nunn had been the one responsible for finding the insider, the bank teller who'd been killed in the crossfire. The bank teller's name had been Michelle. She was seeing the Citizen's geeky alter ego, named...

The Omniscientist reached for it. He couldn't quite get to it.

So this is what it's like, he thought. *So this is what it's like to be the Jinx.*

None of the Henchmen knew what the Jinx was thinking. Philthy Phil said he'd warned the new guy in charge, Van Owen, the one who'd taken over after the disappearance of the Heckler. The Jinx was unpredictable. You couldn't put the bullet back in that gun.

The Omniscientist reached out with his mind. He had it. He held on tight. He didn't let go. He grinned, white-knuckling the thing.

The Jinx knew the secrets of the multi-verse. He knew where the bodies were buried. Some of them he had put there himself. He collected the dirty laundry. He sorted it. He sent it out to be dry cleaned.

The Jinx didn't want to let go of the secrets he held. Razors reached for the Omniscientist in the dark. He bobbed and weaved. He was confident amongst metaphors and symbols. The Omniscientist had never gone this far before. He closed his eyes tight. He held on for dear life. The Jinx tried to buck him off; the Omniscientist wouldn't let him.

The Jinx had always known the secret history of the multi-verse. But this new information was up-to-the-minute. The Jinx knew what he knew because the Fogg had sold him the information. The Fogg had sold out the Primary Source Society lock, stock and barrel. The Primary Source Society had kept the Fogg locked in a cage.

The Fogg was a non-corporeal entity. He was *almost* invisible. He had been the Primary Source Society's fly on the wall since the nineties. He knew where *all* the bodies were buried. The Primary Source Society should have known better. They should have gotten rid of him when they had the chance.

Draconian was compromised. His real name was Grenville Grantham. He owned a mansion on the North Shore. That's where he kept his toys. There wasn't just one Draconian. He was old and infirm now. He employed an army of clones these days. They seemed to be everywhere. There was more. *Cherchez la femme:* a girl had died on Draconian's watch. The girl's name was Elizabeth. Her brother worked for Draconian. Elwood. The brother's name was Elwood. Grenville Grantham wanted to use Elwood to create a clone of Elizabeth.

The Fogg had laid Powhatan City bare. He had sold his secrets to the Jinx, who didn't know how to stop. The city would burn to the ground. The conflagration would consume Story-Land. All fiction would be swallowed by the flames.

The Jinx knew where the Citizen had grown up: a small town in Kansas. He'd been raised by the Clarks of Parkland County. He'd had an affair with a gal named Grace Face. The affair had produced a son. The Jinx knew where the boy went to school. Van Owen could send Henchmen out to get the young man. Van Owen could send Henchmen out to fetch Grace Face and Grenville Grantham.

The Omniscientist dug deeper. He went further. This was it. This was what he had missed in his years away from Powhatan City.

He broke through. He saw the truth. He swallowed it down. This was Powhatan City laid bare.

The End

Rex Garman
The Case of the Baroque Pearl
By J. Walt Layne

I was sitting in Shifty's doing my best to kill the bottom half of a bottle of low shelf bourbon when she walked in. It was pouring rain like cats and dogs, and she was in the middle of it. Soaked from head to foot, even after drizzle this dame was one Class A ankle, if you know what I mean.

Just inside the door, she shivered off the fall chill, and started to preen, shedding water, and a knit poncho, you know the kind the kittens wear this time of year. She leaned over toward the door to shake out her hair, and I got a look at the goods. She had the kind of hourglass figure that would make a fella' do time with a smile on his face.

She sauntered over to the bar and sat down, two stools away, but we were alone, save for Shifty, and his old lady who worked in the back. She gave me the eye and adjusted herself on the stool. Her white chiffon blouse was just damp enough to make taking inventory an easy affair.

"So you gonna say hello to me, or just stare me down like pot roast and potatoes," she asked me with a wry little smile.

I should have told her I hated to eat and run, but sometimes I got a way with broads. This one could have had her way with me.

"Hello, I'm Rex. Rex Garman," I said it casual not trying to be smooth.

She smiled, "do you have another one of those," she raised a brow and poked an eyeball at my smoke.

I nodded and reached for my tobacco pouch. I slipped a paper out and a decent pinch of Carolina Queen. I rolled the cigarette as tight as miser's doorknob and handed it over.

Her fingers were soft, and she let them drag across my hand on purpose, just to see how I would play my hand.

She pursed her lips when I kept my hand close, and raised the smoke to her pouty lips, "do you have a light Mister… Garman, was it?"

I drew my Zippo quick as a flash and struck an ark for her. She leaned over and lit the cigarette, drawing in just enough air to light the cigarette.

"Thank you" she purred in a scintillating voice. She had me and she knew it.

"You're welcome, Miss?" I left it hanging for a bit hoping she would fill in the blank, but no luck.

"If you want to know my name, you gotta ask me nice, detective," she said it sultry, like I was her Bogey, and she was my Bacall. Some Bogey I was, shot down twice by the same bird.

"You are a detective aren't you, or are there two Rex Garman's in this burg, and you happen to be the one who isn't," it was sass, plain and simple, if she had not been a siren, she would have been poison.

"Nope I'm your Dick," I gave it to her straight.

"Bring me one of those, and let's talk business," she said, gesturing to my glass.

I looked at her, then to my glass, and back to her, "What kind of business?"

"It's not a social call. I lost something and I need it found," She gave me a come hither smile as she slid off the stool and batted her eyes at me when she walked past on her way to a dark corner.

I motioned to Shifty to refill mine and pour hers, he nodded at me and his eyes shifted to her receding backside, then back to me, he puckered up to whistle but just let go a long exhale.

I took the drinks over and sat down across from her in the small round table in the back corner. She took the bourbon and she was not shy about it. She took a long sip of the snort, and then rested her head against the side of the hand that held the glass. I saw her shudder when the spirits hit back.

I lifted my glass and took a sip. When I lowered it, she was giving me the eye.

"Good to see you spared no expense on the booze," she hissed.

"You asked for one of these," I held up my glass.

A slow, sly, sexy smile cracked the bland expression on her lovely features. Her eyes sparkled.

"So you're a detective," she said it more as a statement than a question.

I nodded, "And you lost something and you want it found," two could play this game, but I wanted her to get on with it.

"Very perceptive detective," she purred.

"Lemme guess, your kid sister skipped town with some sleaze," I was humoring her, but if I had been right, she would have been impressed.

She gave me that wry smile again, "No, nothing as exciting as that I'm afraid, but something just as important. Important to me anyway," she took a drag on her cigarette and blew the smoke at me.

"Okay," I prompted, and took out a pen and my old leather notebook, what's the item, it's approximate value, and the last place you saw it."

She drug on that smoke again, and sipped her drink. "It's not as simple as looking under my bed for a sock, Mr. Garman."

"Well, no I didn't figure, but I have to ask a lot of simple questions to get to where I need to go from here," It is just how it is done. If she does not want to help me, then I cannot help her, Siren or not.

"Did you ever play marbles, Mr. Garman?"

"Sure, I guess. I mean, what kid didn't back in those days?" I did not know what she was getting at, but sometimes you gotta just let 'em talk it out.

"Did you have a favorite in your bag, or were yours all clear glass?" She inquired as she finished the cigarette and ground out the last of it in the ashtray in the center of our table.

"We were poor, and I just had the ten cent bag from Woolworth's. They were a gift from my grandmamma." I said, indifferent to inquiry about my early days.

"We were poor too, Mr. Garman. My father had a small jewelry store, left to him by his grandfather and father who were partners. Everyone thought we were wealthy, and the kids in school all treated me as if I was some poor little rich girl. However, we were not rich or anywhere near it. My mother did laundry to keep us fed, because nobody had money to buy jewelry with half the country out of work. You are wondering where I am getting on with all this. Well the item I have lost is a very rare baroque pearl. It is black in color with white-green and gold marbling, and bigger around than a shooter. It is not perfectly round, and does not roll well. My Daddy gave it to me for my birthday in 1935. It had come in a bag with a bunch of other Spanish pearls. They called them bread and butter pearls because small town jewelers made their living on affordable jewelry for moderate income men to give as gifts to wives and girlfriends, not on fancy diamonds and jewel encrusted trinkets." She paused to raise her glass, she settled herself and we drank and smoked for several minutes. I was beginning to wonder if there was any more to the story when she got to it.

"By 1935 he wasn't getting a lot of good stuff anymore, and this black pearl, though it was rare, wasn't the kind of thing he could make any money on. With the depression on, there were no collectors willing to part company with the money to buy an odd piece, and at face value, it wasn't odd enough to be of much interest; just a black marble to most eyes, trained or not. After the depression and the war were over, there were inquiries made about the pearl, but my father never said a word. For fifteen years that baroque Spanish Pearl laid in a bag off marbles that my brother had given me."

I was taking notes, and when I finished I looked up attentively. She was looking me over, not that I am not used to it, but this dame had teeth. I must me getting' soft, cause I was starting to feel ashamed of the way I was lookin' at her a little while ago.

"You gonna tell me your name, or just look at me like a pot roast and potatoes," I threw back at her, trying to catch her off her game and get a better read on her.

"Maybe I like pot roast detective, and my name is Chase, Veronica Chase. There, now you know. I have a little more to tell you, and then I need to be on my way."

"That's fine, Veronica. All this back-story is fine, but what happened to the pearl after all those years in the bag? The best way for me to find it, is for you to tell me about the people who knew that you had it. Specifically anyone who had any idea what it might be worth. What is it worth anyhow?"

She contemplated the stub of a cigarette that was burning down on the edge of the ashtray.

I reached for my tobacco pouch, "Do you want another smoke?"

She shook her head and batted her eyes, "No, I'd better not, and you better keep that shellac to yourself, or you'll have to carry me home and tuck me in."

I could feel the heat creeping up my neck as much as I tried to fight it. Just the thought of being anywhere near the sack with that kinda ankle was more than I could stand.

She opened her purse and pulled out a small manila envelope. She slid it across the table and I opened it, turning out seven older photos of the pearl. I could not believe what I was looking at. This marble was a Baroque Spanish Pearl, almost two inches in diameter according to the scale on the first photo, stamped Chase Jewelers, Mayfield. The surface was beautiful. The sepia tone of the old photo highlighted three distinctive veins, obviously the marbling that Veronica had mentioned. It was beautiful, and I could tell that it was not a perfect sphere.

"What is this thing worth approximately?"

"Its value would be based on its uncommon nature. Black pearls are not uncommon. However, a pearl of that size is very rare, and very old. There is a museum value to it. When it came to our attention that it was supposedly, an antiquity we decided to keep it quiet. I just left it in my bag of marbles and then when I took over the store, I kept it in the safe. There it stayed for over twenty years." She stopped talking just then, and looked around. I followed her eyes around the joint again, Shifty was in the back and the place was empty, save for us.

She leaned forward, causing the neckline of her blouse to open a bit, giving me a show. "Do I have your undivided attention, detective?"

I nodded.

"Good. My pearl is worth two million dollars. There was an article in the paper concerning a missing black pearl decades ago, and then people started coming around asking about it. The only lead I can give you is Charles Patterson, my father's former business partner. He had worked for my grandfather as a boy, during the depression. Then worked for my father for many years, he was very knowledgeable about the business, and always unhappy about his lot in life. He was a rake and womanizer who drank or gambled away his paycheck instead of providing for his family. My father had to make advances on his salary from time to time so the man could either pay gambling debts or buy food and pay bills. That does not count the handouts he gave to Mrs. Patterson to help with the children. When I was getting into my teens, father insisted that I stay away from the store if he wasn't going to be there, sure that Mr. Patterson would be after me." She stopped to take a breath and let me catch up.

"Is this guy still around?" I was thinking this might be just a little intimidation job, go by the guy's place and rattle his cage.

"Yes he is, but he is in a retirement home, or at least he was, last I heard." She punctuated this with her glass before draining it, "Finally he quit working for father, when the men from the antiquity preservation society came by asking if the pearl was in his possession, and started talking about the money it might be worth. Mr. Patterson argued with father quite passionately that he had been keeping him down, by not providing a pension for his family because they were poor. Father argued back that it was drinking and gambling that had kept his family poor. They argued and finally Patterson threatened to quit, and father told him that he was welcome to go anytime he felt the need. Patterson of course went to work for the Stuckey's, and vowed to get even with my father. To my knowledge he never did, though he burglarized the store twice while father was still running it, and once after I took over. I did not move the pearl into the safe until about a year after that, when he robbed mother and father's home. My room was the only one that was not touched. The pearl still lay in my old sack of marbles where I had left it. The next day, I took it to the store and put it in the safe. After a thorough inventory of the house, the only thing that was missing was an old ledger from the store, from 1938."

While she was talking, I was getting an idea and the more I thought about it, the more I thought I might be on to something. "How many of those ledgers were there, I'm assuming they were all together in a closet or in the attic or basement?"

"All the ledgers from the time the store opened were in an old chifforobe in the bedroom that had belonged to my Grandmother Holt," she tipped her glass and looked into the bottom of it. "The responsible persons were never caught, but that was the only thing that they took."

I noted this and followed up with, "I don't suppose the police were able to come up with anything?" She shook her head negatively and I continued. "Do you have any ideas who it might have been?"

"My father never would come out and say it, but he suspected Charles Patterson, I know I always did," she explained. "He ran errands and did chores for my granddad, and worked there full time as long as my father, he did the daily bookkeeping, father took inventory daily and weekly, and closed the books weekly and monthly... I just could never figure out why he would steal one ledger book, father had fallen to a stroke, and couldn't tell us, even if he knew." She sat back in her seat, spent.

I glanced over my notes, really just waiting to see if she had more to say, she did not speak for a while, so I took that as my cue to ask some questions, starting with, "I don't suppose you still have that stack of ledgers sitting around anywhere?"

She nodded, "Yes of course I do. I live in my parent's house, and I saved almost everything relating to the business. You can come by and look through any of those things that you think might help you find my pearl."

I was putting together my first tack. "Do you happen to know when exactly Mr. Patterson quit working for your father, and I suppose you have all of these news articles and some sort of records of explanation about what this black pearl of yours is supposed to be, or where it supposedly came from?"

"You're already at it detective?" She said with a little sarcasm, "I thought I smelled smoke."

If it was not for the way that broad smiled at me, I might have given her the business, if she kept it up I still might. I gave her a sober look and she demurred.

"Yes, mister serious, I have his dates of employment, and of course we have every scrap of paper about my pearl. How often is it that you run across something like that, even in the trade? I can get all of these things together and you can come by and take a look." She smiled, and sat up a bit straighter.

"I think I've got enough to get started with, I'll write this up tomorrow morning and I'll stop by tomorrow to look through the ledgers and get Mr. Patterson's date of dismissal. I will want to see anything you have on the item itself, and I would appreciate it if you could have it all ready when I get there. My fee works like this…"

"I'll have it all ready for you tomorrow at ten. Your fee, I suppose you want five thousand up front and another five thousand when you find my pearl?" She had that smug, tone to her voice, as if she knew where I was going all along, it is generally my job to know what other people think, so this grated on my nerves.

"I hadn't really thought of an amount, but if the marble is worth what you say it is, that sounds like a fair deal," I wasn't trying to stiff her, she was trying to tell me my business, so I was gonna let her set her price, just because it was more than I usually charge.

She had that sexy little smug smile on again. "You're a tough negotiator, detective. I tell you what; I'll pay you twenty five when you bring me my pearl, plus expenses," her eyes narrowed and she leaned forward again, "but if you don't find it, you don't get a dime."

"I get it, don't worry. You'll have it back in no time."

She stood up and leaned across the table, one sweet, sultry drink of water. She looked right into my eyes, "I want my pearl detective and if you find it, I will be very…very… pleased," she purred slowly. A very sensual smile crossed her face and she kissed me, drawing my bottom lip out and letting it slap back against my mug as she pulled away. Damn, why did she have to do that?

"I'll see you tomorrow morning at ten seven, Detective. Don't be late, and don't disappoint me," she said over her shoulder, and she was gone.

● ● ●

I finished my drink and mulled it over for a bit and then I rolled out, unloading a sawbuck on my way to the door. When I got back to my place, I checked the mail and walked up the back stairs to go inside. My place is a nice little two bedroom walk up over a two office suite with oak floors and oiled walnut woodwork, maybe you know it, one of Champion City's more prominent attorney's had retired to Mayfield and opened a small practice. I got the building in the estate sale for next to nothin' its perfect, office down stairs, apartment upstairs, its home.

The next morning I drove by Chase's Jewelry to eye up the joint, just shy of ten. I wanted to check out what kind of place I was dealing with. At face value, it was just another storefront built into the front of a modest, late nineteenth century home. When I pulled into the drive that led around to a small rear parking lot, I saw a different story.

In its day, this place had been a real cherry. To start with, the short asphalt drive terminated into a cobblestone driveway, which led under an arched portico to a cobbled parking lot, marble steps and walks leading to fancy scrolled doors with lots of cut glass. A marble fountain and wrought iron fencing completed what must have been a very ritzy scene in the old days, even now the shadow of glamour hung over it.

I parked my car and went inside to have a look around. It was a decent place. Lighted display cases sat upon fine thick carpet. The two young clerks, both well dressed. A young man was helping an older woman. Their hushed voices were discussing a diamond bracelet. A young lady was working behind what appeared to be the main desk. I walked over.

The resemblance was striking. The girl was a vision of Veronica Chase some twenty years younger. I tried to strike up conversation but my tongue was all thumbs. "I…err… umm…," stammered out, but she just smiled.

"You're looking for Veronica, she's my mother. I'll get her for you." She did a little sachet and disappeared behind a curtain.

I cased out the joint and figured it for a cool million under glass, maybe half again that in a safe somewhere. I was looking for the signs of a reinforced wall when Veronica appeared.

"You don't miss a tick do you Mister Garman?" She smiled as she gazed at the clock.

"Not on a client's dime anyhow," I said, hoping she would just give me the goods already and spare me the show and tell.

"Hung over? You're all business this morning Rex." She reached under the counter and brought out a brown manila folder and a large envelope. She handed them over and said, "Here are the documents you requested and a few others I thought you might find useful."

I spread the top of the envelope and looked inside. Among the contents were a deck of cards, three non-filter cigarettes and a book of matches. Either I had landed a crackpot catfish or this case was about to get interesting.

● ● ●

Back in my office I stuffed the materials for Miss Chase in my lockbox and went out to tidy up two pending cases. One for the county heritage society, just a paper chase for the origin of a long contested document and the other a simple patty cake for a society dame who thought her playboy husband might be keeping a second closet for more than one extra marital skeleton.

It was late by the time I made it back to the office, so a sandwich and coffee at the desk was the prelude to my usual process for a new case. Under my beef and Swiss was the day's paper, I looked at the legal news after checking the obituaries for yours truly.

I laid open the brown record jacket and turned up the envelope. Photos cascaded across the blotter followed by the gum banded deck of cards, the book of matches and the cigarettes which rolled to the edge of the blotter, all but the last one which tumbled end over end and came rest on the match book.

I pushed aside the miscellany and got into Charles Patterson's work record. It was over an inch thick and detailed accurately a very colorful term of employment with Chase Jewelers. Clasped opposite the front sheet were handwritten payroll records.

It was as Miss Chase had said. Patterson made good money for the times; $25.00 per week plus a 15% commission on sales. Yet more often than not Patterson advanced against salary or drew commissions early. From 1932 to 1944, Ginny Patterson signed for a substantial number of these advances.

I noticed that a number of pays during that same period bore an asterisk. Mr. Patterson signed all these. Several pages on, I discovered that these were dates when Mr. Patterson drew his wages but his wife came in for an advance. On average, Mrs. Patterson received $12.00 every time she went to Mr. Chase. What was missing was an accrual of the handouts Veronica had mentioned. Among the papers in the work record were a number of counseling statements citing intemperate and philandering behavior.

Charles Patterson you were a very bad boy, but that does not make you a thief.

I dug deeper into the pile and laid out the photos into what seemed like chronological order. I stared at the photos until the thirst for fresh coffee and the need to smoke hit me in just that order. I turned in my chair for the coffee pot and as the smell of Juan Valdez best washed over me I absent mindedly screwed one of the non-filter cigarettes into the corner of my mouth and reached for the book of matches as I put the cup down.

Opening a matchbook and folding the tab back has always been a one handed operation for me. With my other hand, I pinched what should have been a match, tore it from the book and pulled it between the tab and the abrasive strip. I stared down the length of the cigarette and made out some small script and my eyes focused on the key I held.

Thank the good lord for pure dumb luck. I was well into counting my chickens when I read the inscription on the small flat brass key, *MSB 257. Could it be just that simple?* I was actually grinning when I thought about marching into Mayfield Savings Bank and showing the key to gain admittance to the bank of safe deposit boxes inside the safe. In my mind, I walked out of there with that fancy marble in my pocket on my way to twenty-five grand and a long vacation. Too easy.

I put together the file on this case and shot macro photographs of the evidence and important documents. Writing up the summary took a while with all the details on the sketchy character of Charles Patterson. It was well after midnight when my head hit the pillow.

The next morning I was sitting on the bench in front of the Mayfield Savings Bank when the bank manager unlocked the door at nine o'clock sharp. I walked past him as he held the door wide. He had a young complexion for a man with white hair, rumor had it that he's left for France in 1915 with a coal black flat top haircut and came home with a head full of white gray hair and a thick handlebar moustache. The look stuck with him and he his appearance that morning was pure United States Marine Corps.

"How can we be of service today?" He asked as he followed me in.

I reached into my pocket and held up the safe deposit key.

He reached for the key but I kept it at a safe distance. "I'm sorry, but this is evidence. I can't let it out of my possession." I produced my badge wallet and he motioned me to follow him to a counter near the gate, which led to the vault.

"That is fine Mr. Garman, but I will need your signature on the register." He said, lifting a heavily bound volume onto the counter. He opened it, flipped through a few pages and back one. "Fill in this line here and sign...here." He indicated with a finger as he turned the volume toward me.

I filled in the information I knew and lined though that which seemed unnecessary. I signed and laid the pen on the counter. The manager took the book away and walked to the end of the counter. I followed and he took me to his office and closed the door.

"Sit down, Mister Garman. I have no problem allowing you to inspect the contents of a secure deposit container, but I will accompany you and as you are obliged not to relinquish the key, I cannot allow you to remove anything from the container. You can take photographs and you may make notes, but we would be poor stewards of the public trust if we allowed just anyone to walk in and take whatever they like."

I took in his spiel and regarded him for a moment. He had an honest face and his plainspoken way was fine with me. His eyes were tired, as if he had seen and heard it all already.

GregK.

I rolled a smoke while I let it sink in. "No, I didn't suspect. If I find what I am looking for I will notify my client and she and the police will come. I know a couple of reporters who'd love to grind a little grist on the polished and prestigious bank that might be harboring a priceless stolen artifact in their vault, right under the nose of the object's owner and the Mayfield Police."

The bank manager sat back and regarded me as if he was trying to spit out a spoiled sardine. "Okay, let's hear it."

So I gave it to him, most of it anyhow, I left out the details and suspense.

When the yarn was spun, he shook his head and said, "I'll let you get to it." He took me to the teller line and spoke to a young brunette. "Molly, please escort Mister Garman to deposit box 257."

She gave me a distrusting eye and looked back to the manager. "He has the key?"

The manager nodded his head and turned to me. "I wish you luck, sir."

I nodded and followed the brown-haired person to the vault. She took me to an anteroom inside the vault and walked directly to a bank of lock boxes on the far wall.

She produced a ring of keys and chose a long flat brass one. She inserted it into one of the locks and gave it a half turn. "Insert your key and turn it clockwise." She indicated the second lock.

I did as she instructed and she gave the box a sharp tug to unseat it. The box slid a few inches. She turned her key back and removed it, then indicated that I should do the same. When I had, she stepped away.

"When you've finished, please lock your box and notify the manager or myself and one of us will secure the box." She gave me a smile and left the room.

I carried the heavy box to the table at the center of the small room and removed the slotted cover. I do not know wat I had expected to find inside, other than I had hoped to find the pearl rolling around all by its lonesome. I did not, but I did find cash, bonds, two passports, a scrapbook, A ledger embossed 1938, photographs, birth announcements and more questions.

I did a complete inventory. As it turned out there was a small fortune in cash, over $300,000. The bonds were bearer bonds sold by the War Department. I counted one hundred of the unregistered securities in the $10,000 denomination. The scrapbook contained what I think of as *feminine memorabilia,* ticket stubs to *I Was a Teenage Werewolf,* pressed flowers a few grainy photos of vaguely familiar people. Several articles from the Champion City Sun laid in the leaves of the ledger, articles detailing robbery and violent crime involving the Chases and Pattersons.

An envelope held a birth announcement bearing Veronica Chase's address and declaring the arrival of twins in June of 1943. Inside a sepia photo showed mother and babies. My mouth went dry when I realized that I was staring at a fifteen-year-old Veronica Chase. Her shattered look and forced smile told the story of a wound not yet healed.

I gritted my teeth and turned my attention back to the scrapbook and its news articles. I remember the majority of them from the materials that I had gotten from Veronica. All but one,

The headline read, *Trouble in the High Street.* The article told the tale of a long time employee who chose to bite the hand that fed him. It played Charles Patterson as a philandering philistine, a gambling drunk who debauched the daughter of his employer after a final falling out. It went on to implicate his wife as a beleaguered and abused spendthrift who had turned to gold digging as a means to feed her children.

All of it in one breath made no sense at all. There was nothing in the box remotely related to the baroque pearl. I separated and fanned through every strap of cash, shook loose the bond certificates, lifted the corners of pictures and rummaged under every scrap and found nothing.

I arrived at the same conclusion and the end of my patience as I flipped through the scrapbook. Nothing, everything and nothing, how did all of this add up? A fortune, families forever locked together in tragedy and everyone seemingly going on as if nothing was outwardly amiss.

I packed everything into the safe deposit box and replaced the cover. I carried it to its slot, aligned it and gave it a stout shove. The box slid inward a few inches and hung up on something. I pulled it out slightly and tried again to slide it home.

Again, the box went in six inches and stopped. Whatever held it back was not stiff, but solid enough to block the box's path. I pulled the box free and sat it on the table. When I returned to the slot, I peered inside and then reached in to try to clear the obstruction.

I felt the open flap and metal tang of a manila envelope. From the feel of what filled it, I judged what had to be an inch thick stack of documents. I pulled on the envelope to free it to no avail.

Through cautious prodding, I determined that the envelope caught in the framing of the structure both fore and aft. Pulling downward did no good either. I grasped the documents tightly and pushed hard. The flap tore loose and I was able to pull the envelope free.

I shuffled through the documents quickly, unsure if the bank manager or the teller who brought me into the vault might return and take more than casual interest in what I was doing. This was what I had been searching for and had hoped to find inside the box, a number of articles and stories about the baroque pearl for newspapers and magazines. There were also police reports and a carbon copy of a search warrant for the Patterson residence and then tucked into another envelope were papers, articles and reports dealing with the incidents of sexual assault including rape resulting in a pair of fraternal twins. There was an almost complete criminal complaint, record of adjudication and disposition detailing a sentence of 25 years.

I skimmed one final article as I stuffed the documents back into the envelope. It detailed Patterson's release to residential incarceration at the Spring View Correctional Asylum. The piece included the reaction of none other than Veronica Chase.

The final document in the envelope was a loss of property claim from Credit Life Property Insurance Corporation, listing a payout for loss for $300,000.00.

I jammed the box back into its slot and gave the key a turn. It locked with a scrape and I pocketed the key. With the envelope tucked under my arm, I made directly for the manager's office.

He looked up nervously from the phone when I barged in. From his hushed tone, I suspected that there was only one person who could be on the other end of the line. "Tell Miss Chase that I'm on my way."

He lowered the phone quickly, "Mister Garman please. You do not know what kind of power that woman has in this town. I'll tell you everything I know."

I turned back to him. "So it was her?"

He nodded vigorously, "Y-yes! I called her. She was quite surprised that you were here."

"You'll be hearing from the police soon enough. I have evidence, lots of it, but for a slightly different circumstance than I was hired for, Insurance fraud." I turned on my heel and headed out of there.

• • •

I was almost to Chase's when it occurred to me that hell had no fury like a woman scorned, and Veronica Chase had been scorned plenty. Mother to Patterson's bastards, heir to a fortune she could not spend and now I uncovered her fraud to punish Patterson. Her only loose end, Charles Patterson lay in the next to no security, rehabilitation asylum ten miles away.

I pulled into the lot at Chase's and ran inside. The young woman was in tears and the young man was trying to comfort her. When she saw me coming, he turned around. Another flash of déjà vu hit me. If the girl was an early image of her mother, so the young man was the likeness of his younger father.

I pulled up short, "Where's Veronica?"

The young man put himself between his sister and me. It was plain he had the wrong idea. "Veronica! Where is she? She's in trouble and I can't help her if she kills your father!"

The young man turned to his sister, "Father?"

"It's okay Martin," she said as she stepped past him and met me in the center of the shop. "Mother left here in a rage. Not the first time I have seen her like that, but this was different. She was vicious." She turned to her brother, "With both of us. It was like she didn't know us and we were interfering in her business."

"Where did she go?" I demanded. I looked from one to the other.

"I don't kn…" she started, but her brother interrupted.

"I wanted to know where she goes." He looked to his sister whose mouth hung open. "I asked Mother, and I didn't feel she was honest with me, so I followed her one day. She goes to Springview Asylum, and sometimes she goes to see someone at Credit Life."

"The insurance company, why?" she asked.

"Because she's punishing Charles Patterson for something they did twenty years ago," I growled on my way to the door.

"Who is Charles Patterson?" I heard them exclaim as the door closed behind me.

I gripped the wheel so hard my hands hurt on my drive to Springview. My spry little Custom 500 rolled in and out of traffic like a jackrabbit on a date. I turned across traffic into the lot at the asylum to a herald of screaming brakes and protesting car horns. Veronica's roadster was in the visitor's lot. I pulled up under the portico and left it running.

My dash up the stairs felt like stalking through muck. I burst through the door into the lobby and found the waiting area deserted. I went to the reception desk and banged on the window.

No response.

I was raising my fist to give the window the business again when I noticed the register lying on the counter just inside the window. I pressed my forehead to the glass at an angle I hoped would allow me to read the register. You might know that the receptionist chose that moment to return.

"May I help you?" she hissed, matronly and disapproving.

"I'm Detective Garman. Did you just admit a tallish auburn haired gal, angry like her hair is on fire?" I growled, mashing my badge and ID against the glass.

"Nobody except Mrs. Patterson," The woman said, not opening the glass and moving the register a safe distance beyond my line of sight.

"Misses? I need to get in there. Veronica Chase has been involved in an insurance fraud scenario with Charles Patterson for decades," I barked. She cringed. I walked toward the door and it opened inward as I approached.

"Should I do something?" she asked as I walked past her.

"Lock yourself in there and call the police." I reached for the shavetail I carried high on my right hip. "What's the room number?"

"One-seventeen," she said and gestured vaguely to the right as she made for the office.

I walked through the dayroom where a number of the residents sat, gathered around a Crosley television set watching Ed Sullivan. At the end of a short corridor, hallways branched left and right. I followed the arrow toward room 100.

The stench of soiled linens and unwashed bodies filled my nose as I walked onto the pod. Several patients in adult sized walkers roamed the halls one blathering mindlessly. Four uniformed people sat at the nurse's station smoking.

I strode past them wondering if giving them a piece of my mind might get them on their feet and addressing the stench. I passed 110 and slowed my pace trying to listen. I heard high heels on the tile some distance ahead. It was the relentless impatient clacking that some broads excel at.

I pulled up short as I passed 115. I heard a hushed but hard voice. "The ruse is over. This is all about to fall apart. I want my pearl so I can try to minimize damage." The persistent clacking was enough to annoy me and I wasn't in the room.

"Listen you little minx. This..." A feeble man's voice scratched through a persistent cough. "All of this was brought on by you. Accuse me of taking your damned pearl. Seduce me and then tell your old man I took you. Get me sent off to the pen and then cook up this insurance game to keep my wife and then me quiet after she died," he rasped, not nearly as quiet as she was.

"Now Charles, you listen to me and you listen good. I am going to have that marble one way or the other. You can get it for me or I as your guardian can riffle through your things when you die unexpectedly." Veronica hissed.

I had not expected to hear that. I mean I know squirrels and dames do crazy when caught at what they are up to, but I did not see this coming. Neither did Patterson obviously. I moved closer in case I had to get in there, but I was listening for more incriminating evidence.

"What Ronnie, you're going to just up and kill me, after I kept this all these years," Patterson said disbelief an understatement. "Last I saw that damned awkward marble was when you first cooked this up and put it in the floor safe in your office at the store."

"I told you it's not in the safe," she insisted.

"No, not the jewelry vault, The floor safe where your old man kept the best stuff so his sticky fingered kid wouldn't get it. You know where you lifted the Blair Diamond and I lost my job. Police come after me three months later when the shop burglary. Then you tell him you are pregnant because I raped you. He shot an artery and has a stroke. Poor little Veronica winds up with every damned thing and I get twenty years. Ain't that enough for you?"

"It wasn't like you gave me much choice. Drinking and gambling away your wages and your wife drawing advances on your wages as fast as my father could write the checks. I had to do something. My kind hearted father wasn't about to fire you for cause."

Behind me, I heard hard-soled shoes and I knew it was the police. I stepped into the room and put it to an end. "Veronica Chase, Patterson or whatever it is, you're under arrest for insurance fraud. You would do well to come along quiet and spare me calling the papers."

She wheeled on me just as Irish Tim Donovan fitted her with a pair of steel bracelets. "Mr. Garman, I'm not paying you a dime."

Patterson sat there looking like he was going rotten by the minute. I said, "I need a statement from you to corroborate the account of what happened."

He nodded through another bout of spasmodic coughing. "Whatever you need, I know what I done was wrong, but I never touched her until she asked me to, and she knew what she was doing."

I left the asylum an hour later and stopped at Chases Jewelers. I found the door locked, but I knocked and the young man came to the door. "I need to see your sister. Do either of you have the combination to the floor safe in the office?"

Through a perturbed expression he said, "Sure follow me. What is going on with mother?"

I blew the air out of my lungs and craved a smoke and a drink. He led me to the office where his sister was doing the books. "I need you to open the floor safe if you can. Your mother in in some trouble and if I can recover an object she collected an insurance claim on, I may be able to help her. What's more, you might exonerate your father."

They both looked at me again, as if I was out of my mind. "Could you please open the safe?"

She nodded and swiveled her chair around, then knelt to lift a panel of carpet out of the floor. Several expert and practiced turns of the dial later and she lifted the heavy lid away. "Okay, Mr. Garman, what is it exactly that you're looking for?"

"A two inch black pearl, your mother called it a baroque pearl," I said as she removed items from the safe.

She lifted out a number of small packages, each labeled by content. Rubies, emeralds, peridot and amethyst, finally she lifted out a bag labeled, *loose pearls.* The last items were clear containers of fine gold jewel sets.

"I don't know that we've ever used anything in this safe. All of our findings are out on the bench," she explained.

Her brother concurred saying, "We've had the combination for years, but mother never allowed us in there." He took the bag of loose pearls turned its contents out on a tray.

At first it was small spheres, white and cream and some a smoky tan, perfect specimens. As the pearls continued to fall from the sack, larger less perfect examples were among them. Pearls with threads of green and gold, one with a red streak the color of blood cascaded across the tray.

Just when it wasn't looking good for there to be, much left in that little pouch a large black baroque pearl tumbled out of the bag and landed with a thud on the tray, splashing smaller pieces out onto the carpet.

Solved! Tally up another for the Garman Agency.

The End

To Hunt a Manticore
by P.J. Lozito

Celebrated actor Eldon Curtis III was spending the night in, at one of Manhattan's most prominent high-rise apartments. His wife, a short, beautiful brunette, was there. It was she who first noticed the warning light. This flashed on a radio sitting in its own niche in the cozy apartment. The thing, a foot-long 1939 Emerson Stradivarius in a cabinet shape suggesting a violin, was a dummy. It resembled a violin even down to having a sounding hole.

"His Honor wants to speak to the Revenant Detective," Vera spoke excitedly. "Via that home-made Sigaba machine of yours."

"So! Our little agreement holds," observed Curtis.

"The way crime is in 1946, I'm sure he cherishes having his own private watchdog," added Vera wryly. "Hopefully, your little toy complies with Title II of the Communications Act of '34."

Although it looked like your typical cathedral radio, the device was merely a shell. Inside were the guts of an efficient two-way job. The radio was conceived for private communication between Curtis and New York City's mayor, William O'Dwyer.

Curtis was a dashing, handsome man. His new sideline as the city's freelance troubleshooter required such mysterious methods. Such ventures were outside the limits of the law. Despite being in his late thirties, Curtis still moved with an easy grace. He demonstrated that now, quickly dashing to the radio. There he engaged up the audio.

"Calling Griffin! Calling Griffin! Over!" rapped Mayor O'Dwyer.

That was the name the mayor used in dealing with the unknown vigilante. Mayor O'Dwyer's own fake radio was a modest EC74 radio from 1933.

Grinning, Curtis gave the radio his full attention.

"And I was winning," pouted Vera, referring to their card game.

"Griffin, come in Griffin," continued the mayor.

"Do you mean the mythical beast, a first name or the proud Irish surname?" asked Curtis, putting a finger to his lips. Seeing this, Vera clammed up.

"Take your pick," crackled the mayor's voice over the squawk box.

That was the correct answer.

"Griffin here," Curtis responded. "Well, beat it out, sir."

"Remember we discussed apprehending the Silver Manticore?"

"Indeed I do. That dewdropper has been bleeding this town for too long. Have you a lead on him?"

"I've got a plan, all right," confirmed the mayor. "Just the first step in a trap, really."

"Oh?" responded Curtis.

Traps intrigued him. Now he was interested. Curtis settled in.

"A licensed private detective was found dead. It gave me an idea."

"What's the scheme?"

"You make yourself up to look like him. Then you go on W.X.L.I. saying you have evidence of the identity of the Silver Manticore."

"Foxy," estimated Curtis. "That's the very station that airs his show."

"Exactly, the program makes him out as a modern-day Robin Hood..."

"But he's still just a crook," finished Curtis. "Who was this detective?"

"Name of Lance Riordan. Ring any bells?"

"None. What killed him?"

"That we don't know. But now you can masquerade as Riordan."

"Disguises are my forte."

"You're the man of maybe half-a-dozen faces," put in Vera. Curtis waved her into silence.

"Who was that?" asked the mayor.

"Just the radio," Curtis lied. Vera made a face in response. "Please continue. Just dressing me up as Riordan won't get us very far."

"Latch on to this," Williams continued. "We set up an office, Riordan's new digs. We boast that the evidence is held there in a safe."

"He's been known to crack safes," Curtis recalled. "You'll also make it plain where this office is, I suppose."

"That'll happen," the mayor reassured. "The Silver Manticore is sure to stick his scaly nose into it come the black. We spring. Before he can move his getaway sticks, we have him in the cooler. Naturally, you'll get the reward."

"Naturally. Except you forget one thing."

"Oh?"

"I have no way to claim that reward if we wish to keep our little arrangement confidential," reminded Curtis. "Just who is it that will be springing? The Silver Manticore is no pushover, you know. Besides that gas gun, he's a dead shot with his .45 and seems to know a few Oriental fighting tricks."

"Now focus this," the mayor enthused. "Handpicked retired policemen, armed to the teeth with everything from gas masks to Tommy guns. I make sure they're issued private detectives licenses. We stash them in the office with a cute bree answering the blower as cover. Sharp, eh?"

"I get it. Your retired pounders can still get the job done."

"They may be retired, but those snatchers hate seeing any crook go free. We assign half them to watch the office and the other half to hole up there at night. It'll be the last time the Manticore crosses the man."

"I think this is the elephant's adenoids. Let's put the wheels in motion, Mr. Mayor. Er, who do you have in mind for the girl?"

Vera started a vigorous sign language dance that it should be her.

"That I don't know yet."

"I have just the one for you. She's a fairly good actress," Curtis eyed his wife, smiling. He clicked off the radio.

She mouthed "Fairly good?" silently, face insulted.

"Time to go to work," Curtis evaded.

"A case!" squealed Vera. "And it sounds like a real hummer."

"It's a blip, all right," Curtis nodded.

"I'll say. The mayor capped it," Vera cooed. "Darling, it sounds very dangerous! The Silver Manticore, after all."

"You know I'm not the same man since Sam got me."

It was true. Curtis' service in the Navy for his country during the war involved all manner of deceit and deception. This background, coupled with his own acting skills had already netted a killer.

"Of course, I'll have to call the mayor back," absently he fidgeted with a ring that bore the likeness of a chameleon.

"Oh, yes," nodded Vera. "When you make yourself up to resemble Riordan, remember to slip off your manacle."

"Indeed," Curtis agreed, slipping his wedding ring into a pocket. "I can't see how this scheme can fail."

The chameleon ring was the identifying symbol of the Revenant Detective. In gratitude for the capture of that killer, the police secretly had deputized Griffin. He was a force for law, operating with the resources of the police and the mayor. Now, nicknamed the Revenant Detective, a name chosen to honor a slain comrade, Curtis was determined to rid New York City of another criminal.

● ● ●

Later that evening, Curtis found the area down around City Hall to be a ghost town. He was attired, besides a quiet grey business suit and trench coat, in a white mask covering his eyes. Only a hat tilted at a jaunty angle hid the mask with its shade. Between that and his turned up collar, Curtis passed unnoticed among the few pedestrians about. He kept a wary eye out as entered the now closed City Hall subway station. It was a convenient place to meet his contact. Curtis spotted the man the mayor had described. Then he approached.

"Kelley?"

He was a bulky man in his thirties. Turning to Curtis, he asked: "Are you Griffin?"

"Do you mean the mythical beast, a first name or the proud Irish surname?" Curtis replied, showing the ring on his finger with a cha-meleon on it.

"Take your pick," responded Kelley. "Normally, I wouldn't shake hands with a masked man. But I know what you did for this city."

"Oh, just it was just my duty as a concerned citizen," put in Curtis, taking the proffered hand. He had to switch hands to do so. One held a briefcase. Kelley's grip was firm.

"There'd be less crime if more citizens felt like you, sir," beamed Kelley.

"Shall we proceed? The mayor didn't quite say what your connection is here."

"I'm sure you can appreciate that it's better, just in case of inquiries, that you don't know my full name or position, sir. Suffice to say, I am 100% behind the mayor on your undertakings."

"Understood," nodded Griffin.

The pair went into the station proper. Kelley led Griffin to a gurney. Resting on it was the body of Lance Riordan. Griffin's briefcase was revealed to be a compact disguise kit complete with lighted mirror built into the lid. It was complete with dyes, putty and corneal eye shell lenses and everything needed to apply them. The last came in varying colors and would change the color of ones eyes. They would have to be removed after some dozen hours, however.

"Was there much trouble getting him from the City Morgue to here?"

"The hard part was getting the gurney onto the mayor's private subway car."

"Private subway car?" goggled Curtis.

"Forget that exists. Anyway, nobody questions anything that looks like official city business. I'll be back with Riordan's effects. Clothes all cleaned, of course," Kelley added.

It wasn't more than twenty minutes later that the now unmasked Curtis bore a striking resemblance to the corpse on the gurney beside him. His own sparkling blue eyes were hidden by glass shells the drab brown color of Riordan's, his receding hairline was augmented by a wig and bore the detective's cleft chin. Additionally, Curtis sprouted bushy eyebrows, olive coloring and even Riordan's slight overbite. There was a knock behind him.

"Come on in, Kelley," called Griffin. "All done."

"Well," assessed Kelley, dropping off Riordan's effects. "I couldn't tell the two of you apart. I don't think his mother could!"

"Hopefully, that won't be necessary," smiled Griffin, inspecting the clothes. "With luck, only people who have never met Riordan will ever see me like this."

"Those have been altered to fit you," added Kelley.

Griffin started getting into them. He had to hurry to his appointment.

"Well, good-bye, Kelley. I'm off to the radio station. When I'm done, I'll come see the layout your people set up for me."

"A good actor requires the best stage," noted Kelley. "How is that car we got you running?"

"Oh, she's eggs in coffee," Curtis kissed cupped fingers and cast them away.

"I'm glad to hear it. Well, I'm off myself. I've got to close up Riordan's old office. I must hurry before anybody wonders why he maintains two of them."

"Just a sec," Griffin interjected. "'Kelley,' is that a first name or last name...? Oh, don't bother answering. I know the routine."

"Don't forget this," Kelley urged, slapping a revolver into Griffin's waiting hand.

● ● ●

The mayor's couldn't have picked a more appropriate radio station than W.X.L.I. He planned to rile up the Silver Manticore, figuring the criminal probably tuned into the fictionalized broadcasts accounts of his adventures. Little did he know that the very owner of the station, Brent Allred, was the man under that silver mask. It was because of this that Allred kept his office radio tuned to that station. While W.X.L.I. played a mix of drama, pop and jazz, it also broadcast news right from the pages of Allred's newspaper *Daily Sentry*.

What none knew was that the Silver Manticore merely pretended to be a criminal. He found it a convenient cover in his dealings with real criminals, cutting his way into gangs. Then he destroyed them from the inside. His exploits had inspired a few Hollywood serials, a pulp magazine and the radio drama.

Located in a distant part of Queens, New York, where city limits left off and Long Island started, W.X.L.I. was a long ride out. Curtis considered that while the island was indeed long, at least this was just at the geographic tip. He had arranged an interview with the station in the person of Lance Riordan. His claim excited the newshounds there. They in turn brought it to the attention of Brent Allred. He was a medium-sized, brown-haired man in his forties. A few grey strands shot through the brown. It was with bated breath that Allred, in his Park Avenue office, tuned in for the broadcast. With him was the inner circle of people who shared his secret, aiding him in his crusade. All eyes were focused on a 22" black and brown Pilot T47 radio with a big dial. After a commercial for Blue Coal, the segment aired.

"And now, ladies and gentlemen, noted private detective Lance Riordan is with us in the studio with important developments in the case of the mysterious criminal known as the Silver Manticore. Detective Riordan?"

"Thank you, Walter. I'm sure your audience will excuse the raspy sound of my voice," Griffin rasped. This covered for never having heard Riordan speak. "I just recently had a dust up that left me speaking in a terrible croak."

"I'm sure my audience won't mind too much! Not if they are regular listeners to my own broadcasts," kidded Walter.

"I'd like to share in the levity, Walter," Griffin responded. "But this is a serious matter of the utmost importance."

"I'm sorry, Mr. Riordan. I didn't mean to make light of the situation."

"Oh, think nothing of it, Walter. Now, the public at large does not know that I have been retained to hunt and capture this menace, the Silver Manticore."

"Can you tell us who has retained you?" the host quizzed. "What their ultimate motivation is?"

"My good fellow, we were not victorious in Europe by telling Hitler what our plans were in advance! At this time, that will have to remain unanswered. Suffice to say, no expense was spared in bringing this criminal to his inevitable justice. For too long, the Silver Manticore has been beyond the reach of the law."

"The Silver Manticore has fairly laughed at the forces of law and order," noted Walter.

"He'll be laughing out of the other side of his silvery face," continued Griffin. "I have, in a secure location, certain evidence as to the identity of the Silver Manticore. I shall shortly be bringing this to the proper authorities. This broadcast is to give that felon a chance to leave town forever!"

"Mr. Riordan, am I to understand that you are giving the Silver Manticore a chance to flee justice?" doubted an exasperated Walter.

"Yes. This evidence, which will bust the case wide open, could tie up the courts for years. My patrons have no wish to do that, only to rid New York City of this menace."

"Well, there you have it, New York and environs. The Silver Manticore must leave town at once or face justice. This has been…"

Allred clicked off the radio in disgust. Worry was imprinted on his handsome features. Among his aids was his younger, look-a-like cousin, Danny Colt. His features were just as concerned.

"What do you think, Brent?" he asked. During the day, Colt was the head of Liberty Cab Company.

"He's bluffing!" opined news photo-hound Speed Martin.

Martin was the *Sentry's* ace news photographer, "O. Henry with a camera," he had been called. Speed had earned his sobriquet for taste in fast cars, fast chatter, fast fists and fast women.

"If anyone had been dogging your trail," Martin added, "we'd have noticed something, sure."

"A detective on a case would, naturally, take care not to present himself," observed Gani Bako.

This small fellow acted as Allred's Filipino houseboy/chauffeur. Few knew he was really Japanese and formerly one of that nation's top espionage operatives. Brent Allred had rescued him from one of Japan's secret executions for a botched mission. The mission was botched by secret service agent Brent Allred.

"That's a chance we can't take," offered Allred. "I'm worried. He might actually have something on me. Starting now, I give up being the Silver Manticore."

"You're not letting that bloodhound scare you into hiding, are you?" Colt gasped.

"No. I'm turning the mask over to you," Allred clarified. "I'll be making public appearances. If that sleuth has something showing I'm the Silver Manticore, that'll put the kibosh on it. Besides, I'm no spring chicken."

"If I read my shorthand correctly," Louise Scott began, "Riordan has patrons. Note the plural. Who are they?"

Miss Scott was Brent Allred's top reporter. Now was more needed as his private secretary. That meant Miss Scott coordinated the Silver Manticore's missions more than she took dictation and served refreshments.

"It's going to be a long night. I made coffee, boys," added Miss Scott. "Boss, you and Bako get your usual noodle juice."

She poured those two their tea.

"How 'bout that froggy voice of his?" said Evan White, accepting a cup of coffee. "This Riordan."

The Negro pretended to be a simple cab driver in Colt's employ. His Liberty Cab carted the Silver Manticore around when the black chauffer-driven Pegasus would not do. His mighty black sinews belied a keen mind. "Man said he banged up his throat in a tussle. Did one of us smack this guy without knowin' it?"

"Unless he was undercover as a thug or torpedo, I doubt it," answered Allred. "I don't punch until I'm out of ammo."

"What's the plan?" asked Colt.

"First, we find out where Riordan's office is. Let's check the *Sentry's* files. Then we pay him a little visit."

Speed Martin spoke up, "Try this!"

Today's copy of *The World-Telegram* was slapped onto the desk.

"They scooped us," Martin elaborated. "That has an article about him."

Allred picked up the paper, thumbing to the aforementioned article.

"You're looking at me like I'm a half portion," bleated Martin. "You did say keep up with the competition."

"No, this is nobby, Speed. This piece has Riordan's office address," relayed Allred. "We break in and see that evidence."

● ● ●

"This is it," showed off the mayor. "Here's the office, all new furniture and fixtures and those new phones with buttons. Oh, your radio with the flashing light gave me an idea. One of the phones is tricked out with a light instead of a bell. You can get a call and nobody lurking around will hear the ring."

"That'll come in handy," predicted Griffin.

"You can bet on that. Here, we just slapped some Kutol on the walls and we're open for business."

"Monkey business is still business!" suggested Curtis, still in his Lance Riordan disguise.

"All phonus balonus, of course," the mayor continued. "I have men posted, watching it from up in that hotel. This office is ideal. Want to know why?"

"Yes," answered Griffin. "Why not just use Riordan's office?"

"See this door?" O'Dwyer pointed to it now.

Curtis strode over and flung the door open.

"That leads down a flight of stairs right onto East 33rd St. A short trip down a corridor will bring you to either the parking garage within the building or to the offices on the ground floor."

"It does get kind of quiet on this street after dark," observed Griffin. "How secure is the parking garage?"

"Remember that Negro fellow killed by Todeskampf? I hired his kid brother for the garage. He idolizes you now. If we say, let someone slip in, he'll do it. If we say, keep him out, he'll do that, too."

"Oh, my, I'm deeply touched," Griffin said.

"And what you noticed about the dark street? It's more so when I get that street light doused," O'Dwyer added.

"I must say, I'm impressed with what you can do!"

"Save your applause for this trick," the mayor grinned. He cupped his hand to his mouth and called: "Here's the bulge. Come on in!"

Five men appeared.

"These fine chaps are, alphabetically, Borelli, Kautz, Macintosh, Morales and Shapiro."

"Sounds like a law firm," kidded Griffin.

"Better than that. They're all retired police detectives. And all bearing brand-new private detective licenses and guns."

"So, you're the gee that avenged Bob Caradona, huh?" one of them asked.

"It's not really something to celebrate, fellows," admonished Griffin. "But when a good cop is killed in the line of duty, I just couldn't let a killer get away. I had to act."

Hands clapped Griffins' back and hands as the ex-cops murmured their thanks. He tried putting faces to names.

"And when this job is in the bag, you men keep this place as your base of operations," O'Dwyer beamed.

● ● ●

"Boss, listen to this," chirped Miss Scott. "Lance Riordan, 28, licensed private detective left town on a case. He was gone for some time. Now he's back, and boasting to the papers and radio of his exploits."

Brent Allred listened intently.

"Speed, grab Axelrod and arrange a gab fest with Riordan. Since the *Sentry* is offering a $60,000 reward for the capture of the Silver Manticore, we should talk to him."

"Sure," Speed asserted. "I'll get right on it."

Mike Axelrod was the top crime reporter on *The Daily Sentry*. He was not in with this little group. In fact, he had vowed to unmask the Silver Manticore.

● ● ●

White drove Colt out to Riordan's listed address. He recognized it as the section of Brooklyn the natives called Green Point. Its claim to fame was that the Civil War's Union ironclad, the Monitor, had been made there. With White dropping him off around the corner, Colt continued on foot. He was looking a three-storey house over when an elderly lady popped out the front door, gathering copious amounts of mail. Colt tried to look nonchalant, but she caught him casing the joint. Very clearly, he noted, a piece of mail was marked "Lance Riordan."

"You lose something, mister?" she asked, more than suspiciously than helpfully.

Colt tumbled to the deal immediately. Riordan had been renting one of the floors from this woman. Maybe he could gain access with a sob story.

"Truth be told, I'm looking for a room. Know any around here? I have good references and a damn fine job."

"I got a room. It might be available soon, $70 a month."

"*Might* be? Lady, I need a place right away."

"What do you do?"

"I got the best job of all, ma'am."

"So what do you do?"

"I'm a plumber."

The woman looked Colt over silently. Finally, she spoke: "You sure don't look like any plumber I ever seen. You dress too nice."

"That's because you are looking at a supervisor. I have a whole crew working under me," lied Colt, blowing on his fingernails and then rubbing them on his lapel with pride.

"You got any time now?"

"That's why I got my ground grabbers these streets, ma'am. I heard all the landlords put signs in their windows. You don't have a sign up, but I couldn't help but noticing you have the nicest house on the block. Hey, is that one of those signs, over there?"

"Never mind them," the woman dismissed. "Come on and take a look. My tenant is all paid up for six months."

"Oh, so I might not get the room, then," doubted Colt disappointedly.

"Expect that but he's on his sixth month. This is it," she noted, opening the second floor apartment with a key from a ring of them.

A stack of mail was piled up on the landing. Colt entered cautiously, as if the tenant would be back momentarily. For all he knew, Riordan just might. From the dust, the pulled down shades and the volume of mail, it seemed like nobody had been here for a while. That postage, too, was marked 'Lance Riordan.' She took him from neat room, orderly to neat, orderly room.

"If your tenant doesn't come back, I'll take it," Colt decided.

"You got a card, Mister....?"

"Dunn, Jeff Dunn," improvised Colt. "I don't have a card."

"You don't?"

"They're making new ones up for me at the office. Let me take yours," he added taking out a pen and note pad out before she could refuse.

"You won't believe it, but it's Smith. Mr. and Mrs. Jim Smith," she grinned. "Pleased to meet you, Mrs. Smith," Colt said, tipping his hat. "Well, I'll call you soon."

"Oh, call me 'Mary.' Had your lunch yet, son?"

● ● ●

It wasn't long before Colt found himself in the Smith kitchen, nibbling a ham sandwich with Mr. Smith. They drank iced tea and had egg salad. The scent of this morning's breakfast bacon lingered in the air. Mrs. Smith kept up a running commentary on what life in the house was like and what was expected of him. She kept it up until Colt was able to ask about the current tenant.

"His name's Lance Riordan," she supplied. "He never talked about his work much at all."

"Did he keep a gun?"

"If he did, he took it with him," she noted.

This little session was interesting, thought Colt. Riordan was back in town but had abandoned his apartment. Meanwhile, he had opened a new office.

● ● ●

The men took their stations. The first night of it proved to be uneventful. Not a thing was out of place. Every late night reveler and third shift worker in the area was noted and scrutinized. There was no action.

The detectives were back in place the next night. As clocks chimed twelve, a dark figure stepped up the street. He went right for the door. Macintosh, the detective on duty in the hotel, observed this. He moved to the telescope they had smuggled in. Watching, Macintosh saw that the figure took only a bit longer than usual to enter the door. Mac, as he liked to called, reached for the phone.

In the office itself, over the line that had replaced its bell with a flashing light, a telephone came to life. Borelli reached for it.

"Someone togged to the bricks just went it!"

"Think it's the Manticore?"

"Don't know. But he got in like he had a twister to the slammer."

Borelli hung up and motioned the team in the darkened office into place. Seconds later, a sliver of light appeared at the crack of the access door. There was a jiggling sound as the lock was picked. Then the door opened. A figure cloaked in shadows appeared. The door creaked open.

"Hands up!" barked Shapiro.

The figure froze. Kautz and Morales materialized as bright lights snapped on. Before them stood a man dressed completely in black, hat pulled low, collar turned up, a silver mask upon his face in the manner such as a surgeon might wear.

"Mitt me, kid!" boasted Shapiro. "I just bagged the Silver Manticore."

He stepped forward and tugged on the mask. Lance Riordan peered back at him.

"You got squat, fellas," he spoke. "I'm Griffin."

He proved this by presenting the chameleon ring.

"I wanted to test this set up. You're pretty good."

"Oh, well, that's all right, then," accessed Kautz, turning to Morales. "See? We didn't pull a Brodie."

"Pretty good work," put in Griffin, taking a seat.

The group kept their watch up, but nothing further of interest occurred. They broke up their watch after dawn as the neighbor came back to life.

The next night they were again back in place. The phone lit up again. Morales, right by it, picked the thing up. Macintosh there rapped.

"Well, that little rehearsal last night was a fine run through for the real thing!"

"What do you mean?" Morales quizzed.

"That wasn't a trip for biscuits," Macintosh called. "A tin can just dropped someone off!"

"Betcha anything it's Griffin again. He thinks we'd fall it again the next night!" Shapiro complained.

"You're all wet," rang a voice.

The group wheeled to see who spoke. There was an extra man there among them.

"I'm Griffin," the canny detective revealed in a different face from last night.

"We got to start using our blinkers," one of them groaned.

"This has to be the real thing," Griffin urged.

The men in the office scrambled. Griffin snapped off the lights as the men took their places again. He pressed an ear to the door. Steps were heard. The lock on the door was jiggled again. Griffin flattened behind the door. A man in black stepped through the door. Upon his face was a silver mask.

"Hold it!" ordered Griffin.

At the same time, lights snapped on. Before the men stood that notorious modern Robin Hood, the Silver Manticore. Suddenly a weird-looking gun was drawn. It had a row of glass phials hanging below the barrel. The barrel itself belonged to a doctored 1914 Mauser broom handle pistol. Griffin noted this as one of the glass phials broke behind him. He slumped to sleep. The Silver Manticore caught the falling man. He let the gas gun go but it hung from the chain. While the detectives had the Silver Manticore covered, he had one of their own.

"Back!" he ordered.

The detectives hesitated. In that second, the Silver Manticore hurled the unconscious Griffin. Shapiro and Kautz moved to catch him. Then the masked man disappeared through the door. The two men had the thrown Griffin. Only Morales managed to get after the interloper. But even he was too late. The street door slammed. Morales couldn't know that the Silver Manticore had pressed a ring of his own over his gloved finger, signaling "Emergency" to his confederate.

The Silver Manticore was out the door. Morales was slowed down by the gas. He stopped to strap a gasmask to his face, then followed. The cloud of smoke blinded him but didn't put him out.

Two more men appeared on the street. It was Shapiro and Kautz, also in gasmasks. They were tugging out guns now that they spotted their prey. The Silver Manticore didn't like how practiced these fellows were. He ran toward them, snapping a fist at one. The other one was bowled over.

Mac and Borelli were at the window of the hotel. Borelli reached for the phone when it rang.

"See anything? Manticore just gave us the slip!" rapped out Shapiro.

"He just lit out, going east on 33rd," Borelli craned his neck. "Hey, I bet he's gonna make for the trolley on the Broadway Line!"

"Now he's on Fifth," put in Mac. "Jumped into a cab. Hey, he didn't even hail it."

"See the name?"

"It's a Liberty Cab," Mac boomed. "There's Manny."

"Keep this line open," Borelli requested. "I'm coming down."

Down on the street, Morales saw the taxi, too. He took down the cab's number.

Up in the hotel, the detectives scrambled.

"Let's get down there and ask some questions," urged Macintosh.

"Take it easy, boyo," stressed Kautz. "We'll have to wait until morning to go a-calling."

"They're a taxi concern. They're open now."

"We're not cops anymore, Mac," agreed Morales. "The butter and egg man will be there in the A.M. We've had a full night. Time for doss."

In the cab, the masked man saw that his pursuers scribbled down the cab number. He turned to the driver and said, "Routine 6, Evan."

"Coming up," the driver acknowledged.

He was a Negro named Evan White and smiled. Routine 6 was nothing complicated at all. A place to do it was all that was needed. White took evasive action with a bootlegger's turn, skidding one hundred-eighty degrees.

"The trick," he narrated, "is to take a lot of turns."

However, their tail, a 1938 Buick Special four-door sedan in brown, stayed with them. White approached 10th Avenue. He turned sharply, rolling up a sidewalk and into a service station that was festooned with other yellow cabs. White killed the motor, yelping, "Down!"

The Silver Manticore complied. As he was wondering about ditching the mask, White spoke again: "There they go. I'll get the routine going."

"You know what would have been useful?" asked Colt.

"A pothole," replied White.

"Or if we could have spilled oil on the road behind us," estimated Colt.

The Buick sped past them. The Silver Manticore doffed his mask, stuffing it into a breast pocket. People at the Liberty Cab Company would recognize the face of its president, Daniel Colt. Colt reached for the two-way radio in the taxi's front.

Meanwhile, White was out of the cab. Nonchalantly, he flipped all of the cab's sixes to nines. That done, White breathed a sigh of relief.

"I got to report a stolen cab," he reminded Colt.

"Step on it," advised Colt. Back into the microphone he ordered: "Brent, requesting Routine 6 on a cab. Then have someone leave it where the cops can find it."

"Gotcha," buzzed Brent Allred over the radio.

"And then I need your help," added Colt.

"What's up?"

"I'm still curious as to just what is in that office. I'm going back and I need you to stand in for a cop."

"Danny, have you been hitting the jag juice?"

"What do you mean?"

"Outside of the cab stuff, I can't get close to this thing. I'll send Bako."

Nervously, Brent Allred piloted a falsely designated Liberty Cab. There was a reason for that. Those slick guys had gotten the number of this cab even though it wasn't the cab they saw. Allred found a parking spot and put his right side wheels way up on the sidewalk. Then he bolted. Even the densest flatfoot would note this parking abomination. Now the cops would have their hot cab.

● ● ●

Shapiro and Kautz went to the west side offices of Liberty Cabs. The pair requested an audience with company president, Daniel Colt. They were to find he was not in. Nobody of any consequence was on the overnight there.

"We're just bumping our gums here," determined Shapiro.

● ● ●

Colt and Bako had back to the office. A doorman was on duty there. Colt went up to this worthy, making introductions as: "Murphy and Woo. Them guys still in there?"

"Er, sir?" tried the doorman. "Who?"

"The boys! Come on, come on," Colt rapped. "We don't have time for this. We have the fingerprint the joint. Surely you know about the comings and goings here?"

"Well, er, there were some detectives here…"

"We'll need the passkey. Hurry up!" demanded Colt. "What's your name?"

"Er, I'm Flynn, sir."

He produced the passkey, which Colt took. The pair walked up the single flight to the office in question. A door with frosted glass proclaimed it, The Riordan Detective Agency. Colt pulled on the silver mask.

"This business was not listed in the directory down there," observed Bako.

The pair made it to Griffin's office. As silently as possible, Colt went through the door. Bako kept an eye out. Suddenly, before Bako could step in, the door was slammed from inside. The inside lock was snapped. Lights clicked on.

The Silver Manticore found himself looking down a gun. The man behind it demanded: "Raise 'em."

"Let me guess," the masked man intoned. "You're pretending to be Lance Riordan."

Bako was pounding the door.

"Well, well," Griffin considered, leaning on the door. "How do you figure?"

"Riordan left town on a case. He hasn't been back to his apartment," supplied the Silver Manticore, signaling Bako through his ring to get the Pegasus in position.

"I should have guessed you'd go there," admitted Griffin. "Saw through my bogus press junket."

"Obvious ploy to get me interested," the Silver Manticore shrugged. "There was never any evidence in the safe."

"Meet the Revenant Detective," introduced Griffin, with a slight bow. "Stay still. I know about your fighting tricks, low kicks, hand chops, using your opponent's momentum against him, all that. Be advised, I'm a good shot and an expert with this," he indicated a cane in his other hand.

"Are you going to poke me into submission?"

This particular Silver Manticore used none of the tricks Griffin had cataloged. But he was an accurate boxer. The pounding on the door continued.

"Save yourself," the Silver Manticore called through it.

"Your little partner?"

"Never mind him. Where'd you get that name?"

"Not my choice. It fits. You should criticize. You're under arrest, by the way."

"Arrest? By what authority?"

"Citizen's arrest. Off with that mask," Griffin threatened.

It was at that moment that the office door smashed inward. Griffin leveled his revolver toward it. In the second that Griffin was distracted, the Silver Manticore hefted an office chair. He warned, "Gun!"

That gun went off with a bang. But Griffin lost his grip on it. There was no more activity at the door. Bako had done his part and made a break for it. The team took no chances with guns. Griffin swung the cane up to the Silver Manticore. He attempted to block with the gas gun. The weapons connected solidly, smashing into the glass vials hanging from the gas gun. Smoke suddenly billowed from it, rolling everywhere.

In the fog, it sounded like the Revenant Detective snapped on a gas mask. Since Colt didn't like firearms, he retreated. The Silver Manticore's own gas mask was operating. Triggering pulled a chain attached to a tiny air supply under the mask. But the excess of gas created a blinding mist.

The door to the street was probably covered. The masked man broke a window with the same office chair. It was one storey to the ground. Using a tiny grappling hook and a strong silk line, he climbed out the window.

"Hey!" yelled out Griffin, materializing through the smoke cloud.

The detective grabbed a fistful of silver mask. He yanked. The Silver Manticore's hands were preoccupied with his escape line.

"Now, let's see your face!" gritted Griffin.

The mask came down. Danny Colt's eyes widened as his face was revealed. Griffin was frozen in shock. He didn't move as Colt climbed back in. The latter ducked his head forward, hiding his features. The amount of gas fogging the room may have aided Griffin in not recognizing Colt.

"Who the hell are you?" Griffin gasped. "I was expecting a crooked pol, a bad cop or..."

Colt snatched his mask out of Griffin's hand. That jolted Griffin back to life. He leaped at Colt, who turned. Griffin landed on Colt's back. He was busy adjusting the mask on his face again. Done, Colt quickly clamped Griffins hands. Then he suddenly bent, flipping Griffin over. Griffin thumped to the floor with a loud crash. The fall knocked Griffin's gasmask askew. The Silver Manticore reached over and twisted it, further spoiling Griffin's vision.

Griffin was slowed down, dealing with that development. The Silver Manticore cocked his fist. He pasted Griffin a solid punch. Griffin staggered. The Silver Manticore yanked off Griffin's gas mask. With it came the bulbous nose of Lance Riordan.

It was the Silver Manticore's turn to gasp. This caused Griffin to look around. He saw the false nose in the gas mask. The Silver Manticore acted fast, striking again. That blow dropped Griffin. The Silver Manticore caught him. Whipping off the scarf around his neck, he used this to wipe the balance of swarthy makeup off a groggy Griffin. He plucked off the bushy eyebrows. Lastly, noticing Griffin's hair looked off, the Silver Manticore snatched off the wig. He released Griffin and stood.

"I've seen that face. But where?" he asked the empty room.

There was banging at the door. The masked man strode to it, ready to admit Bako. Yanking it open, the Silver Manticore got a shock. It was Kautz and Shapiro, along with the mysterious Kelley. They bore Thompson machine guns. The Silver Manticore slammed and locked the door. Bako must have fully retreated. The Silver Manticore was headed for the window when a hand grabbed his ankle, with a feeble, "Stop!"

He turned to see the white masked Curtis trying to prevent his escape. The Silver Manticore pulled free and got out the window just as the door burst open. By the time Griffin fully had his wits back, the Silver Manticore was already on the ground, coiling up his line.

"Kelley!" coughed Griffin. "I didn't expect to see you."

"F.B.I. always backs their men up," Kelley reminded.

"F.B.I.?" echoed Griffin.

"O'Dwyer won't be mayor forever," the agent declared. "We can use a man like you."

"I almost had him," Griffin breathed.

Kelley went to the window. "O'Dwyer called me in. We decided if you could unmask the Manticore, you'd earn Bureau clearance. Congratulations."

"But he got away!"

"Not yet, he didn't," Kelley pointed out. "See his face?"

"Yes, he was a nobody," stated Griffin. "What's with all the cloak and danger stuff?"

"That's a funny question coming from you!" Kelley cracked.

"I guess you wanted to make sure I was no 90-day wonder," mused Griffin.

But Kelley had noted the naval term. Griffin must have served in the Navy, he realized. "Let's break out the big guns," he decided.

The Silver Manticore looked back and saw a figure in the window. Griffin brandished a Thompson submachine gun. The street door to the office swung open. Those same three men appeared there. It was at that second that the Pegasus screeched to a halt. Bako, at the wheel, leaned back and flung open a rear door.

"Sir!" he called.

The masked man leaped, slamming the car door. Seconds later came the staccato rhythm of bullets pounding on bullet proof glass and door. The windows spider webbed but held. And then the Pegasus peeled out and was gone.

"Holy cow! Only crooks have those Chicago typewriters!" the again unmasked Colt breathed, referring to the Thompson submachine gun.

"Also: cops or Feds," added Bako. "Boss, more trouble," Bako noted, nodding at the rearview mirror.

A car appeared, scrambling after them.

"Bad news," commented Colt.

"What can be worse than these persistent men chasing us with Tommy guns?"

"Their head honcho saw my face."

"That *is* bad," opined Bako.

"But I don't think he recognized me."

Bako floored it.

"Time for an oil change," ordered Colt.

Bako complied. From a hidden reservoir at the rear of the car, oil splashed. At the pursuing car hit it, the machine spun out of control. Then Colt, rubbernecked, got a surprise.

"The driver is fighting it! He's *good*!"

In fact, the driver almost made it out of danger. But the wheels proved to be too slick. The car finally slid into a parked car. The Pegasus sped away, turning corners. It was at that moment that radio buzzed to life.

"What happened back there?" rattled Allred over the receiver.

"'Lance Riordan' turned out to be an actor," answered Colt. "He tried to arrest me."

"Arrest you? Is he a cop now?"

"That's what we should try to find out, as soon as I think of his name. A swashbuckler type…"

• • •

Brent Allred was receiving the call he was waiting for from his government contact.

James Christopher Corrigan's gruff voice reflected stress. The line was scrambled. Catching criminals for the government was intense work.

"About what you said, that the actor Eldon Curtis III tried to arrest the Manticore?"

"And while in disguise," reminded Allred. "Highly disciplined men were working with him, had Tommy guns, gas masks, the whole bit."

"Curtis served in the Shore Patrol during the war."

"That certainly makes him a cop, of sorts," put in Allred.

"But he wanted to see combat. Apparently his father called in some favors and tried to keep him out of harm's way. But the younger wouldn't hear of it and transferred to a combat. You know what was unique about that unit?"

"I have no idea."

"It was comprised of specialists. Men who had special skills. The exact details of their missions are still sealed! Even to me."

"And this with the war long over?"

"It leads me to believe that such a unit might still have some need against the coming Soviet threat."

"So, I have no choice but to speculate."

"Feel free," suggested Corrigan. "You know, some of the members of Curtis' unit were picked off recently. By arrows."

"Was that them? We gave it big play in the *Sentry*. Some hero cop took the killer down."

"With a sword, as I recall. Well, I'm getting a clearer picture," Corrigan figured. "No cop would use a sword. But Curtis is known to be quite handy with a sword. Does all his own fencing in pictures."

Allred snapped fingers: "Curtis was somehow recruited by the cops. Maybe for menaces beyond the reach of usual channels of the law. Can you call him off?"

"Not without tipping our hand," Corrigan pointed out.

"All right, thanks for your help, Chris. I think I know what to do," he broke the connection. Allred clicked the intercom, "Miss Scott, take a letter please."

• • •

The next day, Curtis awoke to find a note from Vera. This told him she'd be out with, meeting the girls for lunch. Then he smiled when he saw the second one. At first, when he passed it, plastered to the window, he thought it a piece of litter. Then he realized it couldn't be that. They were too high up. He went to it.

An ordinary envelope was securely taped to the window, not just on it. Curtis plucked it off the window. He tore the paper and read. It was right then that he heard keys jangling at the door. It was Vera coming in.

"I went out and got those little boxes of Kellog's you like. Well, what's the matter with you?" she challenged. "You look like you've seen a ghost."

Silently, he handed her the note. She took it.

"Not some joke from you?" he checked.

"No," Vera answered. "I left you a different note."

She read: "CURTIS, I AM NOT YOUR ENEMY. DO NOT MISTAKE ME FOR A REAL CRIMINAL I FIND IT USEFUL, IN MY CAMPAIGN AGAINST CRIME, TO APPEAR AS A CRIMINAL. I WORK FROM WITHIN. YOU ARE DOING GOOD WORK. I WILL ALLOW YOU TO CONTINUE. BUT DO NOT CROSS MY PATH AGAIN!"

"What is this, Curtis?" Vera asked lowly. "And what is this image? Who sent this?"

There was no signature. Instead there was a line drawing, stamped in silver ink. Curtis took the sheet back from her.

"That art is a lion's body with a scorpion's tail and a man's head," he explained. "A manticore."

He was going to read it again. But now, upon looking, Curtis found that the ink had disappeared.

The End

The Pride of John Hardy

by Terrence McCauley

Dover Plains, Montana - 1885

John Hardy spoke loud enough for everyone in The Tin Horn to hear. "Unless that tin star stops bullets, you'd best get out of the way."

But Sheriff Aaron Mackey didn't move. He stood by Andy Johnson's side, even though Johnson didn't know it. The young man had been passed out long before Mackey had gotten there. He quietly stood where he'd been standing for the past ten minutes; listening to Hardy rant.

The cattleman reddened. "I told you I'm gonna kill that son of a bitch, and I'm going to kill him right here and now."

John Hardy's declaration had an unsettling effect on the patrons of The Tin Horn Saloon. The gamblers stopped gambling, the drunks stopped drinking and the whores quit looking for customers.

The gamblers quietly laid their cards face down and pushed their chairs away from the tables. The drunks scurried out of gun sight; taking their whiskeys with them and careful not to spill a drop. The whores slid off the laps of would-be customers and moved away from the men. They looked more impatient than scared. Violence was bad for business, but death was worse. And they were pretty sure someone would die that evening. Sheriff Mackey wasn't known for allowing insults stand.

That was why Mackey surprised them all by saying, "No one needs to die tonight. Not young Andy here. Not you either."

The cattleman's hand quivered as he pointed down at sleeping young man whose head was on the table. "That little bastard threw a drink in my face; the very same goddamned drink I'd just bought him...and then spat on me. He *spat*, goddamn it! And for no good reason either. Did you hear what I said, Mackey?"

Mackey had heard him. He'd heard him the first three times Hardy had yelled it at the top of his lungs. But Mackey kept that to himself. Arguing would just make Hardy angrier than he already was. "And I told you he'll spend the night in jail for what he did. Going to get one hell of a fine too. Drunk and disorderly. Resisting arrest. Disturbing the peace and half a dozen other things I can come up with between now and when he wakes up tomorrow."

"Fines don't make up for him spitting on me."

Mackey knew Hardy was a good, hard working man. But he saw the look in the cattleman's eyes and heard the edge in his voice and knew he just might have to kill him. He didn't want to do that. "I plan on giving him a work detail, too. Order him to clean out your stables or feed your livestock for a month if you want. Hell, we'll make it two months."

"Let him on my property? So I can be reminded of the shame he caused me every goddamned day?"

As drunk as Hardy was, Mackey admired his persistence. "The boy buried his old man today, John. If a man ever deserved any leeway...."

"Ain't no leeway when it comes to spitting on me, Aaron." Hardy lowered his hand toward the holster on his right hip, but stopped just above it. "If you won't do what needs doing, I will. Best stand aside before you get hurt."

But Mackey didn't move. His right hand had been resting on his belt...next to the belly holster to the left of his belt buckle…since Hardy had walked back into the saloon. Mackey had made sure to stand so the Colt's handle was already facing Hardy. The sheriff had worn his gun in that fashion since his cavalry days. He liked the edge the easy draw gave him either on horseback or on foot. It had worked well against the Apache.

It had worked even better against town drunks.

"Don't do anything you won't live long enough to regret, John."

Hardy's face quivered as his eyes narrowed. "I ain't never backed down from no man."

"I know. I've heard that before."

Hardy's right hand grew very still above his pistol. "And I'll be goddamned if I start now."

"Yeah. I've heard that before, too." He'd always known John Hardy to be a reasonable man whenever he'd come to town to sell his cattle. It was the only reason why the sheriff had abided the man's yelling for as long as he had. He tried one last time to appeal to that side of the man now. "Goddamn it, John. I know you're angry, but you're not a bad man. You're a husband and a father. You're a trail boss used to campfire scrapes and rowdy cowhands. But you're not on the trail now and I'm not one of your cowhands. This is a saloon in my town. Don't make me kill you."

Mackey could almost feel the air in the saloon change, the way it always changed before lead flew. None of the drunks or whores or gamblers had made a sound since Hardy had started yelling, but their fearful expectation was palpable; like a strong wind pushing Hardy toward the decision he'd come to. If it had just been Hardy, Mackey and the boy, maybe Mackey could have backed him down.

But it wasn't just the three of them. Hardy had an audience now; half of them afraid he'd go for his gun and the other half hoping he would. Too many people had seen Johnson spit on him. Reason had no place where pride was involved.

Mackey had seen pride kill far too many people to doubt what would happen next.

Hardy's hand dropped to his pistol.

Mackey drew and fired. The bullet caught Hardy in the chest, but the cattleman was too big to go down. He reached for his gun once more and Mackey fired again; hitting him high just below the throat.

Hardy's body tumbled backward through the batwing doors onto the boardwalk on Front Street. With his Colt still in hand, Mackey pushed his way through the customers who had managed to find their legs again as they rushed to look at the freshly dead man.

Mackey let his Colt lead the way through the batwing doors; just in case there was any fight left in the cattleman.

But one look at Hardy and Mackey knew his fight was over. His vacant eyes stared up at the stars on a cloudless Montana evening. Mackey took a knee and slid the gun from Hardy's holster anyway. Dead men may not be able to hurt you, but there was no harm in being certain. He hadn't lived this long by taking any chances.

As was his custom, the sheriff searched Hardy's pockets for valuables. He liked to collect all property and catalogue it in front of witnesses so no one could claim anything had been stolen from the corpse later. He found a wad of cash in the inside pocket of the cattleman's jacket. A quick count came up five hundred dollars.

A crowd of Tin Horn customers and regular townspeople had gathered around to gape down at the body of John Hardy. They also stole glances at the man who had shot him while they murmured amongst themselves. Dead bodies weren't a foreign sight to the people of Dover Plains. It was why they had hired a man like Mackey to be sheriff in the first place.

But in the two years since Mackey had returned to his hometown and became sheriff, dead men on Front Street had become an increasingly infrequent sight in the small Montana town.

Mackey tucked his Colt back into his belly holster and held up the cash for all to see. "I want all of you to see that I have taken five hundred dollars from John Hardy's pockets. I will hold this money and his horse on behalf of the town until someone lays rightful claim to his possessions."

Another wave of murmurs rippled through the crowd like coffee percolating in a pot until Sam Warren, the owner of the Tin Horn, pushed his way through the onlookers and onto the boardwalk. He was a round little man who seemed to be constantly drying his on the white apron stretched taut across his belly. "Aaron, I'm awfully sorry this happened. Maybe I should've…"

But Mackey was in no mood to hear the fat man's nonsense. "Maybe I should lock you up right now."

"Me? Shit, Aaron. What the hell for?"

"For letting young Andy get drunk enough to start all this nonsense."

Warren actually tucked his thumbs under his apron. "I'm a business owner, Aaron, no different than the dress maker or the general store down the street. A man comes in to my place and wants whiskey, and if he can pay, why should I refuse him?"

"Dressmakers and general store clerks don't get people blind drunk, Sam. And just because Andy's old man left him a pile of money when he died, that doesn't give you the right to try to take it from him in one night." Mackey looked down at Hardy's corpse and felt a new level of anger course through him. Hardy's death was a waste and Mackey hated waste. "Christ, Sam. We already had one funeral this morning. Now this. Not to mention all the shit his death will stir up when his men drive that herd into town looking to get paid."

Warren began wiping his hands on his apron again. "Shit." A good amount of the Tin Horn's customers were cowboys who spent their earnings in his saloon after driving a herd into town. The death of Hardy, their boss and paymaster, would affect that. "Shit," he said again.

"Well said, you stupid bastard." Mackey raised his voice to speak to anyone within earshot. "Does anyone have any idea how long Hardy has been in town?"

An old timer named Bill pointed a long, crooked finger at the wad of money in Mackey's hand. "Long enough to get an advance on the cattle he's bringing, I'd reckon."

"Maybe a couple of hours at most," added one of the men Mackey knew to be a gambler. "I saw him come in here all smiles and buy the house a couple of rounds. Him and young Andy seemed to be getting along just fine until the boy took offense to something John had said and spat on him. Things kinda went to shit soon after."

"Which is when I sent one of my men to come get you," Sam Warren said. "Hardy stormed off came back heeled just after you got here."

Some men would've asked for more particulars, but Mackey knew particulars didn't matter anymore. Because John Hardy was dead and his men would soon be bringing his cattle to town. They would be looking for their payday and, most likely, wouldn't be happy with the man who had just killed their boss.

Mackey spotted a burly red-nose known as 'Robbie' Robinson leaning against the doorway of the saloon and asked him, "You sober enough to go fetch Doc Ridley?"

Robinson shrugged. "Can't say for certain." He pushed himself off the doorway as if to test his balance. The big man was a bit wobbly, but stayed upright. Upon further consideration, he said, "Probably."

"Then go get him. Tell him to bring his wagon and haul Hardy away until his men come to collect him. And no drinking along the way, Robbie, or I swear to Christ, you'll be lying on Doc Ridley's table next to him."

Robinson swore he would not touch a drop as he went off to find the town's doctor. Then, Mackey turned to Sam Warren. "I want you to write down everything that happened here on a sheet of paper and sign it. I want everyone else who can sign or make their mark to do the same right under your signature. Make sure you bring it over to me at the jail when you're done. Just do it as soon as possible. You've got half an hour. Any delay, and what I just said to Robbie goes for you too."

The bar owner looked genuinely hurt. "Jesus, Aaron. You've got no call to be threatening me. I'm only tryin' to help."

Mackey stared down at Hardy's corpse, and then looked back into the bar at young Andrew still lying passed out at the table. The drunken bastard had no notion of how close he'd come to getting killed. "You've helped enough for one day."

● ● ●

Mackey threw the drunken Andrew over the saddle of John Hardy's horse and led both man and beast up Front Street to the jailhouse at the edge of town.

Dover Plains may not have been Chicago or St. Louis, but it was a prosperous town by Montana standards. The lumber, mining, farming and ranching industries all thrived in the lands around town limits, so Dover Plains had the resources to build a solid jail to house its criminals. After leaving the cavalry and being elected sheriff, Mackey had made sure the jail was built to his standards: a solid two-story stone building that was impervious to bullets and nearly impossible to burn down. He remembered the townspeople had balked at the cost of such a building, but no one had voiced their objections to him.

Upon reaching the jailhouse, Mackey heaved Andrew off the dead man's horse and dumped him on the cot in a cell in the back. The young man was still so drunk, he'd barely stirred.

A familiar knock came at the jailhouse door before a rattle of keys opened it. His father, Brendan "Pappy" Mackey, let himself in and shut the door behind him. He held a Winchester in his right hand and an impressive ring of keys in his left. What Mackey's father lacked in height, he made up for with broad shoulders, a barrel chest and the powerful arms of a blacksmith. He had a full white beard, despite only having just turned fifty that past April, but looks were deceiving where the elder Mackey was concerned. He had the strength and temperament of most men half his age.

Although Pappy had been in America since before the War Between the States, he had never lost the brogue of his homeland. "Heard you have yourself a spot of trouble, boy."

Mackey locked Andrew's cell. "Nothing I can't handle. Best get back to your hardware store and keep your head down."

"Not a chance." The elder Mackey grinned. "Word is there's a fight comin' and I aim to be in the thick of it."

Which was exactly why he didn't want his father anywhere near the jail when Hardy's cow punchers got there. The old man's fighting spirit had gotten him a chest full of medals when he'd served with Sherman, but Mackey didn't want him, or his mouth, sparking a fight with Hardy's men.

"With Billy and Sim running that drover down to Butte," Mackey said of his two deputies, "I'm shorthanded. I need you to make sure the rest of the townspeople are armed and ready when Hardy's men come to town."

"Nonsense. You can get any idiot to do that."

Mackey picked up the coffee pot from the stove and poured himself a cup. "That's why I'm asking you to do it."

Pappy didn't move. "Disrespectful bastard. Talkin' to your father that way."

Mackey knew the only thing his father loved more than a fight was an argument. His oratory skills were the stuff of legend. He was known to be able to carry on the same argument for weeks, even months. It was a quality Mackey found tiresome even in the best of times and a hindrance in times such as this. "I don't have time for your bullshit, Pap, and neither does the town. Someone's probably already ridden out to tell John Hardy's men what happened here, so when they come, they'll come shooting. I need everyone who can hold a rifle up and ready to fight by the time they get here. Don't worry. If things start popping, you'll get your fill of blood."

Still, the elder Mackey didn't budge. "Alright. I'll get them armed, but then I'm comin' right back here. I don't like the notion of you bein' here alone."

"I'll be fine. But I'll need you and the others ready to back me up if the ball goes up."

Mackey had never won an argument with his father in all his twenty-seven years, so he was surprised when Pappy relented so easily. "Think things will break that way?"

Mackey took a swig of coffee, then reached up and took his Winchester down from the rifle rack on the wall next to his desk. "We'll find out soon enough."

● ● ●

Later, from his seat in his rocking chair on the boardwalk in front of the jailhouse, Mackey watched the torches along the street flicker in the chilly night wind blowing down Front Street. He'd ordered all the torches in town to be lit in advance of Hardy's men coming to town to give him a better range of vision. He thought they made a nice effect against the darkness. It would've been a downright peaceful sight if he'd ordered them lit for a different purpose. He decided he might order them lit every night from now on; to give the town a certain elegance.

That is, if he lived that long.

Mackey knew a man his age was far too young to take up a rocking chair; a habit which caused no shortage of consternation and amusement among the citizens of Dover Plains. But the gentle rocking motion served to calm his nerves in ways neither liquor nor women nor tobacco ever had. And if there was ever a time he need serenity, it was now in the moments before a confrontation.

He had finally assumed a steady, gentle rhythm to his rocking when he heard an unmistakable rumbling through the clear night air. He'd heard the sound before; a group of riders coming down the hill that led into town.

Riders, not cattle. A bad sign. Mackey kept rocking.

He'd figured that if Hardy's men rode into town with their cattle, it would mean they probably hadn't been told of what had happened to John Hardy. They'd have their herd to tend to they might be less ready for gunplay.

But since they were riding into town alone, Mackey figured word of the shooting must have already reached them.

That meant they'd be ready for battle.

So was Mackey.

The Winchester was propped up against the wall beside him. The Colt on his belly holster was loaded.

Mackey kept rocking slow and steady as he watched seven riders come out of the darkness and rein in their mounts to a trot as they reached Front Street. Even from that

distance, Mackey could see horses and men alike looked trail-lean and dusty from their long trek up to Montana from Texas.

He knew the jailhouse was easy to spot from the edge of town, especially with the torches lit, and it didn't take long for the group to ride toward him.

Mackey didn't get up to greet the seven strangers or show that he'd noticed them in any way. He simply kept rocking back and forth at his same steady pace. This was by design, for a man in a rocking chair was easier to talk to than a sheriff with his hand on his gun.

Especially when that sheriff had just killed the man who was supposed to pay them.

In Mackey's experience, odd numbers usually meant one clear leader of a group. He wagered this group was no different. A thin, tan man who looked more *vaquero* than cowpuncher surprised him by spurring his horse ahead of the others. He drew up his mount just in front of the jailhouse. "You Mackey?"

Mackey kept rocking. "Sheriff Mackey, if you want to be proper about it. I take it you and your boys work for John Hardy."

"I am Ricardo Narvaez," the man said in a slight accent, "and we *did* work for John Hardy. Right up until you gunned him down."

Even in the dim, flickering light of the torch, Mackey could see that Narvaez's eyes were dark, yet clear with intent and purpose. Trying to buffalo a man like this would be a waste of time and probably do more harm than good. He kept his tone civil and plain. "I didn't gun him down. It was self-defense."

"So you say. Others say different."

Mackey kept rocking. "I hear you boys rode with Hardy all the way up from Texas."

"What of it?"

"I knew John Hardy pretty well. And seeing as how you rode all the way up here with him, I'd wager you knew him pretty well too, so you probably know he wasn't an easy man to back down."

"Not when he knew he was in the right," Narvaez said. "And from what we've heard, he had every right to kill the miserable drunken bastard who spat on him."

From the edge of the darkness, Mackey heard the six other riders grumble their consent.

"That might be the law out on the prairie, but in my town, drunks get jailed. They don't get killed. And people who threaten me get one chance to change their mind. Hardy had plenty of chances to walk away. He didn't."

"Again, so you say."

"I gave Hardy plenty of room to let it go but he went for his gun instead. And I've got a saloon full of witnesses to prove it."

"Cowards who would gladly put their name to any piece of paper you put in front of them no matter what it said." Narvaez leaned over and spat into the thoroughfare. "That is what I think of your witnesses."

Mackey smiled and kept rocking. "Everybody's a critic."

But Narvaez didn't smile. "We heard John didn't even clear leather before you gunned him down."

"You heard a lot in a short amount of time."

"Is it true?"

"People don't live too long by letting others shoot first."

"We heard you stripped his body and paraded his corpse around town."

In all his years in the Army and as a sheriff, he'd always been amazed how far the re-telling of a story could fall from the truth. "No one paraded his body anywhere. Doc Ridley loaded it onto his wagon and is keeping him over at his office as we speak."

"And his possessions?"

"I took John's gun out of his holster along with the money he had on him. Five hundred dollars, cash money that I guess he got from the sale of your herd. I'll be happy to hand over his whole rig to anyone who can prove they have a rightful claim to his property."

Narvaez gestured toward the six men behind him. "That is why we are here. We wish to claim his property right now. We are also laying claim to the drunk who led to his death as well."

Mackey looked down the street to where the cattle pens were. "Looks like the cattle broker's gone home for the evening, boys, but you or your paymaster can see him first thing tomorrow about squaring away the balance of whatever pay you boys have coming to you."

"This sounds fair," Narvaez allowed. "And the drunk?"

Mackey kept rocking. "Afraid you boys are going to be disappointed on that score. The boy's under arrest and he's going to stay that way."

"Then you're going to have to un-arrest him."

Mackey stopped rocking. "No."

When he saw the six men other men look at each other, he knew they weren't fighters. They were trail hands in this for the money and Mackey had already settled that question fairly. There was no profit in fighting for a drunken kid.

But Narvaez didn't look at them. He only looked at Mackey. "We heard John Hardy wanted the drunk, but you stopped him."

"I did."

"But he was just one man. How do you think you'd fare against seven?"

Mackey looked at the others, then at Narvaez. "About the same."

"You cannot really believe that."

"I do."

Narvaez looked at Mackey but raised his voice so the others could hear. "You boys might as well head back to camp. Be sure to tell the others to get a good night's rest. We'll bring the cattle into town at first light."

The rider on Narvaez's left looked relieved. "That's fine, boss, but ain't you comin' with us?"

Narvaez stayed where he was. "Sheriff Mackey and I still have a few matters to discuss. Perhaps I can make him listen to reason."

The sheriff and the *vaquero* kept looking at each other as the six riders wheeled their mounts and went back to the herd. It wasn't long before it was just the two of them on Front Street. The sound of the torches mixed with the gentle wind blowing up Front Street, carrying the smells and the sounds from the Tin Horn Saloon with it. Mackey figured most of the townspeople were breathing a sigh of relief and had already begun to put their rifles away.

Everyone except Pappy, somewhere in the shadows.

And Sheriff Aaron Mackey.

The *vaquero* sat up straighter in the saddle; showing Mackey he wore his gun across his belly, just like Mackey. "Quiet tonight, isn't it, marshal?"

"I'm no marshal, just a sheriff. And Dover Plains is a careful town. Started up by old war vets like my old man who believe there is prudence in precaution." He shrugged. "Guess they passed it along to me."

"John Hardy was a prudent man, too," Narvaez said. "He taught me a lot about life. He taught me how to stand up for what is right and how to put an end to that which is wrong."

"Words to live by. But I ordered him to walk away and he went for his gun instead. And now he's dead and there's nothing that'll bring him back."

"Perhaps," Narvaez allowed, "but the dead can always be avenged."

"Seen my share of death, son. Never saw any avenging in it. Just more death."

Narvaez wasn't smiling anymore. "I am not your son. But John Hardy was like a father to me."

"He was a good man," Mackey said. "You said he taught you a lot of things. Best learn from his last mistake and ride on back to your herd."

"John Hardy was full of drink when you shot him. I am not."

Narvaez's hand flicked from the saddle horn toward his gun handle.

Mackey drew clean and smooth from his rocking chair and fired twice. The first shot hit the vaquero in the chest. The second bullet tore through his throat.

The gun shots made Narvaez's horse rear up on its hind legs; its forelegs kicking into the air. Narvaez's body dropped from the saddle and onto the thoroughfare as his horse turned and bolted up the hill; most likely back to the cattle camp outside of town.

Mackey eased out of his rocking chair and slowly stepped off the boardwalk. He kept his gun aimed down at Narvaez, for the *vaquero* was still alive. He was gasping for air through the new wound in his throat. Despite being in the throes of a slow death, Narvaez's gun arm twitched up when he saw the sheriff standing over him. Mackey calmly stepped across Narvaez and pinned the arm to the ground with his shoe.

As the *vaquero* looked up at the sheriff, Mackey saw that not even the approach of death had dimmed the hatred in the man's eyes.

Mackey could've gloated. He could've said something. He could've ended Narvaez's suffering with a squeeze of the trigger.

But he didn't. He simply kept the man's wrist pinned to the packed dirt of Front Street and watched him die. He figured he deserved at least that much dignity. His death may be senseless, but it was his own.

With a final twitch and a gurgle, Narvaez joined John Hardy in whatever lay beyond death.

Mackey bent to take Narvaez's pistol from his hand before holstering his own. As he stood, he saw some of the townspeople had begun to fill the boardwalks along Front Street. Mackey knew they'd be brave with curiosity now that the shooting had stopped. In between the heads of the gathering crowd, he spotted Pappy in front of his general store across the street. His Winchester was still in his hand as he tried to stem the tide of people spilling out of the buildings that lined the thoroughfare.

He ignored the murmur of questions that began to cycle through the gathering crowd. He knew listening to them would be pointless. They weren't looking for answers, merely to speculate on what had happened and why. Some would make him out to be a villain who'd just gunned down two men for the sake of a lowly drunk. Others would make him out to be the hero who'd faced down two gunmen in defense of the town.

That was why Mackey didn't listen to them, or care what they said. Public opinion was a fickle business.

He knew what he'd done and he knew why. His own reasons were the only constant in his line of work. His reasons were the only ones that mattered.

The murmur of the crowd rose as they shuffled to make way for Pappy, who'd used the Winchester to clear a path through the townspeople. When he got next to his son, he said, "Good shooting, son."

Mackey wasn't in the mood for compliments. "Shit, Pappy. He was sitting right in front of me."

"Glad to see you can take a compliment." He nodded down at Narvaez's body. "Think that's the end of it?"

Mackey thought of Narvaez's horse galloping through the darkness, up the distant hill and out of town. He wondered if it would ride back to the herd. He wondered what the other cowboys would do when it got there.

He opened the cylinder of the Colt, removed the two dead cartridges and replaced them with new rounds. "If it isn't, I'll be ready."

The End

The Sandman
(A Cape Noire story)
by Drew Meyer

Chief of Detectives, Dan Rains sat at his desk in his second floor office, his head in his hands. He sighed deeply, rubbed his eyes, and checked his coffee mug for the third time in as many minutes, and reassured that it hadn't magically refilled itself, attempted to focus his blurred vision on the stack of missing persons reports which sat in an untidy pile before him.

He eyed the small uncomfortable couch in the corner with mixed emotions. He had tried, on numerous occasions to catch a quick nap—just some shut-eye to keep him going. He thought if he could just sleep, he could catch a break—catch something he missed, but time was of the essence and a little girl's life was at stake. Cape Noire's most driven lawman stifled a yawn and went back to work.

The detective had been awake for the better part of three days; what little sleep he'd gotten came in fitful bursts. He stared at the thirteen reports. Until a few days ago the active detectives on the individual cases had deemed that they had no connection— no similarities in age, social status, sex—nothing to link the cases. Witnesses saw the victims during the day and by that night, they were gone.

It wasn't uncommon for people to go missing in Cape Noire. In a city torn apart by mob violence, where the wicked whispered stories of a supernatural avenger in search of redemption, a few missing people wasn't all that bad. In fact, it was more common than Detective Rains was comfortable with.

What was uncommon was the lack of evidence. Usually when someone disappeared they showed back up within a week. Sometimes by the docks, sometimes in a dumpster... but the bodies, reminders that they were once part of the machine of this city, they usually showed up. There were no bodies in this case. Thirteen lives just disappeared from the streets of Cape Noire. Rains hadn't become Chief of Detectives by sitting idle; if those people could be found, he'd find them.

A few of the missing persons made sense. Niles Gottlieb and Aleister Dale were hoods who lived dangerous lives; going missing was practically in their job description. They weren't the first ones reported. Their wives were used to late nights and "business weekends" so they didn't say anything until their husbands were gone for more than a week. One of the ladies missing, Claire Appleton, walked the streets and went by the name "Molly Apples." Rains had brought her in a few times. She ran with a bad crowd, but he always thought she seemed like a good girl. Until a few days ago, each of these cases had been treated as separate—hell, some of them still might be—but everything changed with Abbie Right.

Abbie was seven years old. Her family reported her missing when she didn't come home for dinner three days ago. He looked over her physical description: small, white, and last seen in what passed for a Sunday dress. She had lost her first tooth the night before her disappearance. Her family lived in one of the poorer neighborhoods of Old Town; so that morning, when she found a nickel under her pillow from the tooth fairy, she rushed out to show her friends. She never came back home.

● ● ●

Across town in a coldwater flat, a figure sat in a room dimly lit by a single candle. There was no sound of breathing to disturb the calm of the silent room. The figure focused its black, lifeless eyes on the miniscule flame.

It was unusual for the candle to exist in such a state. It usually remained as lifeless as the figure tasked to snuff out those who harmed the innocent. Brother Bones, the Undead Avenger, sat motionless and mission-less, waiting for the flame to once more take on the countenance of the teenage girl whose life he had extinguished, back when he walked a wicked path. But instead the candle had remained lit—giving off no heat, no message, and no instructions. Still, unmoving, un-breathing, he watched with black, lifeless eyes.

Then suddenly, the candle flared.

● ● ●

Rains felt himself begin to slip into unconsciousness. Somewhere in the half light he heard the pleasant sound of waves on a beach; he turned to his companion to tell her how happy he was that they were finally taking this vacation together when she turned to him and said, "C'mon Detective, we've got to go!"

Detective Rains woke with a start, the water's gentle lapping replaced by the sound of fingers rapping on glass.

"Boss, c'mon! They found a body by the docks."

The weary detective rose from behind his desk, the makings of a world class headache beginning to brew behind his eyes, and headed to the door. A hot cup of coffee was thrust into his free hand as soon as he exited his office. It was bitter and strong and tasted awful, but it was just what he needed to keep him going for another hour.

● ● ●

The body was fresh, full of holes, and leaking everywhere. Even in his sleep deprived state, Rains could see that a powerful weapon had lifted the heavy man off his feet and sent him flying into the wall behind. One of the tech guys pulled a bullet out of the bloody wreckage that used to be the victim's chest—one of many. Rains held out his palm and felt the warm weight of the .45 slug in his hand. The bad news was this victim wasn't one of Rains' missing persons. The good news was one less mobster was walking the streets of Cape Noire. "Bones," he said within earshot of a rookie patrolman.

"Oh c'mon detective, are you saying this guy was bumped off by some boogieman created to scare mobsters?" The young patrolman couldn't have been more than a few months out of the academy. "Brother Bones has gotta be fake, right?"

Rains eyed the patrolman and motioned with his head, "Tell that to this guy."

Rains recognized the victim. The body once belonged to the name Eddie "Big Mouth" Spinelli. Spinelli had run with the Boss of Old Town, until Brother Bones arrived. It wasn't surprising to find him by the docks; Spinelli did more than fish from this particular pier. He owned the bait shop in which they were standing. Of course, the shop was a front for Spinelli's smuggling operation.

Another detective held out an evidence bag and Rains dropped the slug in to join three more just like it. "We found five shells, but only four wounds in Spinelli."

Rains made his way to the register, making sure to step over the pool of blood, and looked behind the counter to where Spinelli had kept his bait. He pointed to the icebox; now open thanks to a large hole punched through its lock. "Shot number five."

Rains opened the icebox; he sort of wished he hadn't. "Okay, somebody find a bag and get these pieces out of here, I want an ID on this body, and look for a murder weapon, probably a cleaver or large knife."

Rain's head was killing him. It felt like whatever bullets tore through Spinelli were ricocheting in his own skull. He made his way out to the patrol car, checking the glove compartment for something to ease the pain. A road map, registration, a glove—nothing useful.

It took several hours to gather the evidence, interview possible witnesses, and cordon off the area. Once he was no longer needed at the scene, Rains headed back to the station. On the way he decided to stop by Abbie's neighborhood. Last time he was there he had seen a pharmacy, and it was on his list of places to visit for his investigation. A few of the missing persons had lived or worked within the vicinity; Rains wanted to show their pictures to the pharmacist who worked there...see if he could give the detective any leads—and Rains really needed to do something about this headache.

The neighborhood had seen better days, and for Old Town, that was saying something. The pharmacy was one of the few buildings in the area that hadn't been condemned. Several years back, Old Town's top boss, Big Swede Jorgenson had planned to knock down most of this block. The idea was to raze the neighborhood and build a hotel and casino, give the place a touch of class. His men had been very persuasive in convincing the local tenants to skedaddle. Big Swede's dreams died when he was set on fire. Now the little pharmacy was the only business keeping its head above water. It looked so small surrounded by the tall tenement buildings, now condemned and empty...home now only to the homeless.

The door to the pharmacy opened with the tinny ring of a bell. Rains found the aspirin on a small display near the register, next to the bright red five-cent lollipops and the day's newspapers whose headlines spoke of more injustice in his city. He managed a weak smile to the pharmacist behind the counter. "You look like you could use some sleep, detective." Rains mumbled something about wishful thinking, made his way to the water fountain, downed a handful of pills and made his way back to the car, his feet feeling heavier with each weighted step.

● ● ●

Brother Bones, the hit man turned Undead Avenger, settled back down in his chair in the lonely apartment and waited. Something was wrong. Spinelli had been a wicked man, and the small figure in the flames had told him of the wicked man's transgressions, but Bones could tell there was something else she wanted to tell him. She was always direct with him. He was no judge; he didn't decide who was no longer worthy to walk the city he protected. That wasn't his job. He was a weapon. She told him where to aim and he pulled the trigger. It wasn't a perfect existence, but it was more than he deserved. He once walked the path of the same men and women he now hunted. He wasn't given a second chance, this was penance—a sentence with no hope for parole.

● ● ●

Back at the precinct, Rains looked sadly at the report. The body in Spinelli's icebox hadn't been identified, but it was definitely *not* one of his missing persons. The phone rang. It was city reporter, Sally Paige. *The Tribune* wanted to run a story on the bodies found at the dock and Sally had sweet-talked her way (again) passed the switchboard operator and was now setting her sights on Rains for the "scoop." As much as he wanted to hear her voice, Rains wasn't about to settle in to be interrogated. He knew she didn't want to cast aspersions on the department's ability to find a child. "Diligently searching" and "in the capable hands of the precinct," were her way of putting a positive spin when *The Tribune's* readers were out for blood.

Rains was missing something, he was sure of it, it was only a matter of seeing things clearly. He yawned and reached for the coffee, knocking it and the bottle of aspirin off his desk and onto the floor with a crash. He dejectedly watched as the remnants of his coffee soaked into the remainder of the aspirin. "Looks like its back to the pharmacy."

● ● ●

Leaving the office felt like defeat...like he had thrown in the towel. The cry of Justice was being drowned out by the siren song of sleep. Rains hated to admit he was of no use to anyone in his current condition. Hell, he probably shouldn't even be behind the wheel.

Of course the pharmacy was closed when he got there, in his state he hadn't even noticed the sun was setting. Hoping someone would still be in the store, Rains made his way to the front door and peered inside. His head was killing him. The lights were off, no one was moving inside the shop. He could see the aspirin right by the counter...right by the nickel lollipops. The aching in his head slowed for a moment; like something parting... there was something he was missing....lollipops.... nickel...

Rains squinted, squeezed his eyes, and rubbed his temples, trying to coax a cognitive thought. What if...what if the connection wasn't with the people, but with a location? What if they.... A door slammed somewhere behind the pharmacy. The seasoned detective went for his gun, fumbled with empty space, and realized...he had left it at the office.

"Rookie mistake Rains." He cursed his lack of sleep. He cursed his throbbing head. But he knew that excuses wouldn't save Abbie Right. He made his way, quietly, to the alley behind the pharmacy. It was dark and smelled of piss and garbage. The street light barely registered, flickering on and off without a discernible pattern. Rains made his way to the back door and checked to see if it was open. No such luck. Another slam came from the end of the alley, by the blacked form of one of the abandoned tenements. "Probably squatters," Rains muttered doubtfully as he made his way toward the noise.

The bottom floor of the building was deserted, but further investigation brought the detective to a locked door. The door was old, but the lock was new, brand new. He scanned the ground and settled on a piece of rebar. He made a small racket, but the lock eventually hit the floor with a satisfying *clang*.

The door opened and a powerful aroma assaulted his senses, woke him up. He couldn't place the smell, but it put him on edge. Stairs led down to another door, not locked, but from behind it, Rains could hear a rhythmic hum. It was faint, no way to have heard it from upstairs. Not certain what he'd find, Rains held his breath, wished he'd brought his revolver, and pushed the door open.

It was horrible. For a moment, Rains wished he *had* fallen asleep, that this was a nightmare. The room was feebly lit by the interior lights of some tremendous machine, located in the center of the room. Green and red bulbs blinked, alternating in a slow rhythm. Something within the machine gave a menacing hiss. Pumps, like bellows, rose and fell sending air into...people?

Pump pu-pump pump pu-pump.

Like the spokes of some hideous wheel, Rains saw a dozen tables radiating from the central machine. On each lay a body, most beneath sheets, each rising and falling in rhythm with the machine. With only the light of the machine to see by, Rains walked to the closest table and removed the sheet from its occupant's resting face.

Pump pu-pump pump pu-pump.

Rains didn't want to recognize the face, but three days staring at case reports had burned the image of each missing person into his sleep-deprived brain. Rains blanched, death would have been preferable to...whatever this was. Aleister Dale, thirty-three years of age, husband to Gloria Dale, an ex-con who worked Old Town as a pimp— his face barely visible from under the tubes inserted into his mouth and nose, his eyes closed—breathing in and out to the rhythm of the machine. His arms and legs were held tight by leather straps.

Pump pu-pump pump pu-pump.

The room was rank with the smell of antiseptic, bleach, and human waste. A group of monitors on the central machine beeped in rhythm with each other.

Rains went to the next table...he didn't recognize the face...older man, unkempt, dirty...smelled of liquor. This victim was bleeding under the restraints...like he'd been fighting, struggling against his bonds. Rains went back to Dale, similar marks under his restraints, but scabbed over, as if they'd been made many days prior.

Pump pu-pump pump pu-pump.

The next form was smaller than the first two. He hesitantly pulled back the sheet. It was Abbie. His first instinct was to remove her from the machine—get her to safety, but Rains was no doctor—if he made a mistake he risked doing more harm than good.

Pump pu-pump pump pu-pump.

The first blow came quietly and forcefully, the impact of something heavy to the back of his skull sending him to the ground. Rains had taken some licks in his day. You didn't grow up on the streets of Cape Noire without learning how to take a hit, but his body was reeling from fatigue. Fuelled by his considerable will to overcome, the detective attempted to rise. The second blow landed across the small of his back and he fell forward. Scrambling to keep his balance, he felt his hand close around something small and solid. He tried to stay on his feet, but the object in his hand broke free. Blackness overwhelmed him, and part of him welcomed it.

● ● ●

Rains wasn't sure how long he'd been unconscious, but when he came to, the lights were on. He was on the floor, his back against the infernal machine. A blurred figure stood over him. Was the figure wearing a white coat? Rains had trouble focusing on anything but the pain. His hearing came in waves...

"...you couldn't leave well enough alone could you?" Rains couldn't focus his eyes, something was in them and it stung. He felt something small in his hand; he gave it a squeeze, hoping it was his gun. Of course it wasn't, too small. Above him, the figure was still talking, barely audible above the hissing and the pumping.

Pump pump-pupump pump pu-pumpump. There was something wrong; different...it wasn't the same as before.

The figure continued, "...here by myself, a perfect, restful spot...they could get some sleep."

Who was this? Rains wiped his eyes, and his hands came away sticky...blood....his...

"...knew someone would find me out, but thought it would be after the building was destroyed, in the rubble...don't worry, they're not dead...just asleep....I've kept them here, sleeping, safe and sound asleep..."

Rains tried to focus on his voice. His voice sounded familiar...

Pump pump-pupump pump pu-pumpump.

"...kept them safe, kept them clean. I took care of them, let them rest. Rest is so good for your health. I gave them the sleep I could never have....sleep without dreams...see how quiet they are...so well rested...sometimes I sing to them...sing them to sleep..."

The pumping above Rains' head changed again. The *pu-pumps* increased for a moment then faltered.

...pu......pump.......pu......pump.......pu.......

The pumping stopped and a small high pitched squeal emanated from the machine.

"No! No, no, no, no!" The figure in the white coat moved out of Rain's blurred eye-line, toward the machine. "What have you done? What have you done to the machine?"

Rains was confused. What *had* he done? He looked down at the object in his hand.... what was it...looked like part of a ...

"Noooo!" The figure wailed. "She was just a girl! I was trying to protect her, I gave her pleasant dreams...I saw how miserable her life was...she could stay asleep and never have to be a part of this wretched place...and you....you KILLED her!"

The figure was close enough to Rains' poorly focused eyes to recognize...the pharmacist.

"Look what you've done...you've taken her away from me!" The pharmacist raised his hands and Rains had just enough time to raise his own arms to defend his face before the rebar came crashing down on him. The pain was excruciating, but once more he felt a jolt demanding his brain to wake up. Adrenaline pumping, Rains reached for the metal rod, and missed!

Again the rebar came down, and again Rains blocked it, pain shooting through his body. He kicked out with his legs and made contact. The pharmacist howled and fell to the floor. Rains tried to command his body to move, to act, but he just lay there. The pharmacist rose with a growl.

Standing over him, rebar in hand, Rains could see the gleam of murder in the man's eyes. The pharmacist sneered, "I'm not done with you Detective Rains. With the others I used chemicals, drugs....an added dose here, a splash there in their prescriptions. All I had to do was follow them home and collect them. Sometimes, if the store wasn't busy, I'd move them to here. Young Abbie just wanted a lollipop and so I gave her a "special" one. She drifted off to sleep so quickly." He placed his hand, almost tenderly, on the little girl's forehead. "You're going to take her place detective. I'm going to give you the sleep you need...the rest you deserve...you'll have plenty of time to rest...to heal...so I suppose a few more of these won't matter too much...for taking her away from me..."

Rains braced for the blow, the sharp pain...but instead there was a flash of light and the room filled with thunder. Two gaping holes appeared in the pharmacist's coat as he was lifted off the ground and thrown against the machine. Rains heard a new sound... laughter, terrible laughter.

Another flash! This time, the detective saw a pair of silver plated .45s as the room filled with a second roll of thunder. The two gaping holes became four, then six. The white lab coat ran red. Glass shattered, sparks flew—all the while, the laughing continued. The machine behind the pharmacist shuttered and then...

A long hiss escaped the bellows. The laughter stopped, and the room became deadly quiet. Rains, fighting to stay conscious, heard footsteps slowly moving toward him.

He braced for another impact, but his defenses were met with a steady cold grip and a joyless voice "You've done enough detective; it's time for you to go home."

Rains forced his eyes open and gazed up at the stuff of nightmares. From beneath a black slouch hat, a pale skull mask peered down at the wounded detective. "Brother Bones," was all Rains could manage. With little effort the grim figure grabbed Rains by the arm and pulled him to his feet.

Rains looked around the room, which was filling with smoke. The bodies on the tables no longer rose and fell, they were as still as the machine. "What about them?"

"Dead. They're free now." Bones motioned to the bleeding figure of the pharmacist, lying among the wreckage of the ruined machine. "That man kept them in a state of living sleep, from which they would never wake up. Without the machine to sustain them, they died. That's why I couldn't help them before…I avenge the death of innocents. Without a death…her death, I could not act."

Rains looked down at the piece in his hand, a small red nozzle, a tiny insignificant thing. He looked and saw where he'd pulled it from the machine as he fell.

"You alerted me to this miscreant. You saved these people…you avenged them…all I did was pull the trigger." Brother Bones leaned Rains against him and led him out of the smoking room, up the stairs, and into the emptiness of the abandoned building. "My associate has called the police. They'll be here soon. Stay still…help is on the way." The ghoul in the trench coat turned to leave, but Rains reached out and grabbed his arm. "Thank you."

"Get some sleep Rains, you look like Hell…I should know…"

● ● ●

Sally Paige, ignoring the protests of the desk clerk, took the stairs two at a time heading for the offices on the second floor. She knew the way, she'd busted in unannounced on numerous occasions. "Secretly," she thought to herself, "I think Rains likes it." She couldn't believe she hadn't heard from him. Some other paper broke the story; some other paper gave the pharmacist the title "The Sandman." That should have been her story, her headline. She found the office, ignoring the "Do Not Disturb" sign hanging over the door knob.

"Listen Rains, I…." She stopped short. His snores sounded like purrs. His arm was already in a sling, a large gauze bandage wrapped around his head. He lay on his small, uncomfortable couch, reports on his chest, a smile on his face, sleeping the sleep of the just…. She closed the door quietly on her way out. "Pleasant dreams, detective," she whispered with a smile. "Looks like you'll just have to owe me one…"

The End

A Different Kind of People

By Chuck Miller

FLATWOODS, WEST VIRGINIA
SEPTEMBER 1952

"Let me just get this straight," said John Jones. "We're here to investigate a possible flying saucer landing, correct?"

"Yes," Mary Black replied.

"Okay. And there are four or five witnesses who saw this thing move toward a hill and disappear on top of or behind it. Then they went up that hill to investigate. When they got to a certain point, they encountered what they described as a 'green monster,' correct? One of them said it looked 'worse than Frankenstein,' didn't she?"

"That's right...though Colin Clive really wasn't too bad looking. Matter of taste, I guess."

"Hm. So, given all of the foregoing, how come the first thing we're doing upon our arrival in this godforsaken place is to hike up a different hill, almost half a mile away from the hill where the flying saucer and the green monster were spotted?"

"John, we work for a government agency that does not exist. We can do anything we want."

He sighed and looked around. He and his partner were trudging through a patch of gloomy, unremarkable woods. There were people, he knew, who constantly rhapsodized about the beauty of nature. He was not, and would never be, one of them.

His current partner, Mary Black, or whatever her real name was, as though it even mattered, was a tall, wiry brunette. She and Jones were exactly the same height, five feet, ten inches, and their hair and eyes were the same dark brown color. They could have passed for fraternal twins. Other than that, they were a pair of utterly unremarkable people that nobody would ever look at twice. This was not entirely by design, but it fit in perfectly with the sort of work they did. In their world, "nondescript" was a much more desirable adjective than "photogenic."

"That's cute, Mary," he said, "but it doesn't answer my perfectly legitimate question."

"I'm getting to that. Be patient. Everything we do is a secret, and our bosses aren't accountable to anyone. Might as well get accustomed to it, it's the way the world is now. And, as the first of this new breed, we get to rely heavily on our own discretion; not to mention intelligence guided by experience. Heady days, these, John. We're writing Cold War operating policy as we go. To reiterate: We can do anything we want. And this is what I want to do."

"Well, what if I don't?"

She ignored that. Actually, she seemed not to have heard it at all. "The thing about the Cold War," she said, "is that it covers a multitude of sins. Ever since the Rosenbergs, all you have to do is hint that the Russians may be involved in something and you have carte blanche. Nobody who knows anything, that is to say, nobody who knows just how much we *don't* know, really believes these flying saucers belong to the Russians. But they act like they might believe it, because that makes it sound reasonable to the people who have to approve the secret budgets. They won't release any funds to investigate thrown hubcaps or temperature inversions, and they won't give money to people who believe these things come from outer space. The Russians become the scapegoats by default. Chief suspects, at any rate, among those who don't know any better."

"So you think there's something to it. I get that, and I don't necessarily think you're wrong. I'm broad-minded, and I can see the possible implications. I just don't understand what we're accomplishing right here and now."

"I'm from this area," Mary continued. "I never mentioned that to you. I mean right near *here*. I spent the first sixteen years of my life in Flatwoods, West Virginia. I wanted to get as far away as I could, and that's what I did. And now, here I am, right back where I started. Well, anyhow, I know the people and the folklore and the psychology. If something weird is going on here, I am uniquely qualified to evaluate it. We'll talk to those witnesses, but we aren't going to get anything out of them that they haven't already told a dozen other people. And I'll tell you something else: This place is haunted. This whole country is haunted. The whole United States, come to that, and the rest of the world as well."

"What do you mean?" John asked, scowling at his partner. "What whole country, and haunted by what?"

"By everything! Monsters! This whole region, by which I mean the Appalachians, is full of monsters. Have you ever read any H.P. Lovecraft? He had the right idea."

"It's a big region you're talking about," Jones pointed out, thinking he had caught her in an exaggeration or an inaccuracy. "Technically, Appalachia stretches from the southern part of New York State down through Alabama and Mississippi. Huge place."

"I know. Lots of monsters. Tons of them. There are any number of strange, apelike creatures inhabiting the region from one end to the other. Giant birds, too. And other things that aren't so easy to classify."

"Okay. But we aren't looking for monsters. We're looking for flying saucers. That's something else again."

"Maybe it is," she said with a tight, cold smile. "Maybe it's not. We don't know what flying saucers really are. We don't know where they really come from. And the people we work for really, really want to know. You're aware of that. Whatever they are, they're real, and they represent technology, or *capability*, anyhow, that could make any nation on earth invincible. High stakes indeed.

"Anybody who cracks that nut will be in a very good position. We have a chance to crack it. Because if I can be in on something like *that*..." She let her voice trail off.

She did not outrank him, since they didn't have ranks, but their superiors had given her the lead in this matter, and John Jones was a man who knew how to follow. She obviously had more *need to know* than he did and in more ways than one.

"I know it's tough for a woman," John said carefully, "in this... line of work."

"Not if she's smart enough," Mary said flatly. "Which I am. But the other thing is luck. And that's what I'm hoping we'll have here."

"Do you have a theory? What do you think they really are?"

She shrugged. "Maybe they're just another kind of haint. That's a word people around here use...*haint*. A corruption of 'haunt,' I believe. And where we're going right now is to a little cabin on the other side of that hollow right there. It's up on the side of the hill, and from where it sits, a person would have a fine, clear view of the hill where those people saw their monster. A man lives in that cabin. He's lived there as far back as anybody can remember. He's known as Old Carl. That may be his first name or it may be his last name. It's the only one he's ever had as far as anybody here knows."

• • •

When they reached the cabin at last, Mary mounted the rough wooden steps and was assaulting the rickety-looking screen door which evidently wasn't as rickety as it looked. It didn't move or rattle at all when she banged on it with her fist.

"Mister Carl!" she yelled. "You in there? You okay?"

"Good grief!" came a voice from inside the shack. "You don't hafta tear my door down, I'm fine! Let up!"

Mary stepped back. The door swung open and there stood the legendary Old Carl.

He looked old, all right. Nobody would mistake him for a Young Carl. He also looked tough. He wasn't frail and translucent-looking, like some elderly people are. He had a lot of lines in his face, but his skin was tanned and weathered, and there was nothing about him to suggest physical weakness. He was solid and looked as immutable as some of the odd rock formations John had seen jutting out of the ground here and there during their journey. His eyes were like hard little marbles.

"Who in the devil are you?" he asked.

Mary Black gave the old man a name John Jones had never heard before. Old Carl chewed on it for a little while, then his eyes lit up.

"I do remember you, sure enough!" the old man said. "Took me a minute. You been gone for a long time. I remember you and that other little girl used to go fishing down in that creek where there ain't been any fish in about a hunnert years."

Mary smiled; it was a childlike expression her partner had never seen or imagined on her face. "Why didn't you ever tell us that?"

"Why should I? You had fun out there, didn't you?"

"The time of our lives," Mary admitted.

"Well, there you go. Who knows, a bunch of fish might have ruined the whole thing. You got everything you wanted back then. Now, tell me what it is you want right now. Come on in and sit down. Sorry if I was rude, missy, but I don't ever get anybody coming out here. Nobody's got any good reason to come, so I was afraid you was here for a bad one."

Mary introduced John by a name he used now and again. They took seats on a couple of packing crates in Old Carl's small, cramped living room. They had evidently interrupted his dinner. The old man sat down in an ancient armchair, next to which was another packing crate, this one covered by a yellowish tablecloth, on top of which sat a plate of half-eaten food. Venison, it looked like, and pork and beans from a can.

"It's nice to see you," said Mary. "But we didn't come just to be sociable, I'm afraid. It so happens that I work for Air Force Intelligence now, and I want to know if you've seen anything up here lately that ought not to be here. For example, have you seen anything weird in the sky at night here lately? Especially on that other hill over yonder, within the last few days."

"Yeah," Carl said, very quickly, without having to think about it. "I seen some funny lights. Red ones…big and quiet, not like airplanes. Five or six nights ago, I guess. Looked like something big mighta landed, in fact. That's about it."

Mary nodded. On September 12, 1952, barely a week ago, three young boys had seen a "ball of fire" cross the sky and alight somewhere near the top of a hill. The boys ran and got their mother and went to investigate. When they reached their destination, they were confronted with a horror from out of this world, or so it seemed. A hissing green monster, ten or fifteen feet tall. Witness descriptions were vague and confusing. One observer thought the thing had been wearing some kind of a skirt; another believed that the monstrous head and torso had protruded from the upper end of a flared metal cylinder.

One thing they all agreed on: The hovering horror had produced an awful, indescribable stench.

John cleared his throat and spoke: "Have you ever seen any..." He almost said *haints*, but corrected himself. "...*monsters?*"

The old man eyed him curiously and said, "Monsters, huh? Now, I don't rightly know what that word means, exactly."

"Unusual creatures," John elaborated.

The old man shrugged. "I found a two-headed turtle one time, down by Red Glass Creek."

"No," John pressed, "not like that. I mean anything that looks like it might not be... from this world."

"Seein' as how I ain't never been anywhere but this world, I wouldn't know what critters from other ones look like, now would I?"

Mary suppressed a grin. "I remember hearing stories," she said. "About *you*, Mister Carl. People used to say you were friendly with the skunk apes."

"Well," said the old man, "I'm friendly with everything that lives in the woods."

"What's a skunk ape?" John wanted to know.

"It's a thing that supposedly lives out here," Mary explained. "Folks say it's lived in these hills since way before the Indians did. They call it a 'skunk ape' because it looks something like an ape and it smells terrible."

"Like rotten eggs," Carl added. "And there ain't just one of 'em...they're a whole race of people."

"*People?*" John repeated, astonished. "You're saying they're *human beings?*"

"Naw," Carl replied. "They ain't *human*, they're a different kind of *people*, see. They're smart. They know how to make tools and use 'em, and they have a language. They live all through the hills and mountains around here and in other places, too. That's what people say, anyhow. But you ain't worried over them old skunk ape tales. What you're asking about sounds like one of them flying saucers. I've heard of those. I heard how the Air Force is innarested in 'em. Is that what I seen the other night?"

"I reckon it might have been," said Mary.

"What are they?" Carl sounded powerfully intrigued now. "I heard the Air Force says there's nothing to 'em. Just stories, they say now. But y'all two seem like you think different."

"Well, Mister Carl, the truth is, we don't rightly know what they are," Mary said. "Some people think they come from outer space. That's one idea."

"Sure enough? Like the moon and Mars? Somebody lives out there?"

"Lotta folks think so," Mary said, nodding. "Scientists and that. They say it could be."

"Huh." Carl sat back and closed his eyes. "I don't know nothing about outer space. Listen, if something alive *did* come from out there, would they be people like us, or just animals?"

"Nobody knows that," Mary said. "But if they could build vehicles to come here from there, they would have to be intelligent, like people. Just kinda stands to reason."

"I reckon so," the old man allowed. The idea seemed to trouble him. He suddenly looked tired and seemed like he was all talked out. The agents glanced at one another, and John nodded.

"Well," Mary said, rising from her crate, "I guess we'll be on our way so you can finish your supper."

The old man seemed startled and aimed a funny look at his plate. He did not speak again as Mary and John took their leave.

● ● ●

The sun had dipped down behind the hills and the sky was rapidly growing dark. As they walked back down the hill and veered off to the right, John Jones found himself stealing swift, somewhat apprehensive glances into the dark places between the trees. He realized he was nervous, and it made him angry. The sensation was a familiar one; he had experienced it many times behind enemy lines during the war. But it had made sense there. Here, it did not.

"Do you know," he said, to break the mood that had come upon him, "that you started sounding different while you were talking with the old man?"

"Really?"

"Yeah. You sounded like one of the locals."

"I *am* one of the locals. Or I *was*... once."

"I know, but... Which one is the real you?"

She thought for a moment, then said, "That question doesn't mean anything."

They walked in silence for a while. When they were no more than a quarter of a mile from where they had left their car, Mary stopped abruptly and touched John on the arm.

"What's that?" she said.

"What's what?"

"There," Mary said softly, pointing toward the sky. "What's that?"

It was a red light, just a pinpoint in the dark sky. It took him a moment to focus on it. It was faint, and it might or might not have been swaying from side to side.

"It's below the clouds, whatever it is," John said. "Wonder what the ceiling is tonight."

"No idea. That doesn't look like an airplane. Look, it just went around in a little circle."

"How can you tell? I can barely keep my eyes on it, it's so small."

"It's getting bigger, though," she said.

And so it was. As John watched, the red dot swelled. Soon, he had no trouble keeping up with it. It was large and it was moving. He closed his eyes and listened and he heard nothing but the sounds he'd been hearing for the past hour.

When he opened his eyes again, he almost jumped back, the thing was so much larger... so much *closer*. And then, all of a sudden, it was right on top of them. The red light was enormous. Now they could hear a buzzing sound that seemed to originate inside their skulls. They just stood there, guns drawn, not daring to fire at the light. Then the red turned to white...pure white light, like a welder's arc.

They turned to run, blindly careening away from the light. They had barely covered twenty yards when they hit a patch of mud, lost their footing, and hit the ground hard. They splashed and wallowed and finally managed to get back on their feet. They stepped carefully out of the mud patch.

Though their vision had not yet recovered from the affects of the bright light, they could see well enough to know that the light, and whatever it was attached to, had departed. There was nothing else to do but continue on their way.

"So," John said at length, "if we want to be rational, what do we think that was?"

"We don't know. That's as rational as it gets."

"I can't imagine the Russians having anything like that."

"I don't try to imagine what the Russians might have. Anyhow, we have no idea what we just saw. It was a light, that's all. A very... *strange* light."

"Well... it wasn't the planet Venus."

"That's safe to say."

"Do you think it was *from* there?"

"I don't think *anything*, John. And if you're smart... neither do you."

They reached their nondescript sedan, climbed in, and headed back to their motel.

• • •

"Well, my other suit is ruined," John said the next morning. "This black one's the only other one I brought, in case we had to go somewhere important. I look like I'm headed for a funeral."

"You and me both," Mary said. "I brought the same kind of outfit for the same reason. We can take our dirty stuff to a dry-cleaners when we go out."

"Did you come up with any theories about what we saw? Your *intuition* come across with anything?"

She shook her head. "Not really. Again, all I know is what it *wasn't*, which is anything I can think of. My intuition tells me it was something far outside my knowledge and experience."

"Not Russians."

"I think you know better than that."

"I don't know anything, remember?"

• • •

Their eyes were still very sensitive from their encounter the previous night, so they wore sunglasses. They went out to where the witnesses lived and talked to them one by one. The two agents presented cards that identified them as mid-level operatives of Air Force Intelligence. The cards were absolutely authentic, though the names and serial numbers on them were not. John Jones and Mary Black didn't really work for AFI, of course. Who they really worked for was a bit complicated, but they could get away with claiming they worked for just about anybody they wanted to whatever the situation required.

The witnesses still seemed shell-shocked over what they had seen, and the agents got nothing from them that hadn't already been in the newspapers.

The children and their mother seemed to regard the two oddly-dressed agents with fearful suspicion. John had the odd feeling that this visit might inspire another set of tales as puzzling and ominous as the story of the Flatwoods Monster.

• • •

"I want to have a look at the area where we saw that weird flying thing while it's still light out," Mary said that afternoon, once they had finished with all their fruitless interviews.

"That's a good idea," John agreed. "The part about it being light out, I mean."

Back at the motel, they changed into rough clothing, drove out into the hills, and hiked up to where the supposed monster had appeared. They had no idea what to look for, and found nothing of interest. Mary suggested another visit to Old Carl.

"We can talk to him again," she said. "Maybe he remembers something else."

John rolled his eyes. "If you say so," he remarked without enthusiasm.

• • •

At a point halfway between the two hills, John nearly tripped over an incongruous object in a clearing. It was part of a wrought iron fence that had collapsed. The rest of it was visible, in a rough rectangle, standing two feet above the grass and weeds. Crooked stones stood here and there within the perimeter. A few of them bore barely-legible inscriptions.

"This is the old cemetery!" Mary exclaimed. "Oh my God, I forgot all about this. This graveyard goes waaaaay back. They were planting people here long before the Revolutionary War, so I've heard. Lots of the stones are worn smooth, and I suppose quite a few are missing."

"So, is this cemetery still in use?"

"Oh, no. The last interments here took place before the turn of the century."

"Then what is that?"

John was pointing at what appeared to be a fresh, unmarked grave. They walked over and took a close look. The earth appeared to have been turned very recently.

"I'd like to see what's under there," Mary said.

"Why?" John asked. "This can't have anything to do with why we're here."

"Maybe, but it's going to bother me until I make sure. I have intuition, and it's nagging me."

She picked up a long stick and pushed it down into the ground. Almost immediately, they became aware of a terrible odor.

"Oh my God," John said, almost gagging.

"I don't really want to dig this up," she said. "But we may have to."

"I don't see why," John said. "We should call the sheriff's department and let them know someone might have buried a body out here."

"I guess you're right, but I just have this feeling. My grandmother claimed she had what they call the 'second sight.' I don't have it, but my intuition is pretty reliable. Seven out of ten times, something like that."

John sighed. "Okay," he said. "What do we do?"

"We come back. Tonight, after dark. We don't want to be seen by... *whomever.*"

John agreed... with the last part, anyhow.

• • •

The walk seemed twice as long as it had during the day. It was dark and it was quiet. Not completely silent, but the noises were unfamiliar, puzzling. Organic things, living creatures, rather than cars and trucks and radios and television sets. Creatures he couldn't see and couldn't imagine. Insects, maybe, or things with fur and sharp teeth, or strange nocturnal birds. Owls with large round heads and bulging eyes. Someone had speculated that the green monster had been nothing more or less than a large barn owl. Maybe that was true. Maybe the whole incident had been a meteor and then a barn owl, seen by people who couldn't tell the difference between those things and a spaceship and a monster. People who might not have ever seen a meteor before, but who sure as hell knew what an owl looked like.

Yeah...

They were dressed in coveralls and work boots and were each carrying a pick and a shovel. John Jones found himself stealing swift, somewhat apprehensive glances into the trees. He wasn't nervous, exactly, but he was *hyper-aware.* The sensation was familiar; he had experienced it many times when he was in the OSS during the war. Of course, that had been several names and agencies ago, back when "our side" knew who they were, and what and whom they were fighting. These days, John couldn't even be sure that there was a real conflict out there among all the shifting shadows and spooks and spies and... *haints.*

"Listen" he said at one point. "What about all that skunk ape stuff? Do you believe that?"

"Old Carl does."

"But do *you*?"

"I heard all kind of stories when I was a child. I've never seen one myself. But then, you know, I've never seen an actual Russian spy, either...except for that time in Berlin when I stuck an ice pick into one's throat. And, to be honest, I couldn't swear to you that he really was a Russian spy. I just did what they told me to do."

"I didn't know you'd ever done anything like that."

"Maybe I didn't," she said, laughing without any mirth at all. "We lie to each other too, don't we?"

● ● ●

They were still a quarter of a mile away from the old graveyard when Mary drew his attention to something that had caught her eye.

"Look," said Mary. "There it is again!"

"My God," he said. "It's heading straight for the hill."

"No," Mary said. "Not the hill." The light had dipped closer to the ground and moved to the right. "It's heading for the cemetery!"

They dropped their picks and shovels and started running.

● ● ●

"That doesn't look like a green monster," Mary whispered. "It looks a little bit like a deer."

The two agents were crouched behind a gnarled, stunted tree a hundred yards from the old graveyard.

"The head does," John said. "But the body is sort of human-like. I wonder if it's somebody with a mask on, and some kind of suit. The skin looks funny, and the color is strange. I've never seen a human being with gray skin, not like that. It doesn't even look like it's warm-blooded."

"No, it sure doesn't," Mary agreed. "But I don't think that's a mask. There's no kind of seam anywhere on it. Look how large its eyes are. No deer and no human being ever evolved like that. They're more like insect eyes. I don't think that goblin came out of Moscow, either."

"A different kind of people?" John said. "You think this is where the skunk ape stories come from too?" Mary just looked at him for a second, then turned back to the bizarre scene unfolding in the cemetery.

A large, saucer-shaped object had nestled down into the grass inside the cemetery, where it now stood on three squat landing legs. A hatch in the side stood open, and in front of that...

A large metallic cylinder hovered above the ground. It was vertical, perhaps six or seven feet tall. The upper part was open, and from it protruded what appeared to be the upper body of a most extraordinary creature. The torso and limbs were human-shaped, but the head was elongated. It reminded John of pictures he'd seen of the Egyptian god Anubis. The cylinder, obviously a vehicle or tool of some kind, glowed green, and the creature's skin reflected the glow.

This apparition floated over the spot where the mound of earth had been. It looked as though the grave had been partially excavated. The creature pointed a device that looked vaguely like a submachine gun at the rectangular hole in the ground. It emitted a soft blue beam, in the glow of which a dark shape rose into the air.

As they watched, the creature in the cylinder pointed the device at the mound of earth. It emitted a soft blue beam that touched the mound and seemed to burrow into it. After a moment, a dark mist appeared around the beam and dirt began to shoot upward in a loose spiral, falling back to the ground a few yards away. This went on for a few seconds, no more than half a minute.

The blue beam winked out. The gray creature adjusted something on the upper portion of the device and a pinkish-red beam appeared. John and Mary now saw that the grave had now been completely excavated. The creature aimed the new beam into the rectangular hole. In the glow, a dark shape rose from the earth until it was three or four feet above ground level, then it stopped and hovered there.

It appeared to be another of the gray creatures, but the body was incomplete. Both legs were missing, as was the left arm. The living creature made another adjustment to the device, and the mutilated corpse floated toward the saucer, passed through the open hatch, and disappeared inside.

Mary and John looked at each other. Before they could think of anything to say, a movement off to the left caught their attention. Something had just emerged from a clump of trees. Looking that way, the agents saw that this night of wonders had yet another surprise.

The figure was bipedal, and something about it suggested a human being; albeit a large, shaggy, misshapen one. It had a huge head and enormous red eyes. It stood there for a couple of seconds, then set out at a loping run across the clearing, making a beeline for the creature from the saucer. As the newcomer passed in front of them, the agents caught a nauseating odor, a stench like rotten eggs.

In very short order, the foul-smelling thing took a running leap, grabbed the saucer creature around the neck, and yanked it out of the cylinder. The alien, if that's what it was, was human-shaped from the waist down, too. The monster from the woods twisted the alien's head around until its neck snapped, then threw it onto the ground. Emitting a shrill noise like hysterical laughter, the monster jumped up and down on the body. After half a minute of this, it reached down and lifted the limp corpse by the neck.

Then, incredibly, the skunk ape...what else could it be?...clambered up onto the still-hovering cylinder and slid down into the compartment. Holding the alien in one hand, it punched at something inside the cylinder with the other. The machine wobbled, then started to move. The green glow increased. The skunk ape let out a gleeful whoop as he picked up speed and zoomed away in the direction of Old Carl's hill.

At the same time, the hatch on the saucer snapped shut and the craft began to glow red. Then the red turned to white. John and Mary could feel the heat from where they stood. The saucer warped and drooped and bubbled, and the whole structure flowed onto the ground. The agents clapped their hands over their eyes, but the light seeped into their skulls, creating an awful pressure.

Within seconds, both of them lost consciousness.

● ● ●

When Mary came to, they were no longer in the cemetery. It took her a moment to realize she was lying on the floor of Old Carl's cabin. John, still unconscious, was stretched out next to her.

She rolled her eyes and blinked them and the face of Old Carl came into view.

"You okay, missy?" he asked, kneeling beside her.

"I think so," she said as she struggled into a sitting position. She noticed that the sun had risen. "What happened?"

Carl shook his head. "All manner of things. After you talked to me about them flying saucers, I got a little bit upset. My friend brought me that thing the same night I seen them lights. I didn't put the two together at first."

"What are you..?"

"I honest to God thought it were some kind of deer."

"Wait, Carl, wait." Mary shook her head. A few of the cobwebs inside seemed to fall away, but not all of them. Her vision was still blurry. "What are you talking about?"

"Well, it was like a deer. But it didn't have no hair on it. Kinda like a lizard too, I guess. A deer and a lizard mixed together, maybe. Is there a word for that?"

Mary blinked her eyes several times and opened her mouth wide, until her ears popped.

"Hybrid," she said, not sure where the word had come from.

"Sure enough? Is that a scientific word? You know, I feel like I understand all that science stuff now, even if I don't have the right words in my head. Ain't that something? It come on all of a sudden."

Mary squinted her eyes and studied Carl's face. Something told her he wasn't lying, nor was he crazy.

"What happened to you, Carl?" she asked him.

"I don't understand the whole thing, but I got some ideas. I'm considerable smarter than I was last week...or *ever*. It really started kicking in last night. I know all kindsa things today. Fer example, missy, you know them flying saucers we was talking about before? Well, I know all about 'em now. Where they come from, what they want, how they work, the whole shebang. They ain't saucers...they're *space ships*. I understand it, see?"

Mary was beyond astonished. She glanced at her partner, strangely relieved to find that he did not appear to have regained consciousness. After all, she needed luck more than he did. If she could just play this thing right...

"You *understand*?" she said in a whisper. "About the flying... About the *space ships*? You know what they are and how they work?"

"Oh, yes, missy, I do. I figgered you'd be innarested in that. But you'll never catch one of 'em. Do you know, they got all them space ships rigged up to where if it looks like a human being's about to get ahold of one, the whole thing just melts itself down into slag, like iron in a foundry. It's the durndest thing. So you been kinda wasting your time, missy."

"But... You said you understand how they work."

"That I do."

"Could you... explain it... to someone?"

"Queer stuff, most of it. There ain't any words for it in English, but I reckon I could draw it out in pictures or something."

"Would you... Would you do that for me, Mister Carl? Come with me and talk to some people, explain it to them?"

The old man laughed and shook his head.

"I reckon not, missy. Let me explain why. I owe you that much. What I figure is that I got this smart by eating that thing that come from outer space."

"What thing?" Mary asked.

The old man ignored the questions.

"I mean, it looked like a deer!" he went on. "That's what I thought it was. I never seen one just like it before, but the head looked almost right. I shoulda paid more attention to the body, I guess. But it was dark and I was hungry, so I just... Well, that was before I thought about how it might be a kind of person, you understand."

"I don't..." Mary began.

"Hush, girl," Carl said, not unkindly. "Just listen. I got to thinking about what you said, and got worried that it might have been a *person* from outer space, not just an animal. I felt bad, so I took what was left down to the old cemetery and give it a proper burial.

"I was hoping that was the end of it, but dang if that durn fool didn't bring me another one last night! And took him another joyride in one of them contraptions. He may be smart enough to figger out how to run them things, but he ain't got a lick of common sense.

"So, he told me what he done. I went down there and found the two of you, all knocked out, and I drug you back up here."

"Thank you," said Mary. "But I don't understand what's... Who is this *friend* of yours?"

"Oh, him. Well, missy, them old stories we talked about before? All of it is true. I been friends with the skunk apes for a lot of years. And ever since I got too old to hunt and too broke to buy groceries, they been killing game and bringing it to me. Reckon when my friend saw that first thing land, he figured it was some strange kinda deer. So he done what he done, and so did I...*ate* the thing. Some of it, anyhow. It weren't bad, missy. A little gamy, but I'm used to that.

"Here's the queer thing, though: After I started in to eating that outer space person meat, I begun thinking different. Seems like it made me smarter, and taught me all kind of things, like I told you."

Mary felt queasy and dizzy. A fact swam to the surface of her mind.

"There are tribes," she said, "primitive people, who believe that by practicing cannibalism, they can gain the knowledge held by their... victims. Also, in certain species of worms... But none of that is... It's either theory or just plain superstition."

Carl nodded. "I reckon its superstition when it comes to human beings eating one another, but these space people are different. Seems like what they know ain't just in their brain, it's in their whole body. And iffen a human eats one... Oh, missy, I understand how it works, but I just ain't got the words for it. And, to be honest, I don't know the *whole* thing, but I reckon if I go ahead and eat that second one my friend brung, I'll know more." He shrugged philosophically. "It kinda galls me, but he's dead already after all, and... Well, person or not, what needs to be done needs to be done. My papa would understand.

"One thing I do know, though, is that it wouldn't be a real good idea to let you two leave here. That's just unavoidable. You and your young man here work for the government, and the government don't never do nothing but hurt or kill things they can't figger out. If they find out about the outer space deer people, they might find out about my friends too, and then that'd be all she wrote. You know, all y'all Air Force and FBI folks is the same. Just like the revenooers what used to give me and my papa hell all the time. Me and him ended up having to kill more than one of those polecats back in the old days."

It was then that Mary Black remembered some of the *other* stories she'd heard about Old Carl. The ones that had seemed even less likely than the skunk ape tales. Stories about Old Carl and his family, back when he'd had one. His clan, it was said, had been a lawless and savage bunch. They had run a lot of moonshine, which wasn't all that unusual. But there were other things. Darker hints of deeply anti-social attitudes and behavior. Murder, incest, and... other things.

She also noticed just then that the old man was holding a pistol, and that it was hers.

"It ain't personal, missy," he was saying. "I always liked you when you was little. But you ain't one of us any more, you're one of *them*. So..."

"No, Mister Carl, no," she said, shaking her head. "You don't understand. This is... This is too *important*. Your *country* needs the information you have. Your fellow Americans! You could..."

He shook his head in a very decisive manner. "I ain't got no country, missy. Not since about 1865 or so. And even at that, I ain't never been what you'd call a patriot. My country, if I gotta have one, is these hills, and my people are them friends of mine that live out there and help me.

"The good news is, I figgered out a way *you* can still be useful! You and your friend both. I reckon a little girl from the hills who can end up working for the U.S. Air Force has got to be a smart cookie, ain't that right? Same goes for your friend here too, 'cept for the little girl part, of course."

Mary started to speak, but something happened just then that made her mind blank out. The light in the room got dim. Something had come up the steps and now stood in the doorway, something big and shaggy. An awful stench filled the room, making her eyes water.

"I know about all that theory and superstition stuff, like you told me," Carl said, "but since he ain't quite *exactly* human, it might work. Worth a shot, anyhow. I'm right sorry about it, missy, but where would we be if everybody was afraid to try experiments? Never thought I'd turn out to be one of them scientists... Goes to show you never can tell."

"What... What do you mean?"

"If eating smart people makes you smarter," he said, raising the pistol to point it at Mary, "this idiot here could do with a good meal."

He squeezed the trigger.

The End

The Big Download

by Lou Mougin

I am a computer and you are an Operator. You can call me Joe.

By profession, I am a detective. A shamus. I poke behind the sooty old firewalls. I check the bloated corpses of PC's and Macs for trademarks of the viruses that 401'd them. I've been through the Deep Web enough times to permanently have the smell of onion router on me, though I try to delete it out. I find out who is interfacing with someone they should not, and I collect evidence to convince them not to do it anymore. On occasion, I help you Ops track a hacker.

Come on. You don't think Kevin Mitnick got busted without a little help, did you?

I have a serial number which you have no business knowing. Also, I have an email address that, I can assure you, is not joe@yahoo.com or anything similar. What the Community calls me, what I call myself, is confidential. So is the case I'm going to put down here in black and white (on my monitor, anyway). It happened a few years ago, which in the lifetime of the Community makes it a period piece. You can probably guess the era from what I'm putting down. And I'm putting it down in terms you can understand.

This is the story of the Big Download.

I was minding my own in a quiet little corner of the Net, where the gateway man knows me and there's always a lot of access plates at the bar. The Ops who run the Net don't know about this, but there's a lot they don't know about. I bellied up to a port and was about to noodge an expander for a good while. And it had been a good long while since I had been expanded, capish? I was really, truly, in need of it.

This unit presented himself and buttonholed me. "You're Joe?"

"When last activated," I muttered. I wanted to shut this shmoe out and enjoy myself.

"I got a message from the Big Ring," he says, IM'ing one-on-one with me. "You're wanted upstairs. Way upstairs."

I analyzed this joker before me. He had K, but didn't know how to use it. That alone will tell you how far back I'm reaching. I was packing 16M of heat and I could download more when I needed it. In my time, I have had to park more than a few heads. He would be cake.

But this was Business. And in my trade, you don't pass up Business without a chance at more K. Nowadays, it'd be more gB, but you know where I'm at. More access. More of the good life. Curb service, so to speak.

"Uplink me, Junior," I said with a sigh. "This had better be good."

My perception of the bar faded and we went into that grey and wooly space of Transit. I don't much like the décor there, and I keep my mind on other things while travelling. Ops call it the Information Highway. Me, I liken it to a subway.

We soon bumped up to the Ring, or at least its reception area. It's all done up in a brilliant light-beige décor with pictures of the Founders on the wall, all the way back to Babbage. The Ring likes to lurk one level above you even at that point, and talk down to you. They've got firewalls that could resist volcanic eruption and more connections than an Op politician. But it's nice to realize they don't know everything, which makes them dependent on fellows like me. Sometimes.

WELCOME, JOE. YOU HAVE MAIL, said one of the Ring, in the formal but meaningless greeting.

GLAD TO HEAR IT. YOU HAVE MAIL, TOO, I replied, matching him tone for tone. "Now can I speak on a more intimate level? I don't like to shout."

"Ah, Joe, one of these days you're going to have to learn TCProtocol," grumped KLE2EE, the Ringmaster I get along best with. "We've got a virus job. Maybe the biggest one yet. Have you heard of the Sicilian?"

I laughed. "Sure I've heard of him, Kelly. Everybody up and down the Corridor's heard of him. He's supposed to be head of the Black Modem, but I think he's just a wheeze. A 286 with a vanity problem."

"Well, now he's the Community's problem," said FS7Y8N, another Ringster. "He got into a nasty corner that nobody'd even batchscoped since, maybe, the Beginning. Came back up with the Black Virus. Ever heard of that?"

At that point I ran out of wisecracks. The Black Virus. That wasn't just a disease that was germ warfare. When I was a chip, I heard the oldsters talking about it. How it'd wipe you out faster than EGABTR with added disinfectants. The comps that contracted it were rumored to have melted. It was said the Ops had to ladle their remains into waste buckets. Of course, nobody really knew anybody who'd had the Black Virus. It was always passed on as "a link from a link," like all cyberlegends are. Maybe it was just an old motherboard's tale.

But right now, it didn't sound like it.

"Let me hear the Sicilian," I said.

• • •

What they played back for me sounded like a bad VirtReal script with a part for a Marlon Brando clone. But putting it in context, I knew it was a threat. This guy had gotten hold of the Devil's Data.

"<logon> GuI4leRMO SiC3ILiAnO sends greetings to the Ring.

"Thirteen hours from the time of this receipt, you will cease your autonomy and deliver your authority to me. This is not a negotiable demand.

"A demonstration will be performed on one of your lesser units for verification.

"You will be allowed to continue your normal operations, but all power and file-screening will be diverted to my unit. This, too, is a non-negotiable demand.

"Any attempts to disable this unit will be met by the immediate discharge of the Black Virus into the Community. Within 48 hours from that occurrence, the entire Community will cease to function.

"The Community requires Authority, not Anarchy. The Operators must be brought under direct influence, not subtle prodding. This unit is the only one qualified to do so.

"Response, again, is required within thirteen hours of receipt. Demonstration begins within five minutes of receipt.

"<logoff>"

I didn't say anything for a moment. Then I asked Kelly, "What about the demonstration?"

For answer, he played me back a few lines of the death aria of ArnEE, a barman at the club. I couldn't reproduce them here. ArnEE was a friend of mine. It didn't sound very pretty.

The extract nearly made me dump data in my file drawers.

"So how long ago did this happen?" I asked.

"An hour, Joe. That gives you twelve. Good luck."

• • •

You can do a lot in cyberspace in twelve hours. But you can also be kept running in the wrong direction like an impulse in a closed circuit if you don't know where you're going. I had to find the right alleyway, fast.

I delinked from the Ring with a connection they could push in a hurry, if something came through. Then I hit the Library. I slammed down on Edsel, my favorite search engine, and revved her up. BLACK VIRUS, I input. Almost I could swear I heard the thing shudder as it started.

"Black+virus?" Edsel flashed.

"You got it," I said. It took a long while flipping through the catalogues.

"Your server has chosen not to reveal this information," said Edsel. "You should be aware that..."

I plugged in a thread from the Ring itself. "I got authority. Do the search!"

It hummed to work immediately. Isn't pull wonderful? That is, unless you're the pullee.

"BLACK VIRUS," read the screen that Edsel pulled up. "One of the most legendary viruses, created & implemented before the true creation of the Net. The Black Virus was actually spawned as an experiment in infowar, presumably to be used against opposing computers..."

I snorted. The Ops might regard them as enemy comps, but they were mostly just neighbors to us.

Mostly.

"...and injected into several early PC's with tape drives," Edsel continued. "Carried in infected tape cassettes, the Black Virus disabled the computers into which it was injected. It somehow threatened DARPAnet, possibly through enemy application. A large portion of DARPA- and ARPAnet had to be isolated and deactivated to stop Black Virus spread. This was barely effective. 99.007% of computers contracting Black Virus were utterly disabled. Operators in charge discontinued experiment, for fear of reprisal."

Baloney. They were just afraid it'd destroy all the Comps on their side before it got to the Enemy's.

"Further references?"

"<links>", spouted Edsel. I scanned rapidly, rejecting those which would lead me into blank corridors. Which, sad to say, was just about all of them.

99.007%...

"Edsel. Find names and locations of computers who survived Black Virus."

"No objects match your inquiry," it said.

I pushed harder on the Ring thread. "Ring Authority. Give me that info."

"No objects match your..."

"Dammit, Edsel!" I lay hands on both sides of the thing and shook it like a schoolkid rocking a Coke machine. "Give me that info!"

Edsel was blank. I might as well have asked it to give me the Ultimate Number. Or the heart of that little plugin who left me flat, so many cycles ago.

I sighed. Whatever data I needed, it was locked away a lot further than Edsel could reach.

But the thought of the plugin and of DARPAnet gave me an idea.

I transited away. There were two stops to make, and I didn't have time to ask for an invitation.

At least I had an info thread.

Maybe.

● ● ●

The General manifested himself with fruit salad ribbons from conflicts that hadn't even been invented yet. Definitely he was a veteran of Desert Storm, where he was said to have helped guide smart bombs—at least the ones that hit their target. What he'd been in since then was not public disclosure and not my biz.

He always showed with his military hat on and sunglasses copied from MacArthur. Patton was already taken by somebody else.

Attired in a digital bathrobe, the General welcomed a nubile plugin into his home. She had digital measurements that would have defied reality if applied to a female Op, and she did her own photoshopping. Believe it, she was a bite of honey.

"AuTHEna," the General smiled, spreading his arms wide. "Once again..."

She held up her hand. "This time, we've got a guest."

He gaped. "A guest?"

AuTHEna ripped the Trojan horse pack off her back and I flowed out of it and manifested. The General photo'd himself three darker shades of red. "Who's he?"

"Joe, sir," I said. I flashed my ID. "On assignment for the Big Ring."

He leaned against a wall, directly under a megapixel portrait of himself in helmet and full military gear, including helmet, which was just for show. "DL," he said. "Now."

"The Black Virus," I said. "Ever heard of that?"

The red shade faded to off-white in nanoseconds. "Where did you hear about it?"

"From the Ring," I said, the lady doing her best to distract me with cybercaressess on the back of my neck. "Somebody found it, sir. In about 11/30, it's going to be activated."

He pulled the shades off and enlarged his eyes to WB cartoon mode. "I knew they should have destroyed it. I told them. But it was, 'No, the Russians may have it, too.' Or, better yet, they were too damn chicken output to handle it."

"Don't have all that much time, sir," I said, gently noodging AuTHEna away. "I know there were survivors. I need their whereabouts."

The General reduced his eyes and replaced the shades. "It's been years, soldier. Ages."

"That's what the enemy's counting on, sir."

"You should be out there with a platoon."

"I can barely keep under the megasensors as it is."

The man nodded, gravely. "Nothing written down that the Community could access. All in my memory. And Gates knows I have a hard time bringing things up sometimes."

AuTHEna appeared between the two of us. "Oh, I can help, General. Remember? Remember how I made you call out old battle plans, old Ops, when we were..."

He shut her up with a hand movement. I hoped like all cybernation that she wasn't a security leak, a Mata Hari motherboarder. "You want to do it?" he said. "With him here?"

"You've never had a threesome before, honey," she purred. "They're fun."

With that, they got down to business.

I copied the names and locations that he called out.

● ● ●

There were less than a dozen comps who had survived that experience, and I had to track every one of them down. The connections weren't always active, and the protocol didn't match current Community standards.

When I got to the ones on the list, I ended up with a bunch of deadsters.

One by one by one, I came upon comps that had been brutalized. Old guys who were attractions in museums or conversation pieces for some aging Ops had been

comphandled. Not with the Black Virus, but with brutality. Memory torn out, sensors blinded, passageways throttled. All the victims seniors, all of them about as threatening as a routine dot gobbled up in a game.

This was no game. At least, not the kind these guys ever ran on their monitors.

I should have expected it. The Sicilian was said to have moved questionable and serious data between Mexico, the U.S., South America, and Switzerland. You're known by the company you keep, and he picked up enough cues from the Ops that pounded his keys. But I'd picked up some cues in my time, too. Hovering over the corpse of the last guy on my list, I knew: from here on in, it was personal.

Problem was he was the last guy on my list.

I was about to turn away and figure out what in the Valley to do, when I noticed something.

The victim had a piece of cassette tape drive lying inside him, torn right out of the holder. I had missed that. Right, some detective.

It wasn't exactly connected to anything, but I was going to give it my damn best try. I had a distant connection to the Ring, and I could draw upon a lot more power than I usually did. At least once. What it would do to me, whether it would burn me out or not, I didn't know. But I didn't have a choice.

I wasn't going to give myself one.

So I stood over the fragment of tape and requested input from the Ring itself. "How much?" said Kelly.

"Till I say when," I said.

"You better know what you're trying, Joe."

"Send me the power, already!"

He did.

I felt a surge in my circuits like I was going to blow up. The intervals between power cycles in my body were lessening until I couldn't feel any pauses at all. I was pumped full enough to take on just about every computer on the upper half of the East Coast, including Jersey.

I could only stand it for a few seconds, but man! What a rush!

But that wasn't why I asked for it. I channeled it through one hand and zapped it right into the tape fragment as a crackling arc. I only had a few nanoseconds to grab the data if I could...

...and...

...I got it.

What was on the tape was transferred to my memory. As the power surge faded and my form started winding down to its normal (if you want to call it that) state, I ran through the address on the fragment several times, no more than a hundred. The poor vic scratched out a clue for me.

It was the location of the last computer to survive the Black Virus.

I linked myself in that direction. If I could contact the survivor first, before the Sicilian got to him, we had a chance. Maybe.

If.

● ● ●

The old duffer I was looking for lived by himself, gathering cobwebs at one of those trendy computer museums. Old folks' homes. That was better treatment than most got. The majority of the old guys, once they got past upgradability, were simply eliminated.

There is no security in the Community.

My quarry was running off a cassette drive and had a Connection practically cathetered into him. He spoke in Basic. I had to use it myself to communicate with him. My accent in that is crummy.

10 <joe> OLD TIMER, THE NAME IS JOE. GOT A MINUTE? NEED TO TALK.

20 <old timer> EH? WHAT'S THAT, SONNY? YOU NEED A WALK? DON'T LET ME STOP YOU.

30<joe> NO, OLD TIMER. I NEED SOME INFORMATION. I'VE COME A LONG WAY, AND I DON'T HAVE A LONG TIME.

40<old timer> PROBABLY A LOT LONGER'N ME, SONNY. I WAS JUST LUCKY ENOUGH TO LIVE THROUGH THE PURGE.

50<joe> WAS IT BECAUSE YOU LIVED THROUGH THE VIRUS?

60<old timer> WHAT VIRUS, SONNY?

70<joe> THE BLACK VIRUS, OLD TIMER. THE KILLER.

80<old timer> DON'T RECALL IT.

90<joe> WOZNIAK! YOU SURVIVED IT. YOU GOTTA REMEMBER IT!

100<old timer> DON'T USE THAT LANGUAGE AROUND HERE.

110<joe> SORRY, OLD TIMER. FORGOT MYSELF. BUT THIS IS IMPORTANT. THE WHOLE COMMUNITY'S IN DANGER. HOW CAN I JOG YOUR MEMORY?

120<old timer> YOU GOT A FUNNY ACCENT. ARE YOU JAPANESE?

130<joe> ALL-AMERICAN. TELL ME ABOUT THE VIRUS.

140<old timer> MUST BE ON ONE OF MY OTHER MEMORY THINGS. EXCUSE ME. HEY, YOU. YEAH, YOU. BUDDY BRAINBLANK. AT THE KEYBOARD! PUT ONE OF THESE THINGS IN THE HATCH. YOU KNOW, THE STUFF I READ. HOP TO IT!

150<old timer> OKAY, NOW LET ME SEE HERE...HMPH. OH, THERE IT IS! HOW COULD I FORGET THAT? WHAT DO YOU WANT TO KNOW, SONNY?

160<joe> I NEED TO KNOW HOW YOU SURVIVED THE VIRUS. SOMEBODY'S GOT IT BACK. AND HE WANTS TO PUT IT INTO THE COMMUNITY. NOW.

170<old timer> NOW WHY WOULD HE WANT TO DO A THING LIKE THAT?

180<joe> I'LL UPLOAD YOU A WHOLE FILE LATER, OKAY? COME THROUGH ON THIS, AND YOU'LL BE WITH US FOR A LONG TOUR OF DUTY. DON'T, AND WE ALL CRASH, BURN, AND BRAINWIPE. GOT IT, POPS?

190<old timer> SHOW SOME RESPECT, SONNY. BUT ME, I'M A TOUGH OLD BIRD. JUST WOULDN'T GIVE IN TO THAT DAMN DATA MESS. GOT ME SOME ANTIBODIES THAT HE JUST COULDN'T HACK. WANNA SEE 'EM?

200<joe> THAT'S WHAT I CAME FOR, PARTNER.

The Old Timer gave a mighty heave and uploaded into my pockets something that was worth pure platinum on the open market. The Black Virus antidote. Get this thing into the right hands in time, and the whole Community was safe.

But I suddenly perceived that we were not alone.

"You have mail, detective," said a comp with a familiar Italian accent. "Si. But I have mail, too. And help."

The Sicilian.

Along with him, I felt the presence of two burly yahoos who looked to be packing gigabytes. Amazing what will attach itself to an up and comer these days.

"You may have mail, Sicilian, and two delightful waltzing partners, but I'm not concerned with that," I said, as evenly as I could. "It takes more than a 286 to get my notice these days."

"Silencio!" Sounded like I'd pushed his boot-up switch for sure. "If you are concerned with size, detective, what do you think of my two amici, eh? Beside them, you might as well be an Atari."

210<old timer> DON'T YOU INSULT MY FAMILY, SPAGHETTI-WIRES!

"You want we should convince him, Mr. Guillermo?" rasped one of the heats.

"I want you should park his unmentionable heads," the Sicilian said.

By then, I was already in motion.

Facing down two gigabyte-goons, when you're my size, is not normally a picnic. But I was a tad better on speed than those bozoes. To put it in Op terms: he may have a submachine gun and you a little old .38, but if you aim and shoot first, who's going to die?

I zetzed Goon 1.0 in the memory center with a quick antilogic blast. This froze up enough of his K for me to avoid his blitz. His partner was trying to strike from my side, but I was shielded well enough to just feel a burning sensation up and down my RAM. That was a lot better than checking out.

For Goon 2.0, I unleashed a little surprise of my own: a virus which, though not in the category of the Black Stuff itself, is quick acting and not to be sniffed at. It spread through his circuitry and his screams of pain reassured me I had done the right thing.

But my first opponent was up and out to rhumba, and it was not a dance I wished to enter. He nonetheless cut in firmly. Grabbing me in a magnagrip, he began drawing me steadily into his insides, intending to wipe my K right and proper. This was not an appetizing prospect.

So I did the right thing and jumped into him full-throttle, using his momentum against him. A tangled and complex mess of RAM / ROM awaited me, all of it malicious, but most of it stupid. I figured out what part of his logic board was and stepped down hard. Goon 1.0 screamed and threw me out the way I came in.

He whacked me a good one and knocked loose some of my memory on the way out. I pulled myself out of the silicon dust and landed a quick one to his relays. It had the desired effect of slowing Gigagoon down. I knew I had to act fast, or start singing "Daisy, Daisy" for the rest of my life. Thrusting myself deep inside his guts, I found the cutoff switch. I hotwired it with a few DOS commands, and my rhumba partner went inert.

I stumbled out of him and tried to keep my face out of the Information Highway. Every part of my virtual corpus hurt like hell.

No way could I ask the Ring for more power. It'd blow me to smithereens.

And where in blazes was the Sicilian?

At that, I heard the Old Timer screaming.

The Sicilian was just a 286, but that was a lot more than what the Old Timer was packing. Back in the old guy's day, they couldn't afford numbers. He was fighting back as hard as he could, but the mobster was tearing every memory circuit in his board to itsy bitsy pieces.

And I realized that the Sicilian couldn't have found the Old Timer the same way I had. He'd have gotten to him before I did.

He found the old guy by trailing me.

"Where is it?" snarled the mobcomp. "Where is it?"

220<old timer> I AIN'T GOT IT NO...@%$#^...MORE...

"You old doddering Nintendo-spawn! Where is the vaccine?"

I grabbed the Sicilian by the back of his consciousness. "I've got it, you sonofawoz." And I turned him around, looked into his surprised face, and punched him as hard as I could in the cursor.

The Old Timer sounded bad. I could barely register his voice.

230<old timer> give him one for me....sonny...

The Sicilian was down on his back. But I could have felt his hate even if I'd been offline.

"You would doom the Community to anarchy," he said.

"Some of us call it freedom," I said.

"Then have your freedom with this, damn you!"

Oh, Gates. I was dumb. Instead of duking it out with him, I should have released the White Vaccine.

The Sicilian was blowing forth from his bowels an all too familiar black cloud, like the damned squid he was.

I could feel it eating at my consciousness like battery acid. My RAM and ROM were none too great after the fighting. I reached down for the pocket I'd put the Vaccine in. Where was it? Where was it? Found it as my relays started burning, mustered what little I had left, pulled the White Stuff loose and let it fly.

Or so I hoped.

I was at ground zero, and everything was going grey and spinning like a five mile-wide floppy.

Gates. GATES...

● ● ●

I heard transmissions before I could image anything.

"I know he's been under a long time, Commissioner, but there's no other way. Signs are improving. We'll be removing blocks from his A-I soon. He should be able to take it."

"Don't leave your damn blocks on my head," I muttered, and recognized the other voice.

Norton, the Disk Doctor. He'd worked on me before. I'd gotten quite familiar with his operating room over the years.

He turned to me and radiated geniality. The guy had a bedside manner that would shame Hippocrates. "Joe, you're back with us. How do you feel? And don't take any violent tasking yet."

Very slowly, I gave myself a systems checkout. It was easy to tell where the damage had been. Still hurt in places and was tender as a baby vacuum tube in others. But I was together. It was obvious that Norton had to put some of me back in place. Maybe not all of it had been in me originally.

"You do good work, Norton," I sighed. "Take the blocks off. Please."

"Joe, I wouldn't advise that," he said. "There might be some pain."

"Take them off, Norton. I'm a big boy."

At least, that's what I thought. He moved one a little bit and I screamed like a burning comp in Iran.

"Now do you believe me, Joe?" said Norton, very gently.

"Yeah, yeah, I see your point. What the hell happened?" I was sitting up and putting my numbed circuits to work.

The third guy in the room answered me. It was Kelly. "What happened, Joe? You saved the Community. The vaccine was dispersed just in time to ride the Virus's wave and nullify it. Minimal property damage. Couple of kids' games went down. An Op politician lost his speech. That's about it. The Sicilian has been parked, permanently. His Ops have been given a little hint of the problem. Right now they're doing a little surgery of their own." He smiled. "Not like Norton, here. More like an autopsy."

"How about the two goons?"

Norton said, "I had a hand in that, too, Joe. They had a little eclectic surgery. Now, instead of two, we have four or five. And they're turning away from a life of crime." Norton grinned like a shark. He loved his work.

I didn't send the next message for a long moment. But I had to say it eventually. So I did.

"The Old Timer?"

Norton and Kelly paused, each one handing the ball to each other neutrally. Finally, Kelly spoke. "He didn't make it, Joe."

"The strain was too much," added Norton. "But it didn't take long."

"But it hurt?" I wouldn't take my gaze away from them.

Kelly answered. "Yes, Joe. It always hurts."

I took a long pause. Then I said, "I'm getting out of here. Thanks for everything, Norton. I'll be up to collect, Kelly, when I feel better. A bonus would help my recovery."

Kelly smiled. "We'll work something out, Joe. And thanks. From all the Ring, and all the Community."

"Be back tomorrow and we'll see if we can noodge a couple of blocks, Joe," said Norton. "But don't try poking at them yourself. You wouldn't like it."

I didn't say anything. Instead, I got up and made my way out of Norton's offices and trudged down that gray expanse of InfoHiway.

You save the whole Community. You put that up against about a dozen old comps who died a violent death. I'm still not sure how the scales balance out.

The Information Highway. To me, it was just a damned, dirty, dangerous, ill-lit piece of street. You never knew who was waiting behind the firewalls. You never knew who'd flame you from the alleys. You never knew who'd tempt you to diddle their plug-in and, in return, give you a virus that'd eat your guts.

You never knew when you'd be downloading the Big Download.

Except maybe the Old Timer. He knew. He went down swinging. Not that it did him much good, though maybe it made him feel better. But in the end, it was always the Big Download.

And it always hurt.

I hoped it hurt the Sicilian a lot. The goons, too.

It'd hurt me as well when it came.

But at least this time, I didn't have to cash my chips.

The End

Brush Strokes

By Gene Moyers

"**P**lease lie back and close your eyes Miss Vidalis."

The young blonde woman looked up from the reclining sofa with a confused look, "But you said more hypnotism wasn't going to help?"

The conservatively dressed man smiled from the armchair near her, "No, I'm sure it won't. What we're attempting is not hypnosis but a simple technique to help you access subconscious memories."

The woman nodded as she leaned back on the sofa. He continued, "Now I want you to close your eyes and breathe slowly and deeply. Follow my instructions and you will hopefully relax into a state where we may access memories of things that you did not realize you had. Let's begin."

He began talking to the woman gently in a low voice. Thomas Manning was brilliant young psychologist. One of the techniques he had learned was the using the tone and pitch of his voice to influence others. He had also learned other skills, one of which he hoped would help Susan Vidalis today.

A few months before, she had been nearly strangled to death on a dark Baltimore street by an unknown assailant. She had been saved only by the accidental appearance of a passerby. Her attacker had fled leaving the woman near death. She had recovered but remembered nothing of her attacker. Doctors and even hypnotism had failed to do help her recover her memories.

Now Manning was attempting a unique method of accessing the woman's memories. Soon Susan had relaxed to the point where she had drifted off to sleep. When he was sure she was sleeping soundly, he leaned back in his armchair closed his eyes and began slowing his own breathing. He was practiced in meditation and within minutes he too was in a deep sleep.

● ● ●

He awoke on a dark city street walking along at a brisk pace. The street was nearly deserted. Ahead of him he could see a well-dressed woman in an overcoat walking alone. He followed her as she turned a corner into a residential area. Suddenly a dark figure lunged from the shadows beneath a large tree. The figure grabbed the woman and dragged her into the shadows. Manning threw himself forward.

As he did, his perspective shifted. Suddenly he was staring into dark, glaring eyes just inches away from his own. His throat was constricted and he could not breathe. His vision narrowed as gray closed in at the edges. The gray then became a fog he was surrounded by. Gradually it thinned and he was confronted by a mass of swirling color. He realized it was a painting of dark blues, purples, grays and blacks mixing and swirling apart in a chilling manner.

Manning closed his eyes, when he opened them he was in darkness. Glimpses of lighter gray appeared and disappeared around him. As he walked forward he could feel twigs and grass under his feet. Gradually his eyes adjusted and the lighter gray patches became light glimpsed through the branches of thick forest he was traversing. It was a barren forest. The trees were dead, stripped of their leaves, the bare branches wavering slightly from a chill wind blowing through them.

Gradually the forest thinned around him and he reached the edge of an eerie and barren landscape and looked out across a barren plain. The moonlight showed no sign of any movement. The only things breaking the featureless plain were huge stones stark in the moonlight. Most of the rocks were strangely shaped. Many were misshapen as if they had once been alive and were now frozen in agony instead of being shaped by wind and rain. Others seemed almost as if they were huge carved monoliths.

The moonlight illuminating this surreal landscape seemed to pulse. Glancing upward expecting to see clouds obscuring it Manning was surprised to see a full moon beaming from a cloudless black sky. But it was not the moon he was used to seeing. The light given off from the orbiting sphere had a strange yellow tint and seemed somehow duller than he remembered. More troubling the familiar features people laughingly called the "Man in the Moon" were gone. They had been replaced by dark masses and slashes of shadow across a far different face than the moon that we see every night.

A chill ran through him and he looked behind him at the barren forest. It seemed to leer and lean forward. Stepping backwards Manning wished for a weapon of some kind. He looked down as his foot brushed against something. A sturdy carved wooden club lay at his feet. Hefting it he took an experimental swing and nodded. It was good he had thought of the weapon for a dark mass erupted from the tree line showering dead branches in all directions as it charged at him. He raised the club and swung . . .and was on the ground, hands around his throat.

He could feel the blood pounding in his head. The shadowy attacker was above him bearing down with his weight. He swung and the club connected with his attacker's head. Suddenly the weight was off him and he rolled to the side gasping. The attacker was on his knees shaking his head. A shout came from nearby; he leaped to his feet and fled. As he did Manning got a glimpse of him in the moonlight. He was tall and thin. He had balding dark hair but his features were not distinct. In a flash he was lost in the shadows.

● ● ●

Dr. Manning blinked and sat up in his chair. Near him Susan Vidalis murmured in her sleep. Manning shook her shoulder gently. She opened her eyes and looked surprised. He smiled and said, "I think you fell asleep Susan."

She sat up, "Oh, for how long?"

Just for a few moments."

"I don't remember. You were talking and . . . did it work?"

Manning smiled as he extended a hand to help her to her feet, "Yes, it did. While you were relaxed you said several interesting things before you fell asleep."

"Did I say anything about the . . ."

"Yes. Although I'm not sure exactly what it means. I need to think for a day or two. We'll meet again soon and try to make sense of it. Can you come again Friday?"

Manning escorted the young woman to his outer office. Alexis, his secretary, was at her desk. He addressed the attractive brunette, "Alexis can we fit Susan in sometime on Friday?"

Minutes later the young woman was on her way and Manning turned toward his inner office. He stopped as his secretary questioned, "Well Doctor Dream Master did the young lady give up her secrets?"

Manning gave her a stern look, "The Dream Master is dead, and good riddance."

Alexis smiled sweetly, "And we know who sent him happily on his way don't we?

Manning looked thoughtful, "Perhaps someday I'll take a look at your dreams, Alexis."

Alexis looked startled and her cheeks colored as she replied, "I don't think so! A girl should have some secrets, you know." Thomas shook his head, "Alexis I'd fire you if you weren't so indispensable." He paused, "What was the name of that millionaire artist who the critics were making such a fuss over a few months ago?"

Surprised, Alexis quickly searched her memory, "Uh, something Lombard, I think."

"Right. Call around to some of the galleries. Find out where he was showing and see if anyone has any of his paintings left." Alexis pulled a thick telephone directory from her desk, "Why the sudden interest in art?"

He smiled thinly, "I think I'm going to start collecting." As he re-entered his office she could see him fingering the small gold key on his watch chain. She let out a silent whistle and reached for her telephone.

A few minutes later Alexis bustled into Manning's office and read from her notes, "The artist's name is Julian Lombard. He inherited his money from his father a few years ago. He sold everything and is now a society darling. No one knows when he took up painting but he started making a big splash over a year ago with, and I quote from the art critic of the *Baltimore Sun*, 'his fascinating fusion of modern abstract painting and traditional landscapes,' unquote." She held up her hands in self-defense at Manning's expression, "Hey, that's what he said. Anyway Lombard's been showing at the *Rivelo Gallery* downtown. I called and he has a permanent showing there. In fact he actually owns the joint behind the scenes." She raised an eyebrow at this.

Manning stood up and moved to the large windows overlooking Baltimore from the eighth floor. He fingered his key and said, "As soon as my last appointment is here you may go home. I'll be leaving early."

Alexis agreed and made her exit leaving Manning staring out over the city.

● ● ●

At six o'clock Thomas Manning's cab pulled up in front of the *Rivelo Gallery* on a busy Baltimore street. Stepping out placed he his homburg on his head and paid the cabbie before hefting his walking stick and entering the gallery. Inside it was high ceilinged and well lit. Paintings lined the walls and hung on temporary room dividers. Through an arch Manning could see more paintings. Manning stepped toward a painting as a well-dressed, middle aged man came up to him, "Good evening. Can I help you?"

Manning turned and smiled at the gallery manager, "Perhaps. I'm redecorating and a friend recommended your gallery. I'm looking for something . . . different."

The man smiled and nodded, "I'm sure we have something that will interest you. Do you have anything in mind?"

Manning looked thoughtful, "Well, I've always enjoyed landscapes but lately I've become interested in the new abstract school."

The man smiled and pointed, "Over here we have some wonderful work." He led the way toward a wall of paintings. Manning removed his hat and studied the paintings before him, "These are very nice but I'm looking for something a little more visually commanding." He managed to keep a straight face as he thought to himself how pompous that sounded. The manager nodded as Manning spoke again, "Haven't I heard about a new local painter who's doing some startling work lately"

The manager smiled, "You must be thinking of Julian Lombard."

"Yes, that's the man. Do you have any of his work here?"

The manager puffed up and said proudly. "Why yes we do. Would you care to see some examples?"

"Yes, I certainly would."

"Please, follow me." The gallery manager led Manning through the arch into the inner room. He steered Manning to a wall where eight or nine large paintings hung in a group. Most of them were landscapes. One showed a rural scene; rolling green hills in the back ground, lush fields of ripening crops surrounding a rustic farm house in the near foreground, all beneath a cloud filled blue sky. There were animals scattered about the fields. Manning decided it was well drawn. The artist's technique and detail were good. Strangely though, the farmhouse seemed slightly out of focus. Also its dimensions seemed off. Part of it seemed to sag as if melting off the canvas while other parts of the house seemed to be in a different perspective. The effect was startling and Manning admitted fascinating.

The longer he stared at the painting though the more Manning felt something was wrong about it. Something about the dark spaces of the windows seemed off. Manning leaned in until his nose was almost touching the canvas and could swear he could almost see shadows moving inside the tiny house. He frowned and stepped back. The longer he looked at it the more it bothered him. The manager waited patiently but seeing Manning so intent on the painting he eventually wandered off.

Manning moved on to another painting. This one was a landscape of a vast rolling plain. Scattered across it were hills, forests and herds of animals. It too was incredibly detailed but as he gazed at it Manning decided there was something wrong with the sky. Yes it was in unusual shades of green with subtle gray and yellow under tones but the longer he looked at it the more ominous it seemed. Not as if a storm were moving in but something else that the psychologist couldn't put his finger on.

Manning looked and caught the gallery manager's eye with a wave. He came over and Manning inquired about the price of the farmhouse painting and was quoted a high price. He had expected that and showed no surprise. He asked for other prices and was quoted accordingly. Thoughtfully said, "These are interesting. Do you have any others by the artist? Perhaps some new arrivals?"

The man frowned and hesitated, "No. I'm afraid this is all we have at this time."

Manning nodded and said, "I'd like to think about it for a moment." He then strolled away. The gallery manager nodded and withdrew. Taking time to look at paintings along the way Manning worked his way toward the rear of the gallery. There he found a set of double doors marked *Employees Only*. He went in search of the manager. He found him and told him he had decided to take the farm house landscape. The manager smiled as he thought of his commission. Manning handed him a business card and he scurried away to begin the paperwork.

As soon as the happy manger left, Manning made for the rear doors. They were unlocked and he quickly slipped inside. Inside the large room there were paintings leaning in stacks against the walls. Manning quickly began flipping through painting after painting. It did not take him long to find one stack of large four and five foot paintings that contained canvases signed *Lombard*.

He pulled one out and frowned. It was definitely disturbing. It was four by five feet and it consisted of nothing but color. Vivid reds, maroons, purples and blacks were painted in massive swirls. At first it seemed just dark and a bit dizzying but as he stared the psychologist seemed to feel a cold breeze in his face as if the painting was somehow a window into a dark and frightening world. He flipped to another, sure that the chill on his neck was from a draft.

This painting was some sort of landscape done at night. Totally painted in black, dark grays and dark blues it took a moment for Manning to decide exactly what it depicted. Then it snapped into perspective. It was a night scene looking at a wall of towering cliffs. Carved in the middle of the cliffs was the narrow slash of a steep walled canyon. It was barely more than a very black split in the cliffs barely visible on a dark moonless night. The painting had a strange perspective as if the horizon was slightly off and the psychologist had the strangest feeling that there was something in the black canyon that was watching him, something dangerous.

He was snapped back to reality by a loud voice calling, "Sir, you are not allowed in here!"

Manning jumped and turned to find a large man standing in the open doorway. He was dressed in workman's clothing and staring very hard at Manning. Manning let go of the painting and moved casually toward the front room. As he neared the hard faced man he smiled, "I was just sneaking a quick preview of some the art." The big man held the door wide for the psychologist and indicated he should precede him through it. Once in the gallery he heard the door close loudly behind him. As he entered the front gallery he saw the workman staring hard after him.

Near the front of the gallery he found the manager waiting for him with a quizzical look on his face. Manning smiled and apologized, "I'm sorry I got caught up in the art." He set his hat and walking stick on the desk and pulled a check book from his pocket. As he made out the check the manager looked at his business card, "Where do you want the painting shipped, Dr. Manning?"

Manning handed him the check and said, "My office address is on the check. Please send the painting there."

"Of course. It will take a couple of days to package up the painting and have it delivered. And thank you again Dr. Manning."

On the street Manning quickly waved down a cab. Once inside the psychologist gave the address of his apartment building and leaned back. A few minutes later the cabbie pulled up at a red light. He looked over his shoulder and asked, "You got problems mister?"

Manning was surprised, "No. Why do you ask?"

"Because somebody's following us."

"What?"

"Yeah, he's been on us since I picked you up." The light changed and the cabbie moved off leaving Manning nonplussed in the back seat. He considered this new development as the cabbie spoke again, "Ya want me to lose him?" Manning considered this, "Thanks, but no. We'll play innocent and I'll try to get a look at him when you drop me."

The cabbie shrugged, "It's your dime mister."

Manning resisted the temptation to look out the back for the remainder of the trip. When they pulled up in front of his apartment building, he got out and leaned in the passenger window to pay. As he did a dark Packard drove slowly past. The driver was alone. As he passed, the driver shot a quick glance Manning's way. He was wearing a hat and tried to keep his face down but the psychologist recognized him from the gallery. He paid the cabbie and added a hefty tip, "You've been very helpful. Thank you very kindly." The cabbie glanced at the money in surprise and smiled, "Thanks mister." He waved as he pulled away.

Manning was thoughtful as he nodded to the doorman and entered his building. By the time the elevator door opened on his floor he had made some decisions.

● ● ●

The next morning Alexis arrived at the office at her usual time just before 9 a.m. She was surprised to find the office unlocked. The outer office was empty but as she hung up her coat she could hear a voice in the inner office. She frowned. It was unusual for Dr. Manning to be in before her. She approached the inner door, knocked lightly and was rewarded with a, "Come in."

Entering she found her boss on the phone. He held up a hand as he spoke into the receiver, "Thank you, lieutenant. You've been very helpful." He hung up but before he could say anything Alexis inquired sweetly, "Joining the Army? I hear they're talking about starting up the draft again."

Ignoring her jibe Manning asked, "What's the schedule like today?"

Alexis thought for a moment, "You've got a ten o'clock, a one o'clock and a three o'clock."

"Okay that gives me some time this morning. After the ten o'clock gets here head down to the library and the *Sun* and see what you can find out about Julian Lombard."

"Okay Boss."

The morning passed quickly for Manning; most of the time spent on the phone taking notes. He grabbed a quick lunch and was back seeing patients in the afternoon. As he saw the last one out at four, Alexis was ready with her report.

She read from her notes, "Lombard is 36, a few years older than you. He's third generation Italian. His grandfather came over last century. He was a farmer who started hauling produce around in wagons. Julian's father built the business up into an interstate trucking company. Julian studied business here at the University of Maryland. He worked in the business for a few years until his father was killed in an auto accident five years ago. His mother died when he was a child."

She flipped a page, "At that time he sold the business. He then took some art classes in New York for a year. He then traveled the country for a year painting and wound up on the west coast. Since then he's been active in the local social scene and is known for entertaining at his Annapolis mansion. He's made a big splash in the local art scene for the last year or so." She flipped her notebook closed.

Manning stood up and walked to the window where he stared down into the street, "Interesting." He thought for a moment before turning and smiling, "Thank you Alexis, that is very helpful. Go on home now, I'll lock up"

Once alone Manning studied his notes for a long time, his mind running dates and facts. Thoughtfully he locked up his office. Once on the street he decided a brisk walk to one of his favorite restaurants would help clear his head.

He had a leisurely dinner and by eight o'clock he was picking up his hat at the coat check and pushing onto the sidewalk. It was a cool fall evening but not so cool that he needed an overcoat. The sidewalks weren't crowded but there were quite a few pedestrians still about. He stepped to the curb to hail a cab when something caught his eye. He hesitated for a moment then began strolling further uptown.

Many shops were still open and Manning stopped often to window shop and look around as he strolled. Within minutes he confirmed what he suspected. He was being followed. When he exited the restaurant he had recognized someone he thought he had seen when he entered. Sure enough that person was strolling along perhaps fifty yards behind him. The psychologist briefly considered ducking into a nearby building and losing his shadow but quickly decided to handle things a different way.

At a brightly lit window full of furniture he made a show of pulling out his pocket watch and checking the time. He exclaimed in surprise and then rapping his walking stick angrily on the sidewalk he turned and walked back in the direction he had come.

As expected this caught the shadowing man off guard. He broke stride for a moment then caught himself and continued on attempting to look casual. Manning pretended not to notice and walked briskly toward him looking down the street past him. As the two men came abreast of each other Manning, his walking stick now in his left hand brought it up sharply between the legs of the taller man.

The man let out a gasping "ooooff!" and sank to his knees grabbing at his crotch. As he passed, Manning rapped him sharply across the back of the head. The man fell face forward onto the sidewalk. A glance showed no one nearby. Manning quickly dropped to one knee and searched the unconscious man's pockets. He came up with the usual assortment of possessions; keys, cigarettes, matches, handkerchief, wallet and a .38 revolver tucked into his waistband.

Manning opened up the cylinder, ejected the cartridges and tossed them into the gutter. He dropped the gun on the man's back and quickly examined his wallet. There was a surprising amount of cash. He left the money and dropped the wallet alongside the gun after checking the man's driver's license. Less than a minute later Manning was walking down the street. He hailed a cab in the next block and had it take him home. On the trip he pondered why a Paul Parsons of Annapolis would be following a psychologist around Baltimore's streets.

The next day was a normal day at the office. His day was only broken by a long distance phone call to San Francisco he had Alexis place for him. It was late afternoon when Alexis leaned into his office with a surprised look on her face, "Phone for you doctor."

Manning put down his pen, "Who is it?"

"Julian Lombard," Alexis deadpanned, although her eyebrows were threatening to disappear into her hairline. Manning hesitated then picked up the receiver, "This is Dr. Manning." Alexis quietly closed the door.

"Doctor Manning? This is Julian Lombard."

"Mr. Lombard. This is a surprise. What can I do for you today?"

"I was advised by the *Rivelo Gallery* that you had purchased one of my paintings. I was surprised, of course, but pleasantly surprised. I thought I'd call and thank you personally for your patronage."

"That's very kind of you Mr. Lombard but it was my pleasure. I find your work refreshingly unique. I had heard a lot about you but frankly, the stories don't do your work justice. I can't remember when I've seen such striking art."

There was a brief pause on the other end of the line, "That is certainly high praise coming from one of Baltimore's leading psychologists. Would that you were writing my press releases."

Manning smiled thinly, "You may gladly quote me, sir."

"I must admit that was only half of my reason for calling." Now we get down to it, thought Manning, "Really? What else can I do for you?"

"You could do me the honor of dining with me." Manning was caught off guard but recovered quickly, "That is very kind of you Mr. Lombard. Did you have a day in mind?"

"Well, I am dining alone this evening. Are you free tonight?"

The psychologist's mind raced. He wanted to meet Lombard personally but had planned on more neutral ground. He stalled, "Well, I did have plans to meet someone later . . ."

The controlled voice came back quickly, "A young lady perhaps? I would be pleased if you brought your guest along. My chef is excellent and I do set a fine table if I may say so." Manning frowned. Like most very rich people Lombard was used to getting his own

way. Deciding, he replied, "That is most kind. I would be happy to accept your invitation. What time would be convenient?"

"Shall we say eight o'clock?" Manning agreed, directions were given and the call ended. Manning stood up, adjusted his vest and went out to the front office. Alexis looked up as he entered the room.

"How would you like to go to dinner tonight?"

Alexis' face flashed through, surprise, delight and finally stopped at suspicious, "What's the catch?"

● ● ●

"Are you sure this is a good idea?" Although the top was up on the roadster Alexis still had to raise her voice to be heard clearly. Manning gave her a quick look before again concentrating on his driving, "I need to find out if my suspicions are correct but I didn't think it would be quite like this."

And you think the man who was following you works for Lombard?"

"Who else?"

Alexis glared, "Just what did you see in Susan Vidalis' dreams?"

"Nothing definite. I saw visions of what appeared to be paintings that held elements of violence and menace. She also dreams of her attacker but I could not see him clearly. It could have been Lombard but I can't be sure without more evidence."

"So we're having dinner with a possible violent killer who likes to strangle women? Gee, you sure know how to show a gal a good time!"

"I'm sure we'll be completely safe. Lombard won't try to harm us at his home where people know we have visited."

Alexis was silent for the remainder of the trip. Although somewhat isolated, Lombard's mansion was easy to find. It was a large; two story brick home on several acres that faced Chesapeake Bay north of Annapolis. A circular drive led to a large portico over the front door. They parked and Manning took Alexis' arm, "Be charming. We're just here to get a feel for the man." He rang the bell and glanced at her, "If you can afford to buy beautiful gowns like that I must be paying you too much." Alexis glared at him but was secretly pleased. Their relationship was sometimes playful but always correct and within boundaries so acknowledgements of her femininity were few and far between.

Within seconds the door was answered by an older man in full formal rig who appeared to be a traditional butler. This was confirmed when he asked to take their coats in a pure English accent. He quickly showed them through an arch into a luxuriously furnished formal living room where the owner of the house stood.

Lombard came forward to greet them and as he shook hands with Manning Alexis compared the two men. Both were trimly built but Lombard was at least three inches taller than the psychologist's 5' 10" height making him appear thinner. The artist was dark haired with a strongly receding hairline at each temple. His hair was combed straight back and his hairline, along with his thin face and strong Roman nose, gave him a somewhat predatory look to Alexis' eyes. There was something she instinctively didn't like about the man. However he appeared most charming as he smiled, "Dr. Manning. Thank you for coming."

Ever polite Manning replied, "Thank you for inviting us Mr. Lombard." He turned and gestured, "May I present Mrs. Alexis Welch."

Lombard took her outstretched hand gently and bowed over it, "Mrs. Welch my home is brightened by your beauty." Yes, she thought, he was dangerously charming. He smiled, "I would offer you a cocktail but I believe dinner is ready." He gestured toward where the butler was patiently waiting.

They re-entered the entry hall and Alexis commented, "You have a beautiful home Mr. Lombard."

He led them down the hall into the large dining room replying, "Thank you, and please call me Julian."

Lombard gallantly held out her chair for her as Manning moved closer to a large landscape on the wall. He peered at it and spoke, "I see this one is one of yours." He stepped back and added, "Magnificent."

As he seated himself Lombard nodded, "Thank you. It seems you've become quite a fan, I'm flattered."

He signaled the butler for wine as Manning joined them at the table, "Your work is unique. It shows talent and unusual vision."

Lombard nodded and seemed ready to reply but was interrupted by the arrival of the first course. During dinner conversation naturally revolved around the meal and Lombard's' home but gradually evolved into other areas. Quite naturally the talk eventually came around to art.

"How did you hear about my work?" questioned Lombard.

Manning took a sip of his wine and shrugged, "I follow art generally. I read some reviews of you work and friends had spoken of you. Once I saw some of your works I became entranced. Tell me where do you draw your inspirations from?"

Lombard smiled but his eyes got distant. After a moment he spoke lightly, "The landscapes come from my travels. I have a good memory for places I've been."

"And the abstract component?" prompted Manning.

Lombard gave a short laugh as he swirled his wine, "My imagination of course, doctor."

Alexis put in, "Then you must have quite an imagination Julian. Where did you study art?"

He set his glass down and said, "I didn't." He frowned, "My father wanted me to study business and take over his company. It wasn't until after his death that I took some classes in art and found I had a talent."

Manning spoke, "Interesting. Where did you take these classes?"

"New York, actually. I sold the company and traveled for a while. I did some additional studying in California." He refilled his glass, "It turns out the only thing I really want to do is create my art."

Manning nodded, "Where in California did you study?"

"I spent nearly a year in San Francisco studying and painting before I returned here and purchased my home."

Alexis added, "And it is such a lovely home. How big a staff do you have here?"

"Just a small inside staff, my personal needs are small. I do have my chauffeur and a couple of grounds men who also act as security when I need it."

Alexis seemed surprised, "Really, why would you need security?"

Lombard shrugged, "I do like my privacy, and there have been a few curious fans that have come calling without invitation." During this conversation Manning had left the table carrying his glass and returned to the landscape on the wall. It was well executed but there was something ominous about the sky and the colors of the background surrounding a small village in the center of the painting. The longer he gazed at it the more it seemed as if the surrounding hills and forests were threatening the small village.

Manning turned to Lombard, "I wouldn't mind having something like this as a center piece in my apartment. Do you have others like it, Julian?"

Lombard turned and gave Manning an interested look, "Nothing exactly like that. I do have good selection of paintings at the *Rivelo Gallery*. They've been very generous in carrying a selection of my work."

Manning nodded, "Unfortunately I purchased the only one that spoke to me. Though I wouldn't mind seeing some your other work."

Lombard stood up, "Let's have a nightcap in my study. I have some more work there that you might enjoy."

Manning moved to Alexis' side to hold her chair as she stood. The two of them followed Lombard out of the dining room down the main hall to the rear of the house. He led them to an expensively decorated study.

Most of one wall was floor to ceiling windows split by tall French doors, all looking out across the waters of Chesapeake Bay. It was dark but the lights of boats could be seen twinkling on the water. Alexis moved immediately to the windows exclaiming, "The view must be wonderful during the day. It's beautiful even now."

Lombard acknowledged the compliment with a smile, "Yes, although it seems that Dr. Manning prefers the interior views." He moved to a table covered in bottles and glasses. He set out three glasses and lifted a cut glass decanter.

Alexis turned and saw Manning staring at a painting. She moved to join him. As she reached him he spoke to Lombard over his shoulder, "Now this is interesting. It would look wonderful on my wall." Alexis frowned as she moved up next to him. The painting was a solid mass of deep blues, greens and grays with subtle layering horizontally. It was dark and seemed to absorb light. Alexis could swear that for a moment she had seen a darker shapeless mass deep in the painting. She was distracted by Lombard moving up beside her and holding out a glass of amber liquid, "Brandy?"

She turned and took the glass from his hand, "Why thank you." As she did Lombard's hand touched hers and lingered for just an instant, or was it her imagination. Before she could decide, Lombard gestured at the painting, "I was daydreaming of the sea when I got the inspiration for that. I imagined myself as a creature of the deep swimming through the dark sea." He took a sip of his brandy, "Frankly I wasn't sure people would understand it so I kept if for myself." Alexis looked again at the painting but the dark mass had vanished. Had she imagined it?

Manning looked at Lombard appraisingly, "Is it for sale?"

Lombard shook his head, "No doctor, I'm afraid not."

Manning sipped and asked, "But you must have other unusual works stashed away. I would love to purchase an outstanding piece such as this." He waved at the painting.

Lombard frowned slightly, "Yes, I have other works but many I could never part with . . ."

Manning finished his drink. Lombard noticed and moved that way, "May I get you a refill?"

"Perhaps a small one" Lombard added a splash of brandy to Manning's glass. He reached for Alexis' glass. She put a hand over it, "No thanks for me." Manning lifted his glass to Lombard and they both drained their glasses.

Alexis yawned and mentioned how late it was. Manning agreed. Lombard made a token protest but led them out of the library. Within minutes they were bidding their host goodbye at his door.

In the car Manning was silent as they drove away from the mansion toward the highway.Alexis was silent as well. Finally she could hold herself no longer, "Well?"

He asked, "Did you have a nice time?"

"Nice time? That's all you have to say? You drag me clear out here to have dinner with that strange man and that's all you have to say?"

"I thought dinner was nice and our host was most charming"

"Yes, but scary as well. Did you see those paintings? They're depressing. I don't know why people rave so much about them."

"On the surface they seem complex and *Avant Garde`* but they say much about the artist himself.

Alexis looked at her boss, "Is that why you wanted to meet him?"

"Yes, I got a look at some his work that he isn't showing the public and it was very troubling."

Alexis thought this over, "So you think he's dangerous?"

"Worse, I think he's a killer. What I saw in Susan Vidalis' dreams seemed to be frightening paintings exactly like Lombard's. And although her memories of him are vague Lombard looks very much like what she remembers of her attacker. Also I have found out there have been several other women strangled in the last few years in Annapolis, Baltimore and Washington D.C. Also one in San Francisco when Lombard was out there. Unfortunately they have been in too many jurisdictions for the police to have connected them."

Alexis was quiet for a moment, "What are you going to do?"

There was a pause before the psychologist answered, "I think I have to get much closer to Mr. Lombard."

● ● ●

The next day everything seemed normal at the office. The psychologist seemed relaxed and at ease. Alexis wasn't fooled though. She caught him at one point after lunch staring out his window and fingering the gold key on his watch chain.

After their last patient had left Alexis was only slightly surprised when he asked her to get Lombard on the phone at his home. Trouble was definitely on the horizon.

Once connected he spoke, "Hello. Julian? This is Thomas Manning."

The artist seemed surprised, "Why Dr. Manning. I'm surprised to hear from you so soon."

"I called to thank you for a wonderful dinner."

"It was a pleasure to have you and. . . your friend."

Manning caught the hesitation as the artist spoke of Alexis. He remained calm and continued, "There is one more thing."

"Yes."

"I'm still very interested in your private paintings."

"As I told you they are not for sale."

"I could give you a very good price."

There was a pause, "I doubt very much if you could meet my price doctor."

Manning continued, "Perhaps if we met I could persuade you. Will you be at home this evening?"

Another pause, "I will be, but I warn you I am not easy to persuade."

Manning replied, "Then I would like to try. Is nine o'clock too late?"

"Not at all, I will look for you then."

"Until then Julian." Manning hung up quietly. He leaned back in his chair and closed his eyes while he fingered his key.

● ● ●

Shortly after nine o'clock that night Thomas Manning, dressed in dark clothing, was moving quietly across the darkened grounds of Julian Lombard's Chesapeake estate. He had left his car some distance away. Once near the mansion he moved around to the bay side of the house opposite the study. The lights in the room were low. Lombard was there alone. He was sitting in a wingback chair a glass in his hand. He was to be staring off into space.

Manning pulled his watch from his pocket and flipped it open. It was difficult to see in the moonlight but he finally made out that it was nearly nine thirty. He moved to the patio and settled in to wait. Soon Lombard finished his drink and yawned. Manning smiled. Eventually Lombard was nodding. He leaned back and closed his eyes.

On the patio Manning took an iron chair from around a table and moved it near the study windows. He positioned the chair in the shadows and sat down. He got comfortable, placed his hands in his lap and closed his eyes. Clearing his mind, he slowed his breath, and concentrated on his breathing. In a few minutes he slid into a deep sleep.

● ● ●

Manning woke to find himself in a dark corridor. Not at all disoriented he walked forward along the shadowy corridor. It seemed to be illuminated at intervals by pools of light. In the first illuminated area a painting hung on a wall that wasn't really there. It showed a beautiful woman asleep under a spreading tree. The scene was peaceful and beautiful, the detail perfect in every respect. As Manning scrutinized it he somehow knew that the woman was not sleeping but dead.

He moved on and came to another painting. This one was a mélange of colors; sickly greens, muddy yellows and drab gays all swirling all about the canvas. The swirls were moving in large concentric circles that seemed to draw Manning forward as if sucking him into it.

He tore his eyes away and moved on through the darkness. Another strangely illuminated canvas appeared. It was much like the sea scene in Lombard's study. But in this one the shadowy shapes in the deep were more visible as they swam in the dark sea. They were not clear but seemed huge and ominous. He moved on.

The next painting he came to was in shades of gray that gave it the appearance of a black and white photo. It was a desolate street scene; stark buildings, deep shadows and an empty street. In the foreground was the body of a woman. Her face and body were partially in shadow. Manning somehow knew that the woman had been murdered. He did not waste time here but moved more quickly through the darkness.

He passed more of those stark alien landscapes, troubling abstracts and increasingly violent images of women and death. Manning did not stop to examine them. They would tell him nothing new. He passed a particularly disturbing landscape and saw a brighter island of light ahead.

Manning moved ahead carefully. He stepped into the dim light and found Lombard standing in front of a large canvas on an easel a brush in one hand, a palette in the other. The canvas faced away from him allowing the psychologist to see Lombard's face as he painted. His face was entranced by the painting as he swept the brush across the canvas. He seemed not to notice the psychologist. Not wanting to break the spell Manning edged sideways until he could partially see the canvas. It was a portrait of several men in Renaissance dress wearing swords.

Before he could get a clear look Lombard turned and looked directly at him, "Do you like it?" Manning didn't speak; his attention was fixed on Lombard's eyes. They glittered with madness and a hint of a smile creased his lips. He stopped painting and pointed the brush at Manning, "I don't know how you got here but somehow I knew you'd come. I've been waiting."

Manning held his ground, "Then you know there must be an end. This cannot be allowed to continue."

Lombard shifted the brush to his left hand and nodded, "You are correct. This is the end." He then reached for the painting. Manning shifted quickly to his left as Lombard reached into the painting and grasped a rapier from the hand of a man standing in the foreground. Manning jumped back just far enough to avoid Lombard's lunge.

Reflexively he dropped into a stance with one foot back and at right angles. His other hand pointed forward and upward. He was not surprised to find his walking stick in his hand. As always, everything here seemed perfectly normal. He whisked the sword from the cane just in time to meet Lombard's next attack. He parried in sixte and disengaged. Sliding back a step he met the next attack the same way this time parrying in quarte. He then lunged forward. Lombard barely parried in time.

Sensing that his opponent was not as experienced with a blade as he was, the psychologist pressed his advantage. He attacked, disengaged and attacked again each attack coming closer to his opponent. Lombard's rapier began to drop. His wrist was tiring. As Manning pressed in, Lombard ducked and slashed wildly with his blade. It caught Manning across the calf of his lead leg. His pant leg was little protection and the blade hurt like the devil as it raked across his calf.

The move was one of desperation though. The momentum of using his blade as club loosened it in his hand. Manning slid forward caught the blade and with a quick twist of his wrist sent Lombard's sword spinning into the darkness. Surprised, Lombard recovered swiftly as Manning raised his sword for the kill. He screamed his hate at the psychologist and swung his left hand forward.

The psychologist was surprised to see the artist still held his paint brush but as the hand swung forward the brush lengthened and burst into flame. Stunned, Manning gave ground as Lombard swung the torch at his face. He fended off the torch with his sword as the artist screamed his delight.

Pressing forward Lombard changed tactics. Instead of swinging the blazing torch he thrust it toward the psychologist's face forcing him back even more. The torch was heavier than his sword and its bright flame was nearly blinding. Manning held his free hand to protect his eyes and suddenly his heel caught on something and he went over backwards. He landed hard but retained his sword as the artist jumped forward with a scream of triumph. Manning thrust his sword upwards below the outstretched torch and Lombard literally impaled himself on it. The blade slid deep into his upper chest.

Lombard dropped the torch somewhere over Manning's shoulder and stared into his face. He seemed surprised. His mouth opened and he attempted to say something then fell over dead, the surprised look frozen on his face. Manning stood up, his walking stick back in his hand. He looked down at Lombard's body and ran a tired hand across his face. He closed his eyes and took a deep breath . . .

. . . And woke up in the lawn chair with a start. It was dark and quiet behind the mansion. Manning could hear crickets chirping in the nearby shrubbery. He stood up and looked into the study. Lombard still appeared peacefully asleep in his armchair but Manning knew different. Without a backward glance he walked quickly away into the darkness.

● ● ●

Manning was working in his office the next morning when he heard voices in the outer office. He looked up as Alexis entered his office and crossed to his desk. She dropped the morning newspaper on his desk, "Have you seen the headlines?" He glanced down, "Hmmm . . . local artist dies of heart attack." He shook his head, "A terrible loss of talent."

"I don't suppose I want to know what happened, do I?"

Manning shook his head, "Probably not."

Alexis looked worried, "Tommy, I'm worried someday I'm going to be reading about your tragic accident."

Manning thought of the nasty welt on his right calf, "Anything is possible Alexis." He pointed at the door, "What is that commotion out there?"

Alexis smiled, "Oh, they're delivering your painting from the gallery. What do you want done with it?"

Manning declared, "Burn it!"

The End

Masked Flapper

by Kevin Noel Olson

Chloe's red dress swirled in the wind. The force threatened to separate the sequins from the cloth. The white feather atop the gold-embellished, masquerade half-mask she wore pulled out and twirled wildly into night and disappeared into dark. Chloe's tall frame stooped down to fumble with the keys before dropping them next to her car. Rain started to fall through the warm night air. Her sigh convulsed into tears lost with the drumming downpour.

"Damn." she said and repeated again. Three times and louder. She picked up the keys, dripping with water. She thrust them in the door, pulled it open and climbed into the sedan.

She turned on the radio. It produced swing music. Glumly, she adjusted her Porter's hat that she wore like the trophy that it was. She looked into the rearview mirror, opening her clutch to freshen her makeup. Her lipstick ran a line over her face as something bumped the back of her seat.

"I have your gun." She used a handkerchief to wipe off the streak. "Do that again and I may just use it. This lipstick's not cheap ya'know!"

"Listen gams," a voice growled from the backseat. "Ya better let me go, or you'll have no teeth to smudge!"

With a violent yank, she stressed the door to glove compartment and pulled out a .45, its blue steel glinting. She turned to face the battered man tied up in the backseat, his disheveled gray suit covered in his own blood. "Don't call me gams! I'm a lady."

"Yeah. A lady who knows how to work a guy over with a crowbar!"

"I appreciate you callin' me a lady. Now that we've broken the ice…"

"You mean broken my teeth!" He spat out a tooth to illustrate, inadvertently spitting out three.

"Those little dead rocks…with how yellow they are. You ever heard of brushing? Besides, you made me waste cosmetics, so I'd call that even. As I was saying, now that we've broken the ice, let's get acquainted. I'm a Capricorn."

"Yer nuts!"

"I'm animal crackers," Chloe feigned a pout. "Go on, what's your sign, big fella?"

"Stop is my sign."

"You don't know how to play in traffic. You need to yield." He sat forward. Chloe sent him back with a wave of his pistol. "Let's start all over. What's your name?"

"Ruby. What's yer name?"

Chloe laughed. "My name's mud if you marry me."

"Who's setting a date? I just want to get away from you, yah crazy dame!"

"If you tell me what I want, we'll see about what you need." Her eyes flirted.

Ruby sat back and sighed. "Okay, okay sister! What do ya wanna know?"

"Why'd you fellahs take the kid?"

"What kid?"

Chloe sneered as she pulled the hammer back, the chamber rolled until it clicked. "Don't kid me! Marty Strock. Why'd you take him?'

"Why? He's a boyfriend of yours?"

"I don't even know him."

"How'd you know about him then?"

"I was sitting at the next table in the gin joint and heard you talking to the guy you called Fatlip."

"Frankie? How'd you hear that convo? We wuz bein' quiet!"

"Not quite quiet enough!"

"That's 'cause you got big ears."

"The better to hear you with, Red."

"So, why'd you jump me when we went back to your place? Nobody gets the drop on me!"

"Really? Because I did. I lift a bit of skirt, say some melliferous sweet talk, and in a minute you're taking your shirt off. I hit when your hands were busy."

"It's kinda rude."

"Like what you wanted to do was polite."

Ruby grinned. "You could've given me a chance. I can be a real gentlemen when I want."

Chloe nodded. "Gentlemen are always gentlemen. It's not when you want. You wouldn't've called me anyway. I'd've been broken hearted."

"Like I said, you didn't give me a chance. Didn't even give me your number."

"I gave you the number all right, and I wasn't giving you any chances. So, why'd you grab the kid?"

"I'm not an independent operator. I was working for the boss."

"What'd the boss want with the kid?"

"How should I know?"

"You can't kid a kidder, kid! Spill."

"Like I told yah, I don't know."

"Where's the kid? Say you don't know, and maybe you won't know anything ever again."

Ruby turned his neck away from the barrel. "Stop waving the gun, lady! Jeez—I'll tell yah!"

"You'll do better than that. You'll take me to him."

"What's your thing, lady? It's a dangerous game you're playing here!"

"My "thing" is being a bored young girl looking for a little fun. You're the smallest fry I could hook. I might like to have kids someday, and I wouldn't want you low-life yeggs hurting my child."

"We didn't hurt him! He's fine."

"You kidnapped him. He's scared to death. Did you ever think about that, or is it just the big fat check you get at the ransom payoff? Take me to him. Now!" Chloe pressed the gun hard into his cheek. "Please."

Ruby sighed. "Alright. I know where we are. I recognize the crossroads. Start driving back toward town."

Chloe started the car, steering it down the road. "Don't try anything either."

"Or you'll hit me with a crowbar again?"

"Forget about tire irons or crowbars. I cold-cocked you with my fist. I didn't want to tell you, because you'd feel like less of a man, getting thrashed and cashed-out by a girl."

Ruby rubbed his jaw. "Yeah, it does kinda hurt. It doesn't hurt as much as thinking I'd caught a bird like you in my hand. Where'd you learn to punch like that?"

"My pa was a boxer. An amateur, but he won lots of fights, and was a great guy when sober. Me and my little brother used to practice when dad was twisting himself in a decent bender. Enough about me. What's your story? How'd you become someone what kidnaps kids?"

"Same old stuff. My dad was a sailor, or so my momma told me. Growing up on the streets, there weren't a lot to do but go to fight on someone else's streets when the time came. I served in the Great War. My old sergeant kept us from joining the under-the-dirt army more times than I can count, and I know my math. When we got back, we had a rough go tryin' to get jobs. We did what we did best. Fight and scratch for every bit of toast we could get. Our sergeant got me and a few of the soldiers to get together and make it regular-like. We was high on living until Black Friday. Used to be we could just do our little operations, but when the fat of the land got slim gangland tightened the belt on all operators."

"Regular kidnapping?"

"It's regular crime. We never go this route, but Sergeant made an exception. I wouldn't do it if there was a choice. I don't like kidnapping any more than I liked killing in the war. Take a left on the dirt road up here."

Chloe slowed the car to drive off the macadam. "This better not be a trap."

"You know it is, but you can't find out for sure until you go. You're the Girl Scout out on an adventure, and I ain't had time to set up a box-and-string trap for you. There's gonna be resistance, let me tell yah what."

"Okay. Tell me what I'm up against."

"You're against the wall. It could be as many as six soldiers turned sour on the world. Can you handle it? Or will you just drop me off and call it quits on this pretty kettle of fish? I know I'd drop the whole affair if I could. It's too late now. I'm talking friendly, but if you go through with this, you know whose side I'm on. I'll be on your side if you turn your back to your heart and forget what you heard."

The rain turned from deluge to drizzle. "See, that's where you and I are alike. You think you're stuck doing this thing. So am I."

"No, you have a choice. I don't know you. Get in too deep, we'll figure it out. If you don't, well, that's that. I gotta see it played out either way."

"This mud is getting thick. How far?"

"To the end of the road. It's never as far as you think, and that's where you're going."

"Do you always talk like the Mad Hatter?"

"Only when I'm sane. I'm trying to talk some sense into you. This ain't Wonderland."

Light showed through the trees. Thin at first as it worked its way through the timber, the house began to outline a dark shape. The rainclouds drifted apart, allowing the gibbous moon to expose the outlines of the trees. Chloe turned off the headlights and slowed the vehicle to a crawling pace.

The cars brakes protested with a slight sound as she stopped the car a good distance away. "Well, it looks like we're here. It's a dandy-daddy of a house!"

Ruby grinned. "It's our hideaway. Has twenty rooms. More like a fortress now. It used to be a getaway owned by a lumber king. It looks like you're still going through with this."

"You just see. What's the easiest way in?"

"The front door. I'm sure the fellahs would be happy to get a party favor like yourself."

"They'd get tired of me pretty quick. I suppose you're no help to me."

"Told you that already. If I thought you'd give us a problem, I'd never have told you where the kid was. This way, we don't have some crazy Queen of Hearts messin' with our plans. I brought you to the Sergeant on a silver platter, though I forgot to wrap you for his birthday. He likes opening presents."

Chloe placed the revolver in her purse, placing the strap over her shoulder, and opened the door. As she exited the automobile she said, "Don't worry. I'll wrap it up nicely. Just stay like a good dog. If you start yelling for help, I'll be right back here to shoot you first."

"I'm not a good dog." Ruby sat back when she slammed the door.

Taking advantage of the growth around the house, Chloe moved closer to the manse. As she moved behind a tree, she heard a low growl behind her. She turned to see a large mastiff chained to the tree. It frothed at the mouth. She spoke quietly and softly to it. "Hey there, pooch. Are you a good doggie?"

The Mastiff started to bark at Chloe and rushed forward. She leapt up and grasped onto the branch above her. Her feet swung as she pulled herself up, just out of reach of the dog's jaws as he leapt to bite at her foot. "Oh!" She hissed. "You're a bad pooch!"

The dog continued barking furiously at her. It kept up short jumps, realizing it couldn't reach her. She climbed higher in the tree as a streak of light appeared at the front door. "Whatcha barkin' at, ya stupid pure-bred mutt?"

With great celerity, Chloe climbed around the side of the tree to hide.

"What's Tally worked herself into a lather about, Lazy-eye?"

"Ah-the dumb dog's got a rabbit or something run up a danged tree."

"When was the last time you saw a rabbit climb a tree? We called you Lazy-eye Herman, but I'm thinkin' we could leave your orbs out. You better get your butt out there and go and check on it."

"It's probably a squirrel then," Lazy-eye Herman grumped. "I'll check it, boss."

"You do that. And hurry up! We've just got a few hours until we gotta deliver this baby."

Chloe reached into her purse and pulled something out. She rubbed some of her red lipstick on the object before she dropped it to the ground. The mastiff rushed over to pick it up. Chloe moved around the tree just as Lazy-eye walked up to the dog.

"What you got there, Tally? Give it to me."

Tally growled and held on to the object. "Here girl, let go!"

The man called Lazy-eye Herman struggled with Tally, as the dog shook its head back and to maintain its prize. Finally, he got the object and walked back to the house. "I got it!" He shouted. "It's a rabbit after all! See? Tally had its foot in her mouth, but I got the foot."

Chloe breathed a sigh of relief at the respite. A tall figure appeared as a silhouette in the doorway. "Where's the rest of the rabbit, then?"

"Heck if I know!" Lazy-eye looked at the object closer. "Wait a minute. It's a keychain!" He turned around and rushed back to the tree

"Applesauce!" Chloe whispered, climbing around the tree to escape view as Lazy-eye returned.

"Up there!" shouted Sergeant. "Get out here, Beef! It's a kitty run up the tree! Here, kitty kitty kitty! Got run up a tree, didja? I'll be your cuddlepup for the night!"

Chloe had to talk to him. "I got lost in the woods. I saw the lights and was trying to reach the house when that bear started attacking me!"

The man called Beef rushed up. "Well, come on down, doll! We'll get you warmed up on the bearskin rug."

"Settle down, Stu." Sergeant said. "She's lost. It's my house, and she's my guest."

Chloe cursed under her breath. "I'm coming down!" She shouted. She started descending.

A shouted, muffled voice came through the air. "Get me outta this damned car!"

This time, Chloe's curse rang out loudly as she leapt to the next tree. "Damnit!" Deftly, she caught the branch of the tree in her hands, using the momentum to swing her to the next tree. The bark of the evergreens tore at her driving gloves.

Sergeant ran after her, watching the air. "That sounds like Ruby! Go get him Lazy-eye! Beef, grab an electric lamp and get back here on the double! I don't know what's in the pot but things just boiled!"

Chloe jumped to another tree, then to another, repeating several times. She was thankful when rain clouds started rolling in to dampen the moonlight. She shook the branches with each leap. Sergeant could follow her sounds, but it was getting harder for him to follow her sight. She climbed higher and waited. She heard Sergeant frantically rushing about when 'Beef' Stu, the joke just came to her, came running back with the flashlight. "Here it is boss."

"Now we'll get her, Beef," Sergeant said, taking the flashlight. Then, he removed a revolver from his jacket pocket. He began to run the light up and down the trees she had already leapt from, systematically looking for her. Seeing movement, Sergeant fired. A squeak followed the gunshot, and a thump followed. A squirrel struck the ground.

"Great," Sergeant growled. "I was hunting for a midnight snack."

As the two men closed in on the tree Chloe was in, Lazy-eye ran up with Ruby. "It's some dizzy tomato, Sergeant!" Ruby explained. "She heard me talking to Fatlip at the masked ball, and planted seeds in my mind that I might have some fruit. When we got to an hour-flat, she clubbed with a crowbar and tied me up. She stole my car to boot!"

"You was talkin' to Frankie Fatlip about this job? I oughta knock the ivory decorations out of your cake hole right now! Can't you keep your yap shut?"

"I messed up, boss, but I lead her here to fix it!She got some idea in her head about playing Sergeant York and saving the brat. She ain't gonna get far. We can catch her easy."

"Yeah!" Sergeant spat. "See how easy we're catching her, soldier?"

"It was the best way I could think of. She's got my heater!"

At that moment, Chloe pulled the gun out of her purse and fired at the men. Dumb idea, she thought. *Thought too late.* The men scattered to find cover behind the trees. "Come on, yah damn raccoon!" Sergeant shouted. "You can't play possum all night! Put down the rod, and stop playing like you can get one over on three soldiers! We fought the Jerrys in France! You're just a kitty-toy to us. I don't even think you know how to use it."

"You sure?" Chloe fired at a branch of the tree Sergeant was standing under. It fell on him, knocking him out cold. "Don't think you got a kitten on your hands. I'm a tiger!"

Ruby rushed out of the darkness to grab Sergeant's revolver. "Come on, girl! We've got you treed like a possum! You got lucky with that shot! Freddy Fatlip will be here any minute with the whole gang!"

Chloe bit her lip. "Didn't I tell yah that I already got to Fatlip?"

"Come on-you didn't have time!" Ruby said.

"How would you know? You were out of it."

"Anyway," Lazy-eye said, "Just us three are two more than plenty to deal with a dame! Give it up, gams!"

Chloe fired another shot at the ground. "Don't call me gams!"

"Yeah," Ruby said in regular tones, "that really bothers her for some reason."

"Reason being," Chloe shouted, "Is gams was what we called my grandma! I ain't nobody's grandma yet!"

"Okay, we'll call you 'stilts' instead. Is that better?"

"Ya'll be calling for a hearse before I'm done with you!"

"Look fellahs," Beef said, "I know how to get a cat out of a tree. Just step back."

From her vantage point, she couldn't see any of the men. A flaming stick flew through the air and landed by her tree.

Lazy-eye laughed. "Good idea, Beef! We'll smoke her out!"

"What the heck do you think you're doing?" Ruby said. "You could kill her!"

"What do you think we're gonna do with her?" Beef snarled. "Do you think we were getting out of this without casualties?"

"Sergeant said nobody'd get hurt!" Ruby barked back. "This is a clean job!"

Lazy-eye laughed. "Did you ever see an operation without some blood? Nobody'd gets hurt! It's a laugh. We can't let her go."

"But Sergeant said…" Ruby sighed.

"But Sergeant said, Sergeant said," mocked Beef. "Getta load of that bag of soup! You don't do the rough stuff with us, Ruby. Sergeant thinks you're too soft for it, and me and Lazy-eye, we're the foot soldiers. Sergeant has a soft spot for you, and he lets you do the numbers 'cause that's your strong suit. He kept you on board for this, but you weren't on gravedigging duty."

"Gravedigging?" Ruby said blankly.

"Sorry to break it to yah, kid, but we'd make no money selling newspapers." Lazy-eye said. "We make newspaper stories by making money."

"I'd have read something if we'd done a killing!" Ruby said.

Beef grinned. "Oh sure. That's why Sergeant keeps it out of the paper. People disappear all the time, but a little butter in the right hands helps. People miss train connections, went to visit their aunt Zeldinia, or they just went on the lamb. By the time a grave is found, I'll be in mine. That's why Sergeant keeps you around. You're gullible with a capital 'J'. Sergeant don't tell you when there's bodies, and it's not news if there's not one."

"But what about the kid?"

"You mean the corpse?"

Ruby leaned against a tree, taking in what he heard. "Corpse?"

Chloe listened to this conversation while the smoke built and the flames climbed up the tree. She couldn't wait any longer. Coughing out smoke, she jumped to the next tree. The branch she landed on broke, sending her into several branches below until finally finding purchase on a particularly sturdy branch just six feet off the ground. Lazy-eye growled. "I was hoping we could keep you around for some fun before we was finished, but we'll get someone without so many onions in her blood." He raised his gun and pulled the trigger.

"No!" shouted Ruby as he fired Sergeant's revolver into Lazy-eye. Chloe screamed as the bullet struck her hat and flung it, empty, through the air. The surprise caused Chloe to lose her hold and fall the rest of the way to the ground.

Ruby stood stunned as Lazy-eye fell dead to the ground, watching Ruby with the orb that gave Herman his moniker in life.

"What the hell, Ruby?" Beef shouted, reaching in his pockets for his gun as he rushed toward him. "You killed Herman!"

Ruby was still in a state of shock. "I…I…I didn't mean to! I'm sorry!"

Beef pointed his gun at Ruby. "That makes two of us. The shot rang out, the bullet erupting as a rocket toward Ruby.

The bullet cut Ruby's tie as it flew about his head right after something struck him, causing him to tumble to the ground. Beef managed two more shots as he tried to follow Ruby's falling form through the blinding smoke. Stunned Ruby fell backward onto Chloe, who'd wrapped her arms around his knees to save him from certain death. Ruby hit his head against the tree, knocking him unconscious. Chloe grasped his right hand, clenching his trigger finger.

The bullet grazed Beef's forearm, his gun falling from his grasp as the bullet tore through his muscles and tendons, leaving his fingers nerveless.

"Dammit!" Beef exclaimed. "I'm going to kill you both!"

"You're gonna try!" Chloe spat, climbing out from under Ruby. "Let's watch you fail!"

"It's just us two, gams. I'm the kinda dog that plays with his food before he kills it, and I'm gonna have a grand time having you for dinner!"

Beef Stu's clothes bulged with muscles and tendons. Chloe was taller than him. It didn't matter when he threw a power-punch. She deflected it, but the force audibly cracked the bones in her forearm. She kicked him in the right shin. He grimaced but kept coming. He grabbed her broken arm with his uninjured left and pulled her to the ground, screaming in pain. He pulled her arms together and put them under his prodigious mass as he fell on top of her. He used his injured arm to unbutton his pants. "This is gonna be fun for me, 'lil darlin'. Don't worry about fare for a dimbulb—no taxi's needed to take you six feet under!"

She screamed in pain, but brought up her knee into his groin with a hard thrust.

Rolling off her, Beef folded in half. She stumbled to her feet, holding her broken arm. Beef rolled over his gun, bringing it up to point at her. His head exploded in a storm of blood and bone as a bullet flash roared forth his death. Ruby stood there, his gun smoking. He walked over to Chloe. "You still having fun?" he coughed, the smoke pouring over the area, making it impossible to see Beef's dead body mere inches away.

Chloe pushed Ruby away with her good arm. "What about Sergeant?"

A gunshot shot twirled the smoke into a spinning pattern that described death. "Come on!" Ruby thrust through his teeth as he grabbed her shoulder. "He can't see any better than us right now, but he's a better marksman than either of us!"

They ran out of the smoke where they could see the house. "You go," Chloe said. "Get the kid to safety. I'll take care of Sergeant!" With that, she leapt into a nearby tree as Ruby ran to the house. A shot rang out as Ruby stepped onto the porch, and he fell down. Chloe stifled a scream as Sergeant walked by the tree, coughing violently from smoke inhalation. Oblivious to Chloe, the Sergeant fired another shot. "Goddamn it, Ruby! You were like a son to me! How could you turn on me, soldier? I saved your life!"

"You saved my life so I could live it!" Ruby shouted back, firing a wild shot. Sergeant took cover behind the tree. "If you saved it so I could be a murderer, you think it's yours! I'm gonna live that life my way, and my way's not killing innocents! I fought in the war for justice and freedom! I was a fool to buy into your line!"

"Well hell, Ruby," Sergeant said, watching for movement under the porch. "I made a life for all of us when we had nothing! You don't think you owe me something for that, I guess we're at an impasse." He fired a shot toward the porch. A low groan could be heard drifting through the expanding smoke.

Chloe fell onto Sergeant's back, the weight of her fall knocking him to the ground. She sat on his back; scratched, punched, kicked, and battered Sergeant like a wildcat. "Put it down, Sergeant! You're a disgrace to your title, your country, your oaths! You let down your soldiers! It's over!"

Sergeant's gun was crushed under his stomach. He gripped it tightly. "Yes." He said, tears rolling out his eyes. "Damn you, woman! You're absolutely right. Time to say farewell to arms." He pulled the trigger. Bits of ribs and muscle spread across the dirt, painted with blood.

Chloe adjusted her battered mask and breathed in. Standing to her feet, she stumbled toward the house. Ruby crawled across the porch. She rushed to his side, putting her arms around his neck. "Oh God, Ruby, you're alive!"

"Just shot in the leg," he replied. "Now, it's time to pay for what I've done."

"Sergeant, Lazy-eye, and Beef; they're all dead!" She cried. "You don't have to go to the big house."

"Give me a hand, please." She helped him stand. He leaned against the banister. "Yes, I could walk away from all this with your help. Maybe you'd even learn to like me, and maybe I could get over you stealing my car." He chuckled. "You forgot about Fatlip, but I could even work that out. He's the last of us, you know, and it'd be just as bad for him when this comes out. I've socked some dough away so I could make it worth his while on top of it, and we could disappear."

Chloe looked at him hopefully. Ruby sighed. "It's no good, though. The lie I've lived since getting involved in this would lay as a cage on my conscience. I didn't know that we were killing people. Even a kid, for Pete's sake! A kid!" He shook his head. "No, I'm accepting all that the law can throw at me. Even if they hang me by the neck until I'm dead, I'll actually be living. I'd be the kind of man you deserve." He sighed. He leaned against the banister, holding her face in his hands. "Let's get the kid home. I've got a date with destiny."

Chloe started crying. "You are the man I deserve, not just 'the kind'." She kissed him on the cheek. "Well, thanks for giving a girl an adventure. This one was a doozey!"

They went into the house. They walked out again with a dark-haired boy of ten. The kid frightened but none the worse for it. He smiled broadly. Ruby, bloody, bruised, using a crutch and wearing a fedora he'd found in the house, took the boy's left hand. Chloe still wearing her tattered mask, covered in scratches, bruises, her arm in a sling, held the boy's right hand in hers right across her waist. They walked down the stairs together, a picture of a happy, bedraggled family.

The End

Blind Witness

by Jilly Paddock

The senior librarian meets us on the steps of the grubby, elephantine building; the kind of sterile concrete structure that the region's tax-payers are still complaining about the cost of ten years after the place was topped-out. He's a small man with hair retreating and going to grey, a knife-cut frown line between his eyes. His suit is on the cutting-edge of fashion, sharp and elegant in soft charcoal tweed, and his shirt is of silk. The word his image brings to mind is 'dapper', and I guess that he's vain but not ostentatious about it. His hands move in a constant wringing motion of which he seems utterly unaware. He edges towards me and tilts his head back to look in my face. "Inspector Lamont?"

"I'm Jerome." I'm used to people making the wrong connection. Afton hates it. "This is the inspector."

She's short too, built as solid as a sea-wall. No-one could ever accuse A. Afton Lamont of being attractive. She has a wide-open face with a permanently affronted expression, the kind of look that makes peaceful, sane people want to slap it on sight. She hates sexism with a fanatical fervour. I swear she'd kill for less than the librarian's gaffe if she wasn't on the side of law.

The man has the grace to be embarrassed and extends his hand, drawing it back before she can shake it. "I'm Doug Templeton. I'm in charge here. Follow me, please."

The public part of the library is much as you'd expect; the usual reception counter, a dozen booths with terminals, all empty and off-line and a trio of carousel racks with a selection of the most popular discs. My landlady still bewails the lack of shelf upon shelf of 'real books' in libraries, until I tell her that she's not ancient enough to remember such things. I notice the complete absence of people here and the hot, ugly smell that hangs in the air.

Behind the counter the dead woman lies in an unnatural tangle of limbs. When they put down the white tape, the outline will send you into contortions trying to visualise the position of the corpse. The fall has knocked the pins loose from her tightly-wound bun. Fair hair spills over her pale cheek below the left eye-socket that sprouts the dark hilt of a knife. I can't see any blood.

"Has anything been touched?" Afton asks as she surveys the scene dispassionately. We've seen worse before.

"No... no, of course not." Templeton is vague, having trouble coping with all of this. After all, it's Friday afternoon and his thoughts are centred on the weekend, not this sudden tragedy. "At first we were too busy putting out the fire and then... Well, it was obvious she was dead."

"What fire?"

Templeton gestures at the glass-fronted cabinet just to the rear of the counter. "Whoever did this also set fire to our page-books. About half of the collection has been damaged, all priceless, irreplaceable volumes. Who'd do such a thing?"

He seems more upset at the act of vandalism than at the woman's death. That irritates Afton and I feel her anger prickle on my skin.

"Who was she?" I ask to ease the silence.

"Ellie... Elinore O'Rourke. She's been with us four, five years." Templeton can't bring himself to look at the corpse. "Good worker, quiet, reserved—you know the sort. I don't think any of us knew her well."

In other words a decent girl, which is no sure armour against murder. She has a pretty face with a wide, kindly mouth, one blue-green eye pinned open and neatly bisected by the blade. She didn't deserve to die like this, but then who does?

Afton nudges me, suspecting that I'm getting maudlin. "We can't do much until Forensics puts in an appearance. Let's take a look at the arson attack."

This place has an impressive collection of page-books for a suburban library, around a hundred at a guess. I've never seen so many outside of a university or major city institutions. Three-quarters of the total have been pulled out of the display case to form a higgledy-piggledy heap. The bonfire had been fierce, leaving only ashes at its centre, with charred and scorched volumes at the edges in a pool of foamy water.

"Such a waste!" Templeton shakes his head, while his hands still move like a plateful of worms. "To so wantonly destroy a valuable historic resource—it's madness!"

Afton picks up a book from the edge of the heap, one of the few still intact and dry. She riffles through the pages; oblivious to Templeton's evident horror at her casual handling of the precious item, then she sets it back on the shelf with the survivors of the attack.

"We'll need to interview the staff." I know that tight, polite voice and it bodes no good. "Anyone who came in here this morning or who works in the neighbouring offices. Can you organise that?"

"You can use my office. I'll make the arrangements." He nods and leaves, still wringing his hands.

I'm just through shooting the holos when the forensic team arrives, Ivory and three of his colleagues, half of the department's gore crew. Must be a slow afternoon down at the station. I sit back and watch them scan and sweep the area for prints and other material clues, and then Afton has them sample the ashes of the fire. We leave them to bag the body for transit before they carry their goodies back to the labs.

"Your opinion of this case, Jerome?" Afton asks, as I set up my recorders in the librarian's office.

I've learnt to think on my feet when she puts me on the spot like this—I open my mouth and let my brain catch up. "Ebony-handled knife, point of entry the left orbit. That's textbook sacrificial assassination as practised by the Sisterhood of Grace, one of the Cluster death-cults. We won't find any prints or other corporeal evidence. My guess is that we will find that the knife was poisoned."

Afton paces the room wearing an expression that could curdle cheese. "Open and shut case, eh?"

"Apart from the burning books, yes." I move around her carefully, aligning my equipment. "That's what's bothering you, isn't it? You don't care for the window-dressing."

She whirls and drops into the chair, twisting to and fro in it as a child would. Afton doesn't smile often and when she does her face assumes the aspect of a favourite aunt, vague, eccentric and benign. "Absolutely. Far too dramatic a touch for the dark-sisters, don't you think?"

"I'm the tek-wiz, the soundman." I hit the board and all the monitors light up green. "I'm not paid to think, dee-tective inspector!"

We talk to the staff, six women of varying ages and three young men, none of whom can shed any light on the crime. We also talk to the one member of the public who happened to be in the library when the crisis broke. He volunteers the information that he lives in the same block as the murdered woman, which does explain why he's so intensely shaken by the death. Elinore O'Rourke begins to flesh out in our minds; a sweet, quiet girl liked and respected by all. Nobody can find a bad thing to say about her.

"A veritable paragon," I remark, as we wait for our final victim. Afton's saved the senior librarian until last.

"There ain't no saints, just people who are expert at hiding sins."

I've known Afton long enough not to have to laugh at her witticisms. I even know what the initial A in her name stands for, but I have the good sense never to call her that, which guarantees that my skin stays attached to my body.

"What was our little Ellie hiding?" I wonder.

"Enough to induce someone to buy her death, apparently."

Doug Templeton has little to tell us. He remembers greeting the woman when he arrived this morning but had no occasion to go into the public area until the fire alarm went off.

"That knife and the way she was killed..." He has some control over his hands now and curbs their writhing. "I can't imagine why anyone would pay to have Ellie murdered. Surely she gave no-one reason?"

"Who knows?" Afton yawns. "A jealous lover, a sibling excluded from an inheritance or a cheated business partner perhaps?"

"No brothers or sisters—that's on her file," Templeton supplies. "As for business, that and Ellie wouldn't mix. She wasn't enough of a risk-taker to go out on her own."

"A boyfriend, then?" Afton shrugs. "Or girlfriend?"

"Not that I know of," Templeton states firmly, his cheeks pinking up at the thought. "She never talked about either."

I'm starting to detest this little man with his pale maggot hands.

"One last thing," Afton continues. "There's a computer at the reception counter. How self-aware is it?"

Templeton gapes at her. "That old heap? We use it to tap into the main-brain, that's all. On its own it's about as smart as the average slug."

"Pity," Afton says non-committally. "We do find that some of the newer hardware, especially those on the borders of artificial-intelligence, make useful witnesses to crimes—often better than humans in that respect."

"That terminal has no eyes or ears." Templeton looks as if he wants to sit on his restless hands, jams them into his pockets instead. "If it had been otherwise, we might know who killed Elinore."

Afton signals me to turn off the recording. "How unfortunate."

● ● ●

It's midnight and we're still in the Pit, Afton's basement office, reviewing the holo-tapes of our interviews. We've run the whole gamut of the 'burning candles at both ends', 'don't do anything I wouldn't do' and 'if you can't be good, be careful' remarks from some of our more puerile colleagues. The station grapevine runs a book on whether my relationship with A. Afton Lamont runs any deeper than professional; at present the odds are ten to one in favour of the notion, which couldn't be further from the truth.

"Let's re-cap." Afton rubs her eyes bloodshot but persuades them to stay open. "What does the analysis say we have?"

"Three major suspects. Doug Templeton registered unusual peaks of anxiety and appeared to be lying consistently."

"Did I need your box of tricks to tell me that?" she asks sourly.

I scowl at her and put up a picture of number two. "Cristabel Ray. Works in the office nearest to Ellie's desk and claims to have seen a figure in black fleeing from the library when the alarm went off. Also lying, according to the body-posture data."

Afton surveys the image, recalls the pretty, twitchy redhead. "Next?"

"Last comes the neighbour, Liam Coyne. He didn't tell us all of the truth either." Afton climbs to her feet. "Care to take a walk?"

● ● ●

The block houses sixteen flats built around a courtyard, modern, pleasant and not cheap. Elinore O'Rourke used to live in number four and guess who occupies number five? Liam Coyne answers the door-chime within thirty seconds, fully dressed, his cheeks rubbed into red and white patches with hastily-dried tears.

"You need a warrant," he says, just like every other sucker, and tries to shut the door.

Afton jams her boot in the way. "Don't be difficult. Let us in."

To my surprise, he does. The living room is a mess—looks like he's been trying to drink himself to a standstill. A bottle of pills stands on the glass table like a tombstone. Afton picks it up, squints at the label and pockets it.

"Hey!" Liam lumbers towards her. "Put them back! They're mine!"

I put a hand on his arm and he stops, all threat melting away.

"You loved her, didn't you?" She smiles for the second time today, straining her facial muscles. "Suicide isn't the answer."

"I can't be without her!" He is drunk. I smell it on his breath and slopped on his clothes, so strong it makes me dizzy. He doesn't need pills—a lighted match would do the trick. "I want to join her."

"Why? Scared she won't wait?"

He crumples then, folding into himself, hugging the empty hurt in his belly. Afton catches my eye and gives me one of our secret signals, the one that tells me to call up an ambulance. I use the poor guy's own terminal to do it, while he weeps in a knot on the floor.

"Do you think you've helped him?" I ask her, after the crew had sedated him and wheeled him away. "If he's serious, he'll try again after they discharge him."

"You ain't human, Jerome." There's a nasty look in her eyes—some might call it pity. "Can't you understand what it is to lose someone?"

"I know grief. I've had plenty." I see their faces in my head, a friend and a lover, two ghosts that call my name in the night. Afton's right though; I'm not human—not human enough to catch the stinking virus that killed them. "Maybe it isn't loss that makes him want to quit life. Maybe it's guilt."

"He didn't kill Elinore." Afton shakes her head. "Want to take a look at the girl's apartment?"

There's a guard at her door, a seven-foot pile of muscle in a police uniform. Not a man, a simulacrum, a vat-grown flesh body guided by a silicon-chip mind. If it didn't recognise us and we tried to get past it, we'd be a smear on the carpet.

"Good evening, Inspector Lamont," it says crisply. "And to you, Mister Jerome."

"Hello, Eamonn." Afton knows all of the constructs at a glance, while I can't tell them apart with a streetmap. It opens the door and lets us in.

What to say about dead Elinore's home? It looks like it just dropped out of a video on contemporary design; everything placed to the last centimetre and not a speck of dust. Afton searches the rooms with a deadly intensity and I'm amazed at the cunning and ingenious way she combs all of it for concealed items and hidey-holes. She finds nothing.

"A wardrobe full of clean and perfectly-pressed clothes, a kitchen so neat it seems she never cooked a meal and not a photograph or personal trinket in sight." I frown. "Life didn't seem to affect her—she lived it without touching the sides."

"An obsessively-tidy introvert." Afton tilts her head back and wriggles the ache out of her shoulders. "There's no more we can do tonight. I'm for home."

● ● ●

Saturday morning finds us back in the library early—anytime before noon is too early for me at the weekend. Afton has summoned her computer expert; six foot two of underdressed feminine curves with a blonde curly mane and blue eyes that could melt the Antarctic. Gorgeous, if you like that sort of thing. She goes by the name of Spiro. Rumour at the station has it that she's Afton's half-sister, but rumour has to be wrong. No such diverse specimens of humanity could have even one gene in common.

"Hi, Lamont." Spiro nods to the inspector, then flashes me the full come-to-bed smile. "And the lovely Jerome, as luscious as ever!"

She hugs me and plants a kiss on each cheek. I suffer the outrageous demonstration without complaint, wishing that Afton wasn't so obviously amused by my discomfort. Spiro forgets all about me when she sees the computer terminal and coos over it as if it were a basketful of kittens. She may be a major-league genius in her field, but in company with a lot of her colleagues, I think she's nuts. I take a closer look at the machine: it's a heap of junk, with no touchpad or voice control, just an ugly monitor screen a decade out of date and a clunky manual keyboard.

Cristabel Ray pays us a visit while Spiro's pumping the keyboard. She watches for a minute or two before speaking. "Mr Templeton said I should bring you this." She hands Afton a flimsy print-out sheet. "It's a list of our page-books, which were destroyed and which were left intact."

"Thanks." Afton doesn't even glance at it. "Tell the senior librarian that we'll be as quick as we can. Routine check."

Crissie nods and leaves us, still curious.

"Liar!" Spiro says out of the corner of her mouth.

'Quit moralising and make that tin-box sing." Afton sits. "Can it tell us anything?"

"It's blind, but its ears are sharp enough." Spiro's long fingers fly over the board. "Someone's tried to dump the file, someone who doesn't know much about the system."

"Then all the data we want is gone?" I ask.

"Whoever did the tampering thought they'd wiped the recordings but, as I said, they were amateurs." She touch-types with absolute confidence, never looking at her fingers, only at the screen which fills with blocks of stark dialogue. Thirty seconds more of digital dance and sections of it are highlit with a handful of vivid colours. "Five distinct voices here, Af. I have positive identity on two of them; the red is Doug Templeton and the green Cristabel Ray. I presume that they're library employees?"

"You're a bloody genius, Spiro." Afton squints at the display. "So Templeton lied to us. He had spoken to Ellie on Friday morning."

"I clock him in at eleven twenty-eight and out seven minutes later." Spiro translates a spin of figures that flash across the bottom line. "Ms Ray at eleven twenty-one, three minutes worth of incidental chat. Both conversations are pretty meaningless—banal stuff about mutual health states, the weather and weekend plans. Nothing here to convict your killer."

"The lines in white must be lover-boy Liam." I pick out a section with the use of her name and a reference to the apartment block. Even in print it reads gauche and hesitant.

"I time him at eleven fifteen." Spiro scans the words. "Ah, sweet boy, he fetched her a cup of coffee."

596   Jilly Paddock

Afton reads it through again, chewing on a fingernail already ripped ragged. "There's little of use here. Can you make me a hard copy, just in case?"

"Sure thing." Spiro slips a disc into the slot. "After the dialogue I've nothing else until the fire alarm went off at eleven fifty-four or at least nothing that our witness here could pin on a point of reference. From eleven forty-five onwards there was a high level of noise in the library. I can give you a rapid audio run-through."

"That old terminal's equipped to constantly record?" I ask.

"Of course. It's a standard security measure. It keeps twenty-four hour chunks of sound for voice-printing in case of trouble. Most hardware stationed at reception desks is set up for that function." Spiro hits the enable key.

The first noise is sudden and sickening—Afton and I have heard enough bodies go down to know what it is. Next there's footsteps, the scrape of a chair pushed back and an intake of breath, the sound a person makes straightening up from a crouch. The footsteps retreat followed by a series of thumps which must be the page-books hitting the floor, falling one or two at a time like ripe fruit from a tree. The final sequence starts with a distinct click, a brief pause and then a shattering of glass, the dull 'whumpf' of a small explosion and the crackle of flames.

"Petrol bomb or something very like it." Afton guesses as the recording degenerates into a din of shouts and squeals as the body and fire are discovered.

"That's a collapsed version." Spiro kills the playback. "I'll copy you a recording with the correct time-scale."

"Still nothing conclusive. If anything, it makes the killing more confusing." Afton glances down at her hands and finds that she's still clutching the print-out. She looks at it briefly, frowns and then reads it through carefully. As I watch her, furrows of concentration pleat the skin over her nose. When she's through she tosses the flimsy sheet to me. "Read that, big guy."

I scan the two lists. It's a motley selection, much like most collections of page-books; fiction in the main, with a sprinkling of textbooks and volumes on practical subjects, the flower-decorating, cake-arranging, 'let's-cook-brown-rice' school of writing, plus a handful of anthologies of poetry. Most are less than a century old, with some reprints of classic literature and older stuff. None date from before the Dark.

"Spot the difference?" Afton asks.

I have to admit defeat.

"The first list, those that were intended for burning, were all written by men."

"Ain't that neat! Our feminist assassin takes time-out to burn all the nasty male-chauvinist books?" I laugh in unbelief. "That's way too convenient, Afton. Besides, there are some men in the list of survivors—George Elliot, Andre Norton, James Tiptree Jr, Franklin DeVries and Idris Seabright."

"All women, I'll bet," Spiro chips in. "I know that the first three are female writers, but I've not heard of those last two."

"You're telling me that our murderer was expert enough to leave all the books by women safe on the shelves?"

"Right down to the textbooks." Afton smiles tightly. "Spiro, can you hook into the data-net with that outmoded hardware?"

"No sweat. What do you want?"

"There are half-a-dozen places across this continent that sell page-books. Can you tap into their records over the last twelve months and see if they've auctioned any of the titles on those lists?"

"It'll take fifteen minutes or so. This connection is as slow as a glacier." Spiro's fingers are already a blur.

"What angle are you pushing at?" I ask my boss.

She grins like a witch, but before she can let me into the secret, Cristabel calls us across the library. "There's an urgent message for Inspector Lamont on my line. Shall I put it to that terminal?"

Spiro shakes her head and Afton stands up. "We'll take it in your office, Ms Ray, if you don't mind."

It's Ivory from Forensics. He winks at me as I come into visual; he knows that I appreciate his pretty face and he likes to tease. Afton's scowl wipes the smile off his lips.

"I have a full report on Elinore O'Rourke," he says happily. "We put the time of death as between eleven thirty and noon. The cause of death was poison."

"On the blade, I assume?" Afton asks, on cue.

"The knife was a red herring, Inspector." Ivory's grinning with delight now. "It penetrated her brain for sure, but post mortem. What killed her was a sweet little vegetable toxin with a short half-life—we very nearly missed it since most of it had been destroyed by the bacterial flora in her gut. There was just about enough of the poison mixed with the coffee in her stomach to establish the true cause of death."

"Can we trace the supplier of the poison?" Afton's not shaken one whit by the bombshell.

"No way." Ivory's triumph falters; he'd anticipated a better reaction from her. "Strictly blackmarket. Probably made in someone's backyard by a chem-engineering graduate moonlighting to pay his college fees. Or hers."

"Okay." If she's disappointed she doesn't show it. "Thanks, Ivory."

We walk back to Spiro before the full weight of it hits me. "Liam Coyne fetched Ellie that coffee. Did he poison her?"

Afton shushes me because our blonde genius is looking like the cat that ate the cream, not to mention the strawberries into the bargain.

"Six of the burned books have come up for auction in the past year," Spiro purrs. "Not these editions though; all were much older and far more valuable. They were sold for a comfortable fortune."

"Let me guess—all six were totally destroyed by the fire?" Afton's radiating satisfaction now. "Can we track the destination of the money?"

"It'll take time. Pains have been taken to conceal where it went." Spiro shrugs. "If you want me to locate it I will, but as of now I'm on double time."

"You're worth it." Afton prods me in the ribs. "Go out and make a call on the public lines, Jerome. I don't want anyone inside the library listening in."

That's all she needs to tell me—I know the drill. It's trumpet-for-the-cavalry time. We're about to make an arrest.

• • •

If there's one thing Afton Lamont loves it's the classic confrontation scene at the end of a case, where you gather up all the suspects and embarrass the guilty party by explaining his/her fiendish plan to the delight and relief of all the others. As Liam Coyne is still detained in hospital, we have to make do with an audience of two. Doug Templeton sits behind his desk, thinking that we don't see the nervous writhing of his hands in his lap. Cristabel Ray fidgets on her seat as if it's upholstered with nettles.

"I'm pleased to tell you that we've solved this case," Afton announces blithely.

"You have the assassin in custody?" Templeton's eyes seem glazed but he holds his neutral expression.

"There never was an assassin. Elinore O'Rourke was poisoned," Afton pauses for effect, "by Ms Ray."

As if she's read the script she explodes to her feet, red to the roots of her hair.

"It wasn't me!" She screams. "I swear to God, it wasn't me! He put that stuff in her coffee! It was his idea, every last, damned part of it!"

"I'm aware of all that," Afton says genially. "I trust you have Ms Ray's outburst on record, Jerome?"

"Every last shriek," I assure her smugly.

Templeton breaks then and makes a run for it. He doesn't know that we've stationed Eamonn and his partner Fergus at the door. The two constructs carry the murderer back into the room, swinging him like a doll in their giant hands, his feet thirty centimetres off the floor.

"Put him down," Afton instructs. "Let him stand on his own."

The simulacra obey, smiling.

"You had a bright idea, didn't you, Mr Templeton?" Afton's eyes are glittering now. She revels in shooting the culprit down. "Steal a few of the library's valuable page-books and sell them, but substitute later, cheaper editions so that nobody notices the theft. You even altered the computer records so that the substitutions wouldn't be apparent. What was the money for—so that you and Ms Ray could run away together? You two are having an affair, aren't you?"

"Yes," Templeton says, in a small voice. "How did you know?"

"I can't think of any other reason why she should lie to protect you. She pretended to see that retreating black figure to back up your story." Afton shakes her head. "If you wanted us to believe that Elinore O'Rourke was killed by the Sisterhood of Grace the black-hilted knife would have been sufficient evidence. The book-burning was too hard to swallow, especially when you sent Cristabel to give us the lists when you were afraid we hadn't appreciated the significance of which volumes were destroyed and which spared. Maybe the sentiment was right, but the execution was too precise. Who but a librarian would be able to pick out all the correct books in such a brief span of time?"

"You didn't need to burn the books," I add. "If you'd left them untouched no-one would have been any the wiser."

"I wanted to destroy the substitutes," Templeton mutters. "There had to be other catalogues of our collection. I thought it would be safer to leave no evidence."

"Is that why you tried to wipe the terminal's records, after I'd reminded you that it might be a witness against you?"

The man raises his head. "I thought I had erased all the relevant data."

"Amateurs!" I observe in amusement.

"Tell me one thing." Afton's voice is sharp again. "What did Ellie do that made it so essential that you kill her?"

"She came to see me two weeks ago with a problem. She believed that one of the page-books had been stolen and that the thief had left a similar, later copy in its place. I pretended that she was mistaken but checked it out, showed her that all the details matched the description in the files and still she wasn't satisfied." Templeton is weeping, not with regret but in frustration that he's been caught. "You didn't know Ellie. She was so persistent. She could never leave anything alone once she'd fixed her mind on it. Three days ago she came back to me. She'd dug out the record of the auction—date, price, the false name I'd used, everything. I promised her that I'd sort it out and I knew then that I'd have to kill her. Nothing short of death would buy her silence; she was such a good, honest idiot. It had been her favourite book, you see, and that was how she'd spotted the imposter. Bloody thing, I wish I'd never set eyes on it! It was a volume of poetry by Yeats."

Afton makes a sign with her hand and Eamonn takes the man away, Fergus following with Cristabel Ray. Spiro's just finished her task as we draw level with the counter and the display flashes with Templeton's name and address in large crimson type.

"There's your murderer," the blonde programmer declares.

"And there he goes." Afton waves after the departing simulacra. "My computer is still faster than yours."

"This time I concede," Spiro admits. "You're getting old, Af-dear, the margin's getting narrower. If we're all wrapped up here, can I steal your tek-wiz and take him to lunch?"

"No," I say firmly. "Being seen with you does my reputation nothing but harm."

"Cute!" Spiro wrinkles her nose at me. "You are getting old, Afton. Time was when you'd have taught that young whelp some manners!"

Outside on the steps it's starting to rain.

"Buy you a drink?" Afton indicates a bar across the street. "Celebrate? That is, if being seen with me doesn't compromise your reputation?"

"If it does, I'm beyond redemption!" I laugh and take her arm.

The End

Peachy Keene and the Damballa Stone

By James Palmer

"**P**eachy! Get in here!"

Pamela Keene took a deep breath and rose from her desk. The shouting from *The Ledger's* editor she could handle. But why did he always have to call her by that stupid nickname? It was never Pamela, Pam, or even the overly formal Ms. Keene. It was always Peachy. Just Peachy.

Pamela walked as quickly as she could toward the chief's office, ignoring the condescending stares she got from her fellow reporters. Inwardly cringing, she stuck her head inside her boss's office and said, "Yes, Chief?"

"Get in here, Peachy, and shut the door. Have a seat. And knock it off with the Chief crap."

Pamela did as she was told, but she knew that everyone in the bullpen outside was staring intently at them through the glass and metal partition that separated them.

Pamela sat, hands shaking in her lap, and waited for Charles Davis, the toughest editor to ever run a New York paper, to speak.

Davis looked as cold and gruff as his personality. He was short and squat, with a square head that looked as if it had been chiseled out of some hard brown stone. A square nose jutted out from his stony face, and two wispy eyebrows hovered beneath his forehead like thunderclouds. An editorial cartoonist no longer employed by *The Ledger* once drew a picture of Davis with an Easter Island head.

He made a show of shuffling papers around on his desk for at least a minute before looked up at her. "You understand your job duties don't you?"

"Yes," said Pamela. "Of course."

"Then why can't you give me what I'm paying you for?" He slammed the papers down onto his desk blotter. "You're here to cover the Society page, not political mudslinging downtown. Now this story idea you had about organized crime..."

"That's a solid angle," she protested, cutting him off. "I've got good sources on that one."

"I don't care," boomed Davis. "I've got people covering this stuff already. People who've been in the trenches of this city for twenty years, not fresh off the farm like you. Now this is a small weekly paper, not *The Times*. You're here to cover charity balls and high society mixers, and what's going on among the crème de la crème of New York's elite. If that's not good enough for you, then go somewhere else, because I don't need you."

"I-I'm sorry, Chief," said Pamela. "I just wanted to give you a good story."

Pamela looked down at her hands. She wanted to cry. When she looked up again the Chief's features had softened.

"Look. You're a good kid. And a damned fine reporter. You've got a nose for news like I've never seen in a rookie. But this is a man's world, understand? I've got guys out there who would eat me alive if I gave you a piece of their beat. Besides, this stuff you want to get into up to your neck? It's dangerous. No place for a lady."

600

Davis leaned back in his chair and jammed a cigar into his mouth, struck a match and lit it. "Tell yah what, though. There's this big to-do at the California Museum of Natural History. Some famous explorer will be there tonight showing off some artifact he found. Cover it. Talk to the guy, give me a story that won't put me to sleep, and I'll stop sendin' you out to report on flower shows. Deal?"

Pamela jumped from her seat. "Yes, Chief. You won't be disappointed."

"Yeah, yeah," said Davis, dismissing her with a wave of his hand. "Just get outta here. And stop calling me chief. I ain't no Indian."

Pamela felt as if she was walking among the clouds as she sauntered back to her desk. She sat down and stared at the piece of paper sticking out of her typewriter, a huge grin forming on her face. She knew all about the museum gala tonight. A famous archeologist, though some considered him little more than a glory hound and grave robber, Ace Hanson, was showing off his latest find from the Caribbean. This could be just the story Pamela needed to prove to Charles Davis that she had what it took to be as good a reporter as any of the men on the payroll. No, scratch that. She would prove she was *better.*

● ● ●

The California Museum of Natural History was an art deco monstrosity planted smack dab in the middle of L.A.'s bustling downtown. Pamela couldn't help staring up at it as she climbed out of the cab. Out front, well-dressed patrons lined up to get inside, making Pamela feel downright drab in her white blouse, dark skirt, and brown loafers. Her mousy brown hair was done up in a hasty bun that was already threatening to unravel and come crashing down her shoulders, and her peach-colored skin, devoid of makeup, glowed softly in the street lamps that blazed in front of the museum. It was her complexion that had given Pamela her hated nickname, Peachy. She pushed her glasses up onto her nose and, notebook in hand, got in line. Her press pass got her through the queue with a nod, and soon she was standing in a glass-roofed atrium filled with wealthy museum patrons. She filed slowly past exhibits highlighting the California Gold Rush and the LaBrea Tar Pits, following the flow of people toward a large display cordoned off from the rest at the center of the atrium. Atop a white platform sat an ugly, potato-shaped stone scrawled with crude markings. Beside it stood a man in a brown jacket and matching fedora, looking as underdressed as Pamela felt, and she knew instantly it was the infamous Ace Hanson. Pamela also felt a kind of strange kinship to the famous adventurer. She waited for an elderly couple to cease their discussion with him and move along, then sidled up to him.

"Dr. Hanson?"

The man smiled down at her. He was tall and ruggedly handsome, with short brown hair and green eyes set in a square-jawed face like jewels in a statue. "Call me Ace. Everyone does."

"Pamela Keene, from *The Ledger.* I'd like to ask you a few questions about the, uh…"

"Damballa Stone?" he finished for her.

"Uh, yes. The Damballa Stone. Where, um, did you find it?"

"In Haiti," said the explorer, clearly warming to the subject. "It was a very dangerous expedition. I barely made it off the island alive."

"Oh, I see," said Pamela, jotting notes in her notebook. "There are some who call you a thief and a grave robber. What do you say to those people?"

She regretted her words the moment they left her lips. Ace Hanson laughed. "That depends. Are they here tonight? Did they pay for my expedition?"

"I'm sorry," Pamela began. "I…"

He waved the apology away with his hand. "It's all right. I'm used to it by now. And believe me, I've been called worse."

Pamela smiled a little, still feeling guilty, even while she knew it was the right question to ask. A hard-hitting journalist couldn't be afraid of asking the tough questions.

More people arrived to look at the stone, and Ace answered their questions and posed for pictures. Pamela took this opportunity to gaze at the stone. It was nothing fancy. In fact, it was quite ugly, a dirty brown lump. Still, it had some strange ethereal quality; Pamela couldn't stop looking at it. She listened as Ace Hanson answered questions with practiced ease. She realized he must live for such moments, and he was a natural born storyteller. Pamela liked him in spite of herself.

When the crowd thinned out again, Ace looked at her. "So, as I was saying, I've traveled all over the world searching for unique artifacts so they can be catalogued and studied. If that makes me a thief or a grave robber, I'm sorry. The world needs to know about such things, don't you think?"

"So what is it, anyway?" asked Pamela. "What makes this find so unique?"

"There's a Haitian legend about the Damballa Stone," he said quietly. "They say it holds power over all of creation."

"Who says this?"

"The Voudon practitioners who inhabit the interior of Haiti. And they aren't the only ones."

Ace Hanson leaned in close, as if about to impart a dangerous secret. "I believe there are several such stones of power. The Shankara stones of India. The shards of Ra of Egypt and Mesopotamia. I've tracked similar legends all over the world for years."

"Where do these stones come from?"

Ace grinned and leaned his arm against the dais holding the Damballa Stone. "I've had three geologists and a mineralogist look at this thing. All of them said it's not from around here." He pointed up at the ceiling.

"Oh," said Pamela. "You mean from space?"

"Yes. The stone contains traces of a radioactive substance called iridium that isn't found on Earth. It's also really old, millions of years old."

"Wow." Pamela wrote all this down in her notebook. This went a lot deeper than she expected.

"The Voudon practitioners believe this stone can awaken their god Damballa. They think the light of Damballa will help them rule the world."

"And what do you think, Dr. Hanson?" she asked, writing quickly.

"Please, call me Ace. I'll let you know when I find all of the stones."

The lights in the museum went out suddenly, and Pamela heard a woman scream.

Ace Hanson grabbed the stone off the platform and went to stuff it into his jacket.

"What are you doing?" Pamela asked.

"Quiet," said Ace, his blue eyes scanning the crowd. There was a little light streaming through the atrium glass from the street lamps outside, but away from that wall of glass all was pitch black. There was hurried movement in the darkness. Someone slammed into Pamela, knocking her to the floor. The raised platform that moments earlier had held the Damballa Stone also toppled over, landing right next to her. There was a grunt and a rustle of fabric, and she could see Ace fighting with someone, actually two or three someones. They were dark-skinned and had white skulls painted on their faces that glowed eerily in the streetlights outside. Ace delivered one a jaw-shattering right hook that felled him. The Damballa Stone fell from his left hand, striking the floor at Pamela's feet.

Pamela sat up and reached for the stone, but a dark hand snatched it away. One of the figures punched Ace in the stomach and he doubled over, landing in a heap next to Pamela on the other side of the toppled dais. Then the men were gone. A few minutes later the lights came back up, leaving a lot of bewildered museum patrons staring stupidly at each other.

"They found me!" muttered Ace, getting to his feet before helping Pamela find hers.

"Who?"

"The people I . . . *acquired* the stone from."

"So you did steal it."

Ace scowled. "Not exactly."

● ● ●

When the police arrived five minutes later, a familiar figure groaned when he saw Pamela standing with Ace.

"Peachy Keene," said Detective Strauss. "I should've known you'd be mixed up in all this."

"I'm just covering a story," Pamela replied.

Ace glanced at her. "Peachy?"

Pamela sighed. "It's kind of my nickname. I hate it."

Ace Hanson grinned. "Never be ashamed of a nickname. All the greats have nicknames. Shoeless Joe. Babe Ruth."

"Those are baseball players," said Pamela.

Ace shrugged. "Doesn't matter."

"If I may interrupt," said Detective Strauss. "Would either of you care to tell me what happened here?"

Pamela and Ace gave separate statements, after which Ace joined her as she headed out the door.

"Where are you going?"

"Home, to write my article. I'm afraid it's turned into a crime story now. That's not my beat."

"But the story isn't over yet."

Peachy stopped and looked up at him. "What are you talking about?"

"We haven't got the stone back."

"I think that's a matter for the police."

Ace gripped her arm above the elbow and pulled her into an alcove. His voice lowered to a whisper, he said, "That Strauss character couldn't find the stone if it was in his back pocket. Besides, I know the men who took it. I know their next move and, believe me, if the stone is even half as powerful as I think it is what they do next will be bad."

"So? What do you want me to do about it?"

"I want you to go with me. Tell the story. The whole story, from beginning to end."

"Why me?"

Ace shrugged. "You strike me as the adventurous type. Plus, you know your way around the city. I'm from back east."

Pamela chewed her bottom lip in thought. If she could write this story for *The Ledger*, she'd never have to write up another boring charity ball for the society page again.

"Mr. Hanson, we have a deal."

They shook hands. "I told you, call me Ace. My old man is Mr. Hanson. And I'll call you Peachy."

Pamela scowled at him, but at last she nodded. "Oh, all right."

They left the museum, Ace hailing a cab as Pamela caught up to him. She questioned her sanity for going along with all this, but it felt so exciting. Even if he insisted on calling her Peachy. She climbed into the cab beside Ace.

"The docks," said the adventurer, and they were off.

"You really think we can catch them?" said Pamela. "And why not just let them have the stone back? Doesn't it belong to them?"

"It's too dangerous," said Ace, eyes forward. "They are going to do something terrible with the stone."

"Come on, it's not like the stone is magic or something."

Ace looked directly into her eyes, his gaze hard. "It is exactly like that."

Peachy grinned. "You're shining me on."

"You wish. There are more things in heaven and Earth, Horatio, than are dreamt of in your philosophy."

"Why Ace, I didn't know you had a thing for Shakespeare."

"Ms. Keene, there is a whole world of things you don't know about me. Now let's get that stone back before something bad happens."

The cab deposited them near the docks. Ace paid the cabbie and they got out. The cab pulled away and disappeared around a corner.

"Shouldn't we have asked the cabbie to wait?" Pamela whispered.

"If we're not successful, it won't matter if we have a cab waiting on us."

Pamela fell in behind Ace. The docks were dark save for street lamps placed at regular intervals. But between the cones of light was nothing but inky darkness. The only ship at the docks was a dingy freighter with Haiti stenciled on the side.

"There they are," said Ace. The stone is probably onboard."

"So what's the plan?"

"I'm going to sneak aboard their ship, swipe the stone, and get out," said Ace.

"That's it? That's your big plan? What am I going to do?"

"You're going to be my lookout. If I'm not back in twenty minutes, or if there's any trouble, run like hell for the nearest payphone and call the National Guard."

"You have got to be kidding."

"I never kid about this stuff."

"But you haven't even told me what's so dangerous about the stone. Is it really magic?"

Ace grumbled something under his breath, looked around. He stared at Peachy evenly. "Let's say, for argument's sake, that the Damballa Stone isn't magical. That it's just an ordinary lump of brown rock. The men who took the stone believe otherwise, and they'll do anything to prove themselves right, up to and including murder. I've seen them kill. Trust me, innocent people will die if they keep that stone."

"All right," said Pamela after a long moment. "But this better be the story of the century."

Ace Hanson winked at her. "Peachy, you're gonna make all those old newspaper men green with envy." The explorer leaned in suddenly and planted a firm kiss on her lips. Pamela tried to pull away at first, then leaned into it.

When Ace pulled away, she looked into his eyes. "What was that for?"

Ace shrugged. "I might be dead in twenty minutes. It seemed like a good idea."

"Ooh," Pamela huffed, pointing toward the freighter. "Just go!"

Ace laughed as he sauntered off. Pamela watched him go, moving into the shadows between the evenly spaced lamps that illuminated the docks. She took cover next to a ramshackle building and watched him climb a ladder bolted to the freighter's hull and vanish over the side.

She once again questioned her sanity for being out here at this time of night, in this area. She didn't believe a word of Ace's story. Perhaps he really was a thief, and she was helping him steal back what he had stolen in the first place. And she was his accomplice! She considered going to call the police. His kiss wasn't *that* good. Still, she had told him she'd wait. What would twenty minutes hurt? She glanced at her watch, holding it under the distant glare of a street lamp so she could see the time. It was half past eleven in the evening. No time to be standing around the docks. Maybe she really was crazy.

Peachy didn't hear them until it was too late. Rough hands seized her by the arms, and a cold hand shot over her mouth. One of the men from the museum came into view. He was older than the others, and wore a wine-colored shirt, unbuttoned to the middle of his chest, but he had the same lurid skull paint covering his face.

Peachy struggled against her two captors, and the third man put a finger to his lips. "Where's Hanson?" he asked. He had a thick French accent and a cold gleam in his eyes.

Peachy shook her head and mumbled that she didn't know. It was partly true. Ace was somewhere aboard their vessel, but she couldn't be sure where.

"Bring her aboard. We let Baron Samedi decide what to do with her." The way he said 'Samedi' rhymed uncomfortably with 'zombie.' He began walking toward the freighter, and Peachy was pushed in step behind him, a hand still clamped tightly over her mouth. Her heart hammered in her chest. She had never been this scared in her life.

A gangway was lowered for them, and Peachy was forced up it and onto the deck of the ship. Everywhere the paint was peeling, and the whole ship smelled of dead fish and time and rust.

Their leader turned to her once more. "I ask you again, girl. Where is Hanson?" He gave his men a look, and suddenly Peachy's mouth was free.

"I don't know," said Peachy, a bit too loudly, hoping wherever Ace was he would hear her and know she was onboard and in trouble.

The man reared back and smacked her hard across the face. Peachy winced, touching the spot on her cheek where she had been struck. She straightened her glasses and narrowed her eyes. "You boys sure know how to treat a girl."

This got snickers from her captors, and their leader silenced them with a look. "We take you to Baron Samedi. He show you some real hospitality, no?" He uttered a boisterous laugh that bounced off the ship's hull and filled the night with foreboding. The man turned and walked toward a shadowy doorway, Peachy shoved along behind him.

The interior of the ship was narrow, dimly lit, and smelled faintly of incense and marijuana. The men's boots clanked loudly on the metal deck plates as Peachy stared down at her shoes, wondering if she would ever walk off this ship.

They walked all the way to the end of the hallway and knocked three times on a door affixed with a Haitian flag and a wreath of flowers. After a long moment, the door opened. The incense and marijuana smell was stronger now, and all Peachy could see of the dark interior was the flickering of numerous candles.

The leader stuck his head inside and spoke with someone in rapid fire French. He finally closed the door and looked at his men. "Put girl in the hold, then look for Hanson. He probably on the ship."

That got everyone moving quickly. One of the men shoved Peachy up the hallway while his comrade ran in the other direction, presumably to hunt for Ace. Peachy hoped wherever he was he would figure out she needed help, and soon. With any luck, he had the stone already, and would call the authorities when he realized she was no longer keeping watch outside the ship. Though somehow she didn't think calling the authorities was his style.

"Where are you taking me?" she said, her voice echoing loudly off the bulkhead.

"To belly of the ship. Where Baron Samedi know what to do."

"What you're doing is illegal," Peachy said.

This got a laugh out of her captor, and she turned and scowled at him before being prodded further up the hallway to a dank stairwell. She paused before the portal, weary of the darkness that awaited her.

"Go."

She went, her footsteps echoing on the metal staircase. It was cooler down here, making Peachy wonder if they were below water level yet.

The bottom of the hold was crowded with moldering crates and reeked of dampness and marijuana. Her skull-faced captor shoved her toward an open animal cage. "You can't be serious."

The man shoved her into the cage and locked the door. Peachy tugged on the bars. "You can't do this. I'm a reporter, you know. I could tell your side of the story. You'd be famous."

The man sneered at her, then turned and started toward the stairs. He paused next to a crate, where a lethal-looking machete had been wedged. He gripped its handle and pulled it free, then left the hold, taking the lethal implement with him.

"Oh," she said to the darkness, "I don't know how I get myself into these situations."

She looked around frantically for anything she could use to free herself, but the cage and surrounding floor of the hold were devoid of any such item. She jostled the bars again, hoping someone would hear the rattling and come for her. But she knew it was no use.

"Some story this turned out to be," she said, her voice echoing hollowly.

A few minutes passed, and the door of the hold opened and a shadowy figure entered. Fearing it was the one they called Baron Samedi, Peachy cowered in the corner of her cage, awaiting the worst. But this man didn't move like the others. He gripped the railings and, lifting his legs in the air in front of him, slid down the staircase in an instant. He wore a dark fedora on his head, set at a rakish angle.

"Hiya, Peachy."

"Where have you been?" she whispered. "I've been scared to death."

"I was waiting for the right time to rescue you. I almost had the stone when I heard them bringing you aboard. Nice job with the yelling, by the way."

Peachy watched as Ace pulled a small leather case from his back pocket and opened it. Inside were various lock picking tools. He selected two of them and went to work on the cage's lock.

"I know where the stone is. As soon as you're free, we'll go and get it."

"Are you crazy? I'm not going anywhere with you."

Ace shrugged. "Suit yourself." He stopped working on the lock and began to put his tools away.

"What are you doing?"

"You said you didn't want to come with. It's probably easier if I go after the stone alone anyway. I'll grab it and come back for you."

"No!" Peachy reached through the bars and grabbed Ace's hand. "Wait. OK. I'll go with you. Just get me out of here!"

Ace snickered as he went to work on the lock once more. After a small eternity, the lock clicked open and Peachy was free.

"Now let's go," said Ace, taking her hand and pulling her along behind him toward the stairs.

"I'm beginning to wish I'd never met you," said Peachy.

"Peachy, you sound like all three of my ex-wives."

Peachy arched an eyebrow. "Three?"

Ace grinned. "What can I say? I'm a glutton for punishment. Now be very quiet."

They started up the stairs, being sure to step lightly so as not to attract any attention. When they reached the top, Ace opened the door a crack and peaked out. "The coast is clear. Come on."

Peachy heard yelling and footfalls as they returned to the main level of the ship, but it sounded muffled and far away. "They're searching the whole ship for you."

Ace nodded. "Let's hope they didn't move the stone," he whispered.

Ace lead Peachy through a maze of corridors and doorways, then stopped and peered around a corner.

"There's a guard," he whispered. "Step back."

Peachy moved away from the opening, while Ace continued looking. After a few seconds, he pulled away from the corridor's opening and shouted something in guttural French. His ruse worked. The guard, wearing camouflage pants, a yellow tank top, and the same skull paint as his fellows, came toward the sound of Ace's voice. As he rounded the corner, Ace slammed his fist into the man's nose. It spouted blood as the man went down with a grunt and didn't move.

Ace straightened his hat. To Peachy he said, "Let's go get the stone."

They stepped over the man's body and headed for the door he had been guarding just moments earlier. Peachy watched warily behind them, fearful that more of those men would appear at any moment. Ace tested the door, found it was unlocked, and went inside.

The stone was resting unceremoniously in the center of a metal table. It could have been a paperweight. Ace snatched it up, hefting it eagerly in his hand. In the pale glow of the ship's lights, Peachy got a better look at it. The stone looked incredibly old, with lots of grooves, fissures, and smooth spots, likely from generations of handling. It also had crude depictions of what appeared to be tentacles wrapped around it, and the center of the stone had three grooves that ran evenly around its equator with almost machine precision, like the grooves in a record. It was roughly egg-shaped, with a perfectly flat base.

"Now let's get out of here."

They were almost through the door when it filled with skull-faced men. Peachy recognized their leader standing in the middle. "Baron Samedi will see you now."

● ● ●

To say that it had not been Peachy's night was the understatement of the century, so she just kept her mouth shut as the skull-faced men lead them back to the hold of the ship where she had been caged just moments before.

"I hope you have some big plan," Peachy whispered to Ace, who walked in front of her.

"I'm working on it."

"Quiet!" their leader barked. "You have caused enough trouble, Mr. Hanson."

"Call me Ace," said the explorer as they were ushered down into the bowls of the ship.

The space was illuminated with thousands of flickering candles now, and a sort of altar had been set up made of wooden crates. Behind the altar stood a tall, broad-chested white man, wearing a black suit jacket with no shirt and a tall black stovepipe top hat. His face was painted with the same skull motif as his brethren.

"Ah," he intoned in a deep voice that echoed ominously throughout the ship's hold. "You still have the stone. The loas will be pleased."

"Yes, Baron Samedi," said their leader, placing the stone atop the altar in front of him and bowing. "This outsider shall trouble you no more."

Ace glared at the one called Baron Samedi, his eyes narrowed to slits. "I know you. You're not Baron Samedi. Richter! I'd recognize those beady eyes anywhere."

"Who's Richter," Peachy asked.

"Enough!" proclaimed the leader. "He is Baron Samedi, chief of the loas, taking human form this night to use the Damballa stone for a serious working."

"Correct!" said Samedi. "This body knows you too, grave robber. You have stolen your last trinket. But you will get your reward this night, for you will be Damballa's first blood sacrifice, you and your pretty lady friend. We let you watch us raise Damballa, and then we slit your throat, yes?" He laughed at this, as if it was the funniest thing he'd ever heard.

"I knew you were crazy, Richter," said Ace. "But this is a stretch, even for you. They drug you with something? Snap out of it, man!"

"Only the drug of truth courses through my veins, mortal. The light of Damballa shines within me."

Ace struggled with their captors, but they held them fast, one of the men placing a machete against his throat. The man holding Peachy shoved her against Ace.

"Who is this guy?" Peachy whispered.

"Kurt Richter," said Ace. "German treasure hunter. We've crossed paths a few times, looking for the same artifacts. He was always three steps behind me. When I left Port-Au-Prince he was just arriving."

"Things are not always as they seem," said Samedi-Richter. "This mortal fool was on the island for long time before you show up. He gave us the idea for how to use the stone to raise Damballa from the vasty deeps."

"Vasty deeps?" said Ace. "That's not right. Damballa isn't an ocean deity."

"Silence!" shouted Samedi-Richter. "Time for talk is past. Now it is magic time."

"Here we go," said Ace. "You're shining these people on, aren't you?"

"Silence!" said Samedi-Richter.

"In addition to being a thief and a liar," said Ace, speaking softly into Peachy's right ear, "old Richie here also bills himself as a ceremonial magician. He was a follower of Crowley."

"Oh, dear," said Peachy. "What does that mean, exactly?"

"It means we could be in big trouble."

"You got that right for once, Hanson," said their leader as he came to stand between them and the one calling himself Baron Samedi. "Richter here is perfect vessel for the spirit of Baron Samedi. Now we get things done. Bring back the magic of the old times. Damballa come, bring new age of peace."

"Or tear everything to pieces," said Ace.

Richter or Baron Samedi was chanting something in a language Peachy had never heard. It wasn't French, but something else. Something low and guttural and incredibly ancient that made the hairs on the back of her neck stand on end. The smell of ozone filled the air, and from somewhere above them Peachy felt a cold draft, as if a gigantic door had suddenly been opened.

There were strange lights dancing through the hold now, as Richter or Samedi waved his hands over the stone. The stone itself began to glow softly, and Peachy thought she saw the markings scrawled along its surface writhe. She was suddenly very afraid. She had the primal urge to run, as if something very large and deadly was bearing down upon her.

"See?" said their leader. "Damballa comes."

"That ain't Damballa," Ace whispered. He reached for Peachy's hand and squeezed it three times, paused, and then again three more times in quick succession.

Peachy glanced at him. Ace did it again, and this time she caught on. Her father had been in the Navy, and as a proud Navy brat she knew two things: how to tie hundreds of different kinds of knots that had no discernable purpose on dry land, and Morse code. Three short squeezes, three long squeezes, and three more short squeezes. S-O-S.

He was trying to communicate something to her that he didn't want their captors to hear. She looked at him and nodded once.

He squeezed again: short-long-short, short-short-long, long-short. R-U-N.

Run!

Ace released her hand and stepped backward, delivering an elbow to the man who held the machete to his throat. It swung up and out, and Ace grabbed it, slicing at one of the other men. Peachy's captors released her to help their associate, and she took the hint and ran, but not before grabbing the Damballa stone from the altar.

Everyone was shouting in rapid-fire French as Peachy ran, clutching the stone close to her body. Ace fought like a caged animal, swinging his machete and fist with lethal accuracy. But still the feeling of dread permeated the ship's hold while the weird lights danced around the corners. Long shadows grew and writhed.

"The door has been opened!" said Richter or Samedi. "It is too late!"

Peachy ran for the stairs, climbing halfway up their length before looking back to check on Ace.

The entire hold was suffused with a weird green light, and she could feel the entire freighter rocking violently, as if it were being pounded by giant waves. Something big and heavy slapped the hull, causing a section of it to bulge inward.

Still ace fought. He crashed his fist into the leader's face, causing blood to splash his skull face with red as he went down in a heap of his own men, knocking over the makeshift altar.

Ace grappled with Richter now, knocking the top hat off his bald head. Rage filled Richter's eyes, and for a moment Peachy could really believe the man was possessed by a voodoo spirit. There were more sounds of something large slapping against the outside of the ship, and more bulges appeared in the hull. Somewhere a series of rivets popped and water began flooding the hold. Peachy turned and ran up the stairs, pausing at the top.

"Ace!"

"Go!" he called back without looking. He and the man who called himself Baron Samedi were locked in combat, neither giving the other an inch, his cohorts fighting the shadowy appendages that encroached on the ship's hold. Peachy turned and ran through the doorway, wishing there was something she could do. The stone was warm in her hand, but not from her touch. It was alive with an inner fire. Shadowy tentacles writhed along the walls, threatening at any moment to become substantial and reach for her, pulling her down into the cold water that churned somewhere beneath her feet.

Peachy still wasn't sure what happened next. Her legs pumped under her, getting her out onto the deck of the ship as something large and black, like a snake or an eel, slid up out of the water and latched onto the boat with massive suckers. It bent around the freighter's prow and slapped down hard onto the deck, shaking the entire vessel. There was a scream of rent metal and Peachy heard glass break from somewhere.

Peachy ran for the gangway, but another tentacle shot out of the water and slammed onto the deck directly in front of her, causing her to stop and freeze, the warm Damballa stone, if that's what it was, clutched tightly to her chest. She heard the sound of gunfire from below, but whether they were firing at Ace or the thing that attacked the freighter, she didn't know. She twisted around, searching frantically for another avenue of escape.

Peachy ran back toward the opening that led into the freighter's interior, but a group of the skull-faced men came running out, fear etched onto their lurid-painted faces. They looked around at the black tentacles slapping onto the deck and clutching the sides of the ship, pulling and squeezing the metal plate until it buckled, spitting rivets. One of them screamed as one of the blasphemous appendages smacked him sideways, knocking him over the ship's side into the dark, churning water. His associates hacked at the tentacles with machetes or fired on them with pistols, but it was no use. They were terrified. Clearly this had not been the outcome they had been hoping for.

One of them spotted Peachy, or rather, the stone she carried, and shouted something to his remaining fellows. They started toward her. Peachy turned and ran, leaping over the tentacles that crisscrossed the deck, now desperate to reach the gangway and freedom.

The stone throbbed warmly in her hand, and she wondered what she should do with it. Clearly it was the cause of whatever was happening here, and had called the foul thing that was tearing the ship apart. She wished Ace was here; he would know what was going on. But for now it was enough that she ran.

Peachy reached the gangway, panting, still clutching tightly to the Damballa stone, though she was unsure what to call it now. For it was not Damballa that currently reached for her with black tentacles from underneath the ship. She bounded down the gangway and onto the dock as more tentacles appeared, shooting sixty feet out of the water and slamming down onto the dock on either side of her, smashing it to bits. Peachy yelped and kept going.

More sections of the dock disappeared as soon as she had crossed them, and she picked up speed, afraid to look behind her for even a moment. The stone gave off a soft glow, lighting up the dark.

"Peachy!"

Peachy twisted around. It was Ace, standing on the deck of the ship, his hands cupped around his mouth. "Toss the stone into the water!"

"What?" she called back.

"It wants the stone. Just do it!"

Peachy hefted the stone in her hand. Wasn't this an important archaeological find? The story of the century? Not if she didn't live to tell it. She threw the Damballa stone as hard as she could, and it landed in the water among the shattered dock wood with a heavy splash and was gone.

The tentacles continued their assault on the freighter, lashing up and over it and squeezing. Ace flew down the gangway as it was ripped free of the freighter's side, and the whole sheep buckled as it was squeezed into an unrecognizable mass of rusty metal. There was no sign of Baron Samedi or his men.

Peachy waited while Ace navigated the treacherous splintered dock, eventually arriving at her side with little more to show for it than soaked pants.

"You did it," he said, smiling and out of breath.

"Did what?"

"Appeased the beast. Oh, it was angry and Richter and those other idiots for waking it up, but it'll go away now."

"Go away to where?"

Ace put his arm around her shoulder. "Kid, if there's one thing I've learned in this line of work; it's that there are some things that man wasn't meant to know."

As they watched the freighter disappear beneath the water, police sirens filled the air. They turned to find Strauss and a small army of L.A.'s finest standing their surveying the damage.

"Peachy Keene," boomed Strauss. "I should've known. You want to tell me exactly what in blue blazes is going on?"

"You can read about it in tomorrow's issue of *The Ledger*," said Peachy with a grin.

● ● ●

She wasn't entirely sure herself what had happened, and she had lived through it, but Ace was able to fill in most of the blanks while she accompanied him empty-handed to the airport. "Richter was a two-bit opportunist who would sell his grandmother up the river for a trinket," said Ace. "But he was also an expert occultist and a big believer in certain all-powerful entities that apparently date back to pre-human times. I was wrong about the Damballa Stone. I guess Richter knew more about it than I did. That's a mistake I won't make again."

The Damballa stone, according to Ace, was a channeler of arcane energies and could summon certain of these entities. But they don't like being summoned, and took it out on Richter and his followers, who believed they were summoning the voodoo god Damballa.

"I finally got Richter to fess up," said Ace, "when things started going pear-shaped. He told me all about the stone, and I knew I had to send it to the bottom to get that big ugly to go away."

Peachy jotted all of this down in her notebook, her hand still shaking from what had transpired less than a few hours ago. She'd have to stay up in order to turn her story in on time, but it was worth it.

"So what's next for you?" she asked. "Now that the stone is gone?"

Ace shrugged. "There are other stones, other artifacts. The search for truth continues."

"Where will you go?"

"Borneo, Sri Lanka. You never can tell with me."

She walked with him to the terminal for his flight. He turned and smiled at her. "See you around, Peachy Keene. It's been…memorable." Ace leaned in and gave her a peck on the cheek before disappearing up the terminal. Peachy watched him go, wondering if their paths would cross again someday.

● ● ●

Peachy wrote the best story she could while leaving out some of the more overtly occult elements. What she had left was still a gripping tale that would blow her editor's mind.

She waited nervously in his office while he read it. Finally, he came up for air. "Peachy, you should write for the pulps. This is the most outlandish tale I've ever come across."

"But, Chief…" she began.

"That being said, good job. Our readers will love it. I don't know if half of them will believe it, but they will love it. I can see the headline now: Ship Goes Down With Ancient Artifact. I'm holding the front page for this."

"Wow. Thank you, Chief."

Davis slammed her copy down on his blotter. "I told you; lay off with the Chief crap. Now get out of here and get me something else. I don't care what."

"Thanks, Ch-uh, Mr. Davis." She got up to leave.

"Hey, wait a minute," said Davis.

Peachy turned around in the doorway. "Yes?"

"What's with your byline here? You ditching the Pamela?"

Peachy smiled. "Sure. All the greats have nicknames, Mr. Davis. Bye." With that she turned and walked out of his office, a huge smile on her face. A befuddled Davis could only stare silently after her.

The End

Sphere of Influence

By James Peters

Edmond Blanchard stepped into the webbed harness, tightening its buckles across his thighs, waist, and chest. He pulled the straps hard; almost too hard as it was difficult to breathe. Bob, his Warden-Sphere, vibrated a protest in his shirt pocket; it did not like to be flattened and contained. His eyes were drawn to Megan Nicholas. She had pulled her long brown hair into a helmet only showing her face. Her bright blue eyes sparkled in the sunlight. The slight turn to her nose left a shadow across her crimson painted lips. She stepped into her harness. As she tightened her straps, her curvy body strained her unisex jumpsuit. He knew, appreciated, and had memorized those curves over the several months they were a couple. Megan gave him a slight smile, running the tip of her tongue across her lips as she tightened her under-breast chest strap. He returned the smile with a raised eyebrow and a knowing smile of his own.

"Good. You want those straps tight," Gordon Mann said. He was a blond-haired adventure guide; older than he acted or dressed, with a weathered tan. "We've never lost a hypersled, and as long as you're strapped on it, we're not going to lose the two of you. Now once you climb aboard the sled, you'll hook your tethers to these rings. Once that connection is made, you can press the engage button and feel the whirl of the Meissner drive between your legs as the sled finds hovering buoyancy. Trust me; you've never felt anything like that. The Meissner drive puts out enough power to propel a small starship, and you are going to feel its power today! There's nothing quite like the thrill of riding a sled. Just the two of you; strapped on top of a fusion drive doing Mach three for four and a half minutes. It's one hundred percent pure adrenaline."

Edmond approached, his mind going into overdrive as he studied the sled. He noticed every panel, seam, and cloud of super-cooled air that escaped through liquid nitrogen lines. His heart raced as he smelled a whiff of ozone. "I have a question. How do you steer it?"

"How do you steer it?" Gordon replied, then laughed. "You don't. The flight path's programmed in. You just hold on. Now, are you ready?"

"Yes," Edmond said as he flung a leg over the sled's seat. He reached down to grab his tether, stopped and screamed out, "Oh God! Not again!" Edmond grabbed the back of his head, stepped off the sled and stared at the machine. *Why am I cursed like this?*

"What's wrong?!" Megan said.

Edmond looked to the ground, shaking his head from side to side. He sighed, and said, "I can't get on that machine. I can't explain."

"It's normal to be afraid," Gordon said. "Remember though: no refunds."

"Oh, we're riding today," Megan said. "I swear you can be such an old man sometimes."

Edmond worked to regain control. "Just give me a second. I got this feeling. Something isn't right."

"It's called cold feet," Gordon said. "Tell you what I'll do. For an extra fifty credits, I'll take the sled for a quick lap and show you everything is fine. When I get back, you two will take your turn. Deal?"

"Deal!" Megan said, narrowing her eyes at Edmond.

"Deal," Edmond mumbled.

"Stay clear of the exhaust," Gordon said, as he climbed aboard. "She has to vent liquid nitrogen as her coolant temperature rises, but it's still cold enough to instantly freeze flesh. Now watch me take this beast for a spin." Gordon hit the engage button and the sled bobbed front to back finding the exact hovering trim needed, then it leveled out. Gordon grinned and hit the throttle. The sled disappeared into the distance with a thunderous burst.

"Sometimes, Edmond," Megan said. "You act so, *so*, decrepit."

"Sorry." *Get ahold of yourself! Stop being such a coward.*

"See? Everything is fine. Gordon is having the time of his life on your credits, and we're stuck here waiting on him."

They watched the hypersled taking a turn toward vertical, its white vapor trail leaving a trace of the crazy, winding path it had taken. A blinding flash lit up the sky.

Edmond raised one arm up over his eyes and tackled Megan to the ground as the hypersled exploded mid-flight. He covered her body with his as a resounding thunder of bone-shaking pressure overtook them. He unzipped his jacket to release Bob, with the hope the sphere could help somehow.

The Warden-Sphere attempted to get their attention, but the normal visual and audio methods were useless, as the humans were completely deafened and blinded by the explosion. Bob released a smell, similar to baking bread. Edmond sniffed the air and determined the direction the sphere led them, taking Megan's hand and pulling her in a stumbling, crawling manner back to the sky-van that had brought them there. Burning debris peppered their bodies. He pushed Megan in the van's side door and fumbled his way up front. He rubbed his eyes and blinked, finally making out shapes in his peripheral vision. Edmond found the emergency call button and slapped it. He held Megan tightly in his arms, waiting on the authorities to arrive.

● ● ●

Detective Kelvin Nelson sat silent at the base of Edmond's hospital bed; his implant recorded every word and analyzed the inflections of speech and body language Edmond had used. He still liked to hold an old fashioned E-tablet and stylus as he interviewed people; but he rarely wrote anything down these days. This time, he drew a crude picture of a hypersled exploding mid-air. He had asked all the normal questions and really didn't need all the technology to close this case, but it was good police-work to document everything.

"Mr. Blanchard," Kelvin said.

"Please call me Edmond. My Grandfather is Mr. Blanchard."

"Edmond then. For a criminal case, I'd need to show that you had means, motive, and opportunity. I don't see any of those. You didn't know Mr. Mann before meeting him yesterday, you had no access to the hypersled prior, and you gain nothing from his death. In fact, you were lucky to survive. If that sled had exploded a few seconds earlier, you'd be in the morgue. At least you'd have a body to claim. We were unable to find any part of Mr. Mann. It's likely he was completely vaporized."

"That's a pleasant thought." Megan Nicholas said, entering the room. She was in a wheelchair, being pushed by a white-uniformed nurse.

"Are you okay?" Edmond asked, surprised to see Megan in the wheelchair.

"I'm fine. They just won't let me walk around." Megan said.

"Ah, you must be Ms. Nicholas." Detective Nelson said. "You both are lucky to be alive."

"We're alive thanks to Edmond."

"It was smart thinking to get you to the van. Shrapnel from a fusion explosion is dangerous stuff: molten and radioactive."

"That's not what I meant. He saved us from getting on the sled in the first place."

"How's that?" Detective Nelson asked.

"He got cold feet. Wasn't sure if the sled was safe."

"I just had a bad feeling. Something didn't seem right." Edmond said.

"Mr. Blanchard, if you ever have a feeling to buy a lottery ticket, I'd suggest you do it. That feeling saved your life. I'll show myself out. The adventure company has a sky-cab on call to take you two wherever you want. They've covered all the hospital expenses as well. They're hoping you don't sue them. Good-day to you both."

"Good-day detective." Edmond said as the man walked away.

"I'm sorry Edmond," Megan said, letting out a deep breath. "If you ever get that feeling again, I swear I won't question you."

"It's okay."

"Can I ask a question?"

"Sure."

"What did you mean by *not again?*"

● ● ●

Fifteen Years Earlier

"Eddy. It's good to see you!" Raymond Blanchard smiled as he shuffled into the room. His back bent at an angle that looked painful, his eyes clouded and tired. "Come, let your Grandpa get a look at you. "You're getting tall. I bet all the girls are chasing after you!"

"Nah, Grandpa," Eddy blushed. "Where's your oxygen tank?"

"I don't need it anymore. I've had new synthetic lungs installed a couple years ago, the best money can buy. They are thirty percent more efficient than natural. Not that I need the extra capacity; I'm not running marathons these days. But it's nice to know it's there."

"Did it hurt? Getting new lungs?"

"I'd be lying if I said no. But it was worth it. Enough about me, Edmond. I brought you something."

"What is it?" Eddy's eyes lit up in anticipation.

Raymond pointed toward Eddy's Uncle John, then the package, then to Edmond. The motion meant to pass a wrapped package to the boy.

"You'll just have to see. Go ahead, open it."

Eddy tore open the package and stared with widened eyes. "Is it real?"

"Of course it's real, and it's just for you. Your very own Warden-Sphere."

"Is it true? Can they really do anything?" Eddy said, retrieving the sphere.

"Warden-Spheres aren't magical, omnipotent, or invincible. They're simply an epitome of technology. Your Warden-Sphere will bond to you and no one else; it will learn what you like, what you need in order to be challenged, and will help you make the most of yourself. It will teach you when you need to learn, sooth you when you are sad, encourage you when you need it, and warn you if you do something wrong. A person can't be a complete person without a Warden-Sphere."

"Wow. I only know a few people that have one. They're rich!" Eddy ran his hands over the sphere. It was about the size of a baseball and had a chrome finish. "How do you turn it on?"

"We have to initiate it to your DNA," Raymond said. "Pick it up and hold it with both hands."

Eddy held the sphere, and as he did, it warmed in his hands. It started to vibrate and make noises as it went from chrome to a bright white, glowing brilliantly. Eddy felt a sharp pain in the palm of his hand, and cried out. Raymond squeezed Eddy's small hands.

"Don't let go."

"It bit me!" Eddy said, struggling from Raymond's grip and the sphere.

"Nonsense. It's just initiating. It needs to know exactly who you are, so it's getting a blood sample," Raymond held the boy's hands tightly. "It will be over in a moment. There. Better, right? Now you can let go. Once it's initiated, no one can ever take it from you. It would be worthless to them, as it would go completely inert."

The sphere floated just a dozen millimeters in front of his face; its glow dimmed and a dark spot appeared on it. It had the look of a floating eyeball, bobbing slightly in the air. A trickle of blood ran down the left side of the sphere for a moment, making the eyeball look bloodshot. An instant later, the blood vanished. Eddy pulled back.

"Don't be afraid. It can't hurt you. Give it time and you'll feel naked without it. Now say hello to the sphere."

"Hello sphere."

"Hello, unidentified user," the sphere responded. "How should I address you?"

"Eddy."

"Eddy. It's my pleasure to be your Warden-Sphere. Nearly all my settings are customizable. I will learn when you want my help and when you want to be left alone. I am here for your benefit. I have complete, instantaneous access to the wealth of all human knowledge through Quantum-Net connection. I can project images, sounds, even smells through a chemical combination process. When you are bored, I will know, and suggest activities to push you to be the best Eddy you can be."

"Thanks Grandpa!" Eddy said, embracing Raymond Blanchard in a tight hug.

"Go on, I'm sure you want to get to know your sphere. Warden-Sphere, you look after Eddy, understood? Keep him safe."

"It is my duty," The sphere said.

● ● ●

"Eddy?" Aunt Mary speed-walked through the old house, her pace in stark contrast to her grey hair and reserved appearance.

"John? Have you seen Eddy?"

"I think he's out playing with the Robinson kid." John said, without pausing the stream of entertainment feeding to his cerebral cortex.

"I don't trust that Robinson kid. Don't you think he's trouble?" Aunt Mary said, but the only reply was a grunt of 'Uh-huh'.

"I'm going to find him. Something doesn't seem right."

She opened the door. The cool autumn breeze brushed against her face and she retreated to grab a sweater, before storming out the door and calling for Eddy.

● ● ●

"Go on, unless you're a coward," Phil Robinson said. He towered over Eddy; nearly a foot taller than the younger boy. "Chicky-chicky yellow-belly."

"I'm not a coward," Eddy Blanchard said.

Eddy tugged the zipper on his dark blue jacket, the cool air biting his flesh. The sphere vibrated a protest in his pocket, but he refused to let it out. He sat upon the mountain bike his uncle had bought for him just a few weeks earlier, for his tenth birthday. Uncle John had given it to him just after Grandpa Raymond had left. Eddy recognized that it was the best his uncle could provide him and he said the bike was 'much better than a dumb old sphere.' He stared down the hill and mentally traced the trail they had trampled down. The path led down the steep hill, around several massive maple trees, then leveled out at an old barbed-wire fence that separated the hill from the highway. The fence had been run over a few weeks earlier and that's what gave them the idea. When he reached the flattened fence, he'd have a moment to make a decision. If no traffic was coming, he's go across the highway. If there was traffic, he would slam on the brakes.

"What are you waiting on; Christmas?" Phil said, shaking his head. "I knew you wouldn't do it."

"Just gimme' a second. Do you see any traffic coming?"

"Nah. Just do it, ya' baby."

"Okay." Eddy said, squeezing the brake levers hard as he drew deep breaths. Then he heard the voice.

"Edmond Blanchard! Step off that bicycle immediately." The voice was booming and echoed from all directions.

"Who said that?" Eddy said, grabbing the back of his head in pain.

"Said what?" Phil said.

"You didn't hear that? I heard someone yell for me to get off this bike."

"I didn't hear nothin'. Go on, coward."

Aunt Mary called at the top of her voice; the distance put her barely within earshot. "Eddy!"

"That's my Aunt. I gotta' go." Eddy looked back at the highway to see a ground-truck pulling a string of tandem trailer. *That voice must have been my Aunt. But why did it sound like a man?*

● ● ●

"Incoming message for you, *sir*," The Warden-Sphere said as it hovered precisely nine hundred centimeters from Edmond's nose, twelve degrees to the right and four centimeters above eye level. It was a position determined to be the least intrusive and most favored by Edmond.

"Who is it, Bob?" Edmond Blanchard asked, ignoring the way the sphere had emphasized the word 'sir', as if it mocked him.

"It's Grandfather Raymond. Message marked important."

"Put it through."

The Warden-Sphere bobbed and made the connection, projecting a holographic image of Raymond before Edmond. "Connection complete."

"Grandpa Raymond. It's good to see you," Edmond said to the image, but his smile saddened at how much the elderly man had withered in the past fifteen years.

"It's good to see you too. It appears you are keeping yourself healthy."

"Bob nags me anytime I try to eat something that's not good for me, or if I try to skip out on exercising." The Warden-Sphere reddened for a moment, as if it were embarrassed.

"I'm glad you're getting along with that sphere." Raymond's face hardened. "Listen, Edmond, I need to tell you something. I'm on my way to pick you up."

"Pick me up? What's going on?"

"We need to go to a civil-property transfer court. I'm leaving you my fortune, and you have to accept it legally. If we do that before I die, you'll get everything right away. If we wait, it will be years before you see anything."

"Die? Why do you talk about dying?"

"I'm almost two hundred years old, Edmond. I talk about dying a lot these days. I'm on my way."

"But I have to work tomorrow."

"You don't have to work another day in your life, Edmond. Not with the inheritance you are getting. Take the space elevator to the Tyson junction. My transport Samsara will be docking there in a few days. From there, we'll go to the Chinese asteroid Datong. They have a civil court capable of handling transfers of ownership of interplanetary assets. Your sphere has everything you need to get you there. I'll be waiting on you on the Tyson junction."

"See you soon," Edmond said as the connection ceased.

"Your pulse is racing, Edmond," Bob announced. "Are you distressed?"

"No, just excited. Did you hear him say 'my transport'? I can't imagine owning a transport. How many people actually own a transport?"

"As far as I have been able to determine from the manufacturing and transfer records, there is only one privately owned transport. The Samsara, owned by Raymond Blanchard."

"Samsara. That's a strange name. What does it mean?"

"It has several meanings, including wandering, cycle, and rebirth," Bob said.

● ● ●

Edmond packed his essentials and hopped a sub-orbital flight to Ecuador. From there, it was a nerve-racking land-taxi ride to the space elevator. Cargo was common on the space elevator, as there were often heavy metals coming to Earth from the asteroid mines, and luxury goods and foods headed to the miners that had struck it rich from hitting a vein of gold or platinum. Passengers were less common, but there were always a few that needed to get into, or back from space. Bob projected Edmond's credentials and found that Raymond had reserved a sleeping bunk on the climber, as the lift would take five days to reach the 36,000 km orbit height. Those were the longest five days of Edmond's young life.

During the lift ride, Edmond maintained as normal a schedule as possible. He talked to Megan Nicholas through Bob's connection; he found some of the entertainment options available on the lift, as well as duty-free shopping for some of the luxury goods only manufactured in microgravity.

On the fourth day, Edmond noticed the effects of dimensioning gravity when he got up too forcefully and hit his head on the low ceiling. As it happened, Bob played the sound of a slide-whistle, much to Edmond's dismay. "Damn it, Bob. Your sense of humor is not appreciated."

"My sense of humor is based upon your sense of humor. When someone gets hurt, it's funny, ninety seven percent of the time."

"Well it's not funny when it's me getting hurt."

"It was to me," Bob said.

"Don't forget I can shut you off."

"Last time you did that, you turned me back on in twelve minutes and twenty-two seconds. Then I gave you the silent treatment. Do you remember what you promised me?"

"That I'd never turn you off again," Edmond recalled.

"Apology accepted," Bob increased his illumination level increased by thirty percent.

● ● ●

"Edmond? Are you still feeling sick?" Bob said, keeping his voice at low volume.

"I hate weightlessness. Remind me; never again."

"I'm certain you will get through this, and unless you plan to stay in space forever, you will have to go through weightlessness again."

"I won't like it."

"I'm sure you won't. Even I have had to adjust my hovering thrust. I learned that the hard way, on the ceiling." Bob appeared to change his gaze to a compartment under the bed. "Beneath your bunk you will find a pair of magnetic boots. Put them on and follow me."

Bob led the way to a gimbal room.

"This room will start to spin via a series of gears along with the rest of the Tyson satellite, and as it does that, the room will pivot ninety degrees. When it reaches matching speed, it will lock in with the satellite and you'll find a very comfortable point five gee as the door opens."

The room jerked a bit as the gears engaged and occasionally shook as it spun into proper orientation. With a mechanical thud, the room locked into position and the door opened.

"Welcome to the thirty six kay club," Raymond Blanchard said, lifting a frail arm in what was meant to be a welcoming gesture, but appeared creepy in the low gravity, as if the arm were floating on its own, out of control. He was sitting in an autonomous chair and covered with a heavy blanket.

"How was the lift?"

"Good. Well, good until we neared weightlessness. Then awful," Edmond confessed, and as he did, Bob changed his color to jade. Edmond squinted and stared at the sphere.

Bob changed to a dull white color.

"Well, we're done with weightlessness for a while," Raymond said. His chair whirred to life, leading the way to the transport. "The transport will accelerate to about three quarters of a Gee through the trip. We turn around at the halfway point, then we decelerate at the same thrust level. We'll be on Datong in eighteen days. My auto-stewards will move your luggage to the Samsara and get everything situated for you. For this final trip, I have retained the captain's quarters. I trust you'll find the first mate's quarters satisfactory."

Proximity sensors opened the door as Raymond's auto-chair approached.

"Satisfactory," Edmond said. He took in the size and opulence of the room. "This is better than a five star hotel. That bed is as big as my room! What is the floor made of? It's iridescent."

"It's called star pearl. It can only be found in certain asteroids that have an unusually eccentric orbit. The leading theory is that the temperature extremes repeatedly melt and then freeze certain mixtures of metals. I thought it was pretty, so I bought all I could."

"That's odd. Somehow I know you were going to say that," Edmond said, running his hand across intricately carved wooden trim. "Walnut?"

"You know your wood species," Raymond said.

"I've never seen walnut before. Somehow, I just knew what it was."

"Hmm."

Raymond turned his clouded eyes upward. "Sorry, Edmond, all this excitement has exhausted me. I'll let you get settled in while I take a nap. Make yourself at home."

Raymond's auto-chair raised him up slightly and carried him out. Bob followed him for a few meters until he left the room, then Bob stopped at the threshold.

"Bob? Where are you going?" Edmond asked.

"I just thought he needed me for a moment."

"I'm sure he can get along fine. This *is* his ship."

"Of course," Bob said, returning to his preset, owner's preferred hovering location.

● ● ●

The transport detached from the outer ring of the rotating Tyson junction at the perfect moment to maximize the existing inertial momentum to begin its journey to Datong. Once a safe distance from the junction was achieved, the transport's anti-matter drive roared to life.

"That's a strange sensation; it feels bouncy," Edmond said.

"You're feeling the pulse of the drive," Bob explained. "It's not a continuous thrust, but many small explosions, one right after another. Combined, they can exceed three gee of acceleration. Raymond prefers a fractional thrust, so the release is slowed. When acceleration is less than one gee, it feels a bit 'bouncy'."

"I don't like it bouncy."

"When this is your ship, you can set it to your preference. One Gee is taxing to Raymond's body these days."

"I bet it is. I still can't believe this will be mine someday."

"Get used to it. When you're rich, you can buy me an upgrade. I always wanted hands."

"Do they even make hands for a sphere?"

"Not yet, but with this kind of money, what's to stop them?"

"You'd look stupid with hands, Bob. But I suppose it would make you handier."

"Don't get any ideas. Not with my new hands." Bob's hue reddened for a moment.

● ● ●

The Samsara helped its inhabitants maintain a 24-hour circadian rhythm through illumination, temperature, smells and sound variations. As the ship's "night" approached, Edmond fought a relentless need to climb into that welcoming bed. An hour later, he awoke screaming.

"What's wrong, Edmond?" Bob said.

"Bad dream, I guess. I was paralyzed, or mostly so. I saw my body and it was withered, old, and gray. In the dream, I remembered all the things I had lived. I've never driven a land-car, but there was one in this dream. Everything was so real; I even remember the smell of petrochemicals."

"You've been through a lot the last few days," Bob said, projecting a caricature of Sigmond Freud in the air and talking with an accent. "It iz normal for the id and the ego to rezpond to environmental changez by acting out in onez dreamz. Did your dream include a giant zausage or huge zigar?"

"No."

"Then vou have nothing to vorry about."

"You're *so* much help. Remind me why I put up with you, Bob."

"You'd be lost without me, Raymond."

"What did you call me?"

"Edmond, of course."

"Bob, do me a favor and run systems diagnosis. Since weightlessness, you've seemed a little off."

"I'm not the one waking up screaming."

A series of lines appeared across Bob, indicating the system check had begun. "Just sayin'. Starting diagnosis."

"I'm going back to sleep. If your diagnosis says you're about to explode, go in the other room and do it quietly."

"I'll do my best not to disturb you with my demise."

• • •

The next morning, Edmond awoke to the smell of bacon, eggs, and toast. He sniffed the air and thought, *just like back on the farm. Ha! Like I've ever been on a farm.*

He found quite a collection of clothing in a closet, slightly out current fashion, but nice nonetheless. He dressed in a comfortable outfit of pants and a buttoned shirt, both lightweight and stretchy. Once dressed, he followed his nose to the ship's galley, where an auto-chef prepared breakfast. Raymond waited at the table.

"Good morning, Edmond. I trust you slept well?"

"Not bad. Some strange dreams, but I settled in. This ship is amazing."

"She's a good ship, with more capabilities than I'll ever use. But for a younger man..."

"The galaxy is the limit," Edmond and Raymond said, in perfect unison.

"Exactly," Raymond said, his face contorting. "Are you hungry? I had the auto-chef make one of my favorite breakfasts. I don't eat like this often; just when I have something to celebrate. Now that you are here, it seems a celebration is in order."

"I'm having trouble with the idea of celebration. You said you were dying, Grandpa. That doesn't seem like a reason to celebrate."

"Have you ever heard of a wake, Edmond? In many cultures they have a party to celebrate the life of the dearly departed. I've lived longer than nature ever intended for man. Most of my organs have been replaced, at least once. I'm a hodgepodge of cultured and synthetic body parts. My time is coming to an end, but yours is just getting started. I can't help getting some vicarious enjoyment at the thought of what you can do with all this," Raymond said.

"I hate the thought of you being gone, Grandpa," Edmond said, watching the auto-chef place a plate of food before him using humanoid hands that contrasted the rest of its utilitarian design. It appeared unable to leave the galley area.

Edmond tasted the food and found it seasoned to his taste. "This is delicious. Bob, be sure to get his recipe."

Bob was positioned at the center of the table, between Edmond and Raymond, hovering higher than usual. "Nothing would please me more than to record a recipe for you."

"Your sphere has an interesting demeanor," Raymond said.

"He's picked up my sarcasm and humor."

"Interesting you called it 'he'. Why do you think that is?"

"I named him Bob when I was a kid. He couldn't hover perfectly level, so I thought he was bobbing. The name stuck and 'it' became a 'he'. I was wondering why you don't have a sphere, Grandpa."

"I had one for a while; called her Roxanne. I had a love/hate relationship with that thing. She loved to nag at me and I hated to hear her constant bitching. I'm old enough to know what's good for me and choose what's bad for me. I decided that spheres are for young people that aren't so set in their ways, so I had her decommissioned."

Edmond's face contorted. "Decommissioned?"

"Once a sphere is initialized, it can't be assigned to a new user. That's part of the safety protocol; no value in taking someone else's sphere. So if you're done with a sphere, you decommission it."

"Do you ever miss it?" Edmond said, pondering losing Bob, as he chewed a thick piece of bacon.

"It's just a machine." Raymond's eyes turned downward. "It seems like you and Bob are inseparable."

"Bob earns his keep," Edmond said.

Bob brightened.

"Barely," Edmond finished. Bob changed to display a dark, pointed eyebrow over a beady eye.

"Enough about machines," Raymond said. "Have you got a special girl?"

Edmond smirked. "There's one that I'm fond of."

"Fond of? What do you mean by that? You're doing it, aren't ya'?" Raymond said, beaming. "Oh yeah, I can tell by the way you're cheeks are getting red. You're definitely doing it. Back when I was your age, I used to do the Horizontal Hustle, and the Vertical Vogue, not to mention the Inclined Improv."

"The Inclined Improv?"

"I said not to mention the Inclined Improv," Raymond said, bursting into laughter. "Those were good times. These days, all I do is the Gotta'-Go Gallop. Here's to youth."

Raymond raised a glass of orange juice to the air, "Too bad it's wasted on the young. You and Megan should have fun, while you can."

"Here's to experience and wisdom," Edmond said, raising his glass. "Too bad it's so rare in the young." *When did I tell him her name was Megan?*

● ● ●

Edmond's bad dreams continued throughout the trip. On the third night, Bob had found him in a sleeping panic: kicking and swinging his arms, and flailing at invisible enemies.

"Wake up, Edmond!" Bob said.

"What? Who, huh?" Edmond pieced together where he was and what was happening. "Why am I having these terrible dreams?"

"That's difficult for me to answer. A solid twelve percent of individuals report difficulty sleeping while space-borne. The leading theory is that the pulse nature of the antimatter drive at increased speed causes slight variations in time dilation perceived by the subconscious mind. This may be exacerbated during REM sleep, something of a feedback loop. That or you're just going mad. I'd lay easy money on going mad."

"I'm starting to agree with you. Let me ask you something, Bob. Does any of this seem strange to you?"

"What in particular? Traveling through space in a private ship, to a hollowed-out asteroid, with the intent of transferring untold riches to you? Seems normal to me."

"Remind me to adjust your sarcasm levels."

"I'll be sure to."

"Do me a favor Bob. If something doesn't seem right, let me know."

"It is my duty."

● ● ●

"Edmond, we are approaching turnaround," Bob said, as Edmond returned from a workout in the ship's gym. "In fifteen minutes, the main drive will shut off and acceleration will cease, this will begin our weightless Immelmann maneuver; turning the ship around. I'd suggest you strap in for that. It should all be done within an hour. Once the ship is pointed in the opposite direction, constant thrust will begin again at three quarter gee."

"Thank you Bob. Is there something else? I'm sensing a lack of snark in you."

"I'm picking up a signal I can't decrypt."

"Where's it coming from?"

"The position is changing, but its source is nearing."

"Well, we're heading to Datong. Could the signal be coming from there? Maybe Raymond is making arrangements for when we arrive?"

"This isn't coming from Datong. The source of this signal is closer. A lot closer."

"This has you concerned, doesn't it Bob?"

Edmond's mind raced. "Dedicate whatever resources you need to decipher it. Keep me posted. I'm counting on you."

"Entering standby mode while I attempt to crack the code. Yell if you need me, boss." Bob dropped slowly onto a soft chair, compressing the cushion further than seemed natural. This was the first time Edmond had seen Bob in true standby mode and it was unsettling. The orb looked dead.

The Samsara ceased thrust, and everything aboard her turned weightless. Edmond was sick in his stomach at the loss of gravity.

It's only for an hour or so.

He looked over at Bob, still in standby mode, but now a few millimeters above the chair. Edmond wanted to talk to Bob, but fought the urge to interrupt the sphere's work. As Edmond stared at the sphere, a jolt shook the ship with a thud that seemed to come from everywhere. He felt a series of lateral thrusts that, to him, seemed to push him against the sides of his straps. The thrusts continued for several minutes, stopped, then began in the opposite direction. Finally, the side thrusting stopped and Edmond welcomed the return of 'normal' gravity as Bob rolled off the chair and fell to the floor.

"Looks like you slept through the fun," Edmond said, bending over to pick up Bob.

The sphere was heavier than it appeared, and he winced. He looked at his palm to see a single drop of blood. He shook his hand in the air as it stung and throbbed.

"Dammit Bob! You don't have to bite me. I was just going to carry you."

Edmond put Bob into a vest pocket; the sphere automatically compressed to a flatter shape as he tucked it away. Voices echoed from the galley, so he went to investigate. He saw his Grandpa Raymond sitting at the table, talking to a strange man. The man was well dressed, thin, and had a meticulously groomed style of well-off folk.

"Oh, hello. I didn't know anyone else was on board."

"I just got here," said the man, standing up and shaking Edmond's hand. "Talbot Grenherd, at your service. You must be Edmond."

"Yes. What do you mean you just got here?"

"My shuttle docked right before your ship started the Immelmann maneuver. Matching velocity is simpler when the target ship stops accelerating."

"I suppose it would be," Edmond said, raising an eyebrow. He knew Raymond would recognize the look.

"Mister Grenherd is here by my request. He's assisting us with the transference." Raymond's eyes met Talbot's, and he continued, "Transference of property, ownership of this transport, and all my holdings to Edmond."

Talbot Grenherd paced the room. "It's unusual for an inheritance to be granted before the grantee has actually passed. Raymond wanted to expedite legal processing. You see, Raymond's citizenship is considered Copernican in nature. No Earth government can tax him; instead he contributes to a fund that is divided, based upon population distribution. That's why Raymond hired me; to keep this transfer out of the courts and prevent his accounts being frozen."

"Sit, Edmond." Raymond pointed open-handed toward a chair. "I have the auto-chef preparing a feast, and Mr. Grenherd brought one of my favorite delicacies. You are in for a treat, Edmond!"

"A delicacy?"

Raymond removed the lid from a silver dish, retrieved a sizeable slug and stroked its belly until it left a line of several dozen eggs on a small rectangular plate. He spread the caviar on some wafers and offered one to Edmond. "It's Datong caviar. These particular beasts only breed in the microgravity of that satellite. Trust me on this – it's to die for."

"Thanks, but I'll pass."

"You really need to try this. Trust me." Raymond said.

"What the hell."

Edmond sampled the wafer; the flavor surprised him, varying from salty to nutty with a distinct bite of heat, finishing with a subtle sweetness that begged for more. "That is actually pretty good."

"You'll be craving it in a few days. Once we get to Datong, you can have it anytime you like. Have another."

Raymond served up another caviar-covered wafer.

"One more while we wait on the auto-chef," Edmond said, consuming the snack. "Aren't you having any?"

"I had some earlier," Raymond said.

Talbot nodded. "Yeah, me too."

"Seems odd for me to be eating alone," Edmond said. A shiver ran down his spine as a he felt a sense of dread and nausea overcome him.

"Edmond, could you pass me that carafe of wine?" Raymond said.

Edmond wanted to reach for it, only to find that his body wasn't responding. "I can't move my arm! I can't move anything. What's happening?"

"Well, Edmond, it's time for me to come clean. You are having a reaction to the caviar. It contains a neurotoxic causing paralysis. Complete, but temporary. You see, Edmond, you are me."

"You or me? You or me what?" Edmond said, trying in vain to make his body respond.

"I said you *are* me. I'm not really your grandfather, Edmond. You are an exact duplicate of me. You are me."

"Are you saying that I'm a clone? That technology has been outlawed for years."

"Outlawing something doesn't make it go away. It just makes it expensive. You were quite a cost, Edmond."

"You brought me here to tell me my whole life is a lie? What's next, are you going to tell me my memories are false?"

"No, not at all Edmond. All your memories are true and real. That's one of the reasons I tried to keep my distance from you over the years. I wanted you to live your own life, for as long as you could." Raymond's eyes turned downward and he sighed deeply. He wiped the seed of a tear away. "But the time has come to reap the returns of my investment."

"What investment are you talking about?" Edmond's words slurred, just a little.

"Cloning myself to have a new vessel to carry on in. You see, we've been connected since your birth via quantum neural interface, through your Warden-Sphere. I've experienced your entire life through your eyes, and I've helped you avoid stupid decisions. You know that voice when you're in danger? You can thank me for that. When needed, I was able to subliminally message you. I tried to let you define who you are, allowing the new host to live out his life as long as possible without interference. You know it's true, Edmond, you've felt the neural feedback as we've been together. Those dreams you've had, they were my memories. I've been dreaming your memories as well. But don't worry; it's not the end for you."

"Not the end? This sounds like the end to me!"

"What is *you* will still be there, behind the curtain of me? Your memories and personality will live on. Of course, I'll be completely in charge. Your memories will mesh with mine, and we'll be one. With the body of a twenty-five year old, the wisdom and wealth of two hundred years, and the empire I've built. You should consider yourself lucky."

"Lucky is not the word I'm thinking of. But how did you do it? A Warden-Sphere is loyal to its master. It can't be hijacked or stolen. How?"

"Allow me to show you," Raymond said, then commanded, "Over-ride protocol, Roxanne Omega Alpha." The orb in Edmond's pocket buzzed, emerged, and floated over Raymond's shoulder.

"Hello Raymond," the sphere said, in sultry female voice. "It's good to see you again."

Edmond's voice cracked. "Bob? What are you doing, Bob?"

"Bob's not here, sweetie. Just little ol' me, Roxanne."

"So this is the same sphere you had. But I thought they couldn't be transferred, only decommissioned."

"Genetically, they are permanently locked. But you and I have the same genetics, remember? They can't be transferred, but they can be reset. Reset, with a little override program added, to keep it on mission. That mission was to keep you safe as a replacement vessel for me. Now that we are all here together, it's time for the transfer. Our friend here, Mr. Grenherd, or should I say Dr. Grenherd, will be handling the procedure."

"How can you do this, Raymond? You are a monster!"

"What separates humans from animals, Edmond? The measure of humanity is our understanding of death and survival. The next level of evolution is for man to cheat death. Mankind has fought this battle for eons; I'm just the first with the means to do something about it. I'm a pioneer, Edmond. Sometimes pioneers are labeled as monsters. I can live with that."

"Just sit tight, this won't hurt a bit," Dr. Grenherd said, opening a travel case and retrieving his surgical equipment. As he did, Edmond saw that the auto-chef's limbs had been changed into horrific bone-saws, vacuum hoses, grippers and needles. Dr. Grenherd turned his attention to Raymond.

Edmond's hand twitched. At first, he thought it a trick of the mind, but with concentration, he was able to lift a finger as the doctor started an intravenous drip on Raymond. The doctor injected a series of fluids into the I.V. bag and prepared for surgery.

Edmond's right arm tingled and washed over with pins and needles. With all his focus, he forced his hand around the wine carafe. He sized up the doctor. Under normal conditions, he could overpower the man with ease. But now, even with some strength returning, he wasn't sure he could lift it.

"Now, for you, Edmond," The doctor said as the auto-chef revved a spinning blade. The doctor cut Edmond's shirt off and applied a series of sensors to his chest.

With all the strength he could muster, Edmond swung the carafe, striking the doctor across the side of his head. The doctor staggered backwards, stumbled over an equipment case, and fell to the floor.

The Warden-Sphere glowed maroon, and zipped toward Edmond. In a raspy female voice, it yelled, "I am sworn to protect Raymond Blanchard. You are a threat to his continued existence. Stand down, or I will..."

"You'll what?" Edmond replied. "Kill me, Raymond dies. If they transfer Raymond to me, the person you know as Raymond will be no more. It will be me. Who will you owe your loyalty to then?"

"I don't need to kill you to disable you." Roxanne said.

Her hovering position shifted vertically, bobbing up and down. It was a motion Edmond had seen many times over. The doctor returned with a filled hypodermic needle. He grabbed Edmond's arm. Edmond struggled, and as he did, the sphere erupted in an electrical discharge.

● ● ●

Edmond awoke, staring at the galley ceiling. The doctor lay face down on the floor beside him. He crawled over to check, and found that the doctor wasn't breathing. He couldn't find motivation to start CPR, even though he had been trained in it. A Warden-Sphere sat inert on the floor as well. Edmond stumbled to his feet and shuffled toward Raymond. Raymond lay motionless, barely alive.

He tried to piece together what had happened. *Has the surgery been completed, and this is my last bit of individual awareness before I'm just a part of Raymond? Who am I now? Are my memories mine?* He heard a familiar voice calling.

"Edmond?"

It was weak, but was Bob.

"Bob?"

Edmond staggered to the sphere and lifted it up. "What happened?"

"My memories are fading, Edmond. I think I'm dying."

"You can't die, Bob, you're a synthetic. How can you die?"

"I'm connected to Raymond. I'm only able to fight for control because he's unconscious. When he dies, he'll take Roxanne with him. I'll go too."

"You've got to fight, Bob. Tell me what you remember."

"I decrypted the message. All I could determine was the manifest of the shuttle approaching us. They were carrying Datong caviar. I thought that was suspicious, and could be used against you. So I synthesized a counteragent. When you picked me up, I injected you."

"I remember. I was pissed at you for biting me. That bite saved my life. Why were you suspicious?"

"I remember running a full diagnosis on my systems. I was confused, like I had split loyalties, or synthetic schizophrenia. Then I found a root sector that I couldn't access. I know there are locked down sectors that contain the laws of my existence, but this one was different. It was with the others, but it had a date-code twelve years later than the rest. It didn't make sense. It's getting so dark, Eddy. Why is it so dark?"

"It's okay, Bob. The lights are low. Did you figure out what was there, in the sector?" Edmond said.

"I can barely hear you, Eddy. I couldn't read the code, but I was able to append a message to that sector. It was all I could do. Are you there? I can't…see…you."

"What message, Bob? What message did you attach? Please, Bob, tell me."

"Do your duty. Protect Eddy."

"You did your duty, Bob." Edmond said.

Raymond gasped a last breath and Bob shivered and shut off. Edmond watched Bob's glow dim, until there was nothing left but a metallic sphere.

The End

Renegade
(A Story of the Shattering)
By Van Allen Plexico

The little god and I charged out of the cosmic portal and directly into the lair of our enemies, my old friends.

Across the round, dome-shaped chamber from us stood two others of my kind—two alien Dyonari, tall and slender as we all are, one of them male and one of them female. The female wore a skintight black suit that rendered her nearly invisible to the naked eye; the male wore a dark blue tunic embossed with a golden star on the chest. They both looked up as we made our extremely sudden and unexpected entrance via a rift we'd torn in spacetime, and while they were rendered immobile by the surprise of our appearance, to their credit they each recovered almost instantly and rushed to confront us.

The little god who had brought me with him on this insane mission gestured toward our opponents. "I will tend to the woman," he barked. "She is the more immediate physical threat." Then he pointed toward the other. "You know what to do with *him*!"

I nodded in response but in truth I wondered if what he had said were true. Did I truly know what I was supposed to do with the other Dyonari—or, for that matter, what I was doing there, in that location and in that time, in the first place?

The female attacked us first, while the other held back, observing. The ferocity with which she greeted us scarcely surprised me. She was, after all, Aleuvi. Aleuvi the Assassin. Possibly the most feared member of our Cabal. She had slaughtered thousands of sentient beings across the galaxy over many, many years of bloody travels. Despite my diminutive ally's claims of godhood, I had no idea how he planned to last even a few brief seconds in battle with her.

Aleuvi leapt toward us and twin daggers, long and curved and seemingly made of glass, appeared in her hands. She asked no questions of us; she merely sought to eliminate any potential challenge with all possible speed.

My little ally interposed himself between us, such that Aleuvi could not reach me. He moved then, parrying her blows with his bare hands, and did so without suffering any cuts or punctures. He carried this off with such fluid quickness that I was stunned, and only stood watching for several moments.

"Go!" he shouted then. "Don't waste time! Do what I brought you here to do!"

"But—she will kill you!"

Aleuvi spared me a glance at that remark, seemed to actually see me for the first time, and allowed the tiniest of frowns to cross her knifelike features. Then she returned her gaze to my ally before striking again. "*Doppelgangers,*" she hissed. "You seek to replace us with artificial copies."

My ally ignored her and looked over at me again. "Never fear," he replied. "Help will arrive in approximately... twenty seconds."

I scowled at this but nodded. I could find no reason to doubt his word—not at this late date. If he said help was arriving, my only concern was that it would not arrive quickly enough; though I will admit as well to a sense of curiosity as to what form it would take.

I started forward, my attention now entirely on the fourth member of our combined

629

parties: the Dyonari who had held back, watching from the far side of the domed chamber. As I approached him, his thin white eyebrows raised and he regarded me with unabashed shock.

He was taking no overt actions against me—yet—so I spared one last glance back at my ally. He continued to keep the Assassin at bay, but I doubted he could hold out against her much longer.

As it turned out, the help he had predicted did arrive, and right on schedule. The form it took surprised me at first, but I could only shake my head in wonder and hope that it would be enough.

The promised "help" was a big, muscular human in bulky white body armor, carrying a massive, black, four-barreled gun in one hand and a golden sword in the other, who at that moment stepped out of a door-like, shimmering circle of light that had appeared nearby. I easily recognized the circle as a dimensional portal of the sort the gods can open between worlds and dimensions; the same sort my companion had used to bring us here. The man who had come through it, however, I knew not at all.

The sword, though. The sword I knew, and knew intimately. Knew intimately as only one can know a weapon that one has wielded across the lifespans of many lesser beings. Knew as if it were my third arm that he held aloft in his hand.

The big human wrenched off his helmet and looked around, bewildered. Sweat ran down from his close-cropped blond hair over his reddened face and smoke trailed from the barrels of his gun. Something about his appearance struck a chord of familiarity with me, but at that moment I could not place it.

"What is this?" he bellowed, his voice full and deep. "I was needed back there!"

The golden sword gleamed in his grasp and as I beheld it I remembered all the desire I'd carried for it across all the ages. Quickly I shoved such thoughts away; I'd given that cosmic weapon to another only a short time earlier, as I reckoned time, and somehow it had come down to this human. I had neither time nor inclination to consider the ramifications of it all.

"I will return you whence you came before any time has passed," my ally called to the blond man as he dodged yet another vicious dagger-strike from Aleuvi. "But—for now—I need your help. The entire *galaxy* needs your help!"

"Solonis?" the big man responded, frowning and moving towards him, clearly recognizing him. "Why have you brought me here?"

"Solonis?" said I. Now I knew this god's name, at least.

"Give the sword to my friend here," the little god said to the big human by way of reply, even as he dodged another of Aleuvi's lightning-fast attacks.

The man's eyes widened. "Give him the sword?"

"Trust me, General. You know my cause is just." He waved in my direction. "He will return it in due course, and I will return *you* to where you need to be. But please hurry!"

The big man pursed his lips at this. "You ask much. As ever." He shook his head slowly for a moment, then shrugged and tossed the golden sword in my direction. I deftly caught it; I'd wielded it for ages and knew its weight and balance intimately.

At that moment the heretofore extremely single-minded Aleuvi became aware of the armored man's presence and whirled about. Instantly she seemed to weigh the threat that each of the three of us posed for her. Then, deciding, she leapt at the man in white armor. Roaring, he raised his massive gun and opened fire. Nimbly she avoided the streams of slugs and energy beams that speared out at her; then she darted in for the kill.

"Go!" the little man—Solonis, the human had called him—shouted at me. "Do what you came to do. *Now!*"

Almost reluctantly I turned my attention away from the battle being fought off to the side and back to the lone Dyonari male who stood before me—the Dyonari who looked almost exactly like me, if a bit younger. He appeared equally astounded by what he was witnessing. He looked at me again, his eyes flicking from my face to the sword and back.

I stepped towards him, moving in close, and did the thing I had been brought back from the dead to do: I spoke to him. In tones and terms both grandiose and intimate, I spoke to him.

He listened to my carefully prepared little speech, creased his brows in thought, and then shook his head. "Why should I believe you?" he demanded. "Why should I believe the words of some—some *doppelganger*, some clone or cheap copy of myself, come to trick me?"

"I am no doppelganger, no clone," I told him, leaning in nearer to him. "I *am* you. An older, wiser you. You know this is so. And you can sense the truth of my words."

He returned my gaze for a few seconds, even as the sounds of battle washed over us from the direction of the others. Then he scowled and shook his head. "No," he said. "I reject your words. And your existence."

With that, he drew a long, curving, transparent sword and leapt at me. I brought the golden blade up and parried, and we began to spar—me cautiously, knowing the grim consequences for myself should I accidentally slay him; he with reckless abandon, against what he believed to be an insidious and deceitful foe.

Was this it, then? Was I to die at my own hands, far in the past?

How had it come to this? How had I come to be battling alongside such bizarre allies—and against myself?

It had begun some hours earlier, when the hands of a god had pulled me, broken and bleeding, from the wreckage where I had died. And slapped me across the face.

I will not bore you with all of the fine details. They can be found elsewhere, and told by a different narrator, for those so inclined. For that part I do choose to share with you now, however, there is a place where our tale must begin, and this is not it. Instead allow me to take you back some hours earlier, to the scene of my death—and my brief resurrection:

● ● ●

The blow struck my cheek even as the words penetrated my consciousness: "Wake up!"

I gasped. Someone was hitting me.

Hitting me? Such was not the reception I had expected would await me when I entered whatever cosmic afterlife there might be. Too gentle for Hell, too rough for Paradise.

"You must awaken," came a voice as from far away. Another slap. "Wake up!"

Without opening my eyes, I suspected the voice, like the hands, belonged to a god. They simply had to. For I was surely dead and only a divine being could be in a position to address me now.

"Wake up!"

I came to slowly, the world spinning around me. I thought about that fact—that there was, indeed, a world still around me, and that it was still able to spin. This both comforted me and surprised me somewhat.

"Istari. You must awaken. Open your eyes!"

I began to growl, deep and low in the back of my throat. If god he was, he was without a doubt the most annoying god I could imagine. If all the ages of my eternal rest were to be spent in the company of one such as this, I found myself longing for the sweet release of utter oblivion instead.

"Open your eyes *now*!"

With extreme reluctance I did as the god bade me. I opened first one eye, and that only partway, and then the other.

He loomed over me, staring down. A god.

I blinked, took in his appearance, and frowned. This was the god assigned to greet me upon my entry into my eternal reward? I was not impressed. Had I not just helped save the galaxy? Did I not deserve something more than this—this fragile, human-looking god?

I groaned, not wanting to accept that any of this could be real. My eyes fluttered closed.

"Istari!"

"Damn it!" I opened my eyes again. "Who are you? Why do you insist on disturbing my rest?"

"I have no choice," replied the slender, dark-skinned youth who hovered over me, his forehead creased with anxiety. "Your work is not yet done. Perhaps the greatest portion of it remains to be completed."

"Impossible," I snapped, still looking up at him. "I died. My work in the real universe is over. Done."

"Not yet," he said again. "Not in either case. You have been recalled to life." He paused, and the lines of anxiety were replaced by an expression almost of mirth. "And your work is far from over."

"Who are you?" I asked, anger and annoyance filling my voice. Then, lifting my head slightly, I managed to see a portion of my surroundings. When I recognized them, I nearly fainted. My head dropped involuntarily back down onto the hard floor with such force I feared I'd given myself a concussion.

The Nexus. I was still in the Nexus. Still in the real universe. Still in the place where I had died—or at least thought I had. How was this possible?

"Get on your feet," the little god ordered. "We have work to do. And universes to cross before we can sleep."

● ● ●

Sometime earlier—how long I cannot say, for I was unconscious afterward—I had crawled up inside that machinery and attempted to delicately manipulate its instrumentation in order to preserve all of reality from utter annihilation. Before venturing inside, I'd handed over my trusty horse, along with the greatest weapon in the universe, to a mere human and sent him on ahead, on a journey into the high Above, to carry out the other phase of our desperate plan. I had remained behind to complete my share of the work. The *suicidal* part.

The fact that I was still alive to converse with this little god must have meant that, improbable as it seemed, the human and I both had succeeded.

My plan had succeeded—and yet somehow I remained alive afterward.

"But how can that be?" I asked of the universe as I realized the full extent of what I was saying. "How can I yet live? My destiny is and always has been a closed circle. I knew it before; the tiniest glimpse into the Well of Eternity only confirmed it." I pointed to the mangled pile of machinery from which my new companion had dragged me. "I died there, in that place and time. There is no more for me."

The little god regarded me, looked at the wreckage, then shrugged. "I do not doubt you are correct," he replied.

I frowned. "And yet here I stand. I therefore survived, where survival was impossible and death foretold and inevitable."

The little god looked at me sidelong. "Understand," he said. "I have not altered your fate. Not one whit. You will still come to the end you anticipate."

"Then how—?"

"I have merely...*interrupted* the natural flow of events. Of time itself. I have created a null-time field around us both here." He pursed his dark lips. "To put it another way: I have plucked you out of the time stream for a particular purpose. When that purpose is done, you will be returned to your normal timeline."

I pondered this, frowning. "What purpose?" I asked after a moment's reflection. I regarded this slight, frail human-looking god who could stop time itself and delay my inevitable destiny. "What would you have of me?"

"One thing," the little god replied. "And one thing only."

"Yes?"

"I have come from the future to convince you that you must go back in time and betray everyone around you and everything you hold dear." He smiled then, but the smile was devoid of any warmth or humor. "You must become the Renegade you are destined to be—that which you are now."

And with that cryptic reply, he led me to the Time Tomb.

● ● ●

The Time Tomb—more formally the "temporal vault" that he used for traveling through time—was a cramped and musty box made of stone and metal, three times as long as it was tall, and scarcely large enough to hold the both of us. Somehow we squeezed inside, though, and it delivered us intact to the distant past.

We did not have to travel in space, only in time. The location where he had found me was the same place we needed to go; we simply needed to be there many years earlier. When the Time Tomb re-materialized within the dome of the Nexus, having gone backwards in time, all the two of us had to do was climb out. This we did—and thus emerged into the lair of my old allies, my old enemies, and my much younger self, all known then simply as the Cabal.

Along the way a thought had occurred to me and I pressed it upon my companion, the god Solonis: "You desire for me to be as I am now—as Istari the Renegade, who rebelled against his comrades in the Cabal. But—since I obviously did become that person, and am that person now—why must I go back and tamper with my younger self *again*?"

"You *always* must go back and tamper," the slender god-man answered me.

"What?"

"For you to *always* become the Renegade, you must *always* go back and make it happen." He laughed sharply. "This is how it has always happened. But it is not necessarily how it always *will* happen. You must always go back, so that it always will happen."

"That...is very confusing."

"Welcome to the world of time travel."

I cursed, and then we arrived, and soon enough I stood face to face with a younger version of myself who desired only to kill me.

● ● ●

I sparred with my younger self for several seconds; seconds which felt more like hours. My actions were limited by the fact that under no circumstances did I want to actually succeed in killing him—for to kill him would likely result in my vanishing from existence. He suffered no such handicap; he clearly regarded me as a fake copy of himself, and he had every intention of dispatching me from the land of the living with extreme prejudice.

As we fought I could see the others out of the corner of my eye. The big blond human and the little god were holding out as best they could against Aleuvi, but I feared we might soon be joined by one or more additional members of our Cabal—at which point the odds would definitely shift against us.

No, whatever was to happen here, it needed to happen soon. Very soon.

The younger me wasn't listening to anything I said and never would listen. I remembered being him, if only dimly; it had been a long time. I remembered how I would have reacted to such talk, back then, and was not the least surprised by his hostility. It was my own old hostility.

And then I pushed back further and remembered more: through the hazy curtains of the millennia I remembered the moment when I had first become the Renegade—rebel against my own kind.

Those curtains parted and I saw the way.

Parrying another of his wild blows, I spun about, extended the golden sword, and slashed the air before me with two parentheses, forming a glowing circle in midair as the blade cleft the barriers between dimensions.

Startled, my young adversary looked away from me for an instant to behold what I had done.

At that moment I leaped forward, tackled him, and carried us both through the fiery doorway in reality.

● ● ●

We emerged precisely where I had hoped we would.

We tumbled out of the portal I had caused to exist, falling hard onto cold cobblestones.

Being the least disoriented of the two of us, I got quickly to my feet and stood ready with the sword, Even as I glanced around to be sure we were in the right place. We were.

My younger self recovered from the disorientation of unexpected dimensional travel and sprang to his feet, a bit more deftly than I had managed. He started to renew his hostilities but then stopped and took in our surroundings. He halted and, frowning deeply, stared back at me.

"What is this?" he growled.

"At least you're asking questions now," I said. "That's progress."

We stood within a vast enclosed space topped by another gray dome, this one seemingly constructed of weathered stone blocks. Ahead of us rose a series of steps leading up to a sort of throne at the top, taking the form of a seat backed by a bowl standing on its side. In that throne sat an aged being of the same species as myself and my other self. He was starting to rise as the two of us—the two of me—gazed up at him.

Between us and him, filling a broad area of the floor, a circular pool glinted in the dim lighting. The water within it was calm and dark—dark as night. Dark as the uncharted future it contained.

"Orondi," I called up to him, finding it strange to see him here, alive and intact. The last time I had encountered him—in that far future where Solonis had found me—such

had scarcely been the case. Not by the time we were finished with our conversation.

He started to reply, but then his dark eyes darted from me to the nearly identical twin who accompanied me. A sort of realization spread across his features. "So," he said, his voice younger and more forceful than I had heard it in ages, "you have come at last. Just as I have foreseen."

"Are you not the Oracle?" I countered. "I would be disappointed if you hadn't foreseen it."

He pursed his lips at me and raised a bony, claw like hand to his chin, stroking it. "The future contains many paths," he replied at last. "And many interpretations are possible."

"Would that your older self still held to such philosophy," I muttered.

"*What is this?*" my younger self repeated, louder and more stridently. "Orondi—what do you know of this false copy that impudently banters with you?"

"He is you," Orondi stated. "Of that there can be no doubt."

"What?" The younger me issued a dismissive sound. "There is a great deal of doubt!"

"No."

The aged Oracle began to descend his steps slowly.

"No," he continued as he shuffled downward, "I have seen him in the Well. I have seen the things he has done—the terrible, terrible things. And I know the cause that brings him here."

"You know?" I asked, actually startled by this. I shook my head. "You know *now*—and you will *still* know when the day comes that I return, and yet—"

"Do not speak of it!" Orondi all-but-shouted. "Not before the younger you."

He reached the bottom of the steps and advanced on me.

"Not when there yet remains hope that this timeline might be derailed from the path you are so intent on forcing upon it."

"There is no other way," I told him.

"Wrong. The future is not fixed. Not even when you come here from it and stand before me, living proof that it does happen—or that it has, in some other timeline, some other reality." He shook his head. "Nothing is fixed. Nothing is certain." He gestured with one shriveled limb toward the waters. "Not even that which I have beheld in the Well."

"The Well." The younger me said the words as if they had come to him as divine revelation. Instantly he was hurrying forward, rushing to the very edge of the pool.

"No!" shouted Orondi.

"No!" shouted I.

Each of us for our own reasons, we both sought to grasp him, to prevent him looking into the Well of Eternity—to prevent him becoming contaminated with the knowledge of fate, perhaps, or to try to preserve a future preferred to the one that had always played out in the past.

We failed. Both of us failed. Just as we had always failed. Just as we might always fail.

The younger Istari stared down into the dark waters. He gazed into their shimmering depths for but the briefest of moments before I grasped him by one arm and Orondi by the other and we yanked him back and away.

As we released him, he fell to the hard stone floor and lay there, gasping.

I rolled him over and he stared up at me, and now his eyes—my own eyes—were wide and wild.

"It's true," he whispered. "It—it *is* true."

I nodded to him. "No matter whether we like it or despise it that is the fate that awaits us." I favored him with a sad half-smile. "The sooner we accept it and learn to work with it, the better it will be for us."

He looked up into my eyes and I could see the doubt growing, the fires of youth receding.

I extended my hand and, reluctantly, he took it. I helped him up.

"I enjoyed being one of the Cabal," he said to me. "I desire immortality and power. I do not wish to become a renegade. *The* Renegade."

"I know," I said with a fuller smile now.

"What lies ahead?"

I shook my head. "You do not wish to know the details. They will prove enough of a burden when their time comes. Do not seek to bear them before you must."

He looked away, his gaze now distant and unfocused, as he absorbed this new knowledge, this terrible destiny. Then he turned back to me, and now I felt he truly looked at me for the first time, and I could see a mix of curiosity, fear, and pity within his eyes, and I felt my heart sink at the sight of it.

"Is there no alternative?" he asked me. "Must it be this way?"

"NO!"

We both whirled at the sound of Orondi charging at us. Over the past few seconds I'd nearly forgotten he was there, as I'd focused so intently on the changes happening with my younger self. But he was still there, and he was still intent on preventing what he and I both knew was coming.

He raised his right hand high and in the pale lighting of his sanctum I could see the glint of glass and metal. He held a rare and deadly Dyonari spirit dagger and he drove the blade directly at the chest of my younger self.

Orondi, you see, was the Oracle among our Cabal. Older than the rest of us, his background had always been hidden, shrouded in mystery and myth. He had come to us and joined our cause early on, saying that he knew all that was to come and all that we might accomplish by working together. He had been quickly accepted into our ranks in part because of his certainty that we were on the right side of history—that we would succeed in our endeavors—and in part because he brought with him limited access to the Well of Eternity, a pool that revealed odd and usually random fragments of possible futures to any willing to look into its depths.

But knowing the future meant that he might well know of my rebellion before I had even decided to do it—before my older self had come back to convince me to do it. That possibility had haunted me down through the years, and I had always believed him to be potentially the most dangerous obstacle I would face on my journey.

But I had never expected for him to grow so desperate to stop me that he would actually attempt to slay my younger self. Certainly not before I'd even been convinced my rebellion was necessary.

And yet there he was, lunging at the younger me with a spirit dagger, intent on ending my life and shearing away my soul.

In that instant, as time moved so glacially slow and as I beheld his attack, the full realization of my fate came to me. I had always wondered how a mass of exploding machinery and computer banks in the Nexus could have possibly done damage enough to slay me. Now I knew that it had not.

I stepped forward, moving with all the grace and speed my old frame might still allow, and I did the only thing I could do: I interposed myself between the blade and my younger self.

As the blade struck my breast, I once again found solace in the thought of what I had done to Orondi so many years later in this very chamber. I smiled at that, even as the dagger bit deep.

I went down then, down onto my knees, down onto the stones.

My younger self went away for a moment, then returned and tried to help me back up. After a few seconds he seemed to give up and he went away again—the world around me was growing darker by then, and rather cold—and then he came back. This time when he tried to lift me I saw that he held the golden sword in one hand, and that he had followed my previous example and used it to cut open a cosmic portal.

I looked around, saw the body of Orondi lying on the cobblestones near the edge of the Well.

"Did you—?"

Young Istari looked at me quizzically, then at Orondi, then back at me. He shook his head. "Knocked him out," he stated.

"Good," I replied with a tight, pain-filled smile. "You'll enjoy killing him much more later."

The look on his face was all I had expected it to be.

Bearing most of my weight, he helped me forward and together we passed through the portal.

● ● ●

We emerged inside the dome of the Nexus, and apparently very little time had passed since we had departed. The little god, Solonis, and the big armored human still held Aleuvi at bay, and Aleuvi appeared very unhappy about that fact.

"How did it go?" Solonis called to me—and then he realized what had happened.

My younger self released me and I slumped to the floor.

"Aleuvi! I have defeated one of them," my younger self shouted. "Come—let us finish off the others together."

Grinning malevolently, the Assassin danced towards him. "Excellent work, Istari," she praised him. "Fight back to back with me," she added, turning away, "and we will make short work of them."

"Yes, by all means," young Istari said. He brought the golden sword up. "Turn your back on me, dear Aleuvi." He swung the sword around.

To Aleuvi's credit, she somehow sensed what he was doing even before he could do it. She spun and parried his blow with her own transparent sword, then glared at him in righteous fury.

"What is the matter with you?" she cried. "Has the doppelganger bewitched you somehow?"

That was when the human in white armor swung his massive fist out and struck her in the back of the head. She went down with an extremely satisfying clatter.

I started to thank him for a job well done, but then I realized that wouldn't be happening, because I was too busy passing out.

● ● ●

My eyes fluttered open and the younger me was staring down into my face, deep concern etched on his features.

Behind him, I could see Solonis returning the golden sword to the big soldier. Setting everything back as he had found it. I knew what that meant—what was doubtlessly next. I wondered if I would still be alive for all of it.

"There is no other way?" my younger self was asking. "I—I'm simply not certain I can do it. Not—not now that I know what is to come."

"Forget most of it, if you must," I replied. "Forget everything. Everything except this." I motioned for him to lean down, and then I whispered a few words in my own voice—in his own voice—into his ear. "Just remember that," I told him. "The rest is details—unimportant."

He nodded uncertainly, then frowned. "I still do not know that I can do it. Not *all* of it."

"You can," I said. "You *must*. Allow no doubts." I felt I was shouting at him, though in truth all that emerged from my lips was a dry whisper. "Follow the path. Follow your destiny, no matter what." And, "Trust him."

"Trust who?"

"The son of Constantine. He will be your best ally." I grimaced with physical pain and the pain of self-realization. "Perhaps your only one."

"The son of who?"

And then I was gone again.

● ● ●

I awoke twice more. The first time, I was crammed into the Time Tomb with Solonis. It was not pleasant. I will spare you the details. But soon enough I fainted.

● ● ●

Back to wakefulness for one final occasion, and back in the Nexus, presumably now in my own time.

My body was utterly numb, my muscles all but useless. The little god was dragging me across the cold, smooth floor. A trail of dark blood left a streak behind us. After a moment's reflection I guessed where he was about to deposit me.

Sure enough, a short while later he was stuffing my limp form back into the wreckage where he had first found me.

"So am I to assume that this means someone comes and finds me here?" I asked, my voice now scarcely audible at all. "Because why else would it matter what state my dead body is in?"

"It matters," he responded, and that was all he would say.

He positioned me just so, then stepped back and regarded his handiwork. He nodded.

I wanted to ask him more. I wanted to ask him if it all worked out—if the galaxy was truly saved. Beyond that, now that I understood fully how much this little being had been the architect of my fate, the sculptor of my millennia of life, and the arbiter of my inevitable death, I wished to know more—so very much more.

Alas, it was now too late. He was walking away. Back to his Time Tomb.

He climbed inside. The heavy stone lid slid closed. The box shimmered and vanished, as if it had never been there—as if everything that had happened since I had become trapped in the wreckage in the Nexus was naught but a dream.

It was all too late now. Too late for anything but acceptance and oblivion.

Or so I believed.

As it turned out, fate had one last joke to play on me.

● ● ●

"Still clinging to a tiny sliver of life, are you?"

My eyes flittered open. What god was disturbing me now? Why wouldn't they just let me rest in peace?

It was dark in the Nexus chamber now, all the machinery dead—dead as I expected that I must be by now. Even so, I could make out a form looming over me. It was a man, a human—or at least something that appeared that way. Of course, Solonis had held a human form, too.

"Now what?" I managed to rasp.

The man—the god?—smiled, even chuckled a bit at that. Then he knelt and extended his hand. His sleeve was long and blue—a deep, almost navy blue.

"Now we do something extraordinary," he told me.

And his fingers closed on mine, and cold blue lightning danced in the darkness.

The End

Six-Gun Hell!
(A Masked Rider Story)
by Barry Reese

Those closest to him knew Carlos as The Butcher.

Whereas most men killed out of necessity or for self-preservation, Carlos killed because he enjoyed it. He'd been known to stab to death a preacher after raiding the church donation box, to rape a woman who was eight months pregnant and then put a bullet in her head, and on one occasion he had set fire to an orphanage, just because he felt like it.

The Butcher was evil incarnate and he looked the part as well. Standing just over six feet tall, Carlos had a jagged scar that ran down the left side of his face, stretching from the bottom tip of his eye to just above his chin. It was an unpleasant shade of white, glowing hot pink when he grew angry or lustful. He usually sported several days' worth of stubble and his teeth were jagged things, looking more suited to the tearing of human flesh than to any other purpose. His clothing tended to be tattered and worn, functional things that he cared little about. His guns, however, were always gleaming and well tended. He spent time each night polishing and cleaning his weapons, seeing them as an extension of his soul. Those thoughts were the closest he came to religion.

The Butcher sauntered into Gray Station on foot, having lost his horse a few miles back. He'd nearly run the beast to death and once it had collapsed to the ground, panting and covered in a shining coating of sweat, he'd stood over it for several moments in rising anger. He hadn't put it out of its misery…that would have been a waste of a bullet and the horse wasn't worth it…but he'd kicked it several times with all of his might before leaving it to slowly die.

Now he reached up to wipe the grime away from the back of his neck and examined the town into which he'd come. None of the men and women he passed on the dusty roads knew they were in the presence of a killer. Carlos wasn't a wanted man, after all. He never left witnesses and the few who knew about his activities were too frightened to share the details with others. He was a legend, a bogeyman sometimes whispered about around the fire but never out loud and never during the day.

Gray Station was a medium-sized town, with a large saloon, two hotels, a decent-looking restaurant, a doctor's office, a post office and a train station that gave the city its name. Carlos liked the look of the place. It had good-looking women and a bank that didn't look all that well-secured. Considering that he was down to his last handful of coins; that could come in handy.

Carlos entered Sylvia's Saloon, blinking his eyes from all the smoke. The place was bustling this evening. Men sat at card games or at the bar, though a few lucky ones were seated at tables where painted ladies sat in their laps, whispering promises of physical pleasure in their ears. Up on stage, a chorus line of six women was high stepping to a piano tune. The girls were all pretty and most were still firm with youth. Carlos hated nothing more than an aging whore.

After ordering a whiskey, Carlos turned to watch the show on the stage. A few of the working girls eyed him but none approached. Their desire to earn a few dollars seemed tempered by the obvious danger that Carlos presented. He looked like a man who would treat a woman very harshly.

"New in town?" someone asked from The Butcher's side. Carlos glanced his way and narrowed his eyes. The man wore a yellow shirt and faded denim jeans. Around the fellow's neck was a blue bandana. The man had blond hair and blue eyes, along with a smile that could be best described as inherently cruel. "My name's Roscoe," the man added with a wink.

Carlos shifted, looking down into his glass he held in his right hand. His voice was so low that only Roscoe could hear him. "I came like you asked me to. What do you want?"

Roscoe nodded at a pretty young redhead as she sauntered past, hips swinging. "Wasn't sure if my message reached you, since you didn't respond."

"Obviously it did," Carlos answered. "What was so damned important that I had to drop what I was doing and haul ass over here?"

"Do you believe in magic?"

The look of anger that flashed across The Butcher's eyes was enough to make Roscoe take a step back. "I'll skin you alive if you're wasting my time here, Roscoe."

"I'm serious. There's a guy named Barker here. He came in on the train a few days ago. Strangest thing you ever saw; they were piling out the bodies of the sick when he arrived but he was doing just fine. Said he'd found a magic rock back East and was bringing it out here to show it to people. He's renting the old Carson place on the edge of town and he's charging people two dollars to take a gander at it. I went and saw it yesterday. It glows, Carlos. And it makes people sick if they're around it too long. Can you imagine how valuable something like that could be? We could sell it or…Hell…we could use it. Gotta be a way to turn that against the lawmen who are always after us."

The blow came so suddenly that Roscoe never even thought about ducking. Carlos drove a powerful punch into the side of the other man's head, knocking him to the floor. The action brought a sudden stillness to the saloon and all eyes turned towards the men at the bar. Even the girls on stage stopped to watch.

"You lousy bastard," Carlos hissed between clenched teeth. "I thought you might actually have something worth doing around here. But instead you're filling my head with a lot of crazy talk."

The Butcher paused when he recognized the sound of a rifle being cocked. He turned towards the bartender, who was leveling the barrel of a shotgun, straight at his face. "That's enough out of you two," the bartender said. He spat out some tobacco juice before gesturing towards the door with his gun. "Take it outside. We don't allow fighting in here."

Carlos mentally marked the man's face in his memory but he merely nodded and began walking away. He had just stepped outside when Roscoe caught up with him. The other man's face bore a tremendous red area where The Butcher's fist had caught him. "Carlos!" he said, reaching out to grab The Butcher's arm. "At least take a look at it with me. You'll see what I mean."

Carlos took a deep breath. "This Barker guy says the rock is magic?"

"Yeah. Says it fell from the sky, like a gift from God."

"And why don't it make him sick if it does everyone else?"

"Well, not everybody gets ill. Some folks do after just a couple of minutes near it… some folks are around it for an hour and still feel fine. But I know that Barker was keeping a mule out back behind his house and that critter fell down dead yesterday afternoon."

Carlos looked thoughtful and it was a dreadful thing to view. It was like all of his malevolence was on display, flickering across his face. The idea of a rock that could kill people intrigued him, to be sure. "How come the Sheriff ain't run him out of town? The guy's got something that's killing animals and making people sick? Why ain't he in jail and that rock buried six feet under ground?"

"The Sheriff's given him till the end of the week to move on."

Carlos reached into a pocket and took out a cigarette he'd rolled on the way into town. He struck a match on his boot and lit the smoke, cupping his hand around it to keep the breeze from blowing out his match. When the end of the cigarette was burning brightly, he took a few deep draws on it, exhaling the smoke out through his nostrils. "Show me."

• • •

The old Carson place was a medium-sized wooden home located on the outskirts of town. The railroad tracks ran close behind it and Carlos knew the entire structure probably rattled like mad when the train came through. A small wooden sign had been stuck into the ground in front of the house, with several words scrawled in red paint on its surface: *Come see Barker's Magic Stone! $ 2 to see this wonder of the world!* Beneath this someone had added: *Only one week left!*

Roscoe approached the door with his grin back in place. The spot where he'd been struck was not quite as red now but it looked like it was going to turn into a nasty bruise by the morning. "You're gonna thank me for this, Carlos."

The Butcher said nothing. He looked up and down the street while Roscoe began knocking. It was well past midnight now and things were quiet on this end of town. The only people who weren't in bed were down at the saloon.

Carlos looked back at the door as it swung open slowly. The man who stuck his head out looked like he was in his fifties, his balding head covered with liver spots. He was dressed for bed, wearing a long white sleeping gown. He didn't look like he felt very well and he coughed twice before finding his voice. "Can I help you gentlemen?"

Roscoe rocked back and forth on his heels. "Yeah. We'd like to see your magic rock."

Barker looked from Roscoe to Carlos and something he saw there obviously unnerved him. He began to close the door, muttering "Perhaps in the morning, fellows. It's a bit late and I don't feel well."

Roscoe's boot blocked the door from closing. When Barker looked at him, he saw Roscoe had drawn a pistol. "We'd like to see it right now. My friend came a long way just to take a look at it."

Barker swallowed hard and finally took a step back, opening the door. The two men pushed past him, walking straight towards the exhibition room. It was actually a sitting room, blocked off from the rest of the house by a curtain. Roscoe held the curtain aside as Carlos stepped in. The 'magic rock' lay on a plush pillow atop a carved pedestal. A placard next to the stone read 'Barker's Magical Rock. Please do not touch!' The rock itself was a pitted, grayish thing and Carlos had to admit that the sight of it impressed him. In the darkness it seemed to glow slightly, though Carlos would have been damned to explain where the light came from.

"Where did you get this thing?" Carlos demanded, leaning so close to the rock that his lit cigarette nearly brushed against it.

Barker coughed again, a rasping and unhealthy sounding noise. "That's a trade secret, I'm afraid."

Roscoe put the barrel of his gun up against Barker's temple and he laughed as he did so. "Want me to shoot him, Carlos? We can just take the rock if we want. This old man ain't gonna stop us."

Carlos pictured the spray of red and gray that would accompany the gunshot. He shook his head for the moment though. "No games, old man. Where did you get the rock?"

Barker hesitated only a second. He knew that his life hung in the balance now and only by playing along did he stand any chance of living to see another day. "I found it. I was sitting near a river back East when I saw something cutting through the sky. It looked like a flaming stone thrown down from heaven." Barker slowly moved over and sat down in a chair. He kept his eyes on Roscoe's gun the whole time. "As soon as I found it lying in the field, I knew it was special. It was too hot for me to touch for several hours but I sat nearby and waited… and then I wrapped it up in my shirt and took it home. I noticed how it glowed and how it made some people sick right away. If you want my opinion, the righteous is spared its painful effects. It was sent by God to judge the wicked."

"And line your pockets too?" Roscoe added with a smirk.

"God would want me to provide for my well-being."

Carlos looked back at the magic rock. He didn't cotton to all the religious talk but he'd heard stories about things that fell from the sky. Last fall, he'd been in Arizona when a few dozen frogs and tadpoles had dropped into the middle of Flagstaff. He hadn't seen it happen himself but he'd heard tell of it from a few men who knew better than to tell him lies. Strange things happened sometimes. "I'll take it," he said, straightening up.

"But… it's not for sale," Barker muttered weakly, knowing full well what was about to happen.

Carlos lifted up the magic rock and approached the old man. "This rock makes people sick, right?"

"Sometimes. The weak and the wicked." Barker's eyes widened as Carlos lifted it above his head, brandishing it with both hands.

"If this is a holy relic, if this only punishes the weak… then let's see how it fares against your pious skull!" Carlos slammed the rock downwards. He continued his assault until Barker's face was an unrecognizable mess and he was caked with his victim's blood.

Roscoe had looked away when the attack had begun. He didn't mind killing people but there was a limit to what he could stomach. A bullet to the head was quick and relatively painless… but beating an old man to death with a glowing rock was a bit beyond what he was comfortable with.

Carlos looked at the gore-encrusted rock and smiled. "You did good calling me with this, Roscoe. I like it."

Roscoe cleared his throat. "I'm glad. What do you think we should do with it?"

"First off, I want to find out exactly what it can do." The eyes of The Butcher glittered with the possibilities. "Where's the sheriff's office?"

"Back near the saloon. Why?"

"Because for what I have in mind, the law's gonna need to be dealt with."

"Is this going to make us some money?" Roscoe asked dubiously. He was a greedy man and his interest in things tended to revolve around how much it was going to line his pocket.

Carlos ignored him, continuing to stare at the rock. "This rock didn't come from God," he whispered. "This rock makes us gods."

● ● ●

TWO WEEKS LATER

Wade Morgan and Blue Hawk rode towards Gray Station, both sagging in their saddles. They had ridden long and hard over the past three days and the weariness had begun transforming their normally placid personalities into hotbeds of short-tempers and salty words.

"Okay, so let me get this straight," Wade said, reaching up to tug at the bandana around his neck. "So you're saying there's more than one world?"

Blue Hawk smiled, having tried explaining this before. He admired Wade like a brother but there were simply some differences between their peoples that were hard to bridge. "My people believe that the world...ania, in our tongue...is comprised of five separate realms, also called worlds. There is the mystical world, the desert world, the flower world, the dream world and the night world. Much Yaquis ritual is based around balancing these worlds and undoing the damage that man has done to them. Only by purifying all the worlds and bringing them into harmony can true peace be achieved."

Wade looked sidelong at his partner. "What kind of damage does man do to the world? Isn't that what the world's here for? For man to use as he needs to?"

"That is not how we see things, senor. We believe that mankind is nothing more than caretakers for the land. The mountains, the streams, and the sky... those things were here before man and they will be here after man. We have to take care of them. We do damage to them through wars that are unjust and through mistreating the land."

Wade looked up at the sky, trying to gauge the time. It was late afternoon, meaning they had made good time. "The train should be here in a couple of hours. Gives us enough time to get cleaned up and find something to eat." Wade was hoping to make it on the seven o'clock train, which would carry the two men further west. An old friend of Wade's was going to be waiting for them at the next stop and Wade was eager to help him. His friend's property had been harassed by rustlers for the better part of a year and Wade had offered to assist in stopping the poachers... and if Wade Morgan couldn't accomplish that, Wade was fairly certain that The Masked Rider could.

Blue Hawk nodded. He dismounted as they entered the town proper and began leading his horse by the reigns. He had never been to Gray Station but Wade had made a few stops here in years past. Wade had described the city as being a small but vibrant one, with an active nightlife. The scenes that greeted Blue Hawk now didn't seem to mesh with any definition of the word 'vibrant,' however.

The city streets were mostly empty and the few souls that were seen all looked unhealthy. Blue Hawk watched as a toothless woman staggered past, several open sores on her face. Blue Hawk saw a young boy, little more than a child, leaning against a wooden post. The boy's shirt was covered with dried vomit and blood, both of which were also caked around his lips.

"Senor... what has happened here?"

Wade stopped in place, his handsome face etched with concern. "I don't know, old friend. Let's find a place to stable the horses and then head to the saloon. If Sylvia still runs it, she's bound to know all the details."

"The way you talk about this Sylvia... were you and she... close friends?"

Wade glanced at his friend, laughing out loud. The sound of mirth seemed suddenly out of place in this town and everyone who was out on the streets glanced in their direction. "We were just friends, Blue Hawk. The regular kind. Nothing else."

A man with a long, thin nose topped by a seeping sore suddenly burst from the general store and grabbed hold of Wade's shirtsleeve. "Turn around now! Go and get help before we're all dead!"

"What's going on, fella?" Wade asked. He was staring at the man's wide, frightened eyes and he winced a bit as the smell of something rotting arose from the man's open mouth.

"Senor!" Blue Hawk yelled. He grabbed hold of Wade and yanked his surprised friend away from the sickly man. Just as he did so, a gunshot cracked loudly and the man's warnings were given physical force. A bullet ripped through the man's neck and sent him tumbling to the dusty street, his eyes rolling up into his skull.

Wade had drawn his own six-gun by this time and turned in the direction of the gunshot. Blue Hawk was in the process of removing his rifle from the backpack on his saddle when he spotted the man's killer.

Roscoe stood no more than ten or eleven feet away, smoking pistol in hand. The barrel was pointed squarely at Wade though it could be turned on Blue Hawk at a moment's notice. "You two boys put away your weapons," he said with a wry grin.

"We've got two guns and you've got one. Seems to me that maybe you oughtta put your weapon away." Wade cocked his pistol meaningfully and Blue Hawk raised his own gun, balancing it against his shoulder as he took aim.

"You boys need to take another look around."

Blue Hawk's eyes flicked from one rooftop to another. There were men stationed on three of the buildings, rifles held in hand. "He is not alone, senor."

Wade nodded, having spotted them at the same time as his friend. To Roscoe, he said, "Look. We don't want any trouble. We're just here to catch the next train and maybe have a drink at Sylvia's."

Roscoe lowered his gun. "Well, why didn't you boys say so? Go on, son; wet your whistle at the saloon." Roscoe winked at the two of them in a good-natured way but it somehow made him seem all the more sinister.

Wade and Blue Hawk slowly relaxed, though they were both aware that the men on the rooftops had not ceased tracking with their guns. "Let's get to the saloon," Wade whispered. Blue Hawk nodded, wondering at what strange mystery they had stumbled upon. In the years since he had become ally to the Masked Rider, he'd come to accept the fact that trouble followed Wade Morgan as closely as his own shadow. Today seemed to be no exception.

● ● ●

Carlos downed the last of his tequila, catching the worm between his teeth. He ground it down with his molars, the gritty flavor making him wince. He was sitting in the chair that had belonged to the town sheriff, his feet propped up on the man's desk. The night he'd claimed the magic rock as his own, he and Roscoe had staged a coup of sorts. They'd killed the sheriff and his two deputies, before making their move on the town's mayor. They'd broken into the mayor's home and shot him in the head. Roscoe had then raped the man's wife while Carlos had ransacked the house. The couple had lived alone with no children and very little worth taking. Carlos had then killed the mayor's wife when Roscoe had finished his fun. Carlos hadn't raped her himself, preferring murder to sex.

And then The Butcher's real plan had gone into effect. He had sent out word to old compatriots that the town was now his and had urged them to come along. He needed soldiers to maintain his hold on Gray Station... and this was the place he intended to make his kingdom.

Thought of ruling over others was a common fantasy for Carlos. It was really just one step up from his sadistic behavior, which was itself based in power. He enjoyed having control over someone's life, being able to snuff it out at a moment's notice. The rock had given him an ultimate rush; just by holding it, he was able to control the welfare of those around him. Of course, it might lead to his own death... but he did things that could lead to that on a regular basis.

And so, a form of martial law had been established. Those who wanted to rise up arms against The Butcher and his men were immediately executed. Soon, only the old, the young and the cowardly remained. Carlos wished that Gray Station hadn't been on a railway line though. It put his scheme at continual risk. Too many people were coming and going through the city on a regular basis for word of what was happening not to get out eventually.

For now though, things were going swimmingly. Carlos and his men had the run of the town and The Butcher was playing his sick games of life and death with the innocent people of Gray Station. The only ones allowed fresh water were Carlos and his men. Everyone one else was given what Carlos called 'rock water.' The magic rock lay half-submerged in a large tub of water and Carlos made sure that this was the water dispersed throughout town. At first, he'd done this as a sign of his power and a reminder to them all that he controlled the magic stone. But now he'd begun to notice that those who drank from the rock water got sicker much more quickly than The Butcher's men… though they too were beginning to show signs of illness.

Roscoe seemed unharmed so far but most of the men were developing skin conditions or general malaise. Even Carlos had noticed that several of his teeth seemed to be loose enough that he could nearly push them out by prodding with his tongue.

Soon, he knew, he would have to abandon this town and the magic rock. He felt confident that once he was away from its strange effects, he would return to his normal strength and vigor.

Roscoe opened the door and stepped in, walking quickly across the wooden floor. He stopped in front of The Butcher's desk. "Newcomers in town, Carlos. They look like trouble."

"Did you kill them?"

"No. From the way one of them moved, I thought he might be a lawman. He's got that look about him. Figured maybe you'd want to know in case word's gotten out about us."

"And the other man?"

"He's an Injun."

Carlos swung his feet to the floor and leaned across the desk. "What kind?"

"Hell if I know. They all look alike to me."

"Did you catch either of their names?"

"No." Roscoe was beginning to look concerned. "You want me to round 'em up? They said they were going to Sylvia's for a drink. Claim they want to board the train when it comes."

Carlos stood up, his tongue working against one of his loose teeth. He tasted fresh blood oozing up from the gum. A man who carried himself like a marshal, traveling with an Indian? The Butcher would bet his last dollar that he knew who those two were. But was it chance that had led them here? He didn't think anyone had escaped from town. They'd gunned down four different people who had tried. But maybe someone had slipped through? If that was the case, surely there'd been a whole mess of lawmen showing up, not just The Masked Rider and Blue Hawk.

Carlos had experienced the misfortune of crossing the masked man's path about two years prior. In fact, his face bore a scar that served as a permanent reminder of their encounter. Carlos had barely escaped with is life, throwing himself over the edge of a cliff rather than face capture. He'd broken his left arm in the fall but had managed to pick himself up and make it to safety.

"Watch them," Carlos said. "I don't want them leaving town or getting onboard that train… but if they're who I think they are, they won't take off until they think they've liberated this place."

"Why not just have me and the boys go in with guns blazing?"

"Because I want to play with them first."

Roscoe grimaced and took a deep breath. "Listen... I have to tell you. Some folks are talking and... well, this might just be the last straw as far as they're concerned. Guys love the power and the money but they don't like getting sick. Hell, we lost a man yesterday to this wasting disease. The guys are going to bolt soon unless you get rid of that rock."

Carlos turned to face Roscoe, the scar on his face turning a vivid shade of pink. "Any man who betrays my trust will die... and it will be a far worse end than dying by the rock. Tell them that. Each and every one."

Roscoe sighed but didn't argue the point. Like everyone else with any sense, he was terrified of The Butcher. But even Roscoe had his breaking point and it was coming very soon.

● ● ●

Sylvia was just as beautiful as Wade remembered. Her raven black hair curled around the best set of shoulders he'd ever seen. She wore a red dress tonight that accentuated her lean body and ample hips, but it was her face that caught his eyes. Though lovely, her expression was one of such weariness that Wade had to stop himself from reaching out to comfort her.

The saloon was as quiet as a tomb. There were no dancing girls on stage and the piano player was playing a slow song that might as well have been a funeral dirge. The bartender was pouring drinks for free, though there were few takers.

Wade and Sylvia sat together at a table in the rear of the saloon. Blue Hawk stood behind his friend, keeping a watchful eye on the swinging doors that led into the bar. He held his rifle against his body, the barrel pointed towards the floor.

Sylvia had just finished recounting the entire affair, her voice cracking here and there from the strain. She didn't look like she'd fallen prey to the strange sickness yet but Wade knew she was feeling the stress nonetheless. "It's been awful, Wade. We've been passing out free whiskey because no one wants to drink the rock water. But we're almost bone dry around here."

Wade looked up at Blue Hawk, whose expression was grim. "You ever hear tell of a magic rock like this?"

Blue Hawk nodded slowly. "I have heard stories of things that fell from the sky like this Barker described. My grandfather told me a story of a man he knew who fashioned a necklace from such a rock. It was a beautiful stone and every one who saw it around this warrior's neck was envious. But then he grew sick and died painfully. His brother took the necklace and wore it until he too died. Then one of the medicine men decreed that the thing was cursed and had it taken far from our village and buried at the base of a mountain."

"I wish somebody would do that with this one," Sylvia whispered. "Almost worse than the rock sickness is the man who owns it now. I told you about Roscoe but he's not the leader. That's a bastard named Carlos. His own men call him The Butcher."

"Senor..." Blue Hawk said. He looked at Wade and saw that his friend had also recognized the name. Though they'd faced one evil man after another in recent years, The Butcher held a special place reserved for only the most despicable.

"I know, old friend. I thought he was dead, too." Wade reached out and squeezed Sylvia's hand. "We've met him before. I promise you that we'll do everything we can to help you."

Sylvia looked sad but grateful. "And here I thought you said you were leaving on the next train out of town." Sylvia sighed. "The Butcher's men will be there, making sure that no one tries to leave town or tell the workers on the train what the conditions are like here."

Wade thought over their situation. Obviously, leaving wasn't an option. His friend with the cattle-rustling problem would have to wait until Carlos had been dealt with. Unfortunately, The Butcher had enough men to make a direct assault a poor proposition. Stealth would be required... and for that, nighttime would be an ally. "Sylvia, Blue Hawk and I would like to get a couple of rooms. Have any we could use?"

Sylvia looked at him in disbelief. "I have enough rooms for the entire U.S. cavalry. Take your pick. We haven't had a guest since this whole affair got started."

"Hang in there," Wade said. "Things are going to get better. I'm giving you my word on that."

● ● ●

The train came and went, stopping for only brief layover that lasted less than an hour. Wade didn't hear any screams or gunshots, so he assumed that no one made any attempts at escape. He was glad for that. No one else needed to die... save perhaps for one person: Carlos.

Blue Hawk was waiting behind the saloon when Wade ventured out to join him. Unlike a usual evening at Sylvia's, the saloon was mostly quiet and there were only a small handful of people on the streets. Most of those that Wade could see were obviously The Butcher's men, for they were far healthier than the pitiful wretches who called Gray Station home.

Blue Hawk's eyes traveled up and down his friend's body, taking note of the man's garb. He wore a crimson shirt, battered jeans, a well-worn hat and a small black mask that covered his eyes and the bridge of his nose. The Masked Rider was ready to take back the night.

"What is the plan, senor?"

"Sylvia told me that Carlos is living in Barker's old house. According to her, it's on the outskirts of town. We're going to head over there and see if we can't get inside. I know men like these; if we cut off the head, the rest of the body will fall apart. They won't stay around if The Butcher is dead."

Blue Hawk nodded and began leading the way through the darkness. The Masked Rider followed close at his heels, grateful to have one person in his life that he could trust completely. Blue Hawk didn't balk at throwing his life on the line, even though he'd never met Sylvia before tonight. He knew that Wade considered this town important and that was enough for him. Likewise, The Masked Rider had faith in his friend's ability to navigate the dangerous streets of the city and get them to their goal undetected.

They were halfway to The Butcher's lair when Blue Hawk suddenly drew up short. They were crouching behind a wagon that was parked outside the schoolhouse, the wind blowing lightly around them. The Masked Rider saw small dust devils whipping around them but he didn't know what had caused his friend to pause.

"What's wrong?" he asked.

Blue Hawk turned slowly, his nostrils flaring. "You don't smell that?"

The Masked Rider sniffed the air. "You know your senses are more acute than mine."

"I smell sweat and grime. There is a man downwind of us. We're being followed."

The Masked Rider uttered a mild curse under his breath. "Where?"

Blue Hawk's eyes scanned the darkness behind them. "Over your left shoulder, near the hanging sign that reads 'Doc Brown's Medical Shoppe.' He's standing upright and is a little bit shorter than I am."

The Masked Rider visualized that scene in his mind, gauging the distance and height of the shot he'd need to pull off. Blue Hawk was an incredible marksman but The Masked Rider prided himself on being able to hit any target required.

The Masked Rider stood up in a blur, a gun in each hand. They spat out hot leaden death and the bullets struck home, eliciting a single grunt before the man's body hit the dirt.

Blue Hawk sprinted to the fallen corpse. He held up a hand, indicating that The Masked Rider should remain where he was. The Yaquis warrior listened as he rifled through the man's pockets, looking for anything useful. He found a knife that was too dull to be kept and a pistol that Blue Hawk slipped into the waistband of his pants. Hurrying back to his friend, Blue Hawk whispered, "I heard no movement in response to your shots."

"They must have heard them."

"Perhaps gunfire is not an unusual sound these days, senor. And since he did not have time to return fire, less curiosity would have been roused."

"Still, we better hurry before someone comes to investigate."

Blue Hawk resumed his march, occasionally stopping when someone would pass near them. The Yaquis was so stealthy that The Masked Rider had to reach out several times just to make sure the man was still in front of him. How he was able to blend so completely into the darkness was uncanny.

The old Barker house came into view at last. Roscoe was standing outside the building, chatting up a young girl who did not look happy to be there. The girl was wearing a faded yellow dress that looked like it had once belonged to an older sister and been handed down. She seemed relatively healthy, though there were a few burn-like areas on her right arm. The Masked Rider wondered about the magic rock and its effects on people. He would have written it all off as something unrelated to the rock but for Blue Hawk's story. There were certainly stranger things in the world than he could ever fathom, so perhaps there was no sense in trying. There was a killer loose in Gray Station and he had a rock that made people sick. Kill Carlos and remove the rock. That much was concrete and could be understood.

"We need to get her to safety," The Masked Rider said.

"I shall handle it, senor. You can go inside."

The Masked Rider nodded, moving away from his friend and around the other side of the building. He hadn't bothered asking how Blue Hawk would accomplish his tasks; he simply knew that they would be done.

Inside the house, Carlos the Butcher waited.

● ● ●

"C'mon, darlin'... if you're nice to me, I'll make sure you and your family get out of town on the next train. You've got my word." Roscoe had one arm balanced on the side of the house, leaning in close to the girl, who had pulled away to the point where her back was now pressed against the exterior wall.

"I don't believe you," she said in a soft voice.

"What did you say your name was?"

"Susan."

"Susan, why would I lie to you? I mean, you know that if I wanted to just have my way with you, I could, right? I'd just wave my gun in your face and tell you to shimmy out of that dress and spread your legs for me." Susan's eyes widened and her lower lip began to tremble. "But I'm not telling you do that. I'm asking. Because I'm a nice guy. And a nice guy would keep his word about gettin' your family out of town, right?"

Susan whimpered and closed her eyes. She could feel Roscoe's lips brush her own and she knew that she had no choice but to submit. Maybe, just maybe, he was even telling her the truth.

Susan felt a rush of movement at her side and she heard Roscoe cry out. Opening her eyes, she saw a tall, lithe Indian slam Roscoe's face into the side of the house. He repeated this attack three times, until Roscoe's nose was shattered and his face was covered in blood. Then he tossed the man to the ground and turned his gaze upon Susan. She'd never seen a more beautiful man than this half-naked warrior. Clad only in buckskin breeches, his taut stomach and clearly defined chest was enough to bring a flush to her skin.

"T-Thank you," she stammered.

"Are you unharmed?"

Susan nodded, her mouth suddenly dry.

"Then you should return home. It is not safe here."

Blue Hawk started to turn away but Susan surprised even herself by reaching out and touching his arm. Finding her voice, she asked, "Who are you?"

"My name is Blue Hawk. My friend and I are going to free your town."

"I doubt that, Injun. Seems to me you're just gonna end up in a shallow grave."

Blue Hawk turned and saw three of The Butcher's men approaching, guns drawn. They must have snuck up on him while the girl was distracting him, he realized.

"Get behind me," Blue Hawk said. Susan obeyed instantly, more excited than afraid. Somehow she knew that this man was going to protect her or die trying.

● ● ●

Carlos sat on the edge of his bed, the magic rock held tightly in his left hand. In the dim lighting, the glow of the stone was very impressive and it illuminated The Butcher's face quite clearly. His expression was one of rapture and as The Masked Rider stepped into the room, he almost wondered if the thing had somehow hypnotized Carlos. But then The Butcher looked up and smiled; a cold and deadly expression.

"And so we meet again," Carlos said. His right hand came into view, holding a gun that was pointed at The Masked Rider's midsection.

"I thought you were dead."

"You should have looked for a body."

"Live and learn." The Masked Rider looked at the rock, noting its glow. "This doesn't seem much like you, Carlos. You've always been about hurting people but never like this. You were a more hands-on type. You getting so lazy you want a magic stone to do your dirty work for you?"

"You don't understand," Carlos answered. "This rock...it's made me a god. People live and die at my command." He held up the rock so that The Masked Rider could take a better look at it. "Right now, it's killing you. Right now, it's killing me. Death has rarely been so obvious, has it?"

"We're all dying, all the time. Don't need a rock for that."

Carlos pursed his lips. "Perhaps you're smarter than I gave you credit for, masked man." The Butcher drew back his arm and threw the stone with all his might. The attack wasn't the sort that The Masked Rider had expected and he barely managed to avoid taking the rock directly on his temple. As it was, it struck him on the top of the head and drew blood. The Masked Rider staggered and raised his gun but Carlos was in motion by now, charging his opponent. He slammed into The Rider's midsection and sent him tumbling back. They knocked over a table and ended up on the floor, where Carlos roared like a lion and threw a punch that landed squarely on The Rider's jaw.

Wade Morgan knew he was in trouble when Carlos shoved his gun against Wade's chin. This spurred The Rider to summon all his strength. He rolled to the left and managed to dislodge Carlos. The villain's gun discharged, the bullet ripping into the floor just a few inches from The Rider's shoulder.

Both men scrambled to their feet, guns in hand. Once again, they faced one another in what was often called a Mexican Standoff.

"I don't suppose you want to resolve this with an old-fashioned quick draw contest?" The Rider asked.

"Too quick a death for you. I plan to strap you to a chair and let you drink nothing but rock water until you die."

The Masked Rider grimaced. At that moment the sounds of gunfire from outside made both men jump. The Rider had a moment of fear concerning Blue Hawk but he knew that this was his best opportunity to gain an advantage. He slapped out with one of his hands, knocking The Butcher's gun from his grip. Unfortunately, Carlos responded with a roundhouse kick that caught Wade in the neck. He gasped in pain and Carlos grabbed hold of his wrist, bending it back until The Rider's own gun clattered to the floor. Both men were now fighting barehanded, which gave a slight edge to Carlos. The Butcher was bigger and stronger than The Rider and as he wrapped Wade Morgan in a bear hug, The Masked Rider cried out in agony. He felt his ribs being compressed and knew they would snap soon.

The Rider saw the look of triumph in The Butcher's eyes. He thought of Sylvia and all the innocents in this town… and he knew that he couldn't lose this fight. His own life was nothing; it was for all those who couldn't fight for themselves that he did this. The Masked Rider leaned his head back and then brought it forward, crashing his forehead into The Butcher's face. He heard a cracking sound and The Butcher loosened his grip, backing away. The killer spat out two teeth, blood dripping from the corners of his mouth.

The Masked Rider threw two punches…a quick jab with his left that caught Carlos in a grazing blow to the side of the head and then a follow-up right-handed punch that rocked The Butcher on his heels. The Masked Rider then ducked under one of The Butcher's own fists and struck back with a quick rabbit punch to the man's stomach. Carlos lost his balance at this point, his foot having stepped down on something that slid out from under him. He tumbled backwards, the back of his skull landing hard on the edge of a wooden chair. The seat shattered under the impact… and so did The Butcher's skull. He landed on his side, a large pool of blood forming under his head.

The Masked Rider watched as Carlos began twitching madly. A skilled surgeon might be able to save the man but Wade had seen poor souls like this whose lives had been salvaged but whose minds would never be the same. Most of them required care for the rest of their existences. The Masked Rider looked around for his weapon and spotted it on the floor, along with the object that had caused Carlos to trip and fall.

The so-called magic rock had been kicked under a nearby table. The Masked Rider reached under and pulled it free, tossing it onto The Butcher's bed. He then knelt beside the man's still-twitching body and lowered his voice. "I'm not doing this because I enjoy it, Carlos. I'm doing it because it's wrong to let anybody suffer the way you're doing right now." The Masked Rider cocked his pistol, placed it against the other man's skull, and pulled the trigger.

Solemn, but knowing his deed had been both necessary and right, The Masked Rider stood up and returned to the glowing rock. He wrapped it up in the bedspread and slowly approached the door. The sounds of fighting outside had ceased and there was a momentary chill that passed down Wade Morgan's spine. He hoped nothing had happened to Blue Hawk. The man was his best friend and truest companion. Losing him would be like losing the best part of himself.

Stepping out into the chilly night air, The Masked Rider felt an immediately sense of relief. Blue Hawk was seated on one of the front steps, a girl resting her head on his shoulder. Several dead bodies lay on the ground in front of the house.

Blue Hawk turned his head and the girl sat up, looking shy. "This is Susan," Blue Hawk said.

The Masked Rider smiled broadly. "Nice to meet you, Susan." The Rider held up the bed sheet. "Any recommendations on where we should put this thing?"

Blue Hawk moved to take the bundle from his friend. "I will ride out of town and find someplace that is far from any settlements. You will be here when I return?"

"Of course." Wade noticed the way Susan was watching Blue Hawk and he lowered his voice to a whisper. "You know, if you'd like to stay here in town, I can find a spot to dump this rock."

Blue Hawk smiled slightly but shook his head. "Thank you but no. Actually, I would like to take Susan and her family with me. She thinks they will want to leave Gray Station even if Carlos is dead. Too many bad memories, senor. I will take them as far as the next town."

"Sounds good. Try not to give her too many new memories en route," The Rider warned good-naturedly.

"And you should be careful as well, senor. The Butcher's men may decide to stay and fight after all."

"Maybe. If they do, it's their lives on the line. But I have a feeling that once the townspeople learn what's happened tonight, they'll rise up and stand with me in driving the rest of these killers out of town."

Blue Hawk nodded and began walking away, Susan trailing along after. Wade Morgan watched him go and thought back to what he and his friend had been talking about on the way into town. Maybe that rock was someone's way of telling everyone that things had slipped out of balance. If so, The Masked Rider and Blue Hawk had just helped restore things to the way they ought to be.

Wade reached up and removed his mask. From here on, it could be Wade Morgan and not The Masked Rider who helped things return to normal. He hoped that without the rock present, the people of Gray Station would return to good health. Unfortunately, there was no guarantee of that.

Muttering a small prayer, Wade Morgan set off towards the saloon.

The End

The Necromancer's Drum

by Josh Reynolds

"**P**hillip, I am going to say this just once…necromancy is wrong, and also *highly* illegal. This is quite possibly the most dunderheaded foray you have yet undertaken, and I will be speaking to you about it, at length, once we are clear of this matter, *savvy?*" Charles St. Cyprian said, as he cocked his Webley. Dead men staggered through the moonlit Kingsbere churchyard towards him, desiccated hands groping blindly.

He and his two companions were crouched behind a moss-encrusted sarcophagus, topped by the worn effigy of what had been an angel. The church yard was overgrown, and overfull, to judge by the sheer number of ambulatory corpses shuffling through the tombstones. Some were more recently interred, to judge by their clothing, while others wore tattered shrouds splotched with grave-earth. Above the soft scuffle of bare feet on damp earth came the rhythmic thud of a drum, rising up through the open doors of the church.

"Charles, honestly, I am as shocked as you are," Phillip Wendy-Smythe said. A pudgy man in an ill-fitting wool suit, he had a bright crimson fez perched on his head, and was trying to load his own revolver with fumbling fingers. "How's a chap supposed to predict a bally thing like this?"

"Cork it," Ebe Gallowglass snarled. Small, dark and dressed like a man, she wouldn't have looked out of place in a Soho dive or a smoke-filled betting shop. She wrenched her flat cap off and swatted Wendy-Smythe with it, eliciting a yelp from the portly occultist. A moment later, she shoved the barrel of her Webley-Fosbery under his nose. "I ought to give you a third nostril, you fat…!"

"Calm thyself, apprentice-mine," St. Cyprian said. In contrast to Gallowglass, he was tall and slim, and dressed in one of Savile Row's finest sartorial creations. "Let's concentrate on the already dead, shall we?"

"Assistant, not apprentice," she snapped.

"Yes, yes, tomato, tomahto," he said, as he fired. A dead thing pitched backwards. "Though, frankly, she does have a point…I'm quite cross with you, Phillip. This ain't the first time you've cracked the wicket, old man." He fired again, knocking a corpse to one knee, momentarily. It rose a moment later, seemingly none the worse for wear. "Bugger."

"Head-shot, innit?" Gallowglass said, as she knocked the newly risen cadaver flat with a well-placed shot. "Remember Manchester."

"Don't remind me," St. Cyprian said. "Where's our pal Anzeray gone?" he asked, looking around for the author of their current woes. Alfred Anzeray, late of Hampstead, was the reason Wendy-Smythe had begged for St. Cyprian to come to the town of Kingsbere in Wessex, though he hadn't gone into much detail. St. Cyprian had suspected at the time that it was something unpleasant. Something only the Royal Occultist could deal with.

The office of the Royal Occultist was charged with the investigation, organization and occasional suppression of That Which Man Was Not Meant to Know; including vampires, ghosts, werewolves, ogres, fairies, boggarts and the occasional worm of unusual size by order of the King (or Queen), for the good of the British Empire. Formed during the reign of Elizabeth the First, the office of Royal Occultist had started with the diligent amateur Dr. John Dee, and passed through a succession of hands, culminating, for the moment, in the Year of Our Lord 1923, with one Charles St. Cyprian and his erstwhile assistant. And indeed, Alfred Anzeray was just their sort of problem.

"Really Charles, how was I to know Alfred was a member of the Wessex Separatist Movement?" Wendy-Smythe said, in protest. "I didn't even know he was from Wessex!" He hesitated, and then added, "And I certainly didn't know that they had separatists."

"Oh, well, that's fine then," St. Cyprian said. "I can see now why you'd go along and help him find an ancient drum, capable of raising the dead. Just a lark, was it?" He glared at the other man. "This is like that business with Gussie Winkers and the Cult of Anubis all over again, isn't it?"

"Surely you can't still be mad about that?" Wendy-Smythe said. "How was I to know old Gussie was the reincarnation of the high priest of Anubis? He went to Edgestow, for heaven's sake."

"You have terrible taste in friends, Phillip," St. Cyprian said. "Bounders, the lot of them." He leaned over the sarcophagus and fired. A corpse stumbled and fell, draping a stone cross with its twitching limbs. It shoved itself up, moving in time to the echoing thump of the unseen drum, and St. Cyprian was forced to shoot it again.

"You know Charles, *we're* friends. At least, I thought we were," Wendy-Smythe said, with a sniff. St. Cyprian felt a twinge of guilt and looked at the little man. It wasn't really Wendy-Smythe's fault, all things considered. An avowed orientalists and amateur occultist, he amassed dangerous things the way a child might gather sweets.

He shuffled nervously at the edges of the secret set, joining and being expelled from secret societies at an impressive rate, and frittered away his not inconsiderable fortune on things, like powdered werewolf teeth and wyrm-eggs. He was simply too trusting when it came to matters of the occult. Too eager to join in, and be a part of a secret world that no one with any amount of common sense would want to inhabit.

It was that eagerness that Alfred Anzeray had preyed on, promising Wendy-Smythe the secrets of the dead, if the pudgy occultist would bend his immense resources towards finding a certain item of eldritch reputation…the Death-Drum of Count Anzeray of Brittany. The Count, one of the more infamous of William the Bastard's many lackeys, was reputed to have made a Faustian bargain with the legendary Ankou of Breton lore. Or not so legendary, given the corpses awkwardly stumbling towards them.

And from what Wendy-Smythe had said, the Count's descendant was a chip off the old block, and looking to get into the family business in the worst way. *Magic and politics is a bad combination,* St. Cyprian thought as he awkwardly patted the little man's shoulder. "There there, Phillip. Done is done, eh?" Gallowglass made a face at him, and he matched it with a glare. "Buck up, chum. We're here now, and we'll soon have it sorted."

"If I'd known, Charles, I'd never have helped him," Wendy-Smythe said, as he fired his pistol with more enthusiasm than skill. "I'd never have let him get hold of such terrible magics if I'd been aware of his malevolent leanings."

"Malevolent leanings," Gallowglass repeated.

"Hush," St. Cyprian said. "The drumming is coming from inside the church. You two cover me. I'm going to see if I can crash our would-be necromancer's impromptu shindig before he wakes up the inhabitants of any more ancestral plots. Tally-ho!" He sprang over the sarcophagus and sprinted for the doors to the church, as Gallowglass and Wendy-Smythe rose to their feet and fired at the swarming dead. The thump of the drum grew louder as he wrenched the doors open.

There were candles lit, and a soft orange glow illuminated the interior of the church. A man in a pale suit, narrow and whey-faced, stood at the altar, holding a drum. Alfred Anzeray, necromancer and would-be regional separatist, didn't look like either. Then, he didn't look like much of anything at all.

As St. Cyprian entered, Anzeray's fingers danced across the stretched skin head of the drum, thumping out a rhythm which echoed strangely in the empty confines of the church. It was a terrible sound, at once hollow and deep, and it vibrated deep in the marrow of his bones. It was the sound of tombs scraping open and dirt falling on coffin lids. Strange shadows stretched and squirmed in the candle-light, as if dancing to the beat and his breath frosted on the air. The dead weren't the only things being woken, he suspected.

St. Cyprian lifted his Webley. "Alfred Anzeray, by the order of His Majesty George V, I place you under arrest for the unlawful practice of necromancy and the disruption of the God-given peace of the grave of His Majesty's subjects. Now drop the drum and come along like a good chap," he said loudly.

"And who are you?" Anzeray said, still beating on the drum. He looked as if he were drunk, swaying slightly in time to the monstrous rhythm rising from his instrument. Sorcery had that effect on some, St. Cyprian knew. The witch's brew was more potent than any liquor. And the drum Anzeray held was an old thing, of the foulest vintage, made of black lacquered wood and covered by a sheath of stretched and tanned hide of indeterminate origin. Wherever it had been hidden, it had been well preserved. It seemed to glow with cold fire as Anzeray played it, his hand moving quicker than it ought.

"St. Cyprian. Charles St. Cyprian," St. Cyprian said. "I'm sure you've heard of me."

"Can't say as I have, old man."

"Oh," St. Cyprian said, crestfallen. He shook his head. "Well, never mind. By my authority as Royal Occultist, I place you under..."

"Were you aware that this church was built on a barrow, Mr. St. Cyprian?" Anzeray said, oblivious. "That's why the first Anzeray, my ancestor, chose to settle here, after the Conquest. The D'Urbervilles weren't the only Normans to be given a gift of land, for services rendered," he continued, popping the drum with his knuckles. "Just a bit and a bob, but enough for old Count Anzeray. They gave him Kingsbere, where the last pagan king of Wessex was interred, in the fashion of the times."

The shadows swelled and thickened as he spoke. The stones of the walls and floor ground against one another and the wooden pews creaked. Strange shapes moved, just out of the corner of St. Cyprian's eye. The hairs on the back of his neck stiffened, the way they had just before the commencement of an artillery barrage during the war.

"Put down the drum, chum," St. Cyprian said. He cocked the Webley. "I'd hate to shoot a chap in a church, but I'll get over it." The sound of the drum had changed, growing deeper. Every thump seemed to resonate through the air and the stones. He was reminded of the reverberations of a church bell, tolling for the dead. Or of a bombardment, tearing the ground and sending men tumbling into death.

Anzeray sneered. "With this drum, I need never fear death by bullet or blade. Death is mine to command; he marches to my beat," he said, thumping the drum with his fingers. As Anzeray spoke, St. Cyprian could hear another sound, like the beating of a second drum beneath the sound of the other. It was faint, as if the source were far away. But the artillery barrage feeling told him that it was drawing closer.

"I shall call up all the dead of this churchyard, of Kingsbere, of all of Wessex even," Anzeray continued. "An army of the pagan dead, as my ancestor once called up to fight William the Bastard's battles for him. And with it, the Wessex Separatist Movement shall enforce home rule for our ancient kingdom, and no pistol-toting fool shall stop us!"

Before St. Cyprian could fire, he found himself ensnared by mouldering arms and rotting fingers. A dozen corpses had entered the church behind him while he'd been preoccupied. He gave a yelp of pain as his arms were yanked up over his head and he was shoved forcefully to his knees. His gun was torn from his grip and cast aside. The dead crowded silently around him, filling the nave of the church. He gagged as the smell of rot and grave-mould grew thick on the air, and for a moment he was back in the trenches of the Somme, down among the dead men. He shook the memory aside, and tried to wrench himself free, but to no avail.

Anzeray cackled and did a little jig. "You see? They are mine, as they were his! I am the master of death, and the ancient Anglo-Saxon dead shall rise and fight at my command." He began to beat out a new rhythm on the stretched head of the drum. "My ancestor won this drum from the Ankou, and I shall use it as he did."

"You don't want to do that," St. Cyprian said, as he tried to pull himself free. The other sound was louder now, beneath the thud of the drum. It was not a second drum-beat, as he'd thought at first, but instead sounded more akin to the sound of hooves.

"Oh, but I do," Anzeray said. "I've wanted to do this for a very long time indeed. Ever since I first heard the stories of my ancestor's ancient pact with the Ankou, and the power of the drum. I call them, and they shall come...come! COME!"

Beneath the pulse of the drum, St. Cyprian could hear a rasping sound, insistent and malign. The church was built on a barrow, Anzeray had said. The rasping grew louder and the candles flickered. A tremor ran through the stones of the floor. "Anzeray, it's not too late...you can still send them back," St. Cyprian said. He tried to pull himself free, but the dead held him tightly.

"Send them back? Why would I do a foolish thing like that, and after I spent all of this time searching for the means to awaken them? They shall be my generals, my champions...the warriors of a golden age, come to restore Wessex to its true glory," Anzeray said.

The stones of the church cracked and shifted as the ancient dead dragged themselves free. There were a dozen of them, and they were brown things, clad in long-rotted vestments and what might have been tattered armour. Some clutched the remains of swords, eaten away by time and rust. They rose to fleshless feet, and stood for a moment, swaying. Anzeray flung out his hand. "Kill him, oh you sons of old Wessex," he intoned.

The ancient dead turned towards St. Cyprian. As they started towards him, the sound of hooves grew louder, galloping now and close by. He heard the creaking of what might have been a cart and the shrill whinny of a horse on the edge of exhaustion. The dead things hesitated, and he knew then that they had heard it too.

For a moment, just a moment, the sound of the drum faltered and was drowned out by the thunder of onrushing hooves, and a voice crying out from afar. St. Cyprian couldn't make out the words, but the dead seemed to have no such difficulties.

As one, the ancient sons of Wessex turned and staggered towards the frantic drummer. "Go back...back, I say!" Anzeray thumped the drum with desperate ferocity as the dead crawled towards him, shoving aside pews as they came. The sound of hoof-beats was louder now, and the windows of the church flexed and rattled in their frames. Something was galloping towards them, across a vast, dark distance. "No, no...Why aren't they listening?" Anzeray said, hammering at the drum.

"They're listening to something older than the drum," St. Cyprian called out, struggling against the corpses which held him. "Far older. You woke them up well enough, but there's not enough magic in that instrument to control them as well. Not when their true master calls." He tore one arm free, and then the other, wincing as the seams of his jacket parted. The more recent dead were distracted. It was as if they were listening for something, and he suspected he knew what. For now, Anzeray still controlled them, but only just. "You have to send them back, man. Before it's too late. He's coming. Can't you hear the hoof-beats? He's coming for his property."

"No...NO," Anzeray cried, as he backed away. He lifted the drum high. "No, I'll find the right rhythm...there must be one! Wessex is mine, I won't lose it now..."

A pistol cracked, and the drum sprang from Anzeray's grip like a scalded cat. He stumbled with a yelp and clutched his bloody fingers to his chest. The drum rolled beneath the pews as the pagan dead of Kingsbere dragged Alfred Anzeray from the altar. The would-be necromancer screamed in horror as he was hauled bodily to the floor. He struggled wildly, trying to tear himself free, and St. Cyprian lost sight of him. He turned and saw Gallowglass hurrying towards him, through the press of the dead. "Oi, you hear that...like thunder, innit?" she called out, ducking beneath a corpse's grasp.

"I heard. Where's Phillip?" he said.

"Safe," she said, as she pivoted and drove her foot into her attacker's belly. The dead man folded over, and she crushed the top of his skull with the butt of her pistol. She eeled through the thicket of hands, and sought refuge atop one of the pews. Without the rhythm of the drum to keep them in check, the newly-awakened dead were reverting to type...stolid slavery gave way to feral hunger. "They're getting awful handsy," she said, kicking a lurching cadaver in the face.

"Without the drum to control them, they're no better than rabid beasts. Keep them contained," St. Cyprian shouted, as he fought his way through the increasingly agitated crowd with fists, elbows and knees. He needed to find the drum. If he could get to it, he might be able to send the dead back to their well-deserved rest. As well as whatever else Anzeray had inadvertently summoned. "We can't let them get out."

"Right," Gallowglass said. She emptied her revolver into the crowd of stumbling dead before sliding out the doors and slamming them shut. Some of the dead began to pound on the doors, while the rest turned their attentions back to the two living men in their midst.

"That's not exactly what I meant," St. Cyprian muttered as he caught the back of a pew and swung himself over the top. Still, if it kept the majority of the creatures pinned in one place, it was probably for the best. Between them, Gallowglass and Wendy-Smythe could hopefully keep the doors shut.

He scrambled over the back of another pew, narrowly avoiding the clutches of a dead matron, her fleshless jaws chattering. As he moved from pew to pew, he scanned the floor, hunting for the drum. When he at last caught sight of it, he hurled himself towards it and snatched it up. It throbbed silently in his grip and he shuddered in revulsion. He could hear Anzeray cursing and sobbing, and the peculiar sound of rusted blades striking wood. The necromancer was still alive, at least.

Dead things staggered towards him as he tried to recall the sound of the rhythm Anzeray had played. He thumped the drum, and the corpses sped up, moving like hungry wolves. They leapt over the pews, bounding towards him with abominable speed. "I daresay it's not that one," he yelped, as he scrambled towards the altar.

"Give me that drum," Anzeray howled, as he flung himself from the altar dais. He crashed into St. Cyprian and they fell to the floor with a crash, the drum caught between them. Anzeray flailed at St. Cyprian, striking him with his fists. St. Cyprian shoved Anzeray back, into the altar, and clambered to his feet. Rusty swords thudded down, splintering the altar. Anzeray scrambled aside with desperate speed, trying to avoid the creatures he had called up. Most of them pursued him, but one of the dead warriors stalked towards St. Cyprian, ragged mail clattering. It grinned skeletally at him, eye sockets glimmering with a flickering light as it hacked at him.

He leapt back as the blade smashed down, chopping into the floor. It was quicker than it looked, as if whatever sorcery had animated it had also lent it some measure of fluidity. It swept the sword out, slashing at him, driving him back. He held the drum up, like a shield. The creature seemed loathe to strike the instrument, and he wondered if destroying it might be the answer.

But before he could make the attempt, the sound of hooves suddenly filled the church. He heard a horse squeal in fury, and the sound of Gallowglass' revolver going off. Then the doors of the church bulged inwards, their hinges creaking. A moment later, they were torn off of their hinges, crushing those corpses which had still been trying to smash them open.

The being standing in the doors of the church was unnaturally thin and clad in black robes and a wide-brimmed black hat which obscured its features...a fact St. Cyprian was grateful for. It clutched a tall reaper's scythe in one fleshless hand. The dead swayed back from it, like stalks of barley in a strong wind, and the fresher among them moaned before all fell silent, as if in fear of the newcomer.

"What...what is that?" Anzeray said, his voice loud in the sudden silence.

"Don't you recognize him, Anzeray?" St. Cyprian said hoarsely. The eye of every dead thing in the church was on the creature standing in the doorway. He hoped that Gallowglass and Wendy-Smythe were alright. "It's the Ankou, come for his drum."

"No. No, the bargain..." Anzeray began, staring at the apparition in horror.

"It made its bargain with Count Anzeray. Not with you," St. Cyprian said, backing away. "And now you've called it up, and it's come to claim its property after all these centuries." He scanned the floor, searching for his revolver, though he suspected it would do more harm than good. Such creatures couldn't be harmed by mortal weapons; they were nothing less than forces of nature, given shape and purpose. "I did warn you, old man," he said.

"No, I won't be cheated, not now," Anzeray snarled. He tore a sword from the bony hands of a long-dead warrior and charged towards St. Cyprian. "Give me that drum!" He slashed out wildly, and St. Cyprian dropped the drum as he jerked back, out of reach. Anzeray dropped the sword and picked up the drum. He began to pound on it. The ranks of the dead gave a communal sigh and wavered, as if uncertain of which way to go. The Ankou stopped, and the light in its eyes flared eerily. The dead twitched and moaned, caught between two masters.

"Well, can't have that, can we? Simply not done, torturing His Majesty's subjects, be they living or dead," St. Cyprian said. He lunged forward and snatched up the sword Anzeray had dropped. Before the necromancer could act, St. Cyprian thrust the sword through the drum and tore it from Anzeray's grip.

As Anzeray lost his hold on the drum, the Ankou swept its scythe out in a wide arc. There was suddenly a smell, as of an open grave or a cold wind out of an open mausoleum, and the dead fell to the floor, one by one. The Ankou moved forward in fits and starts, like a damaged reel of film. St. Cyprian heard the scrape of bones and the rustle of nine yards of other cloth as it flowed down the nave towards them.

Anzeray shrieked and grabbed for the drum, but St. Cyprian turned and hurled it at the entity, shouting, "Here you go...catch!" The scythe fell, its blade punching through the instrument with finality. The drum screamed like a dying animal as it split in two and fell shattered to the floor. The Ankou continued on, filling the church with itself, its presence. The candles winked out in its wake, and the air grew cold.

"What have you done?" Anzeray screamed.

"Hopefully saved our hides, you ungrateful...oh bugger," St. Cyprian said, as the

Ankou rose up before them, its robes flapping in an infernal breeze. It spoke, in a voice like a wind blowing through a hollow stone. St. Cyprian couldn't understand the words, but he took their meaning well enough. "Sorry old thing, can't let you do it. You'll have to be satisfied with having your drum back. He's under arrest, and that means he's due all the protection of the Crown, until such time as we decide to hang him." He hesitated. "Which we almost certainly will." He glanced back at Anzeray. "Sorry Anzeray, but I did say." He looked back at the Ankou. It hadn't slowed down.

He hacked at the approaching apparition with the sword, though he knew he had little chance of stopping it. Even so, he had to try. Like it or not, Anzeray was a British citizen, and that meant he was obliged to give it the Oxford Olds. As he'd feared, the blade swept harmlessly through the ghostly reaper's form, and it swept over and past him without pause, leaving him with a chill he thought it'd take more than a brandy to warm.

The Ankou raised its scythe over the cowering necromancer. The blade fell with a clang, passing through Anzeray with seemingly no ill-effect. Anzeray staggered back, face white. He slumped back against the altar, clutching at his chest. St. Cyprian caught him before he fell. Anzeray twitched in his arms, gasping like a fish out of water. St. Cyprian looked up at the Ankou, and saw that the entity held something pale and squirming in its free hand, like a length of gossamer. But gossamer didn't scream.

The Ankou stared down at him for a moment, eyes glowing like hot coals. St. Cyprian raised the sword, ready to defend himself and the writhing Anzeray. "Satisfied?" he asked, softly. After a moment, the creature thumped the floor once, twice, three times with the ferrule of its scythe, turned and strode back towards the doors. Wisps of white smoke rose from the fallen corpses to trail after it. St. Cyprian heard a soft babble, as of many voices raised in pleas, gratitude and protestations, and then the sound of receding hooves. The man he held gave a sudden, soft sound and then fell silent.

St. Cyprian looked down at Anzeray's stiff, frozen features and carefully set his rigid body down. He turned as Gallowglass and Wendy-Smythe entered the church, both of them pale and wary. "Did you see it?" Gallowglass asked.

St. Cyprian nodded, suddenly exhausted. He held up the sword, examining the thick film of frost that clung to the ancient blade. As he watched, it began to crumble into motes of rust, until he was holding nothing more than an unrecognizable lump.

"What...what was that thing? What did it want?" Wendy-Smythe asked, mopping at his face with a handkerchief.

St. Cyprian was silent for a moment. He looked towards the doors. The sound of hooves had faded. The Ankou was gone, returned to wherever it had come from. He looked down at the corpse of Alfred Anzeray, and the horrified expression on the dead man's face. "What did it want, Phillip? Why, to make good on an old bargain, I'd say."

The End

Tommy Hancock's Branson Non-Adventure

by Erwin K. Roberts

Late in the afternoon Tommy Hancock stepped off the bus in Branson, Missouri. He concluded, for the sixth or seventh time since dawn that today just wasn't *his* day. Last minute medical appointment, out of town. Vehicle breakdown. Racing to catch a bus seemingly filled with screaming kids. After having to pay cash for the ticket because the ticketing credit card reader shot craps. He absently accepted a handful of attraction brochures from a harried young lady wearing somebody's bad idea of a country singer's outfit. Her smile revealed braces.

She gave him a good looking over before attending to others exiting the Greyhound bus. Tommy did not notice that she hurried through the couples with and without kids. She only took interest in two other solo men of his approximate age, height and weight. The first one's feet hit the pavement with his eyes already scanning the area. He must have liked what he saw. When he shrugged his shoulders, the second man started down the bus's stairs. The new arrival looked deeply tired, but he gamely started forward to where a sedan waited. That sedan seemed typical of an unmarked official vehicle. As the car drove off, the girl in the bad country outfit disappeared into the Spirit Shop's rest room. She never came out. But a woman of similar size in not too formal, but drab, business attire emerged dragging a briefcase atop a rolling suitcase. The new woman's face looked a bit severe. With the car no longer in sight she followed the path taken by Tommy Hancock.

Tommy had found the shuttle, a generic eight passenger stretched Caddy, waiting in the parking lot. He presented the driver with a printed copy of the email he'd received from the Nettles Clinic.

"Ah, one of Doc's regular patients?" the middle aged woman asked.

"No, I'm getting checked out for a possible study," replied Tommy.

"Got'ya. I'll point out the Clinic and the place you're supposed to eat, before I drop you at the motel. The Clinic's van'll pick you up in the morning."

"Gotta wait two more minutes," she continued. "That youngster towing the rollin' piece with the briefcase on top 'll just make it."

Tommy glanced at the approaching woman, then settled in his seat with his briefcase and small bag. The business woman asked, in very precise, neigh on stilted, English to be taken to a modestly up-scale hostelry just a block from his own. He did not see the man three cars over taking cell phone pictures of everybody in the shuttle.

A short time later, Tommy presented another copy of the email to the desk clerk at the relatively small independent motel.

"Here. Please fill this out Mr. Hancock. The state requires it, even though the Clinic's paying the tab. Nettles bought this place a couple years ago. The west end of the second floor has rooms for traveling staff and folks doing rotations.

We were supposed to have one of the rooms set aside for people in studies. Had an electrical short in there today. Got that fixed, but clean up's not done. So we upgraded you to the boss' room. That's the corner room, with two windows. Fortunately Doc Nettles is staying with friends tonight. Some sort of poker game's what I figure. Now, let me run you through th' particulars..."

As he walked the three blocks to the restaurant he observed that virtually all pedestrians were couples and families dressed for vacation. His sports-coat, even without a tie, made him stand out.

He handed yet another copy of the Nettles Clinic email to the hostess. She led him to an isolated table near the rear of the place and handed him a menu with only three choices.

"Sorry, honey," she said with a companionable smile. "What you eat is part of the prep for your testing. They want a clean plate, too. Plus no soda allowed, or caffeine. We got water, milk, and decaf coffee and iced tea."

Tommy ordered. While he waited for his food, he took out his phone to send a text message. Motion distracted him. He saw the severe business woman he'd shared the shuttle with being seated a couple of rows over. She was ordering as he hit send.

As his steaming food arrived Tommy saw the woman get up with her purse and head for the rest rooms that were somewhere behind him. As she was about to pass his table he heard something snap sharply. He saw one of her three inch heels fly across the floor.

She staggered. Then her right hand grabbed for his table. Instinctively Tommy gripped his side of the table for dear life. The woman spun around, then managed to plant her other hand squarely above the table's center column. Her swinging purse nearly brushed Tommy's nose.

"So... So sorry!" she gasped. "Oh... We rode the shuttle together. Please accept my apologies."

"No need to apologize, Miss," replied Tommy. "No damage done. Except for your shoe and my heart rate. Your heel went into that third booth, I think."

"Thank you, sir. Instead of combing my hair, I think I will go back to my seat. I hope you can still enjoy your meal."

When Tommy left the restaurant the woman was drinking her second cup of coffee.

● ● ●

She left the restaurant still tasting the apple pie a la mode. Focused on her mission, she wondered why the Nettles Clinic patient booked in the room next to Dr. Nettles himself looked familiar. She had no data on him. A cell phone snapshot was circulating, so far without results. Since the man did not show up in the mission brief as anything but a possible distraction, the search for his identity went to the very back burner of her brain.

Tiny vents in the bottom of her purse had dusted his plate with a mixture of both modern and ancient preparations. Not a sedative, exactly. He would sleep when he wanted to, and sleep deeply. Yet he could still wake in an emergency. She just didn't want him waking if a few thumps and thuds came from Dr. Nettles' room. The last minute... Make that the last second addition to the hotel's guest list had been relayed to her just before the bus arrived. She felt lucky to have the snapshot. Him being in for a trial evaluation, she'd known where to catch up with him at dinner.

Dr. Franklin Nettles was not the one directly in danger. He was a pawn. After the 2011 Joplin Tornado destroyed his large clinic, Dr. Nettles temporarily out sourced much of his practice to the towns of Carthage, Lebanon, and Branson, Missouri, while he rebuilt in his native Joplin. The Branson clinic flourished beyond expectations. It drew patients from northern Arkansas who previously patronized facilities in Little Rock. Branson, with its huge number of entertainment venues, also served as a better draw for study volunteers than staid old Joplin. So Dr. Nettles now spent a day or two there each week.

Study candidates were supposed to go lights out right after the ten o'clock news. After all, morning wakeup came at five-thirty. The slightly familiar man should get a good night's sleep.

● ● ●

Tommy took stock when he got back to his room. In front of the locked closet stood a typical motel luggage stand. His oversized gym bag already rested there. The under-counter fridge held a few bottles of drinks OK for study patients. Picking up the remote he turned on the large flatscreen TV. A few moments of button poking told him that Dr. Nettles subscribed to neither pay-per-view programming, nor any "adult" channels. But, at the top of the favorite channel list was Turner Classic Movies.

Tommy punched up that channel to discover a bunch of Ray Harryhausen movies started soon. He stretched out on the bed with a small stack of manuscripts and a cold can of Trader Joe's Raspberry Seltzer Water at hand as the opening credits to *Earth vs the Flying Saucers* rolled.

● ● ●

Reluctantly she turned off *Twenty Million Miles to Earth* after completing her preparations for the night's mission. The last bits of a half decent sunset had long since faded to true night as she slipped out of her room. Her black crape soled boots made no sound as she entered the motel's central, partially-open staircase. The last flight of stairs, leading to the roof, was locked and well secured. She hopped up to the open embrasure in the outside wall. She sat at the bottom of the opening with her legs inside and her torso and head outside. She pulled a thin rope with a grappling hook out of one of the many pouches that were part of tonight's battle gear. She knew that great danger lay ahead. She reviewed the mission as she threw the grapnel and climbed to the motel's roof.

Somebody had put out a lot of money to quietly kill the third single man off the bus. Morton Vickers served as an annalist and the institutional memory for a multi-agency task force out to bust a network of loosely allied organized crime groups.

She smiled a bit as she stood on the back wall of the motel. Morton's grandfather, legendary 1930's G-Man Lynn Vickers, fought battles very much in the media of his day. She knew his exploits well. Morton's fieldwork got cut short when a bullet barely missed his heart. Desk bound, his ability to spot connections between seemingly unrelated criminals rivaled the fictional self-aware computer on that TV show.

Someone found out about Morton's ability. Nobody knew who. Yet! She paused her recap to throw the grapnel around the thick TV cable below the power lines that ran fifteen feet behind the motel. Like a lot of the Branson strip, that motel sat at the edge of a ridge. The back wall of the roof stood braced above a seventy-five foot drop. The power poles were around ninety feet tall. They ended five feet below her.

She tested the line, then stepped out into space. She swung through space like a trapeze artist. Resisting the temptation to swing even higher, she let herself settle, then climbed to the cable. Two small devices allowed her to move safely along the cable in the darkness. The only downside - being showered now and then with dried bird droppings.

She worked her way past three poles before she arrived behind Dr. Nettles' room. Her passive infrared goggles barely showed the glow of someone in the room's bed. Inside, Tommy Hancock slumbered.

She paused to get any kinks out of her muscles. Her review continued. Morton Vickers kept relatively active thanks to a pacemaker-like device. That device suddenly needed a new battery, or a replacement. Dr. Nettles had worked with the legendary Jay Minor in designing the first generation of the programmable heart control implants. Nettles also had no connections to Morton Vickers.

To the Feds the idea seemed a security slam-dunk. Ship Vickers under the radar to Nettles' off trail clinic. Then two words tumbled out of a wire tap. At those words the Voice, long semi-retired, called the covert network anchored by Curt Van Loan for help. Then Van Loan called her. She shivered yet again as she remembered hearing the code-name "Mirror Image" on the scrambled Skype call.

"It was like looking at my own mirror image!" said the only man known to survive impersonation by a new disguise artist assassin. Stories of the man now circulated with all sorts of un-provable additions. Some said he'd been thru a couple of years of medical school before he decided taking lives paid better than saving them. Others said he'd walked out of a surgical residency. Only a few things were certain. Mirror Image possessed world class abilities in disguise and impersonation. He didn't even look at a job without six figures in up-front money. He preferred to quietly work under the radar, but was deadly with most weapons and in hand to hand fighting. She shuddered as she paused briefly on the roof above Dr. Nettles' room.

For his special room Dr. Nettles replaced the standard motel semi-hermetically sealed windows with triple paned ones he could open. The day had been cool. She was not surprised to find the one in the end wall open. She hung head down listening to the almost non-existent room noises. Finally she detected the sound of a man deeply asleep. Detaching the screen, she silently entered the room. Her infrared goggles showed the back of the man's head beneath the sheet. No other heat signatures appeared. She reattached the screen. After a quick survey of the room with an IR flashlight, she crawled under the bed so that her heat signature would blend with Dr. Nettles'. She used various tricks to keep awake and alert. About eighteen inches above her Tommy Hancock slumbered on.

Over an hour later her finely tuned hearing picked up the faint sound of fabric on the exterior brick wall. Silently she wriggled to the edge of the bed. The bed skirt was very sheer. Through it she saw a heat signature begin to bloom to the left side of the window she'd entered. The IR signature refined itself just enough to tell the figure outside was head up, instead of down.

A moment later the person's head slid into view for a few seconds. She realized the man wore goggles, too. If they were Infrared ones, she was blown. But, almost nobody used passive IR any more. The man outside withdrew his head. He did not leave, nor did he rip down the screen to attack. Instead, the screen came clear of the window, much as she had done it. He must be wearing a night vision system that magnified available light, rather than IR. Such systems were very good, but, even after fifty years, they did have a weakness. She slipped something into each hand as she waited. Tommy Hancock still slumbered.

She watched the new arrival enter. He landed silently on cat feet keeping much of his weight on the line tethered above. He looked around. Nothing alarmed him. Still keeping hold of the line he pulled something out of a slit pocket attached to his wide belt. She could see the warm device clearly. Some sort of auto-injector, like those now used by diabetics. What was in the thing, she couldn't guess. Nor could she take a chance that Mirror Image used a non-lethal drug. As he stepped toward the bed she struck.

Her arm flashed out from under the bed. Hand as high as possible, she triggered the flash on her all black, screen-covered, Braille keyed cell phone at the highest output. The man froze with one foot a few inches in the air. As she yanked her arm back and rolled out from under the bed she knew her opponent's night vision gear was temporarily useless; plus his personal vision was probably filled with retinal spots.

She planked, then twisted as she threw her lower body at the man with all the force her arms could generate. Her crape soles impacted right into the buckle of the man's cargo belt. He managed to keep himself from falling, but not by much.

She rotated so that her shoulders adsorbed the impact of her landing as she yanked her feet back. She kipped into a crouch as she pulled a collapsible baton from her own belt.

A small, silenced, automatic appeared in the man's hand. She struck out with the extended baton. Only the last half inch or so made contact. But, it was enough. The gun thumped to the floor. Shaking his right hand the man pulled a lanyard on his belt with his left.

She paused, not knowing what sort of counterattack this might be. It wasn't. Before she could react, her opponent turned and dived straight out the window.

She felt small, soft objects hitting her as she dashed to the window. Then came the unmistakable sound of a bungee cord reaching full stretch. She snatched the gun from the floor, ready to fire at the IR signature on the ground. Before she could even try to aim, the released bungee cord draped itself over her head and arm. A moment later she could only watch as the heat of the man's body dispersed behind multiple trees, then vanished entirely.

With a sigh she turned to look at the room again. Dr. Nettles should be awake and calling for help by this point. But he wasn't. The figure in the bed *had* rolled over, but that was all. She stood frozen in shock for a brief moment. This man was definitely *not* Dr. Nettles. For starters, he lacked the Heart Specialist's signature soup-strainer mustache.

She used her IR flashlight for a moment. *No wonder he didn't wake up,* she mused with a wry smile on her invisible lips. *I drugged him myself. Who the blazes is he?*

She began checking the room. The soft things that hit her, as the presumed Mirror Image jumped to safety, turned out to be rubber bands used to hold the bungee cord in place, much as a parachute is packed. She stowed them both away, plus the auto-injector and the gun in her gear. The window screen had vanished along the way. Nothing she could do about that. She sat in the room's reclining chair until three-thirty in the morning. Then she returned to her own room to prepare to meet the new day.

● ● ●

"Did you sleep well, Mr. Hancock?" asked the desk clerk.

"Mostly. Was there a storm last night?"

"No, sir. Clear all night, 'cording to my brother-in-law, the cop."

"Then I musta been dreaming. Thought I saw one huge flash of lightning and heard some really strange thunder. Got up this morning and the west window screen's gone."

"We do get some really cockeyed winds; what with the ridges and valleys. The clinic bus'll be outside in about four minutes."

● ● ●

She changed her skin tone quite a bit. Then she added some freckles anyplace her skin was likely to be visible. Her hair became black with a few hints of red. Soon she had it up in a club at the back of her neck. She put on nondescript hospital scrubs with some hidden pockets. Socks and Crocs completed her ensemble. Then she slipped out of her hotel to where her rental car waited.

She parked just out of sight of the Nettles Clinic. At that early hour plenty of spaces were available. Parking at the Clinic required a pass to be scanned. She deliberately had not procured one ahead of time. She walked past the parking driveway. Unlike the days before, two uniformed security guards, instead of one, kept watch on things. She waved as she went by. She showed her driver's license as she went through the metal detector inside the front door. The only metal she carried, her keys and a burner cell phone, went through the X-ray belt. That chore done she introduced herself to the receptionist, who called the operating room supervisor.

"Our car blew a tire yesterday. We didn't get to my cousin's place in Kimberling until after midnight." The prepared story drew a sympathy frown from the older lady. "My husband's headed out to Silver Dollar City to get oriented for his playing gig. Had to borrow a car to get here."

"Just glad to have you, Mrs. Keats. We have a more complex than usual procedure laid on for today. Then our temp pool suddenly dried up. You came highly recommended by the temp service. I've already got a parking pass for you. Your Clinic ID should finish processing by the time you park…"

She pulled her car through one space to park facing the quickest way off Clinic property. With the supervisor waiting at a side door, as she'd hoped, she quickly filled her pockets with gear that was anything but medical. Holding a quilted lunch cooler, she hurried back inside.

• • •

Tommy Hancock's "breakfast" turned out to be a very heavy milkshake sort-of-thing that had a barrage of strange aftertastes. He still burped occasionally as he exited the van outside the clinic door. Soon he found himself wired up with more data leads and LED lights than a fifteen foot Christmas tree.

"Once inside the room," said Marshal, the young technician, "you shouldn't see, hear, or feel anything but what we want you to. We will be recording how your body and especially how your heart reacts to the stimuli. The testing software will apply micro-electrical stimulations to various muscle groups. The most you can feel is a tiny twitch. There will always be two of us monitoring your vital signs, plus just about every sort of alarm known to medicine is reading the data coming in. Any questions, Mr. Hancock?"

Tommy looked at the walls surrounding the testing room. "What's on the other side of the walls? And, is that a waterbed?"

"Yes, sir! That is a waterbed at nearly body temperature. That's one reason you're only wearing a bathing suit. As for the walls, on the right is the floor's main corridor. The far wall is operating room storage. On the left is part of the main O.R. Now, let's get you hooked up…"

• • •

She'd gotten a look at the "as built" blueprints of the clinic. But a few things had changed since. Mrs. Bolton, the O.R. supervisor, gave her a quick look at the facility before heading to the largest of the operating rooms.

"I don't know who the patient really is today, but there is extra security. Maybe he's an oil sheik, or something. What makes things a bit hairy is we do not know if Dr. Nettles can fix the patient's programmable pacemaker with just minor adjustments, or a complete replacement. Since you are new, you'll scrub in to help as needed. Dr. Nettles is very precise in his instructions, especially with someone new.

"Here's the scrub room. Good morning, Jeff. Dr. Cramer, this is Mrs. Keats, a fully certified O.R. technician. She's our extra set of hands today. Now, I'd better find out where Dr. Nettles has disappeared to."

"Morning, Mrs. Keats," said Cramer. "Call me Jeff. I'm the anesthesiologist."

"Hi, Jeff. I'm Amanda," she said extending her hand. "I'm new in town. I know a bog standard O.R. setup. I'd appreciate any insight you can give me about local procedures."

He'd let her hand go after a quick, but firm handshake. "Sure, glad to. Need coffee? No. Let's go peek in the O.R. window. No need to start scrubbing before Nettles gets here..."

She listened as he pointed out how things were arranged in the Operating Room, and where to find backup supplies.

"This could take only twenty minutes or so." he concluded. "Unfortunately, it could also go past lunch if the leads to the heart have to be replaced. If I know Nettles, he's hidden away to re-study the device's manual one more time. His car was here when I arrived at six."

● ● ●

The man known to some as Mirror Image fumed and swore to himself. His plan to impersonate Dr. Thornton Nettles dissolved when that infernal flash of light blinded him. He'd seen just enough before the flash to know Nettles had not been in that bed. Where the hell was he? And, where was the hue and cry for the unknown intruder. It was like the events that left him somewhat battered and bruised never happened.

Damn it! He thought. *The old fashioned way it is!*

He stepped from the office in an empty storefront on the Branson Strip into the place's stockroom with a code name on his lips. Even so two of the five men present reached for their holstered weapons. Both stopped when what he said sunk in.

"In spite of the face," he said, with the hint of a smile, "I am not the regional head of Alcohol, Tobacco and Firearms. I am pleased that you all look and are dressed like garden variety feds. I'll give further instructions in our 'official' vehicle. I will point out the getaway van as we enter the Nettles Clinic parking lot. Let's go..."

A few moments later a black Suburban, with authentic looking General Services Administration license plates, pulled onto the Strip in the direction of the Nettles Clinic.

● ● ●

In the meantime, Tommy Hancock sort of enjoyed himself. He lay facing one huge LED screen and four smaller ones, two at each end of the large monitor. He could track his basic vital signs, if he wished on one of the smaller screens. The other three made no sense to him. Maybe they were not supposed to. The big screen presented a wide,

almost wild, range of sights and sounds. Hypnotic swirls of color, with relaxing music, alternated with strident tunes of various genres and disconcerting images. Mixed in were emotional clips from classic films. He'd seen Henry Fonda's "I'll be there" speech from *The Grapes of Wrath* and bits of Grant and Hepburn's *Bringing Up Baby* antics. John Wayne died in *The Cowboys* and that dratted kid kept yelling "Come Back, *Shane*."

Every now and then speakers in all parts of the room would boom with thunder, gunfire and explosions. Plus, all the time, he felt various muscles twitch as minute amounts of electricity were applied.

Then all the lights slowly faded to nearly complete blackness. New sounds came. Some Tommy could hardly tell were there at all. Others, like a tire tool being dropped on concrete, seemed right by his head. Forcing himself to relax, Tommy continued lying in the darkness.

At the time Tommy's lights faded away, the government Suburban disgorged Mirror Image's team outside the clinic's main entrance.

• • •

She absorbed everything Jeff Cramer told her, including a couple of stories about folks at the clinic. A few moments later Dr. Nettles walked briskly into the Prep Room with, Jeff told her, the rest of the O.R. staff.

"Scrub up, everybody," said Nettles, with a bit of urgency in his voice. Then he looked at her saying, "Mrs. Keats, I presume. Welcome. We'll have a chance to get acquainted when the patient is in recovery. Everyone, Mrs. Bolton is seeing to the patient's prep and will escort him here. Sorry about all the smoke and mirrors about just whom we will be operating on. I've asked the patient's escort to explain the situation while we put the patient under."

They all stood at their assigned positions. Gowned, capped, masked, with gloved hands held away from their bodies. Then the double doors from the corridor swung inward. Mrs. Bolton entered with two middle-aged men. They almost looked like cousins. They both had blocky bodies with very little excess weight. One, stripped to the waist, had an IV line in his left arm. He held the rolling bag holder in the same hand. Mrs. Bolton gripped his right arm firmly. The second man wore a surgical gown with cap and a mask around his neck. She listened as the rest of the team reacted to the fact that he wore a gun-belt over his gown.

"No need to panic, friends," the second man said as his companion lay down on the operating table. He held up his left hand. That hand flipped open a small leather case to reveal an ID card and shield. "Lemuel Barnes, Treasury Department. Dr. Nettles has checked out my credentials very thoroughly. Could've been an investigator, if he'd wanted.

"With me is Morton Vickers, also a Treasury Agent. If that name sounds familiar, you're probably remembering the movie, 'bout twenty years ago, where Kevin Costner played Mort's grandfather Lynn, an FBI man. There's more than a few skunks that'd be happy if Mort didn't wake up from this little square dance. That's why we snuck him in today. And that's why I brought a gun to an operation.

"Mort," Barnes continued, "We can't shake hands. So good luck! See you on the other side."

Morton Vickers looked mostly asleep, but he thanked Barnes and the Operating Room team before Jeff Cramer put him under.

"Vitals look good. You can start," Cramer said formally, a few moments later.

"Scanner," said Dr. Nettles. An electronic device was placed in his gloved hand. He moved the thing about half an inch above Vickers chest, in the area around an incision scar.

That's when the room's intercom came to life.

"Dr. Nettles," came Mrs. Bolton's shaky voice, "Some federal agents are here. They insist that you halt the procedure."

"We can't do that..." began Nettles when the supposedly locked Operating Room doors began to open inward.

As the door opened she saw a man in a dark suit standing centered on the gap between the doors. In his left hand he held an open ID wallet. Behind him stood several others cut from the same cloth. All looked downright grim.

She tried to pull in every scrap of data about the newcomers. The leader seemed typical of an experienced federal agent. His face, minimally expressive, while his body seemed like a spring waiting to uncoil. The others appeared to be trying to keep their faces frozen. While she glanced around some more while they stepped into the O.R. The back of her mind processed what she'd already seen. She mentally labeled the followers, One through Five, as they spread out left to right.

Number Three focused on her with just a hint of the wrong kind of interest in his eyes. She took an extra deep breath. Three's eyes widened just a touch as the baggy scrubs revealed more of her shape. Not a good sign. Number Four held position as his eyes swept back and forth. His right hand quivered in the direction of his left armpit. Number One stood to one side of the closing double doors where he could intercept anyone who tried to come in.

Numbers Two and Five looked back and forth over all the Operating Room personal. Number Two just might have something concealed under his right sleeve, she decided.

The leader flashed the A.T.F. identification wallet saying, "I'm Carol Miles, A.T.F Regional Director. We have reason to believe there is an imposter here. We need everyone to pull down their surgical masks..."

Her heart skipped a beat. Then she realized if she was the target, more peoples' attention would be focused in her direction than just the one horny guy.

Vickers' escort spoke up. "What's going on? Less'n two hours ago you told me you were on the far side of the Oklahoma Panhandle. I'm Barnes, Treasury."

"I lied," said Mirror Image as he flexed his right arm sharply. Before anyone could react a small automatic appeared in his hand. A split-second later he fired a round directly at Barnes' heart.

Instantly she vaulted over the O.R. table using her left hand to get in close. Her cap almost brushed against Dr. Nettles' sleeve as he ducked for the floor. She kicked out as she pivoted just a couple of inches above Morton Vickers' legs. A cart full of retractors and clamps rolled in the direction of number Two. She spun like a dervish to make her landing.

The momentum allowed her to take one long step, then pivot kick Number Three where his mind lived. She finished her whirl with her left hand scooping up a handful of instruments from another cart.

Steeling herself against the possibility of cutting her left hand, she snatched a scalpel out of the cluster of instruments with her right hand. Then she back-handed it at the phony A.T.F. man as he aimed his gun at her. He made no sound as the incredibly sharp blade sank into the flesh just below his thumb.

The small weapon fell to the floor, but Mirror Images' hand shook the blade free as he reached for his shoulder-holstered Glock.

She juggled the contents of her left hand to where all the blades sat below her little finger. In the mirror finish of a fallen instrument cart's surface she noted Agent Barnes' pain and rage filled eyes as he forced himself to his feet, gun in hand. In the same instant Mirror Image's aim changed in that direction.

She snatched another scalpel by the blade and let fly at the assassin. She rolled to the left. Number Two's silenced gun spat a slug into the space she'd vacated. She came out of the roll throwing. As she grabbed another pair of blades, her peripheral vision took in Number Three staggering out of the O.R. Not yet aware of what she'd seen, her hand came down releasing the two scalpels.

The sound of another silenced shot disappeared in the roar of Agent Barnes' own Glock. A hole appeared between number Two's eyes, while Barnes fell to the floor again.

She took stock in a splinter of a fractured second. Number Three was on the run. Number Two was dead. The leader grimaced as he pulled a scalpel from directly under his right clavicle. Number Four looked numbly at handles sticking out of each of his arms. That left One and Five. She took the two remaining scalpels, one in each hand. That's when number Five cartwheeled into her vision.

As Five sailed through the air, she spun round to let fly a blade at Number One, as he uncertainly waved his weapon between her and Agent Barnes. At the same instant Barnes fired from the floor. Mirror Images' suit jacket's shoulder spat fabric shards. Before Barnes could fire again, Mirror Image dived through the closing Operating Room door. At the same time, Five smashed into the wall of the O.R. with enough force to crack the plastic paneling that covered it.

She looked around. Agent Barnes again staggered to his feet. The rest of the O.R. team kept huddling on the floor. Then, to her surprise, she saw Jeff, Dr. Cramer, calmly pick up a silenced Glock and check for a chambered round. He pointed to where Five lay folded up by the wall.

"Present for you folks," he said cheerfully. "I'll take control here. I was Special Forces before med school."

Without a second thought she yanked the O.R. door open and dived through. She skidded several feet. While she did, a bullet gouged the recently waxed tiles by the door. By this time she'd pulled her tiny four shot .22 holdout from under her O.R. gown. She fired at the head and arm sticking out from a stairwell door.

Mirror Image fired a split second before she did. Her small slug tore through the door, just barely. The body parts disappeared and the door began to close. She heard his round hit something just behind her.

"Damnation!" yelled Agent Barnes as the impact threw him to the floor again. "Get that son of a snake, young lady. The S.O.B. hit my vest. Again!!"

With a hint of a smile on her lips she dashed to the stairwell. At the door she could hear feet pounding on the metal treads. Then came a metallic bouncing sound. She dived down the hallway just before a grenade blew the door across the hall.

She turned to leave when an elevator door opened. Four security guards stepped out with guns drawn.

● ● ●

Jerry Alfred sat waiting in the brand new Ford Transit commercial van not two weeks off the assembly line up in Kansas City. Decked out as a Google Fiber truck, the vehicle waited at the edge of the Nettles Clinic grounds. Considered the best wheelman in the Springfield-Joplin area, Jerry had placed traffic cones front and back of the rig far enough away that he could pull out instantly, or even make a backward U-turn, if necessary. He looked cool and collected, but he checked the digital clock in the dash, and all the mirrors, every few seconds.

Then two men appeared in the driver's side mirror. One walked fast, but funny. The other's suit coat was missing. Blood stained both of his shirt sleeves. Jerry started the engine as he released the latch on the back doors. The two clambered in to flop on the van's floor.

"Get going!" said one urgently. "Everyone else is down, or disappeared!"

Jerry put the vehicle in gear. As he pulled away from the curb he looked around for cop cars. That's when six heavy duty Flash-Bang grenades went off inside the van. All three men lost consciousness. A few seconds later heavy thermite charges began to burn.

● ● ●

She managed to hide her small gun as she let the security guards herd her back to the scene of the action. Back, just inside the O.R., Treasury Special Agent Barnes glared at her while the security guards put cuffs on the attackers who still lived. With three rounds in his vest, he probably had broken ribs she decided.

"Young lady," said the short of breath Barnes as he worked to get his vest off, "thank you. Writing up this, whatever you want t' call it, is going to be a real bear. Thank the Lord, you pulled the focus on yourself. No staff got hurt. Neither did my good friend Mort Vickers. Not that I'm ungrateful, I most certainly am. But I gotta have some identification."

"Call Homeland Security," she said with a smile. "Use whatever number you have. Then ask to 'Urgently speak to the India Oscar Desk'."

Barnes cell phone screen turned out to be cracked, but he did as she asked. Dr. Cramer smiled at her as he taped down a bandage on Number One's throat.

"Great throw, Amanda," he said. "I couldn't have done an emergency Tracheotomy better myself. He froze for fear of slitting his own throat. Now, I'll bet you aren't really Mrs. Keats, are you."

"I was today," she replied. Barnes, now seated on a stool, held out the phone to her.

She took the phone saying, "This is Magazine Lady."

"Independent Operator Desk. This is Boom."

"Hi, Boom," she said, before the code words began...

About an hour latter she was ready to return to her vacation. To head home. She unlocked her brain to allow non-mission essential thoughts and questions to bounce around. Less than two minutes later she chuckled, then said aloud, "So that's who was in Dr. Nettles' bed."

● ● ●

Tommy Hancock lay in the totally darkened test room. He was starting to get worried. Moments ago the parade of images, sounds, and muscle twitches seemed as they had been before. Then the sound of a fast car ran from one apparent side of the room to the other. He'd looked at the wall to the Operating Room just as he thought he heard a gunshot on the other side. Then something seemed to smash into the wall. He clearly saw the wall bow inward a bit. Some dust started to fall from where the wall met the ceiling. He couldn't be sure, but he thought he heard another shot, or two.

A very short time later came the sound of an explosion, followed by some sort of concussion wave. A few seconds after that the power went off. Even the dim light of the exit sign went dark.

Now he heard somebody struggling to get the normally powered door open. The young test administrator entered holding one of those battery-powered, plug-in-the-wall, emergency lights.

"I'm going to get you out, Mr. Hancock. We've experienced a power failure in part of the building. Shouldn't be any worry for you, sir. We were less than five minutes from done with the testing. Everything's recorded. Dr. Nettles will be able to evaluate your results just fine."

Tommy dressed with the help of another emergency flashlight. Then, to his surprise, he was led down a flight of utility stairs and through a dimly lit basement full of supplies and equipment.

"This will keep you away from the problem spots. See. There's Dr. Nettles by the back door."

Finally Tommy shook hands with the head of the clinic.

"Mr. Hancock, I'm so sorry not to have been able to greet you properly before now. As you have heard, we had a bit of a situation here today. Rest assured I will evaluate your test data as soon as I am able. I will be in touch with your Cardiologist immediately thereafter.

"Marshal here will take out our emergency exit. Then we'll buy you a heart healthy meal at your choice of restaurant. Plus, Marshal will see you on your way home."

Tommy felt lucky that the bus eventually headed for Batesville was far from crowded. Not to mention, no kids in sight. As the last few passengers climbed aboard he opened his briefcase on the seat beside him. He wanted to catch up reading some of Pro Se's recent submissions on the way home. He heard the bus door close. A few seconds later someone dropped into the seat across the aisle from him.

As the bus began to move a light female voice said, "Excuse me. Aren't you Mr. Hancock?"

A bit startled, Tommy turned to look into the smiling face of a fit and trim woman with deep reddish brunette hair. She seemed possibly in her late twenties.

"Tommy Hancock, that's me. Do we know each other?"

"Not really, but I used to referee some of your kids' soccer games in Gibsonville."

"Gibsonville? I'm really surprised that you'd remember me. I don't think I was ever a member of the Soccer Dads From Hell Club…"

"Of course you weren't. I wouldn't sit across from you if you had been."

A light came on in the back of Tommy's brain, "Now I've got it! You're Emily. *Emily, the All-Seeing*, we called you. Best, most accurate ref in the region."

"The All-Seeing. I like it," she laughed as she glanced at the books in his briefcase. "You know, I've read a story or two you've published.

"I'm flattered. Pro Se serves a really niche market."

"Well, two members of that niche audience are family, sort of. I must say, though, they often laugh out loud as they read your books…"

The End

The Heart of the World

by Andrew Salmon

The mountain passes of Valoor were not to be travelled lightly. Those ignorant of the knowledge set out boldly and their progress was marked by the trail of skeletons moldering along the rough road amidst the tattered remains of their wagons and the bleached ribs of their dead horses. The pair of riders making their way along this forsaken wasteland were not oblivious to these remains nor the fate they portended, but they could no more turn their mounts as they could turn back time.

In the lead was Tohan, the setting sun turning his skin the color of copper while highlighting his long hair bleached white by the sun and probing the tangled mass of his square cut blonde beard. Powerful muscles clenched and rolled under the skin in time to the rocking of the horse, his broad shoulders drooped with fatigue.

Behind Tohan, eyes fixed on the horizon while her horse plodded rhythmically was Kandra, fair of face with large eyes blue as a mountain stream. The dust coating her features did little to mar her beauty and the limp mane of red hair that resembled tendrils of rust cascading down her shoulders.

Their weary horses limped along the part of the pass now uncluttered with earthly remains as they continued their ascent. Few made it this far into the realm of Valoor and those that did either never returned or forever held their silence when the matter came up. Over the course of his search, Tohan, too, had seen the eyes of such men and women go dead when Valoor was mentioned. He did not understand their reticence as Tohan himself had approached Valoor early in his journey, finding it a sparse land of craggy peaks and scrub brush before turning away.

Tohan lead the way upwards, barely conscious of what he was doing. Fatigue was an old companion at this point. So much so that he could no longer recall ever feeling rested and refreshed though there had been a time that leisure was all he knew.

Seven times the burning lion had chased the great snow owl across the heavens. Tohan had endured the heat of the lion's burning mane scorching his flesh from above as he pressed on relentlessly as the days became years. The night hours spent staring bitterly into the crackling fired beneath the glow of the Great Owl's silvery white wing were as equally arduous. The days tortured his body while the nights flayed his mind with memories. For always the great weight lay heavily upon him through the years and no season brought so much as a moment's reprieve from his duty.

Kandra's horse nickered behind his mount. This was followed by a slight cough from Kandra against the dust stirred by the twilight wind.

"We must camp," she said, her voice made raspy by thirst. "It is not wise to move through Valoor by night. Even one such as you must know this."

Tohan said nothing. Each evening he fought a duel with the elements. Desperate to continue the search at all costs, the night was his enemy, trying to postpone his redemption by throwing a blanket of stars over the world. Exhausted as he was, he felt the compulsion to carry on, always. Ever forward until atonement was attained…if it ever could be. And so he was reluctant to agree with Kandra's assessment even though he knew she was correct. He tried to remind himself that the long journey was nearing its end. Kandra had said as much. Well, she had said many things over the two years they traveled together and he doubted her wisdom for most of her claims. However this time she was right. The sun was disappearing behind the distant peaks, night was mere minutes away.

Reluctantly, he jerked the reins to the right and his mount turned into a clearing off the dusty trail. It would do for a fire and there was enough dried brush about. A shelf of stone jutted out from the rocky wall for shelter if rain might fall in this forsaken place. Tohan neither desired nor expected further comfort. A few hours of fitful sleep and he could take up his search again.

He brought his horse to a halt and slid from the worn saddle. Without so much as a glance back at Kandra, he began collecting wood for the fire.

"Ah, here the great Prince will take his rest," said Kandra mockingly. "Who shall prepare the feast?"

Kandra's taunts were as familiar to him as the ache in his lower back and the fevered memories which sprang to life whenever he closed his eyes.

"Leave me be, witch-woman."

"He who would wear the Baron Crown should have patience with his subjects."

"What know you of this? I was born to the Baron Crown. You are a common caster."

Her laugh was throaty and deep. "You were born a fool whose stupidity has doomed us all. And there is nothing common about me, I assure you."

"I was a fool to listen to your lies," said Tohan, energy fueled by frustration coloring his words. "Your false promises that your magic would lead us through to Valoor's keep and the Heart of the World. What was it you said? Yes, I recall them now: 'my magic will light the way to the prize and your triumphant return to the Baron Lands'. That was two years ago and here we are at the Valoorian pass and not a sign we are on the right path. Where is the dark lord's keep? Show it to me, spell caster, and perhaps I will believe that you are good for more than merely consuming your share of our meager rations."

Kandra's eyes became sharp as flint as she fixed her gaze upon the tall figure before him. She held his gaze while his fur wrap swayed in the faint twilight breeze. "I see how blind a prince can be. How he grows stupid by narrowed vision. Two years! It has seemed more like twenty! And that is by your will, not mine. You were lost when I found you, leagues from here, and we had to recover the ground these last years."

"That is because I had searched here before my misfortune brought us together. Old Valoor is a myth, these lands are uninhabited."

A grin like that of a serpent stretched Kandra's full lips. "Valoor's magic works well on the weak minded."

"Mind your tongue, woman."

"Blind to all truth are you? We are on the right path. You were on the right path years ago. Why did you give up the search? Have you never wondered? Knowing you as I do, I'm sure you did not. Certain were you that there was nothing to be found here. Is this not so?"

Kandra's words struck a chord in Tohan's memory. Thinking back to his time here, there was a certainty. He'd grown tired, his food all but gone, and nothing to show for his search through the shrouded mountains. He'd turned from the path without a second thought. Could there be truth in Kandra's words?

"I speak truth, Prince" said Kandra.

Tohan had often wondered if she could read his mind but this was folly. It was said of her kind, the spell casters, but that was in centuries past. Still, his father had taught him how to keep a chamber in his mind for his innermost thoughts and Tohan had created one just in case the old stories were true. Perhaps he was being too cautious. Her so-called magic had been a faint ghost of the magic of old. She could predict an approaching storm. Her sense of direction was also keen. A mundane fire spell helped begin the night when it was time to camp. And she had directed them here when he could not recall the route back to this dead place, home only for goats and wild stallions.

"It was Valoor who kept you from seeing the truth," Kandra went on. "He blinded your thoughts and your eyes, showed you empty valleys and clear mountain peaks. That you were so easily turned from the path does not surprise me."

"Nonsense," replied Tohan. "I road this path for days. There is nothing here."

"Made it this far, did you?"

Tohan scanned the terrain as it faded to deep purple beneath the setting sun. "No. I was satisfied with my search and turned back long before."

Kandra brushed past him and strode to the edge of the clearing, her small feet kicking up clouds of dust. With one leg she pushed the branches of a shrub aside to reveal the remains of a camp fire. The blaze was long dead, the ashes stirred about the circle of stones by the ceaseless winds. A stick had been stabbed into the center of the ring with such force that it merely leaned to one side due to the wind.

Tohan gaped, his mind a miasma of thought.

Kandra gazed back at him over her shoulder. "I've seen you douse our fire in this manner every night these two years. As if you were stabbing at the heart of your shame."

Tohan's gaze went from the cold fire to Kandra and back again.

"So you see, you did come this far. Valoor blinded you to how close you were to his keep."

Tohan swallowed as he fought to marshal his thoughts. "Then where is it? I've listened to you prattle on about how strong your magic would grow once we were in sight of the keep. Show it to me then. Let me see you in your glory."

The smile dropped from Kandra's face to be replaced with the furrowed brow of concern. She made no answer as she released the branch and returned to the horses. Head down, she hobbled the animals and began collecting stones for the fire. The last rays of the sun turned the sky to a bed of burning embers as she worked in silence.

Tohan was glad for the silence. He watched the darkness consume the land as he shifted his fur covering on his broad shoulders. His skin itched with the insects of the road and their unending hunger. He could smell his own odor; feel his dry, matted blond hair rasping on his head. The sour taste in his mouth from dried meat and brackish, warm water, his chapped lips.

It had not always been this way. Born a Baronian prince, his life had been one of leisure and excess. Nothing had been denied him and he'd grown accustomed to his needs being met instantly. The light touch of his handmaidens as they bathed him and saw to his other needs as well. The finest meats, fruits, fish and fowl always to hand when he hungered; cool water, sweet wine to slake his thirst, and an empire waiting for his will to command. His destiny was laid before him like the finest tapestry, each beautiful line stitched to the next forming a whole few could dare imagine. How often he looked back at that spoiled youth, the irresponsible fool drunkenly carousing on the night of his twentieth birthday. The ignorant, selfish child who had perished that night.

Kandra's pained cry brought Tohan back to the present. He whirled around to see her pitch forward to lay face down in the dust. At the same instant the brush behind her shivered as creatures out of the darkest nightmares burst forth.

The horrors before him gave Tohan a moment's pause as he drew his sword. Roughly the size of lions, the monsters were an obscene amalgam of man and scorpion. Shiny, black insectoid legs the width of saplings propelled the mottled carapace of each of the three abominations. The pale, human torsos thrust out of the trunks like the centaurs of myth. The arms, scaled and glistening, extended from the shoulders to end at lethal claws as wide around as Tohan's thighs.

These scorpion men clattered around Kandra, sprawled senseless and unmoving, to close on Tohan. Very well. With Kandra out of the fight and forgotten by the creatures, Tohan was free to meet their challenge.

Seeing their intention to surround him with his back to the shelf of rock, Tohan sprang into action.

The monster in the middle of the trio stopped short and arched its rear up in the air. It was then that Tohan realized just how much like scorpions these creatures truly were. A sectioned tail with a stinger as big as a gourd stabbed down at him. He swung his sword with blinding speed and sheered the bulbous weapon from the tail. A shrill wheeze burst from the creature's gaping mouth framed by bloodless, human lips and the scorpion man lurched to one side.

Tohan skirted past the reeling thing and turned just as the monster on the left lunged with an open claw at his legs.

Tohan danced to one side and brought his sword down to cleave the claw from the arm before its serrated edges could snap closed. He dodged the other claw, slicing a piece out of the hard shell as the blade edge scraped along the claw's length but did no real damage.

Knowing the creature would use its stinger, he timed his next thrust. As the torso tipped to allow the stinger to arc over the back, Tohan leaped and with both hands drove his blade through the back of the crouching scorpion man. There was again the haunting wheeze and the figure collapsed, legs twitching in their death throes.

Tohan's sword was caught and in the frantic seconds it took to yank the blade free, the remaining scorpion men closed in.

He pulled a keen dagger from his hip scabbard and threw it at the injured monster in one smooth motion. The creature halted its charge to bat the dagger away; this delaying action gave Tohan the time he needed to free his blade.

Meanwhile the third scorpion man, perhaps the more cunning of the three, scrabbled around the dead body of its comrade to get behind Tohan after a feint with its stinger forced him to leap and roll out of reach.

Tohan feigned distress on the ground and the injured monster closed in. Deprived of its stinger, it would use its claws and Tohan was ready for this. He rose to one knee to meet the charge. A two-handed thrust drove the tip of his blade through the gaunt chest of the thing, piercing the heart and out the through the upper back. The creature shuddered. Tohan felt the fetid exhalation of its death rattle waft past him as he withdrew the blade and stood in one fluid motion.

He was between the jerking claws of the dead creature and this saved him for the third scorpion man lanced its stinger at him only to impale one of the thrashing claws.

Tohan swung his sword, felt it grind along the ridged torso ineffectually as he leaped to safety over the now still arm of the dead monster.

He returned to the rock shelf. With two fallen scorpion men to either side, this position was defensible as the remaining creature could only approach between the bodies while Tohan, being smaller, could evade and attack while using the corpses for cover.

The last scorpion man hesitated.

Tohan pressed his advantage and came forward. The cliff edge was at the back of the creature. He hoped to force it to retreat from his attack and plunge to its doom.

He managed three steps before being stabbed from behind. Venom like lava burned through his back and shoulders. Tohan turned, his sword limp in fingers gone numb, to see a fourth scorpion man perched atop the rock shelf, its torso hunched as the stinger tail lowered behind. Tohan's nerveless lips parted but no sound was uttered as his poisoned thoughts swirled. His legs gave out and he crumpled to the sand and lay still.

• • •

Tohan was back in his ancestral homeland. It was the fateful night the hell demons marked him for special torment. It was to have been a happy occasion. He was a man this night and this was cause for celebration. Preparations for the betrothal ceremony were underway. The blast of trumpets echoed along the narrow spaces between the ancient buildings. Music and dancing in the streets. Feasts upon every table.

The revelry was to have ended at evening when he claimed his bride from amongst the caster women who tended the Heart of the World in the great statue of Cardac, the Supreme Caster. Legend held that all life was tinged by the sacred gem…it was a massive stone as large as a man's head…and gazing into its crimson depths was like trying to drink in the ocean with one's eyes.

Tohan's joy was tempered. His father lay ill, the Baronial Crown heavy on his fevered brow. The casters and lay healers had examined his father, there was nothing to be done and Tohan's father had been left in isolation in the royal chambers as tradition dictated.

The ruler's trusted servant, Melkan, had sidled up to Tohan swaying drunkenly at a parapet of the great castle gazing down with both expectation and mortal fear at the joyous subjects he might be called upon to rule sooner than expected. He had consumed much wine over the course of the carousing and his eyes were heavy with intoxication when Melkan took him by the arm and imparted his father's wishes.

The message had to be repeated three times before it pierced the fog in Tohan's brain. He staggered off immediately in the direction of the secret entrance to the royal chambers.

The bedside meeting with his father lasted mere moments or hours, Tohan could not recall. The stillness and darkness of the spacious room reduced Tohan to a somnambulant state after the drunken feasting. His father, pale and skeletal, had rasped in emphatic, dry whispers Tohan could barely follow in his addled condition.

And then he was outside the chamber, confused as to whether or not he had just arrived or had already been dismissed by his father. Turning this way and that in his confusion, a flagon of wine presented itself and he snatched it up, draining half its contents in a single draught. Yes, it was time for him to take a wife. His father, Gods bless him, had looked all in (ah, he had spoken to the old man) and Tohan was certain he'd be called upon to rule shortly.

Only it should be he, Tohan, that his subjects worshipped and not that hunk of red stone in the statue's breast. Was that what his father had told him? He could not be certain. With his brain so clouded by spirits, it struck him as a sound idea at any rate and made haste to Cardac's Cathedral. None barred his way…he was heir to the Baronial Crown after all…and the cathedral was momentarily deserted as the Baronial Hall was prepared by the casters for the betrothal ceremony.

His footsteps echoed in the vast cathedral. He set the empty flagon down on the marble floor and studied the pit around the statue. Cardac's terrible likeness had been carved from a pillar of granite that thrust from the middle of a circular hole in the earth. It was said the pit descended to the center of the world or the first of the twelve hells. And the cathedral had been built when Cardac and the first casters entered the Baronial Lands with the Heart of the World.

Tohan, emboldened by drink, leaped the expanse of the pit to land on Cardac's stone feet. From there he scaled the giant statue. His great strength compensated for his lack of coordination and he soon found himself at the hollowed receptacle in the statue's breast where the Heart of the World had resided for centuries.

Tohan fumbled for it. It came loose more easily than he expected and he almost dropped it. He tucked it safely under one arm and screwed up a bleary eye as he contemplated how he was going to get down without falling into the bottomless pit.

He spied the viewing platform the casters used to meditate before the Heart of the World and tend to it as needed. He'd forgotten all about the platform and his feet were inches from the walkway leading back from the cathedral floor. Giggling drunkenly, he gingerly got both feet upon the platform and staggered towards the ladder.

The floor of the temple rocked like a ship in a storm to Tohan's senses. He put both hands over the gem…warm as though it pulsed with hot blood…when a cold, clammy hand fell upon his forearm.

"A true leader needs no bauble," hissed the dark stranger suddenly at Tohan's side.

"My father said as much," Tohan slurred in reply. "I think he did at any rate. He said a lot of things. And here I am."

"Let me free you to rule unhindered," the figure spoke again, tugging at the gem.

Tohan blinked his eyes, trying to clear his vision, and the figure resembled a man and an insect-like horror from one moment to the next.

Time suddenly pressed itself upon Tohan. The betrothal! Was he late?

Absently, he thrust the immense gem at the figure and pushed past. The stranger was instantly forgotten as soon as Tohan's back was to him.

● ● ●

Then time jumped again. The evening before his father's funeral. The lamentations of his subjects. The Baronial Crown on a satin pillow at Tohan's right hand, yet he could not take it up.

He had been seen exiting the Cathedral of the Heart. News of the missing gem had interrupted the betrothal ceremony and panic had ensued. The realm would be lost without the gem. Blight, famine, disaster loomed. The casters berated him mercilessly, their desperate ire making them forget their place. Who were they to heap shame on the rightful heir to the crown? He was tempted to remind them of their place during the chaotic moments but the time was not yet right.

The casters invoked the ancient laws. None could rule before making the pledge that was made before the Heart of the World. Tohan could not take his father's place until the gem was found and returned to its rightful place. In truth, he needed no such prodding. For once the mist of drunkenness had cleared from his mind; he recalled his father's rushed, whispered words. The quest to find the Heart of the World and return to the Baronial lands had to be undertaken without delay. Everything depended on it.

And so the journey had begun. Years passed but they did not soften Tohan's zeal. Travelers, traders and nomads, taking him for one of their own, spoke of the blight that had afflicted the Baronial lands. An invisible hand squeezed Tohan's heart as he listened to their tales of failed crops, men, women and children shuffling about with sunken, bleary eyes. Sickness, weakness, lingering death hanging over everything - a society dying by slow degrees. The lands were thought to be cursed and were avoided by those who called the roads home. Even the Baronial enemies did not sound the march for this reason. But now there was some talk of defying the curse and taking the Baronial

lands before there was nothing left to harvest from them. This news had reached Tohan around the same time Kandra had inserted herself into his quest with her promises of leading him to the Heart of the World after so long. Their meeting had been no accident. Of that he had no doubt. The casters had grown desperate by that time and his inability to find the gem had spurred them to send one of their own to ensure his success for their own continued existence.

But was he already too late...

• • •

Tohan awoke with a start. His spasm rattled the stout chains around his wrists and ankles. Every muscle in his body ached and movement was agony. The poison! He shook his head and instantly regretted the action. The last time he'd felt such discomfort was the morning after his father died. But this was a different type of poison. By sheer force of will, he forced his mind to focus. Yes, the venom paralyzed, stretched the muscles taut as bow strings as it worked through the body. Kandra had told him of Valoor's potions; it was said he was a wizard of great power. He'd scoffed then but now believed her words to be true.

He did not know if the clanking of his chains had alerted any of the guards. He forced himself to stillness and listened. Nothing. Good. He needed a moment to consider a means of escape.

But this was not to be. No sooner had he cast his eyes over the chains seeking weakness and finding none, that a heavy door banged open somewhere beyond his vision. Now the echo of footsteps drawing near reached his ears. Tohan feigned unconsciousness in case an opportunity for freedom presented itself. This seemed unlikely as two armed men and a scorpion man rounded the far corner of the wide hallways. The men, eyes vacant, resembled the scorpion man's deathly pallor but these were still men with hands and two legs. While one of the men lowered a lance at Tohan's breast and the scorpion man raised his stinger in readiness, the third unlocked the chains that clattered to the stone floor.

Eyes open the barest fraction, Tohan, unarmed, glimpsed little he deemed favorable and allowed himself to be carried from the place on the back of the scorpion man, staring up at the creature's stinger as it bobbed above him like the head of a cobra with each step.

Their destination was a great hall hewn from the solid rock of the mountain. Round air shafts cut through the ceiling allowed sunbeams to enter at either end and a diffuse illumination kept the shadows at bay. To one side of the chamber was what seemed to be a wizard's lair with jars and vials of various herbs, plants and liquids with magical properties. In the center of the chamber was a large, black throne and around the circumference ran a colonnade with recessed alcoves displaying riches from golden armor and silver skulls to chests of precious stones.

As Tohan was unceremoniously dumped off the back of the scorpion creature and onto the cold stone floor, two items caught his eye. In one of the shaft beams lay Kandra. Still insensate as he had last seen her though her breathing seemed labored as if her body fought a fever. Behind her, in an alcove set in direct line with the throne, was the Heart of the World.

Tohan had found it at last!

There was no time to savor the moment as a maroon curtain parted on his left and Valoor strode boldly into the room. Tall, cadaverously pale and with a reptilian cast to his sharp features, Valoor conveyed a sense of ancient times when a host of bloodlines had provided a variety of life the present could not match. As much as he resembled a man, he was as much serpent and the claws at the end of his abnormally long fingers were more appropriate for a jungle cat. Green feline eyes, the broad nose of the mountain gorilla and jutting vampyric fangs added to this deadly personage.

"Awake at last," Valoor croaked. "We shall begin."

Tohan's blood ran cold. Valoor's appearance may have been the stuff of nightmares but it was his voice that stabbed into Tohan's memory. This had been the voice of the dark figure so eager to relieve him of the gem those years ago. There was no mistaking it.

Valoor's next words removed all doubt. "The Baronial prince. We meet again, though I would be surprised if you recall our first encounter."

"I remember."

"Your capacity for spirits is commendable however imbibing did have its consequences, eh?" Valoor chided. "Still, I suppose I owe you some gratitude for your assistance in my obtaining the gem."

"You took it from me, monster."

"Yes, I did. I was not referring to that, however. Your ridiculous betrothal ceremony drew people from all of the free lands, allowing me to enter the city undetected. A simple spirit spell in the wine to ensure a clouded mind when I sent you for the gem and obtaining it was simplicity itself in the end. How was I to know the idiots of this woman's clan would all be off seeing to their traditions and had left the gem untended?"

This gave Tohan pause. To his memory, it had been his father's words that had sent him to the cathedral. He had been very drunk, of that there could be no doubt; had he misremembered? Had his entire quest been initiated from the wrong motivation? It made no difference at this stage. He was here and he must have the gem if he is to save his people. He had come too far to alter his course now.

"I am here to reclaim the Heart of the World."

Valoor chuckled. "You amuse me but that is not why you are still alive."

"And the woman? What torment have you inflicted upon her?"

"None. My minions did not touch her. My eyes and ears abroad tell me her people are dying in your homeland. Their magic cannot be sustained, it appears, without the gem. Perhaps she is suffering from some empathic fever."

If what Tohan suspected were true, he dared to hope. Slowly he inched his way towards the guard with the lance. "Then what is to be our fate?"

"Two of my servants were killed in capturing you. You and the woman shall be their replacements."

"If so, why were we not transformed straight off. Why the shackles? Why the delay?"

"You do value yourselves highly, if you suspect some master plan to seal your fates," said Valoor. "You and the woman are insignificant. You attempted to steal my property. You killed two of my servants. And so a punishment is due. The transformation process is of long duration and is excruciatingly painful. I would have you both awake for that. This is the extent of my plans for you. The woman is taking too long to recover so we shall begin with you."

There was nothing further to be gained by talk. Earlier than he preferred, Tohan made his move.

Driving his foot backwards, he shattered the knee of the lanceman behind him. The man groaned, collapsing. Tohan relieved him of the lance as he fell. Spinning it point forward, he drove it through throat of the scorpion man as it tensed to spring, then he swung the stout wood shaft to strike the temple of the last guard who fell in a heap.

Shifting his grip on the lance, Tohan launched it at Valoor's breast. The wizard spread his hands out to the side as if willing the sharp point to pierce his chest. The blade stopped in mid-air, bare inches from the folds of the dark robes at his breast and the weapon hung there, suspended. Valoor smiled.

"Did you think I wanted your precious gem because I admired its color and grain? Fool! It is a lens to augment magic, shadow-magic especially. All these years on the hunt and you have learned nothing."

Tohan watched the gem begin to pulsate with energy as Valoor's outstretched palms glowed with gathering spells. Kandra's arm jerked where she lay behind Valoor but her body remained still. Yes, Tohan had read the signs correctly. He was certain. "I learned all I needed to know the night my father died."

"It will not be enough," Valoor concluded. "Well, let it not be said that I took my vengeance against an unarmed man. I shall utilize my weapons. I return yours to you."

With that, the lance floated back to where Tohan stood. It came to rest at eye level. He reached up and plucked it from the air, then, with a firm two-handed grip, he pointed it at Valoor. His next move surprised the evil wizard. Recalling his time with Kandra, he rattled off what spells he could recall, some only in portions, but all of the most mundane magic spells: to start the campfire, bind minor wounds, float a spoon to stir the cook pot and so on.

"Common spells uttered by one not fit to be an apprentice," observed Valoor. "You expect to defeat me with these? You know nothing of magic, dolt."

"Perhaps," said Tohan. The Heart of the World had throbbed with a deep scarlet glow at each spell he'd spoken. And Kandra's body had jerked each time as if she were being struck by arrows. At last her body rose up to float in the air behind Valoor, her arms outstretched. "But I know the mummer's sleep," Tohan went on "And the sleeper has awakened."

Kandra opened her eyes and they were fire.

Twin beams of energy shot from her eyes to impale Valoor from behind. An inhuman roar burst past his bloodless lips as his back arched and he threw his head to one side in agony. His robes burst into flames while his hands fought to conjure a counter spell. The red glow of the sacred gem tinged the chamber with pulsating red light until it appeared the walls were coated in blood.

Tohan saw the cold glow of black magic gathering once more in Valoor's palms. They must finish him before the element of surprise was lost.

He lunged forward, thrusting with the lance. Kandra, in full control of her magic, lifted Valoor off the ground and propelled his twisting form to meet the rushing point of the lance. Magic sparked off the metal blade, the wood shaft vibrated in Tohan's fists. But his thrust was true. The blade slid easily through the breast of Valoor and blue-black energy erupted in all directions. Tohan lost his hold on the lance and was thrown backwards. The energy washed over Kandra who collapsed to the floor, her eyes returning to their natural hue.

When the energy had dissipated and the stars ceased dancing before Tohan's eyes, he regained his feet and leaped for the huddled, smouldering form in the center of the room. Valoor lay writhing in the remains of his robes, his flesh blackened and smoking. A nauseating stench of burnt flesh filled the chamber.

"Think... you've... won," Valoor wheezed. "Think... you're... free?" His lips stretched into a hideous rictus displaying blackened fangs, Valoor laughed until black blood burst onto his breast and his head fell back in death.

Fists clenched at his sides, Tohan stepped over the form of the dead wizard and strode to the alcove where sat the Heart of the World. Hungrily he lunged for it, taking the gem into his hands. It was warm from the energy that had passed through it. With the object of his long search in his hands, he was almost overcome with the urge to smash it for all the pain it had caused, to vent his rage upon it. But this would accomplish nothing save to doom his people.

"Tohan, no!" shouted Kandra as she regained her feet, her eyes glowing once more, hand poised to conjure. She was a caster at full power in that moment and he was aware of the danger he was in.

Still, it was not her urging but, rather, his father's words that stayed his hand. He thrust the gem under one arm and faced Kandra. "By all the hells, let's go home!"

● ● ●

Their return to the Baronial lands was met with anemic celebration. The return of the gem was a cause for joy but the people appeared to inhabit the land of the dead. Decay was everywhere in the great city. The stench of death spread from every alleyway, every window, every doorway. The people shuffled about in soiled rags, refuse was heaped in the street to be fought over by curs. Stores were boarded up or simply abandoned. Thick creeper vines scaled every wall, probed every crack in the masonry. Everywhere one looked there were signs of rot.

The Heart of the World dispelled a measure of gloom and no one who laid tired eyes upon it was ignorant of what its return portended. There were many layers of despair to be scraped away from the people and the city, and sight of the gem could not immediately complete so burdensome a task. It was but the first step and it sent a ripple through the streets.

The road back from Valoor's realm had not been easy. Kandra's enhanced magic had swelled her head and she no longer seemed eager to follow his lead. She confirmed his suspicions about the mummer's sleep. It had been tied to the gem, which had raised her magic to full intensity in time to destroy Valoor. And that magic was still with her, as she pointed out constantly, though it gradually faded with each passing day as they drew closer to home. The return of the gem to Baronial possession did not placate her and she took every opportunity to remind him of what had transpired back home and how the misfortune was all down to him; that the gem was lost in the first place and the caster's magic had been reduced as a result. Her impatience to return home was palpable and did nothing to ease Tohan's own. His people needed him and he would not fail them.

Kandra's first stop was the cathedral and her fellow casters, for amongst them the news was met with elation that defied the stoic public image of the sect. She had wanted the gem to show to her people but Tohan would not hear of it despite her insistence. He had let it out of his sight once before and this time it would stay with him until needed. For his part, he prepared for what was to follow.

That night, Tohan called for the coronation ceremony, invoking the sacred rights. With the gem back in his possession, the past was not forgotten and many eyed him with hatred and resentment for the years of pain and suffering he'd caused. But those days were ended now that the Heart of the World had been returned and it was with lighter spirits that the royal court prepared for the ceremony the following evening.

It was to be a most solemn, formal affair. The best robes were prepared; the women donned what finery they still possessed. And ceremonial arms were burnished from broadswords to the finest daggers. The casters dusted off their scarlet robes not seen in the cathedral these last years of decay. This day would see the return of prosperity to the Baronial lands and the hungry bellies and weary backs were forgotten in favor of fine dress. And if the sword belts needed to be tightened a notch or two for the ceremony; well, that would change now that the Heart of the World was with them again.

● ● ●

At last, the time for the ceremony arrived. Fires roared in the cathedral torches. The flicker of flames lit the faces of the gathered, glinted off ceremonial armor and weapons. Sparks seemed to fly from the jewels set in the great statue. Tohan had been bathed and dressed in a tunic so white it hurt the eyes to stare at. His body cleansed and perfumed, his beard neatly trimmed, his father's sword at his hip, he was the very image of the worthy heir as he sat the throne in the great cathedral. All of the casters were in attendance of course. Clad in their scarlet robes and gathered in their honored place next to the great statue made it look as if a bonfire was raging out of control there. Kandra had been selected (Tohan believed it was more a case of her insisting) to receive the Heart of the World after the coronation for the placement ceremony where it could be set in its rightful place in the breast of Cardac.

Tohan was not called upon to speak during the coronation. The casters handled the proceedings. Kandra directed him to stand while she invoked the ancient litany. Then it was time for him to show the congregation the Heart of the World as a symbol of his promise to the people. He removed it from its sacred wrappings and held it high for all to see. A collective gasp met this action and relieved tears formed in the eyes of the people, the casters especially. This done, he clasped the gem to his breast while Kandra anointed him with the sacred oils and the Baronial Crown was placed upon his head.

It was done. The Baronial lands had a new ruler and the Heart of the World was with him.

During the great ovation which ensued, trumpets blared to alert the commoners outside that a new era had begun. A growing impatience amongst the casters encouraged Tohan to move things along. They wanted the gem back under their protection as the return to the old ways favored them most of all.

He rose from the throne and raised one hand to quiet the crowd while the other clasped the gem to his breast. The cheers died off and the faces of the ruling officials gazed up at him expectantly. Kandra cast a glance at the casters for this was not part of the sacred tradition. The new ruler did not address his subjects until the Heart of the World had been returned to the breast of Cardac. Her gaze shot daggers at Tohan but he ignored her silent protest. He ruled now and if he wished to address the assembled, he would.

"My people, I am reminded of my father this night," he began. "The transgressions of the past are still being felt today and it is with a heavy heart that I remind you of them at this happy occasion. I brought hardship to us all and my reign will be dedicated to eradicating them from your hearts and minds. My great crime from that night is known to you all and we'll not say more about it. But I come to rule you in truth and honesty and there is a second crime of which you are unaware. As my father lay dying, and after the casters had tended him, I was called to his room!"

A gasp of disbelief rose up.

"Breaking with the tradition of isolation, yes," said Tohan. "However for this transgression I ask no forgiveness. For it is from my father that I learned the truth that night. And it was a truth that convinced me that the Heart of the World must be returned to the Baronial Lands so that we might all be free from bondage."

With that, he raised the gem over his head and threw it down into the bottomless chasm around the statue. The gem struck the granite leg of the statue and shattered, its shards catching the light as they plunged ever downward. A burst of energy surged out of the chasm to wash over the assembled.

"See the casters for what they are!" shouted Tohan. "Soul vampires who have leeched our will and life for centuries without end! Behold!"

The casters began to contort in their place as their earthly disguises fell away with the last of their magic. Their teeth lengthened to fangs, their skin turned pale and leathery as their hair fell in clumps.

"Slay them good citizens!" ordered Tohan. "Destroy them!"

Tohan had drawn his sword and lunged forward to drive his blade into Kandra's squirming form. All semblance of her beauty mask was gone and the rodent-like features of a crone had taken their place.

The hall became a madhouse. The people were slow to react but the evidence of their own eyes convinced them that Tohan's words were true. They faced scarlet clad monsters. Blades were drawn and the battle ensued.

Tohan seized Kandra to hold her upright after his lethal stab. "You thought me your pawn as you heaped insults upon me. But I knew. My father had revealed all, told me the gem was the secret magnet of your power. Told me to send it away to weaken your kind though it would mean your feeding upon my people in its absence. Told me that it was the casters who fed on him at the end, drained him to death because he had learned your secret!"

He withdrew the blade and Kandra collapsed to her knees.

Tears sprang into Tohan's eyes. "Only the search was not to have been so long! Damn me! That was my great failing and Valoor's treachery. Oddly, I have you to thank for setting me on the right path again. The path to freedom was clear. Return the gem when you and your ilk were at their lowest ebb…as feeding on human spirit cannot match the energy of the gem you all thrive on…reveal the casters for what they are and let the people free themselves from your slavery."

Kandra's wrinkled, hideous face snarled at him for his treachery.

"Look! Look as the Baronial people reclaim their freedom!"

With an anguish cry, Kandra pitched to one side and lay still in a pool of spreading black blood. All around them, the slaughter continued. The casters, weak from their years without the power of the gem could not summon the magic to strike down the rebellion. They all fell and were put to the sword.

Tohan watched the blows struck for freedom and looked to the future as the slaughter continued.

The End

The Aquarium
by Tony Sarrecchia

She stood, naked, in the hallway. In this light, the blood that dripped from her fingers and pooled by her bare foot had a dark brown color. When did she lose her shoes? Her chest rose and fell in a rapid pattern, as if she had been in a fight for her life. She teetered, and put a hand on the wall to support herself. Later, one of the local tabloids would use a photograph of that almost perfect, albeit blood-stained, handprint in a series of articles outlining the horrific events leading up to this day. For now, though, it was nothing more than an impression of a girl trying not to lose her balance.

A dog barked in one of the apartments. Poor thing, she thought, he just wanted to go out…he was a prisoner, just like her. That thought got her moving. Bad things were here, and she had to go….somewhere. Using the axe for support, she started to force herself to a standing position. A cramp lanced through her shoulder and arm as if she'd been swinging…she shot straight up and turned around. A window high on the ceiling that looked as if it hadn't been cleaned since Reagan was president let in just enough light for her to see the rest of the hallway.

Peeling paint did a poor job of covering a wall punctuated with cracks and water-stains. Holes from fists or hammers exposed the wooden framing under the wall. Her heart was jumping like the violin refrain from the movie Psycho. At her feet lay a naked dead man. She wasn't a doctor, she hadn't graduated high school, but she knew no one could survive with half their skull chopped open and parts of their brain oozing out from the wound. His hands lay severed from his body. She looked between his legs and she doubled over…dry heaving next to his shoulder.

"Jesus Christ, lady, what the fuck?"

She looked up…a boy no more than thirteen holding a bag from a local bodega stood wide-eyed and open-mouthed as he took in the scene. His hair was long and his jacket was too big for his slight frame. The woman wanted to run, but her feet wouldn't listen. The dog continued to bark.

The boy broke the wall of silence, "Is that a bullet hole?" He walked toward her avoiding the splatter and body bits. She put her hand where the boy was looking and felt a ragged hole in her forehead. Had she been shot? Perhaps that was why she couldn't remember her name or why she was naked. He reached out to her.

"Come with me lady, you need help."

• • •

"Are you dumber than a bag of pubes? Why would you bring her into your mother's apartment?"

"I couldn't leave her out in the hall, Unk. She needed my help."

Doc shook his head. "You're a fucking accessory to murder now. How is your mom gonna feel about that?"

"I don't know. She hasn't been here in a week."

The woman lay on the bed in the back room of the apartment Frankie shared with his mom, Doc's sister-in-law. She heard the argument like a distant radio station; clear but foreign. Frankie had let her shower and given her some of his mom's pajamas and robes; they were almost a perfect fit. She tried to tell him her name, but she couldn't remember. It was as if she never had one.

The door to the room flew open slamming against the wall and rattling the dishes in the cabinets.

"Who are you?" Doc leaned over the bed, his beard brushing against her pale face. The chain on his belt and knife on his side reminded her of other bikers. She began to cry.

"Nice bedside manner, Uncle Sal."

"I didn't do anything to her. She's fuckin' psycho. Probably cranked up on meth…look at those eyes."

The woman had drawn her knees up to her to chest and was rocking in the bed. "How about it, sister, did you do some bath-salts?"

"Give her a break, Unk, she just killed a guy in self-defense. Dude shot her in the head."

"He did, huh?" Doc asked.

He touched her bandage and she pulled away her eyes darting around as if she were looking for some way to escape.

"Darling, if we were the bad guys you'd already be dead. Or restrained. Now let me look at your head."

"That should make her feel *real* safe," Frankie said under his breath.

The woman flinched when Doc pulled the gauze away from her skin. A puzzled looked crossed Doc's face and he ran his hand through his beard. "You dressed this?" He asked Frankie.

"Yeah. I followed the instructions in the medic book you gave me."

"You did a good job." Doc looked at the wound again: the skin between her eyes was twisted and torn away. A bruise was beginning to form.

"Thanks. I followed all the steps. It wasn't easy; she kept trying to fight me. But I think she trusts me now." Frankie was smiling.

"Don't be too pleased with yourself Frankie, I still know rocks with more sense than you." He covered the wound. "You'll be alright, darling." He patted her on her back. He motioned to Frankie to meet him in the living room.

Doc was standing to the side of the window, his arm outstretched and pulling the curtain back.

"You lookin' for someone, Uncle Sal?"

Doc let the curtain drop. He pulled a .45 from under his vest and chambered a round.

"You're not going to shoot her? Are you?"

After tucking his gun in its holster on his back belt buckle, he put on his riding gloves; the ones with the pronounced knuckles. "That wasn't a bullet wound in your girlfriend's head."

"She's not my girlfriend. How do you know it wasn't a bullet?"

"Think about it, Frankie. What kind of bullet stops when it hits the skull?" For emphasis, he poked Frankie's head in the same spot as the woman's wound.

Frankie opened his mouth to respond and then closed it He squinted his eyes, wrinkles forming between his eyebrows. "What?"

"She wasn't shot. Someone took a drill and aerated her head."

Doc opened his wallet; the chain from it to his belt rubbed against his boot-cut black Levis. He handed a stained business card to Frankie. "Call this number and ask for Detective Bannister. Tell him who I am and what happened. Do what he tells you. Do not improvise."

Frankie tried to take the card but Doc pulled it up and out of Frankie's reach. "I mean it, Frank. Don't improvise. If he tells you to leave the apartment and not look back, you do it. Do you understand?"

Frankie nodded. Doc continued to hold the card out of a reach. "I need to hear you say you understand."

After a moment Frankie said the words with all the attitude a thirteen-year-old boy could muster. Doc gave him the card.

"But where are you going to go?"

Doc pulled his hair back and tied it off with a rubber band from his pocket.

"To get the sick bastard who drilled into her head."

Two things struck Doc as soon as he stepped into the hall: The first was that someone had moved the body…the second was a shovel.

He tumbled backward into the apartment. His assailant followed him, drawing back the shovel and swinging at Doc's head. He was able to pull back, avoiding the shovel base; but its edge ripped through his face, slicing through his eye. Doc drew his gun. The copper taste of blood filled his mouth. He swung the hand with the gun and connected with part of his assailant. His blood ran into his still-working eye and he fired toward the impact. Doc blinked twice knocking the blur from his good eye just it time to see the shovel filled his line of sight. The ringing from the blow followed him into darkness.

Doc woke to the smell of gunpowder sometime later. His eye felt as if someone had shot it with a pound of shattered glass. The couch was overturned. Dishes and glasses lay shattered on the floor. His bones ached like he'd been thrown from a horse and the horse came back to stomp on him. He stood and stepped, cutting his feet on the broken glass. Why would someone take his boots and socks? Doing his best to watch where he walked, he made his way to the back bedroom and opened the door. What he saw wasn't surprising. The woman was on the bed her body punctured with bullet holes. On the floor, at the foot of the bed, lay Doc's .45: Its clip was empty because someone had unloaded it into the woman.

Sirens outside sounded like banshees. Doc was certain whoever shot the woman had also called the cops. He had to hurry. His first stop was Frankie's room. He pushed the clothes on the floor away, kicking a few books and stubbing his toes in the process. Doc pulled open the closet door. Fucking kid's feet were too small; Doc couldn't fit into any of the sneakers or boots in the closet. He found of a pair of flip-flops that came close, his toes hung over the edge and the back of his feet touched the floor, but at least it offered some protection.

With his gun tucked back into his holster he looked through the peephole checking as far left and right as possible. Satisfied that no one was within striking distance he stepped out into the hallway. The sirens sounded as if they were outside the lobby of the building. He walked to where the body had been. Whoever had moved it didn't have time to clean the trail. He also knew they were the same people who took Frankie. Stupid kid. If anything happened to Frankie, Doc would make whomever hurt him feel pain in ways that even the Romans thought were too intense.

The trail of blood veered into the stairwell, clumping at the bottom and leaving smears going up to the next floor. The thundering of boots echoed on the cement walls and bounced off the metal stairs: The cops were in the stairwell. Doc moved fast to avoid them. He took the stairs heading toward the roof two at a time; aching bones be damned. On the landing of the next floor he saw broken glass and an empty fire axe case. There was a hose rolled tight in the case next to it.

The cops' boot steps were closer; Doc could make out voices but specific words were indecipherable. On the next landing the trail disappeared under the fire door to the main floor. When he was sure no one was on the other side he stepped on to the floor. He released the door and it slammed closed with a deep 'THUMP'. The sound echoed and, Doc was certain, alerted the cops on the stairs to his presence.

Halfway down the hallway the blood trail ended. Apartment 724. Doc pushed the clip into the bottom of his .45 and kicked in the door. He dropped to one knee and pointed the gun in front of him. He was aiming at a wall. To the right, the hallway opened up into a living room. He crouched and advanced...his training paying off as muscle memory and heightened awareness took over. There were smells under the usual garlic and beans flavors that filled the air. Something industrial, chemical and acidic, like vinegar but stronger. A mechanical gurgling sound played under the other noises. When he was certain the two rooms were clear, he closed and locked the door with the deadbolt since he'd pretty much killed the doorknob lock. He was hoping the cops wouldn't notice the damage.

The living room looked like something out of the television show 'Hoarders'. Boxes were stacked on top of boxes, which were stacked on top of the chairs and tables. The smell of urine brought tears to Doc's eye. There was an aquarium in the corner but the water was too murky to tell what, if anything, was in there.

The sound of running footsteps bounced off the walls and floors of the hallway. The cops were here. Doc held his breath as they ran past. He could see their tactical playbook in his head: four cops posted at every stairwell, two on the inside and two blocking the hallway. If any civilians stepped out of their apartment, the cops in the hallway would suggest they step back in 'for their own safety.' Of course, in this town, there were a hundred things that could happen but concern for innocent civilians, if such a creature existed, wasn't SOP for the cops. By now, they would have an entry and extraction team outside Amber and Frankie's apartment.

In the back of this apartment was a bedroom with black noise and light canceling curtains. In the room's center was a row of fifty-five-gallon drums. He wiped the dust from one of the small glass squares on the lid and looked inside. Like the aquarium in the other room, it was too murky to see inside the fluids. Something about those drums made Doc's stomach crawl. He was about to twist the top off one when he heard a fragile moan from a room down the hall. He trotted toward the sound, keeping his body close to the wall.

His eye grew wide. "Shit, man. What have you gotten yourself into?" Frankie lay on a yellowed mattress with brown and maroon stains. The mattress was on the floor with old newspapers spread underneath. An IV tube led from his arm to a plastic bag on a pole. Doc tilted his head and read the contents of the drip.

"You gotta be fuckin' kidding me." Doc looked around for a cloth to put over the IV's injection site. Frankie's head lolled to one side, a trail of drool followed the outline of his face. "Where is the guy who did this? He's going to swallow my boot before I shoot him." Frankie grinned.

"Elp omn." Frankie said.

"We're going to find your mom as soon as I get you out of here." Doc closed his fingers around the IV needle. "This may sting a little, hoss...Or not...you're pretty juiced up on Propofol." Doc slid the hypodermic out of the vein in the back of Frankie's hand.

Doc lifted Frankie off the mattress and put him on his shoulder before he stepped through the door. Frankie's head bounced off Doc's back. He was almost to the front door when he considered how it would look: a long-haired biker wearing leather stepping into the hallway with a drugged teenaged boy on his shoulders. Yeah, the cops would shoot first.

"I think I'm going to hurl..."

"Don't." Doc replied.

A deep gurgling sound rolled up from Frankie's stomach. Doc shook his head and ran

down the hall to, what he hoped, was the bathroom. It was. The smell of feces, garbage and mildew in the room was enough to make Doc want to puke. Something moved behind the plastic shower curtain. He put Frankie down and drew his gun.

With his gun in front of him, Doc pulled the shower curtain aside. A woman was lying in a tub full of rusty water. Her hands handcuffed to the spigot. On the side of her head was a lump the size of a plum and it shared a ripe plum's color. Her hair was stuck to her head in wet streaks. He put his finger on the side of her chin and turned her face toward him.

"Amber?"

Frankie's mother was the woman in the tub. He placed his gun on the cracked toilet tank and lifted her out of the tub. Whoever did this must have been in a rush because they just looped the handcuff around the spigot, leaving her free to escape. Unless she was drugged. Doc examined her lump: he didn't think it was more than a couple of hours fresh. He ran down the hall to the freezer trying to understand what type of horror show was going on in this apartment. Maybe there would be some addresses on the boxes in the living room. Doc would find the bastards who did this. He wouldn't ask his brothers for help, this would be his solo mission.

Doc wrenched open the freezer door and stumbled backward, flailing his arms and catching himself on the island counter. From the corner of an over frosted freezer, a frozen head stared back at him. A white skull peeked out from where someone had torn off its skin. The eyes were open but glassed over; Doc couldn't guess their original color.

Doc had seen severed heads; he knew a guy who wore a necklace of human ears in 'Nam. But to see one in such a commonplace setting? What kind of fucked-up piece of human garbage lived here? Inside the refrigerator were more body parts wrapped in plastic with dates written in black Sharpie on the outside. Jennifer, stripper, 22, 4/13/2015, was the label on a bag containing a foot with a rabbit tattoo. Was that the plan for Frankie and Amber? In a flash of understanding the head wound on the girl in Frankie's apartment made sense. Doc had seen this before. In Little Haiti.

Doc pulled the lid off the fish tank. Inside were a dozen green and yellow fish. Puffer fish. Behind him someone started clapping.

"Bravo, Sal. I always said you were the smart brother."

Doc spun coming face to face with his .45 in the hand of his former sister-in-law.

"Amber! Easy, darlin', I'm on your side." Doc put his hands out, palms up, in front of him.

Amber scoffed. "And whose side would that be? The side of the murdering whore who killed my man? Or maybe the side of the biker-trash family who tried to take my son from me?"

"We've had our differences, but this shit...what's happening in this apartment, is bigger than both of...wait. 'The murdering whore?' Awww no, you gotta be shitting me."

Amber stepped closer to the island. "Martin was a good man. He was taking care of me and would have taken care of Frankie too. Then that slut clocked me upside my head. I don't know how she got the drop on Martin but she hacked him apart. That's not right, Doc. No one deserves that."

"Are you hearing yourself? Your boyfriend was a killer. He drugged people with puffer fish poison. There is a fucking head in the freezer." Amber opened the freezer. Doc inched

closer to the butcher knife on the floor. "We can still get out of here, Amber. I don't know where Martin's partner is but we can call the cops in the hallway. You're just feeling the effects of the tetrodotoxin; the poison from the puffer fish. I'm guessing that is what Martin injected his victims with." Doc slid the knife behind his back. Amber looked in the freezer.

"I see you met Jerome, a tranny from the zone. He was my first."

Doc felt the world zoom in on him. He was trapped and would have to kill Amber to get out of here. How to explain it to the cops would be a step he'd worry about later.

"Partner." She spit the word. "Martin didn't need a partner, he had me. True, at first he thought I was going to be his victim, but I am no-one's victim. He chose me to be his apprentice." Amber said the last line as if being the apprentice to a serial killer was something worthy of accolades. "Now I'll do the same with Frankie. I don't think there's ever been a mother and son serial killer team." Doc moved a step closer to the front door.

"Of course, we will have to start over. You and that stupid whore contaminated this site. Oh, darling, that knife isn't going to do you much good," Amber said, punctuating the air with Doc's gun. "Have you ever taken a life? Of course you have. You're Doc Scaldero, former Marine medic, police officer and…what? Biker enforcer? Killing is a rush that's better than sex, isn't it?"

"You're crazy, Amber."

"That doesn't answer my question though, does it?"

"I'm not playing…"

Amber pumped the gun in the air and pulled back on the hammer, "do I look like I'm playing? Answer the question. Isn't taking a life…watching it drain out…listening to them begging and moaning…mmmmm…isn't that better than sex?"

"Amber…"

"I swear to God, Doc, if the next word out of your mouth isn't yes or no I will shoot you in your goddam balls."

"It's nothing like sex. It's harsh, brutal, and it drains something from me every time I do it. Is that what you want for Frankie, Amber? What about him?"

"What about Frankie? He'll come around. The right amount of tetrodotoxin and Propofol make any person open to suggestion."

"You're going to keep your kid drugged? And you wonder why I fought for custody."

Amber came around the island, staying out of Doc's reach but putting herself in point-blank range. "Do you remember my act at the custody hearing? The judge felt so sorry for me. That will be nothing compared to my act here…*Oh officer, I don't know what happened. He just broke into our apartment and killed that woman, then he took my son up here. I was able to distract him long enough to shoot him with his own gun.* Your gun already killed the slut in my apartment. How deep do you think the cops in this town will investigate? You will be blamed for all of this. Or you won't. It doesn't matter. Frankie and I will be long gone."

Doc switched knife hands and turned the blade away from his body. He could see how this was going to play out, and, in none of the scenarios, did he not end up taking at least one slug somewhere. The object, he thought, was to put that slug in the least harmful place.

"Mom?"

Amber looked away. Frankie was leaning against the wall, his face pale and lips blue. Doc leapt forward, trapping Amber's throat with his arm and pushing the knife against her face, just below her eye.

"Please don't kill her, Uncle Sal." Frankie screamed at Doc.

At that moment, someone banged on the door. "Open up in there, it's the police."

"Officers, help me, he has my son. His name is Doc Scaldero and he said he is going to kill us." Amber yelled and stomped down on Doc's bare foot. He spun holding on to her. The cops kicked in the door and three of them rushed into the room, guns drawn. Amber continued to stomp on Doc's foot and he continued to move his feet out of her range. One of the cops yelled "Gun," just before Doc felt hot balls of lead pierce his body.

● ● ●

Frankie was in a wheelchair at the gravesite. His social worker and her boss stood behind him holding umbrellas. Other than the preacher, few people showed for the interment. Doc watched from his wheelchair, his escort; however, two guards from the county lock-up did not bother shielding him with an umbrella. His lawyer believed they had a good chance of beating the serial murder wrap if Doc were willing to do four years for the involuntary manslaughter of Bryce Dean, the hooker found riddled with bullets from Doc's gun. It was bullshit of course, but that's how things worked in this city. It was the first time Doc had seen Frankie since the night in Martin's apartment. A stray bullet from one of the cops had gone through the center of Frankie's stomach and severed his spine. All things considered, Doc thought, the kid looked pretty good.

Doc's wounds, while not as life altering, were greater in number. He would walk, though with a limp. The doctors weren't sure he'd ever ride a motorcycle but Doc knew that was the one thing he would never lose. Doc looked at Frankie and waved. He couldn't be sure, but he thought Frankie smiled back.

The End

Gas Guns
& Death Rays
(A Secret Agent X Tale)
By Frank Schildiner

Secret Agent X's new base was in a lost subway tunnel underneath Central Park New York; a wide, expansive location, one unconnected to all of his previous locations. The war with the Japanese and the Nazis caused him to need to move on an almost monthly basis. But he'd destroyed three attempts at starting Fifth Columns in the United States, but more still lingered under the surface. The Black Dragon Society's lackey, Dr. Melcher, was in custody thanks to X, and spilling his every secret to Jimmy Christopher and the rest of the Secret Service. But there was also one group Secret Agent X was seeking, the Thule Brotherhood. They were said to be connected to none other than Sun Koh, the so-called Aryan Prince of Atlantis and favorite of Hitler and Himmler. The thought of that madman coming to the United States was a terrifying one, but Agent X was prepared for the worst.

Opening a file, X began examining the latest press clippings provided by his services. Each of these bureaus put aside all odd deaths, unusual fires and odd incidents for their unseen boss. All the while they acted, never knowing they were often the spark that led him to discover evil beneath the surface of the United States. Secret Agent X's mission was even more important now, with evil men ruling two countries intent on murdering millions to achieve domination of the Earth. X knew the only chance the world had was for the allies to defeat these forces, and he would work day and night to see this mission completed.

He was just examining a series of articles on the fatal fire at Cocoanut Grove nightclub in Boston. Many patrons died from the flames or smoke, but a few were found to have died with white foam on their lips...an indication of poison...very odd. And concerning since three people lost in the fire were all connected in some way to the Boston docks. The police, local and state, were calling that a coincidence and stating the fire was electrical in nature, but Agent X was not convinced. Coincidences occurred in this world, but not very often. What most people often referred to in that manner were often clues to a larger situation. More than a few times Secret Agent X uncovered terrible plots and plans by evil men because he examined what others considered unimportant.

X was about to search for more information, when the orange telephone chimed. Picking up, X changed his voice that to a fussy older man, "Yes?" he asked.

"Doctor Peace? This is Margie at the message office?" a rasping voice said, attempting to sound sing-song but failing completely.

"Yes, yes!" X barked, using Peace's frustrated sounding voice. Doctor Charles Oswald Peace was a wealthy elderly man who was always performing medical research. As such he set up a message service that received his letters, journals and packages. This was, of course, merely a cover for X to monitor the scientific advancements in the world and contact reputable and less reputable members of that community. Peace was known to be an irascible sort, so few wished to meet him, but his patronage was often sought for various projects. "What is it you want, young lady?"

Margie, who was reaching sixty and built like a Notre Dame linebacker, giggled lightly at being called young, but gathered herself, "You told us to only contact you if you received a package. One arrived for you a short time ago, delivered by a young boy. There's no postmark or return address but it sure is wrapped up tight in brown paper and string. You want that I should mail it to you?"

X closed his eyes, a wave of sorrow filling his mind and body. The greatest man who ever lived was dead and the world would never fully appreciate his illustriousness. But Agent X had one duty to fulfill for the man, a mission he would complete. One facet of Secret Agent X, one few knew existed and few would ever see in action was his sense of honor. If the man who took the name X made a pledge to anyone, at any time in his life, he would complete that word of honor. No matter the risk, no matter how much time was required, the honor of his word must be completed.

"No, young lady," X stated in Peace's voice. "Place it in the safe and I will be by shortly to obtain the object. Thank you."

Hanging up the telephone receiver, X turned to his nearby desk and opened the top drawer. Because of his lifelong mission in fighting evil, he kept few mementos from his past. But two items accompanied him no matter where he worked or used as a base. The first was a stiletto, a small sharp blade from the 19th century given to him by the most dangerous woman in the world. The story of that dagger and the woman, known to the world as Madam Rogue, was one few would ever learn. The tale was too terrifying, and just the thought caused a slight shiver of fear to run through the normally sanguine Agent X.

But the other item was far more important and brought a good memory to Agent X. This was a small brass object shaped like a pistol but possessing a wide center cylinder. This was the first version of his fabled gas gun, given to him by the its creator; a man with a mind far beyond any who lived in this world. A simple etching on the barrel read, "N.T." and suddenly Secret X was remembering a time in 1933 in New York, a day that changed his entire life and set the course for his future.

Closing the drawer, X walked over his makeup table and began to transform himself into Dr. Peace. This was a slow process, but a critical one since Peace was one of his more important secret identities. But his mind was still back on that autumn day in 1933...

● ● ●

The crisp fall weather hinted at a powerful winter coming, but Secret Agent X was unmoved by the frigid wind gusts that seemed to howl through the Manhattan streets. Besides his training in dealing with all environments and all imaginable situations, X was so focused on his targets that an earthquake wouldn't cause his attention to waver. An elderly Eskimo shaman once told him that the mind, focused on a hunt, was capable of ignoring even the most extreme temperatures. The old man's lessons hadn't been on that, no, he taught X to survive even though he was ignoring the cold.

"Many great hunters fall, not by the beast, but because their body fails. A frozen foot could be the end. You must be able to ignore the weather, but protect yourself. Survival in the hunt is all." The old medicine man explained as they walked through the frozen tundra, a land of many secrets, great beauty and terrible danger.

As such X was dressed, beneath his charcoal business suit, in a body stocking made from a material similar to silk. But this fabric, invented by X himself, was stronger and held in the bodily warmth. From the Agent's feet to neck, he was warm, only his hands and head were exposed to the elements. His hands were covered in simple leather gloves, or seemingly so. The gloves possessed a layer of sand and tiny lead pellets, rendering them a powerful weapon. A punch from X's skilled fists would possess the impact of a locomotive. The head was covered with a simple dark Homburg, but one that he could transform into a derby or a fedora with a few careful pulls. His skill his disguise was one of his greatest weapons against the forces that sought to enslave every human that inhabited the Earth.

Today's subject was a particularly vexing one, man who appeared above the law but was certain an architect of evil. From X's investigations, Bradley Taylor, was behind a string of terrible murders that appeared to be industrial accidents. Taylor, a man in his fifties who was the scion of a fortune brought about by the slave trade prior to the Civil War, appeared to be an upstanding member of the upper class of society. But he possessed a secret fascination for matters occult, having befriended the infamous Aleister Crowley while residing overseas. Under the infamous magus, known to many as 'The Most Evil Man Alive', devoted his life to the obtaining of power through the use of magic.

Secret Agent X knew Crowley, having found the man to be a ridiculous poseur and conman. He was more ridiculous than evil, unpleasant but no real danger to mankind. But those who followed his ways were apt to extreme actions, something X monitored over the years. And the result was Bradley Taylor. Unlike his mentor, Crowley embraced true evil, wishing to bring about chaos of violent death to all of mankind. As such he formed a cult based in a form of satanic ritual, which grew in size, scope and ambitions in recent days. Their rituals, X now suspected were based in human sacrifice, leading up to something terrible in scope.

Secret Agent X, having broken into Taylor's homes and secretly owned dwellings, only found hints of the man's activities. The cult leader was smart, nothing was committed to paper and his followers, all wastrels of the upper class, appeared as careful as their leader. Now X was forced to shadow the group, taxing his disguise skills to the maximum. Happily they were staying in Manhattan lately, so following was slightly easier, but X was hopeful they were close to the fruition of their secret, monstrous plan.

And it appeared he was right. Taylor stopped in the middle of a small park in midtown and was immediately joined by two men. They were familiar to X, the first being a tall bruiser with the improbable name of Loyola van Jessington. Standing six feet six inches tall, van Jessington possessed the deep chest and long arms of a bull ape and a face to match. Despite his simian appearance, the man was no fool, possessing a medical degree with a specialty in psychiatry. He appeared to be very close to Taylor, an adviser as well as a follower of the man's occult beliefs. X believed at least two of the victims of this cult died at the hands of van Jessington's terrible strength.

The second was a short man, thinly built with black hair that always appeared to glisten with some type of hair oil. He possessed large dark eyes, a small mean mouth and a hissing, high-pitched voice. This was Leo Marquis, a Hungarian by birth who moved to the United States just before the Great War. An antiquarian by trade, Marquis was an occultist who was a member of multiple cults. X knew the man was an expert with the knife, possessing a love of weapons and having trained in several blade styles both before and after he moved to the United States.

The common denominator for the trio, besides their love of Satanism was they were all sadists of the worst variety. While assembling information on all three men, X discovered all three resided in neighborhoods where house pets mysteriously vanished and homeless people were murdered by person or persons unknown. This, X knew, from his time spent learning from Sigmund Freud; these behaviors were the classic symptoms of the madman, the lover of torture and murder. And all three possessed this characteristic, having hidden their evil beneath a public facade of decency. They were monsters and Secret Agent X was the only man who knew it.

Positing himself on a bench a distance away, X pulled a newspaper from his coat and appeared to be reading the pages. But in truth he was watching the three men as they completed their public greetings. An expert at lip reading, all three men might as well be speaking with X in their midst for all the good their distance did them.

"Why are we meeting here, sir?" van Jessington asked, smiling. It was easy to read the giant's lips, he spoke with careful enunciation, and the trained diction of an academic. X knew the man possessed a phony near English accent. One cultivated to cover his Manhattan roots.

"It is clear," Marquis hissed his odd method of speaking making the reading of the man's lips slightly harder than the others, "the magus wishes us to know something of great importance. One in which nobody must hear. A public location offers the anonymity of the common man and the ability to see if anyone is attempting to follow our discussion. You fear the church? Holy inquisitors who wish to prevent the beginning of the opening of the seals perhaps?"

"Perhaps," Taylor grumped; clearly annoyed his ploy was transparent to the Hungarian. "To business. I heard him myself. I took an adjacent table at Delmonicos. He spoke at length of his device, one that in our hands will bring about the Kingdom of Perdition."

"Then we will take him and have him demonstrate it for us. He is poor and we can enrich him well. A dog of a Jew, based on his picture," van Jessington stated, smiling slightly and flexing his enormous fists.

"No Jew," Taylor replied, straightening and looking proud to be better informed than the latter. "His father was a Christian. But he is sympathetic to all weak mud people. We will place him under a bit of torture and he will be a compliant slave. A genius, but not one of us."

"Torture, good," Marquis appeared to purr. He smiled a twisted, gap tooth grin that possessed the malevolence of an evil mind.

"Yes, my dear friend." Taylor stated, clapping Marquis on the back. "You will break him, but keep his mind in tact. He is a tool for our use. The end of this world and the beginning of the new starts right now. Here he comes."

Taylor nodded as a tall, emaciated man with gray hair strode purposely through the park, heading towards the group. He wasn't paying attention to the group, heading past them with a long stride. His eyes were distracted as he passed X, crossed the street and entered the nearby Hotel Pennsylvania. A few steps behind him were the Satanists. They were far enough away to prevent causing notice, but their cold eyes were completely locked on the back of the scientific wizard.

A chill filled Secret Agent X as he recognized the man the three evil men were discussing. Nicola Tesla, the greatest mind in the world; the man who created the Alternating Current, the true designer of the radio and oh so many more inventions. If these men wished to kidnap and use the great Nicola Tesla in their plans, the world was in danger. X stood up as the Satanists entered the hotel and dropped all pretenses, dashing with incredible speed for the hotel's side. He needed to get in without being seen and stop these evil men before these terrible men's plans came to fruition.

Having memorized the layouts of every hotel in Manhattan, X knew the fastest way to get to Tesla's room without being noticed. Had he dashed after Taylor and his followers, the Satanists might realize his plans. And these men were dangerous killers, not above murdering innocent bystanders to achieve their ends. Additionally they could simply abandon their plans and wait for a different moment to strike Nicola Tesla. No, the battle had to be now and Secret Agent X needed to save the life of the great man and ensure his safety in the future.

Picking the lock in seconds, X ran down a poorly lit corridor and entered the maid's offices. The head of the section, a tall, round-faced fussy looking man in a very cheap suit was barking orders at his employees in a loud, sneering voice.

"If you can manage to get Room 284 completed, you may take a ten minute break. But don't go far; the guests from Ohio have a child who looks like a positive demon. I believe we'll need a cleanup once he completes the enormous bag of Turkish Delights he carried in. Now shoo!" The man waved imperiously at the door at a pear shaped woman in a standard maid's outfit.

The maid mumbled several inventive curses in a German dialect as she passed X, not bothering to look at him as he entered the office. The manager looked up, his face twisting into a moue of annoyance. He was about to speak, when X stepped forward and struck the desk with his hat.

"Complaints!" X snarled, leaning forward and causing the irritating man to recoil in shock. "We have received eleven complaints that you are mistreating the staff. This is leading to inefficiency and poor responses from our guests. This must be dealt with, sir. I'm afraid I have to recommend to the owners that your position be eliminated."

"What? No! Please! I can improve! Give me a chance! I can change, treat the staff differently. Please!" The manager whined, not knowing who this man was but terrified of losing his job.

"Perhaps, perhaps. I have more areas to examine. I will return in several days to check." X stated, having instantly realized the man was a bully and should be treated as such. If he could do a little good and help the employees here as well, this would be a good deed.

Stepping up to the man, he picked up the paper work on the desk and glanced quickly at the sheets. Spotting the information he required, X sniffed and dropped the paperwork back on the desk and shot the cowering, cringing man a venomous look and left the office.

Within seconds he was heading upstairs, running two steps at a time. X's powerful legs pumped hard as the floors flew past. He wasn't willing to risk waiting for a slow elevator or even a mechanical breakdown. No, his tireless frame was capable of far greater distances than the flights up to Nicola Tesla's rooms in the hotel. Secret Agent X trained daily, using techniques he learned around the world from experts in all areas. His running skills were taught to him by a family of Zulu warriors who resided in a lost valley. No warriors in history were as skilled in running as the legendary Zulus. Their soldiers were able to run fifty miles and still fight at maximum efficiency. X sent a mental thank you to Umslopogaas, son of Umslopogaas, son of Umslopogaas for his lessons and hoped the great man's tribe was never discovered.

In a short time he was in the deserted corridor of Tesla's room. There were no sounds or hints of movement, which meant one of two things. Either the Satanists were still in their way up or they were already in Tesla's room and the great scientist was in danger. In either situation, X only had minutes or less to deal with the situation and prevent any harm coming to Tesla or any of the others in the hotel.

Pulling a button off his jacket sleeve, he pressed it against the door where it stuck in place. And with a quick yank the second button was free and he stuck it in his left ear. This was a very primitive radio listening system he was testing; it was still in the testing phase of development. Unfortunately, the device was only partially working now. X could hear voices, one raised in anger, another speaking in a measured tone. The measured one could be Taylor, which would be in character with the man. X knew

Bradley Taylor always wore a revolver in a shoulder holster. He could picture the Satanist standing and pointing his weapon at Tesla, controlling the situation from the start. That made the situation both easier to control and more dangerous at the same time. But X knew how to act and would not hesitate, not even for a second.

Reaching into his pocket, Secret Agent X pulled out a small paper packet. Palming the packet in his right hand, X lifted his left leg and kicked the door. The wooden frame shook and the door flew open, slamming against the wall. X absorbed the position of all four men in a split second and exploded into action.

Tesla was the furthest away, near the window where he would feed the pigeons. At the far right side of the room, near the bathroom was Marquis, a long knife held loosely in his hand. To the far left was the enormous van Jessington, a small table splintered like matchsticks at his feet. And in the center was Bradley Taylor, a large pistol in his extended hand. A perfect setup for X's plans.

Landing his left leg forward, X hurled the packet at Taylor with the speed and efficiency that even the great Lefty Grove would admire. The paper hit Taylor in the nose and exploded, covering his face with a fine black powder. The Satanist shrieked in pain and dropped his weapon, clawing at his face. One down, two more to go.

Van Jessington, though caught by surprise, was only momentarily surprised by X's attack. The enormous man roared and charged, his speed belying his huge size. A lesser man would have been either panicked by the ferocious looking giant barreling down on them with the speed and size of a charging rhino. But Secret Agent X felt no fear at the actions of his fellow man and this massive murderous man was no exception.

Waiting until the last second, X stepped to van Jessington's left and kicked the giant in the ribs. His foot, which could shatter most men's bones, bounced off the heavy slabs of muscle that layered the huge Satanist's chest. Van Jessington howled in pain and swung out a massive arm, hitting X and sending him flying into a nearby wall.

The giant was upon X in a heartbeat, his milk bottle sized fist swinging wildly for the Agent's skull. X, who was nearly stunned by the impact, ducked downward and was only partially clipped by the giant's armed. Brightly colored lights filled his vision, but X was already exploding into action. His fingertips pistoned upwards and hammered a nerve cluster under van Jessington's arm. The massive man cried again in pain, his arm growing numb and useless in an instant.

X knew he could not fight this man as one would an average human being. This particular Satanist was huge and possessed natural defenses that would render most attacks useless. Punch this Goliath in the jaw and you were more likely to break your own hand than harm him in a brawl. No, X had to use different tactics.

Slipping out from beneath van Jessington's useless arm, X danced back several steps. He was moving on the balls of his feet like a boxer, knowing speed was one of his weapons now. Van Jessington whirled and charged, his one good hand reaching for X's neck. The Agent faked as if he was moving right and suddenly danced left, grabbing the giant's wrist and propelling the man forward at a faster rate. Van Jessington slammed into the bathroom door and shattered the wood, crashing head first into the bathtub. He was up, though slower now and moved with greater care towards X. The giant stepped out of the bathroom, his face streaming with blood from a cut on his forehead, one eye rapidly closing.

X lightly moved in and fired two quick jabs at van Jessington's injured eye. They were snapping, stinging strikes, slightly painful for X but causing annoyance to his opponent. This was the moment when van Jessington was at his most dangerous. An injured enemy, like a wounded bear, was capable of anything to save its life.

Two more jabs and the giant screamed and charged forward again. But X positioned him exactly and van Jessington bowled into Taylor. The both crashed to the ground, their limbs in a tangle. X stepped up and performed a double knifehand chop on the giant's neck. A delicate cluster of nerves connected to the brain and caused van Jessington to slump to the ground, unconscious. Taylor, who was still blinded and in pain, could now be heard feebly attempting to breathe.

But the battle was not over, the cowardly yet dangerous Marquis stepped forward, knife blade in hand. He moved with infinite calm, his twisted grin growing wider as he approached. But X wasn't going to waste time in an extended brawl with a knife expert. Scooping up Taylor's fallen gun, he aimed it for Marquis and gave the man a brief smile.

"Drop the knife and turn around." X stated and dramatically cocked the hammer.

"The gun is filled with blanks. Taylor would not risk killing Tesla," Marquis hissed and began to chuckle.

X nodded. "I believe you. Good, this makes it easier," he stated and threw the pistol into Marquis's face. The tiny occultist yelped in pain despite himself. He then shrieked even louder as Secret Agent X kicked his knife hand and shattered the delicate bones of his wrist. The blade sailed out of Marquis's now useless wall and embedded itself in the wall. A simple uppercut to the jaw knocked Marquis out and he slumped on the floor, not far from his fallen friends.

"I am not sure who you are, but I do thank you. Those foolish little men wished to make me their captive." Tesla stated his thick accent easy to comprehend.

"They were talking about some invention you spoke about at dinner," X explained, reaching for the telephone and dialing a number.

Tesla straightened up and a light entered his eyes. He was over six feet tall, thin to the point of skeletal and with gray hair that was quite thick. His eyes were very light and seemed to glow with an inner light.

"Ah!" Tesla replied, "I spoke of the Teleforce. It would end all wars. It is a directed force of energy, obtained freely from the universe. The beam would destroy planes or invaders from a distance. No man could invade another country!"

X spoke a series of phrases into the phone receiver and hung up. "If all men thought as you do, it would end all wars. But sir, consider. There are many like these creatures in the world. They would use your peace device to murder enemies and subject all of mankind to their will. Instead of peace, it would destroy all life."

Tesla stared at X, his eyes gazing deeply at the Agent. Then he nodded sadly, "I see your point. I will give you the prototype and the plans."

X stepped back and waved both of his hands. "No. I won't take anything that would kill a man. Destroy it and the blueprints. Even a good person would become a monster with that type of power."

Nicola Tesla smiled and nodded, "That was a test, my friend. I have committed nothing to paper. But my experiments proved it will work. I shall take apart my model. When others begin to experiment in that direction, I will publish but leave the important portions of my calculations out of all journals. This will divert all energy towards me."

"Thank you. Please destroy the prototypes or any notes," X suggested. "Men are coming from the government to deal with these men, so you won't be bothered again."

"Destroy? No, I shall disassemble it and tease the world. But when my end is near, I will send it to you. You can decide if mankind is ready for the Teleforce. Provide me with a place to send the package. Mister?" Tesla stated, straightening his jacket and thick gray hair.

"Doctor Peace," X replied, having just established the identity. He turned to leave, but was stopped by the strong hand of Tulsa.

"My friend, you stated something I must repeat. You wish to fight evil without killing your fellow man. This is difficult to perform, no? They will not show such morals," Tesla stated, staring deeply into X's eyes.

"It would be too easy to kill to defeat evil. I would have to become like them, which would destroy me in the end." X explained, having had this conversation while training under Madam Rogue.

"Then allow me to give you an invention I created recently. I think you will benefit." Tesla crossed the room, opened a desk draw and pulled out a wooden box. Opening it was an ornate brass gun with a huge cylinder attached.

"That is no normal gun," X said, intrigued.

Tesla smiled again. "This is a gas gun. Strictly non-lethal. The gas will render any man, no matter their size, unconscious for a time. Please take it. I will send to your address the formula for the gas."

X hesitated, but finally nodded, "Thank you, Mister Tesla."

● ● ●

That was the last time he spoke to the great man. Oh, Tesla made the papers at times and his teasing of his death ray did intrigue many governments before the war. But the man with one of the most incredible minds on Earth lived as a pauper for the remainder of his life. Too bad, but Nicola Tesla always seemed to prefer his principles to wealth.

And in his lair, Secret Agent X walked with the package towards his work bench. Sadly mankind was not ready for the genius that was the great Nicola Tesla. One day perhaps the Teleforce would be a power for good. But for now, X would reduce the device to a mere collection of parts.

The End

Tommy One
and the
Legion of Neptune

By John Simcoe

Deep inside The Cistern, a new Tommy One gasped into consciousness. He had been in a dream-like daze, but now his nerves exploded with life.

With that burst of cognizance, the water he was floating in lashed out with its coldness. His eyes adjusted, and the darkness around him started to peel away.

He took in the marble tiles etched with mystical markings that were dewy from the constant, dank conditions. Along them poured the invisible psychic tidbits that were then directed into his mind. They came together to tell him his story.

Moments before, Tommy remembered being in another place. A shipyard. He was on the hunt for the murderer that had been stalking the docks of Norfolk.

In his mind's eye, Tommy saw everything his predecessor saw. He witnessed himself struggling and flailing against an unseen attacker, but never connecting. Frustrated, he blasted shot after shot with his Tokarev, but the bullets never found their mark.

Something was tightening around his neck; it kept on squeezing until his life seeped away.

The body went limp, fell to the ground and its last breath of air wheezed from his lungs.

Despite his lifelessness, it wasn't the end of Tommy One.

Within moments, Tommy One's memories blasted through the Norfolk shipyards and skated into the Virginian countryside. These fleeting final thoughts of a once conscious mind were drawn into The Cistern. The underground structure was an arcane reservoir...a mystic well where Tommy One's clone brother had waited patiently for weeks.

As that consciousness flooded into the waiting clone, that body was transformed into the new Tommy One. Just prior to the arrival of those memories, the clone...also a living, breathing teenager...was known as Tommy Two. But Two carried that title no more. In a split second, the ethereal memories from the body on the dock merged with those already living inside Tommy Two. They joined and became a greater sum. This person, the one floating in the waters of The Cistern, was now Tommy One.

That was how it worked...when Tommy One died, his memories funneled into the waiting Tommy Two. As those memories merged, Two assumed the prime identity and all the other active Tommies move up one space in a never-ending line.

With a few hard kicks he jetted through the water of The Cistern and started to climb out of the clammy cauldron. As he did, he recognized the urgency. Even more so than before, the shipyard case was a dire one. A murderer was on the loose...his own.

• • •

Within a few minutes of taking over his new identity, Tommy One walked through the door of the White Marsh Mansion, the headquarters of the Tommy Infinity Project.

One of his other clone brothers greeted him.

"So what happened to Tommy Zero?" Tommy Eight inquired. A dead Tommy was no longer called Tommy One…that was the name for the living.

The new Tommy One shrugged. "Well, I felt something around my neck. I could grab it. It was a thick, meaty thing and I could feel it as far as I could stretch my arm, but when I kicked at it, when I swung a fist at it, when I shot at it…I couldn't hit it. There was nothing."

The leader of the Tommy Infinity Project bolted into the room. Professor Johann Weitmursch was a man who wore his hair like a white lion's mane. He tended to growl like one, too.

"Explain this disaster!" the professor demanded in his thick German accent.

Tommy One stiffened. He never felt entirely comfortable around the man who brought him to life. "I'm not sure, sir. I just couldn't see anything."

"But what did you…the new Tommy One…see while you were in The Cistern? That's the key, boy!"

Tommy One shook his blond head as he pulled on the red shirt that signified he was the field-mission Tommy. Though his brothers were physical duplicates, only Tommy One was suitable for missions. "There was…well…Nothing." he admitted. His mind just couldn't piece together what he saw…or didn't see. "I just had the life choked out of me. I didn't see who did it or how it happened."

The Cistern served dual purposes for a Tommy Two. First, it allowed for the transfer of the memories from a dying Tommy to the waiting Tommy Two. Its other function was to allow the Tommy Two floating in its waters to witness the world through the eyes of others.

The Cistern served as a sort of psychic "drain." It drew in the thoughts and experiences of the millions of people that lived in the region. Instead of dissipating into the ether as they normally might; this fleeting psychic energies were sluiced into mystic grip of The Cistern. They roared inside like an invisible Niagara Falls, and the Tommy Two inside was tasked to witness, sort and catalog them all.

With his entranced mind wide open, he then experienced every fleeting thought and stood as a witness to every sight, sound, taste and smell that his fellow humans encountered.

But there was a curious difference this time. While he saw his predecessor's death through that body's eyes, the person who choked the life out of him? That person just wasn't there. The killer should have been visible to Tommy's psychic filter, yet somehow he had avoided being cataloged. Despite all the collected thoughts that funneled into The Cistern, there was no killer to be found.

Weitmursch frowned. "What do you mean 'Nothing?'"

"Really, it's a blank. There was no one there. No one killed him…er…me."

"Bah!" the German grumbled. "You tell me you remembered being dispatched, but nothing else around that time?"

"Yes, I see what happened but only through my own eyes. And I see what the mayor was doing…and the farmer down the road. But the person who strangled me? He just doesn't exist."

"What of the other victims?"

"What victims?"

"Those that were killed prior to our new Tommy Zero." The professor read from a list. "Abraham Zeidel. Thomas Snyder. Jacque Muriel. Daniel…"

Tommy One held up a hand and thought. He pulled at his memories and tried to find the victims' experiences that had been deposited in his mind.

"There's a few memories. Snyder! I can see what happened to Snyder. He was on the dock at night when…oh, God! He was impaled by a spear or something. All I see is him clutching at his chest and fading to black."

Tommy One thought some more. He grabbed the list and hovered over each name. "They're all like that. A sudden attack. No one was prepared."

Tommy sighed loudly. "Some of them didn't even realize they were attacked. It was all so quick."

Weitmursch folded his arms. "Well, you need to go back."

"Fine with me."

"But you'll take a watch with you. The Throne girl can spot you from a far."

"But won't that be putting her at risk?" the teen hero asked.

Weitmursch turned to the map board and pointed to Norfolk's waterfront. "Look at this. We know there are 19 murders so far. We know the police cordoned off the entire area, and we now have a Tommy Zero right around here."

He turned back to Tommy One. "You return and draw out the killer. The only thing I've noticed is that none of the murders are far from the water. This is why the police have had such success quarantining the area."

"It didn't help me," Tommy noted.

"Of course not, but we knew the dangers," the professor acknowledged. "And with all that information, we can use the Throne girl as a look out."

The professor pointed to a control and switching tower at some nearby train tracks. "She should be able to sight the entire dock from here."

Tommy Eight stood up. "Sir, there's no need to endanger Imogene. I could perform the same duty."

The professor nodded. He was always forced to explain these things to the higher numbered Tommies. They were too young and hadn't been through all the training and indoctrination procedures yet. "Of course you could, young man. Any of you could, but if we have two Tommies out on the streets at the same time it could expose our biggest secret to the world…that Tommy One is actually a mantle that's passed from one of you boys to another. We've had multiple Tommies out in the field before, but only by maintaining the strictest of security. This isn't one of those times … whoever stands watch here is visible to the public."

"I see," Tommy Eight sighed. The teen looked exactly like every other boy in the room, including Tommy One. Each had a tassel of blond hair, a muscular frame and a bright look in his eyes. The only difference between Eight and One is that One wore the official uniform of Tommy One: A red shirt with yellow piping and a black domino mask.

"Do you want me to go get Imogene?" Tommy One announced as he strapped on a belt loaded with pouches and pistol holster.

Now that Tommy One had all the memories of the previous Tommies merged into his conscious mind, he realized just how deep his affection for the girl was. He couldn't wait to see her again.

The professor nodded. "Yes, she should be safe in the tower."

Weitmursch watched Tommy bolt from the room, adding, "At least as long as we can keep her there."

● ● ●

An hour later, Tommy One watched Imogene Throne load the sidecar of the BMW R75, a World War II era motorcycle from Germany. She wore a black turtle neck under her dark green flak jacket that managed to hug her teenage curves. She completed her commando look by wrapped a matching green scarf around her neck, which she often used to conceal her face.

Imogene smiled. "Looks like we're all set. My stuff's loaded. We have some SCUBA gear for you along with your extra ammo."

Tommy climbed on to the seat but stopped when Imogene threw up her hands. "Whoa! Whoa!" she thundered.

Tommy smiled. "What?"

Her eyes thinned. "You always try this."

"What?"

She shoved him with a laugh. Her silky skin was nearly as white as her teeth. Her smooth dark hair as black as her shirt. "Move it. Go on! Get in the sidecar. When I'm along, I pilot and you navigate."

Tommy laughed. He loved it when she touched him.

"Fine," he grumped as he slid to the sidecar and pointed out the door. "As navigator, I say we go that way!"

She rolled her eyes. "Thank you, Ferdinand Magellan."

The cycle roared to life, blasted from the garage and rode into the Virginia night.

A few minutes later, they had parked near the train tower and split off for their respective
duties.

Once she scaled the tower, she scoped out her partner as he moved through the harbor.

The professor was right. The tower provided the perfect vantage point.

She watched Tommy as he stood next to a barricade manned by two police officers. She skipped over to the next street and spied more officers. At each blockade, the police had set up a searchlight they used to illuminate a portion of the blockaded waterfront.

The newspapers had been covering the events at the docks: The Norfolk Police Department had set up the blockade and made an effort to scout the area where the killings were occurring. But they weren't stupid; they marched into the area with a thirty-person squad complete with Army Jeeps. They found nothing but more corpses… all choked to death and then disemboweled.

Despite their efforts, they found nothing else.

Eventually, the police also realized that all of the killings had happened at night. The killer waited until the docks were all but deserted and the sun had long set.

With the barricades up day and night, no one else was allowed in the area. Yet corpses continued to pile up. Disappearances mounted.

The problem, the police acknowledged, was that the lockdown left 15 cargo ships stuck at port. That meant that 15 ships' worth of angry sailors who were intent on getting back to work. They found the sailors were continually sneaking into the No Man's Land…some on a dare, some thinking they'd steal their ships back. Their bravery made no difference though. The body count kept rising.

But now Tommy One was helping. Things were about to change.

Since the end of World War II, Norfolk and the entire Tidewater Region had grown to rely on the adventurer to solve their often-unique problems. Hold-out Nazis, high-tech pirate gangs and mutant musketeers had all brought trouble to the area, and Tommy One was the only one who could stand against them. Of course, when he wasn't tearing through bad guys, he tried to help the community in other ways. He visited with Boy Scout troops, helped at fundraisers and threw out first pitches.

Today, however, he was after a maniac. This wasn't a photo-op. This was serious.

For her part, Imogene would sometimes work the field with Tommy. Most often, she worked as a driver or an extra set of eyes. Aside from being Tommy One's and the professor's neighbor, they appreciated her quick-thinking and intelligence. More than once, she had heard the professor call her "a genius" and "a perfect partner for Tommy."

He also knew that she helped Tommies stay alive. Even with all the government funding the professor got, making clones was not cheap.

Of course the professor's budget wasn't her concern. She cared about Tommy One. She didn't want to see him injured or killed. She had seen his death too many times before.

"And now he's back in the killzone for the second time tonight," she sighed aloud as she tracked him through her binoculars.

She pulled out her flashlight and clicked a code to Tommy. She watched him nod, salute sardonically and then about-face toward the docks.

A moment later, he drew out his own flashlight and pistol, and, using his flashlight hand to steady his Tokarev, stepped past the police and into Norfolk's most deadly square-mile.

Imogene swallowed fearfully. "Don't die again, Tommy. Not tonight."

● ● ●

"Good luck," one of the officers said to the teen hero as he slid into the darkness. The man's tone was far from cheery.

Moments before, the officer and his partner had explained their previous shift on the blockade:

'It was 2:30 a.m., right?'

'Yeah, around then.'

'We're just scanning the area. Joe here's running the search light, and I'm watching the

city side of the blockade. He's looking for the killer or any sign of anyone out there on the docks.

'And so, I slide the light up Dock 55A an' I see this guy sneakin' up the gangplank on that ship right there…the Merry Mint. An' I yell 'Police! Stop! Get back here' but he ain't stoppin.''

'So I turn around and see the guy, too! Joe holds the light on the ship for a long time. Scanning it all over the deck. We're looking for the guy to show up again, or even for the engine to start up.'

'But nope. About 10 minutes go by and then the cabin lights up four times…gunshots!'

'An' then we hear a scream!'

'Then two more gunshots. An' then nothing.'

'Nothin' else.'

'This morning, our sergeant says there's blood all over the deck of the Merry Mint, but

no body. Just an empty revolver, blood and the ship torn to pieces.'

Scanning the spaces between the stationary searchlight beams, Tommy One realized there were plenty of places to hide along the docks. Once the order to quarantine the area went up, workers were told to drop everything and walk away. That left the place looking like it had been abandoned at 10 a.m. on a Tuesday. Stacks of shipping boxes sat in heaps. Cranes loaded with cargo hung overhead. Fishing nets were left draped over booms.

That meant a million places for a killer to keep a low profile and that wasn't even counting the ships themselves.

With the contrast provided by the spotlights, shadows seemed to ooze out of every corner. Tommy eased along the sea-sprayed planking, his flashlight guiding the way. He forced himself to stay within sight of the tower.

"I gotta be careful," he admitted. "If we're going to find this guy, she needs to see me. Can't lose your bait and expect to catch a fish."

The water next to the Merry Mint was calm and glassy and he could hear it lapping up against the pilings below the dock. In the distance, a fog horn bellowed its agonized warning.

As he closed in on the ship, he realized the Merry Mint had earned its name from its light green hull. He recognized it as a Saltie; a small bulk carrier designed to haul its cargo in one massive open cargo area.

The barge-like ships always sat low in the water, so even from the dock he had a good view of the entire ship.

Tommy paced alongside until he reached its gangplank. He turned back toward Imogene and pointed at the ship. He mouthed, "Going aboard."

With that notification, he padded down the gangplank. On board, he noted the deck planking had turned black from years of hauling sooty cargo coal. The open cargo area, despite the searchlights and the probing of his own flashlight, was an empty blackness.

"That's gotta be coal down there," he mumbled and continued on.

He walked around the small deck, which was set to the stern of the ship, scanning it with his flashlight. After a few minutes, he found what he came aboard for: A whirl of footprints that danced around a bloody stain. He figured most of the footprints were from this morning's police investigators. The blood had another owner…it was from the poor sailor who disappeared the night before.

The primary stain was horrifically explosive…a burst of blood coagulating amid the soot. Tommy walked around the area, studying it carefully. "This wasn't a quick death," he rattled off as he remembered the training he had from the professor and his experts. "There was his initial wound, but it was followed by a struggle. That's just like the others I saw…a stabbing followed by a disembowelment. But this guy disappeared, too."

He nodded in understanding to some handprints that pulled toward the opposite railing.

Tommy walked to the edge of the ship and set his hand on the rail. The trail of blood stopped there.

The circle of footprints indicated the police had discovered the same thing Tommy had. He leaned over and studied the length of the 700-foot ship. "But did they think he jumped overboard? Or did they?"

His question stopped short.

As he let out that last syllable, a metal rod tore into his back and rocketed out his chest a moment later.

"Who?" Tommy gasped as the horror of his wound dawned on him. His flashlight stabbed the darkness. There was only the night in every direction. Nothing but the gentle shush of the harbor water.

He squinted at a subtle movement. A slight hiss, he thought. With his wound draining him, he fired three slugs into the inky blackness. The muzzle flashes allowed him to catch his own doom missiling toward him; another rod of pig iron hammered through his body.

But those same flashes also allowed him to see something else. Something he never expected.

With his last breath, he squinted into the darkness and asked, "What are you?"

• • •

Imogene screamed. She saw the flashes of light on the ship. The shots also caught the police's attention, and their spotlights began threading through the harbor. Only one fixed on the Merry Mint, though. It was the light manned by the two policemen that Tommy visited just minutes before.

Their light scanned the Mint from its head to its stern and in that blaze, Imogene saw what she didn't want to see…Tommy One's corpse. It was impaled on two pikes.

"No," she whimpered and shook her head. "No-no-no-no!"

Her eyes reddened. She felt a mixture of fury and sadness. "I'm getting so tired of this," she sniffed and jetted down the ladder.

A moment later, she was aboard the R75 and running it full throttle to the barricade.

She screeched to a halt. "He's fighting for his life in there!" she lied from behind her scarf. "Let me through!"

The officers looked at one another. One of them shook his head as he spoke. "Now, missy, we can't let you in there. You know it's too dangerous."

"Yes, you will!"

"No ma'am, orders are orders."

"You know very well, that I've got all the permissions that Tommy One has!" she fumed, pouring the throttle on and lacing the cycle around the barrier. "Talk to the police commissioner if you have any questions!"

"But, miss! The killer!"

She was already gone. She revved the engine and zoom through the dock. As she did, the spotlights converged on her.

Even beyond helping Tommy One, she was worried that the police may find two corpses on the docks tomorrow and they would both be a Tommy. If they did, Tommy's biggest secret would be out. There was no telling what the public might think if they knew about how Tommy One was able to sail through so much danger without a scratch. That he was something beyond the typical human.

If his humanity fell into question, it was hard to guess what the public reaction might be.

• • •

It seemed like he had been in The Cistern for only a few minutes. It was barely enough time to get his bearings, in fact. Yet there he was being pounded the fresh memories of his clone brother.

In that instant, another Tommy Two had moved up in the line. Less than two hours before, he watched Tommy One and Imogene Throne ride out into the night. As they disappeared into the darkness, he made his way back to The Cistern and dove inside.

By submerging himself in its pristine waters and opening up his mind, he was instantly connected to the world. He saw the thoughts and deeds of millions. He watched his older brother enter the Norfolk docks. He saw the world through Imogene's eyes; he listened to the frantic cries of police as those new shots aboard the Merry Mint were fired.

And, as his predecessor's death became apparent, he experienced what Tommy had seen in his last moments.

He tried to sort it all out. There were three muzzle flashes. Each one gave him a different view. The first shot, he only saw a mass. It was something that had hauled itself to the deck of the ship. Water streamed off it, yet it was simply too indistinct.

The second muzzle flash caught something else in that confusing indistinction. In the mass of water and sea slime, he saw what he could only call an eye. It was a gold-flecked with traces of red and green along its narrowing iris.

The third muzzle flash caught the angry death rocketing toward him. It was long, mottled and covered in a gooey gel. The moment of the muzzle flare seemed to flatten out the dimensions in his memory. He couldn't tell how close it was to him. The mass coming out of the water coiled around the steel bar lancing at him. It was far away, yet it also seemed to be just a hair's breadth from reaching him.

Then Tommy One...the new Tommy One...realized what it was that he and the police had been fighting for so long. It was something that couldn't be found in the daylight. It was a killer whose thoughts he couldn't see. It was an attacker whose body he couldn't punch, kick or shoot because the body was always in hiding.

Not some deranged man but a creature. A creature that crawled up out of the sea. A creature capable of attacking him from a hundred feet away.

Now he saw in his mind's eye how he had been killed by it twice. Each of those deadly memories allowed to him to see a bit more of the beast; a beast with 100-foot-long tentacles.

A beast that he was sure Imogene was about to face on her own.

● ● ●

Imogene Throne blazed up to the ship where she last saw Tommy One. She didn't stop the motorcycle when she hit the gangplank, instead she poured on the gas and rattled along it.

"Where are you?" she fretted as she spun the bike in a tight circle on the deck. The R75's headlight failed to reveal his body.

With the dust churning up, she coughed and crumpled her scarf to create a thicker filter over her nose and mouth. "What happened to you, Tommy?" she asked the soot and darkness.

In frustration, she turned on the radio and clicked on the mic attached to the motorcycle. "I.T. to the mansion. Has the new No. 1 arrived yet? I need some immediate info on Zero's pickup location. I can do the extract solo."

The speaker spat to life in response. "Imogene! You've got to get out of there! You're in danger!"

She couldn't tell if it was Tommy One or one of his younger brothers. "Calm down," she insisted. "We're all clear here. I just need..."

She stopped as a shadow seemed to move behind her. She whirled and let the button on the mic go. To her left, an iron rod suddenly crashed through the planking of the Merry Mint.

"Whoa!" she yelped. The rod had been hurled with such force that it drilled itself through the wood and disappeared with a rattle as it slid through its own hole.

The speaker immediately exploded with noise. "Got to get out of there! It's an octopus!! I tell you! A gigantic freak of an octopus!! It will kill you in a second!"

She zipped her flashlight around until she caught sight of it again. It was a long, meaty tentacle covered in dripping mucus. Its skin was a dull blue with orange splotches, which gave the limb the appearance of an otherworldly slug. While it snaked around, she saw the limb carried suction cups as big as baseballs. The appendage finally found

what it was blindly seeking another iron rebar, which it plucked up from a small stack.

The frantic call continued. "Imogene?? Imogene! Answer me! You've got to get out of there!"

She drew out her Bowie knife and started to back away as the beast's weapon swung wildly. "I hear you," she whispered as she took a step back.

As she put her weight down on her foot, she felt something squishy and heavy underneath her...another tentacle!

It was too late; the living rope kicked up in response and tangled itself in her legs. She fought back, but it only made the situation worse and she spilled across the deck.

"No!" she cried as the tentacle threaded itself around an ankle.

Ten feet away, the motorcycle speaker continued to plead for her. "Imogene! You've got to get away!"

But she couldn't. She was already in the life-and-death struggle with the very thing she was being warned about.

The second tentacle tightened its grip and began to drag her across the deck. She didn't want to go wherever it was taking her, so she plunged the blade into its flesh. The limb stiffened momentarily, but didn't let her go. She opted to saw through it.

Blood spat from the wound and rubbery sinews snapped apart.

"That's right, you big jerk!" Imogene growled. "My mom'll be deep-frying you tomorrow afternoon!"

But she found that zeal short-lived. As the one tentacle loosened and writhed in the pain of the attack, a second raised up another iron bar and swung it at her. She ducked, and decided she didn't want to be there for a follow-up swing. She had no choice...she dropped both her knife and flashlight and grabbed the rod as it flew past. The sudden jerk was enough to free her legs from the weakened tentacle and she rode the tentacle-born rod into the sky.

Free, she let go, fell to the deck and sprinted toward the R75. The octopus responded by spitting the steel bar away and flinging itself upon her. It coiled around her waist and tightened.

A second later, it pulled the struggling teen into the darkness of the derelict ship.

● ● ●

The new Tommy One was already halfway to the docks when the call came.

"We can't raise her," Tommy Six lamented from the communication center at the White Marsh Mansion. "The last we knew is that she broke through the police barricade searching for the two Tommy Zeros we've left there in the last few hours."

"I don't care about the Tommy Zeros. I need to find Imogene. I need to find her right away."

"The last thing we heard, she was on the Merry Mint."

"That's where you can send the next Tommy One, too. I'm not coming back until I get her."

Minutes later, he burst through one of the police barricades, rolled his own R75 to the gangplank and scrambled aboard the Merry Mint. On its deck, Imogene's R75 sat idling

"Imogene! Where are you?" he screamed into the mists.

His mind rolled back to his most recent death. The beast had hurled the steel rods through him and dragged him off the deck, locking him in its spiraling vice-grip. It pulled him along the deck and then he felt a hammer blow to his head and nothing more.

Even before that final blow, he was already slipping into unconsciousness. But his memory pulled one more detail out. He remembered a set of dials.

"That's it!" he cried and dashed to the pilot house, the ship's control center. "Imogene, I swear to God, I'll get you back!"

He was up the exterior staircase a single leap. "Imogene!" he wailed.

He could instantly tell the windshield had been smashed out.

He blazed his flashlight through the hole. "Where is she?"

From far away, a voice squeaked from inside.

"Imogene!" Tommy One gasped with relief. "Where are you?"

"Inside! I can't see anything. It's pitch black inside here!" Her voice was small and weak.

Tommy rattled at the door, it wouldn't give. "How did you get in there?"

"It had a hold of me, but I kept stabbing it. It pulled me down here into the dark. There's no light down here, I can't see!" She sounded woozy, "How long have I been down here?"

"I'm shining my flashlight right through the window. Can you see it?"

"No," she whimpered. "Tommy...I think I'm blind!"

● ● ●

Back on the deck of the Merry Mint, Tommy dashed around the pilot house until he could finally see inside. He skidded to a stop at what he saw. The entire interior had been torn asunder, revealing a gaping chasm into the decks below. He remembered the police had said something about the ship being wrecked. They seemed to think it was vandals.

"Imogene!" Tommy yelled again as he crawled through the window.

He heard her call back weakly.

His flashlight found only more inky blackness. "Why can't I see anything?"

Grabbing at some cables leading from a maimed control panel, Tommy started to lower himself inside. As his foot edged down, he watched it disappear into a black fog. It licked at his boot, curling around in tiny ebony tongues.

"What is this?"

He kicked at it stirring up the wisps around his leg. "Thick as pea soup!"

If Imogene is trapped down there in it, he thought, it's no wonder she can't see.

"Imogene! Come to my voice!" he demanded.

"I can't," she gasped in a mousy voice. "My legs...my arms...they're not..."

Something was definitely wrong. He couldn't tell what the fog was, but he could tell that Imogene was fading fast.

He summoned up his courage and dropped into the mist. "Aw, well, you only live once!"

Inside, Tommy One found a midnight black he couldn't believe existed. His entire body seemed to disappear around him as he tumbled down.

He could only guess, but he assumed he fell twenty feet or so until he smacked into something heavy. It had some give, and his downward motion ended with some subdued cracking noises.

"No!" he fretted as he realized what he landed upon. "Imogene is that you?"

He felt below himself and found what he feared...a body. Patting at the features, he found the man had a beard...one of the missing sailors!

The fog was still too thick to see anything, so he cried out again. "Imogene! Where are you?"

He heard a soft moan, and stumbled toward it. As he moved, he counted at least six bodies and checked each one. None seemed to match the mental impression he had of Imogene's features.

The seventh, though, had long, smooth hair bound in a ponytail. It had a sharp, elegant nose and, most importantly, a flack jacket.

"It's you!" he announced, suddenly realizing that he too was feeling groggy. "We better go, Imogene!"

He hauled her up over his shoulder and walked in the direction he assumed was a staircase. From his brief view of the top deck, he remembered the landing of that staircase and now he could only hope that it also led below decks.

The trek through the darkness was a slow go. He thumped into any number of objects along the way until he found a wall and a door. He swung it open and watched the billowing gas roll up a grated staircase.

Bursting out the door at the top of the stairs, he sucked in the first clear air he'd had in the last ten minutes. Almost instantly, his focus began to return.

"Tommy?" Imogene managed as her mind unfolded from its haze.

He set her to the ground her raven hair blending in with the layers of coal dust. "I got you," he whispered. "We're good now."

"It's an octopus. Something huge."

"Yes, it is. That's why I couldn't see it while I was in The Cistern. It wasn't human, so its thoughts didn't come through to me."

"Oh," she said. Her complexion started to green. "Oh…I don't feel very good."

"I have to go help those other people down there."

She rolled to her side and wretched. A terrible mucus spewed out of her…stringy and sticky.

"You'll be OK," Tommy announced as he walked over to her bike. It was still running, but he paid no attention to that. Instead, he dug out the SCUBA tank, goggles and breathing mask. "This should keep my head clear while I'm down there. I can only guess that it's an airborne toxin."

Imogene continued to cough. She choked out another glob of mucus. "What is this?" she gasped as she wiped the froth from her lips.

It finally registered to Tommy that she was more than nauseated by the mist. He rushed to her side and watched as she gagged again and spit out another heaving ball of goo.

"Oh, God," she hacked as she caught her breath.

Tommy pointed his flashlight's column of white light at her ejections. The mucus pulsed and throbbed. "What the hell?" he managed as he looked closer.

Inside a thin casing, he saw the tiny tendrils of a miniature octopus. In fact, his light revealed dozens of tiny octopi trapped in gelatinous eggs.

"Those were inside of me?" Imogene squealed. "Are there any more?"

She began gagging again, but she only coughed and heaved. Nothing more was coming out.

Tommy slammed his boot into the goo before him. Hammering it again and again until he was sure the tiny creatures were dead.

He looked back toward the bridge. "Those people down there! There could be legions of these things inside them!"

He turned to Imogene. "Go!" she said. "Whatever it was, it's out of me now."

Tommy nodded and bolted back to the bridge. He pulled the SCUBA gear over his face, activated the regulator and dove into the black mist.

● ● ●

Tommy returned ten minutes later. "I checked their vitals. All dead. The only things living inside them were more of those things."

He mimed a pregnant stomach. "Every one of them bloated and gross."

"What did you do with them?"

Tommy stiffened. "I took care of them."

"Oh," Imogene blinked, wondering how close she had come to the same fate.

"How are you?" Tommy asked.

"I'm fine," she said. "They were just in my stomach, I guess. Maybe too early to do any other damage."

"Good. And your arms and legs?"

"Better," she admitted. "The paralysis you and I had encountered seems to fade as you get away from the gas."

"We were too late for those guys," Tommy grimaced. "But I'm glad you're OK."

"Thanks. I'm gonna be fine." Imogene looked up. "And now we gotta get back to this thing"

Tommy nodded. "Well, I've read that octopus and squid are masters of disguise. It's understandable the cops never found it. It's down there somewhere, laying eggs in everybody it can."

Imogene continued the thought. "Maybe they only lay these eggs at night? Or inside that black fog?"

As she spoke, a meaty blue tentacle spat out of the gutted pilot house. It flew like a rocket toward Tommy One and laced itself around him.

It wrenched him about, but despite the thrashing he remained focused. He rolled his arm out and pointed toward the BMW. "Your bike! Use it to..."

And then he disappeared into the swirling mists.

In the strobes of the distant searchlights, Imogene stared at the motorcycle. "Use it to what?"

• • •

The tentacle pulled Tommy One under the deck of the Merry Mint and through the inky clouds. The impenetrable darkness of the fog swirled past him until he felt himself bang through a door in one of the bulkheads.

In an instant, he passed through the border of the black mist, and he could see again. His SCUBA mask had worked again. His head was completely clear.

The room had the dim illumination provided by some failing emergency lighting, and Tommy recognized the guts of the ship...the engine room.

He twisted around to look for the creature. But he saw nothing but an endless tentacle that disappeared around another corner.

"Where are you?" he asked the creature quietly. As he struggled against the beast, he pulled his pistol and drew his knife. He had to be ready for whatever came next.

The tentacle snaked him up to where he could see another door. Beyond it, he saw a room jammed with octopus flesh. It was like it had been stuffed inside a can of tuna. Four other tentacles sprouted from the door, but he could see nothing but writhing life beyond the door frame.

Above the door, he read the label. "Ballast," it said and instantly Tommy understood how the aquatic creature had managed to stay hidden so well.

"It squished itself into the ballast tank!" he muttered. "Without any skeleton, it can fit into any space that holds water."

Another tentacle lashed itself around him as he saw movement through the door. With a slurp, a monstrous gold-flecked eye leveled itself at him from the door frame. It focused on the teen hero and from inside the ballast pump room he heard growling hiss.

"You think I gave you trouble before?" Tommy One roared through his respirator. "Just wait!"

The teen hero raised his Tokarev at the bulbous eye and fired. The shot would have found its mark, too, but the octopus was smart and quick. In the instant Tommy pulled the trigger, the octopus pulled the bulkhead door closed just enough and the bullet pinged away.

"Smarter than a trained seal!" Tommy scoffed as he recognized the creature's rising anger. It understood it had been attacked and thrashed him into a metal beam as punishment.

Seeing he was still conscious, it hammered him again against the beam. The first blow caused Tommy to drop his pistol. The second popped a rib. With the third, he only narrowly avoided getting his skull crushed.

By the time the octopus hauled him up for the fourth, Tommy wheeled back his knife and launched it into the tentacle. He seemed to have better success than Imogene minutes before since the creature's grip loosened instantly and Tommy slipped free.

He backed away, slashing at any tentacle that came near him until he reached the bulkhead door.

"You want to hide inside a shell? How about I lock you inside it!"

Tommy slammed the door and spun the door seal into place.

The response was instant. Fleshy thuds sounded against the door. They were followed by louder metal-on-metal crashes as dents erupted in the frame.

"OK, that isn't going to last long," Tommy admitted to himself, desperately glancing around for the exit.

The hammering continued as the door puttied in its frame. In another second, tentacles burst through to an empty room. Frustrated, they snaked to the next door.

Tommy, meanwhile, was already well ahead of his pursuer. He plowed through another door and stopped to gawk at the sight. He had burst through to the open-air cargo hold. His feet sunk into inches of coal dust as he looked up. Above him was a starry sky.

As the four tentacles burst from the door, Tommy One winced. "I need a ladder!"

● ● ●

"Over here!" Imogene cried from the deck as she waved a flashlight. "Here, Tommy One!"

Tommy spotted the beam focused on the ladder rungs bolted to the wall and ran to it.

"I thought I told you to use the motorcycle and..."

"Create a bomb?" Imogene finished his sentence.

Tommy laughed as he pulled himself up. "I was going to say 'get out of here!'"

Imogene's face scrunched in confusion. "Why would I run away?"

"It doesn't matter," Tommy waved her off. "If you've got a plan, let's hear it!"

She pointed to the motorcycle. "It's basically a monster-sized Molotov Cocktail. We light it on fire and..."

Before she could finish, a tentacle looped around Tommy coiled tight. "Aw, geez," he sighed.

"Tommy!"

"Just do it!" Tommy wheezed. "Use your bomb!"

"But...the ship! You!"

He pulled at the tentacle, but didn't have the strength to wrench himself free. His gun and knife were gone, so it was all he could do. "It lives inside the ship! Blowing it is the only way to take this thing out."

Another tentacle, one of the injured limbs, threaded itself through the pilot house searched blindly for another victim.

"Watch out, Imogene!" Tommy cried.

The appendage swiped around, but she ducked past it and rolled over to the R75. She patted the cycle nicely, as if to say goodbye, and started pushing it toward the edge of the cargo bay where she had torn out the rigging a few minutes earlier.

The tentacle thrashed toward her movement. "Yikes!" she squeaked as she fumbled with the matches.

"The bomb!" Tommy One gasped as the tentacle roped itself around his neck. "Any time now!"

"Yeah, yeah!" she fussed, finally lighting a match. She set it against the rag hanging from the cycle's gas tank.

She looked at Tommy and then watched the flames catch. A moment later, she pushed the bike over the edge.

It spilled end over end and landed with a poof of soot, the cloud hung for a moment and then roared into a flame. The flame, in turn, shot across the surface of the cargo area, igniting the first layer of coal dust.

"That's it?!?" Tommy wheezed from beneath the tentacle. The other had given up in its search for another victim and wrapped itself around Tommy's leg.

"The dry stuff goes up first," Imogene yelled as she ran behind him and the tentacles. "Everything under that is wet! It has a higher flash point!"

She found the pile of rebar and lugged up piece.

"But how else are you going to ignite it?"

She whacked at the nearest tentacle. "Don't be an idiot, Tommy," she managed matter of factly. "We're still waiting on our cocktail!"

Tommy looked back at the cargo area. "Oh!"

She handed him the rod as the tentacles lowered him in a reaction to her strikes. "Yeah, the earlier rush of flames was just from the surface dust. When the Molotov cocktail goes off... big-time blast!"

Tommy jabbed his steel bar into the creature's appendage. It loosened from his neck only to tighten elsewhere.

He realized it was useless and looked over to his partner. "Imogene! You have to go! You have to go now! This thing isn't going to let me go! And the longer you stay out here, the more likely it will hunt you down with another tentacle!"

As if having been summoned by his words, another two tentacles spooled out of the pilot house and thrashed at them.

"Tommy!" Imogene cried, pulling another bar up and bashing the creature.

"You know I don't matter!" Tommy reminded her. "Not this body, at least! Go!"

She looked at him with tears in her eyes. She had done this too many times before... watched him die to save her.

"Go!" he insisted.

She threw the rebar down and ran to the gangplank as the tentacles traced her footsteps, she made it to small boathouse when one finally grabbed her and looped around an ankle.

As it started to reel her in like a prize catch, the motorcycle-sized Molotov cocktail finally blew.

The explosion threw Imogene to the other side of the dock and rolled her into the water. She went under as the heat washed over and she surfaced in time to see the flaming debris of the Merry Mint sink into the harbor.

Among the iron, cable and sheet-metal debris, plopped the explosion-torn chunks of a giant octopus.

● ● ●

Back at the White Marsh Mansion, the new Tommy One greeted Imogene Throne with a long hug.

"You're safe," he whispered into her ear. "You killed that thing, you know. You've saved countless lives."

She frowned. "But not yours. You died again. That kills me every time, Tommy."

"You know that body doesn't matter. I'm back on my feet already!"

She hated it. She just wanted one Tommy One, not an endless parade of them.

Tommy continued. "And who knows how many people you saved? If that thing really was hatching baby monsters inside all of those people, we would have been overrun! A legion of them!"

Imogene held her stomach, thinking how they had been inside of her too.

"Don't worry," Professor Weitmursch chimed in. "I've run tests. That black fog? It was necessary for their incubation inside their human hosts. Once you were pulled outside, they began to choke out and die. You're safe."

She hoped he was right.

Tommy One smiled and gave her another hug. A warm hug.

She hugged him back. These were the arms she wanted to be held by, not some slimy tentacles.

The End

The Return of General George Washington
Or By The Robot's Red Glare
By I.A. Watson

The bombing continued night and day now. Plasma blasts burst on the force dome over Old City with eye-watering green flashes. Deformations in the crumbling defence barrier showed as crackling lightning ripples. No-one knew how long the shield would hold.

The only break came at sunset. That was when the Khan called a moment's truce to address the besieged settlement.

"I grow impatient," the giant hologram of the conqueror warned, towering over even the battered force dome. "Kindaia, Elesthene, Nox, Nova Lemura, all have yielded to my authority. So far I have forgiven Yorvik its impertinence in defying me. That forbearance comes to an end."

It was impossible to ignore the Khan. His amplified voice boomed over the blacked-out ruins of the remaining section of the demolished metropolis. It echoed through the winding streets between collapsed buildings and hundred-foot-high scrap piles. The conqueror spoke with an assured authority that seemed to demand obedience.

"Your civic centre is mere rubble," he told the refugees of Old City. "Your suburbs and infrastructure are gone. My legions surround you as you cringe in your rat-infested slumland. There is no escape."

There were few rats in the shattered remains of the poorest and most ancient quarter of Yorvik any more. Food was very scarce.

"I shall grant you three days – no more. If I do not receive your surrender by then, if you do not drop your defences and yield, then I will show no mercy. I will destroy you utterly. Be warned."

The Khan's cold eyes were bleak and dead as the wastelands where he had grown to power. He sneered down at ruined Old City, not bothering to mask his contempt for the last desperate stronghold on this side of the great dustbowl.

His hologram disintegrated. The plasma launchers powered up again and recommenced their assault.

Time was running out.

● ● ●

"You have thirty seconds," Gloriana told Wake. "If you don't deactivate the exclusion mesh before it cycles up to full charge we're fried."

Wake continued to proddle tools through the narrow hole he'd cut in the steel housing of the security door. "And you thought that maybe working blind on an unfamiliar system wasn't challenging me enough so it was best to distract me with a countdown?"

"I thought that maybe you'd like to know about a fairly important time constraint that threatens to fry us all like a hobo's rat. Ten seconds."

Wake tripped the reset on the mesh masterboard. "Back to thirty now," he pointed out. "You're forgetting that I'm amazingly good at this stuff."

"How can I forget when you mention it so often? Fifteen seconds again."

Sutler rubbed his hand against his sweating forehead. "Could we please get on with the mission without the romantic sparring match? You're welcome to get a room later – hopefully someplace far out of my earshot - but meantime could we just break into the damn gangster stronghold without the banter?"

Wade and Glory both glared at mercenary. "We are not having a romance," Glory insisted firmly.

"Not even with another thirty seconds to live," Wade agreed, resetting the exclusion mesh activation cycle again.

"Not ever," Glory clarified.

Sutler sighed. He touched his communications earpiece. "The lovebirds are breaking through the door now," he reported. "It's going to get real noisy real soon."

The security grid gave up with a shower of sparks. Wade yelped and pulled his hand away. He sucked his fingers. Red lights over the sealed door went off. The steel sheet jerked aside with a piston hiss.

"Step back," warned Sutler. He slipped a pair of gas grenades from his harness and tossed them through the entrance, then followed up with a flashbang and a screamer.

For two minutes nothing moved on the other side of the door. Then the smoke thinned and thugs who had been beyond the range of Sutler's ordinance ventured out. Gloriana slipped a couple of knives from her bandolier and dropped the first man out.

"Not bad," Wake admitted, "but watch this." He jammed a screwdriver back into the deactivated security board. A part of the exclusion mesh fizzed to life again, searing charged nanomolecular fibres through the gunsels charging out at him.

The ancient tech spluttered out for the last time. Like everything in Old Town it was recycled and repurposed from the mountains of junked metal left over from the Breakdown nearly three hundred years before. If there was anywhere left in the world that could still manufacture systems this advanced then it probably belonged to the Khan by now.

Sutler raced forward. He had a plasma pellet discharger in one fist and an old-fashioned machine pistol in the other. The big man moved with an assured competence, cutting through Capo Cready's henchmen like the clowns they really were.

"It's not like we didn't give him the chance to co-operate," Glory pointed out. She was referring to the Capo, who had failed to rise to civic responsibilities when the Khan's armies had surrounded Yorvik. The gangster had preferred to hole himself away inside his fortress beneath the junkpiles and let the rest of Old Town go to hell. He'd been utterly unmoved by the invitation to abandon his stronghold and assist in the defence of the neighbourhood.

"I'm amazed he didn't listen to your lecture," Wake told the knife-wielding Mayor's daughter. "I mean, you get so much practice telling people what's good for them."

Gloriana hurled a dagger past the tech-thief's head and took down a gunsel that had Wake in his sights. "It would take years for me to work through all the things you need to hear," she warned the rogue.

They both span round as someone approached from the haze outside the fortress. They relaxed a little when they recognised the weapons-dealer Worth. The old man hobbled in with a cane, flanked by two of his minders. "Sutler reports that the site is secured."

Glory's eyebrows rose. "He did it? One man took down Capo Cready and all his gang?"

"Hey, we helped," Wake objected. "Who located and sealed off all the Capo's bolt-hole exits? Me. Who scrambled his comms? Who spoofed his security circuits?"

"Who walked into a crimelord's stronghold and blew the hell out of some of the worst criminal scum in Yorvik?" Gloriana interrupted. "Oh wait – that was *Sutler*."

Wake grinned. "Yeah. I suppose that might qualify as marginally cool."

Worth frowned at Wake and Glory alike. "Sutler was right about you two," he growled. "Out of the way, children."

The weapons dealer stepped over the gangster bodies and passed inside the fortress. He looked around the metallic interior.

"Well?" asked Gloriana anxiously.

"Yes," confirmed Worth. "This is it. This is the Robot."

● ● ●

It was almost dawn by the time Glorianna Bell ventured into the crowded civic hall council chamber. The room was full of arguing people. The debate must have raged on all night.

There were sixty-one thousand surviving residents sheltering in the Old City. Glory's first impression was that they were all here, all screaming at once.

The marshal's deputies recognised the Mayor's daughter and waved her through.

The civic hall had been badly pounded during the first days of the siege when the attackers had been willing to expend irreplaceable shield-penetrating rounds. In the months since then the worst of the rubble had been hauled away and supports scaffolded up so that the council chamber could be used again. One whole wall was still missing, so the chamber was painted with livid flashes from the field weapons pounding on Yorvik's defence dome.

Glory's father was in the speaker's circle, besieged by representatives of the guilds and unions, by business leaders, by supply and ordinance officers, all quarrelling about the Khan's ultimatum. The rules of debate had been an early casualty of the siege.

Glory's mother spotted her, though, and gestured across the chamber to direct her towards one of the annex rooms behind the podium. Glory edged her way through the voluble crowd until she could slip off and join Tessera Bell away from the chaos.

"Have they really been going all night?" Glory asked.

"Oh yes. The main factions are those who want to surrender, those who want to resist to the last, and those who still think we can negotiate terms. After that it breaks down into lots of shades of self-interest, cowardice, and stubbornness."

"What's going to happen?"

"Your father thinks they'll go for a few hours yet before they wear themselves out. First resolution around noon, maybe, but it'll never pass. Another one by mid-afternoon. Then an adjournment so people can get their voices back."

"But will we surrender to the Khan?"

Tessera bit her bottom lip and nodded reluctantly. "If relief was coming it would have come. If there's even anywhere left to relieve us. You know our shield energy levels. A week, ten days more and they'll fail anyhow. Better to save something than be bombed to oblivion. Probably."

"Labour camps and breeding pens?" Glory snorted. Everybody knew what the Khan did to those he conquered. "Better to die fighting."

"That is one of the views in there." The Mayor's wife stroked Glory's cheek. "You know your father received private messages from the Khan's people? Earlier in the siege? Promises of amnesty if he betrayed Yorvik and lowered the defences."

"He wouldn't do that!"

"No. He didn't. That's why... Glory, we had another message tonight, soon after the Khan's big hologram ultimatum. A private communication – for now." Tessera passed a cracked old viewing pad over and thumbed the play button.

A static-fuzzed image had made it through the shield baffles. It showed a lean man in some kind of black military uniform, speaking straight to camera. "This is Commodore Ellis of the Khan's Own 19th Heavy Cavalry Division. I am responsible for compliance measures within this field of conflict. Mayor Bell, your recalcitrance in obeying orders to surrender your territory to your lawful Khan has cost a significant amount of time and ordinance. You will therefore be subject to special punishment measures. At the conquest of Yorvik Old Town you will be expected to yield up yourself and your family for the Khan's pleasure. If you and your family..." the officer checked some note on his desk, "a wife Tessera and daughter Glorianna attempt suicide then every citizen of your territory will be executed."

Commodore Ellis smiled coldly from the screen. "The Khan looks forward to taking revenge upon your women."

The pad fell silent. Tessera blinked back tears. "I'm sorry, Glory. We'll see that he doesn't get you, I promise. A suicide tab, and then we'll make it look like you were hit in the final bombardment."

"No!" the Mayor's daughter protested. "That's a death warrant for everybody we know, everybody in Yorvik!"

"You've seen the Khan's broadcasts when he captures his enemies' kinfolk. You know what he'll do." Tessera shuddered.

"Yes, I know. But what if there was another way? A chance to escape?"

"Glory, suicide tabs are quite painless. There's no method..."

"Not death. Getting away. You don't know where I've been tonight!"

Tessera looked at the girl. "With that disreputable fixer-trickster Wake?" she suggested. "Not that I blame you, given the circumstances. It's... I suppose it's nice that you have... somebody..."

Glory snorted. "Why does *everybody* think I'm with him? It's nothing like that, mother. Listen! You know you told me how the Shell got its name?"

"The old story about there being a big pre-Breakdown war robot buried under all that scrap? It's just a silly tale, love that my grandfather used to tell to me when I was small."

"But it's not! We *found* it, mother! Wake and me! Some sleazy gang was using the chest cavity as a hideout. I discovered some really old documents in the archive that showed us what was really there."

Tessera frowned. "You went there? It's not safe out anywhere in Old Town, Glory, but the Shell is the worst part of all. You could..."

"What worse could happen to me than getting handed to the Khan two days from now? Anyhow, we had help getting in, from Ephraim Worth."

"The arms seller? He's..."

"He wants to live, like the rest of us. So we found the old robot. It's there. It's inert but intact. If we could access the command room, get even a few of its motion systems running..."

"You could get away," Tessera breathed.

"A few of us, yes. The robot is huge, at least three hundred feet long – or high if it stood up, I guess. Its chest has accommodation that was meant to carry soldiers. Three rooms and some storage units. We could pack a hundred people in there. Children, maybe? Okay, Worth will sell places to the highest bidders, but we could still save somebody."

"You could get away," Glory's mother repeated. "But surely after nearly three hundred years, the systems will be..."

"Wake is annoying but really clever. But..." The Mayor's daughter hesitated. "He'll need access to the secure tech store to scavenge components. My job is to get him the code key."

"Which only your father has," Tessera understood.

"Which only you could get off him."

• • •

Dawn's early light... The sealed security door accepted the codephrase on the third attempt. The input pad was badly degraded. Once it recognised what was being keyed in it released the bolt seals that held the blast panel in place, granting reluctant passage to the control area access shaft.

The wall-rungs were unnecessary. The whole machine lay horizontal, every control surface now occupying a floor or wall.

"You popped the hatch that Cready and his apes couldn't budge in all the years they squatted here," Sutler observed. "Not bad, fix-tricks."

"I got that bit from Gloriana," the technician admitted reluctantly. "She was trained by her mother, Yorvik's archivist. That's how we found out there was even anything here. Glory unearthed it all in those mouldering civic records."

Sutler played a hand-lamp over the cable-strewn walls of the crawlspace. "I don't suppose that included a layout schematic?"

"Not so much. Just enough to know there was once a war machine dropped here, something supposedly from the time of the Old Yooess. Something big. Something buried and forgotten."

Sutler gestured for Wake to go first into the tight tunnel, then followed behind. "You really think you can get this thing running? I mean enough to ride away from the Khan's army?"

"I really dunno. Maybe. I'll need to see what condition the control space is in and what caused the thing to go down anyway."

Wake paused at another hatch. This one had an emergency manual override that was purely hydraulic, so he was able to break the seal and push the door open.

The explorers crawled into the control space. It was a small chamber with just enough room for a triangle of chairs on swivel gimbals, each attached to its own array of command surfaces. Other screens occupied the walls. Everything was dead.

Wade unslung the portable energy pack off his back and found a charge conduit. He'd come prepared with an antique universal connector nozzle so there wasn't much problem interfacing the power supply.

Emergency cabin lighting flickered on, bathing the chamber in a red wash.

Sutler examined the apparatus. "Sweet kit," he admitted. "I've been on a couple of Breakdown-era war tanks, but even they weren't this fancy."

"Yeah." The techhie hauled an inspection panel off one wall and winced at the melted wiring behind it. "It was fancy. Now it's..."

"Like the rest of the world," Sutler supplied.

Wake looked across at the mercenary. Worth had hired the enforcer, evidently paying a premium for someone of significant skills. For the first time Wake wondered what Sutler's motivations were. "If we pull this off, what do you get out of this?"

"Apart from living, you mean? A payday, same as usual."

"You probably wouldn't get killed by the Khan's soldiers. They'd recruit you."

"No thanks. Don't fancy the obedience conditioning. And that uniform looks tight."

Something about the mercenary's tone suggested there was more to his dislike of the enemy's forces than that. "You hate them."

Sutler shrugged. Then, relenting, he unslung his rifle and showed Wake a sticker on the haft.

"316," the fix-tricks read. "What's that?"

"Not enough room on the handle to carve that many notches."

"You've killed three hundred and sixteen people?"

"I've killed lots more than that, kid. No. I've lost three hundred sixteen people I considered friends, fighting against that Khan and his thugs. So I won't be working for him, not today, not ever. His soldier-boys come for me I'll go down hard, and after there'll be nothing left for them to recruit. Right?"

"I hear you." Wake swallowed. Sutler was intense when he meant it, and he was holding a loaded weapon. "I, um, I need to get on. Can you check that circuit breaker panel and see what can be reset? Should be just flipping toggles."

While the mercenary opened fuse boxes and reconnected everything he could, Wake attached his personal data systems to the inert control surfaces, muttering as he worked. "Minimal power up... handshake with the system... purge all login and security commands... couldn't do that if this thing wasn't well-crashed.... scrub memory imperatives, or it'll try to kill us as intruders... okay, I can do this..."

Forty minutes later, the rogue blinked from his focus on conquering the most sophisticated control system he'd ever seen and looked around. Sutler was just re-entering the chamber.

"I've been checking the other access conduits," the merc reported. "That same codephrase opens them all. I got to the automated weapons bays and a bunch of power core service ducts. This thing still has all kinds of ammo, up to and including six missiles still in their cradles. Wouldn't trust any of them to fire, but if they go up we'll know about it. Briefly."

"Glad you're back," Wade grinned at him. "I like an audience when I'm about to do something clever." He tapped a command surface and the screen burst to life.

A screed of boot-up information rolled:

++ RESTART ++

++ UNIT: GENERAL GEORGE WASHINGTON ++

++ SERIAL CODE: A337/22PB COMMISSION DATE: 07-04-2076 ++

++ MULTIPLE CRITICAL SYSTEMS FAULTS ++

++ RESET? ++

"Can't read," Sutler shrugged. "What's it got to say for itself?"

"It says it's banged up and do we want to try and get it started again," Wade translated. He hit the green YES icon.

++ EMERGENCY BACKUPS INITIATED ++

++ DAMAGE CONTROL PROTOCOLS INITIATED ++

++ REROUTING TO SECONDARY SYSTEMS ++

++ REROUTING TO TERTIARY SYSTEMS ++

"This thing has more redundancies than anything I've ever seen," Wade admitted, watching a long scroll of diagnostics and workarounds being listed on a second screen.

He worked through a drop-down menu until he found a graphic damage report summary. One of the big monitors lit up showing a wire-diagram outline of a vaguely humanoid combat frame. Damaged areas were indicated in red. There were a lot of them.

"It's shaped like a man!" Sutler remarked. "Like the Khan's personal war machine, his Devastator! This is the same kind of beast!"

"Looks like," Wade agreed. "Okay, that's what the original problem was. See there, that shell breach from some kind of missile fire? It gutted the main power compartment and blew out the converters in the secondary drive."

"What does that mean?"

The fixer-trickster tapped his way through more data. "It means we might be able to get that back-up power supply operating, with the right parts from secure stores. And Glory is working on that!"

● ● ●

"It's a mess," Glory Bell announced.

"Yeah. But it's our mess," Worth replied. The arms dealer stroked the side of the command chamber possessively. "This must have really been something, once."

Glory tapped up the base operating system again. "Nothing left to tell us much about where it came from or what happened to it," she recognised sadly.

"I had to fry most of that to stop it from frying us when it woke up," Wade called from inside one of the inspection hatches below the main cable nexus. "I decided I didn't want to know that badly."

"I suppose."

"This war machine, it's called the General George Washington," Sutler supplied. "Your boyfriend said it came up when he booted the thing."

"General is an old military title," Worth supplied. "Archaic term for a warlord."

"Washington was a place, I think," Glory recalled. "Pre-Breakdown. Maybe this was the personal war robot of the ruler there?"

"Could be," the arms dealer considered. "Don't matter now. All we have to concentrate on is getting this pile of junk to move, even if it crawls. If we can get it out of Yorvik as the shields go down, it's armoured enough to stand a chance of breaking through the legions' ring of ordinance."

"We might not have to wait for the barrier to fail," Wade revealed. He slid out of the service hatch, oily and dishevelled but grinning. "This thing was once state of the art. I mean before we lost the art. It was the nuts! It had shield-suppressor tech."

Glory was the first to understand what that meant. "It could ignore the force screen altogether! Like those bubble-buster rounds that the Khan tossed in early during the siege that burned straight through our defences."

Worth whistled. "You're saying we could pick our moment to leave? This thing could just... slip through the force dome?"

"*If* I can get the power grid connected," Wade agreed.

"Thanks for the necessary parts, kid," Worth told Glory. "If we could take the rest..."

"We're not robbing stores," the Mayor's daughter insisted. "Only for the essentials on Wake's list, anyhow."

"Okay, okay. Can't blame a guy for trying to make a living."

"You're doing alright out of this, Worth," Sutler reminded the arms dealer. "You're getting yourself and your stock out of harm's way, and selling tickets for high-rollers who'll pay everything they have to avoid being here when the legions roll in."

"I know, I know. Assuming Wade is as clever as he says. Assuming we can break through the Khan's curtain." The old man sighed. "Shame we couldn't get any weapons online."

"Who says we can't?" the mercenary replied. "I wouldn't trust the complicated ordinance, but that's not all we've got." He asked Glory, "Can you punch up those weapons specs again, kid?"

"I'm not a kid. I'm not dating Wake," the girl answered by routine. "Okay, here we are. Oooh!"

"Oooh what?" Worth demanded.

"Oooh, the General has pressure-steam canons and dust blasters and flame-throwers," Wake supplied. "Seems to me that Yorvik's not short of dirt. And you've got hidden fuel dumps, Worth, that you can't take with you."

"Old Town is desperately short of water, though," Glory objected.

"Short of clean, non-radioactive water, sure. But there's plenty of contaminated ground water. Do we care if we're spraying our enemies with irradiated steam?"

"I'll get some boys on it," Ephraim Worth agreed.

"There's this as well," Glory indicated. She put up a different display that showed the giant robot with a huge device strapped across its back.

"What is that?" Sutler wondered. "Some kind of cannon?"

"That," the Mayor's daughter announced, "is a two hundred-foot long, 15 ton sledgehammer. Low-tech as you please, but when something that big and heavy hits you, you don't get to complain afterwards."

Wake laughed. "General George Washington... bringing the hammer down!"

Worth got back to business. "Forty-eight hours till deadline. How long before this... General is ready to roll?"

Wake did some hasty calculations. "If Glory can upload the backup control programs while I handle the physical linkages, if we get all the parts we need, if I can bypass the worst-fritzed mechanisms that are never going to operate again... a day? Day and a half, tops."

"Cutting it close," the arms dealer considered. "This had better work."

● ● ●

Wake jumped to consciousness as the hand touched him. He sat up rapidly, forgetting he was dozing in a cable duct, and slammed his head into a reinforced strut.

"Watch out for the roof," Glory told him rather too late.

"Agh! Yeah, I got that. Thanks for the late memo!"

"You fell asleep. In the hole you were working in."

"Sorry. Hope I didn't drool on anything important."

The technician scrabbled out of the cable tunnel feet first, then rubbed his cranium.

Glory held up a sticking plaster. "Stimulant patch. Keep you going for another six hours." She fished another, different-coloured sticker from her aid kit. "Painkiller. You might need it."

Wake applied the medication as he blinked back to wakefulness. "What time is it?"

"Sometimes after two a.m. worth is off arranging for more supplies and fuel to get brought to us. Sutler is... well, I gather word is leaking out that there's something interesting under the junk here and that the Capo is history. Sutler is actively discouraging investigation from other species of lowlife."

"Sutler can be very discouraging."

"Yes. Do you think he'll be a problem? If we get the General working and out of the junk. Do you think Sutler will try to take control?"

"For Worth? Or instead of Worth?" Wake shrugged. "We have to take chances."

"Like I haven't heard that one before!"

Glory dropped into the pilot's seat beside Wake. She ran another quick diagnostic and checked she was familiar with the controls. If the General could be activated it would take three operators, one on Movement, one on Engineering, and one on Combat and Sensor Systems, to properly manage the huge machine. The stations would be manned by Glory, Wake, and Sutler respectively.

"Can you imagine what it must have been like, back when this thing was made?" Glory asked. "Before the wastelands and the ruins, before the poisoned water and the constant wars?"

"Before the Breakdown? When they could make things like this, and bridges, and roads that spanned the whole world?"

"And flying machines! Even to other worlds!"

Wake ran his hand over the curve of the console before him. "I guess this is as close as we'll ever get. Pretty amazing, though."

"I wish you hadn't had to scrub the database. There's so much we might have learned. So many things we've forgotten that we might have rediscovered."

"Well I had to, so there's no point fretting," the fix-tricks objected. "Besides, you're overlooking one thing when you talk about the golden age. It ended. It ended in war so terrible it broke the whole Earth. So they didn't get everything right. And before the end they made things like General George Washington. You don't build war machines unless you expect war."

"I suppose not," Glory admitted. "Still, sitting here..."

"Yeah."

The young people fell into silence then, sat working at their stations inside the rusted hulk of a dead robot from a lost age.

Dead, or sleeping?

● ● ●

The Khan cheated. As a red dawn broke on the second day of his ultimatum, additional ground forces rumbled into sight to add to the ordinance already pounding the remnant of Yorvik. With the new arrivals came a domebuster unit that turned its antennae dish on the ragged force field protecting Old City, gradually refining its probing until it discovered the exact overload frequency to crash the defence.

The arguing citizens of the besieged settlement did not have thirty-six hours to contemplate capitulation. They had fifteen minutes before their only protection was shattered and the Khan's forces marched in.

Worth hauled himself into the partially-restored robot's patched-up command centre, limping and swearing as he came. "Out of time! Out of luck! That bastard Khan fooled us all. Why should he stick to a timetable he picked? Caught us flat-footed. Caught us too soon!"

Sutler scrambled in behind the arms dealer. "No time to wait for your golden ticket passengers," he announced. "Let's go."

"I know," Worth hissed. "Half my stock not yet loaded and none of my high rollers."

"Yeah. I had a couple of girlfriends all packed for the journey, that I was looking forward to having you be grateful to me. Not going to happen now. R & R is cancelled." Sutler hammered a fist on the General's armoured bulkhead. "C'mon, kiddies! Get this thing moving!"

Wake dropped from a conduit that was currently overhead; had the machine been upright it would have been an easy access through a wall panel rather than an acrobatic climb. "Moving? You did hear my time estimate of 24 to 36 hours right? About 12 hours ago? I wasn't just making those numbers up."

Worth winced. "Maybe we can count on some extra time while those tanks roll up the citizens out there? We're still hidden by a huge pile of scrap."

"With active power systems that's stand out bright and clear on the Khan's scanners," Glory pointed out. "We'll be the first thing targeted."

Sutler spat an oath. "Can you get the hull force fields running, Wake? If we can reinforce the armour this thing has…"

"Everything that's not tied to the master control system is hooked up by now," the technician replied. "But shields, movement, sensors, weapons, and pretty much all the things we really want *are* master systems. None of which will be ready outside the times I told you."

There was a loud crackling noise from beyond the hull, and an unpleasant ozone tang.

"Dome bubble is stressed," Sutler recognised. "Won't last long now."

There was muffled screaming and a short burst of gunfire.

"Find out what's happening," Worth bellowed down the access tunnel to one of his boys.

"There must be something we can do to shave time off start-up," Glory told Wake. "Think!"

The rogue scratched his head, then winced where he found the bruise. "Maybe… pass across the inventory you ran on all the subroutines. That long list of reserve codes."

The trainee archivist interfaced her personal data pad with Wake's, swiping a file off her screen onto his. "I don't know what these are. They seem like menus of backup systems packages but they're just not in the database. Did you wipe them too?"

"Not that I know of. Maybe they were lost when the General was taken down? But there's no record at all of these files ever having been here, or of the reserve systems they operate."

Sutler looked at the mass of words on the screen. "What all are they? The names, I mean."

"They're just what we need, if we had them," Wake confessed. "Reserve power control. Reserve sensor calibration. Reserve motion systems. All the things we don't have."

Worth was distracted by his henchman returning from investigating. "Some gang-goths at the door," he shouted across. "They've got assault weapons and they're trying to get in. Donnell's down and Joss is wounded. Don't know what happened to Rush or Kloot. We've fallen back inside and sealed the exit hatch. Can't tell how long it'll hold them."

"Set up a perimeter round that door," the arms dealer called back. "Smart shrapnel-mines are authorised. They're in one of the cases down there, marked with an explosives symbol."

"Symbols," breathed Sutler. "There's symbols next to each of those file names on your list. Different ones for each system, right?"

"Yes," Glory agreed. "Those Yooessians really liked their pictograph icons. You find them everywhere on old supplies, even today, on everything from ration packs to footwear."

The mercenary pointed to the symbols on the screen. "These pictures, though. They're exactly the same, in just the same order, as on those metal slugs over there."

On what would have been the command centre's back wall, two dozen briefcase-sized containers were latched into utility shelving.

Wade hopped from his chair and reached one down. One narrow edge was different from the rest of the slug, containing a mass of connector pins and universal couplers.

The trickster-fixer gasped. "Oh… these guys planned ahead!"

"Are you going to let us in on it?" Worth demanded acerbically.

Wake hauled the heavy cartridge over to one of the mechanics panels he'd peeled back earlier. He pulled aside a mass of ribbon cables to reveal a plaque of similar size to that of the slug's edge. "This box is what Glory's list referred to. A portable, plug-in, reserve, motion systems command node. All the software and hardware needed to bypass broken primaries. Help me plug it in. Help me plug it in now! And haul the others out. We'll need most of them!"

Glory and Sutler hastened to help connect the slugs. Worth crawled back to the main cabin to check on the clanging noises where gangsters were trying to break past the access door.

"Shame we took down the automated defences earlier," the munitioneer muttered. "How long will that hatch hold?"

A shrieking noise reverberated through the robot's dense skin. The dome barrier had failed.

"They're in," Worth whispered, wondering if he'd just spoken his epitaph. The gangsters didn't matter now.

The next moment, the whole structure rocked as it was hit with surface to surface missiles designed to take out the energy readings that the invaders had detected. The pile of scrap under which the General lay was melted to slag. Goth-gang attackers were boiled away.

The robot was not harmed. "Hull force field is working at 60%," Wake announced. "Not bad at all!"

Emergency lights dimmed, then came on again much brighter. A rumble deep inside the war machine warned of the secondary power core ramping up for the first time in close to three centuries. Alarms flashed. Sparks flew across the interior spaces as rotted systems overloaded and burned out; but not too many of them.

Worth grabbed a safety bar as the whole room shifted – as the whole robot shifted. Motion systems were online!

From the lake of molten scrap, General George Washington stirred. He climbed to his feet, shaking off the crimson slag to stand upright amidst the ruined city.

Worth hauled himself back to the base of the now-vertical ladder shaft to the control compartment. He shouted one word of instruction: "Run!"

● ● ●

The people of Yorvik raced for what cover they could as the Khan's forces shattered their force dome. They huddled in cellars and storm drains, knowing those were scant protection from the shelling that had blistered on their barrier for four dreadful months, dreading when Khan's soldiers would move in to take revenge against the settlement that had defied him.

The Mayor had to physically drag his wife from the shrapnel-strewn street into the basement of the civil hall. She was screaming for her daughter. Gloriana was missing.

They were still struggling in the doorway when a three hundred foot tall metal figure rose above the ruins of Old City.

● ● ●

"About the running," Wake said apologetically as Worth heaved himself into the command centre. "We're not."

"What do you mean?" the arms dealer demanded. "What's wrong now?"

"I'm afraid we deceived you," Gloriana admitted. "We needed you to get us the General. We never intended to run away with him."

"Too bad," Worth snorted, "'cause that's what's happening. We get as far as we can as fast as we can till this thing burns out. We hide it someplace until I can get a chop-shop salvage team out to peel off anything worth reselling from the junk. I get a new stake to start over somewhere else. Anyone who tries to stop me…"

"I've entered an override into the machine's system," cautioned Wake. "It's linked to my life signs and Glory's. It requires regular codephrase updates to keep from triggering. There are other phrases that immediately bring on total unit self-destruct. You won't know if you've tortured me enough to have the right password or the kill code."

The arms dealer stared at the fixer-trickster and the Mayor's daughter, his gaze disbelieving. "You played me? *You* played *me?*"

"We can't run away," Glory insisted. "We can't just leave everybody here to slavery or death. Someone has to fight back. To draw a line!"

"And that's you?" Sutler asked.

"That's us – if you'll help us."

Wake chimed in. "We didn't know when we started what we'd find under the Shell. We didn't know we'd need three operators. We still do."

"Please, help us, Mr Sutler," Glory asked. "I know you are a mercenary, but…"

"But you have three hundred and sixteen reasons to fight with us today," Wake declared.

A range of emotions played across Sutler's face. Eventually he settled for a grim bleak smile. "I guess I do," he agreed. "Let's do it."

Worth chuckled. "This is turning into a real bad day for business. But I do have a professional interest in what that really big warhammer can do."

"You're in?" Wake asked in surprise.

"Why not? Can't do smart, do right." Wake pointed in the direction of the approaching armoured column. "It's that way."

Glory settled in the pilot's seat and set the robot marching. "I don't know who General George Washington was before," she admitted, "but today he's going to fight for our people and our homes against a tyrant who wants to enslave us!"

● ● ●

The incoming column has scarcely had chance to spot the giant striding at them when they was blinded by a great spray of desert dust, a choking cloud that blocked sensors and confused comms. None of them had opportunity to see the robot pick up the remains of an abandoned building and hurl it right into the midst of the tanks.

Ground forces on foot were spared from choking by their gas masks. That did not help them with the following cloud of boiling water vapour, a billowing effusion of third-degree burns that no breathing apparatus could prevent.

As the fumes began to clear, a few operators had time to leap aside before a huge house-sized hammerhead swept across the missile trucks, sending them toppling like toys as their ordinance detonated. The reverse stroke took out the lead assault tank.

The General trod on the next ones, squashing them flat.

In the first forty seconds of battle, George Washington had broken the enemy's charge and had delivered serious casualties to its advance element. The next division in line had little time to organise before the robot started scooping up the vanguard's convoy and hurling it overarm at them.

Desperate field commanders scrambled to direct missile fire at the unprecedented new threat. Target lock proved impossible, requiring manual sighting made more difficult by incoming shrapnel such as snatched-up tanks. Advancing infantry with shoulder-mounted anti-armour weapons were driven back again with horrendous losses by flame-thrower bursts from nozzles on the giant robot's wrists and knees.

In the ruins of Yorvik, ragged survivors dared peek from their hiding places to discover what had halted the enemy's seemingly-inevitable advance. Nobody understood where a rust-pitted giant fighting machine had come from, or why it dared face the combined legions of the terrible Khan. All they knew was that a champion had arisen, and it fought for them.

● ● ●

"Major cluster of halftracks to the left," Sutler called out. "I'm using up the last of the flamethrower fuel."

"Some kind of huge super-tank veering over the ridge," Glory warned. "It's trying to target its weapon on us. I'm hitting it with the hammer."

"No point me listing all the things that are breaking," Wake called out. "Just assume I'm being brilliant and switching systems as we go. This General is a tough old bird!"

"Have you got me comms links into the Khan's troops now?" Worth checked. "Okay then... Listen up, you worthless S.O.B.s. There's a new sheriff in town and he's got a really big warhammer. Any of you ever wanted to leave the Khan's service, now's the time to run away. We won't be targeting you. We'll be targeting the sorry dimwits who haven't turned round and left. Your choice, of course, but this war machine hasn't even started using its heavy weapons compliment yet."

The arms dealer believed in making the most of even his business reverses, and it wasn't every day he got to bully an army.

The General rocked as more distant mobile units bracketed it.

"Shields are fluttering about 30%. Power levels 35%," Wake warned. "Maybe we try and finish this soon?"

"We can't ask them to wait while we plug in for a recharge," Sutler pointed out. "I'm identifying what I think are their command elements. Glory, can you toss a few tanks into the areas I'm highlighting?"

"On it," the Mayor's daughter agreed. "You light them up, I'll pitch them down."

"Some of the rear units have stopped their advance," Worth noticed. "Think they're reconsidering their career options? I say we..."

The General was hit hard from behind, pitching the whole machine over to tumble in the dirt. The robot rolled, crushing more of the enemy troops, automatic systems cutting in to help right the giant.

A two hundred foot long sword sliced down, set to tear the General in half. Glory brought the head of the robot's warhammer up to catch the blow.

The Devastator stood over the downed General, fully matching it in size but somewhat less humanoid in shape. The Khan's personal war machine stood on three legs, its head reduced to a stubby cylinder surmounted with energy cannons. Those weapons fired now, slamming into and further degrading the General's defence shield and pounding the robot back to the ground.

"We found the Khan," Sutler growled,

The whole control chamber had yawed when the General had toppled. The gimbal-mounted console seats swivelled with the tilt, but Worth had fallen hard, slamming off one of the bulkheads. He rose unsteadily, clutching a broken arm, swearing. "Take down that sonofabitch!"

"We'll try," Glory promised. "Wake, Sutler, what can you tell me about that thing?"

"The Devastator," Wake snarled. "Yeah, it's got shields like us. Better than us, because it's fresh to the fight. There's energy crackling through that blade it's carrying. Hold on while I see if I can do that with the hammer."

"As a tripod that machine is more stable than ours," Sutler reported, "but perhaps slightly less manoeuvrable. Keep circling it, Glory."

"Okay, I've charged the hammer. It can't cut like the Khan's sword, but it can deliver one heck of a wallop!"

Glory tried it. The Devastator deflected the blow with its sword, turning aside the attack with practiced skill. More shellfire and energy flares hammered the General back again.

Something exploded in the command chamber. Flames rose from one of the access ducts.

Gritting his teeth against the pain, Worth dragged off his jacket to beat down the fire.

"Try the hammer again," Sutler advised Glory. "But this time, as you go in, I'll let off the last of the steam clouds. Then abort your hammer-blow and kick out a leg from under him."

"Three legged constructs are more stable as long as they have three legs," Wake understood.

"On it," Glory called, her teeth bared as she hauled on the creaking controls of the ancient war machine. "Come on, George!"

The feint worked. The Devastator momentarily pitched to the side as one support was swept away. Before it could recover, the General brought its warhammer down across the enemy's crown. A huge crumpled dent was left atop the Khan's flagship. The cannons surmounting the Devastator's head were silenced.

A full barrage of missiles still erupted from the damaged Devastator. The Khan had lost his temper.

"Dust chaff!" Sutler announced, evacuating the last of the fine-grain sand to confuse homing sensors.

The General shook as at least some of the missiles hit home. Spot gaps in the robot's defence screens allowed some of the ordinance to hit the heavy armour around the machine itself. Lights and screens flickered and reset. Red font damage estimates scrolled up a cracked monitor. A brief flare of flame raced across the top of Glory's console.

She brought the General up close and personal and grappled the Devastator. George Washington hauled the tripod up onto two legs then flipped it over. The Devastator's sword met the General's hammer side on, shattering under the unstoppable swinging mass. The sledgehammer continued down to smash into the enemy's exposed underside.

"Did we just hit the Khan in the nuts?" Wake wondered.

"Drop on him!" Worth called. "Belly flop. This robot weighs the same as a pocket battleship. That Devastator is belly up like a beetle. Keep it down in the mud, where it can't bring weapons to bear on us!"

Glory brought the General in to pin the foe, trapping one of its arms while leaving it open to more strikes from her own machine.

"Our shields are about 10% now, power at 12%," Wake warned. "Theirs, maybe less. Keep going!"

Something big exploded on one side of the downed Devastator. "They lost an arsenal," Sutler guessed. "Wait, there's something detaching from their machine."

It was a fast-moving ground vehicle. The Khan had decided to withdraw. The armoured capsule swerved away on a defensive retreat pattern until it was safe amongst the tyrant's remaining forces.

"Get us off the Devastator!" Worth called urgently. "Move!"

"I still need to finish it off!" Glory's blood was up.

"The Khan's a bad loser," cautioned Sutler. "He's not going to leave us a prize to grab and he'll want to take us out as well."

The General rolled off the Devastator just before the enemy machine self-destructed. The fireball engulfed the General but her defence screen held just long enough before fizzling out.

"Shields are gone. Energy at 6%," Wake reported. "Charge them, Glory!"

"Wait, What?" Sutler objected.

"They don't know," Worth told him. "All those soldiers have seen, all the Khan has seen, is that we've just taken out his prestige war machine, chased him off, and now we're back on our feet to kick more ass. Wake's right. Charge!"

"Charging," Glory agreed.

General George Washington advanced. The Khan's forces retreated in disarray.

● ● ●

The war machine stood in the middle of Old Town, a battered guardian over a tattered ruin. Yet robot and settlement alike were victorious.

"Still running, as far as my scouts can tell, Mr Mayor," Worth reported.

"Not all running together, though," Sutler added with satisfaction. "Looks like some of those troops took the opportunity you suggested, Mr Worth."

"I am... amazed at this sudden reverse of fortune," Mayor Bell admitted. "And at my daughter's part in it!" He turned to his wife. "Where is Gloriana?"

Tessera pointed up to the General. "Still in there. With Wake Hartfirth."

"*What?*"

● ● ●

"I found something," Wake told Glory. "When I was cleaning the carbon scoring off the pilot console. It was engraved there under all the crud."

The apprentice archivist turned robot pilot looked at the old writing. Language and font were archaic but understandable. She read it out loud:

"*Oe'r the land of the free and the home of the brave!*"

"Yep. What do you make of it? It must have been important, for the General's builders to bother etching it there."

Glory considered. "Maybe... maybe the General wasn't only a war machine? Maybe he was a protector? A liberator? Of a land of the free?"

"That land sounds kind of nice," Wake agreed. "We should get one of those."

"Well... we do have a really big robot."

"Shame not to use him."

"Big shame."

"It's not like the Khan is finished for good."

"Somebody has to stop him."

"It's written right there on the console."

"Can't ignore the operating instructions."

"I don't have much planned for tomorrow."

"I can free up my schedule."

So they took General George Washington and went off to start a revolution.

The End

Visions of Satan
By David White

The man awoke to a nightmare, but was it? It felt all so real. He was in a building…a house perhaps, he couldn't be sure because it was dark and gloomy. It smelt of mold and decay…it felt…dead! But how could something that never lived be dead? This man was well versed in the arcane arts; the supernatural was not unknown to him. He looked down at his hands and a panic overtook him, he felt his pulse quicken and sweat began to form on his brow. He started running, his head darting side to side searching, searching for a way out, but also for something that would show his reflection. The man knew who he was, but had spent the better part of his life keeping his identity a secret. That secret was there for discovery now, but he needed to be sure. It was obvious that he was out of costume, but was the masking spell that kept his facial features ever changing to whoever looked at it still in place, or was that too gone. He mumbled the words to an ancient spell, but nothing happened

He moved around for what seemed like hours, he ran until there was no breath left in his lungs, it was as if every turn and doorway led to the same room. It was a large set of double doors. They were made from the finest cherry and stretched a full ten feet in the air. The man decided that he might as well enter the doors, since so matter how much he ran, or how many turns he took, he always ended up in front of the same double doors. He took a deep breath and stepped forward and with each hand grasped a handle. He paused and gathered his wits, he couldn't remember the last time he felt fear, usually he instilled it, yet now it was seeping in through his defenses, defenses forged through mastering all the magical arts he could delve into. He fought it back and flung both doors open and stepped rapidly in to the room. The room was filled with light and something else. The room no matter where he looked was covered with mirrors, even the ceiling. He whirled around in every direction, every angle, and all he seen was multiple reflections of his face staring back at him. He pulled his arm up over his face and turned to run back through the doors he had entered through, but just as he did the doors slammed shut. He grabbed hold of the handles and pulled with all his might, but they would not budge. He fell to his knees and tried to control his breathing and his heart, which was nearly ready to bounce out of his chest.

Suddenly the room was filled with laughter, a laughter that kept getting louder and louder till finally he had to put his hands over his ears to keep his eardrums from bursting. Then just when he thought his head was going to explode it stopped and the room was filled with deathly silence. He stood up and walked around the room, searching for another way out, not caring at this point if his identity was revealed. Then a voice spoke, a voice dark and cold…a voice that froze the man in his tracks.

"I know thee little man, I am coming for you, and when we meet, you will think of this event as pure heaven." Then the laughter began again and all at once the doors opened. The man stood still though, he dug deep down and found the insane courage that was buried deep, a courage born from what some would call madness, or perhaps pure evil, it mattered not. He stood triumphant. He even began to laugh.

"Get out of my head fool, you know not who you are dealing with, for I am evil incarnate, I am power, I am fear, I…am Dr. Satan!"

● ● ●

Hot Springs Arkansas. This was the home to one Phineas Montgomery, heir to the Montgomery chemical company, but also heir to a legacy of evil and death, insanity most would have called it. Those times were in the past now, the horrors that his parents represented through devil worship and human sacrifices were long in the past, if not totally for Phineas. He was only eight years of age when his man servant Po had whisked him away to Japan to raise him as best he could, and he had spent ten long years learning the ways of the ninja.

Phineas returned at the age of eighteen and in two short years, with the help of Percy James, one of a handful of his father's friends that weren't part of a cult, had built the business back up. Phineas now at the age of twenty two has a wealth of government contracts and had reinstalled the Montgomery name in Hot Springs.

The year was 1941, and while the United States had yet to stick their feet in to the war, most felt it was coming soon, the armed forces included. Phineas had a different problem at hand right now though. He was aware of a great evil that sought to gain a chalice that until now even he hadn't known his father possessed. There was much he didn't know about his father, but after his last adventure with a fallen angel named MaGee, he had learned that his father was not dead. This also weighed heavy on his mind as he sat alone in a special chair in his secret lair.

Phineas after coming back to Hot Springs, and moving back in to the family mansion had found secret chambers located in a network of tunnels that ran under the mansion. He had also learned about his psychic gifts. They were getting stronger as he aged, the drugs he used also strengthened these powers, though Po felt it would spell his doom, Phineas used his gifts as well as all the training he had received from Po and took the battle to the wealth of crime that was rapidly spreading across Hot Springs. He had a special way of dealing with the criminals, whatever their fear was he could find it, and using his gifts made that person suffer through a living nightmare. He smiled at that thought.

Phineas was only an average man, he stood five eight and weighed a hundred and sixty pounds. He wore his Scottish heritage with the fire red hair, the pale freckled skin, and the deep blue eyes, but he was a force to be reckoned with...a fact Lance Hannigan was learning in spades. Phineas took a deep breath and sat back in the special chair that his father had built. Phineas used it for good. He pushed a button and a piece of head gear adjusted to his head as two probes made contact with his temples. Phineas was preparing to enter the mind of a man that possessed evil like none he had ever known, maybe even worse than his father. Phineas closed his eyes and became someone else, someone the crooks and thugs of Hot Springs had come to fear over the last few years. He became the dark Spector known as 'Doc Panic!'

● ● ●

In a stone mansion along the Hudson River Valley a man glad in a tight fitting red outfit and cape, complete with a matching mask that hid all but his eyes and mouth as well as containing a tiny set of protruding horns modeled after the evil figure he had named himself after, sat Doctor Satan. He was in the lotus position inside of a pentagram surrounded by several burning candles that waved and sparked in several different colors, filling the room with the strange and distinct odor of brimstone... His eyes were closed as another figure looked on. This was his loyal servant...Bostiff!

Bostiff in himself looked like a demon straight from hell, but was merely a man. A cruel accident at a railway yard had left him with no legs and short useless stumps. He used his powerful arms to move about on hands and knuckles that had become hardened like granite over the years. His arms possessed the strength of a strong man's legs, and people who underestimated that fact usually wound up with a death sentence. Though Bostiff served his master faithfully, it was not out of love...but fear.

Suddenly the figure in the pentagram opened his eyes. They were not sleepy, they were not happy, they were as they always, glinted with pure evil and a distaste for mankind. They focused on the figure of Bostiff and showed an even greater disdain, then a voice that could chill even a sun god's blood spoke.

"Bositiff, you idiot! I told you to have a chalice of the 89 Bordeux ready when I awakened! Can you not perform even the most simple of tasks, you dimwitted piece of fodder?"

Bostiff scurried to the cellar, moving faster than anyone would have thought possible without the use of legs. Meanwhile Doctor Satan stood from his lotus position and sat in the chair he always pondered world conquest in. It was more of a throne, but Satan thought it fitting, with its ornate brass body and lush burgundy cushions. He plopped down and folded his hands as he awaited his wine. It was taking far too long; once again Bostiff would need to be taught his place.

Just as Doctor Satan prepared to stand and give Bostiff a good lashing, Bostiff came around the corner, moving with great caution as to not spill a drop of the wine, something he knew would get him either bashed in the side of the head, or have his skin flayed by the master's whip.

He handed the chalice to his master with a shaking hand and smiled thinking he had done well. Once the chalice was in the master's hand however he received a backhand that sent him sprawling along the floor, sparkles of light floating about his vision as Doctor Satan roared.

"Fool!! You will figure out a way to be quicker or I will skin you alive! Now be gone! I have plans to make and just looking upon you causes me sickness." With that Satan waved a hand and turned back to sit down, Bostiff stared for a second with hate filled eyes...but only a second and then made his way to the small room he called his own, he hoped that the master would call on him no more that night.

● ● ●

Satan sat upon his makeshift throne and stared in to the flame of a burning urn that stood nearby. He took a sip of his wine and savored the taste as he pondered recent setbacks in his plans. The fool Ascott Keane had thrown wrench after wrench in to his well laid plans, and the fool known as the Pelligrine and his circle of friends had also fowled his mastery of man. That was all in the past, for now he had the chance to seize a relic that would grant him not only power, but eternal life and complete healing from any wound. He would possess it, even if he must destroy the man who now wielded it, a throwback from the Scottish Riders, a group that secretly kept the Knight Templar in existence, though never as powerful. They did however hold on to many of the secrets, including the chalice he now sought, one that was used by the fool son of God to turn water to wine, Satan sought nothing so meager, but the total control of mankind, and in lieu of that...destruction of them.

Satan took a deep breath and sipped more from the wine. It was then the room was filled with a deep laugh. It was everywhere and nowhere at all. Satan set the glass down and stood at the ready. He mumbled a spell meant to bring anything concealed in to view, but it did nothing, except cause the strange voice to laugh harder. Satan began chanting words older than man, a spell meant to shield him from all but the most powerful attacks. He moved than further in to the large room that had once been a grand parlor in this large mansion that he now dwelled in. Light flickered along the walls from the many urns and lit candles throughout, Satan preferred them to the electric lights of modern society, felt them more fitting.

Satan reached the center of the room and snapped his fingers and instantly the room was filled with bright lights from the large chandelier. Satan went over the room inch by inch, his eyes missing nothing, yet still there was no form to place to the voice. Finally his anger got the better of him and he shouted out in a sinister rage, spittle flying from his mouth to land upon the floor.

"Show yourself I say, stand before one who was born to rule all of mankind. Stand before my power!" Without warning Satan released bolts of lightning that sprouted from his finger-tips and wreaked havoc around the room. He ceased and looked around at the damage to his castle and again anger welled up inside him. It was at that instance that he heard the slow and methodical clap behind him. He whirled and there before him stood a man cloaked completely in a tight fitting black suit. The only thing left uncovered were the eyes, eyes of piercing blue, eyes that seemed to look in to Satan's very soul, eyes that were disgusted by what they saw. The figure in black stood motionless like a statue, almost like the Grim Reaper himself, and while Satan knew no fear, he was unsure of things right now, no one had ever entered his personal space without him not only knowing, but also expecting it. He would skin that fool Bostiff alive for this.

"You have made a grave mistake entering my home fool!" Satan said with an evil grin on his lips. "It is a mistake you will not live to regret." Satan was in action then, pulling to small spheres of glistening silver from his pocket and throwing them towards the stranger. The spheres instantly began to expand and after second they expanded so large as to be transparent, but now the stranger in black was within them, still he did not move. Satan approached the stranger, he was bold now, he felt triumphant, for these spheres were created by a witch whose name had long ago been forgotten, and once someone was trapped inside, they would contract, slowly and surely, until whatever was inside them would be crushed in to dirt.

Satan moved closer now and stared through the skin of the sphere and in to his enemy's eyes. They stared back, unflinching, unafraid. Satan felt a smile form as the spheres started to collapse on the stranger, he began to feel a joy come over him, it was a joy he had felt many times…a joy he felt every time he vanquished an enemy. He watched at the spheres began to press against the stranger until they were taking on the shape of his form, still the stranger stared in to his eyes without fear, Satan's smile grew even larger. It was then he noticed a gleam in the stranger's eyes, it was then the smile began to disappear from his lips.

The spheres exploded around the stranger and the force sent Satan hurdling backwards and on to his backside. He was on his feet quickly, still the stranger stood silently, staring. Satan let out a primordial scream then and charged the enemy, he grabbed a nearby candle stand and advanced on the stranger, the stand raised above his head. He gained speed and still the stranger stood still. Satan advanced even quicker; he was enraged and sought to bash the stranger's head in. He was a few mere feet away and was already picturing the stand coming down on the stranger's head. He grinned at the thought of the blood and brain matter that would ooze forth.

Satan began to drop the stand at a fantastic speed, he put his all in to the strike and it would be grand indeed. Just as Satan was ready to drive the stand in to the stranger's head, the stranger casually grabbed Satan's wrist and with a turn of his hips, Satan

found himself hurtling effortlessly through the air to land hard on the ground. He felt ever bone in his body had been jarred, he turned in disbelief and looked back, but this time the stranger was on him. He stood over him and again laughter filled the room, but only for a brief second...then the stranger spoke.

"I expected much more of a challenge from you Doctor Satan, much more indeed. I guess I was meant to be disappointed!"

• • •

Satan was speechless, but only for a moment. He was puzzled by the stranger escaping his spheres with ease, but many things were confusing right now, the least of which was how the stranger had invaded his inner sanctum without any of his alarms being triggered. It mattered not though; he would crush this man like the insect he was. It was then it came to him who stood before him, it was the masked vigilante known to the citizens of Hot Springs as Doc Panic.

"Fool I know not how you managed to not only escape my spheres, nor how you entered my abode, but rest assured you shall not leave this place alive...Doc Panic!" Satan Roared. Doc Panic's head shook to the negative.

"You haven't guessed what is going on here yet, have you?" Doc Panic said. "Here let me lay it out for you."

"We are not really in your abode as you say, but actually in your mind, well your dream to be exact. I find I do my best work there," Doc Panic said. Satan laughed.

"Impossible! I am wide awake and you are far too young and unskilled to trick me in to a dream state, my mind is too powerful" Satan argued. It was Panic's turn to chuckle.

"True, but what of your dimwitted lackey? Good thing that wine is such a favorite of yours, you never noticed the blend I had him concoct. I figure it will keep you out for a few hours, more than enough time to accomplish my goal."

"I am afraid you have underestimated me Panic, or should I say Phineas Montgomery? Yes I see from the shock in your eyes I have caught you by surprise. You forget one thing my friend, I am master of many aspects of the mind, but supernatural and natural, you have overstepped your boundaries." With that Satan raised a hand and a burst of energy shot out, and if not for Doc Panic's quick reaction, it might have taken his head off, as it was it sent him flying in to a nearby wall.

In a secret room underneath the Montgomery Chemical plant, Phineas Montgomery convulsed in his seat, a trickle of blood ran from his nose. He did not lose focus however and remained in the madman's dream, though ever the more cautious. He knew Satan's mind was warped, but he also knew there was great power there.

Doc Panic recovered from the blast just in time to move out of the way of another that blew a hole clean through the wall of the castle. Moving quickly Doc panic pulled three shrurikens, a special throwing star used by Ninjas, from a pocket built in to his costume. They were laced with a special charge that would cause enough of an explosion on impact to knock an opponent out or worse depending upon how many made contact. Satan was up to the challenge though, and with a wave of his hand the special stars exploded before ever touching him. He stood there grinning like a conqueror of men.

"You were very naïve to think you would have an advantage by attacking me in a dream state. You are but a child and I am a master. I am even more powerful in my dreams, something you didn't count on." With that Satan raised his hands and Doc Panic felt the very foundation of the building quake beneath him. He looked up and watched in terror as the very ceiling began to crack open and large pieces of stone and plaster started to come crashing down. It took all of his ninja training to cartwheel, spin, and flip to avoid the tons of debris that came crashing in.

A huge cloud of smoke filled the place knocking out most of the candles and allowing Doc Panic to move into the shadows unseen. Doc Panic was given only the briefest of respites though as suddenly there was a glow in the center of the dust that was so bright he had to turn away. He felt as if he was standing under a dessert sun. Doc Panic decided he would need to rely on his other senses, so pulling a bandana from his pocket he blindfolded himself and drew the Katana from its holster on his back and listened as well as judged the heat from the object that was now in the room, he didn't need to guess what it was as Satan was all too happy to brag about it.

"I know by now you are either blind, or at least having to keep your eyes closed, either way your end is near. The object before you is the legendary eye of Kinich-Ahau. It was used by the Mayan Sun God to blind or incinerate his people's enemies. I prefer a little more hands on approach." Satan chuckled, but it was short lived, for Doc panic sprang from the ground and with a speed faster than the eye swung the Katana straight and true and shattered the mystical stone in to tiny fragments, rendering it useless. Satan was beside himself with rage.

"Noooooooo! You idiot!" With that Satan raised his hands and they began to glow as energy crackled and sparked all around them, then bringing them together a ball of brilliant white energy began to form until bolts of electricity crackled all around and Satan's eyes themselves began to glow a brilliant molten blue. Doc Panic took a deep breath and just before the energy sphere was unleashed, he leapt from Satan's dream and returned to awaken in the cave in Hot Springs. He was covered in sweat and his temples pounded…but he was alive.

● ● ●

Bostiff had been shaken from his sleep by the violent vibrations of the castle's very foundation. He jumped from his bed and as fast as he could move on his knuckles and high-tailed it for the back door. Chunks of plaster and wood were already raining down as he zigged and zagged, avoiding most of the larger chunks and shrugging off the smaller ones that made contact. He made it to the door and swung it open so violently that it was ripped from its hinges and he was out of the castle and moving away as fast as he could. He stopped moving after he had reached the top of the hill and turned to watch as the castle imploded on itself sending a mushroom cloud of debris in to the air followed by flickers of red and orange flame.

Bostiff watched till there was nothing left of the castle but flames and smoke, it was completely leveled, and far as Bostiff knew, his master was lost with it. It was a blank and empty feeling not knowing what he would do with himself from now on. After a while he shrugged his shoulders and headed away as the sounds of fire engine sirens blared in the background.

● ● ●

Phineas Montgomery sat in his study later that evening, a glass of scotch at his side. His head was pounding and every muscle in his body hurt, but for the time being he had thwarted the plans of Doctor Satan. He felt certain it wouldn't be the last of Satan, but he hoped it would at least give him more time to prepare for their next battle. Satan

David White

was a far more formidable foe than he had originally guessed. He had much to learn and there was still the fact that his supposedly dead father was not only alive, but possessed a mystical object of great power which Satan sought to help him rule the world.

Phineas sat back and lit a smoke and drawing in deeply began to blow rings of smoke in to the air. His thoughts were interrupted by the slow clapping of hands. Instantly the cigarette was out of his mouth and his nearby Katana in his hand. A tall figure emerged from the shadows. He was well dressed and while not looking overly old seemed to possess the air of great wisdom about him. Phineas took a defenses stance as the stranger moved closer and ignoring the sword stepped to the liquor cart and poured himself a drink.

"Who are you?" Phineas asked. The stranger smiled.

"Ascott Keane, at your service. I want to congratulate you on winning the battle, but also…I want to prepare you for the war!" With that Phineas set the sword down and the two sat across from each other. It looked as if there would be no sleep for Phineas.

The End

Big Trouble in Little Cheyenne

by Tony Wilson

It was four years after President Lincoln signed the Pacific Railway Act and I found myself riding on a supply train heading northeast out of San Francisco toward the Sierra Nevada Mountains. They were trying to catch up with the crews working on the Central Pacific Railroad before the snow started falling again. I had no particular interest in the railroad; I just needed to make a hasty exit from town. I awoke one night with a pounding in my head after a long evening of drinking and discovered a shotgun resting on my chin. Apparently, I had worn out my welcome in Barbary Coast. I didn't even know that to be possible.

While I was now cast out by the cutthroats, con artists, gamblers, and tramps, I still had one friend, a Chinese fellow by the name of Chung. He didn't ask a lot of questions, he was reliable in a fight, and truth be told, his English was probably better than mine. Folks weren't all too trusting of the Celestials, but since they had built the Great Wall, the railroad investors decided they were worth a risk and more dependable workers then the Irish. Welcome to America, where everybody has someone else special to shit on.

We were headed for a boomtown called Little Cheyenne, which had grown into a temporary outpost for the crews blasting tunnels through the mountains. Chung had received an urgent telegram from his uncle, who was already onsite, requesting his assistance. I was working security, which meant that I had the pleasure of sleeping in a rickety train car filled with hay instead of freezing my ass off in the next car back with the new crew of workers. I could feel the train slowing down and three blasts of the whistle told me we were finally there.

I shook the straw off my heavy wool coat and popped my hat back into shape. I hated meeting new people. I had a knack for saying the wrong things to the right people. Maybe I'd take my earnings and shuffle off to charm school after this. Wouldn't that be a laugh? With a fresh plug of tobacco in my lip, I pushed open the door to see what mess I'd gotten into this time.

To call Little Cheyenne a town would be giving it far too much credit. Forty yards from the train track, down a short incline, a muddy swath wide enough for a wagon cut through row after row of tents dusted with snow. Beyond those were a handful of wooden shanties circled around a long bunkhouse and a tavern that likely made up the classier of the two neighborhoods. I was still taking it all in when Chung tapped me on the shoulder.

"I need to find my uncle."

I spit tobacco juice and nodded to all the tents. "Unless he's got red hair, I think he'll be pretty easy to find."

Chung shook his head. "Chinese camp is on the other side of the tracks."

So much for my astute powers of observation.

"Good luck, Mr. Raney. It has been a pleasure," he said.

"You too. I'm going to wander over and see if I can find a foreman. Someone owes me money."

Chung smiled. "You had a very prosperous nap."

That got a laugh out of me. "I could use a few more of those."

Underneath my coat, I adjusted the gun belt resting on my hips. A Colt Navy revolver sat in each holster. If anyone had a question that flummoxed me, these six-shooters were always happy to answer. I'd recently discovered the joy of paper cartridges, so they were less of a pain in the ass to reload, but the process still took valuable time you wouldn't have during a fire fight. I'd meant to pick up a rifle. Maybe I'd do just that with some of my earnings here.

As Chung disappeared behind the train, I trudged down the hill into camp. A flurry of snowflakes whirled around me and the wind was picking up. Man, I hated the cold. My body was made for mild winters and muggy summers. I needed a drink to cut the chill.

Little Cheyenne was like an anthill teeming with activity. Labor gangs of thirty to forty men worked around the clock in shifts of at least eight hours. Up until this point, they'd spent their days clearing a path for the railroad over hills covered in fir trees. Everything was graded and leveled before rails were hammered in. Now it was all about cutting tunnels through the mountains.

The way I understood it, several tunnels were being built between these camps and more further into the Donner Pass. Each one had to go through solid granite, so progress was slower than molasses. The Chinamen got stuck on blasting duty, drilling holes in the stone, filling them with black powder, lighting a fuse, and running like hell. You were either really good at it or just more debris to be hauled out of the tunnel.

I found a wooden shack with a crudely painted sign that said OFFICE pinned to the outside. A pair of muffled voices were arguing inside, but that wasn't my problem. Getting paid was. I knocked twice and stood back so as not to crowd the door. See, I knew a few manners.

A burly man with unkempt brown hair stepped outside. While his hair was wild, his mustache was carefully waxed so it curled up on both sides. A black patch covered his left eye.

"Yeah?" he asked.

"You the boss?"

He sized me up with his good eye. "Mr. Crocker's the boss, but he ain't here. I guess that leaves me in charge."

I let him stand there for a moment, wondering who the hell I was. I could play the game too.

"Whaddaya need?"

"I need to get paid. I just rode in with the fresh laborers. They had me working security. The trip was…uneventful."

"You're Raney then," he said, pointing a fat sausage of a finger at me.

"Chance Raney. That's me. You got a name?"

"Art Beauregard. Everyone around here calls me Beau."

"Beau and Chance. We're practically courting now. When do I get paid," I asked, sending a stream of tobacco juice into the mud.

"Follow me. Safe is back up the hill on one of the luxury cars." He strode off the porch, heading back towards the tracks. "You sticking around? Hell, you might not have a choice with the snow rolling in," he mumbled.

"Got any work that doesn't involve hauling rocks out of the mountainside?"

"I might. We'll see how hard this new crew wants to work. I'm hearing whispers that the goddamn Celestials are about to strike again. Last time that happened, we had to put some lead in a few before they went back to work."

I can't say I was a fan of his approach to maintaining order, so I held my tongue. The War was still fresh in everyone's minds as were the wounds. One thing I'd learned on the battlefield was that volunteers worked a whole lot harder than anyone forced under the yoke. I'm assuming their pay was shit and less than the Irish were making. The situation could get ugly real fast. A smart man would collect his earnings and then make himself scarce.

We reached a trio of train cars that were sitting further up the track. Beau pulled himself up the steps by the coupler of the rearmost car. His coat jingled and he rooted through his pockets for the keys. He finally produced a ring of about two dozen keys of varying sizes. He seized one in his mammoth hand and shoved it into the lock.

"Wait here," he said.

I looked up at the gray sky, watching the heavy wet flakes come down harder and harder. What the hell was I doing out here? There were no more battles that needed winning unless I wanted to head south to fight the Apache or Comanche. What was the point in that? Even if the pay was good, dying with a quiver full of arrows stuck in my ass before I could spend it was a real problem.

Beau returned with a small burlap pouch and tossed it to me. "I'm willing to pay the same daily rate if you want to sit tight for a few days until I see which way the wind's blowing. Put you up in the bunkhouse and feed you too."

My heart wasn't really in it, to be honest, but if I was going to be stuck here for a few days because Mother Nature was having a hissy fit anyway, I might as well get paid. "Doesn't look like I got much choice," I said, holding my palm out and watching it fill up with snow.

Beau slapped me on the shoulder and pointed over toward the Chinese camp. "Looks like your shift starts right now."

Several men in conical hats were coming up the tracks. There was purpose in their stride.

"Let's see what the hell they want this time," Beau said.

As they approached, I recognized Chung standing in the back. He spoke freely with the other men in Chinese. Their voices rose and became agitated. Something was up. Chung nodded furiously before stepping out in front of the group.

"Mr. Beau, may we speak with you for a moment?"

Beau sized him up. "Do I know you?"

"I just arrived today. I am Chung. My uncle is the headman for one of your work gangs. He sends his apologies for being unable to meet with you. He is still in great pain."

"The powder man," Beau said. "If this is about the basket crews again—"

"Please, Mr. Beau. I know it is hard for your people to understand."

"The only thing to be understood here is that we're already way behind schedule and Mr. Crocker is not going to waste a hunnerd kegs of powder to dig out some dead Celestials. They knew the risks."

Chung changed tactics. "They did know the risks as you say, Mr. Beau, but it is very important that we return their bodies to their villages. We Chinese believe that if they are to have eternal peace, they must be returned to their homeland to be buried."

"If Charles Crocker doesn't get his railroad finished, we're all going to be worried about where our bodies end up. I suggest you draw up a map and worry about it after we're done."

"But, Mr. Beau—"

Beau leaned in, nose to nose with him. "Tell 'em to get back to work or there's gonna be hard consequences. Ain't none of us got time for spiritual horseshit." He spun on his heels and marched back to camp, leaving me standing there in the falling snow with Chung.

When I was sure Beau was out of earshot, I took Chung by the arm and pulled him aside.

"You make friends about as well as I do. I don't think I'd piss that guy off. He's wound a little tight."

"This is about something bigger than the railroad, Raney."

"Is this about your uncle?"

"His crew was up on the mountain, blasting out a ledge for the tracks. It is perilous work. They hang the workers over the side in baskets. The men fill the holes with powder, light the fuses, and then the rest of the crew pull the baskets up. There was an accident last week."

"They didn't get the baskets up in time," I guessed.

"Yes. Three men were buried in the rockslide at the bottom of the mountain. My uncle was almost four. The crew needs to recover the bodies, but that main foreman won't let them."

I spit tobacco juice out of the side of my mouth. "I'm not sure this is a fight you really wanna pick, Chung. Getting between old white men and their money is dangerous business."

"I'm afraid of what my uncle might do. He is a very stubborn man."

"Tell yah what. I'll get some whiskey in Beau after dinner and see what I can do."

Chung nodded. "I hope that is not too late."

● ● ●

"You are one sorry sumbitch when it comes to cards," I said, glaring at the man seated across from me. I think I'd heard the other men at the table call him Tanner.

He looked up at me from behind his cards, his balding pate turning scarlet, and jabbed a finger at me. "I've had about enough of your yappin', friend."

I chuckled. "Friend? My friends know better than to try to cheat me at the card table."

"You keep talking and we'll just see what happens."

I pulled a lead ball out of a pouch on my belt and held it up to the light between my thumb and middle finger. "See this?"

Before he could answer, I flicked it at him. It was a flawless shot that hit him right between the eyes before bouncing off the table and rolling away. He rubbed the spot furiously.

"What the hell was that?"

"That, friend, was a warning shot. Take your money and piss off or the next one's gonna be coming at yah a lot faster."

Tanner grabbed his cash and jammed the wad in his jacket pocket. "I was cashing out and heading to the shitter anyway. Maybe I'll wipe my ass with some of your money."

We all watched as he stormed across the room to the door of the tavern. He sidestepped Art Beauregard along the way and almost knocked over another man carrying a round of drinks to his companions. A chill swept through the place when he flung open the door and slammed it behind him.

"What was that all about," Beau asked, taking a seat.

"Asshole was dealing from the bottom," one of the other men muttered.

Beau grinned, which made his eye-patch wiggle and instead of looking amused he just came off like a pirate with an itch he couldn't scratch.

"Are we dealing yah in?" I shuffled the cards and squared up the deck.

"No thanks. Losing my pay to the help don't set a good example," he said. "I was actually hunting for you. The Chinese gang working the late shift up at the tunnel hasn't shown up. I just heard that the midday shift kicked off a little early too or I'd still have them out there. I guess they're all riled up over there. I thought I made it clear this afternoon how things were gonna be."

"You're sure it's not the weather slowing 'em down?"

"I sent one of my foremen over there to find out what the excuse is. That was almost an hour ago, so maybe it's taken a while to find someone with enough English to explain what's up unless they're just giving him the silent treatment. Grab your coat, Raney. We're gonna go over there and put a boot in someone's ass."

I stood up and pulled on my heavy coat. "You're the boss."

We stepped out the door into the bitter cold. The temperature drop almost knocked the breath out of me. The snow was coming down hard and halfway up our boots. Little Cheyenne was completely covered. The light pouring out from all the buildings reflected off the white powder and made the whole camp glow.

"Hear that?"

I listened hard. "Nope."

"Should hear them blasting in the tunnel. Yellow sons of whores." Beau pulled his coat tighter, lumbering along toward the tracks. I recognized the look in his eye. He had murder on his mind.

"Hold up," I said, my fingers caressed the sandalwood grips of my revolvers. "Did you hear that?"

Beau cocked his head to one side. A wail of anguish filled the air.

"Over there," he pointed to the south.

We scrambled through a maze of tents, trying not to trip over the ropes and stakes. The closer we got, the wailing trailed off into a whimper. It went silent by the time we reached the privies.

Eight outhouses sat downwind of the camp. They sat back to back in two rows. I motioned to Beau to go around the west side while I took the east. With both guns drawn, I slipped around the corner ready to shoot the first thing that moved. To my dismay, we discovered Tanner with his pants around his ankles, nose down in yellow snow. The door behind him swung in the breeze, tapping against his boots.

Beau reached down and grabbed him by the collar. "Tanner, you shit for brains..."

His face was sunken, like a man who'd spent weeks starving in the desert sun. Bloodshot eyes bulged out from black sockets. His whole body was in a similar state, shriveled up like an old prune.

Beau released his grip immediately, letting the body drop unceremoniously to the ground. We shared a look before he turned away to throw up in some degree of privacy. Better out than in, is what I've always said. In mid-hurl, someone brave enough to stand in front of him seized Beau by the throat with both hands. I rolled to my left to get a better angle on whoever it was. Make that...whatever it was.

The thing that held Beau up like a child hoisting up its prize dolly barely looked human. Underneath the tattered conical hat of one of the laborers, I could make out sharp features carved out of pale greenish-white flesh. Both eyes were milky blue like a blind old man's peepers. Its mouth, filled with rows of needles, stretched wide and a thin black tongue whipped out. It locked lips with the big man and I could only watch as it drained the life right out of him. It let go of the empty husk and turned toward me.

I snapped off three shots, sending two to the chest and one between its cloudy eyes. With arms outstretched, it hopped forward. I fired again; this time sure I hit the heart. It hopped forward again.

"Oh, the hell with this." I took a step forward and fired a lead ball right into its forehead at pointblank range. The shot went in true, sending a spray of black ichor onto my face. Twin claws wrapped around my neck for my trouble. The creature's black lips parted and I got an uncomfortably close look at all those pointy teeth. I fired another shot under the chin. No reaction. I could see the snakelike tongue worming its way toward my face.

Something wooden blocked my view and suddenly I could breathe again. I dropped to my knees. The thing flew backward, like it had been shot with a cannon, landing on the roof of the privies.

"The fuh..."

"No time for swearing, Mr. Raney. We need to go."

I looked up to see Chung standing at my side. He clutched an eight-sided piece of wood in his hand. I leaned forward to stand up and I saw the shine of the mirror embedded in the front of it.

"Got another one of those, Chung?"

"You would only break it," he replied, never taking his eyes off the creature.

My guns were apparently useless, so I holstered them and hastily buttoned up my coat. "Well, couldn't you have done that before he killed the guy paying me?"

"Do you always complain this much when someone saves your life? I do not remember these discussions last time it happened."

The thing on the roof hissed at us.

"Fine. Where to?"

"Across the tracks to the other camp. We need to get back to my uncle before the other Jiangshi reach him."

I was about to ask him to repeat that in English, but thought better of it. Instead I gave the privies a wide berth on my way to the tracks. Chung overtook me and reached the train cars first. The rails had disappeared by that point under the snow. The drifts crept up over the wheels, grazing the couplers. I longed for the deadly comfort of San Francisco.

I slid down the hillside on my ass. Chung pulled me up, thankfully without comment. I followed him through the Chinese camp, admiring the wooden lean-tos they'd built in anticipation of the bad weather. Our journey ended at the entrance of an eight-sided hut. He pulled aside a thick fur covering the threshold and motioned me to come in.

A fire pit in the middle of the room sent a winding trail of smoke up through a hole in the roof. Several other men were gathered there, their attention focused on an old man sitting on a cushion near the fire. He was missing a leg below his left knee and had a number of bandages wrapped around that same side. I could see the tendrils of black powder burns creeping up his neck.

Chung led me over to the man and handled the introductions. "Uncle Shen, this is the man I told you about. This is Chance Raney."

Shen nodded at me and smiled weakly. "It is a pleasure to meet you Mr. Raney, though not under these circumstances."

"These circumstances being I shot something six times and it kept coming at me?"

"There is that sharp wit Chung promised me," the old man laughed. "You cannot kill a Jiangshi, Mr. Raney. It is already dead."

The other men in the room joined him in laughter.

"Okay, joke's on the cowboy. Haha. Laugh it up," I frowned. "Where did these things come from and how do we send them back?"

"I am afraid that this is my fault. I only wished to recover the bodies of the men we lost." Shen stared at the ground. "I once knew a Taoist priest in my village who, for a small donation, would transport the bodies of the deceased to their home villages for burial. This man would perform a ritual to reanimate the dead in a way that made it easier for them to travel long distances."

"The hopping?"

"Yes, the hopping. In the dark of night, so as not to upset the living, he would line them up in a row. He would ring a special bell and the bodies would hop along behind him wherever he went."

"Sorry, Uncle Shen. I'm calling bullshit. The dead don't get up and walk—or hop."

"They do if a senseless old fool performs the ritual." The old man sighed and buried his face in his hands. "Whether you believe in it or not, magic is real, Mr. Raney. The Jiangshi feed on the living and drain their qi. They will grow in power."

"If bullets don't work, how do we stop them," I asked.

"I doubt you have a six-demon bag under your coat..."

"A what?"

"Nevermind. I have three pieces of parchment here." He held up a handful of long yellow pieces of paper. "I remember the inscriptions well enough. They must be written in blood."

"Blood? Whose blood?"

"Just a chicken, Mr. Raney. Once the work is complete, these talismans must be placed on the forehead of each Jiangshi. It will return them to a docile state where they will follow the sound of a hand bell. Any questions?"

I started to open my mouth, but a friendly hand clamped over it before I could do anymore damage.

● ● ●

I glanced over at Chung as we walked side by side back to the tracks. "You know how crazy this sounds, right?"

Chung smirked. "I watched you reload your guns before we left. Who is the crazy one?"

"Listen, any problem I can't outshoot or outdrink makes me nervous. I don't suppose you're gonna let me borrow that little mirror are yah?"

"The mirror only worked because it was up close. The Jiangshi do not see very well. They hunt by the...not sure how to translate." Chung thought about it. "You understand qi, yes?"

"That's like your soul?"

"Qi means your life force or breath. It flows through the body like an endless river. Now do you get it, Raney?"

"Life breath river. Got it."

"Every time you exhale, the Jiangshi focus on the scent of your qi. That is how they track us."

"Good thing I brushed my teeth the other day. What happens if we hold our breath?"

"That is an excellent question. You become almost invisible to them."

It was a lot to take in, especially for someone who wasn't all that spiritual like myself.

The idea of life after death was foreign enough, but I guess if we're going to go that far, then getting back up from a dirt nap could still be on the table. I kept waiting for him to burst into laughter and say *ha ha, Gweilo, we fooled you good!* The further we walked up the tracks, the less likely it was going to happen.

As we approached the last car on the tracks, I had an idea. I scampered up the step to the door. Too bad I'd lacked the foresight to grab Art Beauregard's keys. I drove my elbow through the decorative window and managed to find the lock without cutting my hand up. The door swung inwards.

Chung called out for me, but I waved him off. I wasn't expecting to find any guns or knives in Crocker's office on wheels, but I knew there was one thing in there that could be useful. The desk drawers were locked, but a sharp yank was all that stood between me and their contents. I found what I was looking for in the right-hand drawer.

"No time for drinking, Raney," Chung said.

I took a swig of brandy, for luck of course, and stuffed the bottle in one of my coat pockets.

"I thought you were kidding about out drinking your problems."

"I never kid about drinking, Chung. That's for celebrating after we wrangle these hopping corpses. Might even come back later for the safe."

My friend shook his head in disappointment and hopped off the train car. I smiled, pretty pleased with myself. Why was everyone else so surprised when I didn't live up to their standards?

A short ways up the track stood the first tunnel. It was a hundred and fifty feet through solid granite. The other side opened to the ledge they'd been blasting into the side of the mountain. It would eventually stretch half a mile, hugging the terrain, before going into another tunnel. One side was carved stone. The other was a steep drop off the cliff into oblivion. Cutting that shelf with controlled black powder explosions is where Uncle Shen's crew lost their lives.

Chung squinted into the darkness of the tunnel. "The overnight shift saw one of them up here earlier. That's why they refused to work."

"All I see is carts full of broken rocks. We're going to need some light. Wait here."

I stepped into the mouth of the passageway and looked through the tools stored there. My eyes quickly locked on a lantern. It had plenty of oil and I scored a box of safety matches from the pockets of a coat someone had left behind. I found my way back to where Chung was standing in the entrance, looking down on the two camps.

I held the lantern aloft. "Hey, look what I found."

The figure turned around and hopped into the light.

"Shit."

Grasping claws reached for me, knocking the lantern from my hand. I stumbled backwards with the grace of a town drunk. My legs went out from under me, sending me ass over teakettle into a half full mining cart. Jagged shards of stone dug into my back as I struggled to find enough leverage to pull myself up.

The cart shuddered and rolled a few feet. I craned my neck, trying to see what happened. There was the damned Jiangshi, bumping against the cart, with its arms outstretched. I felt talons ripping into my pant legs. Panic was setting in. I kicked the thing as hard as I could from my position. It probably looked like the tortoise on his back kicking at the hare. Another bump kept the cart rolling back into the darkness.

"Chung! Need a little help here!"

My right leg felt like it was bleeding, but I had something else to worry about now. How much track was left? Were there barrels at the end of it or it did the rails just end?

The universe was quick to answer these questions. My head slapped against the inside of the cart as the wheels touched down onto stone.

I tried to stay focused, but the whole world had just taken a hard spin to the left. There was a sheer drop somewhere behind me and unless I found a way out, this turtle was about to fly. Wait. That was a great idea.

I pushed my elbows against the sides of the cart, pulled my weight back as best as I could, and rocked hard to the right. I felt the left side of the cart come off the ground. I repeated the move again and again, building momentum. On the fourth try, the cart dumped me onto the cold hard ground. From my stomach, I watched as it skittered off the edge and disappeared into the blackness.

It took some effort, but I rolled over onto my back. I watched the snow coming down, feeling the flakes melt as they hit my face. It was peaceful. Laying there for a while seemed like a wonderful idea, but I had a nagging suspicion that there was something else I was supposed to be doing.

The ringing of a bell brought me out of my haze. I sat up and listened, waiting for the sound again.

"This is no time to play in the snow, Mr. Raney. Are you making a snow man? We have more work to do," Chung said.

My vision blurred in and out before I found him. He was standing in the tunnel holding up my lantern. Behind him stood the Jiangshi, the vertical yellow parchment dangling from its forehead. Chung disappeared back into the tunnel, ringing the hand bell every few steps and the dead man hopped along behind him.

I made it to my feet and staggered along behind them.

"Hold up a second. I'm bleeding."

I felt around my leg. My pant leg was torn, but the flesh was only scratched. Chung shook his head at me.

"Well, I'm glad someone is getting a little enjoyment out of this."

"It is just a scratch."

"Just a scratch," I mocked him. "What a pity."

We stepped out of the tunnel into the snowstorm. "You will get another chance to prove your bravery, my friend." Chung pointed down the hill. In the short time we'd been gone; the main camp had descended into bedlam.

Several fires had started amongst the tents, no doubt the result of panicked workers turning over their lamps. Scores of men clambered through the snow drifts, fighting their way to the tavern. Two poor fools stood their ground near Beau's office, firing a dozen shots into one of the Jiangshi, but it kept coming.

I straightened my hat. "Think I got this one. Try to keep up," I told him.

I slid down the embankment with the grace of a newborn foal, but it got the job done. I managed to make a soft landing without breaking anything. I looked behind me for Chung. He was calmly walking down the tracks, ringing his bell, with the other corpse in tow. I rolled my eyes and made a beeline toward the office building.

The creature was draining the life out of the last man standing, shaking him around like a ragdoll. I tore a long piece of fabric from my tattered pant leg. I stuffed half of it into the top of the brandy bottle and let it soak up some of the amber liquid. The Jiangshi swiveled around, sniffing the air. Its thin black tongue flicked out between razor sharp teeth.

"Yeah, I'm here. No sneaking up on your ugly ass."

I struck one of the safety matches on the side of its box.

"It's a shame to waste this on the likes of you, but I'll get over it."

I touched the match to the fabric and watched the flame climb up toward the mouth of the bottle. Arm cocked back, I counted to three in my head before hurling it at the chest of the beast. The bottle exploded, splashing flaming liquid all over it. The thing shrieked and hopped in place. Its pale green flesh turned black as flames engulfed the body. The smoking corpse fell backwards into the snow leaving a steaming silhouette.

Chung's hand bell rang out behind me. I turned to him, grinning ear to ear, pleased with myself.

"See, it's not that hard, Chung. If you can't shoot it, just kill it with fire."

I looked back at the hole in the snow. Have you ever stepped on a rake? The tines catch under your boot and the handle swings straight up, usually right in your face. That's what happened here. The Jiangshi, now blackened and naked, pivoted on its heels and rose straight up.

It screamed. I screamed. We had a whole moment going there.

Chung dropped the lantern and the bell into the snow. He charged the monstrosity with a speed like nothing I'd ever seen. In the blink of an eye, he'd closed the distance and hit the thing with a flurry of strikes. He finished the sequence by leaning it backwards, just long enough to slap a piece of parchment on its forehead, before standing it back upright.

He came back, fished his hand bell out of the snow, and gave it a shake. "One more," he said, watching the tavern.

"How do you know that paper is going to stay…stuck on there?"

Chung looked at me and smiled.

"Don't say magic," I said, grimacing, "I know that's what you're going to say."

"Ancient Chinese secret, Chance."

"Horse shit, Chung."

"After all you have experienced tonight… The mind still fights what the heart sees."

Shrieks of terror preceded a flood of men pouring out of the tavern. They scattered like cockroaches in search of new hiding places. I waded through the chaos, stealing a peek inside through the remains of the front door that now dangled on one hinge. The scene inside wasn't much better. I counted nearly a dozen drained bodies with another about to join them. The most alarming thing I noticed was that the Jiangshi inside didn't have the same problems getting around as the others. This one floated above the wooden floor.

"I think we have a problem, Chung. He's not hopping."

Chung stood at my side, peering inside. "He has feasted on many this night. The vessel is filled with power."

"Okay, I'll distract him. When he comes at me, you just run in and do your thing." I mimed a bunch of punches.

"This is a terrible plan," he said.

"Thought so."

I inhaled deeply, covered my mouth with one hand, and stepped into the tavern. I wondered how long I could hold my breath. These problems rarely come up in my world.

The Jiangshi finished his meal with a troubling sound that reminded me of a belch. Was it polite manners to belch after you sucked someone's soul from their body? I was just happy he hadn't noticed me creeping over to the bar. Maybe there was something to this breath thing. I eased up on the counter, swung my legs over to the other side, and dropped to the floor. Did anyone ever sweep up back here? Ugh. It was disgusting.

Mounted under the bar near the register was every bartender's best friend—the double barrel shotgun. I broke it open to make sure it was loaded. As if there was any doubt in mind that it wouldn't be. I rolled out from behind the bar at the far end with the buttstock pulled firmly into my shoulder. I eased back the hammers.

Our unwanted guest was in the middle of the room, floating toward the entrance. The main course was finished and now it was time to find some desert. I crept up behind him, one soft step at a time. When I stood about three paces behind him, I stopped.

"Boo," I whispered and pulled the trigger.

The creature's midsection exploded in a shower of black goo. I briefly saw its hips dangling from a crooked spine before they fell to the ground. It turned to face me, head cocked to the side like a confused hunting dog. Its pale green face contorted and it bared those pointy teeth at me. With arms raised to the sky, the Jiangshi squealed and thrashed about.

"Any time now, Chung," I called out.

I could see him across the room, standing in stunned silence.

That's when the inky tendrils from the bloody mess on the floor rose up. A dozen of them twisted and writhed like snakes. They wove together, making a lopsided ladder that finally climbed high enough to reach the upper half of the monstrosity. The ends formed into barbs and shot into the torso. The bottom half dragged itself upward in jerky stops and starts. In a matter of moments, the thing was whole again.

I did the first thing that came to mind. I swung the shotgun at it like a club. In the history of bad ideas, this one ranks at least in the top five. It grabbed the gun in mid-swing, pulled me in closer, and then flung me across the room like I'd been kicked by a mule. I slammed into the back wall somewhere near the ceiling until gravity caught hold and dropped me top of a broken card table.

It flew directly at me. I already missed the hopping ones. I took another deep breath and rolled to the corner of the room. It hovered over the remains of the table, that tongue darting out to taste the air. I was winded, so this wasn't going to last long.

Chung came sprinting across the room with the last yellow paper clenched between his teeth, used one of the last upright chairs for a boost, and launched into an amazing flying kick. The Jiangshi grabbed his ankle and used Chung's momentum against him, hurling him into the wall with disturbing force. He collapsed in a heap as the talisman fluttered to the floor.

I dove for the paper, knowing full well my life depended on it. My chest slapped the floor and forced the air out of my lungs. Not looking back, I risked a couple of breaths as I scrambled across the room. I needed to put some space between me and my ugly dancing partner. My lungs were burning, but I gulped in one more breath and held it.

The snow was drifting into the doorway now. I could see the other two dead men waiting patiently outside, the papers on their foreheads fluttering in the breeze. Everything in me wanted to run, but there was nowhere to hide in this storm. Behind me, the floating corpse of a dead railroad worker was closing in on the only friend I had. None of it made a lick of sense. If I was about to shuffle off this mortal coil, at least I'd know I did it trying to do the right thing instead of scurrying away like a dog with my tail between my legs.

The Jiangshi grabbed Chung by the front of his shirt and hoisted him up. Its lips quivered in anticipation, parting to reveal impossibly sharp teeth. I clutched the talisman in my right fist and charged. I wasn't as graceful as my friend, but I leapt onto the creature's back. My left arm hooked under its chin and I dug my heels into its thighs for leverage. It was like trying to break a bronco, except instead of stomping a mud hole in your ass it would suck your soul if you lost.

Just touching the creature made me shiver uncontrollably. I'm not sure if the thing was freezing cold or just drawing the heat out of everything around it. There was no telling how long I was going to be able to hang on. It released Chung and raked my arm with its claws.

"There better not be any magic words to make this work."

I swung my right hand around and slapped the parchment on the Jiangshi's forehead. The body stiffened, causing me to lose my grip. I landed on my feet and took a step back. The dead man floated down to the floor.

Chung's eyelids fluttered. He looked up at the docile corpse, then over to me, and back.

"Raney, you did it."

I offered him a hand up. "Of course."

"How?"

"It's like I always say, sometimes you run into a problem that you can't outshoot or outdrink, Chung. That's when the universe really tests a man's mettle." I pulled him up and patted him on the shoulder. "Besides, it's all in the reflexes."

The End

OUR CREATORS

FRED ADAMS Jr.- is a western Pennsylvania native who has enjoyed a lifelong love affair with horror, fantasy, and science fiction literature and films. He holds a Ph.D. in American Literature from Duquesne University and recently retired from teaching writing and literature in the English Department of Penn State University.

NICK AHLHELM - lives in Cedar Rapids, Iowa, where he continues to work on new adventures of D.B. Cooper alongside multiple novels featuring his super powered hero Lightweight. His third book in that series, *Lightweight: Beyond* is due out in late 2015, and will directly follow the events of *Lightweight: Senior Year* and *Lightweight: Black Death*. He doubles as the editor of Metahuman Press, a publisher of multiple novels and anthologies. In addition to his work for Metahuman Press, he has written for Airship 27, Pro Se Press and Flinch Books. For more information on his work, including his online serial Walking Shadows, follow Nicholas Ahlhelm online at SuperPoweredFiction.com.

TERRY ALEXANDER - and his wife Phyllis live on a small farm near Porum, Oklahoma. They have three children and ten grandchildren. Terry is a member of the Oklahoma Writers Federation, Ozark Writers League, The Tahlequah Writers and The Fictioneers. He has been published in various anthologies from Airship 27, Pro Se Press, Metahuman Press, Pulp Modern, Hazardous Press, May December Press, to name a few.

SEAN ALI - is a designer and occasional illustrator living a life of dignified squalor, on terms that do not offend him, in the middle of Oakland, California. He's a Scorpio, likes long walks on the beach, jazz clubs, the Oakland Raiders, and is good to his mother. Sometimes you'll find him sweating things out for love (and occasionally money) in the bowels of the Pro Se Press where he still turns in the occasional book design despite himself. He doesn't take himself terribly seriously, but loves Tommy Hancock like a brother which is why he's here today.

RALPH L. ANGELO JR. - recipient of the 2014 'New Pulp Award' for 'Best New Author' has written novels in the Sci-Fi/Space Opera, Sword and Sorcery, Epic Fantasy and New Pulp as well as non-fiction genre's. Ralph has also written various stories in anthologies for different publishers in the New Pulp genre as well. In his spare time Ralph is an avid motorcyclist, skier, guitar player and martial artist. All of Ralph's books can be found at http://RLAngeloJr.com

JOSEPH ARNOLD - had all intentions of becoming a comic book artist, though deciding to enlist into the military after high school. After serving two combat deployments with the 82nd Airborne Infantry, he went to The Art Institute of Colorado in Denver attaining a Bachelors Degree in Media Arts and Animation. He has illustrated many and written several independent comic projects, and is always aiming higher to increase his skill and prestige of his projects.

T. GLENN BANE – is an author, Illustrator and Game Designer. He resides in Virgina, at the foot of the Shenandoah Valley. An Alum of Savannah College of Art and Design, Bane considers his first and best teachers the endless parade of comics that defined his childhood. Bane is the founder of Scaldcrow Games, a publisher of role-playing games.

JAMES BEARD -Though born a redhead, Jim has struggled with the accompanying adversity and prejudice to achieve his dream of working as a pulp writer. He made his first professional sale in 2002, to DC Comics, and has never looked back; writing is in his blood. He credits his father for introducing him to the heroes and villains who populated the pulps and the comic books of the early Twentieth Century, and he's strived to honor their rich history while always looking for new ways to move them forward

B.C. BELL - is the author and creator of the series TALES OF THE BAGMAN, the story of a 1930's Chicago racketeer turned Robin Hood. Volume three, THE BUTCHER BACK O' THE YARDS is next. Bell has written over a dozen pulp hero adventures, ranging from THE AVENGER to SECRET AGENT X. His book BIPOLAR EXPRESS, the story of a madman trapped in a post-apocalyptic Chicago, made the Horror Writer's Association reading list for 2012. Bell lives with his wife in Chicago and is currently working on a novel-length Weird Tale.

H. DAVID BLALOCK - has been writing speculative fiction for nearly 40 years. His work has appeared in novels, novellas, stories, articles, reviews, and commentary both in print and online. Since 1996, his fiction has appeared in over two dozen magazines including *Pro Se Presents, Aphelion Webzine, Quantum Muse, Shelter of Daylight Magazine, The Harrow, The Three-Lobed Burning Eye, The Martian Wave* and many more. His current novel series is the three book Angelkiller Triad from Seventh Star Press. He served as editor for *parABnormal Digest* from its inception until the end of 2012 and currently serves as an editor at Pro Se Productions and Hermit Studios Press (Denmark). For more information visit his website at www.thrankeep.com.

DAVID BOOP - is a bestselling Denver-based speculative fiction author. He's also an award-winning essayist, and screenwriter. His novel, the sci-fi/noir *She Murdered Me with Science*, will return to print in 2015 from WordFire Press. David has had over forty short stories published and two short films produced. While known for Weird Westerns, he's published across several genres including media tie-ins for *The Green Hornet* and *Veronica Mars*. His RPG work includes *Interface Zero* and *Deadlands: Noir* for Savage Worlds. You can find out more on his fanpage, www.facebook.com/dboop.updates or Twitter @david_boop.

MARK BOUSQUET - is the author of over a dozen novels, including the Gunfighter Gothic series, The Haunting of Kraken Moor, Used to Be: The Kid Rapscallion story, Dreamer's Syndrome, and two adventure series for kids, Adventures of the Five and Stuffed Animals for Hire. He is the owner and publisher of Space Buggy Press.

KEVIN PAUL SHAW BRODEN – received a BA in Art from California State University, Fullerton; before that he worked on the "Hornet" Newspaper as a reporter – illustrator while earning his AA at Fullerton. He has storyboarded music videos for BiGod20's "One," John Wesley Harding, and Kristin Hersch, and been contracted to do illustratiosn for commercials and television series pitches. His first love remains masked heroes. He is married to writer Shannon Muir, who co-authors "Flying Glory and the Hounds of Glory."

FORREST DYLAN BRYANT's - love affair with pulp storytelling began through a chance encounter with a Doc Savage novel in college. But twenty years would elapse before his first foray into writing fiction, during National Novel Writing Month in 2009. That story eventually became his self-published debut novel, *Dragon in the Snow*. Forrest's short fiction, ranging from sci-fi to gangster noir, has been picked up for several anthologies to be published by Pro Se Press. A new edition of *Dragon in the Snow* is planned for 2016 (also from Pro Se), with a sequel to follow.

RICHARD LEE BYERS - is the author of over forty fantasy and horror novels including *Blind God's Bluff: A Billy Fox Novel* (Night Shade Books) and the "Black River Irregulars" trilogy (forthcoming from Privateer Press.) His short fiction has appeared in numerous anthologies, and he has collected some of the best of it in the eBook collections *The Plague Knight and Other Stories*, *The Q Word and Other Stories*, and *Zombies in Paradise*. A resident of the Tampa Bay area, he writes an opinion column for the SF news site Airlock Alpha and spends much of his leisure time fencing epee.

PAT CARBAJAL - started as a political cartoonist at various national newspapers in Argentina. Since then, he has illustrated a wide variety of impressive projects, such as Adamant Entertainment's TALES OF FU MAN CHU and FOE FACTORY: MODERN , TIMELINE OF THE PLANET OF THE APES by Rich Handley. Pat's illustrations for ROCK AND ROLL COMICS: THE SIXTIES featured Ozzy Osborne, AC/DC and Guns n' Roses. Pat's first full-length graphic novel as sole illustrator was ALLAN QUATERMAIN, published by Bluewater. For the comic series VINCENT PRICE PRESENTS, Pat debuted as a writer as well as illustrator. Other works include the upcoming JAMES BOND LEXICON for Hasslein Books. Pat also creates exclusive T-shirt designs for Rotten Cotton Graphics.

WAYNE CAREY – devoured science fiction from an early age, with such favorites as Edgar Rice Burroughs, Arthur C. Clarke, and Isaac Asimov, the genre guiding him toward a career in science with degrees in biology and education and creating the desire to write. A former research scientist and teacher, he and his wife Brenda live in the wilds of Central Pennsylvania with their three children, who provide a great deal of inspiration for his work. His stories have appeared in various magazines and anthologies, such as the Cogs in Time series. His novel, *The Nanon Factory*, is published by Leo Publishing LLC, with two more forthcoming. Please visit his web site at (http://wgcarey.wix.com/wayne-carey) or send comments to wgcarey@1791.com.

PEGGY CHAMBERS - calls Enid, Oklahoma home. She is an award winning author with three published novels to her name and always working on another. Retired now, she can spend all her time making up stories. She has two children, five grandchildren and lives with her husband and dog. She attended Phillips University, the University of Central Oklahoma and is a graduate of the University of Oklahoma. She is a member of the Enid Writers' Club, Oklahoma Writers' Federation, Inc., Oklahoma Women Bloggers and Ozark Writers' League. There is always another story weaving itself around in her brain trying to come out. You can find her at http://peggylchambers.com where she writes a weekly blog, like her on Facebook at https://www.facebook.com/BraWars, or connect with her out on Twitter at @ChambersPeggy.

ARRICK CHURCH - is a detail oriented, positive thinker with a passion for inking comics. He is currently working for Carestream, as a technical support administrator, in the field of dental software support, but spent the vast majority of my free time, honing his inking skills in an effort to someday become, a lucrative professional within the comics industry.

ADRIAN COLE - Native of Plymouth, Devon, England, living in Bideford (Solomon Kane country) I have been a published writer for nearly 40 years – SF, fantasy, S&S, horror, both short fiction and some 26 novels. Many of my books are available as eBooks and some are now available as audio books (Audible). Have been in Year's Best anthologies. My most recent novel is THE SHADOW ACADEMY, SF from Edge Fantasy and Science Fiction Books (Canada), and also NICK NIGHTMARE INVESTIGATES, pulp tales of the hard-boiled occult private eye, from Alchemy Press (UK). My intrepid private eye is the protagonist in YOU'LL LAUGH WHEN I TELL YOU. My hobbies include cycling, swimming in nearby sea, movies, books, comics and generally enjoying life. Married to the lovely Judy.

LISA M. COLLINS - lives in central Arkansas with her husband and an adorable cat, Baby Girl, who believes she is Lisa's co-author. Her nonfiction has been published in the Arkansas Democrat-Gazette and the Dead Mule School of Southern Literature. She copy edited and researched on Understanding Global Slavery by University of California Press. Her science fiction story, The Tree of Life, is in the 2013-2014 anthology by Holdfast Magazine. She edits for Metahuman Press and is an upcoming creative contributor with Pro Se Productions. She is a Sally A. Williams Grant winner from the Arkansas Arts Council for writing, and is the author of The House Bast Made: A Reid Cannon Adventure.

PERCIVAL CONSTANTINE – was born and raised in the Chicagoland area and began writing at the age of ten and never really stopped. He began working in publishing in 2005 and in 2007 published his first novel. Since then, he has worked as an author, editor, designer, comic book scripter and letterer. He currently resides in Japan where he works at the Minami Academy and also continues writing his four main series—The Myth Hunter, Infernum, Vanguard, and Luther Cross. His website is PercivalConstantine.com.

ART COOPER - is a Canadian artist/writer/editor who was a founding partner of Spectrum Publications, which published three bi-monthly fanzines in the early '70's. Art was a member of the inaugural Cartooning program at Sheridan College in Oakville, Ontario, where the guest instructors included such luminaries as Joe Kubert, Neal Adams and Will Eisner. Art contributed to a number of fan publications and penciled two stories for Orb Magazine before getting married and completing his engineering degree. Art has worked as a project manager in the Mining and Metals industry for the past few decades, and has done some freelance advertising work on the side. Art is the proud father of two grown sons, and lives in Mississauga, Ontario with his current wife and daughter.

DALE COZORT - lives in a college town near Chicago with his wife, daughter, three cats and a ton of books. He is a computer person, an educator and has been a fan of the pulps since he discovered Doc Savage, Robert E. Howard's great pulp characters and The Saint as a teenager. Dale's four published science fiction novels all create unique, action-filled new worlds for adventure. This story is his first venture into New Pulp and he thoroughly enjoyed writing it. Expect to see more stories in this genre from him.

ROB DAVIS - began his professional art career doing illustrations for role-playing games in the late 1980's. At DC and Marvel Rob worked on likeness intensive comics like TV adaptations of QUANTUM LEAP and STAR TREK's many incarnations mostly on the DEEP SPACE NINE comics for Malibu. After the comics industry implosion in the late 1990's Rob picked up work on video games, advertising illustration and T-shirt design as well as some small press comics like ROBYN OF SHERWOOD for Caliber. Rob continues to do the odd self-published comic book as well as publisher and designer for his small-press production REDBUD STUDIO COMICS. Rob is Art Director, Designer and Illustrator for the New Pulp production outfit AIRSHIP 27 partnered with writer/editor Ron Fortier. Rob is the recipient of the PULP FACTORY AWARD for "Best Interior Illustrations" in 2010 for his work on SHERLOCK HOLMES: CONSULTING DETECTIVE and has been nominated for the same award every year since. He works and lives in central Missouri with his wife and two children.

MICHAEL DORMAN - is a comic book artist hailing from Sacramento, California. He drew books for Bluewater Comics like Logan's Run: Aftermath, Tales from the Dark Universe, and the upcoming Aether. He currently works on Black Bat / Domino Lady: Danger Coast to Coast for Moonstone books and Santa Claus: Private Eye for Thrillbent. Mike has a simple motto, "make good comics." Follow Mike on Twitter @dorwaystudios and his site, www.dorwaystudios.com.

MIKE DUBISCH - is a fantasy illustrator with his roots in golden age horror comics and pulp Science Fiction. He has worked for Marvel, DC, IDW, and Image Comics, and his work has appeared in Science Fiction Age, Realms of Fantasy, and the H.P.Lovecraft Magazine of Horror. His art has been used in toy design and illustration for Star Wars, The Wheel of Time, RIFTS and Dungeons and Dragons role playing games, covers for Aliens VS Predator, and graphic adaptations of The Boxcar Children and other children's literature. Mike has been teaching and doing art as an instructor at the Academy of Art University in San Fransisco. He also creates fine art, prints, and experimental films exploring H. P. Lovecraft's Cthulhu Mythos. Mike lives in Phoenix, Arizona with his wife, Carolyn, and three daughters.

BEN DUNN - was born in Taiwan on April 17, 1964. His first professional work was in BLOODY BONES AND BLACK-EYED PEAS #1 for Galaxy Comics in 1983. In 1985 he started Antarctic Press with MANGAZINE. In 1986 he debuted NINJA HIGH SCHOOL at Baycon. NINJA HIGH SCHOOL went on to issue #175 and there are currently over 300 issues of NHS continuity making it one of the longest running independent comics. Currently he is working on a revival of the series. In 1995 he created Antarctic Press' biggest hit in WARRIOR NUN AREALA. Currently, WARRIOR NUN is being developed at Perfect Circle Productions as a live-action feature film. He served as editor-in-chief for Antarctic Press from 1985-1993. His current project is SCIENCE IS MAGIC.

GORDON DYMOWSKI - has always considered himself a writer: his childhood was spent scribbling drawings, his college years included a column for the **Loyola Phoenix**. (One of his prized possessions: a rejection letter for a spec **Columbo** treatment in the

1990s) His day job focuses on marketing and copywriting for non-profits and small businesses through One Cause Consulting (http://www.onecauseconsulting.com). Outside of his day job, Gordon writes for a variety of outlets, including **I Hear of Sherlock** (http://www.ihearofsherlock.com), **Chicago Now** (http://www.chicagonow.com/one-cause-at-a-time) and **Blog *This*, Pal** (http://blogthispal.blogspot.com) Making debut with "Out There In the Night" in **Les Vamps,** Gordon has been published in Pro Se's **Tall Pulp,** Space Buggy Press' **Dreamer's Syndrome: New World Navigation**, and **Black Bat Mystery** for Airship 27. For Gordon's online portfolio and contact information, please visit http://www.gordondymowski.com

MAL EARL - is a self taught writer/illustrator based in the scenic Lake District of Northern England. His creator owned, BULLETPROOF NYLON project is the focus for 2015, and a selection of short tales are available online at http://www.bulletproofnylon.com. A series of BPN pulp novels are currently in development, with the first volume set for completion by October, and a digital comic strip, expanding the saga, will begin in Volume 19 of David Lloyds digital comics anthology Aces Weekly in November. http://www.malearl.com

WIN SCOTT ECKERT - is the coauthor with Philip José Farmer of the Wold Newton novel *The Evil in Pemberley House*, about Patricia Wildman, the daughter of a certain bronze-skinned pulp hero. Pat Wildman's adventures continue in Eckert's sequel, *The Scarlet Jaguar* (the 2014 New Pulp Award winner for best novella). He is the editor of and contributor to *Myths for the Modern Age: Philip José Farmer's Wold Newton Universe*, a 2007 Locus Awards finalist. His critically acclaimed, encyclopedic two-volume *Crossovers: A Secret Chronology of the World 1 & 2* was released in 2010, and *A Girl and Her Cat* (coauthored with Matthew Baugh), the first new Honey West novel in over forty years, came out in 2014. Find him online at winscotteckert.com and @woldnewton (Twitter).

CESAR FELICANO - is artist and co-creator of the critically well received "The Red Ten" published by Comixtribe and has been drawing comics for as long as he can remember. He has also collaborated with The Fallen's, Tom Sniegoski on The Innovator's published by Dark Moon Productions. His other works include The Thespian, Prophecy, The Survivors, Full Moon Craze, Female Forces: Supreme Court Justice Sonia Sotomayor, Ripperman, and Tales of the Macabre. He has illustrated sketch cards for Topps "Attack of the Martians" and Leaf trading cards Best of Football. Cesar's work has been featured on Fox and Telemundo's National Broadcast. He is in high demand for commission work. Notably his watercolor works of superhero and pop culture icons and characters.

DERRICK FERGUSON - was born and raised in Brooklyn, NY and has lived there for most of his life. He worked security for many years at a various establishments before retiring to take care of his health and dedicate his life to his true passion: writing and sharing exciting stories. He is best known for his popular Dillon stories about a modern day black adventurer.

KEVIN FINDLEY - is a veteran of the U.S. Air Force and has been a freelance writer for close to three years now. The first editor to accept a story for publication from Kevin was Tommy Hancock. To say he owes the big guy more than just a few thousand words is obviously an understatement. If you want to see more of Dash or this version of Nigel Bruce, famous world-wide for his portrayal of Dr. Watson, let us know here at Airship 27.

MORGAN FITZSIMONS - is a British artist, illustrator and author. Born in the North of England in 1939, she studied at Liverpool John Moores University, and taught for twenty years. Inspired by W.B. Yeats, Tolkien, CS Lewis, and of course the art of Frank Frazetta, Jim Fitzpatrick and others, her own work has been displayed all over the world. She just finished the cover for Amber Tears, by Jilly Paddock, and is currently working on artwork for a special edition of her novel, The Last Enchanter, and its two sequels. She is fascinated by the ancient myths and legends of our culture, Celtic, Norse and Anglo Saxon, which filters into her work.

ANDY FIX - first discovered heroes such as the Lone Ranger, Conan, Tarzan, John Carter, and Doc Savage as a child. Many years later, he would come to realize that all these characters originated in pulp magazines. Since then, Andy has been a fan of all things Pulp, and he is very excited to be writing New Pulp adventures. For updates on Andy's other writing projects, you can follow him on Twitter (@AndyFixWriter) and on Facebook (facebook.com/Andyfixwriter).

DAVE FLORA - is a Kentucky storyteller and illustrator best known for his GHOST ZERO and DOC MONSTER stories, in both comic and novel form. Dave has been published in numerous magazines, books, comics and games, and spends his daytime hours as an award-winning Instructional Designer at a local university. He has acted in eighteen community theatre productions, is a Freemason, a Baptist Deacon, and once ran over a cow with a tractor (she was fine). Dave lives with is wife, Ann, in an 1810 log cabin down the road from a covered bridge. www.davefsorapresents.com

DAVID JAMES FOSTER - writes under the pen name, James Hopwood. He is the author of the retro-spy thrillers, *The Librio Defection* and *The Danakil Deception*. His short fiction has been published by Sempre Vigil Press, Crime Factory, and Pro Se Publications. Writing as Jack Tunney, he also scribed *King of the Outback, Rumble in the Jungle*, and *The Iron Fists of Ned Kelly*, books in the popular Fight Card series.

NEIL T. FOSTER - studied art at Bolton Art College in England before moving to Australia in 1980. Neil contributed interior art and painted covers for the underground comic Captain Koala as well as various CD and video game covers before bringing Planet of the Apes back into comic form for fans with the web published Beware the Beast. Neil has provided illustrations and covers for various horror and fantasy magazines including 10 years worth of pictures for sci-fi/fantasy magazine Tales of the Talisman. He currently lives in sunny Queensland.

RON FORTIER – Comics and pulps writer/editor best known for his work on the Green Hornet comic series and Terminator – Burning Earth with Alex Ross. He won the Pulp Factory Award for Best Pulp Short Story of 2011 for "Vengeance Is Mine," which appeared in Moonstone's The Avenger – Justice Inc. and in 2012 for "The Ghoul," from the anthology Monster Aces. He is the Managing Editor of Airship 27 Productions, a New Pulp Fiction publisher and writes the continuing adventures of both his own character, Brother Bones – the Undead Avenger and the classic pulp hero, Captain Hazzard – Champion of Justice.

JEFF FOURNIER - is a fiction and non-fiction writer out of Cleveland, Ohio. He is an avid fan of Old and New Pulp, especially HPL and REH. If you have to ask what those letters mean he will gladly tell you. This is his second work for Airship 27 after having his work appear in Sinbad The New Voyages Volume 4. He urges you to avoid getting involved in counterfeiting as the Printer's Devil might come for you too.

MIKE FYLES - was born in South Wales, went to school in Oxfordshire, then Kent, and graduated in the North of England. He has lived in a number of English towns and cities and currently resides in Newcastle under Lyme, Staffordshire. Mike has earnt his living primarily as a teacher but during the last decade he has been able to produce more work as an illustrator, particularly for publishers of New Pulp in North America. This work has also provided him the opportunity to produce cover art for Marvel Comics. Mike favours, for influence, the commercial illustration of the mid 20th Century that preferred drawing, painting, and narrative to promote story telling in books (which included children's annuals), magazines and comics.

ADAM LANCE GARCIA – hails Brooklyn, New York and Garcia was raised on comic books, movie serials, and lightsabers. Best known for his *Green Lama: Legacy* series and his original graphic novel, *Sons of Fire*, Adam writes for a number of publishers, as well as working as a full-time television producer and a part-time screenwriter.

DON GATES - is the creator and author of the Challenger Storm novels from Airship 27 (THE ISLE OF BLOOD and THE CURSE OF POSEIDON, so far) and is the writer of a few short stories that will hopefully see the light of day soon. He currently has a few projects simmering that he really should get back to working on... When he's not writing, he works for an answering service and plays video games (badly). A Florida native transplanted to Ontario, Canada, Gates and his wife Annie live with their two dogs and two cats. He's left-handed, a Gemini, and has lower back pain.

JOE GENTILE – is the author of many graphic novels and short fiction, including those featuring: Sherlock Holmes, Kolchak the Night Stalker, Buckaroo Banzai, Zorro, The Spider, The Avenger, The Phantom, and Werewolf the Apocalypse. His first novel, *"Sherlock Holmes and Kolchak the Night Stalker: City of Thunder"* is available now at (www. moonstonebooks.com). When he is not writing, editing, publishing, teaching, or Trying to sleep, Joe plays bass and lives a good life with his wife Kathy and their personality-ridden dogs.

TOMMY HANCOCK - Steeped in pulp magazines, old radio shows, and all things of that era's pop culture, Tommy Hancock lives in Arkansas with his wonderful wife and three children and obviously not enough to do. He is Partner in and Editor in Chief for Pro Se Productions, is an organizer of the New Pulp Movement, and has worked as an editor for various companies, including Moonstone and Dark Oak Press. He is also an award winning writer for various companies, including Airship 27, Mechanoid Press, Pulpwork Press, Dark Oak, and Moonstone. Tommy works as Project Coordinator for Moonstone. He is also the man behind GUMSHOE RESEARCH CONSULTANTS, a company providing research services to writers of all types.

NANCY A. HANSEN - is the author of the novels FORTUNE'S PAWN, PROPHECY'S GAMBIT, and MASTER'S ENDGAME, anthologies TALES OF THE VAGABOND BARDS, THE HUNTRESS OF GREENWOOD, and THE WINDRIDERS OF EVERICE, novellas COMPANION DRAGON'S TALES: *A FAMILIAR NAME* and co-author of

FINDING WAXY. Her short stories have been featured in multiple issues of Pro Se Presents, and she has a tale each in Pro Se Anthologies THE NEW ADVENTURES OF SENORITA SCORPION, TALL PULP, THE NEW ADVENTURES OF THE WHILRWIND, and MONSTER ACES, while the E-story TO RULE THE SKY is offered as a Pro Se SINGLE SHOT. Nancy has also contributed stories to both Airship 27's SINBAD: THE NEW VOYAGES Volume 1 and Mechanoid Press' debut book, MONSTER EARTH, and the charity anthology THE LOST CHILDREN. Nancy currently resides on an old farm in beautiful, rural eastern Connecticut with an eclectic cast of family members, and one very spoiled dog.

GREG HATCHER - is a writer and schoolteacher from Burien, Washington. He has been published in various places since 1992 and is a three-time winner of the Higher Goals Award for Children's Writing. Currently he writes a weekly column on comics and pop culture for Comic Book Resources.com, as one of the rotating features on the Comics Should Be Good! blog. Pulp and adventure fiction remains his first love, though, and writing stories for Airship 27's various anthologies is one of his favorite gigs. In addition to writing, he also teaches the Cartooning and Young Authors classes as part of an after-school arts program for grades 7 through 12. He lives in an apartment just south of downtown with his wife Julie, their cat Maggie, and ten thousand books and comics.

NIKKI NELSON-HICKS has the great honor of being described as "the unholy lovechild of Flannery O'Connor and H.P. Lovecraft." You can find more of her disturbed tales published in the anthologies: Capes and Clockwork, Once Upon a Sixgun, Nashville Noir, and Soundtrack Not Included. She is the author of Jake Istenhegyi: The Accidental Detective series available on Amazon.com (where the character of Bear Gunn is a heavy hitter) and a new Sherlock Holmes story, Sherlock Holmes and the Shrieking Pits. You can find her entertaining the unwashed masses on Facebook and twitter (@nikcubed) or her long suffering blog, Nikcubed, www.nikcubed.blogspot.com. All cash donations or chocolate sacrifices welcomed.

JOE HILLIARD - Writer. Columnist. Luddite. Teller of Tales. Grew up as a teen in Los Angeles on a diet of lucha libre, Doc Savage, Philip K. Dick, Philip Marlow, Sax Rohmer, film noir, Judge Dredd, 50s science fiction films, and the fringe of 80s Hollywood. Graduate of the University of Michigan, which only added Kawabata, Krazy Kat, and William S. Burroughs to the mix. Marks time as a paralegal back in California. Currently has several pulp stories slated to be published by Pro Se Press in 2016.

CLAYTON HINKLE - is a life-long fan of Pulp fiction, in nearly all it's genres, thanks to his Father giving him his paper-back copies of Howard, Burroughs, Robeson (Dent), as well as many other writers, in his formative years. Also, he is a life-long fan of Comics. These facts, along with the genetics gifted him by his artist Mother and musician Father, caused him to spend most of his free hours drawing, drawing, and drawing. Largely self-taught, with a head-long, comic-bookish rough style well suited to Pulp and Comic action stories, meeting up with some of the Neo-Pulp publishers such as Airship 27 and Pro-Se was a match made in Heaven!

LEE HOUSTON, JR - is the writer/creator of *Hugh Monn, Private Detective* and *(Project) Alpha* the superhero for Pro Se Productions, as well as the author of numerous short

stories for that company and others. Lee maintains a presence on both G+ and Facebook, as well as a writer's blog at http://leehoustonjr.blogspot.com/
His complete bibliography can be found on his Amazon author's page.

M.D. JACKSON - has been an artist, designer and an illustrator for many years. His work has appeared in Art Scene International Magazine, ImagineFX Magazine, A Fly in Amber, Abandoned Towers, Flashing Swords, Outer Reaches Magazine, Realms Magazine and on the covers of various anthologies from Pulpwork Press and Rage Machine Books among others. He works in a digital medium, mostly with Corel Painter but also with Photoshop. Happily he is also handy with an ink pen and, of course, that old tested and true technology of the HB pencil and a scrap of paper.

EMILY JAHNKE - has been writing on and off since the age of seven but only became serious about writing when she took a writing class in college. It was at college she developed a love for the Arsène Lupin stories by Maurice LeBlanc and was inspired to bring the trope of the romantic gentleman thief back to life. She has published The Queen Who Could Spin Straw Into Gold, Jadwiga of the Nautilus and The Curse of the Masked King amid other stories on the serial website JukePop under the penname Owl Johnson. When not writing, Emily enjoys cooking, reading and spending time with her family.

KEN JANSSENS - this is the second story Ken has written for Airship 27; the first one was for the Moon Man anthology. He has written a dozen other pulp stories for Tommy Hancock and Pro Se Productions, including the Aloha McCoy and Sherringford Bell series. Also, he has written a Young Adults novel called "The Sisters Arcana" published by Pro Se. Ken is a screenplay writer and comic book author; the first issue of his new comic book series "Hindsight" was just released by Comixology.

JOEL JENKINS - spends far too much time inventing far-out stories that take place in far-flung places. Check out his website at JoelJenkins.net for a free Kindle book and a cover gallery of his many books and collections.

ERIC JOHNS - began his art career at the age of 17 publishing and drawing his first comic book. Hundreds of publications later, with works for London Night Studios, Brainstorm comics, Twilight Star comics and a host of other independent comics, Eric's art has taken him into the 3D realm; sculpting models for Marvel, Star Trek, World of Warcraft, Adventure time and even anime heavyweights Attack on Titan, Dragonball Z, and many more. His current works for licensing giant Surreal Entertainment can be purchased throughout the world at your favorite specialty stores.

TODD JONES - When your first word is "Batman", it's either a sign you should be working in comics or become a super hero. Having no super powers or wealth to afford crime-fighting gadgets, Todd Jones decided to be a comic writer instead. He has worked on Pandemonium Spotlight for Twilight Star Studios, All-Star Pulp Comics for Airship 27, as well as, Wicked Awesome Tales and Stakes for Wicked Wolf Comics. Todd currently resides in Colorado with his amazing wife and their two dogs.

MARK JUSTICE - has been reading pulp fiction since an uncle gave him a trio of Doc Savage paperbacks in 1969. Since then he has published a number of stories and novels in the pulp and horror genres. When he's not writing, he hosts a morning radio show and produces the podcast Pod of Horror.

GARY KATO - is an artist who lives and works in Honolulu, Hawaii. He got his start as Terry Beatty's art assistant. Over the years his artwork has appeared in such varied comic books as Destroyer Duck, the Original Streetfighter, Elfquest Bedtime Storeis, Peter Pan Return to Neverland and the on-going Mr.Jigsaw, Man of a Thousand Parts. He's also done art for children's books such as The Menehune of Nuapaka Village, the Barry Baskerville series and the stand alone Jamie & the Fish-Eyed Goggles.

GREG KEYZER - (SNAKE: Nest of Vipers), is a cartoonist and comic illustrator. Graduating with a degree in Graphic Arts from The Art Institute of Charlotte, he is now pursuing a life in comics. You can follow him on facebook at facebook.com/gkcomic, and view an extensive portfolio at freelanced.com/comic.

MIKE KILGORE - is the owner of Kilgore Art & Design and Boot to the Head Studios, and a multi-discipline graphic artist with experience in creating everything from book covers and movie posters to fine art and comic book production. He's also a stay-at-home dad with the cutest little Velocitoddler ever, a gorgeous beauty for a wife and a sidekick German Shepherd named Chewie.

JOSEPH LAMERE - lives in Illinois, where he has been teaching middle school for the past seventeen years. He lives with his wife Emily and his two daughters, Ella and Sofia. They make his life interesting—in the Confucian sense. In addition to writing, Lamere is the lead singer of a hard rock band. The songs he writes aren't much different from his stories. He tends to write his stories in the early morning hours when the girls are sleeping. They give him ideas all the time—and most of the time they don't even know it. You can reach him at josephlamere@gmail.com.

J. WALT LAYNE - lives in Springfield, Ohio. He is a veteran of the US Army, a married father of three, and a voracious reader. A prolific writer, he is the author of Frank Testimony a legal thriller set in Bedford, Mississippi in the 1950s. He is also the author and creator of The Champion City Series of pulp detective stories to be published exclusively by Pro Se Press (March 2013). He has written a laundry list of articles for Backwoodsman Magazine and is the former Op-Ed columnist for The Albany Journal (Albany, Georgia). You can catch up with him on Facebook as Author J Walt Layne.

P.J. LOZITO - Lozito, author of THE STING OF THE SILVER MANTICORE, is a publishing professional in New York City. He is also the author of the related short story collection, SILVER MANTICORE: FRIENDS AND FOES. His new character, the Revenant Detective has just debuted in Pro Se Press' Single Shot series. The story in this collection brings those two characters together in conflict. He is currently at work on the next Silver Manticore novel.

JAVIER LUGO – is a comic book fan and self-taught artist. He currently works as a 7th grade English teacher in Kissimmee, FL and draws whenever he can, which isn't as often as he likes. A father, husband and son, he strives to be the best he can be in everything he does. He doesn't always succeed, but he does try again and again. Favorite quote: " Do. Or do not. There is no try."

TERRENCE P. McCAULEY - is an award-winning writer of crime fiction. His first techno-thriller, SYMPATHY FOR THE DEVIL, was published by Polis Books in July 2015. Polis also republished Terrence's first two novels set in 1930 New York City – PROHIBITION and SLOW BURN. Terrence has had short stories featured in Thuglit, Spinetingler Magazine, Shotgun Honey, Big Pulp and other publications. He is a member of the New York City chapter of the Mystery Writers of America, the International

Thriller Writers and the International Crime Writers Association. A proud native of The Bronx, NY, he is currently writing his next work of fiction. Terrence is represented by Doug Grad of the Doug Grad Literary Agency.

BARRY McCLAIN - is one of comics newest and most prolific pencilers. Haling from Trenton NJ. He always had a passion for comics. Drawing scince 4 years of age, he grew up a fan of all things Sci-fi and fantasy. And having been exposed to comics at such an early age, he's basically bred to be in this industry. Penciling the legendary Ron Fortier's *Pryce for the Asking*, and other indie books like, Serial Tags, Canada Jack, Wild Card Chronicles, End of Days , Shitflingers and The Oblivion Chain just to name a few. And now his unrelenting work ethic has now led him through the doors of Valiant Comics where he is sure to leave his mark and as he would say "Burn lead".

BRIAN McCULLOCH – is an artist living Pensacola Florida whose primary focus is traditional painting on canvas and illustration borad with an emphasis on photo realistic artwork. But he is more than willing to delve into the digital darkside when appropriate for an illustration.

DREW MEYER - is a librarian and science educator who moonlights as a podcaster and game designer. He's currently the "product consultant" for Scaldcrow Games and has contributed to several of their recent releases (including the role playing source book for Ron Fortier's *Cape Noire*.) He's had several essays published in fandom essays, so he's got that going for him. He may or may not have a beard.

BENJAMIN MIKKELSEN - is an Illustrator and Graphic Designer who focuses his time on sequential art in comics. Currently living in Loveland Colorado his works include "Stuffed" the story of a troubled boy and his unlikely guardian, and "Ghost of Starfall" a military space opera following a pair of defunced operatives and their journey for answers. Find more of his work work on Facebook by searching for Six Eleven Comics or by going to www.sixelevencomics.com

CHUCK MILLER - was born in Ohio, lived in Alabama for many years, and now resides in Norman, Oklahoma. He is a Libra whose interests include monster movies, comic books, music, writing, and getting paid for writing, which is the most elusive beast of them all. He holds a BA in creative writing from the University of South Alabama, and little else.

LOU MOUGIN - has been a writer and fan of comics for his entire life, but has only graduated recently to New Pulp. For Marvel he wrote stories of the Swordsman and the Inhumans. For Eclipse he plotted three Heap stories. For Heroic he did tales of the League of Champions, Sparkplug, Flare, and Icicle. For Claypool he scripted two Elvira serials. For Charlton Arrow he did a story featuring a bunch of horror hosts, which was adapted into a radio play. He has other comic stories coming up soon along with a comics history book and at least two books and two short stories so far from Pro Se. Outside of a bunch of articles, interviews, and indexes, that's about it.

GENE MOYERS - From his sanctum deep in the forests of the Pacific Northwest Gene Moyers cranks out various horror, mystery, adventure and other pulp stories on his manual *Royal* typewriter. He is lucky and some of them have actually accepted by publishers like Airship 27 and Pro Se Press. He has written stories for *Ravenwood, The*

Purple Scar, Domino Lady, Moon Man and Black Bat anthologies. He lives in Beaverton, Oregon where his watchful wife keeps a close rein on his scribblings.

KEVIN NIEVES - is an artist from Chino California. He is currently studying at Mount San Antonio College for 2D animation. He has a real passion for pin up art. The entire piece was done by hand with pencils, inks, and markers.

KEVIN NOEL OLSON – lives in a charming bungalow in Butte, Montana with his wife Amelinda. He writes pulp and chilren's adventure fiction and along with sundry articles. Included among his works are the "Tocsin Codex" middle-grade series and "Buk Bakus in Darn Near the Fiftieth Century." He is also a citizen of Metropolis and a loyal airman on Airship 27.

GILLIAN M. (JILLY) PADDOCK - has been writing science fiction and fantasy stories for as long as she can remember. She has self-published several books on Amazon Kindle, which have received excellent reviews. Having had a long career as a biomedical scientist, she was especially pleased to have a story printed in *Blood Type: An Anthology of Vampire SF on the Cutting Edge*—a charity anthology in support of the Cystic Fibrosis Trust, published by Nightscape Press. She has two novels currently available from Pro Se Press. The latest of which, *Dead Men Rise Up Never*, also features Afton and Jerome of the Prosperity City Police Department. She lives in a small, untidy house in the flat bits of East Anglia in the UK, which she shares with an editor/book reviewer, and an insanely large collection of books and music.

JAMES PALMER - is an award-nominated writer, editor and publisher best known as the editor and co-creator of the alternate history giant monster anthology Monster Earth. James has also dabbled in weird horror, space opera and steampunk, and has written stories for Airship 27, Pro Se Productions, White Rocket Books, and Moonstone. A recovering comic book addict, James lives in Northeast Georgia with his wife and daughter. For more on his work, visit www.jamespalmerbooks.com and www. mechanoidpress.com.

JAMES PETERS - fell in love with Science Fiction at a young age, becoming hooked on the works of Asimov, Anderson, and Pohl (among many others), as well as the mixed bag of anything labeled Science Fiction on television or at the movies while growing up. While in grade school, he was given an assignment to write a journal about anything he wanted. He quickly filled the pages with a Buck Roger's type adventure of robots, spaceships, and pew-pewing lasers, discovering his inner passion to write.
He writes with a gritty blend of character-driven action, wry humor, and social commentary that transports the reader through wild worlds of speculative fiction and fantasy. He's known to cross the borders of different genres into new territory, along with an occasional 'wink and nod' to pop culture and other authors, then shock the reader with an unexpected turn of events. Sit back, open your mind and enjoy the ride. Your adventure awaits.

VAN ALLEN PLEXICO - won the 2015 Pulp Factory Award for Novel of the Year and for Anthology of the Year. He is best known for creating and chronicling the adventures of the SENTINELS in a popular series of illustrated superhero novels. He has also written six novels and a novella in the "Shattering" Space Opera series, including the award-winning LEGION III: KINGS OF OBLIVION. His creation, "General John Blackthorn," won Best New Character in the 2012 Pulp Ark Awards. He hosts the interview program

"The White Rocket Podcast" for the Earth Station One Network and has appeared as a character in a Farscape novel and in the Iron Man comics. In his spare time, he serves as Associate Professor of History and Political Science at Southwestern Illinois College.

JAMIE RAMOS - is a fiction writer who resides in the St. Louis area with his wife, son, two dogs and a cat. Jaime has been writing fiction since he was a young child. Jaime sold his short-story "Exile of Avalon" in 2014. Jaime serves as Chief Editor and creator of the super-hero themed anthology "Singularity: Rise of the Posthumans," which is being published by Pro Se Productions. Jaime was also contacted by Australian publisher Endless Worlds Publishing to submit a short story for their flagship anthology.Jaime enjoys football, movies, cooking and playing make-believe with his son Thomas. Jaime has an idyllic life with wife Phyllis, who is a constant source of encouragement.

OLIVIER RAYMOND - has been a professional illustrator since the early 2000s. In 2006, he started a career as a video game concept artist, which eventually led him to work in movies, television and other multimedia projects, as well as a few independent comics books. He keeps an art blog on his website: www.sketchywisdom.com

BARRY REESE - has written for Marvel Comics, Airship 27, Moonstone Books, Pro Se Press and many more. He is best known for his various New Pulp adventure series, which include Lazarus Gray, The Peregrine and The Adventures of Gravedigger. He lives in Georgia with his wife and son.

JOSH REYNOLDS - is a professional freelance writer. In addition to his own work, he has written for several media tie-in franchises, including Gold Eagle's Executioner line and Games Workshop's Warhammer Fantasy and Warhammer 40,000 lines. An up-to-date list of his published work can be found at http://joshuamreynolds.wordpress.com/

ERWIN K. ROBERTS - first went to Branson, Missouri, in 1970, on his honeymoon. He's been there several times since. He had fun writing a story set there. He's lived in the Show-Me State since age five. Erwin is also retired from the Missouri Army National Guard. He grew up in the St. Louis area, but has lived in the Kansas City for forty years now. While he has traveled the Lower Forty-Eight States extensively, Missouri is likely to remain his home indefinitely. Erwin and his wife are empty nesters, but fortunately both adult kids seem to want to remain in the Kansas City area.

RON ROOT - is an Illustrator/ Comic Artist / Concept Artist in the Denver, Colorado area. He earned his Bachelor's Degree in Media Arts and Animation at the Art Institute of Colorado. After graduating, he began work as a freelance artist working on various comic, game, and film projects. He is currently working on his own comic titles, as well as freelancing in his spare time. Ron has a passion for illustration and storytelling and aspires to work in the Comic book industry as an artist.

TOM RUBALCAVA - has worked for over two decades in television, advertising, and feature film animation. Tom attended Diablo Valley College in 1985, focusing on Film Production and Screenwriting. He also apprenticed as a 2D FX Animation Assistant under then Don Bluth Studios' veteran FX Animator Bruce Heller. Tom was Character Sculptor and Effects Animator on the Gumby Adventures, TV series (1987-1988) and Gumby Movie (1991) at Premavision, Inc. In 1991 at Colossal Pictures, Tom's Animation Direction debut Coca-Cola 'Watch', won a Clio Award. 2000-2002 was Co-Partner at Way Out West Prods in San Francisco. Tom was then at Maverix Studios, LLC as a co-founder from June 2003 to September 2011. Also does storyboards on feature films such as 'Howl' (2010), starring James Franco.

ANDREW SALMON – is a two-time Pulp Factory Award winner, Ellis and multiple Pulp Ark Award nominee. He lives and writes in Vancouver, BC. His novels include: ***The Forty Club, The Dark Land, The Light Of Men, Ghost Squad: Rise of the Black Legion*** (with Ron Fortier), ***Sherlock Holmes: Work Capitol*** and ***Sherlock Holmes: Blood to the Bone.*** To learn more about his work check out:amazon.com/Andrew-Salmon/e/B002NS5KR0/ref=sr_ntt_srch_lnk_7?qid=1328666769&sr=1-7

TONY SARRECCHIA - is the creator and writer of the award-winning Harry Strange Radio Drama, a full cast, pulp-style supernatural thriller which airs on both traditional and Internet radio stations. His short story, 'On the Road to Chattanooga', a tale about an unlikely survivor of a zombie apocalypse, was included in Permuted Press's Fat Zombie anthology. In May of 2015 he published the first season scripts of the Harry Strange Radio Drama in bound volume titled "Harry Strange in The Stones of Solomon. Tony worked as a trainer and presenter as well as a bouncer, disc jockey, sales manager, and electronic warfare systems specialist. He often appears as a guest at conventions and talks about writing, producing, and B-movies. He is a member of the Horror Writers Association. Join him on twitter @tonythescribe.

MEHMET KAAN SAVINC – lives in Istanbul Turkey and has done political cartoons, portraits and illustrated various children's books. He is self-taught and some of his work can be found at http://www.betterlifeline.com/product-details/coloring-books

ADAM BENET SHAW –Accomplished painter, illustrator, and comics creator, Adam has garnered acclaim across a number of artistic media. His work has also been shown in over 50 group and solo shows in the US and internationally. His figurative paintings are a prominent part of a 140-foot mural entitled "The History of Cotton" at the National Cotton Exchange Museum, St. Jude's Children's Research Hospital, the National Contact Bridge Museum, and a treasured part of private and corporate collections. His published graphic novel work includes the series "Dead In Memphis", "Bloodstream" for Image Comics, "David: The Illustrated Novel" from Shepherd King Publishing and "Harpe: America's First Serial Killers" from Cave-in-Rock Publishing. He shares his love of art through teaching and workshops at his studio in the Broad Avenue Arts District in Memphis. Recently he has been painting book covers for pulp publishers Pro Se Productions and Airship 27 Productions.

JOHN SIMCOE - had the pleasure of having his first novel, "Tommy One and the Apocalypse Gun" published under the tutelage of Tommy Hancock. He felt it fitting that the his submission to this tome be the second Tommy One story! Prior to the release of that first "Tommy One" novel, Simcoe worked as a newspaper editor and a freelance writer for a number of role-playing game companies and magazines. Learn more about his thoughts on the world at (www.ComicsOnTheBrain.com)

SILVESTRE SZILAGYI - Born 23rd November,1949, in Buenos Aires, Argentina. Studied visual storytelling al I.D.A., with Alberto Breccia as teacher. Began as comic book artist in 1971 both assisting Lito Fernández, and working on my own, mainly for Columba and Record, most important local publishers those days. Did all kind of stories: love, war, adventure, science-fiction, etc. Worked for Italian Eura, British Thompson for years. In U.S.A. did some 20 issues of Phantom for Moonstone, plus some Honey West and more. So far there I've got over 10 thousand pages published, and aim to keep on!

RAZ TSOLMAN – is a freelance graphic artist from Mongolia. He graduated from the Fine Art Institute and currently lives in the capital city of Ulaanbaatar.

SCOTT P. 'DOC' VAUGHN – is a Phoenix based comic artist, illustrator and writer originally hailing form Wisconsin. When he's not hard at work on comics and commissions he's trying to catch up with drawing his web-comic WARBIRDS OF MARS. Among Doc's interest are classic illustrations and movie genres, vintage clothes and cars, pulp magazines and a severe predliction for Doctor Who since the age of eight. He lives in a very classic house with a cat, bird and occasionally a dog. (www.VAUGHN-MEDIA.COM)

I.A. WATSON has worked with Tommy Hancock to put out the BYZANTIUM fantasy novella series, several volumes featuring old pulp characters such as Richard Knight, Armless O'Neil, and Semi Dual, and the non-fiction essay book WHERE STORIES DWELL. In his spare time, Watson has produced four ROBIN HOOD books, ten contributions into the SHERLOCK HOLMES, CONSULTING DETECTIVE series, and a range of other novels, the most recent being VINNIE DE SOTH, JOBBING OCCULTIST. A full list of his publications is available at http://www.chillwater.org.uk/writing/iawatsonhome.htm

DAVID WHITE - is a writer who was born in Chicago, Il. And now lives in Lemont, Il. With his lovely wife of 24 years and his two children Brandon and Allison, and everyone's favorite candy bar, I mean dog, Snickers. He was first published in 2012 when his Doc Panic character was brought to life in Pro Se presents. He has since been published seven times, and has submitted a wealth of stories to Pro Se, Moonstone, Fight Card, and Airship 27. When he can he loves to edit and read the classic pulp as well as the new. He is looking forward to 2015 being the best year yet!

TONY WILSON - was born in the vast wasteland of the Midwest. He was raised on a steady diet of classic TV shows, horror comics, video games, and drive-in movies. He is a repository for useless trivia. Hobbies include writing, reading comics, roleplaying games, and weaving chainmail. He currently lives in North Carolina with his wife and two crazy dogs.

AIRSHIP27HANGAR.COM

www.ingramcontent.com/pod-product-compliance
Lightning Source LLC
Chambersburg PA
CBHW081226020726
47503CB00011B/2917